The World of Fiction

The World of Fiction

David Madden

Louisiana State University

21929

PN
6120.2
.W66
1990

HOLT, RINEHART AND WINSTON, INC.
Fort Worth   Chicago   San Francisco   Philadelphia
Montreal   Toronto   London   Sydney   Tokyo

Publisher/Acquisitions Editor: Charlyce Jones Owen
Developmental Editor: Tod Gross
Project Editor: Michael D. Hinshaw
Production Manager: Kathy Ferguson
Art & Design Supervisor: John Ritland
Cover Illustration: The Image Bank/M. Garland

Copyright Acknowledgments appear on pages 1192–1196.

Library of Congress Cataloging-in-Publication Data

The World of Fiction / [edited by] David Madden.
    p.   cm.
    Includes index.
    ISBN 0-03-014292-X
    1. Short stories.   I. Madden, David, 1933–
PN6120.2.W66   1989
808.83′1—dc20   89-11088
                                      CIP

ISBN: 0-03-014292-X

Address editorial correspondence to: 301 Commerce Street, Suite 3700,
                                    Fort Worth, TX 76102
        Address orders to: 6277 Sea Harbor Drive,
                                    Orlando, FL 32887
                                    1-800-782-4479, or
                                    1-800-433-0001 (in Florida)

Printed in the United States of America

     4 062 9 8 7 6 5 4 3

Holt, Rinehart and Winston, Inc.
The Dryden Press
Saunders College Publishing

PREFACE

This short story anthology is designed for introductory courses in fiction. It is also designed for short story survey and creative writing courses.

The purpose of this anthology is to provide students with a wide range of the finest authors and stories. Most instructors will find that they are already well prepared to teach a majority of these stories. There is a wide variety of stories, a balance of classics and contemporary works, of simple and complex stories, and this anthology enables the instructor to illustrate all the techniques of fiction. Variety of length is another feature of this anthology; most of the works are of average length, but several novellas and a good number of very short stories are also included.

In recent years, editors of short story texts have made decisions to take one of two major approaches: an anthology that favors many stories over pedagogical apparatus or an anthology that favors discussions of the elements and techniques of fiction, with a relatively small number of stories to illustrate those discussions. With Virgil Scott, I took the latter approach in preparing *Studies in the Short Story,* now in its sixth edition.

In *The World of Fiction,* I have chosen to take the other approach, with a major difference: I have tried to enhance a traditional core of fiction selections with an expanded canon that gives just representation to several kinds of writers that have been underrepresented in literature anthologies. *The World of Fiction* may well prove to include the largest selection of ethnic and women writers of any anthology. To enable instructors and students to interpret the history and contemporary experiences of the rapidly growing number of minority students in courses for which this anthology is designed, I have included distinguished stories by Black Americans, Asian Americans, Native Americans, and Hispanic-Americans, along with stories set in Third World countries, South America, Africa, Japan, and Israel. Of the 101 stories gathered here, almost half are by women.

Realizing that many instructors and students tend, or even prefer, not to make use of the questions following each story, while others *do* find discussion aids helpful, I have decided to deal with the issue in a new way. For each story, several questions or observations for re-reading, discussion, and writing are offered at the back of the book. For almost half of the stories, commentaries, such as are traditionally found in a separate Teachers' Manual, are provided. Commentaries are for those stories that raise special thematic or technical problems and also for a selection of stories not often found in anthologies. Several commentaries are offered as examples of the types of critical papers as well. Very basic information about the authors and about publication of the stories is included, along with, in most cases, a list of major works and a few select biographies and critical articles and books.

I have included several tables of contents and indexes that instructors and students may find useful. Some instructors may choose to draw on the Thematic Table of Contents. The "Chronological Index" on the front and back inside covers enables instructors to take an historical approach. A convenient index to titles ends the book. Authors are listed alphabetically in the main Table of Contents.

A handbook guide to reading and writing for students is available: *A Fiction Tutor* uses Flannery O'Connor's "A Good Man is Hard to Find," Ralph Ellison's "Battle Royal," and Katherine Mansfield's "Miss Brill" to illustrate and aid in understanding the elements, techniques and art of fiction, as well as the arts of reading and writing about fiction.

Examination copies of *A Fiction Tutor* can be requested by writing to: English Editor; Holt, Rinehart and Winston, Inc.; 301 Commerce Street; Suite 3700; Fort Worth, Texas, 76102.

ACKNOWLEDGMENTS

On this book, as on many others, Peggy Bach has given me advice I could not have done without.

Thanks are gladly extended to all those students who have helped me test these stories in the classroom.

John R. May, chair of the English department at Louisiana State University, helped in preparation of this book. Ben Bryant assisted in preparation of the manuscript.

While I held the Chair of Excellence at Austin Peay State University, Center for the Performing Arts, Spring 1988, that university provided me with assistance in preparation of the manuscript. Colleen Watt, managing editor of *Zone 3*, and Brenda Carnell assisted me during that time.

Feroza Jussawalla, University of Texas at El Paso, provided advice and biographical information on Third World writers.

Some of the critical material in this book is an adaptation of passages from my earlier text, *Studies in the Short Story*, edited with Virgil Scott.

Finally, I wish to thank the following reviewers for their generous advice and very helpful suggestions:

Walter Anderson, University of California, Los Angeles
Roger Applebee, University of Illinois—Urbana
Victoria Arana-Robinson, Howard University
Olga Asal, Florida State University
Carol Barnes, Kansas State University
Ernest Bufkin, University of Georgia
Peter Carino, Indiana State University
Phillip Castille, University of Houston
Sumita Chaudhery, Schoolcraft College
Tom Collins, University of Arizona
James Cowan, University of North Carolina at Chapel Hill
Raymond Gozzi, University of Massachusetts at Amherst
Richard Harmetz, Los Angeles Trade Technical College
Barbara Haxby, Triton College
William Holtz, University of Missouri—Columbia
Don Kunz, University of Rhode Island
Rosemary Lanshe, Broward Community College
Lee Leeson, Pepperdine University
Susan Lohafer, University of Iowa
Helen Marlboro, DePaul University
Edward Martin, Middlebury College
Noralyn Masselink, Hofstra University
C. L. Proudfit, University of Colorado—Boulder
Margaret Rowe, Purdue University
Betty Townsend, University of Maryland

Baton Rouge   *David Madden*
June 1989   *Louisiana State University*

CONTENTS

Preface v

Thematic Table of Contents xiii

Chinua Achebe, *Civil Peace* 1

Alice Adams, *New Best Friends* 6

Rudolfo Anaya, *The Silence of the Llano* 17

Sherwood Anderson, *Seeds* 31

Maya Angelou, *The Reunion* 37

Margaret Atwood, *Significant Moments in the Life of My Mother* 42

James Baldwin, *Going to Meet the Man* 55

Toni Cade Bambara, *My Man Bovanne* 69

John Barth, *Lost in the Funhouse* 74

Donald Barthelme, *The King of Jazz* 93

Ann Beattie, *Shifting* 97

Saul Bellow, *Looking for Mr. Green* 108

Ambrose Bierce, *An Occurrence at Owl Creek Bridge* 125

Jorge Louis Borges, *The Garden of Forking Paths* 133

Elizabeth Bowen, *The Demon Lover* 141

Kay Boyle, *Rest Cure* 147

Albert Camus, *The Guest* 153

Raymond Carver, *What We Talk About When We Talk About Love* 164

Willa Cather, *Paul's Case* 174

Denise Chavez, *Willow Game* 190

John Cheever, *The Swimmer* 197

Anton Chekhov, *Gooseberries* 207

       The Darling 216

Charles Chesnutt, *The Wife of His Youth* 226

Frank Chin, *Food for All His Dead* 236

Kate Chopin, *The Story of an Hour* 246

Stephen Crane, *The Bride Comes to Yellow Sky* 249

Isak Dinesen, *The Sailor-Boy's Tale* 259

Ralph Ellison, *King of the Bingo Game* 268

                    Flying Home 276

Louise Erdrich, *The Red Convertible* 292

William Faulkner, *A Rose for Emily* 300

                    That Evening Sun 308

F. Scott Fitzgerald, *Babylon Revisited* 322

Richard Ford, *Communist* 339

Ernest J. Gaines, *Just Like A Tree* 352

Mavis Gallant, *Acceptance of Their Ways* 371

Gabriel García Márquez, *A Very Old Man with Enormous Wings* 378

                    Balthazar's Marvelous Afternoon 384

Nadine Gordimer, *The Termitary* 390

                    A Soldier's Embrace 396

Caroline Gordon, *The Last Day in the Field* 408

Graham Greene, *The Destructors* 415

Nathaniel Hawthorne, *The Minister's Black Veil—A Parable*......... 427

Ernest Hemingway, *The Killers* 438

Langston Hughes, *Thank You, M'am*............................. 446

Zora Neal Hurston, *The Gilded Six-Bits* 450

Henry James, *The Beast in the Jungle*............................ 460

Sarah Orne Jewett, *A White Heron*.............................. 495

James Joyce, *The Dead* 504

Franz Kafka, *In the Penal Colony*................................ 537

Maxine Hong Kingston, *No Name Woman* 558

Perri Klass, *Bloomingdale's* 568

Ring Lardner, *Haircut* 573

D. H. Lawrence, *The Rocking Horse Winner*....................... 582

Ursula Le Guin, *The Ones Who Walk Away from Omelas*........... 595

Doris Lessing, *To Room 19* 601

James Alan McPherson, *Gold Coast* 627

Naguib Mahfouz, *The Whisper of Madness* 645

Bernard Malamud, *The Magic Barrel* 650

Katherine Mansfield, *Bliss*..................................... 664

Paule Marshall, *Brooklyn* 675

Guy de Maupassant, *The Necklace* 691

Yukio Mishima, *Patriotism* **698**
N. Scott Momaday, *House Made of Dawn:* Three Sketches............ **717**
Toshio Mori, *Slant-Eyed Americans* **727**
Toni Morrison, *1919* **732**
Alice Munro, *How I Met My Husband* **738**
Joyce Carol Oates, *How I Contemplated the World From the Detroit
    House of Correction and Began My Life Over Again* **752**
Edna O'Brien, *A Journey* **766**
Flannery O'Connor, *The Geranium* **775**
                    Judgement Day **785**
Frank O'Connor, *Guests of the Nation* **800**
Tillie Olsen, *I Stand Here Ironing* **810**
Amos Oz, *Nomad and Viper* **817**
Cynthia Ozick, *The Shawl* **831**
Grace Paley, *A Conversation with My Father* **835**
Dorothy Parker, *Big Blonde* **840**
Ann Petry, *The Witness* **858**
Edgar Allan Poe, *The Fall of the House of Usher* **873**
Katherine Anne Porter, *Flowering Judas* **888**
Jean Rhys, *Mannequin* **898**
Alain Robbe-Grillet, *The Secret Room* **903**
Philip Roth, *The Conversion of the Jews* **907**
Evelyn Scott, *Kalicz* **920**
Leslie Silko, *Yellow Woman* **932**
Isaac Bashevis Singer, *Gimpel the Fool* **941**
John Steinbeck, *The Chrysanthemums* **953**
Peter Taylor, *Rain in the Heart* **962**
James Thurber, *The Secret Life of Walter Mitty* **977**
Leo Tolstoy, *The Three Hermits* **982**
Jean Toomer, *Fern* **988**
John Updike, *A & P*. **992**
Alice Walker, *Everyday Use* **998**
                    Roselily **1006**
Robert Penn Warren, *Blackberry Winter* **1011**
Eudora Welty, *Why I Live at the P.O.*.............................. **1029**
Edith Wharton, *Roman Fever* **1040**
William Carlos Williams, *The Use of Force* **1051**

Virginia Woolf, *Kew Gardens* **1055**
Richard Wright, *The Man Who Was Almost a Man* **1061**
Questions and Commentaries for Discussion and Writing **1071**
Copyright Acknowledgments **1192**
Index of Titles **1197**

THEMATIC
TABLE OF CONTENTS

Note: Some stories may be studied under several headings. There is a pattern in the sequence of the thirteen theme headings, beginning with "Shapes of Love and Hate," moving on to "Male-Female" Relationships," and then on to "The Family and Conflict of Generations," and so on. Within each section, several stories are paired for comparison and contrast.

1. Shapes of Love and Hate

A Journey O'Brien 766
The Story of An Hour Chopin 246
To Room 19 Lessing 601
My Man Bovanne Bambara 69
What We Talk About When We Talk About Love Carver 164
Roman Fever Wharton 1040
Roselily Walker 1006
The Bride Comes To Yellow Sky Crane 249
Thank You, M'am Hughes 446

2. Male-Female Relationships

The Necklace Maupassant 691
Flowering Judas Porter 888
How I Met My Husband Munro 738
The Magic Barrel Malamud 650
Bliss Mansfield 664
Shifting Beattie 97
The Darling Chekhov 216

The Gilded Six-Bits   Hurston **450**

Fern   Toomer **988**

Big Blonde   Parker **840**

3.   The Family and Conflict of Generations

Paul's Case   Cather **174**

The Silence of the Llano   Anaya **17**

That Evening Sun   Faulkner **308**

How I Contemplated the World . . .   Oates **752**

Just Like a Tree   Gaines **352**

A Conversation with My Father   Paley **835**

No Name Woman   Kingston **558**

I Stand Here Ironing   Olsen **810**

Significant Moments in the Life of My Mother   Atwood **42**

Everyday Use   Walker **998**

Food for All His Dead   Chin **236**

The Termitary   Gordimer **390**

House Made of Dawn: Three Sketches   Momaday **717**

4.   Initiation from Innocence to Experience

That Evening Sun   Faulkner **308**

Paul's Case   Cather **174**

1919   Morrison **732**

Blackberry Winter   Warren **1011**

The Rocking Horse Winner   Lawrence **582**

Willow Game   Chavez **190**

The Killers   Hemingway **438**

A White Heron   Jewett **495**

A&P   Updike.. **992**

5.   Friendship and Brotherhood

The Last Day in the Field   Gordon............................. **408**

Just Like a Tree   Gaines **352**

The Guest   Camus **153**

New Best Friends   Adams **6**

Communist   Ford **339**

Guests of the Nation   O'Connor **800**

6. Illusion and Reality

The Necklace Maupassant **691**
Kew Gardens Woolf **1055**
Paul's Case Cather **174**
The Garden of Forking Paths Borges **133**
The Secret Room Robbe-Grillet **903**
Lost in the Funhouse Barth **74**

7. Self-Deception and Self-Discovery

Flowering Judas Porter **888**
How I Contemplated the World . . . Oates **752**
Paul's Case Cather **174**
Gold Coast McPherson **627**
Haircut Lardner **573**
The Chrysanthemums Steinbeck **953**
The Secret Life of Walter Mitty Thurber **977**
The Swimmer Cheever **197**
The Dead Joyce **504**
Gooseberries Chekhov **207**
The Beast in the Jungle James **460**
Balthazar's Marvelous Afternoon García Márquez **384**
Babylon Revisited Fitzgerald **322**
Seeds Anderson **31**
A Rose For Emily Faulkner **300**
That Evening Sun Faulkner **308**
Why I Live at the P.O. Welty **1029**
Rain in the Heart Taylor **962**

8. Alienation

Paul's Case Cather **174**
Gimpel the Fool Singer **941**
The Conversion of the Jews Roth **907**
How I Contemplated the World . . . Oates **752**
Flowering Judas Porter **888**
Kalicz Scott **920**
The Ones Who Walk Away from Omelas Le Guin **595**
Flying Home Ellison **276**

House Made of Dawn: Three Sketches   Momaday 717

Mannequin   Rhys 898

Bloomingdale's   Klass 568

See Section 10: Race Relations

9.   The Individual Against Society

Paul's Case   Cather 174

The Conversion of the Jews   Roth 907

The Guest   Camus 153

1919   Morrison 732

Looking for Mr. Green   Bellow 108

The Whisper of Madness   Mahfouz 645

See Section 10: Race Relations

10.   Race Relations

That Evening Sun   Faulkner 308

1919   Morrison 732

King of the Bingo Game   Ellison 268

Flying Home   Ellison 276

The Reunion   Angelou 37

Just Like a Tree   Gaines 352

Going to Meet the Man   Baldwin 55

Yellow Woman   Silko 932

The Shawl   Ozick 831

Nomad and Viper   Oz 817

The Guest   Camus 153

A Soldier's Embrace   Gordimer 396

Flowering Judas   Porter 888

The Wife of His Youth   Chesnutt 226

The Man Who Was Almost a Man   Wright 1061

The Red Convertible   Erdrich 292

Slant-Eyed Americans   Mori 727

The Geranium   O'Connor 775

Judgement Day   O'Connor 785

The Witness   Petry 858

Brooklyn   Marshall 675

11. Shapes of Violence

The Use of Force   Williams 1051
1919   Morrison 732
How I Contemplated the World . . .   Oates 752
Civil Peace   Achebe 1
The Destructors   Greene 415
The Killers   Hemingway 438
Patriotism   Mishima 698
The Witness   Petry 858

12. Mortality: Death and Old Age

The Last Day in the Field   Gordon................................. 408
The King of Jazz   Barthelme 93
Just Like a Tree   Gaines 352
Acceptance of Their Ways   Gallant 371
An Occurrence at Owl Creek Bridge   Bierce 125
Rest Cure   Boyle 147

13. Man Against Supernatural Forces

Yellow Woman   Silko 932
The Rocking Horse Winner   Lawrence 582
The Demon Lover   Bowen 141
The Sailor-Boy's Tale   Dinesen 259
The Fall of the House of Usher   Poe 873
A Very Old Man with Enormous Wings   García Márquez.............. 378

14. Spiritual Struggles

The Three Hermits   Tolstoy 982
The Minister's Black Veil—A Parable   Hawthorne 427
In the Penal Colony   Kafka 537

11. Shapes of Violence

The Use of Force, Williams 1051
1919, Morrison 758
How I Contemplated the World..., Oates 752
Civil Peace, Achebe 111
The Parsley Garden, Saroyan 418
The Killers, Hemingway 458
Poetonga Mishipa 698
The Kitchen, Ferry 658

12. Mortality: Death and Old Age

The Last Day in the Field, Gordon 808
The King of Jazz, Barthelme 98
Just Tree Tree, Gaines 502
Acceptance of Their Way, Gallant 971
An Occurrence at Owl Creek Bridge, Bierce 128
Rest Cure, Boyle 847

13. Man Against Supernatural Forces

Yellow Woman, Silko 532
The Rocking Horse Winner, Lawrence 582
The Demon Lover, Bowen 111
The Sailor-Boys Tale, Dinesen 558
The Fall of the House of Usher, Poe 858
A Very Old Man with Enormous Wings, García Márquez 378

14. Spiritual Struggles

The Three Hermits, Tolstoy 968
The Minister's Black Veil—A Parable, Hawthorne 427
In the Penal Colony, Kafka 581

Civil Peace

CHINUA ACHEBE

Jonathan Iwegbu counted himself extra-ordinarily lucky. "Happy survival!" meant so much more to him than just a current fashion of greeting old friends in the first hazy days of peace. It went deep to his heart. He had come out of the war with five inestimable blessings—his head, his wife Maria's head and the heads of three out of their four children. As a bonus he also had his old bicycle—a miracle too but naturally not to be compared to the safety of five human heads.

The bicycle had a little history of its own. One day at the height of the war it was commandeered "for urgent military action." Hard as its loss would have been to him he would still have let it go without a thought had he not had some doubts about the genuineness of the officer. It wasn't his disreputable rags, nor the toes peeping out of one blue and one brown canvas shoes, nor yet the two stars of his rank done obviously in a hurry in biro, that troubled Jonathan; many good and heroic soldiers looked the same or worse. It was rather a certain lack of grip and firmness in his manner. So Jonathan, suspecting he might be amenable to influence, rummaged in his raffia bag and produced the two pounds with which he had been going to buy firewood which his wife, Maria, retailed to camp officials for extra stock-fish and corn meal, and got his bicycle back. That night he buried it in the little clearing in the bush where the dead of the camp, including his own youngest son, were buried. When he dug it up again a year later after the surrender all it needed was a little palm-oil greasing. "Nothing puzzles God," he said in wonder.

He put it to immediate use as a taxi and accumulated a small pile of Biafran money ferrying camp officials and their families across the four-mile stretch to the nearest tarred road. His standard charge per trip was six pounds and those who had the money were only glad to be rid of some of it in this way. At the end of a fortnight he had made a small fortune of one hundred and fifteen pounds.

1

Then he made the journey to Enugu and found another miracle waiting for him. It was unbelievable. He rubbed his eyes and looked again and it was still standing there before him. But, needless to say, even that monumental blessing must be accounted also totally inferior to the five heads in the family. This newest miracle was his little house in Ogui Overside. Indeed nothing puzzles God! Only two houses away a huge concrete edifice some wealthy contractor had put up just before the war was a mountain of rubble. And here was Jonathan's little zinc house of no regrets built with mud blocks quite intact! Of course the doors and windows were missing and five sheets off the roof. But what was that? And anyhow he had returned to Enugu early enough to pick up bits of old zinc and wood and soggy sheets of cardboard lying around the neighbourhood before thousands more came out of their forest holes looking for the same things. He got a destitute carpenter with one old hammer, a blunt plane and a few bent and rusty nails in his tool bag to turn this assortment of wood, paper and metal into door and window shutters for five Nigerian shillings or fifty Biafran pounds. He paid the pounds, and moved in with his overjoyed family carrying five heads on their shoulders.

His children picked mangoes near the military cemetery and sold them to soldiers' wives for a few pennies—real pennies this time—and his wife started making breakfast akara balls for neighbours in a hurry to start life again. With his family earnings he took his bicycle to the villages around and bought fresh palm-wine which he mixed generously in his rooms with the water which had recently started running again in the public tap down the road, and opened up a bar for soldiers and other lucky people with good money.

At first he went daily, then every other day and finally once a week, to the offices of the Coal Corporation where he used to be a miner, to find out what was what. The only thing he did find out in the end was that that little house of his was even a greater blessing than he had thought. Some of his fellow ex-miners who had nowhere to return at the end of the day's waiting just slept outside the doors of the offices and cooked what meal they could scrounge together in Bournvita tins. As the weeks lengthened and still nobody could say what was what Jonathan discontinued his weekly visits altogether and faced his palm-wine bar.

But nothing puzzles God. Came the day of the windfall when after five days of endless scuffles in queues and counter-queues in the sun outside the Treasury he had twenty pounds counted into his palms as ex-gratia award for the rebel money he had turned in. It was like Christmas for him and for many others like him when the payments began. They called it (since few could manage its proper official name) *egg-rasher*.

As soon as the pound notes were placed in his palm Jonathan simply closed it tight over them and buried fist and money inside his trouser pocket. He had to be extra careful because he had seen a man a couple of days earlier collapse into near-madness in an instant before that oceanic crowd because no sooner had he got his twenty pounds than some heartless ruffian picked it off him. Though it was not right that a man in such an extremity of agony should be blamed yet many in the queues that day were able to remark quietly on the victim's carelessness, especially after he pulled out the innards of his pocket and revealed a hole in it big enough to pass a thief's head. But of course he had insisted that the money had been in the other pocket, pulling it out too to show its comparative wholeness. So one had to be careful.

Jonathan soon transferred the money to his left hand and pocket so as to leave his right free for shaking hands should the need arise, though by fixing his gaze at such an elevation as to miss all approaching human faces he made sure that the need did not arise, until he got home.

He was normally a heavy sleeper but that night he heard all the neighbourhood noises die down one after another. Even the night watchman who knocked the hour on some metal somewhere in the distance had fallen silent after knocking one o'clock. That must have been the last thought in Jonathan's mind before he was finally carried away himself. He couldn't have been gone for long, though, when he was violently awakened again.

"Who is knocking?" whispered his wife lying beside him on the floor.

"I don't know," he whispered back breathlessly.

The second time the knocking came it was so loud and imperious that the rickety old door could have fallen down.

"Who is knocking?" he asked then, his voice parched and trembling.

"Na tief-man and him people," came the cool reply. "Make you hopen de door." This was followed by the heaviest knocking of all.

Maria was the first to raise the alarm, then he followed and all their children.

"Police-o! Thieves-o! Neighbours-o! Police-o! We are lost! We are dead! Neighbours, are you asleep? Wake up! Police-o!"

This went on for a long time and then stopped suddenly. Perhaps they had scared the thief away. There was total silence. But only for a short while.

"You done finish?" asked the voice outside. "Make we help you small. Oya, everybody!"

"Police-o! Tief-man-o! Neighbours-o! we done loss-o! Police-o! . . ."

There were at least five other voices besides the leader's.

Jonathan and his family were now completely paralysed by terror. Maria and the children sobbed inaudibly like lost souls. Jonathan groaned continuously.

The silence that followed the thieves' alarm vibrated horribly. Jonathan all but begged their leader to speak again and be done with it.

"My frien," said he at long last, "we don try our best for call dem but I tink say dem all done sleep-o . . . So wetin we go do now? Sometaim you wan call soja? Or you wan make we call dem for you? Soja better pass police. No be so?"

"Na so!" replied his men. Jonathan thought he heard even more voices now than before and groaned heavily. His legs were sagging under him and his throat felt like sand-paper.

"My frien, why you no de talk again. I de ask you say you wan make we call soja?"

"No."

"Awrighto. Now make we talk business. We no be bad tief. We no like for make trouble. Trouble done finish. War done finish and all the katakata wey de for inside. No Civil War again. This time na Civil Peace. No be so?"

"Na so!" answered the horrible chorus.

"What do you want from me? I am a poor man. Everything I had went with this war. Why do you come to me? You know people who have money. We . . ."

"Awright! We know say you no get plenty money. But we sef no get even anini. So derefore make you open dis window and give us one hundred pound and we go commot. Orderwise we de come for inside now to show you guitar-boy like dis . . ."

A volley of automatic fire rang through the sky. Maria and the children began to weep aloud again.

"Ah, missisi de cry again. No need for dat. We done talk say we na good tief. We just take our small money and go nwayorly. No molest. Abi we de molest?"

"At all!" sang the chorus.

"My friends," began Jonathan hoarsely. "I hear what you say and I thank you. If I had one hundred pounds . . ."

"Lookia my frien, no be play we come play for your house. If we make mistake and step for inside you no go like am-o. So derefore . . ."

"To God who made me; if you come inside and find one hundred pounds, take it and shoot me and shoot my wife and children. I swear to God. The only money I have in this life is this twenty-pounds *egg-rasher* they gave me today . . ."

"OK. Time de go. Make you open dis window and bring the twenty pound. We go manage am like dat."

There were now loud murmurs of dissent among the chorus: "Na lie de man de lie; e get plenty money . . . Make we go inside and search properly well . . . Wetin be twenty pound? . . ."

"Shurrup!" rang the leader's voice like a lone shot in the sky and silenced the murmuring at once. "Are you dere? Bring the money quick!"

"I am coming," said Jonathan fumbling in the darkness with the key of the small wooden box he kept by his side on the mat.

At the first sign of light as neighbours and others assembled to commiserate with him he was already strapping his five-gallon demijohn to his bicycle carrier and his wife, sweating in the open fire, was turning over akara balls in a wide clay bowl of boiling oil. In the corner his eldest son was rinsing out dregs of yesterday's palm-wine from old beer bottles.

"I count it as nothing," he told his sympathizers, his eyes on the rope he was tying. "What is *egg-rasher*? Did I depend on it last week? Or is it greater than other things that went with the war? I say, let *egg-rasher* perish in the flames! Let it go where everything else has gone. Nothing puzzles God."

New Best Friends

ALICE ADAMS

"The McElroys really don't care about seeing us anymore—aren't you aware of that?" Jonathan Ferris rhetorically and somewhat drunkenly demands of his wife, Sarah Stein.

Evenly she answers him, "Yes, I can see that."

But he stumbles on, insisting, "We're low, *very* low, on their priority list."

"I *know*."

Jonathan and Sarah are finishing dinner, and too much wine, on one of the hottest nights of August—in Hilton, a mid-Southern town, to which they moved (were relocated) six months ago; Jonathan works for a computer corporation. They bought this new fake-Colonial house, out in some scrubby pinewoods, where now, in the sultry, sulfurous paralyzing twilight no needle stirs, and only mosquitoes give evidence of life, buzz-diving against the window screens.

In New York, in their pretty Bleecker Street apartment, with its fern-shaded courtyard, Sarah would have taken Jonathan's view of the recent McElroy behavior as an invitation to the sort of talk they both enjoyed: insights, analyses—and, from Sarah, somewhat literary speculations. Their five-year marriage has always included a great deal of talk, of just this sort.

However, now, as he looks across the stained blond maple table that came, inexorably, with the bargain-priced house, across plates of wilted food that they were too hot and tired to eat—as he focusses on her face Jonathan realizes that Sarah, who never cries, is on the verge of tears; and also that he is too drunk to say anything that would radically revise what he has already said.

Sarah does begin to cry. "I know we're low on their list," she chokes. "But after all we only met them a couple of months before they moved away. And they'd always lived here. They have family, friends. I've always accepted that. I even said it to you. So why do you have to point it out?"

If he could simply get to his feet, could walk around the table and say, I'm sorry, I didn't mean it—then at least temporarily there would be an improvement in the air between them, a lifting of the heavy night's burden. But Jonathan cannot move; it is so hot his shirt is still stuck to his back, as it has been all day. And he is exhausted.

Besides, what he just said about the McElroys (who at first seemed an instrument of salvation; Sarah was crazy about them) is all too true: Hugh and Hattie McElroy, who moved to Santa Fe in June, now are back for the wedding of a son, and Sarah has barely seen them. And she used to see Hattie almost every day. On this visit, though, the McElroys have come to Sarah and Jonathan's once for dinner, and Sarah saw Hattie at a large lunch party (given by Hattie's old friend Popsie Hooker).

Of course, having lived here forever, the McElroys are indeed involved with family and friends, as Sarah has just said. But really, Jonathan now furiously thinks (as Sarah must have thought), at least they could call her; they could meet for tea, or something.

Weeping, Sarah looks blotchy, aged, distorted; her fine, just-not-sharp features are blurred. "Piquant" is the word that Jonathan's mother has found for Sarah's face. "Well, I wouldn't call her pretty, in any conventional way, but her face is so intelligent, so—piquant." To Jonathan, her face is simply that, her own; he is so close to her that he rarely thinks about it, except that a sudden, unexpected sight of her can deeply move him still. She simply looks like a young woman who is crying, almost any young woman.

Thinking this, it occurs to Jonathan that he has never seen another man cry, and he himself would like to weep, at this moment; it is so hot, they are both so unhappy, everything seems lost. He pulls himself together, though, after this frightening thought, and then he remembers that in fact he did see his own father in tears, as he lay dying, in Mass. General Hospital; big heavy tears ran down his father's long lined white face.

"You must think I'm really stupid," Sarah gets out.

No, you're the brightest girl I ever met, Jonathan does not say. Nor does he add, But that was a stupid remark.

Stupid is the last thing that Sarah is, actually, and during their New York married life (before *this*) she had no trouble getting the part-time editorial jobs that she liked, or books to review. Those occupations used to absorb much of Sarah's time, and her plentiful energy, and Jonathan knows that lack of any such work down here contributes to her unhappiness; it is not just disappointment with the McElroys.

In New York, in a vague, optimistic way (they have been generally happy people, for these times), as they discussed the projected move to Hilton, Sarah and Jonathan assured each other that since it was a university town, not just any old backward Southern city, there would be work of some sort available to her, at the university press, or somewhere. Saying which they forgot one crucial fact, which is that in or around any university there are hundreds of readily exploitable bright students' wives, or students, who grasp at all possible, however low-paying, semi-intellectual work.

And so for Sarah there has been little to do, in the too large, uncharming house, which (Jonathan has unhappily recognized) Sarah has been keeping much too clean. All her scrubbing and waxing, her dusting and polishing have a quality of desperation, as well as being out of character; his old busy Sarah was cheerfully untidy, which was quite all right with Jonathan, who did not mind housework.

Unsteadily, they now clear the table and wash up. They go upstairs to bed; they try to sleep, in the thick damp heat.

Sarah and Jonathan's first month in Hilton, February, was terrible for them both. Cold, dark and windy, and wet, a month of almost unrelenting rains, which turned the new red clay roads leading out to their house into tortuous slicks, deeply rutted, with long wide puddles of muddy red water, sometimes just frozen at the edges. Cold damp drafts penetrated their barnlike house; outside, in the woods, everything dripped, boughs sagged, and no birds sang.

March was a little better: not yet spring, none of the promised balmy Southern blue, and no flowers, but at least the weather cleared; and the blustery winds, though cold, helped to dry the roads, and to cleanse the air.

And, one night at dinner, Sarah announced that she had met a really wonderful woman, in a bookstore. "My new best friend," she said, with a tiny, half-apologetic laugh, as Jonathan's heart sank, a little. They both knew her tendency toward somewhat ill-advised enthusiasms: the charming editor who turned out to be a lively alcoholic, given to midnight (and later) phone calls; the smart young film critic who made it instantly clear that she hated all their other friends. The long line of initially wonderful people, the new best friends, who in one way or another became betrayers of Sarah's dreams of friendship.

However, there was another, larger group of friends she'd had for years, who were indeed all that Sarah said they were, smart and loyal and generous and fun. Jonathan liked those friends, now his friends, too. Life with Sarah had, in fact, made him more gregarious, changing him from a solitary, overeducated young man with a boring corporation job, despite an advanced degree in math, into a warmer, friendlier person. Sarah's talkative, cheery friends were among her early charms for Jonathan. He simply wondered at her occasional lapses in judgment.

Hattie McElroy, the new best friend (and the owner, it turned out, of the bookstore where they had met), was very Southern, Sarah said; she was from Hilton. However, except for her accent (which Sarah imitated, very funnily), she did not seem Southern. "She reads so much, I guess it gives her perspective," Sarah said. And, with a small pleased laugh, "She doesn't like it here very much. She says she's so tired of everyone she knows. They're moving to Santa Fe in June. Unfortunately, for me."

After that, all Sarah's days seemed to include a visit to Hattie's bookstore, where Hattie served up mugs of tea, Sarah said, along with "super" gossip about everyone in town. "There's an old group that's unbelievably stuffy," Sarah reported to Jonathan. "People Hattie grew up with. They never even want to meet anyone new. Especially Yankees." And she laughed, happy to have such an exclusive connection with her informative and amusing new friend.

"Any chance you could take over the bookstore when they leave?" asked Jonathan, early on. "Maybe we could buy it?" This was during the period of Sarah's unhappy discovery about the work situation in Hilton, the gradually apparent fact of there being nothing for her.

"Well, the most awful thing. She sold it to a chain, and just before we got here. She feels terrible, but she says there didn't seem any other way out, no one else came around to buy it. And the chain people are even bringing in their own manager." Sarah's laugh was rueful, and her small chin pointed downward as she added, "One more dead end. And damn, it would have been perfect for me."

The next step, Jonathan dimly imagined, would be a party or dinner of some sort at the McElroys', which he could not help mildly dreading, as he remembered the film critic's party, at which not only was almost everyone else gay (that would have been all right, except that some of the women did seem very hostile, to him) but they all smoked—heavily, some of them pipes and cigars—in three tiny rooms on Horatio Street.

However, it was they who were to entertain the McElroys at dinner, Sarah told him. "And I think just the four of us," she added. "That way it's easier, and I can make something great. And besides, who else?"

All true: an imaginative but fluky cook, Sarah did best on a small scale. And, too, the only other people they knew were fellow-transferees, as displaced and possibly as lonely as themselves, but otherwise not especially sympathetic.

The first surprise about Hattie McElroy, that first April night, was her size: she was a very big woman, with wild bleached straw-looking hair and round doll-blue eyes, and about twenty years older than Jonathan would have imagined; Sarah spoke of her as of a contemporary. Hugh McElroy was tall and gray and somewhat dim.

And Hattie was a very funny woman. Over drinks, she started right in with a description of a party she had been to the night before. "I was wearing this perfectly all-right dress, even if it was a tad on the oldish side," Hattie told them, as she sipped at her gin. "And Popsie Hooker—Can you imagine a woman my age, and still called Popsie? We went to Sunday school together, and she hasn't changed one bit. Anyway, Popsie said to me, 'Oh, I just love that dress you're wearing. I was so sorry when they went out of style five years ago.' Can you imagine? Isn't she marvellous? I just love Popsie, I truly do."

For such a big woman, Hattie's laugh was small, a little-girl laugh, but Jonathan found himself drawn to her big friendly teeth, her crazy hair.

Sarah, it then turned out, had met Popsie Hooker; early on in their stay in Hilton she had gone to a luncheon that Popsie gave for the new corporation wives. And, Sarah told Hattie, "She made a little speech that I didn't quite understand. About how she knew we were all very busy, so please not to write any thank-you notes. It was odd, I thought."

Hattie's chuckle increased in volume. "Oh, you don't understand Southern talk, not at all! I can tell you don't. That meant you were all supposed to write notes, and say you just couldn't resist writing, even if she said not to, since her lunch party was just so lovely."

Sarah laughed, too. "Well, dumb me. I took her at her word, and didn't write."

"Well, honey, you'll larn. But I can tell you, it takes near 'bout a lifetime."

Dinner was not one of Sarah's more successful efforts: veal Orloff, one of her specialties, but this time a little burned.

Hattie, though, seemed to think it was wonderful. "Oh, the trouble you must have gone to! And you must have a way with your butcher. I've just never seen veal like this—not down here."

Jonathan felt that she was overdoing it, but then chided himself: Hattie was Southern, after all; that was how they talked. He must not be negative.

"These mushrooms are truly delicious," Hugh McElroy put in. In Jonathan's view, a truer remark. Hugh was a kind and quiet man, who reminded Jonathan of someone; in an instant, to his mild surprise, he realized that it was his own father, whose shy manner had been rather like Hugh's.

A good evening, then. Jonathan could honestly say to Sarah that he liked her new best friends; they could even laugh over a few of the former candidates for that title.

Their return invitation, to a party at the McElroys', was less fun all around: too many people, in a cluttered but surprisingly formal house, on a too hot night in May. But by then it was almost time for the McElroys to leave, and Hattie had explained to Sarah that they just had to have all those people.

"They're really so loved around here," Sarah somewhat tipsily remarked, as they drove home from that party. "It just won't be the same town."

"It's still very pretty," Jonathan reminded her. "Smell the flowers."

The spring that had finally arrived, after so much rain, had seemed a reward for patience, with its extraordinary gifts of roses, azaleas, even gardenias, everywhere blooming, wafting sweetness into the light night air. And out in the woods white lacings of dogwood had appeared.

For some reason ("I can't think why! I must be going plumb crazy!" Hattie had confided to Sarah), Hattie and Hugh had agreed to be photographed over local TV on the day of their departure, and that night, on a news program, there they were: big Hattie, in her navy linen travelling suit, her white teeth all revealed in a grin for the camera, as she clutched an overflowing tote bag and tried to pin on a cluster of pink camellias; and tall Hugh, a shy smile as he waved an envelope of airline tickets.

As, watching, Sarah, who never cried, burst into tears.

And then they were gone, the McElroys. Moved out to New Mexico.

Sarah moped around. Indifferent housekeeping, minimal efforts. She made thrifty, ordinary meals, so unlike her usual adventurous, rather splashy culinary style, and she lost all interest in how she looked. Not that she was ever given to extravagance in those matters, but she used to wash and brush her hair a lot, and she did something to her eyes, some color, that Jonathan now recognized as missing, gone.

She often wrote to the McElroys, and Hattie answered, often; Sarah produced the letters for Jonathan to read at dinner. They contained a lot about the scenery, the desert, and fairly amusing gossip about what Hattie referred to as the Locals. "You would not believe the number of painters here, and the galleries. Seems like there's an opening most every night, and the Local Folk all come out in their fancy silver jewelry and their great big silver belts. Whole lots of the men are fairies, of course, but I just don't care. They're a lot of fun, they are indeed gay people." Funny, longish letters, with the sound of Hattie's voice, always ending with strong protestations of love and friendship. "Oh, we love you and miss you so much, the both of us!" cried out Hattie, on her thin flowered writing paper.

Jonathan observed all this with dark and ragged emotions—Sarah's deep sadness and the occasional cheer that Hattie's letters brought. He cared about Sarah in a permanent and complex way that made her pain his; still, what looked like true mourning for the absent McElroys gave him further pain. He had to wonder: was he jealous of the McElroys? And he had to concede that he was, in a way. He thought, I am not enough for her, and at the same time he recognized the foolishness of that thought. No one is "enough" for anyone, of course not. What Sarah needs is a job, and more friends that she likes; he knew that perfectly well.

And then one night at dinner, near the first of August, came the phone call from Hattie; Jonathan overheard a lot of exclamations and shouts, gasps from Sarah, who came back to the table all breathless, flushed.

"They're here! The McElroys are back, and staying at the Inn. Just for a visit. One of their boys suddenly decided to marry his girlfriend. Isn't that great?"

Well, it turned out not to be great. There was the dinner at Jonathan and Sarah's house, to which the McElroys came late, from another party (and not hungry; one of Sarah's most successful efforts wasted), and they left rather early. "You would not believe the day we have ahead of us tomorrow! And we thought marrying off a son was supposed to be easy." And the luncheon at Popsie Hooker's.

Jonathan and Sarah were not invited to the wedding, a fact initially excused (maybe overexcused) by Sarah: "We're not the Old Guard, not old Hiltonians, and besides, it's the bride's list, not Hattie's, and we don't even know her, or her family."

And then two weeks of the McElroy visit had passed, accurately calculated by Jonathan. Which calculation led to his fatal remarks, over all that wine, about the priorities of the McElroys.

On the morning after that terrible evening, Jonathan and Sarah have breakfast together as usual, but rather sombrely. Hung over, sipping at tea, nibbling at overripe late-summer fruit, Jonathan wonders what he can say, since he cannot exactly deny the truth of his unfortunate words.

At last he brings out "I'm really sorry I said that, about Hattie and Hugh."

Sarah gives him an opaque, level look, and her voice is judicious as she says, "Well, I'm sure you were right."

One of the qualities that Jonathan has always found exciting in Sarah is her ability to surprise him; she rarely behaves in ways that he would have predicted. Nevertheless, having worried intermittently during the day over her sadness, her low spirits and his own recent part in further lowering them, he is delighted (ah, his old astonishing Sarah) to find her all brushed and bright-eyed, happy, when he comes in the door that night.

"Well, I decided that all this moping around like an abandoned person was really silly," she tells him, over cold before-dinner glasses of wine, in the bright hot flower-scented dusk. "And so I just called Hattie, not being accusatory or anything. I just said that I'd really missed seeing her—them."

"Well, *great*." Jonathan is thinking how he admires her; she is fundamentally honest, and brave. And so pretty tonight, her delicately pointed face, her lively brown hair.

"Hattie couldn't have been nicer. She said they'd missed us, of course, but they just got so caught up in this wedding business. It's next Saturday—I'd lost track. They truly haven't had one minute, she told me, and I can believe her. Anyway, they're coming for supper on Sunday night. She

said a post-wedding collapse would be just the best thing they could possibly think of."

"Well, great," Jonathan repeats, although some dim, indefinable misgiving has edged into his mind. How can one evening of friends at dinner be
as terrific as this one will have to be? That question, after moments,
emerges, and with it a darker, more sinister one: suppose it isn't terrific at
all, as the last one was not?

By mid-August, in Hilton, it has been hot for so long that almost all the
flowers have wilted, despite an occasional thundershower. Many people are
away at that time, and in neglected gardens overblown roses shed fat satin
petals onto drying, yellowing grass; in forgotten orchards sweet unpicked
fruit falls and spatters, fermenting, slowly rotting, among tall summer
weeds, in the simmering heat.

The Saturday of the McElroy son's wedding, however, is surprisingly
cool, with an almost New England briskness in the air. That familiar-feeling
air gives Jonathan an irrational flutter of hope: maybe the next night, Sunday, will be a reasonable evening. With the sort of substantive conversation
that he and Sarah are used to, instead of some nutty Southern doubletalk.
With this hope, the thought comes to Jonathan that Hattie imitating Popsie
Hooker is really Hattie speaking her own true language. Dare he voice this
to Sarah, this interesting perception about the nature of mimicry? Probably
not.

Sarah spends a lot of Saturday cooking, so that it can all be served cold
on Sunday night; she makes several pretty vegetable aspics, and a cold mar-
inated beef salad. Frozen lemon soufflé. By Saturday night she is tired, but
she and Jonathan have a pleasant, quiet dinner together. He has helped
her on and off during the day, cutting up various things, and it is he who
makes their dinner: his one specialty, grilled chicken.

Their mood is more peaceful, more affectionate with each other than it
has been for months, Jonathan observes (since before they came down
here? quite possibly).

Outside, in the gathering, lowering dusk, the just perceptibly earlier twilight, fireflies glimmer dimly from the pinewoods. The breeze is just barely
cooler than most of their evening breezes, reminding Jonathan of the approach of fall—in his view, always a season of hope, of bright leaves on college campuses, and new courses offered.

*   *   *

Having worked so much the day before, Sarah and Jonathan have a richly
indolent morning; they laze about. Around noon the phone rings, and
Sarah goes to answer it. Jonathan, nearby, hears her say, "Oh, Hattie. Hi."

A very long pause, and then Sarah's voice, now stiff, all tightened up:

"Well, no, I don't see that as a good idea. We really don't know Popsie—"

Another long pause, as Sarah listens to whatever Hattie is saying, and then, "Of course I understand, I really do. But I just don't think that Jonathan and I—"

A shorter pause, before Sarah says again, "Of course I understand. I do. Well, sure. Give us a call. Well, bye."

As she comes out to where Jonathan stands, waiting for her, Sarah's face is very white, except for her pink-tipped nose—too pink. She says, "One more thing that Hattie, quote, couldn't get out of. A big post-wedding do at Popsie Hooker's. She said of course she knew I'd been working my head off over dinner for them, so why didn't we just put it all in a basket and bring it on over there. They'd come and help." Unconsciously, perhaps, Sarah has perfectly imitated Hattie's inflections—even a few prolonged vowels; the effect is of a devastating irony, at which Jonathan does not smile.

"Jesus" is all he says, staring at Sarah, at her glistening, darkening eyes, as he wonders what he can do.

Sarah rubs one hand across her face, very slowly. She says, "I'm so tired. I think I'll take a nap."

"Good idea. Uh, how about going out to dinner?"

"Well, why not?" Her voice is absolutely level, controlled.

"I'll put some things away," Jonathan offers.

"Oh, good."

In the too small, crowded kitchen, Jonathan neatly packages the food they were to have eaten in freezer paper; he seals up and labels it all. He hesitates at marking the date, such an unhappy reminder, but then he simply writes down the neutral numbers: 8, 19. By the time they get around to these particular packages they will not attach any significance to that date, he thinks (he hopes).

He considers a nap for himself; he, too, is tired, suddenly, but he decides on a walk instead.

The still, hot, scrubby pinewoods beyond their house are now a familiar place to Jonathan; he walks through the plumy, triumphant weeds, the Queen Anne's lace and luxuriant broomstraw, over crumbling, dry red clay. In the golden August sunlight, he considers what he has always recognized (or perhaps simply imagined that he saw) as a particular look of Sundays, in terms of weather. Even if somehow he did not know that it was Sunday, he believes, he could see that it was, in the motes of sunlight. Here, now, today, the light and the stillness have the same qualities of light and stillness as in long-past Sundays in the Boston suburb where he grew up.

Obviously, he next thinks, they will have to leave this place, he and Sarah; it is not working out for them here, nothing is. They will have to go back to New York, look around, resettle. And to his surprise he feels a sort of regret at the thought of leaving this land, all this red clay that he would have said he hated.

Immersed in these and further, more abstract considerations (old mathematical formulas for comfort, and less comforting thoughts about the future of the earth), Jonathan walks for considerably longer than he intended.

Hurrying, as he approaches the house (which already needs new paint, he distractedly notes), Jonathan does not at all know what to expect: Sarah still sleeping (or weeping) in bed? Sarah (unaccountably, horribly) gone?

What he does find, though, on opening the front door, is the living room visibly pulled together, all tidied up: a tray with a small bowl of ice, some salted almonds in another bowl, on the coffee table. And Sarah, prettily dressed, who smiles as she comes toward him. She is carrying a bottle of chilled white wine.

Jonathan first thinks, Oh, the McElroys must have changed their minds, they're coming. But then he sees that next to the ice bowl are two, and only two, glasses.

In a friendly, familiar way he and Sarah kiss, and she asks, "How was your walk?"

"It was good. I liked it. A real Sunday walk."

Later on, he will tell her what he thought about their moving away—and as Jonathan phrases that announcement he considers how odd it is for him to think of New York as "away."

Over their first glass of wine they talk in a neutral but slightly stilted way, the way of people who are postponing an urgent subject; the absence of the McElroys, their broken plans, trivializes any other topic.

At some point, in part to gain time, Jonathan asks her, "Have I seen that dress before?" (He is aware of the "husbandliness" of the question; classically, *they* don't notice.)

Sarah smiles, "Well, actually not. I bought it a couple of months ago. I just haven't worn it." And then, with a recognizable shift in tone, and a tightening of her voice, she plunges in. "Remember that night when you were talking about the McElroys? When you said we weren't so high on their priority list?"

Well, Jesus, of course he remembers, in detail; but Jonathan only says, very flatly, "Yes."

"Well, it's interesting. Of course I've been thinking about them all day, off and on. And what you said. And oh dear, how right you were. I mean, I knew you were *right*—that was partly what I objected to." Saying this, Sarah raises her face in a full look at him, acknowledging past pain.

What can he say? He is quiet, waiting, as she continues.

"But it's interesting, how you put it," she tells him. "How accurately. Prophetic, really. A lot of talk, and those letters! All about wonderful us, how great we are. But when you come right down to it—"

"The bottom line is old friends," Jonathan contributes, tentatively.

Pleased with him, Sarah laughs, or nearly; the sound she makes is closer to a small cough. But "Exactly," she says. "They poke a lot of fun at Popsie Hooker, but the reality is, that's where they are."

He tries again. "Friendships with outsiders don't really count? Does that cut out all Yankees, really?" He is thinking, Maybe we don't have to leave, after all? Maybe Sarah was just settling in? Eventually she will be all right here?

Grasping at only his stated question, about Yankees, Sarah gleefully answers, "Oh, very likely!" and she does laugh. "Because Yankees might do, oh, almost anything at all. You just can't trust a one of them."

As she laughs again, as she looks at Jonathan, he recognizes some obscure and nameless danger in the enthusiastic glitter of her eyes, and he has then the quite irrational thought that she is looking at him as though he were her new best friend.

However, he is able quickly to dismiss that flashed perception, in the happiness of having his old bright strong Sarah restored to him, their old mutually appreciative dialogue continuing.

He asks her, "Well, time to go out to dinner?"

"Oh, yes! Let's go," she says, quickly getting to her feet.

The Silence of the Llano

RUDOLFO A. ANAYA

His name was Rafael, and he lived on a ranch in the lonely and desolate llano. He had no close neighbors; the nearest home was many miles away on the dirt road which led to the small village of Las Animas. Rafael went to the village only once a month for provisions, quickly buying what he needed, never stopping to talk with the other rancheros who came to the general store to buy what they needed and to swap stories.

Long ago, the friends his parents had known stopped visiting Rafael. The people whispered that the silence of the llano had taken Rafael's soul, and they respected his right to live alone. They knew the hurt he suffered. The dirt road which led from the village to his ranch was overgrown with mesquite bushes and the sparse grasses of the flat country. The dry plain was a cruel expanse broken only by gullies and mesas spotted with juniper and piñon trees.

The people of this country knew the loneliness of the llano; they realized that sometimes the silence of the endless plain grew so heavy and oppressive it became unbearable. When a man heard voices in the wind of the llano, he knew it was time to ride to the village just to listen to the voices of other men. They knew that after many days of riding alone under the burning sun and listening only to the moaning wind, a man could begin to talk to himself. When a man heard the sound of his voice in the silence, he sensed the danger in his lonely existence. Then he would ride to his ranch, saddle a fresh horse, explain to his wife that he needed something in the village, a plug of tobacco, perhaps a new knife, or a jar of salve for deworming the cattle. It was a pretense, in his heart each man knew he went to break the hold of the silence.

Las Animas was only a mud-cluster of homes, a general store, a small church, a sparse gathering of life in the wide plain. The old men of the village sat on a bench in front of the store, shaded by the portal in summer, warmed by the southern sun in winter. They talked about the weather, the dry spells they had known as rancheros on the llano, the bad winters, the price of cattle and sheep. They sniffed the air and predicted the coming of the summer rains, and they discussed the news of the latest politics at the county seat.

The men who rode in listened attentively, nodding as they listened to the soft, full words of the old men, rocking back and forth on their boots, taking pleasure in the sounds they heard. Sometimes one of them would buy a bottle and they would drink and laugh and slap each other on the back as friends will do. Then, fortified by this simple act, each man returned home to share what he had heard with his family. Each would lie with his wife in the warm bed of night, the wind moaning softly outside, and he would tell the stories he had heard: so and so had died, someone they knew had married and moved away, the current price of wool and yearlings. The news of a world so far away was like a dream. The wife listened and was also fortified for the long days of loneliness. In adjoining rooms the children listened and heard the muffled sounds of the words and laughter of the father and mother. Later they would speak the words they heard as they cared for the ranch animals or helped the mother in the house, and in this way their own world grew and expanded.

Rafael knew well the silence of the llano. He was only fifteen when his father and mother died in a sudden, deadly blizzard which caught them on the road to Las Animas. Days later, when finally Rafael could break the snowdrifts for the horse, he had found them. There at La Angostura, where the road followed the edge of a deep arroyo, the horses had bolted or the wagon had slipped in the snow and ice. The wagon had overturned, pinning his father beneath the massive weight. His mother lay beside him, holding him in her arms. His father had been a strong man, he could have made a shelter, burned the wagon to survive the night, but pinned as he was he had been helpless and his wife could not lift the weight of the huge wagon. She had held him in her arms, covered both of them with her coat and blankets, but that night they had frozen. It took Rafael all day to dig graves in the frozen ground, then he buried them there, high on the slope of La Angostura where the summer rains would not wash away the graves.

That winter was cruel in other ways. Blizzards swept in from the north and piled the snowdrifts around the house. Snow and wind drove the cattle against the fences where they huddled together and suffocated as the drifts grew. Rafael worked night and day to try to save his animals, and still he lost half of the herd to the punishing storms. Only the constant work and simple words and phrases he remembered his father and mother speaking kept Rafael alive that winter.

Spring came, the land thawed, the calves were born, and the work of a new season began. But first Rafael rode to the place where he had buried his parents. He placed a cross over their common grave, then he rode to the village of Las Animas and told the priest what had happened. The people gathered and a Mass for the dead was prayed. The women cried and the men slapped Rafael on the back and offered their condolences. All grieved, they had lost good friends, but they knew that was the way of death on the llano, swift and sudden. Now the work of spring was on them. The herds had to be rebuilt after the terrible winter, fences needed mending. As the people returned to their work they forgot about Rafael.

But one woman in the village did not forget. She saw the loneliness in his face, she sensed the pain he felt at the loss of his parents. At first she felt pity when she saw him standing in the church alone, then she felt love. She knew about loneliness, she had lost her parents when she was very young and she had lived most of her life in a room at the back of the small adobe church. Her work was to keep the church clean and to take care of the old priest. It was this young woman who reached out and spoke to Rafael, and when he heard her voice he remembered the danger of the silence of the llano. He smiled and spoke to her. Thereafter, on Sundays he began to ride in to visit her. They would sit together during the Mass, and after that they would walk together to the general store where he would buy a small bag of hard sugar candy, and they would sit on the bench in front of the store, eat their candy and talk. The old people of the village as well as those who rode in from distant ranches knew Rafael was courting her, and knew it was good for both of them. The men tipped their hats as they passed by because Rafael was now a man.

Love grew between the young woman and Rafael. One day she said, "You need someone to take care of you. I will go with you." Her voice filled his heart with joy. They talked to the priest, and he married them, and after Mass there was a feast. The women set up tables in front of the church, covering them with their brightest table oil cloths, and they brought food which they served to everyone who had come to the celebration. The men drank whiskey and talked about the good grass growing high on the llano, and about the herds which would grow and multiply. One of the old men of the village brought out his violin, followed by his friend with his accordion. The two men played the old polkas and the varsilonas while the people danced on the hard-packed dirt in front of the church. The fiesta brought the people of the big and lonely llano together.

The violin and accordion music was accompanied by the clapping of hands and the stamping of feet. The dancing was lively and the people were happy. They laughed and congratulated the young couple. They brought gifts, kitchen utensils for the young bride, ranch tools for Rafael, whiskey for everyone who would drink, real whiskey bought in the general store, not the mula some of the men made in their stills. Even Rafael took a drink, his first drink with the men, and he grew flushed and happy with it. He danced every dance with his young wife and everyone could see that his love was deep and devoted. He laughed with the men when they slapped his back and whispered advice for the wedding night. Then the wind began to rise and it started to rain; the first huge drops mixed with the blowing dust. People sought cover, others hitched their wagons and headed home, all calling their goodbyes and buena suerte in the gathering wind. And so Rafael lifted his young bride onto his horse and they waved goodbye to the remaining villagers as they, too, rode away, south, deep into the empty llano, deep into the storm which came rumbling across the sky with thunder and lightning flashes, pushing the cool wind before it.

And that is how the immense silence of the land and the heavy burden of loneliness came to be lifted from Rafael's heart. His young bride had come to share his life and give it meaning and form. Sometimes late at night when the owl called from its perch on the windmill and the coyotes sang in the hills, he would lie awake and feel the presence of her young, thin body next to his. On such nights the stillness of the spring air and her fragrance intoxicated him and made him drunk with happiness; then he would feel compelled to rise and walk out into the night which was bright with the moon and the million stars which swirled overhead in the sky. He breathed the cool air of the llano night, and it was like a liquor which made his head swirl and his heart pound. He was a happy man.

In the morning she arose before him and fixed his coffee and brought it to him, and at first he insisted that it was he who should get up to start the fire in the wood stove because he was used to rising long before the sun and riding in the range while the dawn was alive with its bright colors, but she laughed and told him she would spoil him in the summer and in the winter when it was cold he would be the one to rise and start the fire and bring her coffee in bed. They laughed and talked during those still-dark, early hours of the morning. He told her where he would ride that day and about the work that needed to be done. She, in turn, told him about the curtains she was sewing and the cabinet she was painting and how she would cover each drawer with oil cloth.

He had whitewashed the inside of the small adobe home for her, then plastered the outside walls with mud to keep out the dust which came with the spring winds and the cold which would come with winter. He fixed the roof and patched the leaks, and one night when it rained they didn't have to rise to catch the leaking water in pots and pans. They laughed and were happy. Just as the spring rains made the land green, so his love made her grow, and one morning she quietly whispered in his ear that by Christmas they would have a child.

Her words brought great joy to him. "A child," she had said, and excitement tightened in his throat. That day he didn't work on the range. He had promised her a garden, so he hitched up one of the old horses to his father's plow and he spent all day plowing the soft, sandy earth by the windmill. He spread manure from the corral on the soil and turned it into the earth. He fixed an old pipe leading to the windmill and showed her how to turn it to water the garden. She was pleased. She spent days planting flowers and vegetables. She watered the old, gnarled peach trees near the garden and they burst into a late bloom. She worked the earth with care and by midsummer she was already picking green vegetables to cook with the meat and potatoes. It became a part of his life to stop on the rise above the ranch when he rode in from the range, to pause and watch her working in the garden in the cool of the afternoon. There was something in that image, something which made a mark of permanence on the otherwise empty llano.

Her slender body began to grow heavier. Sometimes he heard her singing, and he knew it was not only to herself she sang or hummed. Sometimes he glanced at her when her gaze was fixed on some distant object, and he realized it was not a distant mesa or cloud she was seeing, but a distant future which was growing in her.

Time flowed past them. He thinned his herds, prepared for the approaching winter, and she gathered the last of the fruits and vegetables. But something was not right. Her excitement of the summer was gone. She began to grow pale and weak. She would rise in the mornings and fix breakfast, then she would have to return to bed and rest. By late December, as the first clouds of winter appeared and the winds from the west blew sharp and cold, she could no longer rise in the mornings. He tried to help, but there was little he could do except sit by her side and keep her silent company while she slept her troubled sleep. A few weeks later a small flow of blood began, as pains and cramps wracked her body. Something was pulling at the child she carried, but it was not the natural rhythm she had expected.

"Go for Doña Rufina," she said, "go for help."

He hitched the wagon and made the long drive into the village, arriving at the break of light to rouse the old partera from her sleep. For many years the old woman had delivered the babies born in the village or in the nearby ranches, and now, as he explained what had happened and the need to hurry, she nodded solemnly. She packed the things she would need, then kneeled at her altar and made the sign of the cross. She prayed to el Santo Niño for help and whispered to the Virgin Mary that she would return when her work was done. Then she turned the small statues to face the wall. Rafael helped her on the wagon, loaded her bags, then used the reins as a whip to drive the horses at a fast trot on their long journey back. They arrived at the ranch as the sun was setting. That night a child was born, a girl, pulled from the womb by the old woman's practiced hands. The old woman placed her mouth to the baby's and pushed in air. The baby gasped, sucked in air and came alive. Doña Rufina smiled as she cleaned the small, squirming body. The sound was good. The cry filled the night, shattering the silence in the room.

"A daughter," the old woman said. "A hard birth." She cleaned away the sheets, made the bed, washed the young wife who lay so pale and quiet on the bed, and when there was nothing more she could do she rolled a cigarette and sat back to smoke and wait. The baby lay quietly at her mother's side, while the breathing of the young mother grew weaker and weaker and the blood which the old woman was powerless to stop continued to flow. By morning she was dead. She had opened her eyes and looked at the small white bundle which lay at her side. She smiled and tried to speak, but there was no strength left. She sighed and closed her eyes.

"She is dead," Doña Rufina said.

"No, no," Rafael moaned. He held his wife in his arms and shook his head in disbelief. "She cannot die, she cannot die," he whispered over and over. Her body, once so warm and full of joy, was now cold and lifeless, and he cursed the forces he didn't understand but which had drawn her into that eternal silence. He would never again hear her voice, never hear her singing in her garden, never see her waving as he came over the rise from the llano. A long time later he allowed Doña Rufina's hands to draw him away. Slowly he took the shovel she handed him and dug the grave beneath the peach trees by the garden, that place of shade she had loved so much in the summer and which now appeared so deserted in the December cold. He buried her, then quickly saddled his horse and rode into the llano. He was gone for days. When he returned, he was pale and haggard from the great emptiness which filled him. Doña Rufina was there, caring for the child, nursing her as best she could with the little milk she could draw from the milk cow they kept in the corral. Although the baby was thin and sick with colic, she was alive. Rafael looked only once at the child, then he turned his back to her. In his mind the child had taken his wife's life, and he didn't care if the baby lived or died. He didn't care if he lived or died. The joy he had known was gone, her soul had been pulled into the silence he felt around him, and his only wish was to be with her. She was out there somewhere, alone and lost on the cold and desolate plain. If he could only hear her voice he was sure he could find her. That was his only thought as he rode out every day across the plain. He rode and listened for her voice in the wind which moaned across the cold landscape, but there was no sound, only the silence. His tortured body was always cold and shivering from the snow and wind, and when the dim sun sank in the west it was his horse which trembled and turned homeward, not he. He would have been content to ride forever, to ride until the cold numbed his body and he could join her in the silence.

When he returned late in the evenings he would eat alone and in silence. He did not speak to the old woman who sat huddled near the stove, holding the baby on her lap, rocking softly back and forth and singing wisps of the old songs. The baby listened, as if she, too, already realized the strangeness of the silent world she had entered. Over them the storms of winter howled and tore at the small home where the three waited for spring in silence. But there was no promise in the spring. When the days grew longer and the earth began to thaw, Rafael threw himself into his work. He separated his herd, branded the new calves, then drove a few yearlings into the village where he sold them for the provisions he needed. But even the silence of the llano carries whispers. People asked about the child and Doña Rufina, and only once did he look at them and say, "My wife is dead." Then he turned away and spoke no more. The people understood his silence and his need to live in it, alone. No more questions were ever asked. He came into the village only when the need for provisions brought him, moving like a ghost, a haunted man, a man the silence of the llano had conquered and claimed. The old people of the village crossed their foreheads and whispered silent prayers when he rode by.

Seven years passed, unheeded in time, unmarked time, change felt only because the seasons changed. Doña Rufina died. During those years she and Rafael had not exchanged a dozen words. She had done what she could for the child, and she had come to love her as her own. Leaving the child behind was the only regret she felt the day she looked out the window and heard the creaking sound in the silence of the day. In the distance, as if in a whirlwind which swirled slowly across the llano, she saw the figure of death riding a creaking cart which moved slowly towards the ranch house. So, she thought, my comadre la muerte comes for me. It is time to leave this earth. She fed the child and put her to bed, then she wrapped herself in a warm quilt and sat by the stove, smoking her last cigarette, quietly rocking back and forth, listening to the creaking of the rocking chair, listening to the moan of the wind which swept across the land. She felt at peace. The chills she had felt the past month left her. She felt light and airy, as if she were entering a pleasant dream. She heard voices, the voices of old friends she had known on the llano, and she saw the faces of the many babies she had delivered during her lifetime. Then she heard a knock on the door. Rafael, who sat at his bed repairing his bridle and oiling the leather, heard her say, "Enter," but he did not look up. He did not hear her last gasp for air. He did not see the dark figure of the old woman who stood at the door, beckoning to Doña Rufina.

When Rafael looked up he saw her head slump forward. He arose and filled a glass with water. He held her head up and touched the water to her lips, but it was no use. He knew she was dead. The wind had forced the door open and it banged against the wall, filling the room with a cold gust, awakening the child who started from her bed. He moved quickly to shut the door, and the room again became dark and silent. One more death, one more burial, and again he returned to his work. Only out there, in the vast space of the llano, could he find something in which he could lose himself.

Only the weather and the seasons marked time for Rafael as he watched over his land and his herd. Summer nights he slept outside, and the galaxies swirling overhead reminded him he was alone. Out there, in that strange darkness, the soul of his wife rested. In the day, when the wind shifted direction, he sometimes thought he heard the whisper of her voice. Other times he thought he saw the outline of her face in the huge clouds which billowed up in the summer. And always he had to drive away the dream and put away the voice or the image, because the memory only increased his sadness. He learned to live alone, completely alone. The seasons changed, the rains came in July and the llano was green, then the summer sun burned it dry, later the cold of winter came with its fury. And all these seasons he survived, moving across the desolate land, hunched over his horse. He was a man who could not allow himself to dream, he rode alone.

II

And the daughter? What of the daughter? The seasons brought growth to her, and she grew into young womanhood. She learned to watch the man who came and went and did not speak, and so she, too, learned to live in her own world. She learned to prepare the food and to sit aside in silence while he ate, to sweep the floor and keep the small house clean, to keep alive the fire in the iron stove, and to wash the clothes with the scrub-board at the water tank by the windmill. In the summer her greatest pleasure was the cool place by the windmill where the water flowed.

The year she was sixteen, during springtime she stood and bathed in the cool water which came clean and cold out of the pipe, and as she stood under the water the numbing sensation reminded her of the first time the blood had come. She had not known what it was: it came without warning, without her knowledge. She had felt a fever in the night, and cramps in her stomach, then in the restlessness of sleep she had awakened and felt the warm flow between her legs. She was not frightened, but she did remember that for the first time she became aware of her father snoring in his sleep on the bed at the other side of the room. She arose quietly, without disturbing him, and walked out into the summer night, going to the watertank where she washed herself. The water which washed her blood splashed and ran into the garden.

That same summer she felt her breasts mature, her hips widen, and when she ran to gather her chickens into the coop for the night she felt a difference in her movement. She did not think or dwell on it, a dark part of her intuition told her that this was a natural element which belonged to the greater mystery of birth which she had seen take place on the llano around her. She had seen her hens seek secret nests to hatch their eggs, and she knew the proud, clucking noises the hens made when they appeared with the small yellow chicks trailing. There was life in the eggs. Once when the herd was being moved and they came to the water tank to drink she had seen the great bull mount one of the cows, and she remembered the whirling of dust and the bellowing which filled the air. Later, the cow would seek a nest and there would be a calf. These things she knew.

Now she was a young woman. When she went to the watertank to bathe she sometimes paused and looked at her reflection in the water. Her face was smooth and oval, dark from the summer sun, as beautiful as the mother she had not known. When she slipped off her blouse and saw how full and firm her breasts had grown and how rosy the nipples appeared, she smiled and touched them and felt a pleasure she couldn't explain. There had been no one to ask about the changes which came into her life. Once a woman and her daughters had come. She saw the wagon coming up on the road, but instead of going out to greet them she ran and hid in the house, watching through parted curtains as the woman and her daughters came and knocked at the door. She could hear them calling in strange words, words she did not know. She huddled in the corner and kept very still until the knocking at the door had ceased, then she edged closer to the window and watched as they climbed back on the wagon, laughing and talking in a strange, exciting way. Long after they were gone she could still smell the foreign, sweet odors they had brought to her doorstep.

After that, no one came. She remembered the words of Doña Rufina and often spoke them aloud just to hear the sound they made as they exploded from her lips. "Lumbre," she said in the morning when she put kindling on the banked ashes in the stove, whispering the word so the man who slept would not hear her. "Agua," she said when she drew water at the well. "Viento de diablo," she hissed to let her chickens know a swirling dust storm was on its way, and when they did not respond she reverted to the language she had learned from them and with a clucking sound she drove them where she wanted. "Tote! Tote!" she called and made the clicking sound for danger when she saw the gray figure of the coyote stalking close to the ranch house. The chickens understood and hurried into the safety of the coop. She learned to imitate the call of the wild doves. In the evening when they came to drink at the water tank she called to them, and they sang back. The roadrunner which came to chase lizards near the windmill learned to cou for her, and the wild sparrows and other birds also heard her call and grew to know her presence. They fed at her feet like chickens. When the milk cow wandered away from the corral she learned to whistle to bring it back. She invented other sounds, other words, words for the seasons and the weather they brought, words for the birds she loved, words for the juniper and piñon and yucca and wild grass which grew on the llano, words for the light of the sun and dark of the night, words which when uttered broke the silence of the long days she spent alone, never words to be shared with the man who came to eat late in the evenings, who came enveloped in silence, his eyes cast down in a bitterness she did not understand. He ate the meals she served in silence, then he smoked a cigarette, then he slept. Their lives were unencumbered by each other's presence, they did not exist for each other, each had learned to live in his own silent world.

But other presences began to appear on the llano, even at this isolated edge of the plain which lay so far beyond the village of Las Animas. Men came during the season of the yellow moon, and they carried the long sticks which made thunder. In that season when the antelope were rutting they came, and she could hear the sound of thunder they made, even feel the panic of the antelopes which ran across the llano. "Hunters!" her father said, and he spat the word like a curse. He did not want them to enter his world, but still they came, not in the silent, horse-drawn wagons, but in an iron wagon which made noise and smoked.

The sound of these men frightened her, life on the llano grew tense as they drew near. One day, five of the hunters drove up to the ranch house in one of their iron wagons. She moved quickly to lock the door, to hide, for she had seen the antelope they had killed hung over the front of their wagon, a beautiful tan colored buck splattered with blood. It was tied with rope and wire, its dry tongue hanging from its mouth, its large eyes still open. The men pounded on the door and called her father's name. She held her breath and peered through the window. She saw them drink from a bottle they passed to each other. They pounded on the door again and fired their rifles into the air, filling the llano with explosive thunder. The acrid smell of burned powder filled the air. The house seemed to shake as they called words she did not understand. "Rafael!" they called. "A virgin daughter!" They roared with laughter as they climbed in their wagon, and the motor shrieked and roared as they drove away. All day the vibration of the noise and awful presence of the men lay over the house, and at night in nightmares she saw the faces of the men, heard their laughter and the sound of the rifle's penetrating roar as it shattered the silence of the llano. Two of them had been young men, broad-shouldered boys who looked at the buck they had killed and smiled. The faces of these strange men drifted through her dreams and she was at once afraid and attracted by them.

One night in her dreams she saw the face of the man who lived there, the man Doña Rufina had told her was to be called father, and she could not understand why he should appear in her dream. When she awoke she heard the owl cry a warning from its perch on the windmill. She hurried outside, saw the dark form of the coyote slinking toward the chicken coop. A snarl hissed in her throat as she threw a rock, and instantly the coyote faded into the night. She waited in the dark, troubled by her dream and by the appearance of the coyote, then she slipped quietly back into the house. She did not want to awaken the man, but he was awake. He, too, had heard the coyote, and had heard her slip out, but he said nothing. In the warm summer night each lay awake, encased in their solitary silence, saying nothing, expecting no words, but aware of each other as animals are aware when another is close by, as she had been aware even in her sleep that the coyote was drawing near.

III

One afternoon Rafael returned home early. He had seen a cloud of dust on the road to his ranch house. It was not the movement of cattle, and it wasn't the dust of the summer dustdevils. The rising dust could only mean there was a car on the road. He cursed under his breath, remembering the signs he had posted on his fence and the chain and lock he had bought in the village to secure his gate. He did not want to be bothered, he would keep everyone away. For a time he continued to repair the fence, using his horse to draw the wire taut, nailing the barbed wire to the cedar posts he had set that morning. The day was warm, he sweated as he worked, but again he paused, something made him restless, uneasy. He wiped his brow and looked towards the ranch house. Perhaps it was only his imagination, he thought, perhaps the whirlwind was only a mirage, a reflection of the strange uneasiness he felt. He looked to the west where two buzzards circled over the coyote he had shot that morning. Soon they would drop to feed. Around him the ants scurried through the dry grass, working their hills as he worked his land. There was the buzz of grasshoppers, the occasional call of prairie dogs, each sound in its turn absorbed into the hum which was the silence of the land. He returned to his work but the image of the cloud of dust returned, the thoughts of strangers on his land filled him with anger and apprehension. The bad feeling grew until he couldn't work. He packed his tools, swung on his horse and rode homeward.

Later, as he sat on his horse at the top of the rise from where he could view his house, the uneasy feeling grew more intense. Something was wrong, someone had come. Around him a strange dark cloud gathered, shutting off the sun, stirring the wind into frenzy. He urged his horse down the slope and rode up to the front door. All was quiet. The girl usually came out to take his horse to the corral where she unsaddled and fed it, but today there was no sight of her. He turned and looked towards the windmill and the plot of ground where he had buried his wife. The pile of rocks which marked her grave was almost covered by wind-swept sand. The peach trees were almost dead. The girl had watered them from time to time, as she had watered the garden, but no one had helped or taught her and so her efforts were poorly rewarded. Only a few flowers survived in the garden, spots of color in the otherwise dry, tawny landscape.

His horse moved uneasily beneath him; he dismounted slowly. The door of the house was ajar, he pushed it open and entered. The room was dark and cool, the curtains at the window were drawn, the fire for the evening meal was not yet started. Outside the first drops of rain fell on the tin roof as the cloud darkened the land. In the room a fly buzzed. Perhaps the girl is not here, he thought, maybe it is just that I am tired and I have come early to rest. He turned toward the bed and saw her. She sat huddled on the bed, her knees drawn up, her arms wrapped around them. She looked at him, her eyes terrified and wild in the dark. He started to turn away but he heard her make a sound, the soft cry of an injured animal.

"Rafael," she moaned as she reached out for him. "Rafael. . . ."

He felt his knees grow weak. She had never used his name before.

At the same time she flung back the crumpled sheet and pointed to the stain of blood. He shook his head, gasped. Her blouse was torn off, red scratch marks scarred her white shoulders, tears glistened in her eyes as she reached out again and whispered his name. "Rafael . . . Rafael. . . ."

Someone had come in that cloud of dust, perhaps a stray vaquero looking for work, perhaps one of the men from the village who knew she was here alone, a man had come in the whirlwind and forced himself into the house. "Oh God. . . ." he groaned as he stepped back, felt the door behind him, saw her rise from the bed, her arms outstretched, the curves of her breasts rising and falling as she gasped for breath and called his name, "Rafael . . . Rafael. . . ." She held out her arms, and he heard his scream echo in the small adobe room which had suddenly become a prison suffocating him. Still the girl came towards him, her eyes dark and piercing, her dark hair falling over her shoulders and throat. With a great effort he found the strength to turn and flee. Outside, he grabbed the reins of his frightened horse, mounted and dug his spurs into the side of the poor creature. Whipping it hard he rode away from the ranch and what he had seen.

Once before he had fled, on the day he buried his wife. He had seen her face then, as he now saw the image of the girl, saw her eyes burning into him, saw the torn blouse, the bed, and most frightening of all, heard her call his name, "Rafael . . . Rafael. . . ." It opened and broke the shell of his silence, it was a wound which brought back the ghost of his wife, the beauty of her features which he now saw again and which blurred into the image of the girl. He spurred the horse until it buckled with fatigue and sent him crashing into the earth. The impact brought a searing pain and the peace of darkness.

He didn't know how long he lay unconscious. When he awoke he touched his throbbing forehead and felt the clotted blood. The pain in his head was intense, but he could walk. Without direction he stumbled across the llano only to find that late in the afternoon when he looked around he saw his ranch house. He approached the water tank to wash the clotted blood from his face, then he stumbled into the tool shed by the corral and tried to sleep. Dusk came, the bats and night hawks flew over the quiet llano, night fell and still he could not sleep. Through the chinks of the weathered boards he could see the house and the light which burned at the window. The girl was awake. All night he stared at the light burning at the window, and in his fever he saw her face again, her pleading eyes, the

curve of her young breasts, her arms as she reached up and called his
name. Why had she called his name? Why? Was it the devil who rode the
whirlwind? Was it the devil who had come to break the silence of the llano?
He groaned and shivered as the call of the owl sounded in the night. He
looked into the darkness and thought he saw the figure of the girl walking
to the water tank. She bathed her shoulders in the cold water, bathed her
body in the moonlight. Then the owl grew still and the figure in the flowing
gown disappeared as the first sign of dawn appeared in the clouds of the
east.

He rose and entered the house, tremulously, unsure of what he would
find. There was food on the table and hot coffee on the stove. She had prepared his breakfast as she had all those years, and now she sat by the window, withdrawn, her face pale and thin. She looked up at him, but he
turned away and sat at the table with his back to her. He tried to eat but the
food choked him. He drank the strong coffee, then he rose and hurried
outside. He cursed as he reeled towards the corral like a drunken man,
then he stopped suddenly and shuddered with a fear he had never known
before. He shook his head in disbelief and raised his hand as if to ward
away the figure sitting at the huge cedar block at the woodpile. It was the
figure of a woman, a woman who called his name and beckoned him. And
for the first time in sixteen years he called out his wife's name.

"Rita," he whispered, "Rita. . . ."

Yes, it was she, he thought, sitting there as she used to, laughing and
teasing while he chopped firewood. He could see her eyes, her smile, hear
her voice. He remembered how he would show off his strength with the
axe, and she would compliment him in a teasing way as she gathered
the chips of piñon and cedar for kindling. "Rita . . ." he whispered, and
moved toward her, but now the figure sitting at the woodblock was the girl,
she sat there, calling his name, smiling and coaxing him as a demon of hell
would entice the sinner into the center of the whirlwind. "No!" he
screamed and grabbed the axe, lifted it, and summoning his remaining
strength he brought it down on the dark heart of the swirling vortex. The
blow split the block in half and splintered the axe handle. He felt the pain
of the vibration numb his arms. The devil is dead, he thought, opened his
eyes, saw only the split block and the splintered axe in front of him. He
shook his head and backed away, crying to God to exorcize the possession
in his tormented soul. And even as he prayed for respite he looked up and
saw the window. Behind the parted curtains he saw her face, his wife, the
girl, the pale face of the woman who haunted him.

Without saddling the horse he mounted and spurred it south. He had to
leave this place, he would ride south until he could ride no more, until he
disappeared into the desert. He would ride into oblivion, and when he was
dead the tightness and pain in his chest and the torturous thoughts would
be gone, then there would be peace. He would die and give himself to the
silence, and in that element he would find rest. But without warning a dark

whirlwind rose before him, and in the midst of the storm he saw a woman. She did not smile, she did not call his name, her horse was the dark clouds which towered over him, the cracking of her whip a fire which filled the sky. Her laughter rumbled across the sky and shook the earth, her shadow swirled around him, blocking out the sun, filling the air with choking dust, driving fear into both man and animal until they turned in a wide circle back towards the ranch house. And when he found himself once again on the small rise by his home, the whirlwind lifted and the woman disappeared. The thunder rumbled in the distance, then was gone, the air grew quiet around him. He could hear himself breathe, he could hear the pounding of his heart. Around him the sun was bright and warm.

He didn't know how long he sat there remembering other times when he had paused at that place to look down at his home. He was startled from his reverie by the slamming of a screen door. He looked and saw the girl walk towards the water tank. He watched her as she pulled the pipe clear of the tank, then she removed her dress and began her bath. Her white skin glistened in the sunlight as the spray of water splashed over her body. Her long, black hair fell over her shoulders to her waist, glistening from the water. He could hear her humming. He remembered his wife bathing there, covering herself with soap foam, and he remembered how he would sit and smoke while she bathed, and his life was full of peace and contentment. She would wrap a towel around her body and come running to sit by his side in the sun, and as she dried her hair they would talk. Her words had filled the silence of that summer. Her words were an extension of the love she had brought him.

And now? He touched his legs to the horse's sides and the horse moved, making its way down the slope towards the water tank. She turned, saw him coming, and she stepped out of the stream of the cascading water to gather a towel around her naked body. She waited quietly. He rode up to her, looked at her, looked for a long time at her face and into her eyes. Then slowly he dismounted and walked to her. She waited in silence. He moved towards her, and with a trembling hand he reached out and touched her wet hair.

"Rita," he said. "Your name is Rita."

She smiled at the sound. She remembered the name from long ago. It was a sound she remembered from Doña Rufina. It was the sound the axe made when it rang against hard cedar wood, and now he, the man who had lived in silence all those years, he had spoken the name.

It was a good sound which brought joy to her heart. This man had come to speak this sound which she remembered. She saw him turn and point at the peach trees at the edge of the garden.

"Your mother is buried over there," he said. "This was her garden. The spring is the time for the garden. I will turn the earth for you. The seeds will grow."

Seeds

SHERWOOD ANDERSON

He was a small man with a beard and was very nervous. I remember how the cords of his neck were drawn taut.

For years he had been trying to cure people of illness by the method called psychoanalysis. The idea was the passion of his life. "I came here because I am tired," he said dejectedly. "My body is not tired but something inside me is old and worn-out. I want joy. For a few days or weeks I would like to forget men and women and the influences that make them the sick things they are."

There is a note that comes into the human voice by which you may know real weariness. It comes when one has been trying with all his heart and soul to think his way along some difficult road of thought. Of a sudden he finds himself unable to go on. Something within him stops. A tiny explosion takes place. He bursts into words and talks, perhaps foolishly. Little side currents of his nature he didn't know were there run out and get themselves expressed. It is at such times that a man boasts, uses big words, makes a fool of himself in general.

And so it was the doctor became shrill. He jumped up from the steps where we had been sitting, talking and walked about. "You come from the West. You have kept away from people. You have preserved yourself—damn you! I haven't—" His voice had indeed become shrill. "I have entered into lives. I have gone beneath the surface of the lives of men and women. Women especially I have studied—our own women, here in America."

"You have loved them?" I suggested.

"Yes," he said. "Yes—you are right there. I have done that. It is the only way I can get at things. I have to try to love. You see how that is? It's the only way. Love must be the beginning of things with me."

I began to sense the depths of his weariness. "We will go swim in the lake," I urged.

31

"I don't want to swim or do any damn plodding thing. I want to run and shout," he declared. "For awhile, for a few hours, I want to be like a dead leaf blown by the winds over these hills. I have one desire and one only— to free myself."

We walked in a dusty country road. I wanted him to know that I thought I understood, so I put the case in my own way.

When he stopped and stared at me I talked. "You are no more and no better than myself," I declared. "You are a dog that has rolled in offal, and because you are not quite a dog you do not like the smell of your own hide."

In turn my voice became shrill. "You blind fool," I cried impatiently. "Men like you are fools. You cannot go along that road. It is given to no man to venture far along the road of lives."

I became passionately in earnest. "The illness you pretend to cure is the universal illness," I said. "The thing you want to do cannot be done. Fool— do you expect love to be understood?"

We stood in the road and looked at each other. The suggestion of a sneer played about the corners of his mouth. He put a hand on my shoulder and shook me. "How smart we are—how aptly we put things!"

He spat the words out and then turned and walked a little away. "You think you understand, but you don't understand," he cried. "What you say can't be done can be done. You're a liar. You cannot be so definite without missing something vague and fine. You miss the whole point. The lives of people are like young trees in a forest. They are being choked by climbing vines. The vines are old thoughts and beliefs planted by dead men. I am myself covered by crawling creeping vines that choke me."

He laughed bitterly. "And that's why I want to run and play," he said. "I want to be a leaf blown by the wind over hills. I want to die and be born again, and I am only a tree covered with vines and slowly dying. I am, you see, weary and want to be made clean. I am an amateur venturing timidly into lives," he concluded. "I am weary and want to be made clean. I am covered by creeping crawling things."

*   *   *

A woman from Iowa came here to Chicago and took a room in a house on the west-side. She was about twenty-seven years old and ostensibly she came to the city to study advanced methods for teaching music.

A certain young man also lived in the west-side house. His room faced a long hall on the second floor of the house and the one taken by the woman was across the hall facing his room.

In regard to the young man—there is something very sweet in his nature. He is a painter but I have often wished he would decide to become a writer. He tells things with understanding and he does not paint brilliantly.

And so the woman from Iowa lived in the west-side house and came home from the city in the evening. She looked like a thousand other women one sees in the streets every day. The only thing that at all made her stand out among the women in the crowds was that she was a little lame. Her right foot was slightly deformed and she walked with a limp. For three months she lived in the house—where she was the only woman except the landlady—and then a feeling in regard to her began to grow up among the men of the house.

The men all said the same thing concerning her. When they met in the hallway at the front of the house they stopped, laughed and whispered. "She wants a lover," they said and winked. "She may not know it but a lover is what she needs."

One knowing Chicago and Chicago men would think that an easy want to be satisfied. I laughed when my friend—whose name is LeRoy—told me the story, but he did not laugh. He shook his head. "It wasn't so easy," he said. "There would be no story were the matter that simple."

LeRoy tried to explain. "Whenever a man approached her she became alarmed," he said. Men kept smiling and speaking to her. They invited her to dinner and to the theatre, but nothing would induce her to walk in the streets with a man. She never went into the streets at night. When a man stopped and tried to talk with her in the hallway she turned her eyes to the floor and then ran into her room. Once a young drygoods clerk who lived there induced her to sit with him on the steps before the house.

He was a sentimental fellow and took hold of her hand. When she began to cry he was alarmed and arose. He put a hand on her shoulder and tried to explain, but under the touch of his fingers her whole body shook with terror. "Don't touch me," she cried, "don't let your hands touch me!" She began to scream and people passing in the street stopped to listen. The drygoods clerk was alarmed and ran upstairs to his own room. He bolted the door and stood listening. "It is a trick," he declared in a trembling voice. "She is trying to make trouble. I did nothing to her. It was an accident and anyway what's the matter? I only touched her arm with my fingers."

Perhaps a dozen times LeRoy has spoken to me of the experience of the Iowa woman in the west-side house. The men there began to hate her. Although she would have nothing to do with them she would not let them alone. In a hundred ways she continually invited approaches that when made she repelled. When she stook naked in the bathroom facing the hallway where the men passed up and down she left the door slightly ajar. There was a couch in the living room downstairs, and when men were present she would sometimes enter and without saying a word throw herself down before them. On the couch she lay with lips drawn slightly apart. Her eyes stared at the ceiling. Her whole physical being seemed to be waiting for something. The sense of her filled the room. The men standing about pretended not to see. They talked loudly. Embarrassment took possession of them and one by one they crept quietly away.

One evening the woman was ordered to leave the house. Someone, perhaps the drygoods clerk, had talked to the landlady and she acted at once. "If you leave tonight I shall like it that much better," LeRoy heard the elder woman's voice saying. She stood in the hallway before the Iowa woman's room. The landlady's voice rang through the house.

LeRoy the painter is tall and lean and his life has been spent in devotion to ideas. The passions of his brain have consumed the passions of his body. His income is small and he has not married. Perhaps he has never had a sweetheart. He is not without physical desire but he is not primarily concerned with desire.

On the evening when the Iowa woman was ordered to leave the west-side house, she waited until she thought the landlady had gone downstairs, and then went into LeRoy's room. It was about eight o'clock and he sat by a window reading a book. The woman did not knock but opened the door. She said nothing but ran across the floor and knelt at his feet. LeRoy said that her twisted foot made her run like a wounded bird, that her eyes were burning and that her breath came in little gasps. "Take me," she said, putting her face down upon his knees and trembling violently. "Take me quickly. There must be a beginning to things. I can't stand the waiting. You must take me at once."

You may be quite sure LeRoy was perplexed by all this. From what he has said I gathered that until that evening he had hardly noticed the woman. I suppose that of all the men in the house he had been the most indifferent to her. In the room something happened. The landlady followed the woman when she ran to LeRoy, and the two women confronted him. The woman from Iowa knelt trembling and frightened at his feet. The landlady was indignant. LeRoy acted on impulse. An inspiration came to him. Putting his hand on the kneeling woman's shoulder he shook her violently. "Now behave yourself," he said quickly. "I will keep my promise." He turned to the landlady and smiled. "We have been engaged to be married," he said. "We have quarrelled. She came here to be near me. She has been unwell and excited. I will take her away. Please don't let yourself be annoyed. I will take her away."

When the woman and LeRoy got out of the house she stopped weeping and put her hand into his. Her fears had all gone away. He found a room for her in another house and then went with her into a park and sat on a bench.

*   *   *

Everything LeRoy has told me concerning this woman strengthens my belief in what I said to the man that day in the mountains. You cannot venture along the road of lives. On the bench he and the woman talked until midnight and he saw and talked with her many times later. Nothing came of it. She went back, I suppose, to her place in the West.

In the place from which she had come the woman had been a teacher of music. She was one of four sisters, all engaged in the same sort of work and, LeRoy says, all quiet capable women. Their father had died when the eldest girl was not yet ten, and five years later the mother died also. The girls had a house and a garden.

In the nature of things I cannot know what the lives of the women were like but of this one may be quite certain—they talked only of women's affairs, thought only of women's affairs. No one of them ever had a lover. For years no man came near the house.

Of them all only the youngest, the one who came to Chicago, was visibly affected by the utterly feminine quality of their lives. It did something to her. All day and every day she taught music to young girls and then went home to the women. When she was twenty-five she began to think and to dream of men. During the day and through the evening she talked with women of women's affairs, and all the time she wanted desperately to be loved by a man. She went to Chicago with that hope in mind. LeRoy explained her attitude in the matter and her strange behavior in the west-side house by saying she had thought too much and acted too little. "The life force within her became decentralized," he declared. "What she wanted she could not achieve. The living force within could not find expression. When it could not get expressed in one way it took another. Sex spread itself out over her body. It permeated the very fibre of her being. At the last she was sex personified, sex become condensed and impersonal. Certain words, the touch of a man's hand, sometimes even the sight of a man passing in the street did something to her."

*   *   *

Yesterday I saw LeRoy and he talked to me again of the woman and her strange and terrible fate.

We walked in the park by the lake. As we went along the figure of the woman kept coming into my mind. An idea came to me.

"You might have been her lover," I said. "That was possible. She was not afraid of you."

LeRoy stopped. Like the doctor who was so sure of his ability to walk into lives he grew angry and scolded. For a moment he stared at me and then a rather odd thing happened. Words said by the other man in the dusty road in the hills came to LeRoy's lips and were said over again. The suggestion of a sneer played about the corners of his mouth. "How smart we are. How aptly we put things," he said.

The voice of the young man who walked with me in the park by the lake in the city became shrill. I sensed the weariness in him. Then he laughed and said quietly and softly, "It isn't so simple. By being sure of yourself you are in danger of losing all of the romance of life. You miss the whole point.

Nothing in life can be settled so definitely. The woman—you see—was like a young tree choked by a climbing vine. The thing that wrapped her about had shut out the light. She was a grotesque as many trees in the forest are grotesques. Her problem was such a difficult one that thinking of it has changed the whole current of my life. At first I was like you. I was quite sure. I thought I would be her lover and settle the matter."

LeRoy turned and walked a little away. Then he came back and took hold of my arm. A passionate earnestness took possession of him. His voice trembled. "She needed a lover, yes, the men in the house were quite right about that," he said. "She needed a lover and at the same time a lover was not what she needed. The need of a lover was, after all, a quite secondary thing. She needed to be loved, to be long and quietly and patiently loved. To be sure she is a grotesque, but then all the people in the world are grotesques. We all need to be loved. What would cure her would cure the rest of us also. The disease she had is, you see, universal. We all want to be loved and the world has no plan for creating our lovers."

LeRoy's voice dropped and he walked beside me in silence. We turned away from the lake and walked under trees. I looked closely at him. The cords of his neck were drawn taut. "I have seen under the shell of life and I am afraid," he mused. "I am myself like the woman. I am covered with creeping crawling vine-like things. I cannot be a lover. I am not subtle or patient enough. I am paying old debts. Old thoughts and beliefs—seeds planted by dead men—spring up in my soul and choke me."

For a long time we walked and LeRoy talked, voicing the thoughts that came into his mind. I listened in silence. His mind struck upon the refrain voiced by the man in the mountains. "I would like to be a dead dry thing," he muttered looking at the leaves scattered over the grass. "I would like to be a leaf blown away by the wind." He looked up and his eyes turned to where among the trees we could see the lake in the distance. "I am weary and want to be made clean. I am a man covered by creeping crawling things. I would like to be dead and blown by the wind over limitless waters," he said. "I want more than anything else in the world to be clean."

The Reunion

MAYA ANGELOU

Nobody could have told me that she'd be out with a black man; out, like going out. But there she was, in 1958, sitting up in the Blue Palm Cafe, when I played the Sunday matinee with Cal Callen's band.

Here's how it was. After we got on the stage, the place was packed, first Cal led us into "D. B. Blues." Of course I know just like everybody else that Cal's got a thing for Lester Young. Maybe because Cal plays the tenor sax, or maybe because he's about as red as Lester Young, or maybe just cause Lester is the Prez. Anybody that's played with Cal knows that the kickoff tune is gotta be "D. B. Blues." So I was ready. We romped.

I'd played with some of those guys, but never all together, but we took off on that tune like we were headed for Birdland in New York City. The audience liked it. Applauded as much as black audiences ever applaud. Black folks act like they are sure that with a little bit of study they could do whatever you're doing on the stage as well as you do it. If not better. So they clap for your luck. Lucky for you that they're not up there to show you where it's really at.

Anyway, after the applause, Cal started to introduce the band. That's his style. Everybody knows that too. After he's through introducing everybody, he's not going to say anything else till the next set, it doesn't matter how many times we play. So he's got a little comedy worked into the introduction patter. He started with Olly, the trumpet man. . . . "And here we have a real Chicagoan . . . by way of Atlanta, Georgia . . . bringing soul to Soulville . . . Mr. Olly Martin."

He went on. I looked out into the audience. People sitting, not listening, or better, listening with one side of their ears and talking with both sides of their mouths. Some couples were making a little love . . . and some whites were there trying hard to act natural . . . like they come to the South Side of Chicago every day or maybe like they live there . . . then I saw her. Saw

Miss Beth Ann Baker, sitting up with her blond self with a big black man
. . . pretty black man. What? White girls, when they look alike, can look so
much alike, I thought maybe it wasn't Beth. I looked again. It was her. I remember too well the turn of her cheek. The sliding way her jaw goes up to
her hair. That was her. I might have missed a few notes, I might have in
fact missed the whole interlude music.

What was she doing in Chicago? On the South Side. And with a black
man? Beth Ann Baker of the Baker Cotton Gin. Miss Cotton Queen Baker
of Georgia . . .

Then I heard Cal get round to me. He saved me for the last. Mainly
'cause I'm female and he can get a little rise out of the audience if he says,
as he did say, "And our piano man is a lady. And what a lady. A cooker and
a looker. Ladies and Gentlemen, I'd like to introduce to you Miss Philomena Jenkins. Folks call her Meanie." I noticed some applause, but mainly
I was watching Beth. She heard my name and she looked right into my
eyes. Her blue ones got as big as my black ones. She recognized me, in fact
in a second we tipped eyelids at each other. Not winking. Just squinting, to
see better. There was something that I couldn't recognize. Something I'd
never seen in all those years in Baker, Georgia. Not panic, and it wasn't
fear. Whatever was in that face seemed familiar, but before I could really
read it, Cal announced our next number. "Round 'bout Midnight."

That used to be my song, for so many reasons. In Baker, the only time I
could practice jazz, in the church, was round 'bout midnight. When the best
chord changes came to me it was generally round 'bout midnight. When
my first lover held me in his arms, it was round 'bout midnight. Usually
when it's time to play that tune I dig right in it. But this time, I was too busy
thinking about Beth and her family . . . and what she was doing in Chicago,
on the South Side, escorted by the grooviest looking cat I'd seen in a long
time. I was really trying to figure it out, then Cal's saxophone pushed it's
way into my figurings. Forced me to remember "Round 'bout Midnight."
Reminded me of the years of loneliness, the doing-without days, the
C.M.E. church, and the old ladies with hands like men and the round 'bout
midnight dreams of crossing over Jordan. Then I took thirty-two bars. My
fingers found the places between the keys where the blues and the truth lay
hiding. I dug out the story of a woman without a man, and a man without
hope. I tried to wedge myself in and lay down in the groove between B-flat
and B-natural. I must of gotten close to it, because the audience brought
me out with their clapping. Even Cal said, "Yeah baby, that's it." I nodded
to him then to the audience and looked around for Beth.

How did she like them apples? What did she think of little Philomena
that used to shake the farts out of her sheets, wash her dirty drawers, pick
up after her slovenly mama? What did she think now? Did she know that I
was still aching from the hurt Georgia put on me? But Beth was gone. So
was her boyfriend.

I had lived with my parents until I was thirteen, in the servants' quarters. A house behind the Baker main house. Daddy was the butler, my mother was the cook, and I went to a segregated school on the other side of town where the other kids called me the Baker Nigger. Momma's nimble fingers were never able to sew away the truth of Beth's hand-me-down and thrown away clothing. I had a lot to say to Beth, and she was gone.

That was a bring-down. I guess what I wanted was to rub her face in "See now, you thought all I would ever be was you and your mama's flunky." And "See now, how folks, even you, pay to listen to me" and "See now, I'm saying something nobody else can say. Not the way I say it, anyway." But her table was empty.

We did the rest of the set. Some of my favorite tunes, "Sophisticated Lady," "Misty," and "Cool Blues." I admit that I never got back into the groove until we did "When Your Lover Has Gone."

After the closing tune, "Lester Leaps In," which Cal set at a tempo like he was trying to catch the last train to Mobile, was over, the audience gave us their usual thank-you, and we were off for a twenty-minute intermission.

Some of the guys went out to turn on and a couple went to tables where they had ladies waiting for them. But I went to the back of the dark smoky bar where even the occasional sunlight from the front door made no difference. My blood was still fluttering in my fingertips, throbbing. If she was listed in the phone directory I would call her. Hello Miss Beth . . . this is Philomena . . . who was your maid, whose whole family worked for you. Or could I say, Hello Beth. Is this Beth? Well, this is Miss Jenkins. I saw you yesterday at the Blue Palm Cafe. I used to know your parents. In fact your mother said my mother was a gem, and my father was a treasure. I used to laugh 'cause your mother drank so much whiskey, but my Momma said, "Judge not, that ye be not judged." Then I found out that your father had three children down in our part of town and they all looked just like you, only prettier. Oh Beth, now . . . now . . . shouldn't have a chip . . . mustn't be bitter . . . She of course would hang up.

Just imagining what I would have said to her cheered me up. I ordered a drink from the bartender and settled back into my reverie. . . . Hello Beth . . . this is a friend from Baker. What were you doing with that black man Sunday? . . .

"Philomena? Remember me?" She stood before me absorbing the light. The drawl was still there. The soft accent rich white girls practice in Georgia to show that they had breeding. I couldn't think of anything to say. Did I remember her? There was no way I could answer the question.

"I asked Willard to wait for me in the car. I wanted to talk to you."

I sipped my drink and looked in the mirror over the bar and wondered what she really wanted. Her reflection wasn't threatening at all.

"I told him that we grew up . . . in the same town."

I was relieved that she hadn't said we grew up together. By the time I was ten, I knew growing up meant going to work. She smiled and I held my drink.

"I'm engaged to Willard and very happy."

I'm proud of my face. It didn't jump up and walk the bar.

She gave a practiced nod to the bartender and ordered a drink. "He teaches high school here on the South Side." Her drink came and she lifted the glass and our eyes met in the mirror. "I met him two years ago in Canada. We are very happy."

Why the hell was she telling me her fairy story? We weren't kin. So she had a black man. Did she think like most whites in mixed marriages that she had done the whole race a favor?

"My parents . . ." her voice became small, whispery. "My parents don't understand. They think I'm with Willard just to spite them. They . . . When's the last time you went home, Mena?" She didn't wait for my answer.

"They hate him. So much, they say they will disown me." Disbelief made her voice strong again. "They said I could never set foot in Baker again." She tried to catch my eyes in the mirror but I looked down at my drink. "I know there's a lot wrong with Baker, but it's my home." The drawl was turning into a whine. "Mother said, now mind you, she has never laid eyes on Willard, she said, if she had dreamed when I was a baby that I would grow up to marry a nig . . . a black man, she'd have choked me to death on her breast. That's a cruel thing for a mother to say. I told her so."

She bent forward and I shifted to see her expression, but her profile was hidden by the blond hair. "He doesn't understand, and me either. He didn't grow up in the South." I thought, no matter where he grew up, he wasn't white and rich and spoiled. "I just wanted to talk to somebody who knew me. Knew Baker. You know, a person can get lonely. . . . I don't see any of my friends, anymore. Do you understand, Mena? My parents gave me everything."

Well, they owned everything.

"Willard is the first thing I ever got for myself. And I'm not going to give him up."

We faced each other for the first time. She sounded like her mother and looked like a ten-year-old just before a tantrum.

"He's mine. He belongs to me."

The musicians were tuning up on the bandstand. I drained my glass and stood.

"Mena, I really enjoyed seeing you again, and talking about old times. I live in New York, but I come to Chicago every other weekend. Say, will you come to our wedding? We haven't set the date yet. Please come. It's going to be here . . . in a black church . . . somewhere."

"Good-bye Beth. Tell your parents I said go to hell and take you with them, just for company."

I sat down at the piano. She still had everything. Her mother would understand the stubbornness and send her off to Paris or the Moon. Her father couldn't deny that black skin was beautiful. She had money and a wonderful-looking man to play with. If she stopped wanting him she could always walk away. She'd still be white.

The band was halfway into the "D. B. Blues" release before I thought, she had the money, but I had the music. She and her parents had had the power to hurt me when I was young, but look, the stuff in me lifted me up high above them. No matter how bad times became, I would always be the song struggling to be heard.

The piano keys were slippery with tears. I know, I sure as hell wasn't crying for myself.

Significant Moments in the Life of My Mother

MARGARET ATWOOD

When my mother was very small, someone gave her a basket of baby chicks for Easter. They all died.

"I didn't know you weren't supposed to pick them up," says my mother. "Poor little things. I laid them out in a row on a board, with their little legs sticking out straight as pokers, and wept over them. I'd loved them to death."

Possibly this story is meant by my mother to illustrate her own stupidity, and also her sentimentality. We are to understand she wouldn't do such a thing now.

Possibly it's a commentary on the nature of love; though, knowing my mother, this is unlikely.

*   *   *

My mother's father was a country doctor. In the days before cars he drove a team of horses and a buggy around his territory, and in the days before snow ploughs he drove a team and a sleigh, through blizzards and rainstorms and in the middle of the night, to arrive at houses lit with oil lamps where water would be boiling on the wood range and flannel sheets warming on the plate rack, to deliver babies who would subsequently be named after him. His office was in the house, and as a child my mother would witness people arriving at the office door, which was reached through the front porch, clutching parts of themselves—thumbs, fingers, toes, ears, noses—which had accidentally been cut off, pressing these severed parts to the raw stumps of their bodies as if they could be stuck there like dough, in the mostly vain hope that my grandfather would be able to sew them back on, heal the gashes made in them by axes, saws, knives, and fate.

My mother and her younger sister would loiter near the closed office door until shooed away. From behind it would come groans, muffled screams, cries for help. For my mother, hospitals have never been glamorous places, and illness offers no respite or holiday. "Never get sick," she says, and means it. She hardly ever does.

Once, though, she almost died. It was when her appendix burst. My grandfather had to do the operation. He said later that he shouldn't have been the person to do it: his hands were shaking too much. This is one of the few admissions of weakness on his part that my mother has ever reported. Mostly he is portrayed as severe and in charge of things. "We all respected him, though," she says. "He was widely respected." (This is a word which has slipped a little in the scale since my mother's youth. It used to outrank *love*.)

It was someone else who told me the story of my grandfather's muskrat farm: how he and one of my mother's uncles fenced in the swamp at the back of their property and invested my mother's maiden aunt's savings in muskrats. The idea was that these muskrats would multiply and eventually be made into muskrat coats, but an adjoining apple farmer washed his spraying equipment upstream, and the muskrats were all killed by the poison, as dead as doornails. This was during the Depression, and it was no joke.

When they were young—this can cover almost anything these days, but I put it at seven or eight—my mother and her sister had a tree house, where they spent some of their time playing dolls' tea parties and so forth. One day they found a box of sweet little bottles outside my grandfather's dispensary. The bottles were being thrown out, and my mother (who has always hated waste) appropriated them for use in their dolls' house. The bottles were full of yellow liquid, which they left in because it looked so pretty. It turned out that these were urine samples.

"We got Hail Columbia for that," says my mother. "But what did we know?"

*   *   *

My mother's family lived in a large white house near an apple orchard, in Nova Scotia. There was a barn and a carriage-house; in the kitchen there was a pantry. My mother can remember the days before commercial bakeries, when flour came in barrels and all the bread was made at home. She can remember the first radio broadcast she ever heard, which was a singing commercial about socks.

In this house there were many rooms. Although I have been there, although I have seen the house with my own eyes, I still don't know how many. Parts of it were closed off, or so it seemed; there were back staircases. Passages led elsewhere. Five children lived in it, two parents, a hired man and a hired girl, whose names and faces kept changing. The structure of the house was hierarchical, with my grandfather at the top, but its secret life—the life of pie crusts, clean sheets, the box of rags in the linen closet, the loaves in the oven—was female. The house, and all the objects in it, crackled with static electricity; undertows washed through it, the air was heavy with things that were known but not spoken. Like a hollow log, a drum, a church, it amplified, so that conversations whispered in it sixty years ago can be half-heard even today.

In this house you had to stay at the table until you had eaten everything on your plate. " 'Think of the starving Armenians,' mother used to say," says my mother. "I didn't see how eating my bread crusts was going to help them out one jot."

It was in this house that I first saw a stalk of oats in a vase, each oat wrapped in the precious silver paper which had been carefully saved from a chocolate box. I thought it was the most wonderful thing I had ever seen, and began saving silver paper myself. But I never got around to wrapping the oats, and in any case I didn't know how. Like many other art forms of vanished civilizations, the techniques for this one have been lost and cannot quite be duplicated.

"We had oranges at Christmas," says my mother. "They came all the way from Florida; they were very expensive. That was the big treat: to find an orange in the toe of your stocking. It's funny to remember how good they tasted, now."

*   *   *

When she was sixteen, my mother had hair so long she could sit on it. Women were bobbing their hair by then; it was getting to be the twenties. My mother's hair was giving her headaches, she says, but my grandfather, who was very strict, forbade her to cut it. She waited until one Saturday when she knew he had an appointment with the dentist.

"In those days there was no freezing," says my mother. "The drill was worked with a foot pedal, and it went *grind, grind, grind*. The dentist himself had brown teeth: he chewed tobacco, and he would spit the tobacco juice into a spittoon while he was working on your teeth."

Here my mother, who is a good mimic, imitates the sounds of the drill and the tobacco juice: "*Rrrrr! Rrrrr! Rrrrr! Phtt! Rrrrr! Rrrrr! Rrrrr! Phtt!* It was always sheer agony. It was a heaven-sent salvation when gas came in."

My mother went into the dentist's office, where my grandfather was sitting in the chair, white with pain. She asked him if she could have her hair cut. He said she could do anything in tarnation as long as she would get out of there and stop pestering him.

"So I went out straight away and had it all chopped off," says my mother jauntily. "He was furious afterwards, but what could he do? He'd given his word."

My own hair reposes in a cardboard box in a steamer trunk in my mother's cellar, where I picture it becoming duller and more brittle with each passing year, and possibly moth-eaten; by now it will look like the faded wreaths of hair in Victorian funeral jewellery. Or it may have developed a dry mildew; inside its tissue-paper wrappings it glows faintly, in the darkness of the trunk. I suspect my mother has forgotten it's in there. It was cut off, much to my relief, when I was twelve and my sister was born. Before that it was in long curls: "Otherwise," says my mother, "it would have been just one big snarl." My mother combed it by winding it around her index finger every morning, but when she was in the hospital my father couldn't cope. "He couldn't get it around his stubby fingers," says my mother. My father looks down at his fingers. They are indeed broad compared with my mother's long elegant ones, which she calls boney. He smiles a pussy-cat smile.

So it was that my hair was sheared off. I sat in the chair in my first beauty parlour and watched it falling, like handfuls of cobwebs, down over my shoulders. From within it my head began to emerge, smaller, denser, my face more angular. I aged five years in fifteen minutes. I knew I could go home now and try out lipstick.

"Your father was upset about it," says my mother, with an air of collusion. She doesn't say this when my father is present. We smile, over the odd reactions of men to hair.

*   *   *

I used to think that my mother, in her earlier days, led a life of sustained hilarity and hair-raising adventure. (That was before I realized that she never put in the long stretches of uneventful time that must have made up much of her life: the stories were just the punctuation.) Horses ran away with her, men offered to, she was continually falling out of trees or off the ridgepoles of barns, or nearly being swept out to sea in rip-tides; or, in a more minor vein, suffering acute embarrassment in trying circumstances.

Churches were especially dangerous. "There was a guest preacher one Sunday," she says. "Of course we had to go to church every Sunday. There he was, in full career, preaching hellfire and damnation"—she pounds an invisible pulpit—"and his full set of false teeth shot out of his mouth—phoop!—just like that. Well, he didn't miss a stride. He stuck his hand up and caught them and popped them back into his mouth, and he kept right on, condemning us all to eternal torment. The pew was shaking! The tears were rolling down our faces, and the worst of it was, we were in the front pew, he was looking right at us. But of course we couldn't laugh out loud: father would have given us Hail Columbia."

Other people's parlours were booby-trapped for her; so were any and all formal social occasions. Zippers sprang apart on her clothes in strategic places, hats were unreliable. The shortage of real elastic during the war demanded constant alertness: underpants then had buttons, and were more taboo and therefore more significant than they are now. "There you would be," she says, "right on the street, and before you knew it they'd be down around your galoshes. The way to do was to step out of them with one foot, then kick them up with your other foot and whip them into your purse. I got quite good at it."

This particular story is told only to a few, but other stories are for general consumption. When she tells them, my mother's face turns to rubber. She takes all the parts, adds the sound effects, waves her hands around in the air. Her eyes gleam, sometimes a little wickedly, for although my mother is sweet and old and a lady, she avoids being a sweet old lady. When people are in danger of mistaking her for one, she flings in something from left field; she refuses to be taken for granted.

But my mother cannot be duped into telling stories when she doesn't want to. If you prompt her, she becomes self-conscious and clams up. Or she will laugh and go out into the kitchen, and shortly after that you will hear the whir of the Mixmaster. Long ago I gave up attempting to make her do tricks at parties. In gatherings of unknown people, she merely listens intently, her head tilted a little, smiling a smile of glazed politeness. The secret is to wait and see what she will say afterwards.

*   *   *

At the age of seventeen my mother went to the Normal School in Truro. This name—"Normal School"—once held a certain magic for me. I thought it had something to do with learning to be normal, which possibly it did, because really it was where you used to go to learn how to be a schoolteacher. Subsequently my mother taught in a one-room school house not far from her home. She rode her horse to and from the school house every day, and saved up the money she earned and sent herself to university with it. My grandfather wouldn't send her: he said she was too frivolous-minded. She liked ice-skating and dancing too much for his taste.

At Normal School my mother boarded with a family that contained several sons in more or less the same age group as the girl boarders. They all ate around a huge dining-room table (which I pictured as being of dark wood, with heavy carved legs, but covered always with a white linen tablecloth), with the mother and father presiding, one at each end. I saw them both as large and pink and beaming.

"The boys were great jokers," says my mother. "They were always up to something." This was desirable in boys: to be great jokers, to be always up to something. My mother adds a key sentence: "We had a lot of fun."

Having fun has always been high on my mother's agenda. She has as much fun as possible, but what she means by this phrase cannot be understood without making an adjustment, an allowance for the great gulf across which this phrase must travel before it reaches us. It comes from another world, which, like the stars that originally sent out the light we see hesitating in the sky above us these nights, may be or is already gone. It is possible to reconstruct the facts of this world—the furniture, the clothing, the ornaments on the mantelpiece, the jugs and basins and even the chamber pots in the bedrooms, but not the emotions, not with the same exactness. So much that is now known and felt must be excluded.

This was a world in which guileless flirtation was possible, because there were many things that were simply not done by nice girls, and more girls were nice then. To fall from niceness was to fall not only from grace: sexual acts, by girls at any rate, had financial consequences. Life was more joyful and innocent then, and at the same time permeated with guilt and terror, or at least the occasions for them, on the most daily level. It was like the Japanese haiku: a limited form, rigid in its perimeters, within which an astonishing freedom was possible.

There are photographs of my mother at this time, taken with three or four other girls, linked arm in arm or with their arms thrown jestingly around each other's necks. Behind them, beyond the sea or the hills or whatever is in the background, is a world already hurtling towards ruin, unknown to them: the theory of relativity has been discovered, acid is accumulating at the roots of trees, the bull-frogs are doomed. But they smile with something that from this distance you could almost call gallantry, their right legs thrust forward in parody of a chorus line.

One of the great amusements for the girl boarders and the sons of the family was amateur theatre. Young people—they were called "young people"—frequently performed in plays, which were put on in the church basement. My mother was a regular actor. (I have a stack of the scripts somewhere about the house, yellowing little booklets with my mother's parts checked in pencil. They are all comedies, and all impenetrable.) "There was no television then," says my mother. "You made your own fun."

For one of these plays a cat was required, and my mother and one of the sons borrowed the family cat. They put it into a canvas bag and drove to the rehearsal (there were cars by then), with my mother holding the cat on her lap. The cat, which must have been frightened, wet itself copiously, through the canvas bag and all over my mother's skirt. At the same time it made the most astonishingly bad smell.

"I was ready to sink through the floorboards," says my mother. "But what could I do? All I could do was sit there. In those days things like that"—she means cat pee, or pee of any sort—"were not mentioned." She means in mixed company.

I think of my mother driven through the night, skirts dripping, overcome with shame, the young man beside her staring straight ahead, pretending not to notice anything. They both feel that this act of unmentionable urination has been done, not by the cat, but by my mother. And so they continue, in a straight line that takes them over the Atlantic and past the curvature of the earth, out through the moon's orbit and into the dark reaches beyond.

Meanwhile, back on earth, my mother says: "I had to throw the skirt out. It was a good skirt, too, but nothing could get rid of the smell."

*   *   *

"I only heard your father swear once," says my mother. My mother herself never swears. When she comes to a place in a story in which swearing is called for, she says "dad-ratted" or "blankety-blank."

"It was when he mashed his thumb, when he was sinking the well, for the pump." This story, I know, takes place before I was born, up north, where there is nothing underneath the trees and their sheddings but sand and bedrock. The well was for a hand pump, which in turn was for the first of the many cabins and houses my parents built together. But since I witnessed later wells being sunk and later hand pumps being installed, I know how it's done. There's a pipe with a point at one end. You pound it into the ground with a sledge hammer, and as it goes down you screw other lengths of pipe onto it, until you hit drinkable water. To keep from ruining the thread on the top end, you hold a block of wood between the sledge hammer and the pipe. Better, you get someone else to hold it for you. This is how my father mashed his thumb: he was doing both the holding and the hammering himself.

"It swelled up like a radish," says my mother. "He had to make a hole in the nail, with his toad-sticker, to ease the pressure. The blood spurted out like pips from a lemon. Later on the whole nail turned purple and black and dropped off. Luckily he grew another one. They say you only get two chances. When he did it though, he turned the air blue for yards around. I didn't even know he knew those words. I don't know where he picked them up." She speaks as if these words are a minor contagious disease, like chicken pox.

Here my father looks modestly down at his plate. For him, there are two worlds: one containing ladies, in which you do not use certain expressions, and another one—consisting of logging camps and other haunts of his youth, and of gatherings of acceptable sorts of men—in which you do. To let the men's world slip over verbally into the ladies' would reveal you as a mannerless boor, but to carry the ladies' world over into the men's brands you a prig and maybe even a pansy. This is the word for it. All of this is well understood between them.

This story illustrates several things: that my father is no pansy, for one; and that my mother behaved properly by being suitably shocked. But my mother's eyes shine with delight while she tells this story. Secretly, she thinks it funny that my father got caught out, even if only once. The thumbnail that fell off is, in any significant way, long forgotten.

* * *

There are some stories which my mother does not tell when there are men present: never at dinner, never at parties. She tells them to women only, usually in the kitchen, when they or we are helping with the dishes or shelling peas, or taking the tops and tails off the string beans, or husking corn. She tells them in a lowered voice, without moving her hands around in the air, and they contain no sound effects. These are stories of romantic betrayals, unwanted pregnancies, illnesses of various horrible kinds, marital infidelities, mental breakdowns, tragic suicides, unpleasant lingering deaths. They are not rich in detail or embroidered with incident: they are stark and factual. The women, their own hands moving among the dirty dishes or the husks of vegetables, nod solemnly.

Some of these stories, it is understood, are not to be passed on to my father, because they would upset him. It is well known that women can deal with this sort of thing better than men can. Men are not to be told anything they might find too painful; the secret depths of human nature, the sordid physicalities, might overwhelm or damage them. For instance, men often faint at the sight of their own blood, to which they are not accustomed. For this reason you should never stand behind one in the line at the Red Cross donor clinic. Men, for some mysterious reason, find life more difficult than women do. (My mother believes this, despite the female bodies, trapped, diseased, disappearing, or abandoned, that litter her stories.) Men must be allowed to play in the sandbox of their choice, as happily as they can, without disturbance; otherwise they get cranky and won't eat their dinners. There are all kinds of things that men are simply not equipped to understand, so why expect it of them? Not everyone shares this belief about men; nevertheless, it has its uses.

"She dug up the shrubs from around the house," says my mother. This story is about a shattered marriage: serious business. My mother's eyes widen. The other women lean forward. "All she left him were the shower curtains." There is a collective sigh, an expelling of breath. My father enters the kitchen, wondering when the tea will be ready, and the women close ranks, turning to him their deceptive blankly smiling faces. Soon afterwards, my mother emerges from the kitchen, carrying the tea pot, and sets it down on the table in its ritual place.

* * *

"I remember the time we almost died," says my mother. Many of her stories begin this way. When she is in a certain mood, we are to understand that our lives have been preserved only by a series of amazing coincidences and strokes of luck; otherwise the entire family, individually or collectively, would be dead as doornails. These stories, in addition to producing adrenalin, serve to reinforce our sense of gratitude. There is the time we almost went over a waterfall, in a canoe, in a fog; the time we almost got caught in a forest fire; the time my father almost got squashed, before my mother's very eyes, by a ridgepole he was lifting into place; the time my brother almost got struck by a bolt of lightning, which went by him so close it knocked him down. "You could hear it sizzle," says my mother.

This is the story of the hay wagon. "Your father was driving," says my mother, "at the speed he usually goes." We read between the lines: *too fast.* "You kids were in the back." I can remember this day, so I can remember how old I was, how old my brother was. We were old enough to think it was funny to annoy my father by singing popular songs of a type he disliked, such as "Mockingbird Hill"; or perhaps we were imitating bagpipe music by holding our noses and humming, while hitting our Adam's apples with the edges of our hands. When we became too irritating my father would say, "Pipe down." We weren't old enough to know that his irritation could be real: we thought it was part of the game.

"We were going down a steep hill," my mother continues, "when a hay wagon pulled out right across the road, at the bottom. Your father put on the brakes, but nothing happened. The brakes were gone! I thought our last moment had come." Luckily the hay wagon continued across the road, and we shot past it, missing it by at least a foot. "My heart was in my mouth," says my mother.

I didn't know until afterwards what had really happened. I was in the back seat, making bagpipe music, oblivious. The scenery was the same as it always was on car trips: my parents' heads, seen from behind, sticking up above the front seat. My father had his hat on, the one he wore to keep things from falling off the trees into his hair. My mother's hand was placed lightly on the back of his neck.

*   *   *

"You had such an acute sense of smell when you were younger," says my mother.

Now we are on more dangerous ground: my mother's childhood is one thing, my own quite another. This is the moment at which I start rattling the silverware, or ask for another cup of tea. "You used to march into houses that were strange to you, and you would say in a loud voice, 'What's that funny smell?' " If there are guests present, they shift a little away from me, conscious of their own emanations, trying not to look at my nose.

"I used to be so embarrassed," says my mother absent-mindedly. Then she shifts gears. "You were such an easy child. You used to get up at six in the morning and play by yourself in the play room, singing away. . . ."

There is a pause. A distant voice, mine, high and silvery, drifts over the space between us. "You used to talk a blue streak. Chatter, chatter, chatter, from morning to night." My mother sighs imperceptibly, as if wondering why I have become so silent, and gets up to poke the fire.

Hoping to change the subject, I ask whether or not the crocuses have come up yet, but she is not to be diverted. "I never had to spank you," she says. "A harsh word, and you would be completely reduced." She looks at me sideways; she isn't sure what I have turned into, or how. "There were just one or two times. Once, when I had to go out and I left your father in charge." (This may be the real point of the story: the inability of men to second-guess small children.) "I came back along the street, and there were you and your brother, throwing mud balls at an old man out of the upstairs window."

We both know whose idea this was. For my mother, the proper construction to be put on this event is that my brother was a hell-raiser and I was his shadow, "easily influenced," as my mother puts it. "You were just putty in my hands."

"Of course, I had to punish both of you equally," she says. Of course. I smile a forgiving smile. The real truth is that I was sneakier than my brother, and got caught less often. No front-line charges into enemy machine-gun nests for me, if they could be at all avoided. My own solitary acts of wickedness were devious and well concealed; it was only in partnership with my brother that I would throw caution to the winds.

"He could wind you around his little finger," says my mother. "Your father made each of you a toy box, and the rule was—" (my mother is good at the devising of rules) "—the rule was that neither of you could take the toys out of the other one's toy box without permission. Otherwise he would have got all your toys away from you. But he got them anyway, mind you. He used to talk you into playing house, and he would pretend to be the baby. Then he would pretend to cry, and when you asked what he wanted, he'd demand whatever it was out of your toy box that he wanted to play with at the moment. You always gave it to him."

I don't remember this, though I do remember staging World War Two on the living-room floor, with armies of stuffed bears and rabbits; but surely some primal patterns were laid down. Have these early toy-box experiences—and "toy box" itself, as a concept, reeks with implications—have they made me suspicious of men who wish to be mothered, yet susceptible to them at the same time? Have I been conditioned to believe that if I am not solicitous, if I am not forthcoming, if I am not a never-ending cornucopia of entertaining delights, they will take their collections of milk-bottle tops and their mangy one-eared teddy bears and go away into the woods by themselves to play snipers? Probably. What my mother thinks was merely cute may have been lethal.

But this is not her only story about my suckiness and gullibility. She follows up with the *coup de grâce*, the tale of the bunny-rabbit cookies.

"It was in Ottawa. I was invited to a government tea," says my mother, and this fact alone should signal an element of horror: my mother hated official functions, to which however she was obliged to go because she was the wife of a civil servant. "I had to drag you kids along; we couldn't afford a lot of babysitters in those days." The hostess had made a whole plateful of decorated cookies for whatever children might be present, and my mother proceeds to describe these: wonderful cookies shaped like bunny rabbits, with faces and clothes of coloured icing, little skirts for the little girl bunny rabbits, little pants for the little boy bunny rabbits.

"You chose one," says my mother. "You went off to a corner with it, by yourself. Mrs. X noticed you and went over. 'Aren't you going to eat your cookie?' she said. 'Oh, no,' you said. 'I'll just sit here and talk to it.' And there you sat, as happy as a clam. But someone had made the mistake of leaving the plate near your brother. When they looked again, there wasn't a single cookie left. He'd eaten every one. He was very sick that night, I can tell you."

Some of my mother's stories defy analysis. What is the moral of this one? That I was a simp is clear enough, but on the other hand it was my brother who got the stomach ache. Is it better to eat your food, in a straightforward materialistic way, and as much of it as possible, or go off into the corner and talk to it? This used to be a favourite of my mother's before I was married, when I would bring what my father referred to as "swains" home for dinner. Along with the dessert, out would come the bunny-rabbit cookie story, and I would cringe and twiddle my spoon while my mother forged blithely on with it. What were the swains supposed to make of it? Were my kindliness and essential femininity being trotted out for their inspection? Were they being told in a roundabout way that I was harmless, that they could expect to be talked to by me, but not devoured? Or was she, in some way, warning them off? Because there is something faintly crazed about my behaviour, some tinge of the kind of person who might be expected to leap up suddenly from the dinner table and shout, "Don't eat that! It's alive!"

There is, however, a difference between symbolism and anecdote. Listening to my mother, I sometimes remember this.

*   *   *

"In my next incarnation," my mother said once, "I'm going to be an archaeologist and go around digging things up." We were sitting on the bed that had once been my brother's, then mine, then my sister's; we were sorting out things from one of the trunks, deciding what could now be given away or thrown out. My mother believes that what you save from the past is mostly a matter of choice.

At that time something wasn't right in the family; someone wasn't happy. My mother was angry: her good cheer was not paying off.

This statement of hers startled me. It was the first time I'd ever heard my mother say that she might have wanted to be something other than what she was. I must have been thirty-five at the time, but it was still shocking and slightly offensive to me to learn that my mother might not have been totally contented fulfilling the role in which fate had cast her: that of being my mother. What thumbsuckers we all are, I thought, when it comes to mothers.

Shortly after this I became a mother myself, and this moment altered for me.

*   *   *

While she was combing my next-to-impossible hair, winding it around her long index finger, yanking out the snarls, my mother used to read me stories. Most of them are still in the house somewhere, but one has vanished. It may have been a library book. It was about a little girl who was so poor she had only one potato left for her supper, and while she was roasting it the potato got up and ran away. There was the usual chase, but I can't remember the ending: a significant lapse.

"That story was one of your favourites," says my mother. She is probably still under the impression that I identified with the little girl, with her hunger and her sense of loss; whereas in reality I identified with the potato.

Early influences are important. It took that one a while to come out; probably until after I went to university and started wearing black stockings and pulling my hair back into a bun, and having pretentions. Gloom set in. Our next-door neighbour, who was interested in wardrobes, tackled my mother: " 'If she would only *do* something about herself,' " my mother quotes, " 'she could be *quite attractive*.' "

"You always kept yourself busy," my mother says charitably, referring to this time. "You always had something cooking. Some project or other."

It is part of my mother's mythology that I am as cheerful and productive as she is, though she admits that these qualities may be occasionally and temporarily concealed. I wasn't allowed much angst around the house. I had to indulge it in the cellar, where my mother wouldn't come upon me brooding and suggest I should go out for a walk, to improve my circulation. This was her answer to any sign, however slight, of creeping despondency. There wasn't a lot that a brisk sprint through dead leaves, howling winds, or sleet couldn't cure.

It was, I knew, the zeitgeist that was afflicting me, and against it such simple remedies were powerless. Like smog I wafted through her days, dankness spreading out from around me. I read modern poetry and histories of Nazi atrocities, and took to drinking coffee. Off in the distance, my mother vacuumed around my feet while I sat in chairs, studying, with car rugs tucked around me, for suddenly I was always cold.

My mother has few stories to tell about these times. What I remember from them is the odd look I would sometimes catch in her eyes. It struck me, for the first time in my life, that my mother might be afraid of me. I could not even reassure her, because I was only dimly aware of the nature of her distress, but there must have been something going on in me that was beyond her: at any time I might open my mouth and out would come a language she had never heard before. I had become a visitant from outer space, a time-traveller come back from the future, bearing news of a great disaster.

Going to Meet the Man

JAMES BALDWIN

"What's the matter?" she asked.

"I don't know," he said, trying to laugh, "I guess I'm tired."

"You've been working too hard," she said. "I keep telling you."

"Well, goddammit, woman," he said. "it's not my fault!" He tried again; he wretchedly failed again. Then he just lay there, silent, angry, and helpless. Excitement filled him just like a toothache, but it refused to enter his flesh. He stroked her breast. This was his wife. He could not ask her to do just a little thing for him, just to help him out, just for a little while, the way he could ask a nigger girl to do it. He lay there, and he sighed. The image of a black girl caused a distant excitement in him, like a far-away light; but, again, the excitement was more like pain; instead of forcing him to act, it made action impossible.

"Go to sleep," she said, gently, "you got a hard day tomorrow."

"Yeah," he said, and rolled over on his side, facing her, one hand still on one breast. "Goddamn the niggers. The black stinking coons. You'd think they'd learn. Wouldn't you think they'd learn? I mean, *wouldn't* you?"

"They going to be out there tomorrow," she said, and took his hand away, "get some sleep."

He lay there, one hand between his legs, staring at the frail sanctuary of his wife. A faint light came from the shutters; the moon was full. Two dogs, far away, were barking at each other, back and forth, insistently, as though they were agreeing to make an appointment. He heard a car coming north on the road and he half sat up, his hand reaching for his holster, which was on a chair near the bed, on top of his pants. The lights hit the shutters and seemed to travel across the room and then went out. The sound of the car slipped away, he heard it hit gravel, then heard it no more. Some liver-lipped students, probably, heading back to that college—but coming from where? His watch said it was two in the morning. They could be coming

55

from anywhere, from out of state most likely, and they would be at the courthouse tomorrow. The niggers were getting ready. Well, they would be ready, too.

He moaned. He wanted to let whatever was in him out; but it wouldn't come out. Goddamn! he said aloud, and turned again, on his side, away from Grace, staring at the shutters. He was a big, healthy man and he had never had any trouble sleeping. And he wasn't old enough yet to have any trouble getting it up—he was only forty-two. And he was a good man, a God-fearing man, he had tried to do his duty all his life, and he had been a deputy sheriff for several years. Nothing had ever bothered him before, certainly not getting it up. Sometimes, sure, like any other man, he knew that he wanted a little more spice than Grace could give him and he would drive over yonder and pick up a black piece or arrest her, it came to the same thing, but he couldn't do that now, no more. There was no telling what might happen once your ass was in the air. And they were low enough to kill a man then, too, every one of them, or the girl herself might do it, right while she was making believe you made her feel so good. The niggers. What had the good Lord Almighty had in mind when he made the niggers? Well. They were pretty good at that, all right. Damn. Damn. Goddamn.

This wasn't helping him to sleep. He turned again, toward Grace again, and moved close to her warm body. He felt something he had never felt before. He felt that he would like to hold her, hold her, hold her, and be buried in her like a child and never have to get up in the morning again and go downtown to face those faces, good Christ, they were ugly! and never have to enter that jail house again and smell that smell and hear that singing; never again feel that filthy, kinky, greasy hair under his hand, never again watch those black breasts leap against the leaping cattle prod, never hear those moans again or watch that blood run down or the fat lips split or the scaled eyes struggle open. They were animals, they were no better than animals, what could be done with people like that? Here they had been in a civilized country for years and they still lived like animals. Their houses were dark, with oil cloth or cardboard in the windows, the smell was enough to make you puke your guts out, and there they sat, a whole tribe, pumping out kids, it looked like, every damn five minutes, and laughing and talking and playing music like they didn't have a care in the world, and he reckoned they didn't, neither, and coming to the door, into the sunlight, just standing there, just looking foolish, not thinking of anything but just getting back to what they were doing, saying, Yes suh, Mr. Jesse. I surely will, Mr. Jesse. Fine weather, Mr. Jesse. Why, I thank you, Mr. Jesse. He had worked for a mail-order house for a while and it had been his job to collect the payments for the stuff they bought. They were too dumb to know that they were being cheated blind, but that was no skin off his ass— he was just supposed to do his job. They would be late—they didn't have the sense to put money aside; but it was easy to scare them, and he never really had any trouble. Hell, they all liked him, the kids used to smile when he came to the door. He gave them candy, sometimes, or chewing gum, and rubbed their rough bullet heads—maybe the candy should have been poisoned. Those kids were grown now. He had had trouble with one of them today.

"There was this nigger today," he said; and stopped; his voice sounded peculiar. He touched Grace. "You awake?" he asked. She mumbled something, impatiently, she was probably telling him to go to sleep. It was all right. He knew that he was not alone.

"What a funny time," he said, "to be thinking about a thing like that— you listening?" She mumbled something again. He rolled over on his back. "This nigger's one of the ringleaders. We had trouble with him before. We must have had him out there at the work farm three or four times. Well, Big Jim C. and some of the boys really had to whip that nigger's ass today." He looked over at Grace; he could not tell whether she was listening or not; and he was afraid to ask again. "They had this line you know, to register"— he laughed, but she did not—"and they wouldn't stay where Big Jim C. wanted them, no, they had to start blocking traffic all around the court house so couldn't nothing or nobody get through, and Big Jim C. told them to disperse and they wouldn't move, they just kept up that singing, and Big Jim C. figured that the others would move if this nigger would move, him being the ring-leader, but he wouldn't move and he wouldn't let the others move, so they had to beat him and a couple of the others and they threw them in the wagon—but *I* didn't see this nigger till I got to the jail. They were still singing and I was supposed to make them stop. Well, I couldn't make them stop for me but I knew he could make them stop. He was lying on the ground jerking and moaning, they had threw him in a cell by himself, and blood was coming out his ears from where Big Jim C. and his boys had whipped him. Wouldn't you think they'd learn? I put the prod to him and he jerked some more and he kind of screamed—but he didn't have much voice left. "You make them stop that singing," I said to him, "you hear me? You make them stop that singing." He acted like he didn't hear me and I put it to him again, under his arms, and he just rolled around on the floor and blood started coming from his mouth. He'd pissed his pants already." He paused. His mouth felt dry and his throat was as rough as sandpaper; as he talked, he began to hurt all over with that peculiar excitement which refused to be released. "You all are going to stop your singing, I said to him, and you are going to stop coming down to the court house and disrupting traffic and molesting the people and keeping us from our duties and keeping doctors from getting to sick white women and getting all them Northerners in this town to give our town a bad name—!" As he said this, he kept prodding the boy, sweat pouring from beneath the helmet he had not yet taken off. The boy rolled around in his own dirt and water and blood and tried to scream again as the prod hit his testicles, but the scream did not come out, only a kind of rattle and a moan. He stopped. He was not supposed to kill the nigger. The cell was filled with a terrible odor. The boy was still. "You hear me?" he called. "You had enough?" The singing went on. "You had enough?" His foot leapt out, he had not known it was going to, and caught the boy flush on the jaw. *Jesus*, he thought, *this ain't no nigger, this is a goddamn bull*, and he screamed again, "You had enough? You going to make them stop that singing now?"

But the boy was out. And now he was shaking worse than the boy had been shaking. He was glad no one could see him. At the same time, he felt very close to a very peculiar, particular joy; something deep in him and deep in his memory was stirred, but whatever was in his memory eluded him. He took off his helmet. He walked to the cell door.

"White man," said the boy, from the floor, behind him.

He stopped. For some reason, he grabbed his privates.

"You remember Old Julia?"

The boy said, from the floor, with his mouth full of blood, and one eye, barely open, glaring like the eye of a cat in the dark, "My grandmother's name was Mrs. Julia Blossom. *Mrs.* Julia Blossom. You going to call our women by their right names yet.—And those kids ain't going to stop singing. We going to keep on singing until every one of you miserable white mothers go stark raving out of your minds." Then he closed the one eye; he spat blood; his head fell back against the floor.

He looked down at the boy, whom he had been seeing, off and on, for more than a year, and suddenly remembered him: Old Julia had been one of his mail-order customers, a nice old woman. He had not seen her for years, he supposed that she must be dead.

He had walked into the yard, the boy had been sitting in a swing. He had smiled at the boy, and asked, "Old Julia home?"

The boy looked at him for a long time before he answered. "Don't no Old Julia live here."

"This is her house. I know her. She's lived here for years."

The boy shook his head. "You might know a Old Julia someplace else, white man. But don't nobody by that name live here."

He watched the boy; the boy watched him. The boy certainly wasn't more than ten. *White man.* He didn't have time to be fooling around with some crazy kid. He yelled, "Hey! Old Julia!"

But only silence answered him. The expression on the boy's face did not change. The sun beat down on them both, still and silent; he had the feeling that he had been caught up in a nightmare, a nightmare dreamed by a child; perhaps one of the nightmares he himself had dreamed as a child. It had that feeling—everything familiar, without undergoing any other change, had been subtly and hideously displaced: the trees, the sun, the patches of grass in the yard, the leaning porch and the weary porch steps and the cardboard in the windows and the black hole of the door which looked like the entrance to a cave, and the eyes of the pickaninny, all, all, were charged with malevolence. *White man.* He looked at the boy. "She's gone out?"

The boy said nothing.

"Well," he said, "tell her I passed by and I'll pass by next week." He started to go; he stopped. "You want some chewing gum?"

The boy got down from the swing and started for the house. He said, "I don't want nothing you got, white man." He walked into the house and closed the door behind him.

Now the boy looked as though he were dead. Jesse wanted to go over to him and pick him up and pistol whip him until the boy's head burst open like a melon. He began to tremble with what he believed was rage, sweat, both cold and hot, raced down his body, the singing filled him as though it were a weird, uncontrollable, monstrous howling rumbling up from the depths of his own belly, he felt an icy fear rise in him and raise him up, and he shouted, he howled, "You lucky we *pump* some white blood into you every once in a while—your women! Here's what I got for all the black bitches in the world—!" Then he was, abruptly, almost too weak to stand; to his bewilderment, his horror, beneath his own fingers, he felt himself violently stiffen—with no warning at all; he dropped his hands and he stared at the boy and he left the cell.

"All that singing they do," he said. "All that singing." He could not remember the first time he had heard it; he had been hearing it all his life. It was the sound with which he was most familiar—though it was also the sound of which he had been least conscious—and it had always contained an obscure comfort. They were singing to God. They were singing for mercy and they hoped to go to heaven, and he had even sometimes felt, when looking into the eyes of some of the old women, a few of the very old men, that they were singing for mercy for his soul, too. Of course he had never thought of their heaven or of what God was, or could be, for them; God was the same for everyone, he supposed, and heaven was where good people went—he supposed. He had never thought much about what it meant to be a good person. He tried to be a good person and treat everybody right: it wasn't his fault if the niggers had taken it into their heads to fight against God and go against the rules laid down in the Bible for everyone to read! Any preacher would tell you that. He was only doing his duty: protecting white people from the niggers and the niggers from themselves. And there were still lots of good niggers around—he had to remember that; they weren't all like that boy this afternoon; and the good niggers must be mighty sad to see what was happening to their people. They would thank him when this was over. In that way they had, the best of them, not quite looking him in the eye, in a low voice, with a little smile: We surely thanks you, Mr. Jesse. From the bottom of our hearts, we thanks you. He smiled. They hadn't all gone crazy. This trouble would pass.—He knew that the young people had changed some of the words to the songs. He had scarcely listened to the words before and he did not listen to them now; but he knew that the words were different; he could hear that much. He did not know if the faces were different, he had never, before this trouble began, watched them as they sang, but he certainly did not like what he saw now. They hated him, and this hatred was blacker than their hearts, blacker than their skins, redder than their blood, and harder, by far, than his club. Each day, each night, he felt worn out, aching, with their smell in his nostrils and filling his lungs, as though he were drowning—drowning in niggers; and it was all to be done again when he awoke. It would never end. It would never end. Perhaps this was what the singing had meant all along. They had not been singing black folks into heaven, they had been singing white folks into hell.

Everyone felt this black suspicion in many ways, but no one knew how to express it. Men much older than he, who had been responsible for law and order much longer than he, were now much quieter than they had been, and the tone of their jokes, in a way that he could not quite put his finger on, had changed. These men were his models, they had been friends to his father, and they had taught him what it meant to be a man. He looked to them for courage now. It wasn't that he didn't know that what he was doing was right—he knew that, nobody had to tell him that; it was only that he missed the ease of former years. But they didn't have much time to hang out with each other these days. They tended to stay close to their families every free minute because nobody knew what might happen next. Explosions rocked the night of their tranquil town. Each time each man wondered silently if perhaps this time the dynamite had not fallen into the wrong hands. They thought that they knew where all the guns were; but they could not possibly know every move that was made in that secret place where the darkies lived. From time to time it was suggested that they form a posse and search the home of every nigger, but they hadn't done it yet. For one thing, this might have brought the bastards from the North down on their backs; for another, although the niggers were scattered throughout the town—down in the hollow near the railroad tracks, way west near the mills, up on the hill, the well-off ones, and some out near the college— nothing seemed to happen in one part of town without the niggers immediately knowing it in the other. This meant that they could not take them by surprise. They rarely mentioned it, but they *knew* that some of the niggers had guns. It stood to reason, as they said, since, after all, some of them had been in the Army. There were niggers in the Army right now and God knows they wouldn't have had any trouble stealing this half-assed government blind—the whole world was doing it, look at the European countries and all those countries in Africa. They made jokes about it—bitter jokes; and they cursed the government in Washington, which had betrayed them; but they had not yet formed a posse. Now, if their town had been laid out

like some towns in the North, where all the niggers lived together in one lo-
cality, they could have gone down and set fire to the houses and brought
about peace that way. If the niggers had all lived in one place, they could
have kept the fire in one place. But the way this town was laid out, the fire
could hardly be controlled. It would spread all over town—and the niggers
would probably be helping it to spread. Still, from time to time, they spoke
of doing it, anyway; so that now there was a real fear among them that
somebody might go crazy and light the match.

They rarely mentioned anything not directly related to the war that they
were fighting, but this had failed to establish between them the unspoken
communication of soldiers during a war. Each man, in the thrilling silence
which sped outward from their exchanges, their laughter, and their anecdotes, seemed wrestling, in various degrees of darkness, with a secret which
he could not articulate to himself, and which, however directly it related to
the war, related yet more surely to his privacy and his past. They could no
longer be sure, after all, that they had all done the same things. They had
never dreamed that their privacy could contain any element of terror,
could threaten, that is, to reveal itself, to the scrutiny of a judgment day,
while remaining unreadable and inaccessible to themselves; nor had they
dreamed that the past, while certainly refusing to be forgotten, could yet so
stubbornly refuse to be remembered. They felt themselves mysteriously set
at naught, as no longer entering into the real concerns of other people—
while here they were, outnumbered, fighting to save the civilized world.
They had thought that people would care—people didn't care; not
enough, anyway, to help them. It would have been a help, really, or at least
a relief, even to have been forced to surrender. Thus they had lost, probably forever, their old and easy connection with each other. They were
forced to depend on each other more and, at the same time, to trust each
other less. Who could tell when one of them might not betray them all, for
money, or for the ease of confession? But no one dared imagine what there
might be to confess. They were soldiers fighting a war, but their relationship to each other was that of accomplices in a crime. They all had to keep
their mouths shut.

I stepped in the river at Jordan.

Out of the darkness of the room, out of nowhere, the line came flying up
at him, with the melody and the beat. He turned wordlessly toward his
sleeping wife.

I stepped in the river at Jordan.

Where had he heard that song?

"Grace," he whispered. "You awake?"

She did not answer. If she was awake, she wanted him to sleep. Her breathing was slow and easy, her body slowly rose and fell.

> *I stepped in the river at Jordan.*
> *The water came to my knees.*

He began to sweat. He felt an overwhelming fear, which yet contained a curious and dreadful pleasure.

> *I stepped in the river at Jordan*
> *The water came to my waist.*

It had been night, as it was now, he was in the car between his mother and his father, sleepy, his head in his mother's lap, sleepy, and yet full of excitement. The singing came from far away, across the dark fields. There were no lights anywhere. They had said good-bye to all the others and turned off on this dark dirt road. They were almost home.

> *I stepped in the river at Jordan,*
> *The water came over my head,*
> *I looked way over to the other side,*
> *He was making up my dying bed!*

"I guess they singing for him," his father said, seeming very weary and subdued now. "Even when they're sad, they sound like they just about to go and tear off a piece." He yawned and leaned across the boy and slapped his wife lightly on the shoulder, allowing his hand to rest there for a moment. "Don't they?"

"Don't talk that way," she said.

"Well, that's what we going to do," he said, "you can make up your mind to that." He started whistling. "You see? When I begin to feel it, I gets kind of musical, too."

> *Oh, Lord! Come on and ease my troubling mind!*

He had a black friend, his age, eight, who lived nearby. His name was Otis. They wrestled together in the dirt. Now the thought of Otis made him sick. He began to shiver. His mother put her arm around him.

"He's tired," she said.

"We'll be home soon," said his father. He began to whistle again.

"We didn't see Otis this morning," Jesse said. He did not know why he said this. His voice, in the darkness of the car, sounded small and accusing.

"You haven't seen Otis for a couple of mornings," his mother said.

That was true. But he was only concerned about *this* morning.

"No," said his father, "I reckon Otis's folks was afraid to let him show himself this morning."

"But Otis didn't do nothing!" Now his voice sounded questioning.

"Otis *can't* do nothing," said his father, "he's too little." The car lights picked up their wooden house, which now solemnly approached them, the lights falling around it like yellow dust. Their dog, chained to a tree, began to bark.

"We just want to make sure Otis don't do nothing," said his father, and stopped the car. He looked down at Jesse. "And you tell him what your Daddy said, you hear?"

"Yes sir," he said.

His father switched off the lights. The dog moaned and pranced, but they ignored him and went inside. He could not sleep. He lay awake, hearing the night sounds, the dog yawning and moaning outside, the sawing of the crickets, the cry of the owl, dogs barking far away, then no sounds at all, just the heavy, endless buzzing of the night. The darkness pressed on his eyelids like a scratchy blanket. He turned, he turned again. He wanted to call his mother, but he knew his father would not like this. He was terribly afraid. Then he heard his father's voice in the other room, low, with a joke in it; but this did not help him, it frightened him more, he knew what was going to happen. He put his head under the blanket, then pushed his head out again, for fear, staring at the dark window. He heard his mother's moan, his father's sigh; he gritted his teeth. Then their bed began to rock. His father's breathing seemed to fill the world.

That morning, before the sun had gathered all its strength, men and women, some flushed and some pale with excitement, came with news. Jesse's father seemed to know what the news was before the first jalopy stopped in the yard, and he ran out, crying, "They got him, then? They got him?"

The first jalopy held eight people, three men and two women and three children. The children were sitting on the laps of the grown-ups. Jesse knew two of them, the two boys; they shyly and uncomfortably greeted each other. He did not know the girl.

"Yes, they got him," said one of the women, the older one, who wore a wide hat and a fancy, faded blue dress. "They found him early this morning."

"How far had he got?" Jesse's father asked.

"He hadn't got no further than Harkness," one of the men said. "Look like he got lost up there in all them trees—or maybe he just got so scared he couldn't move." They all laughed.

"Yes, and you know it's near a graveyard, too," said the younger woman, and they laughed again.

"Is that where they got him now?" asked Jesse's father.

By this time there were three cars piled behind the first one, with everyone looking excited and shining, and Jesse noticed that they were carrying food. It was like a Fourth of July picnic.

"Yeah, that's where he is," said one of the men, "declare, Jesse, you going to keep us here all day long, answering your damn fool questions. Come on, we ain't got no time to waste."

"Don't bother putting up no food," cried a woman from one of the other cars, "we got enough. Just come on."

"Why, thank you," said Jesse's father, "we be right along, then."

"I better get a sweater for the boy," said his mother, "in case it turns cold."

Jesse watched his mother's thin legs cross the yard. He knew that she also wanted to comb her hair a little and maybe put on a better dress, the dress she wore to church. His father guessed this, too, for he yelled behind her, "Now don't you go trying to turn yourself into no movie star. You just come on." But he laughed as he said this, and winked at the men; his wife was younger and prettier than most of the other women. He clapped Jesse on the head and started pulling him toward the car. "You all go on," he said, "I'll be right behind you. Jesse, you go tie up that there dog while I get this car started."

The cars sputtered and coughed and shook; the caravan began to move; bright dust filled the air. As soon as he was tied up, the dog began to bark. Jesse's mother came out of the house, carrying a jacket for his father and a sweater for Jesse. She had put a ribbon in her hair and had an old shawl around her shoulders.

"Put these in the car, son," she said, and handed everything to him. She bent down and stroked the dog, looked to see if there was water in his bowl, then went back up the three porch steps and closed the door.

"Come on," said his father, "ain't nothing in there for nobody to steal." He was sitting in the car, which trembled and belched. The last car of the caravan had disappeared but the sound of singing floated behind them.

Jesse got into the car, sitting close to his father, loving the smell of the car, and the trembling, and the bright day, and the sense of going on a great and unexpected journey. His mother got in and closed the door and the car began to move. Not until then did he ask, "Where are we going? Are we going on a picnic?"

He had a feeling that he knew where they were going, but he was not sure.

"That's right," his father said, "we're going on a picnic. You won't ever forget *this* picnic—!"

"Are we," he asked, after a moment, "going to see the bad nigger—the one that knocked down old Miss Standish?"

"Well, I reckon," said his mother, "that we *might* see him."

He started to ask, *Will a lot of niggers be there? Will Otis be there?*—but he did not ask his question, to which, in a strange and uncomfortable way, he already knew the answer. Their friends, in the other cars, stretched up the road as far as he could see; other cars had joined them; there were cars behind them. They were singing. The sun seemed, suddenly very hot, and he was, at once very happy and a little afraid. He did not quite understand what was happening, and he did not know what to ask—he had no one to ask. He had grown accustomed, for the solution of such mysteries, to go to Otis. He felt that Otis knew everything. But he could not ask Otis about this. Anyway, he had not seen Otis for two days; he had not seen a black face anywhere for more than two days; and he now realized, as they began chugging up the long hill which eventually led to Harkness, that there were no black faces on the road this morning, no black people anywhere. From the houses in which they lived, all along the road, no smoke curled, no life stirred—maybe one or two chickens were to be seen, that was all. There was no one at the windows, no one in the yard, no one sitting on the porches, and the doors were closed. He had come this road many a time and seen women washing in the yard (there were no clothes on the clothes-lines) men working in the fields, children playing in the dust; black men passed them on the road other mornings, other days, on foot, or in wagons, sometimes in cars, tipping their hats, smiling, joking, their teeth a solid white against their skin, their eyes as warm as the sun, the blackness of their skin like dull fire against the white of the blue or the grey of their torn clothes. They passed the nigger church—dead-white, desolate, locked up; and the graveyard, where no one knelt or walked, and he saw no flowers. He wanted to ask, *Where are they? Where are they all?* But he did not dare. As the hill grew steeper, the sun grew colder. He looked at his mother and his father. They looked straight ahead, seeming to be listening to the singing which echoed and echoed in this graveyard silence. They were strangers to him now. They were looking at something he could not see. His father's lips had a strange, cruel curve, he wet his lips from time to time, and swallowed. He was terribly aware of his father's tongue, it was as though he had never seen it before. And his father's body suddenly seemed immense, bigger than a mountain. His eyes, which were grey-green, looked yellow in the sunlight; or at least there was a light in them which he had never seen before. His mother patted her hair and adjusted the ribbon, leaning forward to look into the car mirror. "You look all right," said his father, and laughed. "When that nigger looks at you, he's going to swear he throwed his life away for nothing. Wouldn't be surprised if he don't come back to haunt you." And he laughed again.

The singing now slowly began to cease; and he realized that they were nearing their destination. They had reached a straight, narrow, pebbly road, with trees on either side. The sunlight filtered down on them from a great height, as though they were underwater; and the branches of the trees scraped against the cars with a tearing sound. To the right of them, and beneath them, invisible now, lay the town; and to the left, miles of trees which led to the high mountain range which his ancestors had crossed in order to settle in this valley. Now, all was silent, except for the bumping of the tires against the rocky road, the sputtering of motors, and the sound of a crying child. And they seemed to move more slowly. They were beginning to climb again. He watched the cars ahead as they toiled patiently upward, disappearing into the sunlight of the clearing. Presently, he felt their vehicle also rise, heard his father's changed breathing, the sunlight hit his face, the trees moved away from them, and they were there. As their car crossed the clearing, he looked around. There seemed to be millions, there were certainly hundreds of people in the clearing, staring toward something he could not see. There was a fire. He could not see the flames, but he smelled the smoke. Then they were on the other side of the clearing, among the trees again. His father drove off the road and parked the car behind a great many other cars. He looked down at Jesse.

"You all right?" he asked.

"Yes sir," he said.

"Well, come on, then," his father said. He reached over and opened the door on his mother's side. His mother stepped out first. They followed her into the clearing. At first he was aware only of confusion, of his mother and father greeting and being greeted, himself being handled, hugged, and patted, and told how much he had grown. The wind blew the smoke from the fire across the clearing into his eyes and nose. He could not see over the backs of the people in front of him. The sounds of laughing and cursing and wrath—and something else—rolled in waves from the front of the mob to the back. Those in front expressed their delight at what they saw, and this delight rolled backward, wave upon wave, across the clearing, more acrid than the smoke. His father reached down suddenly and sat Jesse on his shoulders.

Now he saw the fire—of twigs and boxes, piled high; flames made pale orange and yellow and thin as a veil under the steadier light of the sun; grey-blue smoke rolled upward and poured over their heads. Beyond the shifting curtain of fire and smoke, he made out first only a length of gleaming chain, attached to a great limb of the tree; then he saw that this chain bound two black hands together at the wrist, dirty yellow palm facing dirty yellow palm. The smoke poured up; the hands dropped out of sight; a cry went up from the crowd. Then the hands slowly came into view again, pulled upward by the chain. This time he saw the kinky, sweating, bloody head—he had never before seen a head with so much hair on it, hair so black and so tangled that it seemed like another jungle. The head was hanging. He saw the forehead, flat and high, with a kind of arrow of hair in the center, like he had, like his father had; they called it a widow's peak; and the mangled eyebrows, the wide nose, the closed eyes, and the glinting eye lashes and the hanging lips, all streaming with blood and sweat. His hands were straight above his head. All his weight pulled downward from his hands; and he was a big man, a bigger man than his father, and black as an African jungle Cat, and naked. Jesse pulled upward; his father's hands held him firmly by the ankles. He wanted to say something, he did not know what, but nothing he said could have been heard, for now the crowd roared again as a man stepped forward and put more wood on the fire. The flames leapt up. He thought he heard the hanging man scream, but he was not sure. Sweat was pouring from the hair in his armpits, poured down his sides, over his chest, into his navel and his groin. He was lowered again; he was raised again. Now Jesse knew that he heard him scream. The head went back, the mouth wide open, blood bubbling from the mouth; the veins of the neck jumped out; Jesse clung to his father's neck in terror as the cry rolled over the crowd. The cry of all the people rose to answer the dying man's cry. He wanted death to come quickly. They wanted to make death wait: and it was they who held death, now, on a leash which they lengthened little by little. *What did he do?* Jesse wondered. *What did the man do? What did he do?*—but he could not ask his father. He was seated on his father's shoulders, but his father was far away. There were two older men, friends of his father's, raising and lowering the chain; everyone, indiscriminately, seemed to be responsible for the fire. There was no hair left on the nigger's privates, and the eyes, now, were wide open, as white as the eyes of a clown or a doll. The smoke now carried a terrible odor across the clearing, the odor of something burning which was both sweet and rotten.

He turned his head a little and saw the field of faces. He watched his mother's face. Her eyes were very bright, her mouth was open: she was more beautiful than he had ever seen her, and more strange. He began to feel a joy he had never felt before. He watched the hanging, gleaming body, the most beautiful and terrible object he had ever seen till then. One of his father's friends reached up and in his hands he held a knife: and Jesse wished that he had been that man. It was a long, bright knife and the sun seemed to catch it, to play with it, to caress it—it was brighter than the fire. And a wave of laughter swept the crowd. Jesse felt his father's hands on his ankles slip and tighten. The man with the knife walked toward the crowd, smiling slightly; as though this were a signal, silence fell; he heard his mother cough. Then the man with the knife walked up to the hanging body. He turned and smiled again. Now there was a silence all over the field. The hanging head looked up. It seemed fully conscious now, as though the fire had burned out terror and pain. The man with the knife took the nigger's privates in his hand, one hand, still smiling, as though he were weighing them. In the cradle of the one white hand, the nigger's privates seemed as remote as meat being weighed in the scales; but seemed heavier, too, much heavier, and Jesse felt his scrotum tighten; and huge, huge, much bigger than his father's, flaccid, hairless, the largest thing he had ever seen till then, and the blackest. The white hand stretched them, cradled them, caressed them. Then the dying man's eyes looked straight into Jesse's eyes—it could not have been as long as a second, but it seemed longer than a year. Then Jesse screamed, and the crowd screamed as the knife flashed, first up, then down, cutting the dreadful thing away, and the blood came roaring down. Then the crowd rushed forward, tearing at the body with their hands, with knives, with rocks, with stones, howling and cursing. Jesse's head, of its own weight, fell downward toward his father's head. Someone stepped forward and drenched the body with kerosene. Where the man had been, a great sheet of flame appeared. Jesse's father lowered him to the ground.

"Well, I told you," said his father, "you wasn't never going to forget *this* picnic." His father's face was full of sweat, his eyes were very peaceful. At that moment Jesse loved his father more than he had ever loved him. He felt that his father had carried him through a mighty test, had revealed to him a great secret which would be the key to his life forever.

"I reckon," he said. "I reckon."

Jesse's father took him by the hand and, with his mother a little behind them, talking and laughing with the other women, they walked through the crowd, across the clearing. The black body was on the ground, the chain which had held it was being rolled up by one of his father's friends. Whatever the fire had left undone, the hands and the knives and the stones of the people had accomplished. The head was caved in, one eye was torn out, one ear was hanging. But one had to look carefully to realize this, for it was, now, merely, a black charred object on the black, charred ground. He lay spread-eagled with what had been a wound between what had been his legs.

"They going to leave him here, then?" Jesse whispered.

"Yeah," said his father, "they'll come and get him by and by. I reckon we better get over there and get some of that food before it's all gone."

"I reckon," he muttered now to himself, "I reckon." Grace stirred and touched him on the thigh: the moonlight covered her like glory. Something bubbled up in him, his nature again returned to him. He thought of the boy in the cell; he thought of the man in the fire; he thought of the knife and grabbed himself and stroked himself and a terrible sound, something between a high laugh and a howl, came out of him and dragged his sleeping wife up on one elbow. She stared at him in a moonlight which had now grown cold as ice. He thought of the morning and grabbed her, laughing and crying, crying and laughing, and he whispered, as he stroked her, as he took her, "Come on, sugar, I'm going to do you like a nigger, just like a nigger, come on, sugar, and love me just like you'd love a nigger." He thought of the morning as he labored and she moaned, thought of morning as he labored harder than he ever had before, and before his labors had ended, he heard the first cock crow and the dogs begin to bark, and the sound of tires on the gravel road.

My Man Bovanne

TONI CADE BAMBARA

Blind people got a hummin jones if you notice. Which is understandable completely once you been around one and notice what no eyes will force you into to see people, and you get past the first time, which seems to come out of nowhere, and it's like you in church again with fat-chest ladies and old gents gruntin a hum low in the throat to whatever the preacher be saying. Shakey Bee bottom lip all swole up with Sweet Peach and me explainin how come the sweetpotato bread was a dollar-quarter this time stead of dollar regular and he say uh hunh he understand, then he break into this *thizzin* kind of hum which is quiet, but fiercesome just the same if you ain't ready for it. Which I wasn't. But I got used to it and the onliest time I had to say somethin bout it was when he was playin checkers on the stoop one time and he commenst to hummin quite churchy seem to me. So I says, "Look here Shakey Bee, I can't beat you and Jesus too." He stop.

So that's how come I asked My Man Bovanne to dance. He ain't my man mind you, just a nice ole gent from the block that we all know cause he fixes things and the kids like him. Or used to fore Black Power got hold their minds and mess em around till they can't be civil to ole folks. So we at this benefit for my niece's cousin who's runnin for somethin with this Black party somethin or other behind her. And I press up close to dance with Bovanne who blind and I'm hummin and he hummin, chest to chest like talkin. Not jammin my breasts into the man. Wasn't bout tits. Was bout vibrations. And he dug it and asked me what color dress I had on and how my hair was fixed and how I was doin without a man, not nosy but nice-like, and who was at this affair and was the canapes dainty-stingy or healthy enough to get hold of proper. Comfy and cheery is what I'm trying to get across. Touch talkin like the heel of the hand on the tambourine or on a drum.

But right away Joe Lee come up on us and frown for dancin so close to the man. My own son who knows what kind of warm I am about; and don't grown men call me long distance and in the middle of the night for a little Mama comfort? But he frown. Which ain't right since Bovanne can't see and defend himself. Just a nice old man who fixes toasters and busted irons and bicycles and things and changes the lock on my door when my men friends get messy. Nice man. Which is not why they invited him. Grassroots you see. Me and Sister Taylor and the woman who does heads at Mamies and the man from the barber shop, we all there on account of we grassroots. And I ain't never been souther than Brooklyn Battery and no more country than the window box on my fire escape. And just yesterday my kids tellin me to take them countrified rags off my head and be cool. And now can't get Black enough to suit em. So everybody passin sayin My Man Bovanne. Big deal, keep stepping and don't even stop a minute to get the man a drink or one of them cute sandwiches or tell him what's goin on. And him standin there with a smile ready case someone do speak he want to be ready. So that's how come I pull him on the dance floor and we dance squeezin past the tables and chairs and all them coats and people standin round up in each other face talkin bout this and that but got no use for this blind man who mostly fixed skates and skooters for all these folks when they was just kids. So I'm pressed up close and we touch talkin with the hum. And here come my daughter cuttin her eye at me like she do when she tell me about my "apolitical" self like I got hoof and mouf disease and there ain't no hope at all. And I don't pay her no mind and just look up in Bovanne shadow face and tell him his stomach like a drum and he laugh. Laugh real loud. And here come my youngest, Task, with a tap on my elbow like he the third-grade monitor and I'm cuttin up on the line to assembly.

"I was just talkin on the drums," I explained when they hauled me into the kitchen. I figured drums was my best defense. They can get ready for drums what with all this heritage business. And Bovanne stomach just like that drum Task give me when he come back from Africa. You just touch it and it hum thizzim, thizzim. So I stuck to the drum story. "Just drummin that's all."

"Mama, what are you talkin about?"

"She had too much to drink," say Elo to Task cause she don't hardly say nuthin to me direct no more since that ugly argument about my wigs.

"Look here, Mama," say Task, the gentle one. "We just tryin to pull your coat. You were makin a spectacle of yourself out there dancing like that."

"Dancin like what?"

Task run a hand over his left ear like his father for the world and his father before that.

"Like a bitch in heat," say Elo.

"Well uhh, I was goin to say like one of them sex-starved ladies gettin on in years and not too discriminating. Know what I mean?"

I don't answer cause I'll cry. Terrible thing when your own children talk to you like that. Pullin me out the party and hustlin me into some stranger's kitchen in the back of a bar just like the damn police. And ain't like I'm old old. I can still wear me some sleeveless dresses without the meat hangin off my arm. And I keep up with some thangs through my kids. Who ain't kids no more. To hear them tell it. So I don't say nuthin.

"Dancin with that tom," say Elo to Joe Lee, who leanin on the folks' freezer. "His feet can smell a cracker a mile away and go into their shuffle number post haste. And them eyes. He could be a little considerate and put on some shades. Who wants to look into them blown-out fuses that—"

"Is this what they call the generation gap?" I say.

"Generation gap," spits Elo, like I suggested castor oil and fricassee possum in the milk shakes or somethin. "That's a white concept for a white phenomenon. There's no generation gap among Black people. We are a col—"

"Yeh, well never mind," says Joe Lee. "The point is Mama . . . well, it's pride. You embarrass yourself and us too dancin like that."

"I wasn't shame." Then nobody say nuthin. Them standin there in they pretty clothes with drinks in they hands and gangin up on me, and me in the third-degree chair and nary a olive to my name. Felt just like the police got hold to me.

"First of all," Task say, holding up his hand and tickin off the offenses, "the dress. Now that dress is too short, Mama, and too low cut for a woman your age. And Tamu's going to make a speech tonight to kick off the campaign and will be introducin you and expecting you to organize the council of elders—"

"Me? Didn nobody ask me nuthin. You mean Nisi? She change her name?"

"Well, Norton was supposed to tell you about it. Nisi wants to introduce you and then encourage the older folks to form a Council of the Elders to act as an advisory—"

"And you going to be standing there with your boobs out and that wig on your head and that hem up to your ass. And people'll say, 'Ain't that the horny bitch that was grindin with the blind dude?' "

"Elo, be cool a minute," say Task, gettin to the next finger. "And then there's the drinkin. Mama, you know you can't drink cause next thing you know you be laughin loud and carryin on," and he grab another finger for the loudness. "And then there's the dancin. You been tattooed on the man for four records straight and slow draggin even on the fast numbers. How you think that look for a woman your age?"

"What's my age?"

"What?"

"I'm axin you all a simple question. You keep talkin bout what's proper for a woman my age. How old am I anyhow?" And Joe Lee slams his eyes shut and squinches up his face to figure. And Task run a hand over his ear and stare into his glass like the ice cubes goin calculate for him. And Elo just starin at the top of my head like she goin rip the wig off any minute now.

"Is your hair braided up under that thing? If so, why don't you take it off? You always did do a neat cornroll."

"Uh huh," cause I'm think how she couldn't undo her hair fast enough talking bout cornroll so countrified. None of which was the subject. "How old, I say?"

"Sixtee-one or—"

"You a damn lie Joe Lee Peoples."

"And that's another thing," say Task on the fingers.

"You know what you all can kiss," I say, gettin up and brushin the wrinkles out my lap.

"Oh, Mama," Elo say, puttin a hand on my shoulder like she hasn't done since she left home and the hand landin light and not sure it supposed to be there. Which hurt me to my heart. Cause this was the child in our happiness fore Mr. Peoples die. And I carried that child strapped to my chest till she was nearly two. We was close is what I'm tryin to tell you. Cause it was more me in the child than the others. And even after Task it was the girl-child I covered in the night and wept over for no reason at all less it was she was a chub-chub like me and not very pretty, but a warm child. And how did things get to this, that she can't put a sure hand on me and say Mama we love you and care about you and you entitled to enjoy yourself cause you a good woman?

"And then there's Reverend Trent," say Task, glancin from left to right like they hatchin a plot and just now lettin me in on it. "You were suppose to be talking with him tonight, Mama, about giving us his basement for campaign headquarters and—"

"Didn nobody tell me nuthin. If grassroots mean you kept in the dark I can't use it. I really can't. And Reven Trent a fool anyway the way he tore into the widow man up there on Edgecombe cause he wouldn't take in three of them foster children and the woman not even comfy in the ground yet and the man's mind messed up and—"

"Look here," say Task. "What we need is a family conference so we can get all this stuff cleared up and laid out on the table. In the meantime I think we better get back into the other room and tend to business. And in the meantime, Mama, see if you can't get to Reverend Trent and—"

"You want me to belly rub with the Reven, that it?"

"Oh damn," Elo say and go through the swingin door.

"We'll talk about all this at dinner. How's tomorrow night, Joe Lee?" While Joe Lee being self-important I'm wonderin who's doin the cookin and how come nobody ax me if I'm free and do I get a corsage and things like that. Then Joe nod that it's O.K. and he go through the swingin door and just a little hubbub come through from the other room. Then Task smile his smile, lookin just like his daddy, and he leave. And it just me in this stranger's kitchen, which was a mess I wouldn't never let my kitchen look like. Poison you just to look at the pots. Then the door swing the other way and it's My Man Bovanne standin there saying Miss Hazel but lookin at the deep fry and then at the steam table, and most surprised when I come up on him from the other direction and take him on out of there. Pass the folks pushing up toward the stage where Nisi and some other people settin and ready to talk, and folks gettin to the last of the sandwiches and the booze fore they settle down in one spot and listen serious. And I'm thinkin bout tellin Bovanne what a lovely long dress Nisi got on and the earrings and her hair piled up in a cone and the people bout to hear how we all get-tin screwed and gotta form our own party and everybody there listenin and lookin. But instead I just haul the man on out of there, and Joe Lee and his wife look at me like I'm terrible, but they ain't said boo to the man yet. Cause he blind and old and don't nobody there need him since they grown up and don't need they skates fixed no more.

"Where we goin, Miss Hazel?" Him knowin all the time.

"First we gonna buy you some dark sunglasses. Then you comin with me to the supermarket so I can pick up tomorrow's dinner, which is goin to be a grand thing proper and you invited. Then we goin to my house."

"That be fine. I surely would like to rest my feet." Bein cute, but you got to let men play out they little show, blind or not. So he chat on bout how tired he is and how he appreciate me taking him in hand this way. And I'm thinkin I'll have him change the lock on my door first thing. Then I'll give the man a nice warm bath with jasmine leaves in the water and a little Ep-som salt on the sponge to do his back. And then a good rubdown with rose-water and olive oil. Then a cup of lemon tea with a taste in it. And a little talcum, some of that fancy stuff Nisi mother sent over last Christmas. And then a massage, a good face massage round the forehead which is the wor-ryin part. Cause you gots to take care of the older folks. And let them know they still needed to run the mimeo machine and keep the spark plugs clean and fix the mailboxes for folks who might help us get the breakfast pro-gram goin, and the school for the little kids and the campaign and all. Cause old folks is the nation. That what Nisi was sayin and I mean to do my part.

"I imagine you are a very pretty woman, Miss Hazel."

"I surely am," I say just like the hussy my daughter always say I was.

Lost in the Funhouse

JOHN BARTH

For whom is the funhouse fun? Perhaps for lovers. For Ambrose it is *a place of fear and confusion*. He has come to the seashore with his family for the holiday, *the occasion of their visit is Independence Day, the most important secular holiday of the United States of America*. A single straight underline is the manuscript mark for italic type, *which in turn* is the printed equivalent to oral emphasis of words and phrases as well as the customary type for titles of complete works, not to mention. Italics are also employed, in fiction stories especially, for "outside," intrusive, or artificial voices, such as radio announcements, the texts of telegrams and newspaper articles, et cetera. They should be used *sparingly*. If passages originally in roman type are italicized by someone repeating them, it's customary to acknowledge the fact. *Italics mine*.

Ambrose was "at that awkward age." His voice came out high-pitched as a child's if he let himself get carried away; to be on the safe side, therefore, he moved and spoke with *deliberate calm* and *adult gravity*. Talking soberly of unimportant or irrelevant matters and listening consciously to the sound of your own voice are useful habits for maintaining control in this difficult interval. *En route* to Ocean City he sat in the back seat of the family car with his brother Peter, age fifteen, and Magda G——, age fourteen, a pretty girl and exquisite young lady, who lived not far from them on B—— Street in the town of D——, Maryland. Initials, blanks, or both were often substituted for proper names in nineteenth-century fiction to enhance the illusion of reality. It is as if the author felt it necessary to delete the names for reasons of tact or legal liability. Interestingly, as with other aspects of realism, it is an *illusion* that is being enhanced, by purely artificial means. Is it likely, does it violate the principle of verisimilitude, that a thirteen-year-old boy could make such a sophisticated observation? A girl of fourteen is *the psychological coeval* of a boy of fifteen or sixteen; a thirteen-year-old boy, therefore, even one precocious in some other respects, might be three years her *emotional junior*.

Thrice a year—on Memorial, Independence, and Labor Days—the family visits Ocean City for the afternoon and evening. When Ambrose and Peter's father was their age, the excursion was made by train, as mentioned in the novel *The 42nd Parallel* by John Dos Passos. Many families from the same neighborhood used to travel together, with dependent relatives and often with Negro servants; schoolfuls of children swarmed through the railway cars; everyone shared everyone else's Maryland fried chicken, Virginia ham, deviled eggs, potato salad, beaten biscuits, iced tea. Nowadays (that is, in 19—, the year of our story) the journey is made by automobile— more comfortably and quickly though without the extra fun though without the *camaraderie* of a general excursion. It's all part of the deterioration of American life, their father declares; Uncle Karl supposes that when the boys take *their* families to Ocean City for the holidays they'll fly in Autogiros. Their mother, sitting in the middle of the front seat like Magda in the second, only with her arms on the seat-back behind the men's shoulders, wouldn't want the good old days back again, the steaming trains and stuffy long dresses; on the other hand she can do without Autogiros, too, if she has to become a grandmother to fly in them.

Description of physical appearance and mannerisms is one of several standard methods of characterization used by writers of fiction. It is also important to "keep the senses operating"; when a detail from one of the five senses, say visual, is "crossed" with a detail from another, say auditory, the reader's imagination is oriented to the scene, perhaps unconsciously. This procedure may be compared to the way surveyors and navigators determine their positions by two or more compass bearings, a process known as triangulation. The brown hair on Ambrose's mother's forearms gleamed in the sun like. Though right-handed, she took her left arm from the seat-back to press the dashboard cigar lighter for Uncle Karl. When the glass bead in its handle glowed red, the lighter was ready for use. The smell of Uncle Karl's cigar smoke reminded one of. The fragrance of the ocean came strong to the picnic ground where they always stopped for lunch, two miles inland from Ocean City. Having to pause for a full hour almost within sound of the breakers was difficult for Peter and Ambrose when they were younger; even at their present age it was not easy to keep their anticipation, *stimulated by the briny spume*, from turning into short temper. The Irish author James Joyce, in his unusual novel entitled *Ulysses*, now available in this country, uses the adjectives *snot-green* and *scrotum-tightening* to describe the sea. Visual, auditory, tactile, olfactory, gustatory. Peter and Ambrose's father, while steering their black 1936 LaSalle sedan with one hand, could with the other remove the first cigarette from a white pack of Lucky Strikes and, more remarkably, light it with a match forefingered from its book and thumbed against the flint paper without being detached.

The matchbook cover merely advertised U.S. War Bonds and Stamps. A fine metaphor, simile, or other figure of speech, in addition to its obvious "first-order" relevance to the thing it describes, will be seen upon reflection to have a second order of significance: it may be drawn from the *milieu* of the action, for example, or be particularly appropriate to the sensibility of the narrator, even hinting to the reader things of which the narrator is unaware; or it may cast further and subtler lights upon the things it describes, sometimes ironically qualifying the more evident sense of the comparison.

To say that Ambrose's and Peter's mother was *pretty* is to accomplish nothing; the reader may acknowledge the proposition, but his imagination is not engaged. Besides, Magda was also pretty, yet in an altogether different way. Although she lived on B—— Street she had very good manners and did better than average in school. Her figure was very well developed for her age. Her right hand lay casually on the plush upholstery of the seat, very near Ambrose's left leg, on which his own hand rested. The space between their legs, between her right and his left leg, was out of the line of sight of anyone sitting on the other side of Magda, as well as anyone glancing into the rear-view mirror. Uncle Karl's face resembled Peter's—rather, vice versa. Both had dark hair and eyes, short husky statures, deep voices. Magda's left hand was probably in a similar position on her left side. The boys' father is difficult to describe; no particular feature of his appearance or manner stood out. He wore glasses and was principal of a T—— County grade school. Uncle Karl was a masonry contractor.

Although Peter must have known as well as Ambrose that the latter, because of his position in the car, would be first to see the electrical towers of the power plant at V——, the halfway point of their trip, he leaned forward and slightly toward the center of the car and pretended to be looking for them through the flat pinewoods and tuckahoe creeks along the highway. For as long as the boys could remember, "looking for the Towers" had been a feature of the first half of their excursions to Ocean City, "looking for the standpipe" of the second. Though the game was childish, their mother preserved the tradition of rewarding the first to see the Towers with a candy-bar or piece of fruit. She insisted now that Magda play the game; the prize, she said, was "something hard to get nowadays." Ambrose decided not to join in; he sat far back in his seat. Magda, like Peter, leaned forward. Two sets of straps were discernible through the shoulders of her sun dress; the inside right one, a brassiere-strap, was fastened or shortened with a small safety pin. The right armpit of her dress, presumably the left as well, was damp with perspiration. The simple strategy for being first to espy the Towers, which Ambrose had understood by the age of four, was to sit on the right-hand side of the car. Whoever sat there, however, had also to put up with the worst of the sun, and so Ambrose, without mentioning the matter, chose sometimes the one and sometimes the other. Not impossibly Peter had never caught on to the trick, or thought that his brother hadn't simply because Ambrose on occasion preferred shade to a Baby Ruth or tangerine.

The shade-sun situation didn't apply to the front seat, owing to the windshield; if anything the driver got more sun, since the person on the passenger side not only was shadowed below by the door and dashboard but might swing down his sunvisor all the way too.

"Is that them?" Magda asked. Ambrose's mother teased the boys for letting Magda win, insinuating that "somebody [had] a girlfriend." Peter and Ambrose's father reached a long thin arm across their mother to butt his cigarette in the dashboard ashtray, under the lighter. The prize this time for seeing the Towers first was a banana. Their mother bestowed it after chiding their father for wasting a half-smoked cigarette when everything was so scarce. Magda, to take the prize, moved her hand from so near Ambrose's that he could have touched it as though accidentally. She offered to share the prize, things like that were so hard to find, but everyone insisted it was hers alone. Ambrose's mother sang an iambic trimeter couplet from a popular song, femininely rhymed:

> *"What's good is in the Army.*
> *What's left will never harm me."*

Uncle Karl tapped his cigar ash out the ventilator window; some particles were sucked by the slipstream back into the car through the rear window on the passenger side. Magda demonstrated her ability to hold a banana in one hand and peel it with her teeth. She still sat forward; Ambrose pushed his glasses back onto the bridge of his nose with his left hand, which he then negligently let fall to the seat cushion immediately behind her. He even permitted the single hair, gold, on the second joint of his thumb to brush the fabric of her skirt. Should she have sat back at that instant, his hand would have been caught under her.

Plush upholstery prickles uncomfortably through gabardine slacks in the July sun. The function of the *beginning* of a story is to introduce the principal characters, establish their initial relationships, set the scene for the main action, expose the background of the situation if necessary, plant motifs and foreshadowings where appropriate, and initiate the first complication or whatever of the "rising action." Actually, if one imagines a story called "The Funhouse," or "Lost in the Funhouse," the details of the drive to Ocean City don't seem especially relevant. The *beginning* should recount the events between Ambrose's first sight of the funhouse early in the afternoon and his entering it with Magda and Peter in the evening. The *middle* would narrate all relevant events from the time he goes in to the time he loses his way; middles have the double and contradictory function of delaying the climax while at the same time preparing the reader for it and fetching him to it. Then the *ending* would tell what Ambrose does while he's lost,

how he finally finds his way out, and what everybody makes of the experience. So far there's been no real dialogue, very little sensory detail and
nothing in the way of a *theme*. And a long time has gone by already without
anything happening; it makes a person wonder. We haven't even reached
Ocean City yet; we will never get out of the funhouse.

The more closely an author identifies with the narrator, literally or metaphorically, the less advisable it is, as a rule, to use the first-person narrative
viewpoint. Once three years previously the young people *aforementioned*
played Niggers and Masters in the backyard; when it was Ambrose's turn to
be Master and theirs to be Niggers Peter had to go serve his evening papers; Ambrose was afraid to punish Magda alone, but she led him to the
whitewashed Torture Chamber between the woodshed and the privy in the
Slaves Quarters; there she knelt sweating among bamboo rakes and dusty
Mason jars, pleadingly embraced his knees, and while bees droned in the
lattice as if on an ordinary summer afternoon, purchased clemency at a
surprising price set by herself. Doubtless she remembered nothing of this
event; Ambrose on the other hand seemed unable to forget the least detail
of his life. He even recalled how, standing beside himself with awed imper-
sonality in the reeky heat, he'd stared the while at an empty cigar box in
which Uncle Karl kept stone-cutting chisels: beneath the words *El Producto*,
a laureled, loose-toga'd lady regarded the sea from a marble bench; beside
her, forgotten or not yet turned to, was a five-stringed lyre. Her chin reposed on the back of her right hand; her left depended negligently from
the bench-arm. The lower half of scene and lady was peeled away; the
words EXAMINED BY —— were inked there into the wood. Nowadays cigar boxes are made of pasteboard. Ambrose wondered what Magda would
have done, Ambrose wondered what Magda would do when she sat back
on his hand as he resolved she should. Be angry. Make a teasing joke of it.
Give no sign at all. For a long time she leaned forward, playing cow-poker
with Peter against Uncle Karl and Mother and watching for the first sign
of Ocean City. At nearly the same instant, picnic ground and Ocean City
standpipe hove into view; an Amoco filling station on their side of the road
cost Mother and Uncle Karl fifty cows and the game; Magda bounced back,
clapping her right hand on Mother's right arm; Ambrose moved clear "in
the nick of time."

At this rate our hero, at this rate our protagonist will remain in the funhouse forever. Narrative ordinarily consists of alternating dramatization
and summarization. One symptom of nervous tension, paradoxically, is
repeated and violent yawning; neither Peter nor Magda nor Uncle Karl
nor Mother reacted in this manner. Although they were no longer small
children, Peter and Ambrose were each given a dollar to spend on boardwalk amusements in addition to what money of their own they'd brought
along. Magda, too, though she protested she had ample spending money.
The boys' mother made a little scene out of distributing the bills; she pre-

tended that her sons and Magda were small children and cautioned them not to spend the sum too quickly or in one place. Magda promised with a merry laugh and, having both hands free, took the bill with her left. Peter laughed also and pledged in a falsetto to be a good boy. His imitation of a child was not clever. The boys' father was tall and thin, balding, fair-complexioned. Assertions of that sort are not effective; the reader may acknowledge the proposition, but. We should be much farther along than we are; something has gone wrong; not much of the preliminary rambling seems relevant. Yet everyone begins in the same place; how is it that most go along without difficulty but a few lose their way?

"Stay out from under the boardwalk," Uncle Karl growled from the side of his mouth. The boys' mother pushed his shoulder *in mock annoyance*. They were all standing before Fat May the Laughing Lady who advertised the funhouse. Larger than life, Fat May mechanically shook, rocked on her heels, slapped her thighs while recorded laughter—uproarious, female—came amplified from a hidden loudspeaker. It chuckled, wheezed, wept; tried in vain to catch its breath; tittered, groaned, exploded raucous and anew. You couldn't hear it without laughing yourself, no matter how you felt. Father came back from talking to a Coast-Guardsman on duty and reported that the surf was spoiled with crude oil from tankers recently torpedoed offshore. Lumps of it, difficult to remove, made tarry tidelines on the beach and stuck on swimmers. Many bathed in the surf nevertheless and came out speckled; others paid to use a municipal pool and only sunbathed on the beach. We would do the latter. We would do the latter. We would do the latter.

Under the boardwalk, matchbook covers, grainy other things. What is the story's theme? Ambrose is ill. He perspires in the dark passages, candied apples-on-a-stick, delicious-looking, disappointing to eat. Funhouses need men's and ladies' rooms at intervals. Others perhaps have also vomited in corners and corridors; may even have had bowel movements liable to be stepped in in the dark. The word *fuck* suggests suction and/or and/or flatulence. Mother and Father; grandmothers and grandfathers on both sides; great-grandmothers and great-grandfathers on four sides, et cetera. Count a generation as thirty years: in approximately the year when Lord Baltimore was granted charter to the province of Maryland by Charles I, five hundred twelve women—English, Welsh, Bavarian, Swiss—of every class and character, received into themselves the penises the intromittent organs of five hundred twelve men, ditto, in every circumstance and posture, to conceive the five hundred twelve ancestors of the two hundred fifty-six ancestors of the et cetera et cetera et cetera et cetera et cetera et cetera et cetera et cetera of the author, of the narrator, of this story, *Lost in the Funhouse*. In alleyways, ditches, canopy beds, pinewoods, bridal suites, ship's cabins, coach-and-fours, coaches-and-four, sultry toolsheds; on the cold sand under boardwalks, littered with *El Producto* cigar butts, treasured with Lucky Strike cigarette stubs, Coca-Cola caps, gritty turds, cardboard lollipop sticks, matchbook covers warning that A Slip of the Lip Can Sink a Ship. The shluppish whisper, continuous as seawash round the globe, tide-like falls and rises with the circuit of dawn and dusk.

Magda's teeth. She *was* left-handed. Perspiration. They've gone all the way, through, Magda and Peter, they've been waiting for hours with Mother and Uncle Karl while Father searches for his lost son; they draw french-fried potatoes from a paper cup and shake their heads. They've named the children they'll one day have and bring to Ocean City on holidays. Can spermatozoa properly be thought of as male animalcules when there are no female spermatozoa? They grope through hot, dark windings, past Love's Tunnel's fearsome obstacles. Some perhaps lose their way.

Peter suggested then and there that they do the funhouse; he had been through it before, so had Magda, Ambrose hadn't and suggested, his voice cracking on account of Fat May's laughter, that they swim first. All were chuckling, couldn't help it; Ambrose's father, Ambrose's and Peter's father came up grinning like a lunatic with two boxes of syrup-coated popcorn, one for Mother, one for Magda; the men were to help themselves. Ambrose walked on Magda's right; being by nature left-handed, she carried the box in her left hand. Up front the situation was reversed.

"What are you limping for?" Magda inquired of Ambrose. He supposed in a husky tone that his foot had gone to sleep in the car. Her teeth flashed. "Pins and needles?" It was the honeysuckle on the lattice of the former privy that drew the bees. Imagine being stung there. How long is this going to take?

The adults decided to forgo the pool; but Uncle Karl insisted they change into swimsuits and do the beach. "He wants to watch the pretty girls," Peter teased, and ducked behind Magda from Uncle Karl's pretended wrath. "You've got all the pretty girls you need right here," Magda declared, and Mother said: "Now that's the gospel truth." Magda scolded Peter, who reached over her shoulder to sneak some popcorn. "Your brother and father aren't getting any." Uncle Karl wondered if they were going to have fireworks that night, what with the shortages. It wasn't the shortages, Mr. M—— replied; Ocean City had fireworks from pre-war. But it was too risky on account of the enemy submarines, some people thought.

"Don't seem like Fourth of July without fireworks," said Uncle Karl. The inverted tag in dialogue writing is still considered permissible with proper names or epithets, but sounds old-fashioned with personal pronouns. "We'll have 'em again soon enough," predicted the boys' father. Their mother declared she could do without fireworks: they reminded her too much of the real thing. Their father said all the more reason to shoot off a few now and again. Uncle Karl asked *rhetorically* who needed reminding, just look at people's hair and skin.

"The oil, yes," said Mrs. M——.

Ambrose had a pain in his stomach and so didn't swim but enjoyed watching the others. He and his father burned red easily. Magda's figure was exceedingly well developed for her age. She too declined to swim, and got mad, and became angry when Peter attempted to drag her into the pool. She always swam, he insisted; what did she mean not swim? Why did a person come to Ocean City?

"Maybe I want to lay here with Ambrose," Magda teased.

Nobody likes a pedant.

"Aha," said Mother. Peter grabbed Magda by one ankle and ordered Ambrose to grab the other. She squealed and rolled over on the beach blanket. Ambrose pretended to help hold her back. Her tan was darker than even Mother's and Peter's. "Help out, Uncle Karl!" Peter cried. Uncle Karl went to seize the other ankle. Inside the top of her swimsuit, however, you could see the line where the sunburn ended and, when she hunched her shoulders and squealed again, one nipple's auburn edge. Mother made them behave themselves. "*You* should certainly know," she said to Uncle Karl. Archly. "that when a lady says she doesn't feel like swimming, a gentleman doesn't ask questions." Uncle Karl said excuse *him;* Mother winked at Magda; Ambrose blushed; stupid Peter kept saying "Phooey on *feel like!*" and tugging at Magda's ankle; then even he got the point; and cannonballed with a holler into the pool.

"I swear," Magda said, in mock *in feigned* exasperation.

The diving would make a suitable literary symbol. To go off the high board you had to wait in a line along the poolside and up the ladder. Fellows tickled girls and goosed one another and shouted to the ones at the top to hurry up, or razzed them for bellyfloppers. Once on the springboard some took a great while posing or clowning or deciding on a dive or getting up their nerve; others ran right off. Especially among the younger fellows the idea was to strike the funniest pose or do the craziest stunt as you fell, a thing that got harder to do as you kept on and kept on. But whether you hollered *Geronimo!* or *Sieg heil!*, held your nose or "rode a bicycle," pretended to be shot or did a perfect jackknife or changed your mind halfway down and ended up with nothing, it was over in two seconds, after all that wait. Spring, pose, splash. Spring, neat-o, splash. Spring, aw fooey, splash.

The grown-ups had gone on; Ambrose wanted to converse with Magda; she was remarkably well developed for her age; it was said that that came from rubbing with a turkish towel, and there were other theories. Ambrose could think of nothing to say except how good a diver Peter was, who was showing off for her benefit. You could pretty well tell by looking at their bathing suits and arm muscles how far along the different fellows were. Ambrose was glad he hadn't gone in swimming, the cold water shrank you up so. Magda pretended to be uninterested in the diving; she probably weighed as much as he did. If you knew your way around in the funhouse like your own bedroom, you could wait until a girl came along and then slip away without ever getting caught, even if her boyfriend was right with her. She'd think *he* did it! It would be better to be the boyfriend, and act outraged, and tear the funhouse apart.

Not act; *be.*

"He's a master diver," Ambrose said. In feigned admiration. "You really have to slave away at it to get that good." What would it matter anyhow if he asked her right out whether she remembered, even teased her with it as Peter would have?

There's no point in going farther; this isn't getting anybody anywhere; they haven't even come to the funhouse yet. Ambrose is off the track, in some new or old part of the place that's not supposed to be used; he strayed into it by some one-in-a-million chance, like the time the roller-coaster car left the tracks in the nineteen-teens against all the laws of physics and sailed over the boardwalk in the dark. And they can't locate him because they don't know where to look. Even the designer and operator have forgotten this other part, that winds around on itself like a whelk shell. That winds around the right part like the snakes on Mercury's caduceus. Some people, perhaps, don't "hit their stride" until their twenties, when the growing-up business is over and women appreciate other things besides wisecracks and teasing and strutting. Peter didn't have one-tenth the imagination *he* had, not one-tenth. Peter did this naming-their-children thing as a joke, making up names like Aloysius and Murgatroyd, but Ambrose knew *exactly* how it would feel to be married and have children of your own, and be a loving husband and father, and go comfortably to work in the mornings and to bed with your wife at night, and wake up with her there. With a breeze coming through the sash and birds and mockingbirds singing in the Chinese-cigar trees. His eyes watered, there aren't enough ways to say that. He would be quite famous in his line of work. Whether Magda was his wife or not, one evening when he was wise-lined and gray at the temples he'd smile gravely, at a fashionable dinner party and remind her of his youthful passion. The time they went with his family to Ocean City; the *erotic fantasies* he used to have about her. How long ago it seemed, and childish! Yet tender, too, *n'est-ce pas?* Would she have imagined that the world-famous whatever remembered how many strings were on the lyre on the bench beside the girl on the label of the cigar box he'd stared at in the toolshed at age ten while, she, age eleven. Even then he had felt *wise beyond his years;* he'd stroked her hair and said in his deepest voice and correctest English, as to a dear child: "I shall never forget this moment."

But though he had breathed heavily, groaned as if ecstatic, what he'd really felt throughout was an odd detachment, as though someone else were Master. Strive as he might to be transported, he heard his mind take notes upon the scene: *This is what they call* passion. *I am experiencing it.* Many of the digger machines were out of order in the penny arcades and could not be repaired or replaced for the duration. Moreover the prizes, made now in

USA, were less interesting than formerly, pasteboard items for the most part, and some of the machines wouldn't work on white pennies. The gypsy fortune-teller machine might have provided a foreshadowing of the climax of this story if Ambrose had operated it. It was even dilapidateder than most: the silver coating was worn off the brown metal handles, the glass windows around the dummy were cracked and taped, her kerchiefs and silks long-faded. If a man lived by himself, he could take a department-store mannequin with flexible joints and modify her in certain ways. *However:* by the time he was that old he'd have a real woman. There was a machine that stamped your name around a white-metal coin with a star in the middle: A ——. His son would be the second, and when the lad reached thirteen or so he would put a strong arm around his shoulder and tell him calmly: "It is perfectly normal. We have all been through it. It will not last forever." Nobody knew how to be what they were right. He'd smoke a pipe, teach his son how to fish and softcrab, assure him he needn't worry about himself. Magda would certainly give, Magda would certainly yield a great deal of milk, although guilty of occasional solecisms. It don't taste so bad. Suppose the lights came on now!

The day wore on. You think you're yourself, but there are other persons in you. Ambrose gets hard when Ambrose doesn't want to, *and obversely.* Ambrose watches them disagree; Ambrose watches him watch. In the funhouse mirror room you can't see yourself go on forever, because no matter how you stand, your head gets in the way. Even if you had a glass periscope, the image of your eye would cover up the thing you really wanted to see. The police will come; there'll be a story in the papers. That must be where it happened. Unless he can find a surprise exit, an unofficial backdoor or escape hatch opening on an alley, say, and then stroll up to the family in front of the funhouse and ask where everybody's been; *he's* been out of the place for ages. That's just where it happened, in that last lighted room: Peter and Magda found the right exit; he found one that you weren't supposed to find and strayed off into the works somewhere. In a perfect funhouse you'd be able to go only one way, like the divers off the highboard; getting lost would be impossible; the doors and halls would work like minnow traps or the valves in veins.

On account of German U-boats, Ocean City was "browned out": streetlights were shaded on the seaward side; shop-windows and boardwalk amusement places were kept dim, not to silhouette tankers and Libertyships for torpedoing. In a short story about Ocean City, Maryland, during World War II, the author could make use of the image of sailors on leave in the penny arcades and shooting galleries, sighting through the crosshairs of toy machine guns at swastika'd subs, while out in the black Atlantic a U-boat skipper squints through his periscope at real ships outlined by the glow of penny arcades. After dinner the family strolled back to the amusement end of the boardwalk. The boys' father had burnt red as always and was masked with Noxzema, a minstrel in reverse. The grownups stood at the end of the boardwalk where the Hurricane of '33 had cut an inlet from the ocean to Assawoman Bay.

"Pronounced with a long *o*," Uncle Karl reminded Magda with a wink. His shirt sleeves were rolled up; Mother punched his brown biceps with the arrowed heart on it and said his mind was naughty. Fat May's laugh came suddenly from the funhouse, as if she'd just got the joke; the family laughed too at the coincidence. Ambrose went under the boardwalk to search for out-of-town matchbook covers with the aid of his pocket flashlight; he looked out from the edge of the North American continent and wondered how far their laughter carried over the water. Spies in rubber rafts; survivors in lifeboats. If the joke had been beyond his understanding, he could have said: *"The laughter was over his head."* And let the reader see the serious wordplay on second reading.

He turned the flashlight on and then off at once even before the woman whooped. He sprang away, heart athud, dropping the light. What had the man grunted? Perspiration drenched and chilled him by the time he scrambled up to the family. "See anything?" his father asked. His voice wouldn't come; he shrugged and violently brushed sand from his pants legs.

"Let's ride the old flying horses!" Magda cried. I'll never be an author. It's been forever already, everybody's gone home, Ocean City's deserted, the ghost-crabs are tickling across the beach and down the littered cold streets. And the empty halls of clapboard hotels and abandoned funhouses. A tidal wave; an enemy air raid; a monster-crab swelling like an island from the sea. *The inhabitants fled in terror.* Magda clung to his trouser leg; he alone knew the maze's secret. "He gave his life that we might live," said Uncle Karl with a scowl of pain, as he. The fellow's hands had been tattooed; the woman's legs, the woman's fat white legs had. *An astonishing coincidence.* He yearned to tell Peter. He wanted to throw up for excitement. They hadn't even chased him. He wished he were dead.

One possible ending would be to have Ambrose come across another lost person in the dark. They'd match their wits together against the funhouse, struggle like Ulysses past obstacle after obstacle, help and encourage each other. Or a girl. By the time they found the exit they'd be closest friends, sweethearts if it were a girl; they'd know each other's inmost souls, be bound together *by the cement of shared adventure;* then they'd emerge into the light and it would turn out that his friend was a Negro. A blind girl. President Roosevelt's son. Ambrose's former archenemy.

Shortly after the mirror room he'd groped along a musty corridor, his heart already misgiving him at the absence of phosphorescent arrows and other signs. He'd found a crack of light—not a door, it turned out, but a seam between the plyboard wall panels—and squinting up to it, espied a small old man, *in appearance not unlike* the photographs at home of Ambrose's late grandfather, nodding upon a stool beneath a bare, speckled bulb. A crude panel of toggle- and knife-switches hung beside the open fuse box near his head; elsewhere in the little room were wooden levers and ropes belayed to boat cleats. At the time, Ambrose wasn't lost enough to rap or call; later he couldn't find that crack. Now it seemed to him that he'd possibly dozed off for a few minutes somewhere along the way; certainly he was exhausted from the afternoon's sunshine and the evening's problems, he couldn't be sure he hadn't dreamed part or all of the sight. Had an old black wall fan droned like bees and shimmied two flypaper streamers? Had the funhouse operator—gentle, somewhat sad and tired-appearing, in expression not unlike the photographs at home of Ambrose's late Uncle Konrad—murmured in his sleep? Is there really such a person as Ambrose, or is he a figment of the author's imagination? Was it Assawoman Bay or Sinepuxent? Are there other errors of fact in this fiction? Was there another sound besides the little slap slap of thigh on ham, like water sucking at the chine-boards of a skiff?

When you're lost, the smartest thing to do is stay put till you're found, hollering if necessary. But to holler guarantees humiliation as well as rescue; keeping silent permits some saving of face—you can act surprised at the fuss when your rescuers find you and swear you weren't lost, if they do. What's more you might find your own way yet, *however belatedly.*

"Don't tell me your foot's still asleep!" Magda exclaimed as the three young people walked from the inlet to the area set aside for ferris wheels, carrousels, and other carnival rides, they having decided in favor of the vast and ancient merry-go-round instead of the funhouse. What a sentence, everything was wrong from the outset. People don't know what to make of him, he doesn't know what to make of himself, he's only thirteen, *athletically and socially inept,* not astonishingly bright, but there are antennae; he has . . . some sort of receivers in his head; things speak to him, he understands more than he should, the world winks at him through its objects, grabs grinning at his coat. Everybody else is in on some secret he doesn't know; they've forgotten to tell him. Through simple *procrastination* his mother put off his baptism until this year. Everyone else had it done as a baby; he'd assumed the same of himself, as had his mother, so she claimed, until it was time for him to join Grace Methodist-Protestant and the oversight came out. He was mortified, but pitched sleepless through his private catechizing, intimidated by the ancient mysteries, a thirteen year old would never say that, resolved to experience conversion like St. Augustine. When the water touched his brow and Adam's sin left him, he contrived by a strain like defecation to bring tears into his eyes—but felt nothing. There was some simple, radical difference about him; he hoped it was genius, feared it was madness, devoted himself to amiability and inconspicuousness. Alone on the seawall near his house he was seized by the terrifying transports he'd thought to find in toolshed, in Communion-cup. The grass was alive! The town, the river, himself, were not imaginary; time roared in his ears like the wind; the world was *going on!* This part ought to be dramatized. The Irish author James Joyce once wrote. Ambrose M —— is going to scream.

There is no *texture of rendered sensory detail,* for one thing. The faded distorting mirrors beside Fat May; the impossibility of choosing a mount when one had but a single ride on the great carrousel; the *vertigo attendant on his recognition* that Ocean City was worn out, the place of fathers and grandfathers, straw-boatered men and parasoled ladies survived by their amusements. Money spent, the three paused at Peter's insistence beside Fat May to watch the girls get their skirts blown up. The object was to tease Magda, who said: "I swear, Peter M ——, you've got a one-track mind! Amby and me aren't *interested* in such things." In the tumbling-barrel, too, just inside the Devil's-mouth entrance to the funhouse, the girls were upended and their boyfriends and others could see up their dresses if they cared to. Which was the whole point, Ambrose realized. Of the entire funhouse! If you looked around, you noticed that almost all the people on the boardwalk were paired off into couples except the small children; in a way, that was the whole point of Ocean City! If you had X-ray eyes and could see everything going on at that instant under the boardwalk and in all the hotel rooms and cars and alleyways, you'd realize that all that normally *showed,* like restaurants and dance halls and clothing and test-your-strength machines, was merely preparation and intermission. Fat May screamed.

Because he watched the going-ons from the corner of his eye, it was Ambrose who spied the half dollar on the boardwalk near the tumbling-barrel. Losers weepers. The first time he'd heard some people moving through a corridor not far away, just after he'd lost sight of the crack of light, he'd decided not to call to them, for fear they'd guess he was scared and poke fun; it sounded like roughnecks; he'd hoped they'd come by and he could follow in the dark without their knowing. Another time he'd heard just one person, unless he imagined it, bumping along as if on the other side of the plywood; perhaps Peter coming back for him, or Father, or Magda lost too. Or the owner and operator of the funhouse. He'd called out once, as though merrily: "Anybody know where the heck we are?" But the query was too stiff, his voice cracked, when the sounds stopped he was terrified: maybe it was a queer who waited for fellows to get lost, or a longhaired filthy monster that lived in some cranny of the funhouse. He stood rigid for hours it seemed like, scarcely respiring. His future was shockingly clear, in outline. He tried holding his breath to the point of unconsciousness. There ought to be a button you could push to end your life absolutely without pain; disappear in a flick, like turning out a light. He would push it instantly! He despised Uncle Karl. But he despised his father too, for not being what he was supposed to be. Perhaps his father hated *his* father, and so on, and his son would hate him, and so on. Instantly!

Naturally he didn't have nerve enough to ask Magda to go through the funhouse with him. With incredible nerve and to everyone's surprise he invited Magda, quietly and politely, to go through the funhouse with him. "I warn you, I've never been through it before," he added, *laughing easily;* "but I reckon we can manage somehow. The important thing to remember, after all, is that it's meant to be a *fun*house; that is, a place of amusement. If people really got lost or injured or too badly frightened in it, the owner'd go out of business. There'd even be lawsuits. No character in a work of fiction can make a speech this long without interruption or acknowledgment from the other characters."

Mother teased Uncle Karl: "Three's a crowd, I always heard." But actually Ambrose was relieved that Peter now had a quarter too. Nothing was what it looked like. Every instant, under the surface of the Atlantic Ocean, millions of living animals devoured one another. Pilots were falling in flames over Europe; women were being forcibly raped in the South Pacific. His father should have taken him aside and said: "There is a simple secret to getting through the funhouse, as simple as being first to see the Towers. Here it is. Peter does not know it; neither does your Uncle Karl. You and I are different. Not surprisingly, you've often wished you weren't. Don't think I haven't noticed how unhappy your childhood has been! But you'll understand, when I tell you, why it had to be kept secret until now. And you won't regret not being like your brother and your uncle. *On the contrary!*" If you knew all the stories behind all the people on the boardwalk, you'd see that *nothing* was what it looked like. Husbands and wives often hated each other; parents didn't necessarily love their children; et cetera. A child took things for granted because he had nothing to compare his life to and everybody acted as if things were as they should be. Therefore each saw himself as the hero of the story, when the truth might turn out to be that he's the villain, or the coward. And there wasn't one thing you could do about it!

Hunchbacks, fat ladies, fools—that no one chose what he was was unbearable. In the movies he'd meet a beautiful young girl in the funhouse; they'd have hairs-breadth escapes from real dangers; he'd do and say the right things; she also; in the end they'd be lovers; their dialogue lines would match up; he'd be perfectly at ease; she'd not only like him well enough, she'd think he was *marvelous;* she'd lie awake thinking about *him,* instead of vice versa—the way his face looked in different lights and how he stood and exactly what he'd said—and yet that would be only one small episode in his wonderful life, among many many others. Not a *turning point* at all. What had happened in the toolshed was nothing. He hated, he loathed his parents! One reason for not writing a lost-in-the-funhouse story is that either everybody's felt what Ambrose feels, in which case it goes without saying, or else no normal person feels such things, in which case Ambrose is a freak. "Is anything more tiresome, in fiction, than the problems of sensitive adolescents?" And it's all too long and rambling, as if the author. For all a person knows the first time through, the end could be just around any corner; perhaps, *not impossibly* it's been within reach any number of times. On the other hand he may be scarcely past the start, with everything yet to get through, an intolerable idea.

Fill in: His father's raised eyebrows when he announced his decision to do the funhouse with Magda. Ambrose understands now, but didn't then, that his father was wondering whether he knew what the funhouse was *for*—especially since he didn't object, as he should have, when Peter decided to come along too. The ticket-woman, witchlike, mortifying him when inadvertently he gave her his name-coin instead of the half-dollar, then unkindly calling Magda's attention to the birthmark on his temple: "Watch out for him, girlie, he's a marked man!" She wasn't even cruel, he understood, only vulgar and insensitive. Somewhere in the world there was a young woman with such splendid understanding that she'd see him entire, like a poem or story, and find his words so valuable after all that when he confessed his apprehensions she would explain why they were in fact the very things that made him precious to her . . . and to Western Civilization! There was no such girl, the simple truth being. Violent yawns as they approached the mouth. Whispered advice from an old-timer on a bench near the barrel: "Go crabwise and ye'll get an eyeful without upsetting!" Composure vanished at the first pitch: Peter hollered joyously, Magda tumbled, shrieked, clutched her skirt; Ambrose scrambled crabwise, tight-lipped with terror, was soon out, watched his dropped name-coin slide among the couples. Shame-faced he saw that to get through expeditiously was not the point; Peter feigned assistance in order to trip Magda up, shouted "I see Christmas!" when her legs went flying. The old man, his latest betrayer, cackled approval. A dim hall then of black-thread cobwebs and recorded gibber: he took Magda's elbow to steady her against revolving discs set in the slanted floor to throw your feet out from under, and explained to her in a calm, deep voice his theory that each phase of the funhouse was triggered either automatically, by a series of photoelectric devices, or else manually by operators stationed at peepholes. But he lost his voice thrice as the discs unbalanced him; Magda was anyhow squealing; but at one point she clutched him about the waist to keep from falling, and her right cheek pressed for a moment against his belt-buckle. Heroically he drew her up, it was his chance to clutch her close as if for support and say: "I love you." He even put an arm lightly about the small of her back before a sailor-and-girl pitched into them from behind, sorely treading his left big toe and knocking Magda asprawl with them. The sailor's girl was a string-haired hussy with a loud laugh and light blue drawers; Ambrose realized that he wouldn't have said "I love you" anyhow, and was smitten with self-contempt. How much better it would be to be that common sailor! A wiry little Seaman 3rd, the fellow squeezed a girl to each side and stumbled hilarious into the mirror room, closer to Magda in thirty seconds than Ambrose had gotten in thirteen years. She giggled at something the fellow said to Peter; she drew her hair from her eyes with a movement so womanly it struck Ambrose's heart; Peter's smacking her backside then seemed particularly coarse. But Magda made a pleased indignant face and cried, "All right for *you* mister!" and pursued Peter into the maze without a backward glance. The sailor followed after, leisurely, drawing his girl against his hip; Ambrose understood not only that they were all so relieved to be rid of his burdensome company that they didn't even notice his absence, but that he himself shared their relief. Stepping from the treacherous passage at last into the mirror-maze, he saw once again, more clearly than ever, how readily he deceived himself into supposing he was a person. He even foresaw, wincing at his dreadful self-knowledge, that he would repeat the deception, at ever-rarer intervals, all his wretched life, so fearful were the alternatives. Fame, madness, suicide; perhaps all three. It's not believable that so young a boy could articulate that reflection, and in fiction the merely true must always yield to the plausible. Moreover, the symbolism is in places heavy-footed. Yet Ambrose M—— understood, as few adults do, that the famous loneliness of the great was no popular myth but a general truth—furthermore, that it was as much cause as effect.

All the preceding except the last few sentences is exposition that should've been done earlier or interspersed with the present action instead of lumped together. No reader would put up with so much with such *prolixity*. It's interesting that Ambrose's father, though presumably an intelligent man (as indicated by his role as grade-school principal), neither encouraged nor discouraged his sons at all in any way—as if he either didn't care about them or cared all right but didn't know how to act. If this fact should contribute to one of them's becoming a celebrated but wretchedly unhappy scientist, was it a good thing or not? He too might someday face the question; it would be useful to know whether it had tortured his father for years, for example, or never once crossed his mind.

In the maze two important things happened. First, our hero found a name-coin someone else had lost or discarded: *AMBROSE*, suggestive of the famous lightship and of his late grandfather's favorite dessert, which his mother used to prepare on special occasions out of coconut, oranges, grapes, and what else. Second, as he wondered at the endless replication of his image in the mirrors, second, as he *lost himself in the reflection* that the necessity for an observer makes perfect observation impossible, better make him eighteen at least, yet that would render other things unlikely, he heard Peter and Magda chuckling somewhere together in the maze. "Here!" "No, here!" they shouted to each other; Peter said, "Where's Amby?" Magda murmured. "Amb?" Peter called. In a pleased, friendly voice. He didn't reply. The truth was, his brother was a *happy-go-lucky youngster* who'd've been better off with a regular brother of his own, but who seldom complained of his lot and was generally cordial. Ambrose's throat ached; there aren't enough different ways to say that. He stood quietly while the two young people giggled and thumped through the glittering maze, hurrah'd their discovery of its exit, cried out in joyful alarm at what next beset them. Then he set his mouth and followed after, as he supposed, took a wrong turn, strayed into the pass *wherein he lingers yet*.

The action of conventional dramatic narrative may be represented by a diagram called Freitag's Triangle:

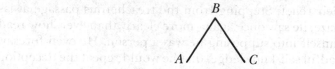

or more accurately by a variant of that diagram:

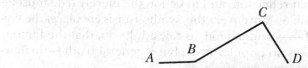

in which *AB* represents the exposition, *B* the introduction of conflict, *BC* the "rising action," complication, or development of the conflict, *C* the climax, or turn of the action, *CD* the dénouement, or resolution of the conflict. While there is no reason to regard this pattern as an absolute necessity, like many other conventions it became conventional because great numbers of people over many years learned by trial and error that it was effective; one ought not to forsake it, therefore, unless one wishes to forsake as well the effect of drama or has clear cause to feel that deliberate violation of the "normal" pattern can better can better effect that effect. This can't go on much longer; it can go on forever. He died telling stories to himself in the dark; years later, when that vast unsuspected area of the funhouse came to light, the first expedition found his skeleton in one of its labyrinthine corridors and mistook it for part of the entertainment. He died of starvation telling himself stories in the dark; but unbeknownst unbeknownst to him, an assistant operator of the funhouse, happening to overhear him, crouched just behind the plyboard partition and wrote down his every word. The operator's daughter, an exquisite young woman with a figure unusually well developed for her age, crouched just behind the partition and transcribed his every word. Though she had never laid eyes on him, she recognized that here was one of Western Culture's truly great imaginations, the eloquence of whose suffering would be an inspiration to unnumbered. And her heart was torn between her love for the misfortunate young man (yes, she loved him, though she had never laid though she knew him only—but how well!—through his words, and the deep, calm voice in which he spoke them) between her love et cetera and her womanly intuition that only in suffering and isolation could he give voice et cetera. Lone dark dying. Quietly she kissed the rough plyboard, and a tear fell upon the page. Where she had written in shorthand *Where she had written in shorthand* Where she had written in shorthand *Where she* et cetera. A long time ago we should have passed the apex of Freitag's Triangle and made brief work of the *dénouement;* the plot doesn't rise by meaningful steps but winds upon itself, digresses, retreats, hesitates, sighs, collapses, expires. The climax of the story must be its protagonist's discovery of a way to get through the funhouse. But he had found none, may have ceased to search.

What relevance does the war have to the story? Should there be fireworks outside or not?

Ambrose wandered, languished, dozed. Now and then he fell into his habit of rehearsing to himself the unadventurous story of his life, narrated from the third-person point of view, from his earliest memory parenthesis of maple leaves stirring in the summer breath of tidewater Maryland end of parenthesis to the present moment. Its principal events, on this telling, would appear to have been *A, B, C,* and *D.*

He imagined himself years hence, successful, married, at ease in the world, the trials of his adolescence far behind him. He has come to the seashore with his family for the holiday: how Ocean City has changed! But at one seldom at one ill-frequented end of the boardwalk a few derelict amusements survive from times gone by: the great carrousel from the turn of the century, with its monstrous griffins and mechanical concert band; the roller coaster rumored since 1916 to have been condemned; the mechanical shooting gallery in which only the image of our enemies changed. His own son laughs with Fat May and wants to know what a funhouse is; Ambrose hugs the sturdy lad close and smiles around his pipestem at his wife.

The family's going home. Mother sits between Father and Uncle Karl, who teases him good-naturedly who chuckles over the fact that the comrade with whom he'd fought his way shoulder to shoulder through the funhouse had turned out to be a blind Negro girl—to their mutual discomfort, as they'd opened their souls. But such are the walls of custom, which even. Whose arm is where? How must it feel. He dreams of a funhouse vaster by far than any yet constructed; but by then they may be out of fashion, like steamboats and excursion trains. Already quaint and seedy: the draperied ladies on the frieze of the carrousel are his father's father's mooncheeked dreams; if he thinks of it more he will vomit his apple-on-a-stick.

He wonders: will he become a regular person? Something has gone wrong; his vaccination didn't take; at the Boy-Scout initiation campfire he only pretended to be deeply moved, as he pretends to this hour that it is not so bad after all in the funhouse, and that he has a little limp. How long will it last? He envisions a truly astonishing funhouse, incredibly complex yet utterly controlled from a great central switchboard like the console of a pipe organ. Nobody had enough imagination. He could design such a place himself, wiring and all, and he's only thirteen years old. He would be its operator: panel lights would show what was up in every cranny of its cunning of its multifarious vastness; a switch-flick would ease this fellow's way, complicate that's, to balance things out; if anyone seemed lost or frightened, all the operator had to do was.

He wishes he had never entered the funhouse. But he has. Then he wishes he were dead. But he's not. Therefore he will construct funhouses for others and be their secret operator—though he would rather be among the lovers for whom funhouses are designed.

The King of Jazz

DONALD BARTHELME

Well I'm the king of jazz now, thought Hokie Mokie to himself as he oiled the slide on his trombone. Hasn't been a 'bone man been king of jazz for many years. But now that Spicy MacLammermoor, the old king, is dead, I guess I'm it. Maybe I better play a few notes out of this window here, to reassure myself.

"Wow!" said somebody standing on the sidewalk. "Did you hear that?"

"I did," said his companion.

"Can you distinguish our great homemade American jazz performers, each from the other?"

"Used to could."

"Then who was that playing?"

"Sounds like Hokie Mokie to me. Those few but perfectly selected notes have the real epiphanic glow."

"The what?"

"The real epiphanic glow, such as is obtained only by artists of the caliber of Hokie Mokie, who's from Pass Christian, Mississippi. He's the king of jazz, now that Spicy MacLammermoor is gone."

Hokie Mokie put his trombone in its trombone case and went to a gig. At the gig everyone fell back before him, bowing.

"Hi Bucky! Hi Zoot! Hi Freddie! Hi George! Hi Thad! Hi Roy! Hi Dexter! Hi Jo! Hi Willie! Hi Greens!"

"What we gonna play, Hokie? You the king of jazz now, you gotta decide."

"How 'bout 'Smoke'?"

"Wow!" everybody said. "Did you hear that? Hokie Mokie can just knock a fella out, just the way he pronounces a word. What a intonation on that boy! God Almighty!"

"I don't want to play 'Smoke,' " somebody said.

93

"Would you repeat that, stranger?"

"I don't want to play 'Smoke.' 'Smoke' is dull. I don't like the changes. I refuse to play 'Smoke.' "

"He refuses to play 'Smoke'! But Hokie Mokie is the king of jazz and he says 'Smoke'!"

"Man, you from outa town or something? What do you mean you refuse to play 'Smoke'? How'd you get on this gig anyhow? Who hired you?"

"I am Hideo Yamaguchi, from Tokyo, Japan."

"Oh, you're one of those Japanese cats, eh?"

"Yes I'm the top trombone man in all of Japan."

"Well you're welcome here until we hear you play. Tell me, is the Tennessee Tea Room still the top jazz place in Tokyo?"

"No, the top jazz place in Tokyo is the Square Box now."

"That's nice. OK, now we gonna play 'Smoke' just like Hokie said. You ready, Hokie? OK, give you four for nothin'. One! Two! Three! Four!"

The two men who had been standing under Hokie's window had followed him into the club. Now they said:

"Good God!"

"Yes, that's Hokie's famous 'English sunrise' way of playing. Playing with lots of rays coming out of it, some red rays, some blue rays, some green rays, some green stemming from a violet center, some olive stemming from a tan center—"

"That young Japanese fellow is pretty good, too."

"Yes, he is pretty good. And he holds his horn in a peculiar way. That's frequently the mark of a superior player."

"Bent over like that with his head between his knees—good God, he's sensational!"

He's sensational, Hokie thought. Maybe I ought to kill him.

But at that moment somebody came in the door pushing in front of him a four-and-one-half-octave marimba. Yes, it was Fat Man Jones, and he began to play even before he was fully in the door.

"What're we playing?"

" 'Billie's Bounce.' "

"That's what I thought it was. What're we in?"

"F."

"That's what I thought we were in. Didn't you use to play with Maynard?"

"Yeah I was on that band for a while until I was in the hospital."

"What for?"

"I was tired."

"What can we add to Hokie's fantastic playing?"

"How 'bout some rain or stars?"

"Maybe that's presumptuous?"

"Ask him if he'd mind."

"You ask him, I'm scared. You don't fool around with the king of jazz. That young Japanese guy's pretty good, too."

"He's sensational."

"You think he's playing in Japanese?"

"Well I don't think it's English."

This trombone's been makin' my neck green for thirty-five years, Hokie thought. How come I got to stand up to yet another challenge, this late in life?

"Well, Hideo—"

"Yes, Mr. Mokie?"

"You did well on both 'Smoke' and 'Billie's Bounce.' You're just about as good as me, I regret to say. In fact, I've decided you're *better* than me. It's a hideous thing to contemplate, but there it is. I have only been the king of jazz for twenty-four hours, but the unforgiving logic of this art demands we bow to Truth, when we hear it."

"Maybe you're mistaken?"

"No, I got ears. I'm not mistaken. Hideo Yamaguchi is the new king of jazz."

"You want to be king emeritus?"

"No, I'm just going to fold up my horn and steal away. This gig is yours, Hideo. You can pick the next tune."

"How 'bout 'Cream'?"

"OK, you heard what Hideo said, it's 'Cream.' You ready, Hideo?"

"Hokie, you don't have to leave. You can play too. Just move a little over to the side there—"

"Thank you, Hideo, that's very gracious of you. I guess I will play a little, since I'm still here. Sotto voce, of course."

"Hideo is wonderful on 'Cream'!"

"Yes, I imagine it's his best tune."

"What's that sound coming in from the side there?"

"Which side?"

"The left."

"You mean that sound that sounds like the cutting edge of life? That sounds like polar bears crossing Arctic ice pans? That sounds like a herd of musk ox in full flight? That sounds like male walruses diving to the bottom of the sea? That sounds like fumaroles smoking on the slopes of Mt. Katmai? That sounds like the wild turkey walking through the deep, soft forest? That sounds like beavers chewing trees in an Appalachian marsh? That sounds like an oyster fungus growing on an aspen trunk? That sounds like a mule deer wandering a montane of the Sierra Nevada? That sounds like prairie dogs kissing? That sounds like witchgrass tumbling or a river meandering? That sounds like manatees munching seaweed at Cape Sable? That sounds like coatimundis moving in packs across the face of Arkansas? That sounds like—"

"Good God, it's Hokie! Even with a cup mute on, he's blowing Hideo right off the stand!"

"Hideo's playing on his knees now! Good God, he's reaching into his belt for a large steel sword—Stop him!"

"Wow! That was the most exciting 'Cream' ever played! Is Hideo all right?"

"Yes, somebody is getting him a glass of water."

"You're my man, Hokie! That was the dadblangedest thing I ever saw!"

"You're the king of jazz once again!"

"Hokie Mokie is the most happening thing there is!"

"Yes, Mr. Hokie sir, I have to admit it, you blew me right off the stand. I see I have many years of work and study before me still."

"That's OK, son. Don't think a thing about it. It happens to the best of us. Or it almost happens to the best of us. Now I want everybody to have a good time because we're gonna play 'Flats.' 'Flats' is next."

"With your permission, sir, I will return to my hotel and pack. I am most grateful for everything I have learned here."

"That's OK, Hideo. Have a nice day. He-he. Now, 'Flats.' "

Shifting

ANN BEATTIE

The woman's name was Natalie and the man's name was Larry. They had been childhood sweethearts; he had first kissed her at an ice-skating party when they were ten. She had been unlacing her skates and had not expected the kiss. He had not expected to do it, either—he had some notion of getting his face out of the wind that was blowing across the iced-over lake, and he found himself ducking his head toward her. Kissing her seemed the natural thing to do. When they graduated from high school he was named "class clown" in the yearbook, but Natalie didn't think of him as being particularly funny. He spent more time than she thought he needed to study chemistry, and he never laughed when she joked. She really did not think of him as funny. They went to the same college, in their hometown, but he left after a year to go to a larger, more impressive university. She took the train to be with him on weekends, or he took the train to see her. When he graduated his parents gave him a car. If they had given it to him when he was still in college, it would have made things much easier. They waited to give it to him until graduation day, forcing him into attending the graduation exercises. He thought his parents were wonderful people, and Natalie liked them in a way, too, but she resented their perfect timing, their careful smiles. They were afraid that he would marry her. Eventually, he did. He had gone on to graduate school after college, and he set a date six months ahead for their wedding so that it would take place after his first-semester final exams. That way he could devote his time to studying for the chemistry exams.

When she married him, he had had the car for eight months. It still smelled like a brand-new car. There was never any clutter in the car. Even the ice scraper was kept in the glove compartment. There was not even a sweater or a lost glove in the back seat. He vacuumed the car every weekend, after washing it at the car wash. On Friday nights, on their way to some cheap restaurant and a dollar movie, he would stop at the car wash, and she would get out so he could vacuum all over the inside of the car. She would lean against the metal wall of the car wash and watch him clean it.

It was expected that she would not become pregnant. She did not. It had also been expected that she would keep their apartment clean, and keep out of the way as much as possible in such close quarters while he was studying. The apartment was messy, though, and when he was studying late at night she would interrupt him and try to talk him into going to sleep. He gave a chemistry-class lecture once a week, and she would often tell him that overpreparing was as bad as underpreparing. She did not know if she believed this, but it was a favorite line of hers. Sometimes he listened to her.

On Tuesdays, when he gave the lecture, she would drop him off at school and then drive to a supermarket to do the week's shopping. Usually she did not make a list before she went shopping, but when she got to the parking lot she would take a tablet out of her purse and write a few items on it, sitting in the car in the cold. Even having a few things written down would stop her from wandering aimlessly in the store and buying things that she would never use. Before this, she had bought several pans and cans of food that she had not used, or that she could have done without. She felt better when she had a list.

She would drop him at school again on Wednesdays, when he had two seminars that together took up all the afternoon. Sometimes she would drive out of town then, to the suburbs, and shop there if any shopping needed to be done. Otherwise, she would go to the art museum, which was not far away but hard to get to by bus. There was one piece of sculpture in there that she wanted very much to touch, but the guard was always nearby. She came so often that in time the guard began to nod hello. She wondered if she could ever persuade the man to turn his head for a few seconds—only that long—so she could stroke the sculpture. Of course she would never dare ask. After wandering through the museum and looking at least twice at the sculpture, she would go to the gift shop and buy a few postcards and then sit on one of the museum benches, padded with black vinyl, with a Calder mobile hanging overhead, and write notes to friends. (She never wrote letters.) She would tuck the postcards in her purse and mail them when she left the museum. But before she left, she often had coffee in the restaurant: she saw mothers and children struggling there, and women dressed in fancy clothes talking with their faces close together, as quietly as lovers.

On Thursdays he took the car. After his class he would drive to visit his parents and his friend Andy, who had been wounded in Vietnam. About once a month she would go with him, but she had to feel up to it. Being with Andy embarrassed her. She had told him not to go to Vietnam—told him that he could prove his patriotism in some other way—and finally, after she and Larry had made a visit together and she had seen Andy in the motorized bed in his parents' house, Larry had agreed that she need not go again. Andy had apologized to her. It embarrassed her that this man, who had been blown sky-high by a land mine and had lost a leg and lost the full use of his arms, would smile up at her ironically and say, "You were right." She also felt as though he wanted to hear what she would say now, and that now he would listen. Now she had nothing to say. Andy would pull himself up, relying on his right arm, which was the stronger, gripping the rails at the side of the bed, and sometimes he would take her hand. His arms were still weak, but the doctors said he would regain complete use of his right arm with time. She had to make an effort not to squeeze his hand when he held hers because she found herself wanting to squeeze energy back into him. She had a morbid curiosity about what it felt like to be blown from the ground—to go up, and to come crashing down. During their visit Larry put on the class-clown act for Andy, telling funny stories and laughing uproariously.

Once or twice Larry had talked Andy into getting in his wheelchair and loaded him into the car and taken him to a bar. Larry called her once, late, pretty drunk, to say that he would not be home that night—that he would sleep at his parents' house. "My God," she said. "Are you going to drive Andy home when you're drunk?" "What the hell else can happen to him?" he said.

Larry's parents blamed her for Larry's not being happy. His mother could only be pleasant with her for a short while, and then she would veil her criticisms by putting them as questions. "I know that one thing that helps enormously is good nutrition," his mother said. "He works so hard that he probably needs quite a few vitamins as well, don't you think?" Larry's father was the sort of man who found hobbies in order to avoid his wife. His hobbies were building model boats, repairing clocks, and photography. He took pictures of himself building the boats and fixing the clocks, and gave the pictures, in cardboard frames, to Natalie and Larry for Christmas and birthday presents. Larry's mother was very anxious to stay on close terms with her son, and she knew that Natalie did not like her very much. Once she had visited them during the week, and Natalie, not knowing what to do with her, had taken her to the museum. She had pointed out the sculpture, and his mother had glanced at it and then ignored it. Natalie hated her for her bad taste. She had bad taste in the sweaters she gave Larry, too, but he wore them. They made him look collegiate. That whole world made her sick.

When Natalie's uncle died and left her his 1965 Volvo, they immediately decided to sell it and use the money for a vacation. They put an ad in the paper, and there were several callers. There were some calls on Tuesday, when Larry was in class, and Natalie found herself putting the people off. She told one woman that the car had too much mileage on it, and mentioned body rust, which it did not have; she told another caller, who was very persistent, that the car was already sold. When Larry returned from school she explained that the phone was off the hook because so many people were calling about the car and she had decided not to sell it after all. They could take a little money from their savings account and go on the trip if he wanted. But she did not want to sell the car. "It's not an automatic shift," he said. "You don't know how to drive it." She told him that she could learn. "It will cost money to insure it," he said, "and it's old and probably not even dependable." She wanted to keep the car. "I know," he said, "but it doesn't make sense. When we have more money, you can have a car. You can have a newer, better car."

The next day she went out to the car, which was parked in the driveway of an old lady next door. Her name was Mrs. Larsen and she no longer drove a car, and she told Natalie she could park their second car there. Natalie opened the car door and got behind the wheel and put her hands on it. The wheel was covered with a flaky yellow-and-black plastic cover. She eased it off. A few pieces of foam rubber stuck to the wheel. She picked them off. Underneath the cover, the wheel was a dull red. She ran her fingers around and around the circle of the wheel. Her cousin Burt had delivered the car—a young opportunist, sixteen years old, who said he would drive it the hundred miles from his house to theirs for twenty dollars and a bus ticket home. She had not even invited him to stay for dinner, and Larry had driven him to the bus station. She wondered if it was Burt's cigarette in the ashtray or her dead uncle's. She could not even remember if her uncle smoked. She was surprised that he had left her his car. The car was much more comfortable than Larry's, and it had a nice smell inside. It smelled a little the way a field smells after a spring rain. She rubbed the side of her head back and forth against the window and then got out of the car and went in to see Mrs. Larsen. The night before, she had suddenly thought of the boy who brought the old lady the evening newspaper every night; he looked old enough to drive, and he would probably know how to shift. Mrs. Larsen agreed with her—she was sure that he could teach her. "Of course, everything has its price," the old lady said.

"I know that. I meant to offer him money," Natalie said, and was surprised, listening to her voice, that she sounded old too.

She took an inventory and made a list of things in their apartment. Larry had met an insurance man one evening while playing basketball at the gym who told him that they should have a list of their possessions, in case of theft. "What's worth anything?" she said when he told her. It was their first argument in almost a year—the first time in a year, anyway, that their voices were raised. He told her that several of the pieces of furniture his grandparents gave them when they got married were antiques, and the man at the gym said that if they weren't going to get them appraised every year, at least they should take snapshots of them and keep the pictures in a safe-deposit box. Larry told her to photograph the pie safe (which she used to store linen), the piano with an inlaid mother-of-pearl decoration on the music rack (neither of them knew how to play), and the table with hand-carved wooden handles and a marble top. He bought her an Instamatic camera at the drugstore, with film and flash bulbs. "Why can't you do it?" she said, and an argument began. He said that she had no respect for his profession and no understanding of the amount of study that went into getting a master's degree in chemistry.

That night he went out to meet two friends at the gym, to shoot baskets. She put the little flashcube into the top of the camera, dropped in the film and closed the back. She went first to the piano. She leaned forward so that she was close enough to see the inlay clearly, but she found that when she was that close the whole piano wouldn't fit into the picture. She decided to take two pictures. Then she photographed the pie safe, with one door open, showing the towels and sheets stacked inside. She did not have a reason for opening the door, except that she remembered a *Perry Mason* show in which detectives photographed everything with the doors hanging open. She photographed the table, lifting the lamp off it first. There were still eight pictures left. She went to the mirror in their bedroom and held the camera above her head, pointing down at an angle, and photographed her image in the mirror. She took off her slacks and sat on the floor and leaned back, aiming the camera down at her legs. Then she stood up and took a picture of her feet, leaning over and aiming down. She put on her favorite record: Stevie Wonder singing "For Once in My Life." She found herself wondering what it would be like to be blind, to have to feel things to see them. She thought about the piece of sculpture in the museum—the two elongated mounds, intertwined, the smooth gray stone as shiny as sea pebbles. She photographed the kitchen, bathroom, bedroom and living room. There was one picture left. She put her left hand on her thigh, palm up, and with some difficulty—with the camera nestled into her neck like a violin—snapped a picture of it with her right hand. The next day would be her first driving lesson.

He came to her door at noon, as he had said he would. He had on a long maroon scarf, which made his deep-blue eyes very striking. She had only seen him from her window when he carried the paper in to the old lady. He was a little nervous. She hoped that it was just the anxiety of any teen-ager confronting an adult. She needed to have him like her. She did not learn about mechanical things easily (Larry had told her that he would have invested in a "real" camera, except that he did not have the time to teach her about it), so she wanted him to be patient. He sat on the footstool in her living room, still in coat and scarf, and told her how a stick shift operated. He moved his hand through the air. The motion he made reminded her of the salute spacemen gave to earthlings in a science-fiction picture she had recently watched on late-night television. She nodded. "How much—" she began, but he interrupted and said, "You can decide what it was worth when you've learned." She was surprised and wondered if he meant to charge a great deal. Would it be her fault and would she have to pay him if he named his price when the lessons were over? But he had an honest face. Perhaps he was just embarrassed to talk about money.

He drove for a few blocks, making her watch his hand on the stick shift. "Feel how the car is going?" he said. "Now you shift." He shifted. The car jumped a little, hummed, moved into gear. It was an old car and didn't shift too easily, he said. She had been sitting forward, so that when he shifted she rocked back hard against the seat—harder than she needed to. Almost unconsciously, she wanted to show him what a good teacher he was. When her turn came to drive, the car stalled. "Take it easy," he said. "Ease up on the clutch. Don't just raise your foot off of it like that." She tried it again. "That's it," he said. She looked at him when the car was in third. He sat in the seat, looking out the window. Snow was expected. It was Thursday. Although Larry was going to visit his parents and would not be back until late Friday afternoon, she decided she would wait until Tuesday for her next lesson. If he came home early, he would find out that she was taking lessons, and she didn't want him to know. She asked the boy, whose name was Michael, whether he thought she would forget all he had taught her in the time between lessons. "You'll remember," he said.

When they returned to the old lady's driveway, the car stalled going up the incline. She had trouble shifting. The boy put his hand over hers and kicked the heel of his hand forward. "You'll have to treat this car a little roughly, I'm afraid," he said. That afternoon, after he left, she made spaghetti sauce, chopping little pieces of pepper and onion and mushroom. When the sauce had cooked down, she called Mrs. Larsen and said that she would bring over dinner. She usually ate with the old lady once a week. The old lady often added a pinch of cinnamon to her food, saying that it brought out the flavor better than salt, and that since she was losing her sense of smell, food had to be strongly flavored for her to taste it. Once she had sprinkled cinnamon on a knockwurst. This time, as they ate, Natalie asked the old lady how much she paid the boy to bring the paper.

"I give him a dollar a week," the old lady said.

"Did he set the price, or did you?"

"He set the price. He told me he wouldn't take much because he has to walk this street to get to his apartment anyway."

"He taught me a lot about the car today," Natalie said.

"He's very handsome, isn't he?" the old lady said.

*   *   *

She asked Larry, "How were your parents?"

"Fine," he said. "But I spent almost all the time with Andy. It's almost his birthday, and he's depressed. We went to see Mose Allison."

"I think it stinks that hardly anyone else ever visits Andy," she said.

"He doesn't make it easy. He tells you everything that's on his mind, and there's no way you can pretend that his troubles don't amount to much. You just have to sit there and nod."

She remembered that Andy's room looked like a gymnasium. There were handgrips and weights scattered on the floor. There was even a psychedelic pink hula hoop that he was to put inside his elbow and then move his arm in circles wide enough to make the hoop spin. He couldn't do it. He would lie in bed with the hoop in back of his neck, and holding the sides, lift his neck off the pillow. His arms were barely strong enough to do that, really, but he could raise his neck with no trouble, so he just pretended that his arms pulling the loop were raising it. His parents thought that it was a special exercise that he had mastered.

"What did you do today?" Larry said now.

"I made spaghetti," she said. She had made it the day before, but she thought that since he was mysterious about the time he spent away from her ("in the lab" and "at the gym" became interchangeable), she did not owe him a straight answer. That day she had dropped off the film and then she had sat at the drugstore counter to have a cup of coffee. She bought some cigarettes, though she had not smoked since high school. She smoked one mentholated cigarette and then threw the pack away in a garbage container outside the drugstore. Her mouth still felt cool inside.

He asked if she had planned anything for the weekend.

"No," she said.

"Let's do something you'd like to do. I'm a little ahead of myself in the lab right now."

That night they ate spaghetti and made plans, and the next day they went for a ride in the country, to a factory where wooden toys were made. In the showroom he made a bear marionette shake and twist. She examined a small rocking horse, rhythmically pushing her finger up and down on the back rung of the rocker to make it rock. When they left they took with them a catalogue of toys they could order. She knew that they would never look at the catalogue again. On their way to the museum he stopped to wash the car. Because it was the weekend there were quite a few cars lined up waiting to go in. They were behind a blue Cadillac that seemed to inch forward of its own accord, without a driver. When the Cadillac moved into the washing area, a tiny man hopped out. He stood on tiptoe to reach the coin box to start the washing machine. She doubted if he was five feet tall.

"Look at that poor son of a bitch," he said.

The little man was washing his car.

"If Andy could get out more," Larry said. "If he could get rid of that feeling he has that he's the only freak . . . I wonder if it wouldn't do him good to come spend a week with us."

"Are you going to take him in the wheelchair to the lab with you?" she said. "I'm not taking care of Andy all day."

His face changed. "Just for a week was all I meant," he said.

"I'm not doing it," she said. She was thinking of the boy, and of the car. She had almost learned how to drive the car.

"Maybe in the warm weather," she said. "When we could go to the park or something."

He said nothing. The little man was rinsing his car. She sat inside when their turn came. She thought that Larry had no right to ask her to take care of Andy. Water flew out of the hose and battered the car. She thought of Andy, in the woods at night, stepping on the land mine, being blown into the air. She wondered if it threw him in an arc, so he ended up somewhere away from where he had been walking, or if it just blasted him straight up, if he went up the way an umbrella opens. Andy had been a wonderful ice skater. They all envied him his long sweeping turns, with his legs somehow neatly together and his body at the perfect angle. She never saw him have an accident on the ice. Never once. She had known Andy, and they had skated at Parker's pond, for eight years before he was drafted.

The night before, as she and Larry were finishing dinner, he had asked her if she intended to vote for Nixon or McGovern in the election. "McGovern," she said. How could he not have known that? She knew then that they were farther apart than she had thought. She hoped that on Election Day she could drive herself to the polls—not go with him and not walk. She planned not to ask the old lady if she wanted to come along because that would be one vote she would keep Nixon from getting.

At the museum she hesitated by the sculpture but did not point it out to him. He didn't look at it. He gazed to the side, above it, at a Francis Bacon painting. He could have shifted his eyes just a little and seen the sculpture, and her, standing and staring.

After three more lessons she could drive the car. The last two times, which were later in the afternoon than her first lesson, they stopped at the drugstore to get the old lady's paper, to save him from having to make the same trip back on foot. When he came out of the drugstore with the paper, after the final lesson, she asked him if he'd like to have a beer to celebrate.

"Sure," he said.

They walked down the street to a bar that was filled with college students. She wondered if Larry ever came to this bar. He had never said that he did.

She and Michael talked. She asked why he wasn't in high school. He told her that he had quit. He was living with his brother, and his brother was teaching him carpentry, which he had been interested in all along. On his napkin he drew a picture of the cabinets and bookshelves he and his brother had spent the last week constructing and installing in the house of two wealthy old sisters. He drummed the side of his thumb against the edge of the table in time with the music. They each drank beer, from heavy glass mugs.

"Mrs. Larsen said your husband was in school," the boy said. "What's he studying?"

She looked up, surprised. Michael had never mentioned her husband to her before. "Chemistry," she said.

"I liked chemistry pretty well," he said. "Some of it."

"My husband doesn't know you've been giving me lessons. I'm just going to tell him that I can drive the stick shift, and surprise him."

"Yeah?" the boy said. "What will he think about that?"

"I don't know," she said. "I don't think he'll like it."

"Why?" the boy said.

His question made her remember that he was sixteen. What she had said would never have provoked another question from an adult. The adult would have nodded or said, "I know."

She shrugged. The boy took a long drink of beer. "I thought it was funny that he didn't teach you himself, when Mrs. Larsen told me you were married," he said.

They had discussed her. She wondered why Mrs. Larsen wouldn't have told her that, because the night she ate dinner with her she had talked to Mrs. Larsen about what an extraordinarily patient teacher Michael was. Had Mrs. Larsen told him that Natalie talked about him?

On the way back to the car she remembered the photographs and went back to the drugstore and picked up the prints. As she took money out of her wallet she remembered that today was the day she would have to pay him. She looked around at him, at the front of the store, where he was flipping through magazines. He was tall and he was wearing a very old black jacket. One end of his long thick maroon scarf was hanging down his back.

"What did you take pictures of?" he said when they were back in the car.

"Furniture. My husband wanted pictures of our furniture, in case it was stolen."

"Why?" he said.

"They say if you have proof that you had valuable things, the insurance company won't hassle you about reimbursing you."

"You have a lot of valuable stuff?" he said.

"My husband thinks so," she said.

A block from the driveway she said, "What do I owe you?"

"Four dollars," he said.

"That's nowhere near enough," she said and looked over at him. He had opened the envelope with the pictures in it while she was driving. He was staring at the picture of her legs. "What's this?" he said.

She turned into the driveway and shut off the engine. She looked at the picture. She could not think what to tell him it was. Her hands and heart felt heavy.

"Wow," the boy said. He laughed. "Never mind. Sorry. I'm not looking at any more of them."

He put the pack of pictures back in the envelope and dropped it on the seat between them.

She tried to think what to say, of some way she could turn the pictures into a joke. She wanted to get out of the car and run. She wanted to stay, not to give him the money, so he would sit there with her. She reached into her purse and took out her wallet and removed four one-dollar bills.

"How many years have you been married?" he asked.

"One," she said. She held the money out to him. He said "Thank you" and leaned across the seat and put his right arm over her shoulder and kissed her. She felt his scarf bunched up against their cheeks. She was amazed at how warm his lips were in the cold car.

He moved his head away and said, "I didn't think you'd mind if I did that." She shook her head no. He unlocked the door and got out.

"I could drive you to your brother's apartment," she said. Her voice sounded hollow. She was extremely embarrassed, but she couldn't let him go.

He got back in the car. "You could drive me and come in for a drink," he said. "My brother's working."

*   *   *

When she got back to the car two hours later she saw a white parking ticket clamped under the windshield wiper, flapping in the wind. When she opened the car door and sank into the seat, she saw that he had left the money, neatly folded, on the floor mat on his side of the car. She did not pick up the money. In a while she started the car. She stalled it twice on the way home. When she had pulled into the driveway she looked at the money for a long time, then left it lying there. She left the car unlocked, hoping the money would be stolen. If it disappeared, she could tell herself that she had paid him. Otherwise she would not know how to deal with the situation.

When she got into the apartment, the phone rang. "I'm at the gym to play basketball," Larry said. "Be home in an hour."

"I was at the drugstore," she said. "See you then."

She examined the pictures. She sat on the sofa and laid them out, the twelve of them, in three rows on the cushion next to her. The picture of the piano was between the picture of her feet and the picture of herself that she had shot by aiming into the mirror. She picked up the four pictures of their furniture and put them on the table. She picked up the others and examined them closely. She began to understand why she had taken them. She had photographed parts of her body, fragments of it, to study the pieces. She had probably done it because she thought so much about Andy's body and the piece that was gone—the leg, below the knee, on his left side. She had had two bourbon-and-waters at the boy's apartment, and drinking always depressed her. She felt very depressed looking at the pictures, so she put them down and went into the bedroom. She undressed. She looked at her body—whole, not a bad figure—in the mirror. It was an automatic reaction with her to close the curtains when she was naked; so she turned quickly and went to the window and did that. She went back to the mirror; the room was darker now and her body looked better. She ran her hands down her sides, wondering if the feel of her skin was anything like the way the sculpture would feel. She was sure that the sculpture would be smoother—her hands would move more quickly down the slopes of it than she wanted—that it would be cool, and that somehow she could feel the grayness of it. Those things seemed preferable to her hands lingering on her body, the imperfection of her skin, the overheated apartment. If she were the piece of sculpture and if she could feel, she would like her sense of isolation.

This was in 1972, in Philadelphia.

Looking for Mr. Green

SAUL BELLOW

Whatsoever thy hand findeth to do, do it with thy might. . . .

Hard work? No, it wasn't really so hard. He wasn't used to walking and stairclimbing, but the physical difficulty of his new job was not what George Grebe felt most. He was delivering relief checks in the Negro district, and although he was a native Chicagoan this was not a part of the city he knew much about—it needed a depression to introduce him to it. No, it wasn't literally hard work, not as reckoned in foot-pounds, but yet he was beginning to feel the strain of it, to grow aware of its peculiar difficulty. He could find the streets and numbers, but the clients were not where they were supposed to be, and he felt like a hunter inexperienced in the camouflage of his game. It was an unfavorable day, too—fall, and cold, dark weather, windy. But, anyway, instead of shells in his deep trenchcoat pocket he had the cardboard of checks, punctured for the spindles of the file, the holes reminding him of the holes in player-piano paper. And he didn't look much like a hunter, either; his was a city figure entirely, belted up in this Irish conspirator's coat. He was slender without being tall, stiff in the back, his legs looking shabby in a pair of old tweed pants gone through and fringy at the cuffs. With this stiffness, he kept his head forward, so that his face was red from the sharpness of the weather; and it was an indoors sort of face with gray eyes that persisted in some kind of thought and yet seemed to avoid definiteness of conclusion. He wore sideburns that surprised you somewhat by the tough curl of the blond hair and the effect of assertion in their length. He was not so mild as he looked, nor so youthful; and nevertheless there was no effort on his part to seem what he was not. He was an educated man; he was a bachelor; he was in some ways simple; without lushing, he liked a drink; his luck had not been good. Nothing was deliberately hidden.

He felt that his luck was better than usual today. When he had reported for work that morning he had expected to be shut up in the relief office at a clerk's job, for he had been hired downtown as a clerk, and he was glad to have, instead, the freedom of the streets and welcomed, at least at first, the vigor of the cold and even the blowing of the hard wind. But on the other hand he was not getting on with the distribution of the checks. It was true that it was a city job; nobody expected you to push too hard at a city job. His supervisor, that young Mr. Raynor, had practically told him that. Still, he wanted to do well at it. For one thing, when he knew how quickly he could deliver a batch of checks, he would know also how much time he could expect to clip for himself. And then, too, the clients would be waiting for their money. That was not the most important consideration, though it certainly mattered to him. No, but he wanted to do well, simply for doing-well's sake, to acquit himself decently of a job because he so rarely had a job to do that required just this sort of energy. Of this peculiar energy he now had a superabundance; once it had started to flow, it flowed all too heavily. And, for the time being anyway, he was balked. He could not find Mr. Green.

So he stood in his big-skirted trenchcoat with a large envelope in his hand and papers showing from his pocket, wondering why people should be so hard to locate who were too feeble or sick to come to the station to collect their own checks. But Raynor had told him that tracking them down was not easy at first and had offerred him some advice on how to proceed. "If you can see the postman, he's your first man to ask, and your best bet. If you can't connect with him, try the stores and tradespeople around. Then the janitor and the neighbors. But you'll find the closer you come to your man the less people will tell you. They don't want to tell you anything."

"Because I'm a stranger."

"Because you're white. We ought to have a Negro doing this, but we don't at the moment, and of course you've got to eat, too, and this is public employment. Jobs have to be made. Oh, that holds for me too. Mind you, I'm not letting myself out. I've got three years of seniority on you, that's all. And a law degree. Otherwise, you might be back of the desk and I might be going out into the field this cold day. The same dough pays us both and for the same, exact, identical reason. What's my law degree got to do with it? But you have to pass out these checks, Mr. Grebe, and it'll help if you're stubborn, so I hope you are."

"Yes, I'm fairly stubborn."

Raynor sketched hard with an eraser in the old dirt of his desk, left-handed, and said, "Sure, what else can you answer to such a question. Anyhow, the trouble you're going to have is that they don't like to give information about anybody. They think you're a plain-clothes dick or an installment collector, or summons-server or something like that. Till you've been seen around the neighborhood for a few months and people know you're only from the relief."

It was dark, ground-freezing, pre-Thanksgiving weather; the wind played hob with the smoke, rushing it down, and Grebe missed his gloves, which he had left in Raynor's office. And no one would admit knowing Green. It was past three o'clock and the postman had made his last delivery. The nearest grocer, himself a Negro, had never heard the name Tulliver Green, or said he hadn't. Grebe was inclined to think that it was true, that he had in the end convinced the man that he wanted only to deliver a check. But he wasn't sure. He needed experience in interpreting looks and signs and, even more, the will not to be put off or denied and even the force to bully if need be. If the grocer did know, he had got rid of him easily. But since most of his trade was with reliefers, why should he prevent the delivery of a check? Maybe Green, or Mrs. Green, if there was a Mrs. Green, patronized another grocer. And was there a Mrs. Green? It was one of Grebe's great handicaps that he hadn't looked at any of the case records. Raynor should have let him read files for a few hours. But he apparently saw no need for that, probably considering the job unimportant. Why prepare systematically to deliver a few checks?

But now it was time to look for the janitor. Grebe took in the building in the wind and gloom of the late November day—trampled, frost-hardened lots on one side; on the other, an automobile junk yard and then the infinite work of Elevated frames, weak-looking, gaping with rubbish fires; two sets of leaning brick porches three stories high and a flight of cement stairs to the cellar. Descending, he entered the underground passage, where he tried the doors until one opened and he found himself in the furnace room. There someone rose toward him and approached, scraping on the coal grit and bending under the canvas-jacketed pipes.

"Are you the janitor?"

"What do you want?"

"I'm looking for a man who's supposed to be living here. Green."

"What Green?"

"Oh, you maybe have more than one Green?" said Grebe with new, pleasant hope. "This is Tulliver Green."

"I don't think I c'n help you, mister. I don't know any."

"A crippled man."

The janitor stood bent before him. Could it be that he was crippled? Oh, God! what if he was. Grebe's gray eyes sought with excited difficulty to see. But no, he was only very short and stooped. A head awakened from meditation, a strong-haired beard, low, wide shoulders. A staleness of sweat and coal rose from his black shirt and the burlap sack he wore as an apron.

"Crippled how?"

Grebe thought and then answered with the light voice of unmixed candor, "I don't know. I've never seen him." This was damaging, but his only other choice was to make a lying guess, and he was not up to it. "I'm delivering checks for the relief to shut-in cases. If he weren't crippled he'd come to collect himself. That's why I said crippled. Bedridden, chair-ridden—is there anybody like that?"

This sort of frankness was one of Grebe's oldest talents, going back to childhood. But it gained him nothing here.

"No suh. I've got four buildin's same as this that I take care of. I don' know all the tenants, leave alone the tenants' tenants. The rooms turn over so fast, people movin' in and out every day. I can't tell you."

The janitor opened his grimy lips but Grebe did not hear him in the piping of the valves and the consuming pull of air to flame in the body of the furnace. He knew, however, what he had said.

"Well, all the same, thanks. Sorry I bothered you. I'll prowl around upstairs again and see if I can turn up someone who knows him."

Once more in the cold air and early darkness he made the short circle from the cellarway to the entrance crowded between the brickwork pillars and began to climb to the third floor. Pieces of plaster ground under his feet; strips of brass tape from which the carpeting had been torn away marked old boundaries at the sides. In the passage, the cold reached him worse than in the street; it touched him to the bone. The hall toilets ran like springs. He thought grimly as he heard the wind burning around the building with a sound like that of the furnace, that this was a great piece of constructed shelter. Then he struck a match in the gloom and searched for names and numbers among the writings and scribbles on the walls. He saw WHOODY-DOODY GO TO JESUS, and zigzags, caricatures, sexual scrawls, and curses. So the sealed rooms of pyramids were also decorated, and the caves of human dawn.

The information on his card was, TULLIVER GREEN—APT 3D. There were no names, however, and no numbers. His shoulders drawn up, tears of cold in his eyes, breathing vapor, he went the length of the corridor and told himself that if he had been lucky enough to have the temperament for it he would bang on one of the doors and bawl out "Tulliver Green!" until he got results. But it wasn't in him to make an uproar and he continued to burn matches, passing the light over the walls. At the rear, in a corner off the hall, he discovered a door he had not seen before and he thought it best to investigate. It sounded empty when he knocked, but a young Negress answered, hardly more than a girl. She opened only a bit, to guard the warmth of the room.

"Yes suh?"

"I'm from the district relief station on Prairie Avenue. I'm looking for a man named Tulliver Green to give him his check. Do you know him?"

No, she didn't; but he thought she had not understood anything of what he had said. She had a dream-bound, dream-blind face, very soft and black, shut off. She wore a man's jacket and pulled the ends together at her throat. Her hair was parted in three directions, at the sides and transversely, standing up at the front in a dull puff.

"Is there somebody around here who might know?"

"I jus' taken this room las' week."

He observed that she shivered, but even her shiver was somnambulistic and there was no sharp consciousness of cold in the big smooth eyes of her handsome face.

"All right, miss, thank you. Thanks," he said, and went to try another place.

Here he was admitted. He was grateful, for the room was warm. It was full of people, and they were silent as he entered—ten people, or a dozen, perhaps more, sitting on benches like a parliament. There was no light, properly speaking, but a tempered darkness that the window gave, and everyone seemed to him enormous, the men padded out in heavy work clothes and winter coats, and the women huge, too, in their sweaters, hats, and old furs. And, besides, bed and bedding, a black cooking range, a piano piled towering to the ceiling with papers, a dining-room table of the old style of prosperous Chicago. Among these people Grebe, with his cold-heightened fresh color and his smaller stature, entered like a schoolboy. Even though he was met with smiles and good will, he knew, before a single word was spoken, that all the currents ran against him and that he would make no headway. Nevertheless he began. "Does anybody here know how I can deliver a check to Mr. Tulliver Green?"

"Green?" It was the man that had let him in who answered. He was in short sleeves, in a checkered shirt, and had a queer, high head, profusely overgrown and long as a shako; the veins entered it strongly from his forehead. "I never heard mention of him. Is this where he live?"

"This is the address they gave me at the station. He's a sick man, and he'll need his check. Can't anybody tell me where to find him?"

He stood his ground and waited for a reply, his crimson wool scarf wound about his neck and drooping outside his trenchcoat, pockets weighted with the block of checks and official forms. They must have realized that he was not a college boy employed afternoons by a bill collector, trying foxily to pass for a relief clerk, recognized that he was an older man who knew himself what need was, who had had more than an average seasoning in hardship. It was evident enough if you looked at the marks under his eyes and at the sides of his mouth.

"Anybody know this sick man?"

"No suh." On all sides he saw heads shaken and smiles of denial. No one knew. And maybe it was true, he considered, standing silent in the earthen, musky human gloom of the place as the rumble continued. But he could never really be sure.

"What's the matter with this man?" said shako-head.

"I've never seen him. All I can tell you is that he can't come in person for his money. It's my first day in this district."

"Maybe they given you the wrong number?"

"I don't believe so. But where else can I ask about him?" He felt that this persistence amused them deeply, and in a way he shared their amusement that he should stand up so tenaciously to them. Though smaller, though slight, he was his own man, he retracted nothing about himself, and he looked back at them, gray-eyed, with amusement and also with a sort of courage. On the bench some man spoke in his throat, the words impossible to catch, and a woman answered with a wild, shrieking laugh, which was quickly cut off.

"Well, so nobody will tell me?"

"Ain't nobody who knows."

"At least, if he lives here, he pays rent to someone. Who manages the building?"

"Greatham Company. That's on Thirty-ninth Street."

Grebe wrote it in his pad. But, in the street again, a sheet of wind-driven paper clinging to his leg while he deliberated what direction to take next, it seemed a feeble lead to follow. Probably this Green didn't rent a flat, but a room. Sometimes there were as many as twenty people in an apartment; the real-estate agent would know only the lessee. And not even the agent could tell you who the renters were. In some places the beds were used in shifts, watchmen or jitney drivers or short-order cooks in night joints turning out after a day's sleep and surrendering their beds to a sister, a nephew, or perhaps a stranger, just off the bus. There were large numbers of newcomers in this terrific, blight-bitten portion of the city between Cottage Grove and Ashland, wandering from house to house and room to room. When you saw them, how could you know them? They didn't carry bundles on their backs or look picturesque. You only saw a man, a Negro, walking in the street or riding in the car, like everyone else, with his thumb closed on a transfer. And therefore how were you supposed to tell? Grebe thought the Greatham agent would only laugh at his question.

But how much it would have simplified the job to be able to say that Green was old, or blind, or consumptive. An hour in the files, taking a few notes, and he needn't have been at such a disadvantage. When Raynor gave him the block of checks he asked, "How much should I know about these people?" Then Raynor had looked as though he were preparing to accuse him of trying to make the job more important than it was. He smiled, because by then they were on fine terms, but nevertheless he had been getting ready to say something like that when the confusion began in the station over Staika and her children.

Grebe had waited a long time for this job. It came to him through the pull of an old schoolmate in the Corporation Counsel's office, never a close friend, but suddenly sympathetic and interested—pleased to show, moreover, how well he had done, how strongly he was coming on even in these miserable times. Well, he was coming through strongly, along with the Democratic administration itself. Grebe had gone to see him in City Hall, and they had had a counter lunch or beers at least once a month for a year, and finally it had been possible to swing the job. He didn't mind being assigned the lowest clerical grade, nor even being a messenger, though Raynor thought he did.

This Raynor was an original sort of guy and Grebe had taken to him immediately. As was proper on the first day, Grebe had come early, but he waited long, for Raynor was late. At last he darted into his cubicle of an office as though he had just jumped from one of those hurtling huge red Indian Avenue cars. His thin, rough face was wind-stung and he was grinning and saying something breathlessly to himself. In his hat, a small fedora, and his coat, the velvet collar a neat fit about his neck, and his silk muffler that set off the nervous twist of his chin, he swayed and turned himself in his swivel chair, feet leaving the ground; so that he pranced a little as he sat. Meanwhile he took Grebe's measure out of his eyes, eyes of an unusual vertical length and slightly sardonic. So the two men sat for a while, saying nothing, while the supervisor raised his hat from his miscombed hair and put it in his lap. His cold-darkened hands were not clean. A steel beam passed through the little makeshift room, from which machine belts once had hung. The building was an old factory.

"I'm younger than you; I hope you won't find it hard taking orders from me," said Raynor. "But I don't make them up, either. You're how old, about?"

"Thirty-five."

"And you thought you'd be inside doing paper work. But it so happens I have to send you out."

"I don't mind."

"And it's mostly a Negro load we have in this district."

"So I thought it would be."

"Fine. You'll get along. *C'est un bon boulot.* Do you know French?"

"Some."

"I thought you'd be a university man."

"Have you been in France?" said Grebe.

"No, that's the French of the Berlitz School. I've been at it for more than a year, just as I'm sure people have been, all over the world, office boys in China and braves in Tanganyika. In fact, I damn well know it. Such is the attractive power of civilization. It's overrated, but what do you want? *Que voulez-vous?* I get *Le Rire* and all the spicy papers, just like in Tanganyika. It must be mystifying, out there. But my reason is that I'm aiming at the diplomatic service. I have a cousin who's a courier, and the way he describes it is awfully attractive. He rides in the wagon-lits and reads books. While we—What did you do before?"

"I sold."

"Where?"

"Canned meat at Stop and Shop. In the basement."

"And before that?"

"Window shades, at Goldblatt's."

"Steady work?"

"No, Thursdays and Saturdays. I also sold shoes."

"You've been a shoe-dog too. Well. And prior to that? Here it is in your folder." He opened the record. "Saint Olaf's College, instructor in classical languages. Fellow, University of Chicago, 1926–1927. I've had Latin, too. Let's trade quotations—'*Dum spiro spero.*' "

" '*Da dextram misero.*' "

" '*Alea jacta est.*' "

" '*Excelsior.*' "

Raynor shouted with laughter, and other workers came to look at him over the partition. Grebe also laughed, feeling pleased and easy. The luxury of fun on a nervous morning.

When they were done and no one was watching or listening, Raynor said rather seriously, "What made you study Latin in the first place? Was it for the priesthood?"

"No."

"Just for the hell of it? For the culture? Oh, the things people think they can pull!" He made his cry hilarious and tragic. "I ran my pants off so I could study for the bar, and I've passed the bar, so I get twelve dollars a week more than you as a bonus for having seen life straight and whole. I'll tell you, as a man of culture, that even though nothing looks to be real, and everything stands for something else, and that thing for another thing, and that thing for a still further one—there ain't any comparison between twenty-five and thirty-seven dollars a week, regardless of the last reality. Don't you think that was clear to your Greeks? They were a thoughtful people, but they didn't part with their slaves."

This was a great deal more than Grebe had looked for in his first interview with his supervisor. He was too shy to show all the astonishment he felt. He laughed a little, aroused, and brushed at the sunbeam that covered his head with its dust. "Do you think my mistake was so terrible?"

"Damn right it was terrible, and you know it now that you've had the whip of hard times laid on your back. You should have been preparing yourself for trouble. Your people must have been well off to send you to the university. Stop me, if I'm stepping on your toes. Did your mother pamper you? Did your father give in to you? Were you brought up tenderly, with permission to go and find out what were the last things that everything else stands for while everybody else labored in the fallen world of appearances?"

"Well, no, it wasn't exactly like that." Grebe smiled. *The fallen world of appearances!* no less. But now it was his turn to deliver a surprise. "We weren't rich. My father was the last genuine English butler in Chicago—"

"Are you kidding?"

"Why should I be?"

"In a livery?"

"In livery. Up on the Gold Coast."

"And he wanted you to be educated like a gentleman?"

"He did not. He sent me to the Armour Institute to study chemical engineering. But when he died I changed schools."

He stopped himself, and considered how quickly Raynor had reached him. In no time he had your valise on the table and all your stuff unpacked. And afterward, in the streets, he was still reviewing how far he might have gone, and how much he might have been led to tell if they had not been interrupted by Mrs. Staika's great noise.

But just then a young woman, one of Raynor's workers, ran into the cubicle exclaiming, "Haven't you heard all the fuss?"

"We haven't heard anything."

"It's Staika, giving out with all her might. The reporters are coming. She said she phoned the papers, and you know she did."

"But what is she up to?" said Raynor.

"She brought her wash and she's ironing it here, with our current, because the relief won't pay her electric bill. She has her ironing board set up by the admitting desk, and her kids are with her, all six. They never are in school more than once a week. She's always dragging them around with her because of her reputation."

"I don't want to miss any of this," said Raynor, jumping up. Grebe, as he followed with the secretary, said, "Who is this Staika?"

"They call her the 'Blood Mother of Federal Street.' She's a professional donor at the hospitals. I think they pay ten dollars a pint. Of course it's no joke, but she makes a very big thing out of it and she and the kids are in the the papers all the time."

A small crowd, staff and clients divided by a plywood barrier, stood in the narrow space of the entrance, and Staika was shouting in a gruff, mannish voice, plunging the iron on the board and slamming it on the metal rest.

"My father and mother came in a steerage, and I was born in our house, Robey by Huron. I'm no dirty immigrant. I'm a U.S. citizen. My husband is a gassed veteran from France with lungs weaker'n paper, that hardly can he go to the toilet by himself. These six children of mine, I have to buy the shoes for their feet with my own blood. Even a lousy little white Communion necktie, that's a couple of drops of blood; a little piece of mosquito veil for my Vadja so she won't be ashamed in church for the other girls, they take my blood for it by Goldblatt. That's how I keep goin'. A fine thing if I had to depend on the relief. And there's plenty of people on the rolls— fakes! There's nothin' *they* can't get, that can go and wrap bacon at Swift and Armour any time. They're lookin' for them by the Yards. They never have to be out of work. Only they rather lay in their lousy beds and eat the public's money." She was not afraid, in a predominantly Negro station, to shout this way about Negroes.

Grebe and Raynor worked themselves forward to get a closer view of the woman. She was flaming with anger and with pleasure at herself, broad and huge, a golden-headed woman who wore a cotton cap laced with pink ribbon. She was barelegged and had on black gym shoes, her Hoover apron was open and her great breasts, not much restrained by a man's undershirt, hampered her arms as she worked at the kid's dress on the ironing board. And the children, silent and white, with a kind of locked obstinacy, in sheepskins and lumberjackets, stood behind her. She had captured the station, and the pleasure this gave her was enormous. Yet her grievances were true grievances. She was telling the truth. But she behaved like a liar. The look of her small eyes was hidden, and while she raged she also seemed to be spinning and planning.

"They send me out college case workers in silk pants to talk me out of what I got comin'. Are they better'n me? Who told them? Fire them. Let 'em go and get married, and then you won't have to cut electric from people's budget."

The chief supervisor, Mr. Ewing, couldn't silence her and he stood with folded arms at the head of his staff, bald, bald-headed, saying to his subordinates like the ex-school principal he was, "Pretty soon she'll be tired and go."

"No she won't," said Raynor to Grebe. "She'll get what she wants. She knows more about the relief even than Ewing. She's been on the rolls for years, and she always gets what she wants because she puts on a noisy show. Ewing knows it. He'll give in soon. He's only saving face. If he gets bad publicity, the Commissioner'll have him on the carpet, downtown. She's got him submerged; she'll submerge everybody in time, and that includes nations and governments."

Grebe replied with his characteristic smile, disagreeing completely. Who would take Staika's orders, and what changes could her yelling ever bring about?

No, what Grebe saw in her, the power that made people listen, was that her cry expressed the war of flesh and blood, perhaps turned a little crazy and certainly ugly, on this place and this condition. And at first, when he went out, the spirit of Staika somehow presided over the whole district for him, and it took color from her; he saw her color, in the spotty curb fires, and the fires under the El, the straight alley of flamy gloom. Later, too, when he went into a tavern for a shot of rye, the sweat of beer, association with West Side Polish streets, made him think of her again.

He wiped the corners of his mouth with his muffler, his handkerchief being inconvenient to reach for, and went out again to get on with the delivery of his checks. The air bit cold and hard and a few flakes of snow formed near him. A train struck by and left a quiver in the frames and a bristling icy hiss over the rails.

Crossing the street, he descended a flight of board steps into a basement grocery, setting off a little bell. It was a dark, long store and it caught you with its stinks of smoked meat, soap, dried peaches, and fish. There was a fire wrinkling and flapping in the little stove, and the proprietor was waiting, an Italian with a long, hollow face and stubborn bristles. He kept his hands warm under his apron.

No, he didn't know Green. You knew people but not names. The same man might not have the same name twice. The police didn't know, either, and mostly didn't care. When somebody was shot or knifed they took the body away and didn't look for the murderer. In the first place, nobody would tell them anything. So they made up a name for the coroner and called it quits. And in the second place, they didn't give a goddamn anyhow. But they couldn't get to the bottom of a thing even if they wanted to. Nobody would get to know even a tenth of what went on among these people. They stabbed and stole, they did every crime and abomination you ever heard of, men and men, women and women, parents and children, worse than the animals. They carried on their own way, and the horrors passed off like a smoke. There was never anything like it in the history of the whole world.

It was a long speech, deepening with every word in its fantasy and passion and becoming increasingly senseless and terrible: a swarm amassed by suggestion and invention, a huge, hugging, despairing knot, a human wheel of heads, legs, bellies, arms, rolling through his shop.

Grebe felt that he must interrupt him. He said sharply, "What are you talking about! All I asked was whether you knew this man."

"That isn't even the half of it. I been here six years. You probably don't want to believe this. But suppose it's true?"

"All the same," said Grebe, "there must be a way to find a person."

The Italian's close-spaced eyes had been queerly concentrated, as were his muscles, while he leaned across the counter trying to convince Grebe. Now he gave up the effort and sat down on his stool. "Oh—I suppose. Once in a while. But I been telling you, even the cops don't get anywhere."

"They're always after somebody. It's not the same thing."

"Well, keep trying if you want. I can't help you."

But he didn't keep trying. He had no more time to spend on Green. He slipped Green's check to the back of the block. The next name on the list was FIELD, WINSTON.

He found the backyard bungalow without the least trouble; it shared a lot with another house, a few feet of yard between. Grebe knew these two-shack arrangements. They had been built in vast numbers in the days before the swamps were filled and the streets raised, and they were all the same—a boardwalk along the fence, well under street level, three or four ball-headed posts for clotheslines, greening wood, dead shingles, and a long, long flight of stairs to the rear door.

A twelve-year-old boy let him into the kitchen, and there the old man was, sitting by the table in a wheel chair.

"Oh, it's d' Government man," he said to the boy when Grebe drew out his checks. "Go bring me my box of papers." He cleared a space on the table.

"Oh, you don't have to go to all that trouble," said Grebe. But Field laid out his papers: Social Security card, relief certification, letters from the state hospital in Manteno, and a naval discharge dated San Diego, 1920.

"That's plenty," Grebe said. "Just sign."

"You got to know who I am," the old man said. "You're from the Government. It's not your check, it's a Government check and you got no business to hand it over till everything is proved."

He loved the ceremony of it, and Grebe made no more objections. Field emptied his box and finished out the circle of cards and letters.

"There's everything I done and been. Just the death certificate and they can close book on me." He said this with a certain happy pride and magnificence. Still he did not sign; he merely held the little pen upright on the golden-green corduroy of his thigh. Grebe did not hurry him. He felt the old man's hunger for conversation.

"I got to get better coal," he said. "I send my little gran'son to the yard with my order and they fill his wagon with screening. The stove ain't made for it. It fall through the grate. The order says Franklin County egg-size coal."

"I'll report it and see what can be done."

"Nothing can be done, I expect. You know and I know. There ain't no little ways to make things better, and the only big thing is money. That's the only sunbeams, money. Nothing is black where it shines, and the only place you see black is where it ain't shining. What we colored have to have is our own rich. There ain't no other way."

Grebe sat, his reddened forehead bridged levelly by his close-cut hair and his cheeks lowered in the wings of his collar—the caked fire shone hard within the isinglass-and-iron frames but the room was not comfortable—sat and listened while the old man unfolded his scheme. This was to create one Negro millionaire a month by subscription. One clever, goodhearted young fellow elected every month would sign a contract to use the money to start a business employing Negroes. This would be advertised by chain letters and word of mouth, and every Negro wage earner would contribute a dollar a month. Within five years there would be sixty millionaires.

"That'll fetch respect," he said with a throat-stopped sound that came out like a foreign syllable. "You got to take and organize all the money that gets thrown away on the policy wheel and horse race. As long as they can take it away from you, they got no respect for you. Money, that's d' sun of human kind!" Field was a Negro of mixed blood, perhaps Cherokee, or Natchez; his skin was reddish. And he sounded, speaking about a golden sun in this dark room, and looked, shaggy and slab-headed, with the mingled blood of his face and broad lips, the little pen still upright in his hand, like one of the underground kings of mythology, old judge Minos himself.

And now he accepted the check and signed. Not to soil the slip, he held

it down with his knuckles. The table budged and creaked, the center of the
gloomy, heathen midden of the kitchen covered with bread, meat, and
cans, and the scramble of papers.

"Don't you think my scheme'd work?"

"It's worth thinking about. Something ought to be done, I agree."

"It'll work if people will do it. That's all. That's the only thing, any time.
When they understand it in the same way, all of them."

"That's true," said Grebe, rising. His glance met the old man's.

"I know you got to go," he said. "Well, God bless you, boy, you ain't been
sly with me. I can tell it in a minute."

He went back through the buried yard. Someone nursed a candle in a
shed, where a man unloaded kindling wood from a sprawl-wheeled baby
buggy and two voices carried on a high conversation. As he came up the
sheltered passage he heard the hard boost of the wind in the branches and
against the house fronts, and then, reaching the sidewalk, he saw the need-
le-eye red of cable towers in the open icy height hundreds of feet above the
river and the factories—those keen points. From here, his view was ob-
structed all the way to the South Branch and its timber banks, and the
cranes beside the water. Rebuilt after the Great Fire, this part of the city
was, not fifty years later, in ruins again, factories boarded up, buildings
deserted or fallen, gaps of prairie between. But it wasn't desolation that this
made you feel, but rather a faltering of organization that set free a huge
energy, an escaped, unattached, unregulated power from the giant raw
place. Not only must people feel it but, it seemed to Grebe, they were compelled to match it. In their very bodies. He no less than others, he realized.
Say that his parents had been servants in their time, whereas he was not
supposed to be one. He thought that they had never done any service like
this, which no one visible asked for, and probably flesh and blood could not
even perform. Nor could anyone show why it should be performed; or see
where the performance would lead. That did not mean that he wanted to
be released from it, he realized with a grimly pensive face. On the contrary.
He had something to do. To be compelled to feel this energy and yet have
no task to do—that was horrible; that was suffering; he knew what that
was. It was now quitting time. Six o'clock. He could go home if he liked, to
his room, that is, to wash in hot water, to pour a drink, lie down on his quilt,
read the paper, eat some liver paste on crackers before going out to dinner.
But to think of this actually made him feel a little sick, as though he had
swallowed hard air. He had six checks left, and he was determined to deliver at least one of these: Mr. Green's check.

So he started again. He had four or five dark blocks to go, past open lots,
condemned houses, old foundations, closed schools, black churches,
mounds, and he reflected that there must be many people alive who had
once seen the neighborhood rebuilt and new. Now there was a second layer
of ruins; centuries of history accomplished through human massing. Num-

bers had given the place forced growth; enormous numbers had also broken it down. Objects once so new, so concrete that it could have occurred to anyone they stood for other things, had crumbled. Therefore, reflected Grebe, the secret of them was out. It was that they stood for themselves by agreement, and were natural and not unnatural by agreement, and when the things themselves collapsed the agreement became visible. What was it, otherwise, that kept cities from looking peculiar? Rome, that was almost permanent, did not give rise to thoughts like these. And was it abidingly real? But in Chicago, where the cycles were so fast and the familiar died out, and again rose changed, and died again in thirty years, you saw the common agreement or covenant, and you were forced to think about appearances and realities. (He remembered Raynor and he smiled. Raynor was a clever boy.) Once you had grasped this, a great many things became intelligible. For instance, why Mr. Field should conceive such a scheme. Of course, if people were to agree to create a millionaire, a real millionaire would come into existence. And if you wanted to know how Mr. Field was inspired to think of this, why, he had within sight of his kitchen window the chart, the very bones of a successful scheme—the El with its blue and green confetti of signals. People consented to pay dimes and ride the crash-box cars, and so it was a success. Yet how absurd it looked; how little reality there was to start with. And yet Yerkes, the great financier who built it, had known that he could get people to agree to do it. Viewed as itself, what a scheme of a scheme it seemed, how close to an appearance. Then why wonder at Mr. Field's idea? He had grasped a principle. And then Grebe remembered, too, that Mr. Yerkes had established the Yerkes Observatory and endowed it with millions. Now how did the notion come to him in his New York museum of a palace or his Aegean-bound yacht to give money to astronomers? Was he awed by the success of his bizarre enterprise and therefore ready to spend money to find out where in the universe being and seeming were identical? Yes, he wanted to know what abides; and whether flesh is Bible grass; and he offered money to be burned in the fire of suns. Okay, then, Grebe thought further, these things exist because people consent to exist with them—we have got so far—and also there is a reality which doesn't depend on consent but within which consent is a game. But what about need, the need that keeps so many vast thousands in position? You tell me that, you *private* little gentleman and *decent* soul—he used these words against himself scornfully. Why is the consent given to misery? And why so painfully ugly? Because there is *something* that is dismal and permanently ugly? Here he sighed and gave it up, and thought it was enough for the present moment that he had a real check in his pocket for a Mr. Green who must be real beyond question. If only his neighbors didn't think they had to conceal him.

This time he stopped at the second floor. He struck a match and found a door. Presently a man answered his knock and Grebe had the check ready and showed it even before he began. "Does Tulliver Green live here? I'm from the relief."

The man narrowed the opening and spoke to someone at his back.

"Does he live here?"

"Uh-uh. No."

"Or anywhere in this building? He's a sick man and he can't come for his dough." He exhibited the check in the light, which was smoky—the air smelled of charred lard—and the man held off the brim of his cap to study it.

"Uh-uh. Never seen the name."

"There's nobody around here that uses crutches?"

He seemed to think, but it was Grebe's impression that he was simply waiting for a decent interval to pass.

"No, suh. Nobody I ever see."

"I've been looking for this man all afternoon"—Grebe spoke out with sudden force—"and I'm going to have to carry this check back to the station. It seems strange not to be able to find a person to give him something when you're looking for him for a good reason. I suppose if I had bad news for him I'd find him quick enough."

There was a responsive motion in the other man's face. "That's right, I reckon."

"It almost doesn't do any good to have a name if you can't be found by it. It doesn't stand for anything. He might as well not have any," he went on, smiling. It was as much of a concession as he could make to his desire to laugh.

"Well, now, there's a little old knot-back man I see once in a while. He might be the one you lookin' for. Downstairs."

"Where? Right side or left? Which door?"

"I don't know which. Thin-face little knot-back with a stick."

But no one answered at any of the doors on the first floor. He went to the end of the corridor, searching by match-light, and found only a stairless exit to the yard, a drop of about six feet. But there was a bungalow near the alley, an old house like Mr. Field's. To jump was unsafe. He ran from the front door, through the underground passage and into the yard. The place was occupied. There was a light through the curtains, upstairs. The name on the ticket under the broken, scoop-shaped mailbox was Green! He exultantly rang the bell and pressed against the locked door. Then the lock clicked faintly and a long staircase opened before him. Someone was slowly coming down—a woman. He had the impression in the weak light that she was shaping her hair as she came, making herself presentable, for he saw her arms raised. But it was for support that they were raised; she was feeling her way downward, down the wall, stumbling. Next he wondered about the pressure of her feet on the treads; she did not seem to be wearing shoes. And it was a freezing stairway. His ring had got her out of bed, perhaps, and she had forgotten to put them on. And then he saw that she was not only shoeless but naked; she was entirely naked, climbing down while she talked to herself, a heavy woman, naked and drunk. She blundered into him. The contact of her breasts, though they touched only his coat, made him go back against the door with a blind shock. See what he had tracked down, in his hunting game!

The woman was saying to herself, furious with insult, "So I cain't —k, huh? I'll show that son-of-a-bitch kin I, cain't I."

What should he do now? Grebe asked himself. Why, he should go. He should turn away and go. He couldn't talk to this woman. He couldn't keep her standing naked in the cold. But when he tried he found himself unable to turn away.

He said, "Is this where Mr. Green lives?"

But she was still talking to herself and did not hear him.

"Is this Mr. Green's house?"

At last she turned her furious drunken glance on him. "What do you want?"

Again her eyes wandered from him; there was a dot of blood in their enraged brilliance. He wondered why she didn't feel the cold.

"I'm from the relief."

"Awright, what?"

"I've got a check for Tulliver Green."

This time she heard him and put out her hand.

"No, no, for *Mr.* Green. He's got to sign," he said. How was he going to get Green's signature tonight!

"I'll take it. He cain't."

He desperately shook his head, thinking of Mr. Field's precautions about identification. "I can't let you have it. It's for him. Are you Mrs. Green?"

"Maybe I is, and maybe I ain't. Who want to know?"

"Is he upstairs?"

"Awright. Take it up yourself, you goddamn fool."

Sure, he was a goddamn fool. Of course he could not go up because Green would probably be drunk and naked, too. And perhaps he would appear on the landing soon. He looked eagerly upward. Under the light was a high narrow brown wall. Empty! It remained empty!

"Hell with you, then!" he heard her cry. To deliver a check for coal and clothes, he was keeping her in the cold. She did not feel it, but his face was burning with frost and self-ridicule. He backed away from her.

"I'll come tomorrow, tell him."

"Ah, hell with you. Don' never come. What you doin' here in the nighttime? Don' come back." She yelled so that he saw the breadth of her tongue. She stood astride in the long cold box of the hall and held on to the banister and the wall. The bungalow itself was shaped something like a box, a clumsy, high box pointing into the freezing air with its sharp, wintry lights.

"If you are Mrs. Green, I'll give you the check," he said, changing his mind.

"Give here, then." She took it, took the pen offered with it in her left hand, and tried to sign the receipt on the wall. He looked around, almost as though to see whether his madness was being observed, and came near believing that someone was standing on a mountain of used tires in the auto-junking shop next door.

"But are you Mrs. Green?" he now thought to ask. But she was already climbing the stairs with the check, and it was too late, if he had made an error, if he was now in trouble, to undo the thing. But he wasn't going to worry about it. Though she might not be Mrs. Green, he was convinced that Mr. Green was upstairs. Whoever she was, the woman stood for Green, whom he was not to see this time. Well, you silly bastard, he said to himself, so you think you found him. So what? Maybe you really did find him— what of it? But it was important that there was a real Mr. Green whom they could not keep him from reaching because he seemed to come as an emissary from hostile appearances. And though the self-ridicule was slow to diminish, and his face still blazed with it, he had, nevertheless, a feeling of elation, too. "For after all," he said, "he *could* be found!"

An Occurrence at Owl Creek Bridge

AMBROSE BIERCE

I

A man stood upon a railroad bridge in Northern Alabama, looking down into the swift waters twenty feet below. The man's hands were behind his back, the wrists bound with a cord. A rope loosely encircled his neck. It was attached to a stout cross-timber above his head, and the slack fell to the level of his knees. Some loose boards laid upon the sleepers supporting the metals of the railway supplied a footing for him and his executioners—two private soldiers of the Federal army, directed by a sergeant, who in civil life may have been a deputy sheriff. At a short remove upon the same temporary platform was an officer in the uniform of his rank, armed. He was a captain. A sentinel at each end of the bridge stood with his rifle in the position known as "support," that is to say, vertical in front of the left shoulder, the hammer resting on the forearm thrown straight across the chest—a formal and unnatural position, enforcing an erect carriage of the body. It did not appear to be the duty of these two men to know what was occurring at the centre of the bridge; they merely blockaded the two ends of the foot plank which traversed it.

Beyond one of the sentinels nobody was in sight; the railroad ran straight away into a forest for a hundred yards, then, curving, was lost to view. Doubtless there was an outpost further along. The other bank of the stream was open ground—a gentle acclivity crowned with a stockade of vertical tree trunks, loop-holed for rifles, with a single embrasure through which protruded the muzzle of a brass cannon commanding the bridge. Midway of the slope between bridge and fort were the spectators—a single company of infantry in line, at "parade rest," the butts of the rifles on the ground, the barrels inclining slightly backward against the right shoulder, the hands crossed upon the stock. A lieutenant stood at the right of the line, the point of his sword upon the ground, his left hand resting upon his right. Excepting the group of four at the centre of the bridge not a man moved. The company faced the bridge, staring stonily, motionless. The sentinels, facing the banks of the stream, might have been statues to adorn the bridge. The captain stood with folded arms, silent, observing the work of his subordinates but making no sign. Death is a dignitary who, when he comes announced, is to be received with formal manifestations of respect, even by those most familiar with him. In the code of military etiquette silence and fixity are forms of deference.

The man who was engaged in being hanged was apparently about thirty-five years of age. He was a civilian, if one might judge from his dress, which was that of a planter. His features were good—a straight nose, firm mouth, broad forehead, from which his long, dark hair was combed straight back, falling behind his ears to the collar of his well-fitting frock coat. He wore a moustache and pointed beard, but no whiskers; his eyes were large and dark grey and had a kindly expression which one would hardly have expected in one whose neck was in the hemp. Evidently this was no vulgar assassin. The liberal military code makes provision for hanging many kinds of people, and gentlemen are not excluded.

The preparations being complete, the two private soldiers stepped aside and each drew away the plank upon which he had been standing. The sergeant turned to the captain, saluted and placed himself immediately behind that officer, who in turn moved apart one pace. These movements left the condemned man and the sergeant standing on the two ends of the same plank, which spanned three of the cross-ties of the bridge. The end upon which the civilian stood almost, but not quite, reached a fourth. This plank had been held in place by the weight of the captain; it was now held by that of the sergeant. At a signal from the former, the latter would step aside, the plank would tilt and the condemned man go down between two ties. The arrangement commended itself to his judgment as simple and effective. His face had not been covered nor his eyes bandaged. He looked a moment at his "unsteadfast footing," then let his gaze wander to the swirling water of the stream racing madly beneath his feet. A piece of dancing driftwood caught his attention and his eyes followed it down the current. How slowly it appeared to move! What a sluggish stream!

He closed his eyes in order to fix his last thoughts upon his wife and children. The water, touched to gold by the early sun, the brooding mists under the banks at some distance down the stream, the fort, the soldiers, the piece of drift—all had distracted him. And now he became conscious of a new disturbance. Striking through the thought of his dear ones was a sound which he could neither ignore nor understand, a sharp, distinct, metallic percussion like the stroke of a blacksmith's hammer upon the anvil; it had the same ringing quality. He wondered what it was, and whether im-measurably distant or near by—it seemed both. Its recurrence was regular, but as slow as the tolling of a death knell. He awaited each stroke with impatience and—he knew not why—apprehension. The intervals of silence grew progressively longer; the delays became maddening. With their greater infrequency the sounds increased in strength and sharpness. They hurt his ear like the thrust of a knife; he feared he would shriek. What he heard was the ticking of his watch.

He unclosed his eyes and saw again the water below him. "If I could free my hands," he thought, "I might throw off the noose and spring into the stream. By diving I could evade the bullets, and, swimming vigorously, reach the bank, take to the woods, and get away home. My home, thank God, is as yet outside their lines; my wife and little ones are still beyond the invader's farthest advance."

As these thoughts, which have here to be set down in words, were flashed into the doomed man's brain rather than evolved from it, the captain nodded to the sergeant. The sergeant stepped aside.

II

Peyton Farquhar was a well-to-do planter, of an old and highly-respected Alabama family. Being a slave owner, and, like other slave owners, a politician, he was naturally an original secessionist and ardently devoted to the Southern cause. Circumstances of an imperious nature which it is unnecessary to relate here, had prevented him from taking service with the gallant army which had fought the disastrous campaigns ending with the fall of Corinth, and he chafed under the inglorious restraint, longing for the release of his energies, the larger life of the soldier, the opportunity for distinction. That opportunity, he felt, would come, as it comes to all in war time. Meanwhile he did what he could. No service was too humble for him to perform in aid of the South, no adventure too perilous for him to undertake if consistent with the character of a civilian who was at heart a soldier, and who in good faith and without too much qualification assented to at least a part of the frankly villainous dictum that all is fair in love and war.

One evening while Farquhar and his wife were sitting on a rustic bench near the entrance to his grounds, a grey-clad soldier rode up to the gate and asked for a drink of water. Mrs. Farquhar was only too happy to serve him with her own white hands. While she was gone to fetch the water, her husband approached the dusty horseman and inquired eagerly for news from the front.

"The Yanks are repairing the railroads," said the man, "and are getting ready for another advance. They have reached the Owl Creek bridge, put it in order, and built a stockade on the other bank. The commandant has issued an order, which is posted everywhere, declaring that any civilian caught interfering with the railroad, its bridges, tunnels, or trains, will be summarily hanged. I saw the order."

"How far is it to the Owl Creek bridge?" Farquhar asked.

"About thirty miles."

"Is there no force on this side the creek?"

"Only a picket post half a mile out, on the railroad, and a single sentinel at this end of the bridge."

"Suppose a man—a civilian and student of hanging—should elude the picket post and perhaps get the better of the sentinel," said Farquhar, smiling, "what could he accomplish?"

The soldier reflected. "I was there a month ago," he replied. "I observed that the flood of last winter had lodged a great quantity of driftwood against the wooden pier at this end of the bridge. It is now dry and would burn like tow."

The lady had now brought the water, which the soldier drank. He thanked her ceremoniously, bowed to her husband, and rode away. An hour later, after nightfall, he repassed the plantation, going northward in the direction from which he had come. He was a Federal scout.

III

As Peyton Farquhar fell straight downward through the bridge, he lost consciousness and was as one already dead. From this state he was awakened—ages later, it seemed to him—by the pain of a sharp pressure upon his throat, followed by a sense of suffocation. Keen, poignant agonies seemed to shoot from his neck downward through every fibre of his body and limbs. These pains appeared to flash along well-defined lines of ramification, and to beat with an inconceivably rapid periodicity. They seemed like streams of pulsating fire heating him to an intolerable temperature. As to his head, he was conscious of nothing but a feeling of fullness—of congestion. These sensations were unaccompanied by thought. The intellectual part of his nature was already effaced; he had power only to feel, and feeling was torment. He was conscious of motion. Encompassed in a luminous cloud, of which he was now merely the fiery heart, without material substance, he swung through unthinkable arcs of oscillation, like a vast pendulum. Then all at once, with terrible suddenness, the light about him shot upward with the noise of a loud plash; a frightful roaring was in his ears, and all was cold and dark. The power of thought was restored; he knew that the rope had broken and he had fallen into the stream. There was no additional strangulation; the noose about his neck was already suffocating him, and kept the water from his lungs. To die of hanging at the bottom of a river—the idea seemed to him ludicrous. He opened his eyes in the blackness and saw above him a gleam of light, but how distant, how inaccessible! He was still sinking, for the light became fainter and fainter until it was a mere glimmer. Then it began to grow and brighten, and he knew that he was rising toward the surface—knew it with reluctance, for he was now very comfortable. "To be hanged and drowned," he thought, "that is not so bad; but I do not wish to be shot. No; I will not be shot; that is not fair."

He was not conscious of an effort, but a sharp pain in his wrist apprised him that he was trying to free his hands. He gave the struggle his attention, as an idler might observe the feat of a juggler, without interest in the out-come. What splendid effort!—what magnificent, what superhuman strength! Oh, that was a fine endeavor! Bravo! The cord fell away; his arms parted and floated upward, the hands dimly seen on each side in the grow-ing light. He watched them with a new interest as first one and then the other pounced upon the noose at his neck. They tore it away and thrust it fiercely aside, its undulations resembling those of a water-snake. "Put it back, put it back!" He thought he shouted these words to his hands, for the undoing of the noose had been succeeded by the direst pang which he had yet experienced. His neck arched horribly; his brain was on fire; his heart, which had been fluttering faintly, gave a great leap, trying to force itself out at his mouth. His whole body was racked and wrenched with an insupport-able anguish! But his disobedient hands gave no heed to the command. They beat the water vigorously with quick, downward strokes, forcing him to the surface. He felt his head emerge; his eyes were blinded by the sun-light; his chest expanded convulsively, and with a supreme and crowning agony his lungs engulfed a great draught of air, which instantly he expelled in a shriek!

He was now in full possession of his physical senses. They were, indeed, preternaturally keen and alert. Something in the awful disturbance of his organic system had so exalted and refined them that they made record of things never before perceived. He felt the ripples upon his face and heard their separate sounds as they struck. He looked at the forest on the bank of the stream, saw the individual trees, the leaves and the veining of each leaf—saw the very insects upon them, the locusts, the brilliant-bodied flies, the grey spiders stretching their webs from twig to twig. He noted the pris-matic colors in all the dewdrops upon a million blades of grass. The hum-ming of the gnats that danced above the eddies of the stream, the beating of the dragon flies' wings, the strokes of the water spiders' legs, like oars which had lifted their boat—all these made audible music. A fish slid along beneath his eyes and he heard the rush of its body parting the water.

He had come to the surface facing down the stream; in a moment the vis-ible world seemed to wheel slowly round, himself the pivotal point, and he saw the bridge, the fort, the soldiers upon the bridge, the captain, the ser-geant, the two privates, his executioners. They were in silhouette against the blue sky. They shouted and gesticulated, pointing at him; the captain had drawn his pistol, but did not fire; the others were unarmed. Their movements were grotesque and horrible, their forms gigantic.

Suddenly he heard a sharp report and something struck the water smartly within a few inches of his head, spattering his face with spray. He heard a second report, and saw one of the sentinels with his rifle at his shoulder, a light cloud of blue smoke rising from the muzzle. The man in the water saw the eye of the man on the bridge gazing into his own through the sights of the rifle. He observed that it was a grey eye, and remembered having read that grey eyes were keenest and that all famous marksmen had them. Nevertheless, this one had missed.

A counter swirl had caught Farquhar and turned him half round; he was again looking into the forest on the bank opposite the fort. The sound of a clear, high voice in a monotonous singsong now rang out behind him and came across the water with a distinctness that pierced and subdued all other sounds, even the beating of the ripples in his ears. Although no soldier, he had frequented camps enough to know the dread significance of that deliberate, drawling, aspirated chant; the lieutenant on shore was taking a part in the morning's work. How coldly and pitilessly—with what an even, calm intonation, presaging and enforcing tranquillity in the men—with what accurately-measured intervals fell those cruel words:

"Attention, company.... Shoulder arms.... Ready.... Aim.... Fire."

Farquhar dived—dived as deeply as he could. The water roared in his ears like the voice of Niagara, yet he heard the dulled thunder of the volley, and rising again toward the surface, met shining bits of metal, singularly flattened, oscillating slowly downward. Some of them touched him on the face and hands, then fell away, continuing their descent. One lodged between his collar and neck; it was uncomfortably warm, and he snatched it out.

As he rose to the surface, gasping for breath, he saw that he had been a long time under water; he was perceptibly farther down stream—nearer to safety. The soldiers had almost finished reloading; the metal ramrods flashed all at once in the sunshine as they were drawn from the barrels, turned in the air, and thrust into their sockets. The two sentinels fired again, independently and ineffectually.

The hunted man saw all this over his shoulder; he was now swimming vigorously with the current. His brain was as energetic as his arms and legs; he thought with the rapidity of lightning.

"The officer," he reasoned, "will not make the martinet's error a second time. It is as easy to dodge a volley as a single shot. He has probably already given the command to fire at will. God help me, I cannot dodge them all!"

An appalling plash within two yards of him, followed by a loud rushing sound, *diminuendo*, which seemed to travel back through the air to the fort and died in an explosion which stirred the very river to its deeps! A rising sheet of water, which curved over him, fell down upon him, blinded him, strangled him! The cannon had taken a hand in the game. As he shook his head free from the commotion of the smitten water, he heard the deflected shot humming through the air ahead, and in an instant it was cracking and smashing the branches in the forest beyond.

"They will not do that again," he thought; "the next time they will use a charge of grape. I must keep my eye upon the gun; the smoke will apprise me—the report arrives too late; it lags behind the missile. It is a good gun."

Suddenly he felt himself whirled round and round—spinning like a top. The water, the banks, the forest, the now distant bridge, fort and men—all were commingled and blurred. Objects were represented by their colors only; circular horizontal streaks of color—that was all he saw. He had been caught in a vortex and was being whirled on with a velocity of advance and gyration which made him giddy and sick. In a few moments he was flung upon the gravel at the foot of the left bank of the stream—the southern bank—and behind a projecting point which concealed him from his ene-mies. The sudden arrest of his motion, the abrasion of one of his hands on the gravel, restored him and he wept with delight. He dug his fingers into the sand, threw it over himself in handfuls and audibly blessed it. It looked like gold, like diamonds, rubies, emeralds; he could think of nothing beau-tiful which it did not resemble. The trees upon the bank were giant garden plants; he noted a definite order in their arrangement, inhaled the fra-grance of their blooms. A strange, roseate light shone through the spaces among their trunks, and the wind made in their branches the music of æolian harps. He had no wish to perfect his escape, was content to remain in that enchanting spot until retaken.

A whizz and rattle of grapeshot among the branches high above his head roused him from his dream. The baffled cannoneer had fired him a ran-dom farewell. He sprang to his feet, rushed up the sloping bank, and plunged into the forest.

All that day he travelled, laying his course by the rounding sun. The for-est seemed interminable; nowhere did he discover a break in it, not even a woodman's road. He had not known that he lived in so wild a region. There was something uncanny in the revelation.

By nightfall he was fatigued, footsore, famishing. The thought of his wife and children urged him on. At last he found a road which led him in what he knew to be the right direction. It was as wide and straight as a city street, yet it seemed untravelled. No fields bordered it, no dwelling any-where. Not so much as the barking of a dog suggested human habitation. The black bodies of the great trees formed a straight wall on both sides, ter-minating on the horizon in a point, like a diagram in a lesson in perspec-tive. Overhead, as he looked up through this rift in the wood, shone great golden stars looking unfamiliar and grouped in strange constellations. He was sure they were arranged in some order which had a secret and malign significance. The wood on either side was full of singular noises, among which—once, twice, and again—he distinctly heard whispers in an unknown tongue.

His neck was in pain, and, lifting his hand to it, he found it horribly swollen. He knew that it had a circle of black where the rope had bruised it. His eyes felt congested; he could no longer close them. His tongue was swollen with thirst; he relieved its fever by thrusting it forward from between his teeth into the cool air. How softly the turf had carpeted the untravelled avenue! He could no longer feel the roadway beneath his feet!

Doubtless, despite his suffering, he fell asleep while walking, for now he sees another scene—perhaps he has merely recovered from a delirium. He stands at the gate of his own home. All is as he left it, and all bright and beautiful in the morning sunshine. He must have travelled the entire night. At he pushes open the gate and passes up the wide white walk, he sees a flutter of female garments; his wife, looking fresh and cool and sweet, steps down from the verandah to meet him. At the bottom of the steps she stands waiting, with a smile of ineffable joy, an attitude of matchless grace and dignity. Ah, how beautiful she is! He springs forward with extended arms. As he is about to clasp her, he feels a stunning blow upon the back of the neck; a blinding white light blazes all about him, with a sound like a shock of a cannon—then all is darkness and silence!

Peyton Farquhar was dead; his body, with a broken neck, swung gently from side to side beneath the timbers of the Owl Creek bridge.

The Garden of Forking Paths

JORGE LUIS BORGES

FOR VICTORIA OCAMPO

Translated by Donald Yates

On page twenty-two of Liddell Hart's *History of World War I* you will read that an attack against the Serre-Montauban line by thirteen British divisions (supported by 1,400 artillery pieces), planned for the 24th of July, 1916, had to be postponed until the morning of the 29th. The torrential rains, Captain Liddell Hart comments, caused this delay, an insignificant one, to be sure.

The following statement, dictated, reread and signed by Dr. Yu Tsun, former professor of English at the *Hochschule* at Tsingtao, throws an unsuspected light over the whole affair. The first two pages of the document are missing.

" . . . and I hung up the receiver. Immediately afterwards, I recognized the voice that had answered in German. It was that of Captain Richard Madden. Madden's presence in Viktor Runeberg's apartment meant the end of our anxieties and—but this seemed, or *should have seemed,* very secondary to me—also the end of our lives. It meant that Runeberg had been arrested or murdered.[1] Before the sun set on that day, I would encounter the same fate. Madden was implacable. Or rather, he was obliged to be so. An Irishman at the service of England, a man accused of laxity and perhaps of treason, how could he fail to seize and be thankful for such a miraculous opportunity: the discovery, capture, maybe even the death of two agents of the German Reich? I went up to my room; absurdly I locked the door and threw myself on my back on the narrow iron cot. Through the window I saw the familiar roofs and the cloud-shaded six o'clock sun. It seemed incredible to me that that day without premonitions or symbols

---

[1] An hypothesis both hateful and odd. The Prussian spy Hans Rabener, alias Viktor Runeberg, attacked with drawn automatic the bearer of the warrant for his arrest, Captain Richard Madden. The latter, in self-defense, inflicted the wound which brought about Runeberg's death. (Borges's note.)

133

should be the one of my inexorable death. In spite of my dead father, in spite of having been a child in a symmetrical garden of Hai Feng, was I—now—going to die? Then I reflected that everything happens to a man precisely *now*. Centuries of centuries and only in the present do things happen; countless men in the air, on the face of the earth and the sea, and all that really is happening is happening to me . . . The almost intolerable recollection of Madden's horselike face banished these wanderings. In the midst of my hatred and terror (it means nothing to me now to speak of terror, now that I have mocked Richard Madden, now that my throat yearns for the noose) it occurred to me that the tumultuous and doubtless happy warrior did not suspect that I possessed the Secret. The name of the exact location of the new British artillery park on the River Ancre. A bird streaked across the gray sky and blindly I translated it into an airplane and that airplane into many (against the French sky) annihilating the artillery station with vertical bombs. If only my mouth, before a bullet shattered it, could cry out that secret name so it could be heard in Germany . . . My human voice was very weak. How might I make it carry to the ear of the Chief? To the ear of that sick and hateful man who knew nothing of Runeberg and me save that we were in Staffordshire and who was waiting in vain for our report in his arid office in Berlin, endlessly examining newspapers . . . I said out loud: *I must flee.* I sat up noiselessly, in a useless perfection of silence, as if Madden were already lying in wait for me. Something—perhaps the mere vain ostentation of proving my resources were nil—made me look through my pockets. I found what I knew I would find. The American watch, the nickel chain and the square coin, the key ring with the incriminating useless keys to Runeberg's apartment, the notebook, a letter which I resolved to destroy immediately (and which I did not destroy), a crown, two shillings and a few pence, the red and blue pencil, the handkerchief, the revolver with one bullet. Absurdly, I took it in my hand and weighed it in order to inspire courage within myself. Vaguely I thought that a pistol report can be heard at a great distance. In ten minutes my plan was perfected. The telephone book listed the name of the only person capable of transmitting the message; he lived in a suburb of Fenton, less than a half hour's train ride away.

I am a cowardly man. I say it now, now that I have carried to its end a plan whose perilous nature no one can deny. I know its execution was terrible. I didn't do it for Germany, no. I care nothing for a barbarous country which imposed upon me the abjection of being a spy. Besides, I know of a man from England—a modest man—who for me is no less great than Goethe. I talked with him for scarcely an hour, but during that hour he was Goethe . . . I did it because I sensed that the Chief somehow feared people of my race—for the innumerable ancestors who merge within me. I wanted to prove to him that a yellow man could save his armies. Besides, I had to flee from Captain Madden. His hands and his voice could call at my door at any moment. I dressed silently, bade farewell to myself in the mirror, went downstairs, scrutinized the peaceful street and went out. The station was not far from my home, but I judged it wise to take a cab. I argued that in this way I ran less risk of being recognized; the fact is that in the deserted street I felt myself visible and vulnerable, infinitely so. I remember that I told the cab driver to stop a short distance before the main entrance. I got out with voluntary, almost painful slowness; I was going to the village of Ashgrove but I bought a ticket for a more distant station. The train left within a very few minutes, at eight-fifty. I hurried; the next one would leave at nine-thirty. There was hardly a soul on the platform. I went through the coaches; I remember a few farmers, a woman dressed in mourning, a young boy who was reading with fervor the *Annals* of Tacitus, a wounded and happy soldier. The coaches jerked forward at last. A man whom I recognized ran in vain to the end of the platform. It was Captain Richard Madden. Shattered, trembling, I shrank into the far corner of the seat, away from the dreaded window.

From this broken state I passed into an almost abject felicity. I told myself that the duel had already begun and that I had won the first encounter by frustrating, even if for forty minutes, even if by a stroke of fate, the attack of my adversary. I argued that this slightest of victories foreshadowed a total victory. I argued (no less fallaciously) that my cowardly felicity proved that I was a man capable of carrying out the adventure successfully. From this weakness I took strength that did not abandon me. I foresee that man will resign himself each day to more atrocious undertakings; soon there will be no one but warriors and brigands; I give them this counsel: *The author of an atrocious undertaking ought to imagine that he has already accomplished it, ought to impose upon himself a future as irrevocable as the past.* Thus I proceeded as my eyes of a man already dead registered the elapsing of the day, which was perhaps the last, and the diffusion of the night. The train ran gently along, amid ash trees. It stopped, almost in the middle of the fields. No one announced the name of the station. "Ashgrove?" I asked a few lads on the platform. "Ashgrove," they replied. I got off.

A lamp enlightened the platform but the faces of the boys were in shadow. One questioned me, "Are you going to Dr. Stephen Albert's house?" Without waiting for my answer, another said, "The house is a long way from here, but you won't get lost if you take this road to the left and at every crossroads turn again to your left." I tossed them a coin (my last), descended a few stone steps and started down the solitary road. It went downhill, slowly. It was of elemental earth; overhead the branches were tangled; the low, full moon seemed to accompany me.

For an instant, I thought that Richard Madden in some way had penetrated my desperate plan. Very quickly, I understood that that was impossible. The instructions to turn always to the left reminded me that such was the common procedure for discovering the central point of certain labyrinths. I have some understanding of labyrinths: not for nothing am I the great grandson of that Ts'ui Pên who was governor of Yunnan and who renounced worldly power in order to write a novel that might be even more populous than the *Hung Lu Meng* and to construct a labyrinth in which all men would become lost. Thirteen years he dedicated to these heterogeneous tasks, but the hand of a stranger murdered him—and his novel was incoherent and no one found the labyrinth. Beneath English trees I meditated on that lost maze: I imagined it inviolate and perfect at the secret crest of a mountain; I imagined it erased by rice fields or beneath the water; I imagined it infinite, no longer composed of octagonal kiosks and returning paths, but of rivers and provinces and kingdoms . . . I thought of a labyrinth of labyrinths, of one sinuous spreading labyrinth that would encompass the past and the future and in some way involve the stars. Absorbed in these illusory images, I forgot my destiny of one pursued. I felt myself to be, for an unknown period of time, an abstract perceiver of the world. The vague, living countryside, the moon, the remains of the day worked on me, as well as the slope of the road which eliminated any possibility of weariness. The afternoon was intimate, infinite. The road descended and forked among the now confused meadows. A high-pitched, almost syllabic music approached and receded in the shifting of the wind, dimmed by leaves and distance. I thought that a man can be an enemy of other men, of the moments of other men, but not of a country; not of fireflies, words, gardens, streams of water, sunsets. Thus I arrived before a tall, rusty gate. Between the iron bars I made out a poplar grove and a pavilion. I understood suddenly two things, the first trivial, the second almost unbelievable: the music came from the pavilion, and the music was Chinese. For precisely that reason I had openly accepted it without paying it any heed. I do not remember whether there was a bell or whether I knocked with my hand. The sparkling of the music continued.

From the rear of the house within a lantern approached: a lantern that the trees sometimes striped and sometimes eclipsed, a paper lantern that had the form of a drum and the color of the moon. A tall man bore it. I didn't see his face for the light blinded me. He opened the door and said slowly, in my own language: "I see that the pious Hsi P'êng persists in correcting my solitude. You no doubt wish to see the garden?"

I recognized the name of one of our consuls and I replied, disconcerted, "The garden?"

"The garden of forking paths."

Something stirred in my memory and I uttered with incomprehensible certainty, "The garden of my ancestor Ts'ui Pên."

"Your ancestor? Your illustrious ancestor? Come in."

The damp path zigzagged like those of my childhood. We came to a library of Eastern and Western books. I recognized bound in yellow silk several volumes of the Lost Encyclopedia, edited by the Third Emperor of the

Luminous Dynasty but never printed. The record on the phonograph revolved next to a bronze phoenix. I also recall a *famille rose* vase and another,
many centuries older, of that shade of blue which our craftsmen copied
from the potters of Persia . . .

Stephen Albert observed me with a smile. He was, as I have said, very
tall, sharp-featured, with gray eyes and a gray beard. He told me that he
had been a missionary in Tientsin "before aspiring to become a Sinologist."

We sat down—I on a long, low divan, he with his back to the window and
a tall circular clock. I calculated that my pursuer, Richard Madden, could
not arrive for at least an hour. My irrevocable determination could wait.

"An astounding fate, that of Ts'ui Pên," Stephen Albert said. "Governor
of his native province, learned in astronomy, in astrology and in the tireless
interpretation of the canonical books, chess player, famous poet and calligrapher—he abandoned all this in order to compose a book and a maze.
He renounced the pleasures of both tyranny and justice, of his populous
couch, of his banquets and even of erudition—all to close himself up for
thirteen years in the Pavilion of the Limpid Solitude. When he died, his
heirs found nothing save chaotic manuscripts. His family, as you may be
aware, wished to condemn them to the fire; but his executor—a Taoist or
Buddhist monk—insisted on their publication."

"We descendants of Ts'ui Pên," I replied, "continue to curse that monk.
Their publication was senseless. The book is an indeterminate heap of contradictory drafts. I examined it once: in the third chapter the hero dies, in
the fourth he is alive. As for the other undertaking of Ts'ui Pên, his labyrinth . . ."

"Here is Ts'ui Pên's labyrinth," he said, indicating a tall lacquered desk.

"An ivory labyrinth!" I exclaimed. "A minimum labyrinth."

"A labyrinth of symbols," he corrected. "An invisible labyrinth of time.
To me, a barbarous Englishman, has been entrusted the revelation of this
diaphanous mystery. After more than a hundred years, the details are irre-
trievable; but it is not hard to conjecture what happened. Ts'ui Pên must
have said once: *I am withdrawing to write a book.* And another time: *I am withdrawing to construct a labyrinth.* Every one imagined two works; to no one did
it occur that the book and the maze were one and the same thing. The Pavilion of the Limpid Solitude stood in the center of a garden that was perhaps intricate; that circumstance could have suggested to the heirs a
physical labyrinth. Ts'ui Pên died; no one in the vast territories that were
his came upon the labyrinth; the confusion of the novel suggested to me
that *it* was the maze. Two circumstances gave me the correct solution of the
problem. One: the curious legend that Ts'ui Pên had planned to create a
labyrinth which would be strictly infinite. The other: a fragment of a letter
I discovered."

Albert rose. He turned his back on me for a moment; he opened a
drawer of the black and gold desk. He faced me and in his hands he held a

sheet of paper that had once been crimson, but was now pink and tenuous and cross-sectioned. The fame of Ts'ui Pên as a calligrapher had been justly won. I read, uncomprehendingly and with fervor, these words written with a minute brush by a man of my blood: *I leave to the various futures (not to all) my garden of forking paths*. Wordlessly, I returned the sheet. Albert continued:

"Before unearthing this letter, I had questioned myself about the ways in which a book can be infinite. I could think of nothing other than a cyclic volume, a circular one. A book whose last page was identical with the first, a book which had the possibility of continuing indefinitely. I remembered too that night which is at the middle of the Thousand and One Nights when Scheherazade (through a magical oversight of the copyist) begins to relate word for word the story of the Thousand and One Nights, establishing the risk of coming once again to the night when she must repeat it, and thus on to infinity. I imagined as well a Platonic, hereditary work, transmitted from father to son, in which each new individual adds a chapter or corrects with pious care the pages of his elders. These conjectures diverted me; but none seemed to correspond, not even remotely, to the contradictory chapters of Ts'ui Pên. In the midst of this perplexity, I received from Oxford the manuscript you have examined. I lingered, naturally, on the sentence: *I leave to the various futures (not to all) my garden of forking paths*. Almost instantly, I understood: 'the garden of forking paths' was the chaotic novel; the phrase 'the various futures (not to all)' suggested to me the forking in time, not in space. A broad rereading of the work confirmed the theory. In all fictional works, each time a man is confronted with several alternatives, he chooses one and eliminates the others; in the fiction of Ts'ui Pên, he chooses—simultaneously—all of them. *He creates*, in this way, diverse futures, diverse times which themselves also proliferate and fork. Here, then, is the explanation of the novel's contradictions. Fang, let us say, has a secret; a stranger calls at his door; Fang resolves to kill him. Naturally, there are several possible outcomes: Fang can kill the intruder, the intruder can kill Fang, they both can escape, they both can die, and so forth. In the work of Ts'ui Pên, all possible outcomes occur; each one is the point of departure for other forkings. Sometimes, the paths of this labyrinth converge: for example, you arrive at this house, but in one of the possible pasts you are my enemy, in another, my friend. If you will resign yourself to my incurable pronunciation, we shall read a few pages."

His face, within the vivid circle of the lamplight, was unquestionably that of an old man, but with something unalterable about it, even immortal. He read with slow precision two versions of the same epic chapter. In the first, an army marches to a battle across a lonely mountain; the horror of the rocks and shadows makes the men undervalue their lives and they gain an easy victory. In the second, the same army traverses a palace where a great festival is taking place; the resplendent battle seems to them a continuation of the celebration and they win the victory. I listened with proper veneration to these ancient narratives, perhaps less admirable in themselves than the fact that they had been created by my blood and were being restored to me by a man of a remote empire, in the course of a desperate adventure, on a Western isle. I remember the last words, repeated in each version like a secret commandment: *Thus fought the heroes, tranquil their admirable hearts, violent their swords, resigned to kill and to die.*

From that moment on, I felt about me and within my dark body an invisible, intangible swarming. Not the swarming of the divergent, parallel and finally coalescent armies, but a more inaccessible, more intimate agitation that they in some manner prefigured. Stephen Albert continued:

"I don't believe that your illustrious ancestor played idly with these variations. I don't consider it credible that he would sacrifice thirteen years to the infinite execution of a rhetorical experiment. In your country, the novel is a subsidiary form of literature; in Ts'ui Pên's time it was a despicable form. Ts'ui Pên was a brilliant novelist, but he was also a man of letters who doubtless did not consider himself a mere novelist. The testimony of his contemporaries proclaims—and his life fully confirms—his metaphysical and mystical interests. Philosophic controversy usurps a good part of the novel. I know that of all problems, none disturbed him so greatly nor worked upon him so much as the abysmal problem of time. Now then, the latter is the only problem that does not figure in the pages of the *Garden*. He does not even use the word that signifies *time*. How do you explain this voluntary omission?"

I proposed several solutions—all unsatisfactory. We discussed them. Finally, Stephen Albert said to me:

"In a riddle whose answer is chess, what is the only prohibited word?"

I thought a moment and replied, "The word *chess*."

"Precisely," said Albert. "*The Garden of Forking Paths* is an enormous riddle, or parable, whose theme is time; this recondite cause prohibits its mention. To omit a word always, to resort to inept metaphors and obvious periphrases, is perhaps the most emphatic way of stressing it. That is the tortuous method preferred, in each of the meanderings of his indefatigable novel, by the oblique Ts'ui Pên. I have compared hundreds of manuscripts, I have corrected the errors that the negligence of the copyists has introduced. I have guessed the plan of this chaos, I have re-established—I believe I have re-established—the primordial organization, I have translated the entire work: it is clear to me that not once does he employ the word 'time.' The explanation is obvious: *The Garden of Forking Paths* is an incomplete, but not false, image of the universe as Ts'ui Pên conceived it. In contrast to Newton and Schopenhauer, your ancestor did not believe in a uniform, absolute time. He believed in an infinite series of times, in a growing dizzying, net of divergent, convergent, and parallel times. This network of times which approached one another, forked, broke off, or were unaware of one another for centuries, embraces *all* possibilities of time. We do not exist in the majority of these times; in some you exist, and not I; in others I, and not you; in others, both of us. In the present one, which a favorable fate has granted me, you have arrived at my house; in another, while crossing the garden, you found me dead; in still another, I utter these same words, but I am a mistake, a ghost."

"In every one," I pronounced, not without a tremble to my voice, "I am grateful to you and revere you for your re-creation of the garden of Ts'ui Pên."

"Not in all," he murmured with a smile. "Time forks perpetually toward innumerable futures. In one of them I am your enemy."

Once again, I felt the swarming sensation of which I have spoken. It seemed to me that the humid garden that surrounded the house was infinitely saturated with invisible persons. Those persons were Albert and I, secret, busy and multiform in other dimensions of time. I raised my eyes and the tenuous nightmare dissolved. In the yellow and black garden there was only one man; but this man was as strong as a statue . . . this man was approaching along the path and he was Captain Richard Madden.

"The future already exists," I replied, "but I am your friend. Could I see the letter again?"

Albert rose. Standing tall, he opened the drawer of the tall desk; for the moment his back was to me. I had readied the revolver. I fired with extreme caution. Albert fell uncomplainingly, immediately. I swear his death was instantaneous—a lightning stroke.

The rest is unreal, insignificant. Madden broke in, arrested me. I have been condemned to the gallows. I have won out abominably; I have communicated to Berlin the secret name of the city they must attack. They bombed it yesterday; I read it in the same papers that offered to England the mystery of the learned Sinologist Stephen Albert who was murdered by a stranger, one Yu Tsun. The Chief had deciphered this mystery. He knew my problem was to indicate (through the uproar of the war) the city called Albert, and that I had found no other means to do so than to kill a man of that name. He does not know (no one can know) my innumerable contrition and weariness.

The Demon Lover

ELIZABETH BOWEN

Towards the end of her day in London Mrs. Drover went round to her shut-up house to look for several things she wanted to take away. Some belonged to herself, some to her family, who were by now used to their country life. It was late August; it had been a steamy, showery day: at the moment the trees down the pavement glittered in an escape of humid yellow afternoon sun. Against the next batch of clouds, already piling up ink-dark, broken chimneys and parapets stood out. In her once familiar street, as in any unused channel, an unfamiliar queerness had silted up; a cat wove itself in and out of railings, but no human eye watched Mrs. Drover's return. Shifting some parcels under her arm, she slowly forced round her latchkey in an unwilling lock, then gave the door, which had warped, a push with her knee. Dead air came out to meet her as she went in.

The staircase window having been boarded up, no light came down into the hall. But one door, she could just see, stood ajar, so she went quickly through into the room and unshuttered the big window in there. Now the prosaic woman, looking about her, was more perplexed than she knew by everything that she saw, by traces of her long former habit of life—the yellow smoke-stain up the white marble mantelpiece, the ring left by a vase on the top of the escritoire; the bruise in the wallpaper where, on the door being thrown open widely, the china handle had always hit the wall. The piano, having gone away to be stored, had left what looked like claw marks on its part of the parquet. Though not much dust had seeped in, each object wore a film of another kind; and, the only ventilation being the chimney, the whole drawing-room smelled of the cold hearth. Mrs. Drover put down her parcels on the escritoire and left the room to proceed upstairs; the things she wanted were in a bedroom chest.

She had been anxious to see how the house was—the part-time caretaker she shared with some neighbours was away this week on his holiday, known

141

to be not yet back. At the best of times he did not look in often, and she was never sure that she trusted him. There were some cracks in the structure, left by the last bombing, on which she was anxious to keep an eye. Not that one could do anything—

A shaft of refracted daylight now lay across the hall. She stopped dead and stared at the hall table—on this lay a letter addressed to her.

She thought first—then the caretaker *must* be back. All the same, who, seeing the house shuttered, would have dropped a letter in at the box? It was not a circular, it was not a bill. And the post office redirected, to the address in the country, everything for her that came through the post. The caretaker (even if he *were* back) did not know she was due in London today—her call here had been planned to be a surprise—so his negligence in the manner of this letter, leaving it to wait in the dusk and the dust, annoyed her. Annoyed, she picked up the letter, which bore no stamp. But it cannot be important, or they would know . . . She took the letter rapidly upstairs with her, without a stop to look at the writing till she reached what had been her bedroom, where she let in light. The room looked over the garden and other gardens: the sun had gone in; as the clouds sharpened and lowered, the trees and rank lawns seemed already to smoke with dark. Her reluctance to look again at the letter came from the fact that she felt intruded upon—and by someone contemptuous of her ways. However, in the tenseness preceding the fall of rain she read it: it was a few lines.

> Dear Kathleen: You will not have forgotten that today is our anniversary, and the day we said. The years have gone by at once slowly and fast. In view of the fact that nothing has changed, I shall rely upon you to keep your promise. I was sorry to see you leave London, but was satisfied that you would be back in time. You may expect me, therefore, at the hour arranged. Until then . . .
>
> K.

Mrs. Drover looked for the date: it was today's. She dropped the letter on to the bed-springs, then picked it up to see the writing again—her lips, beneath the remains of lipstick, beginning to go white. She felt so much the change in her own face that she went to the mirror, polished a clear patch in it and looked at once urgently and stealthily in. She was confronted by a woman of forty-four, with eyes starting out under a hat-brim that had been rather carelessly pulled down. She had not put on any more powder since she left the shop where she ate her solitary tea. The pearls her husband had given her on their marriage hung loose round her now rather thinner throat, slipping in the V of the pink wool jumper her sister knitted last autumn as they sat round the fire. Mrs. Drover's most normal expression was one of controlled worry, but of assent. Since the birth of the third of her little boys, attended by a quite serious illness, she had had an intermittent muscular flicker to the left of her mouth, but in spite of this she could always sustain a manner that was at once energetic and calm.

Turning from her own face as precipitately as she had gone to meet it, she went to the chest where the things were, unlocked it, threw up the lid and knelt to search. But as rain began to come crashing down she could not keep from looking over her shoulder at the stripped bed on which the letter lay. Behind the blanket of rain the clock of the church that still stood struck six—with rapidly heightening apprehension she counted each of the slow strokes. "The hour arranged . . . My God," she said, "*what* hour? How should I . . . ? After twenty-five years . . . ."

The young girl talking to the soldier in the garden had not ever completely seen his face. It was dark; they were saying goodbye under a tree. Now and then—for it felt, from not seeing him at this intense moment, as though she had never seen him at all—she verified his presence for these few moments longer by putting out a hand, which he each time pressed, without very much kindness, and painfully, on to one of the breast buttons of his uniform. That cut of the button on the palm of her hand was, principally what she was to carry away. This was so near the end of a leave from France that she could only wish him already gone. It was August 1916. Being not kissed, being drawn away from and looked at intimidated Kathleen till she imagined spectral glitters in the place of his eyes. Turning away and looking back up the lawn she saw, through branches of trees, the drawing-room window light: she caught a breath for the moment when she could go running back there into the safe arms of her mother and sister, and cry: "What shall I do, what shall I do? He has gone."

Hearing her catch her breath, her fiancé said, without feeling: "Cold?"

"You're going away such a long way."

"Not so far as you think."

"I don't understand?"

"You don't have to," he said. "You will. You know what we said."

"But that was—suppose you—I mean, suppose."

"I shall be with you," he said, "sooner or later. You won't forget that. You need do nothing but wait."

Only a little more than a minute later she was free to run up the silent lawn. Looking in through the window at her mother and sister, who did not for the moment perceive her, she already felt that unnatural promise drive down between her and the rest of all human kind. No other way of having given herself could have made her feel so apart, lost and foresworn. She could not have plighted a more sinister troth.

Kathleen behaved well when, some months later, her fiancé was reported missing, presumed killed. Her family not only supported her but were able to praise her courage without stint because they could not regret, as a husband for her, the man they knew almost nothing about. They hoped she would, in a year or two, console herself—and had it been only a question of consolation things might have gone much straighter ahead. But her trouble, behind just a little grief, was a complete dislocation from everything. She did not reject other lovers, for these failed to appear: for years she failed to attract men—and with the approach of her 'thirties she became natural enough to share her family's anxiousness on this score. She began to put herself out, to wonder; and at thirty-two she was greatly relieved to find herself being courted by William Drover. She married him, and the two of them settled down in this quiet, arboreal part of Kensington: in this house the years piled up, her children were born and they all lived till they were driven out by the bombs of the next war. Her movements as Mrs. Drover were circumscribed, and she dismissed any idea that they were still watched.

As things were—dead or living the letter writer sent her only a threat. Unable, for some minutes, to go on kneeling with her back exposed to the empty room, Mrs. Drover rose from the chest to sit on an upright chair whose back was firmly against the wall. The desuetude of her former bedroom, her married London home's whole air of being a cracked cup from which memory, with its reassuring power, had either evaporated or leaked away, made a crisis—and at just this crisis the letter writer had, knowledgeably, struck. The hollowness of the house this evening cancelled years on years of voices, habits and steps. Through the shut windows she only heard rain fall on the roofs around. To rally herself, she said she was in a mood— and for two or three seconds shutting her eyes, told herself that she had imagined the letter. But she opened them—there it lay on the bed.

On the supernatural side of the letter's entrance she was not permitting her mind to dwell. Who, in London, knew she meant to call at the house to-day? Evidently, however, this had been known. The caretaker, *had* he come back, had had no cause to expect her: he would have taken the letter in his pocket, to forward it, at his own time, through the post. There was no other sign that the caretaker had been in—but, if not? Letters dropped in at doors of deserted houses do not fly or walk to tables in halls. They do not sit on the dust of empty tables with the air of certainty that they will be found. There is needed some human hand—but nobody but the caretaker had a key. Under circumstances she did not care to consider, a house can be entered without a key. It was possible that she was not alone now. She might be being waited for, downstairs. Waited for—until when? Until "the hour arranged". At least that was not six o'clock: six has struck.

She rose from the chair and went over and locked the door.

The thing was, to get out. To fly? No, not that: she had to catch her train. As a woman whose utter dependability was the keystone of her family life she was not willing to return to the country, to her husband, her little boys and her sister, without the objects she had come up to fetch. Resuming work at the chest she set about making up a number of parcels in a rapid, fumbling-decisive way. These, with her shopping parcels, would be too much to carry; these meant a taxi—at the thought of the taxi her heart went up and her normal breathing resumed. I will ring up the taxi now; the taxi cannot come too soon: I shall hear the taxi out there running its engine, till I walk calmly down to it through the hall. I'll ring up—But no: the telephone is cut off . . . She tugged at a knot she had tied wrong.

The idea of flight . . . He was never kind to me, not really. I don't remember him kind at all. Mother said he never considered me. He was set on me, that was what it was—not love. Not love, not meaning a person well. What did he do, to make me promise like that? I can't remember—But she found that she could.

She remembered with such dreadful acuteness that the twenty-five years since then dissolved like smoke and she instinctively looked for the weal left by the button on the palm of her hand. She remembered not only all that he said and did but the complete suspension of *her* existence during that August week. I was not myself—they all told me so at the time. She remembered—but with one white burning blank as where acid has dropped on a photograph: *under no conditions* could she remember his face.

So, wherever he may be waiting, I shall not know him. You have no time to run from a face you do not expect.

The thing was to get to the taxi before any clock struck what could be the hour. She would slip down the street and round the side of the square to where the square gave on the main road. She would return in the taxi, safe, to her own door, and bring the solid driver into the house with her to pick up the parcels from room to room. The idea of the taxi driver made her decisive, bold: she unlocked her door, went to the top of the staircase and listened down.

She heard nothing—but while she was hearing nothing the *passé* air of the staircase was disturbed by a draught that travelled up to her face. It emanated from the basement: down there a door or window was being opened by someone who chose this moment to leave the house.

The rain had stopped; the pavements steamily shone as Mrs. Drover let herself out by inches from her own front door into the empty street. The unoccupied houses opposite continued to meet her look with their damaged stare. Making towards the thoroughfare and the taxi, she tried not to keep looking behind. Indeed, the silence was so intense—one of those creeks of London silence exaggerated this summer by the damage of war—that no tread could have gained on hers unheard. Where her street debouched on the square where people went on living, she grew conscious of, and checked, her unnatural pace. Across the open end of the square two buses impassively passed each other: women, a perambulator, cyclists, a man wheeling a barrow signalized, once again, the ordinary flow of life. At the square's most populous corner should be—and was—the short taxi rank. This evening, only one taxi—but this, although it presented its blank rump, appeared already to be alertly waiting for her. Indeed, without looking round the driver started his engine as she panted up from behind and put her hand on the door. As she did so, the clock struck seven. The taxi faced the main road: to make the trip back to her house it would have to turn—she had settled back on the seat and the taxi *had* turned before she, surprised by its knowing movement, recollected that she had not "said where". She leaned forward to scratch at the glass panel that divided the driver's head from her own.

The driver braked to what was almost a stop, turned round and slid the glass panel back: the jolt of this flung Mrs. Drover forward till her face was almost into the glass. Through the aperture driver and passenger, not six inches between them, remained for an eternity eye to eye. Mrs. Drover's mouth hung open for some seconds before she could issue her first scream. After that she continued to scream freely and to beat with her gloved hands on the glass all round as the taxi, accelerating without mercy, made off with her into the hinterland of deserted streets.

Rest Cure

KAY BOYLE

He sat in the sun with the blanket about him, considering, with his hands lying out like emaciated strangers before him, that today the sun would endure a little longer. Certainly it would survive until the trees below the terrace effaced it, toward four o'clock, like opened parasols. A crime it had been, the invalid thought, turning his head this way and that, to have ever built up one house before another in such a way that one man's habitation cast a shadow upon another's. The whole sloping coast should have been left a wilderness with no order to it, stalked and leafed with the great strong trunks and foliage of these parts. Cactus plants with petals a yard wide and yucca tongues as thick as elephant trunks were sullenly and viciously flourishing all about the house. Upon the terrace had a further attempt at nicety and precision been made: there his wife had seen to it that geraniums were potted into the wooden boxes that stood along the wall.

From his lounging chair he could reach out and, with no effort beyond that of raising the skeleton of his hand, finger the parched stems of the geraniums. The south, and the Mediterranean wind, had blistered them past all belief. They bore their rosy topknots or their soiled white flowers balanced upon their thick Italian heads. There they were, within his reach, a row of weary washerwomen leaning back from the villainous descent of the coast. What parched scions had thrust forth from their stems now served to obliterate in part the vision of the sun. With arms akimbo they surrounded him: thin burned Italian women with their meager bundles of dirty linen on their heads. One after another, with a flicker of irritation for his wife lighting his eye, he fingered them at the waist a moment, and then snapped off each stem. One after another he broke their stalks in two and dropped them away onto the pavings beneath his lounging chair. When he had finished off what plants grew within his reach, he lay back exhausted, sank, thin as an archer's bow, into the depths of his cushions.

147

"They kept the sun off me," he was thinking in absolution.

In spite of the garden and its vegetation, he would have the last drops of sun. He had closed his eyes, and there he lay looking straight ahead of him into the fathomless black pits of his lids. Even here, in the south, in the sun even, the coal mines remained. His nostrils were sick with the smell of them and on his cheeks he felt lingering the slipping mantle of the English fog. He had not seen the mines since he was a young man, but nothing he had ever done between would alter them. There he sat in the sun with his eyes closed, looking into their depths.

Because his father had been a miner, he was thinking, the black of the pits had put some kind of blasphemy on his own blood. He sat with his eyes closed looking directly into the blank awful mines. Against their obscurity he set the icicles of one winter when the war was on, when he had spent his twilights seeking for pine cones under the tall trees in the woods behind the house. In Cornwall. What a vision! How beautiful that year, and many other years, might have been had it not been for the sour thought of war. Every time his heart had lifted for a hillside or a wave, or for the wind blowing, the thought of the turmoil going on had beset and stricken him. It had lain like a burden on his conscience every morning when he was coming awake. The first light moments of day coming had warned him that despite the blood rising in his body, it was no time to rejoice. The war. Ah, yes, the war. After the mines, it had been the war. Whenever he had believed for half a minute in man, then he had remembered that the war was going on.

For a little while one February, it had seemed that the colors set out in Monte Carlo, facing the Casino, would obliterate forever the angry memories his heart had stored away. The great mauve, white, and deep royal bouquets had thrived a week or more, as if rooted in his eyes. Such banks and beds of richly petaled flowers, set thick as thieves or thicker on the cultivated lawns, conveyed the wish. Their artificial physiognomies masked the earth as well as he would have wished his own features to stand guard before his spirit. The invalid lifted his hand and touched his beard. His mouth and chin, he thought with cunning satisfaction, were marvelously concealed.

The sound of his wife's voice speaking in the room that opened behind him onto the terrace roused him a little as he sat pondering in the sun. She seemed to be moving from one long window to another, arranging flowers in the vases, for her voice would come across the pavings, now strong and close, now distant as if turned away, and she was talking to their guest about some sort of shrub or fern. A special kind, the like of which she could find nowhere on the Riviera. It thrived in the cool brisk fogs of their own land, she was saying. Her voice had turned toward him again and was ringing clearly across the terrace.

"Those are beautiful ones you have there now," said the voice of the gentleman.

"Ah, take care!" cried out his wife's voice, somewhat dimmed as though she had again turned toward the room. "I was afraid you had pierced your hand," she said in a moment.

When the invalid opened his eyes, he saw that the sun was even now beginning to glimmer through the upper branches of the trees, was lolling along the prosperous dark upper boughs as if in preparation for descent. Not yet, he thought, not yet. He raised himself on his elbows and scanned the sky. Scarcely three-thirty, surely, he was thinking. The sun can't be going down at once.

"The sun can't be going down yet awhile, can it?" he called out to the house.

He heard the gravel of the pathway sparkling and spitting out from under the soles of their feet as they crossed it, and then his wife's heels and the boots of the guest struck and advanced across the paving stones.

"Oh, oh, the geraniums—" said his wife suddenly by his side.

The guest had raised his head and stood squinting up at the sun.

"I should say it were going down," he said after a moment.

He had deliberately stepped before the rays of it and stood leaning back against the terrace wall. His solid gray head had served to cork the sunlight. Like a wooden stopper, thought the invalid, painted to resemble a man. With the nose of a wooden stopper. And the sightless eyes. And the creases when he speaks or smiles.

"But think what it must be like in Paris now," said the gentleman. "I don't know how you feel, but I can't find words to say how grateful I am for being here." The guest, thought the invalid as he surveyed him, was very conscious of being a guest—of accepting meals, bed, tea, society—and his smile was permanently set beneath his nose.

"Of course you don't know how I feel," said the invalid. He lay looking sourly up at his guest. "Would you mind moving out of the sun?" As the visiting gentleman skipped out of the way, the invalid cleared his throat, dissolved the little pellet of phlegm which had leaped to being on his tongue so as not to spit before them, and sank back into his chair.

"The advantage—or rather *one* of the advantages—of being a writer," said the visiting gentleman with a smile, "is that he can settle down wherever the fancy takes him. Now, a publisher—"

"Why be a publisher?" said the invalid in irritation. He was staring again into the black blank mines.

His wife was squatting and stooping about his chair, gathering up in her dress the butchered geraniums. She said not a word, but crouched there picking them carefully up, one by one. By her side had appeared a little covered basket, and within it rattled a pair of castanets.

"I am sure I can very easily turn these into slips," she said gently, as if speaking to herself. "A little snip in the right place and they'll be as good as new."

"You can make soup out of them," said the invalid bitterly. "What's in the basket," he said, "making a noise?"

"Oh, a *langouste!*" cried out his wife. She had just remembered. "We bought you a *langouste,* alive, at the Beausoleil market. It's as lively as a rig!"

The visiting gentleman burst into laughter. The invalid could hear his gasping with enjoyment by his side.

"I can't bear them alive," said the invalid testily. He lay listening curiously to the animal rattling his jaws and clawing under the basket's lid.

"Oh, but with mayonnaise!" cried his wife. "Tomorrow!"

"Why doesn't Mr. What-do-you-call-him answer the question I put him?" asked the invalid sourly. His mind was possessed with the thought of the visiting man. "I asked him why he was a publisher," said the invalid. What a viper, what a felon, he was thinking, to come and live on me and not give me the satisfaction of a quarrel! He was not a young man, thought the invalid, with his little remains of graying hair, but he had all the endurance and patience of a younger man in the presence of a master. All the smiling and bowing, thought the invalid with contempt, and all the obsequious ways. The man was standing so near to his chair that he could hear his breath whistling through his nostrils. Maybe his eyes were on him, the invalid was thinking. It gave him a turn to think that he was lying there exposed in the sun where the visitor could examine him pore by pore. Hair by hair could the visitor take him in and record him.

"Oh, I beg your pardon," said the gentleman. "I'm afraid I owe you an apology. You see, I'm not accustomed to it."

"To what?" said the invalid sharply. He had flashed his eyes open and looked suspiciously into the publisher's face.

"To seeing you flat on your back," said the gentleman promptly.

"You covered that over very nicely," said the invalid. He clasped his hands across his sunken bosom. "You meant to say something else. You meant to say *death,*" said the invalid calmly. "I heard the first letter of it on your tongue."

He lay back in his chair again with his lids fallen. He could distinctly smell the foul fumes of the pits.

"Elsa," he said, as he lay twitching in the light, "I would like some champagne. *Just because,*" he said, sitting up abruptly, "I've written a few books doesn't mean that you have to keep the truth about me to yourself."

His wife went off across the terrace, leaving the two men together.

"Don't make a mistake," said the invalid, smiling grimly. "Don't make any mistake. I'm not quite finished. Not *quite.* I still have a little more to write about," he said. "Don't you fool yourself, my dear."

"Oh, I flatter myself that I don't," said the gentleman agreeably. "I'm convinced there's an unlimited amount still to come. And I hope to have the honor of publishing some of it. I'm counting on that, you know." He ended on a playful note and looked coyly at the invalid. But every spark of life had suddenly expired in the ill man's face.

"I didn't know the sun would be off the terrace so soon," he said.

His wife had returned and was opening the bottle, carefully and without error, with the end of her pliant thumb. The invalid turned on his side and regarded her: a great strong woman whom he would never forget, never, nor the surprisingly slim crescent of her flexible thumb. All of her fingers, he lay thinking as he watched her, were soft as skeins of silk, and tied in the joints and knuckles by invisible satin bands of faintest rose. And there was the visiting gentleman hovering about her, with his oh-let-me-please-Mrs.-oh-do-let-me-now. But her grip on the neck of the bottle was as tenacious as a snake's. She lifted her head, smiled, and shook it at their guest.

"Oh, no," she said, "I'm doing beautifully."

Just as she spoke the cork flew out and hit the gentleman square in the forehead. After it streamed a geyser of purest gold.

"Oh, oh, oh," cried the invalid. He held out his hands to the golden spray. "Oh, pour it here!" he cried. "Oh, buckets of it going! Oh, pour it over me, Elsa!"

The color had flown into Elsa's face and she was laughing. Softly and breathlessly she ran from glass to glass. There in the stems played the clear living liquid, like a fountain springing upward. Ah, that, ah, that, in the innards of a man, thought the invalid joyfully! Ah, that, springing again and again in the belly and heart! There in the glass it ran, cascaded in needle-points the length of his throat, went whistling to his pulses.

The invalid set down his empty glass.

"Elsa," he said gently, "could I have a little more champagne?"

His wife had risen with the bottle in her hand, but she looked doubtfully at him.

"Do you really think you should?" she asked.

"Yes," said the invalid. He watched the unbelievably pure stuff flowing out all over his glass. "Yes," he said. "Of course. Of course, I should."

A sweet shy look of love had begun to arch in his eyes.

"I'd love to see the *langouste*," he said gently. "Do you think you could let him out and let me see him run around?"

Elsa set down her glass and stooped to lift the cover of the basket. There was the green armored beast lifting its eyes, as if on hinges, to examine the light. Such an expression he had seen before, thought the invalid immediately. There was a startling likeness in those small audacious eyes. Such a look had there been in his father's eyes: that look, and the long smooth mustaches drooping across the wee clefted chin, gave the *langouste* such a look of his father that he exclaimed aloud.

"Be careful," said Elsa. "His claws are tied, but still—"

"I must have him out," said the invalid. He gripped the *langouste* firmly about the hips. He looks like my father, he was thinking. I must have him out where I can see.

In spite of its shackles, the animal contrived to wave his wide pinions in the air as the invalid lifted him up and set him on the rug across his knees. There was the same line of sparkling dew-like substance pearling the *langouste's* lip, the same weak disappointed lip, like the eagle's lip, and the bold suspicious eye. Across the sloping shoulders of the beast lay a sprinkling of brilliant dust, as black as coal dust and quite as luminous. Just as his father had looked coming home at night, with the coal dust showered across his shoulders like a deadly mantle. Just such a deadly cloak of quartz and mica and the rooted roots of fern. Even the queer blue toothless look of his father about the jaws. The invalid took another deep swallow of champagne and let it seep quietly through his flesh and blood. Then he lifted his hand and stroked the *langouste* gently. You've never counted, he was thinking mildly. I've led my life very well without you in it. You better go back to the mines where you belong.

When he lifted up the *langouste* to peer into his face, the arms of the beast fell ludicrously open as if he were seeking to embrace the ailing man. He could see his father very well in him, coming home with the coal dirt all over him in the evening, standing by the door that opened in by halves, opening first the upper half and then the lower, swaying a little as he felt for the latch of the lower half of the door. With the beer he had been drinking, or the dew of the Welsh mist shining on his long mustaches. The invalid gave him a gentle shake and set him down again.

I got on very well without you, he was thinking. He sipped at his champagne and regarded the animal upon his knees. As far as I was concerned you need never have been my father at all. Slowly and warily the wondrous eyes and the feelers of the beast moved in distrust across the invalid's lap and bosom. A lot of good you ever did me, he was thinking, as he watched the *langouste* groping about as if in darkness; he began to think of the glowing miner's lamp his father had worn strapped upon his brow. Feeling about in the dark and choking to death underground, he was thinking impatiently. I might have been anybody's son. The strong shelly odor of the *langouste* was seasoning the air.

"I've got on very well without you," he was thinking bitterly. From his wife's face he gathered that he had spoken aloud. The visiting gentleman looked into the depths of his glass of champagne.

"Don't misunderstand me," said the guest with a forbearing smile. "I'm quite aware of the fact that, long before you met me, you had one of the greatest publics and following of any living writer—"

The invalid looked in bewilderment at his wife's face and at the face of the visiting man. If they scold me, he thought, I am going to cry. He felt his underlip quivering. Scold me! he thought suddenly in indignation. A man with a beard, he thought with a cunning evil gleam narrowing his eye.

"You haven't answered my question," he said aggressively to the visitor. "You haven't answered it yet, have you?"

His hand had fallen against the hard brittle armor of the *langouste's* hide. There were the eyes raised to his and the canny feelers lifted. His fingers closed for comfort about the *langouste's* unwieldy paw. Father, he said in his heart, Father, help me. Father, Father, he said. I don't want to die.

The Guest

ALBERT CAMUS

The schoolmaster was watching the two men climb toward him. One was on horseback, the other on foot. They had not yet tackled the abrupt rise leading to the schoolhouse built on the hillside. The were toiling onward, making slow progress in the snow, among the stones, on the vast expanse of the high, deserted plateau. From time to time the horse stumbled. Without hearing anything yet, he could see the breath issuing from the horse's nostrils. One of the men, at least, knew the region. They were following the trail although it had disappeared days ago under a layer of dirty white snow. The schoolmaster calculated that it would take them half an hour to get onto the hill. It was cold; he went back into the school to get a sweater.

He crossed the empty, frigid classroom. On the blackboard the four rivers of France, drawn with four different colored chalks, had been flowing toward their estuaries for the past three days. Snow had suddenly fallen in mid-October after eight months of drought without the transition of rain, and the twenty pupils, more or less, who lived in the villages scattered over the plateau had stopped coming. With fair weather they would return. Daru now heated only the single room that was his lodging, adjoining the classroom and giving also onto the plateau to the east. Like the class windows, his window looked to the south too. On that side the school was a few kilometers from the point where the plateau began to slope toward the south. In clear weather could be seen the purple mass of the mountain range where the gap opened onto the desert.

Somewhat warmed, Daru returned to the window from which he had first seen the two men. They were no longer visible. Hence they must have tackled the rise. The sky was not so dark, for the snow had stopped falling during the night. The morning had opened with a dirty light which had scarcely become brighter as the ceiling of clouds lifted. At two in the afternoon it seemed as if the day were merely beginning. But still this was better

153

than those three days when the thick snow was falling amidst unbroken darkness with little gusts of wind that rattled the double door of the classroom. Then Daru had spent long hours in his room, leaving it only to go to the shed and feed the chickens or get some coal. Fortunately the delivery truck from Tadjid, the nearest village to the north, had brought his supplies two days before the blizzard. It would return in forty-eight hours.

Besides, he had enough to resist a siege, for the little room was cluttered with bags of wheat that the administration left as a stock to distribute to those of his pupils whose families had suffered from the drought. Actually they had all been victims because they were all poor. Every day Daru would distribute a ration to the children. They had missed it, he knew, during these bad days. Possibly one of the fathers or big brothers would come this afternoon and he could supply them with grain. It was just a matter of carrying them over to the next harvest. Now shiploads of wheat were arriving from France and the worst was over. But it would be hard to forget that poverty, that army of ragged ghosts wandering in the sunlight, the plateaus burned to a cinder month after month, the earth shriveled up little by little, literally scorched, every stone bursting into dust under one's foot. The sheep had died then by thousands and even a few men, here and there, sometimes without anyone's knowing.

In contrast with such poverty, he who lived almost like a monk in his remote schoolhouse, nonetheless satisfied with the little he had and with the rough life, had felt like a lord with his whitewashed walls, his narrow couch, his unpainted shelves, his well, and his weekly provision of water and food. And suddenly this snow, without warning, without the foretaste of rain. This is the way the region was, cruel to live in, even without men—who didn't help matters either. But Daru had been born here. Everywhere else, he felt exiled.

He stepped out onto the terrace in front of the schoolhouse. The two men were now halfway up the slope. He recognized the horseman as Balducci, the old gendarme he had known for a long time. Balducci was holding on the end of a rope an Arab who was walking behind him with hands bound and head lowered. The gendarme waved a greeting to which Daru did not reply, lost as he was in contemplation of the Arab dressed in a faded blue jellaba, his feet in sandals but covered with socks of heavy raw wool, his head surmounted by a narrow, short *chèche*. They were approaching. Balducci was holding back his horse in order not to hurt the Arab, and the group was advancing slowly.

Within earshot, Balducci shouted: "One hour to do the three kilometers from El Ameur!" Daru did not answer. Short and square in his thick sweater, he watched them climb. Not once had the Arab raised his head. "Hello," said Daru when they got up onto the terrace. "Come in and warm up." Balducci painfully got down from his horse without letting go the rope. From under his bristling mustache he smiled at the schoolmaster. His little dark eyes, deep-set under a tanned forehead, and his mouth surrounded with wrinkles made him look attentive and studious. Daru took the bridle, led the horse to the shed, and came back to the two men, who were now waiting for him in the school. He led them into his room. "I am going to heat up the classroom," he said. "We'll be more comfortable there." When he entered the room again, Balducci was on the couch. He had undone the rope tying him to the Arab, who had squatted near the stove. His hands still bound, the *chèche* pushed back on his head, he was looking toward the window. At first Daru noticed only his huge lips, fat, smooth, almost Negroid; yet his nose was straight, his eyes were dark and full of fever. The *chèche* revealed an obstinate forehead and, under the weathered skin now rather discolored by the cold, the whole face had a restless and rebellious look that struck Daru when the Arab, turning his face toward him, looked him straight in the eyes. "Go into the other room," said the schoolmaster, "and I'll make you some mint tea." "Thanks," Balducci said. "What a chore! How I long for retirement." And addressing his prisoner in Arabic: "Come on, you." The Arab got up and, slowly, holding his bound wrists in front of him, went into the classroom.

With the tea, Daru brought a chair. But Balducci was already enthroned on the nearest pupil's desk and the Arab had squatted against the teacher's platform facing the stove, which stood between the desk and the window. When he held out the glass of tea to the prisoner, Daru hesitated at the sight of his bound hands. "He might perhaps be untied." "Sure," said Balducci, "that was for the trip." He started to get to his feet. But Daru, setting the glass on the floor, had knelt beside the Arab. Without saying anything, the Arab watched him with his feverish eyes. Once his hands were free, he rubbed his swollen wrists against each other, took the glass of tea, and sucked up the burning liquid in swift little sips.

"Good," said Daru. "And where are you headed?"

Balducci withdrew his mustache from the tea. "Here, son."

"Odd pupils! And you're spending the night?"

"No. I'm going back to El Ameur. And you will deliver this fellow to Tinguit. He is expected at police headquarters."

Balducci was looking at Daru with a friendly little smile.

"What's this story?" asked the schoolmaster. "Are you pulling my leg?"

"No, son. Those are the orders."

"The orders? I'm not . . . " Daru hesitated, not wanting to hurt the old Corsican. "I mean, that's not my job."

"What! What's the meaning of that? In wartime people do all kinds of jobs."

"Then I'll wait for the declaration of war!"

Balducci nodded.

"O.K. But the orders exist and they concern you too. Things are brewing, it appears. There is talk of a forthcoming revolt. We are mobilized, in a way."

Daru still had his obstinate look.

"Listen, son," Balducci said. "I like you and you must understand. There's only a dozen of us at El Ameur to patrol throughout the whole territory of a small department and I must get back in a hurry. I was told to hand this guy over to you and return without delay. He couldn't be kept there. His village was beginning to stir; they wanted to take him back. You must take him to Tinguit tomorrow before the day is over. Twenty kilometers shouldn't faze a husky fellow like you. After that, all will be over. You'll come back to your pupils and your comfortable life."

Behind the wall the horse could be heard snorting and pawing the earth. Daru was looking out the window. Decidedly, the weather was clearing and the light was increasing over the snowy plateau. When all the snow was melted, the sun would take over again and once more would burn the fields of stone. For days, still, the unchanging sky would shed its dry light on the solitary expanse where nothing had any connection with man.

"After all," he said, turning around toward Balducci, "what did he do?" And, before the gendarme had opened his mouth, he asked: "Does he speak French?"

"No, not a word. We had been looking for him for a month, but they were hiding him. He killed his cousin."

"Is he against us?"

"I don't think so. But you can never be sure."

"Why did he kill?"

"A family squabble, I think. One owed the other grain, it seems. It's not at all clear. In short, he killed his cousin with a billhook. You know, like a sheep, *kreezk!*"

Balducci made the gesture of drawing a blade across his throat and the Arab, his attention attracted, watched him with a sort of anxiety. Daru felt a sudden wrath against the man, against all men with their rotten spite, their tireless hates, their blood lust.

But the kettle was singing on the stove. He served Balducci more tea, hesitated, then served the Arab again, who, a second time, drank avidly. His raised arms made the jellaba fall open and the schoolmaster saw his thin, muscular chest.

"Thanks, kid," Balducci said. "And now, I'm off."

He got up and went toward the Arab, taking a small rope from his pocket.

"What are you doing?" Daru asked dryly.

Balducci, disconcerted, showed him the rope.

"Don't bother."

The old gendarme hesitated. "It's up to you. Of course, you are armed?"

"I have my shotgun."

"Where?"

"In the trunk."

"You ought to have it near your bed."

"Why? I have nothing to fear."

"You're crazy, son. If there's an uprising, no one is safe, we're all in the same boat."

"I'll defend myself. I'll have time to see them coming."

Balducci began to laugh, then suddenly the mustache covered the white teeth.

"You'll have time? O.K. That's just what I was saying. You have always been a little cracked. That's why I like you, my son was like that."

At the same time he took out his revolver and put it on the desk.

"Keep it, I don't need two weapons from here to El Ameur."

The revolver shone against the black paint of the table. When the gendarme turned toward him, the schoolmaster caught the smell of leather and horseflesh.

"Listen, Balducci," Daru said suddenly, "every bit of this disgusts me, and first of all your fellow here. But I won't hand him over. Fight, yes, if I have to. But not that."

The old gendarme stood in front of him and looked at him severely.

"You're being a fool," he said slowly. "I don't like it either. You don't get used to putting a rope on a man even after years of it, and you're even ashamed—yes, ashamed. But you can't let them have their way."

"I won't hand him over," Daru said again.

"It's an order, son, and I repeat it."

"That's right. Repeat to them what I've said to you: I won't hand him over."

Balducci made a visible effort to reflect. He looked at the Arab and at Daru. At last he decided.

"No, I won't tell them anything. If you want to drop us, go ahead; I'll not denounce you. I have an order to deliver the prisoner and I'm doing so. And now you'll just sign this paper for me."

"There's no need. I'll not deny that you left him with me."

"Don't be mean with me. I know you'll tell the truth. You're from hereabouts and you are a man. But you must sign, that's the rule."

Daru opened his drawer, took out a little square bottle of purple ink, the red wooden penholder with the "sergeant-major" pen he used for making models of penmanship, and signed. The gendarme carefully folded the paper and put it into his wallet. Then he moved toward the door.

"I'll see you off," Daru said.

"No," said Balducci. "There's no use being polite. You insulted me."

He looked at the Arab, motionless in the same spot, sniffed peevishly, and turned away toward the door. "Good-by, son," he said. The door shut behind him. Balducci appeared suddenly outside the window and then disappeared. His footsteps were muffled by the snow. The horse stirred on the other side of the wall and several chickens fluttered in fright. A moment later Balducci reappeared outside the window leading the horse by the bridle. He walked toward the little rise without turning around and disappeared from sight with the horse following him. A big stone could be heard bouncing down. Daru walked back toward the prisoner, who, without stirring, never took his eyes off him. "Wait," the schoolmaster said in Arabic and went toward the bedroom. As he was going through the door, he had a second thought, went to the desk, took the revolver, and stuck it in his pocket. Then, without looking back, he went into his room.

For some time he lay on his couch watching the sky gradually close over, listening to the silence. It was this silence that had seemed painful to him during the first days here, after the war. He had requested a post in the little town at the base of the foothills separating the upper plateaus from the desert. There, rocky walls, green and black to the north, pink and lavender to the south, marked the frontier of eternal summer. He had been named to a post farther north, on the plateau itself. In the beginning, the solitude and the silence had been hard for him on these wastelands peopled only by stones. Occasionally, furrows suggested cultivation, but they had been dug to uncover a certain kind of stone good for building. The only plowing here was to harvest rocks. Elsewhere a thin layer of soil accumulated in the hollows would be scraped out to enrich paltry village gardens. This is the way it was: bare rock covered three quarters of the region. Towns sprang up, flourished, then disappeared; men came by, loved one another or fought bitterly, then died. No one in this desert, neither he nor his guest, mattered. And yet, outside this desert neither of them, Daru knew, could have really lived.

When he got up, no noise came from the classroom. He was amazed at the unmixed joy he derived from the mere thought that the Arab might have fled and that he would be alone with no decision to make. But the prisoner was there. He had merely stretched out between the stove and the desk. With eyes open, he was staring at the ceiling. In that position, his thick lips were particularly noticeable, giving him a pouting look. "Come," said Daru. The Arab got up and followed him. In the bedroom, the schoolmaster pointed to a chair near the table under the window. The Arab sat down without taking his eyes off Daru.

"Are you hungry?"

"Yes," the prisoner said.

Daru set the table for two. He took flour and oil, shaped a cake in a frying-pan, and lighted the little stove that functioned on bottled gas. While the cake was cooking, he went out to the shed to get cheese, eggs, dates, and condensed milk. When the cake was done he set it on the window sill to cool, heated some condensed milk diluted with water, and beat up the eggs into an omelette. In one of his motions he knocked against the revolver stuck in his right pocket. He set the bowl down, went into the classroom, and put the revolver in his desk drawer. When he came back to the room, night was falling. He put on the light and served the Arab. "Eat," he said. The Arab took a piece of the cake, lifted it eagerly to his mouth, and stopped short.

"And you?" he asked.

"After you. I'll eat too."

The thick lips opened slightly. The Arab hesitated, then bit into the cake determinedly.

The meal over, the Arab looked at the schoolmaster. "Are you the judge?"

"No, I'm simply keeping you until tomorrow."

"Why do you eat with me?"

"I'm hungry."

The Arab fell silent. Daru got up and went out. He brought back a folding bed from the shed, set it up between the table and the stove, perpendicular to his own bed. From a large suitcase which, upright in a corner, served as a shelf for papers, he took two blankets and arranged them on the camp bed. Then he stopped, felt useless, and sat down on his bed. There was nothing more to do or to get ready. He had to look at this man. He looked at him, therefore, trying to imagine his face bursting with rage. He couldn't do so. He could see nothing but the dark yet shining eyes and the animal mouth.

"Why did you kill him?" he asked in a voice whose hostile tone surprised him.

The Arab looked away.

"He ran away. I ran after him."

He raised his eyes to Daru again and they were full of a sort of woeful interrogation. "Now what will they do to me?"

"Are you afraid?"

He stiffened, turning his eyes away.

"Are you sorry?"

The Arab stared at him openmouthed. Obviously he did not understand. Daru's annoyance was growing. At the same time he felt awkward and self-conscious with his big body wedged between the two beds.

"Lie down there," he said impatiently. "That's your bed."

The Arab didn't move. He called to Daru:

"Tell me!"

The schoolmaster looked at him.

"Is the gendarme coming back tomorrow?"

"I don't know."

"Are you coming with us?"

"I don't know. Why?"

The prisoner got up and stretched out on top of the blankets, his feet toward the window. The light from the electric bulb shone straight into his eyes and he closed them at once.

"Why?" Daru repeated, standing beside the bed.

   The Arab opened his eyes under the blinding light and looked at him, trying not to blink.

"Come with us," he said.

In the middle of the night, Daru was still not asleep. He had gone to bed after undressing completely; he generally slept naked. But when he suddenly realized that he had nothing on, he hesitated. He felt vulnerable and the temptation came to him to put his clothes back on. Then he shrugged his shoulders; after all, he wasn't a child and, if need be, he could break his adversary in two. From his bed he could observe him, lying on his back, still motionless with his eyes closed under the harsh light. When Daru turned out the light, the darkness seemed to coagulate all of a sudden. Little by little, the night came back to life in the window where the starless sky was stirring gently. The schoolmaster soon made out the body lying at his feet. The Arab still did not move, but his eyes seemed open. A faint wind was prowling around the schoolhouse. Perhaps it would drive away the clouds and the sun would reappear.

   During the night the wind increased. The hens fluttered a little and then were silent. The Arab turned over on his side with his back to Daru, who thought he heard him moan. Then he listened for his guest's breathing, become heavier and more regular. He listened to that breath so close to him and mused without being able to go to sleep. In this room where he had been sleeping alone for a year, this presence bothered him. But it bothered him also by imposing on him a sort of brotherhood he knew well but refused to accept in the present circumstances. Men who share the same rooms, soldiers or prisoners, develop a strange alliance as if, having cast off their armor with their clothing, they fraternized every evening, over and above their differences, in the ancient community of dream and fatigue. But Daru shook himself; he didn't like such musings, and it was essential to sleep.

   A little later, however, when the Arab stirred slightly, the schoolmaster was still not asleep. When the prisoner made a second move, he stiffened, on the alert. The Arab was lifting himself slowly on his arms with almost the motion of a sleepwalker. Seated upright in bed, he waited motionless without turning his head toward Daru, as if he were listening attentively. Daru did not stir; it had just occurred to him that the revolver was still in the drawer of his desk. It was better to act at once. Yet he continued to observe the prisoner, who, with the same slithery motion, put his feet on the ground, waited again, then began to stand up slowly. Daru was about to call out to him when the Arab began to walk, in a quite natural but extraordinarily silent way. He was heading toward the door at the end of the room that opened into the shed. He lifted the latch with precaution and went out, pushing the door behind him but without shutting it. Daru had not stirred.

"He is running away," he merely thought. "Good riddance!" Yet he listened attentively. The hens were not fluttering; the guest must be on the plateau. A faint sound of water reached him, and he didn't know what it was until the Arab again stood framed in the doorway, closed the door carefully, and came back to bed without a sound. Then Daru turned his back on him and fell asleep. Still later he seemed, from the depths of his sleep, to hear furtive steps around the schoolhouse. "I'm dreaming! I'm dreaming!" he repeated to himself. And he went on sleeping.

When he awoke, the sky was clear; the loose window let in a cold, pure air. The Arab was asleep, hunched up under the blankets now, his mouth open, utterly relaxed. But when Daru shook him, he started dreadfully, staring at Daru with wild eyes as if he had never seen him and such a frightened expression that the schoolmaster stepped back. "Don't be afraid. It's me. You must eat." The Arab nodded his head and said yes. Calm had returned to his face, but his expression was vacant and listless.

The coffee was ready. They drank it seated together on the folding bed as they munched their pieces of the cake. Then Daru led the Arab under the shed and showed him the faucet where he washed. He went back into the room, folded the blankets and the bed, made his own bed and put the room in order. Then he went through the classroom and out onto the terrace. The sun was already rising in the blue sky; a soft, bright light was bathing the deserted plateau. On the ridge the snow was melting in spots. The stones were about to reappear. Crouched on the edge of the plateau, the schoolmaster looked at the deserted expanse. He thought of Balducci. He had hurt him, for he had sent him off in a way as if he didn't want to be associated with him. He could still hear the gendarme's farewell and, without knowing why, he felt strangely empty and vulnerable. At that moment, from the other side of the schoolhouse, the prisoner coughed. Daru listened to him almost despite himself and then, furious, threw a pebble that whistled through the air before sinking into the snow. That man's stupid crime revolted him, but to hand him over was contrary to honor. Merely thinking of it made him smart with humiliation. And he cursed at one and the same time his own people who had sent him this Arab and the Arab too who had dared to kill and not managed to get away. Daru got up, walked in a circle on the terrace, waited motionless, and then went back into the schoolhouse.

The Arab, leaning over the cement floor of the shed, was washing his teeth with two fingers. Daru looked at him and said: "Come." He went back into the room ahead of the prisoner. He slipped a hunting-jacket on over his sweater and put on walking-shoes. Standing, he waited until the Arab had put on his *chèche* and sandals. They went into the classroom and the schoolmaster pointed to the exit, saying: "Go ahead." The fellow didn't budge. "I'm coming," said Daru. The Arab went out. Daru went back into the room and made a package of pieces of rusk, dates, and sugar. In the classroom, before going out, he hesitated a second in front of his desk, then crossed the threshold and locked the door. "That's the way," he said. He started toward the east, followed by the prisoner. But, a short distance from the schoolhouse, he thought he heard a slight sound behind them. He retraced his steps and examined the surroundings of the house; there was no one there. The Arab watched him without seeming to understand. "Come on," said Daru.

They walked for an hour and rested beside a sharp peak of limestone. The snow was melting faster and faster and the sun was drinking up the puddles at once, rapidly cleaning the plateau, which gradually dried and vibrated like the air itself. When they resumed walking, the ground rang under their feet. From time to time a bird rent the space in front of them with a joyful cry. Daru breathed in deeply the fresh morning light. He felt a sort of rapture before the vast familiar expanse, now almost entirely yellow under its dome of blue sky. They walked an hour more, descending toward the south. They reached a level height made up of crumbly rocks. From there on, the plateau sloped down, eastward, toward a low plain where there were a few spindly trees and, to the south, toward outcroppings of rock that gave the landscape a chaotic look.

Daru surveyed the two directions. There was nothing but the sky on the horizon. Not a man could be seen. He turned toward the Arab, who was looking at him blankly. Daru held out the package to him. "Take it," he said. "There are dates, bread, and sugar. You can hold out for two days. Here are a thousand francs too." The Arab took the package and the money but kept his full hands at chest level as if he didn't know what to do with what was being given him. "Now look," the schoolmaster said as he pointed in the direction of the east, "there's the way to Tinguit. You have a two-hour walk. At Tinguit you'll find the administration and the police. They are expecting you." The Arab looked toward the east, still holding the package and the money against his chest. Daru took his elbow and turned him rather roughly toward the south. At the foot of the height on which they stood could be seen a faint path. "That's the trail across the plateau. In a day's walk from here you'll find pasturelands and the first nomads. They'll take you in and shelter you according to their law." The Arab had now turned toward Daru and a sort of panic was visible in his expression. "Listen," he said. Daru shook his head: "No, be quiet. Now I'm leaving you." He turned his back on him, took two long steps in the direction of the school, looked hesitantly at the motionless Arab, and started off again. For a few minutes he heard nothing but his own step resounding on the cold ground and did not turn his head. A moment later, however, he turned around. The Arab was still there on the edge of the hill, his arms hanging now, and he was looking at the schoolmaster. Daru felt something rise in his throat. But he swore with impatience, waved vaguely, and started off again. There was no longer anyone on the hill.

Daru hesitated. The sun was now rather high in the sky and was beginning to beat down on his head. The schoolmaster retraced his steps, at first
somewhat uncertainly, then with decision. When he reached the little hill,
he was bathed in sweat. He climbed it as fast as he could and stopped, out
of breath, at the top. The rock-fields to the south stood out sharply against
the blue sky, but on the plain to the east a steamy heat was already rising.
And in that slight haze, Daru, with heavy heart, made out the Arab walking
slowly on the road to prison.

A little later, standing before the window of the classroom, the schoolmaster was watching the clear light bathing the whole surface of the plateau, but he hardly saw it. Behind him on the blackboard, among the
winding French rivers, sprawled the clumsily chalked-up words he had just
read: "You handed over our brother. You will pay for this." Daru looked at
the sky, the plateau, and, beyond, the invisible lands stretching all the way
to the sea. In this vast landscape he had loved so much, he was alone.

What We Talk About When We Talk About Love

RAYMOND CARVER

My friend Mel McGinnis was talking. Mel McGinnis is a cardiologist, and sometimes that gives him the right.

The four of us were sitting around his kitchen table drinking gin. Sunlight filled the kitchen from the big window behind the sink. There were Mel and me and his second wife, Teresa—Terri, we called her—and my wife, Laura. We lived in Albuquerque then. But we were all from somewhere else.

There was an ice bucket on the table. The gin and the tonic water kept going around, and we somehow got on the subject of love. Mel thought real love was nothing less than spiritual love. He said he'd spent five years in a seminary before quitting to go to medical school. He said he still looked back on those years in the seminary as the most important years in his life.

Terri said the man she lived with before she lived with Mel loved her so much he tried to kill her. Then Terri said, "He beat me up one night. He dragged me around the living room by my ankles. He kept saying, 'I love you, I love you, you bitch.' He went on dragging me around the living room. My head kept knocking on things." Terri looked around the table. "What do you do with love like that?"

She was a bone-thin woman with a pretty face, dark eyes, and brown hair that hung down her back. She liked necklaces made of turquoise, and long pendant earrings.

"My God, don't be silly. That's not love, and you know it," Mel said. "I don't know what you'd call it, but I sure know you wouldn't call it love."

"Say what you want to, but I know it was," Terri said. "It may sound crazy to you, but it's true just the same. People are different, Mel. Sure, sometimes he may have acted crazy. Okay. But he loved me. In his own way maybe, but he loved me. There was love there, Mel. Don't say there wasn't."

Mel let out his breath. He held his glass and turned to Laura and me. "The man threatened to kill me," Mel said. He finished his drink and reached for the gin bottle. "Terri's a romantic. Terri's of the kick-me-so-I'll-know-you-love-me school. Terri, hon, don't look that way." Mel reached across the table and touched Terri's cheek with his fingers. He grinned at her.

"Now he wants to make up," Terri said.

"Make up what?" Mel said. "What is there to make up? I know what I know. That's all."

"How'd we get started on this subject, anyway?" Terri said. She raised her glass and drank from it. "Mel always has love on his mind," she said. "Don't you, honey?" She smiled. And I thought that was the last of it.

"I just wouldn't call Ed's behavior love. That's all I'm saying, honey," Mel said. "What about you guys?" Mel said to Laura and me. "Does that sound like love to you?"

"I'm the wrong person to ask," I said. "I didn't even know the man. I've only heard his name mentioned in passing. I wouldn't know. You'd have to know the particulars. But I think what you're saying is that love is an absolute."

Mel said, "The kind of love I'm talking about is. The kind of love I'm talking about, you don't try to kill people."

Laura said, "I don't know anything about Ed, or anything about the situation. But who can judge anyone else's situation?"

I touched the back of Laura's hand. She gave me a quick smile. I picked up Laura's hand. It was warm, the nails polished, perfectly manicured. I encircled the broad wrist with my fingers, and I held her.

"When I left, he drank rat poison," Terri said. She clasped her arms with her hands. "They took him to the hospital in Santa Fe. That's where we lived then, about ten miles out. They saved his life. But his gums went crazy from it. I mean they pulled away from his teeth. After that, his teeth stood out like fangs. My God," Terri said. She waited a minute, then let go of her arms and picked up her glass.

"What people won't do!" Laura said.

"He's out of the action now," Mel said. "He's dead."

Mel handed me the saucer of limes. I took a section, squeezed it over my drink, and stirred the ice cubes with my finger.

"It gets worse," Terri said. "He shot himself in the mouth. But he bungled that too. Poor Ed," she said. Terri shook her head.

"Poor Ed nothing," Mel said. "He was dangerous."

Mel was forty-five years old. He was tall and rangy with curly soft hair. His face and arms were brown from the tennis he played. When he was sober, his gestures, all his movements, were precise, very careful.

"He did love me though, Mel. Grant me that," Terri said. "That's all I'm asking. He didn't love me the way you love me. I'm not saying that. But he loved me. You can grant me that, can't you?"

"What do you mean, he bungled it?" I said.

Laura leaned forward with her glass. She put her elbows on the table and held her glass in both hands. She glanced from Mel to Terri and waited with a look of bewilderment on her open face, as if amazed that such things happened to people you were friendly with.

"How'd he bungle it when he killed himself?" I said.

"I'll tell you what happened," Mel said. "He took this twenty-two pistol he'd bought to threaten Terri and me with. Oh, I'm serious, the man was always threatening. You should have seen the way we lived in those days. Like fugitives. I even bought a gun myself. Can you believe it? A guy like me? But I did. I bought one for self-defense and carried it in the glove compartment. Sometimes I'd have to leave the apartment in the middle of the night. To go to the hospital, you know? Terri and I weren't married then, and my first wife had the house and kids, the dog, everything, and Terri and I were living in this apartment here. Sometimes, as I say, I'd get a call in the middle of the night and have to go in to the hospital at two or three in the morning. It'd be dark out there in the parking lot, and I'd break into a sweat before I could even get to my car. I never knew if he was going to come up out of the shrubbery or from behind a car and start shooting. I mean, the man was crazy. He was capable of wiring a bomb, anything. He used to call my service at all hours and say he needed to talk to the doctor, and when I'd return the call, he'd say, 'Son of a bitch, your days are numbered.' Little things like that. It was scary, I'm telling you."

"I still feel sorry for him," Terri said.

"It sounds like a nightmare," Laura said. "But what exactly happened after he shot himself?"

Laura is a legal secretary. We'd met in a professional capacity. Before we knew it, it was a courtship. She's thirty-five, three years younger than I am. In addition to being in love, we like each other and enjoy one another's company. She's easy to be with.

"What happened?" Laura said.

Mel said, "He shot himself in the mouth in his room. Someone heard the shot and told the manager. They came in with a passkey, saw what had happened, and called an ambulance. I happened to be there when they brought him in, alive but past recall. The man lived for three days. His head swelled up to twice the size of a normal head. I'd never seen anything like it, and I hope I never do again. Terri wanted to go in and sit with him when she found out about it. We had a fight over it. I didn't think she should see him like that. I didn't think she should see him, and I still don't."

"Who won the fight?" Laura asked.

"I was in the room with him when he died," Terri said. "He never came up out of it. But I sat with him. He didn't have anyone else."

"He was dangerous," Mel said. "If you call that love, you can have it."

"It was love," Terri said. "Sure, it's abnormal in most people's eyes. But he was willing to die for it. He did die for it."

"I sure as hell wouldn't call it love," Mel said. "I mean, no one knows what he did it for. I've seen a lot of suicides, and I couldn't say anyone ever knew what they did it for."

Mel put his hands behind his neck and tilted his chair back. "I'm not interested in that kind of love," he said. "If that's love, you can have it."

Terri said, "We were afraid. Mel even made a will out and wrote to his brother in California who used to be a Green Beret. Mel told him who to look for if something happened to him."

Terri drank from her glass. She said, "But Mel's right—we lived like fugitives. We were afraid. Mel was, weren't you, honey? I even called the police at one point, but they were no help. They said they couldn't do anything until Ed actually did something. Isn't that a laugh?" Terri said.

She poured the last of the gin into her glass and waggled the bottle. Mel got up from the table and went to the cupboard. He took down another bottle.

"Well, Nick and I know what love is," Laura said. "For us, I mean," Laura said. She bumped my knee with her knee. "You're supposed to say something now," Laura said, and turned her smile on me.

For an answer, I took Laura's hand and raised it to my lips. I made a big production out of kissing her hand. Everyone was amused.

"We're lucky," I said.

"You guys," Terri said. "Stop that now. You're making me sick. You're still on the honeymoon, for God's sake. You're still gaga, for crying out loud. Just wait. How long have you been together now? How long has it been? A year? Longer than a year?"

"Going on a year and a half," Laura said, flushed and smiling.

"Oh, now," Terri said. "Wait awhile."

She held her drink and gazed at Laura.

"I'm only kidding," Terri said.

Mel opened the gin and went around the table with the bottle.

"Here, you guys," he said. "Let's have a toast. I want to propose a toast. A toast to love. To true love," Mel said.

We touched glasses.

"To love," we said.

Outside in the backyard, one of the dogs began to bark. The leaves of the aspen that leaned past the window ticked against the glass. The afternoon sun was like a presence in this room, the spacious light of ease and generosity. We could have been anywhere, somewhere enchanted. We raised our glasses again and grinned at each other like children who had agreed on something forbidden.

"I'll tell you what real love is," Mel said. "I mean, I'll give you a good example. And then you can draw your own conclusions." He poured more gin into his glass. He added an ice cube and a sliver of lime. We waited and sipped our drinks. Laura and I touched knees again. I put a hand on her warm thigh and left it there.

"What do any of us really know about love?" Mel said. "It seems to me we're just beginners at love. We say we love each other and we do, I don't doubt it. I love Terri and Terri loves me, and you guys love each other too. You know the kind of love I'm talking about now. Physical love, that impulse that drives you to someone special, as well as love of the other person's being, his or her essence, as it were. Carnal love and, well, call it sentimental love, the day-to-day caring about the other person. But sometimes I have a hard time accounting for the fact that I must have loved my first wife too. But I did, I know I did. So I suppose I am like Terri in that regard. Terri and Ed." He thought about it and then he went on. "There was a time when I thought I loved my first wife more than life itself. But now I hate her guts. I do. How do you explain that? What happened to that love? What happened to it, is what I'd like to know. I wish someone could tell me. Then there's Ed. Okay, we're back to Ed. He loves Terri so much he tries to kill her and he winds up killing himself." Mel stopped talking and swallowed from his glass. "You guys have been together eighteen months and you love each other. It shows all over you. You glow with it. But you both loved other people before you met each other. You've both been married before, just like us. And you probably loved other people before that too, even. Terri and I have been together five years, been married for four. And the terrible thing, the terrible thing is, but the good thing too, the saving grace you might say, is that if something happened to one of us—excuse me for saying this—but if something happened to one of us tomorrow, I think the other one, the other person, would grieve for a while, you know, but then the surviving party would go out and love again, have someone else soon enough. All this, all of this love we're talking about, it would just be a memory. Maybe not even a memory. Am I wrong? Am I way off base? Because I want you to set me straight if you think I'm wrong. I want to know. I mean, I don't know anything, and I'm the first one to admit it."

"Mel, for God's sake," Terri said. She reached out and took hold of his wrist. "Are you getting drunk? Honey? Are you drunk?"

"Honey, I'm just talking," Mel said. "All right? I don't have to be drunk to say what I think. I mean, we're all just talking, right?" Mel said. He fixed his eyes on her.

"Sweetie, I'm not criticizing," Terri said.

She picked up her glass.

"I'm not on call today," Mel said. "Let me remind you of that. I am not on call," he said.

"Mel, we love you," Laura said.

Mel looked at Laura. He looked at her as if he could not place her, as if she was not the woman she was.

"Love you too, Laura," Mel said. "And you, Nick, love you too. You know something?" Mel said. "You guys are our pals," Mel said.

He picked up his glass.

Mel said, "I was going to tell you about something. I mean, I was going to prove a point. You see, this happened a few months ago, but it's still going on right now, and it ought to make us feel ashamed when we talk like we know what we're talking about when we talk about love."

"Come on now," Terri said. "Don't talk like you're drunk if you're not drunk."

"Just shut up for once in your life," Mel said very quietly. "Will you do me a favor and do that for a minute? So as I was saying, there's this old couple who had this car wreck out on the interstate. A kid hit them and they were all torn to shit and nobody was giving them much chance to pull through."

Terri looked at us and then back at Mel. She seemed anxious, or maybe that's too strong a word.

Mel was handing the bottle around the table.

"I was on call that night," Mel said. "It was May or maybe it was June. Terri and I had just sat down to dinner when the hospital called. There'd been this thing out on the interstate. Drunk kid, teenager, plowed his dad's pickup into this camper with this old couple in it. They were up in their mid-seventies, that couple. The kid—eighteen, nineteen, something—he was DOA. Taken the steering wheel through his sternum. The old couple, they were alive, you understand. I mean, just barely. But they had everything. Multiple fractures, internal injuries, hemorrhaging, contusions, lacerations, the works, and they each of them had themselves concussions. They were in a bad way, believe me. And, of course, their age was two strikes against them. I'd say she was worse off than he was. Ruptured spleen along with everything else. Both kneecaps broken. But they'd been wearing their seatbelts and, God knows, that's what saved them for the time being."

"Folks, this is an advertisement for the National Safety Council," Terri said. "This is your spokesman, Dr. Melvin R. McGinnis, talking." Terri laughed. "Mel," she said, "sometimes you're just too much. But I love you, hon," she said.

"Honey, I love you," Mel said.

He leaned across the table. Terri met him halfway. They kissed.

"Terri's right," Mel said as he settled himself again. "Get those seatbelts on. But seriously, they were in some shape, those oldsters. By the time I got down there, the kid was dead, as I said. He was off in a corner, laid out on a gurney. I took one look at the old couple and told the ER nurse to get me a neurologist and an orthopedic man and a couple of surgeons down there right away."

He drank from his glass. "I'll try to keep this short," he said. "So we took the two of them up to the OR and worked like fuck on them most of the night. They had these incredible reserves, those two. You see that once in a while. So we did everything that could be done, and toward morning we're giving them a fifty-fifty chance, maybe less than that for her. So here they are, still alive the next morning. So, okay, we move them into the ICU, which is where they both kept plugging away at it for two weeks, hitting it better and better on all the scopes. So we transfer them out to their own room."

Mel stopped talking. "Here," he said, "let's drink this cheapo gin the hell up. Then we're going to dinner, right? Terri and I know a new place. That's where we'll go, to this new place we know about. But we're not going until we finish up this cut-rate, lousy gin."

Terri said, "We haven't actually eaten there yet. But it looks good. From the outside, you know."

"I like food," Mel said. "If I had it to do all over again, I'd be a chef, you know? Right, Terri?" Mel said.

He laughed. He fingered the ice in his glass.

"Terri knows," he said. "Terri can tell you. But let me say this. If I could come back again in a different life, a different time and all, you know what? I'd like to come back as a knight. You were pretty safe wearing all that armor. It was all right being a knight until gunpowder and muskets and pistols came along."

"Mel would like to ride a horse and carry a lance," Terri said.

"Carry a woman's scarf with you everywhere," Laura said.

"Or just a woman," Mel said.

"Shame on you," Laura said.

Terri said, "Suppose you came back as a serf. The serfs didn't have it so good in those days," Terri said.

"The serfs never had it good," Mel said. "But I guess even the knights were vessels to someone. Isn't that the way it worked? But then everyone is always a vessel to someone. Isn't that right? Terri? But what I liked about knights, besides their ladies, was that they had that suit of armor, you know, and they couldn't get hurt very easy. No cars in those days, you know? No drunk teenagers to tear into your ass."

"Vassals," Terri said.

"What?" Mel said.

"Vassals," Terri said. "They were called vassals, not vessels."

"Vassals, vessels," Mel said, "what the fuck's the difference? You knew what I meant anyway. All right," Mel said. "So I'm not educated. I learned my stuff. I'm a heart surgeon, sure, but I'm just a mechanic. I go in and I fuck around and I fix things. Shit," Mel said.

"Modesty doesn't become you," Terri said.

"He's just a humble sawbones," I said. "But sometimes they suffocated in all that armor, Mel. They'd even have heart attacks if it got too hot and they were too tired and worn out. I read somewhere that they'd fall off their horses and not be able to get up because they were too tired to stand with all that armor on them. They got trampled by their own horses sometimes."

"That's terrible," Mel said. "That's a terrible thing, Nicky. I guess they'd just lay there and wait until somebody came along and made a shish kebab out of them."

"Some other vessel," Terri said.

"That's right," Mel said. "Some vassal would come along and spear the bastard in the name of love. Or whatever the fuck it was they fought over in those days."

"Same things we fight over these days," Terri said.

Laura said, "Nothing's changed."

The color was still high in Laura's cheeks. Her eyes were bright. She brought her glass to her lips.

Mel poured himself another drink. He looked at the label closely as if studying a long row of numbers. Then he slowly put the bottle down on the table and slowly reached for the tonic water.

"What about the old couple?" Laura said. "You didn't finish that story you started."

Laura was having a hard time lighting her cigarette. Her matches kept going out.

The sunshine inside the room was different now, changing, getting thinner. But the leaves outside the window were still shimmering, and I stared at the pattern they made on the panes and on the Formica counter. They weren't the same patterns, of course.

"What about the old couple?" I said.

"Older but wiser," Terri said.

Mel stared at her.

Terri said, "Go on with your story, hon. I was only kidding. Then what happened?"

"Terri, sometimes," Mel said.

"Please, Mel," Terri said. "Don't always be so serious, sweetie. Can't you take a joke?"

"Where's the joke?" Mel said.

He held his glass and gazed steadily at his wife.

"What happened?" Laura said.

Mel fastened his eyes on Laura. He said, "Laura, if I didn't have Terri and if I didn't love her so much, and if Nick wasn't my best friend, I'd fall in love with you. I'd carry you off, honey," he said.

"Tell your story," Terri said. "Then we'll go to that new place, okay?"

"Okay," Mel said. "Where was I?" he said. He stared at the table and then he began again.

"I dropped in to see each of them every day, sometimes twice a day if I was up doing other calls anyway. Casts and bandages, head to foot, the both of them. You know, you've seen it in the movies. That's just the way they looked, just like in the movies. Little eye-holes and nose-holes and mouth-holes. And she had to have her legs slung up on top of it. Well, the husband was very depressed for the longest while. Even after he found out that his wife was going to pull through, he was still very depressed. Not about the accident, though. I mean, the accident was one thing, but it wasn't every-thing. I'd get up to his mouth-hole, you know, and he'd say no, it wasn't the accident exactly but it was because he couldn't see her through his eye-holes. He said that was what was making him feel so bad. Can you imagine? I'm telling you, the man's heart was breaking because he couldn't turn his goddamn head and see his goddamn wife."

Mel looked around the table and shook his head at what he was going to say.

"I mean, it was killing the old fart just because he couldn't *look* at the fucking woman."

We all looked at Mel.

"Do you see what I'm saying?" he said.

Maybe we were a little drunk by then. I know it was hard keeping things in focus. The light was draining out of the room, going back through the window where it had come from. Yet nobody made a move to get up from the table to turn on the overhead light.

"Listen," Mel said. "Let's finish this fucking gin. There's about enough left here for one shooter all around. Then let's go eat. Let's go to the new place."

"He's depressed," Terri said. "Mel, why don't you take a pill?"

Mel shook his head. "I've taken everything there is."

"We all need a pill now and then," I said.

"Some people are born needing them," Terri said.

She was using her finger to rub at something on the table. Then she stopped rubbing.

"I think I want to call my kids," Mel said. "Is that all right with every-body? I'll call my kids," he said.

Terri said, "What if Marjorie answers the phone? You guys, you've heard us on the subject of Marjorie? Honey, you know you don't want to talk to Marjorie. It'll make you feel even worse."

"I don't want to talk to Marjorie," Mel said. "But I want to talk to my kids."

"There isn't a day goes by that Mel doesn't say he wishes she'd get married again. Or else die," Terri said. "For one thing," Terri said, "she's bankrupting us. Mel says it's just to spite him that she won't get married again. She has a boyfriend who lives with her and the kids, so Mel is supporting the boyfriend too."

"She's allergic to bees," Mel said. "If I'm not praying she'll get married again, I'm praying she'll get herself stung to death by a swarm of fucking bees."

"Shame on you," Laura said.

"Bzzzzzzz," Mel said, turning his fingers into bees and buzzing them at Terri's throat. Then he let his hands drop all the way to his sides.

"She's vicious," Mel said. "Sometimes I think I'll go up there dressed like a beekeeper. You know, that hat that's like a helmet with the plate that comes down over your face, the big gloves, and the padded coat? I'll knock on the door and let loose a hive of bees in the house. But first I'd make sure the kids were out, of course."

He crossed one leg over the other. It seemed to take him a lot of time to do it. Then he put both feet on the floor and leaned forward, elbows on the table, his chin cupped in his hands.

"Maybe I won't call the kids, after all. Maybe it isn't such a hot idea. Maybe we'll just go eat. How does that sound?"

"Sounds fine to me," I said. "Eat or not eat. Or keep drinking. I could head right on out into the sunset."

"What does that mean, honey?" Laura said.

"It just means what I said," I said. "It means I could just keep going. That's all it means."

"I could eat something myself," Laura said. "I don't think I've ever been so hungry in my life. Is there something to nibble on?"

"I'll put out some cheese and crackers," Terri said.

But Terri just sat there. She did not get up to get anything.

Mel turned his glass over. He spilled it out on the table.

"Gin's gone," Mel said.

Terri said, "Now what?"

I could hear my heart beating. I could hear everyone's heart. I could hear the human noise we sat there making, not one of us moving, not even when the room went dark.

Paul's Case

WILLA CATHER

It was Paul's afternoon to appear before the faculty of the Pittsburgh High
School to account for his various misdemeanors. He had been suspended a
week ago, and his father had called at the Principal's office and confessed
his perplexity about his son. Paul entered the faculty room suave and smiling. His clothes were a trifle outgrown, and the tan velvet on the collar of
his open overcoat was frayed and worn; but for all that there was something of the dandy about him, and he wore an opal pin in his neatly knotted
black four-in-hand, and a red carnation in his buttonhole. This latter
adornment the faculty somehow felt was not properly significant of the
contrite spirit befitting a boy under the ban of suspension.

Paul was tall for his age and very thin, with high, cramped shoulders and
a narrow chest. His eyes were remarkable for a certain hysterical brilliancy,
and he continually used them in a conscious, theatrical sort of way, pecu-
liarly offensive in a boy. The pupils were abnormally large, as though he
were addicted to belladonna, but there was a glassy glitter about them
which that drug does not produce.

When questioned by the Principal as to why he was there, Paul stated, politely enough, that he wanted to come back to school. This was a lie, but
Paul was quite accustomed to lying; found it, indeed, indispensable for
overcoming friction. His teachers were asked to state their respective
charges against him, which they did with such a rancour and aggrievedness
as evinced that this was not a usual case. Disorder and impertinence were
among the offences named, yet each of his instructors felt that it was
scarcely possible to put into words the real cause of the trouble, which lay
in a sort of hysterically defiant manner of the boy's; in the contempt which
they all knew he felt for them, and which he seemingly made not the least
effort to conceal. Once, when he had been making a synopsis of a paragraph at the blackboard, his English teacher had stepped to his side and attempted to guide his hand. Paul had started back with a shudder and thrust

his hands violently behind him. The astonished woman could scarcely have been more hurt and embarrassed had he struck at her. The insult was so involuntary and definitely personal as to be unforgettable. In one way and another, he had made all his teachers, men and women alike, conscious of the same feeling of physical aversion. In one class he habitually sat with his hand shading his eyes; in another he always looked out of the window during the recitation; in another he made a running commentary on the lecture, with humorous intent.

His teachers felt this afternoon that his whole attitude was symbolized by his shrug and his flippantly red carnation flower, and they fell upon him without mercy, his English teacher leading the pack. He stood through it smiling, his pale lips parted over his white teeth. (His lips were continually twitching, and he had a habit of raising his eyebrows that was contemptuous and irritating to the last degree.) Older boys than Paul had broken down and shed tears under that ordeal, but his set smile did not once desert him, and his only sign of discomfort was the nervous trembling of the fingers that toyed with the buttons of his overcoat, and an occasional jerking of the other hand which held his hat. Paul was always smiling, always glancing about him, seeming to feel that people might be watching him and trying to detect something. This conscious expression, since it was as far as possible from boyish mirthfulness, was usually attributed to insolence or "smartness."

As the inquisition proceeded, one of his instructors repeated an impertinent remark of the boy's, and the Principal asked him whether he thought that a courteous speech to make to a woman. Paul shrugged his shoulders slightly and his eyebrows twitched.

"I don't know," he replied. "I didn't mean to be polite or impolite, either. I guess it's a sort of way I have, of saying things regardless."

The Principal asked him whether he didn't think that a way it would be well to get rid of. Paul grinned and said he guessed so. When he was told that he could go, he bowed gracefully and went out. His bow was like a repetition of the scandalous red carnation.

His teachers were in despair, and his drawing-master voiced the feeling of them all when he declared there was something about the boy which none of them understood. He added: "I don't really believe that smile of his comes altogether from insolence; there's something sort of haunted about it. The boy is not strong, for one thing. There is something wrong about the fellow."

The drawing-master had come to realize that, in looking at Paul, one saw only his white teeth and the forced animation of his eyes. One warm afternoon the boy had gone to sleep at his drawing-board, and his master had noted with amazement what a white, blue-veined face it was; drawn and wrinkled like an old man's about the eyes, the lips twitching even in his sleep.

His teachers left the building dissatisfied and unhappy; humiliated to have felt so vindictive toward a mere boy, to have uttered this feeling in cutting terms, and to have set each other on, as it were, in the gruesome game of intemperate reproach. One of them remembered having seen a miserable street cat set at bay by a ring of tormentors.

As for Paul, he ran down the hill whistling the Soldiers' Chorus from "Faust," looking behind him now and then to see whether some of his teachers were not there to witness his light-heartedness. As it was now late in the afternoon and Paul was on duty that evening as usher at Carnegie Hall, he decided that he would not go home to supper.

When he reached the concert hall, the doors were not yet open. It was chilly outside, and he decided to go up into the picture gallery—always deserted at this hour—where there were some of Raffelli's gay studies of Paris streets and an airy blue Venetian scene or two that always exhilarated him. He was delighted to find no one in the gallery but the old guard, who sat in the corner, a newspaper on his knee, a black patch over one eye and the other closed. Paul possessed himself of the place and walked confidently up and down, whistling under his breath. After a while he sat down before a blue Rico and lost himself. When he bethought him to look at his watch, it was after seven o'clock, and he rose with a start and ran downstairs, making a face at Augustus Caesar, peering out from the cast-room, and an evil gesture at the Venus of Milo as he passed her on the stairway.

When Paul reached the ushers' dressing-room, half a dozen boys were there already, and he began excitedly to tumble into his uniform. It was one of the few that at all approached fitting, and Paul thought it very becoming—though he knew the tight, straight coat accentuated his narrow chest, about which he was exceedingly sensitive. He was always excited while he dressed, twanging all over to the tuning of the strings and the preliminary flourishes of the horns in the music-room; but tonight he seemed quite beside himself, and he teased and plagued the boys until, telling him that he was crazy, they put him down on the floor and sat on him.

Somewhat calmed by his suppression, Paul dashed out to the front of the house to seat the early comers. He was a model usher. Gracious and smiling he ran up and down the aisles. Nothing was too much trouble for him; he carried messages and brought programmes as though it were his greatest pleasure in life, and all the people in his section thought him a charming boy, feeling that he remembered and admired them. As the house filled, he grew more and more vivacious and animated, and the colour came to his cheeks and lips. It was very much as though this were a great reception and Paul were the host. Just as the musicians came out to take their places, his English teacher arrived with cheques for the seats which a prominent manufacturer had taken for the season. She betrayed some embarrassment when she handed Paul the tickets, and a hauteur which subsequently made her feel very foolish. Paul was startled for a moment, and had the feeling of wanting to put her out; what business had she here among all these fine people and gay colours? He looked her over and decided that she was not appropriately dressed and must be a fool to sit downstairs in such togs. The tickets had probably been sent her out of kindness, he reflected, as he put down a seat for her, and she had about as much right to sit there as he had.

When the symphony began, Paul sank into one of the rear seats with a long sigh of relief, and lost himself as he had done before the Rico. It was not that symphonies, as such, meant anything in particular to Paul, but the first sight of the instruments seemed to free some hilarious spirit within him; something that struggled there like the Genius in the bottle found by the Arab fisherman. He felt a sudden zest of life; the lights danced before his eyes and the concert hall blazed into unimaginable splendour. When the soprano soloist came on, Paul forgot even the nastiness of his teacher's being there, and gave himself up to the peculiar intoxication such personages always had for him. The soloist chanced to be a German woman, by no means in her first youth, and the mother of many children; but she wore a satin gown and a tiara, and she had that indefinable air of achievement, that world-shine upon her, which always blinded Paul to any possible defects.

After a concert was over, Paul was often irritable and wretched until he got to sleep—and tonight he was even more than usually restless. He had the feeling of not being able to let down; of its being impossible to give up this delicious excitement which was the only thing that could be called living at all. During the last number he withdrew and, after hastily changing his clothes in the dressing-room, slipped out to the side door where the singer's carriage stood. Here he began pacing rapidly up and down the walk, waiting to see her come out.

Over yonder the Schenley, in its vacant stretch, loomed big and square through the fine rain, the windows of its twelve stories glowing like those of a lighted cardboard house under a Christmas tree. All the actors and singers of any importance stayed there when they were in Pittsburgh, and a number of the big manufacturers of the place lived there in the winter. Paul had often hung about the hotel, watching the people go in and out, longing to enter and leave schoolmasters and dull care behind him forever.

At last the singer came out, accompanied by the conductor, who helped her into her carriage and closed the door with a cordial *auf wiedersehen*— which set Paul to wondering whether she were not an old sweetheart of his. Paul followed the carriage over to the hotel, walking so rapidly as not to be far from the entrance when the singer alighted and disappeared behind the swinging glass doors which were opened by a Negro in a tall hat and a long coat. In the moment that the door was ajar, it seemed to Paul that he, too, entered. He seemed to feel himself go after her up the steps, into the warm, lighted building, into an exotic, a tropical world of shiny, glistening surfaces and basking ease. He reflected upon the mysterious dishes that were brought into the dining-room, the green bottles in buckets of ice, as he had seen them in the supper-party pictures of the Sunday supplement. A quick gust of wind brought the rain down with sudden vehemence, and Paul was startled to find that he was still outside in the slush of the gravel driveway; that his boots were letting in the water and his scanty overcoat was clinging wet about him; that the lights in front of the concert hall were out, and that the rain was driving in sheets between him and the orange glow of the windows above him. There it was, what he wanted—tangibly before him, like the fairy world of a Christmas pantomime; as the rain beat in his face, Paul wondered whether he were destined always to shiver in the black night outside, looking up at it.

He turned and walked reluctantly toward the car tracks. The end had to come sometime; his father in his night-clothes at the top of the stairs, explanations that did not explain, hastily improvised fictions that were forever tripping him up, his upstairs room and its horrible yellow wallpaper, the creaking bureau with the greasy plush collar-box, and over his painted wooden bed the pictures of George Washington and John Calvin, and the framed motto, 'Feed my Lambs,' which had been worked in red worsted by his mother, whom Paul could not remember.

Half an hour later, Paul alighted from the Negley Avenue car and went slowly down one of the side streets off the main thoroughfare. It was a highly respectable street, where all the houses were exactly alike, and where businessmen of moderate means begot and reared large families of children, all of whom went to Sabbath School and learned the shorter catechism, and were interested in arithmetic; all of whom were as exactly alike as their homes, and of a piece with the monotony in which they lived. Paul never went up Cordelia Street without a shudder of loathing. His home was next to the house of the Cumberland minister. He approached it tonight with the nerveless sense of defeat, the hopeless feeling of sinking back forever into ugliness and commonness that he had always had when he came home. The moment he turned into Cordelia Street he felt the waters close above his head. After each of these orgies of living, he experienced all the physical depression which follows a debauch; the loathing of respectable beds, of common food, of a house permeated by kitchen odours; a shuddering repulsion for the flavourless, colourless mass of every-day existence; a morbid desire for cool things and soft lights and fresh flowers.

The nearer he approached the house, the more absolutely unequal Paul felt to the sight of it all: his ugly sleeping chamber, the old bathroom with the grimy zinc tub, the cracked mirror, the dripping spigots; his father, at the top of the stairs, his hairy legs sticking out from his nightshirt, his feet thrust into carpet slippers. He was so much later than usual that there would certainly be enquiries and reproaches. Paul stopped short before the door. He felt that he could not be accosted by his father tonight, that he could not toss again on that miserable bed. He would not go in. He would tell his father that he had no car-fare, and it was raining so hard he had gone home with one of the boys and stayed all night.

Meanwhile, he was wet and cold. He went around to the back of the house and tried one of the basement windows, found it open, raised it cautiously, and scrambled down the cellar wall to the floor. There he stood, holding his breath, terrified by the noise he had made; but the floor above him was silent, and there was no creak on the stairs. He found a soap-box, and carried it over to the soft ring of light that streamed from the furnace door, and sat down. He was horribly afraid of rats, so he did not try to sleep, but sat looking distrustfully at the dark, still terrified lest he might have awakened his father.

In such reactions, after one of the experiences which made days and nights out of the dreary blanks of the calendar, when his senses were deadened, Paul's head was always singularly clear. Suppose his father had heard him getting in at the window and had come down and shot him for a burglar? Then, again, suppose his father had come down, pistol in hand, and he had cried out in time to save himself, and his father had been horrified to think how nearly he had killed him? Then again, suppose a day should come when his father would remember that night, and wish there had been no warning cry to stay his hand? With this last supposition Paul entertained himself until daybreak.

The following Sunday was fine; the sodden November chill was broken by the last flash of autumnal summer. In the morning Paul had to go to church and Sabbath School, as always. On seasonable Sunday afternoons the burghers of Cordelia Street usually sat out on their front "stoops," and talked to their neighbours on the next stoop, or called to those across the street in neighbourly fashion. The men sat placidly on gay cushions placed upon the steps that led down to the sidewalk, while the women, in their Sunday "waists," sat in rockers on the cramped porches, pretending to be greatly at their ease. The children played in the streets; there were so many of them that the place resembled the recreation grounds of a kindergarten. The men on the steps, all in their shirt-sleeves, their vests unbuttoned, sat with their legs well apart, their stomachs comfortably protruding, and talked of the prices of things, or told anecdotes of the sagacity of their various chiefs and overlords. They occasionally looked over the multitude of squabbling children, listened affectionately to their high-pitched, nasal voices, smiling to see their own proclivities reproduced in their offspring, and interspersed their legends of the iron kings with remarks about their sons' progress at school, their grades in arithmetic, and the amounts they had saved in their toy banks.

On this last Sunday of November, Paul sat all the afternoon on the lowest step of his "stoop," staring into the street, while his sisters, in their rockers, were talking to the minister's daughters next door about how many shirt-waists they had made in the last week, and how many waffles someone had eaten at the last church supper. When the weather was warm, and his father was in a particularly jovial frame of mind, the girls made lemonade, which was always brought out in a red-glass pitcher, ornamented with forget-me-nots in blue enamel. This the girls thought very fine, and the neighbours joked about the suspicious colour of the pitcher.

Today Paul's father, on the top step, was talking to a young man who shifted a restless baby from knee to knee. He happened to be the young man who was daily held up to Paul as a model, and after whom it was his father's dearest hope that he would pattern. This young man was of a ruddy complexion, with a compressed, red mouth, and faded, nearsighted eyes, over which he wore thick spectacles, with gold bows that curved about his ears. He was clerk to one of the magnates of a great steel corporation, and was looked upon in Cordelia Street as a young man with a future. There was a story that, some five years ago—he was now barely twenty-six—he had been a trifle "dissipated," but in order to curb his appetites and save the loss of time and strength that a sowing of wild oats might have entailed, he had taken his chief's advice, oft reiterated to his employees, and at twenty-one had married the first woman whom he could persuade to share his fortunes. She happened to be an angular schoolmistress, much older than he, who also wore thick glasses, and who had now borne him four children, all near-sighted like herself.

The young man was relating how his chief, now cruising in the Mediterranean, kept in touch with all the details of the business, arranging his office hours on his yacht just as though he were at home, and "knocking off work enough to keep two stenographers busy." His father told, in turn, the plan his corporation was considering, of putting in an electric railway plant at Cairo. Paul snapped his teeth; he had an awful apprehension that they might spoil it all before he got there. Yet he rather liked to hear these legends of the iron kings, that were told and retold on Sundays and holidays; these stories of palaces in Venice, yachts on the Mediterranean, and high play at Monte Carlo appealed to his fancy, and he was interested in the triumphs of cash-boys who had become famous though he had no mind for the cash-boy stage.

After supper was over, and he had helped to dry the dishes, Paul nervously asked his father whether he could go to George's to get some help in his geometry, and still more nervously asked for car-fare. This latter request he had to repeat, as his father, on principle, did not like to hear requests for money, whether much or little. He asked Paul whether he could not go to some boy who lived nearer, and told him that he ought not to leave his school work until Sunday; but he gave him the dime. He was not a poor man, but he had a worthy ambition to come up in the world. His only reason for allowing Paul to usher was that he thought a boy ought to be earning a little.

Paul bounded upstairs, scrubbed the greasy odour of the dishwater from his hands with the ill-smelling soap he hated, and then shook over his fingers a few drops of violet water from the bottle he kept hidden in his drawer. He left the house with his geometry conspicuously under his arm, and the moment he got out of Cordelia Street and boarded a downtown car, he shook off the lethargy of two deadening days, and began to live again.

The leading juvenile of the permanent stock company which played at one of the downtown theatres was an acquaintance of Paul's, and the boy had been invited to drop in at the Sunday-night rehearsals whenever he could. For more than a year Paul had spent every available moment loitering about Charley Edward's dressing-room. He had won a place among Edward's following not only because the young actor, who could not afford to employ a dresser, often found him useful, but because he recognized in Paul something akin to what churchmen term "vocation."

It was at the theatre and at Carnegie Hall that Paul really lived; the rest was but a sleep and a forgetting. This was Paul's fairy tale, and it had for him all the allurement of a secret love. The moment he inhaled the gassy, painty, dusty odour behind the scenes, he breathed like a prisoner set free, and felt within him the possibility of doing or saying splendid, brilliant things. The moment the cracked orchestra beat out the overture from *Martha,* or jerked at the serenade from *Rigoletto,* all stupid and ugly things slid from him, and his senses were deliciously, yet delicately fired.

Perhaps it was because, in Paul's world, the natural nearly always wore the guise of ugliness, that a certain element of artificiality seemed to him necessary in beauty. Perhaps it was because his experience of life elsewhere was so full of Sabbath-School picnics, petty economies, wholesome advice as to how to succeed in life, and the unescapable odours of cooking, that he found this existence so alluring, these smartly clad men and women so attractive, that he was so moved by these starry apple orchards that bloomed perennially under the limelight. It would be difficult to put it strongly enough how convincingly the stage entrance of that theatre was for Paul the actual portal of Romance. Certainly none of the company ever suspected it, least of all Charley Edwards. It was very like the old stories that used to float about London of fabulously rich Jews, who had subterranean halls, with palms, and fountains, and soft lamps and richly apparelled women who never saw the disenchanting light of London day. So, in the midst of that smoke-palled city, enamoured of figures and grimy toil, Paul had his secret temple, his wishing-carpet, his bit of blue-and-white Mediterranean shore bathed in perpetual sunshine.

Several of Paul's teachers had a theory that his imagination had been perverted by garish fiction; but the truth was he scarcely ever read at all. The books at home were not such as would either tempt or corrupt a youthful mind, and as for reading the novels that some of his friends urged upon him—well, he got what he wanted much more quickly from music;

any sort of music, from an orchestra to a barrel-organ. He needed only the spark, the indescribable thrill that made his imagination master of his senses, and he could make plots and pictures enough of his own. It was equally true that he was not stage-struck—not, at any rate, in the usual acceptation of that expression. He had no desire to become an actor, any more than he had to become a musician. He felt no necessity to do any of these things; what he wanted was to see, to be in the atmosphere, float on the wave of it, to be carried out, blue league after league, away from everything.

After a night behind the scenes, Paul found the schoolroom more than ever repulsive; the bare floors and naked walls; the prosy men who never wore frock coats, or violets in their buttonholes; the women with their dull gowns, shrill voices, and pitiful seriousness about prepositions that govern the dative. He could not bear to have the other pupils think, for a moment, that he took these people seriously; he must convey to them that he considered it all trivial, and was there only by way of a joke, anyway. He had autographed pictures of all the members of the stock company which he showed his classmates, telling them the most incredible stories of his familiarity with these people, of his acquaintance with the soloists who came to Carnegie Hall, his suppers with them and the flowers he sent them. When these stories lost their effect, and his audience grew listless, he would bid all the boys goodbye, announcing that he was going to travel for a while; going to Naples, to California, to Egypt. Then, next Monday, he would slip back, conscious and nervously smiling; his sister was ill, and he would have to defer his voyage until spring.

Matters went steadily worse with Paul at school. In the itch to let his instructors know how heartily he despised them, and how thoroughly he was appreciated elsewhere, he mentioned once or twice that he had no time to fool with theorems; adding—with a twitch of the eyebrows and a touch of that nervous bravado which so perplexed them—that he was helping the people down at the stock company; they were old friends of his.

The upshot of the matter was that the Principal went to Paul's father, and Paul was taken out of school and put to work. The manager at Carnegie Hall was told to get another usher in his stead; the doorkeeper at the theatre was warned not to admit him to the house; and Charley Edwards remorsefully promised the boy's father not to see him again.

The members of the stock company were vastly amused when some of Paul's stories reached them—especially the women. They were hardworking women, most of them supporting indolent husbands or brothers, and they laughed rather bitterly at having stirred the boy to such fervid and florid inventions. They agreed with the faculty and with his father, that Paul's was a bad case.

The east-bound train was ploughing through a January snowstorm; the dull dawn was beginning to show grey when the engine whistled a mile out of Newark. Paul started up from the seat where he had lain curled in uneasy slumber, rubbed the breath-misted window-glass with his hand, and peered out. The snow was whirling in curling eddies above the white bottom lands, and the drifts lay already deep in the fields and along the fences, while here and there the tall dead grass and dried weed stalks protruded black above it. Lights shone from the scattered houses, and a gang of labourers who stood beside the track waved their lanterns.

Paul had slept very little, and he felt grimy and uncomfortable. He had made the all-night journey in a day coach because he was afraid if he took a Pullman he might be seen by some Pittsburgh business man who had noticed him in Denny and Carson's office. When the whistle woke him, he clutched quickly at his breast pocket, glancing about him with an uncertain smile. But the little, clay-bespattered Italians were still sleeping, the slatternly women across the aisle were in open-mouthed oblivion, and even the crumby, crying babies were for the time stilled. Paul settled back to struggle with his impatience as best he could.

When he arrived at the Jersey City station, he hurried through his breakfast, manifestly ill at ease and keeping a sharp eye about him. After he reached the Twenty-Third Street station, he consulted a cabman, and had himself driven to a men's furnishing establishment which was just opening for the day. He spent upward of two hours there, buying with endless reconsidering and great care. His new street suit he put on in the fitting-room; the frock coat and dress clothes he had bundled into the cab with his new shirts. Then he drove to a hatter's and a shoe house. His next errand was at Tiffany's, where he selected silver-mounted brushes and a scarf-pin. He would not wait to have his silver marked, he said. Lastly, he stopped at a trunk shop on Broadway, and had his purchases packed into various travelling-bags.

It was a little after one o'clock when he drove up to the Waldorf, and, after settling with the cabman, went into the office. He registered from Washington; said his mother and father had been abroad, and that he had come down to await the arrival of their steamer. He told his story plausibly and had no trouble, since he offered to pay for them in advance, in engaging his rooms; a sleeping-room, sitting-room, and bath.

Not once, but a hundred times Paul had planned this entry into New York. He had gone over every detail of it with Charley Edwards, and in his scrapbook at home there were pages of description about New York hotels, cut from the Sunday papers.

When he was shown to his sitting-room on the eighth floor, he saw at a glance that everything was as it should be; there was but one detail in his mental picture that the place did not realize, so he rang for the bell-boy and sent him down for flowers. He moved about nervously until the boy returned, putting away his new linen and fingering it delightedly as he did so. When the flowers came, he put them hastily into water, and then tumbled into a hot bath. Presently he came out of his white bathroom, resplendent in his new silk underwear, and playing with the tassels of his red robe. The snow was whirling so fiercely outside his windows that he could scarcely see across the street; but within, the air was deliciously soft and fragrant. He put the violets and jonquils on the tabouret beside the couch, and threw himself down with a long sigh, covering himself with a Roman blanket. He was thoroughly tired; he had been in such haste, he had stood up to such a strain, covered so much ground in the last twenty-four hours, that he wanted to think how it had all come about. Lulled by the sound of the wind, the warm air, and the cool fragrance of the flowers, he sank into deep, drowsy retrospection.

It had been wonderfully simple; when they had shut him out of the theatre and concert hall, when they had taken away his bone, the whole thing was virtually determined. The rest was a mere matter of opportunity. The only thing that at all surprised him was his own courage—for he realized well enough that he had always been tormented by fear, a sort of apprehensive dread which, of late years, as the meshes of the lies he had told closed about him, had been pulling the muscles of his body tighter and tighter. Until now, he could not remember a time when he had not been dreading something. Even when he was a little boy, it was always there— behind him, or before, or on either side. There had always been the shadowed corner, the dark place into which he dared not look, but from which something seemed always to be watching him—and Paul had done things that were not pretty to watch, he knew.

But now he had a curious sense of relief, as though he had at last thrown down the gauntlet to the thing in the corner.

Yet it was but a day since he had been sulking in the traces; but yesterday afternoon that he had been sent to the bank with Denny and Carson's deposit, as usual—but this time he was instructed to leave the book to be balanced. There was above two thousand dollars in cheques, and nearly a thousand in the banknotes which he had taken from the book and quietly transferred to his pocket. At the bank he had made out a new deposit slip. His nerves had been steady enough to permit of his returning to the office, where he had finished his work and asked for a full day's holiday tomorrow, Saturday, giving a perfectly reasonable pretext. The bank book, he knew, would not be returned before Monday or Tuesday, and his father would be out of town for the next week. From the time he slipped the banknotes into his pocket until he boarded the night train for New York, he had not known a moment's hesitation.

How astonishingly easy it had all been; here he was, the thing done; and this time there would be no awakening, no figure at the top of the stairs. He watched the snowflakes whirling by his window until he fell asleep.

When he awoke, it was four o'clock in the afternoon. He bounded up with a start; one of his precious days gone already! He spent nearly an hour in dressing, watching every stage of his toilet carefully in the mirror. Everything was quite perfect; he was exactly the kind of boy he had always wanted to be.

When he went downstairs, Paul took a carriage and drove up Fifth Avenue toward the Park. The snow had somewhat abated; carriages and tradesmen's wagons were hurrying soundlessly to and fro in the winter twilight; boys in woollen mufflers were shovelling off the doorsteps; the Avenue stages made fine spots of colour against the white street. Here and there on the corners whole flower gardens blooming behind glass windows, against which the snowflakes stuck and melted; violets, roses, carnations, lilies-of-the-valley—somehow vastly more lovely and alluring that they blossomed thus unnaturally in the snow. The Park itself was a wonderful stage winter-piece.

When he returned, the pause of the twilight had ceased, and the tune of the streets had changed. The snow was falling faster, lights streamed from the hotels that reared their many stories fearlessly up into the storm, defying the raging Atlantic winds. A long, black stream of carriages poured down the Avenue, intersected here and there by other streams, tending horizontally. There were a score of cabs about the entrance of his hotel, and his driver had to wait. Boys in livery were running in and out of the awning stretched across the sidewalk, up and down the red velvet carpet laid from the door to the street. Above, about, within it all, was the rumble and roar, the hurry and toss of thousands of human beings as hot for pleasure as himself, and on every side of him towered the glaring affirmation of the omnipotence of wealth.

The boy set his teeth and drew his shoulders together in a spasm of realization; the plot of all dramas, the text of all romances, the nerve-stuff of all sensations was whirling about him like the snowflakes. He burnt like a fagot in a tempest.

When Paul came down to dinner, the music of the orchestra floated up the elevator shaft to greet him. As he stepped into the thronged corridor, he sank back into one of the chairs against the wall to get his breath. The lights, the chatter, the perfumes, the bewildering medley of colour—he had, for a moment, the feeling of not being able to stand it. But only for a moment; these were his own people, he told himself. He went slowly about the corridors, through the writing-rooms, smoking-rooms, reception-rooms, as though he were exploring the chambers of an enchanted palace, built and peopled for him alone.

When he reached the dining-room he sat down at a table near a window. The flowers, the white linen, the many-coloured wine-glasses, the gay toilettes of the women, the low popping of corks, the undulating repetitions of the "Blue Danube" from the orchestra, all flooded Paul's dream with bewildering radiance. When the roseate tinge of his champagne was added—that cold, precious, bubbling stuff that creamed and foamed in his glass—Paul wondered that there were honest men in the world at all. This was what all the world was fighting for, he reflected; this was what all the struggle was about. He doubted the reality of his past. Had he ever known a place called Cordelia Street, a place where fagged-looking businessmen boarded the early car? Mere rivets in a machine they seemed to Paul—sickening men, with combings of children's hair always hanging to their coats, and the smell of cooking in their clothes. Cordelia Street—Ah, that belonged to another time and country! Had he not always been thus, had he not sat here night after night, from as far back as he could remember, looking pensively over just such shimmering textures, and slowly twirling the stem of a glass like this one between his thumb and middle finger? He rather thought he had.

He was not in the least abashed or lonely. He had no especial desire to meet or to know any of these people; all he demanded was the right to look on and conjecture, to watch the pageant. The mere stage properties were all he contended for. Nor was he lonely later in the evening, in his loge at the Opera. He was entirely rid of his nervous misgivings, of his forced aggressiveness, of the imperative desire to show himself different from his surroundings. He felt now that his surroundings explained him. Nobody questioned the purple; he had only to wear it passively. He had only to glance down at his dress coat to reassure himself that here it would be impossible for anyone to humiliate him.

He found it hard to leave his beautiful sitting-room to go to bed that night, and sat long watching the raging storm from his turret window. When he went to sleep, it was with the lights turned on in his bedroom; partly because of his old timidity, and partly so that, if he should wake in the night, there would be no wretched moment of doubt, no horrible suspicion of yellow wallpaper, or of Washington and Calvin above his bed.

On Sunday morning the city was practically snowbound. Paul breakfasted late, and in the afternoon he fell in with a wild San Francisco boy, a freshman at Yale, who said he had run down for a "little flyer" over Sunday. The young man offered to show Paul the night side of the town, and the two boys went off together after dinner, not returning to the hotel until seven o'clock the next morning. They had started out in the confiding warmth of a champagne friendship, but their parting in the elevator was singularly cool. The freshman pulled himself together to make his train, and Paul went to bed. He awoke at two o'clock in the afternoon, very thirsty and dizzy, and rang for ice-water, coffee, and the Pittsburgh papers.

On the part of the hotel management, Paul excited no suspicion. There was this to be said for him, that he wore his spoils with dignity and in no way made himself conspicuous. His chief greediness lay in his ears and eyes, and his excesses were not offensive ones. His dearest pleasures were the grey winter twilights in his sitting-room; his quiet enjoyment of his flowers, his clothes, his wide divan, his cigarette, and his sense of power. He could not remember a time when he had felt so at peace with himself. The mere release from the necessity of petty lying, lying every day and every day, restored his self-respect. He had never lied for pleasure, even at school; but to make himself noticed and admired, to assert his difference from other Cordelia Street boys; and he felt a good deal more manly, more honest, even, now that he had no need for boastful pretensions, now that he could, as his actor friends used to say, "dress the part." It was characteristic that remorse did not occur to him. His golden days went by without a shadow, and he made each as perfect as he could.

On the eighth day after his arrival in New York, he found the whole affair exploited in the Pittsburgh papers, exploited with a wealth of detail which indicated that local news of a sensational nature was at a low ebb. The firm of Denny and Carson announced that the boy's father had refunded the full amount of his theft, and that they had no intention of prosecuting. The Cumberland minister had been interviewed, and expressed his hope of yet reclaiming the motherless lad, and Paul's Sabbath School teacher declared that she would spare no effort to that end. The rumour had reached Pittsburgh that the boy had been seen in a New York hotel, and his father had gone East to find him and bring him home.

Paul had just come in to dress for dinner; he sank into a chair, weak in the knees, and clasped his head in his hands. It was to be worse than jail, even; the tepid waters of Cordelia Street were to close over him finally and forever. The grey monotony stretched before him in hopeless, unrelieved years;—Sabbath School, Young People's Meeting, the yellow-papered room, the damp dish towels; it all rushed back upon him with sickening vividness. He had the old feeling that the orchestra had suddenly stopped, the sinking sensation that the play was over. The sweat broke out on his face, and he sprang to his feet, looked about him with his white, conscious smile, and winked at himself in the mirror. With something of the childish belief in miracles with which he had so often gone to class, all his lessons unlearned, Paul dressed and dashed whistling down the corridor to the elevator.

He had no sooner entered the dining room and caught the measure of the music than his remembrance was lightened by his old elastic power of claiming the moment, mounting with it, and finding it all-sufficient. The glare and glitter about him, the mere scenic accessories had again, and for the last time, their old potency. He would show himself that he was game, he would finish the thing splendidly. He doubted, more than ever, the existence of Cordelia Street, and for the first time he drank his wine recklessly. Was he not, after all, one of these fortunate beings? Was he not still himself, and in his own place? He drummed a nervous accompaniment to the music and looked about him, telling himself over and over that it had paid.

He reflected drowsily, to the swell of the violin and the chill sweetness of his wine, that he might have done it more wisely. He might have caught an outbound steamer and been well out of their clutches before now. But the other side of the world had seemed too far away and too uncertain then; he could not have waited for it; his need had been too sharp. If he had to choose over again, he would do the same thing tomorrow. He looked affectionately about the dining room, now gilded with a soft mist. Ah, it had paid indeed!

Paul was awakened next morning by a painful throbbing in his head and feet. He had thrown himself across the bed without undressing, and had slept with his shoes on. His limbs and hands were lead-heavy, and his tongue and throat were parched. There came upon him one of those fateful attacks of clear-headedness that never occurred except when he was physically exhausted and his nerves hung loose. He lay still and closed his eyes and let the tide of realities wash over him.

His father was in New York; "stopping at some joint or other," he told himself. The memory of successive summers on the front stoop fell upon him like a weight of black water. He had not a hundred dollars left; and he knew now, more than ever, that money was everything, the wall that stood between all he loathed and all he wanted. The thing was winding itself up; he had thought of that on his first glorious day in New York, and had even provided a way to snap the thread. It lay on his dressing-table now; he had got it out last night when he came blindly up from dinner—but the shiny metal hurt his eyes, and he disliked the look of it anyway.

He rose and moved about with a painful effort, succumbing now and again to attacks of nausea. It was the old depression exaggerated; all the world had become Cordelia Street. Yet somehow he was not afraid of anything, was absolutely calm; perhaps because he had looked into the dark corner at last, and knew. It was bad enough, what he saw there; but somehow not so bad as his long fear of it had been. He saw everything clearly now. He had a feeling that he had made the best of it, that he had lived the sort of life he was meant to live, and for half an hour he sat staring at the revolver. But he told himself that was not the way, so he went downstairs and took a cab to the ferry.

When Paul arrived at Newark, he got off the train and took another cab, directing the driver to follow the Pennsylvania tracks out of the town. The snow lay heavy on the roadways and had drifted deep in the open fields. Only here and there the dead grass or dried weed stalks projected, singularly black, above it.

Once well into the country, Paul dismissed the carriage and walked, floundering along the tracks, his mind a medley of irrelevant things. He seemed to hold in his brain an actual picture of everything he had seen that morning. He remembered every feature of both his drivers, the toothless old woman from whom he had bought the red flowers in his coat, the agent from whom he had got his ticket, and all of his fellow-passengers on the ferry. His mind, unable to cope with vital matters near at hand, worked feverishly and deftly at sorting and grouping these images. They made for him a part of the ugliness of the world, of the ache in his head, and the bitter burning on his tongue. He stooped and put a handful of snow into his mouth as he walked, but that, too, seemed hot. When he reached a little hillside, where the tracks ran through a cut some twenty feet below him, he stopped and sat down.

The carnations in his coat were drooping with the cold, he noticed; their red glory over. It occurred to him that all the flowers he had seen in the show windows that first night must have gone the same way, long before this. It was only one splendid breath they had, in spite of their brave mockery at the winter outside the glass. It was a losing game in the end, it seemed, this revolt against the homilies by which the world is run. Paul took one of the blossoms carefully from his coat and scooped a little hole in the snow, where he covered it up. Then he dozed awhile, from his weak condition, seeming insensible to the cold.

The sound of an approaching train woke him and he started to his feet, remembering only his resolution, and afraid lest he should be too late. He stood watching the approaching locomotive, his teeth chattering, his lips drawn away from them in a frightened smile; once or twice he glanced nervously sidewise, as though he were being watched. When the right moment came, he jumped. As he fell, the folly of his haste occurred to him with merciless clearness, the vastness of what he had left undone. There flashed through his brain, clearer than ever before, the blue of Adriatic water, the yellow of Algerian sands.

He felt something strike his chest—his body was being thrown swiftly through the air, on and on, immeasurably far and fast, while his limbs gently relaxed. Then, because the picture-making mechanism was crushed, the disturbing visions flashed into black, and Paul dropped back into the immense design of things.

Willow Game

DENISE CHÁVEZ

I was a child before there was a South. That was before the magic of the East, the beckoning North, or the West's betrayal. For me there was simply Up the street toward the spies' house, next to Old Man W's or there was Down, past the Marking-Off Tree in the vacant lot that was the shortcut between worlds. Down was the passageway to family, the definition of small self as one of the whole, part of a past. Up was in the direction of town, flowers.

Mercy and I would scavenge the neighborhood for flowers that we would lay at Our Lady's feet during those long May Day processions of faith that we so loved. A white satin cloth would be spread in front of the altar. We children would come up one by one and place our flowers on that bridal sheet, our breathless childish fervor heightened by the mystifying scent of flowers, the vision of flowers, the flowers of our offerings. It was this beatific sense of wonder that sent us roaming the street in search of new victims, as our garden had long since been razed, emptied of all future hope.

On our block there were two flower places: Old Man W's and the Strongs. Old Man W was a Greek who worked for the city for many years and who lived with his daughter who was my older sister's friend. Mr. W always seemed eager to give us flowers; they were not as lovely or as abundant as the Strongs' flowers, yet the asking lay calmly with us at Old Man W's.

The Strongs, a misnamed brother-and-sister team who lived together in the largest, most sumptuous house on the block, were secretly referred to by my sister and me as "the spies." A chill of dread would overtake both of us as we'd approach their mansion. We would ring the doorbell and usually the sister would answer. She was a pale woman with a braided halo of wispy white hair who always planted herself possessively in the doorway, her little girl's legs in black laced shoes holding back, sectioning off, craning her inquiry to our shaken selves with a lispy, merciless, "Yes?"

190

I always did the asking. In later years when the street became smaller,
less foreign, and the spies had become, at the least, accepted . . . it was I
who still asked questions, pleaded for flowers to Our Lady, heard the high
piping voices of ecstatic children singing, "Bring flowers of the fairest,
bring flowers of the rarest, from garden and woodland and hillside and
dale. . . . " My refrain floated past the high white walls of the church, across
the Main Street irrigation ditch and up our small street, "Our pure hearts
are swelling, our glad voices telling, the praise of the loveliest Rose of the
Dale. . . ."

One always came down . . .

Down consisted of all the houses past my midway vantage point, including the house across the street, occupied by a couple and their three children, who later became my charges, my baby-sitting responsibilities,
children whose names I have forgotten. This was the house where one day
a used sanitary napkin was ritually burned—a warning to those future furtive random and unconcerned depositors of filth, or so this is what one
read in Mr. Carter's eyes as he raked the offensive item to a pile of leaves
and dramatically set fire to some nameless, faceless woman's woes. I peered
from the trinity of windows cut in our wooden front door and wondered
what all the commotion was about and why everyone seemed so stoically removed, embarrassed or offended. Later I would mournfully peep from the
cyclopian window at the Carter's and wonder why I was there and not
across the street. In my mind I floated Down, past the Marking-Off Tree
with its pitted green fruit, past five or six houses, houses of strangers, "los
desconocidos," as my Grandmother would say, "¿Y pues, quién los parió?"
I would end up at my aunt's house, return, find myself looking at our
house as it was, the porch light shining, the lilies' pale patterns a diadem
crowning our house, there, at night.

The walk from the beginning to the end of the street took no longer than
five to ten minutes, depending on the pace and purpose of the walker. The
walk was short if I was a messenger to my aunt's, or if I was meeting my father, who had recently divorced us and now called sporadically to allow us
to attend to him. The pace may have been the slow, leisurely summer saunter with ice cream or the swirling dust-filled scamper of spring. Our house
was situated in the middle of the block and faced a triangle of trees that became both backdrop and pivot points of this child's tale. The farthest tree,
the Up Tree, was an Apricot Tree that was the property of all the neighborhood children.

The Apricot Tree lay in an empty lot near my cousin's house, the cousin
who always got soap in her nose. Florence was always one of the most popular girls in school and, while I worshipped her, I was glad to have my nose
and not hers. Our mothers would alternate driving us and the Sánchez
boys, one of whom my father nicknamed "Priscilla" because he was always
with the girls, to a small Catholic school that was our genesis. On entering

Florence's house on those days when it was *her* mother's turn, I would inevitably find her bent over the bathroom basin, sneezing. She would yell out, half snottily, half snortingly, "I have soap in my nose!"

Whether the Apricot Tree really belonged to Florence wasn't clear—the tree was the neighborhood's and as such, was as familiar as our own faces, or the faces of our relatives. Her fruit, often abundant, sometimes meager, was public domain. The tree's limbs draped luxuriously across an irrigation ditch whose calm, muddy water flowed all the way from the Río Grande to our small street where it was diverted into channelways that led into the neighborhood's backyards. The fertile water deposited the future seeds of asparagus, weeds and wild flowers, then settled into tufted layers crossed by sticks and stones—hieroglyphic reminders of murky beginnings.

Along with the tree, we children drew power from the penetrating grateful wetness. In return, the tree was resplendent with offerings—there were apricots and more, there were the sturdy compartments, the chambers and tunnelways of dream, the stages of our dramas. "I'm drowning! I'm drowning!" we mocked drowning and were saved at the last moment by a friendly hand, or, "This is the ship and I am the captain!" we exulted having previously transcended death. Much time was spent at the tree, alone or with others. All of us, Priscilla, Soap-in-her-Nose, the two dark boys Up the street, my little sister and I, all of us loved the tree. We would oftentimes find ourselves slipping off from one of those choreless, shoreless days, and with a high surprised "Oh!" we would greet each other's aloneness, there at the tree that embraced us all selflessly.

On returning home we may have wandered alongside the ditch, behind the Wester's house, and near the other vacant lot which housed the second point of the triangle, the Marking-Off Tree, the likes of which may have stood at the edge of the Garden of Eden. It was dried, sad looking. All the years of my growing up it struggled to create a life of its own. The tree passed fruit every few years or so—as old men and women struggle to empty their ravaged bowels. The grey-green balls that it brought forth we used as one uses an empty can, to kick and thrash. The tree was a reference point, offering no shade, but always meditation. It delineated the Up world from the Down. It marked off the nearest point home, without being home; it was a landmark, and as such, occupied our thoughts, not in the way the Apricot Tree did, but in a subtler, more profound way. Seeing the tree was like seeing the same viejito downtown for so long, with his bottle and his wife, and looking into his crusty white-rimmed eyes and thinking: "How much longer?" Tape appears on his neck, the voice box gargles a barking sound and the bruises seem deeper.

There, at that place of recognition and acceptance, you will see the Marking-Off Tree at the edge of my world. I sit on the front porch at twilight. The power is all about me. The great unrest twitters and swells like the erratic chords of small and large birds scaling their way home.

To our left is the Willow Tree, completing this trinity of trees. How to introduce her? I would take the light of unseen eyes and present the sister who lives in France, or her husband who died when he was but thirty. I would show you the best of friends and tell you how clear, how dear. I would recall moments of their eternal charm, their look or stance, the intrinsic quality of their bloom. You would see inside an album a black and white photograph of a man with a wide, ruddy face, in shirtsleeves, holding a plump, squinting child in front of a small tree, a tree too frail for the wild lashes, surely. On the next page an older girl passing a hand through wind-blown hair would look at you, you would feel her gentle beauty, love her form. Next to her a young girl stands, small eyes toward godfather, who stares at the photographer, shaded by a growing-stronger tree. Or then you would be at a birthday party, one of the guests, rimmed in zinnias, cousins surrounding, Soap-in-her-Nose, the two dark boys (younger than in story time) and the others, miniaturized versions of their future selves. Two sisters, with their arms around each other's child-delicate necks, stand out—as the warps and the twinings of the willow background confuse the boys with their whips and the girls with their fans.

In this last photograph one sees two new faces, one shy boy huddled among the girls, the other removed from all contact, sunblinded, lost in leaves.

Next to us lived the Althertons: Rob, Sandy, Ricky and Randy. The history of the house next door was wrought with struggle. Before the Althertons moved in, the Cardozas lived there, with their smiling young boys, senseless boys, demon boys. It was Emmanuel (Mannie) who punched the hole in our plastic swimming pool and Jr. who made us cry. Toward the end of the Cardoza boys' reign, Mrs. C, a small breathless bug-eyed little woman, gave birth to a girl. Mr. C's tile business failed and the family moved to Chiva Town, vacating the house to the Althertons, an alternately histrionically dry and loquacious couple with two boys. Ricky, the oldest, was a tall, tense boy who stalked the Altherton spaces with the natural grace of a wild animal, ready to spring, ears full of sound, eyes taut with anticipation. Young Randy was a plump boy-child with deep, watery eyes that clung to Mrs. Altherton's lumpish self while lean and lanky Papa A ranged the spacious lawn year round in swimming trunks in search of crab grass, weeds, any vestiges of irregularity. Lifting a handful of repugnant weed, he'd wave it in the direction of Sandy, his wife, a pigeon of a woman who cooed, "You don't say . . ."

Jack Spratt shall eat no fat, his wife shall eat no lean, and between them both, you see, they licked the platter clean.

The Altherton yard was very large, centered by a metal pole to which was attached the neighborhood's first tetherball. From our porch where my sister and I sat dressing dolls, we could hear the punch and whirr of balls, the crying and calling out. Ricky would always win, sending Randy racing inside to Mrs. A's side, at which time, having dispatched his odious brother, Ricky would beat and thrash the golden ball around in some sort of crazed and victorious adolescent dance. Randy and Mrs. A would emerge from the house and they would confer with Ricky for a time. Voices were never raised, were always hushed and calm. The two plump ones would then go off, hand in hand, leaving the lean to himself. Ricky would usually stomp away down the neighborhood, flicking off a guiltless willow limb, deleafing it in front of our watchful eyes, leaving behind his confused steps a trail of green, unblinking eyes, the leaves of our tree.

Every once in a while Randy would walk over to us as we sat dressing dolls or patting mud pies, and hesitantly, with that babyish smile of his, ask us to come play ball. We two sisters would cross the barriers of Altherton and joyfully bang the tetherball around with Randy. He played low, was predictable, unlike Ricky, who threw the ball vehemently high, confounding, always confounding. Ricky's games were over quickly, his blows firm, surprising, relentless. Ricky never played with my sister and me. He was godlike and removed, as our older sister, already sealed in some inexplicable anguish of which we children had no understanding. It was Randy who brought us in, called out to us, permitted us to play. And when he was not there to beckon us, it was his lingering generosity and gentleness that pushed us forward into the mysterious Altherton yard, allowing us to risk fear, either of Mr. Altherton and his perennial tan, or Ricky with his senseless animal temper. Often we would find the yard free and would enjoy the tetherball without interruption, other times we would see Ricky stalk by, or hear the rustling approach of clippers, signifying Mr. Altherton's return. If we would sense the vaguest shadow of either spectre, we would run, wildly, madly, safely home, to the world of our Willow where we would huddle and hide in the shelter of green, labyrinthine rooms, abstracting ourselves from the world of Ricky's torment or Mr. Altherton's anxious wanderings.

I have spoken least of all of the Willow Tree, but in speaking of someone dead or gone, what words can reach far enough into the past to secure a vision of someone's smiling face or curious look, who can tame the restless past and show, as I have tried, black and white photographs of small children in front of a tree?

The changes of the Willow were imperceptible at first. Mr. W, the Greek, through an oversight in pronunciation, had always been Mr. V. The spies became individualized when Mr. Strong later became my substitute history teacher and caused a young student to faint. She who was afraid of blood looked up into the professor's nose and saw unmistakable flecks of red. The two dark boys grew up, became wealthy, and my cousin moved away. The irrigation ditch was eventually closed. Only the Willow remained— consoling, substantial. The days became shorter and divided the brothers while the sisters grew closer.

Ricky, now a rampaging, consumed adolescent, continued his thoughtless forays, which included absently ripping off willow limbs and discarding them on our sidewalk. "He's six years older than Randy," said my mother, that dark mother who hid in the trees, "he hates his brother, he just never got over Randy's birth. You love your sister, don't you?" "Yes, mother," I would say.

It was not long after Ricky's emerging manhood that the Willow began to ail, even as I watched it. I knew it was hurting. The tree began to look bare. The limbs were lifeless, in anguish, and there was no discernible reason. The solid, green rooms of our child's play collapsed, the passageways became cavernous hallways, the rivers of grass dried and there was no shade. The tree was dying. My mother became concerned. I don't know what my little sister thought; she was a year younger than I. She probably thought as I did, for at that time she held me close as model and heroine, and enveloped me with her love, something Randy was never able to do for his older brother, that bewildered boy.

It wasn't until years later (although the knowledge was there, admitted, seen) that my mother told me that one day she went outside to see Ricky standing on a ladder under our Willow. He had a pair of scissors in his hands and was cutting whole branches off the tree and throwing them to one side. Mother said, "What are you doing, Ricky?" He replied, "I'm cutting the tree." "Do you realize that you're killing it?" she responded calmly. It is here that the interpretation breaks down, where the photographs fade into grey wash, and I momentarily forget what Ricky's reply was, that day, so many years ago, as the limbs of our Willow fell about him, cascading tears, willow reminders past the face of my mother, who stood solemnly and without horror.

Later, when there was no recourse but to cut down the tree, Regino Suárez, the neighborhood handyman, and his son were called in.

Regino and his son had difficulty with the tree; she refused to come out of the earth. When her roots were ripped up, there lay a cavity of dirt, an enormous aching hole, like a tooth gone, the sides impressed with myriad twistings and turnings. The trunk was moved to the side of the house, where it remained until several years ago, when it was cut up for firewood, and even then, part of the stump was left. Throughout the rest of grade school, high school, and college—until I went away, returned, went away—the Willow stump remained underneath the window of my old room. Often I would look out and see it there, or on thoughtful walks, I would go outside near the Altherton's old house, now sealed by a tall concrete wall, and I would feel the aging hardness of the Willow's flesh.

That painful, furrowed space was left in the front yard, where once the Willow had been. It filled my eyes, my sister's eyes, my mother's eyes. The wall of trees, backdrop of the traveling me, that triangle of trees—the Apricot Tree, the Marking-Off Tree, the Willow Tree—was no longer.

One day Ricky disappeared and we were told that he'd been sent to a home for sick boys.

As children one felt dull, leaden aches that were voiceless cries and were incommunicable. The place they sprung from seemed so desolate and uninhabited and did not touch on anything tangible or transferable. To carry pain around as a child does, in that particular place, that worldless, grey corridor, and to be unable to find the syllables with which to vent one's sorrow, one's horror . . . surely this is insufferable anguish, the most insufferable. Being unable to see, yet able, willing, yet unwilling . . . to comprehend. A child's sorrow is a place that cannot be visited by others. Always the going back is solitary, and the little sisters, however much they love you, were never really very near, and the mothers, well, they stand as I said before, solemnly, without horror, removed from children by their understanding.

I am left with recollections of pain, of loss, with holes to be filled. Time, like trees, withstands the winters, bursts forth new leaves from the dried old sorrows—who knows when and why—and shelters us with the shade of later compassions, loves, although at the time the heart is seared so badly that the hope of all future flowerings is gone.

Much later, after the death of the Willow, I was walking to school when a young boy came up to me and punched me in the stomach. I doubled over, crawled back to Sister Elaine's room, unable to tell her of my recent attack, unprovoked, thoughtless, insane. What could I say to her? To my mother and father? What can I say to you? All has been told. The shreds of magic living, like the silken, green ropes of the Willow's branches, dissolved about me, and I was beyond myself, a child no longer. I was filled with immense sadness, the burning of snow in a desert land of consistent warmth.

I walked outside and the same experience repeated itself; oh, not the same form, but yes, the attack. I was the same child, you see, mouthing pacifications, incantations . . . "Bring flowers of the fairest, bring flowers of the rarest. It's okay, from garden and woodland and hillside and dale. Our pure hearts are swelling. It's all right, our glad voices are telling, please, the praise of the loveliest rose of the dale."

Jack Spratt could eat no fat, his wife could eat no lean, and between them both, you see, they licked the platter clean . . .

My mother planted a willow several years ago, so that if you sit on the porch and face left you will see it, thriving. It's not in the same spot as its predecessor, too far right, but of course, the leveling was never done, and how was Regino to know? The Apricot Tree died, the Marking-Off Tree is fruitless now, relieved from its round of senseless birthings. This willow tree is new, with its particular joys. It stands in the center of the block . . . between.

The Swimmer

JOHN CHEEVER

It was one of those midsummer Sundays when everyone sits around saying, "I *drank* too much last night." You might have heard it whispered by the parishioners leaving church, heard it from the lips of the priest himself, struggling with his cassock in the *vestiarium,* heard it from the golf links and the tennis courts, heard it from the wildlife preserve where the leader of the Audubon group was suffering from a terrible hangover. "I *drank* too much," said Donald Westerhazy. "We all *drank* too much," said Lucinda Merrill. "It must have been the wine," said Helen Westerhazy. "I *drank* too much of that claret."

This was at the edge of the Westerhazys' pool. The pool, fed by an artesian well with a high iron content, was a pale shade of green. It was a fine day. In the west there was a massive stand of cumulus cloud so like a city seen from a distance—from the bow of an approaching ship—that it might have had a name. Lisbon. Hackensack. The sun was hot. Neddy Merrill sat by the green water, one hand in it, one around a glass of gin. He was a slender man—he seemed to have the especial slenderness of youth—and while he was far from young he had slid down his banister that morning and given the bronze backside of Aphrodite on the hall table a smack, as he jogged toward the smell of coffee in his dining room. He might have been compared to a summer's day, particularly the last hours of one, and while he lacked a tennis racket or a sail bag the impression was definitely one of youth, sport, and clement weather. He had been swimming and now he was breathing deeply, stertorously as if he could gulp into his lungs the components of that moment, the heat of the sun, the intenseness of his pleasure. It all seemed to flow into his chest. His own house stood in Bullet Park, eight miles to the south, where his four beautiful daughters would have had their lunch and might be playing tennis. Then it occurred to him that by taking a dogleg to the southwest he could reach his home by water.

His life was not confining and the delight he took in this observation could not be explained by its suggestion of escape. He seemed to see, with a cartographer's eye, that string of swimming pools, that quasi-subterranean stream that curved across the county. He had made a discovery, a contribution to modern geography; he would name the stream Lucinda after his wife. He was not a practical joker nor was he a fool but he was determinedly original and had a vague and modest idea of himself as a legendary figure. The day was beautiful and it seemed to him that a long swim might enlarge and celebrate its beauty.

He took off a sweater that was hung over his shoulders and dove in. He had an inexplicable contempt for men who did not hurl themselves into pools. He swam a choppy crawl, breathing either with every stroke or every fourth stroke and counting somewhere well in the back of his mind the one-two one-two of a flutter kick. It was not a serviceable stroke for long distances but the domestication of swimming had saddled the sport with some customs and in his part of the world a crawl was customary. To be embraced and sustained by the light green water was less a pleasure, it seemed, than the resumption of a natural condition, and he would have liked to swim without trunks, but this was not possible, considering his project. He hoisted himself up on the far curb—he never used the ladder—and started across the lawn. When Lucinda asked where he was going he said he was going to swim home.

The only maps and charts he had to go by were remembered or imaginary but these were clear enough. First there were the Grahams, the Hammers, the Lears, the Howlands, and the Crosscups. He would cross Ditmar Street to the Bunkers and come, after a short portage, to the Levys, the Welchers, and the public pool in Lancaster. Then there were the Hallorans, the Sachses, the Biswangers, Shirley Adams, the Gilmartins, and the Clydes. The day was lovely, and that he lived in a world so generously supplied with water seemed like a clemency, a beneficence. His heart was high and he ran across the grass. Making his way home by an uncommon route gave him the feeling that he was a pilgrim, an explorer, a man with a destiny, and he knew that he would find friends all along the way; friends would line the banks of the Lucinda River.

He went through a hedge that separated the Westerhazys' land from the Grahams', walked under some flowering apple trees, passed the shed that housed their pump and filter, and came out at the Grahams' pool. "Why, Neddy," Mrs. Graham said, "what a marvelous surprise. I've been trying to get you on the phone all morning. Here, let me get you a drink." He saw then, like any explorer, that the hospitable customs and traditions of the natives would have to be handled with diplomacy if he was ever going to reach his destination. He did not want to mystify or seem rude to the Grahams nor did he have the time to linger there. He swam the length of their pool and joined them in the sun and was rescued, a few minutes later, by the arrival of two carloads of friends from Connecticut. During the uproarious reunions he was able to slip away. He went down by the front of the Grahams' house, stepped over a thorny hedge, and crossed a vacant lot to the Hammers'. Mrs. Hammer, looking up from her roses, saw him swim by although she wasn't quite sure who it was. The Lears heard him splashing past the open windows of their living room. The Howlands and the Crosscups were away. After leaving the Howlands' he crossed Ditmar Street and started for the Bunkers', where he could hear, even at that distance, the noise of a party.

The water refracted the sound of voices and laughter and seemed to suspend it in midair. The Bunkers' pool was on a rise and he climbed some stairs to a terrace where twenty-five or thirty men and women were drinking. The only person in the water was Rusty Towers, who floated there on a rubber raft. Oh, how bonny and lush were the banks of the Lucinda River! Prosperous men and women gathered by the sapphire-colored waters while caterer's men in white coats passed them cold gin. Overhead a red de Haviland trainer was circling around and around and around in the sky with something like the glee of a child in a swing. Ned felt a passing affection for the scene, a tenderness for the gathering, as if it was something he might touch. In the distance he heard thunder. As soon as Enid Bunker saw him she began to scream: "Oh, look who's here! What a marvelous surprise! When Lucinda said that you couldn't come I thought I'd *die*." She made her way to him through the crowd, and when they had finished kissing she led him to the bar, a progress that was slowed by the fact that he stopped to kiss eight or ten other women and shake the hands of as many men. A smiling bartender he had seen at a hundred parties gave him a gin and tonic and he stood by the bar for a moment, anxious not to get stuck in any conversation that would delay his voyage. When he seemed about to be surrounded he dove in and swam close to the side to avoid colliding with Rusty's raft. At the far end of the pool he bypassed the Tomlinsons with a broad smile and jogged up the garden path. The gravel cut his feet but this was the only unpleasantness. The party was confined to the pool, and as he went toward the house he heard the brilliant, watery sound of voices fade, heard the noise of a radio from the Bunkers' kitchen, where someone was listening to a ball game. Sunday afternoon. He made his way through the parked cars and down the grassy border of their driveway to Alewives Lane. He did not want to be seen on the road in his bathing trunks but there was no traffic and he made the short distance to the Levys' driveway, marked with a PRIVATE PROPERTY sign and a green tube for *The New York Times*. All the doors and windows of the big house were open but there were no signs of life; not even a dog barked. He went around the side of the house to the pool and saw that the Levys had only recently left. Glasses and bottles and dishes of nuts were on a table at the deep end, where there was a bathhouse or gazebo, hung with Japanese lanterns. After swimming the pool he got himself a glass and poured a drink. It was his fourth or fifth drink and he had swum nearly half the length of the Lucinda River. He felt tired, clean, and pleased at that moment to be alone; pleased with everything.

It would storm. The stand of cumulus cloud—that city—had risen and darkened, and while he sat there he heard the percussiveness of thunder again. The de Haviland trainer was still circling overhead and it seemed to Ned that he could almost hear the pilot laugh with pleasure in the afternoon; but when there was another peal of thunder he took off for home. A train whistle blew and he wondered what time it had gotten to be. Four? Five? He thought of the provincial station at that hour, where a waiter, his tuxedo concealed by a raincoat, a dwarf with some flowers wrapped in newspaper, and a woman who had been crying would be waiting for the local. It was suddenly growing dark; it was that moment when the pin-headed birds seem to organize their song into some acute and knowledge-able recognition of the storm's approach. Then there was a fine noise of rushing water from the crown of an oak at his back, as if a spigot there had been turned. Then the noise of fountains came from the crowns of all the tall trees. Why did he love storms, what was the meaning of his excitement when the door sprang open and the rain wind fled rudely up the stairs, why had the simple task of shutting the windows of an old house seemed fitting and urgent, why did the first watery notes of a storm wind have for him the unmistakable sound of good news, cheer, glad tidings? Then there was an explosion, a smell of cordite, and rain lashed the Japanese lanterns that Mrs. Levy had bought in Kyoto the year before last, or was it the year before that?

He stayed in the Levys' gazebo until the storm had passed. The rain had cooled the air and he shivered. The force of the wind had stripped a maple of its red and yellow leaves and scattered them over the grass and the water. Since it was midsummer the tree must be blighted, and yet he felt a peculiar sadness at this sign of autumn. He braced his shoulders, emptied his glass, and started for the Welchers' pool. This meant crossing the Lind-leys' riding ring and he was surprised to find it overgrown with grass and all the jumps dismantled. He wondered if the Lindleys had sold their horses or gone away for the summer and put them out to board. He seemed to remember having heard something about the Lindleys and their horses but the memory was unclear. On he went, barefoot through the wet grass, to the Welchers' where he found their pool was dry.

This breach in his chain of water disappointed him absurdly, and he felt like some explorer who seeks a torrential headwater and finds a dead stream. He was disappointed and mystified. It was common enough to go away for the summer but no one ever drained his pool. The Welchers had definitely gone away. The pool furniture was folded, stacked, and covered with a tarpaulin. The bathhouse was locked. All the windows of the house were shut, and when he went around to the driveway in front he saw a FOR SALE sign nailed to a tree. When had he last heard from the Welchers— when, that is, had he and Lucinda last regretted an invitation to dine with them? It seemed only a week or so ago. Was his memory failing or had he so disciplined it in the repression of unpleasant facts that he had damaged his sense of the truth? Then in the distance he heard the sound of a tennis game. This cheered him, cleared away all his apprehensions and let him regard the overcast sky and the cold air with indifference. This was the day that Neddy Merrill swam across the county. That was the day! He started off then for his most difficult portage.

Had you gone for a Sunday afternoon ride that day you might have seen him, close to naked, standing on the shoulders of Route 424, waiting for a chance to cross. You might have wondered if he was the victim of foul play, had his car broken down, or was he merely a fool. Standing barefoot in the deposits of the highway—beer cans, rags, and blowout patches—exposed to all kinds of ridicule, he seemed pitiful. He had known when he started that this was a part of his journey—it had been on his maps—but confronted with the lines of traffic, worming through the summery light, he found himself unprepared. He was laughed at, jeered at, a beer can was thrown at him, and he had no dignity or humor to bring to the situation. He could have gone back, back to the Westerhazys', where Lucinda would still be sitting in the sun. He had signed nothing, vowed nothing, pledged nothing, not even to himself. Why, believing as he did, that all human obduracy was susceptible to common sense, was he unable to turn back? Why was he determined to complete his journey even if it meant putting his life in danger? At what point had this prank, this joke, this piece of horseplay become serious? He could not go back, he could not even recall with any clearness the green water at the Westerhazys', the sense of inhaling the day's components, the friendly and relaxed voices saying that they had *drunk* too much. In the space of an hour, more or less, he had covered a distance that made his return impossible.

An old man, tooling down the highway at fifteen miles an hour, let him get to the middle of the road, where there was a grass divider. Here he was exposed to the ridicule of the northbound traffic, but after ten or fifteen minutes he was able to cross. From here he had only a short walk to the Recreation Center at the edge of the village of Lancaster, where there were some handball courts and a public pool.

The effect of the water on voices, the illusion of brilliance and suspense, was the same here as it had been at the Bunkers' but the sounds here were louder, harsher, and more shrill, and as soon as he entered the crowded enclosure he was confronted with regimentation. "ALL SWIMMERS MUST TAKE A SHOWER BEFORE USING THE POOL. ALL SWIMMERS MUST WEAR THEIR

IDENTIFICATION DISKS." He took a shower, washed his feet in a cloudy and bitter solution, and made his way to the edge of the water. It stank of chlorine and looked to him like a sink. A pair of lifeguards in a pair of towers blew police whistles at what seemed to be regular intervals and abused the swimmers through a public address system. Neddy remembered the sapphire water at the Bunkers' with longing and thought that he might contaminate himself—damage his own prosperousness and charm—by swimming in this murk, but he reminded himself that he was an explorer, a pilgrim, and that this was merely a stagnant bend in the Lucinda River. He dove, scowling with distaste, into the chlorine and had to swim with his head above water to avoid collisions, but even so he was bumped into, splashed, and jostled. When he got to the shallow end both lifeguards were shouting at him: "Hey, you, you without the identification disk, get outa the water." He did, but they had no way of pursuing him and he went through the reek of suntan oil and chlorine out through the hurricane fence and passed the handball courts. By crossing the road he entered the wooded part of the Halloran estate. The woods were not cleared and the footing was treacherous and difficult until he reached the lawn and the clipped beech hedge that encircled their pool.

The Hallorans were friends, an elderly couple of enormous wealth who seemed to bask in the suspicion that they might be Communists. They were zealous reformers but they were not Communists, and yet when they were accused, as they sometimes were, of subversion, it seemed to gratify and excite them. Their beech hedge was yellow and he guessed this had been blighted like the Levys' maple. He called hullo, hullo, to warn the Hallorans of his approach, to palliate his invasion of their privacy. The Hallorans, for reasons that had never been explained to him, did not wear bathing suits. No explanations were in order, really. Their nakedness was a detail in their uncompromising zeal for reform and he stepped politely out of his trunks before he went through the opening in the hedge.

Mrs. Halloran, a stout woman with white hair and a serene face, was reading the *Times*. Mr. Halloran was taking beech leaves out of the water with a scoop. They seemed not surprised or displeased to see him. Their pool was perhaps the oldest in the country, a fieldstone rectangle, fed by a brook. It had no filter or pump and its waters were the opaque gold of the stream.

"I'm swimming across the county," Ned said.

"Why, I didn't know one could," exclaimed Mrs. Halloran.

"Well, I've made it from the Westerhazys'," Ned said. "That must be about four miles."

He left his trunks at the deep end, walked to the shallow end, and swam this stretch. As he was pulling himself out of the water he heard Mrs. Halloran say, "We've been *terribly* sorry to hear about all your misfortunes, Neddy."

"My misfortunes?" Ned asked. "I don't know what you mean."

"Why, we heard that you'd sold the house and that your poor children
. . ."

"I don't recall having sold the house," Ned said, "and the girls are at
home."

"Yes," Mrs. Halloran sighed. "Yes . . ." Her voice filled the air with an
unseasonable melancholy and Ned spoke briskly. "Thank you for the
swim."

"Well, have a nice trip," said Mrs. Halloran.

Beyond the hedge he pulled on his trunks and fastened them. They were
loose and he wondered if, during the space of an afternoon, he could have
lost some weight. He was cold and he was tired and the naked Hallorans
and their dark water had depressed him. The swim was too much for his
strength but how could he have guessed this, sliding down the banister that
morning and sitting in the Westerhazys' sun? His arms were lame. His legs
felt rubbery and ached at the joints. The worst of it was the cold in his
bones and the feeling that he might never be warm again. Leaves were falling down around him and he smelled wood smoke on the wind. Who
would be burning wood at this time of year?

He needed a drink. Whiskey would warm him, pick him up, carry him
through the last of his journey, refresh his feeling that it was original and
valorous to swim across the county. Channel swimmers took brandy. He
needed a stimulant. He crossed the lawn in front of the Hallorans' house
and went down a little path to where they had built a house for their only
daughter, Helen, and her husband, Eric Sachs. The Sachses' pool was small
and he found Helen and her husband there.

"Oh, *Neddy*," Helen said. "Did you lunch at Mother's?"

"Not *really*," Ned said. "I *did* stop to see your parents." This seemed to be
explanation enough. "I'm terribly sorry to break in on you like this but I've
taken a chill and I wonder if you'd give me a drink."

"Why, I'd *love* to," Helen said, "but there hasn't been anything in this
house to drink since Eric's operation. That was three years ago."

Was he losing his memory, had his gift for concealing painful facts let
him forget that he had sold his house, that his children were in trouble, and
that his friend had been ill? His eyes slipped from Eric's face to his abdomen, where he saw three pale, sutured scars, two of them at least a foot
long. Gone was his navel, and what, Neddy thought, would the roving
hand, bed-checking one's gifts at 3 A.M., make of a belly with no navel, no
link to birth, this breach in the succession?

"I'm sure you can get a drink at the Biswangers'," Helen said. "They're
having an enormous do. You can hear it from here. Listen!"

She raised her head and from across the road, the lawns, the gardens,
the woods, the fields, he heard again the brilliant noise of voices over water.
"Well, I'll get wet," he said, still feeling that he had no freedom of choice

about his means of travel. He dove into the Sachses' cold water and, gasping, close to drowning, made his way from one end of the pool to the other. "Lucinda and I want *terribly* to see you," he said over his shoulder, his face set toward the Biswangers.' "We're sorry it's been so long and we'll call you *very* soon."

He crossed some fields to the Biswangers' and the sounds of revelry there. They would be honored to give him a drink, they would be happy to give him a drink. The Biswangers invited him and Lucinda for dinner four times a year, six weeks in advance. They were always rebuffed and yet they continued to send out their invitations, unwilling to comprehend the rigid and undemocratic realities of their society. They were the sort of people who discussed the price of things at cocktails, exchanged market tips during dinner, and after dinner told dirty stories to mixed company. They did not belong to Neddy's set—they were not even on Lucinda's Christmas-card list. He went toward their pool with feelings of indifference, charity, and some unease, since it seemed to be getting dark and these were the longest days of the year. The party when he joined it was noisy and large. Grace Biswanger was the kind of hostess who asked the optometrist, the veterinarian, the real-estate dealer, and the dentist. No one was swimming and the twilight, reflected on the water of the pool, had a wintry gleam. There was a bar and he started for this. When Grace Biswanger saw him she came toward him, not affectionately as he had every right to expect, but bellicosely.

"Why, this party has everything," she said loudly, "including a gate crasher."

She could not deal him a social blow—there was no question about this and he did not flinch. "As a gate crasher," he asked politely, "do I rate a drink?"

"Suit yourself," she said. "You don't seem to pay much attention to invitations."

She turned her back on him and joined some guests, and he went to the bar and ordered a whiskey. The bartender served him but he served him rudely. His was a world in which the caterer's men kept the social score, and to be rebuffed by a part-time barkeep meant that he had suffered some loss of social esteem. Or perhaps the man was new and uninformed. Then he heard Grace at his back say: "They went for broke overnight—nothing but income—and he showed up drunk one Sunday and asked us to loan him five thousand dollars. . . ." She was always talking about money. It was worse than eating your peas off a knife. He dove into the pool, swam its length and went away.

The next pool on his list, the last but two, belonged to his old mistress, Shirley Adams. If he had suffered any injuries at the Biswangers' they would be cured here. Love—sexual roughhouse in fact—was the supreme elixir, the pain killer, the brightly colored pill that would put the spring back into his step, the joy of life in his heart. They had had an affair last week, last month, last year. He couldn't remember. It was he who had broken it off, his was the upper hand, and he stepped through the gate of the wall that surrounded her pool with nothing so considered as self-confidence. It seemed in a way to be his pool, as the lover, particularly the illicit lover, enjoys the possessions of his mistress with an authority unknown to holy matrimony. She was there, her hair the color of brass, but her figure, at the edge of the lighted, cerulean water, excited in him no profound memories. It had been, he thought, a lighthearted affair, although she had wept when he broke it off. She seemed confused to see him and he wondered if she was still wounded. Would she, God forbid, weep again?

"What do you want?" she asked.

"I'm swimming across the county."

"Good Christ. Will you ever grow up?"

"What's the matter?"

"If you've come here for money," she said, "I won't give you another cent."

"You could give me a drink."

"I could but I won't. I'm not alone."

"Well, I'm on my way."

He dove in and swam the pool, but when he tried to haul himself up onto the curb he found that the strength in his arms and shoulders had gone, and he paddled to the ladder and climbed out. Looking over his shoulder he saw, in the lighted bathhouse, a young man. Going out onto the dark lawn he smelled chrysanthemums or marigolds—some stubborn autumnal fragrance—on the night air, strong as gas. Looking overhead he saw that the stars had come out, but why should he seem to see Andromeda, Cepheus, and Cassiopeia? What had become of the constellations of midsummer? He began to cry.

It was probably the first time in his adult life that he had ever cried, certainly the first time in his life that he had ever felt so miserable, cold, tired, and bewildered. He could not understand the rudeness of the caterer's barkeep or the rudeness of a mistress who had come to him on her knees and showered his trousers with tears. He had swum too long, he had been immersed too long, and his nose and his throat were sore from the water. What he needed then was a drink, some company, and some clean, dry clothes, and while he could have cut directly across the road to his home he went on to the Gilmartins' pool. Here, for the first time in his life, he did not dive but went down the steps into the icy water and swam a hobbled sidestroke that he might have learned as a youth. He staggered with fatigue on his way to the Clydes' and paddled the length of their pool, stopping again and again with his hand on the curb to rest. He climbed up the ladder and wondered if he had the strength to get home. He had done what he wanted, he had swum the county, but he was so stupefied with exhaustion that his triumph seemed vague. Stooped, holding on to the gateposts for support, he turned up the driveway of his own house.

The place was dark. Was it so late that they had all gone to bed? Had Lucinda stayed at the Westerhazys' for supper? Had the girls joined her there or gone someplace else? Hadn't they agreed, as they usually did on Sunday, to regret all their invitations and stay at home? He tried the garage doors to see what cars were in but the doors were locked and rust came off the handles onto his hands. Going toward the house, he saw that the force of the thunderstorm had knocked one of the rain gutters loose. It hung down over the front door like an umbrella rib, but it could be fixed in the morning. The house was locked, and he thought that the stupid cook or the stupid maid must have locked the place up until he remembered that it had been some time since they had employed a maid or a cook. He shouted, pounded on the door, tried to force it with his shoulder, and then, looking in at the windows, saw that the place was empty.

Gooseberries

ANTON CHEKHOV

The whole sky had been overcast with rain-clouds from early morning; it was a still day, not hot, but heavy, as it is in gray dull weather when the clouds have been hanging over the country for a long while, when one expects rain and it does not come. Ivan Ivanovich, the veterinary surgeon, and Burkin, the high school teacher, were already tired from walking, and the fields seemed to them endless. Far ahead of them they could just see the windmills of the village of Mironositskoe; on the right stretched a row of hillocks which disappeared in the distance behind the village, and they both knew that this was the bank of the river, that there were meadows, green willows, homesteads there, and that if one stood on one of the hillocks one could see from it the same vast plain, telegraph-wires, and a train which in the distance looked like a crawling caterpillar, and that in clear weather one could even see the town. Now, in still weather, when all nature seemed mild and dreamy, Ivan Ivanovich and Burkin were filled with love of the country-side, and both thought how great, how beautiful a land it was.

"Last time we were in Prokofy's barn," said Burkin, "you were about to tell me a story."

"Yes; I meant to tell you about my brother."

Ivan Ivanovich heaved a deep sigh and lighted a pipe to begin to tell his story, but just at that moment the rain began. And five minutes later heavy rain came down, covering the sky, and it was hard to tell when it would be over. Ivan Ivanovich and Burkin stopped in hesitation; the dogs, already drenched, stood with their tails between their legs gazing at them feelingly.

"We must take shelter somewhere," said Burkin. "Let us go to Alehin's; it's close by."

"Come along."

They turned aside and walked through mown fields, sometimes going straight forward, sometimes turning to the right, till they came out on the road. Soon they saw poplars, a garden, then the red roofs of barns; there was a gleam of the river, and the view opened onto a broad expanse of water with a windmill and a white bathhouse: this was Sofino, where Alehin lived.

The watermill was at work, drowning the sound of the rain; the dam was shaking. Here wet horses with drooping heads were standing near their carts, and men were walking about covered with sacks. It was damp, muddy, and desolate; the water looked cold and malignant. Ivan Ivanovich and Burkin were already conscious of a feeling of wetness, messiness, and discomfort all over; their feet were heavy with mud, and when, crossing the dam, they went up to the barns, they were silent, as though they were angry with one another.

In one of the barns there was the sound of a winnowing machine, the door was open, and clouds of dust were coming from it. In the doorway was standing Alehin himself, a man of forty, tall and stout, with long hair, more like a professor or an artist than a landowner. He had on a white shirt that badly needed washing, a rope for a belt, drawers instead of trousers, and his boots, too, were plastered up with mud and straw. His eyes and nose were black with dust. He recognized Ivan Ivanovich and Burkin, and was apparently much delighted to see them.

"Go into the house, gentlemen," he said, smiling; "I'll come directly, this minute."

It was a big two-storied house. Alehin lived in the lower story, with arched ceilings and little windows, where the bailiffs had once lived; here everything was plain, and there was a smell of rye bread, cheap vodka, and harness. He went upstairs into the best rooms only on rare occasions, when visitors came. Ivan Ivanovich and Burkin were met in the house by a maid-servant, a young woman so beautiful that they both stood still and looked at one another.

"You can't imagine how delighted I am to see you, my friends," said Alehin, going into the hall with them. "It is a surprise! Pelageya," he said, addressing the girl, "give our visitors something to change into. And, by the way, I will change too. Only I must first go and wash, for I almost think I have not washed since spring. Wouldn't you like to come into the bath-house? And meanwhile they will get things ready here."

Beautiful Pelageya, looking so refined and soft, brought them towels and soap, and Alehin went to the bathhouse with his guests.

"It's a long time since I had a wash," he said, undressing. "I have got a nice bathhouse, as you see—my father built it—but I somehow never have time to wash."

He sat down on the steps and soaped his long hair and his neck, and the water round him turned brown.

"Yes, I must say," said Ivan Ivanovich meaningly, looking at his head.

"It's a long time since I washed . . ." said Alehin with embarrassment, giving himself a second soaping, and the water near him turned dark blue, like ink.

Ivan Ivanovich went outside, plunged into the water with a loud splash, and swam in the rain, flinging his arms out wide. He stirred the water into waves which set the white lilies bobbing up and down; he swam to the very middle of the millpond and dived, and came up a minute later in another place, and swam on, and kept on diving, trying to touch bottom.

"Oh, my goodness!" he repeated continually, enjoying himself thoroughly. "Oh, my goodness!" He swam to the mill, talked to the peasants there, then returned and lay on his back in the middle of the pond, turning his face to the rain. Burkin and Alehin were dressed and ready to go, but he still went on swimming and diving. "Oh, my goodness! . . ." he said. "Oh, Lord, have mercy on me! . . ."

"That's enough!" Burkin shouted to him.

They went back to the house. And only when the lamp was lighted in the big drawing-room upstairs, and Burkin and Ivan Ivanovich, attired in silk dressing-gowns and warm slippers, were sitting in armchairs; and Alehin, washed and combed, in a new coat, was walking about the drawing-room, evidently enjoying the feeling of warmth, cleanliness, dry clothes, and light shoes; and when lovely Pelageya, stepping noiselessly on the carpet and smiling softly, handed tea and jam on a tray—only then Ivan Ivanovich began on his story, and it seemed as though not only Burkin and Alehin were listening, but also the ladies, young and old, and the officers who looked down upon them sternly and calmly from their gold frames.

"There are two of us brothers," he began—"I, Ivan Ivanovich, and my brother, Nikolay Ivanovich, two years younger. I went in for a learned profession and became a veterinary surgeon, while Nikolay sat in a government office from the time he was nineteen. Our father, Chimsha-Himalaisky, was the son of a private, but he himself rose to be an officer and left us a little estate and the rank of nobility. After his death the little estate went in debts and legal expenses; but, anyway, we had spent our childhood running wild in the country. Like peasant children, we passed our days and nights in the fields and the woods, looked after horses, stripped the bark off the trees, fished and so on . . . And, you know, whoever has once in his life caught perch or has seen the migrating of the thrushes in autumn, watched how they float in flocks over the village on bright, cool days, he will never be a real townsman, and will have a yearning for freedom to the day of his death. My brother was miserable in the government office. Years passed by, and he went on sitting in the same place, went on writing the same papers and thinking of one and the same thing— how to get into the country. And this yearning by degrees passed into a definite desire, into a dream of buying himself a little farm somewhere on the banks of a river or a lake.

"He was a gentle, good-natured fellow, and I was fond of him, but I never sympathized with this desire to shut himself up for the rest of his life in a little farm of his own. It's the correct thing to say that a man needs no more than six feet of earth. But six feet is what a corpse needs, not a man. And they say, too, now, that if our intellectual classes are attracted to the land and yearn for a farm, it's a good thing. But these farms are just the same as six feet of earth. To retreat from town, from the struggle, from the bustle of life, to retreat and bury oneself in one's farm—it's not life, it's egoism, laziness, it's monasticism of a sort, but monasticism without good works. A man does not need six feet of earth or a farm, but the whole globe, all nature, where he can have room to display all the qualities and peculiarities of his free spirit.

"My brother Nikolay, sitting in his government office, dreamed of how he would eat his own cabbages, which would fill the whole yard with such a savory smell, take his meals on the green grass, sleep in the sun, sit for whole hours on the seat by the gate gazing at the fields and the forest. Gardening books and the agricultural hints in calendars were his delight, his favorite spiritual sustenance; he enjoyed reading newspapers, too, but the only things he read in them were the advertisements of so many acres of arable land and a grass meadow with farmhouses and buildings, a river, a garden, a mill and millponds, for sale. And his imagination pictured the garden-paths, flowers and fruit, starling cotes, the carp in the pond, and all that sort of thing, you know. These imaginary pictures were of different kinds according to the advertisements which he came across, but for some reason in every one of them he always had to have gooseberries. He could not imagine a homestead, he could not picture an idyllic nook, without gooseberries.

" 'Country life has its conveniences,' he would sometimes say. 'You sit on the veranda and you drink tea, while your ducks swim on the pond, there is a delicious smell everywhere, and . . . and the gooseberries are growing.'

"He used to draw a map of his property, and in every map there were the same things—(a) house for the family, (b) servants' quarters, (c) kitchen-garden, (d) gooseberry-bushes. He lived parsimoniously, was frugal in food and drink, his clothes were beyond description; he looked like a beggar, but kept on saving and putting money in the bank. He grew fearfully avaricious. I did not like to look at him, and I used to give him something and send him presents for Christmas and Easter, but he used to save that too. Once a man is absorbed by an idea there is no doing anything with him.

"Years passed: he was transferred to another province. He was over forty, and he was still reading the advertisements in the papers and saving up. Then I heard he was married. Still with the same object of buying a farm and having gooseberries, he married an elderly and ugly widow without a trace of feeling for her, simply because she had filthy lucre. He went on living frugally after marrying her, and kept her short of food, while he put her money in the bank in his name.

"Her first husband had been a postmaster, and with him she was accustomed to pies and homemade wines, while with her second husband she did not get enough black bread; she began to pine away with this sort of life, and three years later she gave up her soul to God. And I need hardly say that my brother never for one moment imagined that he was responsible for her death. Money, like vodka, makes a man queer. In our town there was a merchant who, before he died, ordered a plateful of honey and ate up all his money and lottery tickets with the honey, so that no one might get the benefit of it. While I was inspecting cattle at a railway-station a cattle dealer fell under an engine and had his leg cut off. We carried him into the waiting room, the blood was flowing—it was a horrible thing—and he kept asking them to look for his leg and was very much worried about it; there were twenty roubles in the boot on the leg that had been cut off, and he was afraid they would be lost."

"That's a story from a different opera," said Burkin.

"After his wife's death," Ivan Ivanovich went on, after thinking for half a minute, "my brother began looking out for an estate for himself. Of course, you may look about for five years and yet end by making a mistake, and buying something quite different from what you have dreamed of. My brother Nikolay bought through an agent a mortgaged estate of three hundred and thirty acres, with a house for the family, with servants' quarters, with a park, but with no orchard, no gooseberry-bushes, and no duck-pond; there was a river, but the water in it was the color of coffee, because on one side of the estate there was a brickyard and on the other a factory for burning bones. But Nikolay Ivanovich did not grieve much; he ordered twenty gooseberry-bushes, planted them, and began living as a country gentleman.

"Last year I went to pay him a visit. I thought I would go and see what it was like. In his letters my brother called his estate 'Chumbaroklov Waste, alias Himalaiskoe.' I reached 'alias Himalaiskoe' in the afternoon. It was hot. Eveywhere there were ditches, fences, hedges, fir-trees planted in rows, and there was no knowing how to get to the yard, where to put one's horse. I went up to the house, and was met by a fat red dog that looked like a pig. It wanted to bark, but was too lazy. The cook, a fat, barefooted woman, came out of the kitchen, and she, too, looked like a pig, and said that her master was resting. I went in to see my brother. He was sitting up in bed with a quilt over his legs; he had grown older, fatter, wrinkled; his cheeks, his nose, and his mouth all stuck out—he looked as though he might begin grunting into the quilt at any moment.

"We embraced each other, and shed tears of joy and of sadness at the thought that we had once been young and now were both gray-headed and near the grave. He dressed, and led me out to show me the estate.

" 'Well, how are you getting on here?' I asked.

" 'Oh, all right, thank God; I am getting on very well.'

"He was no more a poor timid clerk, but a real landowner, a gentleman. He was already accustomed to it, had grown used to it, and liked it. He ate a great deal, went to the bathhouse, was growing stout, was already at law with the village commune and both factories, and was very much offended when the peasants did not call him 'your Honor.' And he concerned himself with the salvation of his soul in a substantial, gentlemanly manner, and performed deeds of charity, not simply, but with an air of consequence. And what deeds of charity! He treated the peasants for every sort of disease with soda and castor oil, and on his name-day had a thanksgiving service in the middle of the village, and then treated the peasants to a gallon of vodka—he thought that was the thing to do. Oh, those horrible gallons of vodka! One day the fat landowner hauls the peasants up before the district captain for trespass, and next day, in honor of a holiday, treats them to a gallon of vodka, and they drink and shout 'Hurrah!' and when they are drunk bow down to his feet. A change of life for the better and being well fed and idle develop in a Russian the most insolent self-conceit. Nikolay Ivanovich, who at one time in the government office was afraid to have any views of his own, now could say nothing that was not gospel truth, and uttered such truths in the tone of a prime minister. 'Education is essential, but for the peasants it is premature.' 'Corporal punishment is harmful as a rule, but in some cases it is necessary and there is nothing to take its place.'

" 'I know the peasants and understand how to treat them,' he would say. 'The peasants like me. I need only to hold up my little finger and the peasants will do anything I like.'

"And all this, observe, was uttered with a wise, benevolent smile. He repeated twenty times over 'We noblemen,' 'I as a noble'; obviously he did not remember that our grandfather was a peasant, and our father a soldier. Even our surname Chimsha-Himalaisky, in reality so incongruous, seemed to him now melodious, distinguished, and very agreeable.

"But the point just now is not he, but myself. I want to tell you about the change that took place in me during the brief hours I spent at his country place. In the evening, when we were drinking tea, the cook put on the table a plateful of gooseberries. They were not bought, but his own gooseberries, gathered for the first time since the bushes were planted. Nikolay Ivanovich laughed and looked for a minute in silence at the gooseberries, with tears in his eyes; he could not speak for excitement. Then he put one gooseberry in his mouth, looked at me with the triumph of a child who has at last received his favorite toy, and said:

" 'How delicious!'

"And he ate them greedily, continually repeating, 'Ah, how delicious! Do taste them!'

"They were sour and unripe, but, as Pushkin says:

> *Dearer to us the falsehood that exalts*
> *Than hosts of baser truths.*

"I saw a happy man whose cherished dream was so obviously fulfilled, who had attained his object in life, who had gained what he wanted, who was satisfied with his fate and himself. There is always, for some reason, an element of sadness mingled with my thoughts of human happiness, and, on this occasion, at the sight of a happy man I was overcome by an oppressive feeling that was close upon despair. It was particularly oppressive at night. A bed was made up for me in the room next to my brother's bedroom, and I could hear that he was awake, and that he kept getting up and going to the plate of gooseberries and taking one. I reflected how many satisfied, happy people there really are! What an overwhelming force it is! You look at life: the insolence and idleness of the strong, the ignorance and brutishness of the weak, incredible poverty all about us, overcrowding, degeneration, drunkenness, hypocrisy, lying ... Yet all is calm and stillness in the houses and in the streets; of the fifty thousand living in a town, there is not one who would cry out, who would give vent to his indignation aloud. We see the people going to market for provisions, eating by day, sleeping by night, talking their silly nonsense, getting married, growing old, serenely escorting their dead to the cemetery; but we do not see and we do not hear those who suffer, and what is terrible in life goes on somewhere behind the scenes ... Everything is quiet and peaceful, and nothing protests but mute statistics: so many people gone out of their minds, so many gallons of vodka drunk, so many children dead from malnutrition ... And this order of things is evidently necessary; evidently the happy man only feels at ease because the unhappy bear their burden in silence, and without that silence happiness would be impossible. It's a case of general hypnotism. There ought to be behind the door of every happy, contented man someone standing with a hammer continually reminding him with a tap that there are unhappy people; that however happy he may be, life will show him her jaws sooner or later, trouble will come for him—disease, poverty, losses, and no one will see or hear, just as now he neither sees nor hears others. But there is no man with a hammer; the happy man lives at his ease, the trivial daily cares faintly agitate him like the wind in the aspen tree—and all goes well.

"That night I realized that I, too, was happy and contented," Ivan Ivanovich went on, getting up. "I, too, at dinner and at the hunt liked to lay down the law on life and religion, and the way to manage the peasantry. I, too, used to say that science was light, that culture was essential, but for the simple people reading and writing was enough for the time. Freedom is a blessing, I used to say; we can no more do without it than without air, but we must wait a little. Yes, I used to talk like that, and now I ask, 'For what reason are we to wait?'" asked Ivan Ivanovich, looking angrily at Burkin. "Why wait, I ask you? What grounds have we for waiting? I shall be told, it can't be done all at once; every idea takes shape in life gradually, in its due time. But who is it says that? Where is the proof that it's right? You will fall back upon the natural order of things, the uniformity of phenomena; but is there order and uniformity in the fact that I, a living, thinking man, stand over a chasm and wait for it to close of itself, or to fill up with mud at the very time when perhaps I might leap over it or build a bridge across it? And again, wait for the sake of what? Wait till there's no strength to live? And meanwhile one must live, and one wants to live!

"I went away from my brother's early in the morning, and ever since then it has been unbearable for me to be among people. I am oppressed by peace and quiet; I am afraid to look at the windows, for there is no spectacle more painful to me now than the sight of a happy family sitting round the table drinking tea. I am old and am not fit for the struggle; I am not even capable of hatred; I can only grieve inwardly, feel irritated and vexed; but at night my head is hot from the rush of ideas, and I cannot sleep . . . Ah, if I were young!"

Ivan Ivanovich walked backwards and forwards in excitement, and repeated: "If I were young!"

He suddenly went up to Alehin and began pressing first one of his hands and then the other.

"Pavel Konstantinovich," he said in an imploring voice, "don't be calm and contented, don't let yourself be put to sleep! While you are young, strong, confident, be not weary in well-doing! There is no happiness, and there ought not to be; but if there is a meaning and an object in life, that meaning and object is not our happiness, but something greater and more rational. Do good!"

And all this Ivan Ivanovich said with a pitiful, imploring smile, as though he were asking him a personal favor.

Then all three sat in armchairs at different ends of the drawing-room and were silent. Ivan Ivanovich's story had not satisfied either Burkin or Alehin. When the generals and ladies gazed down from their gilt frames, looking in the dusk as though they were alive, it was dreary to listen to the story of the poor clerk who ate gooseberries. They felt inclined for some reason to talk about elegant people, about women. And their sitting in the drawing-room where everything—the chandeliers in their covers, the armchairs, and the carpet under their feet—reminded them that those very people who were now looking down from their frames had once moved about, sat, drunk tea in this room, and the fact that lovely Pelageya was moving noiselessly about was better than any story.

Alehin was fearfully sleepy; he had got up early, before three o'clock in the morning, to look after his work, and now his eyes were closing; but he was afraid his visitors might tell some interesting story after he had gone, and he lingered on. He did not go into the question whether what Ivan Ivanovich had just said was right and true. His visitors did not talk of groats, nor of hay, nor of tar, but of something that had no direct bearing on his life, and he was glad and wanted them to go on.

"It's bedtime, though," said Burkin, getting up. "Allow me to wish you good night."

Alehin said good night and went downstairs to his own domain, while the visitors remained upstairs. They were both taken for the night to a big room where there stood two old wooden beds decorated with carvings, and in the corner was an ivory crucifix. The big cool beds, which had been made by the lovely Pelageya, smelt agreeably of clean linen.

Ivan Ivanovich undressed in silence and got into bed.

"Lord forgive us sinners!" he said, and put his head under the quilt.

His pipe lying on the table smelt strongly of stale tobacco, and Burkin could not sleep for a long while, and kept wondering where the oppressive smell came from.

The rain was pattering on the windowpanes all night.

The Darling

ANTON CHEKHOV

Olenka, the daughter of the retired collegiate assessor, Plemyanniakov, was sitting in her back porch, lost in thought. It was hot, the flies were persistent and teasing, and it was pleasant to reflect that it would soon be evening. Dark rainclouds were gathering from the east, and bringing from time to time a breath of moisture in the air.

Kukin, who was the manager of an open-air theatre called the Tivoli, and who lived in the lodge, was standing in the middle of the garden looking at the sky.

"Again!" he observed despairingly. "It's going to rain again! Rain every day, as though to spite me! I might as well hang myself! It's ruin! Fearful losses every day."

He flung up his hands, and went on, addressing Olenka:

"There! that's the life we lead, Olga Semyonovna. It's enough to make one cry. One works and does one's utmost; one wears oneself out, getting no sleep at night, and racks one's brain what to do for the best. And then what happens? To begin with, one's public is ignorant, boorish. I give them the very best operetta, a dainty masque, first-rate music-hall artists. But do you suppose that's what they want! They don't understand anything of that sort. They want a clown; what they ask for is vulgarity. And then look at the weather! Almost every evening it rains. It started on the tenth of May, and it's kept it up all May and June. It's simply awful! The public doesn't come, but I've to pay the rent just the same, and pay the artists."

The next evening the clouds would gather again, and Kukin would say with an hysterical laugh:

"Well, rain away, then! Flood the garden, drown me! Damn my luck in this world and the next! Let the artists have me up! Send me to prison!— to Siberia!—the scaffold! Ha, ha, ha!"

And next day the same thing.

Olenka listened to Kukin with silent gravity, and sometimes tears came into her eyes. In the end his misfortunes touched her; she grew to love him. He was a small thin man, with a yellow face, and curls combed forward on his forehead. He spoke in a thin tenor; as he talked his mouth worked on one side, and there was always an expression of despair on his face; yet he aroused a deep and genuine affection in her. She was always fond of some-one, and could not exist without loving. In earlier days she had loved her papa, who now sat in a darkened room, breathing with difficulty; she had loved her aunt who used to come every other year from Bryansk; and be-fore that, when she was at school, she had loved her French master. She was a gentle, soft-hearted, compassionate girl, with mild, tender eyes and very good health. At the sight of her full rosy cheeks, her soft white neck and a little dark mole on it, and the kind, naive smile, which came into her face when she listened to anything pleasant, men thought, "Yes, not half bad," and smiled too, while lady visitors could not refrain from seizing her hand in the middle of a conversation, exclaiming in a gush of delight, "You darling!"

The house in which she had lived from her birth upwards, and which was left her in her father's will, was at the extreme end of the town, not far from the Tivoli. In the evenings and at night she could hear the band play-ing, and the crackling and banging of fireworks, and it seemed to her that it was Kukin struggling with his destiny, storming the entrenchments of his chief foe, the indifferent public; there was a sweet thrill at her heart, she had no desire to sleep, and when he returned home at daybreak, she tapped softly at her bedroom window, and showing him only her face and one shoulder through the curtain, she gave him a friendly smile. . . .

He proposed to her, and they were married. And when he had a closer view of her neck and her plump, fine shoulders, he threw up his hands, and said:

"You darling!"

He was happy, but as it rained on the day and night of his wedding, his face still retained an expression of despair.

They got on very well together. She used to sit in his office, to look after things in the Tivoli, to put down the accounts and pay the wages. And her rosy cheeks, her sweet, naive, radiant smile, were to be seen now at the of-fice window, now in the refreshment bar or behind the scenes at the thea-tre. And already she used to say to her acquaintances that the theatre was the chief and most important thing in life, and that it was only through the drama that one could derive true enjoyment and become cultivated and humane.

"But do you suppose the public understands that?" she used to say. "What they want is a clown. Yesterday we gave 'Faust Inside Out,' and al-most all the boxes were empty; but if Vanitchka and I had been producing some vulgar thing, I assure you the theatre would have been packed. To-morrow Vanitchka and I are doing 'Orpheus in Hell.' Do come."

And what Kukin said about the theatre and the actors she repeated. Like him she despised the public for their ignorance and their indifference to art; she took part in the rehearsals, she corrected the actors, she kept an eye on the behaviour of the musicians, and when there was an unfavourable notice in the local paper, she shed tears, and then went to the editor's office to set things right.

The actors were fond of her and used to call her "Vanitchka and I," and "the darling"; she was sorry for them and used to lend them small sums of money, and if they deceived her, she used to shed a few tears in private, but did not complain to her husband.

They got on well in the winter too. They took the theatre in the town for the whole winter, and let it for short terms to a Little Russian company, or to a conjurer, or to a local dramatic society. Olenka grew stouter, and was always beaming with satisfaction, while Kukin grew thinner and yellower, and continually complained of their terrible losses, although he had not done badly all the winter. He used to cough at night, and she used to give him hot raspberry tea or limeflower water, to rub him with eau-de-Cologne and to wrap him in her warm shawls.

"You're such a sweet pet!" she used to say with perfect sincerity, stroking his hair. "You're such a pretty dear!"

Towards Lent he went to Moscow to collect a new troupe, and without him she could not sleep, but sat all night at her window, looking at the stars, and she compared herself with the hens, who are awake all night and uneasy when the cock is not in the hen-house. Kukin was detained in Moscow, and wrote that he would be back at Easter, adding some instructions about the Tivoli. But on the Sunday before Easter, late in the evening, came a sudden ominous knock at the gate; someone was hammering on the gate as though on a barrel—boom, boom, boom! The drowsy cook went flopping with her bare feet through the puddles, as she ran to open the gate.

"Please open," said someone outside in a thick bass. "There is a telegram for you."

Olenka had received telegrams from her husband before, but this time for some reason she felt numb with terror. With shaking hands she opened the telegram and read as follows:

"Ivan Petrovich died suddenly to-day. Awaiting immate instructions fufuneral Tuesday."

That was how it was written in the telegram—"fufuneral," and the utterly incomprehensible word "immate." It was signed by the stage manager of the operatic company.

"My darling!" sobbed Olenka. "Vanitchka, my precious, my darling! Why did I ever meet you! Why did I know you and love you! Your poor heart-broken Olenka is all alone without you!"

Kukin's funeral took place on Tuesday in Moscow, Olenka returned home on Wednesday, and as soon as she got indoors she threw herself on her bed and sobbed so loudly that it could be heard next door, and in the street.

"Poor darling!" the neighbours said, as they crossed themselves. "Olga Semyonovna, poor darling! How she does take on!"

Three months later Olenka was coming home from mass, melancholy and in deep mourning. It happened that one of her neighbours, Vassily Andreitch Pustovalov, returning home from church, walked back beside her. He was the manager at Babakayev's, the timber merchant's. He wore a straw hat, a white waistcoat, and a gold watchchain, and looked more like a country gentleman than a man in trade.

"Everything happens as it is ordained, Olga Semyonovna," he said gravely, with a sympathetic note in his voice; "and if any of our dear ones die, it must be because it is the will of God, so we ought to have fortitude and bear it submissively."

After seeing Olenka to her gate, he said good-bye and went on. All day afterwards she heard his sedately dignified voice, and whenever she shut her eyes she saw his dark beard. She liked him very much. And apparently she had made an impression on him too, for not long afterwards an elderly lady, with whom she was only slightly acquainted, came to drink coffee with her, and as soon as she was seated at table began to talk about Pustovalov, saying that he was an excellent man whom one could thoroughly depend upon, and that any girl would be glad to marry him. Three days later Pustovalov came himself. He did not stay long, only about ten minutes, and he did not say much, but when he left, Olenka loved him—loved him so much that she lay awake all night in a perfect fever, and in the morning she sent for the elderly lady. The match was quickly arranged, and then came the wedding.

Pustovalov and Olenka got on very well together when they were married.

Usually he sat in the office till dinner-time, then he went out on business, while Olenka took his place, and sat in the office till evening, making up accounts and booking orders.

"Timber gets dearer every year; the price rises twenty per cent," she would say to her customers and friends. "Only fancy we used to sell local timber, and now Vassitchka always has to go for wood to the Mogilev district. And the freight!" she would add, covering her cheeks with her hands in horror. "The freight!"

It seemed to her that she had been in the timber trade for ages and ages, and that the most important and necessary thing in life was timber; and there was something intimate and touching to her in the very sound of words such as "baulk," "post," "beam," "pole," "scantling," "batten," "lath," "plank," etc.

At night when she was asleep she dreamed of perfect mountains of planks and boards, and long strings of wagons, carting timber somewhere far away. She dreamed that a whole regiment of six-inch beams forty feet high, standing on end, was marching upon the timber-yard; that logs, beams, and boards knocked together with the resounding crash of dry wood, kept falling and getting up again, piling themselves on each other. Olenka cried out in her sleep, and Pustovalov said to her tenderly: "Olenka, what's the matter, darling? Cross yourself!"

Her husband's ideas were hers. If he thought the room was too hot, or that business was slack, she thought the same. Her husband did not care for entertainments, and on holidays he stayed at home. She did likewise.

"You are always at home or in the office," her friends said to her. "You should go to the theatre, darling, or to the circus."

"Vassitchka and I have no time to go to theatres," she would answer sedately. "We have no time for nonsense. What's the use of these theatres?"

On Saturdays Pustovalov and she used to go to the evening service; on holidays to early mass, and they walked side by side with softened faces as they came home from church. There was a pleasant fragrance about them both, and her silk dress rustled agreeably. At home they drank tea, with fancy bread and jams of various kinds, and afterwards they ate pie. Every day at twelve o'clock there was a savoury smell of beetroot soup and of mutton or duck in their yard, and on fast-days of fish, and no one could pass the gate without feeling hungry. In the office the samovar was always boiling, and customers were regaled with tea and cracknels. Once a week the couple went to the baths and returned side by side, both red in the face.

"Yes, we have nothing to complain of, thank God," Olenka used to say to her acquaintances. "I wish everyone were as well off as Vassitchka and I,"

When Pustovalov went away to buy wood in the Mogilev district, she missed him dreadfully, lay awake and cried. A young veterinary surgeon in the army, called Smirnin, to whom they had let their lodge, used sometimes to come in in the evening. He used to talk to her and play cards with her, and this entertained her in her husband's absence. She was particularly interested in what he told her of his home life. He was married and had a little boy, but was separated from his wife because she had been unfaithful to him, and now he hated her and used to send her forty roubles a month for the maintenance of their son. And hearing of all this, Olenka sighed and shook her head. She was sorry for him.

"Well, God keep you," she used to say to him at parting, as she lighted him down the stairs with a candle. "Thank you for coming to cheer me up, and may the Mother of God give you health."

And she always expressed herself with the same sedateness and dignity, the same reasonableness, in imitation of her husband. As the veterinary surgeon was disappearing behind the door below, she would say:

"You know, Vladimir Platonitch, you'd better make it up with your wife.

You should forgive her for the sake of your son. You may be sure the little fellow understands."

And when Pustovalov came back, she told him in a low voice about the veterinary surgeon and his unhappy home life, and both sighed and shook their heads and talked about the boy, who, no doubt, missed his father, and by some strange connection of ideas, they went up to the holy ikons, bowed to the ground before them and prayed that God would give them children.

And so the Pustovalovs lived for six years quietly and peaceably in love and complete harmony.

But behold! one winter day after drinking hot tea in the office, Vassily Andreitch went out into the yard without his cap on to see about sending off some timber, caught cold and was taken ill. He had the best doctors, but he grew worse and died after four months' illness. And Olenka was a widow once more.

"I've nobody now you've left me, my darling," she sobbed, after her husband's funeral. "How can I live without you, in wretchedness and misery! Pity me, good people, all alone in the world!"

She went about dressed in black with long "weepers," and gave up wearing hat and gloves for good. She hardly ever went out, except to church, or to her husband's grave, and led the life of a nun. It was not till six months later that she took off the weepers and opened the shutters of the windows. She was sometimes seen in the mornings, going with her cook to market for provisions, but what went on in her house and how she lived now could only be surmised. People guessed, from seeing her drinking tea in her garden with the veterinary surgeon, who read the newspaper aloud to her, and from the fact that, meeting a lady she knew at the post-office, she said to her:

"There is no proper veterinary inspection in our town, and that's the cause of all sorts of epidemics. One is always hearing of people's getting infection from the milk supply, or catching disease from horses and cows. The health of domestic animals ought to be as well cared for as the health of human beings."

She repeated the veterinary surgeon's words, and was of the same opinion as he about everything. It was evident that she could not live a year without some attachment, and had found new happiness in the lodge. In anyone else this would have been censured, but no one could think ill of Olenka; everything she did was so natural. Neither she nor the veterinary surgeon said anything to other people of the change in their relations, and tried, indeed, to conceal it, but without success, for Olenka could not keep a secret. When he had visitors, men serving in his regiment, and she poured out tea or served the supper, she would begin talking of the cattle plague, of the foot and mouth disease, and of the municipal slaughter-houses. He was dreadfully embarrassed, and when the guests had gone, he would seize her by the hand and hiss angrily:

"I've asked you before not to talk about what you don't understand. When we veterinary surgeons are talking among ourselves, please don't put your word in. It's really annoying."

And she would look at him with astonishment and dismay, and ask him in alarm: "But, Voloditchka, what *am* I to talk about?"

And with tears in her eyes she would embrace him, begging him not to be angry, and they were both happy.

But this happiness did not last long. The veterinary surgeon departed, departed for ever with his regiment, when it was transferred to a distant place—to Siberia, it may be. And Olenka was left alone.

Now she was absolutely alone. Her father had long been dead, and his armchair lay in the attic, covered with dust and lame of one leg. She got thinner and plainer, and when people met her in the street they did not look at her as they used to, and did not smile to her; evidently her best years were over and left behind, and now a new sort of life had begun for her, which did not bear thinking about. In the evening Olenka sat in the porch, and heard the band playing and the fireworks popping in the Tivoli, but now the sound stirred no response. She looked into her yard without interest, thought of nothing, wished for nothing, and afterwards, when night came on she went to bed and dreamed of her empty yard. She ate and drank as it were unwillingly.

And what was worst of all, she had no opinions of any sort. She saw the objects about her and understood what she saw, but could not form any opinion about them, and did not know what to talk about. And how awful it is not to have any opinions! One sees a bottle, for instance, or the rain, or a peasant driving in his cart, but what the bottle is for, or the rain, or the peasant, and what is the meaning of it, one can't say, and could not even for a thousand roubles. When she had Kukin, or Pustovalov, or the veterinary surgeon, Olenka could explain everything, and give her opinion about anything you like but now there was the same emptiness in her brain and in her heart as there was in her yard outside. And it was as harsh and as bitter as wormwood in the mouth.

Little by little the town grew in all directions. The road became a street, and where the Tivoli and the timber-yard had been, there were new turnings and houses. How rapidly time passes! Olenka's house grew dingy, the roof got rusty, the shed sank on one side, and the whole yard was overgrown with docks and stinging-nettles. Olenka herself had grown plain and elderly; in summer she sat in the porch, and her soul, as before, was empty and dreary and full of bitterness. In winter she sat at her window and looked at the snow. When she caught the scent of spring, or heard the chime of the church bells, a sudden rush of memories from the past came over her, there was a tender ache in her heart, and her eyes brimmed over with tears; but this was only for a minute, and then came emptiness again and the sense of the futility of life. The black kitten, Briska, rubbed against her and purred softly, but Olenka was not touched by these feline caresses.

That was not what she needed. She wanted a love that would absorb her whole being, her whole soul and reason—that would give her ideas and an object in life, and would warm her old blood. And she would shake the kitten off her skirt and say with vexation:

"Get along; I don't want you!"

And so it was, day after day and year after year, and no joy, and no opinions. Whatever Mavra, the cook, said she accepted.

One hot July day, towards evening, just as the cattle were being driven by, and the whole yard was full of dust, someone suddenly knocked at the gate. Olenka went to open it herself and was dumbfounded when she looked out: she saw Smirnin, the veterinary surgeon, grey-headed, and dressed as a civilian. She suddenly remembered everything. She could not help crying and letting her head fall on his breast without uttering a word, and in the violence of her feeling she did not notice how they both walked into the house and sat down to tea.

"My dear Vladimir Platonitch! What fate has brought you?" she muttered, trembling with joy.

"I want to settle here for good, Olga Semyonovna," he told her. "I have resigned my post, and have come to settle down and try my luck on my own account. Besides, it's time for my boy to go to school. He's a big boy. I am reconciled with my wife, you know."

"Where is she?" asked Olenka.

"She's at the hotel with the boy, and I'm looking for lodgings."

"Good gracious, my dear soul! Lodgings! Why not have my house? Why shouldn't that suit you? Why, my goodness, I wouldn't take any rent!" cried Olenka in a flutter, beginning to cry again. "You live here, and the lodge will do nicely for me. Oh dear! how glad I am!"

Next day the roof was painted and the walls were whitewashed, and Olenka, with her arms akimbo, walked about the yard giving directions. Her face was beaming with her old smile, and she was brisk and alert as though she had waked from a long sleep. The veterinary's wife arrived—a thin, plain lady, with short hair and a peevish expression. With her was her little Sasha, a boy of ten, small for his age, blue-eyed, chubby, with dimples in his cheeks. And scarcely had the boy walked into the yard when he ran after the cat, and at once there was the sound of his gay, joyous laugh.

"Is that your puss, auntie?" he asked Olenka. "When she has little ones, do give us a kitten. Mamma is awfully afraid of mice."

Olenka talked to him, and gave him tea. Her heart warmed and there was a sweet ache in her bosom, as though the boy had been her own child. And when he sat at the table in the evening, going over his lessons, she looked at him with deep tenderness and pity as she murmured to herself:

"You pretty pet! . . . . my precious! . . . Such a fair little thing, and so clever."

" 'An island is a piece of land which is entirely surrounded by water,' " he read aloud.

"An island is a piece of land," she repeated, and this was the first opinion to which she gave utterance with positive conviction after so many years of silence and dearth of ideas.

Now she had opinions of her own, and at supper she talked to Sasha's parents, saying how difficult the lessons were at the high schools, but that yet the high school was better than a commercial one, since with a high school education all careers were open to one, such as being a doctor or an engineer.

Sasha began going to the high school. His mother departed to Harkov to her sister's and did not return; his father used to go off every day to inspect cattle, and would often be away from home for three days together, and it seemed to Olenka as though Sasha was entirely abandoned, that he was not wanted at home, that he was being starved, and she carried him off to her lodge and gave him a little room there.

And for six months Sasha had lived in the lodge with her. Every morning Olenka came into his bedroom and found him fast asleep, sleeping noiselessly with his hand under his cheek. She was sorry to wake him.

"Sashenka," she would say mournfully, "get up, darling. It's time for school."

He would get up, dress and say his prayers, and then sit down to breakfast, drink three glasses of tea, and eat two large cracknels and half a buttered roll. All this time he was hardly awake and a little ill-humoured in consequence.

"You don't quite know your fable, Sashenka," Olenka would say, looking at him as though he were about to set off on a long journey. "What a lot of trouble I have with you! You must work and do your best, darling, and obey your teachers."

"Oh, do leave me alone!" Sasha would say.

Then he would go down the street to school, a little figure, wearing a big cap and carrying a satchel on his shoulder. Olenka would follow him noiselessly.

"Sashenka!" she would call after him, and she would pop into his hand a date or a caramel. When he reached the street where the school was, he would feel ashamed of being followed by a tall, stout woman; he would turn round and say:

"You'd better go home, auntie. I can go the rest of the way alone."

She would stand still and look after him fixedly till he had disappeared at the school-gate.

Ah, how she loved him! Of her former attachments not one had been so deep; never had her soul surrendered to any feeling so spontaneously, so disinterestedly, and so joyously as now that her maternal instincts were aroused. For this little boy with the dimple in his cheek and the big school cap, she would have given her whole life, she would have given it with joy and tears of tenderness. Why? Who can tell why?

When she had seen the last of Sasha, she returned home, contented and serene, brimming over with love; her face, which had grown younger during the last six months, smiled and beamed; people meeting her looked at her with pleasure.

"Good-morning, Olga Semyonovna, darling. How are you, darling?"

"The lessons at the high school are very difficult now," she would relate at the market. "It's too much; in the first class yesterday they gave him a fable to learn by heart, and a Latin translation and a problem. You know it's too much for a little chap."

And she would begin talking about the teachers, the lessons, and the school books, saying just what Sasha said.

At three o'clock they had dinner together: in the evening they learned their lessons together and cried. When she put him to bed, she would stay a long time making the cross over him and murmuring a prayer; then she would go to bed and dream of that far-away misty future when Sasha would finish his studies and become a doctor or an engineer, would have a big house of his own with horses and a carriage, would get married and have children. . . . She would fall asleep still thinking of the same thing, and tears would run down her cheeks from her closed eyes, while the black cat lay purring beside her: "Mrr, mrr, mrr."

Suddenly there would come a loud knock at the gate.

Olenka would wake up breathless with alarm, her heart throbbing. Half a minute later would come another knock.

"It must be a telegram from Harkov," she would think, beginning to tremble from head to foot. "Sasha's mother is sending for him from Harkov. . . . Oh, mercy on us!"

She was in despair. Her head, her hands, and her feet would turn chill, and she would feel that she was the most unhappy woman in the world. But another minute would pass, voices would be heard: it would turn out to be the veterinary surgeon coming home from the club.

"Well, thank God!" she would think.

And gradually the load in her heart would pass off, and she would feel at ease. She would go back to bed thinking of Sasha, who lay sound asleep in the next room, sometimes crying out in his sleep.

"I'll give it you! Get away! Shut up!"

The Wife Of His Youth

CHARLES CHESNUTT

I

Mr. Ryder was going to give a ball. There were several reasons why this was an opportune time for such an event.

Mr. Ryder might aptly be called the dean of the Blue Veins. The original Blue Veins were a little society of colored persons organized in a Northern city shortly after the war. Its purpose was to establish and maintain correct social standards among a people whose social condition presented almost unlimited room for improvement. By accident, combined perhaps with some natural affinity, the society consisted of individuals who were, generally speaking, more white than black. Some envious outsider made the suggestion that no one was eligible for membership who was not white enough to show blue veins. The suggestion was readily adopted by those who were not of the favored few, and since that time the society, though possessing a longer and more pretentious name, had been known far and wide as the "Blue Vein Society," and its members as the "Blue Veins."

The Blue Veins did not allow that any such requirement existed for admission to their circle, but, on the contrary, declared that character and culture were the only things considered; and that if most of their members were light colored, it was because such persons, as a rule, had had better opportunities to qualify themselves for membership. Opinions differed, too, as to the usefulness of the society. There were those who had been known to assail it violently as a glaring example of the very prejudice from which the colored race had suffered most; and later, when such critics had succeeded in getting on the inside, they had been heard to maintain with zeal and earnestness that the society was a lifeboat, an anchor, a bulwark and a shield,—a pillar of cloud by day and of fire by night, to guide their people through the social wilderness. Another alleged prerequisite for

226

Blue Vein membership was that of free birth; and while there was really no such requirement, it is doubtless true that very few of the members would have been unable to meet it if there had been. If there were one or two of the older members who had come up from the South and from slavery, their history presented enough romantic circumstances to rob their servile origin of its grosser aspects.

While there were no such tests of eligibility, it is true that the Blue Veins had their notions on these subjects, and that not all of them were equally liberal in regard to the things they collectively disclaimed. Mr. Ryder was one of the most conservative. Though he had not been among the founders of the society, but had come in some years later, his genius for social leadership was such that he had speedily become its recognized adviser and head, the custodian of its standards, and the preserver of its traditions. He shaped its social policy, was active in providing for its entertainment, and when the interest fell off, as it sometimes did, he fanned the embers until they burst again into a cheerful flame.

There were still other reasons for his popularity. While he was not as white as some of the Blue Veins, his appearance was such as to confer distinction upon them. His features were of a refined type, his hair was almost straight; he was always neatly dressed; his manners were irreproachable, and his morals above suspicion. He had come to Groveland a young man, and obtaining employment in the office of a railroad company as messenger had in time worked himself up to the position of stationery clerk, having charge of the distribution of the office supplies for the whole company. Although the lack of early training had hindered the orderly development of a naturally fine mind, it had not prevented him from doing a great deal of reading or from forming decidedly literary tastes. Poetry was his passion. He could repeat whole pages of the great English poets; and if his pronunciation was sometimes faulty, his eye, his voice, his gestures, would respond to the changing sentiment with a precision that revealed a poetic soul and disarmed criticism. He was economical, and had saved money; he owned and occupied a very comfortable house on a respectable street. His residence was handsomely furnished, containing among other things a good library, especially rich in poetry, a piano, and some choice engravings. He generally shared his house with some young couple, who looked after his wants and were company for him; for Mr. Ryder was a single man. In the early days of his connection with the Blue Veins he had been regarded as quite a catch, and young ladies and their mothers had manœuvred with much ingenuity to capture him. Not, however, until Mrs. Molly Dixon visited Groveland had any woman ever made him wish to change his condition to that of a married man.

Mrs. Dixon had come to Groveland from Washington in the spring, and before the summer was over she had won Mr. Ryder's heart. She possessed many attractive qualities. She was much younger than he; in fact, he was old enough to have been her father, though no one knew exactly how old he was. She was whiter than he, and better educated. She had moved in the best colored society of the country, at Washington, and had taught in the schools of that city. Such a superior person had been eagerly welcomed to the Blue Vein Society, and had taken a leading part in its activities. Mr. Ryder had at first been attracted by her charms of person, for she was very good looking and not over twenty-five; then by her refined manners and the vivacity of her wit. Her husband had been a government clerk, and at his death had left a considerable life insurance. She was visiting friends in Groveland, and, finding the town and the people to her liking, had prolonged her stay indefinitely. She had not seemed displeased at Mr. Ryder's attentions, but on the contrary had given him every proper encouragement; indeed, a younger and less cautious man would long since have spoken. But he had made up his mind, and had only to determine the time when he would ask her to be his wife. He decided to give a ball in her honor, and at some time during the evening of the ball to offer her his heart and hand. He had no special fears about the outcome, but, with a little touch of romance, he wanted the surroundings to be in harmony with his own feelings when he should have received the answer he expected.

Mr. Ryder resolved that this ball should mark an epoch in the social history of Groveland. He knew, of course,—no one could know better,—the entertainments that had taken place in past years, and what must be done to surpass them. His ball must be worthy of the lady in whose honor it was to be given, and must, by the quality of its guests, set an example for the future. He had observed of late a growing liberality, almost a laxity, in social matters, even among members of his own set, and had several times been forced to meet in a social way persons whose complexions and callings in life were hardly up to the standards which he considered proper for the society to maintain. He had a theory of his own.

"I have no race prejudice," he would say, "but we people of mixed blood are ground between the upper and the nether millstone. Our fate lies between absorption by the white race and extinction in the black. The one doesn't want us yet, but may take us in time. The other would welcome us, but it would be for us a backward step. 'With malice towards none, with charity for all,' we must do the best we can for ourselves and those who are to follow us. Self-preservation is the first law of nature."

His ball would serve by its exclusiveness to counteract leveling tendencies, and his marriage with Mrs. Dixon would help to further the upward process of absorption he had been wishing and waiting for.

II

The ball was to take place on Friday night. The house had been put in order, the carpets covered with canvas, the halls and stairs decorated with palms and potted plants; and in the afternoon Mr. Ryder sat on his front porch, which the shade of a vine running up over a wire netting made a cool and pleasant lounging place. He expected to respond to the toast "The Ladies" at the supper, and from a volume of Tennyson—his favorite poet—was fortifying himself with apt quotations. The volume was open at "A Dream of Fair Women." His eyes fell on these lines, and he read them aloud to judge better of their effect:—

> "At length I saw a lady within call,
>   Stiller than chisell'd marble, standing there;
> A daughter of the gods, divinely tall,
>   And most divinely fair."

He marked the verse, and turning the page read the stanza beginning,—

> "O sweet pale Margaret,
>   O rare pale Margaret."

He weighed the passage a moment, and decided that it would not do. Mrs. Dixon was the palest lady he expected at the ball, and she was of a rather ruddy complexion, and of lively disposition and buxom build. So he ran over the leaves until his eye rested on the description of Queen Guinevere:—

> "She seem'd a part of joyous Spring:
>   A gown of grass-green silk she wore,
>   Buckled with golden clasps before;
> A light-green tuft of plumes she bore
>   Closed in a golden ring.

*   *   *

> "She look'd so lovely, as she sway'd
>   The rein with dainty finger-tips,
> A man had given all other bliss,
>   And all his worldly worth for this,
> To waste his whole heart in one kiss
>   Upon her perfect lips."

As Mr. Ryder murmured these words audibly, with an appreciative thrill, he heard the latch of his gate click, and a light footfall sounding on the steps. He turned his head, and saw a woman standing before his door.

She was a little woman, not five feet tall, and proportioned to her height. Although she stood erect, and looked around her with very bright and restless eyes, she seemed quite old; for her face was crossed and recrossed with a hundred wrinkles, and around the edges of her bonnet could be seen protruding here and there a tuft of short gray wool. She wore a blue calico gown of ancient cut, a little red shawl fastened around her shoulders with an old-fashioned brass brooch, and a large bonnet profusely ornamented with faded red and yellow artificial flowers. And she was very black,—so black that her toothless gums, revealed when she opened her mouth to speak, were not red, but blue. She looked like a bit of the old plantation life, summoned up from the past by the wave of a magician's wand, as the poet's fancy had called into being the gracious shapes of which Mr. Ryder had just been reading.

He rose from his chair and came over to where she stood.

"Good-afternoon, madam," he said.

"Good-evenin', suh," she answered, ducking suddenly with a quaint curtsy. Her voice was shrill and piping, but softened somewhat by age. "Is dis yere whar Mistuh Ryduh lib, suh?" she asked, looking around her doubtfully, and glancing into the open windows, through which some of the preparations for the evening were visible.

"Yes," he replied, with an air of kindly patronage, unconsciously flattered by her manner, "I am Mr. Ryder. Did you want to see me?"

"Yas, suh, ef I ain't 'sturbin' of you too much."

"Not at all. Have a seat over here behind the vine, where it is cool. What can I do for you?"

" 'Scuse me, suh," she continued, when she had sat down on the edge of a chair, " 'scuse me, suh, I's lookin for my husban'. I heerd you wuz a big man an' had libbed heah a long time, an' I 'lowed you wouldn't min' ef I'd come roun' an' ax you ef you'd ever heerd of a merlatter man by de name er Sam Taylor 'quirin' roun' in de chu'ches ermongs' de people fer his wife 'Liza Jane?"

Mr. Ryder seemed to think for a moment.

"There used to be many such cases right after the war," he said, "but it has been so long that I have forgotten them. There are very few now. But tell me your story, and it may refresh my memory."

She sat back farther in her chair so as to be more comfortable, and folded her withered hands in her lap.

"My name's 'Liza," she began, " 'Liza Jane. W'en I wuz young I us'ter b'long ter Marse Bob Smif, down in ole Missoura. I wuz bawn down dere. W'en I wuz a gal I wuz married ter a man named Jim. But Jim died, an' after dat I married a merlatter man named Sam Taylor. Sam wuz freebawn, but his mammy and daddy died, an' de w'ite folks 'prenticed him ter my marster fer ter work fer 'im 'tel he wuz growed up. Sam worked in de fiel', an' I wuz de cook. One day Ma'y Ann, ole miss's maid, came rushin' out ter de kitchen, an' says she, ' 'Liza Jane, ole marse gwine sell yo' Sam down de ribber.'

" 'Go way f'm yere,' says I; 'my husban' 's free!'

" 'Don' make no diff'ence. I heerd ole marse tell ole miss he wuz gwine take yo' Sam 'way wid 'im ter-morrow, fer he needed money, an' he knowed whar he could git a t'ousan' dollars fer Sam an' no questions axed.'

"W'en Sam come home f'm de fiel' dat night, I tole him 'bout ole marse gwine steal 'im, an' Sam run erway. His time wuz mos' up, an' he swo' dat w'en he wuz twenty-one he would come back an' he'p me run erway, er else save up de money ter buy my freedom. An' I know he'd 'a' done it, fer he thought a heap er me, Sam did. But w'en he come back he did n' fin' me, fer I wuz n' dere. Ole marse had heerd dat I warned Sam, so he had me whip' an' sol' down de ribber.

"Den de wah broke out, an' w'en it wuz ober de cullud folks wuz scattered. I went back ter de ole home; but Sam wuz n' dere, an' I could n' l'arn nuffin' 'bout 'im. But I knowed he'd be'n dere to look fer me an' had n' foun' me, an' had gone erway ter hunt fer me.

"I's be'n lookin' fer 'im eber sence," she added simply, as though twenty-five years were but a couple of weeks, "an' I knows he's be'n lookin' fer me. Fer he sot a heap er sto' by me, Sam did, an' I know he's be'n huntin' fer me all dese years,—'less'n he's be'n sick er sump'n, so he could n' work, er out'n his head, so he could n' 'member his promise. I went back down de ribber, fer I 'lowed he'd gone down dere lookin' fer me. I's be'n ter Noo Orleans, an' Atlanty, an' Charleston, an' Richmon'; an' w'en I'd be'n all ober de Souf I come ter de Norf. Fer I knows I'll fin' 'im some er dese days," she added softly, "er he'll fin' me, an' den we'll bofe be as happy in freedom as we wuz in de ole days befo' de wah." A smile stole over her withered countenance as she paused a moment, and her bright eyes softened into a faraway look.

This was the substance of the old woman's story. She had wandered a little here and there. Mr. Ryder was looking at her curiously when she finished.

"How have you lived all these years?" he asked.

"Cookin', suh. I's a good cook. Does you know anybody w'at needs a good cook, suh? I's stoppin' wid a cullud fam'ly roun' de corner yonder 'tel I kin git a place."

"Do you really expect to find your husband? He may be dead long ago."

She shook her head emphatically. "Oh no, he ain' dead. De signs an' de tokens tells me. I dremp three nights runnin' on'y dis las' week dat I foun' him."

"He may have married another woman. Your slave marriage would not have prevented him, for you never lived with him after the war, and without that your marriage does n't count."

"Would n' make no diff'ence wid Sam. He would n' marry no yuther 'ooman 'tel he foun' out 'bout me. I knows it," she added. "Sump'n 's be'n tellin' me all dese years dat I's gwine fin' Sam 'fo' I dies."

"Perhaps he's outgrown you, and climbed up in the world where he would n't care to have you find him."

"No, indeed, suh," she replied, "Sam ain' dat kin' er man. He wuz good ter me, Sam wuz, but he wuz n' much good ter nobody e'se, fer he wuz one er de triflin'es' han's on de plantation. I 'spec's ter haf ter suppo't 'im w'en I fin' 'im, fer he nebber would work 'less'n he had ter. But den he wuz free, an' he did n' git no pay fer his work, an' I don' blame 'im much. Mebbe he's done better sence he run erway, but I ain' 'spectin' much."

"You may have passed him on the street a hundred times during the twenty-five years, and not have known him; time works great changes."

She smiled incredulously. "I'd know 'im 'mongs' a hund'ed men. Fer dey wuz n' no yuther merlatter man like my man Sam, an' I could n' be mistook. I's toted his picture roun' wid me twenty-five years."

"May I see it?" asked Mr. Ryder. "It might help me to remember whether I have seen the original."

As she drew a small parcel from her bosom he saw that it was fastened to a string that went around her neck. Removing several wrappers, she brought to light an old-fashioned daguerrotype in a black case. He looked long and intently at the portrait. It was faded with time, but the features were still distinct, and it was easy to see what manner of man it had represented.

He closed the case, and with a slow movement handed it back to her.

"I don't know of any man in town who goes by that name," he said, "nor have I heard of any one making such inquiries. But if you will leave me your address, I will give the matter some attention, and if I find out anything I will let you know."

She gave him the number of a house in the neighborhood, and went away, after thanking him warmly.

He wrote the address on the fly-leaf of the volume of Tennyson, and, when she had gone, rose to his feet and stood looking after her curiously. As she walked down the street with mincing step, he saw several persons whom she passed turn and look back at her with a smile of kindly amusement. When she had turned the corner, he went upstairs to his bedroom, and stood for a long time before the mirror of his dressing-case, gazing thoughtfully at the reflection of his own face.

III

At eight o'clock the ballroom was a blaze of light and the guests had begun to assemble; for there was a literary programme and some routine business of the society to be gone through with before the dancing. A black servant in evening dress waited at the door and directed the guests to the dressing-rooms.

The occasion was long memorable among the colored people of the city; not alone for the dress and display, but for the high average of intelligence and culture that distinguished the gathering as a whole. There were a number of school-teachers, several young doctors, three or four lawyers, some professional singers, an editor, a lieutenant in the United States Army spending his furlough in the city, and others in various polite callings; these were colored, though most of them would not have attracted even a casual glance because of any marked difference from white people. Most of the ladies were in evening costume, and dress coats and dancing pumps were the rule among the men. A band of string music, stationed in an alcove behind a row of palms, played popular airs while the guests were gathering.

The dancing began at half past nine. At eleven o'clock supper was served. Mr. Ryder had left the ballroom some little time before the intermission, but reappeared at the suppertable. The spread was worthy of the occasion, and the guests did full justice to it. When the coffee had been served, the toastmaster, Mr. Solomon Sadler, rapped for order. He made a brief introductory speech, complimenting host and guests, and then presented in their order the toasts of the evening. They were responded to with a very fair display of after-dinner wit.

"The last toast," said the toastmaster, when he reached the end of the list, "is one which must appeal to us all. There is no one of us of the sterner sex who is not at some time dependent upon woman,—in infancy for protection, in manhood for companionship, in old age for care and comforting. Our good host has been trying to live alone, but the fair faces I see around me to-night prove that he too is largely dependent upon the gentler sex for most that makes life worth living,—the society and love of friends,—and rumor is at fault if he does not soon yield entire subjection to one of them. Mr. Ryder will now respond to the toast,—The Ladies."

There was a pensive look in Mr. Ryder's eyes as he took the floor and adjusted his eyeglasses. He began by speaking of woman as the gift of Heaven to man, and after some general observations on the relations of the sexes he said: "But perhaps the quality which most distinguishes woman is her fidelity and devotion to those she loves. History is full of examples, but has recorded none more striking than one which only to-day came under my notice.

He then related, simply but effectively, the story told by his visitor of the afternoon. He gave it in the same soft dialect, which came readily to his lips, while the company listened attentively and sympathetically. For the story had awakened a responsive thrill in many hearts. There were some present who had seen and others who had heard their fathers and grandfathers tell, the wrongs and sufferings of this past generation, and all of them still felt, in their darker moments, the shadow hanging over them. Mr. Ryder went on:—

"Such devotion and confidence are rare even among women. There are many who would have searched a year, some who would have waited five years, a few who might have hoped ten years; but for twenty-five years this woman has retained her affection for and her faith in a man she has not seen or heard of in all that time.

"She came to me to-day in the hope that I might be able to help her find this long-lost husband. And when she was gone I gave my fancy rein, and imagined a case I will put to you.

"Suppose that this husband, soon after his escape, had learned that his wife had been sold away, and that such inquiries as he could make brought no information of her whereabouts. Suppose that he was young, and she much older than he; that he was light, and she was black; that their marriage was a slave marriage, and legally binding only if they chose to make it so after the war. Suppose, too, that he made his way to the North, as some of us have done, and there, where he had larger opportunities, had improved them, and had in the course of all these years grown to be as different from the ignorant boy who ran away from fear of slavery as the day is from the night. Suppose, even, that he had qualified himself, by industry, by thrift, and by study, to win the friendship and be considered worthy the society of such people as these I see around me to-night, gracing my board and filling my heart with gladness; for I am old enough to remember the day when such a gathering would not have been possible in this land. Suppose, too, that, as the years went by, this man's memory of the past grew more and more indistinct, until at last it was rarely, except in his dreams, that any image of this bygone period rose before his mind. And then suppose that accident should bring to his knowledge the fact that the wife of his youth, the wife he had left behind him,—not one who had walked by his side and kept pace with him in his upward struggle, but one upon whom advancing years and a laborious life had set their mark,—was alive and seeking him, but that he was absolutely safe from recognition or discovery, unless he chose to reveal himself. My friends, what would the man do? I will presume that he was one who loved honor, and tried to deal justly with all men. I will even carry the case further, and suppose that perhaps he had set his heart upon another, whom he had hoped to call his own. What would he do, or rather what ought he to do, in such a crisis of a lifetime?

"It seemed to me that he might hesitate, and I imagined that I was an old friend, a near friend, and that he had come to me for advice; and I argued the case with him. I tried to discuss it impartially. After we had looked upon the matter from every point of view, I said to him, in words that we all know:—

> 'This above all: to thine own self be true,
> And it must follow, as the night the day,
> Thou canst not then be false to any man.'

Then, finally, I put the question to him, 'Shall you acknowledge her?'

"And now, ladies and gentlemen, friends and companions, I ask you, what should he have done?"

There was something in Mr. Ryder's voice that stirred the hearts of those who sat around him. It suggested more than mere sympathy with an imaginary situation; it seemed rather in the nature of a personal appeal. It was observed, too, that his look rested more especially upon Mrs. Dixon, with a mingled expression of renunciation and inquiry.

She had listened, with parted lips and streaming eyes. She was the first to speak: "He should have acknowledged her."

"Yes," they all echoed, "he should have acknowledged her."

"My friends and companions," responded Mr. Ryder, "I thank you, one and all. It is the answer I expected, for I knew your hearts."

He turned and walked toward the closed door of an adjoining room, while every eye followed him in wondering curiosity. He came back in a moment, leading by the hand his visitor of the afternoon, who stood startled and trembling at the sudden plunge into this scene of brilliant gayety. She was neatly dressed in gray, and wore the white cap of an elderly woman.

"Ladies and gentlemen," he said, "this is the woman, and I am the man, whose story I have told you. Permit me to introduce to you the wife of my youth."

Food for All His Dead

FRANK CHIN

"Jus' forty-fie year 'go, Doctah Sun Yat-sen free China from da Manchus. Dats' why all us Chinee, alla ovah da woil, are celebrate Octob' tan or da Doubloo Tan . . . !"

The shouted voice came through the open bathroom window. The shouting and music was still loud after rising through the night's dry air; white moths jumped on the air, danced through the window over the voice, and lighted quickly on the wet sink, newly reddened from his father's attack. Johnny's arms were around his father's belly, holding the man upright against the edge of the sink to keep the man's mouth high enough to spit lung blood into the drain. . . .

The man's belly shrank and filled against Johnny's arms as the man breathed and spat, breathed and spat, the belly shrinking and filling. The breaths and bodies against each other shook with horrible rhythms that could not be numbed out of Johnny's mind. "Pride," Johnny thought, "pa's pride for his reputation for doing things . . . except dying. He's not proud of dying, so it's a secret between father and son. . . ." At the beginning of the man's death, when he had been Johnny's father, still commanding and large, saying, "Help me. I'm dying; don't tell," and removing his jacket and walking to the bathroom. Then came the grin—pressed lips twisted up into the cheeks—hiding the gathering blood and drool. Johnny had cried then, knowing his father would die. But now the man seemed to have been always dying and Johnny always waiting, waiting with what he felt was a coward's loyalty to the dying, for he helped the man hide his bleeding and was sick himself, knowing he was not waiting for the man to die but waiting for the time after death when he could relax.

". . . free from da yoke of Manchu slab'ry, in'epen'ence, no moah queue on da head! Da's wha'fo' dis big a parade! An' here, in San Francisco, alla us Chinee-'mellican 're pwowd! . . ."

236

"It's all gone . . . . I can't spit any more. Get my shirt, boy. I'm going to make a speech tonight. . . . ." The man slipped from the arms of the boy and sat on the toilet lid and closed his mouth. His bare chest shone as if washed with dirty cooking oil and looked as if he should have been chilled, not sweating, among the cold porcelain and tile of the bathroom.

To the sound of herded drums and cymbals, Johnny wiped the sweat from his father's soft body and dressed him without speaking. He was full of the heat of wanting to cry for his father but would not.

His father was heavier outside the house.

They staggered each other across the alleyway to the edge of Portsmouth Square. They stood together at the end of the slight hill, their feet just off the concrete onto the melted fishbone grass, and could see the brightly lit reviewing stand, and they saw over the heads of the crowd, the dark crowd of people standing in puddles of each other, moving like oily things and bugs floating on a tide; to their left, under trees, children played and shouted on swings and slides; some ran toward Johnny and his father and crouched behind their legs to hide from giggling girls. And they could see the street and the parade beyond the crowd. The man stood away from the boy but held tight to Johnny's arm. The man swallowed a greasy sound and grinned. "I almost feel I'm not dying now. Parades are like that. I used to dance the Lion Dance in China, boy. I was always in the parades."

Johnny glanced at his father and saw the man's eyes staring wide with the skin around the eyes stretching for the eyes to open wider, and Johnny patted his father's shoulder and watched the shadows of children running across the white sand of the play area. He was afraid of watching his father die here; the man was no longer like his father or a man; perhaps it was the parade. But the waiting, the lies and waiting, waiting so long with a flesh going to death that the person was no longer real as a life but a parody of live things, grinning. The man was a fish drying and shrinking inside its skin on the sand, crazy, mimicking swimming, Johnny thought, but a fish could be lifted and slapped against a stone, thrown to cats; for his father, Johnny could only wait and help the man stay alive without helping him die. "That's probably where you got the disease," Johnny said.

"Where, boy?"

"Back in China."

"No, I got it here. I was never sick for one day in China." The man began walking down the hill toward the crowd. "Back in China. . . . ."

They walked down the hill, the man's legs falling into steps with his body jerking after his falling legs; Johnny held his father, held the man back to keep him from falling over his own feet. The man's breath chanted dry and powdered out of his mouth and nostrils to the rhythm of the drums, and his eyes stared far ahead into the parade; his lips opened and showed brick-colored teeth in his grin. "Not so fast, *ah-bah!*" Johnny shouted and pulled at his father's arm. He was always frightened at the man's surges of nervous life.

"Don't run," Johnny said, feeling his father's muscles stretch as he pulled Johnny down the hill toward the crowd. "Stop running, pa!" And his father was running and breathing out fog into the hot night and sweating dirty oil, and trembling his fleshy rump inside his baggy trousers, dancing in stumbles with dead senses. "Pa, not so fast, dammit! You're going to have another attack! Slow down!"

"I can't stop, boy."

They were in the shadow of the crowd now, and children chased around them.

"Look! There they are!" the man said.

"Dere you're, ladies and genullmans! Eben da lion are bow in respack to us tonigh'!"

The crowd clapped and whistled, and boys shoved forward to see. Old women, roundbacked in their black overcoats, lifted their heads to smile; they stood together and nodded, looking like clumps of huge beetles with white faces.

"Closer to the platform, boy; that's where I belong," the man said. He leaned against Johnny's shoulder and coughed out of his nostrils. Johnny heard the man swallow and cringed. The man was grinning again, his eyes anxious, the small orbs jumping scared spiders all over the sockets. "Aren't you happy you came, boy? Look at all the people."

"Take time to catch your breath, *ah-bah.* Don't talk. It's wrong for you to be here anyhow."

"Nothing's wrong, boy; don't you see all your people happy tonight? As long as . . ." he swallowed and put his head against Johnny's cheek, then made a sound something like laughter, "as I've been here . . . do you understand my Chinese?" Then slowly in English, catching quick breaths between his words, "I be here, allabody say dere chillren're gonna leab Chinatong and go way, but 'snot so, huh?" His voice was low, a guttural monotone. "Look a'em all; dey still be Chinee. I taught da feller dat teach dem to dance how to do dat dancer boy. Johnny? dis're you home, here, an' I know you gat tire, but alla you fran's here, an' dey likee you." His face was speaking close to Johnny and chilled the boy's face with hot breath.

The boy did not look at his father talking to him but stared stiffly out to the street, watching the glistening arms of boys jerking the bamboo skeletons of silk-hided lions over their heads. His father was trying to save him again, Johnny thought, trying to be close like he had been to him how long ago when his father was a hero from the war. The man spoke as if he had saved his life to talk to his son now, tonight, here among the eyes and sounds of Chinese.

"I'm sorry, *ah-bah,* I can't help it . . ." was all Johnny could answer sincerely. He knew it would be cruel to say, "Pa, I don't want to be a curiosity

like the rest of the Chinese here. I want to be something by myself," so he
did not, not only because of the old man, but because he was not certain he
believed himself; it had been easy to believe his own shouted words when
he was younger and safe with his parents; it had been easy not to like what
he had then—when he knew he could stay; then, when the man was fat
and not dying, they were separate and could argue, but not now; now he
was favored with the man's secret; they were horribly bound together now.
The old man was dying and still believing in the old ways, still sure—even
brave, perhaps—and that meant something to Johnny.

"An' you see dam bow in respack now, an' da's good lucks to ev'eybody!"

The lion dancers passed, followed by a red convertible with boys beating a
huge drum on the back seat.

Johnny knew the parades; the lion dancers led the wait for the coming of
the long dragon, and the end. The ends of the parades with the dragon
were the most exciting, were the loudest moment before the chase down
the streets to keep the dragon in sight. He was half aware of the air becoming brittle with the noise of the dances and the crowd, and, with his father
now, was almost happy, almost anxious, dull, the way he felt when he was
tired and staring in a mirror, slowly realizing that he was looking at his own
personal reflection; he felt pleased and depressed, as if he had just prayed
for something.

"You know," the man said, "I wan' you to be somebody here. Be doctor,
mak' moneys and halp da Chinee, or lawyer, or edgenerer, make moneys
and halp, and people're respack you." He patted the boy's chest. "You tall
me now you won' leab here when I die, hokay?"

"I don't know, pa." The boy looked down to the trampled grass between
his feet and shrugged off what he did not want to say. They were hopeless
to each other now. He looked over his shoulder to his father and could not
answer the chilled face, and they stared a close moment onto each other
and were private, holding each other and waiting.

Policemen on motorcycles moved close to the feet of the crowd to move
them back. The boys wearing black-and-red silk trousers and white sweat-
shirts, coaxing the clumsy dragon forward with bells and shafts, could be
seen now; they were dancing and shouting past the reviewing stand. The
dragon's glowing head lurched side to side, rose and fell, its jaw dangling
after the goading boys. As the dragon writhed and twisted about itself, boys
jumped in and out from under its head and belly to keep the dragon fresh.

"Maybe I'm not Chinese, pa! Maybe I'm just a Chinese accident. You're
the only one that seems to care that I'm Chinese." The man glared at the
boy and did not listen. "Pa, most of the people I don't like are Chinese.
They even *laugh* with accents, Christ!" He turned his head from the man,

sorry for what he said. It was too late to apologize. "You dare to talk to your father like that?" the man shouted in Chinese. He stood back from the boy, raised himself and slapped him, whining through his teeth as his arm swung heavily toward the boy's cheek. "You're no son of mine! No son! I'm ashamed of you!"

The shape of the bamboo skeleton was a shadow within the thinly painted silk of the dragon, and the boys were shouting inside.

"Pa, *ah-bah*, I'm sorry."

"Get me up to the platform; I gotta make a speech."

"Pa, you've got to go home."

"I'm not dead yet; you'll do as I say."

"All right, I'll help you up because you won't let me help you home. But I'll leave you up there, pa. I'll leave you for ma and sister to bring home."

"From da Pres'den, of da United State' 'mellica! 'To alla ob da Chinee-'mellican on da celebrate ob dere liberate from da Manchu. . . .' "

"I'm trying to make you go home for your own good."

"You're trying to kill me with disgrace. All right, leave me. Get out of my house, too."

"Pa, I'm trying to help you. You're dying!" The boy reached for his father, but the man stepped away. "You'll kill ma by not letting her take care of you."

"Your mother's up on the platform waiting for me."

"Because she doesn't know how bad you are. I do. I have a right to make you go home."

"It's my home, not yours. Leave me alone." The man walked the few steps to the edge of the platform and called his wife. She came down and helped him up. She glanced out but did not see Johnny in the crowd. Her cheeks were made up very pink and her lipstick was still fresh; she looked very young next to Johnny's father, but her hands were old, and seemed older because of the bright nail polish and jade bracelet.

Johnny knew what his father would tell his mother and knew he would have to trust them to be happy without him. Perhaps he meant he would have to trust himself to be happy without them . . . the feeling would pass; he would wait and apologize to them both, and he would not have to leave, perhaps. Everything seemed wrong, all wrong, yet everyone, in his own way, was right. He turned quickly and walked out of the crowd to the children's play area. He sat on a bench and stretched his legs straight out in front of him. The dark old women in black coats stood by on the edges of the play area watching the nightbleached faces of children flash in and out of the light as they ran through each other's shadows. Above him, Johnny could hear the sound of pigeons in the trees. Chinatown was the same and he hated it now. Before, when he was younger, and went shopping with his mother, he had enjoyed the smells of the shops and seeing colored toys between the legs of walking people; he had been proud to look up and see his mother staring at the numbers on the scales that weighed meat, to see the shopkeepers smile and nod at her. And at night, he had played here, like the children chasing each other in front of him now.

"What'sa wrong, Johnny? Tire? He had not seen the girl standing in front of him. He sat up straight and smiled. "You draw more pitchers on napkin for me tonigh'?"

"No, I was with pa." He shrugged. "You still got the napkins, huh?"

"I tole you I want dem. I'm keeping 'em." She wore a short white coat over her red *cheongsam,* and her hair shook down over her face from the wind.

"I wanta walk," he said. "You wanta walk?"

"I gotta gat home before twalve."

"Me too."

"I'll walk for you dan, okay?" She smiled and reached a hand down for him.

"You'll walk *with* me, not *for* me. You're not a dog." He stood and took her hand. He enjoyed the girl; she listened to him; he did not care if she understood what he said or knew what he wanted to say. She listened to him, would listen with her eyes staring with a wide frog's stare until he stopped speaking, then her body would raise and she would sigh a curl of girl's voice and say, "You talk so nice. . . ."

The tail of an embroidered dragon showed under her white coat and seemed to sway as her thigh moved. "You didn' come take me to the parade, Johnny?"

"I was with pa." Johnny smiled. The girl's hand was dryfeeling, cold and dry like a skin of tissue-paper-covered flesh. They walked slowly, rocking forward and back as they stepped up the hill. "I'm always with pa, huh?" he said bitterly. "I'm sorry."

" 'sall right. Is he still dying?"

"Everyone's dying here; it's called the American's common cold."

"Don' talk you colleger stuff to me! I don' unnerstan' it, Johnny."

"He's still dying . . . always. I mean, sometimes I think he won't die or is lying and isn't dying."

"Wou'n't that be good, if he weren't dying? And if it was all a joke? You could all laugh after."

"I don't know, Sharon!" He whined on the girl's name and loosened her hand, but she held.

"Johnny?"

"Yeah?"

"What'll you do if he dies?"

Johnny did not look at the girl as he answered, but lifted his head to glance at the street full of lights and people walking between moving cars.

Grant Avenue. He could smell incense and caged squabs, the dank smell of damp fish heaped on tile from the shops now. "I think I'd leave. I know what that sounds like, like I'm waiting for him to die so I can leave; maybe it's so. Sometimes I think I'd kill him to stop all this waiting and lifting him to the sink and keeping it a secret. But I won't do that."

"You won' do that . . . ." Sharon said.

"An' now, I like to presan' da Pres'den ob da Chinee Benabolen'. . . ."

"My father," Johnny said.

The girl clapped her hands over her ears to keep her hair from jumping in the wind. "You father?" she said.

"I don't think so," Johnny said. They walked close to the walls, stepped almost into doorways to allow crowding people to pass them going down the hill toward the voice. They smelled grease and urine of open hallways, and heard music like birds being strangled as they walked over iron gratings.

"You don't think so what?" Sharon asked, pulling him toward the crowd.

"I don't think so what you said you didn't think so. . . ." He giggled, "I'm sort of funny tonight. I was up all last night listening to my father practice his speech in the toilet and helping him bleed when he got mad. And this morning I started to go to classes and fell asleep on the bus; so I didn't go to classes, and I'm still awake. I'm not tired but kind of stupid with no sleep, dig, Sharon?"

The girl smiled and said, "I dig, Johnny. You the same way every time I see you almos'."

"And I hear myself talking all this stupid stuff, but it's sort of great, you know? Because I have to listen to what I'm saying or I'll miss it."

"My mother say you cute."

They were near the top of the street now, standing in front of a wall stand with a fold-down shelf covered with Chinese magazines, nickel comic books, postcards, and Japanese souvenirs of Chinatown. Johnny, feeling ridiculous with air between his joints and his cheeks tingling with the anxious motion of the crowd, realized he was tired, then realized he was staring at the boy sitting at the wall stand and staring at the boy's leather cap.

"What are you loo' at, huh?" the boy said in a girl's voice. Sharon pulled at Johnny and giggled. Johnny giggled and relaxed to feeling drunk and said, "Are you really Chinese?"

"What're you ting, I'm a Negro soy sauce chicken?"

"Don't you know there's no such thing as a real Chinaman in all of America? That all we are are American Indians cashing in on a fad?"

"Fad? Don' call me a fad. You fad youselv."

"No, you're not Chinese, don't you understand? You see it all started when a bunch of Indians wanted to quit being Indians and fighting the cavalry and all, so they left the reservation, see?"

"In'ian?"

"And they saw that there was this big kick about Chinamen, so they braided their hair into queues and opened up laundries and restaurants and started reading Margaret Mead and Confucius and Pearl Buck and became respectable Chinamen and gained some self-respect."

"Chinamong! You battah not say Chinamong."

"But the reservation instinct stuck, years of tradition, you see? Something about needing more than one Indian to pull off a good rain dance or something, so they made Chinatown! And here we are!"

He glanced around him and grinned. Sharon was laughing, her shoulders hopping up and down. The boy blinked, then pulled his cap lower over his eyes. "It's all right to come out now, you see?" Johnny said. "Indians are back in vogue and the Chinese kick is wearing out. . . ." He laughed until he saw the boy's confused face. "Aww nuts," he said, "this is no fun."

He walked after Sharon through the crowd, not feeling the shoulders and women's hips knocking against him. "I'd like to get outta here so quick, Sharon; I wish I had something to do! What do I do here? What does anybody do here? I'm bored! My mother's a respected woman because she can tell how much monosodium glutamate is in a dish by smelling it, and because she knows how to use a spittoon in a restaurant. Everybody's Chinese here, Sharon."

"Sure!" the girl laughed and hopped to kiss his cheek. "Didn' you like that?"

"Sure, I liked it, but I'm explaining something. You know, nobody shoulda let me grow up and go to any school outside of Chinatown." They walked slowly, twisting to allow swaggering men to pass. "Then, maybe everything would be all right now, you see? I'm stupid, I don't know what I'm talking about. I shouldn't go to parades and see all those kids. I remember when I was a kid. Man, then I knew everything. I knew all my aunts were beautiful, and all my cousins were small, and all my uncles were heroes from the war and the strongest guys in the world that smoked cigars and swore, and my grandmother was a queen of women." He nodded to himself. "I really had it made then, really, and I knew more then than I do now."

"What'd'ya mean? You smart now! You didn't know how to coun' or spall, or nothin'; now you in colleger."

"I had something then, you know? I didn't have to ask about anything; it was all there; I didn't have questions; I knew who I was responsible to, who I should love, who I was afraid of, and all my dogs were smart."

"You lucky, you had a dog!" The girl smiled.

"And all the girls wanted to be nurses; it was fine! Now, I'm just what a kid should be—stupid, embarrassed. I don't know who can tell me anything.

"Here, in Chinatown, I'm undoubtedly the most enlightened, the smartest fortune cookie ever baked to a golden brown, but out there . . . God!"

He pointed down to the end of Grant Avenue, past ornamented lamps of Chinatown to the tall buildings of San Francisco, "Here, I'm fine—and bored stiff. Out there—Oh, hell, what'm I talking about. You don't know either; I try to tell my father, and he doesn't know, and he's smarter'n you."

"If you don't like stupids, why'd you talk to me so much?"

"Because I like you. You're the only thing I know that doesn't fight me. . . . You know I think I've scared myself into liking this place for a while. See what you've done by walking with me? You've made me a good Chinese for my parents again. I think I'll sell firecrackers." He was dizzy now, overwhelmed by the sound of too many feet and clicking lights. "I even like you, Sharon!" He swung her arm and threw her ahead of him and heard her laugh. "My grandmother didn't read English until she watched television and read 'The End'; that's pretty funny, what a kick!" They laughed at each other and ran among the shoulders of the crowd, shouting "Congratulations!" in Chinese into the shops, "Congratulations!" to a bald man with long hair growing down the edges of his head.

"Johnny, stop! You hurt my wrist!"

It was an innocent kiss in her hallway, her eyes closed so tight the lashes shrank and twitched like insect legs, and her lips puckered long, a dry kiss with closed lips. "Good night, Johnny . . . John," she said. And he waved and watched her standing in the hallway, disappearing as he walked down the stairs; then, out of sight, he ran home.

He opened the door to the apartment and hoped that his father had forgotten. "Fine speech, pa!" he shouted.

His little sister came out of her room, walking on the toes of her long pajamas. "Brother? Brother, *ah-bah*, he's sick!" she said. She looked straight up to Johnny as she spoke and nodded. Johnny stepped past his sister and ran to the bathroom and opened the door. His mother was holding the man up to the sink with one hand and holding his head with the other. The man's mess spattered over her *cheongsam*. The room, the man, everything, was uglier because of his mother's misery in her bright *cheongsam*. "Ah-bah?" Johnny said gently as if calling the man from sleep for dinner. They did not turn. He stepped up behind the woman. "I can do that, *ah-mah;* I'm a little stronger than you."

"Don't you touch him! You!" She spoke with her cheek against the man's back and her eyes closed. "He told me what you did, what you said, and you're killing him! If you want to leave, just go! Stop killing this man!"

"Not me, ma. He's been like this a long time. I've been helping him almost every night. He told me not to tell you."

"You think I don't know? I've seen you in here with him when I wanted to use the bathroom at night, and I've crept back to bed without saying anything because I know your father's pride. And you want to go and break it in a single night! First it's your telling everybody how good you are! Now go and murder your father. . . ."

"Ma, I'm sorry. He asked me, and I tried to make him understand. What do you want me to do, lie? I'll call a doctor."

"Get out; you said you're going to leave, so get out," the man said, lifting his head.

"I'll stay, ma, *ah-bah*, I'll stay."

"It's too late," his mother said. "I don't want you here." The time was wrong . . . nobody's fault that his father was dying; perhaps, if his father was not dying out of his mouth, Johnny could have argued and left or stayed, but now, he could not stay without hate. "Ma, I said I'm calling a doctor. . . ."

After the doctor came, Johnny went to his room and cried loudly, pulling the sheets from his bed and kicking at the wall until his foot became numb. He shouted his hate for his father and ignorant mother into his pillow until his face was wet with tears. His sister stood next to his bed and watched him, patting his ankle and saying over and over, "Brother, don't cry, brother. . . ."

Johnny sat up and held the small girl against him. "Be a good girl," he said. "You're going to have my big room now. I'm moving across the bay to school." He spoke very quietly to his sister against the sound of their father's spitting.

Sharon held his sister's elbow and marched behind Johnny and his mother. A band played in front of the coffin, and over the coffin was a large photograph of the dead man. Johnny had a miniature of the photograph in his wallet and would always carry it there. Without being told, he had dressed and was marching now beside his mother behind the coffin and the smell of sweet flowers. It was a parade of black coats and hats, and they all wore sunglasses against the sun; the sky was green, seen through the glasses, and the boys playing in Portsmouth Square had green shadows about them. A few people stopped on the street and watched.

The Story of an Hour

KATE CHOPIN

Knowing that Mrs. Mallard was afflicted with a heart trouble, great care was taken to break to her as gently as possible the news of her husband's death.

It was her sister Josephine who told her, in broken sentences; veiled hints that revealed in half concealing. Her husband's friend Richards was there, too, near her. It was he who had been in the newspaper office when intelligence of the railroad disaster was received, with Brently Mallard's name leading the list of "killed." He had only taken the time to assure himself of its truth by a second telegram, and had hastened to forestall any less careful, less tender friend in bearing the sad message.

She did not hear the story as many women have heard the same, with a paralyzed inability to accept its significance. She wept at once, with sudden, wild abandonment, in her sister's arms. When the storm of grief had spent itself she went away to her room alone. She would have no one follow her.

There stood, facing the open window, a comfortable, roomy armchair. Into this she sank, pressed down by a physical exhaustion that haunted her body and seemed to reach into her soul.

She could see in the open square before her house the tops of trees that were all aquiver with new spring life. The delicious breath of rain was in the air. In the street below a peddler was crying his wares. The notes of a distant song which some one was singing reached her faintly, and countless sparrows were twittering in the eaves.

There were patches of blue sky showing here and there through the clouds that had met and piled one above the other in the west facing her window.

She sat with her head thrown back upon the cushion of the chair, quite motionless, except when a sob came up into her throat and shook her, as a child who has cried itself to sleep continues to sob in its dreams.

She was young, with a fair, calm face, whose lines bespoke repression and even a certain strength. But now there was a dull stare in her eyes, whose gaze was fixed away off yonder on one of those patches of blue sky. It was not a glance of reflection, but rather indicated a suspension of intelligent thought.

There was something coming to her and she was waiting for it, fearfully. What was it? She did not know; it was too subtle and elusive to name. But she felt it, creeping out of the sky, reaching toward her through the sounds, the scents, the color that filled the air.

Now her bosom rose and fell tumultuously. She was beginning to recognize this thing that was approaching to possess her, and she was striving to beat it back with her will—as powerless as her two white slender hands would have been.

When she abandoned herself a little whispered word escaped her slightly parted lips. She said it over and over under her breath: "free, free, free!" The vacant stare and the look of terror that had followed it went from her eyes. They stayed keen and bright. Her pulses beat fast, and the coursing blood warmed and relaxed every inch of her body.

She did not stop to ask if it were or were not a monstrous joy that held her. A clear and exalted perception enabled her to dismiss the suggestion as trivial.

She knew that she would weep again when she saw the kind, tender hands folded in death; the face that had never looked save with love upon her, fixed and gray and dead. But she saw beyond that bitter moment a long procession of years to come that would belong to her absolutely. And she opened and spread her arms out to them in welcome.

There would be no one to live for her during those coming years; she would live for herself. There would be no powerful will bending hers in that blind persistence with which men and women believe they have a right to impose a private will upon a fellow-creature. A kind intention or a cruel intention made the act seem no less a crime as she looked upon it in that brief moment of illumination.

And yet she had loved him—sometimes. Often she had not. What did it matter! What could love, the unsolved mystery, count for in face of this possession of self-assertion which she suddenly recognized as the strongest impulse of her being!

"Free! Body and soul free!" she kept whispering.

Josephine was kneeling before the closed door with her lips to the keyhole, imploring for admission. "Louise, open the door! I beg; open the door—you will make yourself ill. What are you doing, Louise? For heaven's sake open the door."

"Go away. I am not making myself ill." No; she was drinking in a very elixir of life through that open window.

Her fancy was running riot along those days ahead of her. Spring days, and summer days, and all sorts of days that would be her own. She breathed a quick prayer that life might be long. It was only yesterday she had thought with a shudder that life might be long.

She arose at length and opened the door to her sister's importunities. There was a feverish triumph in her eyes, and she carried herself unwittingly like a goddess of Victory. She clasped her sister's waist, and together they descended the stairs. Richards stood waiting for them at the bottom.

Someone was opening the front door with a latchkey. It was Brently Mallard who entered, a little travel-stained, composedly carrying his grip-sack and umbrella. He had been far from the scene of accident, and did not even know there had been one. He stood amazed at Josephine's piercing cry; at Richards' quick motion to screen him from the view of his wife.

But Richards was too late.

When the doctors came they said she had died of heart disease—of joy that kills.

The Bride Comes to Yellow Sky

STEPHEN CRANE

I

The great Pullman was whirling onward with such dignity of motion that a glance from the window seemed simply to prove that the plains of Texas were pouring eastward. Vast flats of green grass, dull-hued spaces of mesquit and cactus, little groups of frame houses, woods of light and tender trees, all were sweeping into the east, sweeping over the horizon, a precipice.

A newly married pair had boarded this coach at San Antonio. The man's face was reddened from many days in the wind and sun, and a direct result of his new black clothes was that his brick-colored hands were constantly performing in a most conscious fashion. From time to time he looked down respectfully at his attire. He sat with a hand on each knee, like a man waiting in a barber's shop. The glances he devoted to other passengers were furtive and shy.

The bride was not pretty, nor was she very young. She wore a dress of blue cashmere, with small reservations of velvet here and there, and with steel buttons abounding. She continually twisted her head to regard her puff sleeves, very stiff, straight, and high. They embarrassed her. It was quite apparent that she had cooked, and that she expected to cook, dutifully. The blushes caused by the careless scrutiny of some passengers as she had entered the car were strange to see upon this plain, under-class countenance, which was drawn in placid, almost emotionless lines.

They were evidently very happy. "Ever been in a parlor car before?" he asked, smiling with delight.

"No," she answered; "I never was. It's fine, ain't it?"

"Great! And then after a while we'll go forward to the diner, and get a big lay-out. Finest meal in the world. Charge a dollar."

249

"Oh, do they?" cried the bride. "Charge a dollar? Why, that's too much—for us—ain't it, Jack?"

"Not this trip, anyhow," he answered bravely. "We're going to go the whole thing."

Later he explained to her about the trains. "You see, it's a thousand miles from one end of Texas to the other; and this train runs right across it, and never stops but four times." He had the pride of an owner. He pointed out to her the dazzling fittings of the coach; and in truth her eyes opened wider as she contemplated the sea-green figured velvet, the shining brass, silver, and glass, the wood that gleamed as darkly brilliant as the surface of a pool of oil. At one end a bronze figure sturdily held a support for a separated chamber, and at convenient places on the ceiling were frescos in olive and silver.

To the minds of the pair, their surroundings reflected the glory of their marriage that morning in San Antonio; this was the environment of their new estate; and the man's face in particular beamed with an elation that made him appear ridiculous to the Negro porter. This individual at times surveyed them from afar with an amused and superior grin. On other occasions he bullied them with skill in ways that did not make it exactly plain to them that they were being bullied. He subtly used all the manners of the most unconquerable kind of snobbery. He oppressed them; but of this oppression they had small knowledge, and they speedily forgot that infrequently a number of travellers covered them with stares of derisive enjoyment. Historically there was supposed to be something infinitely humorous in their situation.

"We are due in Yellow Sky at 3:42," he said, looking tenderly into her eyes.

"Oh, are we?" she said, as if she had not been aware of it. To evince surprise at her husband's statement was part of her wifely amiability. She took from a pocket a little silver watch; and as she held it before her, and stared at it with a frown of attention, the new husband's face shone.

"I bought it in San Anton' from a friend of mine," he told her gleefully.

"It's seventeen minutes past twelve," she said, looking up at him with a kind of shy and clumsy coquetry. A passenger, noting this play, grew excessively sardonic, and winked at himself in one of the numerous mirrors.

At last they went to the dining car. Two rows of Negro waiters, in glowing white suits, surveyed their entrance with the interest, and also the equanimity, of men who had been forewarned. The pair fell to the lot of a waiter who happened to feel pleasure in steering them through their meal. He viewed them with the manner of a fatherly pilot, his countenance radiant with benevolence. The patronage, entwined with the ordinary deference, was not plain to them. And yet, as they returned to their coach, they showed in their faces a sense of escape.

To the left, miles down a long purple slope, was a little ribbon of mist where moved the keening Rio Grande. The train was approaching it at an angle, and the apex was Yellow Sky. Presently it was apparent that, as the distance from Yellow Sky grew shorter, the husband became commensurately restless. His brick-red hands were most insistent in their prominence. Occasionally he was even rather absent-minded and far-away when the bride leaned forward and addressed him.

As a matter of truth, Jack Potter was beginning to find the shadow of a deed weighed upon him like a leaden slab. He, the town marshal of Yellow Sky, a man known, liked, and feared in his corner, a prominent person, had gone to San Antonio to meet a girl he believed he loved, and there, after the usual prayers, had actually induced her to marry him, without consulting Yellow Sky for any part of the transaction. He was now bringing his bride before an innocent and unsuspecting community.

Of course people in Yellow Sky married as it pleased them, in accordance with a general custom; but such was Potter's thought of his duty to his friends, or of their idea of his duty, or of an unspoken form which does not control men in these matters, that he felt he was heinous. He had committed an extraordinary crime. Face to face with this girl in San Antonio, and spurred by his sharp impulse, he had gone headlong over all the social hedges. At San Antonio he was like a man hidden in the dark. A knife to sever any friendly duty, any form, was easy to his hand in that remote city. But the hour of Yellow Sky, the hour of daylight—was approaching.

He knew full well that his marriage was an important thing to his town. It could only be exceeded by the burning of the new hotel. His friends could not forgive him. Frequently he had reflected on the advisability of telling them by telegraph, but a new cowardice had been upon him. He feared to do it. And now the train was hurrying him toward a scene of amazement, glee, and reproach. He glanced out of the window at the line of haze swinging slowly in toward the train.

Yellow Sky had a kind of brass band, which played painfully, to the delight of the populace. He laughed without heart as he thought of it. If the citizens could dream of his prospective arrival with his bride, they would parade the band at the station and escort them, amid cheers and laughing congratulations, to his adobe home.

He resolved that he would use all the devices of speed and plains-craft in making the journey from the station to his house. Once within that safe citadel, he could issue some sort of vocal bulletin, and then not go among the citizens until they had time to wear off a little of their enthusiasm.

The bride looked anxiously at him. "What's worrying you, Jack?"

He laughed again. "I'm not worrying, girl; I'm only thinking of Yellow Sky."

She flushed in comprehension.

A sense of mutual guilt invaded their minds and developed a finer tenderness. They looked at each other with eyes softly aglow. But Potter often laughed the same nervous laugh; the flush upon the bride's face seemed quite permanent.

The traitor to the feelings of Yellow Sky narrowly watched the speeding landscape. "We're nearly there," he said.

Presently the porter came and announced the proximity of Potter's home. He held a brush in his hand, and, with all his airy superiority gone, he brushed Potter's new clothes as the latter slowly turned this way and that way. Potter fumbled out a coin and gave it to the porter, as he had seen others do. It was a heavy and muscle-bound business, as that of a man shoeing his first horse.

The porter took their bag, and as the train began to slow they moved forward to the hooded platform of the car. Presently the two engines and their long string of coaches rushed into the station of Yellow Sky.

"They have to take water here," said Potter, from a constricted throat and in mournful cadence, as one announcing death. Before the train stopped his eye had swept the length of the platform, and he was glad and astonished to see there was none upon it but the station-agent, who, with a slightly hurried and anxious air, was walking toward the water-tanks. When the train had halted, the porter alighted first, and placed in position a little temporary step.

"Come on, girl," said Potter, hoarsely. As he helped her down they each laughed on a false note. He took the bag from the negro, and bade his wife cling to his arm. As they slunk rapidly away, his hang-dog glance perceived that they were unloading the two trunks, and also that the station-agent, far ahead near the baggage-car, had turned and was running toward him, making gestures. He laughed, and groaned as he laughed, when he noted the first effect of his marital bliss upon Yellow Sky. He gripped his wife's arm firmly to his side, and they fled. Behind them the porter stood, chuckling fatuously.

II

The California express on the Southern Railway was due at Yellow Sky in twenty-one minutes. There were six men at the bar of the Weary Gentleman saloon. One was a drummer who talked a great deal and rapidly; three were Texans who did not care to talk at that time; and two were Mexican sheep-herders, who did not talk as a general practice in the Weary Gentleman saloon. The barkeeper's dog lay on the board walk that crossed in front of the door. His head was on his paws, and he glanced drowsily here and there with the constant vigilance of a dog that is kicked on occasion. Across the sandy street were some vivid green grass-plots, so wonderful in appearance, amid the sands that burned near them in a blazing sun, that they caused a doubt in the mind. They exactly resembled the grass mats used to represent lawns on the stage. At the cooler end of the railway station, a man without a coat sat in a tilted chair and smoked his pipe. The fresh-cut bank of the Rio Grande circled near the town, and there could be seen beyond it a great plum-colored plain of mesquit.

Save for the busy drummer and his companions in the saloon, Yellow Sky was dozing. The new-comer leaned gracefully upon the bar, and recited many tales with a confidence of a bard who has come upon a new field.

"—and at the moment that the old man fell downstairs with the bureau in his arms, the old woman was coming up with two scuttles of coal, and of course—"

The drummer's tale was interrupted by a young man who suddenly appeared in the open door. He cried: "Scratchy Wilson's drunk, and has turned loose with both hands." The two Mexicans at once set down their glasses and faded out of the rear entrance of the saloon.

The drummer, innocent and jocular, answered: "All right, old man. S'pose he has? Come in and have a drink, anyhow."

But the information had made such an obvious cleft in every skull in the room that the drummer was obliged to see its importance. All had become instantly solemn. "Say," said he, mystified, "what is this?" His three companions made the introductory gesture of eloquent speech; but the young man at the door forestalled them.

"It means, my friend," he answered, as he came into the saloon, "that for the next two hours this town won't be a health resort."

The barkeeper went to the door, and locked and barred it; reaching out of the window, he pulled in heavy wooden shutters, and barred them. Immediately a solemn, chapel-like gloom was upon the place. The drummer was looking from one to another.

"But say," he cried, "what is this, anyhow? You don't mean there is going to be a gunfight?"

"Don't know whether there'll be a fight or not," answered one man, grimly; "but there'll be some shootin'—some good shootin'."

The young man who had warned them waved his hand. "Oh, there'll be a fight fast enough, if any one wants it. Anybody can get a fight out there in the street. There's a fight just waiting."

The drummer seemed to be swayed between the interest of a foreigner and a perception of personal danger.

"What did you say his name was?" he asked.

"Scratchy Wilson," they answered in chorus.

"And will he kill anybody? What are you going to do? Does this happen often? Does he rampage around like this once a week or so? Can he break in that door?"

"No; he can't break down that door," replied the barkeeper. "He's tried it three times. But when he comes you'd better lay down on the floor, stranger. He's dead sure to shoot at it, and a bullet may come through."

Thereafter the drummer kept a strict eye on the door. The time had not yet been called for him to hug the floor, but, as a minor precaution, he sidled near to the wall. "Will he kill anybody?" he said again.

The men laughed low and scornfully at the question.

"He's out to shoot, and he's out for trouble. Don't see any good in experimentin' with him."

"But what do you do in a case like this? What would you do?"

A man responded: "Why, he and Jack Potter—"

"But," in chorus the other men interrupted, "Jack Potter's in San Anton'."

"Well, who is he? What's he got to do with it?"

"Oh, he's the town marshal. He goes out and fights Scratchy when he gets on one of these tears."

"Wow!" said the drummer, mopping his brow. "Nice job he's got."

The voices had toned away to mere whisperings. The drummer wished to ask further questions, which were born of an increasing anxiety and bewilderment; but when he attempted them, the men merely looked at him in irritation and motioned him to remain silent. A tense waiting hush was upon them. In the deep shadows of the room their eyes shone as they listened for sounds from the street. One man made three gestures at the barkeeper; and the latter, moving like a ghost, handed him a glass and a bottle. The man poured a full glass of whiskey, and set down the bottle noiselessly. He gulped the whiskey in a swallow, and turned again toward the door in immovable silence. The drummer saw that the barkeeper, without a sound, had taken a Winchester from beneath the bar. Later he saw this individual beckoning to him, so he tiptoed across the room.

"You better come with me back of the bar."

"No, thanks," said the drummer, perspiring; "I'd rather be where I can make a break for the back door."

Whereupon the man of bottles made a kindly but peremptory gesture. The drummer obeyed it, and finding himself seated on a box with his head below the level of the bar, balm was laid upon his soul at sight of various zinc and copper fittings that bore a resemblance to armor-plate. The barkeeper took a seat comfortably upon an adjacent box.

"You see," he whispered, "this here Scratchy Wilson is a wonder with a gun—a perfect wonder; and when he goes on the war-trail, we hunt our holes—naturally. He's about the last one of the old gang that used to hang out along the river here. He's a terror when he's drunk. When he's sober he's all right—kind of simple—wouldn't hurt a fly—nicest fellow in town. But when he's drunk—whoo!"

There were periods of stillness. "I wish Jack Potter was back from San Anton'," said the barkeeper. 'He shot Wilson up once—in the leg—and he would sail in and pull out the kinks in this thing."

Presently they heard from a distance the sound of a shot, followed by three wild yowls. It instantly removed a bond from the men in the darkened saloon. There was a shuffling of feet. They looked at each other. "Here he comes," they said.

III

A man in a maroon-colored flannel shirt, which had been purchased for purposes of decoration, and made principally by some Jewish women on the East Side of New York, rounded a corner and walked into the middle of the main street of Yellow Sky. In either hand the man held a long, heavy, blue-black revolver. Often he yelled, and these cries ran through a semblance of a deserted village, shrilly flying over the roofs in a volume that seemed to have no relation to the ordinary vocal strength of a man. It was as if the surrounding stillness formed the arch of a tomb over him. These cries of ferocious challenge rang against walls of silence. And his boots had red tops with gilded imprints, of the kind beloved in winter by little sledding boys on the hillsides of New England.

The man's face flamed in a rage begot of whiskey. His eyes, rolling, and yet keen for ambush, hunted the still doorways and windows. He walked with the creeping movement of the midnight cat. As it occurred to him, he roared menacing information. The long revolvers in his hands were as easy as straws; they were moved with an electric swiftness. The little fingers of each hand played sometimes in a musician's way. Plain from the low collar of the shirt, the cords of his neck straightened and sank, straightened and sank, as passion moved him. The only sounds were his terrible invitations. The calm adobes preserved their demeanor at the passing of this small thing in the middle of the street.

There was no offer of fight—no offer of fight. The man called to the sky. There were no attractions. He bellowed and fumed and swayed his revolvers here and everywhere.

The dog of the barkeeper of the Weary Gentleman saloon had not appreciated the advance of events. He yet lay dozing in front of his master's door. At sight of the dog, the man paused and raised his revolver humorously. At sight of the man, the dog sprang up and walked diagonally away, with a sullen head, and growling. The man yelled, and the dog broke into a gallop. As it was about to enter an alley, there was a loud noise, a whistling, and something spat the ground directly before it. The dog screamed, and, wheeling in terror, galloped headlong in a new direction. Again there was a noise, a whistling, and sand was kicked viciously before it. Fearstricken, the dog turned and flurried like an animal in a pen. The man stood laughing, his weapons at his hips.

Ultimately the man was attracted by the closed door of the Weary Gentleman saloon. He went to it and, hammering with a revolver, demanded drink.

The door remaining imperturbable, he picked a bit of paper from the walk, and nailed it to the framework with a knife. He then turned his back contemptuously upon this popular resort and, walking to the opposite side of the street and spinning there on his heel quickly and lithely, fired at the bit of paper. He missed it by a half-inch. He swore at himself, and went away. Later he comfortably fusilladed the windows of his most intimate friend. The man was playing with this town; it was a toy for him.

But still there was no offer of fight. The name of Jack Potter, his ancient antagonist, entered his mind, and he concluded that it would be a glad thing if he should go to Potter's house, and by bombardment induce him to come out and fight. He moved in the direction of his desire, chanting Apache scalpmusic.

When he arrived at it, Potter's house presented the same still front as had the other adobes. Taking up a strategic position, the man howled a challenge. But this house regarded him as might a great stone god. It gave no sign. After a decent wait, the man howled further challenges, mingling with them wonderful epithets.

Presently there came the spectacle of a man churning himself into deepest rage over the immobility of a house. He fumed at it as the winter wind attacks a prairie cabin in the North. To the distance there should have gone the sound of a tumult like the fighting of two hundred Mexicans. As necessity bade him, he paused for breath or to reload his revolvers.

IV

Potter and his bride walked sheepishly and with speed. Sometimes they laughed together shamefacedly and low.

"Next corner, dear," he said finally.

They put forth the efforts of a pair walking bowed against a strong wind. Potter was about to raise a finger to point the first appearance of the new home when, as they circled the corner, they came face to face with a man in a maroon-colored shirt, who was feverishly pushing cartridges into a large revolver. Upon the instant the man dropped his revolver to the ground and, like lightning, whipped another from its holster. The second weapon was aimed at the bridegroom's chest.

There was a silence. Potter's mouth seemed to be merely a grave for his tongue. He exhibited an instinct to at once loosen his arm from the woman's grip, and he dropped the bag to the sand. As for the bride, her face had gone as yellow as old cloth. She was a slave to hideous rites, gazing at the apparitional snake.

The two men faced each other at a distance of three paces. He of the revolver smiled with a new and quiet ferocity.

"Tried to sneak up on me," he said. "Tried to sneak up on me!" His eyes grew more baleful. As Potter made a slight movement, the man thrust his revolver venomously forward. "No; don't you do it, Jack Potter. Don't you move a finger toward a gun just yet. Don't you move an eyelash. The time has come for me to settle with you, and I'm goin' to do it my own way, and loaf along with no interferin'. So if you don't want a gun bent on you, just mind what I tell you."

Potter looked at his enemy. "I ain't got a gun on me, Scratchy," he said. "Honest, I ain't." He was stiffening and steadying, but yet somewhere at the back of his mind a vision of the Pullman floated: the sea-green figured velvet, the shining brass, silver, and glass, the wood that gleamed as darkly brilliant as the surface of a pool of oil—all the glory of the marriage, the environment of the new estate. "You know I fight when it comes to fighting, Scratchy Wilson; but I ain't got a gun on me. You'll have to do all the shootin' yourself."

His enemy's face went livid. He stepped forward, and lashed his weapon to and fro before Potter's chest. "Don't you tell me you ain't got no gun on you, you whelp. Don't tell me no lie like that. There ain't a man in Texas ever seen you without no gun. Don't take me for no kid." His eyes blazed with light, and his throat worked like a pump.

"I ain't takin' you for no kid," answered Potter. His heels had not moved an inch backward. "I'm takin' you for a damn fool. I tell you I ain't got a gun, and I ain't. If you're goin' to shoot me up, you better begin now; you'll never get a chance like this again."

So much enforced reasoning had told on Wilson's rage; he was calmer. "If you ain't got a gun, why ain't you got a gun?" he sneered. "Been to Sunday-school?"

"I ain't got a gun because I've just come from San Anton' with my wife. I'm married," said Potter. "And if I'd thought there was going to be any galoots like you prowling round when I brought my wife home, I'd had a gun, and don't you forget it."

"Married!" said Scratchy, not at all comprehending.

"Yes, married. I'm married," said Potter, distinctly.

"Married?" said Scratchy. Seemingly for the first time, he saw the drooping, drowning woman at the other man's side. "No!" he said. He was like a creature allowed a glimpse of another world. He moved a pace backward, and his arm, with the revolver, dropped to his side. "Is this the lady?" he asked.

"Yes; this is the lady," answered Potter.

There was another period of silence.

"Well," said Wilson at last, slowly, "I s'pose it's all off now."

"It's all off if you say so, Scratchy. You know I didn't make the trouble." Potter lifted his valise.

"Well, I 'low it's off, Jack," said Wilson. He was looking at the ground. "Married!" He was not a student of chivalry; it was merely that in the presence of this foreign condition he was a simple child of the earlier plains. He picked up his starboard revolver, and, placing both weapons in their holsters, he went away. His feet made funnel-shaped tracks in the heavy sand.

The Sailor-Boy's Tale

ISAK DINESEN

The barque *Charlotte* was on her way from Marseille to Athens, in grey weather, on a high sea, after three days' heavy gale. A small sailor-boy, named Simon, stood on the wet, swinging deck, held on to a shroud, and looked up towards the drifting clouds, and to the upper top-gallant yard of the main mast.

A bird, that had sought refuge upon the mast, had got her feet tangled in some loose tackle-yarn of the halliard, and high up there, struggled to get free. The boy on the deck could see her wings flapping and her head turning from side to side.

Through his own experience of life he had come to the conviction that in this world everyone must look after himself, and expect no help from others. But the mute, deadly fight kept him fascinated for more than an hour. He wondered what kind of bird it would be. These last days a number of birds had come to settle in the barque's rigging: swallows, quails, and a pair of peregrine falcons; he believed that this bird was a peregrine falcon. He remembered how, many years ago, in his own country and near his home, he had once seen a peregrine falcon quite close, sitting on a stone and flying straight up from it. Perhaps this was the same bird. He thought: "That bird is like me. Then she was there, and now she is here."

At that a fellow-feeling rose in him, a sense of common tragedy; he stood looking at the bird with his heart in his mouth. There were none of the sailors about to make fun of him; he began to think out how he might go up by the shrouds to help the falcon out. He brushed his hair back and pulled up his sleeves, gave the deck round him a great glance, and climbed up. He had to stop a couple of times in the swaying rigging.

It was indeed, he found when he got to the top of the mast, a peregrine falcon. As his head was on a level with hers, she gave up her struggle, and looked at him with a pair of angry, desperate yellow eyes. He had to take

259

hold of her with one hand while he got his knife out, and cut off the tackle-yarn. He was scared as he looked down, but at the same time he felt that he had been ordered up by nobody, but that this was his own venture, and this gave him a proud, steadying sensation, as if the sea and the sky, the ship, the bird and himself were all one. Just as he had freed the falcon, she hacked him on the thumb, so that the blood ran, and he nearly let her go. He grew angry with her, and gave her a clout on the head, then he put her inside his jacket, and climbed down again.

When he reached the deck the mate and the cook were standing there, looking up; they roared to him to ask what he had had to do in the mast. He was so tired that the tears were in his eyes. He took the falcon out and showed her to them, and she kept still within his hands. They laughed and walked off. Simon set the falcon down, stood back and watched her. After a while he reflected that she might not be able to get up from the slippery deck, so he caught her once more, walked away with her and placed her upon a bolt of canvas. A little after she began to trim her feathers, made two or three sharp jerks forward, and then suddenly flew off. The boy could follow her flight above the troughs of the grey sea. He thought: "There flies my falcon."

When the *Charlotte* came home, Simon signed aboard another ship, and two years later he was a light hand on the schooner *Hebe* lying at Bodø, high up on the coast of Norway, to buy herrings.

To the great herring markets of Bodø ships came together from all corners of the world; here were Swedish, Finnish and Russian boats, a forest of masts, and on shore a turbulent, irregular display of life, with many languages spoken, and mighty fists. On the shore booths had been set up, and the Lapps, small, yellow people, noiseless in their movements, with watchful eyes, whom Simon had never seen before, came down to sell bead-embroidered leather-goods. It was April, the sky and the sea were so clear that it was difficult to hold one's eyes up against them—salt, infinitely wide, and filled with bird-shrieks—as if someone were incessantly whetting invisible knives, on all sides, high up in Heaven.

Simon was amazed at the lightness of these April evenings. He knew no geography, and did not assign it to the latitude, but he took it as a sign of an unwonted good-will in the Universe, a favour. Simon had been small for his age all his life, but this last winter he had grown, and had become strong of limb. That good luck, he felt, must spring from the very same source as the sweetness of the weather, from a new benevolence in the world. He had been in need of such encouragement, for he was timid by nature; now he asked for no more. The rest he felt to be his own affair. He went about slowly, and proudly.

One evening he was ashore with land-leave, and walked up to the booth of a small Russian trader, a Jew who sold gold watches. All the sailors knew that his watches were made from bad metal, and would not go, still they bought them, and paraded them about. Simon looked at these watches for a long time, but did not buy. The old Jew had divers goods in his shop, and amongst others a case of oranges. Simon had tasted oranges on his journeys; he bought one and took it with him. He meant to go up on a hill, from where he could see the sea, and suck it there.

As he walked on, and had got to the outskirts of the place, he saw a little girl in a blue frock, standing at the other side of a fence and looking at him. She was thirteen or fourteen years old, as slim as an eel, but with a round, clear, freckled face, and a pair of long plaits. The two looked at one another.

"Who are you looking out for?" Simon asked, to say something. The girl's face broke into an ecstatic, presumptuous smile. "For the man I am going to marry, of course," she said. Something in her countenance made the boy confident and happy; he grinned a little at her. "That will perhaps be me," he said. "Ha, ha," said the girl, "he is a few years older than you, I can tell you." "Why," said Simon, "you are not grown up yourself." The little girl shook her head solemnly. "Nay," she said, "but when I grow up I will be exceedingly beautiful, and wear brown shoes with heels, and a hat." "Will you have an orange?" asked Simon, who could give her none of the things she had named. She looked at the orange and at him. "They are very good to eat," said he. "Why do you not eat it yourself then?" she asked. "I have eaten so many already," said he, "when I was in Athens. Here I had to pay a mark for it." "What is your name?" asked she. "My name is Simon," said he. "What is yours?" "Nora," said the girl. "What do you want for your orange now, Simon?"

When he heard his name in her mouth Simon grew bold. "Will you give me a kiss for the orange?" he asked. Nora looked at him gravely for a moment. "Yes," she said, "I should not mind giving you a kiss." He grew as warm as if he had been running quickly. When she stretched out her hand for the orange he took hold of it. At that moment somebody in the house called out for her. "That is my father," said she, and tried to give him back the orange, but he would not take it. "Then come again tomorrow," she said quickly, "then I will give you a kiss." At that she slipped off. He stood and looked after her, and a little later went back to his ship.

Simon was not in the habit of making plans for the future, and now he did not know whether he would be going back to her or not.

The following evening he had to stay aboard, as the other sailors were going ashore, and he did not mind that either. He meant to sit on the deck with the ship's dog, Balthasar, and to practice upon a concertina that he had purchased some time ago. The pale evening was all round him, the sky was faintly roseate, the sea was quite calm, like milk-and-water, only in the wake of the boats going inshore it broke into streaks of vivid indigo. Simon sat and played; after a while his own music began to speak to him so strongly that he stopped, got up and looked upwards. Then he saw that the full moon was sitting high on the sky.

The sky was so light that she hardly seemed needed there; it was as if she

had turned up by a caprice of her own. She was round, demure and presumptuous. At that he knew that he must go ashore, whatever it was to cost
him. But he did not know how to get away since the others had taken the
yawl with them. He stood on the deck for a long time, a small lonely figure
of a sailor-boy on a boat, when he caught sight of a yawl coming in from a
ship farther out, and hailed her. He found that it was the Russian crew
from the boat named *Anna*, going ashore. When he could make himself understood to them, they took him with them; they first asked him for money
for his fare, then laughing, gave it back to him. He thought: "These people
will be believing that I am going in to town, wenching." And then he felt,
with some pride, that they were right, although at the same time they were
infinitely wrong, and knew nothing about anything.

When they came ashore they invited him to come in and drink in their
company, and he would not refuse, because they had helped him. One of
the Russians was a giant, as big as a bear; he told Simon that his name was
Ivan. He got drunk at once, and then fell upon the boy with a bear-like
affection, pawed him, smiled and laughed into his face, made him a present of a gold watch-chain, and kissed him on both cheeks. At that Simon reflected that he also ought to give Nora a present when they met again, and
as soon as he could get away from the Russians he walked up to a booth that
he knew of, and bought a small blue silk handkerchief, the same colour as
her eyes.

It was Saturday evening, and there were many people amongst the
houses; they came in long rows, some of them singing, all keen to have
some fun that night. Simon, in the midst of this rich, bawling life under the
clear moon, felt his head light with the flight from the ship and the strong
drinks. He crammed the handkerchief in his pocket; it was silk, which he
had never touched before, a present for his girl.

He could not remember the path up to Nora's house, lost his way, and
came back to where he had started. Then he grew deadly afraid that he
should be too late, and began to run. In a small passage between two wood-
den huts he ran straight into a big man, and found that it was Ivan once
more. The Russian folded his arms round him and held him. "Good!
Good!" he cried in high glee, "I have found you, my little chicken. I have
looked for you everywhere, and poor Ivan has wept because he lost his
friend." "Let me go, Ivan," cried Simon. "Oho," said Ivan, "I shall go with
you and get you what you want. My heart and my money are all yours; I
have been seventeen years old myself, a little lamb of God, and I want to be
so again tonight." "Let me go," cried Simon, "I am in a hurry." Ivan held
him so that it hurt, and patted him with his other hand. "I feel it, I feel it,"
he said. "Now trust me, my little friend. Nothing shall part you and me, I
hear the others coming; we will have such a night together as you will remember when you are an old grandpapa."

Suddenly he crushed the boy to him, like a bear that carries off a sheep.

The odious sensation of male bodily warmth and the bulk of a man close to him made the lean boy mad. He thought of Nora waiting, like a slender ship in the dim air, and of himself, here, in the hot embrace of a hairy animal. He struck Ivan with all his might. "I shall kill you, Ivan," he cried out, "if you do not let me go." "Oh, you will be thankful to me later on," said Ivan, and began to sing. Simon fumbled in his pocket for his knife, got it opened. He could not lift his hand, but he drove the knife, furiously, in under the big man's arm. Almost immediately he felt the blood spouting out, and running down in his sleeve. Ivan stopped short in the song, let go his hold of the boy and gave two long deep grunts. The next second he tumbled down to his knees. "Poor Ivan, poor Ivan," he groaned. He fell straight on his face. At that moment Simon heard the other sailors coming along, singing, in the bystreet.

He stood still for a minute, wiped his knife, and watched the blood spread into a dark pool underneath the big body. Then he ran. As he stopped for a second to choose his way, he heard the sailors behind him scream out over their dead comrade. He thought: "I must get down to the sea, where I can wash my hand." But at the same time he ran the other way. After a little while he found himself on the path that he had walked on the day before, and it seemed as familiar to him, as if he had walked it many hundred times in his life.

He slackened his pace to look round, and suddenly saw Nora standing on the other side of the fence; she was quite close to him when he caught sight of her in the moonlight. Wavering and out of breath he sank down on his knees. For a moment he could not speak. The little girl looked down at him. "Good evening, Simon," she said in her small coy voice. "I have waited for you a long time," and after a moment she added: "I have eaten your orange."

"Oh, Nora," cried the boy. "I have killed a man." She stared at him, but did not move. "Why did you kill a man?" she asked after a moment. "To get here," said Simon. "Because he tried to stop me. But he was my friend." Slowly he got on to his feet. "He loved me!" the boy cried out, and at that burst into tears. "Yes," said she slowly and thoughtfully. "Yes, because you must be here in time." "Can you hide me?" he asked. "For they are after me." "Nay," said Nora, "I cannot hide you. For my father is the parson here at Bodø, and he would be sure to hand you over to them if he knew that you had killed a man." "Then," said Simon, "give me something to wipe my hands on." "What is the matter with your hands?" she asked, and took a little step forward. He stretched out his hands to her. "Is that your own blood?" she asked. "No," said he, "it is his." She took the step back again. "Do you hate me now?" he asked. "No, I do not hate you," said she. "But do put your hands at your back."

As he did so she came up close to him, at the other side of the fence, and clasped her arms round his neck. She pressed her young body to his, and kissed him tenderly. He felt her face, cool as the moonlight, upon his own, and when she released him, his head swam, and he did not know if the kiss had lasted a second or an hour. Nora stood up straight, her eyes wide open. "Now," she said slowly and proudly, "I promise you that I will never marry anybody, as long as I live." The boy kept standing with his hands on his back, as if she had tied them there. "And now," she said, "you must run, for they are coming." They looked at one another. "Do not forget Nora," said she. He turned and ran.

He leapt over a fence, and when he was down amongst the houses he walked. He did not know at all where to go. As he came to a house, from where music and noise streamed out, he slowly went through the door. The room was full of people; they were dancing in here. A lamp hung from the ceiling, and shone down on them, the air was thick and brown with dust rising from the floor. There were some women in the room, but many of the men danced with each other, and gravely or laughingly stamped the floor. A moment after Simon had come in the crowd withdrew to the walls to clear the floor for two sailors, who were showing a dance from their own country.

Simon thought: "Now, very soon, the men from the boat will come round to look for their comrade's murderer, and from my hands they will know that I have done it." These five minutes during which he stood by the wall of the dancing-room, in the midst of the gay, sweating dancers, were of great significance to the boy. He himself felt it, as if during this time he grew up, and became like other people. He did not entreat his destiny, nor complain. Here he was, he had killed a man, and had kissed a girl. He did not demand any more from life, nor did life now demand more from him. He was Simon, a man like the men round him, and going to die, as all men are going to die.

He only became aware of what was going on outside him, when he saw a woman had come in, and was standing in the midst of the cleared floor, looking round her. She was a short, broad old woman, in the clothes of the Lapps, and she took her stand with such majesty and fierceness as if she owned the whole place. It was obvious that most of the people knew her, and were a little afraid of her, although a few laughed; the din of the dancing room stopped when she spoke.

"Where is my son?" she asked in a high shrill voice, like a bird's. The next moment her eyes fell on Simon himself, and she steered through the crowd, which opened up before her, stretched out her old skinny, dark hand, and took him by the elbow. "Come home with me now," she said. 'You need not dance here tonight. You may be dancing a high enough dance soon."

Simon drew back, for he thought that she was drunk. But as she looked him straight in the face with her yellow eyes, it seemed to him that he had met her before, and that he might do well in listening to her. The old woman pulled him with her across the floor, and he followed her without a word. "Do not birch your boy too badly, Sunniva," one of the men in the room cried to her. "He has done no harm, he only wanted to look at the dance."

At the same moment as they came out through the door there was an alarm in the street, a flock of people came running down it, and one of them as he turned into the house, knocked against Simon, looked at him and the old woman, and ran on.

While the two walked along the street, the old woman lifted up her skirt, and put the hem of it into the boy's hand. "Wipe your hand on my skirt," she said. They had not gone far before they came to a small wooden house, and stopped; the door to it was so low that they must bend to get through it. As the Lapp-woman went in before Simon, still holding on to his arm, the boy looked up for a moment. The night had grown misty; there was a wide ring round the moon.

The old woman's room was narrow and dark, with but one small window to it; a lantern stood on the floor and lighted it up dimly. It was all filled with reindeer skins and wolf skins, and with reindeer horns, such as the Lapps use to make their carved buttons and knife-handles, and the air in here was rank and stifling. As soon as they were in, the woman turned to Simon, took hold of his head, and with her crooked fingers parted his hair and combed it down in Lapp fashion. She clapped a Lapp cap on him and stood back to glance at him. "Sit down on my stool, now," she said. "But first take out your knife." She was so commanding in voice and manner that the boy could not but choose to do as she told him; he sat down on the stool, and he could not take his eyes off her face, which was flat and brown, and as if smeared with dirt in its net of fine wrinkles. As he sat there he heard many people come along outside, and stop by the house; then someone knocked at the door, waited a moment and knocked again. The old woman stood and listened, as still as a mouse.

"Nay," said the boy and got up. "This is no good, for it is me that they are after. It will be better for you to let me go out to them." "Give me your knife," she said. When he handed it to her, she stuck it straight into her thumb, so that the blood spouted out, and she let it drip all over her skirt. "Come in, then," she cried.

The door opened, and two Russian sailors came and stood in the opening; there were more people outside. "Has anybody come in here?" they asked. "We are after a man who has killed our mate, but he has run away from us. Have you seen or heard anybody this way?" The old Lapp-woman turned upon them, and her eyes shone like gold in the lamplight. "Have I seen or heard anyone?" she cried, "I have heard you shriek murder all over the town. You frightened me, and my poor silly boy there, so that I cut my thumb as I was ripping the skin-rug that I sew. The boy is too scared to help me, and the rug is ruined. I shall make you pay me for that. If you are looking for a murderer, come in and search my house for me, and I shall know you when we meet again." She was so furious that she danced where she stood, and jerked her head like an angry bird of prey.

The Russian came in, looked round the room, and at her and her blood-stained hand and skirt. "Do not put a curse on us now, Sunniva," he said timidly. "We know that you can do many things when you like. Here is a mark to pay you for the blood you have spilled." She stretched out her hand, and he placed a piece of money in it. She spat on it. "Then go, and there shall be no bad blood between us," said Sunniva, and shut the door after them. She stuck her thumb in her mouth, and chuckled a little.

The boy got up from his stool, stood up before her and stared into her face. He felt as if he were swaying high up in the air, with but a small hold. "Why have you helped me?" he asked her. "Do you not know?" she answered. "Have you not recognised me yet? But you will remember the peregrine falcon which was caught in the tackle-yarn of your boat, the *Charlotte,* as she sailed in the Mediterranean. That day you climbed up by the shrouds of the top-gallant-mast to help her out, in a stiff wind, and with a high sea. That falcon was me. We Lapps often fly in such a manner, to see the world. When I first met you I was on my way to Africa, to see my younger sister and her children. She is a falcon too, when she chooses. By that time she was living at Takaunga, within an old ruined tower, which down there they call a minaret." She swarthed a corner of her skirt round her thumb, and bit at it, "We do not forget," she said. "I hacked your thumb, when you took hold of me; it is only fair that I should cut my thumb for you tonight."

She came close to him, and gently rubbed her two brown, claw-like fingers against his forehead. "So you are a boy," she said, "who will kill a man rather than be late to meet your sweetheart? We hold together, the females of this earth. I shall mark your forehead now, so that girls will know of that, when they look at you, and they will like you for it." She played with the boy's hair, and twisted it round her finger.

"Listen now, my little bird," said she. "My great grandson's brother-in-law is lying with his boat by the landing-place at this moment; he is to take a consignment of skins out to a Danish boat. He will bring you back to your boat, in time, before your mates come. The *Hebe* is sailing tomorrow morning, is it not so? But when you are aboard, give him back my cap for me." She took up his knife, wiped it in her skirt and handed it to him. "Here is your knife," she said. "You will stick it into no more men; you will not need to, for from now you will sail the seas like a faithful seaman. We have enough trouble with our sons as it is."

The bewildered boy began to stammer his thanks to her. "Wait," said she, "I shall make you a cup of coffee, to bring back your wits, while I wash your jacket." She went and rattled an old copper kettle upon the fireplace. After a while she handed him a hot, strong, black drink in a cup without a handle to it. "You have drunk with Sunniva now," she said; "you have drunk down a little wisdom, so that in the future all your thoughts shall not fall like rain-drops into the salt sea."

When he had finished and set down the cup, she led him to the door and opened it for him. He was so surprised to see that it was almost clear morning. The house was so high up that the boy could see the sea from it, and a milky mist about it. He gave her his hand to say good-bye.

She stared into his face. "We do not forget," she said. "And you, you knocked me on the head there, high up in the mast. I shall give you that blow back." With that she smacked him on the ear as hard as she could, so that his head swam. "Now we are quits," she said, gave him a great, mischie-vous, shining glance, and a little push down the doorstep, and nodded to him.

In this way the sailor-boy got back to his ship, which was to sail the next morning, and lived to tell the story.

King of the Bingo Game

RALPH ELLISON

The woman in front of him was eating roasted peanuts that smelled so good that he could barely contain his hunger. He could not even sleep and wished they'd hurry and begin the bingo game. There, on his right, two fellows were drinking wine out of a bottle wrapped in a paper bag, and he could hear soft gurgling in the dark. His stomach gave a low, gnawing growl. "If this was down South," he thought, "all I'd have to do is lean over and say, 'Lady, gimme a few of those peanuts, please ma'am,' and she'd pass me the bag and never think nothing of it." Or he could ask the fellows for a drink in the same way. Folks down South stuck together that way; they didn't even have to know you. But up here it was different. Ask somebody for something, and they'd think you were crazy. Well, I ain't crazy. I'm just broke, 'cause I got no birth certificate to get a job, and Laura 'bout to die 'cause we got no money for a doctor. But I ain't crazy. And yet a pinpoint of doubt was focused in his mind as he glanced toward the screen and saw the hero stealthily entering a dark room and sending the beam of a flashlight along a wall of bookcases. This is where he finds the trapdoor, he remembered. The man would pass abruptly through the wall and find the girl tied to a bed, her legs and arms spread wide, and her clothing torn to rags. He laughed softly to himself. He had seen the picture three times, and this was one of the best scenes.

On his right the fellow whispered wide eyed to his companion, "Man, look a-yonder!"

"Damn!"

"Wouldn't I like to have her tied up like that . . ."

"Hey! That fool's letting her loose!"

"Aw, man, he loves her."

"Love or no love!"

The man moved impatiently beside him, and he tried to involve himself in the scene. But Laura was on his mind. Tiring quickly of watching the pic-

ture he looked back to where the white beam filtered from the projection
room above the balcony. It started small and grew large, specks of dust
dancing in its whiteness as it reached the screen. It was strange how the
beam always landed right on the screen and didn't mess up and fall somewhere else. But they had it all fixed. Everything was fixed. Now suppose
when they showed that girl with her dress torn the girl started taking off
the rest of her clothes, and when the guy came in he didn't untie her but
kept her there and went to taking off his own clothes? *That* would be something to see. If a picture got out of hand like that those guys up there would
go nuts. Yeah, and there'd be so many folks in here you couldn't find a seat
for nine months! A strange sensation played over his skin. He shuddered.
Yesterday he'd seen a bedbug on a woman's neck as they walked out into
the bright street. But exploring his thigh through a hole in his pocket he
found only goose pimples and old scars.

The bottle gurgled again. He closed his eyes. Now a dreamy music was
accompanying the film and train whistles were sounding in the distance,
and he was a boy again walking along a railroad trestle down South, and
seeing the train coming, and running back as fast as he could go, and hearing the whistle blowing, and getting off the trestle to solid ground just in
time, with the earth trembling beneath his feet, and feeling relieved as he
ran down the cinder-strewn embankment onto the highway, and looking
back and seeing with terror that the train had left the track and was following him right down the middle of the street, and all the white people laughing as he ran screaming . . .

"Wake up there, buddy! What the hell do you mean hollering like that?
Can't you see we trying to enjoy this here picture?"

He stared at the man with gratitude.

"I'm sorry, old man," he said. "I musta been dreaming."

"Well, here, have a drink. And don't be making no noise like that,
damn!"

His hands trembled as he tilted his head. It was not wine, but whiskey.
Cold rye whiskey. He took a deep swoller, decided it was better not to take
another, and handed the bottle back to its owner.

"Thanks, old man," he said.

Now he felt the cold whiskey breaking a warm path straight through the
middle of him, growing hotter and sharper as it moved. He had not eaten
all day, and it made him light-headed. The smell of the peanuts stabbed
him like a knife, and he got up and found a seat in the middle aisle. But no
sooner did he sit than he saw a row of intense-faced young girls, and got up
again, thinking, "You chicks musta been Lindy-hopping somewhere." He
found a seat several rows ahead as the lights came on, and he saw the
screen disappear behind a heavy red and gold curtain; then the curtain rising, and the man with the microphone and a uniformed attendant coming
on the stage.

He felt for his bingo cards, smiling. The guy at the door wouldn't like it if he knew about his having *five* cards. Well, not everyone played the bingo game; and even with five cards he didn't have much of a chance. For Laura, though, he had to have faith. He studied the cards, each with its different numerals, punching the free center hole in each and spreading them neatly across his lap; and when the lights faded he sat slouched in his seat so that he could look from his cards to the bingo wheel with but a quick shifting of his eyes.

Ahead, at the end of the darkness, the man with the microphone was pressing a button attached to a long cord and spinning the bingo wheel and calling out the number each time the wheel came to rest. And each time the voice rang out his finger raced over the cards for the number. With five cards he had to move fast. He became nervous; there were too many cards, and the man went too fast with his grating voice. Perhaps he should just se-lect one and throw the others away. But he was afraid. He became warm. Wonder how much Laura's doctor would cost? Damn that, watch the cards! And with despair he heard the man call three in a row which he missed on all five cards. This way he'd never win . . . .

When he saw the row of holes punched across the third card, he sat para-lyzed and heard the man call three more numbers before he stumbled for-ward, screaming.

"Bingo! Bingo!"

"Let that fool up there," someone called.

"Get up there, man!"

He stumbled down the aisle and up the steps to the stage into a light so sharp and bright that for a moment it blinded him, and he felt that he had moved into the spell of some strange, mysterious power. Yet it was as famil-iar as the sun, and he knew it was the perfectly familiar bingo.

The man with the microphone was saying something to the audience as he held out his card. A cold light flashed from the man's finger as the card left his hand. His knees trembled. The man stepped closer, checking the card against the numbers chalked on the board. Suppose he had made a mistake? The pomade on the man's hair made him feel faint, and he backed away. But the man was checking the card over the microphone now, and he had to stay. He stood tense, listening.

"Under the O, forty-four," the man chanted. "Under the I, seven. Under the G, three. Under the B, ninety-six. Under the N, thirteen!"

His breath came easier as the man smiled at the audience.

"Yessir, ladies and gentlemen, he's one of the chosen people!"

The audience rippled with laughter and applause.

"Step right up to the front of the stage."

He moved slowly forward, wishing that the light was not so bright.

"To win to-night's jackpot of $36.90 the wheel must stop between the double zero, understand?"

He nodded, knowing the ritual from the many days and nights he had watched the winners march across the stage to press the button that controlled the spinning wheel and receive the prizes. And now he followed the instructions as though he'd crossed the slippery stage a million prizewinning times.

The man was making some kind of a joke, and he nodded vacantly. So tense had he become that he felt a sudden desire to cry and shook it away. He felt vaguely that his whole life was determined by the bingo wheel; not only that which would happen now that he was at last before it, but all that had gone before, since his birth, and his mother's birth and the birth of his father. It had always been there, even though he had not been aware of it, handing out the unlucky cards and numbers of his days. The feeling persisted, and he started quickly away. I better get down from here before I make a fool of myself, he thought.

"Here, boy," the man called. "You haven't started yet."

Someone laughed as he went hesitantly back.

"Are you all reet?"

He grinned at the man's jive talk, but no words would come, and he knew it was not a convincing grin. For suddenly he knew that he stood on the slippery brink of some terrible embarrassment.

"Where are you from, boy?" the man asked.

"Down South."

"He's from down South, ladies and gentlemen," the man said. "Where from? Speak right into the mike."

"Rocky Mont," he said. "Rock' Mont, North Car'lina."

"So you decided to come down off that mountain to the U. S.," the man laughed. He felt that the man was making a fool of him, but then something cold was placed in his hand, and the lights were no longer behind him.

Standing before the wheel he felt alone, but that was somehow right, and he remembered his plan. He would give the wheel a short quick twirl. Just a touch of the button. He had watched it many times, and always it came close to double zero when it was short and quick. He steeled himself; the fear had left, and he felt a profound sense of promise, as though he were about to be repaid for all the things he'd suffered all his life. Trembling, he pressed the button. There was a whirl of lights, and in a second he realized with finality that though he wanted to, he could not stop. It was as though he held a high-powered line in his naked hand. His nerves tightened. As the wheel increased its speed it seemed to draw him more and more into its power, as though it held his fate; and with it came a deep need to submit, to whirl, to lose himself in its swirl of color. He could not stop it now. So let it be.

The button rested snugly in his palm where the man had placed it. And now he became aware of the man beside him, advising him through the microphone, while behind the shadowy audience hummed with noisy voices. He shifted his feet. There was still that feeling of helplessness within him, making part of him desire to turn back, even now that the jackpot was right in his hand. He squeezed the button until his fist ached. Then, like the sudden shriek of a subway whistle, a doubt tore through his head. Suppose he did not spin the wheel long enough? What could he do, and how could he tell? And then he knew, even as he wondered, that as long as he pressed the button, he could control the jackpot. He and only he could determine whether or not it was to be his. Not even the man with the microphone could do anything about it now. He felt drunk. Then, as though he had come down from a high hill into a valley of people, he heard the audience yelling.

"Come down from there, you jerk!"

"Let somebody else have a chance . . ."

"Ole Jack thinks he done found the end of the rainbow . . ."

The last voice was not unfriendly, and he turned and smiled dreamily into the yelling mouths. Then he turned his back squarely on them.

"Don't take too long, boy," a voice said.

He nodded. They were yelling behind him. Those folks did not understand what had happened to him. They had been playing the bingo game day in and night out for years, trying to win rent money or hamburger change. But not one of those wise guys had discovered this wonderful thing. He watched the wheel whirling past the numbers and experienced a burst of exaltation: This is God! This is the really truly God! He said it aloud, "This is God!"

He said it with such absolute conviction that he feared he would fall fainting into the footlights. But the crowd yelled so loud that they could not hear. Those fools, he thought. I'm here trying to tell them the most wonderful secret in the world, and they're yelling like they gone crazy. A hand fell upon his shoulder.

"You'll have to make a choice now, boy. You've taken too long."

He brushed the hand violently away.

"Leave me alone, man. I know what I'm doing!"

The man looked surprised and held on to the microphone for support. And because he did not wish to hurt the man's feelings he smiled, realizing with a sudden pang that there was no way of explaining to the man just why he had to stand there pressing the button forever.

"Come here," he called tiredly.

The man approached, rolling the heavy microphone across the stage.

"Anybody can play this bingo game, right?" he said.

"Sure, but . . ."

He smiled, feeling inclined to be patient with this slick looking white man with his blue shirt and his sharp gabardine suit.

"That's what I thought," he said. "Anybody can win the jackpot as long as they get the lucky number, right?"

"That's the rule, but after all . . ."

"That's what I thought," he said. "And the big prize goes to the man who knows how to win it?"

The man nodded speechlessly.

"Well then, go on over there and watch me win like I want to. I ain't going to hurt nobody," he said, "and I'll show you how to win. I mean to show the whole world how it's got to be done."

And because he understood, he smiled again to let the man know that he held nothing against him for being white and impatient. Then he refused to see the man any longer and stood pressing the button, the voices of the crowd reaching him like sounds in distant streets. Let them yell. All the Negroes down there were just ashamed because he was black like them. He smiled inwardly, knowing how it was. Most of the time he was ashamed of what Negroes did himself. Well, let them be ashamed for something this time. Like him. He was like a long thin black wire that was being stretched and wound upon the bingo wheel; wound until he wanted to scream; wound, but this time himself controlling the winding and the sadness and the shame, and because he did, Laura would be all right. Suddenly the lights flickered. He staggered backwards. Had something gone wrong? All this noise. Didn't they know that although he controlled the wheel, it also controlled him, and unless he pressed the button forever and forever and ever it would stop, leaving him high and dry, dry and high on this hard slippery hill and Laura dead? There was only one chance; he had to do whatever the wheel demanded. And gripping the button in despair, he discovered with surprise that it imparted a nervous energy. His spine tingled. He felt a certain power.

Now he faced the raging crowd with defiance, its screams penetrating his eardrums like trumpets shrieking from a juke-box. The vague faces glowing in the bingo lights gave him a sense of himself that he had never known before. He was running the show, by God! They had to react to him, for he was their luck. This is *me*, he thought. Let the bastards yell. Then someone was laughing inside him, and he realized that somehow he had forgotten his own name. It was a sad, lost feeling to lose your name, and a crazy thing to do. That name had been given him by the white man who had owned his grandfather a long lost time ago down South. But maybe those wise guys knew his name.

"Who am I?" he screamed.

"Hurry up and bingo, you jerk!"

They didn't know either, he thought sadly. They didn't even know their own names, they were all poor nameless bastards. Well, he didn't need that old name; he was reborn. For as long as he pressed the button he was The-man-who-pressed-the-button-who-held-the-prize-who-was-the-King-of-Bingo. That was the way it was, and he'd have to press the button even if nobody understood, even though Laura did not understand.

"Live!" he shouted.

The audience quieted like the dying of a huge fan.

"Live, Laura, baby. I got holt of it now, sugar. Live!"

He screamed it, tears streaming down his face. "I got nobody but YOU!"

The screams tore from his very guts. He felt as though the rush of blood to his head would burst out in baseball seams of small red droplets, like a head beaten by police clubs. Bending over he saw a trickle of blood splashing the toe of his shoe. With his free hand he searched his head. It was his nose. God, suppose something has gone wrong? He felt that the whole audience had somehow entered him and was stamping its feet in his stomach and he was unable to throw them out. They wanted the prize, that was it. They wanted the secret for themselves. But they'd never get it; he would keep the bingo wheel whirling forever, and Laura would be safe in the wheel. But would she? It had to be, because if she were not safe the wheel would cease to turn; it could not go on. He had to get away, *vomit* all, and his mind formed an image of himself running with Laura in his arms down the tracks of the subway just ahead of an A train, running desperately *vomit* with people screaming for him to come out but knowing no way of leaving the tracks because to stop would bring the train crushing down upon him and to attempt to leave across the other tracks would mean to run into a hot third rail as high as his waist which threw blue sparks that blinded his eyes until he could hardly see.

He heard singing and the audience was clapping its hands.

> *Shoot the liquor to him, Jim, boy!*
> *Clap-clap-clap*
> *Well a-calla the cop*
> *He's blowing his top!*
> *Shoot the liquor to him, Jim, boy!*

Bitter anger grew within him at the singing. They think I'm crazy. Well let 'em laugh. I'll do what I got to do.

He was standing in an attitude of intense listening when he saw that they were watching something on the stage behind him. He felt weak. But when he turned he saw no one. If only his thumb did not ache so. Now they were applauding. And for a moment he thought that the wheel had stopped. But that was impossible, his thumb still pressed the button. Then he saw them. Two men in uniform beckoned from the end of the stage. They were coming toward him, walking in step, slowly, like a tap-dance team returning for a third encore. But their shoulders shot forward, and he backed away, looking wildly about. There was nothing to fight them with. He had only the long black cord which led to a plug somewhere back stage, and he couldn't use that because it operated the bingo wheel. He backed slowly, fixing the men with his eyes as his lips stretched over his teeth in a tight, fixed grin; moved toward the end of the stage and realizing that he couldn't go much further, for suddenly the cord became taut and he couldn't afford to break the cord. But he had to do something. The audience was howling. Suddenly he stopped dead, seeing the men halt, their legs lifted as in an interrupted step of a slow-motion dance. There was nothing to do but run in the other direction and he dashed forward, slipping and sliding. The men fell back, surprised. He struck out violently going past.

"Grab him!"

He ran, but all too quickly the cord tightened, resistingly, and he turned and ran back again. This time he slipped them, and discovered by running in a circle before the wheel he could keep the cord from tightening. But this way he had to flail his arms to keep the men away. Why couldn't they leave a man alone? He ran, circling.

"Ring down the curtain," someone yelled. But they couldn't do that. If they did the wheel flashing from the projection room would be cut off. But they had him before he could tell them so, trying to pry open his fist, and he was wrestling and trying to bring his knees into the fight and holding on to the button, for it was his life. And now he was down, seeing a foot coming down, crushing his wrist cruelly, down, as he saw the wheel whirling serenely above.

"I can't give it up," he screamed. Then quietly, in a confidential tone, "Boys, I really can't give it up."

It landed hard against his head. And in the blank moment they had it away from him, completely now. He fought them trying to pull him up from the stage as he watched the wheel spin slowly to a stop. Without surprise he saw it rest at double zero.

"You see," he pointed bitterly.

"Sure, boy, sure, it's O.K.," one of the men said smiling.

And seeing the man bow his head to someone he could not see, he felt very, very happy; he would receive what all the winners received.

But as he warmed in the justice of the man's tight smile he did not see the man's slow wink, nor see the bow-legged man behind him step clear of the swiftly descending curtain and set himself for a blow. He only felt the dull pain exploding in his skull, and he knew even as it slipped out of him that his luck had run out on the stage.

Flying Home

RALPH ELLISON

When Todd came to, he saw two faces suspended above him in a sun so hot and blinding that he could not tell if they were black or white. He stirred, feeling a pain that burned as though his whole body had been laid open to the sun which glared into his eyes. For a moment an old fear of being touched by white hands seized him. Then the very sharpness of the pain began slowly to clear his head. Sounds came to him dimly. He done come to. Who are they? he thought. Naw he ain't, I coulda sworn he was white. Then he heard clearly:

"You hurt bad?"

Something within him uncoiled. It was a Negro sound.

"He's still out," he heard.

"Give 'im time. . . . Say, son, you hurt bad?"

Was he? There was that awful pain. He lay rigid, hearing their breathing and trying to weave a meaning between them and his being stretched painfully upon the ground. He watched them warily, his mind traveling back over a painful distance. Jagged scenes, swiftly unfolding as in a movie trailer, reeled through his mind, and he saw himself piloting a tailspinning plane and landing and landing and falling from the cockpit and trying to stand. Then, as in a great silence, he remembered the sound of crunching bone, and now, looking up into the anxious faces of an old Negro man and a boy from where he lay in the same field, the memory sickened him and he wanted to remember no more.

"How you feel, son?"

Todd hesitated, as though to answer would be to admit an inacceptable weakness. Then, "It's my ankle," he said.

"Which one?"

"The left."

With a sense of remoteness he watched the old man bend and remove his boot, feeling the pressure ease.

276

"That any better?"

"A lot. Thank you."

He had the sensation of discussing something else, that his concern was with some far more important thing, which for some reason escaped him.

"You done broke it bad," the old man said. "We have to get you to a doctor."

He felt that he had been thrown into a tailspin. He looked at his watch; how long had he been here? He knew there was but one important thing in the world, to get the plane back to the field before his officers were displeased.

"Help me up," he said. "Into the ship."

"But it's broke too bad. . . ."

"Give me your arm!"

"But, son . . ."

Clutching the old man's arm he pulled himself up, keeping his left leg clear, thinking, "I'd never make him understand," as the leather-smooth face came parallel with his own.

"Now, let's see."

He pushed the old man back, hearing a bird's insistent shrill. He swayed giddily. Blackness washed over him, like infinity.

"You best sit down."

"No, I'm O.K."

"But, son. You jus' gonna make it worse. . . ."

It was a fact that everything in him cried out to deny, even against the flaming pain in his ankle. He would have to try again.

"You mess with that ankle they have to cut your foot off," he heard.

Holding his breath, he started up again. It pained so badly that he had to bite his lips to keep from crying out and he allowed them to help him down with a pang of despair.

"It's best you take it easy. We gon' git you a doctor."

Of all the luck, he thought. Of all the rotten luck, now I have done it. The fumes of high-octane gasoline clung in the heat, taunting him.

"We kin ride him into town on old Ned," the boy said.

Ned? He turned, seeing the boy point toward an ox team browsing where the buried blade of a plow marked the end of a furrow. Thoughts of himself riding an ox through the town, past streets full of white faces, down the concrete runways of the airfield made swift images of humiliation in his mind. With a pang he remembered his girl's last letter. "Todd," she had written, "I don't need the papers to tell me you had the intelligence to fly. And I have always known you to be as brave as anyone else. The papers annoy me. Don't you be contented to prove over and over again that you're brave or skillful just because you're black, Todd. I think they keep beating that dead horse because they don't want to say why you boys are not yet fighting. I'm really disappointed, Todd. Anyone with brains can learn to fly, but then what? What about using it, and who will you use it for? I wish, dear, you'd write about this. I sometimes think they're playing a trick on us. It's very humiliating. . . ." He wiped cold sweat from his face, thinking, What does she know of humiliation? She's never been down South. Now the humiliation would come. When you must have them judge you, knowing that they never accept your mistakes as your own, but hold it against your whole race—that was humiliation. Yes, and humiliation was when you could never be simply yourself, when you were always a part of this old black ignorant man. Sure, he's all right. Nice and kind and helpful. But he's not you. Well, there's one humiliation I can spare myself.

"No," he said, "I have orders not to leave the ship. . . ."

"Aw," the old man said. Then turning to the boy, "Teddy, then you better hustle down to Mister Graves and get him to come. . . ."

"No, wait!" he protested before he was fully aware. Graves might be white. "Just have him get word to the field, please. They'll take care of the rest."

He saw the boy leave, running.

"How far does he have to go?"

"Might' nigh a mile."

He rested back, looking at the dusty face of his watch. But now they know something has happened, he thought. In the ship there was a perfectly good radio, but it was useless. The old fellow would never operate it. That buzzard knocked me back a hundred years, he thought. Irony danced within him like the gnats circling the old man's head. With all I've learned I'm dependent upon this "peasant's" sense of time and space. His leg throbbed. In the plane, instead of time being measured by the rhythms of pain and a kid's legs, the instruments would have told him at a glance. Twisting upon his elbows he saw where dust had powdered the plane's fuselage, feeling the lump form in his throat that was always there when he thought of flight. It's crouched there, he thought, like the abandoned shell of a locust. I'm naked without it. Not a machine, a suit of clothes you wear. And with a sudden embarrassment and wonder he whispered, "It's the only dignity I have. . . ."

He saw the old man watching, his torn overalls clinging limply to him in the heat. He felt a sharp need to tell the old man what he felt. But that would be meaningless. If I tried to explain why I need to fly back, he'd think I was simply afraid of white officers. But it's more than fear . . . a sense of anguish clung to him like the veil of sweat that hugged his face. He watched the old man, hearing him humming snatches of a tune as he admired the plane. He felt a furtive sense of resentment. Such old men often came to the field to watch the pilots with childish eyes. At first it had made him proud; they had been a meaningful part of a new experience. But soon he realized they did not understand his accomplishments and they came to shame and embarrass him, like the distasteful praise of an idiot. A part of the meaning of flying had gone then, and he had not been able to regain it. If I were a prizefighter I would be more human, he thought. Not a monkey doing tricks, but a man. They were pleased simply that he was a Negro who could fly, and that was not enough. He felt cut off from them by age, by understanding, by sensibility, by technology and by his need to measure himself against the mirror of other men's appreciation. Somehow he felt betrayed, as he had when as a child he grew to discover that his father was dead. Now for him any real appreciation lay with his white officers; and with them he could never be sure. Between ignorant black men and condescending whites, his course of flight seemed mapped by the nature of things away from all needed and natural landmarks. Under some sealed orders, couched in ever more technical and mysterious terms, his path curved swiftly away from both the shame the old man symbolized and the cloudy terrain of white men's regard. Flying blind, he knew but one point of landing and there he would receive his wings. After that the enemy would appreciate his skill and he would assume his deepest meaning, he thought sadly, neither from those who condescended nor from those who praised without understanding, but from the enemy who would recognize his manhood and skill in terms of hate. . . ."

He sighed, seeing the oxen making queer, prehistoric shadows against the dry brown earth.

"You just take it easy, son," the old man soothed. "That boy won't take long. Crazy as he is about airplanes."

"I can wait," he said.

"What kinda airplane you call this here'n?"

"An Advanced Trainer," he said, seeing the old man smile. His fingers were like gnarled dark wood against the metal as he touched the low-slung wing.

"'Bout how fast can she fly?"

"Over two hundred an hour."

"Lawd! That's so fast I bet it don't seem like you moving!"

Holding himself rigid, Todd opened his flying suit. The shade had gone and he lay in a ball of fire.

"You mind if I take a look inside? I was always curious to see. . . ."

"Help yourself. Just don't touch anything."

He heard him climb upon the metal wing, grunting. Now the questions would start. Well, so you don't have to think to answer. . . .

He saw the old man looking over into the cockpit, his eyes bright as a child's.

"You must have to know a lot to work all these here things."

He was silent, seeing him step down and kneel beside him.

"Son, how come you want to fly way up there in the air?"

Because it's the most meaningful act in the world . . . because it makes me less like you, he thought.

But he said: "Because I like it, I guess. It's as good a way to fight and die as I know."

"Yeah? I guess you right," the old man said. "But how long you think before they gonna let you all fight?"

He tensed. This was the question all Negroes asked, put with the same timid hopefulness and longing that always opened a greater void within him than that he had felt beneath the plane the first time he had flown. He felt light-headed. It came to him suddenly that there was something sinister about the conversation, that he was flying unwillingly into unsafe and uncharted regions. If he could only be insulting and tell this old man who was trying to help him to shut up!

"I bet you one thing . . ."

"Yes?"

"That you was plenty scared coming down."

He did not answer. Like a dog on a trail the old man seemed to smell out his fears and he felt anger bubble within him.

"You sho' scared me. When I seen you coming down in that thing with it a-rollin' and a-jumpin' like a pitchin' hoss, I thought sho' you was a goner. I almost had me a stroke!"

He saw the old man grinning, "Ever'thin's been happening round here this morning, come to think of it."

"Like what?" he asked.

"Well, first thing I know, here come two white fellers looking for Mister Rudolph, that's Mister Graves's cousin. That got me worked up right away. . . ."

"Why?"

"Why? 'Cause he done broke outta the crazy house, that's why. He liable to kill somebody," he said. "They oughta have him by now though. Then here you come. First I think it's one of them white boys. Then doggone if you don't fall outta there. Lawd, I'd done heard about you boys but I haven't never seen one o' you-all. Cain't tell you how it felt to see somebody what look like me in a airplane!"

The old man talked on, the sound streaming around Todd's thoughts like air flowing over the fuselage of a flying plane. You were a fool, he thought, remembering how before the spin the sun had blazed bright against the billboard signs beyond the town, and how a boy's blue kite had bloomed beneath him, tugging gently in the wind like a strange, odd-shaped flower. He had once flown such kites himself and tried to find the boy at the end of the invisible cord. But he had been flying too high and too fast. He had climbed steeply away in exultation. Too steeply, he thought. And one of the first rules you learn is that if the angle of thrust is too steep the plane goes into a spin. And then, instead of pulling out of it and going into a dive you let a buzzard panic you. A lousy buzzard!

"Son, what made all that blood on the glass?"

"A buzzard," he said, remembering how the blood and feathers had sprayed back against the hatch. It had been as though he had flown into a storm of blood and blackness.

"Well, I declare! They's lots of 'em around here. They after dead things. Don't eat nothing what's alive."

"A little bit more and he would have made a meal out of me," Todd said grimly.

"They bad luck all right. Teddy's got a name for 'em, calls 'em jimcrows," the old man laughed.

"It's a damned good name."

"They the damnedest birds. Once I seen a hoss all stretched out like he was sick, you know. So I hollers, 'Gid up from there, suh!' Just to make sho! An' doggone, son, if I don't see two ole jimcrows come flying right up outa that hoss's insides! Yessuh! The sun was shinin' on 'em and they couldn't a been no greasier if they'd been eating barbecue."

Todd thought he would vomit, his stomach quivered.

"You made that up," he said.

"Nawsuh! Saw him just like I see you."

"Well, I'm glad it was you."

"You see lots a funny things down here, son."

"No, I'll let you see them," he said.

"By the way, the white folks round here don't like to see you boys up there in the sky. They ever bother you?"

"No."

"Well, they'd like to."

"Someone always wants to bother someone else," Todd said. "How do you know?"

"I just know."

"Well," he said defensively, "no one has bothered us."

Blood pounded in his ears as he looked away into space. He tensed, seeing a black spot in the sky, and strained to confirm what he could not clearly see.

"What does that look like to you?" he asked excitedly.

"Just another bad luck, son."

Then he saw the movement of wings with disappointment. It was gliding smoothly down, wings outspread, tail feathers gripping the air, down swiftly—gone behind the green screen of trees. It was like a bird he had imagined there, only the sloping branches of the pines remained, sharp against the pale stretch of sky. He lay barely breathing and stared at the point where it had disappeared, caught in a spell of loathing and admiration. Why did they make them so disgusting and yet teach them to fly so well? It's like when I was up in heaven, he heard, starting.

The old man was chuckling, rubbing his stubbled chin.

"What did you say?"

"Sho', I died and went to heaven . . . maybe by time I tell you about it they be done come after you."

"I hope so," he said wearily.

"You boys ever sit around and swap lies?"

"Not often. Is this going to be one?"

"Well, I ain't so sho', on account of it took place when I was dead."

The old man paused, "That wasn't no lie 'bout the buzzards, though."

"All right," he said.

"Sho' you want to hear 'bout heaven?"

"Please," he answered, resting his head upon his arm.

"Well, I went to heaven and right away started to sproutin' me some wings. Six good ones, they was. Just like them the white angels had. I couldn't hardly believe it. I was so glad that I went off on some clouds by myself and tried 'em out. You know, 'cause I didn't want to make a fool outta myself the first thing. . . ."

It's an old tale, Todd thought. Told me years ago. Had forgotten. But at least it will keep him from talking about buzzards.

He closed his eyes, listening.

". . . First thing I done was to git up on a low cloud and jump off. And doggone, boy, if them wings didn't work! First I tried the right; then I tried the left; then I tried 'em both together. Then Lawd, I started to move on out among the folks. I let 'em see me. . . ."

He saw the old man gesturing flight with his arms, his face full of mock pride as he indicated an imaginary crowd, thinking, It'll be in the newspapers, as he heard, " . . . so I went and found me some colored angels— somehow I didn't believe I was an angel till I seen a real black one, ha, yes! Then I was sho'—but they tole me I better come down 'cause us colored folks had to wear a special kin' a harness when we flew. That was how come they wasn't flyin'. Oh yes, an' you had to be extra strong for a black man even, to fly with one of them harnesses. . . ."

This is a new turn, Todd thought, what's he driving at?

"So I said to myself, I ain't gonna be bothered with no harness! Oh naw! 'Cause if God let you sprout wings you oughta have sense enough not to let nobody make you wear something what gits in the way of flyin'. So I starts to flyin'. Heck, son," he chuckled, his eyes twinkling, "you know I had to let eve'ybody know that old Jefferson could fly good as anybody else. And I could too, fly smooth as a bird! I could even loop-the-loop—only I had to make sho' to keep my long white robe down roun' my ankles. . . ."

Todd felt uneasy. He wanted to laugh at the joke, but his body refused, as of an independent will. He felt as he had as a child when after he had chewed a sugar-coated pill which his mother had given him, she had laughed at his efforts to remove the terrible taste.

". . . Well," he heard, "I was doing all right 'til I got to speeding. Found out I could fan up a right strong breeze, I could fly so fast. I could do all

kin'sa stunts too. I started flying up to the stars and divin' down and zoom-
ing roun' the moon. Man, I like to scare the devil outa some ole white angels. I was raisin' hell. Not that I meant any harm, son. But I was just
feeling good. It was so good to know I was free at last. I accidentally
knocked the tips offa some stars and they tell me I caused a storm and a
coupla lynchings down here in Macon County—though I swear I believe
them boys what said that was making up lies on me. . . ."

He's mocking me, Todd thought angrily. He thinks it's a joke. Grinning
down at me . . . His throat was dry. He looked at his watch; why the hell
didn't they come? Since they had to, why? One day I was flying down one
of them heavenly streets. You got yourself into it, Todd thought. Like Jo-
nah in the whale.

"Justa throwin' feathers in everybody's face. An' ole Saint Peter called me
in. Said, 'Jefferson, tell me two things, what you doin' flyin' without a harness; an' how come you flyin' so fast?' So I tole him I was flyin' without a
harness 'cause it got in my way, but I couldn'ta been flyin' so fast, 'cause I
wasn't usin' but one wing. Saint Peter said, 'You wasn't flyin' with but one
wing?' 'Yessuh,' I says, scared-like. So he says, 'Well, since you got sucha extra fine pair of wings you can leave off yo' harness awhile. But from now on
none of that there one-wing flyin', 'cause you gittin' up too damn much
speed!' "

And with one mouth full of bad teeth you're making too damned much
talk, thought Todd. Why don't I send him after the boy? His body ached
from the hard ground and seeking to shift his position he twisted his ankle
and hated himself for crying out.

"It gittin' worse?"

"I . . . I twisted it," he groaned.

"Try not to think about it, son. That's what I do."

He bit his lip, fighting pain with counter-pain as the voice resumed its
rhythmical droning. Jefferson seemed caught in his own creation.

". . . After all that trouble I just floated roun' heaven in slow motion. But
I forgot, like colored folks will do, and got to flyin' with one wing again.
This time I was restin' my old broken arm and got to flyin' fast enough to
shame the devil. I was comin' so fast, Lawd, I got myself called befo' ole
Saint Peter again. He said, 'Jeff, didn't I warn you 'bout that speedin'?'
'Yessuh,' I says, 'but it was an accident.' He looked at me sad-like and shook
his head and I knowed I was gone. He said, 'Jeff, you and that speedin' is a
danger to the heavenly community. If I was to let you keep on flyin',
heaven wouldn't be nothin' but uproar. Jeff, you got to go!' Son, I argued
and pleaded with that old white man, but it didn't do a bit of good. They
rushed me straight to them pearly gates and gimme a parachute and a map
of the state of Alabama . . ."

Todd heard him laughing so that he could hardly speak, making a screen
between them upon which his humiliation glowed like fire.

"Maybe you'd better stop awhile," he said, his voice unreal.

"Ain't much more," Jefferson laughed. "When they gimme the parachute ole Saint Peter ask me if I wanted to say a few words before I went. I felt so bad I couldn't hardly look at him, specially with all them white angels standin' around. Then somebody laughed and made me mad. So I tole him, 'Well, you done took my wings. And you puttin' me out. You got charge of things so's I can't do nothin' about it. But you got to admit just this: While I was up here I was the flyinest sonofabitch what ever hit heaven!' "

At the burst of laughter Todd felt such an intense humiliation that only great violence would wash it away. The laughter which shook the old man like a boiling purge set up vibrations of guilt within him which not even the intricate machinery of the plane would have been adequate to transform and he heard himself screaming, "Why do you laugh at me this way?"

He hated himself at that moment, but he had lost control. He saw Jefferson's mouth fall open, "What—?"

"Answer me!"

His blood pounded as though it would surely burst his temples and he tried to reach the old man and fell, screaming, "Can I help it because they won't let us actually fly? Maybe we are a bunch of buzzards feeding on a dead horse, but we can hope to be eagles, can't we? Can't we?"

He fell back, exhausted, his ankle pounding. The saliva was like straw in his mouth. If he had the strength he would strangle this old man. This grinning, gray-headed clown who made him feel as he felt when watched by the white officers at the field. And yet this old man had neither power, prestige, rank nor technique. Nothing that could rid him of this terrible feeling. He watched him, seeing his face struggle to express a turmoil of feeling.

"What you mean, son? What you talking 'bout . . . ?"

"Go away. Go tell your tales to the white folks."

"But I didn't mean nothing like that. . . . I . . . I wasn't tryin' to hurt your feelings. . . ."

"Please. Get the hell away from me!"

"But I didn't, son. I didn't mean all them things-a-tall."

Todd shook as with a chill, searching Jefferson's face for a trace of the mockery he had seen there. But now the face was somber and tired and old. He was confused. He could not be sure that there had ever been laughter there, that Jefferson had ever really laughed in his whole life. He saw Jefferson reach out to touch him and shrank away, wondering if anything except the pain, now causing his vision to waver, was real. Perhaps he had imagined it all.

"Don't let it get you down, son," the voice said pensively.

He heard Jefferson sigh wearily, as though he felt more than he could say. His anger ebbed, leaving only the pain.

"I'm sorry," he mumbled.

"You just wore out with pain, was all. . . ."

He saw him through a blur, smiling. And for a second he felt the embarrassed silence of understanding flutter between them.

"What you was doin' flyin' over this section, son? Wasn't you scared they might shoot you for a cow?"

Todd tensed. Was he being laughed at again? But before he could decide, the pain shook him and a part of him was lying calmly behind the screen of pain that had fallen between them, recalling the first time he had ever seen a plane. It was as though an endless series of hangars had been shaken ajar in the air base of his memory and from each, like a young wasp emerging from its cell, arose the memory of a plane.

The first time I ever saw a plane I was very small and planes were new in the world. I was four-and-a-half and the only plane that I had ever seen was a model suspended from the ceiling of the automobile exhibit at the State Fair. But I did not know that it was only a model. I did not know how large a real plane was, nor how expensive. To me it was a fascinating toy, complete in itself, which my mother said could only be owned by rich little white boys. I stood rigid with admiration, my head straining backwards as I watched the gray little plane describing arcs above the gleaming tops of the automobiles. And I vowed that, rich or poor, someday I would own such a toy. My mother had to drag me out of the exhibit and not even the merry-go-round, the Ferris wheel, or the racing horses could hold my attention for the rest of the Fair. I was too busy imitating the tiny drone of the plane with my lips, and imitating with my hands the motion, swift and circling, that it made in flight.

After that I no longer used the pieces of lumber that lay about our back yard to construct wagons and autos . . . now it was used for airplanes. I built biplanes, using pieces of board for wings, a small box for the fuselage, another piece of wood for the rudder. The trip to the Fair had brought something new into my small world. I asked my mother repeatedly when the Fair would come back again. I'd lie in the grass and watch the sky, and each fighting bird became a soaring plane. I would have been good a year just to have seen a plane again. I became a nuisance to everyone with my questions about airplanes. But planes were new to the old folks, too, and there was little that they could tell me. Only my uncle knew some of the answers. And better still, he could carve propellers from pieces of wood that would whirl rapidly in the wind, wobbling noisily upon oiled nails.

I wanted a plane more than I'd wanted anything; more than I wanted the red wagon with rubber tires, more than the train that ran on a track with its train of cars. I asked my mother over and over again:

"Mamma?"

"What do you want, boy?" she'd say.

"Mamma, will you get mad if I ask you?" I'd say.

"What do you want now? I ain't got time to be answering a lot of fool questions. What you want?"

"Mamma, when you gonna get me one . . . ?" I'd ask.

"Get you one what?" she'd say.

"You know, Mamma; what I been asking you. . . ."

"Boy," she'd say, "if you don't want a spanking you better come on an' tell me what you talking about so I can get on with my work."

"Aw, Mamma, you know. . . ."

"What I just tell you?" she'd say.

"I mean when you gonna buy me a airplane."

"AIRPLANE! Boy, is you crazy? How many times I have to tell you to stop that foolishness. I done told you them things cost too much. I bet I'm gon' wham the living daylight out of you if you don't quit worrying me 'bout them things!"

But this did not stop me, and a few days later I'd try all over again.

Then one day a strange thing happened. It was spring and for some reason I had been hot and irritable all morning. It was a beautiful spring. I could feel it as I played barefoot in the backyard. Blossoms hung from the thorny black locust trees like clusters of fragrant white grapes. Butterflies flickered in the sunlight above the short new dew-wet grass. I had gone in the house for bread and butter and coming out I heard a steady unfamiliar drone. It was unlike anything I had ever heard before. I tried to place the sound. It was no use. It was a sensation like that I had when searching for my father's watch, heard ticking unseen in a room. It made me feel as though I had forgotten to perform some task that my mother had ordered . . . then I located it, overhead. In the sky, flying quite low and about a hundred yards off was a plane! It came so slowly that it seemed barely to move. My mouth hung wide; my bread and butter fell into the dirt. I wanted to jump up and down and cheer. And when the idea struck I trembled with excitement: "Some little white boy's plane's done flew away and all I got to do is stretch out my hands and it'll be mine!" It was a little plane like that at the Fair, flying no higher than the eaves of our roof. Seeing it come steadily forward I felt the world grow warm with promise. I opened the screen and climbed over it and clung there, waiting. I would catch the plane as it came over and swing down fast and run into the house before anyone could see me. Then no one could come to claim the plane. It droned nearer. Then when it hung like a silver cross in the blue directly above me I stretched out my hand and grabbed. It was like sticking my finger through a soap bubble. The plane flew on, as though I had simply blown my breath after it. I grabbed again, frantically, trying to catch the tail. My fingers clutched the air and disappointment surged tight and hard in my throat. Giving one last desperate grasp, I strained forward. My fingers ripped from the screen. I was falling. The ground burst hard against me. I drummed the earth with my heels and when my breath returned, I lay there bawling.

My mother rushed through the door.

"What's the matter, chile! What on earth is wrong with you?"

"It's gone! It's gone!"

"What gone?"

"The airplane . . ."

"Airplane?"

"Yessum, jus' like the one at the Fair. . . . I . . . I tried to stop it an' it kep' right on going. . . ."

"When, boy?"

"Just now," I cried, through my tears.

"Where it go, boy, what way?"

"Yonder, there . . ."

She scanned the sky, her arms akimbo and her checkered apron flapping in the wind as I pointed to the fading plane. Finally she looked down at me, slowly shaking her head.

"It's gone! It's gone!" I cried.

"Boy, is you a fool?" she said. "Don't you see that there's a real airplane 'stead of one of them toy ones?"

"Real . . . ?" I forgot to cry. "Real?"

"Yass, real. Don't you know that thing you reaching for is bigger'n a auto? You here trying to reach for it and I bet it's flying 'bout two hundred miles higher'n this roof." She was disgusted with me. "You come on in this house before somebody else sees what a fool you done turned out to be. You must think these here lil ole arms of you'n is mighty long. . . ."

I was carried into the house and undressed for bed and the doctor was called. I cried bitterly, as much from the disappointment of finding the plane so far beyond my reach as from the pain.

When the doctor came I heard my mother telling him about the plane and asking if anything was wrong with my mind. He explained that I had had a fever for several hours. But I was kept in bed for a week and I constantly saw the plane in my sleep, flying just beyond my fingertips, sailing so slowly that it seemed barely to move. And each time I'd reach out to grab it I'd miss and through each dream I'd hear my grandma warning:

> *Young man, young man*
> *Yo' arms too short*
> *To box with God. . . .*

"Hey, son!"

At first he did not know where he was and looked at the old man pointing, with blurred eyes.

"Ain't that one of you-all's airplanes coming after you?"

As his vision cleared he saw a small black shape above a distant field, soaring through waves of heat. But he could not be sure and with the pain

he feared that somehow a horrible recurring fantasy of being split in twain
by the whirling blades of a propeller had come true.

"You think he sees us?" he heard.

"See? I hope so."

"He's coming like a bat outa hell!"

Straining, he heard the faint sound of a motor and hoped it would soon
be over.

"How you feeling?"

"Like a nightmare," he said.

"Hey, he's done curved back the other way!"

"Maybe he saw us," he said. "Maybe he's gone to send out the ambulance
and ground crew." And, he thought with despair, maybe he didn't even see
us.

"Where did you send the boy?"

"Down to Mister Graves," Jefferson said. "Man what owns this land."

"Do you think he phoned?"

Jefferson looked at him quickly.

"Aw sho'. Dabney Graves is got a bad name on accounta them killings but
he'll call though. . . ."

"What killings?"

"Them five fellers . . . ain't you heard?" he asked with surprise.

"No."

"Everybody knows 'bout Dabney Graves, especially the colored. He done
killed enough of us."

Todd had the sensation of being caught in a white neighborhood after
dark.

"What did they do?" he asked.

"Thought they was men," Jefferson said. "An' some he owed money, like
he do me. . . ."

"But why do you stay here?"

"You black, son."

"I know, but . . ."

"You have to come by the white folks, too."

He turned away from Jefferson's eyes, at once consoled and accused.
And I'll have to come by them soon, he thought with despair. Closing his
eyes, he heard Jefferson's voice as the sun burned blood-red upon his lips.

"I got nowhere to go," Jefferson said, "an' they'd come after me if I did.
But Dabney Graves is a funny fellow. He's all the time making jokes. He
can be mean as hell, then he's liable to turn right around and back the colored against the white folks. I seen him do it. But me, I hates him for that
more'n anything else. 'Cause just as soon as he gits tired helping a man he
don't care what happens to him. He just leaves him stone cold. And then
the other white folks is double hard on anybody he done helped. For him
it's just a joke. He don't give a hilla beans for nobody—but hisself. . . ."

Todd listened to the thread of detachment in the old man's voice. It was as though he held his words arm's length before him to avoid their destructive meaning.

"He'd just as soon do you a favor and then turn right around and have you strung up. Me, I stays outa his way 'cause down here that's what you gotta do."

If my ankle would only ease for a while, he thought. The closer I spin toward the earth the blacker I become, flashed through his mind. Sweat ran into his eyes and he was sure that he would never see the plane if his head continued whirling. He tried to see Jefferson, what it was that Jefferson held in his hand? It was a little black man, another Jefferson! A little black Jefferson that shook with fits of belly-laughter while the other Jefferson looked on with detachment. Then Jefferson looked up from the thing in his hand and turned to speak, but Todd was far away, searching the sky for a plane in a hot dry land on a day and age he had long forgotten. He was going mysteriously with his mother through empty streets where black faces peered from behind drawn shades and someone was rapping at a window and he was looking back to see a hand and a frightened face frantically beckoning from a cracked door and his mother was looking down the empty perspective of the street and shaking her head and hurrying him along and at first it was only a flash he saw and a motor was droning as through the sun-glare he saw it gleaming silver as it circled and he was seeing a burst like a puff of white smoke and hearing his mother yell, Come along, boy, I got no time for them fool airplanes, I got no time, and he saw it a second time, the plane flying high, and the burst appeared suddenly and fell slowly, billowing out and sparkling like fireworks and he was watching and being hurried along as the air filled with a flurry of white pinwheeling cards that caught in the wind and scattered over the rooftops and into the gutters and a woman was running and snatching a card and reading it and screaming and he darted into the shower, grabbing as in winter he grabbed for snowflakes and bounding away at his mother's, Come on here, boy! Come on, I say! and he was watching as she took the card away, seeing her face grow puzzled and turning taut as her voice quavered, "Niggers Stay From The Polls," and died to a moan of terror as he saw the eyeless sockets of a white hood staring at him from the card and above he saw the plane spiraling gracefully, agleam in the sun like a fiery sword. And seeing it soar he was caught, transfixed between a terrible horror and a horrible fascination.

The sun was not so high now, and Jefferson was calling and gradually he saw three figures moving across the curving roll of the field.

"Look like some doctors, all dressed in white," said Jefferson.

They're coming at last, Todd thought. And he felt such a release of tension within him that he thought he would faint. But no sooner did he close his eyes than he was seized and he was struggling with three white men who were forcing his arms into some kind of coat. It was too much for him, his arms were pinned to his sides and as the pain blazed in his eyes, he realized that it was a straightjacket. What filthy joke was this?

"That oughta hold him, Mister Graves," he heard.

His total energies seemed focused in his eyes as he searched their faces. That was Graves; the other two wore hospital uniforms. He was poised between two poles of fear and hate as he heard the one called Graves saying, "He looks kinda purty in that there suit, boys. I'm glad you dropped by."

"This boy ain't crazy, Mister Graves," one of the others said. "He needs a doctor, not us. Don't see how you led us way out here anyway. It might be a joke to you, but your cousin Rudolph liable to kill somebody. White folks or niggers, don't make no difference. . . ."

Todd saw the man turn red with anger. Graves looked down upon him, chuckling.

"This nigguh belongs in a straitjacket, too, boys. I knowed that the minit Jeff's kid said something 'bout a nigguh flyer. You all know you cain't let the nigguh git up that high without his going crazy. The nigguh brain ain't built right for high altitudes. . . ."

Todd watched the drawling red face, feeling that all the unnamed horror and obscenities that he had ever imagined stood materialized before him.

"Let's git outta here," one of the attendants said.

Todd saw the other reach toward him, realizing for the first time that he lay upon a stretcher as he yelled.

"Don't put your hands on me!"

They drew back, surprised.

"What's that you say, nigguh?" asked Graves.

He did not answer and thought that Graves's foot was aimed at his head. It landed on his chest and he could hardly breathe. He coughed helplessly, seeing Graves's lips stretch taut over his yellow teeth, and tried to shift his head. It was as though a half-dead fly was dragging slowly across his face and a bomb seemed to burst within him. Blasts of hot, hysterical laughter tore from his chest, causing his eyes to pop and he felt that the veins in his neck would surely burst. And then a part of him stood behind it all, watching the surprise in Graves's red face and his own hysteria. He thought he would never stop, he would laugh himself to death. It rang in his ears like Jefferson's laughter and he looked for him, centering his eyes desperately upon his face, as though somehow he had become his sole salvation in an insane world of outrage and humiliation. It brought a certain relief. He was suddenly aware that although his body was still contorted it was an echo that no longer rang in his ears. He heard Jefferson's voice with gratitude.

"Mister Graves, the Army done tole him not to leave his airplane."

"Nigguh, Army or no, you gittin' off my land! That airplane can stay 'cause it was paid for by taxpayers' money. But you gittin' off. An' dead or alive, it don't make no difference to me."

Todd was beyond it now, lost in a world of anguish.

"Jeff," Graves said, "you and Teddy come and grab holt. I want you to take this here black eagle over to that nigguh airfield and leave him."

Jefferson and the boy approached him silently. He looked away, realizing and doubting at once that only they could release him from his overpowering sense of isolation.

They bent for the stretcher. One of the attendants moved toward Teddy.

"Think you can manage it, boy?"

"I think I can, suh," Teddy said.

"Well, you better go behind them, and let yo' pa go ahead so's to keep that leg elevated."

He saw the white men walking ahead as Jefferson and the boy carried him along in silence. Then they were pausing and he felt a hand wiping his face; then he was moving again. And it was as though he had been lifted out of his isolation, back into the world of men. A new current of communication flowed between the man and boy and himself. They moved him gently. Far away he heard a mockingbird liquidly calling. He raised his eyes, seeing a buzzard poised unmoving in space. For a moment the whole afternoon seemed suspended and he waited for the horror to seize him again. Then like a song within his head he heard the boy's soft humming and saw the dark bird glide into the sun and glow like a bird of flaming gold.

The Red Convertible

LOUISE ERDRICH

LYMAN LAMARTINE

I was the first one to drive a convertible on my reservation. And of course it was red, a red Olds. I owned that car along with my brother Henry Junior. We owned it together until his boots filled with water on a windy night and he bought out my share. Now Henry owns the whole car, and his youngest brother Lyman (that's myself), Lyman walks everywhere he goes.

How did I earn enough money to buy my share in the first place? My own talent was I could always make money. I had a touch for it, unusual in a Chippewa. From the first I was different that way, and everyone recognized it. I was the only kid they let in the American Legion Hall to shine shoes, for example, and one Christmas I sold spiritual bouquets for the mission door to door. The nuns let me keep a percentage. Once I started, it seemed the more money I made the easier the money came. Everyone encouraged it. When I was fifteen I got a job washing dishes at the Joliet Café, and that was where my first big break happened.

It wasn't long before I was promoted to bussing tables, and then the short-order cook quit and I was hired to take her place. No sooner than you know it I was managing the Joliet. The rest is history. I went on managing. I soon became part owner, and of course there was no stopping me then. It wasn't long before the whole thing was mine.

After I'd owned the Joliet for one year, it blew over in the worst tornado ever seen around here. The whole operation was smashed to bits. A total loss. The fryalator was up in a tree, the grill torn in half like it was paper. I was only sixteen. I had it all in my mother's name, and I lost it quick, but before I lost it I had every one of my relatives, and their relatives, to dinner, and I also bought that red Olds I mentioned, along with Henry.

The first time we saw it! I'll tell you when we first saw it. We had gotten a ride up to Winnipeg, and both of us had money. Don't ask me why, because we never mentioned a car or anything, we just had all our money. Mine was cash, a big bankroll from the Joliet's insurance. Henry had two checks—a week's extra pay for being laid off, and his regular check from the Jewel Bearing Plant.

We were walking down Portage anyway, seeing the sights, when we saw it. There it was, parked, large as life. Really as *if* it was alive. I thought of the word *repose,* because the car wasn't simply stopped, parked, or whatever. That car reposed, calm and gleaming, a FOR SALE sign in its left front window. Then, before we had thought it over at all, the car belonged to us and our pockets were empty. We had just enough money for gas back home.

We went places in that car, me and Henry. We took off driving all one whole summer. We started off toward the Little Knife River and Mandaree in Fort Berthold and then we found ourselves down in Wakpala somehow, and then suddenly we were over in Montana on the Rocky Boys, and yet the summer was not even half over. Some people hang on to details when they travel, but we didn't let them bother us and just lived our everyday lives here to there.

I do remember this one place with willows. I remember I laid under those trees and it was comfortable. So comfortable. The branches bent down all around me like a tent or a stable. And quiet, it was quiet, even though there was a powwow close enough so I could see it going on. The air was not too still, not too windy either. When the dust rises up and hangs in the air around the dancers like that, I feel good. Henry was asleep with his arms thrown wide. Later on, he woke up and we started driving again. We were somewhere in Montana, or maybe on the Blood Reserve—it could have been anywhere. Anyway it was where we met the girl.

All her hair was in buns around her ears, that's the first thing I noticed about her. She was posed alongside the road with her arm out, so we stopped. That girl was short, so short her lumber shirt looked comical on her, like a nightgown. She had jeans on and fancy moccasins and she carried a little suitcase.

"Hop on in," says Henry. So she climbs in between us.

"We'll take you home," I says. "Where do you live?"

"Chicken," she says.

"Where the hell's that?" I ask her.

"Alaska."

"Okay," says Henry, and we drive.

We got up there and never wanted to leave. The sun doesn't truly set there in summer, and the night is more a soft dusk. You might doze off, sometimes, but before you know it you're up again, like an animal in nature. You never feel like you have to sleep hard or put away the world. And things would grow up there. One day just dirt or moss, the next day flowers and long grass. The girl's name was Susy. Her family really took to us. They fed us and put us up. We had our own tent to live in by their house, and the kids would be in and out of there all day and night. They couldn't get over me and Henry being brothers, we looked so different. We told them we knew we had the same mother, anyway.

One night Susy came in to visit us. We sat around in the tent talking of this thing and that. The season was changing. It was getting darker by that time, and the cold was even getting just a little mean. I told her it was time for us to go. She stood up on a chair.

"You never seen my hair," Susy said.

That was true. She was standing on a chair, but still, when she unclipped her buns the hair reached all the way to the ground. Our eyes opened. You couldn't tell how much hair she had when it was rolled up so neatly. Then my brother Henry did something funny. He went up to the chair and said, "Jump on my shoulders." So she did that, and her hair reached down past his waist, and he started twirling, this way and that, so her hair was flung out from side to side.

"I always wondered what it was like to have long pretty hair," Henry says. Well we laughed. It was a funny sight, the way he did it. The next morning we got up and took leave of those people.

On to greener pastures, as they say. It was down through Spokane and across Idaho then Montana and very soon we were racing the weather right along under the Canadian border through Columbus, Des Lacs, and then we were in Bottineau County and soon home. We'd made most of the trip, that summer, without putting up the car hood at all. We got home just in time, it turned out, for the army to remember Henry had signed up to join it.

I don't wonder that the army was so glad to get my brother that they turned him into a Marine. He was built like a brick outhouse anyway. We liked to tease him that they really wanted him for his Indian nose. He had a nose big and sharp as a hatchet, like the nose on Red Tomahawk, the Indian who killed Sitting Bull, whose profile is on signs all along the North Dakota highways. Henry went off to training camp, came home once during Christmas, then the next thing you know we got an overseas letter from him. It was 1970, and he said he was stationed up in northern hill country. Whereabouts I did not know. He wasn't such a hot letter writer, and only got off two before the enemy caught him. I could never keep it straight, which direction those good Vietnam soldiers were from.

I wrote him back several times, even though I didn't know if those letters would get through. I kept him informed all about the car. Most of the time

I had it up on blocks in the yard or half taken apart, because that long trip did a hard job on it under the hood.

I always had good luck with numbers, and never worried about the draft myself. I never even had to think about what my number was. But Henry was never lucky in the same way as me. It was at least three years before Henry came home. By then I guess the whole war was solved in the government's mind, but for him it would keep on going. In those years I'd put his car into almost perfect shape. I always thought of it as his car while he was gone, even though when he left he said, "Now it's yours," and threw me his key.

"Thanks for the extra key," I'd say. "I'll put it up in your drawer just in case I need it." He laughed.

When he came home, though, Henry was very different, and I'll say this: the change was no good. You could hardly expect him to change for the better, I know. But he was quiet, so quiet, and never comfortable sitting still anywhere but always up and moving around. I thought back to times we'd sat still for whole afternoons, never moving a muscle, just shifting our weight along the ground, talking to whoever sat with us, watching things. He'd always had a joke, then, too, and now you couldn't get him to laugh, or when he did it was more the sound of a man choking, a sound that stopped up the throats of other people around him. They got to leaving him alone most of the time, and I didn't blame them. It was a fact: Henry was jumpy and mean.

I'd bought a color TV set for my mom and the rest of us while Henry was away. Money still came very easy. I was sorry I'd ever bought it though, because of Henry. I was also sorry I'd bought color, because with black-and-white the pictures seem older and farther away. But what are you going to do? He sat in front of it, watching it, and that was the only time he was completely still. But it was the kind of stillness that you see in a rabbit when it freezes and before it will bolt. He was not easy. He sat in his chair gripping the armrests with all his might, as if the chair itself was moving at a high speed and if he let go at all he would rocket forward and maybe crash right through the set.

Once I was in the room watching TV with Henry and I heard his teeth click at something. I looked over, and he'd bitten through his lip. Blood was going down his chin. I tell you right then I wanted to smash that tube to pieces. I went over to it but Henry must have known what I was up to. He rushed from his chair and shoved me out of the way, against the wall. I told myself he didn't know what he was doing.

My mom came in, turned the set off real quiet, and told us she had made something for supper. So we went and sat down. There was still blood going down Henry's chin, but he didn't notice it and no one said anything, even though every time he took a bite of his bread his blood fell onto it until he was eating his own blood mixed in with the food.

* * *

While Henry was not around we talked about what was going to happen to him. There were no Indian doctors on the reservation, and my mom was afraid of trusting Old Man Pillager because he courted her long ago and was jealous of her husbands. He might take revenge through her son. We were afraid that if we brought Henry to a regular hospital they would keep him.

"They don't fix them in those places," Mom said; "they just give them drugs."

"We wouldn't get him there in the first place," I agreed, "so let's just forget about it."

Then I thought about the car.

Henry had not even looked at the car since he'd gotten home, though like I said, it was in tip-top condition and ready to drive. I thought the car might bring the old Henry back somehow. So I bided my time and waited for my chance to interest him in the vehicle.

One night Henry was off somewhere. I took myself a hammer. I went out to that car and I did a number on its underside. Whacked it up. Bent the tail pipe double. Ripped the muffler loose. By the time I was done with the car it looked worse than any typical Indian car that has been driven all its life on reservation roads, which they always say are like government promises—full of holes. It just about hurt me, I'll tell you that! I threw dirt in the carburetor and I ripped all the electric tape off the seats. I made it look just as beat up as I could. Then I sat back and waited for Henry to find it.

Still, it took him over a month. That was all right, because it was just getting warm enough, not melting, but warm enough to work outside.

"Lyman," he said, walking in one day, "that red car looks like shit."

"Well it's old," I says. "You got to expect that."

"No way!" says Henry. "That car's a classic! But you went and ran the piss right out of it, Lyman, and you know it don't deserve that. I kept that car in A-one shape. You don't remember. You're too young. But when I left, that car was running like a watch. Now I don't even know if I can get it to start again, let alone get it anywhere near its old condition."

"Well you try," I said, like I was getting mad, "but I say it's a piece of junk."

Then I walked out before he could realize I knew he'd strung together more than six words at once.

After that I thought he'd freeze himself to death working on that car. He was out there all day, and at night he rigged up a little lamp, ran a cord out the window, and had himself some light to see by while he worked. He was better than he had been before, but that's still not saying much. It was easier for him to do the things the rest of us did. He ate more slowly and didn't jump up and down during the meal to get this or that or look out the window. I put my hand in the back of the TV set, I admit, and fiddled around with it good, so that it was almost impossible now to get a clear picture. He didn't look at it very often anyway. He was always out with that car or going off to get parts for it. By the time it was really melting outside, he had it fixed.

I had been feeling down in the dumps about Henry around this time. We had always been together before. Henry and Lyman. But he was such a loner now that I didn't know how to take it. So I jumped at the chance one day when Henry seemed friendly. It's not that he smiled or anything. He just said, "Let's take that old shitbox for a spin." Just the way he said it made me think he could be coming around.

We went out to the car. It was spring. The sun was shining very bright. My only sister, Bonita, who was just eleven years old, came out and made us stand together for a picture. Henry leaned his elbow on the red car's windshield, and he took his other arm and put it over my shoulder, very carefully, as though it was heavy for him to lift and he didn't want to bring the weight down all at once.

"Smile," Bonita said, and he did.

That picture, I never look at it anymore. A few months ago, I don't know why, I got his picture out and tacked it on the wall. I felt good about Henry at the time, close to him. I felt good having his picture on the wall, until one night when I was looking at television. I was a little drunk and stoned. I looked up at the wall and Henry was staring at me. I don't know what it was, but his smile had changed, or maybe it was gone. All I know is I couldn't stay in the same room with that picture. I was shaking. I got up, closed the door, and went into the kitchen. A little later my friend Ray came over and we both went back into that room. We put the picture in a brown bag, folded the bag over and over tightly, then put it way back in a closet.

I still see that picture now, as if it tugs at me, whenever I pass that closet door. The picture is very clear in my mind. It was so sunny that day Henry had to squint against the glare. Or maybe the camera Bonita held flashed like a mirror, blinding him, before she snapped the picture. My face is right out in the sun, big and round. But he might have drawn back, because the shadows on his face are deep as holes. There are two shadows curved like little hooks around the ends of his smile, as if to frame it and try to keep it there—that one, first smile that looked like it might have hurt his face. He has his field jacket on and the worn-in clothes he'd come back in and kept wearing ever since. After Bonita took the picture, she went into the house and we got into the car. There was a full cooler in the trunk. We started off, east, toward Pembina and the Red River because Henry said he wanted to see the high water.

The trip over there was beautiful. When everything starts changing, drying up, clearing off, you feel like your whole life is starting. Henry felt it, too. The top was down and the car hummed like a top. He'd really put it back

in shape, even the tape on the seats was very carefully put down and glued
back in layers. It's not that he smiled again or even joked, but his face
looked to me as if it was clear, more peaceful. It looked as though he wasn't
thinking of anything in particular except the bare fields and windbreaks
and houses we were passing.

The river was high and full of winter trash when we got there. The sun
was still out, but it was colder by the river. There were still little clumps of
dirty snow here and there on the banks. The water hadn't gone over the
banks yet, but it would, you could tell. It was just at its limit, hard swollen
glossy like an old gray scar. We made ourselves a fire, and we sat down and
watched the current go. As I watched it I felt something squeezing inside
me and tightening and trying to let go all at the same time. I knew I was not
just feeling it myself; I knew I was feeling what Henry was going through
at that moment. Except that I couldn't stand it, the closing and opening. I
jumped to my feet. I took Henry by the shoulders and I started shaking
him. "Wake up," I says, "wake up, wake up, wake up!" I didn't know what
had come over me. I sat down beside him again.

His face was totally white and hard. Then it broke, like stones break all of
a sudden when water boils up inside them.

"I know it," he says. "I know it. I can't help it. It's no use."

We start talking. He said he knew what I'd done with the car. It was obvious it had been whacked out of shape and not just neglected. He said he
wanted to give the car to me for good now, it was no use. He said he'd fixed
it just to give it back and I should take it.

"No way," I says, "I don't want it."

"That's okay," he says, "you take it."

"I don't want it, though," I says back to him, and then to emphasize, just
to emphasize, you understand, I touch his shoulder. He slaps my hand off.

"Take that car," he says.

"No," I say, "make me," I say, and then he grabs my jacket and rips the
arm loose. That jacket is a class act, suede with tags and zippers. I push
Henry backwards, off the log. He jumps up and bowls me over. We go
down in a clinch and come up swinging hard, for all we're worth, with our
fists. He socks my jaw so hard I feel like it swings loose. Then I'm at his rib-
cage and land a good one under his chin so his head snaps back. He's daz-
zled. He looks at me and I look at him and then his eyes are full of tears and
blood and at first I think he's crying. But no, he's laughing. "Ha! Ha!" he
says. "Ha! Ha! Take good care of it."

"Okay," I says, "okay, no problem. Ha! Ha!"

I can't help it, and I start laughing, too. My face feels fat and strange, and
after a while I get a beer from the cooler in the trunk, and when I hand it
to Henry he takes his shirt and wipes my germs off. "Hoof-and-mouth disease," he says. For some reason this cracks me up, and so we're really laughing for a while, and then we drink all the rest of the beers one by one and

throw them in the river and see how far, how fast, the current takes them before they fill up and sink.

"You want to go on back?" I ask after a while. "Maybe we could snag a couple nice Kashpaw girls."

He says nothing. But I can tell his mood is turning again.

"They're all crazy, the girls up here, every damn one of them."

"You're crazy too," I say, to jolly him up. "Crazy Lamartine boys!"

He looks as though he will take this wrong at first. His face twists, then clears, and he jumps up on his feet. "That's right!" he says. "Crazier 'n hell. Crazy Indians!"

I think it's the old Henry again. He throws off his jacket and starts swinging his legs out from the knees like a fancy dancer. He's down doing something between a grouse dance and a bunny hop, no kind of dance I ever saw before, but neither has anyone else on all this green growing earth. He's wild. He wants to pitch whoopee! He's up and at me and all over. All this time I'm laughing so hard, so hard my belly is getting tied up in a knot.

"Got to cool me off!" he shouts all of a sudden. Then he runs over to the river and jumps in.

There's boards and other things in the current. It's so high. No sound comes from the river after the splash he makes, so I run right over. I look around. It's getting dark. I see he's halfway across the water already, and I know he didn't swim there but the current took him. It's far. I hear his voice, though, very clearly across it.

"My boots are filling," he says.

He says this in a normal voice, like he just noticed and he doesn't know what to think of it. Then he's gone. A branch comes by. Another branch. And I go in.

By the time I get out of the river, off the snag I pulled myself onto, the sun is down. I walk back to the car, turn on the high beams, and drive it up the bank. I put it in first gear and then I take my foot off the clutch. I get out, close the door, and watch it plow softly into the water. The headlights reach in as they go down, searching, still lighted even after the water swirls over the back end. I wait. The wires short out. It is all finally dark. And then there is only the water, the sound of it going and running and going and running and running.

A Rose for Emily

WILLIAM FAULKNER

I

When Miss Emily Grierson died, our whole town went to her funeral: the men through a sort of respectful affection for a fallen monument, the women mostly out of curiosity to see the inside of her house, which no one save an old manservant—a combined gardener and cook—had seen in at least ten years.

It was a big, squarish frame house that had once been white, decorated with cupolas and spires and scrolled balconies in the heavily lightsome style of the seventies, set on what had once been our most select street. But garages and cotton gins had encroached and obliterated even the august names of that neighborhood; only Miss Emily's house was left, lifting its stubborn and coquettish decay above the cotton wagons and the gasoline pumps—an eyesore among eyesores. And now Miss Emily had gone to join the representatives of those august names where they lay in the cedar-bemused cemetery among the ranked and anonymous graves of Union and Confederate soldiers who fell at the battle of Jefferson.

Alive, Miss Emily had been a tradition, a duty, and a care; a sort of hereditary obligation upon the town, dating from that day in 1894 when Colonel Sartoris, the mayor—he who fathered the edict that no Negro woman should appear on the streets without an apron—remitted her taxes, the dispensation dating from the death of her father on into perpetuity. Not that Miss Emily would have accepted charity. Colonel Sartoris invented an involved tale to the effect that Miss Emily's father had loaned money to the town, which the town, as a matter of business, preferred this way of repaying. Only a man of Colonel Sartoris' generation and thought could have invented it, and only a woman could have believed it.

When the next generation, with its more modern ideas, became mayors and aldermen, this arrangement created some little dissatisfaction. On the first of the year they mailed her a tax notice. February came, and there was no reply. They wrote her a formal letter, asking her to call at the sheriff's office at her convenience. A week later the mayor wrote her himself, offering to call or to send his car for her, and received in reply a note on paper of an archaic shape, in a thin, flowing calligraphy in faded ink, to the effect that she no longer went out at all. The tax notice was also enclosed, without comment.

They called a special meeting of the Board of Aldermen. A deputation waited upon her, knocked at the door through which no visitor had passed since she ceased giving china-painting lessons eight or ten years earlier. They were admitted by the old Negro into a dim hall from which a stairway mounted into still more shadow. It smelled of dust and disuse—a close, dank smell. The Negro led them into the parlor. It was furnished in heavy, leather-covered furniture. When the Negro opened the blinds of one window, they could see that the leather was cracked; and when they sat down, a faint dust rose sluggishly about their thighs, spinning with slow motes in the single sun-ray. On a tarnished gilt easel before the fireplace stood a crayon portrait of Miss Emily's father.

They rose when she entered—a small, fat woman in black, with a thin gold chain descending to her waist and vanishing into her belt, leaning on an ebony cane with a tarnished gold head. Her skeleton was small and spare; perhaps that was why what would have been merely plumpness in another was obesity in her. She looked bloated, like a body long submerged in motionless water, and of that pallid hue. Her eyes, lost in the fatty ridges of her face, looked like two small pieces of coal pressed into a lump of dough as they moved from one face to another while the visitors stated their errand.

She did not ask them to sit. She just stood in the door and listened quietly until the spokesman came to a stumbling halt. Then they could hear the invisible watch ticking at the end of the gold chain.

Her voice was dry and cold. "I have no taxes in Jefferson. Colonel Sartoris explained it to me. Perhaps one of you can gain access to the city records and satisfy yourselves."

"But we have. We are the city authorities, Miss Emily. Didn't you get a notice from the sheriff, signed by him?"

"I received a paper, yes," Miss Emily said. "Perhaps he considers himself the sheriff. . . . I have no taxes in Jefferson."

"But there is nothing on the books to show that, you see. We must go by the—"

"See Colonel Sartoris. I have no taxes in Jefferson."

"But, Miss Emily—"

"See Colonel Sartoris." (Colonel Sartoris had been dead almost ten years.) "I have no taxes in Jefferson. Tobe!" The Negro appeared. "Show these gentlemen out."

II

So she vanquished them, horse and foot, just as she had vanquished their fathers thirty years before about the smell. That was two years after her father's death and a short time after her sweetheart—the one we believed would marry her—had deserted her. After her father's death she went out very little; after her sweetheart went away, people hardly saw her at all. A few of the ladies had the temerity to call, but were not received, and the only sign of life about the place was the Negro man—a young man then—going in and out with a market basket.

"Just as if a man—any man—could keep a kitchen properly," the ladies said; so they were not surprised when the smell developed. It was another link between the gross, teeming world and the high and mighty Griersons.

A neighbor, a woman, complained to the mayor, Judge Stevens, eighty years old.

"But what will you have me do about it, madam?" he said.

"Why, send her word to stop it," the woman said. "Isn't there a law?"

"I'm sure that won't be necessary," Judge Stevens said. "It's probably just a snake or a rat that nigger of hers killed in the yard. I'll speak to him about it."

The next day he received two more complaints, one from a man who came in diffident deprecation. "We really must do something about it, Judge. I'd be the last one in the world to bother Miss Emily, but we've got to do something." That night the Board of Aldermen met—three graybeards and one younger man, a member of the rising generation.

"It's simple enough," he said. "Send her word to have her place cleaned up. Give her a certain time to do it in, and if she don't. . . ."

"Dammit, sir," Judge Stevens said, "will you accuse a lady to her face of smelling bad?"

So the next night, after midnight, four men crossed Miss Emily's lawn and slunk about the house like burglars, sniffing along the base of the brickwork and at the cellar openings while one of them performed a regular sowing motion with his hand out of a sack slung from his shoulder. They broke open the cellar door and sprinkled lime there, and in all the outbuildings. As they recrossed the lawn, a window that had been dark was lighted and Miss Emily sat in it, the light behind her, and her upright torso motionless as that of an idol. They crept quietly across the lawn and into the shadow of the locusts that lined the street. After a week or two the smell went away.

That was when people had begun to feel really sorry for her. People in our town, remembering how old lady Wyatt, her great-aunt, had gone completely crazy at last, believed that the Griersons held themselves a little too high for what they really were. None of the young men were quite good enough for Miss Emily and such. We had long thought of them as a tab-

leau, Miss Emily a slender figure in white in the background, her father a
spraddled silhouette in the foreground, his back to her and clutching a
horsewhip, the two of them framed by the backflung front door. So when
she got to be thirty and was still single, we were not pleased exactly, but vin-
dicated; even with insanity in the family she wouldn't have turned down all
of her chances if they had really materialized.

When her father died, it got about that the house was all that was left to
her; and in a way, people were glad. At last they could pity Miss Emily. Being left alone, and a pauper, she had become humanized. Now she too
would know the old thrill and the old despair of a penny more or less.

The day after his death all the ladies prepared to call at the house and offer condolence and aid, as is our custom. Miss Emily met them at the door,
dressed as usual and with no trace of grief on her face. She told them that
her father was not dead. She did that for three days, with the ministers calling on her, and the doctors, trying to persuade her to let them dispose of
the body. Just as they were about to resort to law and force, she broke
down, and they buried her father quickly.

We did not say she was crazy then. We believed she had to do that. We
remembered all the young men her father had driven away, and we knew
that with nothing left, she would have to cling to that which had robbed
her, as people will.

III

She was sick for a long time. When we saw her again, her hair was cut short,
making her look like a girl, with a vague resemblance to those angels in colored church windows—sort of tragic and serene.

The town had just let the contracts for paving the sidewalks, and in the
summer after her father's death they began the work. The construction
company came with niggers and mules and machinery, and a foreman
named Homer Barron, a Yankee—a big, dark, ready man, with a big voice
and eyes lighter than his face. The little boys would follow in groups to
hear him cuss the niggers, and the niggers singing in time to the rise and
fall of picks. Pretty soon he knew everybody in town. Whenever you heard
a lot of laughing anywhere about the square, Homer Barron would be in
the center of the group. Presently, we began to see him and Miss Emily on
Sunday afternoons driving in the yellow-wheeled buggy and the matched
team of bays from the livery stable.

At first we were glad that Miss Emily would have an interest, because the
ladies all said, "Of course a Grierson would not think seriously of a North-
erner, a day laborer." But there were still others, older people, who said
that even grief could not cause a real lady to forget noblesse oblige—without
calling it noblesse oblige. They just said, "Poor Emily. Her kinsfolk should

come to her." She had some kin in Alabama; but years ago her father had fallen out with them over the estate of old lady Wyatt, the crazy woman, and there was no communication between the two families. They had not even been represented at the funeral.

And as soon as the old people said, "Poor Emily," the whispering began. "Do you suppose it's really so?" they said to one another. "Of course it is. What else could. . . ." This behind their hands; rustling of craned silk and satin behind jalousies closed upon the sun of Sunday afternoon as the thin, swift clop-clop-clop of the matched team passed: "Poor Emily."

She carried her head high enough—even when we believed that she was fallen. It was as if she demanded more than ever the recognition of her dignity as the last Grierson; as if it had wanted that touch of earthiness to reaffirm her imperviousness. Like when she bought the rat poison, the arsenic. That was over a year after they had begun to say "Poor Emily," and while the two female cousins were visiting her.

"I want some poison," she said to the druggist. She was only thirty then, still a slight woman, though thinner than usual, with cold, haughty black eyes in a face the flesh of which was strained across the temples and about the eyesockets as you imagine a lighthouse-keeper's face ought to look. "I want some poison," she said.

"Yes, Miss Emily. What kind? For rats and such? I'd recom ——"

"I want the best you have. I don't care what kind."

The druggist named several. "They'll kill anything up to an elephant. But what you want is ——"

"Arsenic," Miss Emily said. "Is that a good one?"

"Is . . . arsenic? Yes, ma'am. But what you want ——"

"I want arsenic."

The druggist looked down at her. She looked back at him, erect, her face like a strained flag. "Why, of course," the druggist said. "If that's what you want. But the law requires you to tell what you are going to use it for."

Miss Emily just stared at him, her head tilted back in order to look him eye for eye, until he looked away and went and got the arsenic and wrapped it up. The Negro delivery boy brought her the package; the druggist didn't come back. When she opened the package at home there was written on the box, under the skull and bones: "For rats."

IV

So the next day we all said, "She will kill herself"; and we said it would be the best thing. When she had first begun to be seen with Homer Barron, we had said, "She will marry him." Then we said, "She will persuade him yet," because Homer himself had remarked—he liked men, and it was known that he drank with the younger men in the Elks' Club—that he was not a marrying man. Later we said, "Poor Emily" behind the jalousies as they passed on Sunday afternoon in the glittering buggy, Miss Emily with her head high and Homer Barron with his hat cocked and a cigar in his teeth, reins and whip in a yellow glove.

Then some of the ladies began to say that it was a disgrace to the town and a bad example to the young people. The men did not want to interfere, but at last the ladies forced the Baptist minister—Miss Emily's people were Episcopal—to call upon her. He would never divulge what happened during that interview, but he refused to go back again. The next Sunday they again drove about the streets, and the following day the minister's wife wrote to Miss Emily's relations in Alabama.

So she had blood-kin under her roof again and we sat back to watch developments. At first nothing happened. Then we were sure that they were to be married. We learned that Miss Emily had been to the jeweler's and ordered a man's toilet set in silver, with the letters H.B. on each piece. Two days later we learned that she had bought a complete outfit of men's clothing, including a nightshift, and we said, "They are married." We were really glad. We were glad because the two female cousins were even more Grierson than Miss Emily had ever been.

So we were not surprised when Homer Barron—the streets had been finished some time since—was gone. We were a little disappointed that there was not a public blowing-off, but we believed that he had gone on to prepare for Miss Emily's coming, or to give her a chance to get rid of the cousins. (By that time it was a cabal, and we were all Miss Emily's allies to help circumvent the cousins.) Sure enough, after another week they departed. And, as we had expected all along, within three days Homer Barron was back in town. A neighbor saw the Negro man admit him at the kitchen door at dusk one evening.

And that was the last we saw of Homer Barron. And of Miss Emily for some time. The Negro man went in and out with the market basket, but the front door remained closed. Now and then we would see her at the window for a moment, as the men did that night when they sprinkled the lime, but for almost six months she did not appear on the streets. Then we knew that this was to be expected too; as if that quality of her father which had thwarted her woman's life so many times had been too virulent and too furious to die.

When we next saw Miss Emily, she had grown fat and her hair was turning gray. During the next few years it grew grayer and grayer until it attained an even pepper-and-salt iron-gray, when it ceased turning. Up to the day of her death at seventy-four it was still that vigorous iron-gray, like the hair of an active man.

From that time on her front door remained closed, save during a period of six or seven years, when she was about forty, during which she gave lessons in china-painting. She fitted up a studio in one of the downstairs rooms, where the daughters and granddaughters of Colonel Sartoris' contemporaries were sent to her with the same regularity and in the same spirit that they were sent to church on Sundays with a twenty-five-cent piece for the collection plate. Meanwhile her taxes had been remitted.

Then the newer generation became the backbone and the spirit of the town, and the painting pupils grew up and fell away and did not send their children to her with boxes of color and tedious brushes and pictures cut from the ladies' magazines. The front door closed upon the last one and remained closed for good. When the town got free postal delivery, Miss Emily alone refused to let them fasten the metal numbers above her door and attach a mailbox to it. She would not listen to them.

Daily, monthly, yearly we watched the Negro grow grayer and more stooped, going in and out with the market basket. Each December we sent her a tax notice, which would be returned by the post office a week later, unclaimed. Now and then we would see her in one of the downstairs windows—she had evidently shut up the top floor of the house—like the carven torso of an idol in a niche, looking or not looking at us, we could never tell which. Thus she passed from generation to generation—dear, inescapable, impervious, tranquil, and perverse.

And so she died. Fell ill in the house filled with dust and shadows, with only a doddering Negro man to wait on her. We did not even know she was sick; we had long since given up trying to get any information from the Negro. He talked to no one, probably not even to her, for his voice had grown harsh and rusty, as if from disuse.

She died in one of the downstairs rooms, in a heavy walnut bed with a curtain, her gray head propped on a pillow yellow and moldy with age and lack of sunlight.

V

The Negro met the first of the ladies at the front door and let them in, with their hushed, sibilant voices and their quick, curious glances, and then he disappeared. He walked right through the house and out the back and was not seen again.

The two female cousins came at once. They held the funeral on the second day, with the town coming to look at Miss Emily beneath a mass of bought flowers, with the crayon face of her father musing profoundly above the bier and the ladies sibilant and macabre; and the very old men—some in their brushed Confederate uniforms—on the porch and the lawn, talking of Miss Emily as if she had been a contemporary of theirs, believing that they had danced with her and courted her perhaps, confusing time with its mathematical progression, as the old do, to whom all the past is not a diminishing road but, instead, a huge meadow which no winter ever quite touches, divided from them now by the narrow bottleneck of the most recent decade of years.

Already we knew that there was one room in that region above stairs which no one had seen in forty years, and which would have to be forced. They waited until Miss Emily was decently in the ground before they opened it.

The violence of breaking down the door seemed to fill this room with pervading dust. A thin, acrid pall as of the tomb seemed to lie everywhere upon this room decked and furnished as for a bridal: upon the valance curtains of faded rose color, upon the rose-shaded lights, upon the dressing table, upon the delicate array of crystal and the man's toilet things backed with tarnished silver, silver so tarnished that the monogram was obscured. Among them lay a collar and tie, as if they had just been removed, which, lifted, left upon the surface a pale crescent in the dust. Upon a chair hung the suit, carefully folded; beneath it the two mute shoes and the discarded socks.

The man himself lay in the bed.

For a long while we just stood there, looking down at the profound and fleshless grin. The body had apparently once lain in the attitude of an embrace, but now the long sleep that outlasts love, that conquers even the grimace of love, had cuckolded him. What was left of him, rotted beneath what was left of the nightshirt, had become inextricable from the bed in which he lay; and upon him and upon the pillow beside him lay that even coating of the patient and biding dust.

Then we noticed that in the second pillow was the indentation of a head. One of us lifted something from it, and leaning forward, that faint and invisible dust dry and acrid in the nostrils, we saw a long strand of iron-gray hair.

That Evening Sun

WILLIAM FAULKNER

I

Monday is no different from any other weekday in Jefferson now. The streets are paved now, and the telephone and electric companies are cutting down more and more of the shade trees—the water oaks, the maples and locusts and elms—to make room for iron poles bearing clusters of bloated and ghostly and bloodless grapes, and we have a city laundry which makes the rounds on Monday morning, gathering the bundles of clothes into bright-colored, specially made motorcars: the soiled wearing of a whole week now flees apparitionlike behind alert and irritable electric horns, with a long diminishing noise of rubber and asphalt like tearing silk, and even the Negro women who still take in white people's washing after the old custom, fetch and deliver it in automobiles.

But fifteen years ago, on Monday morning the quiet, dusty, shade streets would be full of Negro women with, balanced on their steady, turbaned heads, bundles of clothes tied up in sheets, almost as large as cotton bales, carried so without touch of hand between the kitchen door of the white house and the blackened washpot beside a cabin door in Negro Hollow.

Nancy would set her bundle on the top of her head, then upon the bundle in turn she would set the black straw sailor hat which she wore winter and summer. She was tall, with a high, sad face sunken a little where her teeth were missing. Sometimes we would go a part of the way down the lane and across the pasture with her, to watch the balanced bundle and the hat that never bobbed nor wavered, even she walked down into the ditch and up to the other side and stooped through the fence. She would go down on her hands and knees and crawl through the gap, her head rigid, uptilted, the bundle steady as a rock or a balloon, and rise to her feet again and go on.

308

Sometimes the husbands of the washing women would fetch and deliver the clothes, but Jesus never did that for Nancy, even before Father told him to stay away from our house, even when Dilsey was sick and Nancy would come to cook for us.

And then about half the time we'd have to go down the lane to Nancy's cabin and tell her to come on and cook breakfast. We would stop at the ditch, because Father told us to not have anything to do with Jesus—he was a short black man, with a razor scar down his face—and we would throw rocks at Nancy's house until she came to the door, leaning her head around it without any clothes on.

"What yawl mean, chunking my house?" Nancy said. "What you little devils mean?"

"Father says for you to come on and get breakfast," Caddy said. "Father says it's over a half an hour now, and you've got to come this minute."

"I ain't studying no breakfast," Nancy said. "I going to get my sleep out."

"I bet you're drunk," Jason said. "Father says you're drunk. Are you drunk, Nancy?"

"Who says I is?" Nancy said. "I got to get my sleep out. I ain't studying no breakfast."

So after a while we quit chunking the cabin and went back home. When she finally came, it was too late for me to go to school. So we thought it was whiskey until that day they arrested her again and they were taking her to jail and they passed Mr. Stovall. He was the cashier in the bank and a deacon in the Baptist church, and Nancy began to say:

"When you going to pay me, white man? When you going to pay me, white man? It's been three times now since you paid me a cent—" Mr. Stovall knocked her down, but she kept on saying, "When you going to pay me, white man? It's been three times now since—" until Mr. Stovall kicked her in the mouth with his heel and the marshal caught Mr. Stovall back, and Nancy lying in the street, laughing. She turned her head and spat out some blood and teeth and said, "It's been three times now since he paid me a cent."

That was how she lost her teeth, and all that day they told about Nancy and Mr. Stovall, and all that night the ones that passed the jail could hear Nancy singing and yelling. They could see her hands holding to the window bars, and a lot of them stopped along the fence, listening to her and to the jailer trying to make her stop. She didn't shut up until almost daylight, when the jailer began to hear a bumping and scraping upstairs and he went up there and found Nancy hanging from the window bar. He said that it was cocaine and not whiskey, because no nigger would try to commit suicide unless he was full of cocaine, because a nigger full of cocaine wasn't a nigger any longer.

The jailer cut her down and revived her; then he beat her, whipped her. She had hung herself with her dress. She had fixed it all right, but when they arrested her she didn't have on anything except a dress and so she didn't have anything to tie her hands with and she couldn't make her hands let go of the window ledge. So the jailer heard the noise and ran up there and found Nancy hanging from the window, stark naked, her belly already swelling out a little, like a little balloon.

When Dilsey was sick in her cabin and Nancy was cooking for us, we could see her apron swelling out; that was before Father told Jesus to stay away from the house. Jesus was in the kitchen, sitting behind the stove, with his razor scar on his black face like a piece of dirty string. He said it was a watermelon that Nancy had under her dress.

"It never come off of your vine, though," Nancy said.

"Off of what vine?" Caddy said.

"I can cut down the vine it did come off of," Jesus said.

"What makes you want to talk like that before these chillen?" Nancy said. "Whyn't you go on to work? You done et. You want Mr. Jason to catch you hanging around his kitchen, talking that way before these chillen?"

"Talking what way?" Caddy said. "What vine?"

"I can't hang around white man's kitchen," Jesus said. "But white man can hang around mine. White man can come in my house, but I can't stop him. When white man want to come in my house, I ain't got no house. I can't stop him, but he can't kick me outen it. He can't do that."

Dilsey was still sick in her cabin. Father told Jesus to stay off our place. Dilsey was still sick. It was a long time. We were in the library after supper.

"Isn't Nancy through in the kitchen yet?" Mother said. "It seems to me that she has had plenty of time to have finished the dishes."

"Let Quentin go and see," Father said. "Go and see if Nancy is through, Quentin. Tell her she can go on home."

I went to the kitchen. Nancy was through. The dishes were put away and the fire was out. Nancy was sitting in a chair, close to the cold stove. She looked at me.

"Mother wants to know if you are through," I said.

"Yes," Nancy said. She looked at me. "I done finished." She looked at me.

"What is it?" I said. "What is it?"

"I ain't nothing but a nigger," Nancy said. "It ain't none of my fault."

She looked at me, sitting in the chair before the cold stove, the sailor hat on her head. I went back to the library. It was the cold stove and all, when you think of a kitchen being warm and busy and cheerful. And with a cold stove and the dishes all put away, and nobody wanting to eat at that hour.

"Is she through?" Mother said.

"Yessum," I said.

"What is she doing?" Mother said.

"She's not doing anything. She's through."

"I'll go and see," Father said.

"Maybe she's waiting for Jesus to come and take her home," Caddy said.

"Jesus is gone," I said. Nancy told us how one morning she woke up and Jesus was gone.

"He quit me," Nancy said. "Done gone to Memphis, I reckon. Dodging them city *po*-lice for a while, I reckon."

"And a good riddance," Father said. "I hope he stays there."

"Nancy's scaired of the dark," Jason said.

"So are you," Caddy said.

"I'm not," Jason said.

"Scairy cat," Caddy said.

"I'm not," Jason said.

"You, Candace!" Mother said. Father came back.

"I am going to walk down the lane with Nancy," he said. "She says that Jesus is back."

"Has she seen him?" Mother said.

"No. Some Negro sent her word that he was back in town. I won't be long."

"You'll leave me alone, to take Nancy home?" Mother said. "Is her safety more precious to you than mine?"

"I won't be long," Father said.

"You'll leave these children unprotected, with that Negro about?"

"I'm going too," Caddy said. "Let me go, Father."

"What would he do with them, if he were unfortunate enough to have them?" Father said.

"I want to go, too," Jason said.

"Jason!" Mother said. She was speaking to Father. You could tell that by the way she said the name. Like she believed that all day Father had been trying to think of doing the thing she wouldn't like the most, and that she knew all the time that after a while he would think of it. I stayed quiet, because Father and I both knew that Mother would want him to make me stay with her if she just thought of it in time. So Father didn't look at me. I was the oldest. I was nine and Caddy was seven and Jason was five.

"Nonsense," Father said. "We won't be long."

Nancy had her hat on. We came to the lane. "Jesus always been good to me," Nancy said. "Whenever he had two dollars, one of them was mine." We walked in the lane. "If I can just get through the lane," Nancy said, "I be all right then."

The lane was always dark. "This is where Jason got scaired on Hallow'en," Caddy said.

"I didn't," Jason said.

"Can't Aunt Rachel do anything with him?" Father said. Aunt Rachel was old. She lived in a cabin beyond Nancy's, by herself. She had white hair and she smoked a pipe in the door, all day long; she didn't work any more. They said she was Jesus' mother. Sometimes she said she was and sometimes she said she wasn't any kin to Jesus.

"Yes, you did," Caddy said. "You were scairder than Frony. You were scairder than T.P. even. Scairder than niggers."

"Can't nobody do nothing with him," Nancy said. "He say I done woke up the devil in him and ain't but one thing going to lay it down again."

"Well, he's gone now," Father said. "There's nothing for you to be afraid of now. And if you'd just let white men alone."

"Let what white men alone?" Caddy said. "How let them alone?"

"He ain't gone nowhere," Nancy said. "I can feel him. I can feel him now, in this lane. He hearing us talk, every word, hid somewhere, waiting. I ain't seen him, and I ain't going to see him again but once more, with that razor in his mouth. That razor on that string down his back, inside his shirt. And then I ain't going to be even surprised."

"I wasn't scaired," Jason said.

"If you'd behave yourself, you'd have kept out of this," Father said. "But it's all right now. He's probably in Saint Louis now. Probably got another wife by now and forgot all about you."

"If he has, I better not find out about it," Nancy said. "I'd stand there right over them, and every time he wropped her, I'd cut that arm off. I'd cut his head off and I'd slit her belly and I'd shove—"

"Hush," Father said.

"Slit whose belly, Nancy?" Caddy said.

"I wasn't scaired," Jason said. "I'd walk right down this lane by myself."

"Yah," Caddy said. "You wouldn't dare to put your foot down in it if we were not here too."

II

Dilsey was still sick, so we took Nancy home every night until Mother said, "How much longer is this going on? I to be left alone in this big house while you take home a frightened Negro?"

We fixed a pallet in the kitchen for Nancy. One night we waked up, hearing the sound. It was not singing and it was not crying, coming up the dark stairs. There was a light in Mother's room and we heard Father going down the hall, down the back stairs, and Caddy and I went into the hall. The floor was cold. Our toes curled away from it while we listened to the sound. It was like singing and it wasn't like singing, like the sound the Negroes make. Then it stopped and we heard Father going down the back stairs, and we went to the head of the stairs. Then the sound began again, in the stairway, not loud, and we could see Nancy's eyes halfway up the stairs, against the wall. They looked like cat's eyes do, like a big cat against the wall, watching us. When we came down the steps to where she was, she quit making the sound again, and we stood there until Father came back up from the kitchen, with his pistol in his hand. He went back down with Nancy and they came back with Nancy's pallet.

We spread the pallet in our room. After the light in Mother's room went off, we could see Nancy's eyes again. "Nancy," Caddy whispered, "are you asleep, Nancy?"

Nancy whispered something. It was oh or no. I don't know which. Like nobody had made it, like it came from nowhere and went nowhere, until it was like Nancy was not there at all; that I had looked so hard at her eyes on the stairs that they had got printed on my eyeballs, like the sun does when you have closed your eyes and there is no sun. "Jesus," Nancy whispered. "Jesus."

"Was it Jesus?" Caddy said. "Did he try to come into the kitchen?"

"Jesus," Nancy said. Like this: Jeeeeeeeeeeeeeeeesus, until the sound went out, like a match or a candle does.

"It's the other Jesus she means," I said.

"Can you see us, Nancy?" Caddy whispered. "Can you see our eyes too?"

"I ain't nothing but a nigger," Nancy said. "God knows. God knows."

"What did you see down there in the kitchen?" Caddy whispered. "What tried to get in?"

"God knows," Nancy said. We could see her eyes. "God knows."

Dilsey got well. She cooked dinner. "You'd better stay in bed a day or two longer," Father said.

"What for?" Dilsey said. "If I had been a day later, this place would be to rack and ruin. Get on out of here now, and let me get my kitchen straight again."

Dilsey cooked supper too. And that night, just before dark, Nancy came into the kitchen.

"How do you know he's back?" Dilsey said. "You ain't seen him."

"Jesus is a nigger," Jason said.

"I can feel him," Nancy said. "I can feel him laying yonder in the ditch."

"Tonight?" Dilsey said. "Is he there tonight?"

"Dilsey's a nigger too," Jason said.

"You try to eat something," Dilsey said.

"I don't want nothing," Nancy said.

"I ain't a nigger," Jason said.

"Drink some coffee," Dilsey said. She poured a cup of coffee for Nancy. "Do you know he's out there tonight? How come you know it's tonight?"

"I know," Nancy said. "He's there, waiting. I know. I done lived with him too long. I know what he is fixing to do fore he know it himself."

"Drink some coffee," Dilsey said. Nancy held the cup to her mouth and blew into the cup. Her mouth pursed out like a spreading adder's, like a rubber mouth, like she had blown all the color out of her lips with blowing the coffee.

"I ain't a nigger," Jason said. "Are you a nigger, Nancy?"

"I hellborn, child," Nancy said. "I won't be nothing soon. I going back where I come from soon."

III

She began to drink the coffee. While she was drinking, holding the cup in both hands, she began to make the sound again. She made the sound into the cup and the coffee sploshed out onto her hands and her dress. Her eyes looked at us and she sat there, her elbows on her knees, holding the cup in both hands, looking at us across the wet cup, making the sound.

"Look at Nancy," Jason said. "Nancy can't cook for us now. Dilsey's got well now."

"You hush up," Dilsey said. Nancy held the cup in both hands, looking at us, making the sound, like there were two of them: one looking at us and the other making the sound. "Whyn't you let Mr. Jason telefoam the marshal?" Dilsey said. Nancy stopped then, holding the cup in her long brown hands. She tried to drink some coffee again, but it sploshed out of the cup, onto her hands and her dress, and she put the cup down. Jason watched her.

"I can't swallow it," Nancy said. "I swallows but it won't go down me."

"You go down to the cabin," Dilsey said. "Frony will fix you a pallet and I'll be there soon."

"Won't no nigger stop him," Nancy said.

"I ain't a nigger," Jason said. "Am I, Dilsey?"

"I reckon not," Dilsey said. She looked at Nancy. "I don't reckon so. What you going to do, then?"

Nancy looked at us. Her eyes went fast, like she was afraid there wasn't time to look, without hardly moving at all. She looked at us, at all three of us at one time. "You member that night I stayed in yawl's room?" she said. She told about how we waked up early the next morning and played. We had to play quiet, on her pallet, until Father woke up and it was time to get breakfast. "Go and ask your maw to let me stay here tonight," Nancy said. "I won't need no pallet. We can play some more."

Caddy asked Mother. Jason went too. "I can't have Negroes sleeping in the bedrooms," Mother said. Jason cried. He cried until Mother said he couldn't have any dessert for three days if he didn't stop. Then Jason said he would stop if Dilsey would make a chocolate cake. Father was there.

"Why don't you do something about it?" Mother said. "What do we have officers for?"

"Why is Nancy afraid of Jesus?" Caddy said. "Are you afraid of Father, Mother?"

"What could the officers do?" Father said. "If Nancy hasn't seen him, how could the officers find him?"

"Then why is she afraid?" Mother said.

"She says he is there. She says she knows he is there tonight."

"Yet we pay taxes," Mother said. "I must wait here alone in this big house while you take a Negro woman home."

"You know that I am not lying outside with a razor," Father said.

"I'll stop if Dilsey will make a chocolate cake." Jason said. Mother told us to go out and Father said he didn't know if Jason would get a chocolate cake or not, but he knew what Jason was going to get in about a minute. We went back to the kitchen and told Nancy.

"Father said for you to go home and lock the door, and you'll be all right," Caddy said. "All right from what, Nancy? Is Jesus mad at you?" Nancy was holding the coffee cup in her hands again, her elbows on her knees and her hands holding the cup between her knees. She was looking into the cup. "What have you done that made Jesus mad?" Caddy said. Nancy let the cup go. It didn't break on the floor, but the coffee spilled out, and Nancy sat there with her hands still making the shape of the cup. She began to make the sound again, not loud. Not singing and not unsinging. We watched her.

"Here," Dilsey said. "You quit that, now. You get aholt of yourself. You wait here. I going to get Versh to walk home with you." Dilsey went out. We looked at Nancy. Her shoulders kept shaking, but she quit making the sound. We stood and watched her.

"What's Jesus going to do to you?" Caddy said. "He went away."

Nancy looked at us. "We had fun that night I stayed in yawl's room, didn't we?"

"I didn't," Jason said. "I didn't have any fun."

"You were asleep in Mother's room," Caddy said. "You were not there."

"Let's go down to my house and have some more fun," Nancy said.

"Mother won't let us," I said. "It's too late now."

"Don't bother her," Nancy said. "We can tell her in the morning. She won't mind."

"She wouldn't let us," I said.

"Don't ask her now," Nancy said. "Don't bother her now."

"She didn't say we couldn't go," Caddy said.

"We didn't ask," I said.

"If you go, I'll tell," Jason said.

"We'll have fun," Nancy said. "They won't mind, just to my house. I been working for yawl a long time. They won't mind."

"I'm not afraid to go," Caddy said. "Jason is the one that's afraid. He'll tell."

"I'm not," Jason said.

"Yes, you are," Caddy said. "You'll tell."

"I won't tell," Jason said. "I'm not afraid."

"Jason ain't afraid to go with me," Nancy said. "Is you, Jason?"

"Jason is going to tell," Caddy said. The lane was dark. We passed the pasture gate. "I bet if something was to jump out from behind that gate, Jason would holler."

"I wouldn't," Jason said. We walked down the lane. Nancy was talking loud.

"What are you talking so loud for, Nancy?" Caddy said.

"Who; me?" Nancy said. "Listen at Quentin and Caddy and Jason saying I'm talking loud."

"You talk like there was five of us here," Caddy said. "You talk like Father was here too."

"Who; me talking loud, Mr. Jason?" Nancy said.

"Nancy called Jason 'Mister,' " Caddy said.

"Listen how Caddy and Quentin and Jason talk," Nancy said.

"We're not talking loud," Caddy said. "You're the one that's talking like Father—"

"Hush," Nancy said; "hush, Mr. Jason."

"Nancy called Jason 'Mister' aguh—"

"Hush," Nancy said. She was talking loud when we crossed the ditch and stooped through the fence where she used to stoop through with the clothes on her head. Then we came to her house. We were going fast then. She opened the door. The smell of the house was like the lamp and the smell of Nancy was like the wick, like they were waiting for one another to begin to smell. She lit the lamp and closed the door and put the bar up. Then she quit talking loud, looking at us.

"What're we going to do?" Caddy said.

"What do yawl want to do?" Nancy said.

"You said we would have some fun," Caddy said.

There was something about Nancy's house; something you could smell besides Nancy and the house. Jason smelled it, even. "I don't want to stay here," he said. "I want to go home."

"Go home, then," Caddy said.

"I don't want to go by myself," Jason said.

"We're going to have some fun," Nancy said.

"How?" Caddy said.

Nancy stood by the door. She was looking at us, only it was like she had emptied her eyes, like she had quit using them. "What do you want to do?" she said.

"Tell us a story," Caddy said. "Can you tell a story?"

"Yes," Nancy said.

"Tell it," Caddy said. We looked at Nancy. "You don't know any stories."

"Yes," Nancy said. "Yes I do."

She came and sat in a chair before the hearth. There was a little fire there. Nancy built it up, when it was already hot inside. She built a good blaze. She told a story. She talked like her eyes looked, like her eyes watching us and her voice talking to us did not belong to her. Like she was living somewhere else, waiting somewhere else. She was outside the cabin. Her voice was inside and the shape of her, the Nancy that could stoop under a barbed wire fence with a bundle of clothes balanced on her head as though without weight, like a balloon, was there. But that was all. "And so this here queen came walking up to the ditch, where that bad man was hiding. She was walking up to the ditch, and she say, 'If I can just get past this here ditch,' was what she say . . . ."

"What ditch?" Caddy said. "A ditch like that one out there? Why did a queen want to go into a ditch?"

"To get to her house," Nancy said. She looked at us. "She had to cross the ditch to get into her house quick and bar the door."

"Why did she want to go home and bar the door?" Caddy said.

IV

Nancy looked at us. She quit talking. She looked at us. Jason's legs stuck straight out of his pants where he sat on Nancy's lap. "I don't think that's a good story," he said. "I want to go home."

"Maybe we had better," Caddy said. She got up from the floor. "I bet they are looking for us right now." She went toward the door.

"No," Nancy said. "Don't open it." She got up quick and passed Caddy. She didn't touch the door, the wooden bar.

"Why not?" Caddy said.

"Come back to the lamp," Nancy said. "We'll have fun. You don't have to go."

"We ought to go," Caddy said. "Unless we have a lot of fun." She and Nancy came back to the fire, the lamp.

"I want to go home," Jason said. "I'm going to tell."

"I know another story," Nancy said. She stood close to the lamp. She looked at Caddy, like when your eyes looked up at a stick balanced on your nose. She had to look down to see Caddy, but her eyes looked like that, like when you are balancing a stick.

"I won't listen to it," Jason said. "I'll bang on the floor."

"It's a good one," Nancy said. "It's better than the other one."

"What's it about?" Caddy said. Nancy was standing by the lamp. Her hand was on the lamp, against the light, long and brown.

"Your hand is on that hot globe," Caddy said. "Don't it feel hot to your hand?"

Nancy looked at her hand on the lamp chimney. She took her hand away, slow. She stood there, looking at Caddy, wringing her long hand as though it were tied to her wrist with a string.

"Let's do something else," Caddy said.

"I want to go home," Jason said.

"I got some popcorn," Nancy said. She looked at Caddy and then at Jason and then at me and then at Caddy again. "I got some popcorn."

"I don't like popcorn," Jason said. "I'd rather have candy."

Nancy looked at Jason. "You can hold the popper." She was still wringing her hand; it was long and limp and brown.

"All right," Jason said. "I'll stay a while if I can do that. Caddy can't hold it. I'll want to go home again if Caddy holds the popper."

Nancy built up the fire. "Look at Nancy putting her hands in the fire," Caddy said. "What's the matter with you, Nancy?"

"I got popcorn," Nancy said. "I got some." She took the popper from under the bed. It was broken. Jason began to cry.

"Now we can't have any popcorn," he said.

"We ought to go home, anyway," Caddy said. "Come on, Quentin."

"Wait," Nancy said; "wait. I can fix it. Don't you want to help me fix it?"

"I don't think I want any," Caddy said. "It's too late now."

"You help me, Jason," Nancy said. "Don't you want to help me?"

"No," Jason said. "I want to go home."

"Hush," Nancy said; "hush. Watch. Watch me. I can fix it so Jason can hold it and pop the corn." She got a piece of wire and fixed the popper.

"It won't hold good," Caddy said.

"Yes it will," Nancy said. "Yawl watch. Yawl help me shell some corn."

The popcorn was under the bed too. We shelled it into the popper and Nancy helped Jason hold the popper over the fire.

"It's not popping," Jason said. "I want to go home."

"You wait," Nancy said. "It'll begin to pop. We'll have fun then."

She was sitting close to the fire. The lamp was turned up so high it was beginning to smoke. "Why don't you turn it down some?" I said.

"It's all right," Nancy said. "I'll clean it. Yawl wait. The popcorn will start in a minute."

"I don't believe it's going to start," Caddy said. "We ought to start home, anyway. They'll be worried."

"No," Nancy said. "It's going to pop. Dilsey will tell um yawl with me. I been working for yawl long time. They won't mind if yawl at my house. You wait, now. It'll start popping any minute now."

Then Jason got some smoke in his eyes and he began to cry. He dropped the popper into the fire. Nancy got a wet rag and wiped Jason's face, but he didn't stop crying.

"Hush," she said. "Hush." But he didn't hush. Caddy took the popper out of the fire.

"It's burned up," she said. "You'll have to get some more popcorn, Nancy."

"Did you put all of it in?" Nancy said.

"Yes," Caddy said. Nancy looked at Caddy. Then she took the popper and opened it and poured the cinders into her apron and began to sort the grains, her hands long and brown, and we were watching her.

"Haven't you got any more?" Caddy said.

"Yes," Nancy said; "yes. Look. This here ain't burnt. All we need to do is—"

"I want to go home," Jason said. "I'm going to tell."

"Hush," Caddy said. We all listened. Nancy's head was already turned toward the barred door, her eyes filled with red lamplight. "Somebody is coming," Caddy said.

Then Nancy began to make that sound again, not loud, sitting there above the fire, her long hands dangling between her knees; all of a sudden water began to come out on her face in big drops, running down her face, carrying in each one a little turning ball of firelight like a spark until it dropped off her chin. "She's not crying," I said.

"I ain't crying," Nancy said. Her eyes were closed. "I ain't crying. Who is it?"

"I don't know," Caddy said. She went to the door and looked out. "We've got to go now," she said. "Here comes Father."

"I'm going to tell," Jason said. "Yawl made me come."

The water still ran down Nancy's face. She turned in her chair. "Listen. Tell him. Tell him we going to have fun. Tell him I take good care of yawl until in the morning. Tell him to let me come home with yawl and sleep on the floor. Tell him I won't need no pallet. We'll have fun. You member last time how we had so much fun?"

"I didn't have fun," Jason said. "You hurt me. You put smoke in my eyes. I'm going to tell."

V

Father came in. He looked at us. Nancy did not get up.

"Tell him," she said.

"Caddy made us come down here," Jason said. "I didn't want to."

Father came to the fire. Nancy looked up at him. "Can't you go to Aunt Rachel's and stay?" he said. Nancy looked up at Father, her hands between her knees. "He's not here," Father said. "I would have seen him. There's not a soul in sight."

"He in the ditch," Nancy said. "He waiting in the ditch yonder."

"Nonsense," Father said. He looked at Nancy. "Do you know he's there?"

"I got the sign," Nancy said.

"What sign?"

"I got it. It was on the table when I come in. It was a hog-bone, with blood meat still on it, laying by the lamp. He's out there. When yawl walk out that door, I gone."

"Gone where, Nancy?" Caddy said.

"I'm not a tattletale," Jason said.

"Nonsense," Father said.

"He out there," Nancy said. "He looking through that window this minute, waiting for yawl to go. Then I gone."

"Nonsense," Father said. "Lock up your house and we'll take you on to Aunt Rachel's."

" 'Twon't do no good," Nancy said. She didn't look at Father now, but he looked down at her, at her long, limp, moving hands. "Putting it off won't do no good."

"Then what do you want to do?" Father said.

"I don't know," Nancy said. "I can't do nothing. Just put it off. And that don't do no good. I reckon it belong to me. I reckon what I going to get ain't no more than mine."

"Get what?" Caddy said. "What's yours?"

"Nothing," Father said. "You all must get to bed."

"Caddy made me come," Jason said.

"Go on to Aunt Rachel's," Father said.

"It won't do no good," Nancy said. She sat before the fire, her elbows on her knees, her long hands between her knees. "When even your own kitchen wouldn't do no good. When even if I was sleeping on the floor in the room with your chillen, and the next morning there I am, and blood—"

"Hush," Father said. "Lock the door and put out the lamp and go to bed."

"I scaired of the dark," Nancy said. "I scaired for it to happen in the dark."

"You mean you're going to sit right here with the lamp lighted?" Father said. Then Nancy began to make the sound again, sitting before the fire, her long hands between her knees. "Ah, damnation," Father said. "Come along, chillen. It's past bedtime."

"When yawl go home, I gone," Nancy said. She talked quieter now, and her face looked quiet, like her hands. "Anyway, I got my coffin money saved up with Mr. Lovelady." Mr. Lovelady was a short, dirty man who collected the Negro insurance, coming around to the cabins or the kitchens every Saturday morning, to collect fifteen cents. He and his wife lived at the hotel. One morning his wife committed suicide. They had a child, a little girl. He and the child went away. After a week or two he came back alone. We would see him going along the lanes and the back streets on Saturday mornings.

"Nonsense," Father said. "You'll be the first thing I'll see in the kitchen tomorrow morning."

"You'll see what you'll see, I reckon," Nancy said. "But it will take the Lord to say what that will be."

VI

We left her sitting before the fire.

"Come and put the bar up," Father said. But she didn't move. She didn't look at us again, sitting quietly there between the lamp and the fire. From some distance down the lane we could look back and see her through the open door.

"What, Father?" Caddy said. "What's going to happen?"

"Nothing," Father said. Jason was on Father's back so Jason was the tallest of all of us. We went down into the ditch. I looked at it, quiet. I couldn't see much where the moonlight and the shadows tangled.

"If Jesus *is* hid here, he can see us, can't he?" Caddy said.

"He's not there," Father said. "He went away a long time ago."

"You made me come," Jason said, high; against the sky it looked like Father had two heads, a little one and a big one. "I didn't want to."

We went up out of the ditch. We could still see Nancy's house and the open door, but we couldn't see Nancy now, sitting before the fire with the door open, because she was tired. "I just done got tired," she said. "I just a nigger. It ain't no fault of mine."

But we could hear her, because she began just after we came up out of the ditch, the sound that was not singing and not unsinging. "Who will do our washing now, Father?" I said.

"I'm not a nigger," Jason said, high and close above Father's head.

"You're worse," Caddy said, "you are a tattletale. If something was to jump out, you'd be scairder than a nigger."

"I wouldn't," Jason said.

"You'd cry," Caddy said.

"Caddy," Father said.

"I wouldn't!" Jason said.

"Scairy cat," Caddy said.

"Candace!" Father said.

Babylon Revisited

F. SCOTT FITZGERALD

"And where's Mr. Campbell?" Charlie asked.

"Gone to Switzerland. Mr. Campbell's a pretty sick man, Mr. Wales."

"I'm sorry to hear that. And George Hardt?" Charlie inquired.

"Back in America, gone to work."

"And where is the Snow Bird?"

"He was in here last week. Anyway, his friend, Mr. Schaeffer, is in Paris."

Two familiar names from the long list of a year and a half ago. Charlie scribbled an address in his notebook and tore out the page.

"If you see Mr. Schaeffer, give him this," he said. "It's my brother-in-law's address. I haven't settled on a hotel yet."

He was not really disappointed to find Paris was so empty. But the stillness in the Ritz bar was strange and portentous. It was not an American bar any more—he felt polite in it, and not as if he owned it. It had gone back into France. He felt the stillness from the moment he got out of the taxi and saw the doorman, usually in a frenzy of activity at this hour, gossiping with a *chasseur* by the servants' entrance.

Passing through the corridor, he heard only a single, bored voice in the once-clamorous women's room. When he turned into the bar he traveled the twenty feet of green carpet with his eyes fixed straight ahead by old habit; and then, with his foot firmly on the rail, he turned and surveyed the room, encountering only a single pair of eyes that fluttered up from a newspaper in the corner. Charlie asked for the head barman, Paul, who in the latter days of the bull market had come to work in his own custom-built car—disembarking, however, with due nicety at the nearest corner. But Paul was at his country house today and Alix giving him information.

"No, no more," Charlie said. "I'm going slow these days."

Alix congratulated him: "You were going pretty strong a couple of years ago."

"I'll stick to it all right," Charlie assured him. "I've stuck to it for over a year and a half now."

"How do you find conditions in America?"

"I haven't been to America for months. I'm in business in Prague, representing a couple of concerns there. They don't know about me down there."

Alix smiled.

"Remember the night of George Hardt's bachelor dinner here?" said Charlie. "By the way, what's become of Claude Fessenden?"

Alix lowered his voice confidentially: "He's in Paris, but he doesn't come here any more. Paul doesn't allow it. He ran up a bill of thirty thousand francs, charging all his drinks and his lunches, and usually his dinner, for more than a year. And when Paul finally told him he had to pay, he gave him a bad check."

Alix shook his head sadly.

"I don't understand it, such a dandy fellow. Now he's all bloated up—" He made a plump apple of his hands.

Charlie watched a group of strident queens installing themselves in a corner.

"Nothing affects them," he thought. "Stocks rise and fall, people loaf or work, but they go on forever." The place oppressed him. He called for the dice and shook with Alix for the drink.

"Here for long, Mr. Wales?"

"I'm here for four or five days to see my little girl."

"Oh-h! You have a little girl?"

Outside, the fire-red, gas-blue, ghost-green signs shone smokily through the tranquil rain. It was late afternoon and the streets were in movement; the bistros gleamed. At the corner of the Boulevard des Capucines he took a taxi. The Place de la Concorde moved by in pink majesty; they crossed the logical Seine, and Charlie felt the sudden provincial quality of the Left Bank.

Charlie directed his taxi to the Avenue de l'Opéra, which was out of his way. But he wanted to see the blue hour spread over the magnificent façade, and imagine that the cab horns, playing endlessly the first few bars of *Le Plus que Lent*, were the trumpets of the Second Empire. They were closing the iron grill in front of Brentano's Bookstore, and people were already at dinner behind the trim little bourgeois hedge of Duval's. He had never eaten at a really cheap restaurant in Paris. Five-course dinner, four francs fifty, eighteen cents, wine included. For some odd reason he wished that he had.

As they rolled on to the Left Bank, and he felt its sudden provincialism, he thought, "I spoiled this city for myself. I didn't realize it, but the days came along one after another, and then two years were gone, and everything was gone, and I was gone."

He was thirty-five, and good to look at. The Irish mobility of his face was sobered by a deep wrinkle between his eyes. As he rang his brother-in-law's bell in Rue Palatine, the wrinkle deepened till it pulled down his brows; he felt a cramping sensation in his belly. From behind the maid who opened the door darted a lovely little girl of nine who shrieked "Daddy!" and flew up, struggling like a fish, into his arms. She pulled his head around by one ear and set her cheek against his.

"My old pie," he said.

"Oh, daddy, daddy, daddy, daddy, dads, dads, dads!"

She drew him into the salon, where the family waited, a boy and a girl his daughter's age, his sister-in-law and her husband. He greeted Marion with his voice pitched carefully to avoid either feigned enthusiasm or dislike, but her response was more frankly tepid, though she minimized her expression of unalterable distrust by directing her regard toward his child. The two men clasped hands in a friendly way and Lincoln Peters rested his for a moment on Charlie's shoulder.

The room was warm and comfortably American. The three children moved intimately about, playing through the yellow oblongs that led to other rooms; the cheer of six o'clock spoke in the eager smacks of the fire and the sounds of French activity in the kitchen. But Charlie did not relax; his heart sat up rigidly in his body and he drew confidence from his daughter, who from time to time came close to him, holding in his arms the doll he had brought.

"Really extremely well," he declared in answer to Lincoln's question. "There's a lot of business there that isn't moving at all, but we're doing even better than ever. In fact, damn well. I'm bringing my sister over from America next month to keep house for me. My income last year was bigger than it was when I had money. You see, the Czechs——"

His boasting was for a specific purpose; but after a moment, seeing a faint restiveness in Lincoln's eye, he changed the subject:

"Those are fine children of yours, well brought up, good manners."

"We think Honoria's a great little girl too."

Marion Peters came back from the kitchen. She was a tall woman with worried eyes, who had once possessed a fresh American loveliness. Charlie had never been sensitive to it and was always surprised when people spoke of how pretty she had been. From the first there had been an instinctive antipathy between them.

"Well, how do you find Honoria?" she asked.

"Wonderful. I was astonished how much she's grown in ten months. All the children are looking well."

"We haven't had a doctor for a year. How do you like being back in Paris?"

"It seems very funny to see so few Americans around."

"I'm delighted," Marion said vehemently. "Now at least you can go into a store without their assuming you're a millionaire. We've suffered like everybody, but on the whole it's a good deal pleasanter."

"But it was nice while it lasted," Charlie said. "We were a sort of royalty, almost infallible, with a sort of magic around us. In the bar this afternoon"—he stumbled, seeing his mistake—"there wasn't a man I knew."

She looked at him keenly. "I should think you'd have had enough of bars."

"I only stayed a minute. I take one drink every afternoon, and no more."

"Don't you want a cocktail before dinner?" Lincoln asked.

"I take only one drink every afternoon, and I've had that."

"I hope you keep to it," said Marion.

Her dislike was evident in the coldness with which she spoke, but Charlie only smiled; he had larger plans. Her very aggressiveness gave him an advantage, and he knew enough to wait. He wanted them to initiate the discussion of what they knew had brought him to Paris.

At dinner he couldn't decide whether Honoria was most like him or her mother. Fortunate if she didn't combine the traits of both that had brought them to disaster. A great wave of protectiveness went over him. He thought he knew what to do for her. He believed in character; he wanted to jump back a whole generation and trust in character again as the eternally valuable element. Everything else wore out.

He left soon after dinner, but not to go home. He was curious to see Paris by night with clearer and more judicious eyes than those of other days. He bought a *strapontin* for the Casino and watched Josephine Baker go through her chocolate arabesques.

After an hour he left and strolled toward Montmarte, up to the Rue Pigalle into the Place Blanche. The rain had stopped and there were a few people in evening clothes disembarking from taxis in front of cabarets, and *cocottes* prowling singly or in pairs, and many Negroes. He passed a lighted door from which issued music, and stopped with the sense of familiarity; it was Bricktop's, where he had parted with so many hours and so much money. A few doors farther on he found another ancient rendezvous and incautiously put his head inside. Immediately an eager orchestra burst into sound, a pair of professional dancers leaped to their feet and a maître d'hôtel swooped toward him, crying, "Crowd just arriving, sir!" But he withdrew quickly.

"You have to be damn drunk," he thought.

Zelli's was closed, the bleak and sinister cheap hotels surrounding it were dark; up in the Rue Blanche there was more light and a local, colloquial French crowd. The Poet's Cave had disappeared, but the two great mouths of the Café of Heaven and the Café of Hell still yawned—even devoured, as he watched, the meager contents of a tourist bus—a German, a Japanese, and an American couple who glanced at him with frightened eyes.

So much for the effort and ingenuity of Montmartre. All the catering to vice and waste was on an utterly childish scale, and he suddenly realized the meaning of the word "dissipate"—to dissipate into thin air; to make nothing out of something. In the little hours of the night every move from place to place was an enormous human jump, an increase of paying for the privilege of slower and slower motion.

He remembered thousand-franc notes given to an orchestra for playing a single number, hundred-franc notes tossed to a doorman for calling a cab.

But it hadn't been given for nothing.

It had been given, even the most wildly squandered sum, as an offering to destiny that he might not remember the things most worth remembering, the things that now he would always remember—his child taken from his control, his wife escaped to a grave in Vermont.

In the glare of a *brasserie* a woman spoke to him. He bought her some eggs and coffee, and then, eluding her encouraging stare, gave her a twenty-franc note and took a taxi to his hotel.

II

He woke upon a fine fall day—football weather. The depression of yesterday was gone and he liked the people on the streets. At noon he sat opposite Honoria at Le Grand Vatel, the only restaurant he could think of not reminiscent of champagne dinners and long luncheons that began at two and ended in a blurred and vague twilight.

"Now, how about vegetables? Oughtn't you to have some vegetables?"

"Well, yes."

"Here's *épinards* and *chou-fleur* and carrots and *haricots*."

"I'd like *chou-fleur*."

"Wouldn't you like to have two vegetables?"

"I usually only have one at lunch."

The waiter was pretending to be inordinately fond of children. *"Qu'elle est mignonne la petite! Elle parle exactement comme une française."*

"How about dessert? Shall we wait and see?"

The waiter disappeared. Honoria looked at her father expectantly.

"What are we going to do?"

"First, we're going to that toy store in the Rue Saint-Honoré and buy you anything you like. And then we're going to the vaudeville at the Empire."

She hesitated. "I like it about the vaudeville, but not the toy store."

"Why not?"

"Well, you brought me this doll." She had it with her. "And I've got lots of things. And we're not rich any more, are we?"

"We never were. But today you are to have anything you want."

"All right," she agreed resignedly.

When there had been her mother and a French nurse he had been inclined to be strict; now he extended himself, reached out for a new tolerance; he must be both parents to her and not shut any of her out of communication.

"I want to get to know you," he said gravely. "First let me introduce myself. My name is Charles J. Wales, of Prague."

"Oh, daddy!" her voice cracked with laughter.

"And who are you, please?" he persisted, and she accepted a role immediately: "Honoria Wales, Rue Palatine, Paris."

"Married or single?"

"No, not married. Single."

He indicated the doll. "But I see you have a child, madame."

Unwilling to disinherit it, she took it to her heart and thought quickly: "Yes, I've been married, but I'm not married now. My husband is dead."

He went on quickly, "And the child's name?"

"Simone. That's after my best friend at school."

"I'm very pleased that you're doing so well at school."

"I'm third this month," she boasted. "Elsie"—that was her cousin—"is only about eighteenth, and Richard is about at the bottom."

"You like Richard and Elsie, don't you?"

"Oh, yes. I like Richard quite well and I like her all right."

Cautiously and casually he asked: "And Aunt Marion and Uncle Lincoln—which do you like best?"

"Oh, Uncle Lincoln, I guess."

He was increasingly aware of her presence. As they came in, a murmur of ". . . adorable" followed them, and now the people at the next table bent all their silences upon her, staring as if she were something no more conscious than a flower.

"Why don't I live with you?" she asked suddenly. "Because mamma's dead?"

"You must stay here and learn more French. It would have been hard for daddy to take care of you so well."

"I don't really need much taking care of any more. I do everything for myself."

Going out of the restaurant, a man and a woman unexpectedly hailed him.

"Well, the old Wales!"

"Hello there, Lorraine. . . . Dunc."

Sudden ghosts out of the past: Duncan Schaeffer, a friend from college. Lorraine Quarrles, a lovely, pale blond of thirty; one of a crowd who had helped him make months into days in the lavish times of three years ago.

"My husband couldn't come this year," she said, in answer to his question. "We're poor as hell. So he gave me two hundred a month and told me I could do my worst on that. . . . This your little girl?"

"What about coming back and sitting down?" Duncan asked.

"Can't do it." He was glad for an excuse. As always, he felt Lorraine's passionate, provocative attraction, but his own rhythm was different now.

"Well, how about dinner?" she asked.

"I'm not free. Give me your address and let me call you."

"Charlie, I believe you're sober," she said judicially. "I honestly believe he's sober, Dunc. Pinch him and see if he's sober."

Charlie indicated Honoria with his head. They both laughed.

"What's your address?" said Duncan skeptically.

He hesitated, unwilling to give the name of his hotel.

"I'm not settled yet. I'd better call you. We're going to see the vaudeville at the Empire."

"There! That's what I want to do," Lorraine said. "I want to see some clowns and acrobats and jugglers. That's just what we'll do, Dunc."

"We've got to do an errand first," said Charlie. "Perhaps we'll see you there."

"All right, you snob. . . . Good-by, beautiful little girl."

"Good-by."

Honoria bobbed politely.

Somehow, an unwelcome encounter. They liked him because he was functioning, because he was serious; they wanted to see him, because he was stronger than they were now, because they wanted to draw a certain sustenance from his strength.

At the Empire, Honoria proudly refused to sit upon her father's folded coat. She was already an individual with a code of her own, and Charlie was more and more absorbed by the desire of putting a little of himself into her before she crystallized utterly. It was hopeless to try to know her in so short a time.

Between the acts they came upon Duncan and Lorraine in the lobby where the band was playing.

"Have a drink?"

"All right, but not up at the bar. We'll take a table."

"The perfect father."

Listening abstractedly to Lorraine, Charlie watched Honoria's eyes leave their table, and he followed them wistfully about the room, wondering what they saw. He met her glance and she smiled.

"I liked that lemonade," she said.

What had she said? What had he expected? Going home in a taxi afterward, he pulled her over until her head rested against his chest.

"Darling, do you ever think about your mother?"

"Yes, sometimes," she answered vaguely.

"I don't want you to forget her. Have you got a picture of her?"

"Yes, I think so. Anyhow, Aunt Marion has. Why don't you want me to forget her?"

"She loved you very much."

"I loved her too."

They were silent for a moment.

"Daddy, I want to come and live with you," she said suddenly.

His heart leaped; he had wanted it to come like this.

"Aren't you perfectly happy?"

"Yes, but I love you better than anybody. And you love me better than anybody, don't you, now that mummy's dead?"

"Of course I do. But you won't always like me best, honey. You'll grow up and meet somebody your own age and go marry him and forget you ever had a daddy."

"Yes, that's true," she agreed tranquilly.

He didn't go in. He was coming back at nine o'clock and he wanted to keep himself fresh and new for the thing he must say then.

"When you're safe inside, just show yourself in that window."

"All right. Good-by, dads, dads, dads, dads."

He waited in the dark street until she appeared, all warm and glowing, in the window above and kissed her fingers out into the night.

III

They were waiting. Marion sat behind the coffee service in a dignified black dinner dress that just faintly suggested mourning. Lincoln was walking up and down with the animation of one who had already been talking. They were as anxious as he was to get into the question. He opened it almost immediately:

"I suppose you know what I want to see you about—why I really came to Paris."

Marion played with the black stars on her necklace and frowned.

"I'm awfully anxious to have a home," he continued. "And I'm awfully anxious to have Honoria in it. I appreciate your taking in Honoria for her mother's sake, but things have changed now"—he hesitated and then continued more forcibly—"changed radically with me, and I want to ask you to reconsider the matter. It would be silly for me to deny that about three years ago I was acting badly——"

Marion looked up at him with hard eyes.

"—but all that's over. As I told you, I haven't had more than a drink a day for over a year, and I take that drink deliberately, so that the idea of alcohol won't get too big in my imagination. You see the idea?"

"No," said Marion succinctly.

"It's a sort of stunt I set myself. It keeps the matter in proportion."

"I get you," said Lincoln. "You don't want to admit it's got any attraction for you."

"Something like that. Sometimes I forget and don't take it. But I try to take it. Anyhow, I couldn't afford to drink in my position. The people I represent are more than satisfied with what I've done, and I'm bringing my sister over from Burlington to keep house for me, and I want awfully to have Honoria too. You know that even when her mother and I weren't getting along well we never let anything that happened touch Honoria. I know she's fond of me and I know I'm able to take care of her and—well, there you are. How do you feel about it?"

He knew that now he would have to take a beating. It would last an hour or two hours, and it would be difficult, but if he modulated his inevitable resentment to the chastened attitude of the reformed sinner, he might win his point in the end.

Keep your temper, he told himself. You don't want to be justified. You want Honoria.

Lincoln spoke first: "We've been talking it over ever since we got your letter last month. We're happy to have Honoria here. She's a dear little thing, and we're glad to be able to help her, but of course that isn't the question——"

Marion interrupted suddenly. "How long are you going to stay sober, Charlie?" she asked.

"Permanently, I hope."

"How can anybody count on that?"

"You know I never did drink heavily until I gave up business and came over here with nothing to do. Then Helen and I began to run around with——"

"Please leave Helen out of it. I can't bear to hear you talk about her like that."

He stared at her grimly; he had never been certain how fond of each other the sisters were in life.

"My drinking only lasted about a year and a half—from the time we came over until I—collapsed."

"It was time enough."

"It was time enough," he agreed.

"My duty is entirely to Helen," she said. "I try to think what she would have wanted me to do. Frankly, from the night you did that terrible thing you haven't really existed for me. I can't help that. She was my sister."

"Yes."

"When she was dying she asked me to look out for Honoria. If you hadn't been in a sanitarium then, it might have helped matters."

He had no answer.

"I'll never in my life be able to forget the morning when Helen knocked at my door, soaked to the skin and shivering, and said you'd locked her out."

Charlie gripped the sides of the chair. This was more difficult than he expected; he wanted to launch out into a long expostulation and explanation, but he only said. "The night I locked her out—" and she interrupted, "I don't feel up to going over that again."

After a moment's silence Lincoln said: "We're getting off the subject. You want Marion to set aside her legal guardianship and give you Honoria. I think the main point for her is whether she has confidence in you or not."

"I don't blame Marion," Charlie said slowly, "but I think she can have entire confidence in me. I had a good record up to three years ago. Of course, it's within human possibilities I might go wrong any time. But if we wait much longer I'll lose Honoria's childhood and my chance for a home." He shook his head. "I'll simply lose her, don't you see?"

"Yes, I see," said Lincoln.

"Why didn't you think of all this before?" Marion asked.

"I suppose I did, from time to time, but Helen and I were getting along badly. When I consented to the guardianship, I was flat on my back in a sanitarium and the market had cleaned me out. I knew I'd acted badly, and I thought if it would bring any peace to Helen, I'd agree to anything. But now it's different. I'm functioning. I'm behaving damn well, so far as——"

"Please don't swear at me," Marion said.

He looked at her, startled. With each remark the force of her dislike became more and more apparent. She had built up all her fear of life into one wall and faced it toward him. This trivial reproof was possibly the result of some trouble with the cook several hours before. Charlie became increasingly alarmed at leaving Honoria in this atmosphere of hostility against himself; sooner or later it would come out, in a word here, a shake of the head there, and some of that distrust would be irrevocably implanted in Honoria. But he pulled his temper down out of his face and shut it up inside him; he had won a point, for Lincoln realized the absurdity of Marion's remark and asked her lightly since when she had objected to the word "damn."

"Another thing," Charlie said: "I'm able to give her certain advantages now. I'm going to take a French governess to Prague with me. I've got a lease on a new apartment——"

He stopped, realizing that he was blundering. They couldn't be expected to accept with equanimity the fact that his income was again twice as large as their own.

"I suppose you can give her more luxuries than we can," said Marion. "When you were throwing away money we were living along watching every ten francs. . . . I suppose you'll start doing it again."

"Oh, no," he said. "I've learned. I worked hard for ten years, you know—until I got lucky in the market, like so many people. Terribly lucky. It won't happen again."

There was a long silence. All of them felt their nerves straining, and for the first time in a year Charlie wanted a drink. He was sure now that Lincoln Peters wanted him to have his child.

Marion shuddered suddenly; part of her saw that Charlie's feet were

planted on the earth now, and her own maternal feeling recognized the
naturalness of his desire; but she had lived for a long time with a prejudice—a prejudice founded on a curious disbelief in her sister's happiness,
which, in the shock of one terrible night, had turned to hatred for him. It
had all happened at a point in her life where the discouragement of ill
health and adverse circumstances made it necessary for her to believe in
tangible villainy and a tangible villain.

"I can't help what I think!" she cried out suddenly. "How much you were
responsible for Helen's death, I don't know. It's something you'll have to
square with your own conscience."

An electric current of agony surged through him; for a moment he was
almost on his feet, an unuttered sound echoing in his throat. He hung on
to himself for a moment, another moment.

"Hold on there," said Lincoln uncomfortably. "I never thought you were
responsible for that."

"Helen died of heart trouble," Charlie said dully.

"Yes, heart trouble." Marion spoke as if the phrase had another meaning
for her.

Then, in the flatness that followed her outburst, she saw him plainly and
she knew he had somehow arrived at control over the situation. Glancing at
her husband, she found no help from him, and as abruptly as if it were a
matter of no importance, she threw up the sponge.

"Do what you like!" she cried, springing up from her chair. "She's your
child. I'm not the person to stand in your way. I think if it were my child I'd
rather see her—" She managed to check herself. "You two decide it. I can't
stand this. I'm sick. I'm going to bed."

She hurried from the room; after a moment Lincoln said:

"This has been a hard day for her. You know how strongly she feels—"
His voice was almost apologetic: "When a woman gets an idea in her head."

"Of course."

"It's going to be all right. I think she sees now that you—can provide for
the child, and so we can't very well stand in your way or Honoria's way."

"Thank you, Lincoln."

"I'd better go along and see how she is."

"I'm going."

He was still trembling when he reached the street, but a walk down the
Rue Bonaparte to the *quais* set him up, and as he crossed the Seine, fresh
and new by the *quai* lamps, he felt exultant. But back in his room he
couldn't sleep. The image of Helen haunted him. Helen whom he had
loved so until they had senselessly begun to abuse each other's love, tear it
into shreds. On that terrible February night that Marion remembered so
vividly, a slow quarrel had gone on for hours. There was a scene at the
Florida, and then he attempted to take her home, and then she kissed
young Webb at a table; after that there was what she had hysterically said.

When he arrived home alone he turned the key in the lock in wild anger. How could he know she would arrive an hour later alone, that there would be a snow storm in which she wandered about in slippers, too confused to find a taxi? Then the aftermath, her escaping pneumonia by a miracle, and all the attendant horror. They were "reconciled," but that was the beginning of the end, and Marion, who had seen with her own eyes and who imagined it to be one of many scenes from her sister's martyrdom, never forgot.

Going over it again brought Helen nearer, and in the white, soft light that steals upon half sleep near morning he found himself talking to her again. She said that he was perfectly right about Honoria and that she wanted Honoria to be with him. She said she was glad he was being good and doing better. She said a lot of other things—very friendly things—but she was in a swing in a white dress, and swinging faster and faster all the time, so that at the end he could not hear clearly all that she said.

IV

He woke up feeling happy. The door of the world was open again. He made plans, vistas, futures for Honoria and himself, but suddenly he grew sad, remembering all the plans he and Helen had made. She had not planned to die. The present was the thing—work to do and someone to love. But not to love too much, for he knew the injury that a father can do to a daughter or a mother to a son by attaching them too closely: afterward, out in the world, the child would seek in the marriage partner the same blind tenderness and, failing probably to find it, turn against love and life.

It was another bright, crisp day. He called Lincoln Peters at the bank where he worked and asked if he could count on taking Honoria when he left for Prague. Lincoln agreed that there was no reason for delay. One thing—the legal guardianship. Marion wanted to retain that a while longer. She was upset by the whole matter, and it would oil things if she felt that the situation was still in her control for another year. Charlie agreed, wanting only the tangible, visible child.

Then the question of a governess. Charlie sat in a gloomy agency and talked to a cross Béarnaise and to a buxom Breton peasant, neither of whom he could have endured. There were others whom he would see tomorrow.

He lunched with Lincoln Peters at Griffons, trying to keep down his exultation.

"There's nothing quite like your own child," Lincoln said. "But you understand how Marion feels too."

"She's forgotten how hard I worked for seven years there," Charlie said. "She just remembers one night."

"There's another thing," Lincoln hesitated. "While you and Helen were tearing around Europe throwing money away, we were just getting along. I didn't touch any of the prosperity because I never got ahead enough to carry anything but my insurance. I think Marion felt there was some kind of injustice in it—you not even working toward the end, and getting richer and richer."

"It went just as quick as it came," said Charlie.

"Yes, a lot of it stayed in the hands of *chasseurs* and saxophone players and maitres d'hôtel—well, the big party's over now. I just said that to explain Marion's feeling about those crazy years. If you drop in about six o'clock tonight before Marion's too tired, we'll settle the details on the spot."

Back at his hotel, Charlie found a *pneumatique* that had been redirected from the Ritz bar, where Charlie had left his address for the purpose of finding a certain man.

DEAR CHARLIE: You were so strange when we saw you the other day that I wondered if I did something to offend you. If so, I'm not conscious of it. In fact, I have thought about you too much for the last year, and it's always been in the back of my mind that I might see you if I came over here. We *did* have such good times that crazy spring, like the night you and I stole the butcher's tricycle, and the time we tried to call on the president and you had the old derby rim and the wire cane. Everybody seems so old lately, but I don't feel old a bit. Couldn't we get together some time today for old time's sake? I've got a vile hangover for the moment, but will be feeling better this afternoon and will look for you about five in the sweatshop at the Ritz.

Always devotedly,
Lorraine

His first feeling was one of awe that he had actually, in his mature years, stolen a tricycle and pedaled Lorraine all over the Étoile between the small hours and dawn. In retrospect it was a nightmare. Locking out Helen didn't fit in with any other act of his life, but the tricycle incident did—it was one of many. How many weeks or months of dissipation to arrive at that condition of utter irresponsibility?

He tried to picture how Lorraine had appeared to him then—very attractive; Helen was unhappy about it, though she said nothing. Yesterday, in the restaurant, Lorraine had seemed trite, blurred, worn away. He emphatically did not want to see her, and he was glad Alix had not given away his hotel address. It was a relief to think, instead, of Honoria, to think of Sundays spent with her and of saying good morning to her and of knowing she was there in his house at night, drawing her breath in the darkness.

At five he took a taxi and bought presents for all the Peterses—a piquant cloth doll, a box of Roman soldiers, flowers for Marion, big linen handkerchiefs for Lincoln.

He saw, when he arrived in the apartment, that Marion had accepted the inevitable. She greeted him now as though he were a recalcitrant member of the family, rather than a menacing outsider. Honoria had been told she was going; Charlie was glad to see that her tact made her conceal her excessive happiness. Only on his lap did she whisper her delight and the question "When?" before she slipped away with the other children.

He and Marion were alone for a minute in the room, and on an impulse he spoke out boldly:

"Family quarrels are bitter things. They don't go according to any rules. They're not like aches or wounds; they're more like splits in the skin that won't heal because there's not enough material. I wish you and I could be on better terms."

"Some things are hard to forget," she answered. "It's a question of confidence." There was no answer to this and presently she asked, "When do you propose to take her?"

"As soon as I can get a governess. I hoped the day after tomorrow."

"That's impossible. I've got to get her things in shape. Not before Saturday."

He yielded. Coming back into the room, Lincoln offered him a drink.

"I'll take my daily whisky," he said.

It was warm here, it was a home, people together by a fire. The children felt very safe and important; the mother and father were serious, watchful. They had things to do for the children more important than his visit here. A spoonful of medicine was, after all, more important than the strained relations between Marion and himself. They were not dull people, but they were very much in the grip of life and circumstances. He wondered if he couldn't do something to get Lincoln out of his rut at the bank.

A long peal at the doorbell; the *bonne à tout faire* passed through and went down the corridor. The door opened upon another long ring, and then voices, and the three in the salon looked up expectantly; Richard moved to bring the corridor within his range of vision, and Marion rose. Then the maid came back along the corridor, closely followed by the voices, which developed under the light into Duncan Schaeffer and Lorraine Quarrles.

They were gay, they were hilarious, they were roaring with laughter. For a moment Charlie was astounded; unable to understand how they ferreted out the Peterses' address.

"Ah-h-h!" Duncan wagged his finger roguishly at Charlie, "Ah-h-h!"

They both slid down another cascade of laughter. Anxious and at a loss, Charlie shook hands with them quickly and presented them to Lincoln and Marion. Marion nodded, scarcely speaking. She had drawn back a step toward the fire; her little girl stood beside her, and Marion put an arm about her shoulder.

With growing annoyance at the intrusion, Charlie waited for them to explain themselves. After some concentration Duncan said:

"We came to invite you out to dinner. Lorraine and I insist that all this shishi, cagy business 'bout your address got to stop."

Charlie came closer to them, as if to force them backward down the corridor.

"Sorry, but I can't. Tell me where you'll be and I'll phone you in half an hour."

This made no impression. Lorraine sat down suddenly on the side of a chair, and focusing her eyes on Richard, cried, "Oh, what a nice little boy! Come here, little boy." Richard glanced at his mother, but did not move. With a perceptible shrug of her shoulder, Lorraine turned back to Charlie:

"Come and dine. Sure your cousins won' mine. See you so sel'om. Or solemn."

"I can't," said Charlie sharply. "You two have dinner and I'll phone you."

Her voice became suddenly unpleasant. "All right, we'll go. But I remember once when you hammered on my door at four A.M. I was enough of a good sport to give you a drink. Come on, Dunc."

Still in slow motion, with blurred, angry faces, with uncertain feet, they retired along the corridor.

"Good night," Charlie said.

"Good night!" responded Lorraine emphatically.

When he went back into the salon Marion had not moved, only now her son was standing in the circle of her other arm. Lincoln was still swinging Honoria back and forth like a pendulum from side to side.

"What an outrage!" Charlie broke out. "What an absolute outrage!"

Neither of them answered. Charlie dropped into an armchair, picked up his drink, set it down again and said:

"People I haven't seen for two years having the colossal nerve——"

He broke off. Marion had made the sound "Oh!" in one swift, furious breath, turned her body from him with a jerk and left the room.

Lincoln set down Honoria carefully.

"You children go in and start your soup," he said, and when they obeyed, he said to Charlie:

"Marion's not well and she can't stand shocks. That kind of people make her really physically sick."

"I didn't tell them to come here. They wormed your name out of somebody. They deliberately——"

"Well, it's too bad. It doesn't help matters. Excuse me a minute."

Left alone, Charlie sat tense in his chair. In the next room he could hear the children eating, talking in monosyllables, already oblivious to the scene between their elders. He heard a murmur of conversation from a farther room and then the ticking bell of a telephone receiver picked up, and in a panic he moved to the other side of the room and out of earshot.

In a minute Lincoln came back. "Look here, Charlie. I think we'd better call off dinner for tonight. Marion's in bad shape."

"Is she angry with me?"

"Sort of," he said, almost roughly. "She's not strong and——"

"You mean she's changed her mind about Honoria?"

"She's pretty bitter right now. I don't know. You phone me at the bank tomorrow."

"I wish you'd explain to her I never dreamed these people would come here. I'm just as sore as you are."

"I couldn't explain anything to her now."

Charlie got up. He took his coat and hat and started down the corridor. Then he opened the door of the dining room and said in a strange voice, "Good night, children."

Honoria rose and ran around the table to hug him.

"Good night, sweetheart," he said vaguely, and then trying to make his voice more tender, trying to conciliate something, "Good night, dear children."

V

Charlie went directly to the Ritz bar with the furious idea of finding Lorraine and Duncan, but they were not there, and he realized that in any case there was nothing he could do. He had not touched his drink at the Peters, and now he ordered a whisky-and-soda. Paul came over to say hello.

"It's a great change," he said sadly. "We do about half the business we did. So many fellows I hear about back in the States lost everything, maybe not in the first crash, but then in the second. Your friend George Hardt lost every cent, I hear. Are you back in the States?"

"No, I'm in business in Prague."

"I heard that you lost a lot in the crash."

"I did," and he added grimly, "but I lost everything I wanted in the boom."

"Selling short."

"Something like that."

Again the memory of those days swept over him like a nightmare—the people they had met traveling; then people who couldn't add a row of figures or speak a coherent sentence. The little man Helen had consented to dance with at the ship's party, who had insulted her ten feet from the table; the women and girls carried screaming with drink or drugs out of public places——

The men who locked their wives out in the snow, because the snow of twenty-nine wasn't real snow. If you didn't want it to be snow, you just paid some money.

He went to the phone and called the Peterses' apartment; Lincoln answered.

"I called up because this thing is on my mind. Has Marion said anything definite?"

"Marion's sick," Lincoln answered shortly. "I know this thing isn't al-together your fault, but I can't have her go to pieces about it. I'm afraid we'll have to let it slide for six months; I can't take the chance of working her up to this state again."

"I see."

"I'm sorry, Charlie."

He went back to his table. His whisky glass was empty, but he shook his head when Alix looked at it questioningly. There wasn't much he could do now except send Honoria some things; he would send her a lot of things to-morrow. He thought rather angrily that this was just money—he had given so many people money. . . .

"No, no more," he said to another waiter. "What do I owe you?"

He would come back some day; they couldn't make him pay forever. But he wanted his child, and nothing was much good now, beside that fact. He wasn't young any more, with a lot of nice thoughts and dreams to have by himself. He was absolutely sure Helen wouldn't have wanted him to be so alone.

Communist

RICHARD FORD

My mother once had a boyfriend named Glen Baxter. This was in 1961. We—my mother and I—were living in the little house my father had left her up the Sun River, near Victory, Montana, west of Great Falls. My mother was thirty-one at the time. I was sixteen. Glen Baxter was somewhere in the middle, between us, though I cannot be exact about it.

We were living then off the proceeds of my father's life insurance policies, with my mother doing some part-time waitressing work up in Great Falls and going to the bars in the evenings, which I know is where she met Glen Baxter. Sometimes he would come back with her and stay in her room at night, or she would call up from town and explain that she was staying with him in his little place on Lewis Street by the GN yards. She gave me his number every time, but I never called it. I think she probably thought that what she was doing was terrible, but simply couldn't help herself. I thought it was all right, though. Regular life it seemed and still does. She was young, and I knew that even then.

Glen Baxter was a Communist and liked hunting, which he talked about a lot. Pheasants. Ducks. Deer. He killed all of them, he said. He had been to Vietnam as far back as then, and when he was in our house he often talked about shooting the animals over there—monkeys and beautiful parrots—using military guns just for sport. We did not know what Vietnam was then, and Glen, when he talked about that, referred to it only as "the Far East." I think now he must've been in the CIA and been disillusioned by something he saw or found out about and had been thrown out, but that kind of thing did not matter to us. He was a tall, dark-eyed man with thick black hair, and was usually in a good humor. He had gone halfway through college in Peoria, Illinois, he said, where he grew up. But when he was around our life he worked wheat farms as a ditcher, and stayed out of work winters and in the bars drinking with women like my mother, who had work and some money. It is not an uncommon life to lead in Montana.

339

What I want to explain happened in November. We had not been seeing Glen Baxter for some time. Two months had gone by. My mother knew other men, but she came home most days from work and stayed inside watching television in her bedroom and drinking beers. I asked about Glen once, and she said only that she didn't know where he was, and I assumed they had had a fight and that he was gone off on a flyer back to Illinois or Massachusetts, where he said he had relatives. I'll admit that I liked him. He had something on his mind always. He was a labor man as well as a Communist, and liked to say that the country was poisoned by the rich, and strong men would need to bring it to life again, and I liked that because my father had been a labor man, which was why we had a house to live in and money coming through. It was also true that I'd had a few boxing bouts by then—just with town boys and one with an Indian from Choteau—and there were some girlfriends I knew from that. I did not like my mother being around the house so much at night, and I wished Glen Baxter would come back, or that another man would come along and entertain her somewhere else.

At two o'clock on a Saturday, Glen drove up into our yard in a car. He had had a big brown Harley-Davidson that he rode most of the year, in his black-and-red irrigators and a baseball cap turned backwards. But this time he had a car, a blue Nash Ambassador. My mother and I went out on the porch when he stopped inside the olive trees my father had planted as a shelter belt, and my mother had a look on her face of not much pleasure. It was starting to be cold in earnest by then. Snow was down already onto the Fairfield Bench, though on this day a chinook was blowing, and it could as easily have been spring, though the sky above the Divide was turning over in silver and blue clouds of winter.

"We haven't seen you in a long time, I guess," my mother said coldly.

"My little retarded sister died," Glen said, standing at the door of his old car. He was wearing his orange VFW jacket and canvas shoes we called wino shoes, something I had never seen him wear before. He seemed to be in a good humor. "We buried her in Florida near the home."

"That's a good place," my mother said in a voice that meant she was a wronged party in something.

"I want to take this boy hunting today, Aileen," Glen said. "There's snow geese down now. But we have to go right away or they'll be gone to Idaho by tomorrow."

"He doesn't care to go," my mother said.

"Yes I do," I said and looked at her.

My mother frowned at me. "Why do you?"

"Why does he need a reason?" Glen Baxter said and grinned.

"I want him to have one, that's why." She looked at me oddly. "I think Glen's drunk, Les."

"No, I'm not drinking," Glen said, which was hardly ever true. He looked

at both of us, and my mother bit down on the side of her lower lip and
stared at me in a way to make you think she thought something was being
put over on her and she didn't like you for it. She was pretty, though when
she was mad her features were sharpened and less pretty by a long way.
"All right then, I don't care," she said to no one in particular. "Hunt, kill,
maim. Your father did that too." She turned to go back inside.

"Why don't you come with us, Aileen?" Glen was smiling still, pleased.

"To do what?" my mother said. She stopped and pulled a package of cigarettes out of her dress pocket and put one in her mouth.

"It's worth seeing."

"See dead animals?" my mother said.

"These geese are from Sibera, Aileen," Glen said. "They're not like a lot
of geese. Maybe I'll buy us dinner later. What do you say?"

"Buy what with?" my mother said. To tell the truth, I didn't know why
she was so mad at him. I would've thought she'd be glad to see him. But she
just suddenly seemed to hate everything about him.

"I've got some money," Glen said. "Let me spend it on a pretty girl
tonight."

"Find one of those and you're lucky," my mother said, turning away toward the front door.

"I've already found one," Glen Baxter said. But the door slammed behind her, and he looked at me then with a look I think now was helplessness, though I could not see a way to change anything.

My mother sat in the back seat of Glen's Nash and looked out the window
while we drove. My double gun was in the seat between us beside Glen's
Belgian pump, which he kept loaded with five shells in case, he said, he saw
something beside the road he wanted to shoot. I had hunted rabbits before,
and had ground-sluiced pheasants and other birds, but I had never been
on an actual hunt before, one where you drove out to some special place
and did it formally. And I was excited. I had a feeling that something important was about to happen to me and that this would be a day I would always remember.

My mother did not say anything for a long time, and neither did I. We
drove up through Great Falls and out the other side toward Fort Benton,
which was on the benchland where wheat was grown.

"Geese mate for life," my mother said, just out of the blue, as we were
driving. "I hope you know that. They're special birds."

"I know that," Glen said in the front seat. "I have every respect for
them."

"So where were you for three months?" she said. "I'm only curious."

"I was in the Big Hole for a while," Glen said, "and after that I went over
to Douglas, Wyoming."

"What were you planning to do there?" my mother said.

"I wanted to find a job, but it didn't work out."

"I'm going to college," she said suddenly, and this was something I had never heard about before. I turned to look at her, but she was staring out her window and wouldn't see me.

"I knew French once," Glen said. "Rose's pink. Rouge's red." He glanced at me and smiled. "I think that's a wise idea, Aileen. When are you going to start?"

"I don't want Les to think he was raised by crazy people all his life," my mother said.

"Les ought to go himself," Glen said.

"After I go, he will."

"What do you say about that, Les?" Glen said, grinning.

"He says it's just fine," my mother said.

"It's just fine," I said.

Where Glen Baxter took us was out onto the high flat prairie that was disked for wheat and had high, high mountains out to the east, with lower heartbreak hills in between. It was, I remember, a day for blues in the sky, and down in the distance we could see the small town of Floweree and the state highway running past it toward Fort Benton and the high line. We drove out on top of the prairie on a muddy dirt road fenced on both sides, until we had gone about three miles, which is where Glen stopped.

"All right," he said, looking up in the rearview mirror at my mother. "You wouldn't think there was anything here, would you?"

"*We're* here," my mother said. "You brought us here."

"You'll be glad though," Glen said, and seemed confident to me. I had looked around myself but could not see anything. No water or trees, nothing that seemed like a good place to hunt anything. Just wasted land. "There's a big lake out there, Les," Glen said. "You can't see it now from here because it's low. But the geese are there. You'll see."

"It's like the moon out there, I recognize that," my mother said, "only it's worse." She was staring out at the flat, disked wheatland as if she could actually see something in particular and I wanted to know more about it. "How'd you find this place?"

"I came once on the wheat push," Glen said.

"And I'm sure the owner told you just to come back and hunt any time you like and bring anybody you wanted. Come one, come all. Is that it?"

"People shouldn't own land anyway," Glen said. "Anybody should be able to use it."

"Les, Glen's going to poach here," my mother said. "I just want you to know that, because that's a crime and the law will get you for it. If you're a man now, you're going to have to face the consequences."

"That's not true," Glen Baxter said, and looked gloomily out over the steering wheel down the muddy road toward the mountains. Though for myself I believed it was true, and didn't care. I didn't care about anything at that moment except seeing geese fly over me and shooting them down.

"Well, I'm certainly not going out there," my mother said. "I like towns better, and I already have enough trouble."

"That's okay," Glen said. "When the geese lift up you'll get to see them. That's all I wanted. Les and me'll go shoot them, won't we, Les?"

"Yes," I said, and I put my hand on my shotgun, which had been my father's and was heavy as rocks.

"Then we should go on," Glen said, "or we'll waste our light."

We got out of the car with our guns. Glen took off his canvas shoes and put on his pair of black irrigators out of the trunk. Then we crossed the barbed-wire fence and walked out into the high, tilled field toward nothing. I looked back at my mother when we were still not so far away, but I could only see the small, dark top of her head, low in the back seat of the Nash, staring out and thinking what I could not then begin to say.

On the walk toward the lake, Glen began talking to me. I had never been alone with him and knew little about him except what my mother said— that he drank too much, or other times that he was the nicest man she had ever known in the world and that someday a woman would marry him, though she didn't think it would be her. Glen told me as we walked that he wished he had finished college, but that it was too late now, that his mind was too old. He said he had liked "the Far East" very much, and that people there knew how to treat each other, and that he would go back someday but couldn't go now. He said also that he would like to live in Russia for a while and mentioned the names of people who had gone there, names I didn't know. He said it would be hard at first, because it was so different, but that pretty soon anyone would learn to like it and wouldn't want to live anywhere else, and that Russians treated Americans who came to live there like kings. There were Communists everywhere now, he said. You didn't know them, but they were there. Montana had a large number, and he was in touch with all of them. He said that Communists were always in danger and that he had to protect himself all the time. And when he said that he pulled back his VFW jacket and showed me the butt of a pistol he had stuck under his shirt against his bare skin. "There are people who want to kill me right now," he said, "and I would kill a man myself if I thought I had to." And we kept walking. Though in a while he said, "I don't think I know much about you, Les. But I'd like to. What do you like to do?"

"I like to box," I said. "My father did it. It's a good thing to know."

"I suppose you have to protect yourself too," Glen said.

"I know how to," I said.

"Do you like to watch TV?" Glen said, and smiled.

"Not much."

"I love to," Glen said. "I could watch it instead of eating if I had one."

I looked out straight ahead over the green tops of sage that grew at the edge of the disked field, hoping to see the lake Glen said was there. There was an airishness and a sweet smell that I thought might be the place we were going, but I couldn't see it. "How will we hunt these geese?" I said.

"It won't be hard," Glen said. "Most hunting isn't even hunting. It's only shooting. And that's what this will be. In Illinois you would dig holes in the ground to hide in and set out your decoys. Then the geese come to you, over and over again. But we don't have time for that here." He glanced at me. "You have to be sure the first time here."

"How do you know they're here now?" I asked. And I looked toward the Highwood Mountains twenty miles away, half in snow and half dark blue at the bottom. I could see the little town of Floweree then, looking shabby and dimly lighted in the distance. A red bar sign shone. A car moved slowly away from the scattered buildings.

"They always come November first," Glen said.

"Are we going to poach them?"

"Does it make any difference to you?" Glen asked.

"No, it doesn't."

"Well then we aren't," he said.

We walked then for a while without talking. I looked back once to see the Nash far and small in the flat distance. I couldn't see my mother, and I thought that she must've turned on the radio and gone to sleep, which she always did, letting it play all night in her bedroom. Behind the car the sun was nearing the rounded mountains southwest of us, and I knew that when the sun was gone it would be cold. I wished my mother had decided to come along with us, and I thought for a moment of how little I really knew her at all.

Glen walked with me another quarter mile, crossed another barbed-wire fence where sage was growing, then went a hundred yards through wheat-grass and spurge until the ground went up and formed a kind of long hill-ock bunker built by a farmer against the wind. And I realized the lake was just beyond us. I could hear the sound of a car horn blowing and a dog barking all the way down in the town, then the wind seemed to move and all I could hear then and after then were geese. So many geese, from the sound of them, though I still could not see even one. I stood and listened to the high-pitched shouting sound, a sound I had never heard so close, a sound with size to it—though it was not loud. A sound that meant great numbers and that made your chest rise and your shoulders tighten with ex-pectancy. It was a sound to make you feel separate from it and everything else, as if you were of no importance in the grand scheme of things.

"Do you hear them singing?" Glen asked. He held his hand up to make me stand still. And we both listened. "How many do you think, Les, just hearing?"

"A hundred," I said. "More than a hundred."

"Five thousand," Glen said. "More than you can believe when you see them. Go see."

I put down my gun and on my hands and knees crawled up the earthwork through the wheatgrass and thistle until I could see down to the lake and see the geese. And they were there, like a white bandage laid on the water, wide and long and continuous, a white expanse of snow geese, seventy yards from me, on the bank, but stretching onto the lake, which was large itself—a half mile across, with thick tules on the far side and wild plums farther and the blue mountain behind them.

"Do you see the big raft?" Glen said from below me, in a whisper.

"I see it," I said, still looking. It was such a thing to see, a view I had never seen and have not since.

"Are any on the land?" he said.

"Some are in the wheatgrass," I said, "but most are swimming."

"Good," Glen said. "They'll have to fly. But we can't wait for that now."

And I crawled backwards down the heel of land to where Glen was, and my gun. We were losing our light, and the air was purplish and cooling. I looked toward the car but couldn't see it, and I was no longer sure where it was below the lighted sky.

"Where do they fly to?" I said in a whisper, since I did not want anything to be ruined because of what I did or said. It was important to Glen to shoot the geese, and it was important to me.

"To the wheat," he said. "Or else they leave for good. I wish your mother had come, Les. Now she'll be sorry."

I could hear the geese quarreling and shouting on the lake surface. And I wondered if they knew we were here now. "She might be," I said with my heart pounding, but I didn't think she would be much.

It was a simple plan he had. I would stay behind the bunker, and he would crawl, on his belly with his gun through the wheatgrass as near to the geese as he could. Then he would simply stand up and shoot all the ones he could close up, both in the air and on the ground. And when all the others flew up, with luck some would turn toward me as they came into the wind, and then I could shoot them and turn them back to him, and he would shoot them again. He could kill ten, he said, if he was lucky, and I might kill four. It didn't seem hard.

"Don't show them your face," Glen said. "Wait till you think you can touch them, then stand up and shoot. To hesitate is lost in this."

"All right," I said. "I'll try it."

"Shoot one in the head, and then shoot another one," Glen said. "It won't be hard." He patted me on the arm and smiled. Then he took off his VFW jacket and put it on the ground, climbed up the side of the bunker, cradling his shotgun in his arms, and slid on his belly into the dry stalks of yellow grass out of my sight.

Then for the first time in that entire day I was alone. And I didn't mind it. I sat squat down in the grass, loaded my double gun, and took my other two shells out of my pocket to hold. I pushed the safety off and on to see that it was right. The wind rose a little then, scuffed the grass and made me shiver. It was not the warm chinook now, but a wind out of the north, the one geese flew away from if they could.

Then I thought about my mother in the car alone, and how much longer I would stay with her, and what it might mean to her for me to leave. And I wondered when Glen Baxter would die and if someone would kill him, or whether my mother would marry him and how I would feel about it. And though I didn't know why, it occurred to me then that Glen Baxter and I would not be friends when all was said and done, since I didn't care if he ever married my mother or didn't.

Then I thought about boxing and what my father had taught me about it. To tighten your fists hard. To strike out straight from the shoulder and never punch backing up. How to cut a punch by snapping your fist inwards, how to carry your chin low, and to step toward a man when he is falling so you can hit him again. And most important, to keep your eyes open when you are hitting in the face and causing damage, because you need to see what you're doing to encourage yourself, and because it is when you close your eyes that you stop hitting and get hurt badly. "Fly all over your man, Les," my father said. "When you see your chance, fly on him and hit him till he falls." That, I thought, would always be my attitude in things.

And then I heard the geese again, their voices in unison, louder and shouting, as if the wind had changed and put all new sounds in the cold air. And then a *boom.* And I knew Glen was in among them and had stood up to shoot. The noise of geese rose and grew worse, and my fingers burned where I held my gun too tight to the metal, and I put it down and opened my fist to make the burning stop so I could feel the trigger when the moment came. *Boom,* Glen shot again, and I heard him shuck a shell, and all the sounds out beyond the bunker seemed to be rising—the geese, the shots, the air itself going up. *Boom,* Glen shot another time, and I knew he was taking his careful time to make his shots good. And I held my gun and started to crawl up the bunker so as not to be surprised when the geese came over me and I could shoot.

From the top I saw Glen Baxter alone in the wheatgrass field, shooting at a white goose with black tips of wings that was on the ground not far from him, but trying to run and pull into the air. He shot it once more, and it fell over dead with its wings flapping.

Glen looked back at me and his face was distorted and strange. The air around him was full of white rising geese and he seemed to want them all. "Behind you, Les," he yelled at me and pointed. "They're all behind you now." I looked behind me, and there were geese in the air as far as I could see, more than I knew how many, moving so slowly, their wings wide out and working calmly and filling the air with noise, though their voices were not as loud or as shrill as I had thought they would be. And they were very close! Forty feet, some of them. The air around me vibrated and I could kill as many as the times I could shoot—a hundred or a thousand—and I raised my gun, put the muzzle on the head of a white goose and fired. It shuddered in the air, its wide feet sank below its belly, its wings cradled out to hold back air, and it fell straight down and landed with an awful sound, a noise a human would make, a thick, soft, *hump* noise. I looked up again and shot another goose, could hear the pellets hit its chest, but it didn't fall or even break its pattern for flying. *Boom,* Glen shot again. And then again. "Hey," I heard him shout. "Hey, hey." And there were geese flying over me, flying in line after line. I broke my gun and reloaded, and thought to myself as I did: I need confidence here, I need to be sure with this. I pointed at another goose and shot it in the head, and it fell the way the first one had, wings out, its belly down, and with the same thick noise of hitting. Then I sat down in the grass on the bunker and let geese fly over me.

By now the whole raft was in the air, all of it moving in a slow swirl above me and the lake and everywhere, finding the wind and heading out south in long wavering lines that caught the last sun and turned to silver as they gained a distance. It was a thing to see, I will tell you now. Five thousand white geese all in the air around you, making a noise like you have never heard before. And I thought to myself then: This is something I will never see again. I will never forget this. And I was right.

Glen Baxter shot twice more. One shot missed, but with the other he hit a goose flying away from him and knocked it half-falling and -flying into the empty lake not far from shore, where it began to swim as though it was fine and make its noise.

Glen stood in the stubbly grass, looking out at the goose, his gun lowered. "I didn't need to shoot that, did I, Les?"

"I don't know," I said, sitting on the little knoll of land, looking at the goose swimming in the water.

"I don't know why I shoot 'em. They're so beautiful." He looked at me.

"I don't know either," I said.

"Maybe there's nothing else to do with them." Glen stared at the goose again and shook his head. "Maybe this is exactly what they're put on earth for."

I did not know what to say because I did not know what he could mean by that, though what I felt was embarrassment at the great number of geese there were, and a dulled feeling like a hunger because the shooting had stopped and it was over for me now.

Glen began to pick up his geese, and I walked down to my two that had fallen close together and were dead. One had hit with such an impact that its stomach had split and some of its inward parts were knocked out. Though the other looked unhurt, its soft white belly turned up like a pillow, its head and jagged bill teeth and its tiny black eyes looking as if it were alive.

"What's happened to the hunters out here?" I heard a voice speak. It was my mother, standing in her pink dress on the knoll above us, hugging her arms. She was smiling though she was cold. And I realized that I had lost all thought of her in the shooting. "Who did this shooting? Is this your work, Les?"

"No," I said.

"Les is a hunter, though, Aileen," Glen said. "He takes his time." He was holding two white geese by their necks, one in each hand, and he was smiling. He and my mother seemed pleased.

"I see you didn't miss too many," my mother said and smiled. I could tell she admired Glen for his geese, and that she had done some thinking in the car alone. "It *was* wonderful, Glen," she said. "I've never seen anything like that. They were like snow."

"It's worth seeing once, isn't it?" Glen said. "I should've killed more, but I got excited."

My mother looked at me then. "Where's yours, Les?"

"Here," I said and pointed to my two geese on the ground beside me.

My mother nodded in a nice way, and I think she liked everything then and wanted the day to turn out right and for all of us to be happy. "Six, then. You've got six in all."

"One's still out there," I said and motioned where the one goose was swimming in circles on the water.

"Okay," my mother said and put her hand over her eyes to look. "Where is it?"

Glen Baxter looked at me then with a strange smile, a smile that said he wished I had never mentioned anything about the other goose. And I wished I hadn't either. I looked up in the sky and could see the lines of geese by the thousands shining silver in the light, and I wished we could just leave and go home.

"That one's my mistake there," Glen Baxter said and grinned. "I shouldn't have shot that one, Aileen. I got too excited."

My mother looked out on the lake for a minute, then looked at Glen and back again. "Poor goose." She shook her head. "How will you get it, Glen?"

"I can't get that one now," Glen said.

My mother looked at him. "What do you mean?" she said.

"I'm going to leave that one," Glen said.

"Well, no. You can't leave one," my mother said. "You shot it. You have to get it. Isn't that a rule?"

"No," Glen said.

And my mother looked from Glen to me. "Wade out and get it, Glen,"

she said, in a sweet way, and my mother looked young then for some reason, like a young girl, in her flimsy short-sleeved waitress dress, and her
skinny, bare legs in the wheatgrass.

"No," Glen Baxter looked down at his gun and shook his head. And I
didn't know why he wouldn't go, because it would've been easy. The lake
was shallow. And you could tell that anyone could've walked out a long way
before it got deep, and Glen had on his boots.

My mother looked at the white goose, which was not more than thirty
yards from the shore, its head up, moving in slow circles, its wings settled
and relaxed so you could see the black tips. "Wade out and get it, Glenny,
won't you please?" she said. "They're special things."

"You don't understand the world, Aileen," Glen said. "This can happen.
It doesn't matter."

"But that's so cruel, Glen," she said, and a sweet smile came on her lips.

"Raise up your own arms, Leeny," Glen said. "I can't see any angel's
wings, can you Les?" He looked at me, but I looked away.

"Then you go on and get it, Les," my mother said. "You weren't raised by
crazy people." I started to go, but Glen Baxter suddenly grabbed me by my
shoulder and pulled me back hard, so hard his fingers made bruises in my
skin that I saw later.

"Nobody's going," he said. "This is over with now."

And my mother gave Glen a cold look then. "You don't have a heart,
Glen," she said. "There's nothing to love in you. You're just a son of a bitch,
that's all."

And Glen Baxter nodded at my mother as if he understood something
that he had not understood before, but something that he was willing to
know. "Fine," he said, "that's fine." And he took his big pistol out from
against his belly, the big blue revolver I had only seen part of before and
that he said protected him, and he pointed it out at the goose on the water,
his arm straight away from him, and shot and missed. And then he shot
and missed again. The goose made its noise once. And then he hit it dead,
because there was no splash. And then he shot it three times more until the
gun was empty and the goose's head was down and it was floating toward
the middle of the lake where it was empty and dark blue. "Now who has a
heart?" Glen said. But my mother was not there when he turned around.
She had already started back to the car and was almost lost from sight in the
darkness. And Glen smiled at me then and his face had a wild look on it.
"Okay, Les?" he said.

"Okay," I said.

"There're limits to everything, right?"

"I guess so," I said.

"Your mother's a beautiful woman, but she's not the only beautiful
woman in Montana." I did not say anything. And Glen Baxter suddenly
said, "Here," and he held the pistol out at me. "Don't you want this? Don't

you want to shoot me? Nobody thinks they'll die. But I'm ready for it right now." And I did not know what to do then. Though it is true that what I wanted to do was to hit him, hit him as hard in the face as I could, and see him on the ground, bleeding and crying and pleading for me to stop. Only at that moment he looked scared to me, and I had never seen a grown man scared before—though I have seen one since—and I felt sorry for him, as though he were already a dead man. And I did not end up hitting him at all.

A light can go out in the heart. All of this went on years ago, but I still can feel now how sad and remote the world was to me. Glen Baxter, I think now, was not a bad man, only a man scared of something he'd never seen before—something soft in himself—his life going a way he didn't like. A woman with a son. Who could blame him there? I don't know what makes people do what they do or call themselves what they call themselves, only that you have to live someone's life to be the expert.

My mother had tried to see the good side of things, tried to be hopeful in the situation she was handed, tried to look out for us both, and it hadn't worked. It was a strange time in her life then and after that, a time when she had to adjust to being an adult just when she was on the thin edge of things. Too much awareness too early in life was her problem, I think.

And what I felt was only that I had somehow been pushed out into the world, into the real life then, the one I hadn't lived yet. In a year I was gone to hard-rock mining and no-paycheck jobs and not to college. And I have thought more than once about my mother's saying that I had not been raised by crazy people, and I don't know what that could mean or what difference it could make, unless it means that love is a reliable commodity, and even that is not always true, as I have found out.

Late on the night that all this took place I was in bed when I heard my mother say, "Come outside, Les. Come and hear this." And I went out onto the front porch barefoot and in my underwear, where it was warm like spring, and there was a spring mist in the air. I could see the lights of the Fairfield Coach in the distance on its way up to Great Falls.

And I could hear geese, white birds in the sky, flying. They made their high-pitched sound like angry yells, and though I couldn't see them high up, it seemed to me they were everywhere. And my mother looked up and said, "Hear them?" I could smell her hair wet from the shower. "They leave with the moon," she said. "It's still half wild out here."

And I said, "I hear them," and I felt a chill come over my bare chest, and the hair stood up on my arms the way it does before a storm. And for a while we listened.

"When I first married your father, you know, we lived on a street called Bluebird Canyon, in California. And I thought that was the prettiest street and the prettiest name. I suppose no one brings you up like your first love. You don't mind if I say that, do you?" She looked at me hopefully.

"No," I said.

"We have to keep civilization alive somehow." And she pulled her little housecoat together because there was a cold vein in the air, a part of the cold that would be on us the next day. "I don't feel part of things tonight, I guess."

"It's all right," I said.

"Do you know where I'd like to go?" she said.

"No," I said. And I suppose I knew she was angry then, angry with life, but did not want to show me that.

"To the Straits of Juan de Fuca. Wouldn't that be something? Would you like that?"

"I'd like it," I said. And my mother looked off for a minute, as if she could see the Straits of Juan de Fuca out against the line of mountains, see the lights of things alive and a whole new world.

"I know you liked him," she said after a moment. "You and I both suffer fools too well."

"I didn't like him too much," I said. "I didn't really care."

"He'll fall on his face, I'm sure of that," she said. And I didn't say anything because I didn't care about Glen Baxter anymore, and was happy not to talk about him. "Would you tell me something if I asked you? Would you tell me the truth?"

"Yes," I said.

And my mother did not look at me. "Just tell the truth," she said.

"All right," I said.

"Do you think I'm still very feminine? I'm thirty-two years old now. You don't know what that means. But do you think I am?"

And I stood at the edge of the porch, with the olive trees before me, looking straight up into the mist where I could not see geese but could still hear them flying, could almost feel the air move below their white wings. And I felt the way you feel when you are on a trestle all alone and the train is coming, and you know you have to decide. And I said, "Yes, I do." Because that was the truth. And I tried to think of something else then and did not hear what my mother said after that.

And how old was I then? Sixteen. Sixteen is young, but it can also be a grown man. I am forty-one years old now, and I think about that time, without regret, though my mother and I never talked in that way again, and I have not heard her voice now in a long, long time.

Just Like A Tree

ERNEST J. GAINES

I shall not;
I shall not be moved.
I shall not;
I shall not be moved.
Just like a tree that's
planted side the water.
Oh, I shall not be removed.

I made my home in glory;
I shall not be moved.
Made my home in glory;
I shall not be moved.
Just like a tree that's
planted side the water.
Oh, I shall not be removed.

(from an old Negro spiritual)

Chuckkie

Pa hit him on the back and he jeck in the chains like he pulling, but ever'body in the wagon know he ain't, and Pa hit him on the back again. He jeck again like he pulling, but even Big Red know he ain't doing a thing.

"That's why I'm go'n get a horse," Pa say. "He'll kill that other mule. Get up there, Mr. Bascom."

"Oh, let him alone," Grandmon say. "How would you like it if you was pulling a wagon in all that mud?"

Pa don't answer Grandmon; he just hit Mr. Bascom on the back again.

352

"That's right, kill him," Grandmon say. "See where you get mo money to buy another one."

"Get up there, Mr. Bascom," Pa say.

"You hear me talking to you, Emile?" Grandmon say. "You want me to hit you with something?"

"Ma, he ain't pulling," Pa say.

"Leave him alone," Grandmon say.

Pa shake the lines little bit, but Mr. Bascom don't even feel it, and you can see he letting Big Red do all the pulling again. Pa say something kind o' low to hisself, and I can't make out what it is.

I low' my head little bit, 'cause that wind and fine rain was hitting me in the face, and I can feel Mama pressing close to me to keep me warm. She sitting on one side o' me and Pa sitting on the other side o' me, and Grandmon in the back o' me in her setting chair. Pa didn't want to bring the setting chair, telling Grandmon there was two boards in that wagon already and she could sit on one of 'em all by herself if she wanted to, but Grandmon say she was taking her setting chair with her if Pa liked it or not. She say she didn't ride in no wagon on nobody board, and if Pa liked it or not that setting chair was going.

"Let her take her setting chair," Mama say. "What's wrong with taking her setting chair."

"Ehhh, Lord," Pa say, and picked up the setting chair and took it out to the wagon. "I guess I'll have to bring it back in the house, too, when we come back from there."

Grandmon went and clambed in the wagon and moved her setting chair back little bit and sat down and folded her arms, waiting for us to get in, too. I got in and knelt down side her, but Mama told me to come up there and sit on the board side her and Pa so I could stay warm. Soon's I sat down, Pa hit Mr. Bascom on the back, saying what a trifling thing Mr. Bascom was, and soon 's he got some mo' money he was getting rid o' him and getting him a horse.

I raise my head to look see how far we is.

"That's it, yonder," I say.

"Stop pointing," Mama say, "and keep your hand in your pocket."

"Where?" Grandmon say, back there in her setting chair.

"Cross the ditch, yonder," I say.

"Can't see a thing for this rain," Grandmon say.

"Can't hardly see it," I say. "But you can see the light little bit. That chinaball tree standing in the way."

"Poor soul," Grandmon say. "Poor soul."

I know Grandmon was go'n say poor soul, poor soul, 'cause she had been saying poor soul, poor soul ever since she heard Aunt Fe was go'n leave from back there.

Emile

Darn cane crop to finish getting in and only a mule and a half to do it. If I had my way I'd take that shotgun and a load o' buckshots and—but what's the use.

"Get up, Mr. Bascom—please," I say to that little dried-up, long-eared, tobacco-color thing. "Please, come up. Do your share for God sake—if you don't mind. I know it's hard pulling in all that mud, but if you don't do your share, then Big Red'll have to do his and yours, too. Please—"

"Oh, Emile, shut up," Leola say.

"I can't hit him," I say, "or Mama back there'll hit me. So I'll talk to him. Please, Mr. Bascom, if you don't mind it. For my sake. No, not for mine; for God sake. No, not even for His'n; for Big Red sake. A fellow mule just like yourself is. Please, come up."

"Now, you hear that boy blaspheming God in front o' me there," Mama say. "Ehhh, Lord. Keep it up. All this bad weather there like this whole world coming apart—a clap o' thunder come there and knock the fool out you. Just keep it up."

Maybe she right, and I stop. I look at Mr. Bascom there doing nothing, and I just give up. That mule know long 's Ma's alive he go'n do just what he want to do. He know when Pa was dying he told Ma to look after him, and he know no matter what he do, no matter what he don't do, Ma ain't go'n never let me do him anything. Sometimes I even feel Ma care mo' for Mr. Bascom 'an she care for me her own son.

We come up to the gate and I pull back on the lines.

"Whoa up, Big Red," I say. "You don't have to stop, Mr. Bascom. You never started."

I can feel Ma looking at me back there in that setting chair, but she don't say nothing.

"Here," I say to Chuckkie.

He take the lines and I jump down on the ground to open the old beat-up gate. I see Etienne's horse in the yard, and I see Cris new red tractor side the house, shining in the rain. When Ma die, I say to myself, Mr. Bascom you going. Ever'body getting tractors and horses and I'm still stuck with you. You going, brother.

"Can you make it through?" I ask Chuckkie. "That gate ain't too wide."

"I can do it," he say.

"Be sure to make Mr. Bascom pull," I say.

"Emile, you better get back up here and drive 'em through," Leola say. "Chuckkie might break up that wagon."

"No, let him stay down there and give orders," Mama say, back there in that setting chair.

"He can do it," I say. "Come on, Chuckkie Boy."

"Come up, here, mule," Chuckkie say.

And soon 's he say that, Big Red make a lunge for the yard, and Mr. Bas-com don't even move, and 'fore I can bat my eyes I hear "pow-wow; sagg-sagg; pow-wow." But above all the other noise, Leola up there screaming her head off. And Mama—not a word; just sitting there looking at me with her arms still folded.

"Pull Big Red," I say. "Pull Big Red, Chuckkie."

Poor little Chuckkie up there pulling so hard till one of his little arms straight out in back; and Big Red throwing his shoulders and ever'thing else in it, and Mr. Bascom just walking there just 's loose and free like he's suppose to be there just for his good looks. I move out the way just in time to let the wagon go by me, pulling half o' the fence in the yard behind it. I glance up again, and there's Leola still hollering and trying to jump out, but Mama not saying a word—just sitting there in the setting chair with her arms still folded.

"Whoa," I hear little Chuckkie saying. "Whoa up, now."

Somebody open the door and a bunch of people come out on the gallery.

"What the world—?" Etienne say. "Thought the whole place was coming to pieces there."

"Chuckkie had a little trouble coming in the yard," I say.

"Goodness," Etienne say. "Anybody hurt?"

Mama just sit there 'bout ten seconds, then she say something to herself and start clambing out the wagon.

"Let me help you there, Aunt Lou," Etienne say, coming down the steps.

"I can make it," Mama say. When she get on the ground she look at Chuckkie. "Hand me my chair there, boy."

Poor little Chuckkie up there with the lines in one hand, get the chair and hold it to the side, and Etienne catch it just 'fore it fall. Mama start looking at me again, and it look like for at least a hour she stand there look-ing at nobody but me. Then she say, "Ehhh, Lord," like that again, and go inside with Leola and the rest o' the people.

I look back at half o' the fence laying there in the yard, and I jump back on the wagon and guide the mules to the side o' the house. After unhitch-ing 'em and tying 'em to the wheels, I look at Cris pretty red tractor again, and me and Chuckkie go inside. I make sure he kick all the mud off his shoes 'fore he go in the house.

Leola

Sitting over there by the firehalf, trying to look joyful when ever'body there know she ain't. But she trying, you know; smiling and bowing when people say something to her. How can she be joyful, I ask myself; how can she be? Poor thing, she been here all her life—of the most of it, let's say. 'Fore they moved in this house, they lived in one back in the woods 'bout a mile from here. But for the past twenty-five or thirty years, she been right in this one house. I know ever since I been big enough to know people I been seeing her right here.

Aunt Fe, Aunt Fe, Aunt Fe, Aunt Fe: the name's been 'mongst us just like us own family name. Just like the name o' God. Like the name of town— the city. Aunt Fe, Aunt Fe, Aunt Fe, Aunt Fe.

Poor old thing; how many times I done come here and washed her clothes for her when she couldn't do it herself. How many times I done hoed in that garden, ironed her clothes, wrung a chicken neck for her. You count the days in the year and you'll be pretty close. And I didn't mind it a bit. No, I didn't mind it a bit. She there trying to pay me. Proud—Lord, talking 'bout pride. "Here." "No, Aunt Fe; no." "Here; here." "No, Aunt Fe. No. No. What would Mama think if she knowed I took money from you? Aunt Fe, Mama would never forgive me. No. I love doing these things for you. I just wish I could do more." "You so sweet," she would say.

And there, trying to make 'tend she don't mind leaving. Ehhh, Lord.

I hear a bunch o' rattling 'round in the kitchen and I go back there. I see Louise stirring this big pot o' eggnog.

"Louise," I say.

"Leola," she say.

We look at each other and she stir the eggnog again. She know what I'm go'n say next, and she can't even look in my face.

"Louise, I wish there was some other way."

"There's no other way," she say.

"Louise, moving her from here's like moving a tree you been used to in your front yard all your life."

"What else can I do?"

"Oh, Louise, Louise."

"Nothing else, but that."

"Louise, what people go'n do without her here?"

She stir the eggnog and don't answer.

"Louise, us'll take her in with us."

"You all no kin to Auntie. She go with me."

"And us'll never see her again."

She stir the eggnog. Her husband come back in the kitchen and kiss her on the back o' the neck and then look at me and grin. Right from the start I can see I ain't go'n like that nigger.

"Almost ready, Honey?" he say.

"Almost."

He go to the safe and get one o' them bottles of whiskey he got in there and come back to the stove.

"No," Louise say. "Everybody don't like whiskey in it. Add the whiskey after you've poured it up."

"Okay, Hon."

He kiss her on the back o' the neck again. Still don't like the nigger.

Something 'bout him ain't right.

"You one o' the family?" he say.

"Same as one o' the family," I say. "And you?"

He don't like the way I say it, and I don't care if he like it or not. He look at me there a second, and then he kiss her on the ear.

"Un-unnn," she say, stirring the pot.

"I love your ear, Baby," he say.

"Go in the front room and talk with the people," she say.

He kiss her on the other ear. A nigger do all that front o' public got something to hide. He leave the kitchen. I look at Louise.

"Ain't nothing else I can do," she say.

"You sure? You positive?"

"I'm sure. I'm positive," she say.

The front door open and Emile and Chuckkie come in. A minute later Washington and Adrieu come in, too. Adrieu come back in the kitchen there, and I can see she been crying. Aunt Fe is her Godmother, you know.

"How you feel, Adrieu?"

"That weather out there," she say.

"Y'all walked?"

"Yes."

"Us here in the wagon. Y'all can go back with us."

"Y'all the one tore the fence down?" she ask.

"Yes, I guess so. That brother-in-law o' yours in there letting Chuckkie drive that wagon."

"Well, I don't guess it'll matter too much. Nobody go'n be here, anyhow."

And she start crying again. I take her in my arms and pat her on the shoulder, and I look at Louise stirring the eggnog.

"What I'm go'n do and my nan-nane gone? I love her so much."

"Ever'body love her."

"Since my mama died, she been like my mama."

"Shh," I say. "Don't let her hear you. Make her grieve. You don't want her to grieve, now, do you?"

She sniffs there 'gainst my dress few times.

"Oh, Lord," she say. "Lord, have mercy."

"Shhh," I say. "Shh. That's what life's 'bout."

"That ain't what life's 'bout," she say. "It ain't fair. This been her home all her life. These the people she know. She don't know them people she going to. It ain't fair."

"Shhh, Adrieu," I say. "Now, you saying things that ain't your business."

She cry there some mo'.

"Oh, Lord, Lord," she say.

Louise turn from the stove.

" 'Bout ready now," she say, going to the middle door. "James, tell every-body to come back and get some."

James

Let me go on back here and show these country niggers how to have a good time. All they know is talk, talk, talk. Talk so much they make me buggy 'roung here. Damn this weather—wind, rain. Must be a million cracks in this old house.

I go to that old beat-up safe in that corner and get that fifth of Mr. Harper (in the South now; got to say Mister), give the seal one swipe, the stopper one jerk, and head back to that old wood stove. (Man, like, these cats are primitive—goodness. You know what I mean? I mean like wood stoves. Don't mention TV, man, these cats here never heard of that.) I start to dump Mr. Harper in the pot and Baby catches my hand again and say not all of them like it. You ever heard of anything like that? I mean a stud's going to drink eggnog, and he's not going to put whiskey in it. I mean he's going to drink it straight. I mean, you ever heard anything like that? Well, I wasn't pressing none of them on Mr. Harper. I mean me and Mr. Harper get along too well together for me to go around there pressing.

I hold my cup there and let Baby put a few drops of this egg stuff in it, then I jerk my cup back and let Mr. Harper run. Couple of these cats come over (some of them aren't too lame) and set their cups, and I let Mr. Harper run again. Then this cat says he's got 'nough. I let Mr. Harper run for this other stud, and pretty soon he says, "Hold it. Good." Country cat, you know. "Hold it. Good." Real country cat. So I raise the cup to see what Mr. Harper's doing. He's just right. I raise the cup again. Just right, Mr. Harper, just right.

I go to the door with Mr. Harper under my arm and the cup in my hand and I look into the front room where they all are. I mean there's about ninety-nine of them in there. Old ones, young ones, little one, big ones, yellow ones, black ones, brown ones—you name them, brother, and they were there. And what for? Brother, I'll tell you what for. Just because me and Baby was taking this old chick out of these sticks. You ever seen anything like it before? There they are looking sad just because me and Baby was taking this one old chick out of these sticks. Well, I'll tell you where I'd be at this moment if I was one of them. With that weather out there like it is, I'd be under about five blankets with some little warm belly pressing against mine. Brother, you can bet your hat I wouldn't be here. Man, listen to that thing out there. You can hear that rain beating on that old house like grains of rice; and that wind coming through them cracks like it does in those Charlie Chaplin movies. Man, like you know—like whooo-ee; whooo-ee. Man, you talking about some weird cats.

I can feel Mr. Harper starting to massage my wig and I bat my eyes twice and look at the old girl over there. She's still sitting in that funny-looking little old rocking chair, and not saying a word to anybody. Just sitting there looking in the fireplace at them two pieces of wood that isn't giving out enough heat to warm a baby, let alone ninety-nine grown people. I mean, you know, like that sleet's falling out there like all get-up-and-go, and them two pieces of wood are lying there just as dead as the rest of these way-out cats.

One of the old cats—I don't know which one he is—Mose, Sam, or something like that—leans over and pokes in the fire a minute, then a little blaze shoots up, and he raises up, too, looking as satisfied as if he'd just sent a rocket into orbit. I mean these cats are like that. They do these little bitty things, and they feel like they've really done something. Well, back in these sticks, I guess there just isn't nothing big to do.

I feel Mr. Harper touching my skull now—and I notice this little chick passing by me with these two cups of eggnog. She goes over to the fireplace and gives one to each of these old chicks. The one sitting in that setting chair she brought with her from God knows where, and the other cup to the old chick that me and Baby are going to haul from here sometime tomorrow morning. Wait, man, I mean like, you ever heard of anybody going to somebody else house with a chair? I mean, wouldn't you call that an insult at the basest point? I mean, now, like tell me what you think of that? I mean, here I am at my pad, and here you come bringing your own stool. I mean, now, like man, you know. I mean that's an insult at the basest point. I mean, you know . . . you know, like way out . . . .

Mr. Harper, what you doing, boy?—I mean Sir. (Got to watch myself, I'm in the South. Got to keep watching myself.)

This stud touches me on the shoulder and raise his cup and say, "How 'bout a taste?" I know what the stud's talking about, so I let Mr. Harper run for him. But soon 's I let a drop get in, the stud say, " 'Nough," I mean I let about two drops get in, and the stud's got enough. Man, I mean, like you know. I mean these studs are way out. I mean like way back there.

This stud takes a swig of his eggnog and say, "Ahhh." I mean this real down home way of saying "Ahhhh." I mean, man, like, these studs—I notice this little chick passing by me again, and this time she's crying. I mean weeping, you know. And just because this old ninety-nine-year-old chick's packing up and leaving. I mean, you ever heard of anything like that? I mean, here she is as pretty as the day is long and crying because me and Baby are hauling this old chick away. Well, I'd like to make her cry. And I can assure you, brother, it wouldn't be from leaving her.

I turn and look at Baby over there by the stove, pouring eggnog in all these cups. I mean, there're about about twenty of these cats lined up there. And I bet you not half of them will take Mr. Harper along. Some way-out cats, man. Some way-out cats.

I go up to Baby and buss her on the back of the neck and give her a little pat where she likes for me to pat her when we're in the bed. She say, "Uh-uh," but I know she likes it anyhow.

Ben O

I back under the bed and touch the slop jar, and I pull back my leg and back somewhere else, and then I get me a good sight on it. I spin my aggie couple times and sight again and then I shoot. I hit it right squarely in the center and it go flying over the firehalf. I crawl over there to get it and I see 'em all over there drinking they eggnog and they didn't even offer me and Chuckkie none. I find my marble on the bricks, and I go back and tell Chuckkie they over there drinking eggnog.

"You want some?" I say.

"I want shoot marble," Chuckkie say. "Yo' shot."

"I want some eggnog," I say.

"Shoot up, Ben O," he say. "I'm getting cold staying in one place so long. You feel that draft?"

"Coming from that crack under that bed," I say.

"Where?" Chuckkie say, looking for the crack.

"Over by that bed post over there," I say.

"This sure 's a beat-up old house," Chuckkie say.

"I want me some eggnog," I say.

"Well, you ain't getting none," Grandmon say, from the firehalf. "It ain't good for you."

"I can drink eggnog," I say. "How come it ain't good for me? It ain't nothing but eggs and milk. I eat chicken, don't I? I eat beef, don't I?"

Grandmon don't say nothing.

"I want me some eggnog," I say.

Grandmon still don't say no more. Nobody else don't say nothing, neither.

"I want me some eggnog," I say.

"You go'n get a eggnog," Grandmon say. "Just keep that noise up."

"I want me some eggnog," I say; "and I 'tend to get me some eggnog tonight."

Next thing I know, Grandmon done picked up a chip out o' that corner and done sailed it back there where me and Chuckkie is. I duck just in time, and the chip catch old Chuckkie side the head.

"Hey, who that hitting me?" Chuckkie say.

"Move, and you won't get hit," Grandmon say.

I laugh at old Chuckkie over there holding his head, and next thing I know here's Chuckkie done haul back there and hit me in my side. I jump up from there and give him two just to show him how it feel, and he jump up and hit me again. Then we grab each other and start tussling on the floor.

"You, Ben O," I head Grandmon saying. "You, Ben O, cut that out. Y'all cut that out."

But we don't stop, 'cause neither one o' us want be first. Then I feel somebody pulling us apart.

"What I ought to do is whip both o' you," Mrs. Leola say. "Is that what y'all want?"

"No'm," I say.

"Then shake hand."

Me and Chuckkie shake hand.

"Kiss," Mrs. Leola say.

"No'm," I say. "I ain't kissing no boy."

"Kiss him, Chuckkie," she say.

Old Chuckkie kiss me on the jaw.

"Now, kiss him, Ben O."

"I ain't kissing no Chuckkie," I say. "No'm. Uh-uh."

And the next thing I know, Mama done tipped up back o' me and done whop me on the leg with Daddy belt.

"Now, kiss him," she say.

Chuckkie turn his jaw to me and I kiss him. I almost want wipe my mouth. Kissing a boy.

"Now, come back here and get you some eggnog," Mama say.

"That's right, spoil 'em," Grandmon say. "Next thing you know they be drinking from bottles."

"Little eggnog won't hurt 'em, Mama," Mama say.

"That's right," Grandmon say. "Never listen. It's you go'n suffer for it. I be dead and gone, me."

Aunt Clo

Be just like wrapping a chain round a tree and jecking and jecking, and then shifting the chain little bit and jecking and jecking some in that direction, and then shifting it some mo' and jecking and jecking in that direction. Jecking and jecking till you get it loose, and then pulling with all your might. Still it might not be loose enough and you have to back the tractor up some and fix the chain round the tree again and start jecking all over. Jeck, jeck, jeck. Then you hear the roots crying, and then you keep on jecking, and then it give, and you jeck some mo', and then it falls. And not till then that you see what you done done. Not till then you see the big hole in the ground and piece of the taproot still way down in it—a piece you won't never get out no matter if you dig till doomsday. Yeah, you got the tree— least got it down on the ground, but did you get the taproot? No. No, sir, you didn't get the taproot. You stand there and look down in this hole at it and you grab yo' axe and jump down in it and start chopping at the taproot, but do you get the taproot? No. You don't get the taproot, sir. You never get the taproot. But, sir, I tell you what you do get. You get a big hole in the ground, sir, and you get another big hole in the air where the lovely branches been all these years. Yes, sir, that's what you get. The holes, sir, the holes. Two holes, sir, you can't never fill no matter how you try.

So you wrap yo' chain round yo' tree again, sir, and you start dragging it. But the dragging ain't so easy, sir, 'cause she's a heavy old tree—been there a long time, you know—heavy. And you make yo' tractor strain, sir, and the elements work 'gainst you, too, sir, 'cause the elements, they on her side, too, 'cause she part o' the elements, and the elements, they part o' her. So the elements, they do they little share to discourage you—yes, sir, they does. But you will not let the elements stop you. No, sir, you show the elements that they just elements, and man is stronger than elements, and you jeck and jeck on the chain, and soon she start to moving with you, sir, but if you looked over yo' shoulder one second you see her leaving a trail—a trail, sir, that can be seen from miles and miles away. You see her trying to hook her little fine branches in different little cracks, in between pickets, round hills o' grass, round anything they might brush 'gainst. But you is a determined man, sir, and you jeck and you jeck, and she keep on grabbing and trying to hold, but you stronger, sir—course you the strongest—and you finally get her out on the pave road. But what you don't notice, sir, is just 'fore she get on the pave road she leave couple her little branches to remind the people that it ain't her that want leave, but you, sir, that think she ought to. So you just drag her and drag her, sir, and the folks that live in the houses side the pave road, they come out on they gallery and look at her go by, and then they go back in they house and sit by the fire and forget her. So you just go on, sir, and you just go and you go, and for how many days? I don't know. I don't have the least idea. The North to me, sir, is like the elements. It mystify me. But never mind, you finally get there, and then you try to find a place to set her. You look in this corner and you look in that corner, but no corner is good. She kinda stand in the way no matter where you set her. So finally, sir, you say, I just stand her up here a little while and see, and if it don't work out, if she keep getting in the way, I guess we'll just have to take her to the dump.

Chris

Just like him, though, standing up there telling them lies when ever'body else feeling sad. I don't know what you do 'thout people like him. And, yet, you see him there, he sad just like the rest. But he just got to be funny. Crying in the inside, but still got to be funny.

He didn't steal it though. Didn't steal it a bit. His grandpa was just like him. Mat? Mat Jefferson? Just like that. Mat could make you die laughing. 'Member once at a wake. Pa Bully wake. Pa Bully laying up in the coffin dead as a door nail. Ever'body sad and drooping 'round the place. Mat look at that and start his lying. Soon half o' the place laughing. Funniest wake I ever went to, and yet—

Just like now. Look at 'em. Look at 'em laughing. Ten minutes ago you would 'a' thought you was at a funeral. But look at 'em now. Look at her there in that little old chair. How long she had it? Fifty years—a hundred? It ain't a chair no mo'. It's little bit o' her. Just like her arm, just like her leg.

You know I couldn't believe it. I couldn't. Emile passed the house there the other day, right after the bombing, and I was in my yard digging a water drain to let the water out in the road. Emile, he stopped the wagon there 'fore the door. Little Chuckkie, he in there with him with that little rain cap buckled up over his head. I go out to the gate and I say, "Emile, it's the truth?"

"The truth," he say. And just like that he say it. "The truth."

I look at him there, and he looking up the road to keep from looking at me. You know they been pretty close to Aunt Fe ever since they been children. His own mama and Aunt Fe, they been like sisters there together.

Me and him, we talk there little while 'bout the cane cutting, then he say he got to get on to the back. He shake them lines and drive on.

Inside me, my heart feel like it done swole up ten times the size it ought to be. Water come in my eyes, and I got to 'mit I cried right there. Yes, sir, I cried right there by my gate.

Louise come in the room and whisper something to Leola, and they go back in the kitchen. I can hear 'em moving things 'round back there, still getting things together they go'n be taking. If offer me anything, I'd like that big iron pot out there in the yard. Good for boiling water when you killing hog, you know.

You can feel the sadness in the room again. Louise brought it in when she come in and whispered to Leola. Only she didn't take it out when her and Leola left. Ever' pan they move, ever' pot they unhook keep telling you she leaving, she leaving.

Etienne turn over one o' them logs to make the fire pick up some and I see that boy, Lionel, spreading out his hand over the fire. Watch out, I think to myself, here come another lie. People, he just getting started.

Anne-Marie Duvall

"You're not going?"

"I'm not going," he says, turning over the log with the poker. "And if you were in your right mind, you wouldn't go either."

"You just don't understand."

"Oh, I understand. She cooked for your pa. She nursed you when your mama died."

"And I'm trying to pay her back with a seventy-nine cents scarf. Is that too much?"

He is silent, leaning against the mantel, looking down at the fire. The fire throws strange shadows across the big old room. Father looks down at me from against the wall. His eyes do not say go nor stay. But I know what he would do.

"Please go with me, Edward."

"You're wasting your breath."

I look at him a long time, then I get the small package from the coffee table.

"You're still going?"

"I am going."

"Don't call for me if you get bogged down anywhere back there."

I look at him and go out to the garage. The sky is black. The clouds are moving fast and low. A fine drizzle is falling, and the wind coming from the swamps blows in my face. I cannot recall a worse night in all my life.

I hurry into the car and drive out of the yard. The house stands big and black in back of me. Am I angry with Edward? No, I'm not angry with Edward. He's right. I should not go out into this kind of weather. But what he does not understand is I must. Father definitely would have gone if he was alive. Grandfather definitely would have gone also. And therefore, I must. Why? I cannot answer why. Only I must go.

As soon as I turn down that old muddy road I begin to pray. Don't let me go into that ditch, I pray. Don't let me go into that ditch. Please don't let me go into that ditch.

The lights play on the big old trees along the road. Here and there the lights hit a sagging picket fence. But I know I haven't even started yet. She lives far back into the fields. Why? God, why does she have to live so far back? Why couldn't she have lived closer to the front? But the answer to that is as hard for me as is the answer to everything else. It was ordained before I—before father—was born—that she should live back there. So why should I try to understand it now?

The car slides towards the ditch, and I stop it dead and turn the wheel, and then come back into the road again. Thanks, father. I know you're with me. Because it was you who said that I must look after her, didn't you? No, you did not say it directly, father. You said it only with a glance. As grandfather must have said it to you, and as his father must have said it to him.

But now that she's gone, father, now what? I know. I know. Aunt Lou and Aunt Clo.

The lights shine on the dead, wet grass along the road. There's an old pecan tree, looking dead and all alone. I wish I was a little nigger gal so I could pick pecans and eat them under the big old dead tree.

The car hits a rut, but bounces right out of it. I am frightened for a moment, but then I feel better. The windshield wipers are working well, slapping the water away as fast as it hits the glass. If I make the next half mile all right, the rest of the way will be good. It's not much over a mile now.

That was too bad about that bombing—killing that woman and her two children. That poor woman; poor children. What is the answer? What will happen? What do they want? Do they know what they want? Do they really know what they want? Are they positively sure? Have they any idea? Money to buy a car, is that it? If that is all, I pity them. Oh, how I pity them.

Not much farther. Just around that bend and—there's a water hole. Now what?

I stop the car and just look out at the water a minute, then I get out to see how deep it is. The cold wind shoots through my body like needles. Lightning comes from towards the swamps and lights up the place. For a split second the night is as bright as the day. The next second it is blacker than it has ever been.

I look at the water, and I can see that it's too deep for the car. I must turn back or I must walk the rest of the way. I stand there a while wondering what to do. Is it worth it all? Can't I simply send the gift by someone tomorrow morning? But will there be someone tomorrow morning? Suppose she leaves without getting it, then what? What then? Father would never forgive me. Neither would grandfather or great-grandfather either. No, they wouldn't—

The lightning flashes again and I look across the field, and I can see the tree in the yard a quarter of a mile away. I have only one choice. I must walk. I get the package out of the car and stuff it in my coat and start out.

I don't make any progress at first, but then I become a little warmer and I find I like walking. The lightning flashes just in time to show up a puddle of water, and I go around it. But there's no light to show up the second puddle, and I fall flat on my face. For a moment I'm completely blind, then I get slowly to my feet and check the package. It's dry, not harmed. I wash the mud off my raincoat, wash my hands, and start out again.

The house appears in front of me, and as I come into the yard, I can hear the people laughing and talking. Sometimes I think niggers can laugh and joke even if they see somebody beaten to death. I go up on the porch and knock and an old one opens the door for me. I swear, when he sees me he looks as if he's seen a ghost. His mouth drops open, his eyes bulge—I swear.

I go into the old crowded and smelly room, and every one of them looks at me the same way the first one did. All the joking and laughing has stopped. You would think I was the devil in person.

"Done, Lord," I hear her saying over by the fireplace. They move to the side and I can see her sitting in that little rocking chair I bet you she's had

since the beginning of time. "Done, Master," she says. "Child, what you doing in weather like this? Y'all move; let her get to that fire. Y'all move.
Move, now. Let her warm herself."

They start scattering everywhere.

"I'm not cold, Aunt Fe," I say. "I just brought you something—something small—because you're leaving us. I'm going right back."

"Done, Master," she says. Fussing over me just like she's done all her life.
"Done, Master, child, you ain't got no business in a place like this. Get close
to this fire. Get here. Done, Master."

I move closer, and the fire does feel warm and good.

"Done, Lord," she says.

I take out the package and pass it to her. The other niggers gather
around with all kinds of smiles on their faces. Just think of it—a white lady
coming through all of this for one old darky.

She starts to unwrap the package, her bony little fingers working slowly
and deliberately. When she sees the scarf—the seventy-nine cents scarf—
she brings it to her mouth and kisses it.

"Y'all look," she says. "Y'all look. Ain't it the prettiest little scarf y'all ever
did see? Y'all look."

They move around her and look at the scarf. Some of them touch it.

"I go'n put it on right now," she says. "I go'n put it on right now."

She unfolds it and ties it round her head and looks up at everybody and
smiles.

"Thank you, ma'am," she says. "Thank you, ma'am, from the bottom of
my heart."

"Oh, Aunt Fe," I say, kneeling down beside her. "Oh, Aunt Fe."

But I think about the other niggers there looking down at me, and I get
up. But I look into that face again, and I must go back down again. And I
lay my head in that bony old lap, and I cry and I cry, and I don't know how
long. And I feel those old fingers, like death itself, passing over my hair
and my neck. I don't know how long I kneel there crying, and when I stop,
I get out of there as fast as I can.

Etienne

The boy come in, and soon right off they get quiet, blaming the boy. If people could look little farther than the tip of they nose—No, they blame the
boy. Not that they ain't behind the boy what he doing, but they blame him
for what she must do. What they don't know is that the boy didn't start it,
and the people that bombed the house didn't start it, neither. It started a
million years ago. It started when one man envied another man for having
a penny mo' 'an he had, and then the man married a woman to help him
work the field so he could get much 's the other man, but when the other

man saw the man had married a woman to get much 's him, he, himself, he married a woman, too, so he could still have mo'. Then they start having children—not from love; but so the children could help 'em work so they can have mo'. But even with the children one man still had a penny mo' 'an the other, so the other man went and bought him a ox, and the other man did the same—to keep ahead of the other man. And soon the other man had bought him a slave to work the ox so he could get ahead of the other man. But the other man went out and bought him two slaves so he could stay ahead of the other man, and the other man went out and bought him three slaves. And soon they had a thousand slaves apiece, but they still wasn't satisfied. And one day the slaves all rose and kill the masters, but the masters had organized theyself a good police force, and the police force, they come out and kill the two thousand slaves.

So it's not this boy you see standing here 'fore you, 'cause it happened a million years ago. And this boy here 's just doing something the slaves done a million years ago. Just that this boy here ain't doing it they way. 'Stead of raising arms 'gainst the masters, he bow his head.

No, I say; don't blame the boy 'cause she must go. 'Cause when she's dead, and that won't be long after they get her up there, this boy's work will still be going on. She's not the only one that's go'n die from this boy's work. Many mo' of 'em go'n die 'fore it over with. The whole place—ever'thing. A big wind is rising, and when a big wind rise, the sea stirs, and the drop o' water you see laying on top the sea this day won't be there tomorrow, 'cause that's what wind do, and that's what life is. She ain't nothing but one o' these drops o' water laying on top the sea, and what this boy's doing is called the wind . . . and she must be moved. No, don't blame the boy. Go out and blame the wind. No, don't blame him, 'cause tomorrow what he doing today somebody go'n say he ain't done a thing. 'Cause tomorrow will be his time to be turned over just like it's hers today. And after that be somebody else to turn over. And it go'n go like that till it ain't nobody left to turn over.

"Sure, they bombed the house," he say; "because they want us to stop. But if we stopped today, then what good would we have done? What good? They would have just died in vain."

"Maybe if they had bombed your house you wouldn't be so set on keeping this up."

"If they had killed my mother and my brothers and sisters, I'd press just that much harder. I can see you all point. I can see everyone's point. But I can't agree with you. You blame me for this being bombed. You blame me for Aunt Fe's leaving. They died for you and for your children. And I love Aunt Fe as much as anybody in here. Nobody in here love her more than I do. Not one of you." He looks at her. "Don't you believe me, Aunt Fe?"

She nods—that little white scarf still tied round her head.

"How many times have I eaten in your kitchen, Aunt Fe? A thousand times? How many times have I eaten tea cakes and drank milk on your steps, Aunt Fe? A thousand times? How many times have I sat at this same firehalf with you, just the two of us, Aunt Fe? Another thousand times, two thousand times? How many times have I chopped wood for you, chopped grass for you, ran to the store for you? Five thousand? How many times we've walked to church together, Aunt Fe? Gone fishing at the river to-gether—how many thousands of times? I've spent as much time in this house as I've spent in my own. I know every crack in the wall. I know every corner. With my eyes closed, I can go anywhere in here without bumping into anything. How many of you can do that? Not many of you." He looks at her. "Aunt Fe?"

She looks at him.

"Do you think I love you, Aunt Fe?"

She nods.

"I love you, Aunt Fe, as much as I do my own parents. I'm going to miss you as much as I'd miss my own mother if she was to leave me. I'm going to miss you, Aunt Fe, but I'm not going to stop what I've started. You told me a story once, Aunt Fe, about my great-grandpa. Remember? Remember how he died?" She look in the fire and nod.

"Remember how they lynched him? chopped him to pieces?"

She nod.

"Just the two of us were sitting here beside the fire when you told me that. I was so angry I felt like killing. But it was you who told me to get kill-ing out of my head. It was you who told me I would only bring harm to my-self and sadness to the others if I killed. Do you remember that, Aunt Fe?"

She nod, still looking in the fire.

"You were right. We cannot raise our arms. Because it would mean death for ourselves, as well as for the others. But we will do something else. And that's what we will do." He look at the other people. "And if they were to bomb my own mother's house tomorrow, I still wouldn't stop."

"I'm not saying stop," Louise says. "That's up to you. I'm just taking Auntie from here before hers is the next house they get to."

The boy look at Louise, and then at Aunt Fe again. He go to the chair where she sitting.

"Good bye, Aunt Fe," he say, picking up her hand. The hand done shriv-eled up to almost nothing. Look like nothing but loose skin's covering the bones. "I'll miss you," he say.

"Good bye, Emmanuel," she say. She look at him a long time. "God be with you."

He stand there holding the hand a while longer, then he nod his head, and leave the house. The people stir around little bit, but nobody say anything.

Aunt Lou

They tell her good bye, and half of 'em leave the house crying, or want cry, but she just sit there side the firehalf like she don't mind going at all. When Leola ask me if I'm ready to go, I tell her I'm staying right there till Fe leave that house. I tell her I ain't moving one step till she go out that door. I been knowing her for the past fifty some years now, and I ain't 'bout to leave her on her last night here.

That boy, Chuckkie, want stay with me, but I make him go. He follow his mon and pa out the house and soon I hear that wagon turning round. I hear Emile saying something to Mr. Bascom even 'fore that wagon get out the yard. I tell myself, Well, Mr. Bascom, you sure go'n catch it, and me not there to take up for you—and I get up from my chair and go to the door.

"Emile?" I call.

"Whoa," he say.

"You leave that mule 'lone, you hear me?"

"I ain't doing him nothing, Mama," he say.

"Well, you just mind you don't," I say. "I'll sure find out."

"Yes'm," he say. "Come up here, Mr. Bascom."

"Now, you hear that boy, Emile?" I say.

"I'm sorry, Mama," he say. "I didn't mean no harm."

They go out in the road, and I go back to the firehalf and sit down again. Louise stir round in the kitchen a few minutes, then she come in the front where we at. Ever'body else, they gone. That husband o' hers there got drunk long 'fore mid-night, and they had to put him to bed in the other room.

She come there and stand by the fire.

"I'm dead on my feet," she say.

"Why 'on't you go to bed," I say. "I'm go'n be here."

"You all won't need anything?"

"They got wood in that corner?"

"Plenty."

"Then we won't need a thing."

She stand there and warm, and then she say good night and go round the other side.

"Well, Fe?" I say.

"I ain't leaving tomorrow, Lou," she say.

"Course you is," I say. "Up there ain't that bad."

She shake her head. "No, I ain't going nowhere."

I look at her over in her chair, but I don't say nothing. The fire pops in the firehalf, and I look at the fire again. It's a good little fire—not too big, not too little. Just 'nough there to keep the place warm.

"You want sing, Lou?" she say, after a while. "I feel like singing my 'termination song."

"Sure," I say.

She start singing in that little light voice she got there, and I join with her. We sing two choruses, and then she stop.

"My 'termination for Heaven," she say. "Now—now—"

"What's the matter, Fe?" I say.

"Nothing," she say. "I want get in my bed. My gown hanging over there."

I get the gown for her and bring it back to the firehalf. She get out of her dress slowly, like she don't even have 'nough strength to do it. I help her on with her gown, and she kneel down there side the bed and say her prayers. I sit in my chair and look at the fire again.

She pray there a long time—half out loud, half to herself. I look at her there, kneeling down there, little like a little old girl. I see her making some kind o' jecking motion there, but I feel she crying 'cause this her last night here, and 'cause she got to go and leave ever'thing behind. I look at the fire.

She pray there ever so long, and then she start to get up. But she can't make it by herself. I go to help her, and when I put my hand on her shoulder, she say, "Lou; Lou."

I say, "What's the matter, Fe?"

She say, "Lou; Lou."

I feel her shaking in my hand with all her might. Shaking like a person with the chill. Then I hear her taking a long breath—long—longest I ever heard anybody take before. Then she calm down—calm, calm.

"Sleep on, Fe," I say. "When you get up there, tell 'em all I ain't far behind."

Acceptance of Their Ways

MAVIS GALLANT

Prodded by a remark from Mrs. Freeport, Lily Littel got up and fetched the plate of cheese. It was in her to say, "Go get it yourself," but a reputation for coolness held her still. Only the paucity of her income, at which the *Sunday Express* horoscope jeered with its smart talk of pleasure and gain, kept her at Mrs. Freeport's, on the Italian side of the frontier. The coarse and grubby gaiety of the French Riviera would have suited her better, and was not far away; unfortunately it came high. At Mrs. Freeport's, which was cheaper, there was a whiff of infirm nicety to be breathed, a suggestion of regularly aired decay; weakly, because it was respectable, Lily craved that, too. "We seem to have finished with the pudding," said Mrs. Freeport once again, as though she hadn't noticed that Lily was on her feet.

Lily was not Mrs. Freeport's servant, she was her paying guest, but it was a distinction her hostess rarely observed. In imagination, Lily became a punishing statue and raised a heavy marble arm; but then she remembered that this was the New Year. The next day, or the day after that, her dividends would arrive. That meant she could disappear, emerging as a gay holiday Lily up in Nice. Then, Lily thought, turning away from the table, then watch the old tiger! For Mrs. Freeport couldn't live without Lily, not more than a day. She could not stand Italy without the sound of an English voice in the house. In the hush of the dead season, Mrs. Freeport preferred Lily's ironed-out Bayswater to no English at all.

In the time it took her to pick up the cheese and face the table again, Lily had added to her expression a permanent-looking smile. Her eyes, which were a washy blue, were tolerably kind when she was plotting mischief. The week in Nice, desired, became a necessity; Mrs. Freeport needed a scare. She would fear, and then believe, that her most docile boarder, her most pliant errand girl, had gone forever. Stealing into Lily's darkened room, she would count the dresses with trembling hands. She would touch Lily's

371

red with the white dots, her white with the poppies, her green wool with the scarf of mink tails. Mrs. Freeport would also discover—if she carried her snooping that far—the tooled-leather box with Lily's daisy-shaped ear-rings, and the brooch in which a mother-of-pearl pigeon sat on a nest made of Lily's own hair. But Mrs. Freeport would not find the diary, in which Lily had recorded her opinion of so many interesting things, nor would she come upon a single empty bottle. Lily kept her drinking to Nice, where, anonymous in a large hotel, friendly and lavish in a bar, she let herself drown. "Your visits to your sister seem to do you so much good," was Mrs. Freeport's unvarying comment when Lily returned from these excursions, which always followed the arrival of her income. "But you spend far too much money on your sister. You are much too kind." But Lily had no re-grets. Illiberal by circumstance, grudging only because she imitated the be-havior of other women, she became, drunk, an old forgotten Lily-girl, tender and warm, able to shed a happy tear and open a closed fist. She had been cold sober since September.

"Well, there you are," she said, and slapped down the plate of cheese. There was another person at the table, a Mrs. Garnett, who was returning to England the next day. Lily's manner toward the two women combined bullying with servility. Mrs. Freeport, large, in brown chiffon, wearing a hat with a water lily upon it to cover her thinning hair, liked to *feel* served. Lily had been a paid companion once; she had never seen a paradox in the joining of those two words. She simply looked on Mrs. Freeport and Mrs. Garnett as more of that race of ailing, peevish elderly children whose fan-cies and delusions must be humored by the sane.

Mrs. Freeport pursed her lips in acknowledgment of the cheese. Mrs. Garnett, who was reading a book, did nothing at all. Mrs. Garnett had been with them four months. Her blued curls, her laugh, her moist baby's mouth, had the effect on Lily of a stone in the shoe. Mrs. Garnett's hus-band, dead but often mentioned, had evidently liked them saucy and dim in the brain. Now that William Henry was no longer there to protect his wife, she was the victim of the effect of her worrying beauty—a torment to shoe clerks and bus conductors. Italians were dreadful; Mrs. Garnett hardly dared put her wee nose outside the house. "You are a little monkey, Edith!" Mrs. Freeport would sometimes say, bringing her head upward with a jerk, waking out of a sweet dream in time to applaud. Mrs. Garnett would go on telling how she had been jostled on the pavement or offended on a bus. And Lily Littel, who knew—but truly knew—about being fol-lowed and hounded and pleaded with, brought down her thick eyelids and smiled. Talk leads to overconfidence and errors. Lily had guided her life to this quiet shore by knowing when to open her mouth and when to keep it closed.

Mrs. Freeport was not deluded but simply poor. Thirteen years of pen-sion-keeping on a tawdry stretch of Mediterranean coast had done nothing to improve her fortunes and had probably diminished them. Sentiment kept her near Bordighera, where someone precious to her had been buried in the Protestant part of the cemetery. In Lily's opinion, Mrs. Freeport ought to have cleared out long ago, cutting her losses, leaving the servants out of pocket and the grocer unpaid. Lily looked soft; she was round and pink and yellow-haired. The imitation pearls screwed on to her doughy little ears seemed to devour the flesh. But Lily could have bitten a real pearl in two and enjoyed the pieces. Her nature was generous, but an admiration for superior women had led her to cherish herself. An excellent cook, she had dreamed of being a poisoner, but decided to leave that for the loonies; it was no real way to get on. She had a moral program of a sort—thought it wicked to set a poor table, until she learned that the sort of woman she yearned to become was often picky. After that she tried to put it out of her mind. At Mrs. Freeport's she was enrolled in a useful school, for the creed of the house was this: It is pointless to think about anything so temporary as food; coffee grounds can be used many times, and moldy bread, revived in the oven, mashed with raisins and milk, makes a delicious pudding. If Lily had settled for this bleached existence, it was explained by a sentence scrawled over a page of her locked diary: "I live with gentlewomen now." And there was a finality about the statement that implied acceptance of their ways.

Lily removed the fly netting from the cheese. There was her bit left over from luncheon. It was the end of a portion of Dutch so dry it had split. Mrs. Freeport would have the cream cheese, possibly still highly pleasing under its coat of pale fur, while Mrs. Garnett, who was a yoghurt fancier, would require none at all.

"Cheese, Edith," said Mrs. Freeport loudly, and little Mrs. Garnett blinked her doll eyes and smiled: No thank you. Let others thicken their figures and damage their souls.

The cheese was pushed along to Mrs. Freeport, then back to Lily, passing twice under Mrs. Garnett's nose. She did not look up again. She was moving her lips over a particularly absorbing passage in her book. For the last four months, she had been reading the same volume, which was called "Optimism Unlimited." So as not to stain the pretty dust jacket, she had covered it with brown paper, but now even that was becoming soiled. When Mrs. Freeport asked what the book was about, Mrs. Garnett smiled a timid apology and said, "I'm *afraid* it is philosophy." It was, indeed, a new philosophy, counseling restraint in all things, but recommending smiles. Four months of smiles and restraint had left Mrs. Garnett hungry, and, to mark her last evening at Mrs. Freeport's, she had asked for an Italian meal. Mrs. Freeport thought it extravagant—after all, they were still digesting an English Christmas. But little Edith was so sweet when she begged, putting her head to one side, wrinkling her face, that Mrs. Freeport, muttering about monkeys, had given in. The dinner was prepared and served, and Mrs.

Garnett, suddenly remembering about restraint, brought her book to the table and decided not to eat a thing.

It seemed that the late William Henry had found this capriciousness adorable, but Mrs. Freeport's eyes were stones. Lily supposed this was how murders came about—not the hasty, soon regretted sort but the plan that is sown from an insult, a slight, and comes to flower at temperate speed. Mrs. Garnett deserved a reprimand. Lily saw her, without any emotion, doubled in two and shoved in a sack. But did Mrs. Freeport like her friend enough to bother teaching her lessons? Castigation, to Lily, suggested love. Mrs. Garnett and Mrs. Freeport were old friends, and vaguely related. Mrs. Garnett had been coming to Mrs. Freeport's every winter for years, but she left unfinished letters lying about, from which Lily—a great reader—could learn that dear Vanessa was becoming meaner and queerer by the minute. Thinking of Mrs. Freeport as "dear Vanessa" took flexibility, but Lily had that. She was not "Miss" and not "Littel;" she was, or, rather, had been, a Mrs. Cliff Little, who had taken advantage of the disorders of war to get rid of Cliff. He vanished, and his memory grew smaller and faded from the sky. In the bright new day strolled Miss Lily Littel, ready for anything. Then a lonely, fretful widow had taken a fancy to her and, as soon as travel was possible, had taken Lily abroad. There followed eight glorious years of trains and bars and discreet afternoon gambling, of eating éclairs in English-style tearooms, and discovering cafés where bacon and eggs were fried. Oh, the discovery of that sign in Monte Carlo: "Every Friday Sausages and Mashed"! That was the joy of being in foreign lands. One hot afternoon, Lily's employer, hooked by Lily into her stays not an hour before, dropped dead in a cinema lobby in Rome. Her will revealed she had provided for "Miss Littel," for a fox terrier, and for an invalid niece. The provision for the niece prevented the family from coming down on Lily's head; all the same, Lily kept out of England. She had not inspired the death of her employer, but she had nightmares for some time after, as though she had taken the wish for the deed. Her letters were so ambiguous that there was talk in England of an inquest. Lily accompanied the coffin as far as the frontier, for a letter of instructions specified cremation, which Lily understood could take place only in France. The coffin was held up rather a long time at customs, documents went back and forth, and in the end the relatives were glad to hear the last of it. Shortly after that, the fox terrier died, and Lily appropriated his share, feeling that she deserved it. Her employer had been living on overdrafts; there was next to nothing for dog, companion, or niece. Lily stopped having nightmares. She continued to live abroad.

With delicate nibbles, eyes down, Lily ate her cheese. Glancing sidewise, she noticed that Mrs. Garnett had closed the book. She wanted to annoy; she had planned the whole business of the Italian meal, had thought it out beforehand. Their manners were still strange to Lily, although she was a quick pupil. Why not clear the air, have it out? Once again she wondered what the two friends meant to each other. "Like" and "hate" were possibilities she had nearly forgotten when she stopped being Mrs. Cliff and became this curious, two-faced Lily Littel.

Mrs. Freeport's pebbly stare was focussed on her friend's jar of yoghurt. "Sugar?" she cried, giving the cracked basin a shove along the table. Mrs. Garnett pulled it toward her, defiantly. She spoke in a soft, martyred voice, as though Lily weren't there. She said that it was her last evening and it no longer mattered. Mrs. Freeport had made a charge for extra sugar—yes, she had seen it on her bill. Mrs. Garnett asked only to pay and go. She was never coming again.

"I look upon you as essentially greedy." Mrs. Freeport leaned forward, enunciating with care. "You pretend to eat nothing, but I cannot look at a dish after you have served yourself. The *wreck* of the lettuce. The *destruction* of the pudding."

A bottle of wine, adrift and forgotten, stood by Lily's plate. She had not seen it until now. Mrs. Garnett, who was fearless, covered her yoghurt thickly with sugar.

"Like most people who pretend to eat like birds, you manage to keep your strength up," Mrs. Freeport said. "That sugar is the equivalent of a banquet, and you also eat between meals. Your drawers are stuffed with biscuits, and cheese, and chocolate, and heaven knows what."

"Dear Vanessa," Mrs. Garnett said.

"People who make a pretense of eating nothing always stuff furtively," said Mrs. Freeport smoothly. "Secret eating is exactly the same thing as secret drinking."

Lily's years abroad had immunized her to the conversation of gentlewomen, their absorption with money, their deliberate over- or underfeeding, their sudden animal quarrels. She wondered if there remained a great deal more to learn before she could wear their castoff manners as her own. At the reference to secret drinking she looked calm and melancholy. Mrs. Garnett said, "That is most unkind." The yoghurt remained uneaten. Lily sighed, and wondered what would happen if she picked her teeth.

"My change man stopped by today," said Mrs. Garnett, all at once smiling and widening her eyes. How Lily admired that shift of territory—that carrying of banners to another field. She had not learned everything yet. "I *wish* you could have seen his face when he heard I was leaving! There really was no need for his coming, because I'd been in to his office only the week before, and changed all the money I need, and we'd had a lovely chat."

"The odious little money merchant in the bright-yellow automobile?" said Mrs. Freeport.

Mrs. Garnett, who often took up farfetched and untenable arguments, said, "William Henry wanted me to be happy."

"Edith!"

Lily hooked her middle finger around the bottle of wine and pulled it gently toward her. The day after tomorrow was years away. But she did not take her eyes from Mrs. Freeport, whose blazing eyes perfectly matched the small sapphires hanging from her ears. Lily could have matched the expression if she had cared to, but she hadn't arrived at the sapphires yet. Addressing herself, Lily said, "Thanks," softly, and upended the bottle.

"I meant it in a general way," said Mrs. Garnett. "William Henry wanted me to be happy. It was nearly the last thing he said."

"At the time of William Henry's death, he was unable to say anything," said Mrs. Freeport. "William Henry was my first cousin. Don't use him as a platform for your escapades."

Lily took a sip from her glass. Shock! It hadn't been watered—probably in honor of Mrs. Garnett's last meal. But it was sour, thick, and full of silt. "I have always thought a little sugar would improve it," said Lily chattily, but nobody heard.

Mrs. Freeport suddenly conceded that William Henry might have wanted his future widow to be happy. "It was because he spoiled you," she said. "You were vain and silly when he married you, and he made you conceited and foolish. I don't wonder poor William Henry went off his head."

"Off his head?" Mrs. Garnett looked at Lily; calm, courteous Miss Littel was giving herself wine. "We might have general conversation," said Mrs. Garnett, with a significant twitch of face. "Miss Littel has hardly said a word."

"Why?" shouted Mrs. Freeport, throwing her table napkin down. "The meal is over. You refused it. There is no need for conversation of any kind."

She was marvelous, blazing, with that water lily on her head.

Ah, Lily thought, but you should have seen me, in the old days. How I could let fly . . . poor old Cliff.

They moved in single file down the passage and into the sitting room, where, for reasons of economy, the hanging lustre contained one bulb. Lily and Mrs. Freeport settled down directly under it, on a sofa; each had her own newspaper to read, tucked down the side of the cushions. Mrs. Garnett walked about the room. "To think that I shall never see this room again," she said.

"I should hope not," said Mrs. Freeport. She held the paper before her face, but as far as Lily could tell she was not reading it.

"The trouble is"—for Mrs. Garnett could never help giving herself away—"I don't know where to go in the autumn."

"Ask your change man."

"Egypt," said Mrs. Garnett, still walking about. "I had friends who went to Egypt every winter for years and years, and now they have nowhere to go, either."

"Let them stay home," said Mrs. Freeport. "I am trying to read."

"If Egypt continues to carry on, I'm sure I don't know where we shall all be," said Lily. Neither lady took the slightest notice.

"They were perfectly charming people," said Mrs. Garnett, in a complaining way.

"Why don't you do the *Times* crossword, Edith?" said Mrs. Freeport.

From behind them, Mrs. Garnett said, "You know that I can't, and you said that only to make me feel small. But William Henry did it until the very end, which proves, I think, that he was not o.h.h. By o.h.h. I mean *off his head*."

The break in her voice was scarcely more than a quaver, but to the two women on the sofa it was a signal, and they got to their feet. By the time they reached her, Mrs. Garnett was sitting on the floor in hysterics. They helped her up, as they had often done before. She tried to scratch their faces and said they would be sorry when she had died.

Between them, they got her to bed. "Where is her hot-water bottle?" said Mrs. Freeport. "No, not that one. She must have her own—the bottle with the bunny head."

"My yoghurt," said Mrs. Garnett, sobbing. Without her make-up she looked shrunken, as though padding had been removed from her skin.

"Fetch the yoghurt," Mrs. Freeport commanded. She stood over the old friend while she ate the yoghurt, one tiny spoonful at a time. "Now go to sleep," she said.

In the morning, Mrs. Garnett was taken by taxi to the early train. She seemed entirely composed and carried her book. Mrs. Freeport hoped that her journey would be comfortable. She and Lily watched the taxi until it was out of sight on the road, and then, in the bare wintry garden, Mrs. Freeport wept into her hands.

"I've said goodbye to her," she said at last, blowing her nose. "It is the last goodbye. I shall never see her again. I was so horrid to her. And she is so tiny and frail. She might die. I'm convinced of it. She won't survive the summer."

"She has survived every other," said Lily reasonably.

"Next year, she must have the large room with the balcony. I don't know what I was thinking, not to have given it to her. We must begin planning now for next year. She will want a good reading light. Her eyes are so bad. And, you know, we should have chopped her vegetables. She doesn't chew. I'm sure that's at the bottom of the yoghurt affair."

"I'm off to Nice tomorrow," said Lily, the stray. "My sister is expecting me."

"You are so devoted," said Mrs. Freeport, looking wildly for her handkerchief, which had fallen on the gravel path. Her hat was askew. The house was empty. "So devoted . . . I suppose that one day you will want to live in Nice, to be near her. I suppose that day will come."

Instead of answering, Lily set Mrs. Freeport's water lily straight, which was familiar of her; but they were both in such a state, for different reasons, that neither of them thought it strange.

A Very Old Man
with Enormous Wings

GABRIEL GARCÍA MÁRQUEZ

Translated by Gregory Rabassa

On the third day of rain they had killed so many crabs inside the house that Pelayo had to cross his drenched courtyard and throw them into the sea, because the newborn child had a temperature all night and they thought it was due to the stench. The world had been sad since Tuesday. Sea and sky were a single ash-gray thing and the sands of the beach, which on March nights glimmered like powdered light, had become a stew of mud and rotten shellfish. The light was so weak at noon that when Pelayo was coming back to the house after throwing away the crabs, it was hard for him to see what it was that was moving and groaning in the rear of the courtyard. He had to go very close to see that it was an old man, a very old man, lying face down in the mud, who, in spite of his tremendous efforts, couldn't get up, impeded by his enormous wings.

Frightened by that nightmare, Pelayo ran to get Elisenda, his wife, who was putting compresses on the sick child, and he took her to the rear of the courtyard. They both looked at the fallen body with mute stupor. He was dressed like a ragpicker. There were only a few faded hairs left on his bald skull and very few teeth in his mouth, and his pitiful condition of a drenched great-grandfather had taken away any sense of grandeur he might have had. His huge buzzard wings, dirty and half-plucked, were forever entangled in the mud. They looked at him so long and so closely that Pelayo and Elisenda very soon overcame their surprise and in the end found him familiar. Then they dared speak to him, and he anwered in an incomprehensible dialect with a strong sailor's voice. That was how they skipped over the inconvenience of the wings and quite intelligently concluded that he was a lonely castaway from some foreign ship wrecked by the storm. And yet, they called in a neighbor woman who knew everything

378

about life and death to see him, and all she needed was one look to show them their mistake.

"He's an angel," she told them. "He must have been coming for the child, but the poor fellow is so old that the rain knocked him down."

On the following day everyone knew that a flesh-and-blood angel was held captive in Pelayo's house. Against the judgment of the wise neighbor woman, for whom angels in those times were the fugitive survivors of a celestial conspiracy, they did not have the heart to club him to death. Pelayo watched over him all afternoon from the kitchen, armed with his bailiff's club, and before going to bed he dragged him out of the mud and locked him up with the hens in the wire chicken coop. In the middle of the night, when the rain stopped, Pelayo and Elisenda were still killing crabs. A short time afterward the child woke up without a fever and with a desire to eat. Then they felt magnanimous and decided to put the angel on a raft with fresh water and provisions for three days and leave him to his fate on the high seas. But when they went out into the courtyard with the first light of dawn, they found the whole neighborhood in front of the chicken coop having fun with the angel, without the slightest reverence, tossing him things to eat through the openings in the wire as if he weren't a supernatural creature but a circus animal.

Father Gonzaga arrived before seven o'clock, alarmed at the strange news. By that time onlookers less frivolous than those at dawn had already arrived and they were making all kinds of conjectures concerning the captive's future. The simplest among them thought that he should be named mayor of the world. Others of sterner mind felt that he should be promoted to the rank of five-star general in order to win all wars. Some visionaries hoped that he could be put to stud in order to implant on earth a race of winged wise men who could take charge of the universe. But Father Gonzaga, before becoming a priest, had been a robust woodcutter. Standing by the wire, he reviewed his catechism in an instant and asked them to open the door so that he could take a close look at that pitiful man who looked more like a huge decrepit hen among the fascinated chickens. He was lying in a corner drying his open wings in the sunlight among the fruit peels and breakfast leftovers that the early risers had thrown him. Alien to the impertinences of the world, he only lifted his antiquarian eyes and murmured something in his dialect when Father Gonzaga went into the chicken coop and said good morning to him in Latin. The parish priest had his first suspicion of an impostor when he saw that he did not understand the language of God or know how to greet His ministers. Then he noticed that seen close up he was much too human: he had an unbearable smell of the outdoors, the back side of his wings was strewn with parasites and his main feathers had been mistreated by terrestrial winds, and nothing about him measured up to the proud dignity of angels. Then he came out of the chicken coop and in a brief sermon warned the curious against the risks of being ingenuous. He reminded them that the devil had the bad habit of making use of carnival tricks in order to confuse the unwary. He argued that if wings were not the essential element in determining the difference between a hawk and an airplane, they were even less so in the recognition of angels. Nevertheless, he promised to write a letter to his bishop so that the latter would write to his primate so that the latter would write to the Supreme Pontiff in order to get the final verdict from the highest courts.

His prudence fell on sterile hearts. The news of the captive angel spread with such rapidity that after a few hours the courtyard had the bustle of a marketplace and they had to call in troops with fixed bayonets to disperse the mob that was about to knock the house down. Elisenda, her spine all twisted from sweeping up so much marketplace trash, then got the idea of fencing in the yard and charging five cents admission to see the angel.

The curious came from far away. A traveling carnival arrived with a flying acrobat who buzzed over the crowd several times, but no one paid any attention to him because his wings were not those of an angel but, rather, those of a sidereal bat. The most unfortunate invalids on earth came in search of health: a poor woman who since childhood had been counting her heartbeats and had run out of numbers; a Portuguese man who couldn't sleep because the noise of the stars disturbed him; a sleepwalker who got up at night to undo the things he had done while awake; and many others with less serious ailments. In the midst of that shipwreck disorder that made the earth tremble, Pelayo and Elisenda were happy with fatigue, for in less than a week they had crammed their rooms with money and the line of pilgrims waiting their turn to enter still reached beyond the horizon.

The angel was the only one who took no part in his own act. He spent his time trying to get comfortable in his borrowed nest, befuddled by the hellish heat of the oil lamps and sacramental candles that had been placed along the wire. At first they tried to make him eat some mothballs, which, according to the wisdom of the wise neighbor woman, were the food prescribed for angels. But he turned them down, just as he turned down the papal lunches that the penitents brought him, and they never found out whether it was because he was an angel or because he was an old man that in the end he ate nothing but eggplant mush. His only supernatural virtue seemed to be patience. Especially during the first days, when the hens pecked at him, searching for the stellar parasites that proliferated in his wings, and the cripples pulled out feathers to touch their defective parts with, and even the most merciful threw stones at him, trying to get him to rise so they could see him standing. The only time they succeeded in arousing him was when they burned his side with an iron for branding steers, for he had been motionless for so many hours that they thought he was dead. He awoke with a start, ranting in his hermetic language and with tears in his eyes, and he flapped his wings a couple of times, which brought on a whirlwind of chicken dung and lunar dust and a gale of panic that did not seem to be of this world. Although many thought that his reaction had been one not of rage but of pain, from then on they were careful not to annoy him, because the majority understood that his passivity was not that of a hero taking his ease but that of a cataclysm in repose.

Father Gonzaga held back the crowd's frivolity with formulas of maidservant inspiration while awaiting the arrival of a final judgment on the nature of the captive. But the mail from Rome showed no sense of urgency. They spent their time finding out if the prisoner had a navel, if his dialect had any connection with Aramaic, how many times he could fit on the head of a pin, or whether he wasn't just a Norwegian with wings. Those meager letters might have come and gone until the end of time if a providential event had not put an end to the priest's tribulations.

It so happened that during those days, among so many other carnival attractions, there arrived in town the traveling show of the woman who had been changed into a spider for having disobeyed her parents. The admission to see her was not only less than the admission to see the angel, but people were permitted to ask her all manner of questions about her absurd state and to examine her up and down so that no one would ever doubt the truth of her horror. She was a frightful tarantula the size of a ram and with the head of a sad maiden. What was most heart-rending, however, was not her outlandish shape but the sincere affliction with which she recounted the details of her misfortune. While still practically a child she had sneaked out of her parents' house to go to a dance, and while she was coming back through the woods after having danced all night without permission, a fearful thunderclap rent the sky in two and through the crack came the lightning bolt of brimstone that changed her into a spider. Her only nourishment came from the meatballs that charitable souls chose to toss into her mouth. A spectacle like that, full of so much human truth and with such a fearful lesson, was bound to defeat without even trying that of a haughty angel who scarcely deigned to look at mortals. Besides, the few miracles attributed to the angel showed a certain mental disorder, like the blind man who didn't recover his sight but grew three new teeth, or the paralytic who didn't get to walk but almost won the lottery, and the leper whose sores sprouted sunflowers. Those consolation miracles, which were more like mocking fun, had already ruined the angel's reputation when the woman who had been changed into a spider finally crushed him completely. That was how Father Gonzaga was cured forever of his insomnia and Pelayo's courtyard went back to being as empty as during the time it had rained for three days and crabs walked through the bedrooms.

The owners of the house had no reason to lament. With the money they saved they built a two-story mansion with balconies and gardens and high netting so that crabs wouldn't get in during the winter, and with iron bars on the windows so that angels wouldn't get in. Pelayo also set up a rabbit warren close to town and gave up his job as bailiff for good, and Elisenda bought some satin pumps with high heels and many dresses of iridescent silk, the kind worn on Sunday by the most desirable women in those times. The chicken coop was the only thing that didn't receive any attention. If they washed it down with creolin and burned tears of myrrh inside it every so often, it was not in homage to the angel but to drive away the dungheap stench that still hung everywhere like a ghost and was turning the new house into an old one. At first, when the child learned to walk, they were careful that he not get too close to the chicken coop. But then they began to lose their fears and got used to the smell, and before the child got his second teeth he'd gone inside the chicken coop to play, where the wires were falling apart. The angel was no less standoffish with him than with other mortals, but he tolerated the most ingenious infamies with the patience of a dog who had no illusions. They both came down with chicken pox at the same time. The doctor who took care of the child couldn't resist the temptation to listen to the angel's heart, and he found so much whistling in the heart and so many sounds in his kidneys that it seemed impossible for him to be alive. What surprised him most, however, was the logic of his wings. They seemed so natural on that completely human organism that he couldn't understand why other men didn't have them too.

When the child began school it had been some time since the sun and rain had caused the collapse of the chicken coop. The angel went dragging himself about here and there like a stray dying man. They would drive him out of the bedroom with a broom and a moment later find him in the kitchen. He seemed to be in so many places at the same time that they grew to think that he'd been duplicated, that he was reproducing himself all through the house, and the exasperated and unhinged Elisenda shouted that it was awful living in that hell full of angels. He could scarcely eat and his antiquarian eyes had also become so foggy that he went about bumping into posts. All he had left were the bare cannulae of his last feathers. Pelayo threw a blanket over him and extended him the charity of letting him sleep in the shed, and only then did they notice that he had a temperature at night, and was delirious with the tongue twisters of an old Norwegian. That was one of the few times they became alarmed, for they thought he was going to die and not even the wise neighbor woman had been able to tell them what to do with dead angels.

And yet he not only survived his worst winter, but seemed improved with the first sunny days. He remained motionless for several days in the farthest corner of the courtyard, where no one would see him, and at the beginning of December some large, stiff feathers began to grow on his wings, the feathers of a scarecrow, which looked more like another misfortune of decrepitude. But he must have known the reason for those changes, for he was quite careful that no one should notice them, that no one should hear the sea chanteys that he sometimes sang under the stars. One morning Elisenda was cutting some bunches of onions for lunch when a wind that seemed to come from the high seas blew into the kitchen. Then she went to the window and caught the angel in his first attempts at flight. They were so clumsy that his fingernails opened a furrow in the vegetable patch and he was on the point of knocking the shed down with the ungainly flapping that slipped on the light and couldn't get a grip on the air. But he did manage to gain altitude. Elisenda let out a sigh of relief, for herself and for him, when she saw him pass over the last houses, holding himself up in some way with the risky flapping of a senile vulture. She kept watching him even when she was through cutting the onions and she kept on watching until it was no longer possible for her to see him, because then he was no longer an annoyance in her life but an imaginary dot on the horizon of the sea.

Balthazar's Marvelous Afternoon

GABRIEL GARCÍA MÁRQUEZ

Translated by J.S. Bernstein

The cage was finished. Balthazar hung it under the eave, from force of habit, and when he finished lunch everyone was already saying that it was the most beautiful cage in the world. So many people came to see it that a crowd formed in front of the house, and Balthazar had to take it down and close the shop.

"You have to shave," Ursula, his wife, told him. "You look like a Capuchin."

"It's bad to shave after lunch," said Balthazar.

He had two weeks' growth, short, hard, and bristly hair like the mane of a mule, and the general expression of a frightened boy. But it was a false expression. In February he was thirty; he had been living with Ursula for four years, without marrying her and without having children, and life had given him many reasons to be on guard but none to be frightened. He did not even know that for some people the cage he had just made was the most beautiful one in the world. For him, accustomed to making cages since childhood, it had been hardly any more difficult than the others.

"Then rest for a while," said the woman. "With that beard you can't show yourself anywhere."

While he was resting, he had to get out of his hammock several times to show the cage to the neighbors. Ursula had paid little attention to it until then. She was annoyed because her husband had neglected the work of his carpenter's shop to devote himself entirely to the cage, and for two weeks had slept poorly, turning over and muttering incoherencies, and he hadn't thought of shaving. But her annoyance dissolved in the face of the finished cage. When Balthazar woke up from his nap, she had ironed his pants and a shirt; she had put them on a chair near the hammock and had carried the cage to the dining table. She regarded it in silence.

"How much will you charge?" she asked.

"I don't know," Balthazar answered. "I'm going to ask for thirty pesos to see if they'll give me twenty."

"Ask for fifty," said Ursula. "You've lost a lot of sleep in these two weeks. Furthermore, it's rather large. I think it's the biggest cage I've ever seen in my life."

Balthazar began to shave.

"Do you think they'll give me fifty pesos?"

"That's nothing for Mr. Chepe Montiel, and the cage is worth it," said Ursula. "You should ask for sixty."

The house lay in the stifling shadow. It was the first week of April and the heat seemed less bearable because of the chirping of the cicadas. When he finished dressing, Balthazar opened the door to the patio to cool off the house, and a group of children entered the dining room.

The news had spread. Dr. Octavio Giraldo, an old physician, happy with life but tired of his profession, thought about Balthazar's cage while he was eating lunch with his invalid wife. On the inside terrace, where they put the table on hot days, there were many flowerpots and two cages with canaries. His wife liked birds, and she liked them so much that she hated cats because they could eat them up. Thinking about her, Dr. Giraldo went to see a patient that afternoon, and when he returned he went by Balthazar's house to inspect the cage.

There were a lot of people in the dining room. The cage was on display on the table: with its enormous dome of wire, three stories inside, with passageways and compartments especially for eating and sleeping and swings in the space set aside for the birds' recreation, it seemed like a small-scale model of a gigantic ice factory. The doctor inspected it carefully, without touching it, thinking that in effect the cage was better than its reputation, and much more beautiful than any he had ever dreamed of for his wife.

"This is a flight of the imagination," he said. He sought out Balthazar among the group of people and, fixing his maternal eyes on him, added, "You would have been an extraordinary architect."

Balthazar blushed.

"Thank you," he said.

"It's true," said the doctor. He was smoothly and delicately fat, like a woman who had been beautiful in her youth, and he had delicate hands. His voice seemed like that of a priest speaking Latin. "You wouldn't even need to put birds in it," he said, making the cage turn in front of the audience's eyes as if he were auctioning it off. "It would be enough to hang it in the trees so it could sing by itself." He put it back on the table, thought a moment, looking at the cage, and said:

"Fine, then I'll take it."

"It's sold," said Ursula.

"It belongs to the son of Mr. Chepe Montiel," said Balthazar. "He ordered it specially."

The doctor adopted a respectful attitude.

"Did he give you the design?"

"No," said Balthazar. "He said he wanted a large cage, like this one, for a pair of troupials."

The doctor looked at the cage.

"But this isn't for troupials."

"Of course it is, Doctor," said Balthazar, approaching the table. The children surrounded him. "The measurements are carefully calculated," he said, pointing to the different compartments with his forefinger. Then he struck the dome with his knuckles, and the cage filled with resonant chords.

"It's the strongest wire you can find, and each joint is soldered outside and in," he said.

"It's even big enough for a parrot," interrupted one of the children.

"That it is," said Balthazar.

The doctor turned his head.

"Fine, but he didn't give you the design," he said. "He gave you no exact specifications, aside from making it a cage big enough for troupials. Isn't that right?"

"That's right," said Balthazar.

"Then there's no problem," said the doctor. "One thing is a cage big enough for troupials, and another is this cage. There's no proof that this one is the one you were asked to make."

"It's this very one," said Balthazar, confused. "That's why I made it."

The doctor made an impatient gesture.

"You could make another one," said Ursula, looking at her husband. And then, to the doctor: "You're not in any hurry."

"I promised it to my wife for this afternoon," said the doctor.

"I'm very sorry, Doctor," said Balthazar, "but I can't sell you something that's sold already."

The doctor shrugged his shoulders. Drying the sweat from his neck with a handkerchief, he contemplated the cage silently with the fixed, unfocused gaze of one who looks at a ship which is sailing away.

"How much did they pay you for it?"

Balthazar sought out Ursula's eyes without replying.

"Sixty pesos," she said.

The doctor kept looking at the cage. "It's very pretty." He sighed. "Extremely pretty." Then, moving toward the door, he began to fan himself energetically, smiling, and the trace of that episode disappeared forever from his memory.

"Montiel is very rich," he said.

In truth, José Montiel was not as rich as he seemed, but he would have been capable of doing anything to become so. A few blocks from there, in a house crammed with equipment, where no one had ever smelled a smell that couldn't be sold, he remained indifferent to the news of the cage. His

wife, tortured by an obsession with death, closed the doors and windows after lunch and lay for two hours with her eyes opened to the shadow of the
room, while José Montiel took his siesta. The clamor of many voices surprised her there. Then she opened the door to the living room and found
a crowd in front of the house, and Balthazar with the cage in the middle of
the crowd, dressed in white, freshly shaved, with that expression of decorous candor with which the poor approach the houses of the wealthy.

"What a marvelous thing!" José Montiel's wife exclaimed, with a radiant
expression, leading Balthazar inside. "I've never seen anything like it in my
life," she said, and added, annoyed by the crowd which piled up at the
door:

"But bring it inside before they turn the living room into a grandstand."

Balthazar was no stranger to José Montiel's house. On different occasions, because of his skill and forthright way of dealing, he had been called
in to do minor carpentry jobs. But he never felt at ease among the rich. He
used to think about them, about their ugly and argumentative wives, about
their tremendous surgical operations, and he always experienced a feeling
of pity. When he entered their houses, he couldn't move without dragging
his feet.

"Is Pepe home?" he asked.

He had put the cage on the dining-room table.

"He's at school," said José Montiel's wife. "But he shouldn't be long," and
she added, "Montiel is taking a bath."

In reality, José Montiel had not had time to bathe. He was giving himself
an urgent alcohol rub, in order to come out and see what was going on. He
was such a cautious man that he slept without an electric fan so he could
watch over the noises of the house while he slept.

"Adelaide!" he shouted. "What's going on?"

"Come and see what a marvelous thing!" his wife shouted.

José Montiel, obese and hairy, his towel draped around his neck, appeared at the bedroom window.

"What is that?"

"Pepe's cage," said Balthazar.

His wife looked at him perplexedly.

"Whose?"

"Pepe's," replied Balthazar. And then, turning toward José Montiel,
"Pepe ordered it."

Nothing happened at that instant, but Balthazar felt as if someone had
just opened the bathroom door on him. José Montiel came out of the bedroom in his underwear.

"Pepe!" he shouted.

"He's not back," whispered his wife, motionless.

Pepe appeared in the doorway. He was about twelve, and had the same
curved eyelashes and was as quietly pathetic as his mother.

"Come here," José Montiel said to him. "Did you order this?"

The child lowered his head. Grabbing him by the hair, José Montiel forced Pepe to look him in the eye.

"Answer me."

The child bit his lip without replying.

"Montiel," whispered his wife.

José Montiel let the child go and turned toward Balthazar in a fury. "I'm very sorry, Balthazar," he said. "But you should have consulted me before going on. Only to you would it occur to contract with a minor." As he spoke, his face recovered its serenity. He lifted the cage without looking at it and gave it to Balthazar.

"Take it away at once, and try to sell it to whomever you can," he said. "Above all, I beg you not to argue with me." He patted him on the back and explained, "The doctor has forbidden me to get angry."

The child had remained motionless, without blinking, until Balthazar looked at him uncertainly with the cage in his hand. Then he emitted a guttural sound, like a dog's growl, and threw himself on the floor screaming.

José Montiel looked at him, unmoved, while the mother tried to pacify him. "Don't even pick him up," he said. "Let him break his head on the floor, and then put salt and lemon on it so he can rage to his heart's content." The child was shrieking tearlessly while his mother held him by the wrists.

"Leave him alone," José Montiel insisted.

Balthazar observed the child as he would have observed the death throes of a rabid animal. It was almost four o'clock. At that hour, at his house, Ursula was singing a very old song and cutting slices of onion.

"Pepe," said Balthazar.

He approached the child, smiling, and held the cage out to him. The child jumped up, embraced the cage which was almost as big as he was, and stood looking at Balthazar through the wirework without knowing what to say. He hadn't shed one tear.

"Balthazar," said José Montiel softly. "I told you already to take it away."

"Give it back," the woman ordered the child.

"Keep it," said Balthazar. And then, to José Montiel: "After all, that's what I made it for."

José Montiel followed him into the living room.

"Don't be foolish, Balthazar," he was saying, blocking his path. "Take your piece of furniture home and don't be silly. I have no intention of paying you a cent."

"It doesn't matter," said Balthazar. "I made it expressly as a gift for Pepe. I didn't expect to charge anything for it."

As Balthazar made his way through the spectators who were blocking the door, José Montiel was shouting in the middle of the living room. He was very pale and his eyes were beginning to get red.

"Idiot!" he was shouting. "Take your trinket out of here. The last thing we need is for some nobody to give orders in my house. Son of a bitch!"

In the pool hall, Balthazar was received with an ovation. Until that moment, he thought that he had made a better cage than ever before, that he'd had to give it to the son of José Montiel so he wouldn't keep crying, and that none of these things was particularly important. But then he realized that all of this had a certain importance for many people, and he felt a little excited.

"So they gave you fifty pesos for the cage."

"Sixty," said Balthazar.

"Score one for you," someone said. "You're the only one who has managed to get such a pile of money out of Mr. Chepe Montiel. We have to celebrate."

They bought him a beer, and Balthazar responded with a round for everybody. Since it was the first time he had ever been out drinking, by dusk he was completely drunk, and he was talking about a fabulous project of a thousand cages, at sixty pesos each, and then a million cages, till he had sixty million pesos. "We have to make a lot of things to sell to the rich before they die," he was saying, blind drunk. "All of them are sick, and they're going to die. They're so screwed up they can't even get angry any more." For two hours he was paying for the jukebox, which played without interruption. Everybody toasted Balthazar's health, good luck, and fortune, and the death of the rich, but at mealtime they left him alone in the pool hall.

Ursula had waited for him until eight, with a dish of fried meat covered with slices of onion. Someone told her that her husband was in the pool hall, delirious with happiness, buying beers for everyone, but she didn't believe it, because Balthazar had never got drunk. When she went to bed, almost at midnight, Balthazar was in a lighted room where there were little tables, each with four chairs, and an outdoor dance floor, where the plovers were walking around. His face was smeared with rouge, and since he couldn't take one more step, he thought he wanted to lie down with two women in the same bed. He had spent so much that he had had to leave his watch in pawn, with the promise to pay the next day. A moment later, spread-eagled in the street, he realized that his shoes were being taken off, but he didn't want to abandon the happiest dream of his life. The women who passed on their way to five-o'clock Mass didn't dare look at him, thinking he was dead.

The Termitary

NADINE GORDIMER

When you live in a small town far from the world you read about in municipal library books, the advent of repair men in the house is a festival. Daily
life is gaily broken open, improvisation takes over. The living room mas-
querades as a bedroom while the smell of paint in the bedroom makes it
uninhabitable. The secret backs of confident objects (matchwood draped
with cobwebs thickened by dust) are given away when furniture is piled to
the centre of the room. Meals are picnics at which table manners are suspended because the first principle of deportment drummed into children
by their mother—sitting down at table—is missing: there is nowhere to sit.
People are excused eccentricities of dress because no one can find anything
in its place.

A doctor is also a kind of repair man. When he is expected the sheets are
changed and the dog chased off the patient's bed. If a child is sick, she
doesn't have to go to school, she is on holiday, with presents into the bargain—a whole roll of comics tied with newsagent's string, and crayons or
card games. The mother is alone in the house, except for the patient out of
earshot in the sickroom; the other children are at school. Her husband is
away at work. She takes off her apron, combs her hair and puts on a bit of
lipstick to make herself decent for the doctor, setting ready a tea-tray for
two in the quiet privacy of the deserted living-room as for a secret morning
visit from the lover she does not have. After she and the doctor, who smells
intoxicating, coldly sweet because he has just come from the operating theatre, have stood together looking down at the patient and making jolly remarks, he is glad to accept a cup of tea in his busy morning round and their
voices are a murmur and an occasional rise of laughter from behind the
closed living-room door.

Plumber, painter, doctor; with their arrival something has happened
where nothing ever happens; at home: a house with a bungalow face made
of two bow-window eyes on either side of a front-door mouth, in a street in

a gold-mining town of twenty-five thousand people in South Africa in the
1930s.

Once the upright Steinway piano stood alone on the few remaining
boards of a room from which the floor had been ripped. I burst in to look
at the time on the chiming clock that should have been standing on the
mantelpiece and instead flew through the air and found myself jolted down
into a subterranean smell of an earth I'd never smelt before, the earth buried by our house. I was nine years old and the drop broke no bones; the
shock excited me, the thought of that hollow, earth-breaking dark always
beneath our Axminster thrilled me; the importance I gained in my
mother's accounts of how I might so easily have injured myself added to
the sense of occasion usual in the family when there were workmen in.

This time it was not the painters. Mr Strydom and his boys, over whom
my mother raised a quarrel every few years. *I'm not like any other woman. I
haven't got a husband like other women's. The state this house is in. You'd see the
place fall to pieces before you'd lift a finger. Too mean to pay for a lick of paint, and
then when you do you expect it to last ten years. I haven't got a home like other
women.* Workmen were treated as the house-guests we never had; my
mother's friends were neighbours, my father had none, and she wouldn't
give house-room to a spare bed, anyway, because she didn't want his relatives coming. Mr Strydom was served sweet strong tea to his taste many
times a day, while my mother stood by to chat and I followed his skills with
the brush, particularly fascinated when he was doing something he called,
in his Afrikaner's English, 'pulling the line'. This was the free-hand deft-
ness with which he could make a narrow black stripe dividing the lower half
of our passage, painted dark against dirty fingerprints, from the cream upper half. *Yust a sec while I first pull the line, ay.*

Then he would drain his cup so completely that the tea leaves swirled up
and stuck to the sides. This workmanlike thirst, for me, was a foreign custom, sign of the difference between being Afrikaans and English, as we
were, just as I accepted that it must be in accordance with their custom that
the black "boys" drank their tea from jam tins in the yard. But Mr Strydom,
like the doctor, like deaf dapper Mr Waite the electrician, who had drinking bouts because he had been through something called Ypres, and Mr
Hartman who sang to himself in a sad soprano while he tuned the Steinway
upright my mother had brought from her own mother's house, was a recurrent event. The state the house was in, this time, was one without prece-
dent; the men who were in were not repair men. They had been sent for to
exterminate what we called white ants—termites, who were eating our
house away under our feet. A million jaws were devouring steadily night
and day the timber that supported our unchanging routines: one day (if
my mother hadn't done something about it you may be sure no one else
would) that heavy Steinway in its real rosewood case would have crashed
through the floor-boards.

For years my mother had efficiently kicked apart the finely-granulated earth, forming cones perfect as the shape taken by sand that has trickled through an egg-timer, that was piled in our garden by ordinary black ants. My father never did a hand's turn; she herself poured a tar-smelling disinfectant down the ant-holes and emptied into them kettles of boiling water that made the ground break out in a sweat of gleaming, struggling, pinhead creatures in paroxysm. Yet (it was another event) on certain summer evenings after rain we would rush out into the garden to be in the tropical snowfall of millions of transparent wings from what we called flying ants, who appeared from nowhere. We watched while frogs bold with greed hopped onto the verandah to fill their pouched throats with these apparently harmless insects, and our cat ate steadily but with more self-control, spitting out with a shake of her whiskers any fragment of wing she might have taken up by mistake. We did not know that when these creatures shed their four delicate dragon-fly wings (some seemed to struggle like people getting out of coats) and became drab terrestrials, and some idiotically lifted their hindquarters in the air as if they were reacting to injury, they were enacting a nuptial ceremony that, one summer night or another, had ended in one out of these millions being fertilized and making her way under our house to become queen of a whole colony generated and given birth to by herself. Somewhere under our house she was in an endless parturition that would go on until she was found and killed.

The men had been sent for to search out the queen. No evil-smelling poisons, no opening-up of the tunnels more skilfully constructed than the London Underground, the Paris Metro or the New York subway I'd read about, no fumigation such as might do for cockroaches or moles or woodborer beetles, could eradicate termites. No matter how many thousands were killed by my mother, as, in the course of the excavations that tore up the floor-boards of her house, the brittle passages made of grains of earth cemented by a secretion carried in the termites' own bodies were broken, and the inhabitants poured out in a pus of white moving droplets with yellow heads—no matter how many she cast into death agony with her Flit spray, the termitary would at once be repopulated so long as the queen remained, alive, hidden in that inner chamber where her subjects who were also her progeny had walled her in and guarded and tended her.

The three exterminators were one white and two black. All had the red earth of underground clinging to their clothes and skin and hair; their eyes were bloodshot; the nails of their hands, black or white, were outlined in red, their ears rimmed. The long hairs in the nostrils of the white man were coated with red as a bee's legs are yellow with pollen. These men themselves appeared to have been dug up, raw from that clinging earth entombed beneath buildings. Bloodied by their life-long medieval quest, they were ready to take it up once more: the search for a queen. They were said to be very good; my mother was skeptical as she was about the powers of water-diviners with bent twigs or people who got the dead to spell out messages by moving a glass to letters of the alphabet. But what else could she do? My father left it all to her, she had the responsibility.

She didn't like the look of these men. They were so filthy with earth; hands like exposed roots reaching for the tea she brought. She served even the white man with a tin mug.

It was she who insisted they leave a few boards intact under the piano; she knew better than to trust them to move it without damage to the rosewood case. They didn't speak while children watched them at work. The only sound was the pick stopped by the density of the earth under our living-room, and the gasp of the black man who wielded the pick, pulling it free and hurling it back into the earth again. Held off by silence, we children would not go away. We stolidly spent all our free time in witness. Yet in spite of our vigilance, when it happened, when they found her, at last—the queen—we were not there.

My mother was mixing a cake and we had been attracted away to her by that substance of her alchemy that was not the beaten eggs and butter and sugar that went into it, even the lightest stroke of a quick forefinger into the bowl conveyed a coating of fragrant creamy sweetness to the mouth which already had foreknowledge of its utter satisfaction through the scent of vanilla that came not only from the bowl, but from her clothes, her hair, her very skin. Suddenly my mother's dog lifted his twitching lip back over his long teeth and began to bounce towards and back away from the screen door as he did when any stranger approached her. We looked up; the three men had come to the back steps. The white gestured his ochre hand brusquely at one of the blacks, who tramped forward with a child's cardboard shoe-box offered. The lid was on and there were rough air-holes punched in it here and there, just as in the boxes where we had kept silk worms until my mother thought they smelled too musty and threw them away. The white man gestured again; he and my mother for a moment held their hands the same way, his covered with earth, hers with flour. The black man took off the lid.

And there she was, the queen. The smallest child swallowed as if about to retch and ran away to the far side of the kitchen. The rest of us crowded nearer, but my mother made us make way, she wasn't going to be fobbed off with anything but complete satisfaction for her husband's money. We all gazed at an obese, helpless white creature, five inches long, with the tiny, shiny-visored head of an ant at one end. The body was a sort of dropsical sac attached to this head; it had no legs that could be seen, neither could it propel itself by peristaltic action, like a slug or worm. The queen. The queen whose domain, we had seen for ourselves in the galleries and passages that had been uncovered beneath our house, was as big as ours.

The white man spoke. 'That's 'er, missus.'

'You're sure you've got the queen?'

'We got it. That's it.' He gave a professional snigger at ignorance.

Was she alive?—But again the silence of the red-eyed, red-earthed men kept us back; they wouldn't let us daringly put out a finger to touch that body that seemed blown up in sections, like certain party balloons, and that had at once the suggestion of tactile attraction and repugnance—if a finger were to be stroked testingly along that perhaps faintly downy body, sweet creamy stuff might be expected to ooze from it. And in fact, when I found a book in the library called *The Soul of the White Ant*, by Eugène Marais, an Afrikaner like the white man who had found the queen's secret chamber, I read that the children-subjects at certain times draw nourishment from a queen's great body by stroking it so that she exudes her own rich maternal elixir.

'Ughh. Why's she so fat?' The smallest child had come close enough to force himself to look again.

'S'es full of ecks,' the white man said. 'They lays about a million ecks a day.'

'Is it dead?'

But the man only laughed, now that his job was done, and like the show-man's helper at the conclusion of an act, the black man knew to clap the lid back on the shoe-box. There was no way for us to tell; the queen cannot move, she is blind; whether she is underground, the tyrannical prisoner of her subjects who would not have been born and cannot live without her, or whether she is captured and borne away in a shoe-box, she is helpless to evade the consequences of her power.

My mother paid the men out of her housekeeping allowance (but she would have to speak to our father about that) and they nailed back the living-room floor boards and went away, taking the cardboard box with them. My mother had heard that the whole thing was a hoax; these men went from house to house, made the terrible mess they'd left hers in, and produced the same queen time and again, carrying it around with them.

Yet the termites left our house. We never had to have those particular workmen in again. The Axminster carpet was laid once more, the furniture put back in its place, and I had to do the daily half-hour practice on the Steinway that I had been freed of for a week. I read in the book from the library that when the queen dies or is taken away all the termites leave their posts and desert the termitary; some find their way to other communities, thousands die. The termitary with its fungus-gardens for food, its tunnels for conveying water from as much as forty feet underground, its elaborate defence and communications system, is abandoned.

We lived on, above the ruin. The children grew up and left the town; coming back from the war after 1946 and later from visits to Europe and America and the Far East, it bored them to hear the same old stories, to be asked: 'D'you remember Mr Hartman who used to come in to tune the pi-ano? He was asking after you the other day—poor thing, he's crippled with arthritis.' 'D'you remember old Strydom, "pulling the line" . . . how you kids used to laugh. I was quite ashamed . . .' 'D'you remember the time the white ant men were in, and you nearly broke your leg?' Were these events the sum of my mother's life? Why should I remember? I, who—shuddering to look back at those five rooms behind the bow-window eyes and the front-door mouth—have oceans, continents, snowed-in capitals, islands where turtles swim, cathedrals, theatres, palace gardens where people kiss and tramps drink wine—all these to remember. My father grew senile and she put him in a home for his last years. She stayed on, although she said she didn't want to; the house was a burden to her, she had carried the whole responsibility for him, for all of us, all her life. Now she is dead and although I suppose someone else lives in her house, the secret passages, the inner chamber in which she was our queen and our prisoner are sealed up, empty.

A Soldier's Embrace

NADINE GORDIMER

The day the cease-fire was signed she was caught in a crowd. Peasant boys from Europe who had made up the colonial army and freedom fighters whose column had marched into town were staggering about together outside the barracks, not three blocks from her house in whose rooms, for ten years, she had heard the blurred parade-ground bellow of colonial troops being trained to kill and be killed.

The men weren't drunk. They linked and swayed across the street; because all that had come to a stop, everything *had* to come to a stop: they surrounded cars, bicycles, vans, nannies with children, women with loaves of bread or basins of mangoes on their heads, a road gang with picks and shovels, a Coca-Cola truck, an old man with a barrow who bought bottles and bones. They were grinning and laughing amazement. That it could be: there they were, bumping into each other's bodies in joy, looking into each other's rough faces, all eyes crescent-shaped, brimming greeting. The words were in languages not mutually comprehensible, but the cries were new, a whooping and crowing all understood. She was bumped and jostled and she let go, stopped trying to move in any self-determined direction. There were two soldiers in front of her, blocking her off by their clumsy embrace (how do you do it, how do you do what you've never done before) and the embrace opened like a door and took her in—a pink hand with bitten nails grasping her right arm, a black hand with a big-dialled watch and thong bracelet pulling at her left elbow. Their three heads collided gaily, musk of sweat and tang of strong sweet soap clapped a mask to her nose and mouth. They all gasped with delicious shock. They were saying things to each other. She put up an arm round each neck, the rough pile of an army haircut on one side, the soft negro hair on the other, and kissed them both on the cheek. The embrace broke. The crowd wove her away behind backs, arms, jogging heads; she was returned to and took up the will of her direction again—she was walking home from the post office, where she had just sent a telegram to relatives abroad: ALL CALM DON'T WORRY.

The lawyer came back early from his offices because the courts were not sitting although the official celebration holiday was not until next day. He described to his wife the rally before the Town Hall, which he had watched from the office-building balcony. One of the guerilla leaders (not the most important; he on whose head the biggest price had been laid would not venture so soon and deep into the territory so newly won) had spoken for two hours from the balcony of the Town Hall. "Brilliant. Their jaws dropped. Brilliant. They've never heard anything on that level: precise, reasoned—none of them would ever have believed it possible, out of the bush. You should have seen de Poorteer's face. He'd like to be able to get up and open his mouth like that. And be listened to like that. . ." The Governor's handicap did not even bring the sympathy accorded to a stammer; he paused and gulped between words. The blacks had always used a portmanteau name for him that meant the-crane-who-is-trying-to-swallow-the-bullfrog.

One of the members of the black underground organization that could now come out in brass-band support of the freedom fighters had recognized the lawyer across from the official balcony and given him the freedom fighters' salute. The lawyer joked about it, miming, full of pride. "You should have been there—should have seen him, up there in the official party. I told you—really—you ought to have come to town with me this morning."

"And what did you do?" She wanted to assemble all details.

"Oh I gave the salute in return, chaps in the street saluted *me* . . . everybody was doing it. *It was marvellous.* And the police standing by; just to think, last month—only last week—you'd have been arrested."

"Like thumbing your nose at them," she said, smiling.

"Did anything go on around here?"

"Muchanga was afraid to go out all day. He wouldn't even run up to the post office for me!" Their servant had come to them many years ago, from service in the house of her father, a colonial official in the Treasury.

"But there was no excitement?"

She told him: "The soldiers and some freedom fighters mingled outside the barracks. I got caught for a minute or two. They were dancing about; you couldn't get through. All very good-natured.—Oh, I sent the cable."

An accolade, one side a white cheek, the other a black. The white one she kissed on the left cheek, the black one on the right cheek, as if these were two sides of one face.

That vision, version, was like a poster; the sort of thing that was soon peeling off dirty shopfronts and bus shelters while the months of wrangling talks preliminary to the take-over by the black government went by.

To begin with, the cheek was not white but pale or rather sallow, the poor boy's pallor of winter in Europe (that draft must have only just arrived and not yet seen service) with homesick pimples sliced off by the discipline of an army razor. And the cheek was not black but opaque peat-dark, waxed with sweat round the plump contours of the nostril. As if she could return to the moment again, she saw what she had not consciously noted: there had been a narrow pink strip in the darkness near the ear, the sort of tender stripe of healed flesh revealed when a scab is nicked off a little before it is ripe. The scab must have come away that morning: the young man picked at it in the troop carrier or truck (whatever it was the freedom fighters had; the colony had been told for years that they were supplied by the Chinese and Russians indiscriminately) on the way to enter the capital in triumph.

According to newspaper reports, the day would have ended for the two young soldiers in drunkenness and whoring. She was, apparently, not yet too old to belong to the soldier's embrace of all that a land-mine in the bush might have exploded for ever. That was one version of the incident. Another: the opportunity taken by a woman not young enough to be clasped in the arms of the one who (same newspaper, while the war was on, expressing the fears of the colonists for their women) would be expected to rape her.

She considered this version.

She had not kissed on the mouth, she had not sought anonymous lips and tongues in the licence of festival. Yet she had kissed. Watching herself again, she knew that. She had—god knows why—kissed them on either cheek, his left, his right. It was deliberate, if a swift impulse: she had distinctly made the move.

She did not tell what happened not because her husband would suspect licence in her, but because he would see her—born and brought up in the country as the daughter of an enlightened white colonial official, married to a white liberal lawyer well known for his defence of blacks in political trials—as giving free expression to liberal principles.

She had not told, she did not know what had happened.

She thought of a time long ago when a school camp had gone to the sea and immediately on arrival everyone had run down to the beach from the train, tripping and tearing over sand dunes of wild fig, aghast with ecstatic shock at the meeting with the water.

De Poorteer was recalled and the lawyer remarked to one of their black friends, "The crane has choked on the bullfrog. I hear that's what they're saying in the Quarter."

The priest who came from the black slum that had always been known simply by that anonymous term did not respond with any sort of glee. His reserve implied it was easy to celebrate; there were people who "shouted freedom too loud all of a sudden."

The lawyer and his wife understood: Father Mulumbua was one who had shouted freedom when it was dangerous to do so, and gone to prison several times for it, while certain people, now on the Interim Council set up to run the country until the new government took over, had kept silent. He named a few, but reluctantly. Enough to confirm their own suspicions— men who perhaps had made some deal with the colonial power to place its interests first, no matter what sort of government might emerge from the new constitution? Yet when the couple plunged into discussion their friend left them talking to each other while he drank his beer and gazed, frowning as if at a headache or because the sunset light hurt his eyes behind his spectacles, round her huge-leaved tropical plants that bowered the terrace in cool humidity.

They had always been rather proud of their friendship with him, this man in a cassock who wore a clenched fist carved of local ebony as well as a silver cross round his neck. His black face was habitually stern—a high seriousness balanced by sudden splurting laughter when they used to tease him over the fist—but never inattentively ill-at-ease.

"What was the matter?" She answered herself; "I had the feeling he didn't want to come here." She was using a paper handkerchief dipped in gin to wipe greenfly off the back of a pale new leaf that had shaken itself from its folds like a cut-out paper lantern.

"Good lord, he's been here hundreds of times."

"—Before, yes."

What things were they saying?

With the shouting in the street and the swaying of the crowd, the sweet powerful presence that confused the senses so that sound, sight, stink (sweat, cheap soap) ran into one tremendous sensation, she could not make out words that came so easily.

Not even what she herself must have said.

A few wealthy white men who had been boastful in their support of the colonial war and knew they would be marked down by the blacks as arch exploiters, left at once. Good riddance, as the lawyer and his wife remarked. Many ordinary white people who had lived contentedly, without questioning its actions, under the colonial government, now expressed an enthusiastic intention to help build a nation, as the newspapers put it. The lawyer's wife's neighbourhood butcher was one. "I don't mind blacks." He was expansive with her, in his shop that he had occupied for twelve years on a licence available only to white people. "Makes no difference to me who you are so long as you're honest." Next to a chart showing a beast mapped according to the cuts of meat it provided, he had hung a picture of the most important leader of the freedom fighters, expected to be first President. People like the butcher turned out with their babies clutching pennants when the leader drove through the town from the airport.

There were incidents (newspaper euphemism again) in the Quarter. It was to be expected. Political factions, tribally based, who had not fought the war, wanted to share power with the freedom fighters' Party. Muchanga no longer went down to the Quarter on his day off. His friends came to see him and sat privately on their hunkers near the garden compost heap. The ugly mansions of the rich who had fled stood empty on the bluff above the sea, but it was said they would make money out of them yet—they would be bought as ambassadorial residences when independence came, and with it many black and yellow diplomats. Zealots who claimed they belonged to the Party burned shops and houses of the poorer whites who lived, as the lawyer said, "in the inevitable echelon of colonial society", closest to the Quarter. A house in the lawyer's street was noticed by his wife to be accommodating what was certainly one of those families, in the outhouses; green nylon curtains had appeared at the garage window, she reported. The suburb was pleasantly overgrown and well-to-do; no one rich, just white professional people and professors from the university. The barracks was empty now, except for an old man with a stump and a police uniform stripped of insignia, a friend of Muchanga, it turned out, who sat on a beer-crate at the gates. He had lost his job as night-watchman when one of the rich people went away, and was glad to have work.

The street had been perfectly quiet; except for that first day.

The fingernails she sometimes still saw clearly were bitten down until embedded in a thin line of dirt all around, in the pink blunt fingers. The thumb and thick fingertips were turned back coarsely even while grasping her. Such hands had never been allowed to take possession. They were permanently raw, so young, from unloading coal, digging potatoes from the frozen Northern Hemisphere, washing hotel dishes. He had not been killed, and now that day of the cease-fire was over he would be delivered back across the sea to the docks, the stony farm, the scullery of the grand hotel. He would have to do anything he could get. There was unemployment in Europe where he had returned, the army didn't need all the young men any more.

A great friend of the lawyer and his wife, Chipande, was coming home from exile. They heard over the radio he was expected, accompanying the future President as confidential secretary, and they waited to hear from him.

The lawyer put up his feet on the empty chair where the priest had sat, shifting it to a comfortable position by hooking his toes, free in sandals, through the slats. "Imagine, Chipande!" Chipande had been almost a protégé—but they didn't like the term, it smacked of patronage. Tall, cocky, casual Chipande, a boy from the slummiest part of the Quarter, was recommended by the White Fathers' Mission (was it by Father Mulumbua himself?—the lawyer thought so, his wife was not sure they remembered correctly) as a bright kid who wanted to be articled to a lawyer. That was asking a lot, in those days—nine years ago. He never finished his apprenticeship because while he and his employer were soon close friends, and the kid picked up political theories from the books in the house he made free of, he became so involved in politics that he had to skip the country one jump ahead of a detention order signed by the crane-who-was-trying-to-swallow-the-bullfrog.

After two weeks, the lawyer phoned the offices the guerilla-movement-become-Party had set up openly in the town but apparently Chipande had an office in the former colonial secretariat. There he had a secretary of his own; he wasn't easy to reach. The lawyer left a message. The lawyer and his wife saw from the newspaper pictures he hadn't changed much: he had a beard and had adopted the Muslim cap favoured by political circles in exile on the East Coast.

He did come to the house eventually. He had the distracted, insistent friendliness of one who has no time to re-establish intimacy; it must be taken as read. And it must not be displayed. When he remarked on a shortage of accommodation for exiles now become officials, and the lawyer said the house was far too big for two people, he was welcome to move in and regard a self-contained part of it as his private living quarters, he did not answer but went on talking generalities. The lawyer's wife mentioned Father Mulumbua, whom they had not seen since just after the cease-fire. The lawyer added, "There's obviously some sort of big struggle going on, he's fighting for his political life there in the Quarter." "Again," she said, drawing them into a reminder of what had only just become their past.

But Chipande was restlessly following with his gaze the movements of old Muchanga, dragging the hose from plant to plant, careless of the spray; "You remember who this is, Muchanga?" she had said when the visitor arrived, yet although the old man had given, in their own language, the sort of respectful greeting even an elder gives a young man whose clothes and bearing denote rank and authority, he was not in any way overwhelmed nor enthusiastic—perhaps he secretly supported one of the rival factions?

The lawyer spoke of the latest whites to leave the country— people who had got themselves quickly involved in the sort of currency swindle that draws more outrage than any other kind of crime, in a new state fearing the flight of capital: "Let them go, let them go. Good riddance." And he turned to talk of other things—there were so many more important questions to occupy the attention of the three old friends.

But Chipande couldn't stay. Chipande could not stay for supper; his beautiful long velvety black hands with their pale lining (as she thought of the palms) hung impatiently between his knees while he sat forward in the chair, explaining, adamant against persuasion. He should not have been there, even now; he had official business waiting, sometimes he drafted correspondence until one or two in the morning. The lawyer remarked how there hadn't been a proper chance to talk; he wanted to discuss those fellows in the Interim Council Mulumbua was so warily distrustful of— what did Chipande know?

Chipande, already on his feet, said something dismissing and very slightly disparaging, not about the Council members but of Mulumbua—a reference to his connection with the Jesuit missionaries as an influence that "comes through". "But I must make a note to see him sometime."

It seemed that even black men who presented a threat to the Party could be discussed only among black men themselves, now. Chipande put an arm round each of his friends as for the brief official moment of a photograph, left them; he who used to sprawl on the couch arguing half the night before dossing down in the lawyer's pyjamas. "As soon as I'm settled I'll contact you. You'll be around, ay?"

"Oh we'll be around." The lawyer laughed, referring, for his part, to those who were no longer. "Glad to see you're not driving a Mercedes!" he called with reassured affection at the sight of Chipande getting into a modest car. How many times, in the old days, had they agreed on the necessity for African leaders to live simply when they came to power!

On the terrace to which he turned back, Muchanga was doing something extraordinary—wetting a dirty rag with Gilbey's. It was supposed to be his day off, anyway; why was he messing about with the plants when one wanted peace to talk undisturbed?

"Is those thing again, those thing is killing the leaves,"

"For heaven's sake, he could use methylated for that! Any kind of alcohol will do! Why don't you get him some?"

There were shortages of one kind and another in the country, and gin happened to be something in short supply.

Whatever the hand had done in the bush had not coarsened it. It, too, was suède-black, and elegant. The pale lining was hidden against her own skin where the hand grasped her left elbow. Strangely, black does not show toil—she remarked this as one remarks the quality of a fabric. The hand was not as long but as distinguished by beauty as Chipande's. The watch a fine piece of equipment for a fighter. There was something next to it, in fact looped over the strap by the angle of the wrist as the hand grasped. A bit of thong with a few beads knotted where it was joined as a bracelet. Or amulet. Their babies wore such things; often their first and only garment. Grandmothers or mothers attached it as protection. It had worked; he was alive at cease-fire. Some had been too deep in the bush to know, and had been killed after the fighting was over. He had pumped his head wildly and laughingly at whatever it was she—they—had been babbling.

The lawyer had more free time than he'd ever remembered. So many of his clients had left; he was deputed to collect their rents and pay their taxes for them, in the hope that their property wasn't going to be confiscated—there had been alarmist rumours among such people since the day of the cease-fire. But without the rich whites there was little litigation over possessions, whether in the form of the children of dissolved marriages or the houses and cars claimed by divorced wives. The Africans had their own ways of re-solving such redistribution of goods. And a gathering of elders under a tree was sufficient to settle a dispute over boundaries or argue for and against the guilt of a woman accused of adultery. He had had a message, in a round-about way, that he might be asked to be consultant on constitu-tional law to the Party, but nothing seemed to come of it. He took home with him the proposals for the draft constitution he had managed to get hold of. He spent whole afternoons in his study making notes for counter or improved proposals he thought he would send to Chipande or one of the other people he knew in high positions: every time he glanced up, there through his open windows was Muchanga's little company at the bottom of the garden. Once, when he saw they had straggled off, he wandered down himself to clear his head (he got drowsy, as he never did when he used to work twelve hours a day at the office). They ate dried shrimps, from the market: that's what they were doing! The ground was full of bitten-off heads and black eyes on stalks. His wife smiled. "They bring them. Mu-changa won't go near the market since the riot." "It's ridiculous. Who's go-ing to harm him?"

There was even a suggestion that the lawyer might apply for a professor-ship at the university. The chair of the Faculty of Law was vacant, since the students had demanded the expulsion of certain professors engaged dur-ing the colonial regime—in particular of the fuddy-duddy (good riddance) who had gathered dust in the Law chair, and the quite decent young man (pity about him) who had had Political Science. But what professor of Polit-ical Science could expect to survive both a colonial regime and the revolu-tionary regime that defeated it? The lawyer and his wife decided that since he might still be appointed in some consultative capacity to the new govern-ment it would be better to keep out of the university context, where the stu-dents were shouting for Africanization, and even an appointee with his credentials as a fighter of legal battles for blacks against the colonial regime in the past might not escape their ire.

Newspapers sent by friends from over the border gave statistics for the number of what they termed 'refugees' who were entering the neighbouring country. The papers from outside also featured sensationally the inevitable mistakes and misunderstandings, in a new administration, that led to several foreign businessmen being held for investigation by the new regime. For the last fifteen years of colonial rule, Gulf had been drilling for oil in the territory, and just as inevitably it was certain that all sorts of questionable people, from the point of view of the regime's determination not to be exploited preferentially, below the open market for the highest bidder in ideological as well as economic terms, would try to gain concessions.

His wife said, "The butcher's gone."

He was home, reading at his desk; he could spend the day more usefully there than at the office, most of the time. She had left after breakfast with her fisherman's basket that she liked to use for shopping, she wasn't away twenty minutes. "You mean the shop's closed?" There was nothing in the basket. She must have turned and come straight home.

"Gone. It's empty. He's cleared out over the weekend."

She sat down suddenly on the edge of the desk; and after a moment of silence, both laughed shortly, a strange, secret, complicit laugh. "Why, do you think?" "Can't say. He certainly charged, if you wanted a decent cut. But meat's so hard to get, now; I thought it was worth it—justified."

The lawyer raised his eyebrows and pulled down his mouth: "Exactly." They understood; the man probably knew he was marked to run into trouble for profiteering—he must have been paying through the nose for his supplies on the black market, anyway, didn't have much choice.

Shops were being looted by the unemployed and loafers (there had always been a lot of unemployed hanging around for the pickings of the town) who felt the new regime should entitle them to take what they dared not before. Radio and television shops were the most favoured objective for gangs who adopted the freedom fighters' slogans. Transistor radios were the portable luxuries of street life; the new regime issued solemn warnings, over those same radios, that looting and violence would be firmly dealt with but it was difficult for the police to be everywhere at once. Sometimes their actions became street battles, since the struggle with the looters changed character as supporters of the Party's rival political factions joined in with the thieves against the police. It was necessary to be ready to reverse direction, quickly turning down a side street in detour if one encountered such disturbances while driving around town. There were bodies sometimes; both husband and wife had been fortunate enough not to see any close up, so far. A company of the freedom fighters' army was brought down from the north and installed in the barracks to supplement the police force; they patrolled the Quarter, mainly. Muchanga's friend kept his job as gatekeeper although there were armed sentries on guard: the lawyer's wife found that a light touch to mention in letters to relatives in Europe.

"Where'll you go now?"

She slid off the desk and picked up her basket. "Supermarket, I suppose. Or turn vegetarian." He knew that she left the room quickly, smiling, be-

cause she didn't want him to suggest Muchanga ought to be sent to look for
fish in the markets along the wharf in the Quarter. Muchanga was being allowed to indulge in all manner of eccentric refusals; for no reason, unless
out of some curious sentiment about her father?

She avoided walking past the barracks because of the machine guns the
young sentries had in place of rifles. Rifles pointed into the air but machine
guns pointed to the street at the level of different parts of people's bodies,
short and tall, the backsides of babies slung on mothers' backs, the round
heads of children, her fisherman's basket—she knew she was getting like
the others: what she felt was afraid. She wondered what the butcher and
his wife had said to each other. Because he was at least one whom she had
known. He had sold the meat she had bought that these women and their
babies passing her in the street didn't have the money to buy.

It was something quite unexpected and outside their own efforts that decided it. A friend over the border telephoned and offered a place in a lawyers' firm of highest repute there, and some prestige in the world at large,
since the team had defended individuals fighting for freedom of the press
and militant churchmen upholding freedom of conscience on political issues. A telephone call; as simple as that. The friend said (and the lawyer
did not repeat this even to his wife) they would be proud to have a man of
his courage and convictions in the firm. He could be satisfied he would be
able to uphold the liberal principles everyone knew he had always stood
for; there were many whites, in that country still ruled by a white minority,
who deplored the injustices under which their black population suffered
etc. and believed you couldn't ignore the need for peaceful change etc.

His offices presented no problem; something called Africa Seabeds (For-
mosan Chinese who had gained a concession to ship seaweed and dried
shrimps in exchange for rice) took over the lease and the typists. The senior clerks and the current articled clerk (the lawyer had always given a
chance to young blacks, long before other people had come round to it—it
wasn't only the secretary to the President who owed his start to him) he
managed to get employed by the new Trades Union Council; he still knew
a few blacks who remembered the times he had acted for black workers in
disputes with the colonial government. The house would just have to stand
empty, for the time being. It wasn't imposing enough to attract an embassy
but maybe it would do for a Chargé d'Affaires—it was left in the hands of
a half-caste letting agent who was likely to stay put: only whites were allowed in, at the country over the border. Getting money out was going to
be much more difficult than disposing of the house. The lawyer would
have to keep coming back, so long as this remained practicable, hoping to
find a loophole in exchange control regulations.

She was deputed to engage the movers. In their innocence, they had thought it as easy as that! Every large vehicle, let alone a pantechnicon, was commandeered for months ahead. She had no choice but to grease a palm, although it went against her principles, it was condoning a practice they believed a young black state must stamp out before corruption took hold. He would take his entire legal library, for a start; that was the most important possession, to him. Neither was particularly attached to furniture. She did not know what there was she felt she really could not do without. Except the plants. And that was out of the question. She could not even mention it. She did not want to leave her towering plants, mostly natives of South America and not Africa, she supposed, whose aerial tubes pushed along the terrace brick erect tips extending hourly in the growth of the rainy season, whose great leaves turned shields to the spatter of Muchanga's hose glancing off in a shower of harmless arrows, whose two-hand-span trunks were smooth and grooved in one sculptural sweep down their length, or carved by the drop of each dead leaf-stem with concave medallions marking the place and building a pattern at once bold and exquisite. Such things would not travel; they were too big to give away.

The evening she was beginning to pack the books, the telephone rang in the study. Chipande—and he called her by her name, urgently, commandingly—"What is this all about? Is it true, what I hear? Let me just talk to him—"

"Our friend," she said, making a long arm, receiver at the end of it, towards her husband.

"But you can't leave!" Chipande shouted down the phone "*You* can't go! I'm coming round. *Now.*"

She went on packing the legal books while Chipande and her husband were shut up together in the living-room.

"He cried. You know, he actually cried." Her husband stood in the doorway, alone.

"I know—that's what I've always liked so much about them whatever they do. They feel."

The lawyer made a face: there it is, it happened; hard to believe.

"Rushing in here, after nearly a year! I said, but we haven't seen you, all this time . . . he took no notice. Suddenly he starts pressing me to take the university job, raising all sorts of objections, why not this . . . that. And then he really wept, for a moment."

They got on with packing books like builder and mate deftly handling and catching bricks.

And the morning they were to leave it was all done; twenty-one years of life in that house gone quite easily into one pantechnicon. They were quiet with each other, perhaps out of apprehension of the tedious search of their possessions that would take place at the border; it was said that if you struck over-conscientious or officious freedom fighter patrols they would even make you unload a piano, a refrigerator or washing machine. She had bought Muchanga a hawker's licence, a hand-cart, and stocks of small commodities. Now that many small shops owned by white shopkeepers had disappeared, there was an opportunity for humble itinerant black traders. Muchanga had lost his fear of the town. He was proud of what she had done for him and she knew he saw himself as a rich merchant; this was the only sort of freedom he understood, after so many years as a servant. But she also knew, and the lawyer sitting beside her in the car knew she knew, that the shortages of the goods Muchanga could sell from his cart, the sugar and soap and matches and pomade and sunglasses, would soon put him out of business. He promised to come back to the house and look after the plants every week; and he stood waving, as he had done every year when they set off on holiday. She did not know what to call out to him as they drove away. The right words would not come again; whatever they were, she left them behind.

The Last Day in the Field

CAROLINE GORDON

That was the fall when the leaves stayed green so long. We had a drouth in August and the ponds everywhere were dry and the watercourse shrunken. Then in September heavy rains came. Things greened up. It looked like winter was never coming.

"You aren't going to hunt this year, Aleck," Molly said. "Remember how you stayed awake nights last fall with that pain in your leg."

In October light frosts came. In the afternoons when I sat on the back porch going over my fishing tackle I marked their progress on the elderberry bushes that were left standing against the stable fence. The lower, spreading branches had turned yellow and were already sinking to the ground but the leaves in the top clusters still stood up stiff and straight.

"Ah-h, it'll get you yet!" I said, thinking how frost creeps higher and higher out of the ground each night of fall.

The dogs next door felt it and would thrust their noses through the wire fence scenting the wind from the north. When I walked in the back yard they would bound twice their height and whine, for meat scraps Molly said, but it was because they smelled blood on my old hunting coat.

They were almost matched liver-and-white pointers. The big dog had a beautiful, square muzzle and was deep-chested and rangy. The bitch, Judy, had a smaller head and not so good a muzzle but she was springy loined too and had one of the merriest tails I've ever watched.

When Joe Thomas, the boy that owned them, came home from the hardware store he would change his clothes and then come down the back way into the wired enclosure and we would stand there watching the dogs and wondering how they would work. Joe said they were keen as mustard. He was going to take them out the first good Saturday and wanted me to come along.

"I can't make it," I said, "my leg's worse this year than it was last."

408

The fifteenth of November was clear and so warm that we sat out on the porch till nine o'clock. It was still warm when we went to bed towards eleven. The change must have come in the middle of the night. I woke once, hearing the clock strike two, and felt the air cold on my face and thought before I went back to sleep that the weather had broken at last. When I woke again at dawn the cold air was slapping my face hard. I came wide awake, turned over in bed and looked out of the window.

There was a scaly-bark hickory tree growing on the east side of the house. You could see its upper branches from the bedroom window. The leaves had turned yellow a week ago. But yesterday evening when I walked out there in the yard they had still been flat with green streaks showing in them. Now they were curled up tight and a lot of leaves had fallen on to the ground.

I got out of bed quietly so as not to wake Molly, dressed and went down the back way over to the Thomas house. There was no one stirring but I knew which room Joe's was. The window was open and I could hear him snoring. I went up and stuck my head in.

"Hey," I said, "killing frost."

He opened his eyes and looked at me and then his eyes went shut. I reached my arm through the window and shook him. "Get up," I said, "we got to start right away."

He was awake now and out on the floor stretching. I told him to dress and be over at the house as quick as he could. I'd have breakfast ready for us both.

Aunt Martha had a way of leaving fire in the kitchen stove at night. There were red embers there now. I poked the ashes out and piled kindling on top of them. When the flames came up I put some heavier wood on, filled the coffee pot, and put some grease on in a skillet. By the time Joe got there I had coffee ready and some hoe cakes to go with our fried eggs. Joe had brought a thermos bottle. We put the rest of the coffee in it and I found a ham in the pantry and made some sandwiches.

While I was fixing the lunch Joe went down to the lot to hitch up. He was just driving Old Dick out of the stable when I came down the back steps. The dogs knew what was up, all right. They were whining and surging against the fence and Bob, the big dog, thrust his paw through and into the pocket of my hunting coat as I passed. While Joe was snapping on the leashes I got a few handfuls of straw from the rack and put it in the foot of the buggy. It was twelve miles where we were going; the dogs would need to ride warm coming back late.

Joe said he would drive. We got in the buggy and started out, up Seventh Street and on over to College and out through Scufftown. When we got into the nigger section we could see what a killing frost it had been. A light shimmer over all the ground still and the weeds around the cabins dark and matted the way they are when the frost hits them hard and twists them.

We drove on over the Red River bridge and up into the open country. At Jim Gill's place the cows had come up and were standing waiting to be milked but nobody was stirring yet from the house. I looked back from the top of the hill and saw that the frost mists still hung heavy in the bottom and thought it was a good sign. A day like this when the earth is warmer than the air currents is good for the hunter. Scent particles are borne on the warm air and birds will forage far on such a day.

It took us over an hour to get from Gloversville to Spring Creek. Joe wanted to get out as soon as we hit the big bottom there but I held him down and we drove on to the top of the ridge. We got out there, unhitched Old Dick and turned him into one of Rob Fayerlee's pastures—I thought how surprised Rob would be when he saw him grazing there—put our guns together, and started out, the dogs still on leash.

It was rough, broken ground, scrub oak, with a few gum trees and lots of buckberry bushes. One place a patch of corn ran clear up to the top of the ridge. As we passed along between the rows I could see the frost glistening on the north side of the stalks. I knew it was going to be a good day.

I walked over to the brow of the hill. From here you can see off over the whole valley—I've hunted every foot of it in my time—tobacco land, mostly. One or two patches of corn there on the side of the ridge. I thought we might start there and then I knew that wouldn't do. Quail will linger on the roost a cold day and feed in shelter during the morning. It is only in the afternoon that they will work out to the open.

The dogs were whining. Joe bent down and was about to slip their leashes. "Hey, boy," I said, "don't do that."

I turned around and looked down the other side of the ridge. It was better that way. The corn land of the bottoms ran high up on to the hill in several places there and where the corn stopped there were big patches of ironweed and buckberry. I knocked my pipe out on a stump.

"Let's go that way," I said.

Joe was looking at my old buckhorn whistle that I had slung around my neck. "I forgot to bring mine."

"All right," I said, "I'll handle 'em."

He unfastened their collars and cast off. They broke away, racing for the first hundred yards and barking, then suddenly swerved. The big dog took off to the right along the hillside. The bitch, Judy, skirted a belt of corn along the upper bottomlands. I kept my eye on the big dog. A dog that has bird sense will know cover when he sees it. This big Bob was an independent hunter, all right. I could see him moving fast through the scrub oaks, working his way down toward a patch of ironweed. He caught first scent just on the edge of the weed patch and froze with every indication of class, head up, nose stuck out, and tail straight in air. Judy, meanwhile, had been following the line of the corn field. A hundred yards away she caught sight of Bob's point and backed him.

We went up and flushed the birds. They got up in two bunches. I heard Joe's shot while I was in the act of raising my gun and I saw his bird fall not thirty paces from where I stood. I had covered the middle bird of the larger bunch—that's the one led by the boss cock—the way I usually do. He fell, whirling head over heels, driven a little forward by the impact. A well-centered shot. I could tell by the way the feathers fluffed as he tumbled.

The dogs were off through the grass. They had retrieved both birds. Joe stuck his in his pocket. He laughed. "I thought there for a minute you were going to let him get away."

I looked at him but I didn't say anything. It's a wonderful thing to be twenty years old.

The majority of the singles had flown straight ahead to settle in the rank grass that jutted out from the bottomland. Judy got down to work at once but the big dog broke off to the left, wanting to get footloose to find another covey. I thought of how Trecho, the best dog I ever had—the best dog any man ever had—used always to be wanting to do the same thing and I laughed.

"Naw, you don't," I said, "come back here, you scoundrel, and hunt these singles."

He stopped on the edge of a briar patch, looked at me and heeled up promptly. I clucked him out again. He gave me another look. I thought we were beginning to understand each other better. We got some nice points among those singles but we followed that valley along the creek bed and through two or three more corn fields without finding another covey. Joe was disappointed but I wasn't beginning to worry yet; you always make your bag in the afternoon.

It was twelve o'clock by this time, no sign of frost anywhere and the sun beating down steady on the curled-up leaves.

"Come on," I said, "let's go up to Buck's spring and eat."

We walked up the ravine whose bed was still moist with the fall rains and came out at the head of the hollow. They had cleared out some of the trees on the side of the ravine but the spring itself was the same: a deep pool welling up between the roots of an old sycamore. I unwrapped the sandwiches and the piece of cake and laid them on a stump. Joe got the thermos bottle out of his pocket. Something had gone wrong with it and the coffee was stone cold. We were about to drink it that way when Joe saw a good tin can flung down beside the spring. He made a trash fire and we put the coffee in the can and heated it to boiling.

It was warm in the ravine, sheltered from the wind, with the little fire burning. I turned my game leg so that the heat fell full on my knee. Joe had finished his last sandwich and was reaching for the cake.

"Good ham," he said.

"It's John Ferguson's," I told him.

He had got up and was standing over the spring. "Wonder how long this wood'll last, under water this way."

I looked at the sycamore root, green and slick where the thin stream of water poured over it, then my eyes went back to the dogs. They were tired, all right. Judy had gone off to lie down in a cool place at the side of the spring, but the big dog, Bob, lay there, his forepaws stretched out in front of him, never taking his eyes off our faces. I looked at him and thought how different he was from his mate and like some dogs I had known—and men too—who lived only for hunting and could never get enough no matter how long the day. There was something about his head and his markings that reminded one of another dog I used to hunt with a long time ago and I asked the boy who had trained him. He said the old fellow he bought the dogs from had been killed last spring, over in Trigg—Charley Morrison.

Charley Morrison! I remembered how he died, out hunting by himself and the gun had gone off, accidentally they said. Charley had called his dog to him, got blood over him and sent him home. The dog went, all right, but when they got there Charley was dead. Two years ago that was and now I was hunting the last dogs he'd ever trained. . . .

Joe lifted the thermos bottle. "Another cup?"

I held my cup out and he filled it. The coffee was still good and hot. I drank it, standing up, running my eye over the country in front of us. Afternoon is different from morning, more exciting. It isn't only as I say that you'll make your bag in the afternoon, but it takes more figuring. They're fed and rested and when they start out again they'll work in the open and over a wide range.

Joe was stamping out his cigarette: "Let's go."

The dogs were already out of sight but I could see the sedge grass ahead moving and I knew they'd be making for the same thing that took my eye: a spearhead of thicket that ran far out into this open field. We came up over a little rise. There they were, Bob on a point and Judy backing him not fifty feet from the thicket. I saw it was going to be tough shooting. No way to tell whether the birds were between the dog and the thicket or in the thicket itself. Then I saw that the cover was more open along the side of the thicket and I thought that that was the way they'd go if they were in the thicket. But Joe had already broken away to the left. He got too far to the side. The birds flushed to the right and left him standing, flat-footed, without a shot.

He looked sort of foolish and grinned.

I thought I wouldn't say anything and then I found myself speaking: "Trouble with you, you try to out-think the dog."

There was nothing to do about it, though. The chances were that the singles had pitched in the trees below. We went down there. It was hard hunting. The woods were open, the ground everywhere heavily carpeted with leaves. Dead leaves make a tremendous rustle when the dogs surge through them. It takes a good nose to cut scent keenly in such noisy cover. I kept my eye on Bob. He never faltered, getting over the ground in big, springy strides but combing every inch of it. We came to an open place in the woods. Nothing but hickory trees and bramble thickets overhung with trailing vines. Bob passed the first thicket and came to a beautiful point. We went up. He stood perfectly steady but the bird flushed out fifteen or twenty steps ahead of him. I saw it swing to the right, gaining altitude very quickly—woods birds will always cut back to known territory—and it came to me how it would be.

I called to Joe: "Don't shoot yet."

He nodded and raised his gun, following the bird with the barrel. It was directly over the treetops when I gave the word and he shot, scoring a clean kill.

He laughed excitedly as he stuck the bird in his pocket. "My God, man, I didn't know you could take that much time!"

We went on through the open woods. I was thinking about a day I'd had years ago in the woods at Grassdale, with my uncle, James Morris, and his son, Julian. Uncle James had given Julian and me hell for missing just such a shot. I can see him now standing up against a big pine tree, his face red from liquor and his gray hair ruffling in the wind: "*Let him alone! Let him alone!* And establish your lead as he climbs."

Joe was still talking about the shot he'd made. "Lord, I wish I could get another one like that."

"You won't," I said, "we're getting out of the woods now."

We struck a path that led due west and followed it for half a mile. My leg was stiff from the hip down now and every time I brought it over, the pain would start in my knee, Zing! and travel up and settle in the small of my back. I walked with my head down, watching the light catch on the ridges of Joe's brown corduroy trousers and then shift and catch again. Sometimes he would get on ahead and then there would be nothing but the black tree trunks coming up out of the dead leaves.

Joe was talking about some wild land up on the Cumberland. We could get up there on an early train. Have a good day. Might even spend the night. When I didn't answer he turned around: "Man, you're sweating."

I pulled my handkerchief out and wiped my face. "Hot work," I said.

He had stopped and was looking about him. "Used to be a spring somewhere around here."

He had found the path and was off. I sat down on a stump and mopped my face some more. The sun was halfway down through the trees now, the whole west woods ablaze with the light. I sat there and thought that in another hour it would be good and dark and I wished that the day could go on and not end so soon and yet I didn't see how I could make it much farther with my leg the way it was.

Joe was coming up the path with his folding cup full of water. I hadn't thought I was thirsty but the cold water tasted good. We sat there awhile and smoked, then Joe said that we ought to be starting back, that we must be a good piece from the rig by this time.

We set out, working north through the edge of the woods. It was rough going and I was thinking that it would be all I could do to make it back to the rig when we climbed a fence and came out at one end of a long field that sloped down to a wooded ravine. Broken ground, badly gullied and covered with sedge everywhere except where sumac thickets had sprung up—as birdy a place as ever I saw. I looked it over and knew I had to hunt it, leg or no leg, but it would be close work, for me and the dogs too.

I blew them in a bit and we stood there watching them cut up the cover. The sun was down now; there was just enough light left to see the dogs work. The big dog circled the far wall of the basin and came up wind just off the drain, then stiffened to a point. We walked down to it. The birds had obviously run a bit into the scraggly sumac stalks that bordered the ditch. My mind was so much on the dogs I forgot Joe. He took one step too many. The fullest blown bevy of the day roared up through the tangle. It had to be fast work. I raised my gun and scored with the only barrel I had time to peg. Joe shouted; I knew he had got one too.

We stood there trying to figure out which way the singles had gone but they had fanned out too quick for us, excited as we were, and after beating around awhile we gave up and went on.

We came to the rim of the swale, eased over it, crossed the dry creek bed that was drifted thick with leaves, and started up the other side. I had blown in the dogs, thinking there was no use for them to run their heads off now we'd started home, but they didn't come. I walked on a little farther, then I looked back and saw Bob's white shoulders through a tangle of cinnamon vine.

Joe had turned around too. "They've pinned a single out of that last covey," he said.

I looked over at him quick. "Your shot."

He shook his head. "No, you take it."

I limped back and flushed the bird. It went skimming along the buckberry bushes that covered that side of the swale. In the fading light I could hardly make it out and I shot too quick. It swerved over the thicket and I let go with the second barrel. It staggered, then zoomed up. Up, up, up, over the rim of the hill and above the tallest hickories. It hung there for a second, its wings black against the gold light, before, wings still spread, it came whirling down, like an autumn leaf, like the leaves that were everywhere about us, all over the ground.

The Destructors

GRAHAM GREENE

I

It was on the eve of August Bank Holiday that the latest recruit became the leader of the Wormsley Common Gang. No one was surprised except Mike, but Mike at the age of nine was surprised by everything. "If you don't shut your mouth," somebody once said to him, "you'll get a frog down it." After that Mike had kept his teeth tightly clamped except when the surprise was too great.

The new recruit had been with the gang since the beginning of the summer holidays, and there were possibilities about his brooding silence that all recognised. He never wasted a word even to tell his name until that was required of him by the rules. When he said "Trevor" it was a statement of fact, not as it would have been with the others a statement of shame or defiance. Nor did anyone laugh except Mike, who finding himself without support and meeting the dark gaze of the newcomer opened his mouth and was quiet again. There was every reason why T., as he was afterwards referred to, should have been an object of mockery—there was his name (and they substituted the initial because otherwise they had no excuse not to laugh at it), the fact that his father, a former architect and present clerk, had "come down in the world" and that his mother considered herself better than the neighbours. What but an odd quality of danger, of the unpredictable, established him in the gang without any ignoble ceremony of initiation?

The gang met every morning in an impromptu car-park, the site of the last bomb of the first blitz. The leader, who was known as Blackie, claimed to have heard it fall, and no one was precise enough in his dates to point out that he would have been one year old and fast asleep on the down platform of Wormsley Common Underground Station. On one side of the car-park leant the first occupied house, No. 3, of the shattered Northwood Terrace—literally leant, for it had suffered from the blast of the bomb and the side walls were supported on wooden struts. A smaller bomb and some incendiaries had fallen beyond, so that the house stuck up like a jagged tooth and carried on the further wall relics of its neighbour, a dado, the remains of a fireplace. T., whose words were almost confined to voting "Yes" or "No" to the plan of operations proposed each day by Blackie, once startled the whole gang by saying broodingly, "Wren built that house, father says."

"Who's Wren?"

"The man who built St. Paul's."

"Who cares?" Blackie said. "It's only Old Misery's."

Old Misery—whose real name was Thomas—had once been a builder and decorator. He lived alone in the crippled house, doing for himself: once a week you could see him coming back across the common with bread and vegetables, and once as the boys played in the car-park he put his head over the smashed wall of his garden and looked at them.

"Been to the loo," one of the boys said, for it was common knowledge that since the bombs fell something had gone wrong with the pipes of the house and Old Misery was too mean to spend money on the property. He could do the redecorating himself at cost price, but he had never learnt plumbing. The loo was a wooden shed at the bottom of the narrow garden with a star-shaped hole in the door: it had escaped the blast which had smashed the house next door and sucked out the window-frames of No. 3.

The next time the gang became aware of Mr. Thomas was more surprising. Blackie, Mike and a thin yellow boy, who for some reason was called by his surname Summers, met him on the common coming back from the market. Mr. Thomas stopped them. He said glumly, "You belong to the lot that play in the car-park?"

Mike was about to answer when Blackie stopped him. As the leader he had responsibilities. "Suppose we are?" he said ambiguously.

"I got some chocolates," Mr. Thomas said. "Don't like 'em myself. Here you are. Not enough to go round, I don't suppose. There never is," he added with sombre conviction. He handed over three packets of Smarties.

The gang were puzzled and perturbed by this action and tried to explain it away. "Bet someone dropped them and he picked 'em up," somebody suggested.

"Pinched 'em and then got in a bleeding funk," another thought aloud.

"It's a bribe," Summers said. "He wants us to stop bouncing balls on his wall."

"We'll show him we don't take bribes," Blackie said, and they sacrificed the whole morning to the game of bouncing that only Mike was young enough to enjoy. There was no sign from Mr. Thomas.

Next day T. astonished them all. He was late at the rendezvous, and the voting for that day's exploit took place without him. At Blackie's suggestion the gang was to disperse in pairs, take buses at random and see how many free rides could be snatched from unwary conductors (the operation was to be carried out in pairs to avoid cheating). They were drawing lots for their companions when T. arrived.

"Where you been, T.?" Blackie asked. "You can't vote now. You know the rules."

"I've been *there*," T. said. He looked at the ground, as though he had thoughts to hide.

"Where?"

"At Old Misery's." Mike's mouth opened and then hurriedly closed again with a click. He had remembered the frog.

"At Old Misery's?" Blackie said. There was nothing in the rules against it, but he had a sensation that T. was treading on dangerous ground. He asked hopefully, "Did you break in?"

"No. I rang the bell."

"And what did you say?"

"I said I wanted to see his house."

"What did he do?"

"He showed it to me."

"Pinch anything?"

"No."

"What did you do it for then?"

The gang had gathered round: it was as though an impromptu court were about to form and to try some case of deviation. T. said, "It's a beautiful house," and still watching the ground, meeting no one's eyes, he licked his lips first one way, then the other.

"What do you mean, a beautiful house?" Blackie asked with scorn.

"It's got a staircase two hundred years old like a corkscrew. Nothing holds it up."

"What do you mean, nothing holds it up. Does it float?"

"It's to do with opposite forces, Old Misery said."

"What else?"

"There's panelling."

"Like in the Blue Boar?"

"Two hundred years old."

"Is Old Misery two hundred years old?"

Mike laughed suddenly and then was quiet again. The meeting was in a serious mood. For the first time since T. had strolled into the car-park on the first day of the holidays his position was in danger. It only needed a single use of his real name and the gang would be at his heels.

"What did you do it for?" Blackie asked. He was just, he had no jealousy, he was anxious to retain T. in the gang if he could. It was the word "beautiful" that worried him—that belonged to a class world that you could still see parodied at the Wormsley Common Empire by a man wearing a top-hat and a monocle, with a haw-haw accent. He was tempted to say, "My dear

Trevor, old chap," and unleash his hell hounds. "If you'd broken in," he said sadly—that indeed would have been an exploit worthy of the gang.

"This was better," T. said. "I found out things." He continued to stare at his feet, not meeting anybody's eye, as though he were absorbed in some dream he was unwilling—or ashamed—to share.

"What things?"

"Old Misery's going to be away all tomorrow and Bank Holiday."

Blackie said with relief, "You mean we could break in?"

"And pinch things?" somebody asked.

Blackie said, "Nobody's going to pinch things. Breaking in—that's good enough, isn't it? We don't want any court stuff."

"I don't want to pinch anything," T. said. "I've got a better idea."

"What is it?"

T. raised eyes, as grey and disturbed as the drab August day. "We'll pull it down," he said. "We'll destroy it."

Blackie gave a single hoot of laughter and then, like Mike, fell quiet, daunted by the serious implacable gaze. "What'd the police be doing all the time?" he said.

"They'd never know. We'd do it from inside. I've found a way in." He said with a sort of intensity, "We'd be like worms, don't you see, in an apple. When we came out again there'd be nothing there, no staircase, no panels, nothing but just walls, and then we'd make the walls fall down—somehow."

"We'd go to jug," Blackie said.

"Who's to prove? and anyway we wouldn't have pinched anything." He added without the smallest flicker of glee, "There wouldn't be anything to pinch after we'd finished."

"I've never heard of going to prison for breaking things," Summers said.

"There wouldn't be time," Blackie said. "I've seen housebreakers at work."

"There are twelve of us," T. said. "We'd organise."

"None of us know how . . . ."

"I know," T. said. He looked across at Blackie, "Have you got a better plan?"

"Today," Mike said tactlessly, "we're pinching free rides . . . "

"Free rides," T. said. "You can stand down, Blackie, if you'd rather . . . "

"The gang's got to vote."

"Put it up then."

Blackie said uneasily, "It's proposed that tomorrow and Monday we destroy Old Misery's house."

"Here, here," said a fat boy called Joe.

"Who's in favour?"

T. said, "It's carried."

"How do we start?" Summers asked.

"He'll tell you," Blackie said. It was the end of his leadership. He went away to the back of the car-park and began to kick a stone, dribbling it this way and that. There was only one old Morris in the park, for few cars were left there except lorries: without an attendant there was no safety. He took a flying kick at the car and scraped a little paint off the rear mudguard. Beyond, paying no more attention to him than to a stranger, the gang had gathered round T.; Blackie was dimly aware of the fickleness of favour. He thought of going home, of never returning, of letting them all discover the hollowness of T.'s leadership, but suppose after all what T. proposed was possible—nothing like it had ever been done before. The fame of the Wormsley Common car-park gang would surely reach around London. There would be headlines in the papers. Even the grown-up gangs who ran the betting at the all-in wrestling and the barrow-boys would hear with respect of how Old Misery's house had been destroyed. Driven by the pure, simple and altruistic ambition of fame for the gang, Blackie came back to where T. stood in the shadow of Misery's wall.

T. was giving his orders with decision: it was as though this plan had been with him all his life, pondered through the seasons, now in his fifteenth year crystallised with the pain of puberty. "You," he said to Mike, "bring some big nails, the biggest you can find, and a hammer. Anyone else who can better bring a hammer and a screwdriver. We'll need plenty of them. Chisels too. We can't have too many chisels. Can anybody bring a saw?"

"I can," Mike said.

"Not a child's saw," T. said. "A real saw."

Blackie realised he had raised his hand like any ordinary member of the gang.

"Right, you bring one, Blackie. But now there's a difficulty. We want a hacksaw."

"What's a hacksaw?" someone asked.

"You can get 'em at Woolworth's," Summers said.

The fat boy called Joe said gloomily, "I knew it would end in a collection."

"I'll get one myself," T. said. "I don't want your money. But I can't buy a sledge-hammer."

Blackie said, "They are working on No. 15. I know where they'll leave their stuff for Bank Holiday."

"Then that's all," T. said. "We meet here at nine sharp."

"I've got to go to church," Mike said.

"Come over the wall and whistle. We'll let you in."

II

On Sunday morning all were punctual except Blackie, even Mike. Mike had had a stroke of luck. His mother felt ill, his father was tired after Saturday night, and he was told to go to church alone with many warnings of what would happen if he strayed. Blackie had had difficulty in smuggling out the saw, and then in finding the sledge-hammer at the back of No. 15. He approached the house from a lane at the rear of the garden, for fear of the policeman's beat along the main road. The tired evergreens kept off a stormy sun: another wet Bank Holiday was being prepared over the Atlantic, beginning in swirls of dust under the trees. Blackie climbed the wall into Misery's garden.

There was no sign of anybody anywhere. The loo stood like a tomb in a neglected graveyard. The curtains were drawn. The house slept. Blackie lumbered nearer with the saw and the sledge-hammer. Perhaps after all nobody had turned up: the plan had been a wild invention: they had woken wiser. But when he came close to the back door he could hear a confusion of sound, hardly louder than a hive in swarm: a clickety-clack, a bang bang bang, a scraping, a creaking, a sudden painful crack. He thought: it's true, and whistled.

They opened the back door to him and he came in. He had at once the impression of organisation, very different from the old happy-go-lucky ways under his leadership. For a while he wandered up and down stairs looking for T. Nobody addressed him: he had a sense of great urgency, and already he could begin to see the plan. The interior of the house was being carefully demolished without touching the outer walls. Summers with hammer and chisel was ripping out the skirting-boards in the ground floor dining-room: he had already smashed the panels of the door. In the same room Joe was heaving up the parquet blocks, exposing the soft wood floor-boards over the cellar. Coils of wire came out of the damaged skirting and Mike sat happily on the floor, clipping the wires.

On the curved stairs two of the gang were working hard with an inadequate child's saw on the banisters—when they saw Blackie's big saw they signalled for it wordlessly. When he next saw them a quarter of the banisters had been dropped into the hall. He found T. at last in the bathroom—he sat moodily in the least cared-for room in the house, listening to the sounds coming up from below.

"You've really done it," Blackie said with awe. "What's going to happen?"

"We've only just begun," T. said. He looked at the sledge-hammer and gave his instructions. "You stay here and break the bath and the wash-basin. Don't bother about the pipes. They come later."

Mike appeared at the door. "I've finished the wire, T.," he said.

"Good. You've just got to go wandering round now. The kitchen's in the basement. Smash all the china and glass and bottles you can lay hold of. Don't turn on the taps—we don't want a flood—yet. Then go into all the rooms and turn out drawers. If they are locked get one of the others to break them open. Tear up any papers you find and smash all the ornaments. Better take a carving-knife with you from the kitchen. The bedroom's opposite here. Open the pillows and tear up the sheets. That's enough for the moment. And you, Blackie, when you've finished in here crack the plaster in the passage up with your sledge-hammer."

"What are you going to do?" Blackie asked.

"I'm looking for something special," T. said.

It was nearly lunch-time before Blackie had finished and went in search of T. Chaos had advanced. The kitchen was a shambles of broken glass and china. The dining-room was stripped of parquet, the skirting was up, the door had been taken off its hinges, and the destroyers had moved up a floor. Streaks of light came in through the closed shutters where they worked with the seriousness of creators—and destruction after all is a form of creation. A kind of imagination had seen this house as it had now become.

Mike said, "I've got to go home for dinner."

"Who else?" T. asked, but all the others on one excuse or another had brought provisions with them.

They squatted in the ruins of the room and swapped unwanted sandwiches. Half an hour for lunch and they were at work again. By the time Mike returned, they were on the top floor, and by six the superficial damage was completed. The doors were all off, all the skirtings raised, the furniture pillaged and ripped and smashed—no one could have slept in the house except on a bed of broken plaster. T. gave his orders—eight o'clock next morning, and to escape notice they climbed singly over the garden wall, into the car-park. Only Blackie and T. were left: the light had nearly gone, and when they touched a switch, nothing worked—Mike had done his job thoroughly.

"Did you find anything special?" Blackie asked.

T. nodded. "Come over here," he said, "and look." Out of both pockets he drew bundles of pound notes. "Old Misery's savings," he said. "Mike ripped out the mattress, but he missed them."

"What are you going to do? Share them?"

"We aren't thieves," T. said. "Nobody's going to steal anything from this house. I kept these for you and me—a celebration." He knelt down on the floor and counted them out—there were seventy in all. "We'll burn them," he said, "one by one," and taking it in turns they held a note upwards and lit the top corner, so that the flame burnt slowly towards their fingers. The grey ash floated above them and fell on their heads like age. "I'd like to see Old Misery's face when we are through," T. said.

"You hate him a lot?" Blackie asked.

"Of course I don't hate him," T. said. "There'd be no fun if I hated him." The last burning note illuminated his brooding face. "All this hate and love," he said, "it's soft, it's hooey. There's only things, Blackie," and he looked round the room crowded with the unfamiliar shadows of half things, broken things, former things. "I'll race you home, Blackie," he said.

III

Next morning the serious destruction started. Two were missing—Mike and another boy whose parents were off to Southend and Brighton in spite of the slow warm drops that had begun to fall and the rumble of thunder in the estuary like the first guns of the old blitz. "We've got to hurry," T. said.

Summers was restive. "Haven't we done enough?" he said. "I've been given a bob for slot machines. This is like work."

"We've hardly started," T. said. "Why, there's all the floors left, and the stairs. We haven't taken out a single window. You voted like the others. We are going to *destroy* this house. There won't be anything left when we've finished."

They began again on the first floor picking up the top floor-boards next the outer wall, leaving the joints exposed. Then they sawed through the joists and retreated into the hall, as what was left of the floor heeled and sank. They had learnt with practise, and the second floor collapsed more easily. By the evening an odd exhilaration seized them as they looked down the great hollow of the house. They ran risks and made mistakes: when they thought of the windows it was too late to reach them. "Cor," Joe said, and dropped a penny down into the dry rubble-filled well. It cracked and span among the broken glass.

"Why did we start this?" Summers asked with astonishment; T. was already on the ground, digging at the rubble, clearing a space along the outer wall. "Turn on the taps," he said. "It's too dark for anyone to see now, and in the morning it won't matter." The water overtook them on the stairs and fell through the floorless rooms.

It was then they heard Mike's whistle at the back. "Something's wrong," Blackie said. They could hear his urgent breathing as they unlocked the door.

"The bogies?" Summers asked.

"Old Misery," Mike said. "He's on his way." He put his head between his knees and retched. "Ran all the way," he said with pride.

"But why?" T. said. "He told me . . . " He protested with the fury of the child he had never been, "It isn't fair."

"He was down at Southend," Mike said, "and he was on the train coming back. Said it was too cold and wet." He paused and gazed at the water. "My, you've had a storm here. Is the roof leaking?"

"How long will he be?"

"Five minutes. I gave Ma the slip and ran."

"We better clear," Summers said. "We've done enough, anyway."

"Oh no, we haven't. Anybody could do this—" "this" was the shattered hollowed house with nothing left but the walls. Yet walls could be preserved. Façades were valuable. They could build inside again more beautifully than before. This could again be a home. He said angrily, "We've got to finish. Don't move. Let me think."

"There's no time," a boy said.

"There's got to be a way," T. said. "We couldn't have got this far . . ."

"We've done a lot," Blackie said.

"No. No, we haven't. Somebody watch the front."

"We can't do any more."

"He may come in at the back."

"Watch the back too." T. began to plead. "Just give me a minute and I'll fix it. I swear I'll fix it." But his authority had gone with his ambiguity. He was only one of the gang. "Please," he said.

"Please," Summers mimicked him, and then suddenly struck home with the fatal name. "Run along home, Trevor."

T. stood with his back to the rubble like a boxer knocked groggy against the ropes. He had no words as his dreams shook and slid. Then Blackie acted before the gang had time to laugh, pushing Summers backward. "I'll watch the front, T.," he said, and cautiously he opened the shutters of the hall. The grey wet common stretched ahead, and the lamps gleamed in the puddles. "Someone's coming, T. No, it's not him. What's your plan, T.?"

"Tell Mike to go out to the loo and hide close beside it. When he hears me whistle he's got to count ten and start to shout."

"Shout what?"

"Oh, 'Help,' anything."

"You hear, Mike," Blackie said. He was the leader again. He took a quick look between the shutters. "He's coming, T."

"Quick, Mike. The loo. Stay here, Blackie, all of you till I yell."

"Where are you going, T.?"

"Don't worry. I'll see to this. I said I would, didn't I?"

Old Misery came limping off the common. He had mud on his shoes and he stopped to scrape them on the pavement's edge. He didn't want to soil his house, which stood jagged and dark between the bomb-sites, saved so narrowly, as he believed, from destruction. Even the fanlight had been left unbroken by the bomb's blast. Somewhere somebody whistled. Old Misery looked sharply round. He didn't trust whistles. A child was shouting: it seemed to come from his own garden. Then a boy ran into the road from the car-park. "Mr. Thomas," he called, "Mr. Thomas."

"What is it?"

"I'm terribly sorry, Mr. Thomas. One of us got taken short, and we thought you wouldn't mind, and now he can't get out."

"What do you mean, boy?"

"He's got stuck in your loo."

"He'd no business . . . Haven't I seen you before?"

"You showed me your house."

"So I did. So I did. That doesn't give you the right to . . . ."

"Do hurry, Mr. Thomas. He'll suffocate."

"Nonsense. He can't suffocate. Wait till I put my bag in."

"I'll carry your bag."

"Oh no, you don't. I carry my own."

"This way, Mr. Thomas."

"I can't get in the garden that way. I've got to go through the house."

"But you *can* get in the garden this way, Mr. Thomas. We often do."

"You often do?" He followed the boy with a scandalised fascination. "When? What right? . . ."

"Do you see . . . ? the wall's low."

"I'm not going to climb walls into my own garden. It's absurd."

"This is how we do it. One foot here, one foot there, and over." The boy's face peered down, an arm shot out, and Mr. Thomas found his bag taken and deposited on the other side of the wall.

"Give me back my bag," Mr. Thomas said. From the loo a boy yelled and yelled. "I'll call the police."

"Your bag's all right, Mr. Thomas. Look. One foot there. On your right. Now just above. To your left." Mr. Thomas climbed over his own garden wall. "Here's your bag, Mr. Thomas."

"I'll have the wall built up," Mr. Thomas said, "I'll not have you boys coming over here, using my loo." He stumbled on the path, but the boy caught his elbow and supported him. "Thank you, thank you, my boy," he murmured automatically. Somebody shouted again through the dark. "I'm coming, I'm coming," Mr. Thomas called. He said to the boy beside him, "I'm not unreasonable. Been a boy myself. As long as things are done regular. I don't mind you playing round the place Saturday mornings. Sometimes I like company. Only it's got to be regular. One of you asks leave and I say Yes. Sometimes I'll say No. Won't feel like it. And you come in at the front door and out at the back. No garden walls."

"Do get him out, Mr. Thomas."

"He won't come to any harm in my loo," Mr. Thomas said, stumbling slowly down the garden. "Oh, my rheumatics," he said. "Always get 'em on Bank Holiday. I've got to go careful. There's loose stones here. Give me your hand. Do you know what my horoscope said yesterday? 'Abstain from any dealings in first half of week. Danger of serious crash.' That might be on this path," Mr. Thomas said. "They speak in parables and double meanings." He paused at the door of the loo. "What's the matter in there?" he called. There was no reply.

"Perhaps he's fainted," the boy said.

"Not in my loo. Here, you, come out," Mr. Thomas said, and giving a great jerk at the door he nearly fell on his back when it swung easily open. A hand first supported him and then pushed him hard. His head hit the opposite wall and he sat heavily down. His bag hit his feet. A hand whipped the key out of the lock and the door slammed. "Let me out," he called, and heard the key turn in the lock. "A serious crash," he thought, and felt dithery and confused and old.

A voice spoke to him softly through the star-shaped hole in the door.

"Don't worry, Mr. Thomas," it said, "we won't hurt you, not if you stay quiet."

Mr. Thomas put his head between his hands and pondered. He had noticed that there was only one lorry in the car-park, and he felt certain that the driver would not come for it before the morning. Nobody could hear him from the road in front, and the lane at the back was seldom used. Anyone who passed there would be hurrying home and would not pause for what they would certainly take to be drunken cries. And if he did call "Help," who, on a lonely Bank Holiday evening, would have the courage to investigate? Mr. Thomas sat on the loo and pondered with the wisdom of age.

After a while it seemed to him that there were sounds in the silence—they were faint and came from the direction of his house. He stood up and peered through the ventilation-hole—between the cracks in one of the shutters he saw a light, not the light of a lamp, but the wavering light that a candle might give. Then he thought he heard the sound of hammering and scraping and chipping. He thought of burglars—perhaps they had employed the boy as a scout, but why should burglars engage in what sounded more and more like a stealthy form of carpentry? Mr. Thomas let out an experimental yell, but nobody answered. The noise could not even have reached his enemies.

IV

Mike had gone home to bed, but the rest stayed. The question of leadership no longer concerned the gang. With nails, chisels, screwdrivers, anything that was sharp and penetrating they moved around the inner walls worrying at the mortar between the bricks. They started too high, and it was Blackie who hit on the damp course and realised the work could be halved if they weakened the joints immediately above. It was a long, tiring, unamusing job, but at last it was finished. The gutted house stood there balanced on a few inches of mortar between the damp course and the bricks.

There remained the most dangerous task of all, out in the open at the edge of the bomb-site. Summers was sent to watch the road for passers-by, and Mr. Thomas, sitting on the loo, heard clearly now the sound of sawing. It no longer came from his house, and that a little reassured him. He felt less concerned. Perhaps the other noises too had no significance.

A voice spoke to him through the hole. "Mr. Thomas."

"Let me out," Mr. Thomas said sternly.

"Here's a blanket," the voice said, and a long grey sausage was worked through the hole and fell in swathes over Mr. Thomas's head.

"There's nothing personal," the voice said. "We want you to be comfortable to-night."

"To-night," Mr. Thomas repeated incredulously.

"Catch," the voice said. "Penny buns—we've buttered them, and sausage-rolls. We don't want you to starve, Mr. Thomas."

Mr. Thomas pleaded desperately. "A joke's a joke, boy. Let me out and I won't say a thing. I've got rheumatics. I got to sleep comfortable."

"You wouldn't be comfortable, not in your house, you wouldn't. Not now."

"What do you mean, boy?" but the footsteps receded. There was only the silence of night: no sound of sawing. Mr. Thomas tried one more yell, but he was daunted and rebuked by the silence—a long way off an owl hooted and made away again on its muffled flight through the soundless world.

At seven next morning the driver came to fetch his lorry. He climbed into the seat and tried to start the engine. He was vaguely aware of a voice shouting, but it didn't concern him. At last the engine responded and he backed the lorry until it touched the great wooden shore that supported Mr. Thomas's house. That way he could drive right out and down the street without reversing. The lorry moved forward, was momentarily checked as though something were pulling it from behind, and then went on to the sound of a long rumbling crash. The driver was astonished to see bricks bouncing ahead of him, while stones hit the roof of his cab. He put on his brakes. When he climbed out the whole landscape had suddenly altered. There was no house beside the car-park, only a hill of rubble. He went round and examined the back of his car for damage, and found a rope tied there that was still twisted at the other end round part of a wooden strut.

The driver again became aware of somebody shouting. It came from the wooden erection which was the nearest thing to a house in that desolation of broken brick. The driver climbed the smashed wall and unlocked the door. Mr. Thomas came out of the loo. He was wearing a grey blanket to which flakes of pastry adhered. He gave a sobbing cry. "My house," he said. "Where's my house?"

"Search me," the driver said. His eye lit on the remains of a bath and what had once been a dresser and he began to laugh. There wasn't anything left anywhere.

"How dare you laugh," Mr. Thomas said. "It was my house. My house."

"I'm sorry," the driver said, making heroic efforts, but when he remembered the sudden check to his lorry, the crash of bricks falling, he became convulsed again. One moment the house had stood there with such dignity between the bomb-sites like a man in a top hat, and then, bang, crash, there wasn't anything left—not anything. He said, "I'm sorry. I can't help it, Mr. Thomas. There's nothing personal, but you got to admit it's funny."

The Minister's Black Veil— A Parable*

NATHANIEL HAWTHORNE

The sexton stood in the porch of Milford meeting-house, pulling busily at the bell-rope. The old people of the village came stooping along the street. Children, with bright faces, tripped merrily beside their parents, or mimicked a graver gait, in the conscious dignity of their Sunday clothes. Spruce bachelors looked sidelong at the pretty maidens, and fancied that the Sabbath sunshine made them prettier than on week days. When the throng had mostly streamed into the porch, the sexton began to toll the bell, keeping his eye on the Reverend Mr. Hooper's door. The first glimpse of the clergyman's figure was the signal for the bell to cease its summons.

"But what has good Parson Hooper got upon his face?" cried the sexton in astonishment.

All within hearing immediately turned about, and beheld the semblance of Mr. Hooper, pacing slowly his meditative way towards the meeting-house. With one accord they started, expressing more wonder than if some strange minister were coming to dust the cushions of Mr. Hooper's pulpit.

"Are you sure it is our parson?" inquired Goodman Gray of the sexton.

"Of a certainty it is good Mr. Hooper," replied the sexton. "He was to have exchanged pulpits with Parson Shute, of Westbury; but Parson Shute sent to excuse himself yesterday, being to preach a funeral sermon."

The cause of so much amazement may appear sufficiently slight. Mr. Hooper, a gentlemanly person, of about thirty, though still a bachelor, was dressed with due clerical neatness, as if a careful wife had starched his

*Another clergyman in New England, Mr. Joseph Moody, of York, Maine, who died about eighty years since, made himself remarkable by the same eccentricity that is here related of the Reverend Mr. Hooper. In his case, however, the symbol had a different import. In early life he had accidentally killed a beloved friend; and from that day till the hour of his own death, he hid his face from men.

427

band, and brushed the weekly dust from his Sunday's garb. There was but one thing remarkable in his appearance. Swathed about his forehead, and hanging down over his face, so low as to be shaken by his breath, Mr. Hooper had on a black veil. On a nearer view it seemed to consist of two folds of crape, which entirely concealed his features, except the mouth and chin, but probably did not intercept his sight, further than to give a darkened aspect to all living and inanimate things. With this gloomy shade before him, good Mr. Hooper walked onward, at a slow and quiet pace, stooping somewhat, and looking on the ground, as is customary with abstracted men, yet nodding kindly to those of his parishioners who still waited on the meeting-house steps. But so wonder-struck were they that his greeting hardly met with a return.

"I can't really feel as if good Mr. Hooper's face was behind that piece of crape," said the sexton.

"I don't like it," muttered an old woman, as she hobbled into the meeting-house. "He has changed himself into something awful, only by hiding his face."

"Our parson has gone mad!" cried Goodman Gray, following him across the threshold.

A rumor of some unaccountable phenomenon had preceded Mr. Hooper into the meeting-house, and set all the congregation astir. Few could refrain from twisting their heads towards the door; many stood upright, and turned directly about; while several little boys clambered upon the seats, and came down again with a terrible racket. There was a general bustle, a rustling of the women's gowns and shuffling of the men's feet, greatly at variance with that hushed repose which should attend the entrance of the minister. But Mr. Hooper appeared not to notice the perturbation of his people. He entered with an almost noiseless step, bent his head mildly to the pews on each side, and bowed as he passed his oldest parishioner, a white-haired great-grandsire, who occupied an armchair in the centre of the aisle. It was strange to observe how slowly this venerable man became conscious of something singular in the appearance of his pastor. He seemed not fully to partake of the prevailing wonder, till Mr. Hooper had ascended the stairs, and showed himself in the pulpit, face to face with his congregation, except for the black veil. That mysterious emblem was never once withdrawn. It shook with his measured breath as he gave out the psalm; it threw its obscurity between him and the holy page, as he read the Scriptures; and while he prayed, the veil lay heavily on his uplifted countenance. Did he seek to hide it from the dread Being whom he was addressing?

Such was the effect of this simple piece of crape, that more than one woman of delicate nerves was forced to leave the meeting-house. Yet perhaps the pale-faced congregation was almost as fearful a sight to the minister, as his black veil to them.

Mr. Hooper had the reputation of a good preacher, but not an energetic one: he strove to win his people heavenward by mild, persuasive influences, rather than to drive them thither by the thunders of the Word. The sermon which he now delivered was marked by the same characteristics of style and manner as the general series of his pulpit oratory. But there was something, either in the sentiment of the discourse itself, or in the imagination of the auditors, which made it greatly the most powerful effort that they had ever heard from their pastor's lips. It was tinged, rather more darkly than usual, with the gentle gloom of Mr. Hooper's temperament. The subject had reference to secret sin, and those sad mysteries which we hide from our nearest and dearest, and would fain conceal from our own consciousness, even forgetting that the Omniscient can detect them. A subtle power was breathed into his words. Each member of the congregation, the most innocent girl, and the man of hardened breast, felt as if the preacher had crept upon them, behind his awful veil, and discovered their hoarded iniquity of deed or thought. Many spread their clasped hands on their bosoms. There was nothing terrible in what Mr. Hooper said, at least, no violence; and yet, with every tremor of his melancholy voice, the hearers quaked. An unsought pathos came hand in hand with awe. So sensible were the audience of some unwonted attribute in their minister, that they longed for a breath of wind to blow aside the veil, almost believing that a stranger's visage would be discovered, though the form, gesture, and voice were those of Mr. Hooper.

At the close of the services, the people hurried out with indecorous confusion, eager to communicate their pent-up amazement, and conscious of lighter spirits the moment they lost sight of the black veil. Some gathered in little circles, huddled closely together, with their mouths all whispering in the centre: some went homeward alone, wrapt in silent meditation; some talked loudly, and profaned the Sabbath-day with ostentatious laughter. A few shook their sagacious heads, intimating that they could penetrate the mystery; while one or two affirmed that there was no mystery at all, but only that Mr. Hooper's eyes were so weakened by the midnight lamp, as to require a shade. After a brief interval, forth came good Mr. Hooper also, in the rear of his flock. Turning his veiled face from one group to another, he paid due reverence to the hoary heads, saluted the middle aged, with kind dignity as their friend and spiritual guide, greeted the young with mingled authority and love, and laid his hands on the little children's heads to bless them. Such was always his custom on the Sabbath-day. Strange and bewildered looks repaid him for his courtesy. None, as on former occasions, aspired to the honor of walking by their pastor's side. Old Squire Saunders, doubtless by an accidental lapse of memory, neglected to invite Mr. Hooper to his table, where the good clergyman had been wont to bless the food, almost every Sunday since his settlement. He returned, therefore to the parsonage, and, at the moment of closing the door, was observed to look back upon the people, all of whom had their eyes fixed upon the minister. A sad smile gleamed faintly from beneath the black veil, and flickered about his mouth, glimmering as he disappeared.

"How strange," said a lady, "that a simple black veil, such as any woman might wear on her bonnet, should become such a terrible thing on Mr. Hooper's face!"

"Something must surely be amiss with Mr. Hooper's intellects," observed her husband, the physician of the village. "But the strangest part of the affair is the effect of this vagary, even on a sober-minded man like myself. The black veil, though it covers only our pastor's face, throws its influence over his whole person, and makes him ghostlike from head to foot. Do you not feel it so?"

"Truly do I," replied the lady; "and I would not be alone with him for the world. I wonder he is not afraid to be alone with himself!"

"Men sometimes are so," said her husband.

The afternoon service was attended with similar circumstances. At its conclusion, the bell tolled for the funeral of a young lady. The relatives and friends were assembled in the house, and the more distant acquaintances stood about the door, speaking of the good qualities of the deceased, when their talk was interrupted by the appearance of Mr. Hooper, still covered with his black veil. It was now an appropriate emblem. The clergyman stepped into the room where the corpse was laid, and bent over the coffin, to take a last farewell of his deceased parishioner. As he stooped, the veil hung straight from his forehead, so that, if her eyelids had not been closed forever, the dead maiden might have seen his face. Could Mr. Hooper be fearful of her glance, that he so hastily caught back the black veil? A person who watched the interview between the dead and living, scrupled not to affirm, that, at the instant when the clergyman's features were disclosed, the corpse had slightly shuddered, rustling the shroud and muslin cap, though the countenance retained the composure of death. A superstitious old woman was the only witness of this prodigy. From the coffin Mr. Hooper passed into the chamber of the mourners, and thence to the head of the staircase, to make the funeral prayer. It was a tender and heart-dissolving prayer, full of sorrow, yet so imbued with celestial hopes, that the music of a heavenly harp, swept by the fingers of the dead, seemed faintly to be heard among the saddest accents of the minister. The people trembled, though they but darkly understood him, when he prayed that they, and himself, and all of mortal race, might be ready, as he trusted this young maiden had been, for the dreadful hour that should snatch the veil from their faces. The bearers went heavily forth, and the mourners followed, saddening all the street, with the dead before them, and Mr. Hooper in his black veil behind.

"Why do you look back?" said one in the procession to his partner.

"I had a fancy," replied she, "that the minister and the maiden's spirit were walking hand in hand."

"And so had I, at the same moment," said the other.

That night, the handsomest couple in Milford village were to be joined in wedlock. Though reckoned a melancholy man, Mr. Hooper had a placid cheerfulness for such occasions, which often excited a sympathetic smile where livelier merriment would have been thrown away. There was no quality of his disposition which made him more beloved than this. The company at the wedding awaited his arrival with impatience, trusting that the strange awe, which had gathered over him throughout the day, would now be dispelled. But such was not the result. When Mr. Hooper came, the first thing that their eyes rested on was the same horrible black veil, which had added deeper gloom to the funeral, and could portend nothing but evil to the wedding. Such was its immediate effect on the guests that a cloud seemed to have rolled duskily from beneath the black crape, and dimmed the light of the candles. The bridal pair stood up before the minister. But the bride's cold fingers quivered in the tremulous hand of the bridegroom, and her deathlike paleness caused a whisper that the maiden who had been buried a few hours before was come from her grave to be married. If ever another wedding were so dismal, it was that famous one where they tolled the wedding knell. After performing the ceremony, Mr. Hooper raised a glass of wine to his lips, wishing happiness to the new-married couple in a strain of mild pleasantry that ought to have brightened the features of the guests, like a cheerful gleam from the heart. At that instant, catching a glimpse of his figure in the looking-glass, the black veil involved his own spirit in the horror with which it overwhelmed all others. His frame shuddered, his lips grew pale, he spilt the untasted wine upon the carpet, and rushed forth into the darkness. For the Earth, too, had on her Black Veil.

The next day, the whole village of Milford talked of little else than Parson Hooper's black veil. That, and the mystery concealed behind it, supplied a topic for discussion between acquaintances meeting in the street, and good women gossiping at their open windows. It was the first item of news that the tavern-keeper told to his guests. The children babbled of it on their way to school. One imitative little imp covered his face with an old black handkerchief, thereby so affrighting his playmates that the panic seized himself, and he well-nigh lost his wits by his own waggery.

It was remarkable that of all the busybodies and impertinent people in the parish, not one ventured to put the plain question to Mr. Hooper, wherefore he did this thing. Hitherto, whenever there appeared the slightest call for such interference, he had never lacked advisers, nor shown himself averse to be guided by their judgment. If he erred at all, it was by so painful a degree of self-distrust, that even the mildest censure would lead him to consider an indifferent action as a crime. Yet, though so well acquainted with this amiable weakness, no individual among his parishioners chose to make the black veil a subject of friendly remonstrance. There was a feeling of dread, neither plainly confessed nor carefully concealed, which caused each to shift the responsibility upon another, till at length it was found expedient to send a deputation of the church, in order to deal with Mr. Hooper about the mystery, before it should grow into a scandal. Never did an embassy so ill discharge its duties. The minister received them with friendly courtesy, but became silent, after they were seated, leaving to his visitors the whole burden of introducing their important business. The topic, it might be supposed, was obvious enough. There was the black veil swathed round Mr. Hooper's forehead, and concealing every feature above his placid mouth, on which, at times, they could perceive the glimmering of a melancholy smile. But that piece of crape, to their imagination, seemed to hang down before his heart, the symbol of a fearful secret between him and them. Were the veil but cast aside, they might speak freely of it, but not till then. Thus they sat a considerable time, speechless, confused, and shrinking uneasily from Mr. Hooper's eye, which they felt to be fixed upon them with an invisible glance. Finally, the deputies returned abashed to their constituents, pronouncing the matter too weighty to be handled, except by a council of the churches, if, indeed, it might not require a general synod.

But there was one person in the village unappalled by the awe with which the black veil had impressed all beside herself. When the deputies returned without an explanation, or even venturing to demand one, she, with the calm energy of her character, determined to chase away the strange cloud that appeared to be settling round Mr. Hooper, every moment more darkly than before. As his plighted wife, it should be her privilege to know what the black veil concealed. At the minister's first visit, therefore, she entered upon the subject, with a direct simplicity, which made the task easier both for him and her. After he had seated himself, she fixed her eyes steadfastly upon the veil, but could discern nothing of the dreadful gloom that had so overawed the multitude; it was but a double fold of crape, hanging down from his forehead to his mouth, and slightly stirring with his breath.

"No," said she aloud, and smiling, "there is nothing terrible in this piece of crape, except that it hides a face which I am always glad to look upon. Come, good sir, let the sun shine from behind the cloud. First lay aside your black veil: then tell me why you put it on."

Mr. Hooper's smile glimmered faintly.

"There is an hour to come," said he, "when all of us shall cast aside our veils. Take it not amiss, beloved friend, if I wear this piece of crape till then."

"Your words are a mystery, too," returned the young lady. "Take away the veil from them, at least."

"Elizabeth, I will," said he, "so far as my vow may suffer me. Know, then, this veil is a type and a symbol, and I am bound to wear it ever, both in light and darkness, in solitude and before the gaze of multitudes, and as with strangers, so with my familiar friends. No mortal eye will see it withdrawn. This dismal shade must separate me from the world: even you, Elizabeth, can never come behind it!"

"What grievous affliction hath befallen you," she earnestly inquired, "that you should thus darken your eyes forever?"

"If it be a sign of mourning," replied Mr. Hooper, "I perhaps like most other mortals, have sorrows dark enough to be typified by a black veil."

"But what if the world will not believe that it is the type of an innocent sorrow?" urged Elizabeth. "Beloved and respected as you are, there may be whispers, that you hide your face under the consciousness of secret sin. For the sake of your holy office, do away this scandal!"

The color rose into her cheeks as she intimated the nature of the rumors that were already abroad in the village. But Mr. Hooper's mildness did not forsake him. He even smiled again—that same sad smile, which always appeared like a faint glimmering of light, proceeding from the obscurity beneath the veil.

"If I hide my face for sorrow, there is cause enough," he merely replied; "and if I cover it for secret sin, what mortal might not do the same?"

And with this gentle, but unconquerable obstinacy did he resist all her entreaties. At length Elizabeth sat silent. For a few moments she appeared lost in thought, considering, probably, what new methods might be tried to withdraw her lover from so dark a fantasy, which, if it had no other meaning, was perhaps a symptom of mental disease. Though of a firmer character than his own, the tears rolled down her cheeks. But, in an instant, as it were, a new feeling took the place of sorrow: her eyes were fixed insensibly on the black veil, when, like a sudden twilight in the air, its terrors fell around her. She arose, and stood trembling before him.

"And do you feel it then, at last?" said he mournfully.

She made no reply, but covered her eyes with her hand, and turned to leave the room. He rushed forward and caught her arm.

"Have patience with me, Elizabeth!" cried he, passionately. "Do not desert me, though this veil must be between us here on earth. Be mine, and hereafter there shall be no veil over my face, no darkness between our souls! It is but a mortal veil—it is not for eternity! O! you know not how lonely I am, and how frightened, to be alone behind my black veil. Do not leave me in this miserable obscurity forever!"

"Lift the veil but once, and look me in the face," said she.

"Never! It cannot be!" replied Mr. Hooper.

"Then farewell!" said Elizabeth.

She withdrew her arm from his grasp, and slowly departed, pausing at the door, to give one long, shuddering gaze, that seemed almost to penetrate the mystery of the black veil. But, even amid his grief, Mr. Hooper smiled to think that only a material emblem had separated him from happiness, though the horrors, which it shadowed forth, must be drawn darkly between the fondest of lovers.

From that time no attempts were made to remove Mr. Hooper's black veil, or, by a direct appeal, to discover the secret which it was supposed to hide. By persons who claimed a superiority to popular prejudice, it was reckoned merely an eccentric whim, such as often mingles with the sober actions of men otherwise rational, and tinges them all with its own semblance of insanity. But with the multitude good Mr. Hooper was irreparably a bugbear. He could not walk the street with any peace of mind, so conscious was he that the gentle and timid would turn aside to avoid him, and that others would make it a point of hardihood to throw themselves in his way. The impertinence of the latter class compelled him to give up his customary walk at sunset to the burial ground; for when he leaned pensively over the gate, there would always be faces behind the gravestones, peeping at his black veil. A fable went the rounds that the stare of the dead people drove him thence. It grieved him, to the very depth of his kind heart, to observe how the children fled from his approach, breaking up their merriest sports, while his melancholy figure was yet afar off. Their instinctive dread caused him to feel more strongly than aught else, that a preter-natural horror was interwoven with the threads of the black crape. In truth, his own antipathy to the veil was known to be so great, that he never willingly passed before a mirror, nor stooped to drink at a still fountain, lest, in its peaceful bosom, he should be affrighted by himself. This was what gave plausibility to the whispers, that Mr. Hooper's conscience tortured him for some great crime too horrible to be entirely concealed, or otherwise than so obscurely intimated. Thus, from beneath the black veil, there rolled a cloud into the sunshine, an ambiguity of sin or sorrow, which enveloped the poor minister, so that love or sympathy could never reach him. It was said, that ghost and fiend consorted with him there. With self-shudderings and outward terrors, he walked continually in its shadow, groping darkly within his own soul, or gazing through a medium that saddened the whole world. Even the lawless wind, it was believed, respected his dreadful secret, and never blew aside the veil. But still good Mr. Hooper sadly smiled at the pale visages of the worldly throng as he passed by.

Among all its bad influences, the black veil had the one desirable effect, of making its wearer a very efficient clergyman. By the aid of his mysterious emblem—for there was no other apparent cause—he became a man of awful power, over souls that were in agony for sin. His converts always regarded him with a dread peculiar to themselves, affirming, though but figuratively, that, before he brought them to celestial light, they had been with him behind the black veil. Its gloom, indeed, enabled him to sympathize with all dark affections. Dying sinners cried aloud for Mr. Hooper, and would not yield their breath till he appeared; though ever, as he stooped to whisper consolation, they shuddered at the veiled face so near their own. Such were the terrors of the black veil, even when Death had bared his visage! Strangers came long distances to attend service at his church, with the mere idle purpose of gazing at his figure, because it was forbidden them to behold his face. But many were made to quake ere they departed! Once, during Governor Belcher's administration, Mr. Hooper was appointed to preach the election sermon. Covered with his black veil, he stood before the chief magistrate, the council, and the representatives, and wrought so deep an impression, that the legislative measures of that year were characterized by all the gloom and piety of our earliest ancestral sway.

In this manner Mr. Hooper spent a long life, irreproachable in outward act, yet shrouded in dismal suspicions; kind and loving, though unloved, and dimly feared; man apart from men, shunned in their health and joy, but ever summoned to their aid in mortal anguish. As years wore on, shedding their snows above his sable veil, he acquired a name throughout the New England churches, and they called him Father Hooper. Nearly all his parishioners, who were of mature age when he was settled, had been borne away by many a funeral: he had one congregation in the church, and a more crowded one in the churchyard; and having wrought so late into the evening, and done his work so well, it was now good Father Hooper's turn to rest.

Several persons were visible by the shaded candlelight, in the death chamber of the old clergyman. Natural connections he had none. But there was the decorously grave, though unmoved physician, seeking only to mitigate the last pangs of the patient whom he could not save. There were the deacons, and other eminently pious members of his church. There, also, was the Reverend Mr. Clark, of Westbury, a young and zealous divine, who had ridden in haste to pray by the bedside of the expiring minister. There was the nurse, no hired handmaiden of death, but one whose calm affection had endured thus long in secrecy, in solitude, amid the chill of age, and would not perish, even at the dying hour. Who, but Elizabeth! And there lay the hoary head of good Father Hooper upon the death pillow, with the black veil still swathed about his brow, and reaching down over his face, so that each more difficult gasp of his faint breath caused it to stir. All through life that piece of crape had hung between him and the world; it had separated him from cheerful brotherhood and woman's love, and kept him in that saddest of all prisons, his own heart; and still it lay upon his face, as if to deepen the gloom of his darksome chamber, and shade him from the sunshine of eternity.

For some time previous, his mind had been confused, wavering doubtfully between the past and the present, and hovering forward, as it were, at intervals, into the indistinctness of the world to come. There had been feverish turns, which tossed him from side to side, and wore away what little strength he had. But in his most convulsive struggles, and in the wildest vagaries of his intellect, when no other thought retains its sober influence, he still showed an awful solicitude lest the black veil should slip aside. Even if his bewildered soul could have forgotten, there was a faithful woman at his pillow, who, with averted eyes, would have covered that aged face, which she had last beheld in the comeliness of manhood. At length the death-stricken old man lay quietly in the torpor of mental and bodily exhaustion, with an imperceptible pulse, and breath that grew fainter and fainter, except when a long, deep, and irregular inspiration seemed to prelude the flight of his spirit.

The minister of Westbury approached the bedside.

"Venerable Father Hooper," said he, "the moment of your release is at hand. Are you ready for the lifting of the veil that shuts in time from eternity?"

Father Hooper at first replied merely by a feeble motion of his head; then, apprehensive, perhaps, that his meaning might be doubtful, he exerted himself to speak.

"Yea," said he, in faint accents, "my soul hath a patient weariness until that veil be lifted."

"And is it fitting," resumed the Reverend Mr. Clark, "that a man so given to prayer, of such a blameless example, holy in deed and thought, so far as mortal judgment may pronounce; is it fitting that a father in the church should leave a shadow in his memory, that may seem to blacken a life so pure? I pray you, my venerable brother, let not this thing be! Suffer us to be gladdened by your triumphant aspect, as you go to your reward. Before the veil of eternity be lifted, let me cast aside this black veil from your face!"

And thus speaking, the Reverend Mr. Clark bent forward to reveal the mystery of so many years. But, exerting a sudden energy, that made all the beholders stand aghast, Father Hooper snatched both his hands from beneath the bedclothes, and pressed them strongly on the black veil, resolute to struggle, if the minister of Westbury would contend with a dying man.

"Never!" cried the veiled clergyman. "On earth, never!"

"Dark old man!" exclaimed the affrighted minister, "with what horrible crime upon your soul are you now passing to the judgment?"

Father Hooper's breath heaved; it rattled in his throat but, with a mighty effort, grasping forward with his hands, he caught hold of life, and held it back till he should speak. He even raised himself in bed; and there he sat, shivering with the arms of death around him, while the black veil hung down, awful, at that last moment, in the gathered terrors of a lifetime. And yet the faint, sad smile, so often there, now seemed to glimmer from its obscurity, and linger on Father Hooper's lips.

"Why do you tremble at me alone?" cried he, turning his veiled face round the circle of pale spectators. "Tremble also at each other! Have men avoided me, and women shown no pity, and children screamed and fled, only for my black veil? What, but the mystery which it obscurely typifies, has made this piece of crape so awful? When the friend shows his inmost heart to his friend; the lover to his best beloved; when man does not vainly shrink from the eye of his Creator, loathsomely treasuring up the secret of his sin; then deem me a monster; for the symbol beneath which I have lived, and die! I look around me, and, lo! on every visage a Black Veil!"

While his auditors shrank from one another, in mutual affright, Father Hooper fell back upon his pillow, a veiled corpse with a faint smile lingering on the lips. Still veiled, they laid him in his coffin, and a veiled corpse they bore him to the grave. The grass of many years has sprung up and withered on that grave, the burial stone is moss-grown, and good Mr. Hooper's face is dust; but awful is still the thought that it mouldered beneath the Black Veil!

The Killers

ERNEST HEMINGWAY

The door of Henry's lunch-room opened and two men came in. They sat down at the counter.

"What's yours?" George asked them.

"I don't know," one of the men said. "What do you want to eat, Al?"

"I don't know," said Al. "I don't know what I want to eat."

Outside it was getting dark. The street-light came on outside the window. The two men at the counter read the menu. From the other end of the counter Nick Adams watched them. He had been talking to George when they came in.

"I'll have a roast pork tenderloin with apple sauce and mashed potatoes," the first man said.

"It isn't ready yet."

"What the hell do you put it on the card for?"

"That's the dinner," George explained. "You can get that at six o'clock."

George looked at the clock on the wall behind the counter.

"It's five o'clock."

"The clock says twenty minutes past five," the second man said.

"It's twenty minutes fast."

"Oh, to hell with the clock," the first man said. "What have you got to eat?"

"I can give you any kind of sandwiches," George said. "You can have ham and eggs, bacon and eggs, liver and bacon, or a steak."

"Give me chicken croquettes with green peas and cream sauce and mashed potatoes."

"That's the dinner."

"Everything we want's the dinner, eh? That's the way you work it."

"I can give you ham and eggs, bacon and eggs, liver—"

"I'll take ham and eggs," the man called Al said. He wore a derby hat and

438

a black overcoat buttoned across the chest. His face was small and white and he had tight lips. He wore a silk muffler and gloves.

"Give me bacon and eggs," said the other man. He was about the same size as Al. Their faces were different, but they were dressed like twins. Both wore overcoats too tight for them. They sat leaning forward, their elbows on the counter.

"Got anything to drink?" Al asked.

"Silver beer, bevo, ginger-ale," George said.

"I mean you got anything to *drink?*"

"Just those I said."

"This is a hot town," said the other. "What do they call it?"

"Summit."

"Ever hear of it?" Al asked his friend.

"No," said the friend.

"What do you do here nights?" Al asked.

"They eat the dinner," his friend said. "They all come here and eat the big dinner."

"That's right," George said.

"So you think that's right?" Al asked George.

"Sure."

"You're a pretty bright boy, aren't you?"

"Sure," said George.

"Well, you're not," said the other little man. "Is he, Al?"

"He's dumb," said Al. He turned to Nick. "What's your name?"

"Adams."

"Another bright boy," Al said. "Ain't he a bright boy, Max?"

"The town's full of bright boys," Max said.

George put the two platters, one of ham and eggs, the other of bacon and eggs, on the counter. He set down two side dishes of fried potatoes and closed the wicket into the kitchen.

"Which is yours?" he asked Al.

"Don't you remember?"

"Ham and eggs."

"Just a bright boy," Max said. He leaned forward and took the ham and eggs. Both men ate with their gloves on. George watched them eat.

"What are *you* looking it?" Max looked at George.

"Nothing."

"The hell you were. You were looking at me."

"Maybe the boy meant it for a joke, Max," Al said.

George laughed.

"*You* don't have to laugh," Max said to him. "*You* don't have to laugh at all, see?"

"All right," said George.

"So he thinks it's all right." Max turned to Al. "He thinks it's all right.

That's a good one."

"Oh, he's a thinker," Al said. They went on eating.

"What's the bright boy's name down the counter?" Al asked Max.

"Hey, bright boy," Max said to Nick. "You go around on the other side of the counter with your boy friend."

"What's the idea?" Nick asked.

"There isn't any idea."

"You better go around, bright boy," Al said. Nick went around behind the counter.

"What's the idea?" George asked.

"None of your damn business," Al said. "Who's out in the kitchen?"

"The nigger."

"What do you mean the nigger?"

"The nigger that cooks."

"Tell him to come in."

"What's the idea?"

"Tell him to come in."

"Where do you think you are?"

"We know damn well where we are," the man called Max said. "Do we look silly?"

"You talk silly," Al said to him. "What the hell do you argue with this kid for? Listen," he said to George, "tell the nigger to come out here."

"What are you going to do to him?"

"Nothing. Use your head, bright boy. What would we do to a nigger?"

George opened the slit that opened back into the kitchen. "Sam," he called. "Come in here a minute."

The door to the kitchen opened and the nigger came in. "What was it?" he asked. The two men at the counter took a look at him.

"All right, nigger. You stand right there," Al said.

Sam, the nigger, standing in his apron, looked at the two men sitting at the counter. "Yes, sir," he said. Al got down from his stool.

"I'm going back to the kitchen with the nigger and bright boy," he said. "Go on back to the kitchen, nigger. You go with him, bright boy." The little man walked after Nick and Sam, the cook, back into the kitchen. The door shut after them. The man called Max sat at the counter opposite George. He didn't look at George but looked in the mirror that ran along back of the counter. Henry's had been made over from a saloon into a lunch-counter.

"Well, bright boy," Max said, looking into the mirror, "why don't you say something?"

"What's it all about?"

"Hey, Al," Max called, "bright boy wants to know what it's all about."

"Why don't you tell him?" Al's voice came from the kitchen.

"What do you think it's all about?"

"I don't know."

"What do you think?"

Max looked into the mirror all the time he was talking.

"I wouldn't say."

"Hey, Al, bright boy says he wouldn't say what he thinks it's all about."

"I can hear you, all right," Al said from the kitchen. He had propped open the slit that dishes passed through into the kitchen with a catsup bottle. "Listen, bright boy," he said from the kitchen to George. "Stand a little further along the bar. You move a little to the left, Max." He was like a photographer arranging for a group picture.

"Talk to me, bright boy," Max said. "What do you think's going to happen?"

George did not say anything.

"I'll tell you," Max said. "We're going to kill a Swede. Do you know a big Swede named Ole Andreson?"

"Yes."

"He comes here to eat every night, don't he?"

"Sometimes he comes here."

"He comes here at six o'clock, don't he?"

"If he comes."

"We know all that, bright boy," Max said. "Talk about something else. Ever go to the movies?"

"Once in a while."

"You ought to go to the movies more. The movies are fine for a bright boy like you."

"What are you going to kill Ole Andreson for? What did he ever do to you?"

"He never had a chance to do anything to us. He never even seen us."

"And he's only going to see us once," Al said from the kitchen.

"What are you going to kill him for, then?" George asked.

"We're killing him for a friend. Just to oblige a friend, bright boy."

"Shut up," said Al from the kitchen. "You talk too goddam much."

"Well, I got to keep bright boy amused. Don't I, bright boy?"

"You talk too damn much," Al said. "The nigger and my bright boy are amused by themselves. I got them tied up like a couple of girl friends in the convent."

"I suppose you were in a convent?"

"You never know."

"You were in a kosher convent. That's where you were."

George looked up at the clock.

"If anybody comes in you tell them the cook is off, and if they keep after it, you tell them you'll go back and cook yourself. Do you get that, bright boy?"

"All right," George said. "What are you going to do with us afterward?"

"That'll depend," Max said. "That's one of those things you never know at the time."

George looked up at the clock. It was a quarter past six. The door from the street opened. A street-car motorman came in.

"Hello, George," he said. "Can I get supper?"

"Sam's gone out," George said. "He'll be back in about half an hour."

"I'd better go up the street," the motorman said. George looked at the clock. It was twenty minutes past six.

"That was nice, bright boy," Max said. "You're a regular little gentleman."

"He knew I'd blow his head off," Al said from the kitchen.

"No," said Max. "It ain't that. Bright boy is nice. He's a nice boy. I like him."

At six-fifty-five George said: "He's not coming."

Two other people had been in the lunch-room. Once George had gone out to the kitchen and made a ham-and-egg sandwich "to go" that a man wanted to take with him. Inside the kitchen he saw Al, his derby hat tipped back, sitting on a stool beside the wicket with the muzzle of a sawed-off shotgun resting on the ledge. Nick and the cook were back to back in the corner, a towel tied in each of their mouths. George had cooked the sandwich, wrapped it up in oiled paper, put it in a bag, brought it in, and the man had paid for it and gone out.

"Bright boy can do everything," Max said. "He can cook and everything. You'd make some girl a nice wife, bright boy."

"Yes?" George said. "Your friend, Ole Andreson, isn't going to come."

"We'll give him ten minutes," Max said.

Max watched the mirror and the clock. The hands of the clock marked seven o'clock, and then five minutes past seven.

"Come on, Al," said Max. "We better go. He's not coming."

"Better give him five minutes," Al said from the kitchen.

In the five minutes a man came in, and George explained that the cook was sick.

"Why the hell don't you get another cook?" the man asked. "Aren't you running a lunch-counter?" He went out.

"Come on, Al," Max said.

"What about the two bright boys and the nigger?"

"They're all right."

"You think so?"

"Sure. We're through with it."

"I don't like it," said Al. "It's sloppy. You talk too much."

"Oh, what the hell," said Max. "We got to keep amused, haven't we?"

"You talk too much, all the same," Al said. He came out from the kitchen. The cut-off barrels of the shotgun made a slight bulge under the waist of his too tight-fitting overcoat. He straightened his coat with his gloved hands.

"So long, bright boy," he said to George. "You got a lot of luck."

"That's the truth," Max said. "You ought to play the races, bright boy."

The two of them went out the door. George watched them, through the window, pass under the arc light and cross the street. In their tight over-coats and derby hats they looked like a vaudeville team. George went back through the swinging-door into the kitchen and untied Nick and the cook.

"I don't want any more of that," said Sam, the cook. "I don't want any more of that."

Nick stood up. He had never had a towel in his mouth before.

"Say," he said. "What the hell?" He was trying to swagger it off.

"They were going to kill Ole Andreson," George said. "They were going to shoot him when he came in to eat."

"Ole Andreson?"

"Sure."

The cook felt the corners of his mouth with his thumbs.

"They all gone?" he asked.

"Yeah," said George. "They're gone now."

"I don't like it," said the cook. "I don't like any of it at all."

"Listen," George said to Nick. "You better go see Ole Andreson."

"All right."

"You better not have anything to do with it at all," Sam, the cook, said. "You better stay way out of it."

"Don't go if you don't want to," George said.

"Mixing up in this ain't going to get you anywhere," the cook said. "You stay out of it."

"I'll go see him," Nick said to George. "Where does he live?"

The cook turned away.

"Little boys always know what they want to do," he said.

"He lives up at Hirsch's rooming-house," George said to Nick.

"I'll go up there."

Outside the arc-light shone through the bare branches of a tree. Nick walked up the street beside the car-tracks and turned at the next arc-light down a side-street. Three houses up the street was Hirsch's rooming-house. Nick walked up the two steps and pushed the bell. A woman came to the door.

"Is Ole Andreson here?"

"Do you want to see him?"

"Yes, if he's in."

Nick followed the woman up a flight of stairs and back to the end of a corridor. She knocked on the door.

"Who is it?"

"It's somebody to see you, Mr. Andreson," the woman said.

"It's Nick Adams."

"Come in."

Nick opened the door and went into the room. Ole Andreson was lying on the bed with all his clothes on. He had been a heavyweight prizefighter and he was too long for the bed. He lay with his head on two pillows. He did not look at Nick.

"What was it?" he asked.

"I was up at Henry's," Nick said, "and two fellows came in and tied up me and the cook, and they said they were going to kill you."

It sounded silly when he said it. Ole Andreson said nothing.

"They put us out in the kitchen," Nick went on. "They were going to shoot you when you came in to supper."

Ole Andreson looked at the wall and did not say anything.

"George thought I better come and tell you about it."

"There isn't anything I can do about it," Ole Andreson said.

"I'll tell you what they were like."

"I don't want to know what they were like," Ole Andreson said. He looked at the wall. "Thanks for coming to tell me about it."

"That's all right."

Nick looked at the big man lying on the bed.

"Don't you want me to go and see the police?"

"No," Ole Andreson said. "That wouldn't do any good."

"Isn't there something I could do?"

"No. There ain't anything to do."

"Maybe it was just a bluff."

Ole Andreson rolled over toward the wall.

"The only thing is," he said, talking toward the wall, "I just can't make up my mind to go out. I been in here all day."

"Couldn't you get out of town?"

"No," Ole Andreson said. "I'm through with all that running around."

He looked at the wall.

"There ain't anything to do now."

"Couldn't you fix it up some way?"

"No. I got in wrong." He talked in the same flat voice. "There ain't anything to do. After a while I'll make up my mind to go out."

"I better go back and see George," Nick said.

"So long," said Ole Andreson. He did not look toward Nick. "Thanks for coming around."

Nick went out. As he shut the door he saw Ole Andreson with all his clothes on, lying on the bed looking at the wall.

"He's been in his room all day," the landlady said down-stairs. "I guess he don't feel well. I said to him: 'Mr. Andreson, you ought to go out and take a walk on a nice fall day like this,' but he didn't feel like it."

"He doesn't want to go out."

"I'm sorry he don't feel well," the woman said. "He's an awfully nice man. He was in the ring, you know."

"I know it."

"You'd never know it except from the way his face is," the woman said. They stood talking just inside the street door. "He's just as gentle."

"Well, good-night, Mrs. Hirsch," Nick said.

"I'm not Mrs. Hirsch," the woman said. "She owns the place. I just look after it for her. I'm Mrs. Bell."

"Well, good-night, Mrs. Bell," Nick said.

"Good-night," the woman said.

Nick walked up the dark street to the corner under the arc-light, and then along the car-tracks to Henry's eating-house. George was inside, back of the counter.

"Did you see Ole?"

"Yes," said Nick. "He's in his room and he won't go out."

The cook opened the door from the kitchen when he heard Nick's voice.

"I don't even listen to it," he said and shut the door.

"Did you tell him about it?" George asked.

"Sure. I told him but he knows what it's all about."

"What's he going to do?"

"Nothing."

"They'll kill him."

"I guess they will."

"He must have got mixed up in something in Chicago."

"I guess so," said Nick.

"It's a hell of a thing."

"It's an awful thing," Nick said.

They did not say anything. George reached down for a towel and wiped the counter.

"I wonder what he did?" Nick said.

"Double-crossed somebody. That's what they kill them for."

"I'm going to get out of this town," Nick said.

"Yes," said George. "That's a good thing to do."

"I can't stand to think about him waiting in the room and knowing he's going to get it. It's too damned awful."

"Well," said George, "you better not think about it."

Thank You, M'am

LANGSTON HUGHES

She was a large woman with a large purse that had everything in it but a hammer and nails. It had a long strap, and she carried it slung across her shoulder. It was about eleven o'clock at night, dark, and she was walking alone, when a boy ran up behind her and tried to snatch her purse. The strap broke with the sudden single tug the boy gave it from behind. But the boy's weight and the weight of the purse combined caused him to lose his balance. Instead of taking off full blast as he had hoped, the boy fell on his back on the sidewalk and his legs flew up. The large woman simply turned around and kicked him right square in his blue-jeaned sitter. Then she reached down, picked the boy up by his shirt front, and shook him until his teeth rattled.

After that the woman said, "Pick up my pocketbook, boy, and give it here."

She still held him tightly. But she bent down enough to permit him to stoop and pick up her purse. Then she said, "Now ain't you ashamed of yourself?"

Firmly gripped by his shirt front, the boy said, "Yes'm."

The woman said, "What did you want to do it for?"

The boy said, "I didn't aim to."

She said, "You a lie!"

By that time two or three people passed, stopped, turned to look, and some stood watching.

"If I turn you loose, will you run?" asked the woman.

"Yes'm," said the boy.

"Then I won't turn you loose," said the woman. She did not release him.

"Lady, I'm sorry," whispered the boy.

"Um-hum! Your face is dirty. I got a great mind to wash your face for you. Ain't you got nobody home to tell you to wash your face?"

"No'm," said the boy.

"Then it will get washed this evening," said the large woman, starting up the street, dragging the frightened boy behind her.

He looked as if he were fourteen or fifteen, frail and willow-wild, in tennis shoes and blue jeans.

The woman said, "You ought to be my son. I would teach you right from wrong. Least I can do right now is to wash your face. Are you hungry?"

"No'm," said the being-dragged boy. "I just want you to turn me loose."

"Was I bothering *you* when I turned that corner?" asked the woman.

"No'm."

"But you put yourself in contact with *me*," said the woman. "If you think that that contact is not going to last awhile, you got another thought coming. When I get through with you, sir, you are going to remember Mrs. Luella Bates Washington Jones."

Sweat popped out on the boy's face and he began to struggle. Mrs. Jones stopped, jerked him around in front of her, put a half nelson about his neck, and continued to drag him up the street. When she got to her door, she dragged the boy inside, down a hall, and into a large kitchenette-furnished room at the rear of the house. She switched on the light and left the door open. The boy could hear other roomers laughing and talking in the large house. Some of their doors were open, too, so he knew he and the woman were not alone. The woman still had him by the neck in the middle of her room.

She said, "What is your name?"

"Roger," answered the boy.

"Then, Roger, you go to that sink and wash your face," said the woman, whereupon she turned him loose—at last. Roger looked at the door—looked at the woman—looked at the door—*and went to the sink.*

"Let the water run until it gets warm," she said. "Here's a clean towel."

"You gonna take me to jail?" asked the boy, bending over the sink.

"Not with that face, I would not take you nowhere," said the woman. "Here I am trying to get home to cook me a bite to eat, and you snatch my pocketbook! Maybe you ain't been to your supper either, late as it be. Have you?"

"There's nobody home at my house," said the boy.

"Then we'll eat," said the woman. "I believe you're hungry—or been hungry—to try to snatch my pocketbook!"

"I want a pair of blue suede shoes," said the boy.

"Well, you didn't have to snatch *my* pocketbook to get some suede shoes," said Mrs. Luella Bates Washington Jones. "You could of asked me."

"M'am?"

The water dripping from his face, the boy looked at her. There was a long pause. A very long pause. After he had dried his face, and not knowing what else to do, dried it again, the boy turned around, wondering what next. The door was open. He could make a dash for it down the hall. He could run, run, run, *run!*

The woman was sitting on the daybed. After a while she said, "I were young once and I wanted things I could not get."

There was another long pause. The boy's mouth opened. Then he frowned, not knowing he frowned.

The woman said, "Um-hum! You thought I was going to say *but,* didn't you? You thought I was going to say, *but I didn't snatch people's pocketbooks.* Well, I wasn't going to say that." Pause. Silence. "I have done things, too, which I would not tell you, son—neither tell God, if He didn't already know. Everybody's got something in common. So you set down while I fix us something to eat. You might run that comb through your hair so you will look presentable."

In another corner of the room behind a screen was a gas plate and an icebox. Mrs. Jones got up and went behind the screen. The woman did not watch the boy to see if he was going to run now, nor did she watch her purse, which she left behind her on the daybed. But the boy took care to sit on the far side of the room, away from the purse, where he thought she could easily see him out of the corner of her eye if she wanted to. He did not trust the woman *not* to trust him. And he did not want to be mistrusted now.

"Do you need somebody to go to the store," asked the boy, "maybe to get some milk or something?"

"Don't believe I do," said the woman, "unless you just want sweet milk yourself. I was going to make cocoa out of this canned milk I got here."

"That will be fine," said the boy.

She heated some lima beans and ham she had in the icebox, made the cocoa, and set the table. The woman did not ask the boy anything about where he lived, or his folks, or anything else that would embarrass him. Instead, as they ate, she told him about her job in a hotel beauty shop that stayed open late, what the work was like, and how all kinds of women came in and out, blonds, redheads, and Spanish. Then she cut him a half of her ten-cent cake.

"Eat some more, son," she said.

When they were finished eating, she got up and said, "Now here, take this ten dollars and buy yourself some blue suede shoes. And next time, do not make the mistake of latching onto *my* pocketbook *nor nobody else's*—because shoes got by devilish ways will burn your feet. I got to get my rest now. But from here on in, son, I hope you will behave yourself."

She led him down the hall to the front door and opened it. "Good night! Behave yourself, boy!" she said, looking out into the street as he went down the steps.

The boy wanted to say something other than, "Thank you, M'am," to Mrs. Luella Bates Washington Jones, but although his lips moved, he couldn't even say that as he turned at the foot of the barren stoop and looked up at the large woman in the door. Then she shut the door.

The Gilded Six-Bits

ZORA NEAL HURSTON

It was a Negro yard around a Negro house in a Negro settlement that looked to the payroll of the G and G Fertilizer works for its support.

But there was something happy about the place. The front yard was parted in the middle by a sidewalk from gate to doorstep, a sidewalk edged on either side by quart bottles driven neck down to the ground on a slant. A mess of homey flowers planted without a plan but blooming cheerily from their helter-skelter places. The fence and house were whitewashed. The porch and steps scrubbed white.

The front door stood open to the sunshine so that the floor of the front room could finish drying after its weekly scouring. It was Saturday. Everything clean from the front gate to the privy house. Yard raked so that the strokes of the rake would make a pattern. Fresh newspaper cut in fancy-edge on the kitchen shelves.

Missie May was bathing herself in the galvanized washtub in the bedroom. Her dark-brown skin glistened under the soapsuds that skittered down from her wash rag. Her stiff young breasts thrust forward aggressively like broad-based cones with the tips lacquered in black.

She heard men's voices in the distance and glanced at the dollar clock on the dresser.

"Humph! Ah'm way behind time t'day! Joe gointer be heah 'fore Ah git mah clothes on if Ah don't make haste."

She grabbed the clean meal sack at hand and dried herself hurriedly and began to dress. But before she could tie her slippers, there came the ring of singing metal on wood. Nine times.

Missie May grinned with delight. She had not seen the big tall man come stealing in the gate and creep up the walk grinning happily at the joyful mischief he was about to commit. But she knew that it was her husband throwing silver dollars in the door for her to pick up and pile beside her plate at dinner. It was this way every Saturday afternoon. The nine dollars hurled into the open door, he scurried to a hiding place behind the cape jasmine bush and waited.

Missie May promptly appeared at the door in mock alarm.

"Who dat chunkin' money in mah do'way?" she demanded. No answer from the yard. She leaped off the porch and began to search the shrubbery. She peeped under the porch and hung over the gate to look up and down the road. While she did this, the man behind the jasmine darted to the chinaberry tree. She spied him and gave chase.

"Nobody ain't gointer be chunkin' money at me and Ah not do'em nothin'," she shouted in mock anger. He ran around the house with Missie May at his heels. She overtook him at the kitchen door. He ran inside but could not close it after him before she crowded in and locked with him in a rough and tumble. For several minutes the two were a furious mass of male and female energy. Shouting, laughing, twisting, turning, and Joe trying, but not too hard, to get away.

"Missie May, take yo' hand out mah pocket!" Joe shouted out between laughs.

"Ah ain't, Joe, not lessen you gwine gimme whateve' it is good you got in yo' pocket. Turn it go Joe, do Ah'll tear yo' clothes."

"Go on tear 'em. You de one dat pushes de needles round heah. Move yo' hand Missie May."

"Lemme git dat paper sack out yo' pocket. Ah bet its candy kisses."

"Tain't. Move yo' hand. Woman ain't got no business in a man's clothes nohow. Go 'way."

Missie May gouged way down and gave an upward jerk and triumphed.

"Unhhunh! Ah got it. It 'tis so candy kisses. Ah knowed you had somethin' for me in yo' clothes. Now Ah got to see what's in every pocket you got."

Joe smiled indulgently and let his wife go through all of his pockets and take out the things that he had hidden there for her to find. She bore off the chewing gum, the cake of sweet soap, the pocket handkerchief as if she had wrested them from him, as if they had not been bought for the sake of this friendly battle.

"Whew! dat play-fight done got me all warmed up," Joe exclaimed. "Got me some water in de kittle?"

"Yo' water is on de fire and yo' clean things is cross de bed. Hurry up and wash yo'self and git changed so we kin eat. Ah'm hongry." As Missie said this, she bore the steaming kettle into the bedroom.

"You ain't hongry, sugar," Joe contradicted her. "Youse jes's little empty. Ah'm de one whut's hongry. Ah could eat up camp meetin', back off 'ssociation, and drink Jurdan dry. Have it on de table when Ah git out de tub."

"Don't you mess wid mah business, man. You git in yo' clothes. Ah'm a real wife, not no dress and breath. Ah might not look lak one, but if you burn me, you won't git a thing but wife ashes."

Joe splashed in the bedroom and Missie May fanned around in the kitchen. A fresh red and white checked cloth on the table. Big pitcher of buttermilk beaded with pale drops of butter from the churn. Hot fried mullet, crackling bread, ham hocks atop a mound of string beans and new potatoes, and perched on the window-sill a pone of spicy potato pudding.

Very little talk during the meal but that little consisted of banter that pretended to deny affection but in reality flaunted it. Like when Missie May reached for a second helping of the tater pone. Joe snatched it out of her reach. After Missie May had made two or three unsuccessful grabs at the pan, she begged, "Aw, Joe gimme some mo' dat tater pone."

"Nope, sweetenin' is for us men-folks. Y'all pritty li'l frail eels don't need nothin' lak dis. You too sweet already."

"Please, Joe."

"Naw, naw. Ah don't want you to git no sweeter than whut you is already. We goin' down de road al li'l piece t'night so you go put on yo' Sunday-go-to-meetin' things."

Missie May looked at her husband to see if he was playing some prank. "Sho' nuff, Joe?"

"Yeah. We goin' to de ice cream parlor."

"Where de ice cream parlor at, Joe?"

"A new man done come heah from Chicago and he done got a place and took and opened it up for a ice cream parlor, and bein' as it's real swell, Ah wants you to be one de first ladies to walk in dere and have some set down."

"Do Jesus, Ah ain't knowed nothin' bout it. Who de man done it?"

"Mister Otis D. Slemmons, of spots and places—Memphis, Chicago, Jacksonville, Philadelphia and so on."

"Dat heavy-set man wid his mouth full of gold teethes?"

"Yeah. Where did you see 'im at?"

"Ah went down to de sto' tuh git a box of lye and Ah seen 'im standin' on de corner talkin' to some of de mens, and Ah come on back and went to scrubbin' de floor, and he passed and tipped his hat whilst Ah was scourin' de steps. Ah thought never Ah seen *him* befo'."

Joe smiled pleasantly. "Yeah, he's up to date. He got de finest clothes Ah ever seen on a colored man's back."

"Aw, he don't look no better in his clothes than you do in yourn. He got a puzzlegut on 'im and he so chuckle-headed, he got a pone behind his neck."

Joe looked down at his own abdomen and said wistfully, "Wisht Ah had a build on me lak he got. He ain't puzzlegutted, honey. He jes' got a corperation. Dat make 'im look lak a rich white man. All rich mens is got some belly on 'em."

"Ah seen de pitchers of Henry Ford and he's a spare-built man and Rockefeller look lak he ain't got but one gut. But Ford and Rockefeller and

dis Slemmons and all de rest kin be as many-gutted as dey please, ah'm satisfied wid you jes' lak you is, baby. God took pattern after a pine tree and
built you noble. Youse a pritty still man, and if Ah knowed any way to make
you mo' pritty still Ah'd take and do it."

Joe reached over gently and toyed with Missie May's ear. "You jes' say dat
cause you love me, but Ah know Ah can't hold no light to Otis D. Slemmons. Ah ain't never been nowhere and Ah ain't got nothin' but you."

"How you know dat, Joe."

"He tole us so hisself."

"Dat don't make it so. His mouf is cut cross-ways, ain't it? Well, he kin lie
jes' lak anybody els."

"Good Lawd, Missie! You womens sho' is hard to sense into things. He's
got a five-dollar gold piece for a stick-pin and he got a ten-dollar gold piece
on his watch chain and his mouf is jes' crammed full of gold teethes. Sho'
wisht it wuz mine. And whut make it so cool, he got money 'cumulated.
And womens give it all to 'im."

"Ah don't see whut de womens see on 'im. Ah wouldn't give 'im a wind if
de sherff wuz after 'im."

"Well, he tole us how de white womens in Chicago give 'im all dat gold
money. So he don't 'low nobody to touch it at all. Not even put dey finger
on it. Dey tole 'im not to. You kin make 'miration at it, but don't tetch it."

"Whyn't he stay up dere where dey so crazy 'bout 'im?"

"Ah reckon dey done made 'im vast-rich and he wants to travel some. He
say dey wouldn't leave 'im hit a lick of work. He got mo' lady people crazy
'bout him than he kin shake a stick at."

"Joe, Ah hates to see you so dumb. Dat stray nigger jes' tell y'all anything
and y'all b'lieve it."

"Go 'head on now, honey and put on yo' clothes. He talkin' 'bout his
pritty womens—Ah want 'im to see *mine*."

Missie May went off to dress and Joe spent the time trying to make his
stomach punch out like Slemmons middle. He tried the rolling swagger of
the stranger, but found that his tall bone-and-muscle stride fitted ill with it.
He just had time to drop back into his seat before Missie May came in
dressed to go.

On the way home that night Joe was exultant. "Didn't Ah say ole Otis was
swell? Can't he talk Chicago talk? Wuzn't dat funny whut he said when
great big fat ole Ida Armstrong come in? He asted me, " 'Who is dat broad
wid de forty shake?' Dat's a new word. Us always thought forty was a set of
figgers but he showed us where it means a whole heap of things. Sometimes
he don't say forty, he jes' say thirty-eight and two and dat means de same
thing. Know whut he tole me when Ah was payin' for our ice cream? He
say, 'Ah have to hand it to you, Joe. Dat wife of yours is jes' thirty-eight and
two. Yessuh, she's forty!' Ain't he killin'?"

"He'll do in case of a rush. But he sho' is got uh heap uh gold on 'im. Dat's de first time Ah ever seed gold money. It lookted good on him sho' nuff, but it'd look a whole heap better on you."

"Who, me? Missie May was youse crazy! Where would a po' man lak me git gold money from?"

Missie May was silent for a minute, then she said, "Us might find some goin' long de road some time. Us could."

"Who would be losin' gold money 'round heah? We ain't even seen none dese white folks wearin' no gold money on dey watch chain. You must be figgeren' Mister Packard or Mister Cadillac goin' pass through heah . . . "

"You don't know whut been lost 'round heah. Maybe somebody way back in memorial times lost they gold money and went on off and it ain't never been found. And then if we wuz to find it, you could wear some 'thout havin' no gang of womens lak dat Slemmons say he got."

Joe laughed and hugged her. "Don't be so wishful 'bout me. Ah'm satisfied de way Ah is. So long as Ah be yo' husband, ah don't keer 'bout nothin' else. Ah'd ruther all de other womens in de world to be dead than for you to have de toothache. Less we go to bed and git our night rest."

It was Saturday night once more before Joe could parade his wife in Slemmons' ice cream parlor again. He worked the night shift and Saturday was his only night off. Every other evening around six o'clock he left home, and dying dawn saw him hustling home around the lake where the challenging sun flung a flaming sword from east to west across the trembling water.

That was the best part of life—going home to Missie May. Their whitewashed house, the mock battle on Saturday, the dinner and ice cream parlor afterwards, church on Sunday nights when Missie outdressed any woman in town—all, everything was right.

One night around eleven the acid ran out at the G and G. The foreman knocked off the crew and let the steam die down. As Joe rounded the lake on his way home, a lean moon rode the lake in a silver boat. If anybody had asked Joe about the moon on the lake, he would have said he hadn't paid it any attention. But he saw it with his feelings. It made him yearn painfully for Missie. Creation obsessed him. He thought about children. They had been married for more than a year now. They had money put away. They ought to be making little feet for shoes. A little boy child would be about right.

He saw a dim light in the bedroom and decided to come in through the kitchen door. He could wash the fertilizer dust off himself before presenting himself to Missie May. It would be nice for her not to know that he was there until he slipped into his place in bed and hugged her back. She always liked that.

He eased the kitchen door open slowly and silently, but when he went to set his dinner bucket on the table he bumped it into a pile of dishes, and something crashed to the floor. He heard his wife gasp in fright and hurried to reassure her.

"Iss me, honey. Don't get skeered."

There was a quick, large movement in the bedroom. A rustle, a thud, and a stealthy silence. The light went out.

What? Robbers? Murderers? Some varmint attacking his helpless wife, perhaps. He struck a match, threw himself on guard and stepped over the door-sill into the bedroom.

The great belt on the wheel of Time slipped and eternity stood still. By the match light he could see the man's legs fighting with his breeches in his frantic desire to get them on. He had both chance and time to kill the intruder in his helpless condition—half-in and half-out of his pants—but he was too weak to take action. The shapeless enemies of humanity that live in the hours of Time had waylaid Joe. He was assaulted in his weakness. Like Samson awakening after his haircut. So he just opened his mouth and laughed.

The match went out and he struck another and lit the lamp. A howling wind raced across his heart, but underneath its fury he heard his wife sobbing and Slemmons pleading for his life. Offering to buy it with all that he had. "Please, suh, don't kill me. Sixty-two dollars at de sto' gold money."

Joe just stood. Slemmons looked at the window, but it was screened. Joe stood out like a rough-backed mountain between him and the door. Barring him from escape, from sunrise, from life.

He considered a surprise attack upon the big clown that stood there laughing like a chessy cat. But before his fist could travel an inch, Joe's own rushed out to crush him like a battering ram. Then Joe stood over him.

"Git into yo' damn rags, Slemmons, and dat quick."

Slemmons scrambled to his feet and into his vest and coat. As he grabbed his hat, Joe's fury overrode his intentions and he grabbed at Slemmons with his left hand and struck at him with his right. The right landed. The left grazed the front of his vest. Slemmons was knocked a somersault into the kitchen and fled through the open door. Joe found himself alone with Missie May, with the golden watch charm clutched in his left fist. A short bit of broken chain dangled between his fingers.

Missie May was sobbing. Wails of weeping without words. Joe stood, and after awhile she found out that he had something in his hand. And then he stood and felt without thinking and without seeing with his natural eyes. Missie May kept on crying and Joe kept on feeling so much and not knowing what to do with all his feelings, he put Slemmons' watch charm in his pants pocket and took a good laugh and went to bed.

"Missie May, whut you crying for?"

"Cause Ah love you so hard and Ah know you don't love *me* no mo'."

Joe sank his face into the pillow for a spell then he said huskily, "You don't know de feelings of dat yet, Missie May."

"Oh Joe, honey, he said he wuz gointer gimme dat gold money and he jes' kept on after me—"

Joe was very still and silent for a long time. Then he said, "Well, don't cry no mo', Missie May. Ah got yo' gold piece for you."

The hours went past on their rusty ankles. Joe still and quiet on one bed-rail and Missie May wrung dry of sobs on the other. Finally the sun's tide crept upon the shore of night and drowned all its hours. Missie May with her face stiff and streaked towards the window saw the dawn come into her yard. It was day. Nothing more. Joe wouldn't be coming home as usual. No need to fling open the front door and sweep off the porch, making it nice for Joe. Never no more breakfast to cook; no more washing and starching of Joe's jumper-jackets and pants. No more nothing. So why get up?

With this strange man in her bed, she felt embarrassed to get up and dress. She decided to wait till he had dressed and gone. Then she would get up, dress quickly and be gone forever beyond reach of Joe's looks and laughs. But he never moved. Red light turned to yellow, then white.

From beyond the no-man's land between them came a voice. A strange voice that yesterday had been Joe's.

"Missie May, ain't you gonna fix me no breakfus'?"

She sprang out of bed. "Yeah, Joe. Ah didn't reckon you wuz hongry."

No need to die today. Joe needed her for a few more minutes anyhow.

Soon there was a roaring fire in the cook stove. Water bucket full and two chickens killed. Joe loved fried chicken and rice. She didn't deserve a thing and good Joe was letting her cook him some breakfast. She rushed hot biscuits to the table as Joe took his seat.

He ate with his eyes on his plate. No laughter, no banter.

"Missie May, you ain't eatin' yo' breakfus'."

"Ah don't choose none, Ah thank yuh."

His coffee cup was empty. She sprang to refill it. When she turned from the stove and bent to set the cup beside Joe's plate, she saw the yellow coin on the table between them.

She slumped into her seat and wept into her arms.

Presently Joe said calmly, "Missie May, you cry too much. Don't look back lak Lot's wife and turn to salt."

The sun, the hero of every day, the impersonal old man that beams as brightly on death as on birth, came up every morning and raced across the blue dome and dipped into the sea of fire every evening. Water ran down hill and birds nested.

Missie knew why she didn't leave Joe. She couldn't. She loved him too much. But she couldn't understand why Joe didn't leave her. He was polite, even kind at times, but aloof.

There were no more Saturday romps. No ringing silver dollars to stack beside her plate. No pockets to rifle. In fact the yellow coin in his trousers was like a monster hiding in the cave of his pockets to destroy her.

She often wondered if he still had it, but nothing could have induced her to ask nor yet to explore his pockets to see for herself. Its shadow was in the house whether or no.

One night Joe came home around midnight and complained of pains in the back. He asked Missie to rub him down with liniment. It had been three months since Missie had touched his body and it all seemed strange. But she rubbed him. Grateful for the chance. Before morning, youth triumphed and Missie exulted. But the next day, as she joyfully made up their bed, beneath her pillow she found the piece of money with the bit of chain attached.

Alone to herself, she looked at the thing with loathing, but look she must. She took it into her hands with trembling and saw first thing that it was no gold piece. It was a gilded half-dollar. Then she knew why Slemmons had forbidden anyone to touch his gold. He trusted village eyes at a distance not to recognize his stick-pin as a gilded quarter, and his watch charm as a four-bit piece.

She was glad at first that Joe had left it there. Perhaps he was through with her punishment. They were man and wife again. Then another thought came clawing at her. He had come home to buy from her as if she were any woman in the long house. Fifty cents for her love. As if to say that he could pay as well as Slemmons. She slid the coin into his Sunday pants pocket and dressed herself and left his house.

Halfway between her house and the quarters she met her husband's mother, and after a short talk she turned and went back home. If she had not the substance of marriage, she had the outside show. Joe must leave *her*. She let him see she didn't want his gold four-bits too.

She saw no more of the coin for some time though she knew that Joe could not help finding it in his pocket. But his health kept poor, and he came home at least every ten days to be rubbed.

The sun swept around the horizon, trailing its robes of weeks and days. One morning as Joe came in from work, he found Missie May chopping wood. Without a word he took the ax and chopped a huge pile before he stopped.

"You ain't got no business choppin' wood, and you know it."

"How come? Ah been choppin' it for de last longest."

"Ah ain't blind. You makin' feet for shoes."

"Won't you be glad to have a li'l baby chile, Joe?"

"You know dat 'thout astin' me."

"Iss gointer be a boy chile and de very spit of you."

"You reckon, Missie May?"

"Who else could it look lak?"

Joe said nothing, but he thrust his hand deep into his pocket and fingered something there.

It was almost six months later Missie May took to bed and Joe went and got his mother to come wait on the house.

Missie May delivered a fine boy. Her travail was over when Joe came in from work one morning. His mother and the old women were drinking great bowls of coffee around the fire in the kitchen.

The minute Joe came into the room his mother called him aside.

"How did Missie May make out?" he asked quickly.

"Who, dat gal? She strong as a ox. She gointer have plenty mo'. We done fixed her wid de sugar and lard to sweeten her for de nex' one."

Joe stood silent awhile.

"You ain't ast 'bout de baby, Joe. You oughter be mighty proud cause he sho' is de spittin' image of yuh, son. Dat's yourn all right, if you never git another one, dat un is yourn. And you know Ah'm mighty proud too, son, cause Ah never thought well of you marryin' Missie May cause her ma used tuh fan her foot 'round right smart and Ah been mighty skeered dat Missie May wuz gointer git misput on her road."

Joe said nothing. He fooled around the house till late in the day then just before he went to work, he went and stood at the foot of the bed and asked his wife how she felt. He did this every day during the week.

On Saturday he went to Orlando to make his market. It had been a long time since he had done that.

Meat and lard, meal and flour, soap and starch. Cans of corn and tomatoes. All the staples. He fooled around town for awhile and bought bananas and apples. Way after while he went around to the candy store.

"Hellow, Joe," the clerk greeted him. "Ain't seen you in a long time."

"Nope, Ah ain't been heah. Been 'round spots and places."

"Want some of them molasses kisses you always buy?"

"Yessuh." He threw the gilded half-dollar on the counter. "Will dat spend?"

"Whut is it, Joe? Well, I'll be doggone! A gold-plated four-bit piece. Where'd you git it, Joe?"

"Offen a stray nigger dat come through Eatonville. He had it on his watch chain for a charm—goin' 'round making out iss gold money. Ha ha! He had a quarter on his tie pin and it wuz all golded up too. Tryin' to fool people. Makin' out so he so rich and everything. Ha! Ha! Tryin' to tole off folkses wives from home."

"How did you git it, Joe? Did he fool you, too?"

"Who, me? Naw suh! He ain't fooled me none. Know whut Ah done? He come 'round me wid his smart talk. Ah hauled off and knocked 'im down and took his old four-bits 'way from 'im. Gointer buy my wife some good ole 'lasses kisses wid it. Gimme fifty cents worth of dem candy kisses."

"Fifty cents buys a mighty lot of candy kisses, Joe. Why don't you split it up and take some chocolate bars, too. They eat good, too."

"Yessuh, dey do, but Ah wants all dat in kisses. Ah got a li'l boy chile home now. Tain't a week old yet, but he kin suck a sugar tit and maybe eat one them kisses hisself."

Joe got his candy and left the store. The clerk turned to the next customer. "Wisht I could be like these darkies. Laughin' all the time. Nothin' worries 'em."

Back in Eatonville, Joe reached his own front door. There was the ring of singing metal on wood. Fifteen times. Missie couldn't run to the door, but she crept there as quickly as she could.

"Joe Banks, Ah hear you chunkin' money in mah do'way. You wait till Ah got mah strength back and Ah'm gointer fix you for dat."

The Beast in the Jungle

HENRY JAMES

I

What determined the speech that startled him in the course of their encounter scarcely matters, being probably but some words spoken by himself quite without intention—spoken as they lingered and slowly moved together after their renewal of acquaintance. He had been conveyed by friends an hour or two before to the house at which she was staying; the party of visitors at the other house, of whom he was one, and thanks to whom it was his theory, as always, that he was lost in the crowd, had been invited over to luncheon. There had been after luncheon much dispersal, all in the interest of the original motive, a view of Weatherend itself and the fine things, intrinsic features, pictures, heirlooms, treasures of all the arts, that made the place almost famous; and the great rooms were so numerous that guests could wander at their will, hang back from the principal group and in cases where they took such matters with the last seriousness give themselves up to mysterious appreciations and measurements. There were persons to be observed, singly or in couples, bending toward objects in out-of-the-way corners with their hands on their knees and their heads nodding quite as with the emphasis of an excited sense of smell. When they were two they either mingled their sounds of ecstasy or melted into silences of even deeper import, so that there were aspects of the occasion that gave it for Marcher much the air of the "look round," previous to a sale highly advertised, that excites or quenches, as may be, the dream of acquisition. The dream of acquisition at Weatherend would have had to be wild indeed, and John Marcher found himself, among such suggestions, disconcerted almost equally by the presence of those who knew too much and by that of those who knew nothing. The great rooms caused so much poetry and history to press upon him that he needed some straying apart to feel in a

460

proper relation with them, though this impulse was not, as happened, like the gloating of some of his companions, to be compared to the movements of a dog sniffing a cupboard. It had an issue promptly enough in a direction that was not to have been calculated.

It led, briefly, in the course of the October afternoon, to his closer meeting with May Bartram, whose face, a reminder, yet not quite a remembrance, as they sat much separated at a very long table, had begun merely by troubling him rather pleasantly. It affected him as the sequel of something of which he had lost the beginning. He knew it, and for the time quite welcomed it, as a continuation, but didn't know what it continued, which was an interest or an amusement the greater as he was also somehow aware—yet without a direct sign from her—that the young woman herself hadn't lost the thread. She hadn't lost it, but she wouldn't give it back to him, he saw, without some putting forth of his hand for it; and he not only saw that, but saw several things more, things odd enough in the light of the fact at the moment some accident of grouping brought them face to face he was still merely fumbling with the idea that any contact between them in the past would have had no importance. If it had had no importance he scarcely knew why his actual impression of her should so seem to have so much; the answer to which, however, was that in such a life as they all appeared to be leading for the moment one could but take things as they came. He was satisfied, without in the least being able to say why, that this young lady might roughly have ranked in the house as a poor relation; satisfied also that she was not there on a brief visit, but was more or less a part of the establishment—almost a working, a remunerated part. Didn't she enjoy at periods a protection that she paid for by helping, among other services, to show the place and explain it, deal with the tiresome people, answer questions about the dates of the building, the styles of the furniture, the authorship of the pictures, the favourite haunts of the ghost? It wasn't that she looked as if you could have given her shillings—it was impossible to look less so. Yet when she finally drifted toward him, distinctly handsome, though ever so much older—older than when he had seen her before—it might have been as an effect of her guessing that he had, within the couple of hours, devoted more imagination to her than to all the others put together, and had thereby penetrated to a kind of truth that the others were too stupid for. She *was* there on harder terms than any one; she was there as a consequence of things suffered, one way and another, in the interval of years; and she remembered him very much as she was remembered—only a good deal better.

By the time they at last thus came to speech they were alone in one of the rooms—remarkable for a fine portrait over the chimney-place—out of which their friends had passed, and the charm of it was that even before they had spoken they had practically arranged with each other to stay behind for talk. The charm, happily, was in other things too—partly in there being scarce a spot at Weatherend without something to stay behind for. It was in the way the autumn day looked into the high windows as it waned; the way the red light, breaking at the close from under a low sombre sky, reached out in a long shaft and played over old wainscots, old tapestry, old gold, old colour. It was most of all perhaps in the way she came to him as if, since she had been turned on to deal with the simpler sort, he might, should he choose to keep the whole thing down, just take her mild attention for a part of her general business. As soon as he heard her voice, however, the gap was filled up and the missing link supplied; the slight irony he divined in her attitude lost its advantage. He almost jumped at it to get there before her. "I met you years and years ago in Rome. I remember all about it." She confessed to disappointment—she had been so sure he didn't; and to prove how well he did he began to pour forth the particular recollections that popped up as he called for them. Her face and her voice, all at his service now, worked the miracle—the impression operating like the torch of a lamplighter who touches into flame, one by one, a long row of gas-jets. Marcher flattered himself the illumination was brilliant, yet he was really still more pleased on her showing him, with amusement, that in his haste to make everything right he had got most things rather wrong. It hadn't been at Rome—it had been at Naples; and it hadn't been eight years before—it had been more nearly ten. She hadn't been, either, with her uncle and aunt, but with her mother and her brother; in addition to which it was not with the Pembles *he* had been, but with the Boyers, coming down in their company from Rome—a point on which she insisted, a little to his confusion, and as to which she had her evidence in hand. The Boyers she had known, but didn't know the Pembles, though she had heard of them, and it was the people he was with who had made them acquainted. The incident of the thunderstorm that had raged round them with such violence as to drive them for refuge into an excavation—this incident had not occurred at the Palace of the Caesars, but at Pompeii, on an occasion when they had been present there at an important find.

He accepted her amendments, he enjoyed her corrections, though the moral of them was, she pointed out, that he *really* didn't remember the least thing about her; and he only felt it as a drawback that when all was made strictly historic there didn't appear much of anything left. They lingered together still, she neglecting her office—for from the moment he was so clever she had no proper right to him—and both neglecting the house, just waiting as to see if a memory or two more wouldn't again breathe on them. It hadn't taken them many minutes, after all, to put down on the table, like the cards of a pack, those that constituted their respective hands; only what came out was that the pack was unfortunately not perfect—that the past, invoked, invited, encouraged, could give them, naturally, no more than it had. It had made them anciently meet—her at twenty, him at twenty-five; but nothing was so strange, they seemed to say to each other, as that, while so occupied, it hadn't done a little more for them. They looked at each other as with the feeling of an occasion missed; the present would have been so much better if the other, in the far distance, in the foreign land, hadn't been so stupidly meagre. There weren't apparently, all counted, more than a dozen little old things that had succeeded in coming to pass between them; trivialities of youth, simplicities of freshness, stupidities of ignorance, small possible germs, but too deeply buried—too deeply (didn't it seem?) to sprout after so many years. Marcher could only feel he ought to have rendered her some service—saved her from a capsized boat in the Bay or at least recovered her dressing-bag, filched from her cab in the streets of Naples by a lazzarone with a stiletto. Or it would have been nice if he could have been taken with fever all alone at his hotel, and she could have come to look after him, to write to his people, to drive him out in convalescence. *Then* they would be in possession of the something or other that their actual show seemed to lack. It yet somehow presented itself, this show, as too good to be spoiled; so that they were reduced for a few minutes more to wondering a little helplessly why—since they seemed to know a certain number of the same people—their reunion had been so long averted. They didn't use that name for it, but their delay from minute to minute to join the others was a kind of confession that they didn't quite want it to be a failure. Their attempted supposition of reasons for their not having met but showed how little they knew of each other. There came in fact a moment when Marcher felt a positive pang. It was vain to pretend she was an old friend, for all the communities were wanting, in spite of which it was as an old friend that he saw she would have suited him. He had new ones enough—was surrounded with them for instance on the stage of the other house; as a new one he probably wouldn't have so much as noticed her. He would have liked to invent something, get her to make-believe with him that some passage of a romantic or critical kind *had* originally occurred. He was really almost reaching out in imagination—as against time—for something that would do, and saying to himself that if it didn't come this sketch of a fresh start would show for quite awkwardly bungled. They would separate, and now for no second or no third chance. They would have tried and not succeeded. Then it was, just at the turn, as he afterwards made it out to himself, that, everything else failing, she herself decided to take up the case and, as it were, save the situation. He felt as soon as she spoke that she had been consciously keeping back what she said and hoping to get on without it; a scruple in her that immensely touched him when, by the end of three or four minutes more, he was able to measure it. What she brought out, at any rate, quite cleared the air and supplied the link—the link it was so odd he should frivolously have managed to lose.

"You know you told me something I've never forgotten and that again and again has made me think of you since; it was that tremendously hot day when we went to Sorrento, across the bay, for the breeze. What I allude to was what you said to me, on the way back, as we sat under the awning of the boat enjoying the cool. Have you forgotten?"

He had forgotten and was even more surprised than ashamed. But the great thing was that he saw in this no vulgar reminder of any "sweet" speech. The vanity of women had long memories, but she was making no claim on him of a compliment or a mistake. With another woman, a totally different one, he might have feared the recall possibly even of some imbecile "offer." So, in having to say that he had indeed forgotten, he was conscious rather of a loss than of a gain; he already saw an interest in the matter of her mention. "I try to think—but I give it up. Yet I remember the Sorrento day."

"I'm not very sure you do," May Bartram after a moment said; "and I'm not very sure I ought to want you to. It's dreadful to bring a person back at any time to what he was ten years before. If you've lived away from it," she smiled, "so much the better."

"Ah if *you* haven't why should I?" he asked.

"Lived away, you mean, from what I myself was?"

"From what *I* was. I was of course an ass," Marcher went on; "but I would rather know from you just the sort of ass I was than—from the moment you have something in your mind—not know anything."

Still, however, she hesitated. "But if you've completely ceased to be that sort—?"

"Why I can then all the more bear to know. Besides, perhaps I haven't."

"Perhaps. Yet if you haven't," she added, "I should suppose you'd remember. Not indeed that *I* in the least connect with my impression the invidious name you use. If I had only thought you foolish," she explained, "the thing I speak of wouldn't so have remained with me. It was about yourself." She waited as if it might come to him; but as, only meeting her eyes in wonder, he gave no sign, she burnt her ships. "Has it ever happened?"

Then it was that, while he continued to stare, a light broke for him and the blood slowly came to his face, which began to burn with recognition. "Do you mean I told you—?" But he faltered, lest what came to him shouldn't be right, lest he should only give himself away.

"It was something about yourself that it was natural one shouldn't forget—that is if one remembered you at all. That's why I ask you," she smiled, "if the thing you then spoke of has ever come to pass?"

Oh then he saw, but he was lost in wonder and found himself embarrassed. This, he also saw, made her sorry for him, as if her illusion had been a mistake. It took him but a moment, however, to feel it hadn't been, much as it had been a surprise. After the first little shock of it her knowledge on the contrary began, even if rather strangely, to taste sweet to him. She was the only other person in the world then who would have it, and she had had it all these years, while the fact of his having so breathed his secret had unaccountably faded from him. No wonder they couldn't have met as if nothing had happened.

"I judge," he finally said, "that I know what you mean. Only I had strangely enough lost any sense of having taken you so far into my confidence."

"Is it because you've taken so many others as well?"

"I've taken nobody. Not a creature since then."

"So that I'm the only person who knows?"

"The only person in the world."

"Well," she quickly replied, "I myself have never spoken. I've never, never repeated of you what you told me." She looked at him so that he perfectly believed her. Their eyes met over it in such a way that he was without a doubt. "And I never will."

She spoke with an earnestness that, as if almost excessive, put him at ease about her possible derision. Somehow the whole question was a new luxury to him—that is from the moment she was in possession. If she didn't take the sarcastic view she clearly took the sympathetic, and that was what he had had, in all the long time, from no one whomsoever. What he felt was that he couldn't at present have begun to tell her, and yet could profit perhaps exquisitely by the accident of having done so of old. "Please don't then. We're just right as it is."

"Oh I am," she laughed, "if you are!" To which she added: "Then you do still feel in the same way?"

It was impossible he shouldn't take to himself that she was really interested, though it all kept coming as perfect surprise. He had thought of himself so long as abominably alone, and lo he wasn't alone a bit. He hadn't been, it appeared, for an hour—since those moments on the Sorrento boat. It was *she* who had been, he seemed to see as he looked at her—she who had been made so by the graceless fact of his lapse of fidelity. To tell her what he had told her—what had it been but to ask something of her? something that she had given, in her charity, without his having by a remembrance, by a return of the spirit, failing another encounter, so much as thanked her. What he had asked of her had been simply at first not to laugh at him. She had beautifully not done so for ten years, and she was not doing so now. So he had endless gratitude to make up. Only for that he must see just how he had figured to her. "What, exactly, was the account I gave—?"

"Of the way you did feel? Well, it was very simple. You said you had had from your earliest time, as the deepest thing within you, the sense of being kept for something rare and strange, possibly prodigious and terrible, that was sooner or later to happen to you, that you had in your bones the foreboding and the conviction of, and that would perhaps overwhelm you."

"Do you call that very simple?" John Marcher asked.

She thought a moment. "It was perhaps because I seemed, as you spoke, to understand it."

"You do understand it?" he eagerly asked.

Again she kept her kind eyes on him. "You still have the belief?"

"Oh!" he exclaimed helplessly. There was too much to say.

"Whatever it's to be," she clearly made out, "it hasn't yet come."

He shook his head in complete surrender now. "It hasn't yet come. Only, you know, it isn't anything I'm to *do*, to achieve in the world, to be distinguished or admired for. I'm not such an ass as *that*. It would be much better, no doubt, if I were."

"It's to be something you're merely to suffer?"

"Well, say to wait for—to have to meet, to face, to see suddenly break out in my life; possibly destroying all further consciousness, possibly annihilating me; possibly, on the other hand, only altering everything, striking at the root of all my world and leaving me to the consequences, however they shape themselves."

She took this in, but the light in her eyes continued for him not to be that of mockery. "Isn't what you describe perhaps but the expectation—or at any rate the sense of danger, familiar to so many people—of falling in love?"

John Marcher wondered. "Did you ask me that before?"

"No—I wasn't so free-and-easy then. But it's what strikes me now."

"Of course," he said after a moment, "it strikes you. Of course it strikes *me*. Of course what's in store for me may be no more than that. The only thing is," he went on, "that I think if it had been that I should by this time know."

"Do you mean because you've *been* in love?" And then as he but looked at her in silence: "You've been in love, and it hasn't meant such a cataclysm, hasn't proved the great affair?"

"Here I am, you see. It hasn't been overwhelming."

"Then it hasn't been love," said May Bartram.

"Well, I at least thought it was. I took it for that—I've taken it till now. It was agreeable, it was delightful, it was miserable," he explained. "But it wasn't strange. It wasn't what *my* affair's to be."

"You want something all to yourself—something that nobody else knows or *has* known?"

"It isn't a question of what I 'want'—God knows I don't want anything. It's only a question of the apprehension that haunts me—that I live with day by day."

He said this so lucidly and consistently that he could see it further impose itself. If she hadn't been interested before she'd have been interested now. "Is it a sense of coming violence?"

Evidently now too again he liked to talk of it. "I don't think of it as—

when it does come—necessarily violent. I only think of it simply as *the* thing. *The* thing will of itself appear natural."

"Then how will it appear strange?"

Marcher bethought himself. "It won't—to *me*."

"To whom then?"

"Well," he replied, smiling at last, "say to you."

"Oh then I'm to be present?"

"Why you *are* present—since you know."

"I see." She turned it over. "But I mean at the catastrophe."

At this, for a minute, their lightness gave way to their gravity; it was as if the long look they exchanged held them together. "It will only depend on yourself—if you'll watch with me."

"Are you afraid?" she asked.

"Don't leave me *now*," he went on.

"Are you afraid?" she repeated.

"Do you think me simply out of my mind?" he pursued instead of answering. "Do I merely strike you as a harmless lunatic?"

"No," said May Bartram. "I understand you. I believe you."

"You mean you feel how my obsession—poor old thing!—may correspond to some possible reality?"

"To some possible reality."

"Then you *will* watch with me?"

She hesitated, then for the third time put her question. "Are you afraid?"

"Did I tell you I was—at Naples?"

"No, you said nothing about it."

"Then I don't know. And I should *like* to know," said John Marcher. "You'll tell me yourself whether you think so. If you'll watch with me you'll see."

"Very good then." They had been moving by this time across the room, and at the door, before passing out, they paused as for the full wind-up of their understanding. "I'll watch with you," said May Bartram.

II

The fact that she "knew"—knew and yet neither chaffed him nor betrayed him—had in a short time begun to constitute between them a goodly bond, which became more marked when, within the year that followed their afternoon at Weatherend, the opportunities for meeting multiplied. The event that thus promoted these occasions was the death of the ancient lady her great-aunt, under whose wing, since losing her mother, she had to such an extent found shelter, and who, though but the widowed mother of the new successor to the property, had succeeded—thanks to a high tone and a high temper—in not forfeiting the supreme position at the great house.

The deposition of this personage arrived but with her death, which, followed by many changes, made in particular a difference for the young woman in whom Marcher's expert attention had recognised from the first a dependent with a pride that might ache though it didn't bristle. Nothing for a long time had made him easier than the thought that the aching must have been much soothed by Miss Bartram's now finding herself able to set up a small home in London. She had acquired property, to an amount that made that luxury just possible, under her aunt's extremely complicated will, and when the whole matter began to be straightened out, which indeed took time, she let him know that the happy issue was at last in view. He had seen her again before that day, both because she had more than once accompanied the ancient lady to town and because he had paid another visit to the friends who so conveniently made of Weatherend one of the charms of their own hospitality. These friends had taken him back there; he had achieved there again with Miss Bartram some quiet detachment; and he had in London succeeded in persuading her to more than one brief absence from her aunt. They went together, on these latter occasions, to the National Gallery and the South Kensington Museum, where, among vivid reminders, they talked of Italy at large—not now attempting to recover, as at first, the taste of their youth and their ignorance. That recovery, the first day at Weatherend, had served its purpose well, had given them quite enough; so that they were, to Marcher's sense, no longer hovering about the headwaters of their stream, but had felt their boat pushed sharply off and down the current.

They were literally afloat together; for our gentleman this was marked, quite as marked as that the fortunate cause of it was just the buried treasure of her knowledge. He had with his own hands dug up this little hoard, brought to light—that is to within reach of the dim day constituted by their discretions and privacies—the object of value the hiding place of which he had, after putting it into the ground himself, so strangely, so long forgotten. The rare luck of his having again just stumbled on the spot made him indifferent to any other question; he would doubtless have devoted more time to the odd accident of his lapse of memory if he hadn't been moved to devote so much to the sweetness, the comfort, as he felt, for the future, that this accident itself had helped to keep fresh. It had never entered into his plan that any one should "know," and mainly for the reason that it wasn't in him to tell any one. That would have been impossible, for nothing but the amusement of a cold world would have waited on it. Since, however, a mysterious fate had opened his mouth betimes, in spite of him, he would count that a compensation and profit by it to the utmost. That the right person *should* know tempered the asperity of his secret more even than his shyness had permitted him to imagine; and May Bartram was clearly right, because—well, because there she was. Her knowledge simply settled it; he would have been sure enough by this time had she been wrong. There was that in his situation, no doubt, that disposed him too much to see her as a mere confidant, taking all her light for him from the fact—the fact only— of her interest in his predicament; from her mercy, sympathy, seriousness, her consent not to regard him as the funniest of the funny. Aware, in fine, that her price for him was just in her giving him this constant sense of his being admirably spared, he was careful to remember that she had also a life of her own, with things that might happen to *her,* things that in friendship one should likewise take account of. Something fairly remarkable came to pass with him, for that matter, in this connexion—something represented by a certain passage of his consciousness, in the suddenest way, from one extreme to the other.

He had thought himself, so long as nobody knew, the most disinterested person in the world, carrying his concentrated burden, his perpetual suspense, ever so quietly, holding his tongue about it, giving others no glimpse of it nor of its effect upon his life, asking of them no allowance and only making on his side all those that were asked. He hadn't disturbed people with the queerness of their having to know a haunted man, though he had had moments of rather special temptation on hearing them say they were forsooth "unsettled." If they were as unsettled as he was—he who had never been settled for an hour in his life—they would know what it meant. Yet it wasn't, all the same, for him to make them, and he listened to them civilly enough. This was why he had such good—though possibly such rather colourless—manners; this was why, above all, he could regard himself, in a greedy world, as decently—as in fact perhaps even a little sublimely—unselfish. Our point is accordingly that he valued this character quite sufficiently to measure his present danger of letting it lapse, against which he promised himself to be much on his guard. He was quite ready, none the less, to be selfish just a little, since surely no more charming occasion for it had come to him. "Just a little," in a word, was just as much as Miss Bartram, taking one day with another, would let him. He never would be in the least coercive, and would keep well before him the lines on which consideration for her—the very highest—ought to proceed. He would thoroughly establish the heads under which her affairs, her requirements, her peculiarities—he went so far as to give them the latitude of that name—would come into their intercourse. All this naturally was a sign of how much he took the intercourse itself for granted. There was nothing more to be done about *that.* It simply existed; had sprung into being with her first penetrating question to him in the autumn light there at Weatherend. The real form it should have taken on the basis that stood out large was the form of their marrying. But the devil in this was that the very basis itself put marrying out of the question. His conviction, his apprehension, his obsession, in short, wasn't a privilege he could invite a woman to share; and that consequence of it was precisely what was the matter with him. Something or other lay in wait for him, amid the twists and the turns of the months and the years, like a crouching beast in the jungle. It signified little whether the crouching beast were destined to slay him or to be slain. The definite point was the inevitable spring of the creature; and the definite lesson from that was that a man of feeling didn't cause himself to be accompanied by a lady on a tiger hunt. Such was the image under which he had ended by figuring his life.

They had at first, none the less, in the scattered hours spent together, made no allusion to that view of it; which was a sign he was handsomely alert to give that he didn't expect, that he in fact didn't care, always to be talking about it. Such a feature in one's outlook was really like a hump on one's back. The difference it made every minute of the day existed quite independently of discussion. One discussed of course *like* a hunchback, for there was always, if nothing else, the hunchback face. That remained, and she was watching him; but people watched best, as a general thing, in silence, so that such would be predominantly the manner of their vigil. Yet he didn't want, at the same time, to be tense and solemn; tense and solemn was what he imagined he too much showed for with other people. The thing to be, with the one person who knew, was easy and natural—to make the reference rather than be seeming to avoid it, to avoid it rather than be seeming to make it, and to keep it, in any case, familiar, facetious even, rather than pedantic and portentous. Some such consideration as the latter was doubtless in his mind for instance when he wrote pleasantly to Miss Bartram that perhaps the great thing he had so long felt as in the lap of the gods was no more than this circumstance, which touched him so nearly, of her acquiring a house in London. It was the first allusion they had yet again made, needing any other hitherto so little; but when she replied, after having given him the news, that she was by no means satisfied with such a trifle as the climax to so special a suspense, she almost set him wondering if she hadn't even a larger conception of singularity for him than he had for himself. He was at all events destined to become aware little by little, as time went by, that she was all the while looking at his life, judging it, measuring it, in the light of the thing she knew, which grew to be at last, with the consecration of the years, never mentioned between them save as "the real truth" about him. That had always been his own form of reference to it, but she adopted the form so quietly that, looking back at the end of a period, he knew there was no moment at which it was traceable that she had, as he might say, got inside his idea, or exchanged the attitude of beautifully indulging for that of still more beautifully believing him.

It was always open to him to accuse her of seeing him but as the most harmless of maniacs, and this, in the long run—since it covered so much ground—was his easiest description of their friendship. He had a screw loose for her, but she liked him in spite of it and was practically, against the rest of the world, his kind wise keeper, unremunerated but fairly amused and, in the absence of other near ties, not disreputably occupied. The rest of the world of course thought him queer, but she, she only, knew how, and above all why, queer; which was precisely what enabled her to dispose the concealing veil in the right folds. She took his gaiety from him—since it had to pass with them for gaiety—as she took everything else; but she certainly so far justified by her unerring touch his finer sense of the degree to which he had ended by convincing her. *She* at least never spoke of the secret of his life except as "the real truth about you," and she had in fact a wonderful way of making it seem, as such, the secret of her own life too. That was in fine how he so constantly felt her as allowing for him; he couldn't on the whole call it anything else. He allowed himself, but she, exactly, allowed still more; partly because, better placed for a sight of the matter, she traced his unhappy perversion through reaches of its course into which he could scarce follow it. He knew how he felt, but, besides knowing that, she knew how he *looked* as well; he knew each of the things of importance he was insidiously kept from doing, but she could add up the amount they made, understand how much, with a lighter weight on his spirit, he might have done, and thereby established how, clever as he was, he fell short. Above all she was in the secret of the difference between the forms he went through—those of his little office under Government, those of caring for his modest patrimony, for his library, for his garden in the country, for the people in London whose invitations he accepted and repaid—and the detachment that reigned beneath them and that made of all behaviour, all that could in the least be called behaviour, a long act of dissimulation. What it had come to was that he wore a mask painted with the social simper, out of the eyeholes of which there looked eyes of an expression not in the least matching the other features. This the stupid world, even after years, had never more than half-discovered. It was only May Bartram who had, and she achieved, by an art indescribable, the feat of at once—or perhaps it was only alternately—meeting the eyes from in front and mingling her own vision, as from over his shoulder, with their peep through the apertures.

So while they grew older together she did watch with him, and so she let this association give shape and colour to her own existence. Beneath *her* forms as well detachment had learned to sit, and behaviour had become for her, in the social sense, a false account of herself. There was but one account of her that would have been true all the while and that she could give straight to nobody, least of all to John Marcher. Her whole attitude was a virtual statement, but the perception of that only seemed called to take its place for him as one of the many things necessarily crowded out of his consciousness. If she had moreover, like himself, to make sacrifices to their real truth, it was to be granted that her compensation might have affected her as more prompt and more natural. They had long periods, in this London time, during which, when they were together, a stranger might have listened to them without in the least pricking up his ears; on the other hand the real truth was equally liable at any moment to rise to the surface, and the auditor would then have wondered indeed what they were talking about. They had from an early hour made up their mind that society was, luckily, unintelligent, and the margin allowed them by this had fairly become one of their commonplaces. Yet there were still moments when the situation turned almost fresh—usually under the effect of some expression drawn from herself. Her expressions doubtless repeated themselves, but her intervals were generous. "What saves us, you know, is that we answer so completely to so usual an appearance: that of the man and woman whose friendship had become such a daily habit—or almost—as to be at last indispensable." That for instance was a remark she had frequently enough had occasion to make, though she had given it at different times different developments. What we are especially concerned with is the turn it happened to take from her one afternoon when he had come to see her in honour of her birthday. This anniversary had fallen on a Sunday, at a season of thick fog and general outward gloom; but he had brought her his customary offering, having known her now long enough to have established a hundred small traditions. It was one of his proofs to himself, the present he made her on her birthday, that he hadn't sunk into real selfishness. It was mostly nothing more than a small trinket, but it was always fine of its kind, and he was regularly careful to pay for it more than he thought he could afford. "Our habit saves you at least, don't you see? because it makes you, after all, for the vulgar, indistinguishable from other men. What's the most inveterate mark of men in general? Why the capacity to spend endless time with dull women—to spend it I won't say without being bored, but without minding that they are, without being driven off at a tangent by it; which comes to the same thing. I'm your dull woman, a part of the daily bread for which you pray at church. That covers your tracks more than anything."

"And what covers yours?" asked Marcher, whom his dull woman could mostly to this extent amuse. "I see of course what you mean by your saving me, in this way and that, so far as other people are concerned—I've seen it all along. Only what is it that saves you? I often think, you know, of that."

She looked as if she sometimes thought of that too, but rather in a different way. "Where other people, you mean, are concerned?"

"Well, you're really so in with me, you know—as a sort of result of my being so in with yourself. I mean of my having such an immense regard for you, being so tremendously mindful of all you've done for me. I sometimes ask myself if it's quite fair. Fair I mean to have so involved and—since one may say it—interested you. I almost feel as if you hadn't really had time to do anything else."

"Anything else but be interested?" she asked. "Ah what else does one ever want to be? If I've been 'watching' with you, as we long ago agreed I was to do, watching's always in itself an absorption."

"Oh certainly," John Marcher said, "if you hadn't had your curiosity—! Only doesn't it sometimes come to you as time goes on that your curiosity isn't being particularly repaid?"

May Bartram had a pause. "Do you ask that, by any chance, because you feel at all that yours isn't? I mean because you have to wait so long."

Oh he understood what she meant! "For the thing to happen that never does happen? For the beast to jump out? No, I'm just where I was about it. It isn't a matter as to which I can *choose,* I can decide for a change. It isn't one as to which there can be a change. It's in the lap of the gods. One's in the hands of one's law—there one is. As to the form the law will take, the way it will operate, that's its own affair."

"Yes," Miss Bartram replied; "of course one's fate's coming, of course it *has* come in its own form and its own way, all the while. Only, you know, the form and the way in your case were to have been—well, something so exceptional and, as one may say, so particularly *your* own."

Something in this made him look at her with suspicion. "You say 'were to *have* been,' as if in your heart you had begun to doubt."

"Oh!" she vaguely protested.

"As if you believed," he went on, "that nothing will now take place."

She shook her head slowly but rather inscrutably. "You're far from my thought."

He continued to look at her. "What then is the matter with you?"

"Well," she said after another wait, "the matter with me is simply that I'm more sure than ever my curiosity, as you call it, will be but too well repaid."

They were frankly grave now; he had got up from his seat, had turned once more about the little drawing-room to which, year after year, he brought his inevitable topic; in which he had, as he might have said, tasted their intimate community with every sauce, where every object was as familiar to him as the things of his own house and the very carpets were worn with his fitful walk very much as the desks in old counting-houses are worn by the elbows of generations of clerks. The generations of his nervous moods had been at work there, and the place was the written history of his whole middle life. Under the impression of what his friend had just said he knew himself, for some reason, more aware of these things; which made him, after a moment, stop again before her. "Is it possibly that you've grown afraid?"

"Afraid?" He thought, as she repeated the word, that his question had made her, a little, change colour; so that, lest he should have touched on a truth, he explained very kindly: "You remember that that was what you asked *me* long ago—that first day at Weatherend."

"Oh yes, and you told me you didn't know—that I was to see for myself. We've said little about it since, even in so long a time."

"Precisely," Marcher interposed—"quite as if it were too delicate a matter for us to make free with. Quite as if we might find, on pressure, that I *am* afraid. For then," he said, "we shouldn't, should we? quite know what to do."

She had for the time no answer to this question. "There have been days when I thought you were. Only, of course," she added, "there have been days when we have thought almost anything."

"Everything. Oh!" Marcher softly groaned as with a gasp, half-spent, at the face, more uncovered just then than it had been for a long while, of the imagination always with them. It had always had its incalculable moments of glaring out, quite as with the very eyes of the very Beast, and, used as he was to them, they could still draw from him the tribute of a sigh that rose from the depths of his being. All they had thought, first and last, rolled over him; the past seemed to have been reduced to mere barren speculation. This in fact was what the place had just struck him as so full of—the simplification of everything but the state of suspense. That remained only by seeming to hang in the void surrounding it. Even his original fear, if fear it had been, had lost itself in the desert. "I judge, however," he continued, "that you see I'm not afraid now."

"What I see, as I make it out, is that you've achieved something almost unprecedented in the way of getting used to danger. Living with it so long and so closely you've lost your sense of it; you know it's there, but you're indifferent, and you cease even, as of old, to have to whistle in the dark. Considering what the danger is," May Bartram wound up, "I'm bound to say I don't think your attitude could well be surpassed."

John Marcher faintly smiled. "It's heroic?"

"Certainly—call it that."

It was what he would have liked indeed to call it. "I *am* then a man of courage?"

"That's what you were to show me."

He still, however, wondered. "But doesn't the man of courage know what he's afraid of—or *not* afraid of? I don't know *that*, you see. I don't focus it. I can't name it. I only know I'm exposed."

"Yes, but exposed—how shall I say?—so directly. So intimately. That's surely enough."

"Enough to make you feel then—as what we may call the end and the upshot of our watch—that I'm not afraid?"

"You're not afraid. But it isn't," she said, "the end of our watch. That is it isn't the end of yours. You've everything still to see."

"Then why haven't *you?*" he asked. He had had, all along, today, the sense of her keeping something back, and he still had it. As this was his first impression of that it quite made a date. The case was the more marked as she didn't at first answer; which in turn made him go on. "You know something I don't." Then his voice, for that of a man of courage, trembled a little. "You know what's to happen." Her silence, with the face she showed, was almost a confession—it made him sure. "You know, and you're afraid to tell me. It's so bad that you're afraid I'll find out."

All this might be true, for she did look as if, unexpectedly to her, he had crossed some mystic line that she had secretly drawn round her. Yet she might, after all, not have worried; and the real climax was that he himself, at all events, needn't. "You'll never find out."

III

It was all to have made, none the less, as I have said, a date; which came out in the fact that again and again, even after long intervals, other things that passed between them wore in relation to this hour but the character of recalls and results. Its immediate effect had been indeed rather to lighten insistence—almost to provoke a reaction; as if their topic had dropped by its own weight and as if moreover, for that matter, Marcher had been visited by one of his occasional warnings against egotism. He had kept up, he felt, and very decently on the whole, his consciousness of the importance of not being selfish, and it was true that he had never sinned in that direction without promptly enough trying to press the scales the other way. He often repaired his fault, the season permitting, by inviting his friend to accompany him to the opera; and it not infrequently thus happened that, to show he didn't wish her to have but one sort of food for her mind, he was the cause of her appearing there with him a dozen nights in the month. It even happened that, seeing her home at such times, he occasionally went in with her to finish, as he called it, the evening, and, the better to make his point, sat down to the frugal but always careful little supper that awaited his pleasure. His point was made, he thought, by his not eternally insisting with her on himself; made for instance, at such hours, when it befell that, her piano at hand and each of them familiar with it, they went over passages of the opera together. It chanced to be on one of these occasions, however, that he reminded her of her not having answered a certain question he had put to her during the talk that had taken place between them on her last birthday. "What is it that saves *you*?"—saved her, he meant, from that appearance of variation from the usual human type. If he had practically escaped remark, as she pretended, by doing, in the most important particular, what most men do—find the answer to life in patching up an alliance of a sort with a woman no better than himself—how had she escaped it, and how could the alliance, such as it was, since they must suppose it had been more or less noticed, have failed to make her rather positively talked about?

"I never said," May Bartram replied, "that it hadn't made me a good deal talked about."

"Ah well then you're not 'saved.'"

"It hasn't been a question for me. If you've had your woman I've had," she said, "my man."

"And you mean that makes you all right?"

Oh it was always as if there were so much to say! "I don't know why it shouldn't make me—humanly, which is what we're speaking of—as right as it makes you."

"I see," Marcher returned. " 'Humanly,' no doubt, as showing that you're living for something. Not, that is, just for me and my secret."

May Bartram smiled. "I don't pretend it exactly shows that I'm not living for you. It's my intimacy with you that's in question."

He laughed as he saw what she meant. "Yes, but since, as you say, I'm only, so far as people make out, ordinary, you're—aren't you?—no more than ordinary either. You help me to pass for a man like another. So if I *am,* as I understand you, you're not compromised. Is that it?"

She had another of her waits, but she spoke clearly enough. "That's it. It's all that concerns me—to help you to pass for a man like another."

He was careful to acknowledge the remark handsomely. "How kind, how beautiful, you are to me! How shall I ever repay you?"

She had her last grave pause, as if there might be a choice of ways. But she chose. "By going on as you are."

It was into this going on as he was that they relapsed, and really for so long a time that the day inevitably came for a further sounding of their depths. These depths, constantly bridged over by a structure firm enough in spite of its lightness and of its occasional oscillation in the somewhat vertiginous air, invited on occasion, in the interest of their nerves, a dropping of the plummet and a measurement of the abyss. A difference had been made moreover, once for all, by the fact that she had all the while not appeared to feel the need of rebutting his charge of an idea within her that she didn't dare to express—a charge uttered just before one of the fullest of their later discussions ended. It had come up for him then that she "knew" something and that what she knew was bad—too bad to tell him. When he had spoken of it as visibly so bad that she was afraid he might find it out, her reply had left the matter too equivocal to be let alone and yet, for Marcher's special sensibility, almost too formidable again to touch. He circled about it at a distance that alternately narrowed and widened and that still wasn't much affected by the consciousness in him that there was nothing she could "know," after all, any better than he did. She had no source of knowledge he hadn't equally—except of course that she might have finer nerves. That was what women had where they were interested; they made out things, where people were concerned, that the people often couldn't have made out for themselves. Their nerves, their sensibility, their imagination, were conductors and revealers, and the beauty of May Bartram was in particular that she had given herself so to his case. He felt in these days what, oddly enough, he had never felt before, the growth of a dread of losing her by some catastrophe—some catastrophe that yet wouldn't at all be *the* catastrophe: partly because she had almost of a sudden begun to strike him as more useful to him than ever yet, and partly by reason of an appearance of uncertainty in her health, coincident and equally new. It was characteristic of the inner detachment he had hitherto

so successfully cultivated and to which our whole account of him is a reference, it was characteristic that his complications, such as they were, had
never yet seemed so as at this crisis to thicken about him, even to the point
of making him ask himself if he were, by any chance, of a truth, within sight
or sound, within touch or reach, within the immediate jurisdiction, of the
thing that waited.

When the day came, as come it had to, that his friend confessed to him
her fear of a deep disorder in her blood, he felt somehow the shadow of a
change and the chill of a shock. He immediately began to imagine aggra-
vations and disasters, and above all to think of her peril as the direct men-
ace for himself of personal privation. This indeed gave him one of those
partial recoveries of equanimity that were agreeable to him—it showed
him that what was still first in his mind was the loss she herself might suffer.
"What if she should have to die before knowing, before seeing—?" It
would have been brutal, in the early stages of her trouble, to put that question to her; but it had immediately sounded for him to his own concern,
and the possibility was what most made him sorry for her. If she did
"know," moreover, in the sense of her having had some—what should he
think?—mystical irresistible light, this would make the matter not better,
but worse, inasmuch as her original adoption of his own curiosity had quite
become the basis of her life. She had been living to see what would *be* to be
seen, and it would quite lacerate her to have to give up before the accom-
plishment of the vision. These reflexions, as I say, quickened his generosity; yet, make them as he might, he saw himself, with the lapse of the
period, more and more disconcerted. It lapsed for him with a strange
steady sweep, and the oddest oddity was that it gave him, independently of
the threat of much inconvenience, almost the only positive surprise his career, if career it could be called, had yet offered him. She kept the house as
she had never done; he had to go to her to see her—she could meet him
nowhere now, though there was scarce a corner of their loved old London
in which she hadn't in the past, at one time or another, done so; and he
found her always seated by her fire in the deep old-fashioned chair she was
less and less able to leave. He had been struck one day, after an absence exceeding his usual measure, with her suddenly looking much older to him
than he had ever thought of her being; then he recognised that the suddenness was all on his side—he had just simply and suddenly noticed. She
looked older because inevitably, after so many years, she *was* old, or almost;
which was of course true in still greater measure of her companion. If she
was old, or almost, John Marcher assuredly was, and yet it was her showing
of the lesson, not his own, that brought the truth home to him. His surprises began here; when once they had begun they multiplied; they came
rather with a rush: it was as if, in the oddest way in the world, they had all
been kept back, sown in a thick cluster, for the late afternoon of life, the
time at which for people in general the unexpected has died out.

One of them was that he should have caught himself—for he *had* so done—*really* wondering if the great accident would take form now as nothing more than his being condemned to see this charming woman, this admirable friend, pass away from him. He had never so unreservedly qualified her as while confronted in thought with such a possibility; in spite of which there was small doubt for him that as an answer to his long riddle the mere effacement of even so fine a feature of his situation would be an abject anti-climax. It would represent, as connected with his past attitude, a drop of dignity under the shadow of which his existence could only become the most grotesque of failures. He had been far from holding it a failure— long as he had waited for the appearance that was to make it a success. He had waited for quite another thing, not for such a thing as that. The breath of his good faith came short, however, as he recognised how long he had waited, or how long at least his companion had. That she, at all events, might be recorded as having waited in vain—this affected him sharply, and all the more because of his at first having done little more than amuse himself with the idea. It grew more grave as the gravity of her condition grew, and the state of mind it produced in him, which he himself ended by watching as if it had been some definite disfigurement of his outer person, may pass for another of his surprises. This conjoined itself still with another, the really stupefying consciousness of a question that he would have allowed to shape itself had he dared. What did everything mean—what, that is, did *she* mean, she and her vain waiting and her probable death and the soundless admonition of it all—unless that, at this time of day, it was simply, it was overwhelmingly too late? He had never at any stage of his queer consciousness admitted the whisper of such a correction; he had never till within these last few months been so false to his conviction as not to hold that what was to come to him had time, whether *he* struck himself as having it or not. That at last, at last, he certainly hadn't it, to speak of, or had it but in the scantiest measure—such, soon enough, as things went with him, became the inference with which his old obsession had to reckon: and this it was not helped to do by the more and more confirmed appearance that the great vagueness casting the long shadow in which he had lived had, to attest itself, almost no margin left. Since it was in Time that he was to have met his fate, so it was in Time that his fate was to have acted; and as he waked up to the sense of no longer being young, which was exactly the sense of being stale, just as that, in turn, was the sense of being weak, he waked up to another matter beside. It all hung together; they were subject, he and the great vagueness, to an equal and indivisible law. When the possibilities themselves had accordingly turned stale, when the secret of the gods had grown faint, had perhaps even quite evaporated, that, and that only, was failure. It wouldn't have been failure to be bankrupt, dishonoured, pilloried, hanged; it was failure not to be anything. And so in the dark valley into which his path had taken its unlooked-for twist, he wondered not a little as he groped. He didn't care what awful crash might overtake him, with what ignominy or what monstrosity he might yet be associated—since he wasn't after all too utterly old to suffer—if it would only be decently proportionate to the posture he had kept, all his life, in the threatened presence of it. He had but one desire left—that he shouldn't have been "sold."

IV

Then it was that, one afternoon, while the spring of the year was young and new she met all in her own way his frankest betrayal of these alarms. He had gone in late to see her, but evening hadn't settled and she was presented to him in that long fresh light of waning April days which affects us often with a sadness sharper than the greyest hours of autumn. The week had been warm, the spring was supposed to have begun early, and May Bartram sat, for the first time in the year, without a fire; a fact that, to Marcher's sense, gave the scene of which she formed part a smooth and ultimate look, an air of knowing, in its immaculate order and cold meaningless cheer, that it would never see a fire again. Her own aspect—he could scarce have said why—intensified this note. Almost as white as wax, with the marks and signs in her face as numerous and as fine as if they had been etched by a needle, with soft white draperies relieved by a faded green scarf on the delicate tone of which the years had further refined, she was the picture of a serene and exquisite but impenetrable sphinx, whose head, or indeed all whose person, might have been powdered with silver. She was a sphinx, yet with her white petals and green fronds she might have been a lily too—only an artificial lily, wonderfully imitated and constantly kept, without dust or stain, though not exempt from a slight droop and a complexity of faint creases, under some clear glass bell. The perfection of household care, of high polish and finish, always reigned in her rooms, but they now looked most as if everything had been wound up, tucked in, put away, so that she might sit with folded hands and with nothing more to do. She was "out of it," to Marcher's vision; her work was over; she communicated with him as across some gulf or from some island of rest that she had already reached, and it made him feel strangely abandoned. Was it—or rather wasn't it—that if for so long she had been watching with him the answer to their question must have swum into her ken and taken on its name, so that her occupation was verily gone? He had as much as charged her with this in saying to her, many months before, that she even then knew something she was keeping from him. It was a point he had never since ventured to press, vaguely fearing as he did that it might become a difference, perhaps a disagreement, between them. He had in this later time turned nervous, which was what he in all the other years had never been; and the oddity was that his nervousness should have waited till he had begun to doubt, should have held off so long as he was sure. There was something, it seemed to him, that the wrong word would bring down on his head, something that would so at least ease off his tension. But he wanted not to speak the wrong word; that would make everything ugly. He wanted the knowledge he lacked to drop on him, if drop it could, by its own august weight. If she was to forsake him it was surely for her to take leave. This was why he didn't directly ask her again what she knew; but it was also why, approaching the matter from another side, he said to her in the course of his visit: "What do you regard as the very worst that at this time of day *can* happen to me?"

He had asked her that in the past often enough; they had, with the odd irregular rhythm of their intensities and avoidances, exchanged ideas about it and then had seen the ideas washed away by cool intervals, washed like figures traced in sea-sand. It had ever been the mark of their talk that the oldest allusions in it required but a little dismissal and reaction to come out again, sounding for the hour as new. She could thus at present meet his enquiry quite freshly and patiently. "Oh yes, I've repeatedly thought, only it always seemed to me of old that I couldn't quite make up my mind. I thought of dreadful things, between which it was difficult to choose; and so must you have done."

"Rather! I feel now as if I had scarce done anything else. I appear to myself to have spent my life in thinking of nothing *but* dreadful things. A great many of them I've at different times named to you, but there were others I couldn't name."

"They were too, too dreadful?"

"Too, too dreadful—some of them."

She looked at him a minute, and there came to him as he met it an inconsequent sense that her eyes, when one got their full clearness, were still as beautiful as they had been in youth, only beautiful with a strange cold light—a light that somehow was a part of the effect, if it wasn't rather a part of the cause, of the pale hard sweetness of the season and the hour. "And yet," she said at last, "there are horrors we've mentioned."

It deepened the strangeness to see her, as such a figure in such a picture, talk of "horrors," but she was to do in a few minutes something stranger yet—though even of this he was to take the full measure but afterwards—and the note of it already trembled. It was, for the matter of that, one of the signs that her eyes were having again the high flicker of their prime. He had to admit, however, what she said. "Oh yes, there were times when we did go far." He caught himself in the act of speaking as if it all were over. Well, he wished it were; and the consummation depended for him clearly more and more on his friend.

But she had now a soft smile. "Oh far—!"

It was oddly ironic. "Do you mean you're prepared to go further?"

She was frail and ancient and charming as she continued to look at him, yet it was rather as if she had lost the thread. "Do you consider that we went far?"

"Why I thought it the point you were just making—that we *had* looked most things in the face."

"Including each other?" She still smiled. "But you're quite right. We've had together great imaginations, often great fears; but some of them have been unspoken."

"Then the worst—we haven't faced that. I *could* face it, I believe, if I knew what you think it. I feel," he explained, "as if I had lost my power to conceive such things." And he wondered if he looked as blank as he sounded. "It's spent."

"Then why do you assume," she asked, "that mine isn't?"

"Because you've given me signs to the contrary. It isn't a question for you of conceiving, imagining, comparing. It isn't a question now of choosing." At last he came out with it. "You know something I don't. You've shown me that before."

These last words had affected her, he made out in a moment, exceedingly, and she spoke with firmness. "I've shown you, my dear, nothing."

He shook his head. "You can't hide it."

"Oh, oh!" May Bartram sounded over what she couldn't hide. It was almost a smothered groan.

"You admitted it months ago, when I spoke of it to you as of something you were afraid I should find out. Your answer was that I couldn't, that I wouldn't, and I don't pretend I have. But you had something therefore in mind, and I now see how it must have been, how it still is, the possibility that, of all possibilities, has settled itself for you as the worst. This," he went on, "is why I appeal to you. I'm only afraid of ignorance today—I'm not afraid of knowledge." And then as for a while she said nothing: "What makes me sure is that I see in your face and feel here, in this air and amid these appearances, that you're out of it. You've done. You've had your experience. You leave me to my fate."

Well, she listened, motionless and white in her chair, as on a decision to be made, so that her manner was fairly an avowal, though still, with a small fine inner stiffness, an imperfect surrender. "It *would* be the worst," she finally let herself say. "I mean the thing I've never said."

It hushed him a moment. "More monstrous than all the monstrosities we've named?"

"More monstrous. Isn't that what you sufficiently express," she asked, "in calling it the worst?"

Marcher thought. "Assuredly—if you mean, as I do, something that includes all the loss and all the shame that are thinkable."

"It would if it *should* happen," said May Bartram. "What we're speaking of, remember, is only my idea."

"It's your belief," Marcher returned. "That's enough for me. I feel your beliefs are right. Therefore if, having this one, you give me no more light on it, you abandon me."

"No, no!" she repeated. "I'm with you—don't you see?—still." And as to make it more vivid to him she rose from her chair—a movement she seldom risked in these days—and showed herself, all draped and all soft, in her fairness and slimness. "I haven't forsaken you."

It was really, in its effort against weakness, a generous assurance, and had the success of the impulse not, happily, been great, it would have touched him to pain more than to pleasure. But the cold charm in her eyes had spread, as she hovered before him, to all the rest of her person, so that it was for the minute almost a recovery of youth. He couldn't pity her for that; he could only take her as she showed—as capable even yet of helping him. It was as if, at the same time, her light might at any instant go out; wherefore he must make the most of it. There passed before him with intensity the three or four things he wanted most to know; but the question that came of itself to his lips really covered the others. "Then tell me if I shall consciously suffer."

She promptly shook her head. "Never!"

It confirmed the authority he imputed to her, and it produced on him an extraordinary effect. "Well, what's better than that? Do you call that the worst?"

"You think nothing is better?" she asked.

She seemed to mean something so special that he again sharply wondered, though still with the dawn of a prospect of relief. "Why not, if one doesn't *know*?" After which, as their eyes, over his question, met in a silence, the dawn deepened and something to his purpose came prodigiously out of her very face. His own, as he took it in, suddenly flushed to the forehead, and he gasped with the force of a perception to which, on the instant, everything fitted. The sound of his gasp filled the air; then he became articulate. "I see—if I don't suffer!"

In her own look, however, was doubt. "You see what?"

"Why what you mean—what you've always meant."

She again shook her head. "What I mean isn't what I've always meant. It's different."

"It's something new?"

She hung back from it a little. "Something new. It's not what you think. I see what you think."

His divination drew breath then; only her correction might be wrong. "It isn't that I *am* a blockhead?" he asked between faintness and grimness. "It isn't that it's all a mistake?"

"A mistake?" she pityingly echoed. *That* possibility, for her, he saw, would be monstrous; and if she guaranteed him the immunity from pain it would accordingly not be what she had in mind. "Oh no," she declared; "it's nothing of that sort. You've been right."

Yet he couldn't help asking himself if she weren't, thus pressed, speaking but to save him. It seemed to him he should be most in a hole if his history should prove all a platitude. "Are you telling me the truth, so that I shan't have been a bigger idiot than I can bear to know? I *haven't* lived with a vain imagination, in the most besotted illusion? I haven't waited but to see the door shut in my face?"

She shook her head again. "However the case stands *that* isn't the truth. Whatever the reality, it *is* a reality. The door isn't shut. The door's open," said May Bartram.

"Then something's to come?"

She waited once again, always with her cold sweet eyes on him. "It's never too late." She had, with her gliding step, diminished the distance between them, and she stood nearer to him, close to him, a minute, as if still charged with the unspoken. Her movement might have been for some finer emphasis of what she was at once hesitating and deciding to say. He had been standing by the chimneypiece, fireless and sparely adorned, a small perfect old French clock and two morsels of rosy Dresden constituting all its furniture; and her hand grasped the shelf while she kept him waiting, grasped it a little as for support and encouragement. She only kept him waiting, however; that is he only waited. It had become suddenly, from her movement and attitude, beautiful and vivid to him that she had something more to give him; her wasted face delicately shone with it—it glittered almost as with the white lustre of silver in her expression. She was right, incontestably, for what he saw in her face was the truth, and strangely, without consequence, while their talk of it as dreadful was still in the air, she appeared to present it as inordinately soft. This, prompting bewilderment, made him but gape the more gratefully for her revelation, so that they continued for some minutes silent, her face shining at him, her contact imponderably pressing, and his stare all kind but all expectant. The end, none the less, was that what he had expected failed to come to him. Something else took place instead, which seemed to consist at first in the mere closing of her eyes. She gave way at the same instant to a slow fine shudder, and though he remained staring—though he stared in fact but the harder—turned off and regained her chair. It was the end of what she had been intending, but it left him thinking only of that.

"Well, you don't say—?"

She had touched in her passage a bell near the chimney and had sunk back strangely pale. "I'm afraid I'm too ill."

"Too ill to tell me?" It sprang up sharp to him, and almost to his lips, the fear she might die without giving him light. He checked himself in time from so expressing his question, but she answered as if she had heard the words.

"Don't you know—now?"

" 'Now'—?" She had spoken as if some difference had been made within the moment. But her maid, quickly obedient to her bell, was already with them. "I know nothing." And he was afterwards to say to himself that he must have spoken with odious impatience, such an impatience as to show that, supremely disconcerted, he washed his hands of the whole question.

"Oh!" said May Bartram.

"Are you in pain?" he asked as the woman went to her.

"No," said May Bartram.

Her maid, who had put an arm round her as if to take her to her room, fixed on him eyes that appealingly contradicted her; in spite of which, however, he showed once more his mystification. "What then has happened?"

She was once more, with her companion's help, on her feet, and, feeling withdrawal imposed on him, he had blankly found his hat and gloves and had reached the door. Yet he waited for her answer. "What *was* to," she said.

V

He came back the next day, but she was then unable to see him, and as it was literally the first time this had occurred in the long stretch of their acquaintance he turned away, defeated and sore, almost angry—or feeling at least that such a break in their custom was really the beginning of the end—and wandered alone with his thoughts, especially with the one he was least able to keep down. She was dying and he would lose her; she was dying and his life would end. He stopped in the Park, into which he had passed, and stared before him at his recurrent doubt. Away from her the doubt pressed again; in her presence he had believed her, but as he felt his forlornness he threw himself into the explanation that, nearest at hand, had most of a miserable warmth for him and least of a cold torment. She had deceived him to save him—to put him off with something in which he should be able to rest. What could the thing that was to happen to him be, after all, but just this thing that had begun to happen? Her dying, her death, his consequent solitude—*that* was what he had figured as the Beast in the Jungle, that was what had been in the lap of the gods. He had had her word for it as he left her—what else on earth could she have meant? It wasn't a thing of a monstrous order; not a fate rare and distinguished; not a stroke of fortune that overwhelmed and immortalised; it had only the stamp of the common doom. But poor Marcher at this hour judged the common doom sufficient. It would serve his turn, and even as the consummation of infinite waiting he would bend his pride to accept it. He sat down on a bench in the twilight. He hadn't been a fool. Something had *been,* as she had said, to come. Before he rose indeed it had quite struck him that the final fact really matched with the long avenue through which he had had to reach it. As sharing his suspense and as giving herself all, giving her life, to bring it to an end, she had come with him every step of the way. He had lived by her aid, and to leave her behind would be cruelty, damnably to miss her. What could be more overwhelming than that?

Well, he was to know within the week, for though she kept him a while at bay, left him restless and wretched during a series of days on each of which he asked about her only again to have to turn away, she ended his trial by receiving him where she had always received him. Yet she had been brought out at some hazard into the presence of so many of the things that were, consciously, vainly, half their past, and there was scant service left in the gentleness of her mere desire, all too visible, to check his obsession and wind up his long trouble. That was clearly what she wanted, the one thing more for her own peace while she could still put out her hand. He was so affected by her state that, once seated by her chair, he was moved to let everything go; it was she herself therefore who brought him back, took up again, before she dismissed him, her last word of the other time. She showed how she wished to leave their business in order. "I'm not sure you understood. You've nothing to wait for more. It *has* come."

Oh how he looked at her! "Really?"

"Really."

"The thing that, as you said, *was* to?"

"The thing that we began in our youth to watch for."

Face to face with her once more he believed her; it was a claim to which he had so abjectly little to oppose. "You mean that it has come as a positive definite occurrence, with a name and a date?"

"Positive. Definite. I don't know about the 'name,' but oh with a date!"

He found himself again too helplessly at sea. "But come in the night—come and passed me by?"

May Bartram had her strange faint smile. "Oh no, it hasn't passed you by!"

"But if I haven't been aware of it and it hasn't touched me—?"

"Ah your not being aware of it"—and she seemed to hesitate an instant to deal with this—"your not being aware of it is the strangeness *in* the strangeness. It's the wonder *of* the wonder." She spoke as with the softness almost of a sick child, yet now at last, at the end of all, with the perfect straightness of a sibyl. She visibly knew that she knew, and the effect on him was of something co-ordinate, in its high character, with the law that had ruled him. It was the true voice of the law; so on her lips would the law itself have sounded. "It *has* touched you," she went on. "It has done its office. It has made you all its own."

"So utterly without my knowing it?"

"So utterly without your knowing it." His hand, as he leaned to her, was on the arm of her chair, and, dimly smiling always now, she placed her own on it. "It's enough if *I* know it."

"Oh!" he confusedly breathed, as she herself of late so often had done.

"What I long ago said is true. You'll never know now, and I think you ought to be content. You've *had* it," said May Bartram.

"But had what?"

"Why what was to have marked you out. The proof of your law. It has acted. I'm too glad," she then bravely added, "to have been able to see what it's *not*."

He continued to attach his eyes to her, and with the sense that it was all beyond him, and that *she* was too, he would still have sharply challenged her hadn't he so felt it an abuse of her weakness to do more than take devoutly what she gave him, take it hushed as to a revelation. If he did speak, it was out of the fore-knowledge of his loneliness to come. "If you're glad of what it's 'not' it might then have been worse?"

She turned her eyes away, she looked straight before her; with which after a moment: "Well, you know our fears."

He wondered. "It's something then we never feared?"

On this slowly she turned to him. "Did we ever dream, with all our dreams, that we should sit and talk of it thus?"

He tried for a little to make out that they had; but it was as if their dreams, numberless enough, were in solution in some thick cold mist through which thought lost itself. "It might have been that we couldn't talk?"

"Well"—she did her best for him—"not from this side. This, you see," she said, "is the *other* side."

"I think," poor Marcher returned, "that all sides are the same to me." Then, however, as she gently shook her head in correction: "We mightn't, as it were, have got across—?"

"To where we are—no. We're *here*"—she made her weak emphasis.

"And much good does it do us!" was her friend's frank comment.

"It does us the good it can. It does us the good that *it* isn't here. It's past. It's behind," said May Bartram. "Before—" but her voice dropped.

He had got up, not to tire her, but it was hard to combat his yearning. She after all told him nothing but that his light had failed—which he knew well enough without her. "Before—?" he blankly echoed.

"Before, you see, it was always to *come*. That kept it present."

"Oh I don't care what comes now! Besides," Marcher added, "it seems to me I liked it better present, as you say, than I can like it absent with *your* absence."

"Oh mine!"—and her pale hands made light of it.

"With the absence of everything." He had a dreadful sense of standing there before her for—so far as anything but this proved, this bottomless drop was concerned—the last time of their life. It rested on him with a weight he felt he could scarce bear, and this weight it apparently was that still pressed out what remained in him of speakable protest. "I believe you; but I can't begin to pretend I understand. *Nothing*, for me, is past; nothing *will* pass till I pass myself, which I pray my stars may be as soon as possible. Say, however," he added, "that I've eaten my cake, as you contend, to the last crumb—how can the thing I've never felt at all be the thing I was marked out to feel?"

She met him perhaps less directly, but she met him unperturbed. "You take your 'feelings' for granted. You were to suffer your fate. That was not necessarily to know it."

"How in the world—when what is such knowledge but suffering?"

She looked up at him a while in silence. "No—you don't understand."

"I suffer," said John Marcher.

"Don't, don't!"

"How can I help at least *that*?"

"*Don't!*" May Bartram repeated.

She spoke it in a tone so special, in spite of her weakness, that he stared an instant—stared as if some light, hitherto hidden, had shimmered across his vision. Darkness again closed over it, but the gleam had already become for him an idea. "Because I haven't the right—?"

"Don't *know*—when you needn't," she mercifully urged. "You needn't—for we shouldn't."

"Shouldn't?" If he could but know what she meant!

"No—it's too much."

"Too much?" he still asked but, with a mystification that was the next moment of a sudden to give way. Her words, if they meant something, affected him in this light—the light also of her wasted face—as meaning *all*, and the sense of what knowledge had been for herself came over him with a rush which broke through into a question. "Is it of that then you're dying?"

She but watched him, gravely at first, as to see, with this, where he was, and she might have seen something or feared something that moved her sympathy. "I would live for you still—if I could." Her eyes closed for a little, as if, withdrawn into herself, she were for a last time trying. "But I can't!" she said as she raised them again to take leave of him.

She couldn't indeed, as but too promptly and sharply appeared, and he had no vision of her after this that was anything but darkness and doom. They had parted for ever in that strange talk; access to her chamber of pain, rigidly guarded, was almost wholly forbidden him; he was feeling now moreover, in the face of doctors, nurses, the two or three relatives attracted doubtless by the presumption of what she had to "leave," how few were the rights, as they were called in such cases, that he had to put forward, and how odd it might even seem that their intimacy shouldn't have given him more of them. The stupidest fourth cousin had more, even though she had been nothing in such a person's life. She had been a feature of features in *his,* for what else was it to have been so indispensable? Strange beyond saying were the ways of existence, baffling for him the anomaly of his lack, as he felt it to be, of producible claim. A woman might have been, as it were, everything to him, and it might yet present him in no connexion that any one seemed held to recognise. If this was the case in these closing weeks it was the case more sharply on the occasion of the last offices rendered, in the great grey London cemetery, to what had been mortal, to what had been precious, in his friend. The concourse at her grave was not numerous, but he saw himself treated as scarce more nearly concerned with it than if there had been a thousand others. He was in short from this moment face to face with the fact that he was to profit extraordinarily little by the interest May Bartram had taken in him. He couldn't quite have said what he expected, but he hadn't surely expected this approach to a double privation. Not only had her interest failed him, but he seemed to feel himself unattended—and for a reason he couldn't seize—by the distinction, the dignity, the propriety, if nothing else, of the man markedly bereaved. It was as if in the view of society he had not *been* markedly bereaved, as if there still failed some sign or proof of it, and as if none the less his character could never be affirmed nor the deficiency ever made up. There were moments as the weeks went by when he would have liked, by some almost aggressive act, to take his stand on the intimacy of his loss, in order that it *might* be questioned and his retort, to the relief of his spirit, so recorded; but the moments of an irritation more helpless followed fast on these, the moments during which, turning things over with a good conscience but with a bare horizon, he found himself wondering if he oughtn't to have begun, so to speak, further back.

He found himself wondering indeed at many things, and this last speculation had others to keep it company. What could he have done, after all, in her lifetime, without giving them both, as it were, away? He couldn't have made known she was watching him, for that would have published the superstition of the Beast. This was what closed his mouth now—now that the Jungle had been threshed to vacancy and that the Beast had stolen away. It sounded too foolish and too flat; the difference for him in this particular, the extinction in his life of the element of suspense, was such as in fact to surprise him. He could scarce have said what the effect resembled; the abrupt cessation, the positive prohibition, of music perhaps, more than anything else, in some place all adjusted and all accustomed to sonority and to attention. If he could at any rate have conceived lifting the veil from his image at some moment of the past (what had he done, after all, if not lift it to *her?*) so to do this today, to talk to people at large of the Jungle cleared and confide to them that he now felt it as safe, would have been not only to see them listen as to a goodwife's tale, but really to hear himself tell one. What it presently came to in truth was that poor Marcher waded through his beaten grass, where no life stirred, where no breath sounded, where no evil eye seemed to gleam from a possible lair, very much as if vaguely looking for the Beast, and still more as if acutely missing it. He walked about in an existence that had grown strangely more spacious, and, stopping fitfully in places where the undergrowth of life struck him as closer, asked himself yearningly, wondered secretly and sorely, if it would have lurked here or there. It would have at all events *sprung;* what was at least complete was his belief in the truth itself of the assurance given him. The change from his old sense to his new was absolute and final: what was to happen *had* so absolutely and finally happened that he was as little able to know a fear for his future as to know a hope; so absent in short was any question of anything still to come. He was to live entirely with the other question, that of his unidentified past, that of his having to see his fortune impenetrably muffled and masked.

The torment of this vision became then his occupation; he couldn't perhaps have consented to live but for the possibility of guessing. She had told him, his friend, not to guess; she had forbidden him, so far as he might, to know, and she had even in a sort denied the power in him to learn: which were so many things, precisely, to deprive him of rest. It wasn't that he wanted, he argued for fairness, that anything past and done should repeat itself; it was only that he shouldn't, as an anticlimax, have been taken sleeping so sound as not to be able to win back by an effort of thought the lost stuff of consciousness. He declared to himself at moments that he would either win it back or have done with consciousness for ever; he made this idea his one motive in fine, made it so much his passion that none other, to compare with it, seemed ever to have touched him. The lost stuff of consciousness became thus for him as a strayed or stolen child to an unappeasable father; he hunted it up and down very much as if he were knocking at doors and enquiring of the police. This was the spirit in which, inevitably, he set himself to travel; he started on a journey that was to be as long as he could make it; it danced before him that, as the other side of the globe couldn't possibly have less to say to him, it might, by a possibility of suggestion, have more. Before he quitted London, however, he made a pilgrimage to May Bartram's grave, took his way to it through the endless avenues of the grim suburban metropolis, sought it out in the wilderness of tombs, and, though he had come but for the renewal of the act of farewell, found himself, when he had at last stood by it, beguiled into long intensities. He stood for an hour, powerless to turn away and yet powerless to penetrate the darkness of death; fixing with his eyes her inscribed name and date, beating his forehad against the fact of the secret they kept, drawing his breath, while he waited, as if some sense would in pity of him rise from the stones. He kneeled on the stones, however, in vain; they kept what they concealed; and if the face of the tomb did become a face for him it was because her two names became a pair of eyes that didn't know him. He gave them a last long look, but no palest light broke.

VI

He stayed away, after this, for a year; he visited the depths of Asia, spending himself on scenes of romantic interest, of superlative sanctity; but what was present to him everywhere was that for a man who had known what *he* had known the world was vulgar and vain. The state of mind in which he had lived for so many years shone out to him, in reflexion, as a light that coloured and refined, a light beside which the glow of the East was garish and cheap and thin. The terrible truth was that he had lost—with everything else—a distinction as well; the things he saw couldn't help being common when he had become common to look at them. He was simply now one of them himself—he was in the dust, without a peg for the sense of difference; and there were hours when, before the temples of gods and the sepulchres of kings, his spirit turned for nobleness of association to the barely discriminated slab in the London suburb. That had become for him, and more intensely with time and distance, his one witness of a past glory. It was all that was left to him for proof or pride, yet the past glories of Pharaohs were nothing to him as he thought of it. Small wonder then that he came back to it on the morrow of his return. He was drawn there this time as irresistibly as the other, yet with a confidence, almost, that was doubtless the effect of the many months that had elapsed. He had lived, in spite of himself, into his change of feeling, and in wandering over the earth had wandered, as might be said, from the circumference to the centre of his desert. He had settled to his safety and accepted perforce his extinction; figuring to himself, with some colour, in the likeness of certain little old men he remembered to have seen, of whom, all meagre and wizened as they might look, it was related that they had in their time fought twenty duels or been loved by ten princesses. They indeed had been wondrous for others while he was but wondrous for himself; which, however, was exactly the cause of his haste to renew the wonder by getting back, as he might put it, into his own presence. That had quickened his steps and checked his delay. If his visit was prompt it was because he had been separated so long from the part of himself that alone he now valued.

It's accordingly not false to say that he reached his goal with a certain elation and stood there again with a certain assurance. The creature beneath the sod *knew* of his rare experience, so that, strangely now, the place had lost for him its mere blankness of expression. It met him in mildness—not, as before, in mockery; it wore for him the air of conscious greeting that we find, after absence, in things that have closely belonged to us and which seem to confess of themselves to the connexion. The plot of ground, the graven tablet, the tended flowers affected him so as belonging to him that he resembled for the hour a contented landlord reviewing a piece of property. Whatever had happened—well, had happened. He had not come back this time with the vanity of that question, his former worrying "what, *what*?" now practically so spent. Yet he would none the less never again so cut himself off from the spot; he would come back to it every month, for if he did nothing else by its aid he at least held up his head. It thus grew for him, in the oddest way, a positive resource; he carried out his idea of periodical returns, which took their place at last among the most inveterate of his habits. What it all amounted to, oddly enough, was that in his finally so simplified world this garden of death gave him the few square feet of earth on which he could still most live. It was as if, being nothing anywhere else for any one, nothing even for himself, he were just everything here, and if not for a crowd of witnesses or indeed for any witness but John Marcher, then by clear right of the register that he could scan like an open page. The open page was the tomb of his friend, and *there* were the facts of the past, there the truth of his life, there the backward reaches in which he could lose himself. He did this from time to time with such effect that he seemed to wander through the old years with his hand in the arm of a companion who was, in the most extraordinary manner, his other, his younger self; and to wander, which was more extraordinary yet, round and round a third presence—not wandering she, but stationary, still, whose eyes, turning with his revolution, never ceased to follow him, and whose seat was his point, so to speak, of orientation. Thus in short he settled to live—feeding all on the sense that he once *had* lived, and dependent on it not alone for a support but for an identity.

It sufficed him in its way for months and the year elapsed; it would doubtless even have carried him further but for an accident, superficially slight, which moved him, quite in another direction, with a force beyond any of his impressions of Egypt or of India. It was a thing of the merest chance—the turn, as he afterwards felt, of a hair, though he was indeed to live to believe that if light hadn't come to him in this particular fashion it would still have come in another. He was to live to believe this, I say, though he was not to live, I may not less definitely mention, to do much else. We allow him at any rate the benefit of the conviction, struggling up for him at the end, that, whatever might have happened or not happened, he would have come round of himself to the light. The incident of an autumn day had put the match to the train laid from of old by his misery. With the light before him he knew that even of late his ache had only been smothered. It was strangely drugged, but it throbbed; at the touch it began to bleed. And the touch, in the event, was the face of a fellow mortal. This face, one grey afternoon when the leaves were thick in the alleys, looked into Marcher's own, at the cemetery, with an expression like the cut of a blade. He felt it, that is, so deep down that he winced at the steady thrust. The person who so mutely assaulted him was a figure he had noticed, on reaching his own goal, absorbed by a grave a short distance away, a grave apparently fresh, so that the emotion of the visitor would probably match it for frankness. This face alone forbade further attention, though during the time he stayed he remained vaguely conscious of his neighbour, a middle-aged man apparently, in mourning, whose bowed back, among the clustered monuments and mortuary yews, was constantly presented. Marcher's theory that these were elements in contact with which he himself revived, had suffered, on this occasion, it may be granted, a marked, an excessive check. The autumn day was dire for him as none had recently been, and he rested with a heaviness he had not yet known on the low stone table that bore May Bartram's name. He rested without power to move, as if some spring in him, some spell vouchsafed, had suddenly been broken for ever. If he could have done that moment as he wanted he would simply have stretched himself on the slab that was ready to take him, treating it as a place prepared to receive his last sleep. What in all the wide world had he now to keep awake for? He stared before him with the question, and it was then that, as one of the cemetery walks passed near him, he caught the shock of the face.

His neighbour at the other grave had withdrawn, as he himself, with force enough in him, would have done by now, and was advancing along the path on his way to one of the gates. This brought him close, and his pace was slow, so that—and all the more as there was a kind of hunger in his look—the two men were for a minute directly confronted. Marcher knew him at once for one of the deeply stricken—a perception so sharp that nothing else in the picture comparatively lived, neither his dress, his age, nor his presumable character and class; nothing lived but the deep ravage of the features he showed. He *showed* them—that was the point; he was moved, as he passed, by some impulse that was either a signal for sympathy or, more possibly, a challenge to an opposed sorrow. He might already have been aware of our friend, might at some previous hour have noticed in him the smooth habit of the scene, with which the state of his own senses so scantly consorted, and might thereby have been stirred as by an overt discord. What Marcher was at all events conscious of was in the first place that the image of scarred passion presented to him was conscious too—of something that profaned the air; and in the second that, roused, startled, shocked, he was yet the next moment looking after it, as it went, with envy. The most extraordinary thing that had happened to him—though he had given that name to other matters as well—took place, after his immediate vague stare, as a consequence of this impression. The stranger passed, but the raw glare of his grief remained, making our friend wonder in pity what wrong, what wound it expressed, what injury not to be healed. What had the man *had,* to make him by the loss of it so bleed and yet live?

Something—and this reached him with a pang—that *he,* John Marcher, hadn't; the proof of which was precisely John Marcher's arid end. No passion had ever touched him, for this was what passion meant; he had survived and maundered and pined, but where had been *his* deep ravage? The extraordinary thing we speak of was the sudden rush of the result of this question. The sight that had just met his eyes named to him, as in letters of quick flame, something he had utterly, insanely missed, and what he had missed made these things a train of fire, made them mark themselves in an anguish of inward throbs. He had seen *outside* of his life, not learned it within, the way a woman was mourned when she had been loved for herself: such was the force of his conviction of the meaning of the stranger's face, which still flared for him as a smoky torch. It hadn't come to him, the knowledge, on the wings of experience; it had brushed him, jostled him, upset him, with the disrespect of chance, the insolence of accident. Now that the illumination had begun, however, it blazed to the zenith, and what he presently stood there gazing at was the sounded void of his life. He gazed, he drew breath, in pain; he turned in his dismay, and, turning, he had before him in sharper incision than ever the open page of his story. The name on the table smote him as the passage of his neighbour had done, and what it said to him, full in the face, was that *she* was what he had missed. This was the awful thought, the answer to all the past, the vision at the dread clearness of which he grew as cold as the stone beneath him. Everything fell together, confessed, explained, overwhelmed; leaving him most of all stupefied at the blindness he had cherished. The fate he had been marked for he had met with a vengeance—he had emptied the cup to the lees; he had been the man of his time, *the* man, to whom nothing on earth was to have happened. That was the rare stroke—that was his visitation. So he saw it, as we say, in pale horror, while the pieces fitted and fitted. So *she* had seen it while he didn't, and so she served at this hour to drive the truth home. It was the truth, vivid and monstrous, that all the while he had waited the wait was itself his portion. This the companion of his vigil had at a given moment made out, and she had then offered him the chance to baffle his doom. One's doom, however, was never baffled, and on the day she told him his own had come down she had seen him but stupidly stare at the escape she offered him.

The escape would have been to love her; then, *then* he would have lived. *She* had lived—who could say now with what passion?—since she had loved him for himself; whereas he had never thought of her (ah how it hugely glared at him!) but in the chill of his egotism and the light of her use. Her spoken words came back to him—the chain stretched and stretched. The Beast had lurked indeed, and the Beast, at its hour, had sprung it; it had sprung in that twilight of the cold April when, pale, ill, wasted, but all beautiful, and perhaps even then recoverable, she had risen from her chair to stand before him and let him imaginably guess. It had sprung as he didn't guess; it had sprung as she hopelessly turned from him, and the mark, by the time he left her, had fallen where it *was* to fall. He had justified his fear and achieved his fate; he had failed, with the last exactitude, of all he was to fail of; and a moan now rose to his lips as he remembered she had prayed he mightn't know. This horror of waking—*this* was knowledge, knowledge under the breath of which the very tears in his eyes seemed to freeze. Through them, none the less, he tried to fix it and hold it; he kept it there before him so that he might feel the pain. That at least, belated and bitter, had something of the taste of life. But the bitterness suddenly sickened him, and it was as if, horribly, he saw, in the truth, in the cruelty of his image, what had been appointed and done. He saw the Jungle of his life and saw the lurking Beast; then, while he looked, perceived it, as by a stir of the air, rise, huge and hideous, for the leap that was to settle him. His eyes darkened—it was close; and, instinctively turning, in his hallucination, to avoid it, he flung himself, face down, on the tomb.

A White Heron

SARAH ORNE JEWETT

I

The woods were already filled with shadows one June evening, just before eight o'clock, though a bright sunset still glimmered faintly among the trunks of the trees. A little girl was driving home her cow, a plodding, dilatory, provoking creature in her behavior, but a valued companion for all that. They were going away from the western light, and striking deep into the dark woods, but their feet were familiar with the path, and it was no matter whether their eyes could see it or not.

There was hardly a night the summer through when the old cow could be found waiting at the pasture bars; on the contrary, it was her greatest pleasure to hide herself away among the high huckleberry bushes, and though she wore a loud bell she had made the discovery that if one stood perfectly still it would not ring. So Sylvia had to hunt for her until she found her, and call Co'! Co'! with never an answering Moo, until her childish patience was quite spent. If the creature had not given good milk and plenty of it, the case would have seemed very different to her owners. Besides, Sylvia had all the time there was, and very little use to make of it. Sometimes in pleasant weather it was a consolation to look upon the cow's pranks as an intelligent attempt to play hide and seek, and as the child had no playmates she lent herself to this amusement with a good deal of zest. Though this chase had been so long that the wary animal herself had given an unusual signal of her whereabouts, Sylvia had only laughed when she came upon Mistress Moolly at the swamp-side, and urged her affectionately homeward with a twig of birch leaves. The old cow was not inclined to wander farther, she even turned in the right direction for once as they left the pasture, and stepped along the road at a good pace. She was quite ready to be milked now, and seldom stopped to browse. Sylvia wondered what her grandmother would say because they were so late. It was a great while since she had left home at half past five o'clock, but everybody knew the difficulty of making this errand a short one. Mrs. Tilley had chased the horned torment too many summer evenings herself to blame any one else for lingering, and was only thankful as she waited that she had Sylvia, nowadays, to give such valuable assistance. The good woman suspected that Sylvia loitered occasionally on her own account; there never was such a child for straying about out-of-doors since the world was made! Everybody said that it was a good change for a little maid who had tried to grow for eight years in a crowded manufacturing town, but, as for Sylvia herself, it seemed as if she never had been alive at all before she came to live at the farm. She thought often with wistful compassion of a wretched dry geranium that belonged to a town neighbor.

" 'Afraid of folks,' " old Mrs. Tilley said to herself, with a smile, after she had made the unlikely choice of Sylvia from her daughter's houseful of children, and was returning to the farm. " 'Afraid of folks,' they said! I guess she won't be troubled no great with 'em up to the old place!" When they reached the door of the lonely house and stopped to unlock it, and the cat came to purr loudly, and rub against them, a deserted pussy, indeed, but fat with young robins, Sylvia whispered that this was a beautiful place to live in, and she never should wish to go home.

The companions followed the shady wood-road, the cow taking slow steps, and the child very fast ones. The cow stopped long at the brook to drink, as if the pasture were not half a swamp, and Sylvia stood still and waited, letting her bare feet cool themselves in the shoal water, while the great twilight moths struck softly against her. She waded on through the brook as the cow moved away, and listened to the thrushes with a heart that beat fast with pleasure. There was a stirring in the great boughs overhead. They were full of little birds and beasts that seemed to be wide-awake, and going about their world, or else saying good-night to each other in sleepy twitters. Sylvia herself felt sleepy as she walked along. However, it was not much farther to the house, and the air was soft and sweet. She was not often in the woods so late as this, and it made her feel as if she were a part of the gray shadows and the moving leaves. She was just thinking how long it seemed since she first came to the farm a year ago, and wondering if everything went on in the noisy town just the same as when she was there; the thought of the great red-faced boy who used to chase and frighten her made her hurry along the path to escape from the shadow of the trees.

Suddenly this little woods-girl is horror-stricken to hear a clear whistle not very far away. Not a bird's whistle, which would have a sort of friendliness, but a boy's whistle, determined, and somewhat aggressive. Sylvia left the cow to whatever sad fate might await her, and stepped discreetly aside into the bushes, but she was just too late. The enemy had discovered her, and called out in a very cheerful and persuasive tone. "Halloa, little girl, how far is it to the road?" and trembling Sylvia answered almost inaudibly, "A good ways."

She did not dare to look boldly at the tall young man, who carried a gun over his shoulder, but she came out of her bush and again followed the cow, while he walked alongside.

"I have been hunting for some birds," the stranger said kindly, "and I have lost my way, and need a friend very much. Don't be afraid," he added gallantly. "Speak up and tell me what your name is, and whether you think I can spend the night at your house, and go out gunning early in the morning."

Sylvia was more alarmed than before. Would not her grandmother consider her much to blame? But who could have foreseen such an accident as this? It did not appear to be her fault, and she hung her head as if the stem of it were broken, but managed to answer, "Sylvy," with much effort when her companion again asked her name.

Mrs. Tilley was standing in the doorway when the trio came into view. The cow gave a loud moo by way of explanation.

"Yes, you'd better speak up for yourself, you old trial! Where'd she tucked herself away this time, Sylvy?" Sylvia kept an awed silence; she knew by instinct that her grandmother did not comprehend the gravity of the situation. She must be mistaking the stranger for one of the farmer-lads of the region.

The young man stood his gun beside the door, and dropped a heavy game-bag beside it; then he bade Mrs. Tilley good evening, and repeated his wayfarer's story, and asked if he could have a night's lodging.

"Put me anywhere you like," he said. "I must be off early in the morning, before day; but I am very hungry, indeed. You can give me some milk at any rate, that's plain."

"Dear sakes, yes," responded the hostess, whose long slumbering hospitality seemed to be easily awakened. "You might fare better if you went out on the main road a mile or so, but you're welcome to what we've got. I'll milk right off, and you make yourself at home. You can sleep on husks or feathers," she proffered graciously. "I raised them all myself. There's good pasturing for geese just below here towards the ma'sh. Now step round and set a plate for the gentleman, Sylvy!" And Sylvia promptly stepped. She was glad to have something to do, and she was hungry herself.

It was a surprise to find so clean and comfortable a little dwelling in this New England wilderness. The young man had known the horrors of its most primitive housekeeping, and the dreary squalor of that level of society which does not rebel at the companionship of hens. This was the best thrift of an old-fashioned farmstead, though on such a small scale that it seemed like a hermitage. He listened eagerly to the old woman's quaint talk, he watched Sylvia's pale face and shining gray eyes with ever growing enthusiasm, and insisted that this was the best supper he had eaten for a month; then, afterward, the new-made friends sat down in the doorway together while the moon came up.

Soon it would be berry time, and Sylvia was a great help at picking. The cow was a good milker, though a plaguy thing to keep track of, the hostess gossiped frankly, adding presently that she had buried four children, so that Sylvia's mother, and a son (who might be dead) in California were all the children she had left. "Dan, my boy, was a great hand to go gunning," she explained sadly. "I never wanted for pa'tridges or gray squer'ls while he was to home. He's been a great wand'rer, I expect, and he's no hand to write letters. There, I don't blame him, I'd ha' seen the world myself if it had been so I could.

"Sylvia takes after him," the grandmother continued affectionately, after a minute's pause. "There ain't a foot o' ground she don't know her way over, and the wild creatur's counts her one o' themselves. Squer'ls she'll tame to come an' feed right out o' her hands, and all sorts o' birds. Last winter she got the jay-birds to bangeing here, and I believe she'd 'a' scanted herself of her own meals to have plenty to throw out amongst 'em, if I hadn't kep' watch. Anything but crows, I tell her, I'm willin' to help support,—though Dan he went an' tamed one o' them that did seem to have reason same as folks. It was round here a good spell after he went away. Dan an' his father they didn't hitch,—but he never held up his head ag'in after Dan had dared him an' gone off."

The guest did not notice this hint of family sorrows in his eager interest in something else.

"So Sylvy knows all about birds, does she?" he exclaimed, as he looked round at the little girl who sat, very demure but increasingly sleepy, in the moonlight. "I am making a collection of birds myself. I have been at it ever since I was a boy." (Mrs. Tilley smiled.) "There are two or three very rare ones I have been hunting for these five years. I mean to get them on my own ground if they can be found."

"Do you cage 'em up?" asked Mrs. Tilley doubtfully, in response to this enthusiastic announcement.

"Oh, no, they're stuffed and preserved, dozens and dozens of them," said the ornithologist, "and I have shot or snared every one myself. I caught a glimpse of a white heron three miles from here on Saturday, and I have followed it in this direction. They have never been found in this district at all. The little white heron, it is," and he turned again to look at Sylvia with the hope of discovering that the rare bird was one of her acquaintances.

But Sylvia was watching a hop toad in the narrow footpath.

"You would know the heron if you saw it," the stranger continued eagerly. "A queer tall white bird with soft feathers and long thin legs. And it would have a nest perhaps in the top of a high tree, made of sticks, something like a hawk's nest."

Sylvia's heart gave a wild beat; she knew that strange white bird, and had once stolen softly near where it stood in some bright green swamp grass, away over at the other side of the woods. There was an open place where the sunshine always seemed strangely yellow and hot, where tall, nodding rushes grew, and her grandmother had warned her that she might sink in the soft black mud underneath and never be heard of more. Not far beyond were the salt marshes and beyond those was the sea, the sea which Sylvia wondered and dreamed about, but never had looked upon, though its great voice could often be heard above the noise of the woods on stormy nights.

"I can't think of anything I should like so much as to find that heron's nest," the handsome stranger was saying. "I would give ten dollars to anybody who could show it to me," he added desperately, "and I mean to spend my whole vacation hunting for it if need be. Perhaps it was only migrating, or had been chased out of its region by some bird of prey."

Mrs. Tilley gave amazed attention to all this, but Sylvia still watched the toad, not divining, as she might have done at some calmer time, that the creature wished to get to its hole under the doorstep, and was much hindered by the unusual spectators at that hour of the evening. No amount of thought, that night, could decide how many wished-for treasures the ten dollars, so lightly spoken of, would buy.

The next day the young sportsman hovered about the woods, and Sylvia kept him company, having lost her first fear of the friendly lad, who proved to be most kind and sympathetic. He told her many things about the birds and what they knew and where they lived and what they did with themselves. And he gave her a jackknife, which she thought as great a treasure as if she were a desert-islander. All day long he did not once make her troubled or afraid except when he brought down some unsuspecting singing creature from its bough. Sylvia would have liked him vastly better without his gun; she could not understand why he killed the very birds he seemed to like so much. But as the day waned, Sylvia still watched the young man with loving admiration. She had never seen anybody so charming and delightful; the woman's heart, asleep in the child, was vaguely thrilled by a dream of love. Some premonition of that great power stirred and swayed these young foresters who traversed the solemn woodlands with soft-footed silent care. They stopped to listen to a bird's song; they pressed forward again eagerly, parting the branches—speaking to each other rarely and in whispers; the young man going first and Sylvia following, fascinated, a few steps behind, with her gray eyes dark with excitement.

She grieved because the longed-for white heron was elusive, but she did not lead the guest, she only followed, and there was no such thing as speaking first. The sound of her own unquestioned voice would have terrified her—it was hard enough to answer yes or no when there was need of that. At last evening began to fall, and they drove the cow home together, and Sylvia smiled with pleasure when they came to the place where she heard the whistle and was afraid only the night before.

II

Half a mile from home, at the farther edge of the woods, where the land was highest, a great pine-tree stood, the last of its generation. Whether it was left for a boundary mark, or for what reason, no one could say; the woodchoppers who had felled its mates were dead and gone long ago, and a whole forest of sturdy trees, pines and oaks and maples, had grown again. But the stately head of this old pine towered above them all and made a landmark for sea and shore miles and miles away. Sylvia knew it well. She had always believed that whoever climbed to the top of it could see the ocean; and the little girl had often laid her hand on the great rough trunk and looked up wistfully at those dark boughs that the wind always stirred, no matter how hot and still the air might be below. Now she thought of the tree with a new excitement, for why, if one climbed it at break of day, could not one see all the world, and easily discover whence the white heron flew, and mark the place, and find the hidden nest?

What a spirit of adventure, what wild ambition! What fancied triumph and delight and glory for the later morning when she could make known the secret! It was almost too real and too great for the childish heart to bear.

All night the door of the little house stood open, and the whippoorwills came and sang upon the very step. The young sportsman and his old hostess were sound asleep, but Sylvia's great design kept her broad awake and watching. She forgot to think of sleep. The short summer night seemed as long as the winter darkness, and at last when the whippoorwills ceased, and she was afraid the morning would after all come too soon, she stole out of the house and followed the pasture path through the woods, hastening toward the open ground beyond, listening with a sense of comfort and companionship to the drowsy twitter of a half-awakened bird, whose perch she had jarred in passing. Alas, if the great wave of human interest which flooded for the first time this dull little life should sweep away the satisfactions of an existence heart to heart with nature and the dumb life of the forest!

There was the huge tree asleep yet in the paling moonlight, and small and hopeful Sylvia began with utmost bravery to mount to the top of it, with tingling, eager blood coursing the channels of her whole frame, with her bare feet and fingers, that pinched and held like bird's claws to the monstrous ladder reaching up, up, almost to the sky itself. First she must mount the white oak tree that grew alongside, where she was almost lost among the dark branches and the green leaves heavy and wet with dew; a bird fluttered off its nest, and a red squirrel ran to and fro and scolded pettishly at the harmless housebreaker. Sylvia felt her way easily. She had often climbed there, and knew that higher still one of the oak's upper branches chafed against the pine trunk, just where its lower boughs were set close together. There, when she made the dangerous pass from one tree to the other, the great enterprise would really begin.

She crept out along the swaying oak limb at last, and took the daring step across into the old pine-tree. The way was harder than she thought; she must reach far and hold fast, the sharp dry twigs caught and held her and scratched her like angry talons, the pitch made her thin little fingers clumsy and stiff as she went round and round the tree's great stem, higher and higher upward. The sparrows and robins in the woods below were beginning to wake and twitter to the dawn, yet it seemed much lighter there aloft in the pine-tree, and the child knew that she must hurry if her project were to be of any use.

The tree seemed to lengthen itself out as she went up, and to reach farther and farther upward. It was like a great main-mast to the voyaging earth; it must truly have been amazed that morning through all its ponderous frame as it felt this determined spark of human spirit creeping and climbing from higher branch to branch. Who knows how steadily the least twigs held themselves to advantage this light, weak creature on her way! The old pine must have loved his new dependent. More than all the hawks, and bats, and moths, and even the sweet-voiced thrushes, was the brave, beating heart of the solitary gray-eyed child. And the tree stood still and held away the winds that June morning while the dawn grew bright in the east.

Sylvia's face was like a pale star, if one had seen it from the ground, when the last thorny bough was past, and she stood trembling and tired but wholly triumphant, high in the tree-top. Yes, there was the sea with the dawning sun making a golden dazzle over it, and toward that glorious east flew two hawks with slow-moving pinions. How low they looked in the air from that height when before one had only seen them far up, and dark against the blue sky. Their gray feathers were as soft as moths; they seemed only a little way from the tree, and Sylvia felt as if she too could go flying away among the clouds. Westward, the woodlands and farms reached miles and miles into the distance; here and there were church steeples, and white villages; truly it was a vast and awesome world.

The birds sang louder and louder. At last the sun came up bewilderingly bright. Sylvia could see the white sails of ships out at sea, and the clouds that were purple and rose-colored and yellow at first began to fade away.

Where was the white heron's nest in the sea of green branches, and was this wonderful sight and pageant of the world the only reward for having climbed to such a giddy height? Now look down again, Sylvia, where the green marsh is set among the shining birches and dark hemlocks; there where you saw the white heron once you will see him again; look, look! a white spot of him like a single floating feather comes up from the dead hemlock and grows larger, and rises, and comes close at last, and goes by the landmark pine with steady sweep of wing and outstretched slender neck and crested head. And wait! wait! do not move a foot or a finger, little girl, do not send an arrow of light and consciousness from your two eager eyes, for the heron has perched on a pine bough not far beyond yours, and cries back to his mate on the nest, and plumes his feathers for the new day!

The child gives a long sigh a minute later when a company of shouting cat-birds comes also to the tree, and vexed by their fluttering and lawlessness the solemn heron goes away. She knows his secret now, the wild, light, slender bird that floats and wavers, and goes back like an arrow presently to his home in the green world beneath. Then Sylvia, well satisfied, makes her perilous way down again, not daring to look far below the branch she stands on, ready to cry sometimes because her fingers ache and her lamed feet slip. Wondering over and over again what the stranger would say to her, and what he would think when she told him how to find his way straight to the heron's nest.

"Sylvy, Sylvy!" called the busy old grandmother again and again, but nobody answered, and the small husk bed was empty, and Sylvia had disappeared.

The guest waked from a dream, and remembering his day's pleasure hurried to dress himself that it might sooner begin. He was sure from the way the shy little girl looked once or twice yesterday that she had at least seen the white heron, and now she must really be persuaded to tell. Here she comes now, paler than ever, and her worn old frock is torn and tattered, and smeared with pine pitch. The grandmother and the sportsman stand in the door together and question her, and the splendid moment has come to speak of the dead hemlock-tree by the green marsh.

But Sylvia does not speak after all, though the old grandmother fretfully rebukes her, and the young man's kind appealing eyes are looking straight in her own. He can make them rich with money; he has promised it, and they are poor now. He is so well worth making happy, and he waits to hear the story she can tell.

No, she must keep silence! What is it that suddenly forbids her and makes her dumb? Has she been nine years growing, and now, when the great world for the first time puts out a hand to her, must she thrust it aside for a bird's sake? The murmur of the pine's green branches is in her ears, she remembers how the white heron came flying through the golden air and how they watched the sea and the morning together, and Sylvia cannot speak; she cannot tell the heron's secret and give its life away.

Dear loyalty, that suffered a sharp pang as the guest went away disappointed later in the day, that could have served and followed him and loved him as a dog loves! Many a night Sylvia heard the echo of his whistle haunting the pasture path as she came home with the loitering cow. She forgot even her sorrow at the sharp report of his gun and the piteous sight of thrushes and sparrows dropping silent to the ground, their songs hushed and their pretty feathers stained and wet with blood. Were the birds better friends than their hunter might have been,—who can tell? Whatever treasures were lost to her, woodlands and summer-time, remember! Bring your gifts and graces and tell your secrets to this lonely country child!

The Dead

JAMES JOYCE

Lily, the caretaker's daughter, was literally run off her feet. Hardly had she brought one gentleman into the little pantry behind the office on the ground floor and helped him off with his overcoat than the wheezy hall-door bell clanged again and she had to scamper along the bare hallway to let in another guest. It was well for her she had not to attend to the ladies also. But Miss Kate and Miss Julia had thought of that and had converted the bathroom upstairs into a ladies' dressing-room. Miss Kate and Miss Julia were there, gossiping and laughing and fussing, walking after each other to the head of the stairs, peering down over the banisters and calling down to Lily to ask her who had come.

It was always a great affair, the Misses Morkan's annual dance. Everybody who knew them came to it, members of the family, old friends of the family, the members of Julia's choir, any of Kate's pupils that were grown up enough and even some of Mary Jane's pupils too. Never once had it fallen flat. For years and years it had gone off in splendid style as long as anyone could remember; ever since Kate and Julia, after the death of their brother Pat, had left the house in Stoney Batter and taken Mary Jane, their only niece, to live with them in the dark gaunt house on Usher's Island, the upper part of which they had rented from Mr Fulham, the corn-factor on the ground floor. That was a good thirty years ago if it was a day. Mary Jane, who was then a little girl in short clothes, was now the main prop of the household for she had the organ in Haddington Road. She had been through the Academy and gave a pupils' concert every year in the upper room of the Antient Concert Rooms. Many of her pupils belonged to better-class families on the Kingstown and Dalkey line. Old as they were, her aunts also did their share. Julia, though she was quite grey, was still the leading soprano in Adam and Eve's, and Kate, being too feeble to go about much, gave music lessons to beginners on the old square piano in the back room. Lily, the caretaker's daughter, did housemaid's work for them. Though their life was modest they believed in eating well; the best of everything: diamond-bone sirloins, three-shilling tea and the best bottled stout. But Lily seldom made a mistake in the orders so that she got on well with her three mistresses. They were fussy, that was all. But the only thing they would not stand was back answers.

Of course they had good reason to be fussy on such a night. And then it was long after ten o'clock and yet there was no sign of Gabriel and his wife. Besides they were dreadfully afraid that Freddy Malins might turn up screwed. They would not wish for worlds that any of Mary Jane's pupils should see him under the influence; and when he was like that it was sometimes very hard to manage him. Freddy Malins always came late but they wondered what could be keeping Gabriel: and that was what brought them every two minutes to the banisters to ask Lily had Gabriel or Freddy come.

—O, Mr Conroy, said Lily to Gabriel when she opened the door for him, Miss Kate and Miss Julia thought you were never coming. Good-night Mrs Conroy.

—I'll engage they did, said Gabriel, but they forget that my wife here takes three mortal hours to dress herself.

He stood on the mat, scraping the snow from his goloshes, while Lily led his wife to the foot of the stairs and called out:

—Miss Kate, here's Mrs Conroy.

Kate and Julia came toddling down the dark stairs at once. Both of them kissed Gabriel's wife, said she must be perished alive and asked was Gabriel with her.

—Here I am as right as the mail, Aunt Kate! Go on up. I'll follow, called out Gabriel from the dark.

He continued scraping his feet vigorously while the three women went upstairs, laughing, to the ladies' dressing-room. A light fringe of snow lay like a cape on the shoulders of his overcoat and like toecaps on the toes of his goloshes; and, as the buttons of his overcoat slipped with a squeaking noise through the snow-stiffened frieze, a cold fragrant air from out-of-doors escaped from crevices and folds.

—Is it snowing again, Mr Conroy? asked Lily.

She had preceded him into the pantry to help him off with his overcoat. Gabriel smiled at the three syllables she had given his surname and glanced at her. She was a slim, growing girl, pale in complexion and with hay-coloured hair. The gas in the pantry made her look still paler. Gabriel had known her when she was a child and used to sit on the lowest step nursing a rag doll.

—Yes, Lily, he answered, and I think we're in for a night of it.

He looked up at the pantry ceiling, which was shaking with the stamping and shuffling of feet on the floor above, listened for a moment to the piano and then glanced at the girl, who was folding his overcoat carefully at the end of a shelf.

—Tell me, Lily, he said in a friendly tone, do you still go to school?

—O no, sir, she answered. I'm done schooling this year and more.

—O, then, said Gabriel gaily, I suppose we'll be going to your wedding one of these fine days with your young man, eh?

The girl glanced back at him over her shoulder and said with great bitterness:

—The men that is now is only all palaver and what they can get out of you.

Gabriel coloured as if he felt he had made a mistake and, without looking at her, kicked off his goloshes and flicked actively with his muffler at his patent-leather shoes.

He was a stout tallish young man. The high colour of his cheeks pushed upwards even to his forehead where it scattered itself in a few formless patches of pale red; and on his hairless face there scintillated restlessly the polished lenses and the bright gilt rims of the glasses which screened his delicate and restless eyes. His glossy black hair was parted in the middle and brushed in a long curve behind his ears where it curled slightly beneath the groove left by his hat.

When he had flicked lustre into his shoes he stood up and pulled his waistcoat down more tightly on his plump body. Then he took a coin rapidly from his pocket.

—O Lily, he said, thrusting it into her hands, it's Christmastime, isn't it? Just . . . here's a little. . . .

He walked rapidly towards the door.

—O no, sir! cried the girl, following him. Really sir, I wouldn't take it.

—Christmastime! Christmastime! said Gabriel, almost trotting to the stairs and waving his hand to her in deprecation.

The girl, seeing that he had gained the stairs, called out after him:

—Well, thank you, sir.

He waited outside the drawing-room door until the waltz should finish, listening to the skirts that swept against it and to the shuffling of feet. He was still discomposed by the girl's bitter and sudden retort. It had cast a gloom over him which he tried to dispel by arranging his cuffs and the bows of his tie. Then he took from his waistcoat pocket a little paper and glanced at the headings he had made for his speech. He was undecided about the lines from Robert Browning for he feared they would be above the heads of his hearers. Some quotation that they could recognise from Shakespeare or from the Melodies would be better. The indelicate clacking of the men's heels and the shuffling of their soles reminded him that their grade of culture differed from his. He would only make himself ridiculous by quoting poetry to them which they could not understand. They would think that he was airing his superior education. He would fail with them just as he had failed with the girl in the pantry. He had taken up a wrong tone. His whole speech was a mistake from first to last, an utter failure.

Just then his aunts and his wife came out of the ladies' dressing-room. His aunts were two small plainly dressed old women. Aunt Julia was an inch or so the taller. Her hair, drawn low over the tops of her ears, was grey; and grey also, with darker shadows, was her large flaccid face. Though she was stout in build and stood erect her slow eyes and parted lips gave her the appearance of a woman who did not know where she was or where she was going. Aunt Kate was more vivacious. Her face, healthier than her sister's, was all puckers and creases, like a shrivelled red apple, and her hair, braided in the same old-fashioned way, had not lost its ripe nut colour.

They both kissed Gabriel frankly. He was their favourite nephew, the son of their dead elder sister, Ellen, who had married T. J. Conroy of the Port and Docks.

—Gretta tells me you're not going to take a cab back to Monkstown to-night, Gabriel, said Aunt Kate.

—No, said Gabriel, turning to his wife, we had quite enough of that last year, hadn't we. Don't you remember, Aunt Kate, what a cold Gretta got out of it? Cab windows rattling all the way, and the east wind blowing in after we passed Merrion. Very jolly it was. Gretta caught a dreadful cold.

Aunt Kate frowned severely and nodded her head at every word.

—Quite right, Gabriel, quite right, she said. You can't be too careful.

—But as for Gretta there, said Gabriel, she'd walk home in the snow if she were let.

Mrs Conroy laughed.

—Don't mind him, Aunt Kate, she said. He's really an awful bother, what with green shades for Tom's eyes at night and making him do the dumb-bells, and forcing Eva to eat the stirabout. The poor child! And she simply hates the sight of it! . . . . O, but you'll never guess what he makes me wear now!

She broke out into a peal of laughter and glanced at her husband, whose admiring and happy eyes had been wandering from her dress to her face and hair. The two aunts laughed heartily too, for Gabriel's solicitude was a standing joke with them.

—Goloshes! said Mrs Conroy. That's the latest. Whenever it's wet underfoot I must put on my goloshes. To-night even he wanted me to put them on, but I wouldn't. The next thing he'll buy me will be a diving suit.

Gabriel laughed nervously and patted his tie reassuringly while Aunt Kate nearly doubled herself, so heartily did she enjoy the joke. The smile soon faded from Aunt Julia's face and her mirthless eyes were directed towards her nephew's face. After a pause she asked:

—And what are goloshes, Gabriel?

—Goloshes, Julia! exclaimed her sister. Goodness me, don't you know what goloshes are? You wear them over your . . . over your boots, Gretta, isn't it?

—Yes, said Mrs Conroy. Guttapercha things. We both have a pair now. Gabriel says everyone wears them on the continent.

—O, on the continent, murmured Aunt Julia, nodding her head slowly.

Gabriel knitted his brows and said, as if he were slightly angered:

—It's nothing very wonderful but Gretta thinks it very funny because she says the word reminds her of Christy Minstrels.

—But tell me, Gabriel, said Aunt Kate, with brisk tact. Of course, you've seen about the room. Gretta was saying . . .

—O, the room is all right, replied Gabriel, I've taken one in the Gresham.

—To be sure, said Aunt Kate, by far the best thing to do. And the children, Gretta, you're not anxious about them?

—O, for one night, said Mrs Conroy. Besides, Bessie will look after them.

—To be sure, said Aunt Kate again. What a comfort it is to have a girl like that, one you can depend on! There's that Lily, I'm sure I don't know what has come over her lately. She's not the girl she was at all.

Gabriel was about to ask his aunt some questions on this point but she broke off suddenly to gaze after her sister who had wandered down the stairs and was craning her neck over the banisters.

—Now, I ask you, she said, almost testily, where is Julia going? Julia! Julia! Where are you going?

Julia, who had gone halfway down one flight, came back and announced blandly:

—Here's Freddy.

At the same moment a clapping of hands and a final flourish of the pianist told that the waltz had ended. The drawing-room door was opened from within and some couples came out. Aunt Kate drew Gabriel aside hurriedly and whispered into his ear:

—Slip down, Gabriel, like a good fellow and see if he's all right, and don't let him up if he's screwed. I'm sure he's screwed. I'm sure he is.

Gabriel went to the stairs and listened over the banisters. He could hear two persons talking in the pantry. Then he recognised Freddy Malins' laugh. He went down the stairs noisily.

—It's such a relief, said Aunt Kate to Mrs Conroy, that Gabriel is here. I always feel easier in my mind when he's here. . . . Julia, there's Miss Daly and Miss Power will take some refreshment. Thanks for your beautiful waltz, Miss Daly. It made lovely time.

A tall wizen-faced man, with a stiff grizzled moustache and swarthy skin, who was passing out with his partner said:

—And may we have some refreshment, too, Miss Morkan?

—Julia, said Aune Kate summarily, and here's Mr Browne and Miss Furlong. Take them in, Julia, with Miss Daly and Miss Power.

—I'm the man for the ladies, said Mr Browne, pursing his lips until his moustache bristled and smiling in all his wrinkles. You know, Miss Morkan, the reason they are so fond of me is—

He did not finish his sentence, but, seeing that Aunt Kate was out of earshot, at once led the three young ladies into the back room. The middle of the room was occupied by two square tables placed end to end, and on these Aunt Julia and the caretaker were straightening and smoothing a large cloth. On the sideboard were arrayed dishes and plates, and glasses and bundles of knives and forks and spoons. The top of the closed square piano served also as a sideboard for viands and sweets. At a smaller sideboard in one corner two young men were standing, drinking hop-bitters.

Mr Browne led his charges thither and invited them all, in jest, to some ladies' punch, hot, strong and sweet. As they said they never took anything strong he opened three bottles of lemonade for them. Then he asked one of the young men to move aside, and, taking hold of the decanter, filled out for himself a goodly measure of whisky. The young men eyed him respectfully while he took a trial sip.

—God help me, he said, smiling, it's the doctor's orders.

His wizened face broke into a broader smile, and the three young ladies laughed in musical echo to his pleasantry, swaying their bodies to and fro, with nervous jerks of their shoulders. The boldest said:

—O, now, Mr Browne, I'm sure the doctor never ordered anything of the kind.

Mr Browne took another sip of his whisky and said, with sidling mimicry:

—Well, you see, I'm like the famous Mrs Cassidy, who is reported to have said: *Now, Mary Grimes, if I don't take it, make me take it, for I feel I want it.*

His hot face had leaned forward a little too confidentially and he had assumed a very low Dublin accent so that the young ladies, with one instinct, received his speech in silence. Miss Furlong, who was one of Mary Jane's pupils, asked Miss Daly what was the name of the pretty waltz she had played; and Mr Browne, seeing that he was ignored, turned promptly to the two young men who were more appreciative.

A red-faced young woman, dressed in pansy, came into the room, excitedly clapping her hands and crying:

—Quadrilles! Quadrilles!

Close on her heels came Aunt Kate, crying:

—Two gentlemen and three ladies, Mary Jane!

—O, here's Mr Bergin and Mr Kerrigan, said Mary Jane. Mr Kerrigan, will you take Miss Power? Miss Furlong, may I get you a partner, Mr Bergin. O, that'll just do now.

—Three ladies, Mary Jane, said Aunt Kate.

The two young gentlemen asked the ladies if they might have the pleasure, and Mary Jane turned to Miss Daly.

—O, Miss Daly, you're really awfully good, after playing for the last two dances, but really we're so short of ladies to-night.

—I don't mind in the least, Miss Morkan.

—But I've a nice partner for you, Mr Bartell D'Arcy, the tenor. I'll get him to sing later on. All Dublin is raving about him.

—Lovely voice, lovely voice! said Aunt Kate.

As the piano had twice begun the prelude to the first figure Mary Jane led her recruits quickly from the room. They had hardly gone when Aunt Julia wandered slowly into the room, looking behind her at something.

—What is the matter, Julia? asked Aunt Kate anxiously. Who is it?

Julia, who was carrying a column of table-napkins, turned to her sister and said, simply, as if the question had surprised her:

—It's only Freddy, Kate, and Gabriel with him.

In fact right behind her Gabriel could be seen piloting Freddy Malins across the landing. The latter, a young man of about forty, was of Gabriel's size and build, with very round shoulders. His face was fleshy and pallid, touched with colour only at the thick hanging lobes of his ears and at the wide wings of his nose. He had coarse features, a blunt nose, a convex and receding brow, tumid and protruded lips. His heavy-lidded eyes and the disorder of his scanty hair made him look sleepy. He was laughing heartily in a high key at a story which he had been telling Gabriel on the stairs and at the same time rubbing the knuckles of his left fist backwards and forwards into his left eye.

—Good-evening, Freddy, said Aunt Julia.

Freddy Malins bade the Misses Morkan good-evening in what seemed an offhand fashion by reason of the habitual catch in his voice and then, seeing that Mr Browne was grinning at him from the sideboard, crossed the room on rather shaky legs and began to repeat in an undertone the story he had just told to Gabriel.

—He's not so bad, is he? said Aunt Kate to Gabriel.

Gabriel's brows were dark but he raised them quickly and answered:

—O no, hardly noticeable.

—Now, isn't he a terrible fellow! she said. And his poor mother made him take the pledge on New Year's Eve. But come on, Gabriel, into the drawing-room.

Before leaving the room with Gabriel she signalled to Mr Browne by frowning and shaking her forefinger in warning to and fro. Mr Browne nodded in answer and, when she had gone, said to Freddy Malins:

—Now, then, Teddy, I'm going to fill you out a good glass of lemonade just to buck you up.

Freddy Malins, who was nearing the climax of his story, waved the offer aside impatiently but Mr Browne, having first called Freddy Malins' attention to a disarray in his dress, filled out and handed him a full glass of lemonade. Freddy Malin's left hand accepted the glass mechanically, his right hand being engaged in the mechanical readjustment of his dress. Mr Browne, whose face was once more wrinkling with mirth, poured out for himself a glass of whisky while Freddy Malins exploded, before he had well reached the climax of his story in a kink of high-pitched bronchitic laughter and, setting down his untasted and overflowing glass, began to rub the knuckles of his left fist backwards and forwards into his left eye, repeating words of his last phrase as well as his fit of laughter would allow him.

*　　　*　　　*

Gabriel could not listen while Mary Jane was playing her Academy piece, full of runs and difficult passages, to the hushed drawing-room. He liked music but the piece she was playing had no melody for him and he doubted whether it had any melody for the other listeners, though they had begged Mary Jane to play something. Four young men, who had come from the refreshment-room to stand in the doorway at the sound of the piano, had gone away quietly in couples after a few minutes. The only persons who seemed to follow the music were Mary Jane herself, her hands racing along the key-board or lifted from it at the pauses like those of a priestess in momentary imprecation, and Aunt Kate standing at her elbow to turn the page.

Gabriel's eyes, irritated by the floor, which glittered with beeswax under the heavy chandelier, wandered to the wall above the piano. A picture of the balcony scene in *Romeo and Juliet* hung there and beside it was a picture of the two murdered princes in the Tower which Aunt Julia had worked in red, blue and brown wools when she was a girl. Probably in the school they had gone to as girls that kind of work had been taught, for one year his mother had worked for him as a birthday present a waistcoat of purple tabinet, with little foxes' heads upon it, lined with brown satin and having round mulberry buttons. It was strange that his mother had had no musical talent though Aunt Kate used to call her the brains carrier of the Morkan family. Both she and Julia had always seemed a little proud of their serious and matronly sister. Her photograph stood before the pierglass. She held an open book on her knees and was pointing out something in it to Constantine who, dressed in a man-o'-war suit, lay at her feet. It was she who had chosen the names for her sons for she was very sensible of the dignity of family life. Thanks to her, Constantine was now senior curate in Balbriggan and, thanks to her, Gabriel himself had taken his degree in the Royal University. A shadow passed over his face as he remembered her sullen opposition to his marriage. Some slighting phrases she had used still rankled in his memory; she had once spoken of Gretta as being country cute and that was not true of Gretta at all. It was Gretta who had nursed her during all her last long illness in their house at Monkstown.

He knew that Mary Jane must be near the end of her piece for she was playing again the open melody with runs of scales after every bar and while he waited for the end the resentment died down in his heart. The piece ended with a trill of octaves in the treble and a final deep octave in the bass. Great applause greeted Mary Jane as, blushing and rolling up her music nervously, she escaped from the room. The most vigorous clapping came from the four young men in the doorway who had gone away to the refreshment-room at the beginning of the piece but had come back when the piano had stopped.

Lancers were arranged. Gabriel found himself partnered with Miss Ivors. She was a frank-mannered talkative young lady, with a freckled face and prominent brown eyes. She did not wear a low-cut bodice and the large brooch which was fixed in front of her collar bore on it an Irish device.

When they had taken their places she said abruptly:

—I have a crow to pluck with you.

—With me? said Gabriel.

She nodded her head gravely.

—What is it? asked Gabriel, smiling at her solemn manner.

—Who is G. C.? answered Miss Ivors, turning her eyes upon him.

Gabriel coloured and was about to knit his brows, as if he did not understand, when she said bluntly:

—O, innocent Amy! I have found out that you write for *The Daily Express*. Now, aren't you ashamed of yourself?

—Why should I be ashamed of myself? asked Gabriel, blinking his eyes and trying to smile.

—Well, I'm ashamed of you, said Miss Ivors frankly. To say you'd write for a rag like that. I didn't think you were a West Briton.

A look of perplexity appeared on Gabriel's face. It was true that he wrote a literary column every Wednesday in *The Daily Express*, for which he was paid fifteen shillings. But that did not make him a West Briton surely. The books he received for review were almost more welcome than the paltry cheque. He loved to feel the covers and turn over the pages of newly printed books. Nearly every day when his teaching in the college was ended he used to wander down the quays to the second-hand booksellers, to Hickey's on Bachelor's Walk, to Webb's or Massey's on Aston's Quay, or to O'Clohissey's in the by-street. He did not know how to meet her charge. He wanted to say that literature was above politics. But they were friends of many years' standing and their careers had been parallel, first at the University and then as teachers: he could not risk a grandiose phrase with her. He continued blinking his eyes and trying to smile and murmured lamely that he saw nothing political in writing reviews of books.

When their turn to cross had come he was still perplexed and inattentive. Miss Ivors promptly took his hand in a warm grasp and said in a soft friendly tone:

—Of course, I was only joking. Come, we cross now.

When they were together again she spoke of the University question and Gabriel felt more at ease. A friend of hers had shown her his review of Browning's poems. That was how she had found out the secret: but she liked the review immensely. Then she said suddenly:

—O, Mr Conroy, will you come for an excursion to the Aran Isles this summer? We're going to stay there a whole month. It will be splendid out in the Atlantic. You ought to come. Mr Clancy is coming, and Mr Kilkelly and Kathleen Kearney. It would be splendid for Gretta too if she'd come. She's from Connacht, isn't she?

—Her people are, said Gabriel shortly.

—But you will come, won't you? said Miss Ivors, laying her warm hand eagerly on his arm.

—The fact is, said Gabriel, I have already arranged to go—

—Go where? asked Miss Ivors.

—Well, you know, every year I go for a cycling tour with some fellows and so—

—But where? asked Miss Ivors.

—Well, we usually go to France or Belgium or perhaps Germany, said Gabriel awkwardly.

—And why do you go to France and Belgium, said Miss Ivors, instead of visiting your own land?

—Well, said Gabriel, it's partly to keep in touch with the languages and partly for a change.

—And haven't you your own language to keep in touch with—Irish? asked Miss Ivors.

—Well, said Gabriel, if it comes to that, you know, Irish is not my language.

Their neighbours had turned to listen to the cross-examination. Gabriel glanced right and left nervously and tried to keep his good humour under the ordeal which was making a blush invade his forehead.

—And haven't you your own land to visit, continued Miss Ivors, that you know nothing of, your own people, and your own country?

—O, to tell you the truth, retorted Gabriel suddenly, I'm sick of my own country, sick of it!

—Why? asked Miss Ivors.

Gabriel did not answer for his retort had heated him.

—Why? repeated Miss Ivors.

They had to go visiting together and, as he had not answered her, Miss Ivors said warmly:

—Of course, you've no answer.

Gabriel tried to cover his agitation by taking part in the dance with great energy. He avoided her eyes for he had seen a sour expression on her face. But when they met in the long chain he was surprised to feel his hand firmly pressed. She looked at him from under her brows for a moment quizzically until he smiled. Then, just as the chain was about to start again, she stood on tiptoe and whispered into his ear:

—West Briton!

When the lancers were over Gabriel went away to a remote corner of the room where Freddy Malins' mother was sitting. She was a stout feeble old woman with white hair. Her voice had a catch it in like her son's and she stuttered slightly. She had been told that Freddy had come and that he was nearly all right. Gabriel asked her whether she had had a good crossing. She lived with her married daughter in Glasgow and came to Dublin on a visit once a year. She answered placidly that she had had a beautiful crossing and that the captain had been most attentive to her. She spoke also of the beautiful house her daughter kept in Glasgow, and of all the nice friends they had there. While her tongue rambled on Gabriel tried to banish from his mind all memory of the unpleasant incident with Miss Ivors. Of course the girl or woman, or whatever she was, was an enthusiast but there was a time for all things. Perhaps he ought not to have answered her like that. But she had no right to call him a West Briton before people, even in joke. She had tried to make him ridiculous before people, heckling him and staring at him with her rabbit's eyes.

He saw his wife making her way towards him through the waltzing couples. When she reached him she said into his ear:

—Gabriel, Aunt Kate wants to know won't you carve the goose as usual. Miss Daly will carve the ham and I'll do the pudding.

—All right, said Gabriel.

—She's sending in the younger ones first as soon as this waltz is over so that we'll have the table to ourselves.

—Were you dancing? asked Gabriel.

—Of course I was. Didn't you see me? What words had you with Molly Ivors?

—No words. Why? Did she say so?

—Something like that. I'm trying to get that Mr D'Arcy to sing. He's full of conceit, I think.

—There were no words, said Gabriel moodily, only she wanted me to go for a trip to the west of Ireland and I said I wouldn't.

His wife clasped her hands excitedly and gave a little jump.

—O, do go, Gabriel, she cried. I'd love to see Galway again.

—You can go if you like, said Gabriel coldly.

She looked at him for a moment, then turned to Mrs Malins and said:

—There's a nice husband for you, Mrs Malins.

While she was threading her way back across the room Mrs Malins, without adverting to the interruption, went on to tell Gabriel what beautiful places there were in Scotland and beautiful scenery. Her son-in-law brought them every year to the lakes and they used to go fishing. Her son-in-law was a splendid fisher. One day he caught a fish, a beautiful big big fish, and the man in the hotel boiled it for their dinner.

Gabriel hardly heard what she said. Now that supper was coming near he began to think again about his speech and about the quotation. When he saw Freddy Malins coming across the room to visit his mother Gabriel left the chair free for him and retired into the embrasure of the window. The room had already cleared and from the back room came the clatter of plates and knives. Those who still remained in the drawing-room seemed tired of dancing and were conversing quietly in little groups. Gabriel's warm trembling fingers tapped the cold pane of the window. How cool it must be outside! How pleasant it would be to walk out alone, first along by the river and then through the park! The snow would be lying on the branches of the trees and forming a bright cap on the top of the Wellington Monument. How much more pleasant it would be there than at the supper-table!

He ran over the headings of his speech: Irish hospitality, sad memories, the Three Graces, Paris, the quotation from Browning. He repeated to himself a phrase he had written in his review: *One feels that one is listening to a thought-tormented music.* Miss Ivors had praised the review. Was she sincere? Had she really any life of her own behind all her propagandism? There had never been any ill-feeling between them until that night. It unnerved him to think that she would be at the supper-table, looking up at him while he spoke with her critical quizzing eyes. Perhaps she would not be sorry to see him fail in his speech. An idea came into his mind and gave him courage. He would say, alluding to Aunt Kate and Aunt Julia: *Ladies and Gentlemen, the generation which is now on the wane among us may have had its faults but for my part I think it had certain qualities of hospitality, of humour, of humanity, which the new and very serious and hypereducated generation that is growing up around us seems to me to lack.* Very good: that was one for Miss Ivors. What did he care that his aunts were only two ignorant old women?

A murmur in the room attracted his attention. Mr Browne was advancing from the door, gallantly escorting Aunt Julia, who leaned upon his arm, smiling and hanging her head. An irregular musketry of applause escorted her also as far as the piano and then, as Mary Jane seated herself on the stool, and Aunt Julia, no longer smiling, half turned so as to pitch her voice fairly into the room, gradually ceased. Gabriel recognised the prelude. It was that of an old song of Aunt Julia's—*Arrayed for the Bridal.* Her voice, strong and clear in tone, attacked with great spirit the runs which embellish the air and though she sang very rapidly she did not miss even the smallest of the grace notes. To follow the voice, without looking at the singer's face, was to feel and share the excitement of swift and secure flight. Gabriel applauded loudly with all the others at the close of the song and loud applause was borne in from the invisible supper-table. It sounded so genuine that a little colour struggled into Aunt Julia's face as she bent to replace in the music-stand the old leather-bound song-book that had her initials on the cover. Freddy Malins, who had listened with his head perched sideways to hear her better, was still applauding when everyone else had ceased and talking animatedly to his mother who nodded her head gravely and slowly in acquiescence. At last, when he could clap no more, he stood up suddenly and hurried across the room to Aunt Julia whose hand he seized and held in both his hands, shaking it when words failed him or the catch in his voice proved too much for him.

—I was just telling my mother, he said, I never heard you sing so well, never. No, I never heard your voice so good as it is to-night. Now! Would you believe that now? That's the truth. Upon my word and honour that's the truth. I never heard your voice sound so fresh and so . . . so clear and fresh, never.

Aunt Julia smiled broadly and murmured something about compliments as she released her hand from his grasp. Mr Browne extended his open hand towards her and said to those who were near him in the manner of a showman introducing a prodigy to an audience:

—Miss Julia Morkan, my latest discovery!

He was laughing very heartily at this himself when Freddy Malins turned to him and said:

—Well, Browne, if you're serious you might make a worse discovery. All I can say is I never heard her sing half so well as long as I am coming here. And that's the honest truth.

—Neither did I, said Mr Browne. I think her voice has greatly improved.

Aunt Julia shrugged her shoulders and said with meek pride:

—Thirty years ago I hadn't a bad voice as voices go.

—I often told Julia, said Aunt Kate emphatically, that she was simply thrown away in that choir. But she never would be said by me.

She turned as if to appeal to the good sense of the others against a refractory child while Aunt Julia gazed in front of her, a vague smile of reminiscence playing on her face.

—No, continued Aunt Kate, she wouldn't be said or led by anyone, slaving there in that choir night and day, night and day. Six o'clock on Christmas morning! And all for what?

—Well, isn't it for the honour of God, Aunt Kate? asked Mary Jane, twisting round on the piano-stool and smiling.

Aunt Kate turned fiercely on her niece and said:

—I know all about the honour of God, Mary Jane, but I think it's not at all honourable for the pope to turn out the women out of the choirs that have slaved there all their lives and put little whipper-snappers of boys over their heads. I suppose it is for the good of the Church if the pope does it. But it's not just, Mary Jane, and it's not right.

She had worked herself into a passion and would have continued in defence of her sister for it was a sore subject with her but Mary Jane, seeing that all the dancers had come back, intervened pacifically:

—Now, Aunt Kate, you're giving scandal to Mr Browne who is of the other persuasion.

Aunt Kate turned to Mr Browne, who was grinning at this allusion to his religion, and said hastily:

—O, I don't question the pope's being right. I'm only a stupid old woman and I wouldn't presume to do such a thing. But there's such a thing as common everyday politeness and gratitude. And if I were in Julia's place I'd tell that Father Healy straight up to his face . . .

—And besides, Aunt Kate, said Mary Jane, we really are all hungry and when we are hungry we are all very quarrelsome.

—And when we are thirsty we are also quarrelsome, added Mr Browne.

—So that we had better go to supper, said Mary Jane, and finish the discussion afterwards.

On the landing outside the drawing-room Gabriel found his wife and Mary Jane trying to persuade Miss Ivors to stay for supper. But Miss Ivors, who had put on her hat and was buttoning her cloak, would not stay. She did not feel in the least hungry and she had already overstayed her time.

—But only for ten minutes, Molly, said Mrs Conroy. That won't delay you.

—To take a pick itself, said Mary Jane, after all your dancing.

—I really couldn't, said Miss Ivors.

—I am afraid you didn't enjoy yourself at all, said Mary Jane hopelessly.

—Ever so much, I assure you, said Miss Ivors, but you really must let me run off now.

—But how can you get home? asked Mrs Conroy.

—O, it's only two steps up the quay.

Gabriel hesitated a moment and said:

—If you will allow me, Miss Ivors, I'll see you home if you are really obliged to go.

But Miss Ivors broke away from them.

—I won't hear of it, she cried. For goodness sake go in to your suppers and don't mind me. I'm quite well able to take care of myself.

—Well, you're the comical girl, Molly, said Mrs Conroy frankly.

—*Beannacht libh*, cried Miss Ivors, with a laugh, as she ran down the staircase.

Mary Jane gazed after her, a moody puzzled expression on her face, while Mrs Conroy leaned over the banisters to listen for the hall-door. Gabriel asked himself was he the cause of her abrupt departure. But she did not seem to be in ill humour: she had gone away laughing. He stared blankly down the staircase.

At that moment Aunt Kate came toddling out of the supper-room, almost wringing her hands in despair.

—Where is Gabriel? she cried. Where on earth is Gabriel? There's everyone waiting in there, stage to let, and nobody to carve the goose!

—Here I am, Aunt Kate! cried Gabriel, with sudden animation, ready to carve a flock of geese, if necessary.

A fat brown goose lay at one end of the table and at the other end, on a bed of creased paper strewn with sprigs of parsley, lay a great ham, stripped of its outer skin and peppered over with crust crumbs, a neat paper frill round its shin and beside this was a round of spiced beef. Between these rival ends ran parallel lines of side-dishes: two little minsters of jelly, red and yellow; a shallow dish full of blocks of blancmange and red jam, a large green leaf-shaped dish with a stalk-shaped handle, on which lay bunches of purple raisins and peeled almonds, a companion dish on which lay a solid rectangle of Smyrna figs, a dish of custard topped with grated nutmeg, a small bowl full of chocolates and sweets wrapped in gold and silver papers and a glass vase in which stood some tall celery stalks. In the centre of the table there stood, as sentries to a fruit-stand which upheld a pyramid of oranges and American apples, two squat old-fashioned decanters of cut glass, one containing port and the other dark sherry. On the closed square piano a pudding in a huge yellow dish lay in waiting and behind it were three squads of bottles of stout and ale and minerals, drawn up according to the colours of their uniforms, the first two black, with brown and red labels, the third and smallest squad white, with transverse green sashes.

Gabriel took his seat boldly at the head of the table and, having looked to the edge of the carver, plunged his fork firmly into the goose. He felt quite at ease now for he was an expert carver and liked nothing better than to find himself at the head of a well-laden table.

—Miss Furlong, what shall I send you? A wing or a slice of the breast?

—Just a small slice of the breast.

—Miss Higgins, what for you?

—O, anything at all, Mr Conroy.

While Gabriel and Miss Daly exchanged plates of goose and plates of ham and spiced beef Lily went from guest to guest with a dish of hot floury potatoes wrapped in a white napkin. This was Mary Jane's idea and she had also suggested apple sauce for the goose but Aunt Kate had said that plain roast goose without apple sauce had always been good enough for her and she hoped she might never eat worse. Mary Jane waited on her pupils and saw that they got the best slices and Aunt Kate and Aunt Julia opened and carried across from the piano bottles of stout and ale for the gentlemen and bottles of minerals for the ladies. There was a great deal of confusion and laughter and noise, the noise of orders and counter-orders, of knives and forks, of corks and glass-stoppers. Gabriel began to carve second helpings as soon as he had finished the first round without serving himself. Everyone protested loudly so that he compromised by taking a long draught of stout for he had found the carving hot work. Mary Jane settled down quietly to her supper but Aunt Kate and Aunt Julia were still toddling round the table, walking on each other's heels, getting in each other's way and giving each other unheeded orders. Mr Browne begged of them to sit down and eat their suppers and so did Gabriel but they said there was time enough so that, at last, Freddy Malins stood up and, capturing Aunt Kate, plumped her down on her chair amid general laughter.

When everyone had been well served Gabriel said, smiling:

—Now, if anyone wants a little more of what vulgar people call stuffing let him or her speak.

A chorus of voices invited him to begin his own supper and Lily came forward with three potatoes which she had reserved for him.

—Very well, said Gabriel amiably, as he took another preparatory draught, kindly forget my existence, ladies and gentlemen, for a few minutes.

He set to his supper and took no part in the conversation with which the table covered Lily's removal of the plates. The subject of talk was the opera company which was then at the Theatre Royal. Mr Bartell D'Arcy, the tenor, a dark-complexioned young man with a smart moustache, praised very highly the leading contralto of the company but Miss Furlong thought she had a rather vulgar style of production. Freddy Malins said there was a negro chieftain singing in the second part of the Gaiety pantomime who had one of the finest tenor voices he had ever heard.

—Have you heard him? he asked Mr Bartell D'Arcy across the table.

—No, answered Mr Bartell D'Arcy carelessly.

—Because, Freddy Malins explained, now I'd be curious to hear your opinion of him. I think he has a grand voice.

—It takes Teddy to find out the really good things, said Mr Browne familiarly to the table.

—And why couldn't he have a voice too? asked Freddy Malins sharply. Is it because he's only a black?

Nobody answered this question and Mary Jane led the table back to the legitimate opera. One of her pupils had given her a pass for *Mignon*. Of course it was very fine, she said, but it made her think of poor Georgina Burns. Mr Browne could go back farther still, to the old Italian companies that used to come to Dublin—Tietjens, Ilma de Murzka, Campanini, the great Trebelli, Giuglini, Ravelli, Aramburo. Those were the days, he said, when there was something like singing to be heard in Dublin. He told too of how the top gallery of the old Royal used to be packed night after night, of how one night an Italian tenor had sung five encores to *Let Me Like a Soldier Fall*, introducing a high C every time, and of how the gallery boys would sometimes in their enthusiasm unyoke the horses from the carriage of some great *prima donna* and pull her themselves through the streets to her hotel. Why did they never play the grand old operas now, he asked, *Dinorah, Lucrezia Borgia*? Because they could not get the voices to sing them: that was why.

—O, well, said Mr Bartell D'Arcy, I presume there are as good singers today as there were then.

—Where are they? asked Mr Browne defiantly.

—In London, Paris, Milan, said Mr Bartell D'Arcy warmly. I suppose Caruso, for example, is quite as good, if not better than any of the men you have mentioned.

—Maybe so, said Mr Browne. But I may tell you I doubt it strongly.

—O, I'd give anything to hear Caruso sing, said Mary Jane.

—For me, said Aunt Kate, who had been picking a bone, there was only one tenor. To please me, I mean. But I suppose none of you ever heard of him.

—Who was he, Miss Morkan? asked Mr Bartell D'Arcy politely.

—His name, said Aunt Kate, was Parkinson. I heard him when he was in his prime and I think he had then the purest tenor voice that was ever put into a man's throat.

—Strange, said Mr Bartell D'Arcy. I never even heard of him.

—Yes, yes, Miss Morkan is right, said Mr Browne. I remember hearing of old Parkinson but he's too far back for me.

—A beautiful pure sweet mellow English tenor, said Aunt Kate with enthusiasm.

Gabriel having finished, the huge pudding was transferred to the table. The clatter of forks and spoons began again. Gabriel's wife served out spoonfuls of the pudding and passed the plates down the table. Midway down they were held up by Mary Jane, who replenished them with raspberry or orange jelly or with blancmange and jam. The pudding was of Aunt Julia's making and she received praises for it from all quarters. She herself said that it was not quite brown enough.

—Well, I hope, Miss Morkan, said Mr Browne, that I'm brown enough for you because, you know, I'm all brown.

All the gentlemen, except Gabriel, ate some of the pudding out of compliment to Aunt Julia. As Gabriel never ate sweets the celery had been left for him. Freddy Malins also took a stalk of celery and ate it with his pudding. He had been told that celery was a capital thing for the blood and he was just then under doctor's care. Mrs Malins, who had been silent all through the supper, said that her son was going down to Mount Melleray in a week or so. The table then spoke of Mount Melleray, how bracing the air was down there, how hospitable the monks were and how they never asked for a penny-piece from their guests.

—And do you mean to say, asked Mr Browne incredulously, that a chap can go down there and put up there as if it were a hotel and live on the fat of the land and then come away without paying a farthing?

—O, most people give some donation to the monastery when they leave, said Mary Jane.

—I wish we had an institution like that in our Church, said Mr Browne candidly.

He was astonished to hear that the monks never spoke, got up at two in the morning and slept in their coffins. He asked what they did it for.

—That's the rule of the order, said Aunt Kate firmly.

—Yes, but why? asked Mr Browne.

Aunt Kate repeated that it was the rule, that was all. Mr. Browne still seemed not to understand. Freddy Malins explained to him, as best he could, that the monks were trying to make up for the sins committed by all the sinners in the outside world. The explanation was not very clear for Mr Browne grinned and said:

—I like that idea very much but wouldn't a comfortable bed do them as well as a coffin?

—The coffin, said Mary Jane, is to remind them of their last end.

As the subject had grown lugubrious it was buried in a silence of the table during which Mrs Malins could be heard saying to her neighbour in an indistinct undertone:

—They are very good men, the monks, very pious men.

The raisins and almonds and figs and apples and oranges and chocolates and sweets were now passed about the table and Aunt Julia invited all the guests to have either port or sherry. At first Mr Bartell D'Arcy refused to take either but one of his neighbours nudged him and whispered something to him upon which he allowed his glass to be filled. Gradually as the last glasses were being filled the conversation ceased. A pause followed, broken only by the noise of the wine and by unsettlings of chairs. The Misses Morkan, all three, looked down at the tablecloth. Someone coughed once or twice and then a few gentlemen patted the table gently as a signal for silence. The silence came and Gabriel pushed back his chair and stood up.

The patting at once grew louder in encouragement and then ceased altogether. Gabriel leaned his ten trembling fingers on the tablecloth and smiled nervously at the company. Meeting a row of upturned faces he raised his eyes to the chandelier. The piano was playing a waltz tune and he could hear the skirts sweeping against the drawing-room door. People, perhaps, were standing in the snow on the quay outside, gazing up at the lighted windows and listening to the waltz music. The air was pure there. In the distance lay the park where the trees were weighted with snow. The Wellington Monument wore a gleaming cap of snow that flashed westward over the white field of Fifteen Acres.

He began:

—Ladies and Gentlemen.

—It has fallen to my lot this evening, as in years past, to perform a very pleasing task but a task for which I am afraid my poor powers as a speaker are all too inadequate.

—No, no! said Mr Browne.

—But, however that may be, I can only ask you to-night to take the will for the deed and to lend me your attention for a few moments while I endeavour to express to you in words what my feelings are on this occasion.

—Ladies and Gentlemen. It is not the first time that we have gathered together under this hospitable roof, around this hospitable board. It is not the first time that we have been the recipients—or perhaps, I had better say, the victims—of the hospitality of certain good ladies.

He made a circle in the air with his arm and paused. Everyone laughed or smiled at Aunt Kate and Aunt Julia and Mary Jane who all turned crimson with pleasure. Gabriel went on more boldly:

—I feel more strongly with every recurring year that our country has no tradition which does it so much honour and which it should guard so jealously as that of its hospitality. It is a tradition that is unique as far as my experience goes (and I have visited not a few places abroad) among the modern nations. Some would say, perhaps, that with us it is rather a failing than anything to be boasted of. But granted even that, it is, to my mind, a princely failing, and one that I trust will long be cultivated among us. Of one thing, at least, I am sure. As long as this one roof shelters the good ladies aforesaid—and I wish from my heart it may do so for many and many a long year to come—the tradition of genuine warm-hearted courteous Irish hospitality, which our forefathers have handed down to us and which we in turn must hand down to our descendants, is still alive among us.

A hearty murmur of assent ran round the table. It shot through Gabriel's mind that Miss Ivors was not there and that she had gone away discourteously: and he said with confidence in himself:

—Ladies and Gentlemen.

—A new generation is growing up in our midst, a generation actuated by new ideas and new principles. It is serious and enthusiastic for these new ideas and its enthusiasm, even when it is misdirected, is, I believe, in the main sincere. But we are living in a sceptical and, if I may use the phrase, a thought-tormented age: and sometimes I fear that this new generation, educated or hypereducated as it is, will lack those qualities of humanity, of hospitality, of kindly humour which belonged to an older day. Listening to-night to the names of all those great singers of the past it seemed to me, I must confess, that we were living in a less spacious age. Those days might, without exaggeration, be called spacious days: and if they are gone beyond recall let us hope, at least, that in gatherings such as this we shall still speak of them with pride and affection, still cherish in our hearts the memory of those dead and gone great ones whose fame the world will not willingly let die.

—Hear, hear! said Mr Browne loudly.

—But yet, continued Gabriel, his voice falling into a softer inflection, there are always in gatherings such as this sadder thoughts that will recur to our minds: thoughts of the past, of youth, of changes, of absent faces that we miss here tonight. Our path through life is strewn with many such sad memories: and were we to brood upon them always we could not find the heart to go on bravely with our work among the living. We have all of us living duties and living affections which claim, and rightly claim, our strenuous endeavours.

—Therefore, I will not linger on the past. I will not let any gloomy moralising intrude upon us here to-night. Here we are gathered together for a brief moment from the bustle and rush of our everyday routine. We are met here as friends, in the spirit of good-fellowship, as colleagues, also to a certain extent, in the true spirit of *camaraderie,* and as the guests of—what shall I call them?—the Three Graces of the Dublin musical world.

The table burst into applause and laughter at this sally. Aunt Julia vainly asked each of her neighbours in turn to tell her what Gabriel had said.

—He says we are the Three Graces, Aunt Julia, said Mary Jane.

Aunt Julia did not understand but she looked up, smiling, at Gabriel, who continued in the same vein:

—Ladies and Gentlemen.

—I will not attempt to play to-night the part that Paris played on another occasion. I will not attempt to choose between them. The task would be an invidious one and one beyond my poor powers. For when I view them in turn, whether it be our chief hostess herself, whose good heart, whose too good heart, has become a byword with all who know her, or her sister, who seems to be gifted with perennial youth and whose singing must have been a surprise and a revelation to us all to-night, or, last but not least, when I consider our youngest hostess, talented, cheerful, hard-working and the best of nieces, I confess, Ladies and Gentlemen, that I do not know to which of them I should award the prize.

Gabriel glanced down at his aunts and, seeing the large smile on Aunt Julia's face and the tears which had risen to Aunt Kate's eyes, hastened to his close. He raised his glass of port gallantly, while every member of the company fingered a glass expectantly, and said loudly:

—Let us toast them all three together. Let us drink to their health, wealth, long life, happiness and prosperity and may they continue to hold the proud and self-won position which they hold in their profession and the position of honour and affection which they hold in our hearts.

All the guests stood up, glass in hand, and, turning towards the three seated ladies, sang in unison, with Mr Browne as leader:

For they are jolly gay fellows,
For they are jolly gay fellows,
For they are jolly gay fellows,
Which nobody can deny.

Aunt Kate was making frank use of her handkerchief and even Aunt Julia seemed moved. Freddy Malins beat time with his pudding-fork and the singers turned toward one another, as if in melodious conference, while they sang, with emphasis:

Unless he tells a lie,
Unless he tells a lie.

Then, turning once more towards their hostesses, they sang:

For they are jolly gay fellows,
For they are jolly gay fellows,
For they are jolly gay fellows,
Which nobody can deny.

The acclamation which followed was taken up beyond the door of the supper-room by many of the other guests and renewed time after time, Freddy Malins acting as officer with his fork on high.

*   *   *

The piercing morning air came into the hall where they were standing so that Aunt Kate said:

—Close the door, somebody. Mrs Malins will get her death of cold.

—Browne is out there, Aunt Kate, said Mary Jane.

—Browne is everywhere, said Aunt Kate, lowering her voice.

Mary Jane laughed at her tone.

—Really, she said archly, he is very attentive.

—He has been laid on here like the gas, said Aunt Kate in the same tone, all during the Christmas.

She laughed herself this time good-humouredly and then added quickly:

—But tell him to come in, Mary Jane, and close the door. I hope to goodness he didn't hear me.

At that moment the hall-door was opened and Mr Browne came in from the doorstep, laughing as if his heart would break. He was dressed in a long green overcoat with mock astrakhan cuffs and collar and wore on his head an oval fur cap. He pointed down the snow-covered quay from where the sound of shrill prolonged whistling was borne in.

—Teddy will have all the cabs in Dublin out, he said.

Gabriel advanced from the little pantry behind the office, struggling into his overcoat and, looking round the hall, said:

—Gretta not down yet?

—She's getting on her things, Gabriel, said Aunt Kate.

—Who's playing up there? asked Gabriel.

—Nobody. They're all gone.

—O no, Aunt Kate, said Mary Jane. Bartell D'Arcy and Miss O'Callaghan aren't gone yet.

—Someone is strumming at the piano, anyhow, said Gabriel.

Mary Jane glanced at Gabriel and Mr Browne and said with a shiver:

—It makes me feel cold to look at you two gentlemen muffled up like that. I wouldn't like to face your journey home at this hour.

—I'd like nothing better this minute, said Mr Browne stoutly, than a rattling fine walk in the country or a fast drive with a good spanking goer between the shafts.

—We used to have a very good horse and trap at home, said Aunt Julia sadly.

—The never-to-be-forgotten Johnny, said Mary Jane, laughing.

Aunt Kate and Gabriel laughed too.

—Why, what was wonderful about Johnny? asked Mr Browne.

—The late lamented Patrick Morkan, our grandfather, that is, explained Gabriel, commonly known in his later years as the old gentleman, was a glue-boiler.

—O, now, Gabriel, said Aunt Kate, laughing, he had a starch mill.

—Well, glue or starch, said Gabriel, the old gentleman had a horse by the name of Johnny. And Johnny used to work in the old gentleman's mill, walking round and round in order to drive the mill. That was all very well; but now comes the tragic part about Johnny. One fine day the old gentleman thought he'd like to drive out with the quality to a military review in the park.

—The Lord have mercy on his soul, said Aunt Kate compassionately.

—Amen, said Gabriel. So the old gentleman, as I said, harnessed Johnny and put on his very best tall hat and his very best stock collar and drove out in grand style from his ancestral mansion somewhere near Back Lane, I think.

Everyone laughed, even Mrs Malins, at Gabriel's manner and Aunt Kate said:

—O now, Gabriel, he didn't live in Back Lane, really. Only the mill was there.

—Out from the mansion of his forefathers, continued Gabriel, he drove with Johnny. And everything went on beautifully until Johnny came in sight of King Billy's statue: and whether he fell in love with the horse King Billy sits on or whether he thought he was back again in the mill, anyhow he began to walk round the statue.

Gabriel paced in a circle round the hall in his goloshes amid the laughter of the others.

—Round and round he went, said Gabriel, and the old gentleman, who was a very pompous old gentleman, was highly indignant. *Go on, sir! What do you mean, sir? Johnny! Johnny! Most extraordinary conduct! Can't understand the horse!*

The peals of laughter which followed Gabriel's imitation of the incident were interrupted by a resounding knock at the hall-door. Mary Jane ran to open it and let in Freddy Malins. Freddy Malins, with his hat well back on his head and his shoulders humped with cold, was puffing and steaming after his exertions.

—I could only get one cab, he said.

—O, we'll find another along the quay, said Gabriel.

—Yes, said Aunt Kate. Better not keep Mrs Malins standing in the draught.

Mrs Malins was helped down the front steps by her son and Mr Browne and, after many manœuvres, hoisted into the cab. Freddy Malins clambered in after her and spent a long time settling her on the seat, Mr Browne helping him with advice. At last she was settled comfortably and Freddy Malins invited Mr Browne into the cab. There was a good deal of confused talk, and then Mr Browne got into the cab. The cabman settled his rug over his knees, and bent down for the address. The confusion grew greater and the cabman was directed differently by Freddy Malins and Mr Browne, each of whom had his head out through a window of the cab. The difficulty was to know where to drop Mr Browne along the route and Aunt Kate, Aunt Julia and Mary Jane helped the discussion from the doorstep with cross-directions and contradictions and abundance of laughter. As for Freddy Malins he was speechless with laughter. He popped his head in and out of the window every moment, to the great danger of his hat, and told his mother how the discussion was progressing till at last Mr Browne shouted to the bewildered cabman above the din of everybody's laughter:

—Do you know Trinity College?

—Yes, sir, said the cabman.

—Well, drive bang up against Trinity College gates, said Mr Browne, and then we'll tell you where to go. You understand now?

—Yes, sir, said the cabman.

—Make like a bird for Trinity College.

—Right, sir, cried the cabman.

The horse was whipped up and the cab rattled off along the quay amid a chorus of laughter and adieus.

Gabriel had not gone to the door with the others. He was in the dark part of the hall gazing up the staircase. A woman was standing near the top of the first flight, in the shadow also. He could not see her face but he could see the terracotta and salmonpink panels of her skirt which the shadow

made appear black and white. It was his wife. She was leaning on the banisters, listening to something. Gabriel was surprised at her stillness and
strained his ear to listen also. But he could hear little save the noise of
laughter and dispute on the front steps, a few chords struck on the piano
and a few notes of a man's voice singing.

He stood still in the gloom of the hall, trying to catch the air that the voice
was singing and gazing up at his wife. There was grace and mystery in her
attitude as if she were a symbol of something. He asked himself what is a
woman standing on the stairs in the shadow, listening to distant music, a
symbol of. If he were a painter he would paint her in that attitude. Her
blue felt hat would show off the bronze of her hair against the darkness
and the dark panels of her skirt would show off the light ones. *Distant Music*
he would call the picture if he were a painter.

The hall-door was closed; and Aunt Kate, Aunt Julia and Mary Jane
came down the hall, still laughing.

—Well, isn't Freddy terrible? said Mary Jane. He's really terrible.

Gabriel said nothing but pointed up the stairs towards where his wife was
standing. Now that the hall-door was closed the voice and the piano could
be heard more clearly. Gabriel held up his hand for them to be silent. The
song seemed to be in the old Irish tonality and the singer seemed uncertain
both of his words and of his voice. The voice, made plaintive by distance
and by the singer's hoarseness, faintly illuminated the cadence of the air
with words expressing grief:

> *O, the rain falls on my heavy locks*
> *And the dew wets my skin,*
> *My babe lies cold . . .*

—O, exclaimed Mary Jane. It's Bartell D'Arcy singing and he wouldn't
sing all the night. O, I'll get him to sing a song before he goes.

—O do, Mary Jane, said Aunt Kate.

Mary Jane brushed past the others and ran to the staircase but before she
reached it the singing stopped and the piano was closed abruptly.

—O, what a pity! she cried. Is he coming down, Gretta?

Gabriel heard his wife answer yes and saw her come down towards them.
A few steps behind her were Mr Bartell D'Arcy and Miss O'Callaghan.

—O, Mr D'Arcy, cried Mary Jane, it's downright mean of you to break
off like that when we were all in raptures listening to you.

—I have been at him all the evening, said Miss O'Callaghan, and Mrs
Conroy too and he told us he had a dreadful cold and couldn't sing.

—O, Mr D'Arcy, said Aunt Kate, now that was a great fib to tell.

—Can't you see that I'm as hoarse as a crow? said Mr D'Arcy roughly.

He went into the pantry hastily and put on his overcoat. The others,
taken aback by his rude speech, could find nothing to say. Aunt Kate wrin-

kled her brows and made signs to the others to drop the subject. Mr D'Arcy stood swathing his neck carefully and frowning.

—It's the weather, said Aunt Julia, after a pause.

—Yes, everybody has colds, said Aunt Kate readily, everybody.

—They say, said Mary Jane, we haven't had snow like it for thirty years; and I read this morning in the newspapers that the snow is general all over Ireland.

—I love the look of snow, said Aunt Julia sadly.

—So do I, said Miss O'Callaghan. I think Christmas is never really Christmas unless we have the snow on the ground.

—But poor Mr D'Arcy doesn't like the snow, said Aunt Kate, smiling.

Mr D'Arcy came from the pantry, fully swathed and buttoned, and in a repentant tone told them the history of his cold. Everyone gave him advice and said it was a great pity and urged him to be very careful of his throat in the night air. Gabriel watched his wife who did not join in the conversation. She was standing right under the dusty fanlight and the flame of the gas lit up the rich bronze of her hair which he had seen her drying at the fire a few days before. She was in the same attitude and seemed unaware of the talk about her. At last she turned towards them and Gabriel saw that there was colour on her cheeks and that her eyes were shining. A sudden tide of joy went leaping out of his heart.

—Mr D'Arcy, she said, what is the name of that song you were singing?

—It's called *The Lass of Aughrim*, said Mr D'Arcy, but I couldn't remember it properly. Why? Do you know it?

—*The Lass of Aughrim*, she repeated. I couldn't think of the name.

—It's a very nice air, said Mary Jane. I'm sorry you were not in voice tonight.

—Now, Mary Jane, said Aunt Kate, don't annoy Mr D'Arcy. I won't have him annoyed.

Seeing that all were ready to start she shepherded them to the door where good-night was said:

—Well, good-night, Aunt Kate, and thanks for the pleasant evening.

—Good-night, Gabriel. Good-night, Gretta!

—Good-night, Aunt Kate, and thanks ever so much. Good-night, Aunt Julia.

—O, good-night, Gretta, I didn't see you.

—Good-night, Mr D'Arcy. Good-night, Miss O'Callaghan.

—Good-night, Miss Morkan.

—Good-night, again.

—Good-night, all. Safe home.

—Good-night. Good-night.

The morning was still dark. A dull yellow light brooded over the houses and the river; and the sky seemed to be descending. It was slushy underfoot; and only streaks and patches of snow lay on the roofs, on the parapets of the quay and on the area railings. The lamps were still burning redly in the murky air and, across the river, the palace of the Four Courts stood out menacingly against the heavy sky.

She was walking on before him with Mr Bartell D'Arcy, her shoes in a brown parcel tucked under one arm and her hands holding her skirt up from the slush. She had no longer any grace of attitude but Gabriel's eyes were still bright with happiness. The blood went bounding along his veins; and the thoughts went rioting through his brain, proud, joyful, tender, valorous.

She was walking on before him so lightly and so erect that he longed to run after her noiselessly, catch her by the shoulders and say something foolish and affectionate into her ear. She seemed to him so frail that he longed to defend her against something and then to be alone with her. Moments of their secret life together burst like stars upon his memory. A heliotrope evelope was lying beside his breakfast-cup and he was caressing it with his hand. Birds were twittering in the ivy and the sunny web of the curtain was shimmering along the floor: he could not eat for happiness. They were standing on the crowded platform and he was placing a ticket inside the warm palm of her glove. He was standing with her in the cold, looking in through a grated window at a man making bottles in a roaring furnace. It was very cold. Her face, fragrant in the cold air, was quite close to his; and suddenly she called out to the man at the furnace:

—Is the fire hot, sir?

But the man could not hear her with the noise of the furnace. It was just as well. He might have answered rudely.

A wave of yet more tender joy escaped from his heart and went coursing in warm flood along his arteries. Like the tender fires of stars moments of their life together, that no one knew of or would ever know of, broke upon and illumined his memory. He longed to recall to her those moments, to make her forget the years of their dull existence together and remember only their moments of ecstasy. For the years, he felt, had not quenched his soul or hers. Their children, his writing, her household cares had not quenched all their souls' tender fire. In one letter that he had written to her then he had said: *Why is it that words like these seem to me so dull and cold? Is it because there is no word tender enough to be your name?*

Like distant music these words that he had written years before were borne towards him from the past. He longed to be alone with her. When the others had gone away, when he and she were in their room in the hotel, then they would be alone together. He would call her softly:

—Gretta!

Perhaps she would not hear at once: she would be undressing. Then something in his voice would strike her. She would turn and look at him. . . .

At the corner of Winetavern Street they met a cab. He was glad of its rattling noise as it saved him from conversation. She was looking out of the window and seemed tired. The others spoke only a few words, pointing out some building or street. The horse galloped along wearily under the murky morning sky, dragging his old rattling box after his heels, and Gabriel was again in a cab with her, galloping to catch the boat, galloping to their honeymoon.

As the cab drove across O'Connell Bridge Miss O'Callaghan said:

—They say you never cross O'Connell Bridge without seeing a white horse.

—I see a white man this time, said Gabriel.

—Where? asked Mr Bartell D'Arcy.

Gabriel pointed to the statue, on which lay patches of snow. Then he nodded familiarly to it and waved his hand.

—Good-night, Dan, he said gaily.

When the cab drew up before the hotel Gabriel jumped out and, in spite of Mr Bartell D'Arcy's protest, paid the driver. He gave the man a shilling over his fare. The man saluted and said:

—A prosperous New Year to you, sir.

—The same to you, said Gabriel cordially.

She leaned for a moment on his arm in getting out of the cab and while standing at the curbstone, bidding the others good-night. She leaned lightly on his arm, as lightly as when she had danced with him a few hours before. He had felt proud and happy then, happy that she was his, proud of her grace and wifely carriage. But now, after the kindling again of so many memories, the first touch of her body, musical and strange and perfumed, sent through him a keen pang of lust. Under cover of her silence he pressed her arm closely to his side; and, as they stood at the hotel door, he felt that they had escaped from their lives and duties, escaped from home and friends and run away together with wild and radiant hearts to a new adventure.

An old man was dozing in a great hooded chair in the hall. He lit a candle in the office and went before them to the stairs. They followed him in silence, their feet falling in soft thuds on the thickly carpeted stairs. She mounted the stairs behind the porter, her head bowed in the ascent, her frail shoulders curved as with a burden, her skirt girt tightly about her. He could have flung his arms about her hips and held her still for his arms were trembling with desire to seize her and only the stress of his nails against the palms of his hands held the wild impulse of his body in check. The porter halted on the stairs to settle his guttering candle. They halted too on the steps below him. In the silence Gabriel could hear the falling of the molten wax into the tray and the thumping of his own heart against his ribs.

The porter led them along a corridor and opened a door. Then he set his unstable candle down on a toilet-table and asked at what hour they were to be called in the morning.

—Eight, said Gabriel.

The porter pointed to the tap of the electric-light and began a muttered apology but Gabriel cut him short.

—We don't want any light. We have light enough from the street. And I say, he added, pointing to the candle, you might remove that handsome article, like a good man.

The porter took up his candle again, but slowly for he was surprised by such a novel idea. Then he mumbled good-night and went out. Gabriel shot the lock to.

A ghostly light from the street lamp lay in a long shaft from one window to the door. Gabriel threw his overcoat and hat on a couch and crossed the room towards the window. He looked down into the street in order that his emotion might calm a little. Then he turned and leaned against a chest of drawers with his back to the light. She had taken off her hat and cloak and was standing before a large swinging mirror, unhooking her waist. Gabriel paused for a few moments, watching her, and then said:

—Gretta!

She turned away from the mirror slowly and walked along the shaft of light towards him. Her face looked so serious and weary that the words would not pass Gabriel's lips. No, it was not the moment yet.

—You looked tired, he said.

—I am a little, she answered.

—You don't feel ill or weak?

—No, tired: that's all.

She went on to the window and stood there, looking out. Gabriel waited again and then, fearing that diffidence was about to conquer him, he said abruptly:

—By the way, Gretta!

—What is it?

—You know that poor fellow Malins? he said quickly.

—Yes. What about him?

—Well, poor fellow, he's a decent sort of chap after all, continued Gabriel in a false voice. He gave me back that sovereign I lent him and I didn't expect it really. It's a pity he wouldn't keep away from that Browne, because he's not a bad fellow at heart.

He was trembling now with annoyance. Why did she seem so abstracted? He did not know how he could begin. Was she annoyed, too, about something? If she would only turn to him or come to him of her own accord! To take her as she was would be brutal. No, he must see some ardour in her eyes first. He longed to be master of her strange mood.

—When did you lend him the pound? she asked, after a pause.

Gabriel strove to restrain himself from breaking out into brutal language about the sottish Malins and his pound. He longed to cry to her from his soul, to crush her body against his, to overmaster her. But he said:

—O, at Christmas, when he opened that little Christmas-card shop in Henry Street.

He was in such a fever of rage and desire that he did not hear her come from the window. She stood before him for an instant, looking at him strangely. Then, suddenly raising herself on tiptoe and resting her hands lightly on his shoulders, she kissed him.

—You are a very generous person, Gabriel, she said.

Gabriel, trembling with delight at her sudden kiss and at the quaintness of her phrase, put his hands on her hair and began smoothing it back, scarcely touching it with his fingers. The washing had made it fine and brilliant. His heart was brimming over with happiness. Just when he was wishing for it she had come to him of her own accord. Perhaps her thoughts had been running with his. Perhaps she had felt the impetuous desire that was in him and then the yielding mood had come upon her. Now that she had fallen to him so easily he wondered why he had been so diffident.

He stood, holding her head between his hands. Then, slipping one arm swiftly about her body and drawing her towards him, he said softly:

—Gretta dear, what are you thinking about?

She did not answer nor yield wholly to his arm. He said again, softly:

—Tell me what it is, Gretta, I think I know what is the matter. Do I know?

She did not answer at once. Then she said in an outburst of tears:

—O, I am thinking about that song, *The Lass of Aughrim.*

She broke loose from him and ran to the bed and, throwing her arms across the bed-rail, hid her face. Gabriel stood stockstill for a moment in astonishment and then followed her. As he passed in the way of the cheval-glass he caught sight of himself in full length, his broad, well-filled shirt-front, the face whose expression always puzzled him when he saw it in a mirror and his glimmering gilt-rimmed eyeglasses. He halted a few paces from her and said:

—What about the song? Why does that make you cry?

She raised her head from her arms and dried her eyes with the back of her hand like a child. A kinder note than he had intended went into his voice.

—Why, Gretta? he asked.

—I am thinking about a person long ago who used to sing that song.

—And who was the person long ago? asked Gabriel, smiling.

—It was a person I used to know in Galway when I was living with my grandmother, she said.

The smile passed away from Gabriel's face. A dull anger began to gather

again at the back of his mind and the dull fires of his lust began to glow angrily in his veins.

—Someone you were in love with? he asked ironically.

—It was a young boy I used to know, she answered, named Michael
Furey. He used to sing that song, *The Lass of Aughrim*. He was very delicate.

Gabriel was silent. He did not wish her to think that he was interested in
this delicate boy.

—I can see him so plainly, she said after a moment. Such eyes as he had:
big dark eyes! And such an expression in them—an expression!

—O then, you were in love with him? said Gabriel.

—I used to go out walking with him, she said, when I was in Galway.

A thought flew across Gabriel's mind.

—Perhaps that was why you wanted to go to Galway with that Ivors girl?
he said coldly.

She looked at him and asked in surprise:

—What for?

Her eyes made Gabriel feel awkward. He shrugged his shoulders and
said:

—How do I know? To see him perhaps.

She looked away from him along the shaft of light towards the window in
silence.

—He is dead, she said at length. He died when he was only seventeen.
Isn't it a terrible thing to die so young as that?

—What was he? asked Gabriel, still ironically.

—He was in the gasworks, she said.

Gabriel felt humiliated by the failure of his irony and by the evocation of
this figure from the dead, a boy in the gasworks. While he had been full of
memories of their secret life together, full of tenderness and joy and desire,
she had been comparing him in her mind with another. A shameful consciousness of his own person assailed him. He saw himself as a ludicrous
figure, acting as a pennyboy for his aunts, a nervous well-meaning senti-
mentalist, orating to vulgarians and idealising his own clownish lusts, the
pitiable fatuous fellow he had caught a glimpse of in the mirror. Instinctively he turned his back more to the light lest she might see the shame that
burned upon his forehead.

He tried to keep up his tone of cold interrogation but his voice when he
spoke was humble and indifferent.

—I suppose you were in love with this Michael Furey, Gretta, he said.

—I was great with him at that time, she said.

Her voice was veiled and sad. Gabriel, feeling now how vain it would be
to try to lead her whither he had purposed, caressed one of her hands and
said, also sadly:

—And what did he die of so young, Gretta? Consumption, was it?

—I think he died for me, she answered.

A vague terror seized Gabriel at this answer as if, at that hour when he had hoped to triumph, some impalpable and vindictive being was coming against him, gathering forces against him in its vague world. But he shook himself free of it with an effort of reason and continued to caress her hand. He did not question her again for he felt that she would tell him of herself. Her hand was warm and moist: it did not respond to his touch but he continued to caress it just as he had caressed her first letter to him that spring morning.

—It was in the winter, she said, about the beginning of the winter when I was going to leave my grandmother's and come up here to the convent. And he was ill at the time in his lodgings in Galway and wouldn't be let out and his people in Oughterard were written to. He was in decline, they said, or something like that. I never knew rightly.

She paused for a moment and sighed.

—Poor fellow, she said. He was very fond of me and he was such a gentle boy. We used to go out together, walking, you know, Gabriel, like the way they do in the country. He was going to study singing only for his health. He had a very good voice, poor Michael Furey.

—Well; and then? asked Gabriel.

—And then when it came to the time for me to leave Galway and come up to the convent he was much worse and I wouldn't be let see him so I wrote a letter saying I was going up to Dublin and would be back in the summer and hoping he would be better then.

She paused for a moment to get her voice under control and then went on:

—Then the night before I left I was in my grandmother's house in Nuns' Island, packing up, and I heard gravel thrown up against the window. The window was so wet I couldn't see so I ran downstairs as I was and slipped out the back into the garden and there was the poor fellow at the end of the garden, shivering.

—And did you not tell him to go back? asked Gabriel.

—I implored of him to go home at once and told him he would get his death in the rain. But he said he did not want to live. I can see his eyes as well as well! He was standing at the end of the wall where there was a tree.

—And did he go home? asked Gabriel.

—Yes, he went home. And when I was only a week in the convent he died and he was buried in Oughterard where his people came from. O, the day I heard that, that he was dead!

She stopped, choking with sobs, and, overcome by emotion, flung herself face downward on the bed, sobbing in the quilt. Gabriel held her hand for a moment longer, irresolutely, and then, shy of intruding on her grief, let it fall gently and walked quietly to the window.

She was fast asleep.

Gabriel, leaning on his elbow, looked for a few moments unresentfully on her tangled hair and half-open mouth, listening to her deep-drawn breath. So she had had that romance in her life: a man had died for her sake. It hardly pained him now to think how poor a part he, her husband, had played in her life. He watched her while she slept as though he and she had never lived together as man and wife. His curious eyes rested long upon her face and on her hair: and, as he thought of what she must have been then, in that time of her first girlish beauty, a strange friendly pity for her entered his soul. He did not like to say even to himself that her face was no longer beautiful but he knew that it was no longer the face for which Michael Furey had braved death.

Perhaps she had not told him all the story. His eyes moved to the chair over which she had thrown some of her clothes. A petticoat string dangled to the floor. One boot stood upright, its limp upper fallen down: the fellow of it lay upon its side. He wondered at his riot of emotions of an hour before. From what had it proceeded? From his aunt's supper, from his own foolish speech, from the wine and dancing, the merrymaking when saying good-night in the hall, the pleasure of the walk along the river in the snow. Poor Aunt Julia! She, too, would soon be a shade with the shade of Patrick Morkan and his horse. He had caught that haggard look upon her face for a moment when she was singing *Arrayed for the Bridal*. Soon, perhaps, he would be sitting in that same drawing-room, dressed in black, his silk hat on his knees. The blinds would be drawn down and Aunt Kate would be sitting beside him, crying and blowing her nose and telling him how Julia had died. He would cast about in his mind for some words that might console her, and would find only lame and useless ones. Yes, yes: that would happen very soon.

The air of the room chilled his shoulders. He stretched himself cautiously along under the sheets and lay down beside his wife. One by one they were all becoming shades. Better pass boldly into that other world, in the full glory of some passion, than fade and wither dismally with age. He thought of how she who lay beside him had locked in her heart for so many years that image of her lover's eyes when he had told her that he did not wish to live.

Generous tears filled Gabriel's eyes. He had never felt like that himself towards any woman but he knew that such a feeling must be love. The tears gathered more thickly in his eyes and in the partial darkness he imagined he saw the form of a young man standing under a dripping tree. Other forms were near. His soul had approached that region where dwell the vast hosts of the dead. He was conscious of, but could not apprehend, their wayward and flickering existence. His own identity was fading out into a grey impalpable world: the solid world itself which these dead had one time reared and lived in was dissolving and dwindling.

A few light taps upon the pane made him turn to the window. It had begun to snow again. He watched sleepily the flakes, silver and dark, falling obliquely against the lamplight. The time had come for him to set out on his journey westward. Yes, the newspapers were right: snow was general all over Ireland. It was falling on every part of the dark central plain, on the treeless hills, falling softly upon the Bog of Allen and, farther westward, softly falling into the dark mutinous Shannon waves. It was falling, too, upon every part of the lonely churchyard on the hill where Michael Furey lay buried. It lay thickly drifted on the crooked crosses and headstones, on the spears of the little gate, on the barren thorns. His soul swooned slowly as he heard the snow falling faintly through the universe and faintly falling, like the descent of their last end, upon all the living and the dead.

In the Penal Colony

FRANZ KAFKA

"It's a remarkable piece of apparatus," said the officer to the explorer and surveyed with a certain air of admiration the apparatus which was after all quite familiar to him. The explorer seemed to have accepted merely out of politeness the Commandant's invitation to witness the execution of a soldier condemned to death for disobedience and insulting behavior to a superior. Nor did the colony itself betray much interest in this execution. At least, in the small sandy valley, a deep hollow surrounded on all sides by naked crags, there was no one present save the officer, the explorer, the condemned man, who was a stupid-looking wide-mouthed creature with bewildered hair and face, and the soldier who held the heavy chain controlling the small chains locked on the prisoner's ankles, wrists and neck, chains which were themselves attached to each other by communicating links. In any case, the condemned man looked so like a submissive dog that one might have thought he could be left to run free on the surrounding hills and would only need to be whistled for when the execution was due to begin.

The explorer did not much care about the apparatus and walked up and down behind the prisoner with almost visible indifference while the officer made the last adjustments, now creeping beneath the structure, which was bedded deep in the earth, now climbing a ladder to inspect its upper parts. These were tasks that might well have been left to a mechanic, but the officer performed them with great zeal, whether because he was a devoted admirer of the apparatus or because of other reasons the work could be entrusted to no one else. "Ready now!" he called at last and climbed down from the ladder. He looked uncommonly limp, breathed with his mouth wide open and had tucked two fine ladies' handkerchiefs under the collar of his uniform. "These uniforms are too heavy for the tropics, surely," said the explorer, instead of making some inquiry about the apparatus, as the officer had expected. "Of course," said the officer, washing his oily and greasy hands in a bucket of water that stood ready, "but they mean home to us; we don't want to forget about home. Now just have a look at this machine," he added at once, simultaneously drying his hands on a towel and indicating the apparatus. "Up till now a few things still had to be set by hand, but from this moment it works all by itself." The explorer nodded and followed him. The officer, anxious to secure himself against all contingencies, said: "Things sometimes go wrong, of course; I hope that nothing goes wrong today, but we have to allow for the possibility. The machinery should go on working continuously for twelve hours. But if anything does go wrong it will only be some small matter that can be set right at once.

"Won't you take a seat?" he asked finally, drawing a cane chair out from among a heap of them and offering it to the explorer, who could not refuse it. He was now sitting at the edge of a pit, into which he glanced for a fleeting moment. It was not very deep. On one side of the pit the excavated soil had been piled up in a rampart, on the other side of it stood the apparatus. "I don't know," said the officer, "if the Commandant has already explained this apparatus to you." The explorer waved one hand vaguely; the officer asked for nothing better, since now he could explain the apparatus himself. "This apparatus," he said, taking hold of a crank handle and leaning against it, "was invented by our former Commandant. I assisted at the very earliest experiments and had a share in all the work until its completion. But the credit of inventing it belongs to him alone. Have you ever heard of our former Commandant? No? Well, it isn't saying too much if I tell you that the organization of the whole penal colony is his work. We who were his friends knew even before he died that the organization of the colony was so perfect that his successor, even with a thousand new schemes in his head, would find it impossible to alter anything, at least for many years to come. And our prophecy has come true; the new Commandant has had to acknowledge its truth. A pity you never met the old Commandant!—But," the officer interrupted himself, "I am rambling on, and here stands his apparatus before us. It consists, as you see, of three parts. In the course of time each of these parts has acquired a kind of popular nickname. The lower one is called the 'Bed,' the upper one the 'Designer,' and this one here in the middle that moves up and down is called the 'Harrow.'" "The Harrow?" asked the explorer. He had not been listening very attentively, the glare of the sun in the shadeless valley was altogether too strong, it was difficult to collect one's thoughts. All the more did he admire the officer, who in spite of his tight-fitting fulldress uniform coat, amply befrogged and weighed down by epaulettes, was pursuing his subject with such enthusiasm and, besides talking, was still tightening a screw here and there with a spanner. As for the soldier, he seemed to be in much the same condition as the explorer. He had wound the prisoner's chain round both his wrists, propped himself on his rifle, let his head hang and was paying no attention to anything. That did not surprise the explorer, for the officer was speaking French, and certainly neither the soldier nor the prisoner understood a word of French. It was all the more remarkable, therefore, that the prisoner was none the less making an effort to follow the officer's explanations. With a kind of drowsy persistence he directed his gaze wherever the officer pointed a finger, and at the interruption of the explorer's question he, too, as well as the officer, looked round.

"Yes, the Harrow," said the officer, "a good name for it. The needles are set in like the teeth of a harrow and the whole thing works something like a harrow, although its action is limited to one place and contrived with much more artistic skill. Anyhow, you'll soon understand it. On the Bed here the condemned man is laid—I'm going to describe the apparatus first before I set it in motion. Then you'll be able to follow the proceedings better. Besides, one of the cogwheels in the Designer is badly worn; it creaks a lot when it's working, you can hardly hear yourself speak; spare parts, unfortunately, are difficult to get here.—Well, here is the Bed, as I told you. It is completely covered with a layer of cotton wool; you'll find out why later. On this cotton wool the condemned man is laid, face down, quite naked, of course; here are straps for the hands, here for the feet, and here for the neck, to bind him fast. Here at the head of the bed, where the man, as I said, first lays down his face, is this little gag of felt, which can be easily regulated to go straight into his mouth. It is meant to keep him from screaming and biting his tongue. Of course the man is forced to take the felt into his mouth, for otherwise his neck would be broken by the strap." "Is that cotton wool?" asked the explorer, bending forward. "Yes, certainly," said the officer, with a smile. "Feel it for yourself." He took the explorer's hand and guided it over the bed. "It's specially prepared cotton wool; that's why it looks so different; I'll tell you presently what it's for." The explorer already felt a dawning interest in the apparatus; he sheltered his eyes from the sun with one hand and gazed up at the structure. It was a huge affair. The Bed and the Designer were of the same size and looked like two dark wooden chests. The Designer hung about two meters above the Bed; each of them was bound at the corners with four rods of brass that almost flashed out rays in the sunlight. Between the chests shuttled the Harrow on a ribbon of steel.

The officer had scarcely noticed the explorer's previous indifference, but he was now well aware of his dawning interest; so he stopped explaining in order to leave a space of time for quiet observation. The condemned man imitated the explorer; since he could not use a hand to shelter his eyes he gazed upwards without shade.

"Well, the man lies down," said the explorer, leaning back in his chair and crossing his legs.

"Yes," said the officer, pushing his cap back a little and passing one hand over his heated face, "now listen! Both the Bed and the Designer have an electric battery each; the Bed needs one for itself, the Designer for the Harrow. As soon as the man is strapped down, the Bed is set in motion. It quivers in minute, very rapid vibrations, both from side to side and up and down. You will have seen similar apparatus in hospitals; but in our Bed the movements are all precisely calculated; you see, they have to correspond very exactly to the movements of the Harrow. And the Harrow is the instrument for the actual execution of the sentence."

"And how does the sentence run?" asked the explorer.

"You don't know that either?" said the officer in amazement, and bit his lips. "Forgive me if my explanations seem rather incoherent. I do beg your pardon. You see, the Commandant always used to do the explaining; but the new Commandant shirks this duty; yet that such an important visitor"—the explorer tried to deprecate the honor with both hands; the officer, however, insisted—"that such an important visitor should not even be told about the kind of sentence we pass is a new development, which—" He was just on the point of using strong language but checked himself and said only: "I was not informed, it is not my fault. In any case, I am certainly the best person to explain our procedure, since I have here"—he patted his breast pocket—"the relevant drawings made by our former Commandant."

"The Commandant's own drawings?" asked the explorer. "Did he combine everything in himself, then? Was he soldier, judge, mechanic, chemist and draughtsman?"

"Indeed he was," said the officer, nodding assent, with a remote, glassy look. Then he inspected his hands critically; they did not seem clean enough to him for touching the drawings; so he went over to the bucket and washed them again. Then he drew out a small leather wallet and said: "Our sentence does not sound severe. Whatever commandment the prisoner has disobeyed is written upon his body by the Harrow. This prisoner, for instance"—the officer indicated the man—"will have written on his body: HONOR THY SUPERIORS!"

The explorer glanced at the man; he stood, as the officer pointed him out, with bent head, apparently listening with all his ears in an effort to catch what was being said. Yet the movement of his blubber lips, closely pressed together, showed clearly that he could not understand a word. Many questions were troubling the explorer, but at the sight of the prisoner he asked only:

"Does he know his sentence?" "No," said the officer, eager to go on with his exposition, but the explorer interrupted him: "He doesn't know the sentence that has been passed on him?" "No," said the officer again, pausing a moment as if to let the explorer elaborate his question, and then said: "There would be no point in telling him. He'll learn it on his body." The explorer intended to make no answer, but he felt the prisoner's gaze turned on him; it seemed to ask if he approved such goings on. So he bent forward again, having already leaned back in his chair, and put another question: "But surely he knows that he has been sentenced?" "Nor that either," said the officer, smiling at the explorer as if expecting him to make further surprising remarks. "No," said the explorer, wiping his forehead, "then he can't know either whether his defense was effective?" "He has had no chance of putting up a defense," said the officer, turning his eyes away as if speaking to himself and so sparing the explorer the shame of hearing self-evident matters explained. "But he must have had some chance of defending himself," said the explorer, and rose from his seat.

The officer realized that he was in danger of having his exposition of the apparatus held up for a long time; so he went up to the explorer, took him by the arm, waved a hand towards the condemned man, who was standing very straight now that he had so obviously become the center of attention—the soldier had also given the chain a jerk—and said: "This is how the matter stands. I have been appointed judge in this penal colony. Despite my youth. For I was the former Commandant's assistant in all penal matters and know more about the apparatus than anyone. My guiding principle is this: Guilt is never to be doubted. Other courts cannot follow that principle, for they consist of several opinions and have higher courts to scrutinize them. That is not the case here, or at least, it was not the case in the former Commandant's time. The new man has certainly shown some inclination to interfere with my judgments, but so far I have succeeded in fending him off and will go on succeeding. You wanted to have the case explained; it is quite simple, like all of them. A captain reported to me this morning that this man, who had been assigned to him as a servant and sleeps before his door, had been asleep on duty. It is his duty, you see, to get up every time the hour strikes and salute the captain's door. Not an exacting duty, and very necessary, since he has to be a sentry as well as a servant, and must be alert in both functions. Last night the captain wanted to see if the man was doing his duty. He opened the door as the clock struck two and there was his man curled up asleep. He took his riding whip and lashed him across the face. Instead of getting up and begging pardon, the man caught hold of his master's legs, shook him and cried: 'Throw that whip away or I'll eat you alive.'—That's the evidence. The captain came to me an hour ago, I wrote down his statement and appended the sentence to it. Then I had the man put in chains. That was all quite simple. If I had first called the man before me and interrogated him, things would have got into a confused tangle. He would have told lies, and had I exposed these lies he would have backed them up with more lies, and so on and so forth. As it is, I've got him and I won't let him go.—Is that quite clear now? But we're wasting time, the execution should be beginning and I haven't finished explaining the apparatus yet." He pressed the explorer back into his chair, went up again to the apparatus and began: "As you see, the shape of the Harrow corresponds to the human form; here is the harrow for the torso, here are the harrows for the legs. For the head there is only this one small spike. Is that quite clear?" He bent amiably forward towards the explorer, eager to provide the most comprehensive explanations.

The explorer considered the Harrow with a frown. The explanation of the judicial procedure had not satisfied him. He had to remind himself that this was in any case a penal colony where extraordinary measures were needed and that military discipline must be enforced to the last. He also felt that some hope might be set on the new Commandant, who was apparently of a mind to bring in, although gradually, a new kind of procedure which the officer's narrow mind was incapable of understanding. This train of thought prompted his next question: "Will the Commandant attend the execution?" "It is not certain," said the officer, wincing at the direct question, and his friendly expression darkened. "That is just why we have to lose no time. Much as I dislike it, I shall have to cut my explanations short. But of course tomorrow, when the apparatus has been cleaned—its one drawback is that it gets so messy—I can recapitulate all the details. For the present, then, only the essentials.—When the man lies down on the Bed and it begins to vibrate, the Harrow is lowered onto his body. It regulates itself automatically so that the needles barely touch his skin; once contact is made the steel ribbon stiffens immediately into a rigid band. And then the performance begins. An ignorant onlooker would see no difference between one punishment and another. The Harrow appears to do its work with uniform regularity. As it quivers, its points pierce the skin of the body which is itself quivering from the vibration of the Bed. So that the actual progress of the sentence can be watched, the Harrow is made of glass. Getting the needles fixed in the glass was a technical problem, but after many experiments we overcame the difficulty. No trouble was too great for us to take, you see. And now anyone can look through the glass and watch the inscription taking form on the body. Wouldn't you care to come a little nearer and have a look at the needles?"

The explorer got up slowly, walked across and bent over the Harrow. "You see," said the officer, "there are two kinds of needles arranged in multiple patterns. Each long needle has a short one beside it. The long needle does the writing, and the short needle sprays a jet of water to wash away the blood and keep the inscription clear. Blood and water together are then conducted here through small runnels into this main runnel and down a waste pipe into the pit." With his finger the officer traced the exact course taken by the blood and water. To make the picture as vivid as possible he held both hands below the outlet of the waste pipe as if to catch the outflow, and when he did this the explorer drew back his head and feeling behind him with one hand sought to return to his chair. To his horror he found that the condemned man too had obeyed the officer's invitation to examine the Harrow at close quarters and had followed him. He had pulled forward the sleepy soldier with the chain and was bending over the glass. One could see that his uncertain eyes were trying to perceive what the two gentlemen had been looking at, but since he had not understood the explanation he could not make head or tail of it. He was peering this way and that way. He kept running his eyes along the glass. The explorer wanted to drive him away, since what he was doing was probably culpable. But the officer firmly restrained the explorer with one hand and with the other took a clod of earth from the rampart and threw it at the soldier. He opened his eyes with a jerk, saw what the condemned man had dared to do, let his rifle fall, dug his heels into the ground, dragged his prisoner back so that he stumbled and fell immediately, and then stood looking down at him, watching him struggling and rattling in his chains. "Set him on his feet!" yelled the officer, for he noticed that the explorer's attention was being too much distracted by the prisoner. In fact he was even leaning right across the Harrow, without taking any notice of it, intent only on finding out what was happening to the prisoner. "Be careful with him!" cried the officer again. He ran round the apparatus, himself caught the condemned man under the shoulders and with the soldier's help got him up on his feet, which kept slithering from under him.

"Now I know all about it," said the explorer as the officer came back to him. "All except the most important thing," he answered, seizing the explorer's arm and pointing upwards: "In the Designer are all the cogwheels that control the movements of the Harrow, and this machinery is regulated according to the inscription demanded by the sentence. I am still using the guiding plans drawn by the former Commandant. Here they are"—he extracted some sheets from the leather wallet—"but I'm sorry I can't let you handle them; they are my most precious possessions. Just take a seat and I'll hold them in front of you like this, then you'll be able to see everything quite well." He spread out the first sheet of paper. The explorer would have liked to say something appreciative, but all he could see was a labyrinth of lines crossing and re-crossing each other, which covered the paper so thickly that it was difficult to discern the blank spaces between them. "Read it," said the officer. "I can't," said the explorer. "Yet it's clear enough," said the officer. "It's very ingenious," said the explorer evasively, "but I can't make it out." "Yes," said the officer with a laugh, putting the paper away again, "it's no calligraphy for school children. It needs to be studied closely. I'm quite sure that in the end you would understand it too. Of course the script can't be a simple one; it's not supposed to kill a man straight off, but only after an interval of, on an average, twelve hours; the turning point is reckoned to come at the sixth hour. So there have to be lots and lots of flourishes around the actual script; the script itself runs round the body only in a narrow girdle; the rest of the body is reserved for the embellishments. Can you appreciate now the work accomplished by the Harrow and the whole apparatus?—Just watch it!" He ran up the ladder, turned a wheel, called down: "Look out, keep to one side!" and everything started working. If the wheel had not creaked, it would have been marvelous. The officer, as if surprised by the noise of the wheel, shook his fist at it, then spread out his arms in excuse to the explorer and climbed down rapidly to peer at the working of the machine from below. Something perceptible to no one save himself was still not in order; he clambered up again, did something with both hands in the interior of the Designer, then slid down one of the rods, instead of using the ladder, so as to get down quicker, and with the full force of his lungs, to make himself heard at all in the noise, yelled in the explorer's ear: "Can you follow it? The Harrow is beginning to write; when it finishes the first draft of the inscription on the man's back, the layer of cotton wool begins to roll and slowly turns the body over, to give the Harrow fresh space for writing. Meanwhile the raw part that has been written on lies on the cotton wool, which is specially prepared to staunch the bleeding and so makes all ready for a new deepening of the script. Then these teeth at the edge of the Harrow, as the body turns further round, tear the cotton wool away from the wounds, throw it into the pit, and there is more work for the Harrow. So it keeps on writing deeper and deeper for the whole twelve hours. The first six hours the condemned man stays alive almost as before, he suffers only pain. After two hours the felt gag is taken away, for he has no longer strength to scream. Here, into this electrically heated basin at the head of the bed, some warm rice pap is poured, from which the man, if he feels like it, can take as much as his tongue can lap. Not one of them ever misses the chance. I can remember none, and my experience is extensive. Only about the sixth hour does the man lose all desire to eat. I usually kneel down here at that moment and observe what happens. The man rarely swallows his last mouthful, he only rolls it round his mouth and spits it out into the pit. I have to duck just then or he would spit it in my face. But how quiet he grows at just about the sixth hour! Enlightenment comes to the most dull-witted. It begins around the eyes. From there it radiates. A moment that might tempt one to get under the Harrow oneself. Nothing more happens than that the man begins to understand the inscription, he purses his mouth as if he were listening. You have seen how difficult it is to decipher the script with one's eyes; but our man deciphers it with his wounds. To be sure, that is a hard task; he needs six hours to accomplish it. By that time the Harrow has pierced him quite through and casts him into the pit, where he pitches down upon the blood and water and the cotton wool. Then the judgment has been fulfilled, and we, the soldier and I, bury him."

The explorer had inclined his ear to the officer and with his hands in his jacket pockets watched the machine at work. The condemned man watched it too, but uncomprehendingly. He bent forward a little and was intent on the moving needles when the soldier, at a sign from the officer, slashed through his shirt and trousers from behind with a knife, so that they fell off; he tried to catch at his falling clothes to cover his nakedness, but the soldier lifted him into the air and shook the last remnants from him. The officer stopped the machine, and in the sudden silence the condemned man was laid under the Harrow. The chains were loosened and the straps fastened on instead; in the first moment that seemed almost a relief to the prisoner. And now the Harrow was adjusted a little lower, since he was a thin man. When the needle points touched him a shudder ran over his skin; while the soldier was busy strapping his right hand, he flung out his left hand blindly; but it happened to be in the direction towards where the explorer was standing. The officer kept watching the explorer sideways, as if seeking to read from his face the impression made on him by the execution, which had been at least cursorily explained to him.

The wrist strap broke; probably the soldier had drawn it too tight. The officer had to intervene, the soldier held up the broken piece of strap to show him. So the officer went over to him and said, his face still turned towards the explorer: "This is a very complex machine, it can't be helped that things are breaking or giving way here and there; but one must not thereby allow oneself to be diverted in one's general judgment. In any case, this strap is easily made good; I shall simply use a chain; the delicacy of the vibrations for the right arm will of course be a little impaired." And while he fastened the chains, he added: "The resources for maintaining the machine are now very much reduced. Under the former Commandant I had free access to a sum of money set aside entirely for this purpose. There was a store, too, in which spare parts were kept for repairs of all kinds. I confess I have been almost prodigal with them, I mean in the past, not now as the new Commandant pretends, always looking for an excuse to attack our old way of doing things. Now he has taken charge of the machine money himself, and if I send for a new strap they ask for the broken old strap as evidence, and the new strap takes ten days to appear and then is of shoddy material and not much good. But how I am supposed to work the machine without a strap, that's something nobody bothers about."

The explorer thought to himself: It's always a ticklish matter to intervene decisively in other people's affairs. He was neither a member of the penal colony nor a citizen of the state to which it belonged. Were he to denounce this execution or actually try to stop it, they could say to him: You are a foreigner, mind your own business. He could make no answer to that, unless he were to add that he was amazed at himself in this connection, for he traveled only as an observer, with no intention at all of altering other people's methods of administering justice. Yet here he found himself strongly tempted. The injustice of the procedure and the inhumanity of the execution were undeniable. No one could suppose that he had any selfish interest in the matter, for the condemned man was a complete stranger, not a fellow countryman or even at all sympathetic to him. The explorer himself had recommendations from high quarters, had been received here with great courtesy, and the very fact that he had been invited to attend the execution seemed to suggest that his views would be welcome. And this was all the more likely since the Commandant, as he had heard only too plainly, was no upholder of the procedure and maintained an attitude almost of hostility to the officer.

At that moment the explorer heard the officer cry out in rage. He had just, with considerable difficulty, forced the felt gag into the condemned man's mouth when the man in an irresistible access of nausea shut his eyes and vomited. Hastily the officer snatched him away from the gag and tried to hold his head over the pit; but it was too late, the vomit was running all over the machine. "It's all the fault of that Commandant!" cried the officer, senselessly shaking the brass rods in front, "the machine is befouled like a pigsty." With trembling hands he indicated to the explorer what had happened. "Have I not tried for hours at a time to get the Commandant to understand that the prisoner must fast for a whole day before the execution? But our new, mild doctrine thinks otherwise. The Commandant's ladies stuff the man with sugar candy before he's led off. He has lived on stinking fish his whole life long and now he has to eat sugar candy! But it could still be possible, I should have nothing to say against it, but why won't they get me a new felt gag, which I have been begging for the last three months. How should a man not feel sick when he takes a felt gag into his mouth which more than a hundred men have already slobbered and gnawed in their dying moments?"

The condemned man had laid his head down and looked peaceful; the soldier was busy trying to clean the machine with the prisoner's shirt. The officer advanced towards the explorer, who in some vague presentiment fell back a pace, but the officer seized him by the hand, and drew him to one side. "I should like to exchange a few words with you in confidence," he said, "may I?" "Of course," said the explorer, and listened with downcast eyes.

"This procedure and method of execution, which you are now having the opportunity to admire, has at the moment no longer any open adherents in our colony. I am its sole advocate, and at the same time the sole advocate of the old Commandant's tradition. I can no longer reckon on any further extension of the method; it takes all my energy to maintain it as it is. During the old Commandant's lifetime the colony was full of his adherents; his strength of conviction I still have in some measure, but not an atom of his power; consequently the adherents have skulked out of sight, there are still many of them but none of them will admit it. If you were to go into the teahouse today, on execution day, and listen to what is being said, you would perhaps hear only ambiguous remarks. These would all be made by adherents, but under the present Commandant and his present doctrines they are of no use to me. And now I ask you: because of this Commandant and the women who influence him, is such a piece of work, the work of a lifetime"—he pointed to the machine—"to perish? Ought

one to let that happen? Even if one has only come as a stranger to our island for a few days? But there's no time to lose, an attack of some kind is
impending on my function as judge; conferences are already being held in
the Commandant's office from which I am excluded; even your coming
here today seems to me a significant move; they are cowards and use you as
a screen, you, a stranger.—How different an execution was in the old days!
A whole day before the ceremony the valley was packed with people; they
all came only to look on; early in the morning the Commandant appeared
with his ladies; fanfares roused the whole camp; I reported that everything
was in readiness; the assembled company—no high official dared to absent
himself—arranged itself round the machine; this pile of cane chairs is a
miserable survival from that epoch. The machine was freshly cleaned and
glittering, I got new spare parts for almost every execution. Before hundreds of spectators—all of them standing on tiptoe as far as the heights
there—the condemned man was laid under the Harrow by the Commandant himself. What is left today for a common soldier to do was then my
task, the task of the presiding judge, and was an honor for me. And then
the execution began! No discordant noise spoilt the working of the machine. Many did not care to watch it but lay with closed eyes in the sand;
they all knew: Now Justice is being done. In the silence one heard nothing
but the condemned man's sighs, half muffled by the felt gag. Nowadays the
machine can no longer wring from anyone a sigh louder than the felt gag
can stifle; but in those days the writing needles let drop an acid fluid, which
we're no longer permitted to use. Well, and then came the sixth hour! It
was impossible to grant all the requests to be allowed to watch it from near
by. The Commandant in his wisdom ordained that the children should
have the preference; I, of course, because of my office had the privilege of
always being at hand; often enough I would be squatting there with a small
child in either arm. How we all absorbed the look of transfiguration on the
face of the sufferer, how we bathed our cheeks in the radiance of that justice, achieved at last and fading so quickly! What times these were, my comrade!" The officer had obviously forgotten whom he was addressing; he
had embraced the explorer and laid his head on his shoulder. The explorer
was deeply embarrassed, impatiently he stared over the officer's head. The
soldier had finished his cleaning job and was now pouring rice pap from a
pot into the basin. As soon as the condemned man, who seemed to have recovered entirely, noticed this action he began to reach for the rice with his
tongue. The soldier kept pushing him away, since the rice pap was certainly
meant for a later hour, yet it was just as unfitting that the soldier himself
should thrust his dirty hands into the basin and eat out of it before the
other's avid face.

The officer quickly pulled himself together. "I didn't want to upset you,"
he said. "I know it is impossible to make those days credible now. Anyhow,
the machine is still working and it is still effective in itself. It is effective in

itself even though it stands alone in this valley. And the corpse still falls at the last into the pit with an incomprehensibly gentle wafting motion, even although there are no hundreds of people swarming round like flies as formerly. In those days we had to put a strong fence round the pit; it has long since been torn down."

The explorer wanted to withdraw his face from the officer and looked round him at random. The officer thought he was surveying the valley's desolation; so he seized him by the hands, turned him round to meet his eyes, and asked: "Do you realize the shame of it?"

But the explorer said nothing. The officer left him alone for a little; with legs apart, hands on hips, he stood very still, gazing at the ground. Then he smiled encouragingly at the explorer and said: "I was quite near you yesterday when the Commandant gave you the invitation. I heard him giving it. I know the Commandant. I divined at once what he was after. Although he is powerful enough to take measures against me, he doesn't dare to do it yet, but he certainly means to use your verdict against me, the verdict of an illustrious foreigner. He has calculated it carefully: this is your second day on the island, you did not know the old Commandant and his ways, you are conditioned by European ways of thought, perhaps you object on principle to capital punishment in general and to such mechanical instruments of death in particular, besides you will see that the execution has no support from the public, a shabby ceremony—carried out with a machine already somewhat old and worn—now, taking all that into consideration, would it not be likely (so thinks the Commandant) that you might disapprove of my methods? And if you disapprove, you wouldn't conceal the fact (I'm still speaking from the Commandant's point of view), for you are a man to feel confidence in your own well-tried conclusions. True, you have seen and learned to appreciate the peculiarities of many peoples, and so you would not be likely to take a strong line against our proceedings, as you might do in your own country. But the Commandant has no need of that. A casual, even an unguarded remark will be enough. It doesn't even need to represent what you really think, so long as it can be used speciously to serve his purpose. He will try to prompt you with sly questions, of that I am certain. And his ladies will sit around you and prick up their ears; you might be saying something like this: 'In our country we have a different criminal procedure,' or 'In our country the prisoner is interrogated before he is sentenced,' or 'We haven't used torture since the Middle Ages.' All these statements are as true as they seem natural to you, harmless remarks that pass no judgment on my methods. But how would the Commandant react to them? I can see him, our good Commandant, pushing his chair away immediately and rushing onto the balcony, I can see his ladies streaming out after him. I can hear his voice—the ladies call it a voice of thunder—well, and this is what he says: 'A famous Western investigator, sent out to study criminal procedure in all the countries of the world, has just said that our old tradition of administering justice is inhumane. Such a verdict from such a personality makes it impossible for me to countenance these methods any longer. Therefore from this very day I ordain . . .' and so on. You may want to interpose that you never said any such thing, that you never called my methods inhumane; on the contrary your profound experience leads you to believe they are most humane and most in consonance with human dignity, and you admire the machine greatly—but it will be too late; you won't even get onto the balcony, crowded as it will be with ladies; you may try to draw attention to yourself; you may want to scream out; but a lady's hand will close your lips—and I and the work of the old Commandant will be done for."

The explorer had to suppress a smile; so easy, then, was the task he had felt to be so difficult. He said evasively: "You overestimate my influence; the Commandant has read my letters of recommendation, he knows that I am no expert in criminal procedure. If I were to give an opinion, it would be as a private individual, an opinion no more influential than that of any ordinary person, and in any case much less influential than that of the Commandant, who, I am given to understand, has very extensive powers in this penal colony. If his attitude to your procedure is as definitely hostile as you believe, then I fear the end of your tradition is at hand, even without any humble assistance from me."

Had it dawned on the officer at last? No, he still did not understand. He shook his head emphatically, glanced briefly round at the condemned man and the soldier, who both flinched away from the rice, came close up to the explorer and without looking at his face but fixing his eye on some spot on his coat said in a lower voice than before: "You don't know the Commandant; you feel yourself—forgive the expression—a kind of outsider so far as all of us are concerned; yet, believe me, your influence cannot be rated too highly. I was simply delighted when I heard that you were to attend the execution all by yourself. The Commandant arranged it to aim a blow at me, but I shall turn it to my advantage. Without being distracted by lying whispers and contemptuous glances—which could not have been avoided had a crowd of people attended the execution—you have heard my explanations, seen the machine and are now in course of watching the execution. You have doubtless already formed your own judgment; if you still have some small uncertainties the sight of the execution will resolve them. And now I make this request to you: help me against the Commandant!"

The explorer would not let him go on. "How could I do that?" he cried. "It's quite impossible. I can neither help nor hinder you."

"Yes, you can," the officer said. The explorer saw with a certain apprehension that the officer had clenched his fists. "Yes, you can," repeated the officer, still more insistently. "I have a plan that is bound to succeed. You believe your influence is insufficient. I know that it is sufficient. But even granted that you are right, is it not necessary, for the sake of preserving this tradition, to try even what might prove insufficient? Listen to my plan, then. The first thing necessary for you to carry it out is to be as reticent as possible today regarding your verdict on these proceedings. Unless you are asked a direct question you must say nothing at all; but what you do say must be brief and general; let it be remarked that you would prefer not to discuss the matter, that you are out of patience with it, that if you are to let yourself go you would use strong language. I don't ask you to tell any lies; by no means; you should only give curt answers, such as: 'Yes, I saw the execution,' or 'Yes, I had it explained to me.' Just that, nothing more. There are grounds enough for any impatience you betray, although not such as will occur to the Commandant. Of course, he will mistake your meaning and interpret it to please himself. That's what my plan depends on. Tomorrow in the Commandant's office there is to be a large conference of all the high administrative officials, the Commandant presiding. Of course the Commandant is the kind of man to have turned these conferences into public spectacles. He has had a gallery built that is always packed with spectators. I am compelled to take part in the conferences, but they make me sick with disgust. Now, whatever happens, you will certainly be invited to this conference; if you behave today as I suggest the invitation will become an urgent request. But if for some mysterious reason you're not invited, you'll have to ask for an invitation; there's no doubt of your getting it then. So tomorrow you're sitting in the Commandant's box with the ladies. He keeps looking up to make sure you're there. After various trivial and ridiculous matters, brought in merely to impress the audience—mostly harbor works, nothing but harbor works!—our judicial procedure comes up for discussion too. If the Commandant doesn't introduce it, or not soon enough, I'll see that it's mentioned. I'll stand up and report that today's execution has taken place. Quite briefly, only a statement. Such a statement is not usual, but I shall make it. The Commandant thanks me, as always, with an amiable smile, and then he can't restrain himself, he seizes the excellent opportunity. 'It has just been reported,' he will say, or words to that effect, 'that an execution has taken place. I should like merely to add that this execution was witnessed by the famous explorer who has, as you all know, honored our colony so greatly by his visit to us. His presence at today's session of our conference also contributes to the importance of this occasion. Should we not now ask the famous explorer to give us his verdict on our traditional mode of execution and the procedure that leads up to it?' Of course there is loud applause, general agreement, I am more insistent than anyone. The Commandant bows to you and says: 'Then in the name of the assembled company, I put the question to you.' And now you advance to the front of the box. Lay your hands where everyone can see them, or the ladies will catch them and press your fingers.—And then at last you can speak out. I don't know how I'm going to endure the tension of waiting for that moment. Don't put any restraint on yourself when you make your speech, publish the truth aloud, lean over the front of the box, shout, yes, indeed, shout your verdict, your unshakable conviction, at the Commandant. Yet perhaps you wouldn't care to do that, it's not in keeping with your character, in your country perhaps people do these things differently, well, that's all right too, that will be quite as effective, don't even stand up, just say a few words, even in a whisper, so that only the officials beneath you will hear them, that will be quite enough, you don't even need to mention the lack of public support for the execution, the creaking wheel, the broken strap, the filthy gag of felt, no, I'll take all that upon me, and, believe me, if my indictment doesn't drive him out of the conference hall, it will force him to his knees to make the acknowledgment: Old Commandant, I humble myself before you.—That is my plan; will you help me to carry it out? But of course you are willing, what is more, you must." And the officer seized the explorer by both arms and gazed, breathing heavily, into his face. He had shouted the last sentence so loudly that even the soldier and the condemned man were startled into attending; they had not understood a word but they stopped eating and looked over at the explorer, chewing their previous mouthfuls.

From the very beginning the explorer had no doubt about what answer he must give; in his lifetime he had experienced too much to have any uncertainty here; he was fundamentally honorable and unafraid. And yet now, facing the soldier and the condemned man, he did hesitate, for as long as it took to draw one breath. At last, however, he said, as he had to: "No." The officer blinked several times but did not turn his eyes away. "Would you like me to explain?" asked the explorer. The officer nodded wordlessly. "I do not approve of your procedure," said the explorer then, "even before you took me into your confidence—of course I shall never in any circumstances betray your confidence—I was already wondering whether it would be my duty to intervene and whether my intervention would have the slightest chance of success. I realized to whom I ought to turn: to the Commandant, of course. You have made that fact even clearer, but without having strengthened my resolution; on the contrary, your sincere conviction has touched me, even though it cannot influence my judgment."

The officer remained mute, turned to the machine, caught hold of a brass rod, and then, leaning back a little, gazed at the Designer as if to assure himself that all was in order. The soldier and the condemned man seemed to have come to some understanding; the condemned man was making signs to the soldier, difficult though his movements were because of the tight straps; the soldier was bending down to him; the condemned man whispered something and the soldier nodded.

The explorer followed the officer and said: "You don't know yet what I mean to do. I shall tell the Commandant what I think of the procedure, certainly, but not at a public conference, only in private; nor shall I stay here long enough to attend any conference; I am going away early tomorrow morning, or at least embarking on my ship."

It did not look as if the officer had been listening. "So you did not find the procedure convincing," he said to himself and smiled, as an old man smiles at childish nonsense and yet pursues his own meditations behind the smile.

"Then the time has come," he said at last, and suddenly looked at the explorer with bright eyes that held some challenge, some appeal for cooperation. "The time for what?" asked the explorer uneasily, but got no answer.

"You are free," said the officer to the condemned man in the native tongue. The man did not believe it at first. "Yes, you are set free," said the officer. For the first time the condemned man's face woke to real animation. Was it true? Was it only a caprice of the officer's that might change again? Had the foreign explorer begged him off? What was it? One could read these questions on his face. But not for long. Whatever it might be, he wanted to be really free if he might, and he began to struggle so far as the Harrow permitted him.

"You'll burst my straps," cried the officer. "Lie still! We'll soon loosen them." And signing the soldier to help him, he set about doing so. The condemned man laughed wordlessly to himself, now he turned his face left towards the officer, now right towards the soldier, nor did he forget the explorer.

"Draw him out," ordered the officer. Because of the Harrow this had to be done with some care. The condemned man had already torn himself a little in the back through his impatience.

From now on, however, the officer paid hardly any attention to him. He went up to the explorer, pulled out the small leather wallet again, turned over the papers in it, found the one he wanted and showed it to the explorer. "Read it," he said. "I can't," said the explorer, "I told you before that I can't make out these scripts." "Try taking a close look at it," said the officer and came quite near to the explorer so that they might read it together. But when even that proved useless, he outlined the script with his little finger, holding it high above the paper as if the surface dared not be sullied by touch, in order to help the explorer to follow the script in that way. The explorer did make an effort, meaning to please the officer in this respect at least, but he was quite unable to follow. Now the officer began to spell it, letter by letter, and then read out the words. " 'BE JUST!' is what is written there," he said. "Surely you can read it now." The explorer bent so close to the paper that the officer feared he might touch it and drew it farther away; the explorer made no remark, yet it was clear that he still could not decipher it. " 'BE JUST!' is what is written there," said the officer once more. "Maybe," said the explorer, "I am prepared to believe you." "Well, then," said the officer, at least partly satisfied, and climbed up the ladder with the paper; very carefully he laid it inside the Designer and seemed to be changing the disposition of all the cogwheels; it was a troublesome piece of work and must have involved wheels that were extremely small, for sometimes the officer's head vanished altogether from sight inside the Designer, so precisely did he have to regulate the machinery.

The explorer, down below, watched the labor uninterruptedly, his neck grew stiff and his eyes smarted from the glare of sunshine over the sky. The soldier and the condemned man were now busy together. The man's shirt and trousers, which were already lying in the pit, were fished out by the point of the soldier's bayonet. The shirt was abominably dirty and its owner washed it in the bucket of water. When he put on the shirt and trousers both he and the soldier could not help guffawing, for the garments were of course slit up behind. Perhaps the condemned man felt it incumbent on him to amuse the soldier, he turned round and round in his slashed garments before the soldier, who squatted on the ground beating his knees with mirth. All the same, they presently controlled their mirth out of respect for the gentlemen.

When the officer had at length finished his task aloft, he surveyed the machinery in all its details once more, with a smile, but this time shut the lid of the Designer, which had stayed open till now, climbed down, looked into the pit and then at the condemned man, noting with satisfaction that the clothing had been taken out, then went over to wash his hands in the water bucket, perceived too late that it was disgustingly dirty, was unhappy because he could not wash his hands, in the end thrust them into the sand— this alternative did not please him, but he had to put up with it—then stood upright and began to unbutton his uniform jacket. As he did this, the two ladies' handkerchiefs he had tucked under his collar fell into his hands. "Here are your handkerchiefs," he said, and threw them to the condemned man. And to the explorer he said in explanation: "A gift from the ladies."

In spite of the obvious haste with which he was discarding first his uniform jacket and then all his clothing, he handled each garment with loving care, he even ran his fingers caressingly over the silver lace on the jacket and shook a tassel into place. This loving care was certainly out of keeping with the fact that as soon as he had a garment off he flung it at once with a kind of unwilling jerk into the pit. The last thing left to him was his short sword with the sword belt. He drew it out of the scabbard, broke it, then gathered all together, the bits of the sword, the scabbard and the belt, and flung them so violently down that they clattered into the pit.

Now he stood naked there. The explorer bit his lips and said nothing. He knew very well what was going to happen, but had no right to obstruct the officer in anything. If the judicial procedure which the officer cherished were really so near its end—possibly as a result of his own intervention, as to which he felt himself pledged—then the officer was doing the right thing; in his place the explorer would not have acted otherwise.

The soldier and the condemned man did not understand at first what was happening; at first they were not even looking on. The condemned man was gleeful at having got the handkerchiefs back, but he was not allowed to enjoy them for long, since the soldier snatched them with a sudden, unexpected grab. Now the condemned man in turn was trying to twitch them from under the belt where the soldier had tucked them, but the soldier was on his guard. So they were wrestling, half in jest. Only when the officer stood quite naked was their attention caught. The condemned man especially seemed struck with the notion that some great change was impending. What had happened to him was now going to happen to the officer. Perhaps even to the very end. Apparently the foreign explorer had given the order for it. So this was revenge. Although he himself had not suffered to the end, he was to be revenged to the end. A broad, silent grin now appeared on his face and stayed there all the rest of the time.

The officer, however, had turned to the machine. It had been clear enough previously that he understood the machine well, but now it was almost staggering to see how he managed it and how it obeyed him. His hand had only to approach the Harrow for it to rise and sink several times till it was adjusted to the right position for receiving him; he touched only the edge of the Bed and already it was vibrating; the felt gag came to meet his mouth, one could see that the officer was really reluctant to take it but he shrank from it only a moment, soon he submitted and received it. Everything was ready, only the straps hung down at the sides, yet they were obviously unnecessary, the officer did not need to be fastened down. Then the condemned man noticed the loose straps, in his opinion the execution was incomplete unless the straps were buckled, he gestured eagerly to the soldier and they ran together to strap the officer down. The latter had already stretched out one foot to push the lever that started the Designer; he saw the two men coming up; so he drew his foot back and let himself be buckled in. But now he could not reach the lever; neither the soldier nor the condemned man would be able to find it, and the explorer was determined not to lift a finger. It was not necessary; as soon as the straps were fastened the machine began to work; the Bed vibrated, the needles flickered above the skin, the Harrow rose and fell. The explorer had been staring at it quite a while before he remembered that a wheel in the Designer should have been creaking; but everything was quiet, not even the slightest hum could be heard.

Because it was working so silently the machine simply escaped one's attention. The explorer observed the soldier and the condemned man. The latter was the more animated of the two, everything in the machine interested him, now he was bending down and now stretching up on tiptoe, his forefinger was extended all the time pointing out details to the soldier. This annoyed the explorer. He was resolved to stay till the end, but he could not bear the sight of these two. "Go back home," he said. The soldier would have been willing enough, but the condemned man took the order as a punishment. With clasped hands he implored to be allowed to stay, and when the explorer shook his head and would not relent, he even went down on his knees. The explorer saw that it was no use merely giving orders; he was on the point of going over and driving them away. At that moment he heard a noise above him in the Designer. He looked up. Was that cogwheel going to make trouble after all? But it was something quite different. Slowly the lid of the Designer rose up and then clicked wide open. The teeth of a cogwheel showed themselves and rose higher, soon the whole wheel was visible; it was as if some enormous force were squeezing the Designer so that there was no longer room for the wheel; the wheel moved up till it came to the very edge of the Designer, fell down, rolled along the sand a little on its rim and then lay flat. But a second wheel was already rising after it, followed by many others, large and small and indistinguishably minute, the same thing happened to all of them, at every moment one imagined the Designer must now really be empty, but another complex of numerous wheels was already rising into sight, falling down, trundling along the sand and lying flat. This phenomenon made the condemned man completely forget the explorer's command, the cogwheels fascinated him, he was always trying to catch one and at the same time urging the soldier to help, but always drew back his hand in alarm, for another wheel always came hopping along which, at least on its first advance, scared him off.

The explorer, on the other hand, felt greatly troubled; the machine was obviously going to pieces; its silent working was a delusion; he had a feeling that he must now stand by the officer, since the officer was no longer able to look after himself. But while the tumbling cogwheels absorbed his whole attention he had forgotten to keep an eye on the rest of the machine; now that the last cogwheel had left the Designer, however, he bent over the Harrow and had a new and still more unpleasant surprise. The Harrow was not writing, it was only jabbing, and the bed was not turning the body over but only bringing it up quivering against the needles. The explorer wanted to do something, if possible, to bring the whole machine to a standstill, for this was no exquisite torture such as the officer desired, this was plain murder. He stretched out his hands. But at that moment the Harrow rose with the body spitted on it and moved to the side, as it usually did only when the twelfth hour had come. Blood was flowing in a hundred streams, not mingled with water, the water jets too had failed to function. And now the last action failed to fulfil itself, the body did not drop off the long needles, streaming with blood it went on hanging over the pit without falling into it. The Harrow tried to move back to its old position, but as if it had itself noticed that it had not yet got rid of its burden it stuck after all where it was, over the pit. "Come and help!" cried the explorer to the other two, and himself seized the officer's feet. He wanted to push against the feet while the others seized the head from the opposite side and so the officer might be slowly eased off the needles. But the other two could not make up their minds to come; the condemned man actually turned away; the explorer had to go over to them and force them into position at the officer's head. And here, almost against his will, he had to look at the face of the corpse. It was as it had been in life; no sign was visible of the promised redemption; what the others had found in the machine the officer had not found; the lips were firmly pressed together, the eyes were open, with the same expression as in life, the look was calm and convinced, through the forehead went the point of the great iron spike.

As the explorer, with the soldier and the condemned man behind him, reached the first houses of the colony, the soldier pointed to one of them and said: "There is the teahouse."

In the ground floor of the house was a deep, low, cavernous space, its walls and ceiling blackened with smoke. It was open to the road all along its length. Although this teahouse was very little different from the other houses of the colony, which were all very dilapidated, even up to the Commandant's palatial headquarters, it made on the explorer the impression of a historic tradition of some kind, and he felt the power of past days. He went near to it, followed by his companions, right up between the empty tables which stood in the street before it, and breathed the cool, heavy air that came from the interior. "The old man's buried here," said the soldier. "The priest wouldn't let him lie in the churchyard. Nobody knew where to bury him for a while, but in the end they buried him here. The officer never told you about that, for sure, because of course that's what he was most ashamed of. He even tried several times to dig the old man up by night, but he was always chased away." "Where is the grave?" asked the explorer, who found it impossible to believe the soldier. At once both of them, the soldier and the condemned man, ran before him pointing with outstretched hands in the direction where the grave should be. They led the explorer right up to the back wall, where guests were sitting at a few tables. They were apparently dock laborers, strong men with short, glistening, full black beards. None had a jacket, their shirts were torn, they were poor, humble creatures. As the explorer drew near, some of them got up, pressed close to the wall, and stared at him. "It's a foreigner," ran the whisper around him. "He wants to see the grave." They pushed one of the tables aside, and under it there was really a gravestone. It was a simple stone, low enough to be covered by a table. There was an inscription on it in very small letters, the explorer had to kneel down to read it. This was what it said: "Here rests the old Commandant. His adherents, who now must be nameless, have dug this grave and set up this stone. There is a prophecy that after a certain number of years the Commandant will rise again and lead his adherents from this house to recover the colony. Have faith and wait!" When the explorer had read this and risen to his feet he saw all the bystanders around him smiling, as if they too had read the inscription, had found it ridiculous and were expecting him to agree with them. The explorer ignored this, distributed a few coins among them, waiting till the table was pushed over the grave again, quitted the teahouse and made for the harbor.

The soldier and the condemned man had found some acquaintances in the teahouse, who detained them. But they must have soon shaken them off, for the explorer was only halfway down the long flight of steps leading to the boats when they came rushing after him. Probably they wanted to force him at the last minute to take them with him. While he was bargaining below with a ferryman to row him to the steamer, the two of them came headlong down the steps, in silence, for they did not dare to shout. But by the time they reached the foot of the steps the explorer was already in the boat, and the ferryman was just casting off from the shore. They could have jumped into the boat, but the explorer lifted a heavy knotted rope from the floor boards, threatened them with it and so kept them from attempting the leap.

and were expecting him to agree with them. The explorer ignored this, distributed a few coins among them, waiting till the table was pushed over the
grave again, quitted the teahouse, and made for the harbor.

The soldier and the condemned man had found some acquaintances in
the teahouse who detained them, but they must have soon shaken them
off, for the explorer was only halfway down the long flight of steps leading
to the boats when they came rushing after him. Probably they wanted to
force him at the last minute to take them with him. While he was bargaining below with a ferryman to row him to the steamer, the two of them came
headlong down the steps, in silence, for they did not dare to shout. But by
the time they reached the foot of the steps the explorer was already in the
boat, and the ferryman was just casting off from the shore. They could
have jumped into the boat, but the explorer lifted a heavy knotted rope

No Name Woman

MAXINE HONG KINGSTON

"You must not tell anyone," my mother said, "what I am about to tell you.
In China your father had a sister who killed herself. She jumped into the
family well. We say that your father has all brothers because it is as if she
had never been born.

"In 1924 just a few days after our village celebrated seventeen hurry-up
weddings—to make sure that every young man who went 'out on the road'
would responsibly come home—your father and his brothers and your
grandfather and his brothers and your aunt's new husband sailed for
America, the Gold Mountain. It was your grandfather's last trip. Those
lucky enough to get contracts waved good-bye from the decks. They fed
and guarded the stowaways and helped them off in Cuba, New York, Bali,
Hawaii. "We'll meet in California next year," they said. All of them sent
money home.

"I remember looking at your aunt one day when she and I were dressing;
I had not noticed before that she had such a protruding melon of a stomach. But I did not think, 'She's pregnant,' until she began to look like other
pregnant women, her shirt pulling and the white tops of her black pants
showing. She could not have been pregnant, you see, because her husband
had been gone for years. No one said anything. We did not discuss it. In
early summer she was ready to have the child, long after the time when it
could have been possible.

"The village had also been counting. On the night the baby was to be
born the villagers raided our house. Some were crying. Like a great saw,
teeth strung with lights, files of people walked zigzag across our land, tearing the rice. Their lanterns doubled in the disturbed black water, which
drained away through the broken bunds. As the villagers closed in, we
could see that some of them, probably men and women we knew well, wore

558

white masks. The people with long hair hung it over their faces. Women with short hair made it stand up on end. Some had tied white bands around their foreheads, arms, and legs.

"At first they threw mud and rocks at the house. Then they threw eggs and began slaughtering our stock. We could hear the animals scream their deaths—the roosters, the pigs, a last great roar from the ox. Familiar wild heads flared in our night windows; the villagers encircled us. Some of the faces stopped to peer at us, their eyes rushing like searchlights. The hands flattened against the panes, framed heads, and left red prints.

"The villagers broke in the front and the back doors at the same time, even though we had not locked the doors against them. Their knives dripped with the blood of our animals. They smeared blood on the doors and walls. One woman swung a chicken, whose throat she had slit, splattering blood in red arcs about her. We stood together in the middle of our house, in the family hall with the pictures and tables of the ancestors around us, and looked straight ahead.

"At that time the house had only two wings. When the men came back, we would build two more to enclose our courtyard and a third one to begin a second courtyard. The villagers pushed through both wings, even your grandparents' rooms, to find your aunt's, which was also mine until the men returned. From this room a new wing for one of the younger families would grow. They ripped up her clothes and shoes and broke her combs, grinding them underfoot. They tore her work from the loom. They scattered the cooking fire and rolled the new weaving in it. We could hear them in the kitchen breaking our bowls and banging the pots. They overturned the great waist-high earthenware jugs; duck eggs, pickled fruits, vegetables burst out and mixed in acrid torrents. The old woman from the next field swept a broom through the air and loosed the spirits-of-the-broom over our heads. 'Pig.' 'Ghost.' 'Pig,' they sobbed and scolded while they ruined our house.

"When they left, they took sugar and oranges to bless themselves. They cut pieces from the dead animals. Some of them took bowls that were not broken and clothes that were not torn. Afterward we swept up the rice and sewed it back up into sacks. But the smells from the spilled preserves lasted. Your aunt gave birth in the pigsty that night. The next morning when I went for the water, I found her and the baby plugging up the family well.

"Don't let your father know that I told you. He denies her. Now that you have started to menstruate, what happened to her could happen to you. Don't humiliate us. You wouldn't like to be forgotten as if you had never been born. The villagers are watchful."

Whenever she had to warn us about life, my mother told stories that ran like this one, a story to grow up on. She tested our strength to establish realities. Those in the emigrant generations who could not reassert brute survival died young and far from home. Those of us in the first American generations have had to figure out how the invisible world the emigrants built around our childhoods fit in solid America.

The emigrants confused the gods by diverting their curses, misleading them with crooked streets and false names. They must try to confuse their offspring as well, who, I suppose, threaten them in similar ways—always trying to get things straight, always trying to name the unspeakable. The Chinese I know hide their names; sojourners take new names when their lives change and guard their real names with silence.

Chinese-Americans, when you try to understand what things in you are Chinese, how do you separate what is peculiar to childhood, to poverty, insanities, one family, your mother who marked your growing with stories, from what is Chinese? What is Chinese tradition and what is the movies?

If I want to learn what clothes my aunt wore, whether flashy or ordinary, I would have to begin, "Remember Father's drowned-in-the-well sister?" I cannot ask that. My mother has told me once and for all the useful parts. She will add nothing unless powered by Necessity, a riverbank that guides her life. She plants vegetable gardens rather than lawns; she carries the odd-shaped tomatoes home from the fields and eats food left for the gods.

Whenever we did frivolous things, we used up energy; we flew high kites. We children came up off the ground over the melting cones our parents brought home from work and the American movie on New Year's Day—*Oh, You Beautiful Doll* with Betty Grable one year, and *She Wore a Yellow Ribbon* with John Wayne another year. After the one carnival ride each, we paid in guilt; our tired father counted his change on the dark walk home.

Adultery is extravagance. Could people who hatch their own chicks and eat the embryos and the heads for delicacies and boil the feet in vinegar for party food, leaving only the gravel, eating even the gizzard lining—could such people engender a prodigal aunt? To be a woman, to have a daughter in starvation time was a waste enough. My aunt could not have been the lone romantic who gave up everything for sex. Women in the old China did not choose. Some man had commanded her to lie with him and be his secret evil. I wonder whether he masked himself when he joined the raid on her family.

Perhaps she encountered him in the fields or on the mountain where the daughters-in-law collected fuel. Or perhaps he first noticed her in the marketplace. He was not a stranger because the village housed no strangers. She had to have dealings with him other than sex. Perhaps he worked an adjoining field, or he sold her the cloth for the dress she sewed and wore. His demand must have surprised, then terrified her. She obeyed him; she always did as she was told.

When the family found a young man in the next village to be her husband, she stood tractably beside the best rooster, his proxy, and promised before they met that she would be his forever. She was lucky that he was her age and she would be the first wife, an advantage secure now. The night she first saw him, he had sex with her. Then he left for America. She had almost forgotten what he looked like. When she tried to envision him, she only saw the black and white face in the group photograph the men had had taken before leaving.

The other man was not, after all, much different from her husband. They both gave orders: she followed. "If you tell your family, I'll beat you. I'll kill you. Be here again next week." No one talked sex, ever. And she might have separated the rapes from the rest of living if only she did not have to buy her oil from him or gather wood in the same forest. I want her fear to have lasted just as long as rape lasted so that the fear could have been contained. No drawn-out fear. But women at sex hazarded birth and hence lifetimes. The fear did not stop but permeated everywhere. She told the man, "I think I'm pregnant." He organized the raid against her.

On nights when my mother and father talked about their life back home, sometimes they mentioned an "outcast table" whose business they still seemed to be settling, their voices tight. In a commensal tradition, where food is precious, the powerful older people made wrongdoers eat alone. Instead of letting them start separate new lives like the Japanese, who could become samurais and geishas, the Chinese family, faces averted but eyes glowering sideways, hung on to the offenders and fed them leftovers. My aunt must have lived in the same house as my parents and eaten at an outcast table. My mother spoke about the raid as if she had seen it, when she and my aunt, a daughter-in-law to a different household, should not have been living together at all. Daughters-in-law lived with their husbands' parents, not their own; a synonym for marriage in Chinese is "taking a daughter-in-law." Her husband's parents could have sold her, mortgaged her, stoned her. But they had sent her back to her own mother and father, a mysterious act hinting at disgraces not told me. Perhaps they had thrown her out to deflect the avengers.

She was the only daughter; her four brothers went with her father, husband, and uncles "out on the road" and for some years became western men. When the goods were divided among the family, three of the brothers took land, and the youngest, my father, chose an education. After my grandparents gave their daughter away to her husband's family, they had dispensed all the adventure and all the property. They expected her alone to keep the traditional ways, which her brothers, now among the barbarians, could fumble without detection. The heavy, deep-rooted women were to maintain the past against the flood, safe for returning. But the rare urge west had fixed upon our family, and so my aunt crossed boundaries not delineated in space.

The work of preservation demands that the feelings playing about in one's guts not be turned into action. Just watch their passing like cherry blossoms. But perhaps my aunt, my forerunner, caught in a slow life, let dreams grow and fade and after some months or years went toward what persisted. Fear at the enormities of the forbidden kept her desires delicate, wire and bone. She looked at a man because she liked the way the hair was tucked behind his ears, or she liked the question-mark line of a long torso curving at the shoulder and straight at the hip. For warm eyes or a soft voice or a slow walk—that's all—a few hairs, a line, a brightness, a sound, a pace, she gave up family. She offered us up for a charm that vanished with tiredness, a pigtail that didn't toss when the wind died. Why, the wrong lighting could erase the dearest thing about him.

It could very well have been, however, that my aunt did not take subtle enjoyment of her friend, but, a wild woman, kept rollicking company. Imagining her free with sex doesn't fit, though. I don't know any women like that, or men either. Unless I see her life branching into mine, she gives me no ancestral help.

To sustain her being in love, she often worked at herself in the mirror, guessing at the colors and shapes that would interest him, changing them frequently in order to hit on the right combination. She wanted him to look back.

On a farm near the sea, a woman who tended her appearance reaped a reputation for eccentricity. All the married women blunt-cut their hair in flaps about their ears or pulled it back in tight buns. No nonsense. Neither style blew easily into heart-catching tangles. And at their weddings they displayed themselves in their long hair for the last time. "It brushed the backs of my knees," my mother tells me. "It was braided, and even so, it brushed the backs of my knees."

At the mirror my aunt combed individuality into her bob. A bun could have been contrived to escape into black streamers blowing in the wind or in quiet wisps about her face, but only the older women in our picture album wear buns. She brushed her hair back from her forehead, tucking the flaps behind her ears. She looped a piece of thread, knotted into a circle between her index fingers and thumbs, and ran the double strand across her forehead. When she closed her fingers as if she were making a pair of shadow geese bite, the string twisted together catching the little hairs. Then she pulled the thread away from her skin, ripping the hairs out neatly, her eyes watering from the needles of pain. Opening her fingers, she cleaned the thread, then rolled it along her hairline and the tops of her eyebrows. My mother did the same to me and my sisters and herself. I used to believe that the expression "caught by the short hairs" meant a captive held with a depilatory string. It especially hurt at the temples, but my mother said we were lucky we didn't have to have our feet bound when we were seven. Sisters used to sit on their beds and cry together, she said, as their mothers or their slaves removed the bandages for a few minutes each night and let the blood gush back into their veins. I hope that the man my aunt loved appreciated a smooth brow, that he wasn't just a tits-and-ass man.

Once my aunt found a freckle on her chin, at a spot that the almanac said predestined her for unhappiness. She dug it out with a hot needle and washed the wound with peroxide.

More attention to her looks than these pullings of hairs and pickings at spots would have caused gossip among the villagers. They owned work clothes and good clothes, and they wore good clothes for feasting the new seasons. But since a woman combing her hair hexes beginnings, my aunt rarely found an occasion to look her best. Women looked like great sea snails—the corded wood, babies, and laundry they carried were the whorls on their backs. The Chinese did not admire a bent back; goddesses and warriors stood straight. Still there must have been a marvelous freeing of beauty when a worker laid down her burden and stretched and arched.

Such commonplace loveliness, however, was not enough for my aunt. She dreamed of a lover for the fifteen days of New Year's, the time for families to exchange visits, money, and food. She plied her secret comb. And sure enough she cursed the year, the family, the village, and herself.

Even as her hair lured her imminent lover, many other men looked at her. Uncles, cousins, nephews, brothers would have looked, too, had they been home between journeys. Perhaps they had already been restraining their curiosity, and they left, fearful that their glances, like a field of nesting birds, might be startled and caught. Poverty hurt, and that was their first reason for leaving. But another, final reason for leaving the crowded house was the never-said.

She may have been unusually beloved, the precious only daughter, spoiled and mirror gazing because of the affection the family lavished on her. When her husband left, they welcomed the chance to take her back from the in-laws; she could live like the little daughter for just a while longer. There are stories that my grandfather was different from other people, "crazy ever since the little Jap bayoneted him in the head." He used to put his naked penis on the dinner table, laughing. And one day he brought home a baby girl, wrapped up inside his brown western-style greatcoat. He had traded one of his sons, probably my father, the youngest, for her. My grandmother made him trade back. When he finally got a daughter of his own, he doted on her. They must have all loved her, except perhaps my father, the only brother who never went back to China, having once been traded for a girl.

Brothers and sisters, newly men and women, had to efface their sexual color and present plain miens. Disturbing hair and eyes, a smile like no other threatened the ideal of five generations living under one roof. To focus blurs, people shouted face to face and yelled from room to room. The immigrants I know have loud voices, unmodulated to American tones even after years away from the village where they called their friendships out across the fields. I have not been able to stop my mother's screams in public libraries or over telephones. Walking erect (knees straight, toes pointed forward, not pigeon-toed, which is Chinese-feminine) and speaking in an inaudible voice, I have tried to turn myself American-feminine. Chinese communication was loud, public. Only sick people had to whisper. But at the dinner table, where the family members came nearest one another, no one could talk, not the outcasts nor any eaters. Every word that falls from the mouth is a coin lost. Silently they gave and accepted food with both hands. A preoccupied child who took his bowl with one hand got a sideways glare. A complete moment of total attention is due everyone alike. Children and lovers have no singularity here, but my aunt used a secret voice, a separate attentiveness.

She kept the man's name to herself throughout her labor and dying; she did not accuse him that he be punished with her. To save her inseminator's name she gave silent birth.

He may have been somebody in her own household, but intercourse with a man outside the family would have been no less abhorrent. All the village were kinsmen, and the titles shouted in loud country voices never let kinship be forgotten. Any man within visiting distance would have been neutralized as a lover—"brother," "younger brother," "older brother"—one hundred and fifteen relationship titles. Parents researched birth charts probably not so much to assure good fortune as to circumvent incest in a population that has but one hundred surnames. Everybody has eight million relatives. How useless then sexual mannerisms, how dangerous.

As if it came from an atavism deeper than fear, I used to add "brother" silently to boys' names. It hexed the boys, who would or would not ask me to dance, and made them less scary and as familiar and deserving of benevolence as girls.

But, of course, I hexed myself also—no dates. I should have stood up, both arms waving, and shouted out across libraries, "Hey, you! Love me back." I had no idea, though, how to make attraction selective, how to control its direction and magnitude. If I made myself American-pretty so that the five or six Chinese boys in the class fell in love with me, everyone else— the Caucasian, Negro, and Japanese boys—would too. Sisterliness, dignified and honorable, made much more sense.

Attraction eludes control so stubbornly that whole societies designed to organize relationships among people cannot keep order, not even when they bind people to one another from childhood and raise them together. Among the very poor and the wealthy, brothers married their adopted sisters, like doves. Our family allowed some romance, paying adult brides' prices and providing dowries so that their sons and daughters could marry strangers. Marriage promises to turn strangers into friendly relatives—a nation of siblings.

In the village structure, spirits shimmered among the live creatures, balanced and held in equilibrium by time and land. But one human being flaring up into violence could open up a black hole, a maelstrom that pulled in the sky. The frightened villagers, who depended on one another to maintain the real, went to my aunt to show her a personal, physical representation of the break she had made in the "roundness." Misallying couples snapped off the future, which was to be embodied in true offspring. The villagers punished her for acting as if she could have a private life, secret and apart from them.

If my aunt had betrayed the family at a time of large grain yields and peace, when many boys were born, and wings were being built on many houses, perhaps she might have escaped such severe punishment. But the men—hungry, greedy, tired of planting in dry soil, cuckolded—had had to leave the village in order to send food-money home. There were ghost plagues, bandit plagues, wars with the Japanese, floods. My Chinese brother and sister had died of an unknown sickness. Adultery, perhaps only a mistake during good times, became a crime when the village needed food.

The round moon cakes and round doorways, the round tables of graduated size that fit one roundness inside another, round windows and rice bowls—these talismen had lost their power to warn this family of the law: a family must be whole, faithfully keeping the descent line by having sons to feed the old and the dead, who in turn look after the family. The villagers came to show my aunt and her lover-in-hiding a broken house. The villagers were speeding up the circling of events because she was too short-sighted to see that her infidelity had already harmed the village, that waves of consequences would return unpredictably, sometimes in disguise, as now, to hurt her. This roundness had to be made coin-sized so that she would see its circumference: punish her at the birth of her baby. Awaken her to the inexorable. People who refused fatalism because they could invent small resources insisted on culpability. Deny accidents and wrest fault from the stars.

After the villagers left, their lanterns now scattering in various directions toward home, the family broke their silence and cursed her. "Aiaa, we're going to die. Death is coming. Death is coming. Look what you've done. You've killed us. Ghost! Dead ghost! Ghost! You've never been born." She ran out into the fields, far enough from the house so that she could no longer hear their voices, and pressed herself against the earth, her own land no more. When she felt the birth coming, she thought that she had been hurt. Her body seized together. "They've hurt me too much," she thought. "This is gall, and it will kill me." Her forehead and knees against the earth, her body convulsed and then released her onto her back. The black well of sky and stars went out and out and out forever; her body and her complexity seemed to disappear. She was one of the stars, a bright dot in blackness, without home, without a companion, in eternal cold and silence. An agoraphobia rose in her, speeding higher and higher, bigger and bigger; she would not be able to contain it; there would be no end to fear.

Flayed, unprotected against space, she felt pain return, focusing her body. This pain chilled her—a cold, steady kind of surface pain. Inside, spasmodically, the other pain, the pain of the child, heated her. For hours she lay on the ground, alternately body and space. Sometimes a vision of normal comfort obliterated reality: she saw the family in the evening gambling at the dinner table, the young people massaging their elders' backs. She saw them congratulating one another, high joy on the mornings the rice shoots came up. When these pictures burst, the stars drew yet further apart. Black space opened.

She got to her feet to fight better and remembered that old-fashioned women gave birth in their pigsties to fool the jealous, pain-dealing gods, who do not snatch piglets. Before the next spasms could stop her, she ran to the pigsty, each step a rushing out into emptiness. She climbed over the fence and knelt in the dirt. It was good to have a fence enclosing her, a tribal person alone.

Laboring, this woman who had carried her child as a foreign growth that sickened her every day, expelled it at last. She reached down to touch the hot, wet, moving mass, surely smaller than anything human, and could feel that it was human after all—fingers, toes, nails, nose. She pulled it up on to her belly, and it lay curled there, butt in the air, feet precisely tucked one under the other. She opened her loose shirt and buttoned the child inside. After resting, it squirmed and thrashed and she pushed it up to her breast. It turned its head this way and that until it found her nipple. There, it made little snuffling noises. She clenched her teeth at its preciousness, lovely as a young calf, a piglet, a little dog.

She may have gone to the pigsty as a last act of responsibility: she would protect this child as she had protected its father. It would look after her soul, leaving supplies on her grave. But how would this tiny child without family find her grave when there would be no marker for her anywhere, neither in the earth nor the family hall? No one would give her a family hall name. She had taken the child with her into the wastes. At its birth the two of them had felt the same raw pain of separation, a wound that only the family pressing tight could close. A child with no descent line would not soften her life but only trail after her, ghostlike, begging her to give it purpose. At dawn the villagers on their way to the fields would stand around the fence and look.

Full of milk, the little ghost slept. When it awoke, she hardened her breasts against the milk that crying loosens. Toward morning she picked up the baby and walked to the well.

Carrying the baby to the well shows loving. Otherwise abandon it. Turn its face into the mud. Mothers who love their children take them along. It was probably a girl; there is some hope of forgiveness for boys.

"Don't tell anyone you had an aunt. Your father does not want to hear her name. She has never been born." I have believed that sex was unspeakable and words so strong and fathers so frail that "aunt" would do my father mysterious harm. I have thought that my family, having settled among immigrants who had also been their neighbors in the ancestral land, needed to clean their name, and a wrong word would incite the kinspeople even here. But there is more to this silence: they want me to participate in her punishment. And I have.

In the twenty years since I heard this story I have not asked for details nor said my aunt's name; I do not know it. People who can comfort the dead can also chase after them to hurt them further—a reverse ancestor worship. The real punishment was not the raid swiftly inflicted by the villagers, but the family's deliberately forgetting her. Her betrayal so maddened them, they saw to it that she would suffer forever, even after death. Always hungry, always needing, she would have to beg food from other ghosts, snatch and steal it from those whose living descendants give them gifts. She would have to fight the ghosts massed at crossroads for the buns a few thoughtful citizens leave to decoy her away from village and home so that the ancestral spirits could feast unharassed. At peace, they could act like gods, not ghosts, their descent lines providing them with paper suits and dresses, spirit money, paper houses, paper automobiles, chicken, meat, and rice into eternity—essences delivered up in smoke and flames, steam and incense rising from each rice bowl. In an attempt to make the Chinese care for people outside the family, Chairman Mao encourages us now to give our paper replicas to the spirits of outstanding soldiers and workers, no matter whose ancestors they may be. My aunt remains forever hungry. Goods are not distributed evenly among the dead.

My aunt haunts me—her ghost drawn to me because now, after fifty years of neglect, I alone devote pages of paper to her, though not origamied into houses and clothes. I do not think she always means me well. I am telling on her, and she was a spite suicide, drowning herself in the drinking water. The Chinese are always very frightened of the drowned one, whose weeping ghost, wet hair hanging and skin bloated, waits silently by the water to pull down a substitute.

Bloomingdale's

PERRI KLASS

The Paramus branch of Bloomingdale's is holding three afternoon lectures
for local home economics classes. Each afternoon will cover one important
subject for teenage girls: fashion, makeup, and diet and exercise. Since all
the girls will have to miss school those afternoons, they must get their parents to sign permission slips.

The home economics teacher says to the home economics class: "And I
hope you will remember that you are representing our school and dress accordingly. No jeans, please."

"Are other pants okay?" a girl asks.

"I think we'll say double knit is fine, but corduroy is out," the teacher
says, and the girls nod.

There is one girl in the room who looks different. Some are fatter, some
have worse acne, but she is the only one who does not seem to have made
an effort. Her name is Maggie. She is one of very few girls to wear no
makeup, her jeans are baggy, her man's teeshirt is an ugly brown, and her
hair looks a little dirty. The other fat girls wear clothes that the magazines
say will distract attention from their waists, and they take special trouble
with their hair. Just by looking, you could not tell that Maggie is the only
overweight girl who isn't on a perpetual diet, but that's true too. She is sitting next to her best friend, who has also made little obvious effort, but
manages to look quite all right in her jeans and shirt. Maggie's best friend
is thin and her skin is clear. She sits hunched over, covertly doing French
under the desk.

[It is so hard to give any dignity to high school. And I am afraid to tell
you the truth. Because the truth would be I was the fattest, the ugliest, the
one on whom a thousand full skirts, interesting necklines, and layers of
Cover Girl makeup would have been useless. And my best friend was one
of those people who cannot make a graceless move, and her blond hair

swung around her face perfectly, and even her handwriting was beautiful
. . . but the truth would make my story less convincing; you might write it
off as the leftover self-hatred and jealousy of an unhappy teenager, so I will
tone it down to where you will begin to believe me.]

The home economics room is full of sewing machines. They sit around
the sides of the room and wait for the girls to sew. There is a bulletin board
with a poster on it, released by the Simplicity Pattern Company, which
shows six very pretty teenage girls in dresses made from Simplicity patterns. The writing on the bottom of the poster says these are the winners of
Simplicity's "Sew It and Model It Contest" and copies of the poster, along
with rules for next year's contest, are available from Simplicity for seventy-
five cents.

There is another bulletin board with charts of the four basic food groups
on it. That is for the advanced home economics class, in which girls learn
about planning a family's meals. It is coordinated with the senior health
class, in which girls learn about the other kind of family planning.

Maggie shifts down in her chair so her feet sprawl out. Her best friend,
who is artistic, draws a very clever caricature of the teacher and shows it to
Maggie, who grins. The bell rings and they all go off to gym.

Once, a year ago, Maggie dressed up for school. She wore jeans that the
lady in Bamberger's said were just her size, and a flowered shirt with pearly
buttons. The clothes felt very tight. She borrowed some of her mother's
face powder and held her hair back with two matching barrettes. She was
not comfortable that day, but she held a picture of her prettiness in her
mind and moved with care and deliberate grace. Gym period came, and
she faced the full-length mirror in the locker room, and she bulged out of
the clothes and her face looked greasy. It has been so long since then that
probably no one can remember her in anything but the baggy clothes she is
wearing now. Home economics is required, and so is gym.

[In fact, everything we took was required that year, even music, where
the teacher, who wore fake stick-on sideburns, had a special program called
"Jukebox Jury," in which we rated the top ten songs every week, then discussed their musical qualities, and later had to identify lyrics on a test. So
you see, I don't need to exaggerate.]

Maggie comes to school the day of the first trip to Bloomingdale's in a
skirt and teeshirt, and all the girls get on the school bus. Maggie sits with
her best friend, and everybody sings for a while, starting with "Found a
Peanut" and going on to a football song. Maggie knows all the words (that
was their first music lesson) and she lets herself sing softly until she catches
her best friend's eye and feels obliged to giggle. She looks out her window
at Paramus, New Jersey, shopping-center capital of the world. All over Paramus there are enormous shopping malls. Some are enclosed in super-
buildings, with trees along the indoor promenades between the stores.
Waterfalls tumble off the roofs of department stores onto Styrofoam rocks

in lily ponds (the lilies are plastic, as are the frogs crouching on them), and one mall has a bunch of automated plastic cows (life-size) grazing on the Astroturf.

The Bloomingdale's mall is one of the classier ones. Maggie and most of her classmates are more familiar with some of the cheaper stores at the more plebeian malls. The bus parks, the girls climb out and follow the teacher into Bloomingdale's. As they move toward the escalator, they finger the scarves, stroke the tweed blazers, and a few of the daring try a spritz from one of the sample perfume bottles.

Maggie is at the back of the group; she sees the first girls rising into the quiet heights of Bloomingdale's on the escalator. She has always been slightly afraid of up escalators, but she gets on and off without hesitation. The girls are led around the handbag tables and into a small auditorium. It is almost full of other home economics classes; there are just enough seats left. They all sit down. The faces are young and pretty, colored with creams and powders, the bodies are dressed in pastels, the necks are circled by thin gold chains dangling crosses, stars, charms, and hearts onto shirts or into necklines.

[And yet they couldn't *all* have been pretty, could they? I could watch them in the hall at school and see individual flaws. Some of them were beautiful, some were pretty, and some fit in only by virtue of careful attention to detail. But all together, they blended into a pretty group, a group of pretty girls.]

It takes five minutes to quiet the girls down. A woman walks onto the stage and welcomes them all. She is handsome, wearing a dark red suit, and she handles herself easily. She comments on what a nice-looking group they are and how pleased Bloomingdale's is to welcome them. The first topic, she announces, will be fashion. Several Bloomingdale's people come on the stage and talk: the lady from the College Boutique, the man from Teen Sportswear, finally the lady from Lingerie. The girls giggle. "Now," she says, "there is nothing funny about underwear. After all, we're all girls together here." They giggle again.

The Bloomingdale's people pick six pretty girls out of the audience, ask them to come up on the stage, and analyze their clothes. They tell one to put on a blue sweater ("See how it pulls your whole look together?") and another to put on a plastic belt painted to look as if it were made out of linked chewing-gum wrappers ("See how the right accessories highlight your outfit?"), and soon they are all festooned with Bloomingdale's merchandise.

"I bet everyone goes down and buys those things right after the lecture," Maggie whispers to her best friend.

"There'll be thirty people wearing that belt in school tomorrow," whispers her best friend, and they giggle.

The next week they pick six girls and have them take off all their own makeup with cold cream. Then a very effeminate man ("faggy," the girls whisper) with a tie printed to look like gum wrappers applies makeup to them while he explains what he is doing: "brings out" "conceals" "shadows" "plays up" "shapes" "highlights" "brightens" "plucks" and "covers." The six decorated girls then walk around the room so everyone can get a good look, while the man answers questions.

"What can I do about my freckles?"

"My brows never come out even."

"What liner goes well with green eye shadow?"

"Is it better to have your lipstick match your blush exactly?"

Maggie whispers to her best friend, "I dare you to ask how to cover serious birth defects." Maggie thinks makeup looks silly and has never been really tempted to use it, so she is able to laugh. Still, she sometimes imagines she is Cybill Shepherd posing for Cover Girl makeup ads. These are the kinds of fantasies she tries not to have, and she is ashamed of herself for having them. She feels that to daydream about being Cybill Shepherd is just the sort of silly irony she should avoid.

[In case you wonder, I can also still recognize Susie Blakely, and Lauren Hutton, and every other model who ever glowed on the cover of *Mademoiselle* in her autumn-russet cheek gloss and peach-coral lip paint, hair by Sassoon.]

The makeup man produces a little blue plastic thing; it looks like a tiny propeller. When he presses a switch it spins like a fan and he explains that it is a battery-operated eyeliner dryer. Maggie laughs aloud and everyone looks at her.

The third week is diet and exercise. The girls are told to eat fruit instead of candy and to get fresh air during their menstrual periods (giggles). It is suggested that they make a habit of chewing each mouthful of food thirty-two times ("Your jaws will get tired and you won't take so many mouthfuls!"), and that they spend twenty minutes a day doing some simple exercises. To demonstrate the exercises the Bloomingdale's people pick six overweight girls. Maggie sees the woman coming toward her and tries to look both hostile and invisible. The woman picks her, leads her to the stage, where she stands with the five other overweight girls, all embarrassed and fidgeting.

"Lie down on your backs," the woman says. "Now lift your legs off the floor." Maggie does not lift her legs. She lies on her back in the soft Bloomingdale's carpet. The woman says, "Now, we're not trying." She picks up Maggie's ankles, rather gingerly.

Maggie screams. The lady drops her ankles. All the other girls jump up. Maggie lies there. The lady touches her shoulder and Maggie screams again and kicks the carpet. Maggie's teacher hurries up to the stage, and

Maggie is on her feet with bits of lint in her hair. She is so angry that her head burns. She is so angry she wants to spit. She spits at her home economics teacher, who shrieks.

Maggie is standing alone on the stage and crying, and everyone stares at her, and if there is understanding in the eyes of the other five fat girls she does not see it. Maggie wraps her arms around herself and shudders, wishing she were invisible, weightless. She has a sudden tearstained picture of herself flying above Bloomingdale's, holding on to a battery-operated blue plastic propeller.

Haircut

RING LARDNER

I got another barber that comes over from Carterville and helps me out Saturdays, but the rest of the time I can get along all right alone. You can see for yourself that this ain't no New York City and besides that, the most of the boys works all day and don't have no leisure to drop in here and get themselves prettied up.

You're a newcomer, ain't you? I thought I hadn't seen you round before. I hope you like it good enough to stay. As I say, we ain't no New York City or Chicago, but we have pretty good times. Not as good, though, since Jim Kendall got killed. When he was alive, him and Hod Meyers used to keep this town in an uproar. I bet they was more laughin' done here than any town its size in America.

Jim was comical, and Hod was pretty near a match for him. Since Jim's gone, Hod tries to hold his end up just the same as ever, but it's tough goin' when you ain't got nobody to kind of work with.

They used to be plenty fun in here Saturdays. This place is jam-packed Saturdays, from four o'clock on. Jim and Hod would show up right after their supper, round six o'clock. Jim would set himself down in that big chair, nearest the blue spittoon. Whoever had been settin' in that chair, why they'd get up when Jim come in and give it to him.

You'd of thought it was a reserved seat like they have sometimes in a theayter. Hod would generally always stand or walk up and down, or some Saturdays, of course, he'd be settin' in this chair part of the time, gettin' a haircut.

Well, Jim would set there a w'ile without openin' his mouth only to spit, and then finally he'd say to me, "Whitey,"—my right name, that is, my right first name, is Dick, but everybody round here calls me Whitey—Jim would say, "Whitey, your nose looks like a rosebud tonight. You must of been drinkin' some of your aw de cologne."

So I'd say, "No, Jim, but you look like you'd been drinkin' somethin' of that kind or somethin' worse."

Jim would have to laugh at that, but then he'd speak up and say, "No, I ain't had nothin' to drink, but that ain't sayin' I wouldn't like somethin'. I wouldn't even mind if it was wood alcohol."

Then Hod Meyers would say, "Neither would your wife." That would set everybody to laughin' because Jim and his wife wasn't on very good terms. She'd of divorced him only they wasn't no chance to get alimony and she didn't have no way to take care of herself and the kids. She couldn't never understand Jim. He *was* kind of rough, but a good fella at heart.

Him and Hod had all kinds of sport with Milt Sheppard. I don't suppose you've seen Milt. Well, he's got an Adam's apple that looks more like a mushmelon. So I'd be shavin' Milt and when I'd start to shave down here on his neck, Hod would holler, "Hey, Whitey, wait a minute! Before you cut into it, let's make up a pool and see who can guess closest to the number of seeds."

And Jim would say, "If Milt hadn't of been so hoggish, he'd of ordered a half a cantaloupe instead of a whole one and it might not of stuck in his throat."

All the boys would roar at this and Milt himself would force a smile, though the joke was on him. Jim certainly was a card!

There's his shavin' mug, settin' on the shelf, right next to Charley Vail's. "Charles M. Vail." That's the druggist. He comes in regular for his shave, three times a week. And Jim's is the cup next to Charley's. "James H. Kendall." Jim won't need no shavin' mug no more, but I'll leave it there just the same for old time's sake. Jim certainly was a character!

Years ago, Jim used to travel for a canned goods concern over in Carterville. They sold canned goods. Jim had the whole northern half of the State and was on the road five days out of every week. He'd drop in here Saturdays and tell his experiences for that week. It was rich.

I guess he paid more attention to playin' jokes than makin' sales. Finally the concern let him out and he come right home here and told everybody he'd been fired instead of sayin' he'd resigned like most fellas would of.

It was a Saturday and the shop was full and Jim got up out of that chair and says, "Gentlemen, I got an important announcement to make. I been fired from my job."

Well, they asked him if he was in earnest and he said he was and nobody could think of nothin' to say till Jim finally broke the ice himself. He says, "I been sellin' canned goods and now I'm canned goods myself."

You see, the concern he'd been workin' for was a factory that made canned goods. Over in Carterville. And now Jim said he was canned himself. He was certainly a card!

Jim had a great trick that he used to play w'ile he was travelin'. For instance, he'd be ridin' on a train and they'd come to some little town like, well, like, we'll say, like Benton. Jim would look out the train window and read the signs on the stores.

For instance, they'd be a sign, "Henry Smith, Dry Goods." Well, Jim would write down the name and the name of the town and when he got to wherever he was goin' he'd mail back a postal card to Henry Smith at Benton and not sign no name to it, but he'd write on the card, well, somethin' like "Ask your wife about that book agent that spent the afternoon last week," or "Ask your Missus who kept her from gettin' lonesome the last time you was in Carterville." And he'd sign the card, "A Friend."

Of course, he never knew what really come of none of these jokes, but he could picture what *probably* happened and that was enough.

Jim didn't work very steady after he lost his position with the Carterville people. What he did earn, doin' odd jobs round town, why he spent pretty near all of it on gin and his family might of starved if the stores hadn't of carried them along. Jim's wife tried her hand at dressmakin', but they ain't nobody goin' to get rich makin' dresses in this town.

As I say, she'd of divorced Jim, only she seen that she couldn't support herself and the kids and she was always hopin' that some day Jim would cut out his habits and give her more than two or three dollars a week.

They was a time when she would go to whoever he was workin' for and ask them to give her his wages, but after she done this once or twice, he beat her to it by borrowin' most of his pay in advance. He told it all round town, how he had outfoxed his Missus. He certainly was a caution!

But he wasn't satisfied with just outwittin' her. He was sore the way she had acted, tryin' to grab off his pay. And he made up his mind he'd get even. Well, he waited till Evans's Circus was advertised to come to town. Then he told his wife and two kiddies that he was goin' to take them to the circus. The day of the circus, he told them he would get the tickets and meet them outside the entrance to the tent.

Well, he didn't have no intentions of bein' there or buyin' tickets or nothin'. He got full of gin and laid round Wright's poolroom all day. His wife and the kids waited and waited and of course he didn't show up. His wife didn't have a dime with her, or nowhere else, I guess. So she finally had to tell the kids it was all off and they cried like they wasn't never goin' to stop.

Well, it seems, w'ile they was cryin', Doc Stair came along and he asked what was the matter, but Mrs. Kendall was stubborn and wouldn't tell him, but the kids told him and he insisted on takin' them and their mother in the show. Jim found this out afterwards and it was one reason why he had it in for Doc Stair.

Doc Stair come here about a year and a half ago. He's a mighty handsome young fella and his clothes always look like he has them made to order. He goes to Detroit two or three times a year and w'ile he's there he must have a tailor take his measure and them make him a suit to order. They cost pretty near twice as much, but they fit a whole lot better than if you just bought them in a store.

For a w'ile everybody was wonderin' why a young doctor like Doc Stair should come to a town like this where we already got old Doc Gamble and Doc Foote that's both been here for years and all the practice in town was always divided between the two of them.

Then they was a story got round that Doc Stair's gal had throwed him over, a gal up in the Northern Peninsula somewheres, and the reason he come here was to hide himself away and forget it. He said himself that he thought they wasn't nothin' like general practice in a place like ours to fit a man to be a good all round doctor. And that's why he'd came.

Anyways, it wasn't long before he was makin' enough to live on, though they tell me that he never dunned nobody for what they owed him, and the folks here certainly has got the owin' habit, even in my business. If I had all that was comin' to me for just shaves alone, I could go to Carterville and put up at the Mercer for a week and see a different picture every night. For instance, they's old George Purdy—but I guess I shouldn't ought to be gossipin'.

Well, last year, our coroner died of the flu. Ken Beatty, that was his name. He was the coroner. So they had to choose another man to be coroner in his place and they picked Doc Stair. He laughed at first and said he didn't want it, but they made him take it. It ain't no job that anybody would fight for and what a man makes out of it in a year would just about buy seeds for their garden. Doc's the kind, though, that can't say no to nothin' if you keep at him long enough.

But I was goin' to tell you about a poor boy we got here in town—Paul Dickson. He fell out of a tree when he was about ten years old. Lit on his head and it done somethin' to him and he ain't never been right. No harm in him, but just silly. Jim Kendall used to call him cuckoo; that's a name Jim had for anybody that was off their head, only he called people's head their bean. That was another of his gags, callin' head bean and callin' crazy people cuckoo. Only poor Paul ain't crazy, but just silly.

You can imagine that Jim used to have all kinds of fun with Paul. He'd send him to the White Front Garage for a left-handed monkey wrench. Of course they ain't no such a thing as a left-handed monkey wrench.

And once we had a kind of a fair here and they was a baseball game between the fats and the leans and before the game started Jim called Paul over and sent him way down to Schrader's hardware store to get a key for the pitcher's box.

They wasn't nothin' in the way of gags that Jim couldn't think up, when he put his mind to it.

Poor Paul was always kind of suspicious of people, maybe on account of how Jim had kept foolin' him. Paul wouldn't have much to do with anybody only his own mother and Doc Stair and a girl here in town named Julie Gregg. That is, she ain't a girl no more, but pretty near thirty or over.

When Doc first come to town, Paul seemed to feel like here was a real friend and he hung round Doc's office most of the w'ile; the only time he wasn't there was when he'd go home to eat or sleep or when he seen Julie Gregg doin' her shoppin'.

When he looked out Doc's window and seen her, he'd run downstairs and join her and tag along with her to the different stores. The poor boy was crazy about Julie and she always treated him mighty nice and made him feel like he was welcome, though of course it wasn't nothin' but pity on her side.

Doc done all he could to improve Paul's mind and he told me once that he really thought the boy was gettin' better, that they was times when he was as bright and sensible as anybody else.

But I was goin' to tell you about Julie Gregg. Old Man Gregg was in the lumber business, but got to drinkin' and lost the most of his money and when he died, he didn't leave nothin' but the house and just enough insurance for the girl to skimp along on.

Her mother was a kind of a half invalid and didn't hardly ever leave the house. Julie wanted to sell the place and move somewheres else after the old man died, but the mother said she was born here and would die here. It was tough on Julie, as the young people round this town—well, she's too good for them.

She's been away to school and Chicago and New York and different places and they ain't no subject she can't talk on, where you take the rest of the young folks here and you mention anything to them outside of Gloria Swanson or Tommy Meighan and they think you're delirious. Did you see Gloria in Wages of Virtue? You missed somethin'!

Well, Doc Stair hadn't been here more than a week when he come in one day to get shaved and I recognized who he was as he had been pointed out to me, so I told him about my old lady. She's been ailin' for a couple years and either Doc Gamble or Doc Foote, neither one, seemed to be helpin' her. So he said he would come out and see her, but if she was able to get out herself, it would be better to bring her to his office where he could make a completer examination.

So I took her to his office and w'ile I was waitin' for her in the reception room, in come Julie Gregg. When somebody comes in Doc Stair's office, they's a bell that rings in his inside office so as he can tell they's somebody to see him.

So he left my old lady inside and come out to the front office and that's the first time him and Julie met and I guess it was what they call love at first sight. But it wasn't fifty-fifty. This young fella was the slickest lookin' fella she'd ever seen in this town and she went wild over him. To him she was just a young lady that wanted to see the doctor.

She'd came on about the same business I had. Her mother had been doctorin' for years with Doc Gamble and Doc Foote and without no results. So she'd heard they was a new doc in town and decided to give him a try. He promised to call and see her mother that same day.

I said a minute ago that it was love at first sight on her part. I'm not only judgin' by how she acted afterwards but how she looked at him that first day in his office. I ain't no mind reader, but it was wrote all over her face that she was gone.

Now Jim Kendall, besides bein' a jokesmith and a pretty good drinker, well, Jim was quite a lady-killer. I guess he run pretty wild durin' the time he was on the road for them Carterville people, and besides that, he'd had a couple little affairs of the heart right here in town. As I say, his wife could of divorced him, only she couldn't.

But Jim was like the majority of men, and women, too, I guess. He wanted what he couldn't get. He wanted Julie Gregg and worked his head off tryin' to land her. Only he'd of said bean instead of head.

Well, Jim's habits and his jokes didn't appeal to Julie and of course he was a married man, so he didn't have no more chance than, well, than a rabbit. That's an expression of Jim's himself. When somebody didn't have no chance to get elected or somethin', Jim would always say they didn't have no more chance than a rabbit.

He didn't make no bones about how he felt. Right in here, more than once, in front of the whole crowd, he said he was stuck on Julie and anybody that could get her for him was welcome to his house and his wife and kids included. But she wouldn't have nothin' to do with him; wouldn't even speak to him on the street. He finally seen he wasn't gettin' nowheres with his usual line so he decided to try the rough stuff. He went right up to her house one evenin' and when she opened the door he forced his way in and grabbed her. But she broke loose and before he could stop her, she run in the next room and locked the door and phoned to Joe Barnes. Joe's the marshal. Jim could hear who she was phonin' to and he beat it before Joe got there.

Joe was an old friend of Julie's pa. Joe went to Jim the next day and told him what would happen if he ever done it again.

I don't know how the news of this little affair leaked out. Chances is that Joe Barnes told his wife and she told somebody else's wife and they told their husband. Anyways, it did leak out and Hod Meyers had the nerve to kid Jim about it, right here in this shop. Jim didn't deny nothin' and kind of laughed it off and said for us all to wait; that lots of people had tried to make a monkey out of him, but he always got even.

Meanw'ile everybody in town was wise to Julie's bein' wild mad over the

Doc. I don't suppose she had any idear how her face changed when him and her was together; of course she couldn't of, or she'd of kept away from him. And she didn't know that we was all noticin' how many times she made excuses to go up to his office or pass it on the other side of the street and look up in his window to see if he was there. I felt sorry for her and so did most other people.

Hod Meyers kept rubbin' it into Jim about how the Doc had cut him out. Jim didn't pay no attention to the kiddin' and you could see he was plannin' one of his jokes.

One trick Jim had was the knack of changin' his voice. He could make you think he was a girl talkin' and he could mimic any man's voice. To show you how good he was along this line, I'll tell you the joke he played on me once.

You know, in most towns of any size, when a man is dead and needs a shave, why the barber that shaves him soaks him five dollars for the job; that is, he don't soak *him,* but whoever ordered the shave. I just charge three dollars because personally I don't mind much shavin' a dead person. They lay a whole lot stiller than live customers. The only thing is that you don't feel like talkin' to them and you get kind of lonesome.

Well, about the coldest day we ever had here, two years ago last winter, the phone rung at the house w'ile I was home to dinner and I answered the phone and it was a woman's voice and she said she was Mrs. John Scott and her husband was dead and would I come out and shave him.

Old John had always been a good customer of mine. But they live seven miles out in the country, on the Streeter road. Still I didn't see how I could say no.

So I said I would be there, but would have to come in a jitney and it might cost three or four dollars besides the price of the shave. So she, or the voice, it said that was all right, so I got Frank Abbott to drive me out to the place and when I got there, who should open the door but old John himself! He wasn't no more dead than, well, than a rabbit.

It didn't take no private detective to figure out who had played me this little joke. Nobody could of thought it up but Jim Kendall. He certainly was a card!

I tell you this incident just to show you how he could disguise his voice and make you believe it was somebody else talkin'. I'd of swore it was Mrs. Scott had called me. Anyways, some woman.

Well, Jim waited til he had Doc Stair's voice down pat; then he went after revenge.

He called Julie up on a night when he knew Doc was over in Carterville. She never questioned but what it was Doc's voice. Jim said he must see her that night; he couldn't wait no longer to tell her somethin'. She was all excited and told him to come to the house. But he said he was expectin' an important long distance call and wouldn't she please forget her manners for

once and come to his office. He said they couldn't nothin' hurt her and nobody would see her and he just *must* talk to her a little w'ile. Well, poor Julie
fell for it.

Doc always keeps a night light in his office, so it looked to Julie like they
was somebody there.

Meanw'ile Jim Kendall had went to Wright's poolroom, where they was a
whole gang amusin' themselves. The most of them had drank plenty of gin,
and they was a rough bunch even when sober. They was always strong for
Jim's jokes and when he told them to come with him and see some fun they
give up their card games and pool games and followed along.

Doc's office is on the second floor. Right outside his door they's a flight of
stairs leadin' to the floor above. Jim and his gang hid in the dark behind
these stairs.

Well, Julie come up to Doc's door and rung the bell and they was nothin'
doin'. She rung it again and she rung it seven or eight times. Then she tried
the door and found it locked. Then Jim made some kind of a noise and she
heard it and waited a minute, and then she says, "Is that you, Ralph!" Ralph
is Doc's first name.

They was no answer and it must of came to her all of a sudden that she'd
been bunked. She pretty near fell downstairs and the whole gang after her.
They chased her all the way home, hollerin' "Is that you, Ralph?" and "Oh,
Ralphie, dear, is that you?" Jim says he couldn't holler it himself, as he was
laughin' too hard.

Poor Julie! She didn't show up here on Main Street for a long, long time
afterward.

And of course Jim and his gang told everybody in town, everybody but
Doc Stair. They was scared to tell him, and he might of never knowed only
for Paul Dickson. The poor cuckoo, as Jim called him, he was here in the
shop one night when Jim was still gloatin' yet over what he'd done to Julie.
And Paul took in as much of it as he could understand and he run to Doc
with the story.

It's a cinch Doc went up in the air and swore he'd make Jim suffer. But it
was a kind of a delicate thing, because if it got out that he had beat Jim up,
Julie was bound to hear of it and then she'd know that Doc knew and of
course knowin' that he knew would make it worse for her than ever. He was
goin' to do somethin', but it took a lot of figurin'.

Well, it was a couple of days later when Jim was here in the shop again,
and so was the cuckoo. Jim, was goin' duck-shootin' the next day and had
come in lookin' for Hod Meyers to go with him. I happened to know that
Hod had went over to Carterville and wouldn't be home till the end of the
week. So Jim said he hated to go alone and he guessed he would call it off.
Then poor Paul spoke up and said if Jim would take him he would go
along. Jim thought a w'ile and then he said, well, he guessed a half-wit was
better than nothin'.

I suppose he was plottin' to get Paul out in the boat and play some joke on him, like pushin' him in the water. Anyways, he said Paul could go. He asked him had he ever shot a duck and Paul said no, he'd never even had a gun in his hands. So Jim said he could set in the boat and watch him and if he behaved himself, he might lend him his gun for a couple of shots. They made a date to meet in the mornin' and that's the last I seen of Jim alive.

Next mornin', I hadn't been open more than ten minutes when Doc Stair come in. He looked kind of nervous. He asked me had I seen Paul Dickson. I said no, but I knew where he was, out duck-shootin' with Jim Kendall. So Doc says that's what he had heard, and he couldn't understand it because Paul had told him he wouldn't never have no more to do with Jim as long as he lived.

He said Paul had told him about the joke Jim had played on Julie. He said Paul had asked him what he thought of the joke and the Doc had told him that anybody that would do a thing like that ought not to be let live.

I said it had been a kind of a raw thing, but Jim just couldn't resist no kind of a joke, no matter how raw. I said I thought he was all right at heart, but just bubblin' over with mischief. Doc turned and walked out.

At noon he got a phone call from old John Scott. The lake where Jim and Paul had went shootin is on John's place. Paul had came runnin' up to the house a few minutes before and said they'd been an accident. Jim had shot a few ducks and then give the gun to Paul and told him to try his luck. Paul hadn't never handled a gun and he was nervous. He was shakin' so hard that he couldn't control the gun. He let fire and Jim sunk back in the boat, dead.

Doc Stair, bein' the coroner, jumped in Frank Abbott's flivver and rushed out to Scott's farm. Paul and old John was down on the shore of the lake. Paul had rowed the boat to shore, but they'd left the body in it, waitin' for Doc to come.

Doc examined the body and said they might as well fetch it back to town. They was no use leavin' it there or callin' a jury, as it was a plain case of accidental shootin'.

Personally I wouldn't never leave a person shoot a gun in the same boat I was in unless I was sure they knew somethin' about guns. Jim was a sucker to leave a new beginner have his gun, let along a half-wit. It probably served Jim right, what he got. But still we miss him round here. He certainly was a card!

Comb it wet or dry?

The Rocking Horse Winner

D. H. LAWRENCE

There was a woman who was beautiful, who started with all the advantages, yet she had no luck. She married for love, and the love turned to dust. She had bonny children, yet she felt they had been thrust upon her, and she could not love them. They looked at her coldly, as if they were finding fault with her. And hurriedly she felt she must cover up some fault in herself. Yet what it was that she must cover up she never knew. Nevertheless, when her children were present, she always felt the center of her heart go hard. This troubled her, and in her manner she was all the more gentle and anxious for her children, as if she loved them very much. Only she herself knew that at the center of her heart was a hard little place that could not feel love, no, not for anybody. Everybody else said of her: "She is such a good mother. She adores her children." Only she herself, and her children themselves, knew it was not so. They read it in each other's eyes.

There were a boy and two little girls. They lived in a pleasant house, with a garden, and they had discreet servants, and felt themselves superior to anyone in the neighborhood.

Although they lived in style, they felt always an anxiety in the house. There was never enough money. The mother had a small income, and the father had a small income, but not nearly enough for the social position which they had to keep up. The father went into town to some office. But though he had good prospects, these prospects never materialized. There was always the grinding sense of the shortage of money, though the style was always kept up.

At last the mother said: "I will see if *I* can't make something." But she did not know where to begin. She racked her brains, and tried this thing and the other, but could not find anything successful. The failure made deep lines come into her face. Her children were growing up, they would have to go to school. There must be more money, there must be more money. The father, who was always very handsome and expensive in his tastes, seemed as if he never *would* be able to do anything worth doing. And the mother, who had a great belief in herself, did not succeed any better, and her tastes were just as expensive.

And so the house came to be haunted by the unspoken phrase: *There must be more money! There must be more money!* The children could hear it all the time, though nobody said it aloud. They heard it at Christmas, when the expensive and splendid toys filled the nursery. Behind the shining modern rocking horse, behind the smart doll's house, a voice would start whispering: "There *must* be more money! There *must* be more money!" And the children would stop playing, to listen for a moment. They would look into each other's eyes, to see if they had all heard. And each one saw in the eyes of the other two that they too had heard. "There *must* be more money! There *must* be more money!"

It came whispering from the springs of the still-swaying rocking horse, and even the horse, bending his wooden, champing head, heard it. The big doll, sitting so pink and smirking in her new pram, could hear it quite plainly, and seemed to be smirking all the more self-consciously because of it. The foolish puppy, too, that took the place of the teddy bear, he was looking so extraordinarily foolish for no other reason but that he heard the secret whisper all over the house: "There *must* be more money!"

Yet nobody ever said it aloud. The whisper was everywhere, and therefore no one spoke it. Just as no one ever says: "We are breathing!" in spite of the fact that breath is coming and going all the time.

"Mother," said the boy Paul one day, "why don't we keep a car of our own? Why do we always use Uncle's, or else a taxi?"

"Because we're the poor members of the family," said the mother.

"But why *are* we, Mother?"

"Well—I suppose," she said slowly and bitterly, "it's because your father has no luck."

The boy was silent for some time.

"Is luck money, Mother?" he asked rather timidly.

"No, Paul. Not quite. It's what causes you to have money."

"Oh!" said Paul vaguely. "I thought when Uncle Oscar said *filthy lucker*, it meant money."

"*Filthy lucre* does mean money," said the mother. "But it's lucre, not luck."

"Oh!" said the boy. "Then what *is* luck, Mother?"

"It's what causes you to have money. If you're lucky you have money. That's why it's better to be born lucky than rich. If you're rich, you may lose your money. But if you're lucky, you will always get more money."

"Oh! Will you? And is Father not lucky?"

"Very unlucky, I should say," she said bitterly.

The boy watched her with unsure eyes.

"Why?" he asked.

"I don't know. Nobody ever knows why one person is lucky and another unlucky."

"Don't they? Nobody at all? Does *nobody* know?"

"Perhaps God. But He never tells."

"He ought to, then. And aren't you lucky either, Mother?"

"I can't be, if I married an unlucky husband."

"But by yourself, aren't you?"

"I used to think I was, before I married. Now I think I am very unlucky indeed."

"Why?"

"Well—never mind! Perhaps I'm not really," she said.

The child looked at her, to see if she meant it. But he saw, by the lines of her mouth, that she was only trying to hide something from him.

"Well, anyhow," he said stoutly, "I'm a lucky person."

"Why?" said his mother, with a sudden laugh.

He stared at her. He didn't even know why he had said it.

"God told me," he asserted, brazening it out.

"I hope He did, dear!" she said, again with a laugh, but rather bitter.

"He did, Mother!"

"Excellent!" said the mother.

The boy saw she did not believe him; or, rather, that she paid no attention to his assertion. This angered him somewhat, and made him want to compel her attention.

He went off by himself, vaguely, in a childish way, seeking for the clue to "luck." Absorbed, taking no heed of other people, he went about with a sort of stealth, seeking inwardly for luck. He wanted luck, he wanted it, he wanted it. When the two girls were playing dolls in the nursery, he would sit on his big rocking horse, charging madly into space, with a frenzy that made the little girls peer at him uneasily. Wildly the horse careered, the waving dark hair of the boy tossed, his eyes had a strange glare in them. The little girls dared not speak to him.

When he had ridden to the end of his mad little journey, he climbed down and stood in front of his rocking horse, staring fixedly into its lowered face. Its red mouth was slightly open, its big eye was wide and glassy-bright.

Now! he would silently command the snorting steed. Now, take me to where there is luck! Now take me!

And he would slash the horse on the neck with the little whip he had asked Uncle Oscar for. He *knew* the horse could take him to where there was luck, if only he forced it. So he would mount again, and start on his furious ride, hoping at last to get there. He knew he could get there.

"You'll break your horse, Paul!" said the nurse.

"He's always riding like that! I wish he'd leave off!" said his elder sister Joan.

But he only glared down on them in silence. Nurse gave him up. She could make nothing of him. Anyhow he was growing beyond her.

One day his mother and his Uncle Oscar came in when he was on one of his furious rides. He did not speak to them.

"Hallo, you young jockey! Riding a winner?" said his uncle.

"Aren't you growing too big for a rocking horse? You're not a very little boy any longer, you know," said his mother.

But Paul only gave a blue glare from his big, rather close-set eyes. He would speak to nobody when he was in full tilt. His mother watched him with an anxious expression on her face.

At last he suddenly stopped forcing his horse into the mechanical gallop, and slid down.

"Well, I got there!" he announced fiercely, his blue eyes still flaring, and his sturdy long legs straddling apart.

"Where did you get to?" asked his mother.

"Where I wanted to go," he flared back at her.

"That's right son!" said Uncle Oscar. "Don't you stop till you get there. What's the horse's name?"

"He doesn't have a name," said the boy.

"Gets on without all right?" asked the uncle.

"Well, he has different names. He was called Sansovino last week."

"Sansovino, eh? Won the Ascot. How did you know his name?"

"He always talks about horse races with Bassett," said Joan.

The uncle was delighted to find that his small nephew was posted with all the racing news. Bassett, the young gardener, who had been wounded in the left foot in the war and had got his present job through Oscar Cresswell, whose batman he had been, was a perfect blade of the "turf." He lived in the racing events, and the small boy lived with him.

Oscar Cresswell got it all from Bassett.

"Master Paul comes and asks me, so I can't do more than tell him, sir," said Bassett, his face terribly serious, as if he were speaking of religious matters.

"And does he ever put anything on a horse he fancies?"

"Well—I don't want to give him away—he's a young sport, a fine sport, sir. Would you mind asking him himself? He sort of takes a pleasure in it, and perhaps he'd feel I was giving him away, sir, if you don't mind."

Bassett was serious as a church.

The uncle went back to his nephew and took him off for a ride in the car.

"Say, Paul, old man, do you ever put anything on a horse?" the uncle asked.

The boy watched the handsome man closely.

"Why, do you think I oughtn't to?" he parried.

"Not a bit of it! I thought perhaps you might give me a tip for the Lincoln."

The car sped on into the country, going down to Uncle Oscar's place in Hampshire.

"Honor bright?" said the nephew.

"Honor bright, son!" said the uncle.

"Well, then, Daffodil."

"Daffodil! I doubt it, sonny. What about Mirza?"

"I only know the winner," said the boy. "That's Daffodil."

"Daffodil, eh?" There was a pause. Daffodil was an obscure horse comparatively.

"Uncle!"

"Yes, son?"

"You won't let it go any further, will you? I promised Bassett."

"Bassett be damned, old man! What's he got to do with it?"

"We're partners. We've been partners from the first. Uncle, he lent me my first five shillings, which I lost. I promised him, honor bright, it was only between me and him; only you gave me that ten-shilling note I started winning with, so I thought you were lucky. You won't let it go any further, will you?"

The boy gazed at his uncle from those big, hot, blue eyes, set rather close together. The uncle stirred and laughed uneasily.

"Right you are, son! I'll keep your tip private. Daffodil, eh? How much are you putting on him?"

"All except twenty pounds," said the boy. "I keep that in reserve."

The uncle thought it a good joke.

"You keep twenty pounds in reserve, do you, you young romancer? What are you betting, then?"

"I'm betting three hundred," said the boy gravely. "But it's between you and me, Uncle Oscar! Honor bright?"

The uncle burst into a roar of laughter.

"It's between you and me all right, you young Nat Gould," he said, laughing. "But where's your three hundred?"

"Bassett keeps it for me. We're partners."

"You are, are you! And what is Bassett putting on Daffodil?"

"He won't go quite as high as I do, I expect. Perhaps he'll go a hundred and fifty."

"What, pennies?" laughed the uncle.

"Pounds," said the child, with a surprised look at his uncle. "Bassett keeps a bigger reserve than I do."

Between wonder and amusement Uncle Oscar was silent. He pursued the matter no further, but he determined to take his nephew with him to the Lincoln races.

"Now, son," he said, "I'm putting twenty on Mirza, and I'll put five for you on any horse you fancy. What's your pick?"

"Daffodil, Uncle."

"No, not the fiver on Daffodil!"

"I should if it was my own fiver," said the child.

"Good! Good! Right you are! A fiver for me and a fiver for you on Daffodil."

The child had never been to a race meeting before, and his eyes were blue fire. He pursed his mouth tight, and watched. A Frenchman just in front had put his money on Lancelot. Wild with excitement, he flailed his arms up and down, yelling *"Lancelot! Lancelot!"* in his French accent.

Daffodil came in first, Lancelot second, Mirza third. The child, flushed and with eyes blazing, was curiously serene. His uncle brought him four five-pound notes, four to one.

"What am I to do with these?" he cried, waving them before the boy's eyes.

"I suppose we'll talk to Bassett," said the boy. "I expect I have fifteen hundred now; and twenty in reserve; and this twenty."

His uncle studied him for some moments.

"Look here, son!" he said. "You're not serious about Bassett and that fifteen hundred, are you?"

"Yes, I am. But it's between you and me, Uncle. Honor bright!"

"Honor bright all right, son! But I must talk to Bassett."

"If you'd like to be a partner, Uncle, with Bassett and me, we could all be partners. Only, you'd have to promise, honor bright, Uncle, not to let it go beyond us three. Bassett and I are lucky, and you must be lucky, because it was your ten shillings I started winning with. . . ."

Uncle Oscar took both Bassett and Paul into Richmond Park for an afternoon, and there they talked.

"It's like this, you see, sir," Bassett said. "Master Paul would get me talking about racing events, spinning yarns, you know, sir. And he was always keen on knowing if I'd made or if I'd lost. It's about a year since, now, that I put five shillings on Blush of Dawn for him—and we lost. Then the luck turned, with that ten shillings he had from you, that we put on Singhalese. And since then, it's been pretty steady, all things considering. What do you say, Master Paul?"

"We're all right when we're sure," said Paul. "It's when we're not quite sure that we go down."

"Oh, but we're careful then," said Bassett.

"But when are you *sure*?" Uncle Oscar smiled.

"It's Master Paul, sir," said Bassett, in a secret, religious voice. "It's as if he had it from heaven. Like Daffodil, now, for the Lincoln. That was as sure as eggs."

"Did you put anything on Daffodil?" asked Oscar Cresswell.

"Yes, sir. I made my bit."

"And my nephew?"

Bassett was obstinately silent, looking at Paul.

"I made twelve hundred, didn't I, Bassett? I told Uncle I was putting three hundred on Daffodil."

"That's right," said Bassett, nodding.

"But where's the money?" asked the uncle.

"I keep it safe locked up, sir. Master Paul he can have it any minute he likes to ask for it."

"What, fifteen hundred pounds?"

"And twenty! And *forty*, that is, with the twenty he made on the course."

"It's amazing!" said the uncle.

"If Master Paul offers you to be partners, sir, I would, if I were you; if you'll excuse me," said Bassett.

Oscar Cresswell thought about it.

"I'll see the money," he said.

They drove home again, and sure enough, Bassett came round to the garden house with fifteen hundred pounds in notes. The twenty pounds reserve was left with Joe Glee, in the Turf Commission deposit.

"You see, it's all right, Uncle, when I'm *sure!* Then we go strong, for all we're worth. Don't we, Bassett?"

"We do that, Master Paul."

"And when are you sure?" said the uncle, laughing.

"Oh, well, sometimes I'm *absolutely* sure, like about Daffodil," said the boy; "and sometimes I have an idea; and sometimes I haven't even an idea, have I, Bassett? Then we're careful, because we mostly go down."

"You do, do you! And when you're sure, like about Daffodil, what makes you sure, sonny?"

"Oh, well, I don't know," said the boy uneasily. "I'm sure, you know, Uncle; that's all."

"It's as if he had it from heaven, sir," Bassett reiterated.

"I should say so!" said the uncle.

But he became a partner. And when the Leger was coming on, Paul was "sure" about Lively Spark, which was a quite inconsiderable horse. The boy insisted on puttting a thousand on the horse, Bassett went for five hundred, and Oscar Cresswell two hundred. Lively Spark came in first, and the betting had been ten to one against him. Paul had made ten thousand.

"You see," he said, "I was absolutely sure of him."

Even Oscar Cresswell had cleared two thousand.

"Look here, son," he said, "this sort of thing makes me nervous."

"It needn't, Uncle! Perhaps I shan't be sure again for a long time."

"But what are you going to do with your money?" asked the uncle.

"Of course," said the boy. "I started it for Mother. She said she had no luck, because Father is unlucky, so I thought if *I* was lucky, it might stop whispering."

"What might stop whispering?"

"Our house. I *hate* our house for whispering."

"What does it whisper?"

"Why—why"—the boy fidgeted—"why, I don't know. But it's always short of money, you know, Uncle."

"I know it, son, I know it."

"You know people send Mother writs, don't you, Uncle?"

"I'm afraid I do," said the uncle.

"And then the house whispers, like people laughing at you behind your back. It's awful, that is! I thought if I was lucky. . . ."

"You might stop it," added the uncle.

The boy watched him with big blue eyes, that had an uncanny cold fire in them, and he said never a word.

"Well, then!" said the uncle. "What are we doing?"

"I shouldn't like Mother to know I was lucky," said the boy.

"Why not, son?"

"She'd stop me."

"I don't think she would."

"Oh!"—and the boy writhed in an odd way—"I *don't* want her to know, Uncle."

"All right, son! We'll manage it without her knowing."

They managed it very easily. Paul, at the other's suggestion, handed over five thousand pounds to his uncle, who deposited it with the family lawyer, who was then to inform Paul's mother that a relative had put five thousand pounds into his hands, which sum was to be paid out a thousand pounds at a time, on the mother's birthday, for the next five years.

"So she'll have a birthday present of a thousand pounds for five successive years," said Uncle Oscar. "I hope it won't make it all the harder for her later."

Paul's mother had her birthday in November. The house had been "whispering" worse than ever lately, and, even in spite of his luck, Paul could not bear up against it. He was very anxious to see the effect of the birthday letter, telling his mother about the thousand pounds.

When there were no visitors, Paul now took his meals with his parents, as he was beyond the nursery control. His mother went into town nearly every day. She had discovered that she had an odd knack of sketching furs and dress materials, so she worked secretly in the studio of a friend who was the chief artist for the leading drapers. She drew the figures of ladies in furs and ladies in silk and sequins for the newspaper advertisements. This young woman artist earned several thousand pounds a year, but Paul's mother only made several hundreds, and she was again dissatisfied. She so wanted to be first in something, and she did not succeed, even in making sketches for drapery advertisements.

She was down to breakfast on the morning of her birthday. Paul watched her face as she read her letters. He knew the lawyer's letter. As his mother read it, her face hardened and became more expressionless. Then a cold, determined look came on her mouth. She hid the letter under the pile of others, and said not a word about it.

"Didn't you have anything nice in the post for your birthday, Mother?" said Paul.

"Quite moderately nice," she said, her voice cold and absent.

She went away to town without saying more.

But in the afternoon Uncle Oscar appeared. He said Paul's mother had had a long interview with the lawyer, asking if the whole five thousand could not be advanced at once, as she was in debt.

"What do you think, Uncle?" said the boy.

"I leave it to you, son."

"Oh, let her have it, then! We can get some more with the other," said the boy.

"A bird in the hand is worth two in the bush, laddie!" said Uncle Oscar.

"But I'm sure to *know* for the Grand National; or the Lincolnshire; or else the Derby. I'm sure to know for *one* of them," said Paul.

So Uncle Oscar signed the agreement, and Paul's mother touched the whole five thousand. Then something very curious happened. The voices in the house suddenly went mad, like a chorus of frogs on a spring evening. There were certain new furnishings, and Paul had a tutor. He was *really* going to Eton, his father's school, in the following autumn. There were flowers in the winter, and a blossoming of the luxury Paul's mother had been used to. And yet the voices in the house, behind the sprays of mimosa and almond blossom, and from under the piles of iridescent cushions, simply trilled and screamed in a sort of ecstasy: "There *must* be more money! Oh-h-h; there *must* be more money. Oh, now, now-w! Now-w-w—there *must* be more money!—more than ever! More than ever!"

It frightened Paul terribly. He studied away at his Latin and Greek. But his intense hours were spent with Bassett. The Grand National had gone by; he had not "known," and had lost a hundred pounds. Summer was at hand. He was in agony for the Lincoln. But even for the Lincoln he didn't "know," and he lost fifty pounds. He became wild-eyed and strange, as if something were going to explode in him.

"Let it alone, son! Don't you bother about it!" urged Uncle Oscar. But it was as if the boy couldn't really hear what his uncle was saying.

"I've got to know for the Derby! I've got to know for the Derby!" the child reiterated, his big blue eyes blazing with a sort of madness.

His mother noticed how overwrought he was.

"You'd better go to the seaside. Wouldn't you like to go now to the seaside, instead of waiting? I think you'd better," she said, looking down at him anxiously, her heart curiously heavy because of him.

But the child lifted his uncanny blue eyes. "I couldn't possibly go before the Derby, Mother!" he said. "I couldn't possibly!"

"Why not?" she said, her voice becoming heavy when she was opposed. "Why not? You can still go from the seaside to see the Derby with your uncle Oscar, if that's what you wish. No need for you to wait here. Besides, I think you care too much about these races. It's a bad sign. My family has been a gambling family, and you won't know till you grow up how much damage it has done. But it has done damage. I shall have to send Bassett away, and ask Uncle Oscar not to talk racing to you, unless you promise to be reasonable about it; go away to the seaside and forget it. You're all nerves!"

"I'll do what you like, Mother, so long as you don't send me away till after the Derby," the boy said.

"Send you away from where? Just from this house?"

"Yes," he said, gazing at her.

"Why, you curious child, what makes you care about this house so much, suddenly? I never knew you loved it."

He gazed at her without speaking. He had a secret within a secret, something he had not divulged, even to Bassett or to his uncle Oscar.

But his mother, after standing undecided and a little bit sullen for some moments, said:

"Very well, then! Don't go to the seaside till after the Derby, if you don't wish it. But promise me you won't let your nerves go to pieces. Promise you won't think so much about horse racing and *events*, as you call them!"

"Oh, no," said the boy casually. "I won't think much about them, Mother. You needn't worry. I wouldn't worry, Mother, if I were you."

"If you were me and I were you," said the mother, "I wonder what we *should* do!"

"But you know you needn't worry, Mother, don't you?" the boy repeated.

"I should be awfully glad to know it," she said wearily.

"Oh, well, you *can*, you know. I mean, you *ought* to know you needn't worry," he insisted.

"Ought I? Then I'll see about it," she said.

Paul's secret of secrets was his wooden horse, that which had no name. Since he was emancipated from a nurse and a nursery governess, he had had his rocking horse removed to his own bedroom at the top of the house.

"Surely, you're too big for a rocking horse!" his mother had remonstrated.

"Well, you see, Mother, till I can have a *real* horse, I like to have *some* sort of animal about," had been his quaint answer.

"Do you feel he keeps you company?" She laughed.

"Oh, yes! He's very good, he always keeps me company, when I'm there," said Paul.

So the horse, rather shabby, stood in an arrested prance in the boy's bedroom.

The Derby was drawing near, and the boy grew more and more tense. He hardly heard what was spoken to him, he was very frail, and his eyes were really uncanny. His mother had sudden strange seizures of uneasiness about him. Sometimes, for half an hour, she would feel a sudden anxiety about him that was almost anguish. She wanted to rush to him at once, and know he was safe.

Two nights before the Derby, she was at a big party in town, when one of her rushes of anxiety about her boy, her firstborn, gripped her heart till she could hardly speak. She fought with the feeling, might and main, for she believed in common sense. But it was too strong. She had to leave the dance and go downstairs to telephone to the country. The children's nursery governess was terribly surprised and startled at being rung up in the night.

"Are the children all right, Miss Wilmot?"

"Oh, yes, they are quite all right."

"Master Paul? Is he all right?"

"He went to bed as right as a trivet. Shall I run up and look at him?"

"No," said Paul's mother reluctantly. "No! Don't trouble. It's all right. Don't sit up. We shall be home fairly soon." She did not want her son's privacy intruded upon.

"Very good," said the governess.

It was about one o'clock when Paul's mother and father drove up to their house. All was still. Paul's mother went to her room and slipped off her white fur cloak. She had told her maid not to wait up for her. She heard her husband downstairs, mixing a whisky and soda.

And then, because of the strange anxiety at her heart, she stole upstairs to her son's room. Noiselessly she went along the upper corridor. Was there a faint noise? What was it?

She stood, with arrested muscles, outside his door, listening. There was a strange, heavy, and yet not loud noise. Her heart stood still. It was a soundless noise, yet rushing and powerful. Something huge, in violent, hushed motion. What was it? What in God's name was it? She ought to know. She felt that she knew the noise. She knew what it was.

Yet she could not place it. She couldn't say what it was. And on and on it went, like a madness.

Softly, frozen with anxiety and fear, she turned the door handle. The room was dark. Yet in the space near the window, she heard and saw something plunging to and fro. She gazed in fear and amazement.

Then suddenly she switched on the light, and saw her son, in his green pajamas, madly surging on the rocking horse. The blaze of light suddenly lit him up, as he urged the wooden horse, and lit her up, as she stood, blonde, in her dress of pale green and crystal, in the doorway.

"Paul!" she cried. "Whatever are you doing?"

"It's Malabar!" he screamed, in a powerful, strange voice. "It's Malabar!"

His eyes blazed at her for one strange and senseless second, as he ceased urging his wooden horse. Then he fell with a crash to the ground, and she, all her tormented motherhood flooding upon her, rushed to gather him up.

But he was unconscious, and unconscious he remained, with some brain fever. He talked and tossed, and his mother sat stonily by his side.

"Malabar! It's Malabar! Bassett, Bassett, I *know!* It's Malabar!"

So the child cried, trying to get up and urge the rocking horse that gave him his inspiration.

"What does he mean by Malabar?" asked the heart-frozen mother.

"I don't know," said the father stonily.

"What does he mean by Malabar?" she asked her brother Oscar.

"It's one of the horses running for the Derby," was the answer.

And, in spite of himself, Oscar Cresswell spoke to Bassett, and himself put a thousand on Malabar: at fourteen to one.

The third day of the illness was critical: they were waiting for a change. The boy, with his rather long, curly hair, was tossing ceaselessly on the pillow. He neither slept nor regained consciousness, and his eyes were like blue stones. His mother sat, feeling her heart had gone, turned actually into a stone.

In the evening, Oscar Cresswell did not come, but Bassett sent a message, saying could he come up for one moment, just one moment? Paul's mother was very angry at the intrusion, but on second thought she agreed. The boy was the same. Perhaps Bassett might bring him to consciousness.

The gardener, a shortish fellow with a little brown mustache, and sharp little brown eyes, tiptoed into the room, touched his imaginary cap to Paul's mother, and stole to the bedside, staring with glittering, smallish eyes at the tossing, dying child.

"Master Paul!" he whispered. "Master Paul! Malabar came in first all right, a clean win. I did as you told me. You've made over seventy thousand pounds, you have; you've got over eighty thousand. Malabar came in all right, Master Paul."

"Malabar! Malabar! Did I say Malabar, Mother? Did I say Malabar? Do you think I'm lucky, Mother? I knew Malabar, didn't I? Over eighty thousand pounds! I knew, didn't I know I knew? Malabar came in all right. If I ride my horse till I'm sure, then I tell you, Bassett, you can go as high as you like. Did you go for all you were worth, Bassett?"

"I went a thousand on it, Master Paul."

"I never told you, Mother, that if I can ride my horse, and *get there*, then I'm absolutely sure—oh, absolutely! Mother, did I ever tell you? I *am* lucky!"

"No, you never did," said the mother.

But the boy died in the night.

And even as he lay dead, his mother heard her brother's voice saying to her: "My God, Hester, you're eighty-odd thousand to the good, and a poor devil of a son to the bad. But, poor devil, poor devil, he's best gone out of a life where he rides his rocking horse to find a winner."

The Ones Who Walk Away from Omelas

URSULA LE GUIN

With a clamor of bells that set the swallows soaring, the Festival of Summer came to the city. Omelas, bright-towered by the sea. The rigging of the boats in harbor sparkled with flags. In the streets between houses with red roofs and painted walls, between old moss-grown gardens and under avenues of trees, past great parks and public buildings, processions moved. Some were decorous: old people in long stiff robes of mauve and grey, grave master workmen, quiet, merry women carrying their babies and chatting as they walked. In other streets the music beat faster, a shimmering of gong and tambourine, and the people went dancing, the procession was a dance. Children dodged in and out, their high calls rising like the swallows' crossing flights over the music and the singing. All the processions wound towards the north side of the city, where on the great water-meadow called the Green Fields boys and girls, naked in the bright air, with mud-stained feet and ankles and long, lithe arms, exercised their restive horses before the race. The horses wore no gear at all but a halter without bit. Their manes were braided with streamers of silver, gold, and green. They flared their nostrils and pranced and boasted to one another; they were vastly excited, the horse being the only animal who has adopted our ceremonies as his own. Far off to the north and west the mountains stood up half encircling Omelas on her bay. The air of morning was so clear that the snow still crowning the Eighteen Peaks burned with white-gold fire across the miles of sunlit air, under the dark blue of the sky. There was just enough wind to make the banners that marked the racecourse snap and flutter now and then. In the silence of the broad green meadows one could hear the music winding through the city streets, farther and nearer and ever approaching, a cheerful faint sweetness of the air that from time to time trembled and gathered together and broke out into the great joyous clanging of the bells.

Joyous! How is one to tell about joy? How describe the citizens of Omelas?

They were not simple folk, you see, though they were happy. But we do not say the words of cheer much any more. All smiles have become archaic. Given a description such as this one tends to make certain assumptions. Given a description such as this one tends to look next for the King, mounted on a splendid stallion and surrounded by his noble knights, or perhaps in a golden litter borne by great-muscled slaves. But there was no king. They did not use swords, or keep slaves. They were not barbarians. I do not know the rules and laws of their society, but I suspect that they were singularly few. As they did without monarchy and slavery, so they also got on without the stock exchange, the advertisement, the secret police, and the bomb. Yet I repeat that these were not simple folk, not dulcet shepherds, noble savages, bland utopians. They were not less complex than us. The trouble is that we have a bad habit, encouraged by pedants and sophisticates, of considering happiness as something rather stupid. Only pain is intellectual, only evil interesting. This is the treason of the artist: a refusal to admit the banality of evil and the terrible boredom of pain. If you can't lick 'em, join 'em. If it hurts, repeat it. But to praise despair is to condemn delight, to embrace violence is to lose hold of everything else. We have almost lost hold; we can no longer describe a happy man, nor make any celebration of joy. How can I tell you about the people of Omelas? They were not naïve and happy children—though their children were, in fact, happy. They were mature, intelligent, passionate adults whose lives were not wretched. O miracle! but I wish I could describe it better. I wish I could convince you. Omelas sounds in my words like a city in a fairy tale, long ago and far away, once upon a time. Perhaps it would be best if you imagined it as your own fancy bids, assuming it will rise to the occasion, for certainly I cannot suit you all. For instance, how about technology? I think that there would be no cars or helicopters in and above the streets; this follows from the fact that the people of Omelas are happy people. Happiness is based on a just discrimination of what is necessary, what is neither necessary nor destructive, and what is destructive. In the middle category, however—that of the unnecessary but undestructive, that of comfort, luxury, exuberance, etc.—they could perfectly well have central heating, subway trains, washing machines, and all kinds of marvelous devices not yet invented here, floating light-sources, fuelless power, a cure for the common cold. Or they could have none of that: it doesn't matter. As you like it. I incline to think that people from towns up and down the coast have been coming in to Omelas during the last days before the Festival on very fast little trains and double-decked trams and that the train station of Omelas is actually the handsomest building in town, though plainer than the magnificent Farmers' Market. But even granted trains, I fear that Omelas so far strikes some of you as goody-goody. Smiles, bells, parades, horses, bleh. If so, please add an orgy. If an orgy would help, don't hesitate. Let us not, however, have temples from which issue beautiful nude priests and priestesses already half in ecstasy and ready to copulate with any man or woman, lover or stranger, who desires union with the deep godhead of the blood, although that was my first idea. But really it would be better not to have any temples in Omelas—at least, not manned temples. Religion yes, clergy no. Surely the beautiful nudes can just wander about, offering themselves like divine soufflés to the hunger of the needy and the rapture of the flesh. Let them join the processions. Let tambourines be struck above the copulations, and the glory of desire be proclaimed upon the gongs, and (a not unimportant point) let the offspring of these delightful rituals be beloved and looked after by all. One thing I know there is none of in Omelas is guilt. But what else should there be? I thought at first there were no drugs, but that is puritanical. For those who like it, the faint insistent sweetness of *drooz* may perfume the ways of the city, *drooz* which first brings a great lightness and brilliance to the mind and limbs, and then after some hours a dreamy languor, and wonderful visions at last of the very arcana and inmost secrets of the Universe, as well as exciting the pleasure of sex beyond all belief; and it is not habit-forming. For more modest tastes I think there ought to be beer. What else, what else belongs in the joyous city? The sense of victory, surely, the celebration of courage. But as we did without clergy, let us do without soldiers. The joy built upon successful slaughter is not the right kind of joy; it will not do; it is fearful and it is trivial. A boundless and generous contentment, a magnanimous triumph felt not against some outer enemy but in communion with the finest and fairest in the souls of all men everywhere and the splendor of the world's summer: this is what swells the hearts of the people of Omelas, and the victory they celebrate is that of life. I really don't think many of them need to take *drooz*.

Most of the processions have reached the Green Fields by now. A marvelous smell of cooking goes forth from the red and blue tents of the provisioners. The faces of small children are amiably sticky; in the benign grey beard of a man a couple of crumbs of rich pastry are entangled. The youths and girls have mounted their horses and are beginning to group around the starting line of the course. An old woman, small, fat, and laughing, is passing out flowers from a basket, and tall young men wear her flowers in their shining hair. A child of nine or ten sits at the edge of the crowd, alone, playing on a wooden flute. People pause to listen, and they smile, but they do not speak to him, for he never ceases playing and never sees them, his dark eyes wholly rapt in the sweet, thin magic of the tune.

He finishes, and slowly lowers his hands holding the wooden flute.

As if that little private silence were the signal, all at once a trumpet sounds from the pavilion near the starting line: imperious, melancholy, piercing. The horses rear on their slender legs, and some of them neigh in answer. Sober-faced, the young riders stroke the horses' necks and soothe them, whispering, "Quiet, quiet, there my beauty, my hope. . . ." They begin to form in rank along the starting line. The crowds along the racecourse are like a field of grass and flowers in the wind. The Festival of Summer has begun.

Do you believe? Do you accept the festival, the city, the joy? No? Then let me describe one more thing.

In a basement under one of the beautiful public buildings of Omelas, or perhaps in the cellar of one of its spacious private homes, there is a room. It has one locked door, and no window. A little light seeps in dustily between cracks in the boards, secondhand from a cobwebbed window somewhere across the cellar. In one corner of the little room a couple of mops, with stiff, clotted, foul-smelling heads, stand near a rusty bucket. The floor is dirt, a little damp to the touch, as cellar dirt usually is. The room is about three paces long and two wide: a mere broom closet or disused tool room. In the room a child is sitting. It could be a boy or a girl. It looks about six, but actually is nearly ten. It is feeble-minded. Perhaps it was born defective, or perhaps it has become imbecile through fear, malnutrition, and neglect. It picks its nose and occasionally fumbles vaguely with its toes or genitals, as it sits hunched in the corner farthest from the bucket and the two mops. It is afraid of the mops. It finds them horrible. It shuts its eyes, but it knows the mops are still standing there; and the door is locked; and nobody will come. The door is always locked; and nobody ever comes, except that sometimes—the child has no understanding of time or interval—sometimes the door rattles terribly and opens, and a person, or several people, are there. One of them may come in and kick the child to make it stand up. The others never come close, but peer in at it with frightened, disgusted eyes. The food bowl and the water jug are hastily filled, the door is locked, the eyes disappear. The people at the door never say anything, but the child, who has not always lived in the tool room, and can remember sunlight and its mother's voice, sometimes speaks. "I will be good," it says. "Please let me out. I will be good!" They never answer. The child used to scream for help at night, and cry a good deal, but now it only makes a kind of whining, "eh-haa, eh-haa," and it speaks less and less often. It is so thin there are no calves to its legs; its belly protrudes; it lives on a half-bowl of corn meal and grease a day. It is naked. It buttocks and thighs are a mass of festered sores, as it sits in its own excrement continually.

They all know it is there, all the people of Omelas. Some of them have come to see it, others are content merely to know it is there. They all know that it has to be there. Some of them understand why, and some do not, but they all understand that their happiness, the beauty of their city, the tenderness of their friendships, the health of their children, the wisdom of their scholars, the skill of their makers, even the abundance of their harvest and the kindly weathers of their skies, depend wholly on this child's abominable misery.

This is usually explained to children when they are between eight and twelve, whenever they seem capable of understanding; and most of those who come to see the child are young people, though often enough an adult comes, or comes back, to see the child. No matter how well the matter has been explained to them, these young spectators are always shocked and sickened at the sight. They feel disgust, which they had thought themselves superior to. They feel anger, outrage, impotence, despite all the explanations. They would like to do something for the child. But there is nothing they can do. If the child were brought up into the sunlight out of that vile place, if it were cleaned and fed and comforted, that would be a good thing, indeed; but if it were done, in that day and hour all the prosperity and beauty and delight of Omelas would wither and be destroyed. Those are the terms. To exchange all the goodness and grace of every life in Omelas for that single, small improvement: to throw away the happiness of thousands for the chance of the happiness of one: that would be to let guilt within the walls indeed.

The terms are strict and absolute; there may not even be a kind word spoken to the child.

Often the young people go home in tears, or in a tearless rage, when they have seen the child and faced this terrible paradox. They may brood over it for weeks or years. But as time goes on they begin to realize that even if the child could be released, it would not get much good of its freedom: a little vague pleasure of warmth and food, no doubt, but little more. It is too degraded and imbecile to know any real joy. It has been afraid too long ever to be free of fear. Its habits are too uncouth for it to respond to humane treatment. Indeed, after so long it would probably be wretched without walls about it to protect it, and darkness for its eyes, and its own excrement to sit in. Their tears at the bitter injustice dry when they begin to perceive the terrible justice of reality and to accept it. Yet it is their tears and anger, the trying of their generosity and the acceptance of their helplessness, which are perhaps the true source of the splendor of their lives. Theirs is no vapid, irresponsible happiness. They know that they, like the child, are not free. They know compassion. It is the existence of the child, and their knowledge of its existence, that makes possible the nobility of their architecture, the poignancy of their music, the profundity of their science. It is because of the child that they are so gentle with children. They know that if the wretched one were not there snivelling in the dark, the other one, the flute-player, could make no joyful music as the young riders line up in their beauty for the race in the sunlight of the first morning of summer.

Now do you believe in them? Are they not more credible? But there is one more thing to tell, and this is quite incredible.

At times one of the adolescent girls or boys who go to see the child does not go home to weep or rage, does not, in fact, go home at all. Sometimes also a man or woman much older falls silent for a day or two, and then leaves home. These people go out into the street, and walk down the street alone. They keep walking, and walk straight out of the city of Omelas, through the beautiful gates. They keep walking across the farmlands of Omelas. Each one goes alone, youth or girl, man or woman. Night falls; the traveler must pass down village streets, between the houses with yellow-lit windows, and on out into the darkness of the fields. Each alone, they go west or north, towards the mountains. They go on. They leave Omelas, they walk ahead into the darkness, and they do not come back. The place they go towards is a place even less imaginable to most of us than the city of happiness. I cannot describe it at all. It is possible that it does not exist. But they seem to know where they are going, the ones who walk away from Omelas.

To Room 19

DORIS LESSING

This is a story, I suppose, about a failure in intelligence: the Rawlings' marriage was grounded in intelligence.

They were older when they married than most of their married friends: in their well-seasoned late twenties. Both had had a number of affairs, sweet rather than bitter; and when they fell in love—for they did fall in love—had known each other for some time. They joked that they had saved each other "for the real thing." That they had waited so long (but not too long) for this real thing was to them a proof of their sensible discrimination. A good many of their friends had married young, and now (they felt) probably regretted lost opportunities; while others, still unmarried, seemed to them arid, self-doubting, and likely to make desperate or romantic marriages.

Not only they, but others, felt they were well-matched: their friends' delight was an additional proof of their happiness. They had played the same roles, male and female, in this group or set, if such a wide, loosely connected, constantly changing constellation of people could be called a set. They had both become, by virtue of their moderation, their humour, and their abstinence from painful experience, people to whom others came for advice. They could be, and were, relied on. It was one of those cases of a man and a woman linking themselves whom no one else had ever thought of linking, probably because of their similarities. But then everyone exclaimed: Of course! How right! How was it we never thought of it before!

And so they married amid general rejoicing, and because of their foresight and their sense for what was probable, nothing was a surprise to them.

Both had well-paid jobs. Matthew was a subeditor on a large London newspaper, and Susan worked in an advertising firm. He was not the stuff of which editors or publicised journalists are made, but he was much more than "a subeditor," being one of the essential background people who in

601

fact steady, inspire, and make possible the people in the limelight. He was content with this position. Susan had a talent for commercial drawing. She was humorous about the advertisements she was responsible for, but she did not feel strongly about them one way or the other.

Both, before they married, had had pleasant flats, but they felt it unwise to base a marriage on either flat, because it might seem like a submission of personality on the part of the one whose flat it was not. They moved into a new flat in South Kensington on the clear understanding that when their marriage had settled down (a process they knew would not take long, and was in fact more a humorous concession to popular wisdom than what was due to themselves) they would buy a house and start a family.

And this is what happened. They lived in their charming flat for two years, giving parties and going to them, being a popular young married couple, and then Susan became pregnant, she gave up her job, and they bought a house in Richmond. It was typical of this couple that they had a son first, then a daughter, then twins, son and daughter. Everything right, appropriate, and what everyone would wish for, if they could choose. But people did feel these two had chosen; this balanced and sensible family was no more than what was due to them because of their infallible sense for *choosing* right.

And so they lived with their four children in their gardened house in Richmond and were happy. They had everything they had wanted and had planned for.

And yet. . . .

Well, even this was expected, that there must be a certain flatness. . . .

Yes, yes, of course, it was natural they sometimes felt like this. Like what?

Their life seemed to be like a snake biting its tail. Matthew's job for the sake of Susan, children, house, and garden—which caravanserai needed a well-paid job to maintain it. And Susan's practical intelligence for the sake of Matthew, the children, the house, and the garden—which unit would have collapsed in a week without her.

But there was no point about which either could say: "For the sake of *this* is all at rest." Children? But children can't be a centre of life and a reason for being. They can be a thousand things that are delightful, interesting, satisfying, but they can't be a wellspring to live from. Or they shouldn't be. Susan and Matthew knew that well enough.

Matthew's job? Ridiculous. It was an interesting job, but scarcely a reason for living. Matthew took pride in doing it well, but he could hardly be expected to be proud of the newspaper; the newspaper he read, *his* newspaper, was not the one he worked for.

Their love for each other? Well, that was nearest it. If this wasn't a centre, what was? Yes, it was around this point, their love, that the whole extraordinary structure revolved. For extraordinary it certainly was. Both Susan and Matthew had moments of thinking so, of looking in secret disbelief at this thing they had created: marriage, four children, big house, garden, charwomen, friends, cars . . . and this *thing*, this entity, all of it had come into existence, been blown into being out of nowhere, because Susan loved Matthew and Matthew loved Susan. Extraordinary. So that was the central point, the wellspring.

And if one felt that it simply was not strong enough, important enough, to support it all, well whose fault was that? Certainly neither Susan's nor Matthew's. It was in the nature of things. And they sensibly blamed neither themselves nor each other.

On the contrary, they used their intelligence to preserve what they had created from a painful and explosive world: they looked around them, and took lessons. All around them, marriages collapsing, or breaking, or rubbing along (even worse, they felt). They must not make the same mistakes, they must not.

They had avoided the pitfall so many of their friends had fallen into—of buying a house in the country *for the sake of the children,* so that the husband became a weekend husband, a weekend father, and the wife always careful not to ask what went on in the town flat which they called (in joke) a bachelor flat. No, Matthew was a full-time husband, a full-time father, and at night, in the big married bed in the big married bedroom (which had an attractive view of the river), they lay beside each other talking and he told her about his day, and what he had done, and whom he had met; and she told him about her day (not as interesting, but that was not her fault), for both knew of the hidden resentments and deprivations of the woman who has lived her own life—and above all, has earned her own living—and is now dependent on a husband for outside interests and money.

Nor did Susan make the mistake of taking a job for the sake of her independence, which she might very well have done, since her old firm, missing her qualities of humour, balance, and sense, invited her often to go back. Children needed their mother to a certain age, that both parents knew and agreed on; and when these four healthy wisely brought up children were of the right age, Susan would work again, because she knew, and so did he, what happened to women of fifty at the height of their energy and ability, with grownup children who no longer needed their full devotion.

So here was this couple, testing their marriage, looking after it, treating it like a small boat full of helpless people in a very stormy sea. Well, of course, so it was. . . . The storms of the world were bad, but not too close—which is not to say they were selfishly felt: Susan and Matthew were both well-informed and responsible people. And the inner storms and quicksands were understood and charted. So everything was all right. Everything was in order. Yes, things were under control.

So what did it matter if they felt dry, flat? People like themselves, fed on a hundred books (psychological, anthropological, sociological), could scarcely be unprepared for the dry, controlled wistfulness which is the distinguishing mark of the intelligent marriage. Two people, endowed with education, with discrimination, with judgement, linked together voluntarily from their will to be happy together and to be of use to others—one sees them everywhere, one knows them, one even is that thing oneself: sadness because so much is after all so little. These two, unsurprised, turned towards each other with even more courtesy and gentle love: this was life, that two people, no matter how carefully chosen, could not be everything to each other. In fact, even to say so, to think in such a way, was banal; they were ashamed to do it.

It was banal, too, when one night Matthew came home late and confessed he had been to a party, taken a girl home, and slept with her. Susan forgave him, of course. Except that forgiveness is hardly the word. Understanding, yes. But if you understand something, you don't forgive it, you are the thing itself: forgiveness is for what you *don't* understand. Nor had he *confessed*—what sort of word is that?

The whole thing was not important. After all, years ago they had joked: Of course I'm not going to be faithful to you, no one can be faithful to one other person for a whole lifetime. (And there was the word "faithful"—stupid, all these words, stupid, belonging to a savage old world.) But the incident left both of them irritable. Strange, but they were both bad-tempered, annoyed. There was something unassimilable about it.

Making love splendidly after he had come home that night, both had felt that the idea that Myra Jenkins, a pretty girl met at a party, could be even relevant was ridiculous. They had loved each other for over a decade, would love each other for years more. Who, then, was Myra Jenkins?

Except, thought Susan, unaccountably bad-tempered, she was (is?) the first. In ten years. So either the ten years' fidelity was not important, or she isn't. (No, no, there is something wrong with this way of thinking, there must be.) But if she isn't important, presumably it wasn't important either when Matthew and I first went to bed with each other that afternoon whose delight even now (like a very long shadow at sundown) lays a long, wand-like finger over us. (Why did I say sundown?) Well, if what we felt that afternoon was not important, nothing is important, because if it hadn't been for what we felt, we wouldn't be Mr. and Mrs. Rawlings with four children, et cetera, et cetera. The whole thing is *absurd*—for him to have come home and told me was absurd. For him not to have told me was absurd. For me to care or, for that matter, not to care, is absurd . . . and who is Myra Jenkins? Why, no one at all.

There was only one thing to do, and of course these sensible people did it; they put the thing behind them, and consciously, knowing what they were doing, moved forward into a different phase of their marriage, giving thanks for the past good fortune as they did so.

For it was inevitable that the handsome, blond, attractive, manly man, Matthew Rawlings, should be at times tempted (oh, what a word!) by the attractive girls at parties she could not attend because of the four children; and that sometimes he would succumb (a word even more repulsive, if possible) and that she, a goodlooking woman in the big well-tended garden at Richmond, would sometimes be pierced as by an arrow from the sky with bitterness. Except that bitterness was not in order, it was out of court. Did the casual girls touch the marriage? They did not. Rather it was they who knew defeat because of the handsome Matthew Rawlings' marriage body and soul to Susan Rawlings.

In that case why did Susan feel (though luckily not for longer than a few seconds at a time) as if life had become a desert, and that nothing mattered, and that her children were not her own?

Meanwhile her intelligence continued to assert that all was well. What if her Matthew did have an occasional sweet afternoon, the odd affair? For she knew quite well, except in her moments of aridity, that they were very happy, that the affairs were not important.

Perhaps that was the trouble? It was in the nature of things that the adventures and delights could no longer be hers, because of the four children and the big house that needed so much attention. But perhaps she was secretly wishing, and even knowing that she did, that the wildness and the beauty could be his. But he was married to her. She was married to him. They were married inextricably. And therefore the gods could not strike him with the real magic, not really. Well, was it Susan's fault that after he came home from an adventure he looked harassed rather than fulfilled? (In fact, that was how she knew he had been *unfaithful,* because of his sullen air, and his glances at her, similar to hers at him: What is it that I share with this person that shields all delight from me?) But none of it by anybody's fault. (But what did they feel ought to be somebody's fault?) Nobody's fault, nothing to be at fault, no one to blame, no one to offer or to take it . . . and nothing wrong, either, except that Matthew never was really struck, as he wanted to be, by joy; and that Susan was more and more often threatened by emptiness. (It was usually in the garden that she was invaded by this feeling: she was coming to avoid the garden, unless the children or Matthew were with her.) There was no need to use the dramatic words "unfaithful," "forgive," and the rest: intelligence forbade them. Intelligence barred, too, quarrelling, sulking, anger, silences of withdrawal, accusations, and tears. Above all, intelligence forbids tears.

A high price has to be paid for the happy marriage with the four healthy children in the large white gardened house.

And they were paying it, willingly, knowing what they were doing. When they lay side by side or breast to breast in the big civilised bedroom overlooking the wild sullied river, they laughed, often, for no particular reason; but they knew it was really because of these two small people, Susan and Matthew, supporting such an edifice on their intelligent love. The laugh comforted them; it saved them both, though from what, they did not know.

They were now both fortyish. The older children, boy and girl, were ten and eight, at school. The twins, six, were still at home. Susan did not have nurses or girls to help her: childhood is short; and she did not regret the hard work. Often enough she was bored, since small children can be boring; she was often very tired; but she regretted nothing. In another decade, she would turn herself back into being a woman with a life of her own.

Soon the twins would go to school, and they would be away from home from nine until four. These hours, so Susan saw it, would be the preparation for her own slow emancipation away from the role of hub-of-the-family into woman-with-her-own-life. She was already planning for the hours of freedom when all the children would be "off her hands." That was the phrase used by Matthew and by Susan and by their friends, for the moment when the youngest child went off to school. "They'll be off your hands, darling Susan, and you'll have time to yourself." So said Matthew, the intelligent husband, who had often enough commended and consoled Susan, standing by her in spirit during the years when her soul was not her own, as she said, but her children's.

What it amounted to was that Susan saw herself as she had been at twenty-eight, unmarried; and then again somewhere about fifty, blossoming from the root of what she had been twenty years before. As if the essential Susan were in abeyance, as if she were in cold storage. Matthew said something like this to Susan one night: and she agreed that it was true—she did feel something like that. What, then, was this essential Susan? She did not know. Put like that it sounded ridiculous, and she did not really feel it. Anyway, they had a long discussion about the whole thing before going off to sleep in each other's arms.

So the twins went off to their school, two bright affectionate children who had no problems about it, since their older brother and sister had trodden this path so successfully before them. And now Susan was going to be alone in the big house, every day of the school term, except for the daily woman who came in to clean.

It was now, for the first time in this marriage, that something happened which neither of them had foreseen.

This is what happened. She returned, at nine-thirty, from taking the twins to the school by car, looking forward to seven blissful hours of freedom. On the first morning she was simply restless, worrying about the twins "naturally enough" since this was their first day away at school. She was hardly able to contain herself until they came back. Which they did happily, excited by the world of school, looking forward to the next day. And the next day Susan took them, dropped them, came back, and found herself reluctant to enter her big and beautiful home because it was as if something was waiting for her there that she did not wish to confront. Sensibly, however, she parked the car in the garage, entered the house, spoke to Mrs. Parkes, the daily woman, about her duties, and went up to her bedroom. She was possessed by a fever which drove her out again, downstairs, into the kitchen, where Mrs. Parkes was making cake and did not need her, and into the garden. There she sat on a bench and tried to calm herself looking at trees, at a brown glimpse of the river. But she was filled with tension, like a panic: as if an enemy was in the garden with her. She spoke to herself severely, thus: All this is quite natural. First, I spent twelve years of my adult life working, *living my own life*. Then I married, and from the moment I became pregnant for the first time I signed myself over, so to speak, to other people. To the children. Not for one moment in twelve years have I been alone, had time to myself. So now I have to learn to be myself again. That's all.

And she went indoors to help Mrs. Parkes cook and clean, and found some sewing to do for the children. She kept herself occupied every day. At the end of the first term she understood she felt two contrary emotions. First: secret astonishment and dismay that during those weeks when the house was empty of children she had in fact been more occupied (had been careful to keep herself occupied) than ever she had been when the children were around her needing her continual attention. Second: that now she knew the house would be full of them, and for five weeks, she resented the fact she would never be alone. She was already looking back at those hours of sewing, cooking (but by herself) as at a lost freedom which would not be hers for five long weeks. And the two months of term which would succeed the five weeks stretched alluringly open to her—freedom. But what freedom—when in fact she had been so careful *not* to be free of small duties during the last weeks? She looked at herself, Susan Rawlings, sitting in a big chair by the window in the bedroom, sewing shirts or dresses, which she might just as well have bought. She saw herself making cakes for hours at a time in the big family kitchen: yet usually she bought cakes. What she saw was a woman alone, that was true, but she had not felt alone. For instance, Mrs. Parkes was always somewhere in the house. And she did not like being in the garden at all, because of the closeness there of the enemy—irritation, restlessness, emptiness, whatever it was—which keeping her hands occupied made less dangerous for some reason.

Susan did not tell Matthew of these thoughts. They were not sensible. She did not recognise herself in them. What should she say to her dear friend and husband, Matthew? "When I go into the garden, that is, if the children are not there, I feel as if there is an enemy there waiting to invade me." "What enemy, Susan darling?" "Well I don't know, really. . . ." "Perhaps you should see a doctor?"

No, clearly this conversation should not take place. The holidays began and Susan welcomed them. Four children, lively, energetic, intelligent, demanding: she was never, not for a moment of her day, alone. If she was in a room, they would be in the next room, or waiting for her to do something for them; or it would soon be time for lunch or tea, or to take one of them to the dentist. Something to do: five weeks of it, thank goodness.

On the fourth day of these so welcome holidays, she found she was storming with anger at the twins; two shrinking beautiful children who (and this is what checked her) stood hand in hand looking at her with sheer dismayed disbelief. This was their calm mother, shouting at them. And for what? They had come to her with some game, some bit of nonsense. They looked at each other, moved closer for support, and went off hand in hand, leaving Susan holding on to the windowsill of the livingroom, breathing deep, feeling sick. She went to lie down, telling the older children she had a headache. She heard the boy Harry telling the little ones: "It's all right, Mother's got a headache." She heard that *It's all right* with pain.

That night she said to her husband: "Today I shouted at the twins, quite unfairly." She sounded miserable, and he said gently: "Well, what of it?"

"It's more of an adjustment than I thought, their going to school."

"But Susie, Susie darling. . . ." For she was crouched weeping on the bed. He comforted her: "Susan, what is this all about? You shouted at them? What of it? If you shouted at them fifty times a day it wouldn't be more than the little devils deserve." But she wouldn't laugh. She wept. Soon he comforted her with his body. She became calm. Calm, she wondered what was wrong with her, and why she should mind so much that she might, just once, have behaved unjustly with the children. What did it matter? They had forgotten it all long ago: Mother had a headache and everything was all right.

It was a long time later that Susan understood that that night, when she had wept and Matthew had driven the misery out of her with his big solid body, was the last time, ever in their married life, that they had been—to use their mutual language—with each other. And even that was a lie, because she had not told him of her real fears at all.

The five weeks passed, and Susan was in control of herself, and good and kind, and she looked forward to the holidays with a mixture of fear and longing. She did not know what to expect. She took the twins off to school (the elder children took themselves to school) and she returned to the house determined to face the enemy wherever he was, in the house, or the garden or—where?

She was again restless, she was possessed by restlessness. She cooked and sewed and worked as before, day after day, while Mrs. Parkes remonstrated: "Mrs. Rawlings, what's the need for it? I can do that, it's what you pay me for."

And it was so irrational that she checked herself. She would put the car in the garage, go up to her bedroom, and sit, hands in her lap, forcing herself to be quiet. She listened to Mrs. Parkes moving around the house. She looked out into the garden and saw the branches shake the trees. She sat defeating the enemy, restlessness. Emptiness. She ought to be thinking about her life, about herself. But she did not. Or perhaps she could not. As soon as she forced her mind to think about Susan (for what else did she want to be alone for?), it skipped off to thoughts of butter or school clothes. Or it thought of Mrs. Parkes. She realised that she sat listening for the movements of the cleaning woman, following her every turn, bend, thought. She followed her in her mind from kitchen to bathroom, from table to oven, and it was as if the duster, the cleaning cloth, the saucepan, were in her own hand. She would hear herself saying: No, not like that, don't put that there. . . . Yet she did not give a damn what Mrs. Parkes did, or if she did it at all. Yet she could not prevent herself from being conscious of her, every minute. Yes, this was what was wrong with her: she needed, when she was alone, to be really alone, with no one near. She could not endure the knowledge that in ten minutes or in half an hour Mrs. Parkes would call up the stairs: "Mrs. Rawlings, there's no silver polish. Madam, we're out of flour."

So she left her house and went to sit in the garden where she was screened from the house by trees. She waited for the demon to appear and claim her, but he did not.

She was keeping him off, because she had not, after all, come to an end of arranging herself.

She was planning how to be somewhere where Mrs. Parkes would not come after her with a cup of tea, or a demand to be allowed to telephone (always irritating, since Susan did not care who she telephoned or how often), or just a nice talk about something. Yes, she needed a place, or a state of affairs, where it would not be necessary to keep reminding herself: In ten minutes I must telephone Matthew about . . . and at half past three I must leave early for the children because the car needs cleaning. And at ten o'clock tomorrow I must remember. . . . She was possessed with resentment that the seven hours of freedom in every day (during weekdays in the school term) were not free, that never, not for one second, ever, was she free from the pressure of time, from having to remember this or that. She could never forget herself; never really let herself go into forgetfulness.

Resentment. It was poisoning her. (She looked at this emotion and thought it was absurd. Yet she felt it.) She was a prisoner. (She looked at this thought too, and it was no good telling herself it was a ridiculous one.) She must tell Matthew—but what? She was filled with emotions that were utterly ridiculous, that she despised, yet that nevertheless she was feeling so strongly she could not shake them off.

The school holidays came round, and this time they were for nearly two months, and she behaved with a conscious controlled decency that nearly drove her crazy. She would lock herself in the bathroom, and sit on the edge of the bath, breathing deep, trying to let go into some kind of calm. Or she went up into the spare room, usually empty, where no one would expect her to be. She heard the children calling "Mother, Mother," and kept silent, feeling guilty. Or she went to the very end of the garden, by herself, and looked at the slow-moving brown river; she looked at the river and closed her eyes and breathed slow and deep, taking it into her being, into her veins.

Then she returned to the family, wife and mother, smiling and responsible, feeling as if the pressure of these people—four lively children and her husband—were a painful pressure on the surface of her skin, a hand pressing on her brain. She did not once break down into irritation during these holidays, but it was like living out a prison sentence, and when the children went back to school, she sat on a white stone near the flowing river, and she thought: It is not even a year since the twins went to school, since *they were off my hands* (What on earth did I think I meant when I used that stupid phrase?), and yet I'm a different person. I'm simply not myself. I don't understand it.

Yet she had to understand it. For she knew that this structure—big white house, on which the mortgage still cost four hundred a year, a husband, so good and kind and insightful; four children, all doing so nicely; and the garden where she sat; and Mrs. Parkes, the cleaning woman—all this depended on her, and yet she could not understand why, or even what it was she contributed to it.

She said to Matthew in their bedroom: "I think there must be something wrong with me."

And he said: "Surely not, Susan? You look marvellous—you're as lovely as ever."

She looked at the handsome blond man, with his clear, intelligent, blue-eyed face, and thought: Why is it I can't tell him? Why not? And she said: "I need to be alone more than I am."

At which he swung his slow blue gaze at her, and she saw what she had been dreading: Incredulity. Disbelief. And fear. An incredulous blue stare from a stranger who was her husband, as close to her as her own breath.

He said: "But the children are at school and off your hands."

She said to herself: I've got to force myself to say: Yes, but do you realize that I never feel free? There's never a moment I can say to myself: There's nothing I have to remind myself about, nothing I have to do in half an hour, or an hour, or two hours. . . .

But she said: "I don't feel well."

He said: "Perhaps you need a holiday."

She said, appalled: "But not without you, surely?" For she could not imagine herself going off without him. Yet that was what he meant. Seeing her face, he laughed, and opened his arms, and she went into them, thinking: Yes, yes, but why can't I say it? And what is it I have to say?

She tried to tell him, about never being free. And he listened and said: "But Susan, what sort of freedom can you possibly want—short of being dead! Am I ever free? I go to the office, and I have to be there at ten—all right, half past ten, sometimes. And I have to do this or that, don't I. Then I've got to come home at a certain time—I don't mean it, you know I don't—but if I'm not going to be back home at six I telephone you. When can I ever say to myself: I have nothing to be responsible for in the next six hours?"

Susan, hearing this, was remorseful. Because it was true. The good marriage, the house, the children, depended just as much on his voluntary
bondage as it did on hers. But why did he not feel bound? Why didn't he
chafe and become restless? No, there was something really wrong with her
and this proved it.

And that word "bondage"—why had she used it? She had never felt
marriage, or the children, as bondage. Neither had he, or surely they
wouldn't be together lying in each other's arms content after twelve years
of marriage.

No, her state (whatever it was) was irrelevant, nothing to do with her real
good life with her family. She had to accept the fact that, after all, she was
an irrational person and to live with it. Some people had to live with crippled arms, or stammers, or being deaf. She would have to live knowing she
was subject to a state of mind she could not own.

Nevertheless, as a result of this conversation with her husband, there was
a new regime next holidays.

The spare room at the top of the house now had a cardboard sign saying:
PRIVATE! DO NOT DISTURB! on it. (This sign had been drawn in coloured
chalks by the children, after a discussion between the parents in which it
was decided this was psychologically the right thing). The family and Mrs.
Parkes knew this was "Mother's Room" and that she was entitled to her privacy. Many serious conversations took place between Matthew and the children about not taking Mother for granted. Susan overheard the first,
between father and Harry, the older boy, and was surprised at her irritation over it. Surely she could have a room somewhere in that big house and
retire into it without such a fuss being made? Without it being so solemnly
discussed? Why couldn't she simply have announced: "I'm going to fit out
the little top room for myself, and when I'm in it I'm not to be disturbed for
anything short of fire"? Just that, and finished; instead of long earnest discussions. When she heard Harry and Matthew explaining it to the twins
with Mrs. Parkes coming in—"Yes, well, a family sometimes gets on top of
a woman"—she had to go right away to the bottom of the garden until the
devils of exasperation had finished their dance in her blood.

But now there was a room, and she could go there when she liked, she
used it seldom; she felt even more caged there than in her bedroom. One
day she had gone up there after a lunch for ten children she had cooked
and served because Mrs. Parkes was not there, and had sat alone for a while
looking into the garden. She saw the children stream out from the kitchen
and stand looking up at the window where she sat behind the curtains.
They were all—her children and their friends—discussing Mother's
Room. A few minutes later, the chase of the children in some game came
pounding up the stairs, but ended as abruptly as if they had fallen over a
ravine, so sudden was the silence. They had remembered she was there,
and had gone silent in a great gale of "Hush! Shhhhh! Quiet, you'll dis-

turb her. . . ." And they went tiptoeing downstairs like criminal conspirators. When she came down to make tea for them, they all apologised. The twins put their arms around her, from front and back, making a human cage of loving limbs, and promised it would never occur again. "We forgot, Mummy, we forgot all about it!"

What it amounted to was that Mother's Room, and her need for privacy, had become a valuable lesson in respect for other people's rights. Quite soon Susan was going up to the room only because it was a lesson it was a pity to drop. Then she took sewing up there, and the children and Mrs. Parkes came in and out: it had become another family room.

She sighed, and smiled, and resigned herself—she made jokes at her own expense with Matthew over the room. That is, she did from the self she liked, she respected. But at the same time, something inside her howled with impatience, with rage. . . . And she was frightened. One day she found herself kneeling by her bed and praying: "Dear God, keep it away from me, keep him away from me." She meant the devil, for she now thought of it, not caring if she was irrational, as some sort of demon. She imagined him, or it, as a youngish man, or perhaps a middleaged man pretending to be young. Or a man young-looking from immaturity? At any rate, she saw the young-looking face which, when she drew closer, had dry lines about mouth and eyes. He was thinnish, meagre in build. And he had a reddish complexion, and ginger hair. That was he—a gingery, energetic man, and he wore a reddish hairy jacket, unpleasant to the touch.

Well, one day she saw him. She was standing at the bottom of the garden, watching the river ebb past, when she raised her eyes and saw this person, or being, sitting on the white stone bench. He was looking at her, and grinning. In his hand was a long crooked stick, which he had picked off the ground, or broken off the tree above him. He was absent-mindedly, out of absent-minded or freakish impulse of spite, using the stick to stir around in the coils of a blindworm or a grass snake (or some kind of snake-like creature: it was whitish and unhealthy to look at, unpleasant). The snake was twisting about, flinging its coils from side to side in a kind of dance of protest against the teasing prodding stick.

Susan looked at him, thinking: Who is the stranger? What is he doing in our garden? Then she recognised the man around whom her terrors had crystallised. As she did so, he vanished. She made herself walk over to the bench. A shadow from a branch lay across thin emerald grass, moving jerkily over its roughness, and she could see why she had taken it for a snake, lashing and twisting. She went back to the house thinking: Right, then, so I've seen him with my own eyes, so I'm not crazy after all—there *is* a danger because I've seen him. He is lurking in the garden and sometimes even in the house, and he wants to *get into me and to take me over*.

She dreamed of having a room or a place, anywhere, where she could go and sit, by herself, no one knowing where she was.

Once, near Victoria, she found herself outside a news agent that had Rooms to Let advertised. She decided to rent a room, telling no one. Sometimes she could take the train into Richmond and sit alone in it for an hour or two. Yet how could she? A room would cost three or four pounds a week, and she earned no money, and how could she explain to Matthew that she needed such a sum? What for? It did not occur to her that she was taking it for granted she wasn't going to tell him about the room.

Well, it was out of the question, having a room; yet she knew she must.

One day, when a school term was well established, and none of the children had measles or other ailments, and everything seemed in order, she did the shopping early, explained to Mrs. Parkes she was meeting an old school friend, took the train to Victoria, searched until she found a small quiet hotel, and asked for a room for the day. They did not let rooms by the day, the manageress said, looking doubtful, since Susan so obviously was not the kind of woman who needed a room for unrespectable reasons. Susan made a long explanation about not being well, being unable to stop without frequent rests for lying down. At last she was allowed to rent the room provided she paid a full night's price for it. She was taken up by the manageress and a maid, both concerned over the state of her health . . . which must be pretty bad if, living at Richmond (she had signed her name and address in the register), she needed a shelter at Victoria.

The room was ordinary and anonymous, and was just what Susan needed. She put a shilling in the gas fire, and sat, eyes shut, in a dingy armchair with her back to a dingy window. She was alone. She was alone. She was alone. She could feel pressures lifting off her. First the sounds of traffic came very loud; then they seemed to vanish; she might even have slept a little. A knock on the door: it was Miss Townsend, the manageress, bringing her a cup of tea with her own hands, so concerned was she over Susan's long silence and possible illness.

Miss Townsend was a lonely woman of fifty, running this hotel with all the rectitude expected of her, and she sensed in Susan the possibility of understanding companionship. She stayed to talk. Susan found herself in the middle of a fantastic story about her illness, which got more and more impossible as she tried to make it tally with the large house at Richmond, well-off husband, and four children. Suppose she said instead: Miss Townsend, I'm here in your hotel because I need to be alone for a few hours, above all *alone and with no one knowing where I am*. She said it mentally, and saw, mentally, the look that would inevitably come on Miss Townsend's elderly maiden's face. "Miss Townsend, my four children and my husband are driving me insane, do you understand that? Yes, I can see from the gleam of hysteria in your eyes that comes from loneliness controlled but only just contained that I've got everything in the world you've ever longed for. Well, Miss Townsend, I don't want any of it. You can have it, Miss Townsend. I wish I was absolutely alone in the world, like you. Miss Townsend,

I'm besieged by seven devils, Miss Townsend, Miss Townsend, let me stay in your hotel where the devils can't get me. . . ." Instead of saying all this, she described her anaemia, agreed to try Miss Townsend's remedy for it, which was raw liver, minced, between whole-meal bread, and said yes, perhaps it would be better if she stayed at home and let a friend do shopping for her. She paid her bill and left the hotel, defeated.

At home Mrs. Parkes said she didn't really like it, no, not really, when Mrs. Rawlings was away from nine in the morning until five. The teacher had telephoned from school to say Joan's teeth were paining her, and she hadn't known what to say; and what was she to make for the children's tea, Mrs. Rawlings hadn't said.

All this was nonsense, of course. Mrs. Parkes's complaint was that Susan had withdrawn herself spiritually, leaving the burden of the big house on her.

Susan looked back at her day of "freedom" which had resulted in her becoming a friend of the lonely Miss Townsend, and in Mrs. Parkes's remonstrances. Yet she remembered the short blissful hour of being alone, really alone. She was determined to arrange her life, no matter what it cost, so that she could have that solitude more often. An absolute solitude, where no one knew her or cared about her.

But how? She thought of saying to her old employer: I want you to back me up in a story with Matthew that I am doing part-time work for you. The truth is that. . . . But she would have to tell him a lie too, and which lie? She could not say: I want to sit by myself three or four times a week in a rented room. And besides, he knew Matthew, and she could not really ask him to tell lies on her behalf, apart from being bound to think it meant a lover.

Suppose she really took a part-time job, which she could get through fast and efficiently, leaving time for herself. What job? Addressing envelopes? Canvassing?

And there was Mrs. Parkes, working widow, who knew exactly what she was prepared to give to the house, who knew by instinct when her mistress withdrew in spirit from her responsibilities. Mrs. Parkes was one of the servers of this world, but she needed someone to serve. She had to have Mrs. Rawlings, her madam, at the top of the house or in the garden, so that she could come and get support from her: "Yes, the bread's not what it was when I was a girl. . . . Yes, Harry's got a wonderful appetite, I wonder where he puts it all. . . . Yes, it's lucky the twins are so much of a size, they can wear each other's shoes, that's a saving in these hard times. . . . Yes, the cherry jam from Switzerland is not a patch on the jam from Poland, and three times the price. . . ." And so on. That sort of talk Mrs. Parkes must have, every day, or she would leave, not knowing herself why she left.

Susan Rawlings, thinking these thoughts, found that she was prowling through the great thicketed garden like a wild cat: she was walking up the stairs, down the stairs, through the rooms into the garden, along the brown running river, back, up through the house, down again. . . . It was a wonder Mrs. Parkes did not think it strange. But, on the contrary, Mrs. Rawlings could do what she liked, she could stand on her head if she wanted, provided she was *there*. Susan Rawlings prowled and muttered through her house, hating Mrs. Parkes, hating poor Miss Townsend, dreaming of her hour of solitude in the dingy respectability of Miss Townsend's hotel bedroom, and she knew quite well she was mad. Yes, she was mad.

She said to Matthew that she must have a holiday. Matthew agreed with her. This was not as things had been once—how they had talked in each other's arms in the marriage bed. He had, she knew, diagnosed her finally as *unreasonable*. She had become someone outside himself that he had to manage. They were living side by side in this house like two tolerably friendly strangers.

Having told Mrs. Parkes—or rather, asked for her permission—she went off on a walking holiday in Wales. She chose the remotest place she knew of. Every morning the children telephoned her before they went off to school, to encourage and support her, just as they had over Mother's Room. Every evening she telephoned them, spoke to each child in turn, and then to Matthew. Mrs. Parkes, given permission to telephone for instructions or advice, did so every day at lunchtime. When, as happened three times, Mrs. Rawlings was out on the mountainside, Mrs. Parkes asked that she should ring back at such-and-such a time, for she would not be happy in what she was doing without Mrs. Rawlings' blessing.

Susan prowled over wild country with the telephone wire holding her to her duty like a leash. The next time she must telephone, or wait to be telephoned, nailed her to her cross. The mountains themselves seemed trammelled by her unfreedom. Everywhere on the mountains, where she met no one at all, from breakfast time to dusk, excepting sheep, or a shepherd, she came face to face with her own craziness, which might attack her in the broadest valleys, so that they seemed too small, or on a mountain top from which she could see a hundred other mountains and valleys, so that they seemed too low, too small, with the sky pressing down too close. She would stand gazing at a hillside brilliant with ferns and bracken, jewelled with running water, and see nothing but her devil, who lifted inhuman eyes at her from where he leaned negligently on a rock, switching at his ugly yellow boots with a leafy twig.

She returned to her home and family, with the Welsh emptiness at the back of her mind like a promise of freedom.

She told her husband she wanted to have an *au pair* girl.

They were in their bedroom, it was late at night, the children slept. He sat, shirted and slippered, in a chair by the window, looking out. She sat brushing her hair and watching him in the mirror. A time-hallowed scene in the connubial bedroom. He said nothing, while she heard the arguments coming into his mind, only to be rejected because every one was *reasonable*.

"It seems strange to get one now; after all, the children are in school most of the day. Surely the time for you to have help was when you were stuck with them day and night. Why don't you ask Mrs. Parkes to cook for you? She's even offered to—I can understand if you are tired of cooking for six people. But you know that an *au pair* girl means all kinds of problems; it's not like having an ordinary char in during the day. . . ."

Finally he said carefully: "Are you thinking of going back to work?"

"No," she said, "no, not really." She made herself sound vague, rather stupid. She went on brushing her black hair and peering at herself so as to be oblivious of the short uneasy glances her Matthew kept giving her. "Do you think we can't afford it?" she went on vaguely, not at all the old efficient Susan who knew exactly what they could afford.

"It's not that," he said, looking out of the window at dark trees, so as not to look at her. Meanwhile she examined a round, candid, pleasant face with clear dark brows and clear grey eyes. A sensible face. She brushed thick healthy black hair and thought: Yet that's the reflection of a madwoman. How very strange! Much more to the point if what looked back at me was the gingery green-eyed demon with his dry meagre smile. . . . Why wasn't Matthew agreeing? After all, what else could he do? She was breaking her part of the bargain and there was no way of forcing her to keep it: that her spirit, her soul, should live in this house, so that the people in it could grow like plants in water, and Mrs. Parkes remain content in their service. In return for this, he would be a good loving husband, and responsible towards the children. Well, nothing like this had been true of either of them for a long time. He did his duty, perfunctorily; she did not even pretend to do hers. And he had become like other husbands, with his real life in his work and the people he met there, and very likely a serious affair. All this was her fault.

At last he drew heavy curtains, blotting out the trees, and turned to force her attention: "Susan, are you really sure we need a girl?" But she would not meet his appeal at all. She was running the brush over her hair again and again, lifting fine black clouds in a small hiss of electricity. She was peering in and smiling as if she were amused at the clinging hissing hair that followed the brush.

"Yes, I think it would be a good idea, on the whole," she said, with the cunning of a madwoman evading the real point.

In the mirror she could see her Matthew lying on his back, his hands behind his head, staring upwards, his face sad and hard. She felt her heart (the old heart of Susan Rawlings) soften and call out to him. But she set it to be indifferent.

He said: "Susan, the children?" It was an appeal that *almost* reached her. He opened his arms, lifting them palms up, empty. She had only to run across and fling herself into them, onto his hard, warm chest, and melt into herself, into Susan. But she could not. She would not see his lifted arms.

She said vaguely: "Well, surely it'll be even better for them? We'll get a French or a German girl and they'll learn the language."

In the dark she lay beside him, feeling frozen, a stranger. She felt as if Susan had been spirited away. She disliked very much this woman who lay here, cold and indifferent beside a suffering man, but she could not change her.

Next morning she set about getting a girl, and very soon came Sophie Traub from Hamburg, a girl of twenty, laughing, healthy, blue-eyed, intending to learn English. Indeed, she already spoke a good deal. In return for a room—"Mother's Room"—and her food, she undertook to do some light cooking, and to be with the children when Mrs. Rawlings asked. She was an intelligent girl and understood perfectly what was needed. Susan said: "I go off sometimes, for the morning or for the day—well, sometimes the children run home from school, or they ring up, or a teacher rings up. I should be here, really. And there's the daily woman. . . ." And Sophie laughed her deep fruity *Fräulein's* laugh, showed her fine white teeth and her dimples, and said: "You want some person to play mistress of the house sometimes, not so?"

"Yes, that is just so," said Susan, a bit dry, despite herself, thinking in secret fear how easy it was, how much nearer to the end she was than she thought. Healthy Fräulein Traub's instant understanding of their position proved this to be true.

The *au pair* girl, because of her own commonsense, or (as Susan said to herself, with her new inward shudder) because she had been *chosen* so well by Susan, was a success with everyone, the children liking her, Mrs. Parkes forgetting almost at once that she was German, and Matthew finding her "nice to have around the house." For he was now taking things as they came, from the surface of life, withdrawn both as a husband and a father from the household.

One day Susan saw how Sophie and Mrs. Parkes were talking and laughing in the kitchen, and she announced that she would be away until tea time. She knew exactly where to go and what she must look for. She took the District Line to South Kensington, changed to the Circle, got off at Paddington, and walked around looking at the smaller hotels until she was satisfied with one which had FRED'S HOTEL painted on windowpanes that needed cleaning. The facade was a faded shiny yellow, like unhealthy skin. A door at the end of a passage said she must knock; she did, and Fred appeared. He was not at all attractive, not in any way, being fattish, and run-down, and wearing a tasteless striped suit. He had small sharp eyes in a white creased face, and was quite prepared to let Mrs. Jones (she chose the farcical name deliberately, staring him out) have a room three days a week from ten until six. Provided of course that she paid in advance each time she came? Susan produced fifteen shillings (no price had been set by him) and held it out, still fixing him with a bold unblinking challenge she had not known until then she could use at will. Looking at her still, he took up a ten-shilling note from her palm between thumb and forefinger, fingered it; then shuffled up two half-crowns, held out his own palm with these bits of money displayed thereon, and let his gaze lower broodingly at them. They were standing in the passage, a red-shaded light above, bare boards beneath, and a strong smell of floor polish rising about them. He shot his gaze up at her over the still-extended palm, and smiled as if to say: What do you take me for? "I shan't," said Susan, "be using this room for the purposes of making money." He still waited. She added another five shillings, at which he nodded and said: "You pay, and I ask no questions." "Good," said Susan. He now went past her to the stairs, and there waited a moment: the light from the street door being in her eyes, she lost sight of him momentarily. Then she saw a sober-suited, white-faced, white-balding little man trotting up the stairs like a waiter, and she went after him. They proceeded in utter silence up the stairs of this house where no questions were asked—Fred's Hotel, which could afford the freedom for its visitors that poor Miss Townsend's hotel could not. The room was hideous. It had a single window, with thin green brocade curtains, a three-quarter bed that had a cheap green satin bedspread on it, a fireplace with a gas fire and a shilling meter by it, a chest of drawers, and a green wicker armchair.

"Thank you," said Susan, knowing that Fred (if this was Fred, and not George, or Herbert, or Charlie) was looking at her, not so much with curiosity, an emotion he would not own to, for professional reasons, but with a philosophical sense of what was appropriate. Having taken her money and shown her up and agreed to everything, he was clearly disapproving of her for coming here. She did not belong here at all, so his look said. (But she knew, already, how very much she did belong: the room had been waiting for her to join it.) "Would you have me called at five o'clock, please?" and he nodded and went downstairs.

It was twelve in the morning. She was free. She sat in the armchair, she simply sat, she closed her eyes and sat and let herself be alone. She was alone and no one knew where she was. When a knock came on the door she was annoyed, and prepared to show it: but it was Fred himself; it was five o'clock and he was calling her as ordered. He flicked his sharp little eyes over the room—bed, first. It was undisturbed. She might never have been in the room at all. She thanked him, said she would be returning the day after tomorrow, and left. She was back home in time to cook supper, to put the children to bed, to cook a second supper for her husband and herself later. And to welcome Sophie back from the pictures where she had gone with a friend. All these things she did cheerfully, willingly. But she was thinking all the time of the hotel room; she was longing for it with her whole being.

Three times a week. She arrived promptly at ten, looked Fred in the eyes, gave him twenty shillings, followed him up the stairs, went into the room, and shut the door on him with gentle firmness. For Fred, disapproving of her being here at all, was quite ready to let friendship, or at least acquaintanceship, follow his disapproval, if only she would let him. But he was content to go off on her dismissing nod, with the twenty shillings in his hand.

She sat in the armchair and shut her eyes.

What did she *do* in the room? Why, nothing at all. From the chair, when it had rested her, she went to the window, stretching her arms, smiling, treasuring her anonymity, to look out. She was no longer Susan Rawlings, mother of four, wife of Matthew, employer of Mrs. Parkes and of Sophie Traub, with these and those relations with friends, school-teachers, tradesmen. She no longer was mistress of the big white house and garden, owning clothes suitable for this and that activity or occasion. She was Mrs. Jones, and she was alone, and she had no past and no future. Here I am, she thought, after all these years of being married and having children and playing those roles of responsibility—and I'm just the same. Yet there have been times I thought that nothing existed of me except the roles that went with being Mrs. Matthew Rawlings. Yes, here I am, and if I never saw any of my family again, here I would still be . . . how very strange that is! And she leaned on the sill, and looked into the street, loving the men and women who passed, because she did not know them. She looked at the down-trodden buildings over the street, and at the sky, wet and dingy, or sometimes blue, and she felt she had never seen buildings or sky before. And then she went back to the chair, empty, her mind a blank. Sometimes she talked aloud, saying nothing—an exclamation, meaningless, followed by a comment about the floral pattern on the thin rug, or a stain on the green satin coverlet. For the most part, she wool-gathered—what word is there for it?—brooded, wandered, simply went dark, feeling emptiness run deliciously through her veins like the movement of her blood.

This room had become more her own than the house she lived in. One morning she found Fred taking her a flight higher than usual. She stopped, refusing to go up, and demanded her usual room, Number 19. "Well, you'll have to wait half an hour, then," he said. Willingly she descended to the dark disinfectant-smelling hall, and sat waiting until the two, man and woman, came down the stairs, giving her swift indifferent glances before they hurried out into the street, separating at the door. She went up to the room, *her* room, which they had just vacated. It was no less hers, though the windows were set wide open, and a maid was straightening the bed as she came in.

After these days of solitude, it was both easy to play her part as mother and wife, and difficult—because it was so easy: she felt an imposter. She felt as if her shell moved here, with her family, answering to Mummy, Mother, Susan, Mrs. Rawlings. She was surprised no one saw through her, that she wasn't turned out of doors, as a fake. On the contrary, it seemed the children loved her more; Matthew and she "got on" pleasantly, and Mrs. Parkes was happy in her work under (for the most part, it must be confessed) Sophie Traub. At night she lay beside her husband, and they made love again, apparently just as they used to, when they were really married. But she, Susan, or the being who answered so readily and improbably to the name of Susan, was not there: she was in Fred's Hotel, in Paddington, waiting for the easing hours of solitude to begin.

Soon she made a new arrangement with Fred and with Sophie. It was for five days a week. As for the money, five pounds, she simply asked Matthew for it. She saw that she was not even frightened he might ask what for: he would give it to her, she knew that, and yet it was terrifying it could be so, for this close couple, these partners, had once known the destination of every shilling they must spend. He agreed to give her five pounds a week. She asked for just so much, not a penny more. He sounded indifferent about it. It was as if he were paying her, she thought: *paying her off*—yes, that was it. Terror came back for a moment when she understood this, but she stilled it: things had gone too far for that. Now, every week, on Sunday nights, he gave her five pounds, turning away from her before their eyes could meet on the transaction. As for Sophie Traub, she was to be somewhere in or near the house until six at night, after which she was free. She was not to cook, or to clean; she was simply to be there. So she gardened or sewed, and asked friends in, being a person who was bound to have a lot of friends. If the children were sick, she nursed them. If teachers telephoned, she answered them sensibly. For the five daytimes in the school week, she was altogether the mistress of the house.

One night in the bedroom, Matthew asked: "Susan, I don't want to interfere—don't think that, please—but are you sure you are well?"

She was brushing her hair at the mirror. She made two more strokes on either side of her head, before she replied: "Yes, dear, I am sure I am well."

He was again lying on his back, his blond head on his hands, his elbows angled up and part-concealing his face. He said: "Then Susan, I have to ask you this question, though you must understand, I'm not putting any sort of pressure on you." (Susan heard the word "pressure" with dismay, because this was inevitable; of course she could not go on like this.) "Are things going to go on like this?"

"Well," she said, going vague and bright and idiotic again, so as to escape: "Well, I don't see why not."

He was jerking his elbows up and down, in annoyance or in pain, and, looking at him, she saw he had got thin, even gaunt; and restless angry movements were not what she remembered of him. He said: "Do you want a divorce, is that it?"

At this, Susan only with the greatest difficulty stopped herself from laughing: she could hear the bright bubbling laughter she *would* have emitted, had she let herself. He could only mean one thing: she had a lover, and that was why she spent her days in London, as lost to him as if she had vanished to another continent.

Then the small panic set in again: she understood that he hoped she did have a lover, he was begging her to say so, because otherwise it would be too terrifying.

She thought this out as she brushed her hair, watching the fine black stuff fly up to make its little clouds of electricity, hiss, hiss, hiss. Behind her head, across the room, was a blue wall. She realised she was absorbed in watching the black hair making shapes against the blue. She should be answering him. "Do *you* want a divorce, Matthew?"

He said: "That surely isn't the point, is it?"

"You brought it up, I didn't," she said, brightly, suppressing meaningless tinkling laughter.

Next day she asked Fred: "Have enquiries been made for me?"

He hesitated, and she said: "I've been coming here a year now. I've made no trouble, and you've been paid every day. I have a right to be told."

"As a matter of fact, Mrs. Jones, a man did come asking."

"A man from a detective agency?"

"Well, he could have been, couldn't he?"

"I was asking you. . . . Well, what did you tell him?"

"I told him a Mrs. Jones came every weekday from ten until five or six and stayed in Number 19 by herself."

'Describing me?"

"Well, Mrs. Jones, I had no alternative. Put yourself in my place."

"By rights I should deduct what that man gave you for the information."

He raised shocked eyes: she was not the sort of person to make jokes like this! Then he chose to laugh: a pinkish wet slit appeared across his white crinkled face; his eyes positively begged her to laugh, otherwise he might lose some money. She remained grave, looking at him.

He stopped laughing and said: "You want to go up now?"—returning to the familiarity, the comradeship, of the country where no questions are asked, on which (and he knew it) she depended completely.

She went up to sit in her wicker chair. But it was not the same. Her husband had searched her out. (The world had searched her out.) The pressures were on her. She was here with his connivance. He might walk in at any moment, here into Room 19. She imagined the report from the detective agency: "A woman calling herself Mrs. Jones, fitting the description of your wife (et cetera, et cetera, et cetera), stays alone all day in Room No. 19. She insists on this room, waits for it if it is engaged. As far as the proprietor knows, she receives no visitors there, male or female." A report something on these lines Matthew must have received.

Well, of course he was right: things couldn't go on like this. He had put an end to it all simply by sending a detective after her.

She tried to shrink herself back into the shelter of the room, a snail pecked out of its shell and trying to squirm back. But the peace of the room had gone. She was trying to revive it, trying to let go into the dark creative trance (or whatever it was) that she had found there. It was no use, yet she craved for it, she was as ill as a suddenly deprived addict.

Several times she returned to the room, to look for herself there, but instead she found the unnamed spirit of restlessness, a pricking fevered hunger for movement, an irritable self-consciousness that made her brain feel as if it had coloured lights going on and off inside it. Instead of the soft dark that had been the room's air, were now waiting for her demons that made her dash blindly about, muttering words of hate; she was impelling herself from point to point like a moth dashing itself against a window-pane, sliding to the bottom, fluttering off on broken wings, then crashing into the invisible barrier again. And again and again. Soon she was exhausted, and she told Fred that for a while she would not be needing the room, she was going on a holiday. Home she went, to the big white house by the river. The middle of a weekday, and she felt guilty at returning to her own home when not expected. She stood unseen, looking in at the kitchen window. Mrs. Parkes, wearing a discarded floral overall of Susan's, was stooping to slide something into the oven. Sophie, arms folded, was leaning her back against a cupboard and laughing at some joke made by a girl not seen before by Susan—a dark foreign girl, Sophie's visitor. In an armchair Molly, one of the twins, lay curled, sucking her thumb and watching the grownups. She must have some sickness, to be kept from school. The child's listless face, the dark circles under her eyes, hurt Susan: Molly was looking at the three grownups working and talking in exactly the same way Susan looked at the four through the kitchen window: she was remote, shut off from them.

But then, just as Susan imagined herself going in, picking up the little girl, and sitting in an armchair with her, stroking her probably heated forehead, Sophie did just that: she had been standing on one leg, the other knee flexed, its foot set against the wall. Now she let her foot in its ribbon-tied red shoe slide down the wall, stood solid on two feet, clapping her hands before and behind her, and sang a couple of lines in German, so that the child lifted her heavy eyes at her and began to smile. The she walked, or rather skipped, over to the child, swung her up, and let her fall into her lap at the same moment she sat herself. She said "Hopla! Hopla! Molly . . ." and began stroking the dark untidy young head that Molly laid on her shoulder for comfort.

Well. . . . Susan blinked the tears of farewell out of her eyes, and went quietly up through the house to her bedroom. There she sat looking at the river through the trees. She felt at peace, but in a way that was new to her. She had no desire to move, to talk, to do anything at all. The devils that had haunted the house, the garden, were not there; but she knew it was because her soul was in Room 19 in Fred's Hotel; she was not really here at all. It was a sensation that should have been frightening: to sit at her own bedroom window, listening to Sophie's rich young voice sing German nursery songs to her child, listening to Mrs. Parkes clatter and move below, and to know that this had nothing to do with her: she was already out of it.

Later, she made herself go down and say she was home: it was unfair to be here unannounced. She took lunch with Mrs. Parkes, Sophie, Sophie's Italian friend Maria, and her daughter Molly, and felt like a visitor.

A few days later, at bedtime, Matthew said: "Here's your five pounds," and pushed them over at her. Yet he must have known she had not been leaving the house at all.

She shook her head, gave it back to him, and said, in explanation, not in accusation: "As soon as you knew where I was, there was no point."

He nodded, not looking at her. He was turned away from her: thinking, she knew, how best to handle this wife who terrified him.

He said: "I wasn't trying to. . . . It's just that I was worried."

"Yes, I know."

"I must confess that I was beginning to wonder. . . ."

"You thought I had a lover?"

"Yes, I am afraid I did."

She knew that he wished she had. She sat wondering how to say: "For a year now I've been spending all my days in a very sordid hotel room. It's the place where I'm happy. In fact, without it I don't exist." She heard herself saying this, and understood how terrified he was that she might. So instead she said: "Well, perhaps you're not far wrong."

Probably Matthew would think that the hotel proprietor lied: he would want to think so.

"Well," he said, and she could hear his voice spring up, so to speak with relief, "in that case I must confess I've got a bit of an affair on myself."

She said, detached and interested: "Really? Who is she?" and saw Matthew's startled look because of this reaction.

"It's Phil. Phil Hunt."

She had known Phil Hunt well in the old unmarried days. She was thinking: No, she won't do, she's too neurotic and difficult. She's never been happy yet. Sophie's much better. Well, Matthew will see that himself, as sensible as he is.

This line of thought went on in silence, while she said aloud: "It's no point telling you about mine, because you don't know him."

Quick, quick, invent, she thought. Remember how you invented all that nonsense for Miss Townsend.

She began slowly, careful not to contradict herself: "His name is Michael" *(Michael What?)*—"Michael Plant." (What a silly name!) "He's rather like you—in looks, I mean." And indeed, she could imagine herself being touched by no one but Matthew himself. "He's a publisher." (Really? Why?) "He's got a wife already and two children."

She brought out this fantasy, proud of herself.

Matthew said: "Are you two thinking of marrying?"

She said, before she could stop herself: "Good God, *no!*"

She realised, if Matthew wanted to marry Phil Hunt, that this was too emphatic, but apparently it was all right, for his voice sounded relieved as he said: "It is a bit impossible to imagine oneself married to anyone else, isn't it?" With which he pulled her to him, so that her head lay on his shoulder. She turned her face into the dark of his flesh, and listened to the blood pounding through her ears saying: I am alone, I am alone, I am alone.

In the morning Susan lay in bed while he dressed.

He had been thinking things out in the night, because now he said: "Susan, why don't we make a foursome?"

Of course, she said to herself, of course he would be bound to say that. If one is sensible, if one is reasonable, if one never allows oneself a base thought or an envious emotion, naturally one says: Let's make a foursome!

"Why not?" she said.

"We could all meet for lunch. I mean, it's ridiculous, you sneaking off to filthy hotels, and me staying late at the office, and all the lies everyone has to tell."

What on earth did I say his name was?—she panicked, then said: "I think it's a good idea, but Michael is away at the moment. When he comes back, though—and I'm sure you two would like each other."

"He's away, is he? So that's why you've been. . . ." Her husband put his hand to the knot of his tie in a gesture of male coquetry she would not before have associated with him; and he bent to kiss her cheek with the expression that goes with the words: Oh you naughty little puss! And she felt its answering look, naughty and coy, come onto her face.

Inside she was dissolving in horror at them both, at how far they had both sunk from honesty of emotion.

So now she was saddled with a lover, and he had a mistress! How ordinary, how reassuring, how jolly! And now they would make a foursome of it, and go out to theatres and restaurants. After all, the Rawlings could well afford that sort of thing, and presumably the publisher Michael Plant could afford to do himself and his mistress quite well. No, there was nothing to stop the four of them developing the most intricate relationship of civilised tolerance, all enveloped in a charming afterglow of autumnal passion. Perhaps they would all go off on holidays together? She had known people who did. Or perhaps Matthew would draw the line there? Why should he, though, if he was capable of talking about "foursomes" at all?

She lay in the empty bedroom, listening to the car drive off with Matthew in it, off to work. Then she heard the children clattering off to school to the accompaniment of Sophie's cheerfully ringing voice. She slid down into the hollow of the bed, for shelter against her own irrelevance. And she stretched out her hand to the hollow where her husband's body had lain, but found no comfort there: he was not her husband. She curled herself up in a small tight ball under the clothes: she could stay here all day, all week, indeed, all her life.

But in a few days she must produce Michael Plant, and—but how? She must presumably find some agreeable man prepared to impersonate a publisher called Michael Plant. And in return for which she would—what? Well, for one thing they would make love. The idea made her want to cry with sheer exhaustion. Oh no, she had finished with all that—the proof of it was that the words "make love," or even imagining it, trying hard to revive no more than the pleasures of sensuality, let alone affection, or love, made her want to run away and hide from the sheer effort of the thing. . . . Good Lord, why make love at all? Why make love with anyone? Or if you are going to make love, what does it matter who with? Why shouldn't she simply walk into the street, pick up a man, and have a roaring sexual affair with him? Why not? Or even with Fred? What difference did it make?

But she had let herself in for it—an interminable stretch of time with a lover, called Michael, as part of a gallant civilised foursome. Well, she could not, and she would not.

She got up, dressed, went down to find Mrs. Parkes, and asked her for the loan of a pound, since Matthew, she said, had forgotten to leave her money. She exchanged with Mrs. Parkes variations on the theme that husbands are all the same, they don't think, and without saying a word to Sophie, whose voice could be heard upstairs from the telephone, walked to the underground, travelled to South Kensington, changed to the Inner Circle, got out at Paddington, and walked to Fred's Hotel. There she told Fred that she wasn't going on holiday after all, she needed the room. She would have to wait an hour, Fred said. She went to a busy tearoom-cum-restaurant around the corner, and sat watching the people flow in and out the door that kept swinging open and shut, watched them mingle and merge, and separate, felt her being flow into them, into their movement. When the hour was up, she left a half-crown for her pot of tea, and left the place without looking back at it, just as she had left her house, the big, beautiful, white house, without another look, but silently dedicating it to Sophie. She returned to Fred, received the key of Number 19, now free, and ascended the grimy stairs slowly, letting floor after floor fall away below her, keeping her eyes lifted, so that floor after floor descended jerkily to her level of vision, and fell away out of sight.

Number 19 was the same. She saw everything with an acute, narrow, checking glance: the cheap shine of the satin spread, which had been replaced carelessly after the two bodies had finished their convulsions under it; a trace of powder on the glass that topped the chest of drawers; an intense green shade in a fold of the curtain. She stood at the window, looking down, watching people pass and pass and pass until her mind went dark from the constant movement. Then she sat in the wicker chair, letting herself go slack. But she had to be careful, because she did not want, today, to be surprised by Fred's knock at five o'clock.

The demons were not here. They had gone forever, because she was buying her freedom from them. She was slipping already into the dark fructifying dream that seemed to caress her inwardly, like the movement of her blood . . . but she had to think about Matthew first. Should she write a letter for the coroner? But what should she say? She would like to leave him with the look on his face she had seen this morning—banal, admittedly, but at least confidently healthy. Well, that was impossible, one did not look like that with a wife dead from suicide. But how to leave him believing she was dying because of a man—because of the fascinating publisher Michael Plant? Oh, how ridiculous! How absurd! How humiliating! But she decided not to trouble about it, simply not to think about the living. If he wanted to believe she had a lover, he would believe it. And he *did* want to believe it. Even when he had found out that there was no publisher in London called Michael Plant, he would think: Oh poor Susan, she was afraid to give me his real name.

And what did it matter whether he married Phil Hunt or Sophie? Though it ought to be Sophie, who was already the mother of those children . . . and what hypocrisy to sit here worrying about the children, when she was going to leave them because she had not got the energy to stay.

She had about four hours. She spent them delightfully, darkly, sweetly, letting herself slide gently, gently, to the edge of the river. Then, with hardly a break in her consciousness, she got up, pushed the thin rug against the door, made sure the windows were tight shut, put two shillings in the meter, and turned on the gas. For the first time since she had been in the room she lay on the hard bed that smelled stale, that smelled of sweat and sex.

She lay on her back on the green satin cover, but her legs were chilly. She got up, found a blanket folded in the bottom of the chest of drawers, and carefully covered her legs with it. She was quite content lying there, listening to the faint soft hiss of the gas that poured into the room, into her lungs, into her brain, as she drifted off into the dark river.

Gold Coast

JAMES ALAN McPHERSON

That spring, when I had a great deal of potential and no money at all, I took a job as a janitor. That was when I was still very young and spent money very freely, and when, almost every night, I drifted off to sleep lulled by sweet anticipation of that time when my potential would suddenly be realized and there would be capsule biographies of my life on dust jackets of many books, all proclaiming: ". . . He knew life on many levels. From shoeshine boy, free-lance waiter, 3rd cook, janitor, he rose to . . ." I had never been a janitor before and I did not really have to be one and that is why I did it. But now, much later, I think it might have been because it is possible to be a janitor without really becoming one, and at parties or at mixers when asked what it was I did for a living, it was pretty good to hook my thumbs in my vest pockets and say comfortably: "Why, I am an apprentice janitor." The hippies would think it degenerate and really dig me and it made me feel good that people in Philosophy and Law and Business would feel uncomfortable trying to make me feel better about my station while wondering how the hell I had managed to crash the party.

"What's an apprentice janitor?" they would ask.

"I haven't got my card yet," I would reply. "Right now I'm just taking lessons. There's lots of complicated stuff you have to learn before you get your card and your own building."

"What kind of stuff?"

"Human nature, for one thing. *Race* nature, for another."

"Why race?"

"Because," I would say in a low voice looking around lest someone else should overhear, "you have to be able to spot Jews and Negroes who are passing."

"That's terrible," would surely be said then with a hint of indignation.

"It's an art," I would add masterfully.

627

After a good pause I would invariably be asked: "But you're a Negro yourself, how can you keep your own people out?"

At which point I would look terribly disappointed and say: "*I* don't keep them out. But if they get in it's my job to make their stay just as miserable as possible. Things are changing."

Now the speaker would just look at me in disbelief.

"It's Janitorial Objectivity," I would say to finish the thing as the speaker began to edge away. "Don't hate me," I would call after him to his considerable embarrassment. "Somebody has to do it."

It as an old building near Harvard Square. Conrad Aiken had once lived there and in the days of the Gold Coast, before Harvard built its great Houses, it had been a very fine haven for the rich; but that was a world ago and this building was one of the few monuments of that era which had survived. The lobby had a high ceiling with thick redwood beams and it was replete with marble floor, fancy ironwork, and an old-fashioned house telephone that no longer worked. Each apartment had a small fireplace, and even the large bathtubs and chain toilets, when I was having my touch of nature, made me wonder what prominent personage of the past had worn away all the newness. And, being there, I felt a certain affinity toward the rich.

It was a funny building; because the people who lived there made it old. Conveniently placed as it was between the Houses and Harvard Yard, I expected to find it occupied by a company of hippies, hopeful working girls, and assorted graduate students. Instead, there were a majority of old maids, dowagers, asexual middle-aged men, homosexual young men, a few married couples and a teacher. No one was shacking up there, and walking through the quiet halls in the early evening, I sometimes had the urge to knock on a door and expose myself just to hear someone breathe hard for once.

It was a Cambridge spring: down by the Charles happy students were making love while sad-eyed middle-aged men watched them from the bridge. It was a time of activity: Law students were busy sublimating, Business School people were making records of the money they would make, the Harvard Houses were clearing out, and in the Square bearded pot-pushers were setting up their restaurant tables in anticipation of the Summer School faithfuls. There was a change of season in the air, and to comply with its urgings, James Sullivan, the old superintendent, passed his three beaten garbage cans on to me with the charge that I should take up his daily rounds of the six floors, and with unflinching humility, gather whatever scraps the old-maid tenants had refused to husband.

I then became very rich, with my own apartment, a sensitive girl, a stereo, two speakers, one tattered chair, one fork, a job, and the urge to acquire. Having all this and youth besides made me pity Sullivan: he had been in that building thirty years and had its whole history recorded in the little folds of his mind, as his own life was recorded in the wrinkles of his face. All he had to show for his time there was a berserk dog, a wife almost as mad as the dog, three cats, bursitis, acute myopia, and a drinking problem. He was well over seventy and could hardly walk, and his weekly check of twenty-two dollars from the company that managed the building would not support anything. So, out of compromise, he was retired to superintendent of my labor.

My first day as a janitor, while I skillfully lugged my three overflowing cans of garbage out of the building, he sat on his bench in the lobby, faded and old and smoking in patched, loose blue pants. He watched me. He was a chain smoker and I noticed right away that he very carefully dropped all of the ashes and butts on the floor and crushed them under his feet until there was a yellow and gray smear. Then he laboriously pushed the mess under the bench with his shoe, all the while eyeing me like a cat in silence as I hauled the many cans of muck out to the big disposal unit next to the building. When I had finished, he gave me two old plates to help stock my kitchen and his first piece of advice.

"Sit down, for Chrissake, and take a load off your feet," he told me.

I sat on the red bench next to him and accepted the wilted cigarette he offered me from the crushed package he kept in his sweater pocket.

"Now I'll tell you something to help you get along in the building," he said.

I listened attentively.

"If any of these sons-of-bitches ever ask you to do something extra, be sure to charge them for it."

I assured him that I absolutely would.

"If they can afford to live here, they can afford to pay. The bastards."

"Undoubtedly," I assured him again.

"And another thing," he added. "Don't let any of these girls shove any cat shit under your nose. That ain't your job. You tell them to put it in a bag and take it out themselves."

I reminded him that I knew very well my station in life, and that I was not about to haul cat shit or anything of that nature. He looked at me through his thick-lensed glasses. He looked like a cat himself. "That's right," he said at last. "And if they still try to sneak it in the trash be sure to make the bastards pay. They can afford it." He crushed his seventh butt on the floor and scattered the mess some more while he lit up another. "I never hauled out no cat shit in the thirty years I been here and you don't do it either."

"I'm going to wash my hands," I said.

"Remember," he called after me, "don't take no shit from any of them."

I protested once more that, upon my life, I would never, never do it, not even for the prettiest girl in the building. Going up in the elevator, I felt comfortably resolved that I would never do it. There were no pretty girls in the building.

I never found out what he had done before he came there, but I do know that being a janitor in that building was as high as he ever got in life. He had watched two generations of the rich pass the building on their way to the Yard, and he had seen many governors ride white horses thirty times into that same Yard to send sons and daughters of the rich out into life to produce, to acquire, to procreate and to send back sons and daughters so that the cycle would continue. He had watched the cycle from when he had been able to haul the cans out for himself, and now he could not, and he was bitter.

He was Irish, of course, and he took pride in Irish accomplishments when he could have none of his own. He had known Frank O'Connor when that writer had been at Harvard. He told me on many occasions how O'Connor had stopped to talk every day on his way to the Yard. He had also known James Michael Curley, and his most colorful memory of the man was a long ago day when he and James Curley sat in a Boston bar and one of Curley's runners had come in and said: "Hey Jim, Sol Bernstein the Jew wants to see you." And Curley, in his deep, memorial voice had said to James Sullivan: "Let us go forth and meet this Israelite Prince." These were his memories, and I would obediently put aside my garbage cans and laugh with him over the hundred or so colorful, insignificant little details which made up a whole lifetime of living in the basement of Harvard. And although they were of little value to me then, I knew that they were the reflections of a lifetime and the happiest moments he would ever have, being sold to me cheap, as youthful time is cheap, for as little time and interest as I wanted to spend. It was a buyer's market.

II

In those days I believed myself gifted with a boundless perception and attacked my daily garbage route with a gusto superenforced by the happy knowledge that behind each of the fifty or so doors in our building lived a story which could, if I chose to grace it with the magic of my pen, become immortal. I watched my tenants fanatically, noting their perversions, their visitors, and their eating habits. So intense was my search for material that I had to restrain myself from going through their refuse scrap by scrap; but at the topmost layers of muck, without too much hand-soiling in the process, I set my perceptions to work. By late June, however, I had discovered only enough to put together a skimpy, rather naïve Henry Miller novel. The most colorful discoveries being:

1. The lady in #24 was an alumna of Paducah College.
2. The couple in #55 made love at least five hundred times a week and the wife had not yet discovered the pill.
3. The old lady in #36 was still having monthly inconvenience.

4. The two fatsos in #56 consumed nightly an extraordinary amount of chili.
5. The fat man in #54 had two dogs that were married to each other, but he was not married to anyone at all.
6. The middle-aged single man in #63 threw out an awful lot of flowers.

Disturbed by the snail's progress I was making, I confessed my futility to James one day as he sat on his bench chain-smoking and smearing butts on my newly waxed lobby floor. "So you want to know about the tenants?" he said, his cat's eyes flickering over me.

I nodded.

"Well the first thing to notice is how many Jews there are."

"I haven't noticed many Jews," I said.

He eyed me in amazement.

"Well, a few," I said quickly to prevent my treasured perception from being dulled any further.

"A few, hell," he said. "There's more Jews here than anybody."

"How can you tell?"

He gave me that undecided look again. "Where do you think all that garbage comes from?" He nodded feebly toward my bulging cans. I looked just in time to prevent a stray noodle from slipping over the brim. "That's right," he continued. "Jews are the biggest eaters in the world. They eat the best too."

I confessed then that I was of the chicken-soup generation and believed that Jews ate only enough to muster strength for their daily trips to the bank.

"Not so!" he replied emphatically. "You never heard the expression: 'Let's get to the restaurant before the Jews get there'?"

I shook my head sadly.

"You don't know that in certain restaurants they take the free onions and pickles off the tables when they see Jews coming?"

I held my head down in shame over the bounteous heap.

He trudged over to my can and began to turn back the leaves of noodles and crumpled tissues from #47 with his hand. After a few seconds of digging he unmucked an empty paté can. "Look at that," he said triumphantly. "Gourmet stuff, no less."

"That's from #44," I said.

"What else?" he said all-knowingly. "In 1946 a Swedish girl moved in up there and took a Jewish girl for her roommate. Then the Swedish girl moved out and there's been a Jewish Dynasty up there ever since."

I recalled that #44 was occupied by a couple that threw out a good number of S. S. Pierce cans, Chivas Regal bottles, assorted broken records, and back issues of *Evergreen* and the *Realist*.

"You're right," I said.

"Of course," he replied as if there was never any doubt. "I can spot them anywhere, even when they think they're passing." He leaned closer and said in a you-and-me voice: "But don't ever say anything bad about them in public, the Anti-Defamation League will get you."

Just then his wife screamed for him from the second floor, and the dog joined her and beat against the door. He got into the elevator painfully and said: "Don't ever talk about them in public. You don't know who they are and that Defamation League will take everything you got."

Sullivan did not really hate Jews. He was just bitter toward anyone better off than himself. He liked me because I seemed to like hauling garbage and because I listened to him and seemed to respect what he said and seemed to imply, by lingering on even when he repeated himself, that I was eager to take what wisdom he had for no other reason than that I needed it in order to get along.

He lived with his wife on the second floor and his apartment was very dirty because both of them were sick and old, and neither could move very well. His wife swept dirt out into the hall, and two hours after I had mopped and waxed their section of the floor, there was sure to be a layer of dirt, grease, and crushed-scattered tobacco from their door to the end of the hall. There was a smell of dogs and cats and age and death about their door, and I did not ever want to have to go in there for any reason because I feared something about it I cannot name.

Mrs. Sullivan, I found out, was from South Africa. She loved animals much more than people and there was a great deal of pain in her face. She kept little pans of meat posted at strategic points about the building, and I often came across her in the early morning or late at night throwing scraps out of the second-floor window to stray cats. Once, when James was about to throttle a stray mouse in their apartment, she had screamed at him to give the mouse a sporting chance. Whenever she attempted to walk she had to balance herself against a wall or a rail, and she hated the building because it confined her. She also hated James and most of the tenants. On the other hand, she loved the *Johnny Carson Show,* she loved to sit outside on the front steps (because she could get no further unassisted), and she loved to talk to anyone who would stop to listen. She never spoke coherently except when she was cursing James, and then she had a vocabulary like a sailor. She had great, shrill lungs, and her screams, accompanied by the rabid barks of the dog, could be heard all over the building. She was never really clean, her teeth were bad, and the first most pathetic thing in the world was to see her sitting on the steps in the morning watching the world pass, in a stained smock and a fresh summer blue hat she kept just to wear downstairs, with no place in the world to go. James told me, on the many occasions of her screaming, that she was mentally disturbed and could not control herself. The admirable thing about him was that he never lost his temper with her, no matter how rough her curses became and no matter who heard them. And the second most pathetic thing in the world was to see them slowly making their way in Harvard Square, he supporting her, through the hurrying crowds of miniskirted summer girls, J-Pressed Ivy Leaguers, beatniks, and bused Japanese tourists, decked in cameras, who would take pictures of every inch of Harvard Square except them. Once, he told me, a hippie had brushed past them and called back over his shoulder: "Don't break any track records, Mr. and Mrs. Speedy Molasses."

Also on the second floor lived Miss O'Hara, a spinster who hated Sullivan as only an old maid can hate an old man. Across from her lived a very nice, gentle, celibate named Murphy who had once served with Montgomery in North Africa and who was now spending the rest of his life cleaning his little apartment and gossiping with Miss O'Hara. It was an Irish floor.

I never found out just why Miss O'Hara hated the Sullivans with such a passion. Perhaps it was because they were so unkempt and she was so superciliously clean. Perhaps it was because O'Hara had a great deal of Irish pride and they were stereotyped Irish. Perhaps it was because she merely had no reason to like them. She was a fanatic about cleanliness and put out her little bit of garbage wrapped very neatly in yesterday's *Christian Science Monitor* and tied in a bow with a fresh piece of string. Collecting all those little neat packages, I would wonder where she got the string and imagined her at night picking meat-market locks with a hairpin and hobbling off with yards and yards of white cord concealed under the gray sweater she always wore. I could even imagine her back in her little apartment chuckling and rolling the cord into a great white ball by candlelight. Then she would stash it away in her breadbox. Miss O'Hara kept her door slightly open until late at night, and I suspected that she heard everything that went on in the building. I had the feeling that I should never dare to make love with gusto for fear that she would overhear and write down all my happy-time phrases, to be maliciously recounted to me if she were ever provoked.

She had been in the building longer than Sullivan, and I suppose that her greatest ambition in life was to outlive him and then attend his wake with a knitting ball and needles. She had been trying to get him fired for twenty-five years or so and did not know when to quit. On summer nights when I painfully mopped the second floor, she would offer me root beer, apples, or cupcakes while trying to pump me for evidence against him.

"He's just a filthy old man, Robert," she would declare in a little-old-lady whisper. "And don't think you have to clean up those dirty old butts of his. Just report him to the Company."

"Oh, I don't mind," I would tell her, gulping the root beer as fast as possible.

"Well, they're both a couple of lushes, if you ask me. They haven't been sober a day in twenty-five years."

"Well, she's sick too, you know."

"Ha!" She would throw up her hands in disgust. "She's only sick when he doesn't give her the booze."

I fought to keep down a burp. "How long have *you* been here?"

She motioned for me to step out of the hall and into her dark apartment. "Don't tell him,"—she nodded towards Sullivan's door—"but I've been here for thirty-four years." She waited for me to be taken aback. Then she added: "And it was a better building before those two lushes came."

She then offered me an apple, asked five times if the dog's barking bothered me, forced me to take a fudge brownie, said that the cats had wet the floor again last night, got me to dust the top of a large chest too high for her to reach, had me pick up the minute specks of dust which fell from my dustcloth, pressed another root beer on me, and then showed me her family album. As an afterthought, she had me take down a big old picture of her great-grandfather, also too high for her to reach, so that I could dust that too. Then together we picked up the dust from it which might have fallen to the floor. "He's really a filthy old man, Robert," she said in closing, "and don't be afraid to report him to the property manager any time you want."

I assured her that I would do it at the slightest provocation from Sullivan, finally accepted an apple but refused the money she offered, and escaped back to my mopping. Even then she watched me, smiling, from her half-opened door.

"Why does Miss O'Hara hate you?" I asked James once.

He lifted his cigaretted hand and let the long ash fall elegantly to the floor. "That old bitch has been an albatross around my neck ever since I got here," he said. "Don't trust her, Robert. It was her kind that sat around singing hymns and watching them burn saints in this state."

There was never an adequate answer to my question. And even though the dog was noisy and would surely kill someone if it ever got loose, no one could really dislike the old man because of it. The dog was all they had. In his garbage each night, for every wine bottle, there would be an equally empty can of dog food. Some nights he took the brute out for a long walk, when he could barely walk himself, and both of them had to be led back to the building.

III

In those days I had forgotten that I was first of all a black and I had a very lovely girl who was not first of all a black. We were both young and optimistic then, and she believed with me in my potential and liked me partly because of it; and I was happy because she belonged to me and not to the race, which made her special. It made me special too because I did not have to wear a beard or hate or be especially hip or ultra-Ivy Leaguish. I did not have to smoke pot or supply her with it, or be for any other cause at all except myself. I only had to be myself, which pleased me; and I only had to produce, which pleased both of us. Like many of the artistically inclined rich, she wanted to own in someone else what she could not own in herself. But this I did not mind, and I forgave her for it because she forgave me moods and the constant smell of garbage and a great deal of latent hostility. She only minded James Sullivan and all the valuable time I was wasting listening to him rattle on and on. His conversations, she thought, were useless, repetitious, and promised nothing of value to me. She was accustomed to the old-rich whose conversations meandered around a leitmotiv of how well off they were and how much they would leave behind very soon. She was not at all cold, but she had been taught how to tolerate the old-poor and perhaps toss them a greeting in passing. But nothing more.

Sullivan did not like her when I first introduced them because he saw that she was not a hippie and could not be dismissed. It is in the nature of things that liberal people will tolerate two interracial hippies more than they will an intelligent, serious-minded mixed couple. The former liaison is easy to dismiss as the dregs of both races, deserving of each other and the contempt of both races; but the latter poses a threat because there is no immediacy or overpowering sensuality or "you-pick-my-fleas-I'll-pick-yours" apparent on the surface of things, and people, even the most publicly liberal, cannot dismiss it so easily.

"That girl is Irish, isn't she?" he had asked one day in my apartment soon after I had introduced them.

"No," I said definitely.

"What's her name again?"

"Judy Smith," I said, which was not her name at all.

"Well, I can spot it," he said. "She's got Irish blood, all right."

"Everybody's got a little Irish blood," I told him.

He looked at me cattily and craftily from behind his thick lenses. "Well, she's from a good family, I suppose."

"I suppose," I said.

He paused to let some ashes fall to the rug. "They say the Colonel's Lady and Nelly O'Grady are sisters under the skin." Then he added: "Rudyard Kipling."

"That's true," I said with equal innuendo, "that's why you have to maintain a distinction by marrying the Colonel's Lady."

An understanding passed between us then, and we never spoke more on the subject.

Almost every night the cats wet the second floor while Meg Sullivan watched the *Johnny Carson Show* and the dog howled and clawed the door. During commercials Meg would curse James to get out and stop dropping ashes on the floor or to take the dog out or something else, totally unintelligible to those of us on the fourth, fifth and sixth floors. Even after the *Car-*

son Show she would still curse him to get out, until finally he would go down to the basement and put away a bottle or two of wine. There was a steady stench of cat functions in the basement, and with all the grease and dirt, discarded trunks, beer bottles, chairs, old tools and the filthy sofa on which he sometimes slept, seeing him there made me want to cry. He drank the cheapest sherry, the wino kind, straight from the bottle; and on many nights that summer at 2:00 A.M. my phone would ring me out of bed.

"Rob? Jimmy Sullivan here. What are you doing?"

There was nothing suitable to say.

"Come on down to the basement for a drink."

"I have to be at work at eight-thirty," I would protest.

"Can't you have just one drink?" he would say pathetically.

I would carry down my own glass so that I would not have to drink out of the bottle. Looking at him on the sofa, I could not be mad because now I had many records for my stereo, a story that was going well, a girl who believed in me and belonged to me and not to the race, a new set of dishes, and a tomorrow morning with younger people.

"I don't want to burden you unduly," he would always preface.

I would force myself not to look at my watch and say: "Of course not."

"My Meg is not in the best health, you know," he would say, handing the bottle to me.

"She's just old."

"The doctors say she should be in an institution."

"That's no place to be."

"I'm a sick man myself, Rob. I can't take much more. She's crazy."

"Anybody who loves animals can't be crazy."

He took another long draw from the bottle. "I won't live another year. I'll be dead in a year."

"You don't know that."

He looked at me closely, without his glasses, so that I could see the desperation in his eyes. "I just hope Meg goes before I do. I don't want them to put her in an institution after I'm gone."

At 2:00 A.M. with the cat stench in my nose and a glass of bad sherry standing still in my hand because I refused in my mind to touch it, and when all my dreams of greatness were above him and the basement and the building itself, I did not know what to say. The only way I could keep from hating myself was to talk about the AMA or the Medicare program or hippies. He was pure hell on all three. To him, the medical profession was "morally bankrupt," Medicare was a great farce which deprived oldsters like himself of their "rainy-day dollars," and hippies were "dropouts from the human race." He could rage on and on in perfect phrases about all three of his major dislikes, and I had the feeling that because the sentences were so well constructed and well turned, he might have memorized them from something he had read. But then he was extremely well read and it did not matter if he had borrowed a phrase or two from someone else. The ideas were still his own.

It would be 3:00 A.M. before I knew it, and then 3:30, and still he would go on. He hated politicians in general and liked to recount, at these times, his private catalogue of political observations. By the time he got around to Civil Rights it would be 4:00 A.M., and I could not feel sorry or responsible for him at that hour. I would begin to yawn and at first he would just ignore it. Then I would start to edge toward the door, and he would see that he could hold me no longer, not even by declaring that he wanted to be an honorary Negro because he loved the race so much.

"I hope I haven't burdened you unduly," he would say again.

"Of course not," I would say, because it was over then and I could leave him and the smell of the cats there and sometimes I would go out in the cool night and walk around the Yard and be thankful that I was only an assistant janitor, and a transient one at that. Walking in the early dawn and seeing the Summer School fellows sneak out of the girls' dormitories in the Yard gave me a good feeling, and I thought that tomorrow night it would be good to make love myself so that I could be busy when he called.

IV

"Why don't you tell that old man your job doesn't include baby-sitting with him?" Jean told me many times when she came over to visit during the day and found me sleeping.

I would look at her and think to myself about social forces and the pressures massing and poised, waiting to attack us. It was still July then. It was hot and I was working good. "He's just an old man," I said. "Who else would listen to him?"

"You're too soft. As long as you do your work you don't have to be bothered with him."

"He could be a story if I listened long enough."

"There are too many stories about old people."

"No," I said, thinking about us again, "there are just too many people who have no stories."

Sometimes he would come up and she would be there, but I would let him come in anyway, and he would stand in the room looking dirty and uncomfortable, offering some invented reason for having intruded. At these times something silent would pass between them, something I cannot name, which would reduce him to exactly what he was: an old man, come out of his basement to intrude where he was not wanted. But all the time this was being communicated, there would be a surface, friendly conversation between them. And after five minutes or so of being unwelcome, he would apologize for having come, drop a few ashes on the rug and back out the door. Downstairs we could hear his wife screaming.

We endured and aged and August was almost over. Inside the building the cats were still wetting, Meg was still screaming, the dog was getting madder, and Sullivan began to drink during the day. Outside it was hot and lush and green, and the summer girls were wearing shorter miniskirts and no panties and the middle-aged men down by the Charles were going wild on their bridge. Everyone was restless for change, for August is the month when undone summer things must be finished or regretted all through the winter.

V

Being imaginative people, Jean and I played a number of original games. One of them we called "Social Forces," the object of which was to see which side could break us first. We played it with the unknown nightriders who screamed obscenities from passing cars. And because that was her side I would look at her expectantly, but she would laugh and say: "No." We played it at parties with unaware blacks who attempted to enchant her with skillful dances and hip vocabulary, believing her to be community property. She would be polite and aloof, and much later, it then being my turn, she would look at me expectantly. And I would force a smile and say: "No." The last round was played while taking her home in a subway car, on a hot August night, when one side of the car was black and tense and hating and the other side was white and of the same mind. There was not enough room on either side for the two of us to sit and we would not separate; and so we stood, holding on to a steel post through all the stops, feeling all the eyes, between the two sides of the car and the two sides of the world. We aged. And, getting off finally at the stop which was no longer ours, we looked at each other, again expectantly, and there was nothing left to say.

I began to avoid the old man, would not answer the door when I knew it was he who was knocking, and waited until very late at night, when he could not possibly be awake, to haul the trash down. I hated the building then; and I was really a janitor for the first time. I slept a lot and wrote very little. And I did not give a damn about Medicare, the AMA, the building, Meg or the crazy dog. I began to consider moving out.

In that same month, Miss O'Hara finally succeeded in badgering Murphy, the celibate Irishman, and a few other tenants into signing a complaint about the dog. No doubt Murphy signed because he was a nice fellow and women like Miss O'Hara had always dominated him. He did not really mind the dog: he did not really mind anything. She called him "Frank Dear," and I had the feeling that when he came to that place, fresh from

Montgomery's Campaign, he must have had a will of his own; but she had drained it all away, year by year, so that now he would do anything just to be agreeable.

One day soon after the complaint, the Property Manager came around to tell Sullivan that the dog had to be taken away. Miss O'Hara told me the good news later, when she finally got around to my door.

"Well, that crazy dog is gone now, Robert. Those two are enough."

"Where is the dog?" I asked.

"I don't know, but Albert Rustin made them get him out. You should have seen the old drunk's face," she said. "That dirty useless old man."

"You should be at peace now," I said.

"Almost," was her reply. "The best thing would be to get rid of those two old boozers along with the dog."

I congratulated Miss O'Hara again and then went out. I knew that the old man would be drinking and would want to talk. I did not want to talk. But very late that evening he called me on the telephone and caught me in.

"Rob?" he said. "James Sullivan here. Would you come down to my apartment like a good fellow? I want to ask you something important."

I had never been in his apartment before and did not want to go then. But I went down anyway.

They had three rooms, all grimy from corner to corner. There was a peculiar odor in that place I did not want to ever smell again, and his wife was dragging herself around the room talking in mumbles. When she saw me come in the door, she said: "I can't clean it up. I just can't. Look at that window. I can't reach it. I can't keep it clean." She threw up both her hands and held her head down and to the side. "The whole place is dirty and I can't clean it up."

"What do you want?" I said to Sullivan.

"Sit down." He motioned me to a kitchen chair. "Have you changed that bulb on the fifth floor?"

"It's done."

He was silent for a while, drinking from a bottle of sherry, and he offered me some and a dirty glass. "You're the first person who's been here in years," he said. "We couldn't have company because of the dog."

Somewhere in my mind was a note that I should never go into his apartment. But the dog had not been the reason. "Well, he's gone now," I said, fingering the dirty glass of sherry.

He began to cry. "They took my dog away," he said. "It was all I had. How can they take a man's dog away from him?"

There was nothing I could say.

"I couldn't do nothing," he continued. After a while he added: "But I know who it was. It was that old bitch O'Hara. Don't ever trust her, Rob. She smiles in your face but it was her kind that laughed when they burned Joan of Arc in this state."

Seeing him there, crying and making me feel unmanly because I wanted
to touch him or say something warm, also made me eager to be far away
and running hard. "Everybody's got problems," I said. "I don't have a girl
now."

He brightened immediately, and for a while he looked almost happy in
his old cat's eyes. Then he staggered over to my chair and held out his
hand. I did not touch it, and he finally pulled it back. "I know how you
feel," he said. "I know just how you feel."

"Sure," I said.

"But you're a young man, you have a future. But not me. I'll be dead inside of a year."

Just then his wife dragged in to offer me a cigar. They were being hospitable and I forced myself to drink a little of the sherry.

"They took my dog away today," she mumbled. "That's all I had in the
world, my dog."

I looked at the old man. He was drinking from the bottle.

VI

During the first week of September one of the middle-aged men down by
the Charles got tired of looking and tried to take a necking girl away from
her boyfriend. The police hauled him off to jail, and the girl pulled down
her dress tearfully. A few days later another man exposed himself near the
same spot. And that same week a dead body was found on the banks of the
Charles.

The miniskirted brigade had moved out of the Yard and it was quiet and
green and peaceful there. In our building another Jewish couple moved
into #44. They did not eat gourmet stuff and, on occasion, threw out pork-
and-beans cans. But I had lost interest in perception. I now had many records for my stereo, loads of S. S. Pierce stuff, and a small bottle of Chivas
Regal which I never opened. I was working good again and did not miss
other things as much; or at least I told myself that.

The old man was coming up steadily now, at least three times a day, and
I had resigned myself to it. If I refused to let him in he would always come
back later with a missing bulb on the fifth floor. We had taken to buying
cases of beer together, and when he had finished his half, which was very
frequently, he could come up to polish off mine. I began to enjoy talking
about politics, the AMA, Medicare, and hippies, and listening to him recite
from books he had read. I discovered that he was very well read in history,
philosophy, literature, and law. He was extraordinarily fond of saying: "I
am really a cut above being a building superintendent. Circumstances
made me what I am." And even though he was drunk and dirty and it was
very late at night, I believed him and liked him anyway because having him

there was much better than being alone. After he had gone I could sleep and I was not lonely in sleep; and it did not really matter how late I was at work the next morning, because when I really thought about it all, I discovered that nothing really matters except not being old and being alive and having potential to dream about, and not being alone.

Whenever I passed his wife on the steps she would say: "That no-good bastard let them take my dog away." And whenever her husband complained that he was sick she said: "That's good for him. He took my dog away."

Sullivan slept in the basement on the sofa almost every night because his wife would think about the dog after the *Carson Show* and blame him for letting it be taken away. He told her, and then me, that the dog was on a farm in New Hampshire; but that was unlikely because the dog had been near mad, and it did not appease her. It was nearing autumn and she was getting violent. Her screams could be heard for hours though the halls and I knew that beyond her quiet door Miss O'Hara was plotting again. Sullivan now had little cuts and bruises on his face and hands, and one day he said: "Meg is like an albatross around my neck. I wish she was dead. I'm sick myself and I can't take much more. She blames me for the dog and I couldn't help it."

"Why don't you take her out to see the dog?" I said.

"I couldn't help it Rob," he went on. "I'm old and I couldn't help it."

"You ought to just get her out of here for a while."

He looked at me, drunk as usual. "Where would we go? We can't even get past the Square."

There was nothing left to say.

"Honest to God, I couldn't help it," he said. He was not saying it to me.

That night I wrote a letter from a mythical New Hampshire farmer telling them that the dog was very fine and missed them a great deal because he kept trying to run off. I said that the children and all the other dogs liked him and that he was not vicious any more. I wrote that the open air was doing him a lot of good and added that they should feel absolutely free to come up to visit the dog at any time. That same night I gave him the letter.

One evening, some days later, I asked him about it.

"I tried to mail it, I really tried," he said.

"What happened?"

"I went down to the Square and looked for cars with New Hampshire license plates. But I never found anybody."

"That wasn't even necessary, was it?"

"It had to have a New Hampshire postmark. You don't know my Meg."

"Listen," I said. "I have a friend who goes up there. Give me the letter and I'll have him mail it."

He held his head down. "I'll tell you the truth. I carried that letter in my pocket so much it got ragged and dirty and I got tired of carrying it. I finally just tore it up."

Neither one of us said anything for a while.

"If I could have sent it off it would have helped some," he said at last. "I know it would have helped."

"Sure," I said.

"I wouldn't have to ask anybody if I had my strength."

"I know."

"If I had my strength I would have mailed it myself."

"I know," I said.

That night we both drank from his bottle of sherry and it did not matter at all that I did not provide my own glass.

VII

In late September the Cambridge police finally picked up the bearded pot-pusher in the Square. He had been in a restaurant all summer, at the same table, with the same customers flocking around him; but now that summer was over, they picked him up. The leaves were changing. In the early evening students passed the building and Meg, blue-hatted and waiting on the steps, carrying sofas and chairs and coffee tables to their suites in the Houses. Down by the Charles the middle-aged men were catching the last phases of summer sensuality before the grass grew cold and damp, and before the young would be forced indoors to play. I wondered what those hungry, spying men did in the winter or at night when it was too dark to see. Perhaps, I thought, they just stood there and listened.

In our building Miss O'Hara was still listening. She had never stopped. When Meg was outside on the steps it was very quiet and I felt good that Miss O'Hara had to wait a long, long time before she heard anything. The company gave the halls and ceilings a new coat of paint, but it was still old in the building. James Sullivan got his yearly two-week vacation and they went to the Boston Common for six hours: two hours going, two hours sitting on the benches, and two hours coming back. Then they both sat on the steps, watching, and waiting.

At first I wanted to be kind because he was old and dying in a special way and I was young and ambitious. But at night, in my apartment, when I heard his dragging feet in the hall outside and knew that he would be drunk and repetitious and imposing on my privacy, I did not want to be kind any more. There were girls outside and I knew that I could have one now because that desperate look had finally gone somewhere deep inside. I was young and now I did not want to be bothered.

"Did you read about the lousy twelve per cent Social Security increase those bastards in Washington gave us?"

"No."

He would force himself past me, trying to block the door with my body, and into the room. "When those old pricks tell me to count my blessings, I tell them, 'You're not one of them,'" He would seat himself at the table without meeting my eyes. "The cost of living's gone up more than twelve per cent in the last six months."

"I know."

"What unmitigated bastards."

I would try to be busy with something on my desk.

"But the Texas Oil Barons got another depletion allowance."

"They can afford to bribe politicians," I would mumble.

"They tax away our rainy-day dollars and give us a lousy twelve per cent."

"It's tough."

He would know that I did not want to hear any more and he would know that he was making a burden of himself. It made me feel bad that it was so obvious to him, but I could not help myself. It made me feel bad that I disliked him more every time I heard a girl laugh on the street far below my window. So I would nod occasionally and say half-phrases and smile slightly at something witty he was saying for the third time. If I did not offer him a drink he would go sooner and so I gave him Coke when he hinted at how dry he was. Then, when he had finally gone, saying, "I hope I haven't burdened you unduly," I went to bed and hated myself.

VIII

If I am a janitor it is either because I have to be a janitor or because I want to be a janitor. And if I do not have to do it, and if I no longer want to do it, the easiest thing in the world, for a young man, is to step up to something else. Any move away from it is a step up because there is no job more demeaning than that of a janitor. One day I made myself suddenly realize that the three dirty cans would never contain anything of value to me, unless, of course, I decided to gather material for Harold Robbins or freelance for the *Realist*. Neither alternative appealed to me.

Toward dawn one day, during the first part of October, I rented a U-Haul truck and took away two loads of things I had accumulated. The records I packed very carefully, and the stereo I placed on the front seat of the truck beside me. I slipped the Chivas Regal and a picture of Jean under some clothes in a trunk I will not open for a long time. And I left the rug on the floor because it was dirty and too large for my new apartment. I also left the two plates given to me by James Sullivan, for no reason at all. Sometimes I want to go back to get them, but I do not know how to ask for them or explain why I left them in the first place. But sometimes at night, when there is a sleeping girl beside me, I think that I cannot have them again because I am still young and do not want to go back into that building.

I saw him once in the Square walking along very slowly with two shopping bags, and they seemed very heavy. As I came up behind him I saw him put them down and exercise his arms while the crowd moved in two streams around him. I had an instant impulse to offer help and I was close enough to touch him before I stopped. I will never know why I stopped. And after a few seconds of standing behind him and knowing that he was not aware of anything at all except the two heavy bags waiting to be lifted after his arms were sufficiently rested, I moved back into the stream of people which passed on the left of him. I never looked back.

The Whisper of Madness

NAGUIB MAHFOUZ

What is madness?

It seems to be a condition as inscrutable as life and death. You can learn a great deal about it when you look at it from the outside, but its substance and real essence remain a closed secret. Our friend knows now that he stayed for a while as a guest in Khanka. Like all sane people, he can still remember his past life and is fully aware of his present one as well. But, when it comes to remembering about that short period—it was short, thank God—he is completely at a loss and cannot be certain of anything. It was a journey into a marvellous ethereal world filled with mist. Faces from this world float in front of his eyes, but he cannot make out their features. Every time he tries to use his memory to throw some light on them, they fly away and are swallowed up in darkness. Sometimes he hears something which sounds like a whisper, and, if he really concentrates, he can make out the various places where he hears them; until, that is, they run away and leave behind a sense of silence and bewilderment.

That magical period is now lost forever and the pleasures and pain which went with it. Even the people who were alive during that remarkable period have drawn a thick veil of silence and pretended ignorance over it for some undeclared reason. So it has fallen into oblivion without any reliable historian being allowed to record its wonders. How did it happen, I ask myself? When did it happen? How did people realize that someone had lost his reason, and that this person had become an eccentric who had to be kept away from people, like some wild beast?!

He was a quiet man, and this absolute quietness was his own special characteristic. Perhaps that was why he liked to be apathetic and lazy, withdrew from contact with other people and refused to exert himself in any way. That was why he left school at an early age and refused to do any work; he was happy with another fairly good source of income. The thing he liked

645

best was to sit quietly in an isolated seat in the pavement cafe, interlock his hands over his knee, and spend hour after hour sitting there without moving or saying a word. He would sit there with a sleepy look and drooping eyelids, watching the people coming and going. He never got bored, tired or worried; his whole life involved sitting on this particular chair on the pavement and it gave him the greatest pleasure. However, behind this silent and stupid exterior, there was nothing; no warmth or movement deep down inside him or even in his imagination. His quietness was complete, inside and out, mind and body, feelings and imagination. He was a statue of flesh and blood, seeming to watch people as they passed by, but really isolated from life.

Then what?!

In this stagnant, brackish water, there was a sudden strange movement as though someone had thrown a stone into it.

How?!

One day, he was sitting quietly on his seat on the pavement and noticed some workers filling up the whole street in advance of a spectacular parade. They were sprinkling bright yellow sand, much to the delight of the people who were watching. For the first time in his life, something astonished him. Why were they sprinkling sand, he asked himself. It would get blown about and would fill people's nostrils and hurt them. The same people would soon come back, brush it all up and collect it again. So why sprinkle it at all?! Perhaps the whole thing was too paltry to demand questions or justify any feeling of bewilderment. But to him, the question seemed to be the most important truth in his life at that moment. He imagined that he was dealing with one of the greatest problems of the universe. In all this sprinkling followed by sweeping up, with people being hurt in between the two operations, he found a bewildering problem. He even felt like laughing, which was something he rarely did; but this time he laughed and laughed till his eyes were running. This laughter was no mere sudden emotion; in fact, it was the sign of a complete change which brought him out of his terrible silence to a totally new attitude. He spent his day either in a state of bewilderment or else laughing. He kept on talking to himself in a sort of a daze:—"They sprinkle, then they hurt people, then they sweep ... Ha, Ha, Ha!"

Next morning, he had not recovered from his bewilderment. He stood in front of the mirror getting ready to go out. His eyes fell on his tie and he soon felt baffled all over again. Why, he asked himself, did he tie his tie like that? What was the point of a tie? Why do we put ourselves to the trouble of having to choose a color and material? Before he realized it, he was laughing again as he had done the day before. He started looking at the tie in helpless confusion. He looked at the various parts of his outfit with a feeling of rejection and alienation. What was the point, he asked himself, of hiding ourselves in this laughable fashion? Why did we not take these clothes off and throw them on the ground? Why did we not appear as God created us? However, he continued to put his clothes on until he was fully dressed, and then went out of the house as usual.

He no longer felt that compact quietness which had lived peacefully beneath his skin for so long. How could he relax when these heavy clothes were beginning to strangle him in spite of himself?! Yes, in spite of himself. A wave of anger came over him as he hurried along. It annoyed him to have to accept any restrictions in spite of himself. Wasn't mankind free? He thought for a moment and then replied enthusiastically, "Yes, I'm free." Suddenly he felt filled with the spirit of freedom; its light illuminated every part of his soul until he felt overjoyed. Yes, he was free. Freedom came to him like a revelation. He was quite certain about it, and there was no room for doubt. He was free to do what he wished, how he wished, when he wished, without submitting to any force or giving way to any factors internal or external. The problem of free will was solved in one second, and with incredible enthusiasm he rescued it from the heavy tread of pretexts. He had a remarkable feeling of happiness and superiority. He looked disdainfully at people as they strolled along the sides of the road in fetters, powerless to control their own fate, be it good or bad. When they walked, they could not stop; when they stopped, they could not walk. He, on the other hand, could walk when he wished and stop when he wished; even more, he could despise every force, every law, every instinct. This exciting new feeling encouraged him to test out his extraordinary power; he could not resist the call of freedom.

He stopped suddenly as he was walking. "Here I am," he told himself. "I've stopped for no reason at all." He looked around him for a few seconds, and then asked himself whether he could lift his hands up without bothering about anyone else. Then he asked himself again whether he could find the courage to stand on one leg. "Why shouldn't I?" he asked himself. "What is there to hamper my freedom?" he started lifting his left leg as though he were doing a gymnastic exercise; he was concentrating hard and not worrying about anything else as though he were the only person on the road and no one were watching him. A sense of serenity and contentment filled his heart, and he had a feeling of boundless self-confidence. He began to regret the opportunities he had missed all his life when he could have enjoyed his freedom and happiness. He carried on walking as though he was facing life all over again.

On his way to the cafe, he passed by a restaurant where he would sometimes eat his dinner. He noticed a table on the pavement filled with delicious things. A man and woman were sitting at it facing each other; they were both eating and drinking with gusto. A short distance away, a group of street urchins was crouching. They were completely naked except for a few torn rags, and their faces and skin were covered with a thick layer of dust and filth. The disparity between the two groups of people displeased him, and his sense of freedom shared in his displeasure and refused to allow him to walk past the restaurant in haughty disdain. But what could he do? The urchins must eat along with those other people, his heart told him with confidence and conviction. But the others will not give up any of the delicious chicken they have in front of them without a fight, that is certain! If he threw it on the ground, it would get covered in dust. There was no power which could deprive the urchins of having it; so was there anything to stop him carrying out his wish? . . . Go on! Dithering may have been feasible in the old days, but now . . . Quietly, he went up to the table, stretched out his hand to the tray and took the chicken. He then threw it at the feet of the naked children, turned away from the table and proceeded on his way as though he had done nothing wrong. He paid no attention to the yelling and screaming full of the most obscene oaths and curses which pursued him. In fact, he could not help laughing and started doing so uncontrollably till his eyes began to run. He sighed with satisfaction from deep down inside him, and his confidence and happiness and a profound sense of calm came back to him.

He reached the cafe and proceeded to his chair as usual, but this time, he could not interlock his hands over his knees and then abandon himself to his usual silence. His own self would not obey him. He had lost his power to sit still, or else had been cured of the inability to move. You could see it from the way he was sitting there. He was on the point of getting up when, at that very moment, he saw someone who was no stranger to him although they had not been formally introduced. Like him, this man was one of the cafe regulars. He was portly and swaggered along with his head held high in disdain. He looked at the people round him with an arrogant contempt, and every movement he made spoke of vanity and pride. It seemed as though humanity aroused in him the feelings which worms can arouse in the minds of sensitive people. It was as though he were seeing this man for the first time; his ugliness and eccentricity were exposed. The strange laughter which had kept on teasing him for these two days got the better of him. He did not take his eyes off this man and focused in particular on his neck which protruded from the gusset of his shirt, broad, full and enticing. He asked himself whether he could let him pass by in peace?? God forbid! He had met the missionary of freedom and had promised not to let him down in any way. He shrugged his shoulders indifferently and came up to the man till he was almost touching him. He lifted his hand and brought it down on the nape of the man's neck with all the force he could muster. The thump of the blow echoed around. He could not control himself and burst into laughter. However, this experiment did not end quite as innocuously as the previous one. The man turned round and faced towards him with an insane anger written all over his face. He grabbed hold of his collar and pummelled and kicked him till some of the people sitting around pulled them apart. He left the cafe panting. Remarkably enough, he did not feel annoyed or sorry; on the contrary, he felt a strange pleasure which he had never experienced before. His mouth displayed a lingering smile. His heart was overflowing with a vitality and joy which overcame any feeling of pain. He no longer cared about anything except the freedom which he had won in a happy moment of time. He refused to relinguish it for a single second of his life. From then on, he threw himself into an ever-increasing stream of risky experiments with an unbendable will and uncontrollable force. He cuffed people's necks, spat in their faces and kicked them front and back. He did not escape without being punched or cursed on every occasion. His glasses were smashed, the tassel on his *tarbush* was torn, his shirt was ripped and his trousers were spoiled. But he could not be stopped, restrained or turned from his course, fraught with dangers though it was. The smile never left his lips, and the drunkenness which was affecting his besotted heart did not abate. If death itself had blocked his path, he would have plunged into the attack without fear.

Just as the sun was on the point of setting, his wandering eyes noticed a beautiful girl coming towards him with her arm in that of an elegant-looking man. She was strutting along in a thin, transparent dress, and the nipples of her breasts were almost breaking through the material of her silk gown. Her ample bosom caught his eyes and they grew wider as his astonishment increased. The view staggered him. She came closer and closer till she was at arm's length.

His mind—or his madness—was thinking at an imaginary speed. He imagined that he was touching those wayward breasts—some man would be doing it in any case ... so let it be this man. He stood in her way, stretched out his hand with lightning speed and pinched her. Oh dear! What a hail of blows and punches fell on him! Many people joined in but eventually they left him alone! Maybe it was his insane laughter which made them afraid, or perhaps the look in his staring eyes alarmed them. In any case, they left him. So he escaped and was hardly the worse for wear! He was still eager for more adventure. But he took a look at his clothes, and was shocked to find them so torn and ripped. However, instead of feeling sorry for himself, he began to remember what he had been thinking about the day before when he was standing in front of the mirror. A strange look appeared in his eyes, and he started asking himself again why he allowed himself to remain a prisoner in these stupid wrappings which constricted his chest, stomach and legs?! He felt weighed down by them, as though the pressure which they exerted was strangling him. He exploded; he could not stand them any longer. His hands started to tear them off one by one without the slightest pause for thought. He had stripped himself of all his clothes, and stood there as naked as God created him. His strange laughter toyed with him and he guffawed. Then he dashed off on his way ...

The Magic Barrel

BERNARD MALAMUD

Not long ago there lived in uptown New York, in a small, almost meager room, though crowded with books, Leo Finkle, a rabbinical student in the Yeshivah University. Finkle, after six years of study, was to be ordained in June and had been advised by an acquaintance that he might find it easier to win himself a congregation if he were married. Since he had no present prospects of marriage, after two tormented days of turning it over in his mind, he called in Pinye Salzman, a marriage broker whose two-line advertisement he had read in the *Forward*.

The matchmaker appeared one night out of the dark fourth-floor hall-way of the graystone rooming house where Finkle lived, grasping a black, strapped portfolio that had been worn thin with use. Salzman, who had been long in the business, was of slight but dignified build, wearing an old hat, and an overcoat too short and tight for him. He smelled frankly of fish, which he loved to eat, and although he was missing a few teeth, his presence was not displeasing, because of an amiable manner curiously contrasted with mournful eyes. His voice, his lips, his wisp of beard, his bony fingers were animated, but gave him a moment of repose and his mild blue eyes revealed a depth of sadness, a characteristic that put Leo a little at ease although the situation, for him, was inherently tense.

He at once informed Salzman why he had asked him to come, explaining that his home was in Cleveland, and that but for his parents, who had married comparatively late in life, he was alone in the world. He had for six years devoted himself almost entirely to his studies, as a result of which, understandably, he had found himself without time for a social life and the company of young women. Therefore he thought it the better part of trial and error—of embarrassing fumbling—to call in an experienced person to advise him on these matters. He remarked in passing that the function of the marriage broker was ancient and honorable, highly approved in the

Jewish community, because it made practical the necessary without hindering joy. Moreover, his own parents had been brought together by a matchmaker. They had made, if not a financially profitable marriage—since neither had possessed any worldly goods to speak of—at least a successful one in the sense of their everlasting devotion to each other. Salzman listened in embarrassed surprise, sensing a sort of apology. Later, however, he experienced a glow of pride in his work, an emotion that had left him years ago, and he heartily approved of Finkle.

The two went to their business. Leo had led Salzman to the only clear place in the room, a table near a window that overlooked the lamp-lit city. He seated himself at the matchmaker's side but facing him, attempting by an act of will to suppress the unpleasant tickle in his throat. Salzman eagerly unstrapped his portfolio and removed a loose rubber band from a thin packet of much-handled cards. As he flipped through them, a gesture and sound that physically hurt Leo, the student pretended not to see and gazed steadfastly out the window. Although it was still February, winter was on its last legs, signs of which he had for the first time in years begun to notice. He now observed the round white moon, moving high in the sky through a cloud menagerie, and watched with half-open mouth as it penetrated a huge hen, and dropped out of her like an egg laying itself. Salzman, though pretending through eyeglasses he had just slipped on, to be engaged in scanning the writing on the cards, stole occasional glances at the young man's distinguished face, noting with pleasure the long, severe scholar's nose, brown eyes heavy with learning, sensitive yet ascetic lips, and a certain, almost hollow quality of the dark cheeks. He gazed around at shelves upon shelves of books and let out a soft, contented sigh.

When Leo's eyes fell upon the cards, he counted six spread out in Salzman's hand.

"So few?" he asked in disappointment.

"You wouldn't believe me how much cards I got in my office," Salzman replied. "The drawers are already filled to the top, so I keep them now in a barrel, but is every girl good for a new rabbi?"

Leo blushed at this, regretting all he had revealed of himself in a curriculum vitae he had sent to Salzman. He had thought it best to acquaint him with his strict standards and specifications, but in having done so, felt he had told the marriage broker more than was absolutely necessary.

He hesitantly inquired, "Do you keep photographs of your clients on file?"

"First comes family, amount of dowry, also what kind promises," Salzman replied, unbuttoning his tight coat and settling himself in the chair. "After comes pictures, rabbi."

"Call me Mr. Finkle. I'm not yet a rabbi."

Salzman said he would, but instead called him doctor, which he changed to rabbi when Leo was not listening too attentively.

Salzman adjusted his horn-rimmed spectacles, gently cleared his throat and read in an eager voice the contents of the top card:

"Sophie P. Twenty four years. Widow one year. No children. Educated high school and two years college. Father promises eight thousand dollars. Has wonderful wholesale business. Also real estate. On the mother's side comes teachers, also one actor. Well known on Second Avenue."

Leo gazed up in surprise. "Did you say a widow?"

"A widow don't mean spoiled, rabbi. She lived with her husband maybe four months. He was a sick boy she made a mistake to marry him."

"Marrying a widow has never entered my mind."

"This is because you have no experience. A widow, especially if she is young and healthy like this girl, is a wonderful person to marry. She will be thankful to you the rest of her life. Believe me, if I was looking now for a bride, I would marry a widow."

Leo reflected, then shook his head.

Salzman hunched his shoulders in an almost imperceptible gesture of disappointment. He placed the card down on the wooden table and began to read another:

"Lily H. High school teacher. Regular. Not a substitute. Has savings and new Dodge car. Lived in Paris one year. Father is successful dentist thirty-five years. Interested in professional man. Well Americanized family. Wonderful opportunity."

"I knew her personally," said Salzman. "I wish you could see this girl. She is a doll. Also very intelligent. All day you could talk to her about books and theyater and what not. She also knows current events."

"I don't believe you mentioned her age?"

"Her age?" Salzman said, raising his brows. "Her age is thirty-two years."

Leo said after a while. "I'm afraid that seems a little too old."

Salzman let out a laugh. "So how old are you, rabbi?"

"Twenty-seven."

"So what is the difference, tell me, between twenty-seven and thirty-two? My own wife is seven years older than me. So what did I suffer?—Nothing. If Rothschild's a daughter wants to marry you, would you say on account her age, no?"

"Yes," Leo said dryly.

Salzman shook off the no in the yes. "Five years don't mean a thing. I give you my word that when you will live with her for one week, you will forget her age. What does it mean five years—that she lived more and knows more than somebody who is younger? On this girl, God bless you, years are not wasted. Each one that it comes makes better the bargain."

"What subject does she teach in high school?"

"Languages. If you heard the way she speaks French, you will think it is music. I am in the business twenty-five years, and I recommend her with my whole heart. Believe me, I know what I'm talking, rabbi."

"What's on the next card?" Leo said abruptly.

Salzman reluctantly turned up the third card:

"Ruth K. Nineteen years. Honor student. Father offers thirteen thousand cash to the right bridegroom. He is a medical doctor. Stomach specialist with marvelous practice. Brother in law owns own garment business. Particular people."

Salzman looked as if he had read his trump card.

"Did you say nineteen?" Leo asked with interest.

"On the dot."

"Is she attractive?" He blushed. "Pretty?"

Salzman kissed his finger tips. "A little doll. On this I give you my word. Let me call the father tonight and you will see what means pretty."

But Leo was troubled. "You're sure she's that young?"

"This I am positive. The father will show you the birth certificate."

"Are you positive there isn't something wrong with her?" Leo insisted.

"Who says there is wrong?"

"I don't understand why an American girl her age should go to a marriage broker."

A smile spread over Salzman's face.

"So for the same reason you went, she comes."

Leo flushed. "I am pressed for time."

Salzman, realizing he had been tactless, quickly explained. "The father came, not her. He wants she should have the best, so he looks around himself. When we will locate the right boy he will introduce him and encourage. This makes a better marriage than if a young girl without experience takes for herself. I don't have to tell you this."

"But don't you think this young girl believes in love?" Leo spoke uneasily.

Salzman was about to guffaw but caught himself and said soberly, "Love comes with the right person, not before."

Leo parted dry lips but did not speak. Noticing that Salzman had snatched a glance at the next card, he cleverly asked, "How is her health?"

"Perfect," Salzman said, breathing with difficulty. "Of course, she is a little lame on her right foot from an auto accident that it happened to her when she was twelve years, but nobody notices on account she is so brilliant and also beautiful."

Leo got up heavily and went to the window. He felt curiously bitter and upbraided himself for having called in the marriage broker. Finally, he shook his head.

"Why not?" Salzman persisted, the pitch of his voice rising.

"Because I detest stomach specialists."

"So what do you care what is his business? After you marry her do you need him? Who says he must come every Friday night to your house?"

Ashamed of the way the talk was going, Leo dismissed Salzman, who went home with heavy, melancholy eyes.

Though he had felt only relief at the marriage broker's departure, Leo was in low spirits the next day. He explained it as arising from Salzman's failure to produce a suitable bride for him. He did not care for his type of clientele. But when Leo found himself hesitating whether to seek out another matchmaker, one more polished than Pinye, he wondered if it could be—his protestations to the contrary, and although he honored his father and mother—that he did not, in essence, care for the matchmaking institution? This thought he quickly put out of mind yet found himself still upset. All day he ran around in the woods—missed an important appointment, forgot to give out his laundry, walked out of a Broadway cafeteria without paying and had to run back with the ticket in his hand; had even not recognized his landlady in the street when she passed with a friend and courteously called out, "A good evening to you, Doctor Finkle." By nightfall, however, he had regained sufficient calm to sink his nose into a book and there found peace from his thoughts.

Almost at once there came a knock on the door. Before Leo could say enter, Salzman, commercial cupid, was standing in the room. His face was gray and meager, his expression hungry, and he looked as if he would expire on his feet. Yet the marriage broker managed, by some trick of the muscles, to display a broad smile.

"So good evening. I am invited?"

Leo nodded, disturbed to see him again, yet unwilling to ask the man to leave.

Beaming still, Salzman laid his portfolio on the table. "Rabbi, I got for you tonight good news."

"I've asked you not to call me rabbi. I'm still a student."

"Your worries are finished. I have for you a first-class bride."

"Leave me in peace concerning this project." Leo pretended lack of interest.

"The world will dance at your wedding."

"Please, Mr. Salzman, no more."

"But first must come back my strength," Salzman said weakly. He fumbled with the portfolio straps and took out of the leather case an oily paper bag, from which he extracted a hard, seeded roll and a small, smoked white fish. With a quick motion of his hand he stripped the fish out of its skin and began ravenously to chew. "All day in a rush," he muttered.

Leo watched him eat.

"A sliced tomato you have maybe?" Salzman hesitantly inquired.

"No."

The marriage broker shut his eyes and ate. When he had finished he carefully cleaned up the crumbs and rolled up the remains of the fish, in the paper bag. His spectacled eyes roamed the room until he discovered, amid some piles of books, a one-burner gas stove. Lifting his hat and humbly asked, "A glass tea you got, rabbi?"

Conscience-stricken, Leo rose and brewed the tea. He served it with a chunk of lemon and two cubes of lump sugar, delighting Salzman.

After he had drunk his tea, Salzman's strength and good spirits were restored.

"So tell me, rabbi," he said amiably, "you considered some more the three clients I mentioned yesterday?"

"There was no need to consider."

"Why not?"

"None of them suits me."

"What then suits you?"

Leo let it pass because he could only give a confused answer.

Without waiting for a reply, Salzman asked, "You remember this girl I talked to you—the high school teacher?"

"Age thirty-two?"

But, surprisingly, Salzman's face lit in a smile. "Age twenty-nine."

Leo shot him a look. "Reduced from thirty-two?"

"A mistake," Salzman avowed. "I talked today with the dentist. He took me to his safety deposit box and showed me the birth certificate. She was twenty-nine years last August. They made her a party in the mountains where she went for her vacation. When her father spoke to me the first time I forgot to write the age and I told you thirty-two, but now I remember this was a different client, a widow."

"The same one you told me about? I thought she was twenty-four?"

"A different. Am I responsible that the world is filled with widows?"

"No, but I'm not interested in them, nor for that matter, in school teachers."

Salzman pulled his clasped hands to his breast. Looking at the ceiling he devoutly exclaimed, "Yiddishe kinder, what can I say to somebody that he is not interested in high school teachers? So what then you are interested?"

Leo flushed but controlled himself.

"In what else will you be interested," Salzman went on, "if you not interested in this fine girl that she speaks four languages and has personally in the bank ten thousand dollars? Also her father guarantees further twelve thousand. Also she has a new car, wonderful clothes, talks on all subjects, and she will give you a first-class home and children. How near do we come in our life to paradise?"

"If she's so wonderful, why wasn't she married ten years ago?"

"Why?" said Salzman with a heavy laugh. "—Why? Because she is *partikiler*. This is why. She wants the *best*."

Leo was silent, amused at how he had entangled himself. But Salzman had aroused his interest in Lily H., and he began seriously to consider calling on her. When the marriage broker observed how intently Leo's mind was at work on the facts he had supplied, he felt certain they would soon come to an agreement.

*   *   *

Late Saturday afternoon, conscious of Salzman, Leo Finkle walked with Lily Hirschorn along Riverside Drive. He walked briskly and erectly, wearing with distinction the black fedora he had that morning taken with trepidation out of the dusty hat box on his closet shelf, and the heavy black Saturday coat he had thoroughly whisked clean. Leo also owned a walking stick, a present from a distant relative, but quickly put temptation aside and did not use it. Lily, petite and not unpretty, had on something signifying the approach of spring. She was au courant, animatedly, with all sorts of subjects, and he weighed her words and found her surprisingly sound— score another for Salzman, whom he uneasily sensed to be somewhere around, hiding perhaps high in a tree along the street, flashing the lady signals with a pocket mirror; or perhaps a cloven-hoofed Pan, piping nuptial ditties as he danced his invisible way before them, strewing wild buds on the walk and purple grapes in their path, symbolizing fruit of a union, though there was of course still none.

Lily startled Leo by remarking, "I was thinking of Mr. Salzman, a curious figure, wouldn't you say?"

Not certain what to answer, he nodded.

She bravely went on, blushing, "I for one am grateful for his introducing us. Aren't you?"

He courteously replied, "I am."

"I mean," she said with a little laugh—and it was all in good taste, or at least gave the effect of being not in bad—"do you mind that we came together so?"

He was not displeased with her honesty, recognizing that she meant to set the relationship aright, and understanding that it took a certain amount of experience in life, and courage, to want to do it quite that way. One had to have some sort of past to make that kind of beginning.

He said that he did not mind. Salzman's function was traditional and honorable—valuable for what it might achieve, which, he pointed out, was frequently nothing.

Lily agreed with a sigh. They walked on for a while and she said after a long silence, again with a nervous laugh, "Would you mind if I asked you something a little bit personal? Frankly, I find the subject fascinating." Although Leo shrugged, she went on half embarrassedly, "How was it that you came to your calling? I mean was it a sudden passionate inspiration?"

Leo, after a time, slowly replied, "I was always interested in the Law."

"You saw revealed in it the presence of the Highest?"

He nodded and changed the subject. "I understand that you spent a little time in Paris, Miss Hirschorn?"

"Oh, did Mr. Salzman tell you, Rabbi Finkle?" Leo winced but she went on, "It was ages ago and almost forgotten. I remember I had to return for my sister's wedding."

And Lily would not be put off. "When," she asked in a trembly voice, "did you become enamored of God?"

He stared at her. Then it came to him that she was talking not about Leo Finkle, but of a total stranger, some mystical figure, perhaps even passionate prophet that Salzman had dreamed up for her—no relation to the living or dead. Leo trembled with rage and weakness. The trickster had obviously sold her a bill of goods, just as he had him, who'd expected to become acquainted with a young lady of twenty-nine, only to behold, the moment he laid eyes upon her strained and anxious face, a woman past thirty-five and aging rapidly. Only his self control had kept him this long in her presence.

"I am not," he said gravely, "a talented religious person," and in seeking words to go on, found himself possessed by shame and fear. "I think," he said in a strained manner, "that I came to God not because I loved Him, but because I did not."

This confession he spoke harshly because its unexpectedness shook him.

Lily wilted. Leo saw a profusion of loaves of bread go flying like ducks high over his head, not unlike the winged loaves by which he had counted himself to sleep last night. Mercifully, then, it snowed, which he would not put past Salzman's machinations.

He was infuriated with the marriage broker and swore he would throw him out of the room the minute he reappeared. But Salzman did not come that night, and when Leo's anger had subsided, an unaccountable despair grew in its place. At first he thought this was caused by his disappointment in Lily, but before long it became evident that he had involved himself with Salzman without a true knowledge of his own intent. He gradually realized—with an emptiness that seized him with six hands—that he had called in the broker to find him a bride because he was incapable of doing it himself. This terrifying insight he had derived as a result of his meeting and conversation with Lily Hirschorn. Her probing questions had somehow irritated him into revealing—to himself more than her—the true nature of his relationship to God, and from that it had come upon him, with shocking force, that apart from his parents, he had never loved anyone. Or perhaps it went the other way, that he did not love God so well as he might, because he had not loved man. It seemed to Leo that his whole life stood starkly revealed and he saw himself for the first time as he truly was—unloved and loveless. This bitter but somehow not fully unexpected revelation brought him to a point of panic, controlled only by extraordinary effort. He covered his face with his hands and cried.

The week that followed was the worst of his life. He did not eat and lost weight. His beard darkened and grew ragged. He stopped attending seminars and almost never opened a book. He seriously considered leaving the

Yeshivah, although he was deeply troubled at the thought of the loss of all his years of study—saw them like pages torn from a book, strewn over the city—and at the devastating effect of this decision upon his parents. But he had lived without knowledge of himself, and never in the Five Books and all the Commentaries—mea culpa—had the truth been revealed to him. He did not know where to turn, and in all this desolating loneliness there was no *to whom*, although he often thought of Lily but not once could bring himself to go downstairs and make the call. He became touchy and irritable, especially with his landlady, who asked him all manner of personal questions; on the other hand, sensing his own disagreeableness, he waylaid her on the stairs and apologized abjectly, until mortified, she ran from him. Out of this, however, he drew the consolation that he was a Jew and that a Jew suffered. But gradually, as the long and terrible week drew to a close, he regained his composure and some idea of purpose in life: to go on as planned. Although he was imperfect, the ideal was not. As for his quest of a bride, the thought of continuing afflicted him with anxiety and heartburn, yet perhaps with this new knowledge of himself he would be more successful than in the past. Perhaps love would now come to him and a bride to that love. And for this sanctified seeking who needed a Salzman?

The marriage broker, a skeleton with haunted eyes, returned that very night. He looked, withal, the picture of frustrated expectancy—as if he had steadfastly waited the week at Miss Lily Hirschorn's side for a telephone call that never came.

Casually coughing, Salzman came immediately to the point: "So how did you like her?"

Leo's anger rose and he could not refrain from chiding the matchmaker: "Why did you lie to me, Salzman?"

Salzman's pale face went dead white, the world had snowed on him.

"Did you not state that she was twenty-nine?" Leo insisted.

"I give you my word—"

"She was thirty-five, if a day. At *least* thirty-five."

"Of this don't be too sure. Her father told me—"

"Never mind. The worst of it was that you lied to her."

"How did I lie to her, tell me?"

"You told her things about me that weren't true. You made me out to be more, consequently less than I am. She had in mind a totally different person, a sort of semimystical Wonder Rabbi."

"All I said, you was a religious man."

"I can imagine."

Salzman sighed. "This is my weakness that I have," he confessed. "My wife says to me I shouldn't be a salesman, but when I have two fine people that they would be wonderful to be married, I am so happy that I talk too much." He smiled wanly. "This is why Salzman is a poor man."

Leo's anger left him. "Well, Salzman, I'm afraid that's all."

The marriage broker fastened hungry eyes on him.

"You don't want any more a bride?"

"I do," said Leo, "but I have decided to seek her in a different way. I am no longer interested in an arranged marriage. To be frank, I now admit the necessity of premarital love. That is, I want to be in love with the one I marry."

"Love?" said Salzman, astounded. After a moment he remarked, "For us, our love is our life, not for the ladies. In the ghetto they—"

"I know, I know," said Leo. "I've thought of it often. Love, I have said to myself, should be a by-product of living and worship rather than its own end. Yet for myself I find it necessary to establish the level of my need and fulfill it."

Salzman shrugged but answered, "Listen, rabbi, if you want love, this I can find for you also. I have such beautiful clients that you will love them the minute your eyes will see them."

Leo smiled unhappily. "I'm afraid you don't understand."

But Salzman hastily unstrapped his portfolio and withdrew a manila packet from it.

"Pictures," he said, quickly laying the envelope on the table.

Leo called after him to take the pictures away, but as if on the wings of the wind, Salzman had disappeared.

March came. Leo had returned to his regular routine. Although he felt not quite himself yet—lacked energy—he was making plans for a more active social life. Of course it would cost something, but he was an expert in cutting corners; and when there were no corners left he would make circles rounder. All the while Salzman's pictures had lain on the table, gathering dust. Occasionally as Leo sat studying, or enjoying a cup of tea, his eyes fell on the manila envelope, but he never opened it.

The days went by and no social life to speak of developed with a member of the opposite sex—it was difficult, given the circumstances of his situation. One morning Leo toiled up the stairs to his room and stared out the window at the city. Although the day was bright his view of it was dark. For some time he watched the people in the street below hurrying along and then turned with a heavy heart to his little room. On the table was the packet. With a sudden relentless gesture he tore it open. For a half-hour he stood by the table in a state of excitement, examining the photographs of the ladies Salzman had included. Finally, with a deep sigh he put them down. There were six, of varying degrees of attractiveness, but look at them long enough and they all became Lily Hirschorn: all past their prime, all starved behind bright smiles, not a true personality in the lot. Life, despite their frantic yoohooings, had passed them by; they were pictures in a brief case that stank of fish. After a while, however, as Leo attempted to return the photographs into the envelope, he found in it another, a snapshot of the type taken by a machine for a quarter. He gazed at it a moment and let out a cry.

Her face deeply moved him. Why, he could at first not say. It gave him the impression of youth—spring flowers, yet age—a sense of having been used to the bone, wasted; this came from the eyes, which were hauntingly familiar, yet absolutely strange. He had a vivid impression that he had met her before, but try as he might he could not place her although he could almost recall her name, as if he had read it in her own handwriting. No, this couldn't be; he would have remembered her. It was not, he affirmed, that she had an extraordinary beauty—no, though her face was attractive enough; it was that *something* about her moved him. Feature for feature, even some of the ladies of the photographs could do better; but she leaped forth to his heart—had *lived,* or wanted to—more than just wanted, perhaps regretted how she had lived—had somehow deeply suffered: it could be seen in the depths of those reluctant eyes, and from the way the light enclosed and shone from her, and within her, opening realms of possibility: this was her own. Her he desired. His head ached and eyes narrowed with the intensity of his gazing, then as if an obscure fog had blown up in the mind, he experienced fear of her and was aware that he had received an impression, somehow, of evil. He shuddered, saying softly, it is thus with us all. Leo brewed some tea in a small pot and sat sipping it without sugar, to calm himself. But before he had finished drinking, again with excitement he examined the face and found it good: good for Leo Finkle. Only such a one could understand him and help him seek whatever he was seeking. She might, perhaps, love him. How she had happened to be among the discards in Salzman's barrel he could never guess, but he knew he must urgently go find her.

Leo rushed downstairs, grabbed up the Bronx telephone book, and searched for Salzman's home address. He was not listed, nor was his office. Neither was he in the Manhattan book. But Leo remembered having written down the address on a slip of paper after he had read Salzman's advertisement in the "personals" column of the *Forward.* He ran up to his room and tore through his papers, without luck. It was exasperating. Just when he needed the matchmaker he was nowhere to be found. Fortunately Leo remembered to look in his wallet. There on a card he found his name written and a Bronx address. No phone number was listed, the reason—Leo now recalled—he had originally communicated with Salzman by letter. He got on his coat, put a hat on over his skull cap and hurried to the subway station. All the way to the far end of the Bronx he sat on the edge of his seat. He was more than once tempted to take out the picture and see if the girl's face was as he remembered it, but he refrained, allowing the snapshot to remain in his inside coat pocket, content to have her so close. When the train pulled into the station he was waiting at the door and bolted out. He quickly located the street Salzman had advertised.

The building he sought was less than a block from the subway, but it was not an office building, nor even a loft, nor a store in which one could rent office space. It was a very old tenement house. Leo found Salzman's name in pencil on a soiled tag under the bell and climbed three dark flights to his apartment. When he knocked, the door was opened by a thin, asthmatic, gray-haired woman, in felt slippers.

"Yes?" she said, expecting nothing. She listened without listening. He could have sworn he had seen her, too, before but knew it was an illusion.

"Salzman—does he live here? Pinye Salzman," he said, "the matchmaker?"

She stared at him a long minute. "Of course."

He felt embarrassed. "Is he in?"

"No." Her mouth, though left open, offered nothing more.

"The matter is urgent. Can you tell me where his office is?"

"In the air." She pointed upward.

"You mean he has no office?" Leo asked.

"In his socks."

He peered into the apartment. It was sunless and dingy, one large room divided by a half-open curtain, beyond which he could see a sagging metal bed. The near side of a room was crowded with rickety chairs, old bureaus, a three-legged table, racks of cooking utensils, and all the apparatus of a kitchen. But there was no sign of Salzman or his magic barrel, probably also a figment of the imagination. An odor of frying fish made Leo weak to the knees.

"Where is he?" he insisted. "I've got to see your husband."

At length she answered, "So who knows where he is? Every time he thinks a new thought he runs to a different place. Go home, he will find you."

"Tell him Leo Finkle."

She gave no sign she had heard.

He walked downstairs, depressed.

But Salzman, breathless, stood waiting at his door.

Leo was astounded and overjoyed. "How did you get here before me?"

"I rushed."

"Come inside."

They entered. Leo fixed tea, and a sardine sandwich for Salzman. As they were drinking he reached behind him for the packet of pictures and handed them to the marriage broker.

Salzman put down his glass and said expectantly, "You found somebody you like?"

"Not among these."

The marriage broker turned away.

"Here is the one I want." Leo held forth the snapshot.

Salzman slipped on his glasses and took the picture into his trembling hand. He turned ghastly and let out a groan.

"What's the matter?" cried Leo.

"Excuse me. Was an accident this picture. She isn't for you."

Salzman frantically shoved the manila packet into his portfolio. He thrust the snapshot into his pocket and fled down the stairs.

Leo, after momentary paralysis, gave chase and cornered the marriage broker in the vestibule. The landlady made hysterical outcries but neither of them listened.

"Give me back the picture, Salzman."

"No." The pain in his eyes was terrible.

"Tell me who she is then."

"This I can't tell you. Excuse me."

He made to depart, but Leo, forgetting himself, seized the matchmaker by his tight coat and shook him frenziedly.

"Please," sighed Salzman. *"Please."*

Leo ashamedly let him go. "Tell me who she is," he begged. "It's very important for me to know."

"She is not for you. She is a wild one—wild, without shame. This is not a bride for a rabbi."

"What do you mean wild?"

"Like an animal. Like a dog. For her to be poor was a sin. This is why to me she is dead now."

"In God's name, what do you mean?"

"Her I can't introduce to you," Salzman cried.

"Why are you so excited?"

"Why, he asks," Salzman said, bursting into tears. "This is my baby, my Stella, she should burn in hell."

Leo hurried up to bed and hid under the covers. Under the covers he thought his life through. Although he soon fell asleep he could not sleep her out of his mind. He woke, beating his breast. Though he prayed to be rid of her, his prayers went unanswered. Through days of torment he endlessly struggled not to love her; fearing success, he escaped it. He then concluded to convert her to goodness, himself to God. The idea alternately nauseated and exalted him.

He perhaps did not know that he had come to a final decision until he encountered Salzman in a Broadway cafeteria. He was sitting alone at a rear table, sucking the bony remains of a fish. The marriage broker appeared haggard, and transparent to the point of vanishing.

Salzman looked up at first without recognizing him. Leo had grown a pointed beard and his eyes were weighted with wisdom.

"Salzman," he said, "love has at last come to my heart."

"Who can love from a picture?" mocked the marriage broker.

"It is not impossible."

"If you can love her, then you can love anybody. Let me show you some new clients that they just sent me their photographs. One is a little doll."

"Just her I want," Leo murmured.

"Don't be a fool, doctor. Don't bother with her."

"Put me in touch with her, Salzman," Leo said humbly. "Perhaps I can be of service."

Salzman had stopped eating and Leo understood with emotion that it was now arranged.

Leaving the cafeteria, he was, however, afflicted by a tormenting suspicion that Salzman had planned it all to happen this way.

Leo was informed by letter that she would meet him on a certain corner, and she was there one spring night, waiting under a street lamp. He appeared, carrying a small bouquet of violets and rosebuds. Stella stood by the lamp post, smoking. She wore white with red shoes, which fitted his expectations, although in a troubled moment he had imagined the dress red, and only the shoes white. She waited uneasily and shyly. From afar he saw that her eyes—clearly her father's—were filled with desperate innocence. He pictured, in her, his own redemption. Violins and lit candles revolved in the sky. Leo ran forward with flowers outthrust.

Around the corner, Salzman, leaning against a wall, chanted prayers for the dead.

Bliss

KATHERINE MANSFIELD

Although Bertha Young was thirty she still had moments like this when she wanted to run instead of walk, to take dancing steps on and off the pavement, to bowl a hoop, to throw something up in the air and catch it again, or to stand still and laugh at—nothing—at nothing, simply.

What can you do if you are thirty and, turning the corner of your own street, you are overcome, suddenly, by a feeling of bliss—absolute bliss!—as though you'd suddenly swallowed a bright piece of that late afternoon sun and it burned in your bosom, sending out a little shower of sparks into every particle, into every finger and toe? . . .

Oh, is there no way you can express it without being "drunk and disorderly"? How idiotic civilization is! Why be given a body if you have to keep it shut up in a case like a rare, rare fiddle?

"No, that about the fiddle is not quite what I mean," she thought, running up the steps and feeling in her bag for the key—she'd forgotten it, as usual—and rattling the letter-box. "It's not what I mean, because —— Thank you, Mary"—she went into the hall. "Is nurse back?"

"Yes, M'm."

"And has the fruit come?"

"Yes, M'm. Everything's come."

"Bring the fruit up to the dining-room, will you? I'll arrange it before I go upstairs."

It was dusky in the dining-room and quite chilly. But all the same Bertha threw off her coat; she could not bear the tight clasp of it another moment, and the cold air fell on her arms.

But in her bosom there was still that bright glowing place—that shower of little sparks coming from it. It was almost unbearable. She hardly dared to breathe for fear of fanning it higher, and yet she breathed deeply, deeply. She hardly dared to look into the cold mirror—but she did look, and it gave her back a woman, radiant, with smiling, trembling lips, with big, dark eyes and an air of listening, waiting for something . . . divine to happen . . . that she knew must happen . . . infallibly.

Mary brought in the fruit on a tray and with it a glass bowl, and a blue dish, very lovely, with a strange sheen on it as though it had been dipped in milk.

"Shall I turn on the light, M'm?"

"No, thank you. I can see quite well."

There were tangerines and apples stained with strawberry pink. Some yellow pears, smooth as silk, some white grapes covered with a silver bloom and a big cluster of purple ones. These last she had bought to tone in with the new dining-room carpet. Yes, that did sound rather far-fetched and absurd, but it was really why she had bought them. She had thought in the shop: "I must have some purple ones to bring the carpet up to the table." And it had seemed quite sense at the time.

When she had finished with them and had made two pyramids of these bright round shapes, she stood away from the table to get the effect—and it really was most curious. For the dark table seemed to melt into the dusky light and the glass dish and the blue bowl to float in the air. This, of course in her present mood, was so incredibly beautiful. . . . She began to laugh.

"No, no. I'm getting hysterical." And she seized her bag and coat and ran upstairs to the nursery.

Nurse sat at a low table giving Little B her supper after her bath. The baby had on a white flannel gown and a blue woollen jacket, and her dark, fine hair was brushed up into a funny little peak. She looked up when she saw her mother and began to jump.

"Now, my lovey, eat it up like a good girl," said Nurse, setting her lips in a way that Bertha knew, and that meant she had come into the nursery at another wrong moment.

"Has she been good, Nanny?"

"She's been a little sweet all the afternoon," whispered Nanny. "We went to the park and I sat down on a chair and took her out of the pram and a big dog came along and put his head on my knee and she clutched its ear, tugged it. Oh, you should have seen her."

Bertha wanted to ask if it wasn't rather dangerous to let her clutch at a strange dog's ear. But she did not dare to. She stood watching them, her hands by her side, like the poor little girl in front of the rich little girl with the doll.

The baby looked up at her again, stared, and then smiled so charmingly that Bertha couldn't help crying:

"Oh, Nanny, do let me finish giving her her supper while you put the bath things away."

"Well, M'm, she oughtn't to be changed hands while she's eating," said Nanny, still whispering. "It unsettles her; it's very likely to upset her."

How absurd it was. Why have a baby if it has to be kept—not in a case like a rare, rare fiddle—but in another woman's arms?

"Oh, I must!" said she.

Very offended, Nanny handed her over.

"Now, don't excite her after her supper. You know you do, M'm. And I have such a time with her after!"

Thank heaven! Nanny went out of the room with the bath towels.

"Now I've got you to myself, my little precious," said Bertha, as the baby leaned against her.

She ate delightfully, holding up her lips for the spoon and then waving her hands. Sometimes she wouldn't let the spoon go; and sometimes, just as Bertha had filled it, she waved it away to the four winds.

When the soup was finished Bertha turned round to the fire.

"You're nice—you're very nice!" said she, kissing her warm baby. "I'm fond of you. I like you."

And, indeed, she loved Little B so much—her neck as she bent forward, her exquisite toes as they shone transparent in the firelight—that all her feeling of bliss came back again, and again she didn't know how to express it—what to do with it.

"You're wanted on the telephone," said Nanny, coming back in triumph and seizing *her* Little B.

Down she flew. It was Harry.

"Oh, is that you, Ber? Look here. I'll be late. I'll take a taxi and come along as quickly as I can, but get dinner put back ten minutes—will you? All right?"

"Yes, perfectly. Oh, Harry!"

"Yes?"

What had she to say? She'd nothing to say. She only wanted to get in touch with him for a moment. She couldn't absurdly cry: "Hasn't it been a divine day!"

"What is it?" rapped out the little voice.

"Nothing. *Entendu*," said Bertha, and hung up the receiver, thinking how more than idiotic civilization was.

They had people coming to dinner. The Norman Knights—a very sound couple—he was about to start a theater, and she was awfully keen on interior decoration, a young man, Eddie Warren, who had just published a little book of poems and whom everybody was asking to dine, and a "find" of Bertha's called Pearl Fulton. What Miss Fulton did, Bertha didn't know. They had met at the club and Bertha had fallen in love with her, as she always did fall in love with beautiful women who had something strange about them.

The provoking thing was that, though they had been about together and met a number of times and really talked, Bertha couldn't yet make her out. Up to a certain point Miss Fulton was rarely, wonderfully frank, but the certain point was there, and beyond that she would not go.

Was there anything beyond it? Harry said, "No." Voted her dullish, and "cold like all blond women, with a touch, perhaps, of anæmia of the brain." But Bertha wouldn't agree with him; not yet, at any rate.

"No, the way she has of sitting with her head a little on one side, and smiling, has something behind it, Harry, and I must find out what that something is."

"Most likely it's a good stomach," answered Harry.

He made a point of catching Bertha's heels with replies of that kind . . . "liver frozen, my dear girl," or "pure flatulence," or "kidney disease," . . . and so on. For some strange reason Bertha liked this, and almost admired it in him very much.

She went into the drawing room and lighted the fire; then, picking up the cushions, one by one, that Mary had disposed so carefully, she threw them back on to the chairs and the couches. That made all the difference; the room came alive at once. As she was about to throw the last one she surprised herself by suddenly hugging it to her, passionately, passionately. But it did not put out the fire in her bosom. Oh, on the contrary!

The windows of the drawing-room opened on to a balcony overlooking the garden. At the far end, against the wall, there was a tall, slender pear tree in fullest, richest bloom; it stood perfect, as though becalmed against the jade-green sky. Bertha couldn't help feeling, even from this distance, that it had not a single bud or a faded petal. Down below, in the garden beds, the red and yellow tulips, heavy with flowers, seemed to lean upon the dusk. A grey cat, dragging its belly, crept across the lawn, and a black one, its shadow, trailed after. The sight of them, so intent and so quick, gave Bertha a curious shiver.

"What creepy things cats are!" she stammered, and she turned away from the window and began walking up and down. . . .

How strong the jonquils smelled in the warm room. Too strong? Oh, no. And yet, as though overcome, she flung down on a couch and pressed her hands to her eyes.

"I'm too happy—too happy!" she murmured.

And she seemed to see on her eyelids the lovely pear tree with its wide open blossoms as a symbol of her own life.

Really—really—she had everything. She was young. Harry and she were as much in love as ever, and they got on together splendidly and were really good pals. She had an adorable baby. They didn't have to worry about money. They had this absolutely satisfactory house and garden. And

friends—modern, thrilling friends, writers and painters and poets or people keen on social questions—just the kind of friends they wanted. And
then there were books, and there was music, and she had found a wonderful little dressmaker, and they were going abroad in the summer, and their
new cook made the most superb omelettes. . . .

"I'm absurd! Absurd!" She sat up; but she felt quite dizzy, quite drunk. It
must have been the spring.

Yes, it was the spring. Now she was so tired she could not drag herself
upstairs to dress.

A white dress, a string of jade beads, green shoes and stockings. It wasn't
intentional. She had thought of this scheme hours before she stood at the
drawing room window.

Her petals rushed softly into the hall, and she kissed Mrs. Norman
Knight, who was taking off the most amusing orange coat with a procession
of black monkeys round the hem and up the fronts.

". . . Why! Why! Why is the middle-class so stodgy—so utterly without a
sense of humor! My dear, it's only a fluke that I am here at all—Norman
being the protective fluke. For my darling monkeys so upset the train that
it rose to a man and simply ate me with its eyes. Didn't laugh—wasn't
amused—that I should have loved. No, just stared—and bored me
through and through."

"But the cream of it was," said Norman, pressing a large tortoiseshell-
rimmed monocle into his eye, "you don't mind me telling this, Face, do
you?" (In their home and among their friends they called each other Face
and Mug.) "The cream of it was when she, being full fed, turned to the
woman beside her and said: 'Haven't you ever seen a monkey before?' "

"Oh, yes!" Mrs. Norman Knight joined in the laughter. "Wasn't that too
absolutely creamy?"

And a funnier thing still was that now her coat was off she did look like a
very intelligent monkey—who had even made that yellow silk dress out of
scraped banana skins. And her amber earrings; they were like little dangling nuts.

"This is a sad, sad fall!" said Mug, pausing in front of Little B's perambulator. "When the perambulator comes into the hall ——" and he waved the
rest of the quotation away.

The bell rang. It was lean, pale Eddie Warren (as usual) in a state of acute
distress.

"It is the right house, isn't it?" he pleaded.

"Oh, I think so—I hope so," said Bertha brightly.

"I have had such a dreadful experience with a taxi-man; he was most sinister. I couldn't get him to stop. The more I knocked and called the faster he
went. And in the moonlight this bizarre figure with the flattened head crouching over the lit-tle wheel. . . ."

He shuddered, taking off an immense white silk scarf. Bertha noticed
that his socks were white, too—most charming.

"But how dreadful!" she cried.

"Yes, it really was," said Eddie, following her into the drawing room. "I saw myself *driving* through Eternity in a *timeless* taxi."

He knew the Norman Knights. In fact, he was going to write a play for N. K. when the theater scheme came off.

"Well, Warren, how's the play?" said Norman Knight, dropping his monocle and giving his eye a moment in which to rise to the surface before it was screwed down again.

And Mrs. Norman Knight: "Oh, Mr. Warren, what happy socks!"

"I *am* so glad you like them," said he, staring at his feet. "They seem to have got so *much* whiter since the moon rose." And he turned his lean sorrowful young face to Bertha. "There *is* a moon, you know."

She wanted to cry: "I am sure there is—often—often!"

He really was a most attractive person. But so was Face, crouched before the fire in her banana skins, and so was Mug, smoking a cigarette and saying as he flicked the ash: "Why doth the bridegroom tarry?"

"There he is, now."

Bang went the front door open and shut. Harry shouted: "Hullo, you people. Down in five minutes." And they heard him swarm up the stairs. Bertha couldn't help smiling; she knew how he loved doing things at high pressure. What, after all, did an extra five minutes matter? But he would pretend to himself that they mattered beyond measure. And then he would make a great point of coming into the drawing room, extravagantly cool and collected.

Harry had such a zest for life. Oh, how she appreciated it in him. And his passion for fighting—for seeking in everything that came up against him another test of his power and of his courage—that, too, she understood. Even when it made him just occasionally, to other people, who didn't know him well, a little ridiculous perhaps. . . . For there were moments when he rushed into battle where no battle was. . . . She talked and laughed and positively forgot until he had come in (just as she had imagined) that Pearl Fulton had not turned up.

"I wonder if Miss Fulton has forgotten?"

"I expect so," said Harry. "Is she on the 'phone?"

"Ah! There's a taxi, now." And Bertha smiled with that little air of proprietorship that she always assumed while her women finds were new and mysterious. "She lives in taxis."

"She'll run to fat if she does," said Harry coolly, ringing the bell for dinner. "Frightful danger for blond women."

"Harry—don't," warned Bertha, laughing up at him.

Came another tiny moment, while they waited, laughing and talking, just a trifle too much at their ease, a trifle too unaware. And then Miss Fulton, all in silver, with a silver fillet binding her pale blond hair, came in smiling, her head a little on one side.

"Am I late?"

"No, not at all," said Bertha. "Come along." And she took her arm and they moved into the dining-room.

What was there in the touch of that cool arm that could fan—fan—start blazing—blazing—the fire of bliss that Bertha did not know what to do with?

Miss Fulton did not look at her, but then she seldom did look at people directly. Her heavy eyelids lay upon her eyes and the strange half smile came and went upon her lips as though she lived by listening rather than seeing. But Bertha knew, suddenly, as if the longest, most intimate look had passed between them—as if they had said to each other: "You, too?"—that Pearl Fulton, stirring the beautiful red soup in the grey plate, was feeling just what she was feeling.

And the others? Face and Mug, Eddie and Harry, their spoons rising and falling—dabbing their lips with their napkins, crumbling bread, fiddling with the forks and glasses and talking.

"I met her at the Alpha shore—the weirdest little person. She'd not only cut off her hair, but she seemed to have taken a dreadfully good snip off her legs and arms and her neck and her poor little nose as well."

"Isn't she very *liée* with Michael Oat?"

"The man who wrote *Love in False Teeth*?"

"He wants to write a play for me. One act. One man. Decides to commit suicide. Gives all the reasons why he should and why he shouldn't. And just as he has made up his mind either to do it or not to do it—curtain. Not half a bad idea."

"What's he going to call it—'Stomach Trouble'?"

"I *think* I've come across the *same* idea in a lit-tle French review, *quite* unknown in England."

No, they didn't share it. They were dears—dears—and she loved having them there, at her table, and giving them delicious food and wine. In fact, she longed to tell them how delightful they were, and what a decorative group they made, how they seemed to set one another off and how they reminded her of a play by Tchekof!

Harry was enjoying his dinner. It was part of his—well, not his nature, exactly, and certainly not his pose—his—something or other—to talk about food and to glory in his "shameless passion for the white flesh of the lobster" and "the green of pistachio ices—green and cold like the eyelids of Egyptian dancers."

When he looked up at her and said: "Bertha, this is a very admirable *soufflée!*" she almost could have wept with child-like pleasure.

Oh, why did she feel so tender toward the whole world tonight? Everything was good—was right. All that happened seemed to fill again her brimming cup of bliss.

And still, in the back of her mind, there was the pear tree. It would be silver now, in the light of poor dear Eddie's moon, silver as Miss Fulton, who sat there turning a tangerine in her slender fingers that were so pale a light seemed to come from them.

What she simply couldn't make out—what was miraculous—was how she should have guessed Miss Fulton's mood so exactly and so instantly. For she never doubted for a moment that she was right, and yet what had she to go on? Less than nothing.

"I believe this does happen very, very rarely between women. Never between men," thought Bertha. "But while I am making coffee in the drawing-room perhaps she will 'give a sign.' "

What she meant by that she did not know, and what would happen after that she could not imagine.

While she thought like this she saw herself talking and laughing. She had to talk because of her desire to laugh.

"I must laugh or die."

But when she noticed Face's funny little habit of tucking something down the front of her bodice—as if she kept a tiny, secret hoard of nuts there, too—Bertha had to dig her nails into her hands—so as not to laugh too much.

It was over at last. And: "Come and see my new coffee machine," said Bertha.

"We only have a new coffee machine once a fortnight," said Harry. Face took her arm this time; Miss Fulton bent her head and followed after.

The fire had died down in the drawing-room to a red, flickering "nest of baby phoenixes," said Face.

"Don't turn up the light for a moment. It is so lovely." And down she crouched by the fire again. She was always cold . . . . "without her little red flannel jacket, of course," thought Bertha.

At that moment Miss Fulton "gave the sign."

"Have you a garden?" said the cool, sleepy voice.

This was so exquisite on her part that all Bertha could do was to obey. She crossed the room, pulled the curtains apart, and opened those long windows.

"There!" she breathed.

And the two women stood side by side looking at the slender, flowering tree. Although it was so still it seemed, like the flame of a candle, to stretch up, to point, to quiver in the bright air, to grow taller and taller as they gazed—almost to touch the rim of the round, silver moon.

How long did they stand there? Both, as it were, caught in that circle of unearthly light, understanding each other perfectly, creatures of another world, and wondering what they were to do in this one with all this blissful treasure that burned in their bosoms and dropped, in silver flowers, from their hair and hands?

Forever—for a moment? And did Miss Fulton murmur: "Yes, Just *that*." Or did Bertha dream it?

Then the light was snapped on and Face made the coffee and Harry said: "My dear Mrs. Knight, don't ask me about my baby. I never see her. I shan't feel the slightest interest in her until she has a lover," and Mug took his eye out of the conservatory for a moment and then put it under glass again and Eddie Warren drank his coffee and set down the cup with a face of anguish as though he had drunk and seen the spider.

"What I want to do is to give the young men a show. I believe London is simply teeming with first-chop, unwritten plays. What I want to say to 'em is: 'Here's the theater. Fire ahead.' "

"You know, my dear, I am going to decorate a room for the Jacob Nathans. Oh, I am so tempted to do a fried-fish scheme, with the backs of the chairs shaped like frying pans and lovely chip potatoes embroidered all over the curtains."

"The trouble with our young writing men is that they are still too romantic. You can't put out to sea without being seasick and wanting a basin. Well, why won't they have the courage of those basins?"

"A *dreadful* poem about a *girl* who was *violated* by a beggar *without* a nose in the lit-tle wood. . . ."

Miss Fulton sank into the lowest, deepest chair and Harry handed round the cigarettes.

From the way he stood in front of her shaking the silver box and saying abruptly: "Egyptian? Turkish? Virginian? They're all mixed up," Bertha realized that she not only bored him; he really disliked her. And she decided from the way Miss Fulton said: "No, thank you, I won't smoke," that she felt it, too, and was hurt.

"Oh, Harry, don't dislike her. You are quite wrong about her. She's wonderful, wonderful. And, besides, how can you feel so differently about someone who means so much to me? I shall try to tell you when we are in bed tonight what has been happening. What she and I have shared."

At those last words something strange and almost terrifying darted into Bertha's mind. And this something blind and smiling whispered to her: "Soon these people will go. The house will be quiet—quiet. The lights will be out. And you and he will be alone together in the dark room—the warm bed. . . ."

She jumped up from her chair and ran over to the piano.

"What a pity someone does not play!" she cried. "What a pity somebody does not play."

For the first time in her life Bertha Young desired her husband.

Oh, she loved him—she'd been in love with him, of course, in every other way, but just not in that way. And, equally, of course, she'd understood that he was different. They'd discussed it so often. It had worried her dreadfully at first to find that she was so cold, but after a time it had not seemed to matter. They were so frank with each other—such good pals. That was the best of being modern.

But now—ardently! ardently! The word ached in her ardent body! Was this what the feeling of bliss had been leading up to? But then—then——

"My dear," said Mrs. Norman Knight, "you know our shame. We are the victims of time and train. We live in Hampstead. It's been so nice."

"I'll come with you into the hall," said Bertha. "I love having you. But you must not miss the last train. That's so awful, isn't it?"

"Have a whisky, Knight, before you go?" called Harry.

"No, thanks, old chap."

Bertha squeezed his hand for that as she shook it.

"Good night, good-bye," she cried from the top step, feeling that this self of hers was taking leave of them forever.

When she got back into the drawing room the others were on the move.

". . . Then you can come part of the way in my taxi."

"I shall be *so* thankful *not* to have to face *another* drive *alone* after my *dreadful* experience."

"You can get a taxi at the rank just at the end of the street. You won't have to walk more than a few yards."

"That's comfort. I'll go and put on my coat."

Miss Fulton moved toward the hall and Bertha was following when Harry almost pushed past.

"Let me help you."

Bertha knew that he was repenting his rudeness—she let him go. What a boy he was in some ways—so impulsive—so—simple.

And Eddie and she were left by the fire.

"I *wonder* if you have seen Bilks' *new* poem called *Table d'Hôte,*" said Eddie softly. "It's *so* wonderful. In the last Anthology. Have you got a copy? I'd *so* like to *show* it to you. It begins with an *incredibly* beautiful line: 'Why Must it Always be Tomato Soup?' "

"Yes," said Bertha. And she moved noiselessly to a table opposite the drawing room door and Eddie glided noiselessly after her. She picked up the little book and gave it to him; they had not made a sound.

While he looked it up she turned her head toward the hall. And she saw . . . Harry with Miss Fulton's coat in his arms and Miss Fulton with her back turned to him and her head bent. He tossed the coat away, put his hands on her shoulders and turned her violently to him. His lips said: "I adore you," and Miss Fulton laid her moonbeam fingers on his cheeks and smiled her sleepy smile. Harry's nostrils quivered; his lips curled back in a hideous grin while he whispered: "Tomorrow," and with her eyelids Miss Fulton said: "Yes."

"Here it is," said Eddie. " 'Why Must it Always be Tomato Soup?' It's so *deeply* true, don't you feel? Tomato soup is so *dreadfully* eternal."

"If you prefer," said Harry's voice, very loud, from the hall, "I can 'phone you a cab to come to the door."

"Oh, no. It's not necessary," said Miss Fulton, and she came up to Bertha and gave her the slender fingers to hold.

"Good-bye. Thank you so much."

"Good-bye," said Bertha.

Miss Fulton held her hand a moment longer.

"Your lovely pear tree!" she murmured.

And then she was gone, with Eddie following, like the black cat following the grey cat.

"I'll shut up shop," said Harry, extravagantly cool and collected.

"Your lovely pear tree—pear tree—pear tree!"

Bertha simply ran over to the long windows.

"Oh, what is going to happen now?" she cried.

But the pear tree was as lovely as ever and as full of flower and as still.

Brooklyn

PAULE MARSHALL

A summer wind, soaring just before it died, blew the dusk and the first scattered lights of downtown Brooklyn against the shut windows of the classroom, but Professor Max Berman—B.A., 1919, M.A., 1921, New York; Docteur de l'Université, 1930, Paris—alone in the room, did not bother to open the windows to the cooling wind. The heat and airlessness of the room, the perspiration inching its way like an ant around his starched collar were discomforts he enjoyed; they obscured his larger discomfort: the anxiety which chafed his heart and tugged his left eyelid so that he seemed to be winking, roguishly, behind his glasses.

To steady his eye and ease his heart, to fill the time until his students arrived and his first class in years began, he reached for his cigarettes. As always he delayed lighting the cigarette so that his need for it would be greater and, thus, the relief and pleasure it would bring, fuller. For some time he fondled it, his fingers shaping soft, voluptuous gestures, his warped old man's hands looking strangely abandoned on the bare desk and limp as if the bones had been crushed, and so white—except for the tobacco burn on the index and third fingers—it seemed his blood no longer traveled that far.

He lit the cigarette finally and as the smoke swelled his lungs, his eyelid stilled and his lined face lifted, the plume of white hair wafting above his narrow brow; his body—short, blunt, the shoulders slightly bent as if in deference to his sixty-three years—settled back in the chair. Delicately Max Berman crossed his legs and, looking down, examined his shoes for dust. (The shoes were of a very soft, fawn-colored leather and somewhat foppishly pointed at the toe. They had been custom made in France and were his one last indulgence. He wore them in memory of his first wife, a French Jewess from Alsace-Lorraine whom he had met in Paris while lingering over his doctorate and married to avoid returning home. She had been gay,

675

mindless and very excitable—but at night, she had also been capable of a profound stillness as she lay in bed waiting for him to turn to her, and this had always awed and delighted him. She had been a gift—and her death in a car accident had been a judgment on him for never having loved her, for never, indeed, having even allowed her to matter.) Fastidiously Max Berman unbuttoned his jacket and straightened his vest, which had a stain two decades old on the pocket. Through the smoke his veined eyes contemplated other, more pleasurable scenes. With his neatly shod foot swinging and his cigarette at a rakish tilt, he might have been an old *boulevardier* taking the sun and an absinthe before the afternoon's assignation.

A young face, the forehead shiny with earnestness, hung at the half-opened door. "It this French Lit, fifty-four? Camus and Sartre?"

Max Berman winced at the rawness of the voice and the flat "a" in Sartre and said formally, "This is Modern French Literature, number fifty-four, yes, but there is some question as to whether we will take up Messieurs Camus and Sartre this session. They might prove hot work for a summer-evening course. We will probably do Gide and Mauriac, who are considerably more temperate. But come in nonetheless. . . ."

He was the gallant, half rising to bow her to a seat. He knew that she would select the one in the front row directly opposite his desk. At the bell her pen would quiver above her blank notebook, ready to commit his first word—indeed, the clearing of his throat—to paper, and her thin buttocks would begin sliding toward the edge of her chair.

His eyelid twitched with solicitude. He wished that he could have drawn the lids over her fitful eyes and pressed a cool hand to her forehead. She reminded him of what he had been several lifetimes ago: a boy with a pale, plump face and harried eyes, running from the occasional taunts at his yarmulke along the shrill streets of Brownsville in Brooklyn, impeded by the heavy satchel of books which he always carried as proof of his scholarship. He had been proud of his brilliance at school and the Yeshiva, but at the same time he had been secretly troubled by it and resentful, for he could never believe that he had come by it naturally or that it belonged to him alone. Rather, it was like a heavy medal his father had hung around his neck—the chain bruising his flesh—and constantly exhorted him to wear proudly and use well.

The girl gave him an eager and ingratiating smile and he looked away. During his thirty years of teaching, a face similar to hers had crowded his vision whenever he had looked up from a desk. Perhaps it was fitting, he thought, and lighted another cigarette from the first, that she should be present as he tried again at life, unaware that behind his rimless glasses and within his ancient suit, he had been gutted.

He thought of those who had taken the last of his substance—and smiled tolerantly. "The boys of summer," he called them, his inquisitors, who had flailed him with a single question: "Are you now or have you ever been a member of the Communist party?" Max Berman had never taken their question seriously—perhaps because he had never taken his membership in the party seriously—and he had refused to answer. What had disturbed him, though, even when the investigation was over, was the feeling that he had really been under investigation for some other offense which did matter and of which he was guilty; that behind their accusations and charges had lurked another which had not been political but personal. For had he been disloyal to the government? His denial was a short, hawking laugh. Simply, he had never ceased being religious. When his father's God had become useless and even a little embarrassing, he had sought others: his work for a time, then the party. But he had been middle aged when he joined and his faith, which had been so full as a boy, had grown thin. He had come, by then, to distrust all pieties, so that when the purges in Russia during the thirties confirmed his distrust, he had withdrawn into a modest cynicism.

But he had been made to answer for that error. Ten years later his inquisitors had flushed him out from the small community college in upstate New York where he had taught his classes from the same neat pack of notes each semester and had led him bound by subpoena to New York and bandied his name at the hearings until he had been dismissed from his job.

He remembered looking back at the pyres of burning autumn leaves on the campus his last day and feeling that another lifetime had ended—for he had always thought of his life as divided into many small lives, each with its own beginning and end. Like a hired mute, he had been present at each dying and kept the wake and wept professionally as the bier was lowered into the ground. Because of this feeling, he told himself that his final death would be anticlimactic.

After his dismissal he had continued living in the small house he had built near the college, alone except for an occasional visit from a colleague, idle but for some tutoring in French, content with the income he received from the property his parents had left him in Brooklyn—until the visits and tutoring had tapered off and a silence had begun to choke the house, like weeds springing up around a deserted place. He had begun to wonder then if he were still alive. He would wake at night from the recurrent dream of the hearings, where he was being accused of an unstated crime, to listen for his heart, his hand fumbling among the bedclothes to press the place. During the day he would pass repeatedly in front of the mirror with the pretext that he might have forgotten to shave that morning or that something had blown into his eyes. Above all, he had begun to think of his inquisitors with affection and to long for the sound of their voices. They, at least, had assured him of being alive.

As if seeking them out, he had returned to Brooklyn and to the house in Brownsville where he had lived as a boy and had boldly applied for a teaching post without mentioning the investigation. He had finally been offered the class which would begin in five minutes. It wasn't much: a six-week course in the summer evening session of a college without a rating, where classes were held in a converted factory building, a college whose campus took in the bargain department stores, the five-and-dime emporiums and neon-spangled movie houses of downtown Brooklyn.

Through the smoke from his cigarette, Max Berman's eyes—a waning blue that never seemed to focus on any one thing—drifted over the students who had gathered meanwhile. Imbuing them with his own disinterest, he believed that even before the class began, most of them were longing for its end and already anticipating the soft drinks at the soda fountain downstairs and the synthetic dramas at the nearby movie.

They made him sad. He would have liked to have lead them like a Pied Piper back to the safety of their childhoods—all of them: the loud girl with the formidable calves of an athlete who reminded him, uncomfortably, of his second wife (a party member who was always shouting political heresy from some picket line and who had promptly divorced him upon discovering his irreverence); the two sallow-faced young men leaning out the window as if searching for the wind that had died; the slender young woman with crimped black hair who sat very still and apart from the others, her face turned toward the night sky as if to a friend.

Her loneliness interested him. He sensed its depth and his eye paused. He saw then that she was a Negro, a very pale mulatto with skin the color of clear, polished amber and a thin, mild face. She was somewhat older than the others in the room—a schoolteacher from the South, probably, who came north each summer to take courses toward a graduate degree. He felt a fleeting discomfort and irritation: discomfort at the thought that although he had been sinned against as a Jew he still shared in the sin against her and suffered from the same vague guilt, irritation that she recalled his own humiliations: the large ones, such as the fact that despite his brilliance he had been unable to get into a medical school as a young man because of the quota on Jews (not that he had wanted to be a doctor; that had been his father's wish) and had changed his studies from medicine to French; the small ones which had worn him thin: an eye widening imperceptibly as he gave his name, the savage glance which sought the Jewishness in his nose, his chin, in the set of his shoulders, the jokes snuffed into silence at his appearance. . . .

Tired suddenly, his eyelid pulsing, he turned and stared out the window at the gaudy constellation of neon lights. He longed for a drink, a quiet place and then sleep. And to bear him gently into sleep, to stay the terror which bound his heart then reminding him of those oleographs of Christ with the thorns binding his exposed heart—fat drops of blood from one so bloodless—to usher him into sleep, some pleasantly erotic image: a nude in a boudoir scattered with her frilled garments and warmed by her frivolous laugh, with the sun like a voyeur at the half-closed shutters. But this time instead of the usual Rubens nude with thighs like twin portals and a belly like a huge alabaster bowl into which he poured himself, he chose Gauguin's Aita Parari, her languorous form in the straight-back chair, her dark, sloping breasts, her eyes like the sun under shadow.

With the image still on his inner eye, he turned to the Negro girl and appraised her through a blind of cigarette smoke. She was still gazing out at the night sky and something about her fixed stare, her hands stiffly arranged in her lap, the nerve fluttering within the curve of her throat, betrayed a vein of tension within the rock of her calm. It was as if she had fled long ago to a remote region within herself, taking with her all that was most valuable and most vulnerable about herself.

She stirred finally, her slight breasts lifting beneath her flowered summer dress as she breathed deeply—and Max Berman thought again of Gauguin's girl with the dark, sloping breasts. What would this girl with the amber-colored skin be like on a couch in a sunlit room, nude in a straight-back chair? And as the question echoed along each nerve and stilled his breathing, it seemed suddenly that life, which had scorned him for so long, held out her hand again—but still a little beyond his reach. Only the girl, he sensed, could bring him close enough to touch it. She alone was the bridge. So that even while he repeated to himself that he was being presumptuous (for she would surely refuse him) and ridiculous (for even if she did not, what could he do—his performance would be a mere scramble and twitch), he vowed at the same time to have her. The challenge eased the tightness around his heart suddenly; it soothed the damaged muscle of his eye and as the bell rang he rose and said briskly, "Ladies and gentlemen, may I have your attention, please. My name is Max Berman. The course is Modern French Literature, number fifty-four. May I suggest that you check your program cards to see whether you are in the right place at the right time."

Her essay on Gide's *The Immoralist* lay on his desk and the note from the administration informing him, first, that his past political activities had been brought to their attention and then dismissing him at the end of the session weighed the inside pocket of his jacket. The two, her paper and the note, were linked in his mind. Her paper reminded him that the vow he had taken was still an empty one, for the term was half over and he had never once spoken to her (as if she understood his intention she was always late and disappeared as soon as the closing bell rang, leaving him trapped in a clamorous circle of students around his desk), while the note which wrecked his small attempt to start anew suddenly made that vow more urgent. It gave him the edge of desperation he needed to act finally. So that as soon as the bell rang, he returned all the papers but hers, announced that all questions would have to wait until their next meeting and, waving off the students from his desk, called above their protests, "Miss Williams, if you have a moment, I'd like to speak with you briefly about your paper."

She approached his desk like a child who has been cautioned not to talk to strangers, her fingers touching the backs of the chair as if for support, her gaze following the departing students as though she longed to accompany them.

Her slight apprehensiveness pleased him. It suggested a submissiveness which gave him, as he rose uncertainly, a feeling of certainty and command. Her hesitancy was somehow in keeping with the color of her skin. She seemed to bring not only herself but the host of black women whose bodies had been despoiled to make her. He would not only possess her but them also, he thought (not really thought, for he scarcely allowed these thoughts to form before he snuffed them out). Through their collective suffering, which she contained, his own personal suffering would be eased; he would be pardoned for whatever sin it was he had committed against life.

"I hope you weren't unduly alarmed when I didn't return your paper along with the others," he said, and had to look up as she reached the desk. She was taller close up and her eyes, which he had thought were black, were a strong, flecked brown with very small pupils which seemed to shrink now from the sight of him. "But I found it so interesting I wanted to give it to you privately."

"I didn't know what to think," she said, and her voice—he heard it for the first time for she never recited or answered in class—was low, cautious, Southern.

"It was, to say the least, refreshing. It not only showed some original and mature thinking on your part, but it also proved that you've been listening in class—and after twenty-five years and more of teaching it's encouraging to find that some students do listen. If you have a little time I'd like to tell you, more specifically, what I liked about it. . . ."

Talking easily, reassuring her with his professional tone and a deft gesture with his cigarette, he led her from the room as the next class filed in, his hand cupped at her elbow but not touching it, his manner urbane, courtly, kind. They paused on the landing at the end of the long corridor with the stairs piled in steel tiers above and plunging below them. An intimate silence swept up the stairwell in a warm gust and Max Berman said, "I'm curious. Why did you choose *The Immoralist*?"

She started suspiciously, afraid, it seemed, that her answer might expose and endanger the self she guarded so closely within.

"Well," she said finally, her glance reaching down the stairs to the door marked EXIT at the bottom "when you said we could use anything by Gide I decided on *The Immoralist,* since it was the first book I read in the original French when I was in undergraduate school. I didn't understand it then because my French was so weak, I guess, so I always thought about it afterward for some odd reason. I was shocked by what I did understand, of course, but something else about it appealed to me, so when you made the assignment I thought I'd try reading it again. I understood it a little better this time. At least I think so. . . ."

"Your paper proves you did."

She smiled absently, intent on some other thought. Then she said cautiously, but with unexpected force, "You see, to me, the book seems to say that the only way you begin to know what you are and how much you are capable of is by daring to try something, by doing something which tests you. . . ."

"Something bold," he said

"Yes."

"Even sinful."

She paused, questioning this, and then said reluctantly, "Yes, perhaps even sinful."

"The salutary effects of sin, you might say." He gave the little bow.

But she had not heard this; her mind had already leaped ahead. "The only trouble, at least with the character in Gide's book, is that what he finds out about himself is so terrible. He is so unhappy. . . ."

"But at least he knows, poor sinner." And his playful tone went unnoticed.

"Yes," she said with the same startling forcefulness. "And another thing, in finding out what he is, he destroys his wife. It was as if she had to die in order for him to live and know himself. Perhaps in order for a person to live and know himself somebody else must die. Maybe there's always a balancing out. . . . In a way"—and he had to lean close now to hear her—"I believe this."

Max Berman edged back as he glimpsed something move within her abstracted gaze. It was like a strong and restless seed that had taken root in the darkness there and was straining now toward the light. He had not expected so subtle and complex a force beneath her mild exterior and he found it disturbing and dangerous, but fascinating.

"Well, it's a most interesting interpretation," he said. "I don't know if M. Gide would have agreed, but then he's not around to give his opinion. Tell me, where did you do your undergraduate work?"

"At Howard University."

"And you majored in French?"

"Yes."

"Why, if I may ask?" he said gently.

"Well, my mother was from New Orleans and could still speak a little Creole and I got interested in learning to speak French through her, I guess. I teach it now at a junior high school in Richmond. Only the beginner courses because I don't have my master's. You know, *je vais, tu vas, il va* and *Frère Jacques*. It's not very inspiring."

"You should do something about that then, my dear Miss Williams. Perhaps it's time for you, like our friend in Gide, to try something new and bold."

"I know," she said, and her pale hand sketched a vague, despairing gesture. "I thought maybe if I got my master's . . . that's why I decided to come north this summer and start taking some courses. . . ."

Max Berman quickly lighted a cigarette to still the flurry inside him, for the moment he had been awaiting had come. He flicked her paper, which he still held. "Well, you've got the makings of a master's thesis right here. If you like I will suggest some ways for you to expand it sometime. A few pointers from an old pro might help."

He had to turn from her astonished and grateful smile—it was like a child's. He said carefully, "The only problem will be to find a place where we can talk quietly. Regrettably, I don't rate an office. . . ."

"Perhaps we could use one of the empty classrooms," she said.

"That would be much too dismal a setting for a pleasant discussion."

He watched the disappointment wilt her smile and when he spoke he made certain that the same disappointment weighed his voice. "Another difficulty is that the term's half over, which gives us little or no time. But let's not give up. Perhaps we can arrange to meet and talk over a weekend. The only hitch there is that I spend weekends at my place in the country. Of course you're perfectly welcome to come up there. It's only about seventy miles from New York, in the heart of what's very appropriately called the Borsch Circuit, even though, thank God, my place is a good distance away from the borsch. That is, it's very quiet and there's never anybody around except with my permission."

She did not move, yet she seemed to start; she made no sound, yet he thought he heard a bewildered cry. And then she did a strange thing, standing there with the breath sucked into the hollow of her throat and her smile, that had opened to him with such trust, dying—her eyes, her hands faltering up begged him to declare himself.

"There's a lake near the house," he said, "so that when you get tired of talking—or better, listening to me talk—you can take a swim, if you like. I would very much enjoy that sight." And as the nerve tugged at his eyelid, he seemed to wink behind his rimless glasses.

Her sudden, blind step back was like a man groping his way through a strange room in the dark, and instinctively Max Berman reached out to break her fall. Her arms, bare to the shoulder because of the heat (he knew the feel of her skin without even touching it—it would be like a rich, fine-textured cloth which would soothe and hide him in its amber warmth), struck out once to drive him off and then fell limp at her side, and her eyes became vivid and convulsive in her numbed face. She strained toward the stairs and the exit door at the bottom, but she could not move. Nor could she speak. She did not even cry. Her eyes remained dry and dull with disbelief. Only her shoulders trembled as though she was silently weeping inside.

It was as though she had never learned the forms and expressions of anger. The outrage of a lifetime, of her history, was trapped inside her. And she stared at Max Berman with this mute, paralyzing rage. Not really at him but to his side, as if she caught sight of others behind him. And remembering how he had imagined a column of dark women trailing her to his desk, he sensed that she glimpsed a legion of old men with sere flesh and lonely eyes flanking him: "old lechers with a love on every wind . . ."

"I'm sorry, Miss Williams," he said and would have welcomed her insults, for he would have been able, at least, to distill from them some passion and a kind of intimacy. It would have been, in a way, like touching her. "It was only that you are a very attractive young woman and although I'm no longer young"—and he gave a tragic little laugh which sought to dismiss that fact—"I can still appreciate and even desire an attractive woman. But I was wrong. . . ." His self-disgust, overwhelming him finally, choked off his voice. "And so very crude. Forgive me. I can offer no excuse for my behavior other than my approaching senility."

He could not even manage a little marionette bow this time. Quickly he shoved the paper on Gide into her lifeless hand, but it fell, the pages separating, and as he hurried past her downstairs and out the door, he heard the pages scattering like dead leaves on the steps.

She remained away until the night of the final examination, which was also the last meeting of the class. By that time Max Berman, believing that she would not return, had almost succeeded in forgetting her. He was no longer certain of how she looked, for her face had been absorbed into the single, blurred, featureless face of all the women who had ever refused him. So that she startled him as much as a stranger would have when he entered the room that night and found her alone amid a maze of empty chairs, her face turned toward the window as on the first night and her hands serene in her lap. She turned at his footstep and it was as if she had also forgotten all that had passed between them. She waited until he said, "I'm glad you decided to take the examination. I'm sure you won't have any difficulty with it"; then she gave him a nod that was somehow reminiscent of his little bow and turned again to the window.

He was relieved yet puzzled by her composure. It was as if during her three-week absence she had waged and won a decisive contest with herself and was ready now to act. He was wary suddenly and all during the examination he tried to discover what lay behind her strange calm, studying her bent head amid the shifting heads of the other students, her slim hand guiding the pen across the page, her legs—the long bone visible, it seemed, beneath the flesh. Desire flared and quickly died.

"Excuse me, Professor Berman, will you take up Camus and Sartre next semester, maybe?" The girl who sat in front of his desk was standing over him with her earnest smile and finished examination folder.

"That might prove somewhat difficult, since I won't be here."

"No more?"

"No."

"I mean, not even next summer?"

"I doubt it."

"Gee, I'm sorry. I mean, I enjoyed the course and everything."

He bowed his thanks and held his head down until she left. Her compliment, so piteous somehow, brought on the despair he had forced to the dim rear of his mind. He could no longer flee the thought of the exile awaiting him when the class tonight ended. He could either remain in the house in Brooklyn, where the memory of his father's face above the radiance of the Sabbath candles haunted him from the shadows, reminding him of the certainty he had lost and never found again, where the mirrors in his father's room were still shrouded with sheets, as on the day he lay dying and moaning into his beard that his only son was a bad Jew; or he could return to the house in the country, to the silence shrill with loneliness.

The cigarette he was smoking burned his fingers, rousing him and he saw over the pile of examination folders on his desk that the room was empty except for the Negro girl. She had finished—her pen lay aslant the closed folder on her desk—but she had remained in her seat and she was smiling across the room at him—a set, artificial smile that was both cold and threatening. It utterly denuded him and he was wildly angry suddenly that she had seen him give way to despair; he wanted to remind her (he could not stay the thought; it attacked him like an assailant from a dark turn in his mind) that she was only black after all. . . . His head dropped and he almost wept with shame.

The girl stiffened as if she had seen the thought and then the tiny muscles around her mouth quickly arranged the bland smile. She came up to his desk, placed her folder on top of the others and said pleasantly, her eyes like dark, shattered glass that spared Max Berman his reflection, "I've changed my mind. I think I'd like to spend a day at your place in the country if your invitation still holds."

He thought of refusing her, for her voice held neither promise nor passion, but he could not. Her presence, even if it was only for a day, would make his return easier. And there was still the possibility of passion despite her cold manner and the deliberate smile. He thought of how long it had been since he had had someone, of how badly he needed the sleep which followed love and of awakening certain, for the first time in years, of his existence.

"Of course the invitation still holds. I'm driving up tonight."

"I won't be able to come until Sunday," she said firmly. "Is there a train then?"

"Yes, in the morning," he said, and gave her the schedule.

"You'll meet me at the station?"

"Of course. You can't miss my car. It's a very shabby but venerable Chevy."

She smiled stiffly and left, her heels awakening the silence of the empty corridor, the sound reaching back to tap like a warning finger on Max Berman's temple.

The pale sunlight slanting through the windshield lay like a cat on his knees, and the motor of his old Chevy, turning softly under him could have been the humming of its heart. A little distance from the car a log-cabin station house—the logs blackened by the seasons—stood alone against the hills, and the hills, in turn, lifted softly, still green although the summer was ending, into the vague autumn sky.

The morning mist and the pale sun, the green that was still somehow new, made it seem that the season was stirring into life even as it died, and this contradiction pained Max Berman at the same time that it pleased him. For it was his own contradiction after all: his desires which remained those of a young man even as he was dying.

He had been parked for some time in the deserted station, yet his hands were still tensed on the steering wheel and his foot hovered near the accelerator. As soon as he had arrived in the station he had wanted to leave. But like the girl that night on the landing, he was too stiff with tension to move. He could only wait, his eyelid twitching with foreboding, regret, curiosity and hope.

Finally and with no warning the train charged through the fiery green, setting off a tremor underground. Max Berman imagined the girl seated at a window in the train, her hands arranged quietly in her lap and her gaze scanning the hills that were so familiar to him, and yet he could not believe that she was really there. Perhaps her plan had been to disappoint him. She might be in New York or on her way back to Richmond now, laughing at the trick she had played on him. He was convinced of this suddenly, so that even when he saw her walking toward him through the blown steam from under the train, he told himself that she was a mirage created by the steam. Only when she sat beside him in the car, bringing with her, it seemed, an essence she had distilled from the morning air and rubbed into her skin, was he certain of her reality.

"I brought my bathing suit but it's much too cold to swim," she said and gave him the deliberate smile.

He did not see it; he only heard her voice, its warm Southern lilt in the chill, its intimacy in the closed car—and an excitement swept him, cold first and then hot, as if the sun had burst in his blood.

"It's the morning air," he said. "By noon it should be like summer again."

"Is that a promise?"

"Yes."

By noon the cold morning mist had lifted above the hills and below, in the lake valley, the sunlight was a sheer gold net spread out on the grass as if to dry, draped on the trees and flung, glinting, over the lake. Max Berman felt it brush his shoulders gently as he sat by the lake waiting for the girl who had gone up to the house to change into her swimsuit.

He had spent the morning showing her the fields and small wood near his house. During the long walk he had been careful to keep a little apart from her. He would extend a hand as they climbed a rise or when she stepped uncertainly over a rock, but he would not really touch her. He was afraid that at his touch, no matter how slight and casual, her scream would spiral into the morning calm, or worse, his touch would unleash the threatening thing he sensed behind her even smile.

He had talked of her paper and she had listened politely and occasionally even asked a question or made a comment. But all the while detached, distant, drawn within herself as she had been that first night in the classroom. And then halfway down a slope she had paused and, pointing to the canvas tops of her white sneakers, which had become wet and dark from the dew secreted in the grass, she had laughed. The sound, coming so abruptly in the midst of her tense quiet, joined her, it seemed, to the wood and wide fields, to the hills; she shared their simplicity and held within her the same strong current of life. Max Berman had felt privileged suddenly, and humble. He had stopped questioning her smile. He had told himself then that it would not matter even if she stopped and picking up a rock bludgeoned him from behind.

"There's a lake near my home, but it's not like this," the girl said, coming up behind him. "Yours is so dark and serious-looking."

He nodded and followed her gaze out to the lake, where the ripples were long, smooth welts raised by the wind, and across to the other bank, where a group of birches stepped delicately down to the lake and bending over touched the water with their branches as if testing it before they plunged.

The girl came and stood beside him now—and she was like a pale-gold naiad, the spirit of the lake, her eyes reflecting its somber autumnal tone and her body as supple as the birches. She walked slowly into the water, unaware, it seemed, of the sudden passion in his gaze, or perhaps uncaring; and as she walked she held out her arms in what seemed a gesture of invocation (and Max Berman remembered his father with the fringed shawl draped on his outstretched arm as he invoked their God each Sabbath with the same gesture); her head was bent as if she listened for a voice beneath the water's murmurous surface. When the ground gave way she still seemed to be walking and listening, her arms outstretched. The water reached her waist, her small breasts, her shoulders. She lifted her head once, breathed deeply and disappeared.

She stayed down for a long time and when her white cap finally broke the water some distance out, Max Berman felt strangely stranded and deprived. He understood suddenly the profound cleavage between them and the absurdity of his hope. The water between them became the years which separated them. Her white cap was the sign of her purity, while the silt darkening the lake was the flotsam of his failures. Above all, their color— her arms a pale, flashing gold in the sunlit water and his bled white and flaccid with the veins like angry blue penciling—marked the final barrier.

He was sad as they climbed toward the house late that afternoon and troubled. A crow cawed derisively in the bracken, heralding the dusk which would not only end their strange day but would also, he felt, unveil her smile, so that he would learn the reason for her coming. And because he was sad, he said wryly, "I think I should tell you that you've been spending the day with something of an outcast."

"Oh," she said and waited.

He told her of the dismissal, punctuating his words with the little hoarse, deprecating laugh and waving aside the pain with his cigarette. She listened, polite but neutral, and because she remained unmoved, he wanted to confess all the more. So that during dinner and afterward when they sat outside on the porch, he told her of the investigation.

"It was very funny once you saw it from the proper perspective, which I did, of course," he said. "I mean here they were accusing me of crimes I couldn't remember committing and asking me for the names of people with whom I had never associated. It was pure farce. But I made a mistake. I should have done something dramatic or something just as farcical. Bared my breast in the public market place or written a tome on my apostasy, naming names. It would have been a far different story then. Instead of my present ignominy I would have been offered a chairmanship at Yale. . . . No? Well, Brandeis then. I would have been draped in honorary degrees. . . ."

"Well, why didn't you confess?" she said impatiently.

"I've often asked myself the same interesting question, but I haven't come up with a satisfactory answer yet. I suspect, though, that I said nothing because none of it really mattered that much."

"What did matter?" she asked sharply.

He sat back, waiting for the witty answer, but none came, because just then the frame upon which his organs were strung seemed to snap and he felt his heart, his lungs, his vital parts fall in a heap within him. Her question had dealt the severing blow, for it was the same question he understood suddenly that the vague forms in his dream asked repeatedly. It had been the plaintive undercurrent to his father's dying moan, the real accusation behind the charges of his inquisitors at the hearing.

For what had mattered? He gazed through his sudden shock at the night squatting on the porch steps, at the hills asleep like gentle beasts in the darkness, at the black screen of the sky where the events of his life passed in a mute, accusing review—and he saw nothing there to which he had given himself or in which he had truly believed since the belief and dedication of his boyhood.

"Did you hear my question?" she asked, and he was glad that he sat within the shadows clinging to the porch screen and could not be seen.

"Yes, I did," he said faintly, and his eyelid twitched. "But I'm afraid it's another one of those I can't answer satisfactorily." And then he struggled for the old flippancy. "You make an excellent examiner, you know. Far better than my inquisitors."

"What will you do now?" Her voice and cold smile did not spare him.

He shrugged and the motion, a slow, eloquent lifting of the shoulders, brought with it suddenly the weight and memory of his boyhood. It was the familiar gesture of the women hawkers in Belmont Market, of the men standing outside the temple on Saturday mornings, each of them reflecting his image of God in their forbidding black coats and with the black, tumbling beards in which he had always imagined he could hide as in a forest. All this had mattered, he called loudly to himself, and said aloud to the girl, "Let me see if I can answer this one at least. What *will* I do?" He paused and swung his leg so that his foot in the fastidious French shoe caught the light from the house. "Grow flowers and write my memoirs. How's that? That would be the proper way for a gentleman and scholar to retire. Or hire one of those hefty housekeepers who will bully me and when I die in my sleep draw the sheet over my face and call my lawyer. That's somewhat European, but how's that?"

When she said nothing for a long time, he added soberly, "But that's not a fair question for me any more. I leave all such considerations to the young. To you, for that matter. What will you do, my dear Miss Williams?"

It was as if she had been expecting the question and had been readying her answer all the time he had been talking. She leaned forward eagerly and with her face and part of her body fully in the light, she said, "I will do something. I don't know what yet, but something."

Max Berman started back a little. The answer was so unlike her vague, resigned "I know" on the landing that night when he had admonished her to try something new.

He edged back into the darkness and she leaned further into the light, her eyes overwhelming her face and her mouth set in a thin, determined line. "I will do something," she said, bearing down on each word, "because for the first time in my life I feel almost brave."

He glimpsed this new bravery behind her hard gaze and sensed something vital and purposeful, precious, which she had found and guarded like a prize within her center. He wanted it. He would have liked to snatch it and run like a thief. He no longer desired her but it, and starting forward with a sudden envious cry, he caught her arm and drew her close, seeking it.

But he could not get to it. Although she did not pull away her arm, although she made no protest as his face wavered close to hers, he did not really touch her. She held herself and her prize out of his desperate reach and her smile was a knife she pressed to his throat. He saw himself for what he was in her clear, cold gaze: an old man with skin the color and texture of dough that had been kneaded by the years into tragic folds, with faded eyes adrift behind a pair of rimless glasses and the roughened flesh at his throat like a bird's wattles. And as the disgust which he read in her eyes swept him, his hand dropped from her arm. He started to murmur, "Forgive me . . ." when suddenly she caught hold of his wrist, pulling him close again, and he felt the strength which had borne her swiftly through the water earlier hold him now as she said quietly and without passion, "And do you know why, Dr. Berman, I feel almost brave today? Because ever since I can remember my parents were always telling me 'Stay away from white folks. Just leave them alone. You mind your business and they'll mind theirs. Don't go near them.' And they made sure I didn't. My father, who was the principal of a colored grade school in Richmond, used to drive me to and from school every day. When I needed something from downtown my mother would take me and if the white saleslady asked me anything she would answer. . . ."

"And my parents were always telling me, 'Stay away from niggers,' and that meant anybody darker than we were." She held out her arm in the light and Max Berman saw the skin almost as white as his but for the subtle amber shading. Staring at the arm she said tragically, "I was so confused I never really went near anybody. Even when I went away to college I kept to myself. I didn't marry the man I wanted to because he was dark and I knew my parents would disapprove. . . ." She paused, her wistful gaze searching the darkness for the face of the man she refused, it seemed, and not finding it she went on sadly, "So after graduation I returned home and started teaching and I was just as confused and frightened and ashamed as always. When my parents died I went on the same way. And I would have gone on like that the rest of my life if it hadn't been for you, Dr. Berman"—and the sarcasm leaped behind her cold smile. "In a way you did me a favor. You let me know how you—and most of the people like you—see me."

"My dear Miss Williams, I assure you I was not attracted to you because you were colored. . . ." And he broke off, remembering just how acutely aware of her color he had been.

"I'm not interested in your reasons!" she said brutally. "What matters is what it meant to me. I thought about this these last three weeks and about my parents—how wrong they had been, how frightened, and the terrible thing they had done to me . . . And I wasn't confused any longer." Her head lifted, tremulous with her new assurance. "I can do something now! I can begin," she said with her head poised. "Look how I came all the way up here to tell you this to your face. Because how could you harm me? You're so old you're like a cup I could break in my hand." And her hand tightened on his wrist, wrenching the last of his frail life from him, it seemed. Through the quick pain he remembered her saying on the landing that night: "Maybe in order for a person to live someone else must die" and her quiet "I believe this" then. Now her sudden laugh, an infinitely cruel sound in the warm night, confirmed her belief.

Suddenly she was the one who seemed old, indeed ageless. Her touch became mortal and Max Berman saw the darkness that would end his life gathered in her eyes. But even as he sprang back, jerking his arm away, a part of him rushed forward to embrace that darkness, and his cry, wounding the night, held both ecstasy and terror.

"That's all I came for," she said, rising. "You can drive me to the station now."

They drove to the station in silence. Then, just as the girl started from the car, she turned with an ironic, pitiless smile and said, "You know, it's been a nice day, all things considered. It really turned summer again as you said it would. And even though your lake isn't anything like the one near my home, it's almost as nice."

Max Berman bowed to her for the last time, accepting with that gesture his responsibility for her rage, which went deeper than his, and for her anger, which would spur her finally to live. And not only for her, but for all those at last whom he had wronged through his indifference: his father lying in the room of shrouded mirrors, the wives he had never loved, his work which he had never believed in enough and, lastly (even though he knew it was too late and he would not be spared), himself.

Too weary to move, he watched the girl cross to the train which would bear her south, her head lifted as though she carried life as lightly there as if it were a hat made of tulle. When the train departed his numbed eyes followed it until its rear light was like a single firefly in the immense night or the last flickering of his life. Then he drove back through the darkness.

The Necklace

GUY DE MAUPASSANT

She was one of those pretty and charming girls born, as though fate had blundered over her, into a family of artisans. She had no marriage portion, no expectations, no means of getting known, understood, loved, and wedded by a man of wealth and distinction; and she let herself be married off to a little clerk in the Ministry of Education.

Her tastes were simple because she had never been able to afford any other, but she was as unhappy as though she had married beneath her; for women have no caste or class, their beauty, grace, and charm serving them for birth or family. Their natural delicacy, their instinctive elegance, their nimbleness of wit, are their only mark of rank, and put the slum girl on a level with the highest lady in the land.

She suffered endlessly, feeling herself born for every delicacy and luxury. She suffered from the poorness of her house, from its mean walls, worn chairs, and ugly curtains. All these things, of which other women of her class would not even have been aware, tormented and insulted her. The sight of the little Breton girl who came to do the work in her little house aroused heart-broken regrets and hopeless dreams in her mind. She imagined silent antechambers, heavy with Oriental tapestries, lit by torches in lofty bronze sockets, with two tall footmen in knee-breeches sleeping in large arm-chairs, overcome by the heavy warmth of the stove. She imagined vast salons hung with antique silks, exquisite pieces of furniture supporting priceless ornaments, and small, charming, perfumed rooms, created just for little parties of intimate friends, men who were famous and sought after, whose homage roused every other woman's envious longings.

When she sat down for dinner at the round table covered with a three-days-old cloth, opposite her husband, who took the cover off the soup-tureen, exclaiming delightedly: "Aha! Scotch broth! What could be better?" she imagined delicate meals, gleaming silver, tapestries peopling the walls with folk of a past age and strange birds in faery forests; she imagined delicate food served in marvelous dishes, murmured gallantries, listened to with an inscrutable smile as one trifled with the rosy flesh of trout or wings of asparagus chicken.

She had no clothes, no jewels, nothing. And these were the only things she loved; she felt that she was made for them. She had longed so eagerly to charm, to be desired, to be wildly attractive and sought after.

She had a rich friend, an old school friend whom she refused to visit, because she suffered so keenly when she returned home. She would weep whole days, with grief, regret, despair, and misery.

One evening her husband came home with an exultant air, holding a large envelope in his hand.

"Here's something for you," he said.

Swiftly she tore the paper and drew out a printed card on which were these words:

> "The Minister of Education and Madame Ramponneau request the pleasure of the company of Monsieur and Madame Loisel at the Ministry on the evening of Monday, January the 18th."

Instead of being delighted, as her husband hoped, she flung the invitation petulantly across the table, murmuring:

"What do you want me to do with this?"

"Why, darling, I thought you'd be pleased. You never go out, and this is a great occasion. I had tremendous trouble to get it. Every one wants one; it's very select, and very few go to the clerks. You'll see all the really big people there."

She looked at him out of furious eyes, and said impatiently:

"And what do you suppose I am to wear to such an affair?"

He had not thought about it; he stammered:

"Why, the dress you go to the theatre in. It looks very nice, to me. . . ."

He stopped, stupefied and utterly at a loss when he saw that his wife was beginning to cry. Two large tears ran slowly down from the corners of her eyes towards the corner of her mouth.

"What's the matter with you? What's the matter with you?" he faltered.

But with a violent effort she overcame her grief and replied in a calm voice, wiping her wet cheeks:

"Nothing. Only I haven't a dress and so I can't go to this party. Give your invitation to some friend of yours whose wife will be turned out better than I shall."

He was heart-broken.

"Look here, Mathilde," he persisted. "What would be the cost of a suitable dress, which you could use on other occasions as well, something very simple?"

She thought for several seconds, reckoning up prices and also wondering for how large a sum she could ask without bringing upon herself an immediate refusal and an exclamation of horror from the careful-minded clerk.

At last she replied with some hesitation:

"I don't know exactly, but I think I could do it on four hundred francs."

He grew slightly pale, for this was exactly the amount he had been saving for a gun, intending to get a little shooting next summer on the plain of Nanterre with some friends who went lark-shooting there on Sundays.

Nevertheless he said: "Very well. I'll give you four hundred francs. But try and get a really nice dress with the money."

The day of the party drew near, and Madame Loisel seemed sad, uneasy and anxious. Her dress was ready, however. One evening her husband said to her:

"What's the matter with you? You've been very odd for the last three days."

"I'm utterly miserable at not having any jewels, not a single stone, to wear," she replied. "I shall look absolutely no one. I would almost rather not go to the party."

"Wear flowers," he said. "They're very smart at this time of the year. For ten francs you could get two or three gorgeous roses."

She was not convinced.

"No . . . there's nothing so humiliating as looking poor in the middle of a lot of rich women."

"How stupid you are!" exclaimed her husband. "Go and see Madame Forestier and ask her to lend you some jewels. You know her quite well enough for that."

She uttered a cry of delight.

"That's true. I never thought of it."

Next day she went to see her friend and told her her trouble.

Madame Forestier went to her dressing-table, took up a large box, brought it to Madame Loisel, opened it, and said:

"Choose, my dear."

First she saw some bracelets, then a pearl necklace, then a Venetian cross in gold and gems, of exquisite workmanship. She tried the effect of the jewels before the mirror, hesitating, unable to make up her mind to leave them, to give them up. She kept on asking:

"Haven't you anything else?"

"Yes. Look for yourself. I don't know what you would like best."

Suddenly she discovered, in a black satin case, a superb diamond necklace; her heart began to beat covetously. Her hands trembled as she lifted it. She fastened it round her neck, upon her high dress, and remained in ecstasy at the sight of herself.

Then, with hesitation, she asked in anguish:

"Could you lend me this, just this alone?"

"Yes, of course."

She flung herself on her friend's breast, embraced her frenziedly, and went away with her treasure.

The day of the party arrived. Madame Loisel was a success. She was the prettiest woman present, elegant, graceful, smiling, and quite above herself with happiness. All the men stared at her, inquired her name, and asked to be introduced to her. All the Under-Secretaries of State were eager to waltz with her. The Minister noticed her.

She danced madly, ecstatically, drunk with pleasure, with no thought for anything, in the triumph of her beauty, in the pride of her success, in a cloud of happiness made up of this universal homage and admiration, of the desires she had aroused, of the completeness of a victory so dear to her feminine heart.

She left about four o'clock in the morning. Since midnight her husband had been dozing in a deserted little room, in company with three other men whose wives were having a good time.

He threw over her shoulders the garments he had brought for them to go home in, modest everyday clothes, whose poverty clashed with the beauty of the ball-dress. She was conscious of this and was anxious to hurry away, so that she should not be noticed by the other women putting on their costly furs.

Loisel restrained her.

"Wait a little. You'll catch cold in the open. I'm going to fetch a cab."

But she did not listen to him and rapidly descended the staircase. When they were out in the street they could not find a cab; they began to look for one, shouting at the drivers whom they saw passing in the distance.

They walked down towards the Seine, desperate and shivering. At last they found on the quay one of those old night-prowling carriages which are only to be seen in Paris after dark, as though they were ashamed of their shabbiness in the daylight.

It brought them to their door in the Rue des Martyrs, and sadly they walked up to their own apartment. It was the end, for her. As for him, he was thinking that he must be at the office at ten.

She took off the garments in which she had wrapped her shoulders, so as to see herself in all her glory before the mirror. But suddenly she uttered a cry. The necklace was no longer round her neck!

"What's the matter with you?" asked her husband, already half undressed.

She turned towards him in the utmost distress.

"I . . . I . . . I've no longer got Madame Forestier's necklace. . . ."

He started with astonishment.

"What! . . . Impossible!"

They searched in the folds of her dress, in the folds of the coat, in the pockets, everywhere. They could not find it.

"Are you sure that you still had it on when you came away from the ball?" he asked.

"Yes, I touched it in the hall at the Ministry."

"But if you had lost it in the street, we should have heard it fall."

"Yes. Probably we should. Did you take the number of the cab?"

"No. You didn't notice it, did you?"

"No."

They stared at one another, dumbfounded. At last Loisel put on his clothes again.

"I'll go over all the ground we walked," he said, "and see if I can't find it."

And he went out. She remained in her evening clothes, lacking strength to get into bed, huddled on a chair, without volition or power of thought.

Her husband returned about seven. He found nothing.

He went to the police station, to the newspapers, to offer a reward, to the cab companies, everywhere that a ray of hope impelled him.

She waited all day long, in the same state of bewilderment at this fearful catastrophe.

Loisel came home at night, his face lined and pale; he had discovered nothing.

"You must write to your friend," he said. "and tell her that you've broken the clasp of her necklace and are getting it mended. That will give us time to look about us."

She wrote at his dictation.

By the end of the week they had lost all hope.

Loisel, who had aged five years, declared:

"We must see about replacing the diamonds."

Next day they took the box which had held the necklace and went to the jewellers whose name was inside. He consulted his books.

"It was not I who sold this necklace, Madame; I must have merely supplied the clasp."

Then they went from jeweller to jeweller, searching for another necklace like the first, consulting their memories, both ill with remorse and anguish of mind.

In a shop at the Palais-Royal they found a string of diamonds which seemed to them exactly like the one they were looking for. It was worth forty thousand francs. They were allowed to have it for thirty-six thousand.

They begged the jeweller not to sell it for three days. And they arranged matters on the understanding that it would be taken back for thirty-four thousand francs, if the first one were found before the end of February.

Loisel possessed eighteen thousand francs left to him by his father. He intended to borrow the rest.

He did borrow it, getting a thousand from one man, five hundred from another, five louis here, three louis there. He gave notes of hand, entered into ruinous agreements, did business with usurers and the whole tribe of money-lenders. He mortgaged the whole remaining years of his existence, risked his signature without even knowing if he could honour it and, appalled at the agonising face of the future, at the black misery about to fall upon him, at the prospect of every possible physical privation and moral torture, he went to get the new necklace and put down upon the jeweller's counter thirty-six thousand francs.

When Madame Loisel took back the necklace to Madame Forestier, the latter said to her in a chilly voice:

"You ought to have brought it back sooner; I might have needed it."

She did not, as her friend had feared, open the case. If she had noticed the substitution, what would she have thought? What would she have said? Would she not have taken her for a thief?

Madame Loisel came to know the ghastly life of abject poverty. From the very first she played her part heroically. This fearful debt must be paid off. She would pay it. The servant was dismissed. They changed their flat; they took a garret under the roof.

She came to know the heavy work of the house, the hateful duties of the kitchen. She washed the plates, wearing out her pink nails on the coarse pottery and the bottoms of pans. She washed the dirty linen, the shirts and dish-clothes, and hung them out to dry on a string; every morning she took the dustbin down into the street and carried up the water, stopping on each landing to get her breath. And, clad like a poor woman, she went to the fruiterer, to the grocer, to the butcher, a basket on her arm, haggling, insulted, fighting for every wretched halfpenny of her money.

Every month notes had to be paid off, others renewed, time gained.

Her husband worked in the evenings at putting straight a merchant's accounts, and often at night he did copying at two-pence-halfpenny a page.

And this life lasted ten years.

At the end of ten years everything was paid off, everything, usurer's charges and the accumulation of superimposed interest.

Madame Loisel looked old now. She had become like all the other strong, hard, coarse women of poor households. Her hair was badly done, her skirts were awry, her hands were red. She spoke in a shrill voice, and the water slopped all over the floor when she scrubbed it. But sometimes, when he husband was at the office, she sat down by the window and thought of that evening long ago, of the ball at which she had been so beautiful and so much admired.

What would have happened if she had never lost those jewels. Who knows? Who knows? How strange life is, how fickle! How little is needed to ruin or to save!

One Sunday, as she had gone for a walk along the Champs-Élysées to freshen herself after the labours of the week, she caught sight suddenly of a woman who was taking a child out for a walk. It was Madame Forestier, still young, still beautiful, still attractive.

Madame Loisel was conscious of some emotion. Should she speak to her? Yes, certainly. And now that she had paid, she would tell her all. Why not?

She went up to her.

"Good morning, Jeanne."

The other did not recognize her, and was surprised at being thus familiarly addressed by a poor woman.

"But . . . Madame . . ." she stammered. "I don't know . . . you must be making a mistake."

"No . . . I am Mathilde Loisel."

Her friend uttered a cry.

"Oh! . . . my poor Mathilde, how you have changed! . . ."

"Yes, I've had some hard times since I saw you last; and many sorrows . . . and all on your account."

"On my account! . . . How was that?"

"You remember the diamond necklace you lent me for the ball at the Ministry?"

"Yes. Well?"

"Well, I lost it."

"How could you? Why, you brought it back."

"I brought you another one just like it. And for the last ten years we have been paying for it. You realise it wasn't easy for us; we had no money. . . . Well, it's paid for at last, and I'm glad indeed."

Madame Forestier had halted.

"You say you bought a diamond necklace to replace mine?"

"Yes. You hadn't noticed it? They were very much alike."

And she smiled in proud and innocent happiness.

Madame Forestier, deeply moved, took her two hands.

"Oh, my poor Mathilde! But mine was imitation. It was worth at the very most five hundred francs! . . ."

Patriotism

YUKIO MISHIMA

Translated by Geoffrey W. Sargent

I

On the twenty-eighth of February, 1936 (on the third day, that is, of the February 26 Incident), Lieutenant Shinji Takeyama of the Konoe Transport Battalion—profoundly disturbed by the knowledge that his closest colleagues had been with the mutineers from the beginning, and indignant at the imminent prospect of Imperial troops attacking Imperial troops—took his officer's sword and ceremonially disemboweled himself in the eight-mat room of his private residence in the sixth block of Aoba-chō, in Yotsuya Ward. His wife, Reiko, followed him, stabbing herself to death. The lieutenant's farewell note consisted of one sentence: "Long live the Imperial Forces." His wife's, after apologies for her unfilial conduct in thus preceding her parents to the grave, concluded: "The day which, for a soldier's wife, had to come, has come. . . ." The last moments of this heroic and dedicated couple were such as to make the gods themselves weep. The lieutenant's age, it should be noted, was thirty-one, his wife's twenty-three; and it was not half a year since the celebration of their marriage.

II

Those who saw the bride and bridegroom in the commemorative photograph—perhaps no less than those actually present at the lieutenant's wedding—had exclaimed in wonder at the bearing of this handsome couple. The lieutenant, majestic in military uniform, stood protectively beside his bride, his right hand resting upon his sword, his officer's cap held at his left side. His expression was severe, and his dark brows and wide-gazing eyes well conveyed the clear integrity of youth. For the beauty of the bride in her white over-robe no comparisons were adequate. In the eyes, round beneath soft brows, in the slender, finely shaped nose, and in the full lips, there was both sensuousness and refinement. One hand, emerging shyly from a sleeve of the over-robe, held a fan, and the tips of the fingers, clustering delicately, were like the bud of a moonflower.

After the suicide, people would take out this photograph and examine it, and sadly reflect that too often there was a curse on these seemingly flawless unions. Perhaps it was no more than imagination, but looking at the picture after the tragedy it almost seemed as if the two young people before the gold-lacquered screen were gazing, each with equal clarity, at the deaths which lay before them.

Thanks to the good offices of their go-between, Lieutenant General Ozeki, they had been able to set themselves up in a new home at Aoba-chō in Yotsuya. "New home" is perhaps misleading. It was an old three-room rented house backing onto a small garden. As neither the six- nor the four-and-a-half mat room downstairs was favored by the sun, they used the upstairs eight-mat room as both bedroom and guest room. There was no maid, so Reiko was left alone to guard the house in her husband's absence.

The honeymoon trip was dispensed with on the grounds that these were times of national emergency. The two of them had spent the first night of their marriage at this house. Before going to bed, Shinji, sitting erect on the floor with his sword laid before him, had bestowed upon his wife a soldierly lecture. A woman who had become the wife of a soldier should know and resolutely accept that her husband's death might come at any moment. It could be tomorrow. It could be the day after. But, no matter when it came—he asked—was she steadfast in her resolve to accept it? Reiko rose to her feet, pulled open a drawer of the cabinet, and took out what was the most prized of her new possessions, the dagger her mother had given her. Returning to her place, she laid the dagger without a word on the mat before her, just as her husband had laid his sword. A silent understanding was achieved at once, and the lieutenant never again sought to test his wife's resolve.

In the first few months of her marriage Reiko's beauty grew daily more radiant, shining serene like the moon after rain.

As both were possessed of young, vigorous bodies, their relationship was passionate. Nor was this merely a matter of the night. On more than one occasion, returning home straight from maneuvers, and begrudging even the time it took to remove his mud-splashed uniform, the lieutenant had pushed his wife to the floor almost as soon as he had entered the house. Reiko was equally ardent in her response. For a little more or a little less than a month, from the first night of their marriage Reiko knew happiness, and the lieutenant, seeing this, was happy too.

Reiko's body was white and pure, and her swelling breasts conveyed a firm and chaste refusal; but, upon consent, those breasts were lavish with

their intimate, welcoming warmth. Even in bed these two were frighten-
ingly and awesomely serious. In the very midst of wild, intoxicating passion, their hearts were sober and serious.

By day the lieutenant would think of his wife in the brief rest periods between training; and all day long, at home, Reiko would recall the image of
her husband. Even when apart, however, they had only to look at the wedding photograph for their happiness to be once more confirmed. Reiko felt
not the slightest surprise that a man who had been a complete stranger until a few months age should now have become the sun about which her
whole world revolved.

All these things had a moral basis, and were in accordance with the Education Rescript's injunction that "husband and wife should be harmoni-
ous." Not once did Reiko contradict her husband, nor did the lieutenant
ever find reason to scold his wife. On the god shelf below the stairway,
alongside the tablet from the Great Ise Shrine, were set photographs of
their Imperial Majesties, and regularly every morning, before leaving for
duty, the lieutenant would stand with his wife at this hallowed place and together they would bow their heads low. The offering water was renewed
each morning, and the sacred sprig of *sasaki* was always green and fresh.
Their lives were lived beneath the solemn protection of the gods and were
filled with an intense happiness which set every fiber in their bodies
trembling.

III

Although Lord Privy Seal Saitō's house was in their neighborhood, neither
of them heard any noise of gunfire on the morning of February 26. It was
a bugle, sounding muster in the dim, snowy dawn, when the ten-minute
tragedy had already ended, which first disrupted the lieutenant's slumbers.
Leaping at once from his bed, and without speaking a word, the lieutenant
donned his uniform, buckled on the sword held ready for him by his wife,
and hurried swiftly out into the snow-covered streets of the still darkened
morning. He did not return until the evening of the twenty-eighth.

Later, from the radio news, Reiko learned the full extent of this sudden
eruption of violence. Her life throughout the subsequent two days was
lived alone, in complete tranquility and behind locked doors.

In the lieutenant's face, as he hurried silently out into the snowy morning, Reiko had read the determination to die. If her husband did not return, her own decision was made: she too would die. Quietly she attended
to the disposition of her personal possessions. She chose her sets of visiting
kimonos as keepsakes for friends of her schooldays, and she wrote a name
and address on the stiff paper wrapping in which each was folded. Constantly admonished by her husband never to think of the morrow, Reiko

had not even kept a diary and was now denied the pleasure of assiduously rereading her record of the happiness of the past few months and consigning each page to the fire as she did so. Ranged across the top of the radio were a small china dog, a rabbit, a squirrel, a bear, a fox. There were also a small vase and a water pitcher. These comprised Reiko's one and only collection. But it would hardly do, she imagined, to give such things as keepsakes. Nor again would it be quite proper to ask specifically for them to be included in the coffin. It seemed to Reiko, as these thoughts passed through her mind, that the expressions on the small animals' faces grew even more lost and forlorn.

Reiko took the squirrel in her hand and looked at it. And then, her thoughts turning to a realm far beyond these childlike affections, she gazed up into the distance at the great sunlike principle which her husband embodied. She was ready, and happy, to be hurtled along to her destruction in that gleaming sun chariot—but now, for these few moments of solitude, she allowed herself to luxuriate in this innocent attachment to trifles. The time when she had genuinely loved these things, however, was long past. Now she merely loved the memory of having once loved them, and their place in her heart had been filled by more intense passions, by a more frenzied happiness. . . . For Reiko had never, even to herself, thought of those soaring joys of the flesh as a mere pleasure. The February cold, and the icy touch of the china squirrel, had numbed Reiko's slender fingers; yet, even so, in her lower limbs, beneath the ordered repetition of the pattern which crossed the skirt of her trim *meisen* kimono, she could feel now, as she thought of the lieutenant's powerful arms reaching out toward her, a hot moistness of the flesh which defied the snows.

She was not in the least afraid of the death hovering in her mind. Waiting alone at home, Reiko firmly believed that everything her husband was feeling or thinking now, his anguish and distress, was leading her—just as surely as the power in his flesh—to a welcome death. She felt as if her body could melt away with ease and be transformed to the merest fraction of her husband's thought.

Listening to the frequent announcements on the radio, she heard the names of several of her husband's colleagues mentioned among those of the insurgents. This was news of death. She followed the developments closely, wondering anxiously, as the situation became daily more irrevocable, why no Imperial ordinance was sent down, and watching what had at first been taken as a movement to restore the nation's honor come gradually to be branded with the infamous name of mutiny. There was no communication from the regiment. At any moment, it seemed, fighting might commence in the city streets, where the remains of the snow still lay.

Toward sundown on the twenty-eighth Reiko was startled by a furious pounding on the front door. She hurried downstairs. As she pulled with fumbling fingers at the bolt, the shape dimly outlined beyond the frosted-glass panel made no sound, but she knew it was her husband. Reiko had never known the bolt on the sliding door to be so stiff. Still it resisted. The door just would not open.

In a moment, almost before she knew she had succeeded, the lieutenant was standing before her on the cement floor inside the porch, muffled in a khaki greatcoat, his top boots heavy with slush from the street. Closing the door behind him, he returned the bolt once more to its socket. With what significance, Reiko did not understand.

Reiko bowed deeply, but her husband made no response. As he had already unfastened his sword and was about to remove his greatcoat, Reiko moved around behind to assist. The coat, which was cold and damp and had lost the odor of horse dung it normally exuded when exposed to the sun, weighed heavily upon her arm. Draping it across a hanger, and cradling the sword and leather belt in her sleeves, she waited while her husband removed his top boots and then followed behind him into the "living room." This was the six-mat room downstairs.

Seen in the clear light from the lamp, her husband's face, covered with a heavy growth of bristle, was almost unrecognizably wasted and thin. The cheeks were hollow, their luster and resilience gone. In his normal good spirits he would have changed into old clothes as soon as he was home and have pressed her to get supper at once, but now he sat before the table still in his uniform, his head drooping dejectedly. Reiko refrained from asking whether she should prepare the supper.

After an interval the lieutenant spoke.

"I knew nothing. They hadn't asked me to join. Perhaps out of consideration, because I was newly married. Kanō, and Homma too, Yamaguchi."

Reiko recalled momentarily the faces of high-spirited young officers, friends of her husband, who had come to the house occasionally as guests.

"There may be an Imperial ordinance sent down tomorrow. They'll be posted as rebels, I imagine. I shall be in command of a unit with orders to attack them. . . . I can't do it. It's impossible to do a thing like that."

He spoke again.

"They've taken me off guard duty, and I have permission to return home for one night. Tomorrow morning, without question, I must leave to join the attack. I can't do it, Reiko."

Reiko sat erect with lowered eyes. She understood clearly that her husband had spoken of his death. The lieutenant was resolved. Each word, being rooted in death, emerged sharply and with powerful significance against this dark, unmovable background. Although the lieutenant was speaking of his dilemma, already there was no room in his mind for vacillation.

However, there was a clarity, like the clarity of a stream fed from melting snows, in the silence which rested between them. Sitting in his own home after the long two-day ordeal, and looking across at the face of his beautiful wife, the lieutenant was for the first time experiencing true peace of mind. For he had once known, though she said nothing, that his wife divined the resolve which lay beneath his words.

"Well, then . . . ." The lieutenant's eyes opened wide. Despite his exhaustion they were strong and clear, and now for the first time they looked straight into the eyes of his wife. "Tonight I shall cut my stomach."

Reiko did not flinch.

Her round eyes showed tension, as taut as the clang of a bell.

"I am ready," she said. "I ask permission to accompany you."

The lieutenant felt almost mesmerized by the strength in those eyes. His words flowed swiftly and easily, like the utterances of a man in delirium, and it was beyond his understanding how permission in a matter of such weight could be expressed so casually.

"Good. We'll go together. But I want you as a witness, first, for my own suicide. Agreed?"

When this was said a sudden release of abundant happiness welled up in both their hearts. Reiko was deeply affected by the greatness of her husband's trust in her. It was vital for the lieutenant, whatever else might happen, that there should be no irregularity in his death. For that reason there had to be a witness. The fact that he had chosen his wife for this was the first mark of his trust. The second, and even greater mark, was that though he had pledged that they should die together he did not intend to kill his wife first—he had deferred her death to a time when he would no longer be there to verify it. If the lieutenant had been a suspicious husband, he would doubtless, as in the usual suicide pact, have chosen to kill his wife first.

When Reiko said, "I ask permission to accompany you," the lieutenant felt these words to be final fruit of the education which he had himself given his wife, starting on the first night of their marriage, and which had schooled her, when the moment came, to say what had to be said without a shadow of hesitation. This flattered the lieutenant's opinion of himself as a self-reliant man. He was not so romantic or conceited as to imagine that the words were spoken spontaneously, out of love for her husband.

With happiness welling almost too abundantly in their hearts, they could not help smiling at each other. Reiko felt as if she had returned to her wedding night.

Before her eyes was neither pain nor death. She seemed to see only a free and limitless expanse opening out into vast distances.

"The water is hot. Will you take your bath now?"

"Ah yes, of course."

"And supper . . .?"

The words were delivered in such level, domestic tones that the lieutenant came near to thinking, for the fraction of a second, that everything had been a hallucination.

"I don't think we'll need supper. But perhaps you could warm some sake?"

"As you wish."

As Reiko rose and took a *tanzen* gown from the cabinet for after the bath, she purposely directed her husband's attention to the open drawer. The lieutenant rose, crossed to the cabinet, and looked inside. From the ordered array of paper wrappings he read, one by one, the addresses of the keepsakes. There was no grief in the lieutenant's response to this demonstration of heroic resolve. His heart was filled with tenderness. Like a husband who is proudly shown the childish purchases of a young wife, the lieutenant, overwhelmed by affection, lovingly embraced his wife from behind and implanted a kiss upon her neck.

Reiko felt the roughness of the lieutenant's unshaven skin against her neck. This sensation, more than being just a thing of this world, was for Reiko almost the world itself, but now—with the feeling that it was soon to be lost forever—it had freshness beyond all her experience. Each moment had its own vital strength, and the senses in every corner of her body were reawakened. Accepting her husband's caresses from behind, Reiko raised herself on the tips of her toes, letting the vitality seep through her entire body.

"First the bath, and then, after some sake . . . lay out the bedding upstairs, will you?"

The lieutenant whispered the words into his wife's ear. Reiko silently nodded.

Flinging off his uniform, the lieutenant went to the bath. To faint background noises of slopping water Reiko tended the charcoal brazier in the living room and began the preparations for warming the sake.

Taking the *tanzen*, a sash, and some underclothes, she went to the bathroom to ask how the water was. In the midst of a coiling cloud of steam the lieutenant was sitting cross-legged on the floor, shaving, and she could dimly discern the rippling movements of the muscles on his damp, powerful back as they responded to the movement of his arms.

There was nothing to suggest a time of any special significance. Reiko, going busily about her tasks, was preparing side dishes from odds and ends in stock. Her hands did not tremble. If anything, she managed even more efficiently and smoothly than usually. From time to time, it is true, there was a strange throbbing deep within her breast. Like distant lightning, it had a moment of sharp intensity and then vanished without trace. Apart from that, nothing was in any way out of the ordinary.

The lieutenant, shaving in the bathroom, felt his warmed body miraculously healed at last of the desperate tiredness of the days of indecision and filled—in spite of the death which lay ahead—with pleasurable anticipation. The sound of his wife going about her work came to him faintly. A healthy physical craving, submerged for two days, reasserted itself.

The lieutenant was confident there had been no impurity in that joy they had experienced when resolving upon death. They had both sensed at that moment—though not, of course, in any clear and conscious way—that those permissible pleasures which they shared in private were once more beneath the protection of Righteousness and Divine Power, and of a complete and unassailable morality. On looking into each other's eyes and discovering there an honorable death, they had felt themselves safe once more behind steel walls which none could destroy, encased in an impenetrable armor of Beauty and Truth. Thus, so far from seeing any inconsistency or conflict between the urges of his flesh and the sincerity of his patriotism, the lieutenant was even able to regard the two as parts of the same thing.

Thrusting his face close to the dark, cracked, misted wall mirror, the lieutenant shaved himself with great care. This would be his death face. There must be no unsightly blemishes. The clean-shaven face gleamed once more with a youthful luster, seeming to brighten the darkness of the mirror. There was a certain elegance, he even felt, in the association of death with this radiantly healthy face.

Just as it looked now, this would become his death face! Already, in fact, it had half departed from the lieutenant's personal possession and had become the bust above a dead soldier's memorial. As an experiment he closed his eyes tight. Everything was wrapped in blackness, and he was no longer a living, seeing creature.

Returning from the bath, the traces of the shave glowing faintly blue beneath his smooth cheeks, he seated himself beside the now well-kindled charcoal brazier. Busy though Reiko was, he noticed, she had found time lightly to touch up her face. Her cheeks were gay and her lips moist. There was no shadow of sadness to be seen. Truly, the lieutenant felt, as he saw this mark of his young wife's passionate nature, he had chosen the wife he ought to have chosen.

As soon as the lieutenant had drained his sake cup he offered it to Reiko. Reiko had never before tasted sake, but she accepted without hesitation and sipped timidly.

"Come here," the lieutenant said.

Reiko moved to her husband's side and was embraced as she leaned backward across his lap. Her breast was in violent commotion, as if sadness, joy, and the potent sake were mingling and reacting within her. The lieutenant looked down into his wife's face. It was the last face he would see in this world, the last face he would see of his wife. The lieutenant scrutinized the face minutely, with the eyes of a traveler bidding farewell to splendid vistas which he will never revisit. It was a face he could not tire of looking at—the features regular yet not cold, the lips lightly closed with a soft strength. The lieutenant kissed those lips, unthinkingly. And suddenly, though there was not the slightest distortion of the face into the unsightliness of sobbing, he noticed that tears were welling slowly from beneath the long lashes of the closed eyes and brimming over into a glistening stream.

When, a little later, the lieutenant urged that they should move to the up-stairs bedroom, his wife replied that she would follow after taking a bath. Climbing the stairs alone to the bedroom, where the air was already warmed by the gas heater, the lieutenant lay down on the bedding with arms outstretched and legs apart. Even the time at which he lay waiting for his wife to join him was no later and no earlier than usual.

He folded his hands beneath his head and gazed at the dark boards of the ceiling in the dimness beyond the range of the standard lamp. Was it death he was now waiting for? Or a wild ecstasy of the senses? The two seemed to overlap, almost as if the object of this bodily desire was death it-self. But, however that might be, it was certain that never before had the lieutenant tasted such total freedom.

There was the sound of a car outside the window. He could hear the screech of its tires skidding in the snow piled at the side of the street. The sound of its horn re-echoed from near-by walls. . . . Listening to these noises he had the feeling that this house rose like a solitary island in the ocean of a society going as restlessly about its business as ever. All around, vastly and untidily, stretched the country for which he grieved. He was to give his life for it. But would that great country, with which he was pre-pared to remonstrate to the extent of destroying himself, take the slightest heed of his death? He did not know; and it did not matter. His was a battle-field without glory, a battlefield where none could display deeds of valor: it was the front line of the spirit.

Reiko's footsteps sounded on the stairway. The steep stairs in this old house creaked badly. There were fond memories in that creaking, and many a time, while waiting in bed, the lieutenant had listened to its wel-come sound. At the thought that he would hear it no more he listened with intense concentration, striving for every corner of every moment of this precious time to be filled with the sound of those soft footfalls on the creak-ing stairway. The moments seemed transformed to jewels, sparkling with inner light.

Reiko wore a Nagoya sash about the waist of her *yukata*, but as the lieu-tenant reached toward it, its redness sobered by the dimness of the light, Reiko's hand moved to his assistance and the sash fell away, slithering swiftly to the floor. As she stood before him, still in her *yukata*, the lieuten-ant inserted his hands through the side slits beneath each sleeve, intending to embrace her as she was; but at the touch of his finger tips upon the warm naked flesh, and as the armpits closed gently about his hands, his whole body was suddenly aflame.

In a few moments the two lay naked before the glowing gas heater.

Neither spoke the thought, but their hearts, their bodies, and their pounding breasts blazed with the knowledge that this was the very last time.

It was as if the words "The Last Time" were spelled out, in invisible brush-strokes, across every inch of their bodies.

The lieutenant drew his wife close and kissed her vehemently. As their tongues explored each other's mouths, reaching out into the smooth, moist interior, they felt as if the still-unknown agonies of death had tempered their senses to the keenness of red-hot steel. The agonies they could not yet feel, the distant pains of death, had refined their awareness of pleasure.

"This is the last time I shall see your body," said the lieutenant. "Let me look at it closely." And, tilting the shade on the lampstand to one side, he directed the rays along the full length of Reiko's outstretched form.

Reiko lay still with her eyes closed. The light from the low lamp clearly revealed the majestic sweep of her white flesh. The lieutenant, not without a touch of egocentricity, rejoiced that he would never see this beauty crumble in death.

At his leisure, the lieutenant allowed the unforgettable spectacle to engrave itself upon his mind. With one hand he fondled the hair, with the other he softly stroked the magnificent face, implanting kisses here and there where his eyes lingered. The quiet coldness of the high, tapering forehead, the closed eyes with their long lashes beneath faintly etched brows, the set of the finely shaped nose, the gleam of teeth glimpsed between full, regular lips, the soft cheeks and the small, wise chin . . . these things conjured up in the lieutenant's mind the vision of a truly radiant death face, and again and again he pressed his lips tight against the white throat—where Reiko's own hand was soon to strike—and the throat reddened faintly beneath his kisses. Returning to the mouth he laid his lips against it with the gentlest of pressures, and moved them rhythmically over Reiko's with the light rolling motion of a small boat. If he closed his eyes, the world became a rocking cradle.

Wherever the lieutenant's eyes moved his lips faithfully followed. The high, swelling breasts, surmounted by nipples like the buds of a wild cherry, hardened as the lieutenant's lips closed about them. The arms flowed smoothly downward from each side of the breast, tapering toward the wrists, yet losing nothing of their roundness or symmetry, and at their tips were those delicate fingers which had held the fan at the wedding ceremony. One by one, as the lieutenant kissed them, the fingers withdrew behind their neighbor as if in shame. . . . The natural hollow curving between the bosom and the stomach carried in its lines a suggestion not only of softness but of resilient strength, and while it gave forewarning of the rich curves spreading outward from here to the hips it had, in itself, an appearance only of restraint and proper discipline. The whiteness and richness of the stomach and hips was like milk brimming in a great bowl, and the sharply shadowed dip of the navel could have been the fresh impress of a raindrop, fallen there that very moment. Where the shadows gathered more thickly, hair clustered, gentle and sensitive, and as the agitation mounted in the now no longer passive body there hung over this region a scent like the smoldering of fragrant blossoms, growing steadily more pervasive.

At length, in a tremulous voice, Reiko spoke.

"Show me. . . . Let me look too, for the last time."

Never before had he heard from his wife's lips so strong and unequivocal a request. It was as if something which her modesty had wished to keep hidden to the end had suddenly burst its bonds of constraint. The lieutenant obediently lay back and surrendered himself to his wife. Lithely she raised her white, trembling body, and—burning with an innocent desire to return to her husband what he had done for her—placed two white fingers on the lieutenant's eyes, which gazed fixedly up at her, and gently stroked them shut.

Suddenly overwhelmed by tenderness, her cheeks flushed by a dizzying uprush of emotion, Reiko threw her arms about the lieutenant's close-cropped head. The bristly hairs rubbed painfully against her breast, the prominent nose was cold as it dug into her flesh, and his breath was hot. Relaxing her embrace, she gazed down at her husband's masculine face. The severe brows, the closed eyes, the splendid bridge of the nose, the shapely lips drawn firmly together . . . the blue, clean-shaven cheeks reflecting the light and gleaming smoothly. Reiko kissed each of these. She kissed the broad nape of the neck, the strong, erect shoulders, the powerful chest with its twin circles like shields and its russet nipples. In the armpits, deeply shadowed by the ample flesh of the shoulders and chest, a sweet and melancholy odor emanated from the growth of hair, and in the sweetness of this odor was contained, somehow, the essence of young death. The lieutenant's naked skin glowed like a field of barley, and everywhere the muscles showed in sharp relief, converging on the lower abdomen about the small, unassuming navel. Gazing at the youthful, firm stomach, modestly covered by a vigorous growth of hair, Reiko thought of it as it was soon to be, cruelly cut by the sword, and she laid her head upon it, sobbing in pity, and bathed it with kisses.

At the touch of his wife's tears upon his stomach the lieutenant felt ready to endure with courage the cruelest agonies of his suicide.

What ecstasies they experienced after these tender exchanges may well be imagined. The lieutenant raised himself and enfolded his wife in a powerful embrace, her body now limp with exhaustion after her grief and tears. Passionately they held their faces close, rubbing cheek against cheek. Reiko's body was trembling. Their breasts, moist with sweat, were tightly joined, and every inch of the young and beautiful bodies had become so much one with the other that it seemed impossible there should ever again be a separation. Reiko cried out. From the heights they plunged into the abyss, and from the abyss they took wing and soared once more the dizzying heights. The lieutenant panted like the regimental standard-bearer on a route march. . . . As one cycle ended, almost immediately a new wave of passion would be generated, and together—with no trace of fatigue—they would climb again in a single breathless movement to the very summit.

IV

When the lieutenant at last turned away, it was not from weariness. For one thing, he was anxious not to undermine the considerable strength he would need in carrying out his suicide. For another, he would have been sorry to mar the sweetness of these last memories by overindulgence.

Since the lieutenant had clearly desisted, Reiko too, with her usual compliance, followed his example. The two lay naked on their backs, with fingers interlaced, staring fixedly at the dark ceiling. The room was warm from the heater, and even when the sweat had ceased to pour from their bodies they felt no cold. Outside, in the hushed night, the sounds of passing traffic had ceased. Even the noise of the trains and streetcars around Yotsuya station did not penetrate this far. After echoing through the region bounded by the moat, they were lost in the heavily wooded park fronting the broad driveway before Akasaka Palace. It was hard to believe in the tension gripping this whole quarter, where the two factions of the bitterly divided Imperial Army now confronted each other, poised for battle.

Savoring the warmth glowing within themselves, they lay still and recalled the ecstasies they had just known. Each moment of the experience was relived. They remembered the taste of kisses which had never wearied, the touch of naked flesh, episode after episode of dizzying bliss. But already, from the dark boards of the ceiling, the face of death was peering down. These joys had been final, and their bodies would never know them again. Not that joy of this intensity—and the same thought had occurred to them both—was ever likely to be re-experienced, even if they should live on to old age.

The feel of their fingers intertwined—this too would soon be lost. Even the wood-grain patterns they now gazed at on the dark ceiling boards would be taken from them. They could feel death edging in, nearer and nearer. There could be no hesitation now. They must have the courage to reach out to death themselves, and to seize it.

"Well, let's make our preparations," said the lieutenant. The note of determination in the words was unmistakable, but at the same time Reiko had never heard her husband's voice so warm and tender.

After they had risen, a variety of tasks awaited them.

The lieutenant, who had never once before helped with the bedding, now cheerfully slid back the door of the closet, lifted the mattress across the room by himself, and stowed it away inside.

Reiko turned off the gas heater and put away the lamp standard. During the lieutenant's absence she had arranged this room carefully, sweeping and dusting it to a fresh cleanness, and now—if one overlooked the rosewood table drawn into one corner—the eight-mat room gave all the appearance of a reception room ready to welcome an important guest.

"We've seen some drinking here, haven't we? With Kanō and Homma and Noguchi . . . "

"Yes, they were great drinkers, all of them."

"We'll be meeting them before long, in the other world. They'll tease us, I imagine, when they find I've brought you with me."

Descending the stairs, the lieutenant turned to look back into this calm, clean room, now brightly illuminated by the ceiling lamp. There floated across his mind the faces of the young officers who had drunk there, and laughed, and innocently bragged. He had never dreamed then that he would one day cut open his stomach in this room.

In the two rooms downstairs husband and wife busied themselves smoothly and serenely with their respective preparations. The lieutenant went to the toilet, and then to the bathroom to wash. Meanwhile Reiko folded away her husband's padded robe, placed his uniform tunic, his trousers, and a newly cut bleached loincloth in the bathroom, and set out sheets of paper on the living-room table for the farewell notes. Then she removed the lid from the writing box and began rubbing ink from the ink tablet. She had already decided upon the wording of her own note.

Reiko's fingers pressed hard upon the cold gilt letters of the ink tablet, and the water in the shallow well at once darkened, as if a black cloud had spread across it. She stopped thinking that this repeated action, the pressure from her fingers, this rise and fall of faint sound, was all and solely for death. It was a routine domestic task, a simple paring away of time until death should finally stand before her. But somehow, in the increasingly smooth motion of the tablet rubbing on the stone, and in the scent from the thickening ink, there was unspeakable darkness.

Neat in his uniform, which he now wore next to his skin, the lieutenant emerged from the bathroom. Without a word he seated himself at the table, bolt upright, took a brush in his hand, and stared undecidedly at the paper before him.

Reiko took a white silk kimono with her and entered the bathroom. When she reappeared in the living room, clad in the white kimono and with her face lightly made up, the farewell note lay completed on the table beneath the lamp. The thick black brushstrokes said simply:

"Long Live the Imperial Forces—Army Lieutenant Takeyama Shinji."

While Reiko sat opposite him writing her own note, the lieutenant gazed in silence, intensely serious, at the controlled movement of his wife's pale fingers as they manipulated the brush.

With their respective notes in their hands—the lieutenant's sword strapped to his side, Reiko's small dagger thrust into the sash of her white kimono—the two of them stood before the god shelf and silently prayed. Then they put out all the downstairs lights. As he mounted the stairs the lieutenant turned his head and gazed back at the striking, white-clad figure of his wife, climbing behind him, with lowered eyes, from the darkness beneath.

The farewell notes were laid side by side in the alcove of the upstairs room. They wondered whether they ought not to remove the hanging scroll, but since it had been written by their go-between, Lieutenant General Ozeki, and consisted, moreover, of two Chinese characters signifying "Sincerity," they left it where it was. Even if it were to become stained with splashes of blood, they felt that the lieutenant general would understand.

The lieutenant, sitting erect with his back to the alcove, laid his sword on the floor before him.

Reiko sat facing him, a mat's width away. With the rest of her so severely white the touch of rouge on her lips seemed remarkably seductive.

Across the dividing mat they gazed intently into each other's eyes. The lieutenant's sword lay before his knees. Seeing it, Reiko recalled their first night and was overwhelmed with sadness. The lieutenant spoke, in a hoarse voice:

"As I have no second to help me I shall cut deep. It may look unpleasant, but please do not panic. Death of any sort is a fearful thing to watch. You must not be discouraged by what you see. Is that all right?"

"Yes."

Reiko nodded deeply.

Looking at the slender white figure of his wife the lieutenant experienced a bizarre excitement. What he was about to perform was an act in his public capacity as a soldier, something he had never previously shown his wife. It called for a resolution equal to the courage to enter battle; it was a death of no less degree and quality than death in the front line. It was his conduct on the battlefield that he was now to display.

Momentarily the thought led the lieutenant to a strange fantasy. A lonely death on the battlefield, a death beneath the eyes of his beautiful wife . . . in the sensation that he was now to die in these two dimensions, realizing an impossible union of them both, there was sweetness beyond words. This must be the very pinnacle of good fortune, he thought. To have every moment of his death observed by those beautiful eyes—it was like being borne to death on a gentle, fragrant breeze. There was some special favor here. He did not understand precisely what it was, but it was a domain unknown to others: a dispensation granted to no one else had been permitted to himself. In the radiant, bridelike figure of his white-robed wife the lieutenant seemed to see a vision of all those things he had loved and for which he was to lay down his life—the Imperial Household, the Nation, the Army Flag. All these, no less than the wife who sat before him, were presences observing him closely with clear and never-faltering eyes.

Reiko too was gazing intently at her husband, so soon to die, and she thought that never in this world had she seen anything so beautiful. The lieutenant always looked well in uniform, but now, as he comtemplated death with severe brows and firmly closed lips, he revealed what was perhaps masculine beauty at its most superb.

"It's time to go," the lieutenant said at last.

Reiko bent her body low to the mat in a deep bow. She could not raise her face. She did not wish to spoil her make-up with tears, but the tears could not be held back.

When at length she looked up she saw hazily through the tears that her husband had wound a white bandage around the blade of his now unsheathed sword, leaving five or six inches of naked steel showing at the point.

Resting the sword in its cloth wrapping on the mat before him, the lieutenant rose from his knees, resettled himself cross-legged, and unfastened the hooks of his uniform collar. His eyes no longer saw his wife. Slowly, one by one, he undid the flat brass buttons. The dusky brown chest was revealed, and then the stomach. He unclasped his belt and undid the buttons of his trousers. The pure whiteness of the thickly coiled loincloth showed itself. The lieutenant pushed the cloth down with both hands, further to ease his stomach, and then reached for the white-bandaged blade of his sword. With his left hand he massaged his abdomen, glancing downward as he did so.

To reassure himself on the sharpness of his sword's cutting edge the lieutenant folded back the left trouser flap, exposing a little of his thigh, and lightly drew the blade across the skin. Blood welled up in the wound at once, and several streaks of red trickled downward, glistening in the strong light.

It was the first time Reiko had ever seen her husband's blood, and she felt a violent throbbing in her chest. She looked at her husband's face. The lieutenant was looking at the blood with calm appraisal. For a moment—though thinking at the same time that it was hollow comfort—Reiko experienced a sense of relief.

The lieutenant's eyes fixed his wife with an intense, hawk-like stare. Moving the sword around to his front, he raised himself slightly on his hips and let the upper half of his body lean over the sword point. That he was mustering his whole strength was apparent from the angry tension of the uniform at his shoulders. The lieutenant aimed to strike deep into the left of his stomach. His sharp cry pierced the silence of the room.

Despite the effort he had himself put into the blow, the lieutenant had the impression that someone else had struck the side of his stomach agonizingly with a thick rod of iron. For a second or so his head reeled and he had no idea what had happened. The five or six inches of naked point had vanished completely into his flesh, and the white bandage, gripped in his clenched fist, pressed directly against his stomach.

He returned to consciousness. The blade had certainly pierced the wall of the stomach, he thought. His breathing was difficult, his chest thumped violently, and in some far deep region, which he could hardly believe was a part of himself, a fearful and excruciating pain came welling up as if the ground had split open to disgorge a boiling stream of molten rock. The pain came suddenly nearer, with terrifying speed. The lieutenant bit his lower lip and stifled an instinctive moan.

Was this *seppuku*?—he was thinking. It was a sensation of utter chaos, as if the sky had fallen on his head and the world was reeling drunkenly. His will power and courage, which had seemed so robust before he made the incision, had now dwindled to something like a single hairlike thread of steel, and he was assailed by the uneasy feeling that he must advance along this thread, clinging to it with desperation. His clenched fist had grown moist. Looking down, he saw that both his hand and the cloth about the blade were drenched in blood. His loincloth too was dyed a deep red. It struck him as incredible that, amidst this terrible agony, things which could be seen could still be seen, and existing things existed still.

The moment the lieutenant thrust the sword into his left side and she saw the deathly pallor fall across his face, like an abruptly lowered curtain, Reiko had to struggle to prevent herself from rushing to his side. That was the duty her husband had laid upon her. Opposite her, a mat's space away, she could clearly see her husband biting his lip to stifle the pain. The pain was there, with absolute certainty, before her eyes. And Reiko had no means of rescuing him from it.

The sweat glistened on her husband's forehead. The lieutenant closed his eyes, and then opened them again, as if experimenting. The eyes had lost their luster, and seemed innocent and empty like the eyes of a small animal.

The agony before Reiko's eyes burned as strong as the summer sun, utterly remote from the grief which seemed to be tearing herself apart within. The pain grew steadily in stature, stretching upward. Reiko felt that her husband had already become a man in a separate world, a man whose whole being had been resolved into pain, a prisoner in a cage of pain where no hand could reach out to him. But Reiko felt no pain at all. Her grief was not pain. As she thought about this, Reiko began to feel as if someone had raised a cruel wall of glass high between herself and her husband.

Ever since her marriage her husband's existence had been her own existence, and every breath of his had been a breath drawn by herself. But now, while her husband's existence in pain was a vivid reality, Reiko could find in this grief of hers no certain proof at all of her own existence.

With only his right hand on the sword the lieutenant began to cut sideways across his stomach. But as the blade became entangled with the entrails it was pushed constantly outward by their soft resilience; and the lieutenant realized that it would be necessary, as he cut, to use both hands to keep the point pressed deep into his stomach. He pulled the blade across. It did not cut as easily as he had expected. He directed the strength of his whole body into his right hand and pulled again. There was a cut of three or four inches.

The pain spread slowly outward from the inner depths until the whole stomach reverberated. It was like the wild clanging of a bell. Or like a thousand bells which jangled simultaneously at every breath he breathed and every throb of his pulse, rocking his whole being. The lieutenant could no longer stop himself from moaning. But by now the blade had cut its way through to below the navel, and when he noticed this he felt a sense of satisfaction, and a renewal of courage.

The volume of blood had steadily increased, and now it spurted from the wound as if propelled by the beat of the pulse. The mat before the lieutenant was drenched red with splattered blood, and more blood overflowed onto it from pools which gathered in the folds of the lieutenant's khaki trousers. A spot, like a bird, came flying across to Reiko and settled on the lap of her white silk kimono.

By the time the lieutenant had at last drawn the sword across to the right side of his stomach, the blade was already cutting shallow and had revealed its naked tip, slippery with blood and grease. But, suddenly stricken by a fit of vomiting, the lieutenant cried out hoarsely. The vomiting made the fierce pain fiercer still, and the stomach, which had thus far remained firm and compact, how abruptly heaved, opening wide its wound, and the entrails burst through, as if the wound too were vomiting. Seemingly ignorant of their master's suffering, the entrails gave an impression of robust health and almost disagreeable vitality as they slipped smoothly out and spilled over into the crotch. The lieutenant's head dropped, his shoulders heaved, his eyes opened to narrow slits, and a thin trickle of saliva dribbled from his mouth. The gold markings on his epaulettes caught the light and glinted.

Blood was scattered everywhere. The lieutenant was soaked in it to his knees, and he sat now in a crumpled and listless posture, one hand on the floor. A raw smell filled the room. The lieutenant, his head drooping, retched repeatedly, and the movement showed vividly in his shoulders. The blade of the sword, now pushed back by the entrails and exposed to its tip, was still in the lieutenant's right hand.

It would be difficult to imagine a more heroic sight than that of the lieutenant at this moment, as he mustered his strength and flung back his head. The movement was performed with sudden violence, and the back of his head struck with a sharp crack against the alcove pillar. Reiko had been sitting until now with her face lowered, gazing in fascination at the tide of blood advancing toward her knees, but the sound took her by surprise and she looked up.

The lieutenant's face was not the face of a living man. The eyes were hollow, the skin parched, the once so lustrous cheeks and lips the color of dried mud. The right hand alone was moving. Laboriously gripping the sword, it hovered shakily in the air like the hand of a marionette and strove to direct the point at the base of the lieutenant's throat. Reiko watched her husband make this last, most heart-rending, futile exertion. Glistening with blood and grease, the point was thrust at the throat again and again. And each time it missed its aim. The strength to guide it was no longer there. The straying point struck the collar and collar badges. Although its hooks had been unfastened, the stiff military collar had closed together again and was protecting the throat.

Reiko could bear the sight no longer. She tried to go to her husband's help, but she could not stand. She moved through the blood on her knees, and her white skirts grew deep red. Moving to the rear of her husband, she helped no more than by loosening the collar. The quivering blade at last contacted the naked flesh of the throat. At that moment Reiko's impression was that she herself had propelled her husband forward; but that was not the case. It was a movement planned by the lieutenant himself, his last exertion of strength. Abruptly he threw his body at the blade, and the blade pierced his neck, emerging at the nape. There was a tremendous spurt of blood and the lieutenant lay still, cold blue-tinged steel protruding from his neck at the back.

V

Slowly, her socks slippery with blood, Reiko descended the stairway. The upstairs room was now completely still.

Switching on the ground-floor lights, she checked the gas jet and the main gas plug and poured water over the smoldering, half-buried charcoal in the brazier. She stood before the upright mirror in the four-and-a-half-mat room and held up her skirts. The bloodstains made it seem as if a bold, vivid pattern was printed across the lower half of her white kimono. When she sat down before the mirror, she was conscious of the dampness and coldness of her husband's blood in the region of her thighs, and she shivered. Then, for a long while, she lingered over her toilet preparations. She applied the rouge generously to her cheeks, and her lips too she painted heavily. This was no longer make-up to please her husband. It was make-up for the world which she would leave behind, and there was a touch of the magnificent and the spectacular in her brushwork. When she rose, the mat before the mirror was wet with blood. Reiko was not concerned about this.

Returning from the toilet, Reiko stood finally on the cement floor of the porchway. When her husband had bolted the door here last night it had been in preparation for death. For a while she stood immersed in the consideration of a simple problem. Should she now leave the bolt drawn? If she were to lock the door, it could be that the neighbors might not notice their suicide for several days. Reiko did not relish the thought of their two corpses putrifying before discovery. After all, it seemed, it would be best to leave it open. . . . She released the bolt, and also drew open the frosted-glass door a fraction. . . . At once a chill wind blew in. There was no sign of anyone in the midnight streets, and stars glittered ice-cold through the trees in the large house opposite.

Leaving the door as it was, Reiko mounted the stairs. She had walked here and there for some time and her socks were no longer slippery. About halfway up, her nostrils were already assailed by a peculiar smell.

The lieutenant was lying on his face in a sea of blood. The point protruding from his neck seemed to have grown even more prominent than before. Reiko walked heedlessly across the blood. Sitting beside the lieutenant's corpse, she stared intently at the face, which lay on one cheek on the mat. The eyes were opened wide, as if the lieutenant's attention had been attracted by something. She raised the head, folding it in her sleeve, wiped the blood from the lips, and bestowed a last kiss.

Then she rose and took from the closet a new white blanket and a waist cord. To prevent any derangement of her skirts, she wrapped the blanket about her waist and bound it there firmly with the cord.

Reiko sat herself on a spot about one foot distant from the lieutenant's body. Drawing the dagger from her sash, she examined its dully gleaming blade intently, and held it to her tongue. The taste of the polished steel was slightly sweet.

Reiko did not linger. When she thought how the pain which had previously opened such a gulf between herself and her dying husband was now to become a part of her own experience, she saw before her only the joy of herself entering a realm her husband had already made his own. In her husband's agonized face there had been something inexplicable which she was seeing for the first time. Now she would solve the riddle. Reiko sensed that at last she too would be able to taste the true bitterness and sweetness of that great moral principle in which her husband believed. What had until now been tasted only faintly through her husband's example she was about to savor directly with her own tongue.

Reiko rested the point of the blade against the base of her throat. She thrust hard. The wound was only shallow. Her head blazed, and her hands shook uncontrollably. She gave the blade a strong pull sideways. A warm substance flooded into her mouth, and everything before her reddened, in a vision of spouting blood. She gathered her strength and plunged the point of the blade deep into her throat.

Three Sketches from
House Made of Dawn

N. SCOTT MOMADAY

I
THE SPARROW AND THE REED

I'm not sure how it was. He talked about it sometimes, not much. It might have been like this:

The river lies in a valley of hills and fields. The north end of the valley is narrow, and the river runs down from the mountains through a canyon. The sun strikes the canyon floor only a few hours each day, and in winter the snow remains for a long time in the crevices of the walls. There is a town in the valley, and there are ruins of other towns in the canyon. In three directions from the town there are cultivated fields. Most of them lie to the west, across the river, on the slope of the plain. Now and then in winter, great angles of geese fly through the valley, and then the sky and the geese are the same color and the air is hard and damp and smoke rises from the houses of the town. In summer the valley is hot, and birds come to the tamarack on the river. The feathers of blue and yellow birds are prized by the townsmen.

The fields are small and irregular, and from the west mesa they seem an intricate patchwork of arbors and gardens, too numerous for the town. The townsmen work all summer in the fields. When the moon is full they work at night with ancient, handmade plows and hoes, and if the weather is good and the water plentiful they take a good harvest from the fields. They grow the things that can be preserved easily, corn and chili and alfalfa. On the town side of the river there are a few orchards and patches of melons and grapes and squash. Every four or five years there is a harvest of

717

pinons far to the east of the town. That harvest, like the deer in the mountains, is the gift of God.

Early in July, 1946, the old man Francisco drove a team of roan mares near the place where the river bends around a cottonwood. The sun shone on the sand and the river and the leaves of the tree, and waves of heat shimmered from the stones. The colored stones on the bank of the river were small and smooth, and they rubbed together and cracked under the wagon wheels. Once in a while one of the roan mares tossed its head, and the commotion of its dark mane sent a swarm of flies into the air. Downstream the brush grew thick on a sandbar in the river, and there Francisco saw the reed. He turned the mares into the water and stepped down on the bar. A sparrow hung from the reed. It was upside down and its wings were partly open and the feathers at the back of its head lay spread in a tiny ruff. The eyes were neither open nor closed. Francisco drew the reed from the sand and cut loose the horsehair from the sparrow's feet. The bird fell into the water and was carried away in the current. He turned the reed in his hands; it was smooth and nearly translucent, like the spine of an eagle feather, and it had not yet been burned and made brittle by the sun and wind. He had cut the hair too short, and he pulled another from the tail of the near roan and set the snare again. When the reed was curved and strung like a bow, he replaced it carefully in the sand. He laid his forefinger lightly on top of the reed and the reed sprang and the looped end of the hair snapped across his finger and made a white line above the nail. "Si, bien hecho," he said aloud, and without removing the reed from the sand he cocked it again.

The sun rose higher and Francisco urged the mares away from the river. Then he was on the old road to San Ysidro. At times he sang and talked to himself above the noise of the wagon: "Yo heyana oh . . . heyana oh . . . heyana oh . . . Abelito, tarda en venir . . ." The mares pulled easily, with their heads low. He held a vague tension on the lines and settled into the ride by force of habit. A lizard ran across the road in front of the mares and crouched on a large flat rock, its tail curved over the edge. Far away a whirlwind moved toward the river, but it soon spun itself out and the air was again perfectly still.

He was alone on the wagon road. The pavement lay on a higher parallel at the base of the hills to the east. The trucks of the town—and those of the lumbermen from Paliza and Vallecitos—made an endless parade on the highway, but the wagon road was used only by the herdsmen and planters whose fields lay to the south and west. When he came to the place called Seytokwa, Francisco remembered the race for good hunting and harvests. Once he had played a part; he had been rubbed with soot, and he ran on the wagon road at dawn. He ran so hard that he could feel the sweat fly from his head and arms, though it was winter and the air was filled with snow. He ran until his breath burned in his throat and his feet rose and fell in a strange repetition that seemed apart from all his effort. At last he had overtaken Mariano, who was everywhere supposed to be the best of the runners. For a long way Mariano kept just beyond his reach; then, as they drew near to the corrals on the edge of the town, Francisco picked up the pace. He drew even and saw for an instant Mariano's face, wet and contorted in defeat . . . "Se dió por vencido" . . . and he struck it with his hand, leaving a black smear across the mouth and jaw. And Mariano fell and was exhausted. Francisco held his stride all the way to the Middle, and even then he could have run on, for nothing more than the sake of running on. And that year he killed seven bucks and seven does. Some years afterward, when he was no longer young and his legs had been stiffened by disease, he made a pencil drawing on the first page of a ledgerbook which he kept with his store of prayer feathers in the rafters of his room. It was the likeness of a straight, black man running in the snow. Beneath it was the legend 1889.

He crossed the river below the bridge at San Ysidro. The roan mares strained as they brought the wagon up the embankment and onto the pavement. It was nearly noon. The doors of the houses were closed against the heat, and even the usual, naked children who sometimes shouted and made fun of him had gone inside. Here and there a dog, content to have found a little shade, raised its head to look but remained outstretched and quiet. Well before he came to the junction, he could hear the slow whine of tires on the Cuba and Bloomfield road. It was a strange sound; it began at a high and descending pitch, passed, and rose again to become at last inaudible, lost in the near clatter of the rig and the hooves—lost even in the slow, directionless motion of the flies. But it was recurrent; another, and another; and he turned into the intersection and drove on the trading post. He had come about seven miles.

A few minutes past One, the bus came over a rise far down in the plain, and its windows caught for a moment the light of the sun. It grew in his vision until he looked away and limped round in a vague circle and smoothed the front of his new shirt with his hands. "Abelito, Abelito," he repeated under his breath, and he glanced at the wagon and the mares to be sure that everything was in order. He could feel the beat of his heart, and instinctively he drew himself up in the dignity of his age. He heard the sharp wheeze of the brakes as the big bus rolled to a stop in front of the gas pumps, and only then did he give attention to it, as if it had taken him by surprise. The door swung open and Abel stepped heavily to the ground and reeled. He was drunk, and he fell against his grandfather and did not know him. His wet lips hung loose and his eyes were half closed and rolling. Francisco's crippled legs nearly gave way. His good straw hat fell off and he braced himself against the weight of his grandson. Tears came to his eyes, and he knew only that he must laugh and turn away from the faces in the windows of the bus. He held Abel upright and led him to the wagon, listening as the bus at last moved away and its tires began to sing upon the road.

On the way back to the town Abel lay ill in the bed of the wagon and Francisco sat bent to the lines. The mares went a little faster on the way home, and near the bridge a yellow dog came out to challenge them.

II
HOMECOMING

Abel slept through the day and night in his grandfather's house. With the first light of dawn he arose and went out. He walked swiftly through the dark streets of the town and all the dogs began to bark. He passed through the maze of corrals and crossed the highway and climbed the steep escarpment of the hill. Then he was high above the town and he could see the whole of the valley growing light and the far mesas and the sunlight on the crest of the mountain. In the early morning the land lay huge and sluggish, discernible only as a whole, with nothing in relief except its own sheer, brilliant margin as far away as the eye could see, and beyond that the nothingness of the sky. Silence lay like water on the land, and even the frenzy of the dogs below was feeble and a long time in finding the ear.

"Yahah!" he had yelled when he was five years old, and he climbed up on the horse behind Vidal and they went out with Francisco and the others—some in covered wagons, but most on foot and horseback—across the river to the cacique's field. It was a warm spring morning, and he and Vidal ran ahead of the planters over the cool, dark furrows of earth and threw stones at the birds in the gray cottonwoods and elms. Vidal took him to the face of the red mesa and into a narrow box canyon which he had never seen before. The bright red walls were deep, deeper than he could have imagined, and they seemed to close over him. When they came to the end it was dark and cool as a cave. Once he looked up at the crooked line of the sky and saw that a cloud was passing, and its motion seemed to be that of the great leaning walls themselves and he was afraid and cried. When they returned he went to his grandfather and watched him work. It was nearly finished, and the men broke the wall of the ditch, and he stood there watching the foaming brown water creep among the furrows and go into the broken earth.

His mother had come in the wagon with Francisco and she had made oven bread and rabbit stew and coffee and round, blue cornmeal cakes filled with jam, coarse and faintly sweet, like figs. They ate upon the ground in families, all but the cacique and the governor and the other officials of the town, who sat at the place of honor nearest the trees. His father was a Sia, they said, or a Santa Ana, or a Cochiti—an outsider anyway—which made him and his mother and Vidal somehow foreign and strange. Francisco was the man of the family, but even then he was old and going lame. And even then the boy could sense his grandfather's age, just as he knew somehow that his mother was soon going to die of her illness. It was nothing he was told, but he knew it anyway and without understanding, as he knew already the sun's motion and the seasons. He was tired then, and he rode home in the wagon beside his mother and closed his eyes and listened to his grandfather sing. His mother died in October, and for a long time afterward he would not go near her grave, and he remembered that she had been beautiful in a way that he as well as others could see and her voice had been as soft as water.

They called the old woman that, Nicholas teah-whau, because she had a white moustache and a hunched back and she would beg for whisky. She was a Pecos woman, they said, and a witch. She was old the first time he had seen her, and drunk. She had screamed at him some unintelligible curse, appearing out of a cornfield, when as a child he had herded the sheep nearby. And he had run away, hard, until he came to a clump of mesquite on the bank of an arroyo. There he caught his breath and waited for the snake-killer dog to close the flock and follow. Later, when the sheep had filed into the arroyo and from the bank he could see them all, he dropped a little bread for the snake-killer dog, but the dog quivered and laid back its ears. Slowly it backed away and crouched, not looking at him, not looking at anything, but listening. Then he heard the thing itself. He knew even then that it was only the wind, but it was a stranger sound than any he had ever known. And at the same time he saw the hole in the rock where the wind dipped, struck, and rose. It was larger than a rabbit hole and partly concealed by the choke cherry which grew beside it. The moan of the wind grew loud, and it filled him with dread. For the rest of his life it would be for him the particular sound of anguish.

Francisco nudged him awake, and he dressed himself in the bitter cold. He was—how old?—seventeen then, and he had hunted in clear weather like this and risen as early in order to be near the stream at daybreak. Yes, and the first to come was a mule doe, small and longhaired, unsuspecting, but full of latent flight. He brought the rifle up with no sound that he could hear, but the doe's head sprang up and its body stiffened. Then he stood and the doe exploded away. The crack of the rifle reverberated among the trees, and he ran to the place where the ground had been scarcely marked but for the two small tracks against which the doe had driven itself up and out through the branches. But farther on there was blood, and then the doe itself, lying across the trunk of a dead tree with its tongue out and the wound full of hot blood, welling out.

Francisco had already hitched the team to the wagon, and they set out. That was January 1, 1937. The moon and stars were out, and there was yet no sign of the dawn. His face burned with the cold and he huddled over and blew into his hands. And part of the way he ran beside the horses, swinging his arms and scaring them to a trot. At Sia they waited in the house of Juan Medina for the dawn. It was nearly then, and Juan built a fire and gave them coffee. The deer and antelope had already gone into the hills, and the crows were dressing in the kiva. When it was gray outside they went to the Middle, and there were already some people there, Navajos and Domingos in blankets, smoking. The singing had begun. Directly the sun shone and the deer and antelope ran down from the hills and the crows and buffalo and singers came out and began to dance. A lot of men had rifles, and they fired them in the air. He watched the black, half-naked crows, hopping and stooping, and he thought of how cold they must be with the big, gleaming conchos, like ice, pressing into their bellies and backs. But it was all right; it was good, that dance.

Later, when he had drunk some wine, one of Medina's daughters lay down with him out of the town, on a dune by the river. She was laughing all the time, and he too, though the wine had made him nearly sullen and his laughter was put on and there was nothing to it. Her body, when it shuddered and then went limp, was not enough for him and he wanted her again, but she dressed and ran from him and he could not catch her because his legs would not work for him and she stood away and laughed.

You ought to do this and that, Francisco said.

The silent land bore in upon him as, little by little, it got hold of the light and shone. The pale margin of the night receded toward him like a rising drift, and he waited for it. All the rims of color stood out upon the hills, and the hills converged at the mouth of the canyon. That dark cleft might have been a shadow or a pool of smoke; there was nothing to suggest its distance or its depth, but it held the course of the river for twenty or thirty miles. The town lay for a time on the verge of the day; then the spire of the mission gleamed and the Angelus rang and the riverside houses flamed. Still the cold clung to him and the night was at his back. There, to the east, the earth was ashen and the sky on fire. The contour of the black mesa was clean where the sun ranged like a cloud in advance of the solstices.

A car appeared on the hills: it moved in and out of his vision and toward the town and made no sound until it was directly below him. Then it turned into the town and wound through the streets and into the trees at the mission. Roosters began to crow and the townspeople stirred and their thin voices rose on the air. He could smell the sweet wine which kept still to his clothing. He had not eaten in two days, and his mouth tasted of sickness. But the morning was cold and deep, and he rubbed his hands together and felt the blood rise and flow.

He stood for a long time, the land still yielding to the light. He stood without thinking, nor did he move; only his eyes ranged after something he should and should not have seen. The white escarpment dropped under him like the lee of a dune thirty feet to the highway. The last patches of shade vanished from the river bottom and the chill grew dull on the air. He picked his way down the hill and the earth and stones rolled at his feet. He felt a tension at his knees, and then the weight of the sun on his head and hands. The dry light of the valley caught him up, and the land became hard and pale.

III
THE ALBINO

The late afternoon of the *corre de gaio* was still and hot, and there were no clouds in the sky. The river was low, and the grape leaves had begun to curl in the fire of the sun. The pale yellow grass on the river plain was tall, for the cattle and sheep had been taken to graze in the high meadows, and alkali lay like frost in the cracked beds of the irrigation ditches. It was a pale, midsummer day, two or three hours before sundown.

Father Bothene went with his mother and sister out of the rectory. They walked slowly, talking together, along the street which ran up-hill towards the Middle. There were houses along the north side of the street, patches of grapes and corn and melons on the south. There had been no rain in the valley for a long time, and the dust was deep in the street. By one of the houses a thin old man tended his long hair, careless of their passing. He was bent forward, and his hair reached nearly to the ground. His head was cocked, so that the hair hung all together on one side of his face and in front of the shoulder. He brushed slowly the inside of it, downward from the ear, with a bunch of quills. His hands worked easily, intimately, with the coarse, shining hair, in which there was no appearance of softness, except that light moved upon it as on a pouring of oil.

They saw faces in the dark windows and doorways of the houses, half in hiding, watching with wide, solemn eyes. They lagged behind, mother and son, and Angela drew away from them a little. She was among the houses of the town, and there was an excitement all around, a ceaseless murmur under the sound of the drum, lost in back of the walls, apart from the dead, silent light of the afternoon. When she had got too far ahead she waited beside a windmill and a trough, around which there was a muddy, black ring, filled with the tracks of animals. In July the town smelt of animals, and smoke, and sawn lumber, and the sweet, moist smell of bread that has been cut open and left to stand.

When they came to the Middle there was a lot of sound going on. The people of the town had begun to gather along the walls of the houses, and a group of small boys were tumbling on the ground and shouting. The Middle was an ancient place, nearly a hundred yards long and forty wide. The smooth, packed earth was not flat, as it appeared at first to be, but rolling and concave, rising slightly to the walls around it so that there were no edges or angles in the dry clay of the ground and the houses; there were only the soft contours and depressions of things worn down and away in time. From within, the space appeared to be inclosed, but there were narrow passages at the four corners and a wide opening midway along the south side, where once there had been a house; there was now a low, uneven ruin of earthen bricks, nearly indistinguishable from the floor and the back wall of the deep recess. There Angela and the Bothenes entered and turned, waiting, conscious of themselves, to be absorbed in the sound and motion of the town. The oldest houses, those at the west end and on the north side, were tiered two and three storeys high, and clusters of men stood about on the roofs. The drummer was there, on a rooftop, beating still on the drum, slowly, exactly in time, with only a quick, nearly imperceptible motion of the hand, standing perfectly still and even-eyed, old and imperturbable. Just there, in sight of him, the deep vibration of the drum seemed to Angela scarcely louder, deeper, than it had an hour before and a mile away, when she was in a room of the rectory, momentarily alone with it and borne upon it. And it would not have seemed less had she been at the river or among the hills; the drum held sway in the valley, like the breaking of thunder far away, echoing on and on in a region out of time. One has only to take it for granted, she thought, like a storm coming up, and the certain, rare downfall of rain. She pulled away from it and caught sight of window frames, blue and white, ovens like the hives of bees, dogs and flies. Equidistant from the walls of the Middle there was a fresh hole in the ground, about eight inches in diameter, and a small mound of sandy earth.

In a little while the riders came into the west end in groups of three and four, on their best animals. There were seven or eight men and as many boys. They crossed the width of the Middle and doubled back in single file along the wall. Abel rode one of his grandfather's roan, black-maned mares and sat too rigid in the saddle, too careful of the gentle mare. He had put on his old clothes, Levi's and a wide black belt, a gray work shirt and a straw hat with a low crown and wide, rolled brim. His sleeves were rolled high, and his arms and hands were newly sunburned. One of the men was white, and he wore little round colored glasses and rode a fine black horse of good blood. The black horse was high-spirited, and the white man held its head high on the reins and kept the stirrups free of it. He was the last in line, and when he had taken his place with the others in the shade of the wall, an official of the town brought a large white rooster from one of the houses. He placed it in the hole and moved the dirt in upon it until it was buried to the neck. Its white head jerked from side to side, so that its comb and wattles shook and its hackles were spread on the sand. The townspeople laughed to see it so, buried and fearful, its round, unblinking eyes yellow and bright in the dying day. The official moved away and the first horse and rider bolted from the shade. Then one at a time the others rode down upon the rooster and reached for it, holding to the horns of their saddles and leaning sharply down against the shoulders of their mounts. Most of the animals were untrained, and they drew up when their riders leaned. One, then another of the boys fell to the ground, and the townspeople jeered in delight. When it came Abel's turn he made a poor showing, full of caution and gesture. Angela despised him a little; she remembered that, but her attention was spread over the whole, fantastic scene, and she felt herself going limp. With the rush of the first horse all of her senses were struck at once. The sun, low and growing orange, burned on her face and arms; she closed her eyes, but it was there still, the brilliant disorder of motion: the dark and darker gold of the earth and earthen walls and the deep incisions of shade and the vague, violent procession of centaurs. So unintelligible the sharp sound of voices and hooves, the odor of animals and sweat; so empty of meaning it all was, and yet so full of appearance. As I, too, she thought, and when he passed in front of her at a walk, on his way back, she was ready again to deceive. She smiled to him and looked away.

The white man was large and thick-set, powerful and deliberate in his movements. The black horse started fast and ran easily, even as the white man leaned down from it. He got hold of the rooster and took it from the ground. Then he was upright in the saddle, suddenly, without once having shifted the center of his weight from the spine of the running horse. He reined in hard, so that the animal tucked its haunches and its hooves ploughed in the ground. Angela thrilled to see it handled so, as if the white man were its will and all its shivering force drawn to his bow. A perfect commotion, full of symmetry and sound. And yet there was something out of place, some flaw in proportion or design, some mere unnatural thing. She keened to it, and an old fascination returned upon her. The black horse whirled; the white man looked down the Middle towards the other riders and held the rooster up and away in his left hand while its great wings beat the air. He started back on the dancing horse along the south wall, and the townspeople gave him room. Then he faced her, and Angela saw that under his hat the pale yellow hair was thin and cut close to the scalp; the tight skin of the head was visible and pale and pink. The face was huge and mottled white and pink, and the thick, open lips were violet and blue. The flesh of the jowls was loose, and it rode on the bone of the jaws. There were no brows, and the small, round, black glasses lay like pennies close together and flat against the enormous face. He was directly above her for one instant, huge and hideous at the extremity of the terrified bird. It was then her eyes were drawn to the heavy, bloodless hand at the throat of the bird. It was like marble or chert, equal in the composure of stone to the awful frenzy of the bird, and the bright wattles of the bird lay still among the long blue nails, and the comb on the swollen heel of the hand. And then he was past. He rode in among the riders, and they too parted for him, watching to see whom he would choose, wary, on edge. After a long time of playing the game, he rode beside Abel, turned suddenly upon him, and began to flail him with the rooster. Their horses wheeled; the others drew off. Again and again the white man struck him heavily, brutally, upon the chest and shoulders and head, and Abel threw up his hands, but the great bird fell upon them and beat them down. He was unused to the game, and the white man was too quick for him. The roan mare lunged, but it was hemmed in against the wall; the black horse lay close against it, keeping it off balance, coiled and wild in its eyes. The white man leaned and struck, back and forth, with only the malice of the act itself, careless, undetermined, almost composed in some final, preeminent sense. Then the bird was dead, and still he swung it down and across, and the neck of the bird was broken and the flesh torn open and the blood splashed everywhere about. The mare hopped and squatted and reared, and Abel hung on. The black horse stood its ground, cutting off every line of retreat, pressing upon the terrified mare. It was all a dream, a tumultuous shadow, and before it, the fading red glare of the sun on bits of silver and panes of glass and softer on the glowing, absorbent walls of the town. Then the feathers and flesh and entrails of the bird were scattered about on the ground, and the dogs crept near and crouched, and it was finished. Here and there the townswomen threw water to finish it in sacrifice.

It is in keeping, she thought afterwards, this vain convalescence. She was weary, and her feet slipped down in the sand of the street, and it was nearly beyond her to walk. Like this, her body had been left to recover without her when once, having wept, she had lain with David; and it had been the same sacrificial hour of the day. She had been too tired for guilt and gladness, and she lay for a long time on the edge of sleep, empty of the least desire, in the warm current of her blood. Like this, though she couldn't then have known—the sheer black land above the trees, the scarlet sky and the quarter-moon.

Slant-Eyed Americans

TOSHIO MORI

My mother was commenting on the fine California weather. It was Sunday noon, December 7. We were having our lunch, and I had the radio going. "Let's take the afternoon off and go to the city," I said to Mother.

"All right. We shall go," she said dreamily. "Ah, four months ago my boy left Hayward to join the army, and a fine send-off he had. Our good friends—ah, I shall never forget the day of his departure."

"We'll visit some of our friends in Oakland and then take in a movie," I said. "Care to come along, Papa?"

Father shook his head. "No, I'll stay home and take it easy."

"That's his heaven," Mother commented. "To stay home, read the papers over and over, and smoke his Bull Durham."

I laughed. Suddenly the musical program was cut off as a special announcement came over the air: At 7:25 a.m. this morning a squadron of Japanese bombing planes attacked Pearl Habor. The battle is still in progress.

"What's this? Listen to the announcement," I cried, going to the radio.

Abruptly the announcement stopped and the musicale continued.

"What is it?" Mother asked. "What has happened?"

"The radio reports that the Japanese planes attacked Hawaii this morning," I said incredulously. "It couldn't be true."

"It must be a mistake. Couldn't it have been a part of a play?" asked Mother.

I dialed other stations. Several minutes later one of the stations confirmed the bulletin.

"It must be true," Father said quietly.

I said, "Japan has declared war on the United States and Great Britain."

The room became quiet but for the special bulletin coming in every now and then.

727

"It cannot be true, yet it must be so," Father said over and over.

"Can it be one of those programs scaring the people about invasion?" Mother asked me.

"No, I'm sure this is a news report," I replied.

Mother's last ray of hope paled and her eyes became dull. "Why did it have to happen? The common people in Japan don't want war, and we don't want war. Here the people are peace-loving. Why cannot the peoples of the earth live together peacefully?"

"Since Japan declared war on the United States it'll mean that you parents of American citizens have become enemy aliens," I said.

"Enemy aliens," my mother whispered.

Night came but sleep did not come. We sat up late in the night hoping against hope that some good news would come, retracting the news of vicious attack and open hostilities.

"This is very bad for the people with Japanese faces," I said.

Father slowly shook his head.

"What shall we do?" asked Mother.

"What can we do?" Father said helplessly.

At the flower market next morning the growers were present but the buyers were scarce. The place looked empty and deserted. "Our business is shot to pieces," one of the boys said.

"Who'll buy flowers now?" another called.

Don Haley, the seedsman, came over looking bewildered. "I suppose you don't need seeds now."

We shook our heads.

"It looks bad," I said. "Will it affect your business?"

"Flower seed sale will drop but the vegetable seeds will move quicker," Don said. "I think I'll have to put more time on the vegetable seeds."

Nobu Hiramatsu who had been thinking of building another greenhouse joined us. He had plans to grow more carnations and expand his business.

"What's going to happen to your plans, Nobu?" asked one of the boys.

"Nothing. I'm going to sit tight and see how the things turn out," he said.

"Flowers and war don't go together," Don said. "You cannot concentrate too much on beauty when destruction is going about you."

"Sure, pretty soon we'll raise vegetables instead of flowers," Grasselli said.

A moment later the market opened and we went back to the table to sell our flowers. Several buyers came in and purchased a little. The flowers didn't move at all. Just as I was about to leave the place I met Tom Yamashita, the Nisei gardener with a future.

"What are you doing here, Tom? What's the matter with your work?" I asked as I noticed his pale face.

"I was too sick with yesterday's news so I didn't work," he said. "This is the end. I am done for."

"No, you're not. Buck up, Tom," I cried. "You have a good future, don't lose hope."

"Sometimes I feel all right. You are an American, I tell myself. Devote your energy and life to the American way of life. Long before this my mind was made up to become a true American. This morning my Caucasian American friends sympathized with me. I felt good and was grateful. Our opportunity has come to express ourselves and act. We are Americans in thought and action. I felt like leaping to work. Then I got sick again because I got to thinking that Japan was the country that attacked the United States. I wanted to bury myself for shame."

I put my hand on his shoulder. "We all feel the same way, Tom. We're human so we flounder around awhile when an unexpected and big problem confronts us, but now that situation has to be passed by. We can't live in the same stage long. We have to move along, face the reality no matter what's in store for us."

Tom stood silently.

"Let's go to my house and take the afternoon off," I suggested. "We'll face a new world tomorrow morning with boldness and strength. What do you say, Tom?"

"All right," Tom agreed.

At home Mother was anxiously waiting for me. When she saw Tom with me her eyes brightened. Tom Yamashita was a favorite of my mother's.

"Look, a telegram from Kazuo!" she cried to me, holding up an envelope. "Read it and tell me what he says."

I tore it open and read. "He wants us to send $45 for train fare. He has a good chance for a furlough."

Mother fairly leaped in the air with the news. She had not seen my brother for four months. "How wonderful! This can happen only in America."

Suddenly she noticed Tom looking glum, and pushed him in the house. "Cheer up, Tom. This is no time for young folks to despair. Roll up your sleeves and get to work. America needs you."

Tom smiled for the first time and looked at me.

"See, Tom?" I said. "She's quick to recover. Yesterday she was wilted, and she's seventy-three."

"Tom, did you go to your gardens today?" she asked him.

"No."

"Why not?" she asked, and then added quickly. "You young men should work hard all the more, keeping up the normal routine of life. You ought to know, Tom, that if everybody dropped their work everything would go to seed. Who's going to take care of the gardens if you won't?"

Tom kept still.

Mother poured tea and brought the cookies. "Don't worry about your old folks. We have stayed here to belong to the American way of life. Time will tell our true purpose. We remained in America for permanence—not for temporary convenience. We common people need not fear."

"I guess you are right," Tom agreed.

"And America is right. She cannot fail. Her principles will stand the test of time and tyranny. Someday aggression will be outlawed by all nations."

Mother left the room to prepare the dinner. Tom got up and began to walk up and down the room. Several times he looked out the window and watched the wind blow over the field.

"Yes, if the gardens are ruined I'll rebuild them," he said. "I'll take charge of every garden in the city. All the gardens of America for that matter. I'll rebuild them as fast as the enemies wreck them. We'll have nature on our side and you cannot crush nature."

I smiled and nodded. "Good for you! Tomorrow we'll get up early in the morning and work, sweat, and create. Let's shake on it."

We solemnly shook hands, and by the grip of his fingers I knew he was ready to lay down his life for America and for his gardens.

"No word from him yet," Mother said worriedly. "He should have arrived yesterday. What's happened to him?"

It was eight in the evening, and we had had no word from my brother for several days.

"He's not coming home tonight. It's too late now," I said. "He should have arrived in Oakland this morning at the latest."

Our work had piled up and we had to work late into the night. There were still some pompons to bunch. Faintly the phone rang in the house.

"The phone!" cried Mother excitedly. "It's Kazuo, sure enough."

In the flurry of several minutes I answered the phone, greeted my brother, and was on my way to San Leandro to drive him home. On the way I tried to think of the many things I wanted to say. From the moment I spotted him waiting on the corner I could not say the thing I wanted to. I took his bag and he got in the car, and for some time we did not say anything. Then I asked him how the weather had been in Texas and how he had been.

"We were waiting for you since yesterday," I said. "Mother is home getting the supper ready. You haven't eaten yet, have you?"

He shook his head. "The train was late getting into Los Angeles. We were eight hours behind time and I should have reached San Francisco this morning around eight."

Reaching home it was the same way. Mother could not say anything. "We have nothing special tonight, wish we had something good."

"Anything would do, Mama," my brother said.

Father sat in the room reading the papers but his eyes were over the sheet and his hands were trembling. Mother scurried about getting his supper ready. I sat across the table from my brother, and in the silence which was action I watched the wave of emotions in the room. My brother was aware of it too. He sat there without a word, but I knew he understood. Not many years ago he was the baby of the family, having never been away from home. Now he was on his own, his quiet confidence actually making him appear larger. Keep up the fire, that was his company's motto. It was evident that he was a soldier. He had gone beyond life and death matter, where the true soldiers of war or peace must travel, and had returned.

For five short days we went about our daily task, picking and bunching the flowers for Christmas, eating heavy meals, and visiting the intimates. It was as if we were waiting for the hour of his departure, the time being so short. Every minute was crowded with privacy, friends, and nursery work. Too soon the time for his train came but the family had little to talk.

"'Kazuo, don't worry about home or me," Mother said as we rode into town.

"Take care of yourself," my brother told her.

At the 16th Street Station Mother's close friend was waiting for us. She came to bid my brother good-bye. We had fifteen minutes to wait. My brother bought a copy of *The Coast* to see if his cartoons were in.

"Are you in this month's issue?" I asked.

"I haven't seen it yet," he said, leafing the pages. "Yes, I'm in. Here it is."

"Good!" I said. "Keep trying hard. Someday peace will come, and when you return laughter will reign once again."

My mother showed his cartoon to her friend. The train came in and we got up. It was a long one. We rushed to the Los Angeles-bound coach.

Mother's friend shook hands with my brother. "Give your best to America. Our people's honor depend on you Nisei soldiers."

My brother nodded and then glanced at Mother. For a moment her eyes twinkled and she nodded. He waved good-bye from the platform. Once inside the train we lost him. When the train began to move my mother cried, "Why doesn't he pull up the shades and look out? Others are doing it."

We stood and watched until the last of the train was lost in the night of darkness.

1919

TONI MORRISON

Except for World War II, nothing ever interfered with the celebration of
National Suicide Day. It had taken place every January third since 1920, although Shadrack, its founder, was for many years the only celebrant.
Blasted and permanently astonished by the events of 1917, he had returned to Medallion handsome but ravaged, and even the most fastidious
people in the town sometimes caught themselves dreaming of what he must
have been like a few years back before he went off to war. A young man of
hardly twenty, his head full of nothing and his mouth recalling the taste of
lipstick, Shadrack had found himself in December, 1917, running with his
comrades across a field in France. It was his first encounter with the enemy
and he didn't know whether his company was running toward them or
away. For several days they had been marching, keeping close to a stream
that was frozen at its edges. At one point they crossed it, and no sooner had
he stepped foot on the other side than the day was adangle with shouts and
explosions. Shellfire was all around him, and though he knew that this was
something called *it,* he could not muster up the proper feeling—the feeling
that would accommodate *it.* He expected to be terrified or exhilarated—to
feel *something* very strong. In fact, he felt only the bite of a nail in his boot,
which pierced the ball of his foot whenever he came down on it. The day
was cold enough to make his breath visible, and he wondered for a moment
at the purity and whiteness of his own breath among the dirty, gray explosions surrounding him. He ran, bayonet fixed, deep in the great sweep of
men flying across this field. Wincing at the pain in his foot, he turned his
head a little to the right and saw the face of a soldier near him fly off. Before he could register shock, the rest of the soldier's head disappeared under the inverted soup bowl of his helmet. But stubbornly, taking no
direction from the brain, the body of the headless soldier ran on, with energy and grace, ignoring altogether the drip and slide of brain tissue down
its back.

*　　*　　*

When Shadrack opened his eyes he was propped up in a small bed. Before him on a tray was a large tin plate divided into three triangles. In one triangle was rice, in another meat, and in the third stewed tomatoes. A small round depression held a cup of whitish liquid. Shadrack stared at the soft colors that filled these triangles: the lumpy whiteness of rice, the quivering blood tomatoes, the grayish-brown meat. All their repugnance was contained in the neat balance of the triangles—a balance that soothed him, transferred some of its equilibrium to him. Thus reassured that the white, the red and the brown would stay where they were—would not explode or burst forth from their restricted zones—he suddenly felt hungry and looked around for his hands. His glance was cautious at first, for he had to be very careful—anything could be anywhere. Then he noticed two lumps beneath the beige blanket on either side of his hips. With extreme care he lifted one arm and was relieved to find his hand attached to his wrist. He tried the other and found it also. Slowly he directed one hand toward the cup and, just as he was about to spread his fingers, they began to grow in higgledy-piggledy fashion like Jack's beanstalk all over the tray and the bed. With a shriek he closed his eyes and thrust his huge growing hands under the covers. Once out of sight they seemed to shrink back to their normal size. But the yell had brought a male nurse.

"Private? We're not going to have any trouble today, are we? Are we, Private?"

Shadrack looked up at a balding man dressed in a green-cotton jacket and trousers. His hair was parted low on the right side so that some twenty or thirty yellow hairs could discreetly cover the nakedness of his head.

"Come on. Pick up that spoon. Pick it up, Private. Nobody is going to feed you forever."

Sweat slid from Shadrack's armpits down his sides. He could not bear to see his hands grow again and he was frightened of the voice in the apple-green suit.

"Pick it up, I said. There's no point to this . . . ." The nurse reached under the cover for Shadrack's wrist to pull out the monstrous hand. Shadrack jerked it back and overturned the tray. In panic he raised himself to his knees and tried to fling off and away his terrible fingers, but succeeded only in knocking the nurse into the next bed.

When they bound Shadrack into a straitjacket, he was both relieved and grateful, for his hands were at last hidden and confined to whatever size they had attained.

Laced and silent in his small bed, he tried to tie the loose cords in his mind. He wanted desperately to see his own face and connect it with the word "private"—the word the nurse (and the others who helped bind him) had called him. "Private" he thought was something secret, and he wondered why they looked at him and called him a secret. Still, if his hands behaved as they had done, what might he expect from his face? The fear and

longing were too much for him, so he began to think of other things. That
is, he let his mind slip into whatever cave mouths of memory it chose.

He saw a window that looked out on a river which he knew was full of
fish. Someone was speaking softly just outside the door . . . . Shadrack's earlier violence had coincided with a memorandum from the hospital execu-
tive staff in reference to the distribution of patients in high-risk areas.
There was clearly a demand for space. The priority of the violence earned
Shadrack his release, $217 in cash, a full suit of clothes and copies of very
official-looking papers.

When he stepped out of the hospital door the grounds overwhelmed
him: the cropped shrubbery, the edged lawns, the undeviating walks. Shadrack looked at the cement stretches: each one leading clearheadedly to
some presumably desirable destination. There were no fences, no warnings, no obstacles at all between concrete and green grass, so one could easily ignore the tidy sweep of stone and cut out in another direction—a
direction of one's own.

Shadrack stood at the foot of the hospital steps watching the heads of
trees tossing ruefully but harmlessly, since their trunks were rooted too
deeply in the earth to threaten him. Only the walks made him uneasy. He
shifted his weight, wondering how he could get to the gate without stepping on the concrete. While plotting his course—where he would have to
leap, where to skirt a clump of bushes—a loud guffaw startled him. Two
men were going up the steps. Then he noticed that there were many people about, and that he was just now seeing them, or else they had just materialized. They were thin slips, like paper dolls floating down the walks.
Some were seated in chairs with wheels, propelled by other paper figures
from behind. All seemed to be smoking, and their arms and legs curved in
the breeze. A good high wind would pull them up and away and they
would land perhaps among the tops of the trees.

Shadrack took the plunge. Four steps and he was on the grass heading
for the gate. He kept his head down to avoid seeing the paper people
swerving and bending here and there, and he lost his way. When he looked
up, he was standing by a low red building separated from the main building by a covered walkway. From somewhere came a sweetish smell which
reminded him of something painful. He looked around for the gate and
saw that he had gone directly away from it in his complicated journey over
the grass. Just to the left of the low building was a graveled driveway that
appeared to lead outside the grounds. He trotted quickly to it and left, at
last, a haven of more than a year, only eight days of which he fully recollected.

Once on the road, he headed west. The long stay in the hospital had left
him weak—too weak to walk steadily on the gravel shoulders of the road.
He shuffled, grew dizzy, stopped for breath, started again, stumbling and
sweating but refusing to wipe his temples, still afraid to look at his hands.

Passengers in dark, square cars shuttered their eyes at what they took to be a drunken man.

The sun was already directly over his head when he came to a town. A few blocks of shaded streets and he was already at its heart—a pretty, quietly regulated downtown.

Exhausted, his feet clotted with pain, he sat down at the curbside to take off his shoes. He closed his eyes to avoid seeing his hands and fumbled with the laces of the heavy high-topped shoes. The nurse had tied them into a double knot, the way one does for children, and Shadrack, long unaccustomed to the manipulation of intricate things, could not get them loose. Uncoordinated, his fingernails tore away at the knots. He fought a rising hysteria that was not merely anxiety to free his aching feet; his very life depended on the release of the knots. Suddenly without raising his eyelids, he began to cry. Twenty-two years old, weak, hot, frightened, not daring to acknowledge the fact that he didn't even know who or what he was . . . with no past, no language, no tribe, no source, no address book, no comb, no pencil, no clock, no pocket handkerchief, no rug, no bed, no can opener, no faded postcard, no soap, no key, no tobacco pouch, no soiled underwear and nothing nothing nothing to do . . . he was sure of one thing only: the unchecked monstrosity of his hands. He cried soundlessly at the curbside of a small Midwestern town wondering where the window was, and the river, and the soft voices just outside the door . . .

Through his tears he saw the fingers joining the laces, tentatively at first, then rapidly. The four fingers of each hand fused into the fabric, knotted themselves and zig-zagged in and out of the tiny eyeholes.

By the time the police drove up, Shadrack was suffering from a blinding headache, which was not abated by the comfort he felt when the policemen pulled his hands away from what he thought was a permanent entanglement with his shoelaces. They took him to jail, booked him for vagrancy and intoxication, and locked him in a cell. Lying on a cot, Shadrack could only stare helplessly at the wall, so paralyzing was the pain in his head. He lay in this agony for a long while and then realized he was staring at the painted-over letters of a command to fuck himself. He studied the phrase as the pain in his head subsided.

Like moonlight stealing under a window shade an idea insinuated itself: his earlier desire to see his own face. He looked for a mirror; there was none. Finally, keeping his hands carefully behind his back he made his way to the toilet bowl and peeped in. The water was unevenly lit by the sun so he could make nothing out. Returning to his cot he took the blanket and covered his head, rendering the water dark enough to see his reflection. There in the toilet water he saw a grave black face. A black so definite, so unequivocal, it astonished him. He had been harboring a skittish apprehension that he was not real—that he didn't exist at all. But when the blackness greeted him with its indisputable presence, he wanted nothing more.

In his joy he took the risk of letting one edge of the blanket drop and glanced at his hands. They were still. Courteously still.

Shadrack rose and returned to the cot, where he fell into the first sleep of his new life. A sleep deeper than the hospital drugs; deeper than the pits of plums, steadier than the condor's wing; more tranquil than the curve of eggs.

The sheriff looked through the bars at the young man with the matted hair. He had read through his prisoner's papers and hailed a farmer. When Shadrack awoke, the sheriff handed him back his papers and escorted him to the back of a wagon. Shadrack got in and in less than three hours he was back in Medallion, for he had been only twenty-two miles from his window, his river, and his soft voices just outside the door.

In the back of the wagon, supported by sacks of squash and hills of pumpkins, Shadrack began a struggle that was to last for twelve days, a struggle to order and focus experience. It had to do with making a place for fear as a way of controlling it. He knew the smell of death and was terrified of it, for he could not anticipate it. It was not death or dying that frightened him, but the unexpectedness of both. In sorting it all out, he hit on the notion that if one day a year were devoted to it, everybody could get it out of the way and the rest of the year would be safe and free. In this manner he instituted National Suicide Day.

On the third day of the new year, he walked through the Bottom down Carpenter's Road with a cowbell and a hangman's rope calling the people together. Telling them that this was their only chance to kill themselves or each other.

At first the people in the town were frightened; they knew Shadrack was crazy but that did not mean that he didn't have any sense or, even more important, that he had no power. His eyes were so wild, his hair so long and matted, his voice was so full of authority and thunder that he caused panic on the first, or Charter, National Suicide Day in 1920. The next one, in 1921, was less frightening but still worrisome. The people had seen him a year now in between. He lived in a shack on the riverbank that had once belonged to his grandfather long time dead. On Tuesday and Friday he sold the fish he had caught that morning, the rest of the week he was drunk, loud, obscene, funny and outrageous. But he never touched anybody, never fought, never caressed. Once the people understood the boundaries and nature of his madness, they could fit him, so to speak, into the scheme of things.

Then, on subsequent National Suicide Days, the grown people looked out from behind the curtains as he rang his bell; a few stragglers increased their speed, and little children screamed and ran. The tetter heads tried goading him (although he was only four or five years older than they) but not for long, for his curses were stingingly personal.

As time went along, the people took less notice of these January thirds, or rather they thought they did, thought they had no attitudes or feelings one way or another about Shadrack's annual solitary parade. In fact they had simply stood remarking on the holiday because they had absorbed it into their thoughts, into their language, into their lives.

Someone said to a friend, "You sure was a long time delivering that baby. How long was you in labor?"

And the friend answered, " 'Bout three days. The pains started on Suicide Day and kept up till the following Sunday. All my boys is Sunday boys."

Some lover said to his bride-to-be, "Let's do it after New Years, 'stead of before. I get paid New Year's Eve."

And his sweetheart answered, "OK, but make sure it ain't on Suicide Day. I ain't 'bout to be listening to no cowbells whilst the weddin's going on."

Somebody's grandmother said her hens always started a laying of double yolks right after Suicide Day.

The Reverend Deal took it up, saying the same folks who had sense enough to avoid Shadrack's call were the ones who insisted on drinking themselves to death or womanizing themselves to death. "May's well go on with Shad and save the Lamb the trouble of redemption."

Easily, quietly, Suicide Day became a part of the fabric of life up in the Bottom of Medallion, Ohio.

How I Met My Husband

ALICE MUNRO

We heard the plane come over at noon, roaring through the radio news, and we were sure it was going to hit the house, so we all ran out into the yard. We saw it coming in over the treetops, all red and silver, the first close-up plane I ever saw. Mrs. Peebles screamed.

"Crash landing," their little boy said. Joey was his name.

"It's okay," said Dr. Peebles. "He knows what he's doing." Dr. Peebles was only an animal doctor, but had a calming way of talking, like any doctor.

This was my first job—working for Dr. and Mrs. Peebles, who had bought an old house out on the Fifth Line, about five miles out of town. It was just when the trend was starting of town people buying up old farms, not to work them but to live on them.

We watched the plane land across the road, where the fairgrounds used to be. It did make a good landing field, nice and level for the old race track, and the barns and display sheds torn down now for scrap lumber so there was nothing in the way. Even the old grandstand bays had burned.

"All right," said Mrs. Peebles, snappy as she always was when she got over her nerves. "Let's go back in the house. Let's not stand here gawking like a set of farmers."

She didn't say that to hurt my feelings. It never occurred to her.

I was just setting the dessert down when Loretta Bird arrived, out of breath, at the screen door.

"I thought it was going to crash into the house and kill youse all!"

She lived on the next place and the Peebleses thought she was a country-woman, they didn't know the difference. She and her husband didn't farm, he worked on the roads and had a bad name for drinking. They had seven children and couldn't get credit at the HiWay Grocery. The Peebleses made her welcome, not knowing any better, as I say, and offered her dessert.

738

Dessert was never anything to write home about, at their place. A dish of Jello-O or sliced bananas or fruit out of a tin. "Have a house without a pie, be ashamed until you die," my mother used to say, but Mrs. Peebles operated differently.

Loretta Bird saw me getting the can of peaches.

"Oh, never mind," she said."I haven't got the right kind of a stomach to trust what comes out of those tins, I can only eat home canning."

I could have slapped her. I bet she never put down fruit in her life.

"I know what he's landed here for," she said. "He's got permission to use the fairgrounds and take people up for rides. It costs a dollar. It's the same fellow who was over at Palmerston last week and was up the lakeshore before that. I wouldn't go up, if you paid me."

"I'd jump at the chance," Dr. Peebles said. "I'd like to see this neighborhood from the air."

Mrs. Peebles said she would just as soon see it from the ground. Joey said he wanted to go and Heather did, too. Joey was nine and Heather was seven.

"Would you, Edie?" Heather said.

I said I didn't know. I was scared, but I never admitted that, especially in front of children I was taking care of.

"People are going to be coming out here in their cars raising dust and trampling your property, if I was you I would complain." Loretta said. She hooked her legs around the chair rung and I knew we were in for a lengthy visit. After Dr. Peebles went back to his office or out on his next call and Mrs. Peebles went for her nap, she would hang around me while I was trying to do the dishes. She would pass remarks about the Peebleses in their own house.

"She wouldn't find time to lay down in the middle of the day, if she had seven kids like I got."

She asked me did they fight and did they keep things in the dresser drawer not to have babies with. She said it was a sin if they did. I pretended I didn't know what she was talking about.

I was fifteen and away from home for the first time. My parents had made the effort and sent me to high school for a year, but I didn't like it. I was shy of strangers and the work was hard, they didn't make it nice for you or explain the way they do now. At the end of the year the averages were published in the paper, and mine came out at the very bottom, 37 percent. My father said that's enough and I didn't blame him. The last thing I wanted, anyway, was to go on and end up teaching school. It happened the very day the paper came out with my disgrace on it, Dr. Peebles was staying at our place for dinner, having just helped one of our cows have twins, and he said I looked smart to him and his wife was looking for a girl to help. He said she felt tied down, with the two children, out in the country. I guess she would, my mother said, being polite, though I could tell from her face she was wondering what on earth it would be like to have only two children and no barn work, and then to be complaining.

When I went home I would describe to them the work I had to do, and it made everybody laugh. Mrs. Peebles had an automatic washer and dryer, the first I ever saw. I have had those in my own home for such a long time now it's hard to remember how much of a miracle it was to me, not having to struggle with the wringer and hang up and haul down. Let alone not having to heat water. Then there was practically no baking. Mrs. Peebles said she couldn't make pie crust, the most amazing thing I ever heard a woman admit. I could, of course, and I could make light biscuits and a white cake and dark cake, but they didn't want it, she said they watched their figures. The only thing I didn't like about working there, in fact, was feeling half hungry a lot of the time. I used to bring back a box of dough-nuts made out at home, and hide them under my bed. The children found out, and I didn't mind sharing, but I thought I better bind them to secrecy.

The day after the plane landed Mrs. Peebles put both children in the car and drove over to Chesley, to get their hair cut. There was a good woman then at Chesley for doing hair. She got hers done at the same place, Mrs. Peebles did, and that meant they would be gone a good while. She had to pick a day Dr. Peebles wasn't going out into the country, she didn't have her own car. Cars were still in short supply then, after the war.

I loved being left in the house alone, to do my work at leisure. The kitchen was all white and bright yellow, with fluorescent lights. That was before they ever thought of making the appliances all different colors and doing the cupboards like dark old wood and hiding the lighting. I loved light. I loved the double sink. So would anybody new-come from washing dishes in a dishpan with a rag-plugged hole on an oilcloth-covered table by light of a coal-oil lamp. I kept everything shining.

The bathroom too. I had a bath in there once a week. They wouldn't have minded if I took one oftener, but to me it seemed like asking too much, or maybe risking making it less wonderful. The basin and the tub and the toilet were all pink, and there were glass doors with flamingoes painted on them, to shut off the tub. The light had a rosy cast and the mat sank under your feet like snow, except that it was warm. The mirror was three-way. With the mirror all steamed up and the air like a perfume cloud, from things I was allowed to use, I stood up on the side of the tub and ad-mired myself naked, from three directions. Sometimes I thought about the way we lived out at home and the way we lived here and how one way was so hard to imagine when you were living the other way. But I thought it was still a lot easier, living the way we lived at home, to picture something like this, the painted flamingoes and the warmth and the soft mat, than it was anybody knowing only things like this to picture how it was the other way. And why was that?

I was through my jobs in no time, and had the vegetables peeled for sup-per and sitting in cold water besides. Then I went into Mrs. Peebles' bed-

room. I had been in there plenty of times, cleaning, and I always took a
good look in her closet, at the clothes she had hanging there. I wouldn't
have looked in her drawers, but a closet is open to anybody. That's a lie. I
would have looked in drawers, but I would have felt worse doing it and
been more scared she could tell.

Some clothes in her closet she wore all the time. I was quite familiar with
them. Others she never put on, they were pushed to the back. I was disappointed to see no wedding dress. But there was one long dress I could just
see the skirt of, and I was hungering to see the rest. Now I took note of
where it hung and lifted it out. It was satin, a lovely weight on my arm, light
bluish-green in color, almost silvery. It has a fitted, pointed waist and a full
skirt and an off-the-shoulder fold hiding the little sleeves.

Next thing was easy. I got out of my own things and slipped it on. I was
slimmer at fifteen than anybody would believe who knows me now and the
fit was beautiful. I didn't, of course, have a strapless bra on, which was what
it needed, I just had to slide my straps down my arms under the material.
Then I tried pinning up my hair, to get the effect. One thing led to another. I put on rouge and lipstick and eyebrow pencil from her dresser.
The heat of the day and the weight of the satin and all the excitement made
me thirsty, and I went out to the kitchen, got-up as I was, to get a glass of
ginger ale with ice cubes from the refrigerator. The Peebleses drank ginger
ale, or fruit drinks, all day, like water, and I was getting so I did too. Also
there was no limit on ice cubes, which I was so fond of I would even put
them in a glass of milk.

I turned from putting the ice tray back and saw a man watching me
through the screen. It was the luckiest thing in the world I didn't spill the
ginger ale down the front of me then and there.

"I never meant to scare you. I knocked but you were getting the ice out,
you didn't hear me."

I couldn't see what he looked like, he was dark the way somebody is
pressed up against a screen door with the bright daylight behind them. I
only knew he wasn't from around here.

"I'm from the plane over there. My name is Chris Watters and what I was
wondering was if I could use that pump."

There was a pump in the yard. That was the way the people used to get
their water. Now I noticed he was carrying a pail.

"You're welcome," I said. "I can get it from the tap and save you pumping." I guess I wanted him to know we had piped water, didn't pump ourselves.

"I don't mind the exercise." He didn't move, though, and finally he said,
"Were you going to a dance?"

Seeing a stranger there had made me entirely forget how I was dressed.

"Or is that the way ladies around here generally get dressed up in the afternoon?"

I didn't know how to joke back then. I was too embarrassed.

"You live here? Are you the lady of the house?"

"I'm the hired girl."

Some people change when they find that out, their whole way of looking at you and speaking to you changes, but his didn't.

"Well, I just wanted to tell you you look very nice. I was so surprised when I looked in the door and saw you. Just because you looked so nice and beautiful."

I wasn't even old enough then to realize how out of the common it is, for a man to say something like that to a woman, or somebody he is treating like a woman. For a man to say a word like *beautiful*. I wasn't old enough to realize or to say anything back, or in fact to do anything but wish he would go away. Not that I didn't like him, but just that it upset me so, having him look at me, and me trying to think of something to say.

He must have understood. He said good-bye, and thanked me, and went and started filling his pail from the pump. I stood behind the Venetian blinds in the dining room, watching him. When he had gone, I went into the bedroom and took the dress off and put it back in the same place. I dressed in my own clothes and took my hair down and washed my face, wiping it on Kleenex, which I threw in the wastebasket.

The Peebleses asked me what kind of man he was. Young, middle-aged, short, tall? I couldn't say.

"Good-looking?" Dr. Peebles teased me.

I couldn't think a thing but that he would be coming to get his water again, he would be talking to Dr. or Mrs. Peebles, making friends with them, and he would mention seeing me that first afternoon, dressed up. Why not mention it? He would think it was funny. And no idea of the trouble it would get me into.

After supper the Peebleses drove into town to go to a movie. She wanted to go somewhere with her hair fresh done. I sat in my bright kitchen wondering what to do, knowing I would never sleep. Mrs. Peebles might not fire me, when she found out, but it would give her a different feeling about me altogether. This was the first place I ever worked but I already had picked up things about the way people feel when you are working for them. They like to think you aren't curious. Not just that you aren't dishonest, that isn't enough. They like to feel you don't notice things, that you don't think or wonder about anything but what they liked to eat and how they liked things ironed, and so on. I don't mean they weren't kind to me, because they were. They had me eat my meals with them (to tell the truth I expected to, I didn't know there were families who don't) and sometimes they took me along in the car. But all the same.

I went up and checked on the children being asleep and then I went out. I had to do it. I crossed the road and went in the old fairgrounds gate. The plane looked unnatural sitting there, and shining with the moon. Off at the far side of the fairgrounds, where the bush was taking over, I saw his tent.

He was sitting outside it smoking a cigarette. He saw me coming.

"Hello, were you looking for a plane ride? I don't start taking people up till tomorrow." Then he looked again and said, "Oh, it's you. I didn't know you without your long dress on."

My heart was knocking away, my tongue was dried up. I had to say something. But I couldn't. My throat was closed and I was like a deaf-and-dumb.

"Did you want a ride? Sit down. Have a cigarette."

I couldn't even shake my head to say no, so he gave me one.

"Put it in your mouth or I can't light it. It's a good thing I'm used to shy ladies."

I did. It wasn't the first time I had smoked a cigarette, actually. My girl-friend out home Muriel Lowe, used to steal them from her brother.

"Look at your hand shaking. Did you just want to have a chat, or what?"

In one bust I said, "I wisht you wouldn't say anything about that dress."

"What dress? Oh, the long dress."

"It's Mrs. Peebles'."

"Whose? Oh, the lady you work for? Is that it? She wasn't home so you got dressed up in her dress, eh? You got dressed up and played queen. I don't blame you. You're not smoking the cigarette right. Don't just puff. Draw it in. Did anybody ever show you how to inhale? Are you scared I'll tell on you? Is that it?"

I was so ashamed at having to ask him to connive this way I couldn't nod. I just looked at him and he saw *yes*.

"Well I won't. I won't in the slightest way mention it or embarrass you. I give you my word of honor."

Then he changed the subject, to help me out, seeing I couldn't even thank him.

"What do you think of this sign?"

It was a board sign lying practically at my feet.

SEE THE WORLD FROM THE SKY. ADULTS $1.00, CHILDREN 50¢. QUALIFIED PILOT.

"My old sign was getting pretty beat up, I thought I'd make a new one. That's what I've been doing with my time today."

The lettering wasn't all that handsome, I thought. I could have done a better one in half an hour.

"I'm not an expert at sign making."

"It's very good," I said.

"I don't need it for publicity, word of mouth is usually enough. I turned away two carloads tonight. I felt like taking it easy. I didn't tell them ladies were dropping in to visit me."

Now I remembered the children and I was scared again, in case one of them had waked up and called me and I wasn't there.

"Do you have to go so soon?"

I remembered some manners. "Thank you for the cigarette."

"Don't forget. You have my word of honor."

I tore off across the fairgrounds, scared I'd see the car heading home from town. My sense of time was mixed up, I didn't know how long I'd been out of the house. But it was all right, it wasn't late, the children were asleep. I got in bed myself and lay thinking what a lucky end to the day, after all, and among things to be grateful for I could be grateful Loretta Bird hadn't been the one who caught me.

The yard and borders didn't get trampled, it wasn't as bad as that. All the same it seemed very public, around the house. The sign was on the fairgrounds gate. People came mostly after supper but a good many in the afternoon, too. The Bird children all came without fifty cents between them and hung on the gate. We got used to the excitement of the plane coming in and taking off, it wasn't excitement anymore. I never went over, after that one time, but would see him when he came to get his water. I would be out on the steps doing sitting-down work, like preparing vegetables, if I could.

"Why don't you come over? I'll take you up in my plane."

"I'm saving my money," I said, because I couldn't think of anything else.

"For what? For getting married?"

I shook my head.

"I'll take you up for free if you come sometime when it's slack. I thought you would come, and have another cigarette."

I made a face to hush him, because you never could tell when the children would be sneaking around the porch, or Mrs. Peebles herself listening in the house. Sometimes she came out and had a conversation with him. He told her things he hadn't bothered to tell me. But then I hadn't thought to ask. He told her he had been in the war, that was where he learned to fly a plane, and now he couldn't settle down to ordinary life, this was what he liked. She said she couldn't imagine anybody liking such a thing. Though sometimes, she said, she was almost bored enough to try anything herself, she wasn't brought up to living in the country. It's all my husband's idea, she said. This was news to me.

"Maybe you ought to give flying lessons," she said.

"Would you take them?"

She just laughed.

Sunday was a busy flying day in spite of it being preached against from two pulpits. We were all sitting out watching. Joey and Heather were over on the fence with the Bird kids. Their father had said they could go, after their mother saying all week they couldn't.

A car came down the road past the parked cars and pulled up right in the drive. It was Loretta Bird who got out, all importance, and on the driver's side another woman got out, more sedately. She was wearing sunglasses.

"This is a lady looking for the man that flies the plane," Loretta Bird said. "I heard her inquire in the hotel coffee shop where I was having a Coke and I brought her out."

"I'm sorry to bother you," the lady said. "I'm Alice Kelling, Mr. Waters' fiancée."

This Alice Kelling had on a pair of brown and white checked slacks and a yellow top. Her bust looked to me rather low and bumpy. She had a worried face. Her hair had had a permanent, but had grown out, and she wore a yellow band to keep it off her face. Nothing in the least pretty or even young-looking about her. But you could tell from how she talked she was from the city, or educated, or both.

Dr. Peebles stood up and introduced himself and his wife and me and asked her to be seated.

"He's up in the air right now, but you're welcome to sit and wait. He gets his water here and he hasn't been yet. He'll probably take his break about five."

"That is him, then?" said Alice Kelling, wrinkling and straining at the sky.

"He's not in the habit of running out on you, taking a different name?" Dr. Peebles laughed. He was the one, not his wife, to offer iced tea. Then she sent me into the kitchen to fix it. She smiled. She was wearing sunglasses too.

"He never mentioned his fiancée," she said.

I loved fixing iced tea with lots of ice and slices of lemon in tall glasses. I ought to have mentioned before, Dr. Peebles was an abstainer, at least around the house, or I wouldn't have been allowed to take the place. I had to fix a glass for Loretta Bird to, though it galled me, and when I went out she had settled in my lawn chair, leaving me the steps.

"I knew you was a nurse when I first heard you in that coffee shop."

"How would you know a thing like that?"

"I get my hunches about people. Was that how you met him, nursing?"

"Chris? Well yes. Yes, it was."

"Oh, were you overseas?" said Mrs. Peebles.

"No, it was before he went overseas. I nursed him when he was stationed at Centralia and had a ruptured appendix. We got engaged and then he went overseas. My, this is refreshing, after a long drive."

"He'll be glad to see you," Dr. Peebles said. "It's a rackety kind of life, isn't it, not staying one place long enough to really make friends."

"Youse've had a long engagement," Loretta Bird said.

Alice Kelling passed that over. "I was going to get a room at the hotel, but when I was offered directions I came on out. Do you think I could phone them?"

"No need," Dr. Peebles said. "You're five miles away from him if you stay at the hotel. Here, you're right across the road. Stay with us. We've got rooms on rooms, look at this big house."

Asking people to stay, just like that, is certainly a country thing, and maybe seemed natural to him now, but not to Mrs. Peebles, from the way she said, oh yes, we have plenty of room. Or to Alice Kelling, who kept protesting, but let herself be worn down. I got the feeling it was a temptation to her, to be that close. I was trying for a look at her ring. Her nails were painted red, her fingers were freckled and wrinkled. It was a tiny stone. Muriel Lowe's cousin had one twice as big.

Chris came to get his water, late in the afternoon just as Dr. Peebles had predicted. He must have recognized the car from a way off. He came smiling.

"Here I am chasing after you to see what you're up to," called Alice Kelling. She got up and went to meet him and they kissed, just touched, in front of us.

"You're going to spend a lot on gas that way," Chris said.

Dr. Peebles invited Chris to stay for supper, since he had already put up the sign that said: NO MORE RIDES TILL 7 P.M. Mrs. Peebles wanted it served in the yard, in spite of the bugs. One thing strange to anybody from the country is this eating outside. I had made a potato salad earlier and she had made a jellied salad, that was one thing she could do, so it was just a matter of getting those out, and some sliced meat and cucumbers and fresh leaf lettuce. Loretta Bird hung around for some time saying, "Oh, well, I guess I better get home to those yappers," and, "It's so nice just sitting here, I sure hate to get up," but nobody invited her, I was relieved to see, and finally she had to go.

That night after rides were finished Alice Kelling and Chris went off somewhere in her car. I lay awake till they got back. When I saw the car lights sweep my ceiling I got up to look down on them through the slats of my blind. I don't know what I thought I was going to see. Muriel Lowe and I used to sleep on her front veranda and watch her sister and her sister's boy friend saying good night. Afterward we couldn't get to sleep, for longing for somebody to kiss us and rub up against us and we would talk about suppose you were out in a boat with a boy and he wouldn't bring you in to shore unless you did it, or what if somebody got you trapped in a barn, you would have to, wouldn't you, it wouldn't be your fault. Muriel said her two girl cousins used to try with a toilet paper roll that one of them was a boy. We wouldn't do anything like that; just lay and wondered.

All that happened was that Chris got out of the car on one side and she got out on the other and they walked off separately—him toward the fairgrounds and her toward the house. I got back in bed and imagined about me coming home with him, not like that.

Next morning Alice Kelling got up late and I fixed a grapefruit for her the way I had learned and Mrs. Peebles sat down with her to visit and have another cup of coffee. Mrs. Peebles seemed pleased enough now, having company. Alice Kelling said she guessed she better get used to putting in a day just watching Chris take off and come down, and Mrs. Peebles said she didn't know if she should suggest it because Alice Kelling was the one with the car, but the lake was only twenty-five miles away and what a good day for a picnic.

Alice Kelling took her up on the idea and by eleven o'clock they were in the car, with Joey and Heather and a sandwich lunch I had made. The only thing was that Chris hadn't come down, and she wanted to tell him where they were going.

"Edie'll go over and tell him," Mrs. Peebles said. "There's no problem."

Alice Kelling wrinkled her face and agreed.

"Be sure and tell him we'll be back by five!"

I didn't see that he would be concerned about knowing this right away, and I thought of him eating whatever he ate over there, alone, cooking on his camp stove, so I got to work and mixed up a crumb cake and baked it, in between the other work I had to do; then, when it was a bit cooled, wrapped it in a tea towel. I didn't do anything to myself but take off my apron and comb my hair. I would like to have put some makeup on, but I was too afraid it would remind him of the way he first saw me, and that would humiliate me all over again.

He had come and put another sign on the gate: NO RIDES THIS P.M. APOLOGIES. I worried that he wasn't feeling well. No sign of him outside and the tent flap was down. I knocked on the pole.

"Come in," he said, in a voice that would just as soon have said *Stay out*.

I lifted the flap.

"Oh, it's you. I'm sorry. I didn't know it was you."

He had been just sitting on the side of the bed, smoking. Why not at least sit and smoke in the fresh air?

"I brought a cake and hope you're not sick," I said.

"Why would I be sick? Oh—that sign. That's all right. I'm just tired of talking to people. I don't mean you. Have a seat." He pinned back the tent flap. "Get some fresh air in here."

I sat on the edge of the bed, there was no place else. It was one of those fold-up cots, really: I remembered and gave him his fiancée's message.

He ate some of the cake. "Good."

"Put the rest away for when you're hungry later."

"I'll tell you a secret. I won't be around here much longer."

"Are you getting married?"

"Ha ha. What time did you say they'd be back?"

"Five o'clock."

"Well, by that time this place will have seen the last of me. A plane can get further than a car." He unwrapped the cake and ate another piece of it, absent-mindedly.

"Now you'll be thirsty."

"There's some water in the pail."

"It won't be very cold. I could bring some fresh. I could bring some ice from the refrigerator."

"No," he said. "I don't want you to go. I want a nice long time of saying good-bye to you."

He put the cake away carefully and sat beside me and started those little kisses, so soft, I can't ever let myself think about them, such kindness in his face and lovely kisses, all over my eyelids and neck and ears, all over, then me kissing back as well as I could (I had only kissed a boy on a dare before, and kissed my own arms for practice) and we lay back on the cot and pressed together, just gently, and he did some other things, not bad things or not in a bad way. It was lovely in the tent, that smell of grass and hot tent cloth with the sun beating down on it, and he said, "I wouldn't do you any harm for the world." Once, when he had rolled on top of me and we were sort of rocking together on the cot, he said softly, "Oh, no," and freed himself and jumped up and got the water pail. He splashed some of it on his neck and face, and the little bit left, on me lying there.

"That's to cool us off, miss."

When we said good-bye I wasn't at all sad, because he held my face and said "I'm going to write you a letter. I'll tell you where I am and maybe you can come and see me. Would you like that? Okay then. You wait." I was really glad I think to get away from him, it was like he was piling presents on me I couldn't get the pleasure of till I considered them alone.

No consternation at first about the plane being gone. They thought he had taken somebody up, and I didn't enlighten them. Dr. Peebles had phoned he had to go to the country, so there was just us having supper, and then Loretta Bird thrusting her head in the door and saying, "I see he's took off."

"What?" said Alice Kelling, and pushed back her chair.

"The kids come and told me this afternoon he was taking down his tent. Did he think he'd run through all the business there was around here? He didn't take off without letting you know, did he?"

"He'll send me word," Alice Kelling said. "He'll probably phone tonight. He's terribly restless, since the war."

"Edie, he didn't mention to you, did he?" Mrs. Peebles said. "When you took over the message?"

"Yes," I said. So far so true.

"Well why didn't you say?" All of them were looking at me. "Did he say where he was going?"

"He said he might try Bayfield," I said. What made me tell such a lie? I didn't intend it.

"Bayfield, how far is that?" said Alice Kelling.

Mrs. Peebles said, "Thirty, thirty-five miles."

"That's not far. Oh, well, that's really not far at all. It's on the lake, isn't it?"

You'd think I'd be ashamed of myself, setting her on the wrong track. I did it to give him more time, whatever time he needed. I lied for him, and also, I have to admit, for me. Women should stick together and not do things like that. I see that now, but didn't then. I never thought of myself as being in any way like her, or coming to the same troubles, ever.

She hadn't taken her eyes off me. I thought she suspected my lie.

"When did he mention this to you?"

"Earlier."

"When you were over at the plane?"

"Yes."

"You must've stayed and had a chat." She smiled at me, not a nice smile. "You must've stayed and had a little visit with him."

"I took a cake," I said, thinking that telling some truth would spare me telling the rest.

"We didn't have a cake," said Mrs. Peebles rather sharply.

"I baked one."

Alice Kelling said, "That was very friendly of you."

"Did you get permission," said Loretta Bird. "You never know what these girls'll do next," she said. "It's not they mean harm so much, as they're ignorant."

"The cake is neither here nor there," Mrs. Peebles broke in. "Edie, I wasn't aware you knew Chris that well." I didn't know what to say.

"I'm not surprised," Alice Kelling said in a high voice. "I knew by the look of her as soon as I saw her. We get them at the hospital all the time." She looked hard at me with her stretched smile. "Having their babies. We have to put them in a special ward because of their diseases. Little country tramps. Fourteen and fifteen years old. You should see the babies they have, too."

"There was a bad woman here in town had a baby that pus was running out of its eyes," Loretta Bird put in.

"Wait a minute," said Mrs. Peebles. "What is this talk? Edie. What about you and Mr. Watters? Were you intimate with him?"

"Yes," I said. I was thinking of us lying on the cot and kissing, wasn't that intimate? And I would never deny it.

They were all one minute quiet, even Loretta Bird.

"Well," said Mrs. Peebles. "I am surprised. I think I need a cigarette. This is the first of any such tendencies I've seen in her," she said, speaking to Alice Kelling, but Alice Kelling was looking at me.

"Loose little bitch." Tears ran down her face. "Loose little bitch, aren't you? I knew as soon as I saw you. Men despise girls like you. He just made use of you and went off, you know that, don't you? Girls like you are just nothing, they're just public conveniences, just filthy little rags!"

"Oh, now," said Mrs. Peebles.

"Filthy," Alice Kelling sobbed. "Filthy little rags!"

"Don't get yourself upset," Loretta Bird said. She was swollen up with pleasure at being in on this scene. "Men are all the same."

"Edie, I'm very surprised," Mrs. Peebles said. "I thought your parents were so strict. You don't want to have a baby, do you?"

I'm still ashamed of what happened next. I lost control, just like a six-year-old, I started howling. "You don't get a baby from just doing that!"

"You see. Some of them are that ignorant," Loretta Bird said.

But Mrs. Peebles jumped up and caught my arms and shook me.

"Calm down. Don't get hysterical. Calm down. Stop crying. Listen to me. Listen. I'm wondering, if you know what being intimate means. Now tell me. What did you think it meant?"

"Kissing," I howled.

She let go. "Oh, Edie. Stop it. Don't be silly. It's all right. It's all a misunderstanding. Being intimate means a lot more than that. Oh, I *wondered*."

"She's trying to cover up, now," said Alice Kelling. "Yes. She's not so stupid. She sees she got herself in trouble."

"I believe her," Mrs. Peebles said. "This is an awful scene."

"Well there is one way to find out," said Alice Kelling, getting up. "After all, I am a nurse."

Mrs. Peebles drew a breath and said, "No. No. Go to your room, Edie. And stop that noise. This is too disgusting."

I heard the car start in a little while. I tried to stop crying, pulling back each wave as it started over me. Finally I succeeded, and lay heaving on the bed.

Mrs. Peebles came and stood in the doorway.

"She's gone," she said. "That Bird woman too. Of course, you know you should never have gone near that man and that is the cause of all this trouble. I have a headache. As soon as you can, go and wash your face in cold water and get at the dishes and we will not say any more about this."

Nor we didn't. I didn't figure out till years later the extent of what I had been saved from. Mrs. Peebles was not very friendly to me afterward, but she was fair. Not very friendly is the wrong way of describing what she was. She had never been very friendly. It was just that now she had to see me all the time and it got on her nerves, a little.

As for me, I put it all out of my mind like a bad dream and concentrated on waiting for my letter. The mail came every day except Sunday, between one-thirty and two in the afternoon, a good time for me because Mrs. Peebles was always having her nap. I would get the kitchen all cleaned and then go up to the mailbox and sit in the grass, waiting. I was perfectly happy, waiting, I forgot all about Alice Kelling and her misery and awful talk and Mrs. Peebles and her chilliness and the embarrassment of whether she told Dr. Peebles and the face of Loretta Bird, getting her fill of other people's troubles. I was always smiling when the mailman got there, and continued smiling even after he gave me the mail and I saw today wasn't the day. The mailman was a Carmichael. I knew by his face because there are a lot of Carmichaels living out by us and so many of them have a sort of sticking-out top lip. So I asked his name (he was a young man, shy, but good-humored, anybody could ask him anything) and then I said, "I knew by your face!" He was pleased by that and always glad to see me and got a little less shy. "You've got the smile I've been waiting on all day!" he used to holler out the car window.

It never crossed my mind for a long time a letter might not come. I believed in it coming just like I believed the sun would rise in the morning. I just put off my hope from day to day, and there was the goldenrod out around the mailbox and the children gone back to school, and the leaves turning, and I was wearing a sweater when I went to wait. One day walking back with the hydro bill stuck in my hand, that was all, looking across at the fairgrounds with the full-blown milkweed and dark teasels, so much like fall, it just struck me: *No letter was ever going to come.* It was an impossible idea to get used to. No, not impossible. If I thought about Chris's face when he said he was going to write to me, it was impossible, but if I forgot that and thought about the actual tin mailbox, empty, it was plain and true. I kept on going to meet the mail, but my heart was heavy now like a lump of lead. I only smiled because I thought of the mailman counting on it, and he didn't have an easy life, with the winter driving ahead.

Till it came to me one day there were women doing this with their lives, all over. There were women just waiting and waiting by mailboxes for one letter or another. I imagined me making this journey day after day and year after year, and my hair starting to go gray, and I thought, I was never made to go on like that. So I stopped meeting the mail. If there were women all through life waiting, and women busy and not waiting, I knew which I had to be. Even though there might be things the second kind of women have to pass up and never know about, it still is better.

I was surprised when the mailman phoned the Peebleses' place in the evening and asked for me. He said he missed me. He asked if I would like to go to Goderich, where some well-known movie was on, I forget now what. So I said yes, and I went out with him for two years and he asked me to marry him, and we were engaged a year more while I got my things together, and then we did marry. He always tells the children the story of how I went after him by sitting by the mailbox every day, and naturally I laugh and let him, because I like for people to think what pleases them and makes them happy.

How I Contemplated the World From the Detroit House of Correction and Began My Life Over Again

JOYCE CAROL OATES

*Notes for an Essay for an English Class at Baldwin
Country Day School; Poking Around in Debris;
Disgust and Curiosity; A Revelation of the Meaning of Life;
A Happy Ending . . .*

I. EVENTS

1. The girl (myself) is walking through Branden's, that excellent store. Suburb of a large famous city that is a symbol for large famous American cities. The event sneaks up on the girl, who believes she is herding it along with a small fixed smile, a girl of fifteen, innocently experienced. She dawdles in a certain style by a counter of costume jewelry. Rings, earrings, necklaces. Prices from $5 to $50, all within reach. All ugly. She eases over to the glove counter, where everything is ugly too. In her close-fitted coat with its black fur collar she contemplates the luxury of Branden's, which she has known for many years: its many mild pale lights, easy on the eye and the soul, its elaborate tinkly decorations, its women shoppers with their excellent shoes and coats and hairdos, all dawdling gracefully, in no hurry.

Who was ever in a hurry here?

2. The girl seated at home. A small library, paneled walls of oak. Someone is talking to me. An earnest, husky, female voice drives itself against my

ears, nervous, frightened, groping around my heart, saying, "If you wanted gloves, why didn't you say so? Why didn't you ask for them?" That store, Branden's, is owned by Raymond Forrest who lives on Du Maurier Drive. We live on Sioux Drive. Raymond Forrest. A handsome man? An ugly man? A man of fifty or sixty, with gray hair, or a man of forty with earnest, courteous eyes, a good golf game; who is Raymond Forrest, this man who is my salvation? Father has been talking to him. Father is not his physician; Dr. Berg is his physician. Father and Dr. Berg refer patients to each other. There is a connection. Mother plays bridge with . . . On Mondays and Wednesdays our maid Billie works at . . . The strings draw together in a cat's cradle, making a net to save you when you fall. . . .

3. *Harriet Arnold's.* A small shop, better than Branden's. Mother in her black coat, I in my close-fitted blue coat. Shopping. Now look at this, isn't this cute, do you want this, why don't you want this, try this on, take this with you to the fitting room, take this also, what's wrong with you, what can I do for you, why are you so strange . . . ? "I wanted to steal but not to buy," I don't tell her. The girl droops along in her coat and gloves and leather boots, her eyes scan the horizon, which is pastel pink and decorated like Branden's, tasteful walls and modern ceilings with graceful glimmering lights.

4. Weeks later, the girl at a bus stop. Two o'clock in the afternoon, a Tuesday; obviously she has walked out of school.

5. The girl stepping down from a bus. Afternoon, weather changing to colder. Detroit. Pavement and closed-up stores; grillwork over the windows of a pawnshop. What is a pawnshop, exactly?

II. CHARACTERS

1. The girl stands five feet five inches tall. An ordinary height. Baldwin Country Day School draws them up to that height. She dreams along the corridors and presses her face against the Thermoplex glass. No frost or steam can ever form on that glass. A smudge of grease from her forehead . . . could she be boiled down to grease? She wears her hair loose and long and straight in suburban teen-age style, 1968. Eyes smudged with pencil, dark brown. Brown hair. Vague green eyes. A pretty girl? An ugly girl? She sings to herself under her breath, idling in the corridor, thinking of her many secrets (the thirty dollars she once took from the purse of a friend's mother, just for fun, the basement window she smashed in her own house just for fun) and thinking of her brother who is at Susquehanna Boys'

Academy, an excellent preparatory school in Maine, remembering him unclearly . . . he has long manic hair and a squeaking voice and he looks like one of the popular teen-age singers of 1968, one of those in a group, *The Certain Forces, The Way Out, The Maniacs Responsible*. The girl in her turn looks like one of those fieldsful of girls who listen to the boys' singing, dreaming and mooning restlessly, breaking into high sullen laughter, innocently experienced.

2. The mother. A Midwestern woman of Detroit and suburbs. Belongs to the Detroit Athletic Club. Also the Detroit Golf Club. Also the Bloomfield Hills Country Club. The Village Women's Club at which lectures are given each winter on Genet and Sartre and James Baldwin, by the Director of the Adult Education Program at Wayne State University. . . . The Bloomfield Art Association. Also the Founders Society of the Detroit Institute of Arts. Also . . . Oh, she is in perpetual motion, this lady, hair like blown-up gold and finer than gold, hair and fingers and body of inestimable grace. Heavy weighs the gold on the back of her hairbrush and hand mirror. Heavy heavy the candlesticks in the dining room. Very heavy is the big car, a Lincoln, long and black, that on one cool autumn day split a squirrel's body in two unequal parts.

3. The father. Dr. ——. He belongs to the same clubs as #2. A player of squash and golf; he has a golfer's umbrella of stripes. Candy stripes. In his mouth nothing turns to sugar, however; saliva works no miracles here. His doctoring is of the slightly sick. The sick are sent elsewhere (to Dr. Berg?), the deathly sick are sent back for more tests and their bills are sent to their homes, the unsick are sent to Dr. Coronet (Isabel, a lady), an excellent psychiatrist for unsick people who angrily believe they are sick and want to do something about it. If they demand a male psychiatrist, the unsick are sent by Dr. —— (my father) to Dr. Lowenstein, a male psychiatrist, excellent and expensive, with a limited practice.

4. Clarita. She is twenty, twenty-five, she is thirty or more? Pretty, ugly, what? She is a woman lounging by the side of a road, in jeans and a sweater, hitchhiking, or she is slouched on a stool at a counter in some roadside diner. A hard line of jaw. Curious eyes. Amused eyes. Behind her eyes processions move, funeral pageants, cartoons. She says, "I never can figure out why girls like you bum around down here. What are you looking for anyway?" An odor of tobacco about her. Unwashed underclothes, or no underclothes, unwashed skin, gritty toes, hair long and falling into strands, not recently washed.

5. Simon. In this city the weather changes abruptly, so Simon's weather changes abruptly. He sleeps through the afternoon. He sleeps through the morning. Rising, he gropes around for something to get him going, for a cigarette or a pill to drive him out to the street, where the temperature is hovering around 35°. Why doesn't it drop? Why, why doesn't the cold clean air come down from Canada; will he have to go up into Canada to get it? will he have to leave the Country of his Birth and sink into Canada's frosty fields . . . ? Will the F.B.I. (which he dreams about constantly) chase him over the Canadian border on foot, hounded out in a blizzard of broken glass and horns . . . ?

"Once I was Huckleberry Finn," Simon says, "but now I am Roderick Usher." Beset by frenzies and fears, this man who makes my spine go cold, he takes green pills, yellow pills, pills of white and capsules of dark blue and green . . . he takes other things I may not mention, for what if Simon seeks me out and climbs into my girl's bedroom here in Bloomfield Hills and strangles me, what then . . . ? (As I write this I begin to shiver. Why do I shiver? I am now sixteen and sixteen is not an age for shivering.) It comes from Simon, who is always cold.

III. WORLD EVENTS

Nothing.

IV. PEOPLE AND CIRCUMSTANCES CONTRIBUTING TO THIS DELINQUENCY

Nothing.

V. SIOUX DRIVE

George, Clyde G. 240 Sioux. A manufacturer's representative; children, a dog, a wife. Georgian with the usual columns. You think of the White House, then of Thomas Jefferson, then your mind goes blank on the white pillars and you think of nothing. Norris, Ralph W. 246 Sioux. Public relations. Colonial. Bay window, brick, stone, concrete, wood, green shutters, sidewalk, lantern, grass, trees, blacktop drive, two children, one of them my classmate Esther (Esther Norris) at Baldwin. Wife, cars. Ramsey, Michael D. 250 Sioux. Colonial. Big living room, thirty by twenty-five, fireplaces in living room, library, recreation room, paneled walls wet bar five bathrooms five bedrooms two lavatories central air conditioning automatic sprinkler automatic garage door three children one wife two cars a breakfast room a patio a large fenced lot fourteen trees a front door with a brass knocker never knocked. Next is our house. Classic contemporary. Traditional modern. Attached garage, attached Florida room, attached patio, attached pool and cabana, attached roof. A front door mail slot through which pour *Time Magazine, Fortune, Life, Business Week,* the *Wall Street Journal,* the *New York Times,* the *New Yorker,* the *Saturday Review, M.D., Modern Medicine, Disease of the Month* . . . and also. . . . And in addition to all this, a quiet sealed letter from Baldwin saying: *Your daughter is not doing work compatible with her performance on the Stanford-Binet.* . . . And your son is not doing well, not well at all, very sad. Where is your son anyway? Once he stole trick-and-treat candy from some six-year-old kids, he himself being a robust ten. The beginning. Now your daughter steals. In the Village Pharmacy she made off with, yes she did, don't deny it, she made off with a copy of *Pageant Magazine* for no reason, she swiped a roll of Life Savers in a green wrapper and was in no need of saving her life or even in need of sucking candy; when she was no more than eight years old she stole, don't blush, she stole a package of Tums only because it was out on the counter and available, and the nice lady behind the counter (now dead) said nothing. . . . Sioux Drive. Maples, oaks, elms. Diseased elms cut down. Sioux Drive runs into Roosevelt Drive. Slow, turning lanes, not streets, all drives and lanes and ways and passes. A private police force. Quiet private police, in unmarked cars. Cruising on Saturday evenings with paternal smiles for the residents who are streaming in and out of houses, going to and from parties, a thousand parties, slightly staggering, the women in their furs alighting from automobiles bought of Ford and General Motors and Chrysler, very heavy automobiles. No foreign cars. Detroit. In 275 Sioux, down the block in that magnificent French-Normandy mansion, lives —— himself, who has the C—— account itself, imagine that! Look at where he lives and look at the enormous trees and chimneys, imagine his many fireplaces, imagine his wife and children, imagine his wife's hair, imagine her fingernails, imagine her bathtub of smooth clean glowing pink, imagine their embraces, his trouser pockets filled with odd coins and keys and dust and peanuts, imagine their ecstasy on Sioux Drive, imagine their income tax returns, imagine their little boy's pride in his experimental car, a scaled down C——, as he roars round the neighborhood on the sidewalks frightening dogs and Negro maids, oh imagine all these things, imagine everything, let your mind roar out all over Sioux Drive and Du Maurier Drive and Roosevelt Drive and Ticonderoga Pass and Burning Bush Way and Lincolnshire Pass and Lois Lane.

When spring comes, its winds blow nothing to Sioux Drive, no odors of hollyhocks or forsythia, nothing Sioux Drive doesn't already possess, everything is planted and performing. The weather vanes, had they weather vanes, don't have to turn with the wind, don't have to contend with the weather. There is no weather.

VI. DETROIT

There is always weather in Detroit. Detroit's temperature is always 32°. Fast-falling temperatures. Slow-rising temperatures. Wind from the north-northeast four to forty miles an hour, small-craft warnings, partly cloudy today and Wednesday changing to partly sunny through Thursday . . . small warnings of frost, soot warnings, traffic warnings, hazardous lake conditions for small craft and swimmers, restless Negro gangs, restless cloud formations, restless temperatures aching to fall out the very bottom of the thermometer or shoot up over the top and boil everything over in red mercury.

Detroit's temperature is 32°. Fast-falling temperatures. Slow-rising temperatures. Wind from the north-northeast four to forty miles an hour. . . .

VII. EVENTS

1. The girl's heart is pounding. In her pocket is a pair of gloves! In a plastic bag! Airproof breathproof plastic bag, gloves selling for twenty-five dollars on Branden's counter! In her pocket! Shoplifted! . . . In her purse is a blue comb, not very clean. In her purse is a leather billfold (a birthday present from her grandmother in Philadelphia) with snapshots of the family in clean plastic windows, in the billfold are bills, she doesn't know how many bills. . . . In her purse is an ominous note from her friend Tykie *What's this about Joe H. and the kids hanging around at Louise's Sat. night? You heard anything?* . . . passed in French class. In her purse is a lot of dirty yellow Kleenex, but her mother's heart would break to see such very dirty Kleenex, and at the bottom of her purse are brown hairpins and safety pins and a broken pencil and a ballpoint pen (blue) stolen from somewhere forgotten and a purse-size compact of Cover Girl Make-Up, Ivory Rose. . . . Her lipstick is Broken Heart, a corrupt pink; her fingers are trembling like crazy; her teeth are beginning to chatter; her insides are alive; her eyes glow in her head; she is saying to her mother's astonished face *I want to steal but not to buy.*

2. At Clarita's. Day or night? What room is this? A bed, a regular bed, and a mattress on the floor nearby. Wallpaper hanging in strips. Clarita says she tore it like that with her teeth. She was fighting a barbaric tribe that

night, high from some pills; she was battling for her life with men wearing helmets of heavy iron and their faces no more than Christian crosses to breathe through, every one of those bastards looking like her lover Simon, who seems to breathe with great difficulty through the slits of mouth and nostrils in his face. Clarita has never heard of Sioux Drive. Raymond For- rest cuts no ice with her, nor does the C—— account and its millions; Har- vard Business School could be at the corner of Vernor and 12th Street for all she cares, and Vietnam might have sunk by now into the Dead Sea un- der its tons of debris, for all the amazement she could show . . . her face is overworked, overwrought, at the age of twenty (thirty?) it is already ex- hausted but fanciful and ready for a laugh. Clarita says mournfully to me *Honey somebody is going to turn you out let me give you warning.* In a movie shown on late television Clarita is not a mess like this but a nurse, with short neat hair and a dedicated look, in love with her doctor and her doctor's pa- tients and their diseases, enamored of needles and sponges and rubbing alcohol. . . . Or no: she is a private secretary. Robert Cummings is her boss. She helps him with fantastic plots, the canned audience laughs, no, the au- dience doesn't laugh because nothing is funny, instead her boss is Robert Taylor and they are not boss and secretary but husband and wife, she is threatened by a young starlet, she is grim, handsome, wifely, a good com- panion for a good man. . . . She is Claudette Colbert. Her sister too is Clau- dette Colbert. They are twins, identical. Her husband Charles Boyer is a very rich handsome man and her sister, Claudette Colbert, is plotting her death in order to take her place as the rich man's wife, no one will know be- cause they are *twins.* . . . All these marvelous lives Clarita might have lived, but she fell out the bottom at the age of thirteen. At the age when I was packing my overnight case for a slumber party at Toni Deshield's she was tearing filthy sheets off a bed and scratching up a rash on her arms. . . . Thirteen is uncommonly young for a white girl in Detroit, Miss Brock of the Detroit House of Correction said in a sad newspaper interview for the *Detroit News;* fifteen and sixteen are more likely. Eleven, twelve, thirteen are not surprising in colored . . . they are more precocious. What can we do? Taxes are rising and the tax base is falling. The temperature rises slowly but falls rapidly. Everything is falling out the bottom, Woodward Avenue is filthy. Livernois Avenue is filthy! Scraps of paper flutter in the air like pi- geons, dirt flies up and hits you right in the eye, oh Detroit is breaking up into dangerous bits of newspaper and dirt, watch out. . . .

Clarita's apartment is over a restaurant. Simon her lover emerges from the cracks at dark. Mrs. Olesko, a neighbor of Clarita's, an aged white wisp of a woman, doesn't complain but sniffs with contentment at Clarita's noisy life and doesn't tell the cops, hating cops, when the cops arrive. I should give more fake names, more blanks, instead of telling all these secrets. I my- self am a secret; I am a minor.

3. My father reads a paper at a medical convention in Los Angeles. There he is, on the edge of the North American continent, when the un-marked detective put his hand so gently on my arm in the aisle of Branden's and said, "Miss, would you like to step over here for a minute?"

And where was he when Clarita put her hand on my arm, that wintry dark sulphurous aching day in Detroit, in the company of closed-down barber shops, closed-down diners, closed-down movie houses, homes, windows, basements, faces . . . she put her hand on my arm and said, "Honey, are you looking for somebody down here?"

And was he home worrying about me, gone for two weeks solid, when they carried me off . . . ? It took three of them to get me in the police cruiser, so they said, and they put more than their hands on my arm.

4. I work on this lesson. My English teacher is Mr. Forest, who is from Michigan State. Not handsome, Mr. Forest, and his name is plain, unlike Raymond Forrest's, but he is sweet and rodentlike, he has conferred with the principal and my parents, and everything is fixed . . . treat her as if nothing has happened, a new start, begin again, only sixteen years old, what a shame, how did it happen?—nothing happened, nothing could have happened, a slight physiological modification known only to a gynecologist or to Dr. Coronet. I work on my lesson, I sit in my pink room. I look around the room with my sad pink eyes. I sigh, I dawdle, I pause. I eat up time. I am limp and happy to be home, I am sixteen years old suddenly, my head hangs heavy as a pumpkin on my shoulders, and my hair has just been cut by Mr. Faye at the Crystal Salon and is said to be very becoming.

(Simon too put his hand on my arm and said, "Honey, you have got to come with me," and in his six-by-six room we got to know each other. Would I go back to Simon again? Would I lie down with him in all that filth and craziness? Over and over again.

a Clarita is being betrayed as in front of a Cunningham Drug Store she is nervously eying a colored man who may or may not have money, or a nervous white boy of twenty with sideburns and an Appalachian look, who may or may not have a knife hidden in his jacket pocket, or a husky red-faced man of friendly countenance who may or may not be a member of the Vice Squad out for an early twilight walk.)

I work on my lesson for Mr. Forest. I have filled up eleven pages. Words pour out of me and won't stop. I want to tell everything . . . what was the song Simon was always humming, and who was Simon's friend in a very new trench coat with an old high school graduation ring on his finger . . . ? Simon's bearded friend? When I was down too low for him, Simon kicked me out and gave me to him for three days, I think, on Fourteenth Street in Detroit, an airy room of cold cruel drafts with newspapers on the floor. . . . Do I really remember that or am I piercing it together from what they told me? Did they tell the truth? Did they know much of the truth?

VIII. CHARACTERS

1. Wednesdays after school, at four; Saturday mornings at ten. Mother drives me to Dr. Coronet. Ferns in the office, plastic or real, they look the same. Dr. Coronet is queenly, an elegant nicotine-stained lady who would have studied with Freud had circumstances not prevented it, a bit of a Catholic, ready to offer you some mystery if your teeth will ache too much without it. Highly recommended by Father! Forty dollars an hour, Father's forty dollars! Progress! Looking up! Looking better! That new haircut is so becoming, says Dr. Coronet herself, showing how normal she is for a woman with an I.Q. of 180 and many advanced degrees.

2. Mother. A lady in a brown suede coat. Boots of shiny black material, black gloves, a black fur hat. She would be humiliated could she know that of all the people in the world it is my ex-lover Simon who walks most like her . . . self-conscious and unreal, listening to distant music, a little bowleg-ged with craftiness. . . .

3. Father. Tying a necktie. In a hurry. On my first evening home he put his hand on my arm and said, "Honey, we're going to forget all about this."

4. Simon. Outside, a plane is crossing the sky, in here we're in a hurry. Morning. It must be morning. The girl is half out of her mind, whimpering and vague; Simon her dear friend is wretched this morning . . . he is wretched with morning itself . . . he forces her to give him an injection with that needle she knows is filthy, she had a dread of needles and surgical in-struments and the odor of things that are to be sent into the blood, thinking somehow of her father. . . . This is a bad morning, Simon says that his mind is being twisted out of shape, and so he submits to the needle that he usually scorns and bites his lip with his yellowish teeth, his face going very pale. *Ah baby!* he says in his soft mocking voice, which with all women is a mockery of love, *do it like this—Slowly—*And the girl, terrified, almost drops the precious needle but manages to turn it up to the light from the window . . . is it an extension of herself then? She can give him this gift then? I *wish you wouldn't do this to me,* she says, wise in her terror, because it seems to her that Simon's danger—in a few minutes he may be dead—is a way of press-ing her against him that is more powerful than any other embrace. She has

to work over his arm, the knotted corded veins of his arm, her forehead wet with perspiration as she pushes and releases the needle, staring at that mixture of liquid now stained with Simon's bright blood. . . . When the drug hits him she can feel it herself, she feels that magic that is more than any woman can give him, striking the back of his head and making his face stretch as if with the impact of a terrible sun. . . . She tries to embrace him but he pushes her aside and stumbles to his feet. *Jesus Christ,* he says. . . .

5. Princess, a Negro girl of eighteen. What is her charge? She is closed-mouthed about it, shrewd and silent, you know that no one had to wrestle her to the sidewalk to get her in here; she came with dignity. In the recreation room she sits reading *Nancy Drew and the Jewel Box Mystery,* which inspires in her face tiny wrinkles of alarm and interest: what a face! Light brown skin, heavy shaded eyes, heavy eyelashes, a serious sinister dark brow, graceful fingers, graceful wristbones, graceful legs, lips, tongue, a sugar-sweet voice, a leggy stride more masculine than Simon's and my mother's, decked out in a dirty white blouse and dirty white slacks; vaguely nautical is Princess' style. . . . At breakfast she is in charge of clearing the table and leans over me, saying, *Honey you sure you ate enough?*

6. The girl lies sleepless, wondering. Why here, why not there? Why Bloomfield Hills and not jail? Why jail and not her pink room? Why downtown Detroit and not Sioux Drive? What is the difference? Is Simon all the difference? The girl's head is a parade of wonders. She is nearly sixteen, her breath is marvelous with wonders, not long ago she was coloring with crayons and now she is smearing the landscape with paints that won't come off and won't come off her fingers either. She says to the matron *I am not talking about anything,* not because everyone has warned her not to talk but because, because she will not talk; because she won't say anything about Simon, who is her secret. And she says to the matron, *I won't go home,* up until that night in the lavatory when everything was changed. . . . "No, I won't go home I want to stay here," she says, listening to her own words with amazement, thinking that weeds might climb everywhere over that marvelous $180,000 house and dinosaurs might return to muddy the beige carpeting, but never never will she reconcile four o'clock in the morning in Detroit with eight o'clock breakfasts in Bloomfield Hills. . . . oh, she aches still for Simon's hands and his caressing breath, though he gave her little pleasure, he took everything from her (five-dollar bills, ten-dollar bills, passed into her numb hands by men and taken out of her hands by Simon) until she herself was passed into the hands of other men, police, when Simon evidently got tired of her and her hysteria. . . . *No, I won't go home, I don't want to be bailed out.* The girl thinks as a *Stubborn and Wayward Child* (one of several charges lodged against her), and the matron understands

her crazy white-rimmed eyes that are seeking out some new violence that will keep her in jail, should someone threaten to let her out. Such children try to strangle the matrons, the attendants, or one another . . . they want the locks locked forever, the doors nailed shut . . . and this girl is no different up until that night her mind is changed for her. . . .

IX. THAT NIGHT

Princess and Dolly, a little white girl of maybe fifteen, hardy however as a sergeant and in the House of Correction for armed robbery, corner her in the lavatory at the farthest sink and the other girls look away and file out to bed, leaving her. God, how she is beaten up! Why is she beaten up? Why do they pound her, why such hatred? Princess vents all the hatred of a thousand silent Detroit winters on her body, this girl whose body belongs to me, fiercely she rides across the Midwestern plains on this girl's tender bruised body . . . revenge on the oppressed minorities of America! revenge on the slaughtered Indians! revenge on the female sex, on the male sex, revenge on Bloomfield Hills, revenge revenge. . . .

X. DETROIT

In Detroit, weather weighs heavily upon everyone. The sky looms large. The horizon shimmers in smoke. Downtown the buildings are imprecise in the haze. Perpetual haze. Perpetual motion inside the haze. Across the choppy river is the city of Windsor, in Canada. Part of the continent has bunched up here and is bulging outward, at the tip of Detroit; a cold hard rain is forever falling on the expressways. . . . Shoppers shop grimly, their cars are not parked in safe places, their windshields may be smashed and graceful ebony hands may drag them out through their shatterproof smashed windshields, crying, *Revenge for the Indians!* Ah, they all fear leaving Hudson's and being dragged to the very tip of the city and thrown off the parking roof of Cobo Hall, that expensive tomb, into the river. . . .

XI. CHARACTERS WE ARE FOREVER ENTWINED WITH

1. Simon drew me into his tender rotting arms and breathed gravity into me. Then I came to earth, weighed down. He said, *You are such a little girl,* and he weighed me down with his delight. In the palms of his hands were teeth marks from his previous life experiences. He was thirty-five, they said. Imagine Simon in this room, in my pink room: he is about six feet tall

and stoops slightly, in a feline cautious way, always thinking, always on guard, with his scuffed light suede shoes and his clothes that are anyone's clothes, slightly rumpled ordinary clothes that ordinary men might wear to not-bad jobs. Simon has fair long hair, curly hair, spent languid curls that are like . . . exactly like the curls of wood shavings to the touch, I am trying to be exact . . . and he smells of unheated mornings and coffee and too many pills coating his tongue with a faint green-white scum. . . . Dear Simon, who would be panicked in this room and in this house (right now Billie is vacuuming next door in my parents' room; a vacuum cleaner's roar is a sign of all good things), Simon who is said to have come from a home not much different from this, years ago, fleeing all the carpeting and the polished banisters . . . Simon has a deathly face, only desperate people fall in love with it. His face is bony and cautious, the bones of his cheeks prominent as if with the rigidity of his ceaseless thinking, plotting, for he has to make money out of girls to whom money means nothing, they're so far gone they can hardly count it, and in a sense money means nothing to him either except as a way of keeping on with his life. *Each Day's Proud Struggle,* the title of a novel we could read at jail. . . . Each day he needs a certain amount of money. He devours it. It wasn't love he uncoiled in me with his hollowed-out eyes and his courteous smile, that remnant of a prosperous past, but a dark terror that needed to press itself flat against him, or against another man . . . but he was the first, he came over to me and took my arm, a claim. We struggled on the stairs and I said, *Let me loose, you're hurting my neck, my face,* it was such a surprise that my skin hurt where he rubbed it, and afterward we lay face to face and he breathed everything into me. In the end I think he turned me in.

2. Raymond Forrest. I just read this morning that Raymond Forrest's father, the chairman of the board at ——, died of a heart attack on a plane bound for London. I would like to write Raymond Forrest a note of sympathy. I would like to thank him for not pressing charges against me one hundred years ago, saving me, being so generous . . . well, men like Raymond Forrest are generous men, not like Simon. I would like to write him a letter telling of my love, or of some other emotion that is positive and healthy. Not like Simon and his poetry, which he scrawled down when he was high and never changed a word . . . but when I try to think of something to say, it is Simon's language that comes back to me, caught in my head like a bad song, it is always Simon's language:

> *There is no reality only dreams*
> *Your neck may get snapped when you wake*
> *My love is drawn to some violent end*
> *She keeps wanting to get away*
> *My love is heading downward*

And I am heading upward
She is going to crash on the sidewalk
And I am going to dissolve into the clouds

XII. EVENTS

1. Out of the hospital, bruised and saddened and converted, with Princess' grunts still tangled in my hair . . . and Father in his overcoat, looking like a prince himself, come to carry me off. Up the expressway and out north to home. Jesus Christ, but the air is thinner and cleaner here. Monumental houses. Heartbreaking sidewalks, so clean.

2. Weeping in the living room. The ceiling is two stories high and two chandeliers hang from it. Weeping, weeping, though Billie the maid is *probably listening*. I will never leave home again. Never. Never leave home. Never leave this home again, never.

3. Sugar doughnuts for breakfast. The toaster is very shiny and my face is distorted in it. Is that my face?

4. The car is turning in the driveway. Father brings me home. Mother embraces me. Sunlight breaks in movieland patches on the roof of our traditional-contemporary home, which was designed for the famous automotive stylist whose identity, if I told you the name of the famous car he designed, you would all know, so I can't tell you because my teeth chatter at the thought of being sued . . . or having someone climb into my bedroom window with a rope to strangle me. . . . The car turns up the blacktop drive. The house opens to me like a doll's house, so lovely in the sunlight, the big living room beckons to me with its walls falling away in a delirium of joy at my return, Billie the maid is *no doubt* listening from the kitchen as I burst into tears and the hysteria Simon got so sick of. Convulsed in Father's arms, I say I will never leave again, never, why did I leave, where did I go, what happened, my mind is gone wrong, my body is one big bruise, my backbone was sucked dry, it wasn't the men who hurt me and Simon never hurt me but only those girls . . . my God, how they hurt me . . . I will never leave home again. . . . The car is perpetually turning up the drive and I am perpetually breaking down in the living room and we are perpetually taking the right exit from the expressway (Lahser Road) and the wall of the rest room is perpetually banging against my head and perpetually are Simon's hands moving across my body and adding everything up and so too are Father's hands on my shaking bruised back, far from the surface of my skin on the surface of my good blue cashmere coat (dry-cleaned for my

release). . . . I weep for all the money here, for God in gold and beige carpeting, for the beauty of chandeliers and the miracle of a clean polished gleaming toaster and faucets that run both hot and cold water, and I tell them, *I will never leave home, this is my home, I love everything here, I am in love with everything here. . . .*

I am home.

A Journey

EDNA O'BRIEN

February the twenty-second. Not far away was the honking of waterfowl from the pond in Battersea Park. The wrong side of London, some said, but she liked it, found it homely; the big power station was her landmark, as once upon a time a straggle of blue hills in Ireland had been.

The morning was cold, the ice had clawed at the window and left its telltale marks—long jagged lines, criss-cross lines, scrawls, lines at war with one another, lines bent on torment. It was still like twilight in the bedroom, and yet she wakened with alertness and her heart was as warm as a little ball of knitting wool. He was deep in a trough of sleep, impervious to nudging, to hitting, to pounding. He was beautiful. His hair like a halo was arced around his head—beautiful hair, not quite brown, not quite red, not quite gold, of the same darkness as gunmetal but with strands of brightness. Oh Christ, he'll think he's in his own house with his own woman, she thought as his eyelids flickered and he peered through. But he didn't. He knew where he was and said how glad he was to be there, and drawing her toward him he held her and squeezed her out like a bit of old washing.

They were off to Scotland, where he had to deliver a lecture to some students at a technical college, and later to a group of men—fellow-unionists who worked in the shipyards. "We're going a-travelling," she said, almost worried.

"Yes, pet," he said.

At any rate he hadn't changed his mind yet. He was a bit of a vacillator.

She made the coffee while he contemplated getting up, and from the kitchen she kept urging him, saying how they would be late, how he must please bestir himself. For some reason she was reminded of her wedding morning; both mornings had a feeling of unrealness, plus the same uncertainty and the same anxiety about being late. But that was a long time ago.

766

That was over, and dry in the mouth like a pod or a desiccated seed. This was this.

Why do I love him, this man upstairs, this Boyce, she thought. A workingman, a man unaccustomed to a woman like her, a man shy and moody and inarticulate.

Not that speech was what mattered between people. She learned that the very day she had accosted him on a train a few weeks before. A young man. She saw him and simply had to touch the newspaper he was scanning, flick it delicately with her finger; and he stared across at her and very quietly received her into his being, but without a word, without even a face-saving hello.

"I can't say things," he had said, and then breathed out quickly and nervously as if it had cost him a lot to admit it. He was like a hound, a little whippet. To venture loving him was like crossing the Rubicon—also daft. Also dicey. A journey of pain. She had no idea then how extensive that journey would be. A good man? Maybe. Maybe not. She was looking for reasons to unlove him. When he came down to the kitchen, he almost but didn't smile. There was such a tentativeness about him. Is it always going to be like this, she thought, spilling the coffee, slopping it in the saucer, and then nervously dumping the brown granular mass from a strainer onto an ashtray, and for no reason.

"I have no composure," she said. From him a wan smile. Would her buying the tickets be all right, would he look away while she paid, would it be an auspicious trip? She took his hand and warmed it and said she never wanted to do aught else, and he said not to say such things, not to say them, but in fact they were only a skimming of the real things she was longing to say. Years divided them, class divided them, position divided them. He wanted to give her a present and couldn't in case it wasn't swish enough. He bought perfume off a hawker in Oxford Circus, offered it to her, and then took it back. Probably gave it to Madge, his woman, put it down on the table along with his pay packet. Or maybe left it on a dressing table, if they had one. A tender moment? All these unknowns divided them. The morning she was getting married he was pruning trees in an English park, earning a smallish sum and living with a woman who had four children. He had always lived with some woman or another but insisted that he wasn't a philanderer, wasn't. He lived with Madge now, drank two pints of beer every evening, cuddled his baby girl, and smoked forty cigarettes a day.

In the taxi, he whispered to her to please not look at him like that, and at the airport he spent the bulk of the waiting time in the gents'. She wondered if there was a barber's in there, or if perhaps he had done a disappearance act, like people on their wedding day who do not show up at the altar rails. In fact, he had bought a plastic hairbrush to straighten his hair for the journey because it had got tangled in the night. Afterward, he put it in her travel bag. Did she need a travel bag? How long were they to stay? No knowing. They were terribly near and they were not near. No outsider could guess the relationship. In the plane, the hostess tried hard to flirt with him, said she'd seen him on television, but he skirted the subject by asking for a light. He was very active in his union and often appeared in television debates; at private meetings, he exhorted the members to think hard for themselves, to forget race and creed but to be on the side of their fellow-workers and to rope in new ones. He had made quite a reputation for himself by reading them cases from history, clippings from old newspapers, making them realize how they had been ill-treated for hundreds of years. He was a scaffolder like his father before him, but he had left Belfast soon after his parents died. His brothers and sisters were scattered.

When they got to the city destination, he suddenly suggested that she dump her bag in a safety locker, and she knew then that she shouldn't have brought it, that possibly they would not be staying overnight. Walking up the street of Edinburgh with a bitter breeze in their faces, she pointed to a castle that looked like a dungeon and asked him what he thought of it. Not much. He didn't think much—that was his answer. What did he do? Dream, daydream, imagine, forget? The leaves in the municipal flower bed were blowing and shivered like tatters, but the soil was a beautiful flaky black. They happened to be passing a funeral parlor and she asked if he preferred burial or cremation, but about that, too, he was indifferent. It made no matter. They should still be in bed, under covers, drowsed. She linked him and he jerked his arm away, saying those who knew him knew the woman he lived with and he would not like to appear knavish. They were halfway up the hill, and there was between them now one of those little swords of silence that are always slicing love—that kind of love.

"If Madge knew about this, she'd be immeasurably hurt," he said.

But Madge will know, she thought but did not say. She said instead that it was colder up north, that they were not far from the sea, and didn't he detect bits of hail in the wind? He saw her sadness, traced it lightly with his finger, traced the near-tears and the little pouch under the lids. He said, "You're a terrible woman altogether," to which she replied, "You're not a bad bloke," and they laughed. He was supposed to have travelled by train the night before, the very night he slept with her and had his hair pulled from the roots, like a bush brought away from a hillside. How good a liar was he, and how strong a man? He had crossed the street ahead of her, and to make amends he waited for her by the lights and watched her, admiring, as she came toward him, watched her walk, her lovely legs, her long, incongruous skirt, and watched the effect she had on others—one of shock, as if she were undressed or carrying some sort of invisible torch. He spoke of it—her poise—and even referred to an ancient queen.

"It's not that it's not pleasant holding your arm," he said, and took her elbow, feeling the wobble of the funny bone. Then he had to make a phone call, and soon they were going somewhere in a taxi, and the back streets of Edinburgh were not unlike the back streets of any other town—a bit black, a bit decrepit, pub fronts being washed down.

He's afraid of me, she thought. And I'm afraid of him. Fear is corrosive, and she felt certain that the woman he lived with was much more adept at living and arguing than she was. Probably would insist that he bring in the coal or clean out the ashes or share his last cigarette, would put her cards on the table. For a moment she was seized with a desire to see them together, and had the terrible idea that she would call at their place as a door-to-door saleswoman with a little attaché case full of cleaning stuffs, so she would have to go in and show her wares. She would see their kitchen and their pram and the baby in it, she would see how disposed they were to one another. But that would not be necessary, because he was leaving, because he had told her that between him and the woman it was all over; it had all gone dry and flaccid. When Boyce looked at her then, it was a true felt look and laden with sweetness—white, mesmerizing, like the blossom that hangs from the cherry tree.

Before addressing the students, he called on some friends. Even that was furtive—he didn't knock; he whistled some sort of code through the letter box. In the big, sparsely furnished room there was a pregnant cat—marmalade—and the leftovers of a breakfast, and a man and a woman who had obviously just tumbled out of their bed. She thought, This is how it should be. When, through a crack in the door, catching a glimpse of their big tossed bed and the dented pillows without pillow slips, she ached to go in and lie there, she knew that the sight of it had permeated her consciousness and it was a longing she would always feel. That longing was replaced by a stitch in the chest, then a lot of stitches, and then something like a lump in the back of the mouth—something sad that would not dissolve. Would he live with her, as he had said? Would he do it? Would he forsake everything—fear, respectability, safeness, the woman, the child? The questions were like pendulums swinging this way and that. The answers would swing, too.

The woman she had just met was called Ita and the man was called Jim the Limb. He had some defect in his right arm. They were plump and radiant, what with their night and their big breakfast and now a fresh pot of tea. They were chain smokers. Ita said her fur coat and the marmalade cat were alike, and Boyce said that was a wrong thing to say. But there was no wrong thing so far as she was concerned. She just wanted them to welcome her in, to accept her. When they taked about the union and the various men and the weekly meetings, when they discussed a rally that was to take place in London, she thought, Let me be one of you, let me put aside my old stupid flitting life, let me take part, let me in. Her life was not exactly soignée and she, too, had lived in poor rooms and ridden a ridiculous bicycle and swapped old shoes for other old shoes, but she seemed not to belong, because she had bettered herself—had done it on her own, and now that she was a graphic designer she designed alone. Also, these people in the union were townspeople; they all had lived in small steep town houses, slept two or three or four to a bed, sparred, lived in and out of one another's pockets, knew familiarity well enough to know that it was tolerable.

Ita announced that she was not going to the factory that morning, said dammit, the bloody sweatshop, and told of two women who were fired because they had gone deaf from the machines and weren't able to hear proper.

Instantly Boyce said they must fight it. They were a clan. Yet when he winked at *her* he seemed to be saying something else, something ambiguous, like "I see you there, I am not forsaking you"—or was he saying "Look how influential I am, look at me"? A word he often used was "big shot." Maybe he had dreams of being a big shot? Just before the four of them left the house for the college, he went for the third time to the lavatory, and she believed he had gone to be sick. Yet when he stood on the small ladder platform, holding up a faulty loudspeaker, brandishing it, making jokes about it—calling it Big Brother—he seemed to be utterly in his element. He spoke without notes, he spoke freely, telling the crowd of his background in Belfast, his father's work at the shipyards, his having to emigrate, his job in London, the lads, the way this fellow or that fellow had got nabbed, and though what he had to say was about discrimination, he made it all funny. When questions were put after he had finished, it was clear that he had cajoled them all, except for one dissenter—an aristocratic-looking boy in a dress suit, a boy who seemed to be on the brink of a nervous breakdown. Even with him he dealt deftly. He replied without any venom, and when the dissenter was booed and told to belt up, he said "Aach" to his friends who were heckling. The hat was passed around—a navy college cap—into which coins were tossed from all corners of the room. She hesitated, not knowing whether to give a lot or a little and wanting only to do the right thing. She gave a pound note, and afterward in the refectory to which they had all repaired she saw a girl hand him ten pounds and thought how the collection must have been to foot his expenses.

Ita and Jim decided to accompany them to Glasgow, where he was conducting the same sort of meeting in the evening, in a public hall. Getting to the station late, as they did, he said, "Let's jump in here," and ushered them into a first-class carriage, though their tickets were for second. When the ticket-collector came, she paid the difference, knowing that he had chosen the first because he felt it was where she belonged. They couldn't hear one another for the rattle of the train, the shunting of other carriages, and a whipping wind that lashed through a broken window. He dozed; sometimes, coming awake, he nudged her with his shoe. The ladies sat on one side, the men opposite, and Ita was whispering to her in her ear, saying how when she met Jim they had gone to bed for an entire week. Boyce looked at the women whispering and tittering and he seemed to like that, and there was a satisfaction in the way he lolled.

By the time they got to the station they were all hungry. "Starving you I am," he said to her as he asked a porter for the name of a restaurant. "A French joint," he said. As they were settling down in the garish room, Ita tripped over the flex of the table lamp and Jim glowered with embarrassment, said this wasn't home—not by a long shot. They dived into the basket of bread, calling for butter, butter. Boyce made jokes about the wine, sniffed it, and asked if for sure it was the best vintage. She fed him with her fingers the little potato sticks on her plate. He accepted them as if they were matches, then gobbled them down, and the others knew what they had suspected—that this pair were lovers. Jim said they looked like two people in a snapshot, and they smiled as if they *were*, and their faces scanned one another as if in a beautiful daze.

At the meeting, he gave the same spiel, except that it had to be shortened, and this he did by omitting one anecdote about a man who was sent to jail for speaking Gaelic in the northern province of his own country. There was a collection here, too, and the amount was much higher, because the bulk of the audience were workingmen, and proud to contribute.

From the hall they went with a group to a big ramshackle room at the top of a large house in the north side of the city. In the front hall there were dozens of milk bottles, and in the back hall two or three bicycles jumbled together. He had bought a bottle of whiskey, and in the kitchen off the big room she heated a kettle to make a hot punch for him because his throat was sore. He came out to the kitchen and told her what a grand person she was, and he kissed her stealthily. The kitchen was a shambles, and although at first intending to tidy it a bit, all she did was scald two cups and a tumbler for his punch. Some had hot whiskey, some had cold; she had hers laced in a cup of tea. They all talked, interrupting one another, joking, having inside conversation about meetings they'd been to and other meetings to which they'd sent hecklers, and demonstrations that they were planning to have, and all their supporters in France, Italy, and throughout Europe.

She looked up at the light shade, wrinkled plastic as big as a beach ball, and decorated with a lot of fishes. She felt useless. The designs she made were simple and geometric and somewhat moving, but at that moment they seemed irrelevant. They had no relation to these people, to their conversa-

tion, to their curious kind of bantering anger. She remembered nights on
end when she had striven to make a shape or a design that would go
straight to the quick of someone's being, she had gruelled over it—but to
these people it would be a piece of folly. The place was unkempt, but still it
was a place. Above the window, several brass rings had come off their
hooks and the heavy velvet curtain gaped. He was being witty. Someone
had said that there were more ways than one of killing a cat, and he had intervened to say that the word was "skinning." That was the first flicker of
cruelty she had seen in him. She was sitting next him on the divan bed, she
leaning back against the wall slightly out of the melee, he pressing forward
making the odd joke. He said that at forty he might find his true vocation
in life, and feared it might be as a whiz kid. There was a rocking chair in
which one of the men sat, and several easy chairs with stained and torn upholstery, their springs dipping down to variable degrees, depending on the
weight and pranks of the sitters. Sometimes a girl with plaits would rush
over and sit on her man's knee and pull his beard and then the springs
dropped like the inside of a broken melodeon. If only he and she could be
that unreserved.

Then he was missing—out on the landing, using the phone. She knew
they had missed the last plane back to London, and long ago had missed
the last train, and that they would have to kip down somewhere, and she
thought how awful if it had to be in the center of town, in the freezing cold,
on a bench. Ita asked her if they were perhaps going to make a touring holiday, and she said no but couldn't add to that, couldn't gloss the reply with
some extra little piece of information. When he came back to the room, he
told her that a taxi was on its way.

"I don't know where we're heading for—a wonderland," he said, shaking hands with Ita, and then he said cheers to the room at large.

The hotel was close to the airport—a modern building made of concrete
cubes, like something built by a child, and with vertical slits for windows.
They might be turned away. He went in whistling. She waited, one foot on
the step of the taxi and one on the footpath, and said an involuntary
prayer. She saw him handing over money, then beckoning for her to come
in. He had signed the register, and in the lift, as he fondled her, he told her
the false name that he had used. It was a nice name—Egan. In the bedroom they thought of whiskey, but they were too tired, and shy all over
again, and neither of them imperious enough to give an order while the
other was listening.

"I know you better now," he said. She wondered at what precise moment in
the day he had come to know her better. Had he crept in on her like a little
invisible camera and knew that he knew her and would know her for all
time? Maybe some non-moment, when she walked gauchely toward the la-

dies' room, or when asked her second name she hesitated, in case by giving
a name she should compromise him. She apologized for not talking more,
and he said that that was what was lovely about her, and he apologized for
giving the same lecture twice, and for all the stupid things that got said.
Then he trotted around naked, getting his tiny transistor from his overcoat
pocket, studying the hotel clock—a square face set into the bedside table—
fiddling with the various lights. He had never stayed in a hotel before, and
it was then he told her that there would be a refund if in the morning they
didn't eat breakfast. He had paid. His earnings for the day had been swallowed up by the payment.

"I'll refund you," she said, and he said what rot, and in the dark they
were together again—together like spare limbs, like rag dolls or bits of mo-
torcar tire, bits of themselves, together, effortless and full of harmony, as if
they had grown that way, always were and always would be. But she
couldn't ask for a pledge. It had to come from him. He was thinking of
leaving London, changing jobs, going back home to Belfast. Well, wherever
he went she was going too. He had brought everything to a head, everything she had wanted to feel—love and pity and softness and passion and
patience and barefaced jealousy. They went to sleep talking, then half talking, voices trailing away like tendrils, sleepy voices, sleepy brains, sleepy
bodies, talking, not talking, dumb.

"I love you, I love you." He said it the very moment that the hotel clock
triggered off, and the doubts and the endless cups of coffee and the bulging ashtrays were all sweet reminds of a day in which the fates changed. He
said he dearly wished that they could lie there for hours on end and have
coffee and papers sent up, and lie there and let the bloody airplanes and
the bloody world go by.

But why were they hurrying? It was a Saturday and he had no work.

"I'll say goodbye here," he said, and he kissed her and pulled the lapel of
her fur coat up around her neck so that she wouldn't feel the cold.

"But we're going together," she said.

He said yes, but they would be in public places and they would not be
able to say goodbye—not intimately. He kissed her.

"We will be together?" she said.

"It will take time," he said.

"How long?'" she asked.

"Months, years . . ."

They were ready to go.

In the plane, they talked first about mushrooms, and she said how mushrooms were reputed to be magic, and then she asked him if he had wanted
a son rather than a daughter, and he said no, a daughter, and smiled at the
thought of his little one. He read four of the morning papers—read them,

reread them, combed the small news items that were put in at the last minute, and got printing ink all over his hands. The edges of the paper sometimes jutted against her nose or her eyes or her forehead, and without turning he would say, "Sorry, love." To live with, he would be all right—silent at times, undemonstrative, then all of a sudden touching as an infant. Every slight gesture of his, every "Sorry, love" tore at some place in her gut.

In London, a bus was waiting on the tarmac, right next to the landed plane. He said they needn't bother rushing, and as a result they were very nearly not taken at all. The steward looked down the aisle of the bus, put up a finger to say that there was room for only one, and then in the end grumpily let them both enter. They had to sit separately, with an aisle between them, and she began to revert to her cursed superstitions, such as if they passed a white gate all would be well.

At the terminus, he had to make a phone call, and she could see him, although she had not meant to look, gesticulating fiercely in the glass booth. When he came out, he was biting his thumb. After a while he said he was late, that the woman had had to stay home from work, that he was in the wrong again. She saw it clearly, cruelly—as clear and as cruel as the lines of ice that had claimed the windowpane. Claims. Responsibility. "Be here, be here."

They walked up the street toward the Underground station. No matter how she carried it, the travel bag bumped against her, or, when she changed hands, against him. Boyce said she was never to tell anyone. She said she wasn't likely to go spouting it, and he said why the frown, why spoil everything with a frown like that? It went out like a shooting star—the sense of peace, the suffusion, the near-happiness. He asked her to hang on while he got cigarettes, and then, plunging into the dark passage that led to the Underground, he saw her hesitate and said did she always take taxis? They kissed. It was a dark, unpropitious passage but a real kiss. Their mouths clung, the skin of their lips would not be parted; she felt that they might fall into a trance in order not to terminate it. He was as helpless then as a schoolboy, and his eyes as pathetic as watered ink.

"If I must, if I must talk to you, may I?" she asked.

He looked at her bitterly. He was like a chisel. "I can't promise anything," he said, and repeated it. Then he was gone, doing a little hop through the turnstile and omitting to get a ticket. She walked on, the bag bumping off the calf of her leg; soon, when she had enough composure, she would hail a taxi. Would he go? Would he come back? What would he do? It was like a door that had just come ajar and anything could happen to it; it could shut tight or open a fraction or fly wide in a burst. She thought of the bigness and wonder of destiny; meeting him had been a fluke, and this now was a fluke, and so was the future, and they would be together or not be together as life the gaffer thought fit.

The Geranium

FLANNERY O'CONNOR

Old Dudley folded into the chair he was gradually molding to his own shape and looked out the window fifteen feet away into another window framed by blackened red brick. He was waiting for the geranium. They put it out every morning about ten and they took it in at five-thirty. Mrs. Carson back home had a geranium in her window. There were plenty of geraniums at home, better looking geraniums. Ours are sho nuff geraniums, Old Dudley thought, not any er this pale pink business with green, paper bows. The geranium they would put in the window reminded him of the Grisby boy at home who had polio and had to be wheeled out every morning and left in the sun to blink. Lutisha could have taken that geranium and stuck it in the ground and had something worth looking at in a few weeks. Those people across the alley had no business with one. They set it out and let the hot sun bake it all day and they put it so near the ledge the wind could almost knock it over. They had no business with it, no business with it. It shouldn't have been there. Old Dudley felt his throat knotting up. Lutish could root anything. Rabie too. His throat was drawn taut. He laid his head back and tried to clear his mind. There wasn't much he could think of to think about that didn't do his throat that way.

His daughter came in. "Don't you want to go out for a walk?" she asked. She looked provoked.

He didn't answer her.

"Well?"

"No." He wondered how long she was going to stand there. She made his eyes feel like his throat. They'd get watery and she'd see. She had seen before and had looked sorry for him. She'd looked sorry for herself too; but she could er saved herself, Old Dudley thought, if she'd just have let him alone—let him stay where he was back home and not be so taken up with her damn duty. She moved out of the room leaving an audible sigh to crawl over him and remind him again of that one minute—that wasn't her fault at all—when suddenly he had wanted to go to New York to live with her.

He could have got out of going. He could have been stubborn and told her he'd spend his life where he'd always spent it, send him or not send him the money every month, he'd get along with his pension and odd jobs. Keep her damn money—she needed it worse than he did. She would have been glad to have had her duty disposed of like that. Then she could have said if he died without his children near him, it was his own fault; if he got sick and there wasn't anybody to take care of him, well, he'd asked for it, she could have said. But there was that thing inside him that had wanted to see New York. He had been to Atlanta once when he was a boy and he had seen New York in a picture show. "Big Town Rhythm" it was. Big towns were important places. The thing inside him had sneaked up on him for just one instant. The place like he'd seen in the picture show had room for him! It was an important place and it had room for him! He'd said, yes, he'd go.

He must have been sick when he said it. He couldn't have been well and said it. He had been sick and she had been so taken up with her damn duty, she had wangled it out of him. Why did she have to come down there in the first place to pester him? He had been doing all right. There was his pension that could feed him and odd jobs that kept him his room in the boarding house.

The window in that room showed him the river—thick and red as it struggled over rocks and around curves. He tried to think how it was besides red and slow. He added green blotches for trees on either side of it and a brown spot for trash somewhere upstream. He and Rabie had fished it in a flat-bottom boat every Wednesday. Rabie knew the river up and down for twenty miles. There wasn't another nigger in Coa County that knew it like he did. He loved the river, but it hadn't meant anything to Old Dudley. The fish were what he was after. He liked to come in at night with a long string of them and slap them down in the sink. "Few fish I got," he'd say. It took a man to get those fish, the old girls at the boarding house always said. He and Rabie would start out early Wednesday morning and fish all day. Rabie would find the spots and row; Old Dudley always caught them. Rabie didn't care much about catching them—he just loved the river. "Ain't no use settin' yo' line down dere, boss," he'd say, "ain't no fish dere. Dis ol' riber ain't hidin' none nowhere 'round hyar, nawsuh," and he would giggle and shift the boat downstream. That was Rabie. He could steal cleaner than a weasel but he knew where the fish were. Old Dudley always gave him the little ones.

Old Dudley had lived upstairs in the corner room of the boarding house ever since his wife died in '22. He protected the old ladies. He was the man in the house and he did the things a man in the house was supposed to do. It was a dull occupation at night when the old girls crabbed and crocheted in the parlor and the man in the house had to listen and judge the sparrow-like wars that rasped and twittered intermittently. But in the daytime there was Rabie. Rabie and Lutisha lived down in the basement. Lutish cooked and Rabie took care of the cleaning and the vegetable garden; but he was sharp at sneaking off with half his work done and going to help Old Dudley with some current project—building a hen house or painting a door. He liked to listen, he liked to hear about Atlanta when Old Dudley had been there and about how guns were put together on the inside and all the other things the old man knew.

Sometimes at night they would go 'possum hunting. They never got a 'possum but Old Dudley liked to get away from the ladies once in a while and hunting was a good excuse. Rabie didn't like 'possum hunting. They never got a 'possum; they never even treed one; and besides, he was mostly a water nigger. "We ain't gonna go huntin' no 'possum tonight, is we, boss? I got a lil' business I wants tuh tend tuh," he'd say when Old Dudley would start talking about hounds and guns. "Whose chickens you gonna steal to-night?" Dudley would grin. "I reckon I be huntin' 'possum tonight," Rabie'd sigh.

Old Dudley would get out his gun and take it apart and, as Rabie cleaned the pieces, would explain the mechanism to him. Then he'd put it together again. Rabie always marveled at the way he could put it together again. Old Dudley would have liked to have explained New York to Rabie. If he could have showed it to Rabie, it wouldn't have been so big—he wouldn't have felt pressed down every time he went out in it. "It ain't so big," he would have said. "Don't let it get you down, Rabie. It's just like any other city and cities ain't all that complicated."

But they were. New York was swishing and jamming one minute and dirty and dead the next. His daughter didn't even live in a house. She lived in a building—the middle in a row of buildings all alike, all blackened-red and gray with rasp-mouthed people hanging out their windows looking at other windows and other people just like them looking back. Inside you could go up and you could go down and there were just halls that re-minded you of tape measures strung out with a door every inch. He re-membered he'd been dazed by the building the first week. He'd wake up expecting the halls to have changed in the night and he'd look out the door and there they stretched like dog runs. The streets were the same way. He wondered where he'd be if he walked to the end of one of them. One night he dreamed he did and ended at the end of the building—nowhere.

The next week he had become more conscious of the daughter and son-in-law and their boy—no place to be out of their way. The son-in-law was a queer one. He drove a truck and came in only on the weekends. He said "nah" for "no" and he'd never heard of a 'possum. Old Dudley slept in the room with the boy who was sixteen and couldn't be talked to. But some-times when the daughter and Old Dudley were alone in the apartment, she would sit down and talk to him. First she had to think of something to say. Usually it gave out before what she considered was the proper time to get up and do something else, so he would have to say something. He always tried to think of something he hadn't said before. She never listened the second time. She was seeing that her father spent his last years with his own family and not in a decayed boarding house full of old women whose heads jiggled. She was doing her duty. She had brothers and sisters who were not.

Once she took him shopping with her but he was too slow. They went in a "subway"—a railroad underneath the ground like a big cave. People boiled out of trains and up steps and over into the streets. They rolled off the street and down steps and into trains—black and white and yellow all mixed up like vegetables in soup. Everything was boiling. The trains swished in from tunnels, up canals, and all of a sudden stopped. The people coming out pushed through the people coming in and a noise rang and the train swooped off again. Old Dudley and the daughter had to go in three different ones before they got where they were going. He wondered why people ever went out of their houses. He felt like his tongue had slipped down in his stomach. She held him by the coat sleeve and pulled him through the people.

They went on an overhead train too. She called it an "El." They had to go up on a high platform to catch it. Old Dudley looked over the rail and could see the people rushing and the automobiles rushing under him. He felt sick. He put one hand on the rail and sank down on the wooden floor of the platform. The daughter screamed and pulled him over from the edge. "Do you want to fall off and kill yourself?" she shouted.

Through a crack in the boards he could see the cars swimming in the street. "I don't care," he murmured, "I don't care if I do or not."

"Come on," she said, "you'll feel better when we get home."

"Home?" he repeated. The cars moved in a rhythm below him.

"Come on," she said, "here it comes; we've just got time to make it." They'd just had time to make all of them.

They made that one. They came back to the building and the apartment. The apartment was too tight. There was no place to be where there wasn't somebody else. The kitchen opened into the bathroom and the bathroom opened into everything else and you were always where you started from. At home there was upstairs and the basement and the river and down town in front of Fraziers . . . damn his throat.

The geranium was late today. It was ten-thirty. They usually had it out by ten-fifteen.

Somewhere down the hall a woman shrilled something unintelligible out to the street; a radio was bleating the worn music to a soap serial; and a garbage can crashed down a fire-escape. The door to the next apartment slammed and a sharp footstep clipped down the hall. "That would be the nigger," Old Dudley muttered. "The nigger with the shiny shoes." He had

been there a week when the nigger moved in. That Thursday he was looking out the door at the dog run halls when this nigger went into the next
apartment. He had on a grey, pin-stripe suit and a tan tie. His collar was
stiff and white and made a clear-cut line next to his neck. His shoes were
shiny tan—they matched his tie and his skin. Old Dudley scratched his
head. He hadn't known the kind of people that would live thick in a building could afford servants. He chuckled. Lot of good a nigger in a Sunday
suit would do them. Maybe this nigger would know the country around
here—or maybe how to get to it. They might could hunt. They might could
find them a stream somewhere. He shut the door and went to the daughter's room. "Hey!" he shouted, "the folks next door got 'em a nigger. Must
be gonna clean for them. You reckon they gonna keep him every day?"

She looked up from making the bed. "What are you talking about?"

"I say they got 'em a servant next door—a nigger—all dressed up in a
Sunday suit."

She walked to the other side of the bed. "You must be crazy," she said.
"The next apartment is vacant and besides, nobody around here can afford
any servant."

"I tell you I saw him," Old Dudley snickered. "Going right in there with
a tie and a white collar on—and sharp-toed shoes."

"If he went in there, he's looking at it for himself," she muttered. She
went to the dresser and started fidgeting with things.

Old Dudley laughed. She could be right funny when she wanted to.
"Well," he said, "I think I'll go over and see what day he gets off. Maybe I
can convince him he likes to fish," and he'd slapped his pocket to make the
two quarters jingle. Before he got out in the hall good, she came tearing behind him and pulled him in. "Can't you hear?" she yelled. "I meant what I
said. He's renting that himself if he went in there. Don't you go asking him
any questions or saying anything to him. I don't want any trouble with
niggers."

"You mean," Old Dudley murmured, "he's gonna live next door to you?"

She shrugged. "I suppose he is. And you tend to your own business," she
added. "Don't have anything to do with him."

That's just the way she'd said it. Like he didn't have any sense at all. But
he'd told her off then. He'd stated his say and she knew what he meant.
"You ain't been raised that way!" he'd said thundery-like. "You ain't been
raised to live tight with niggers that think they're just as good as you, and
you think I'd go messin' around with one er that kind! If you think I want
anything to do with them, you're crazy." He had had to slow down then because his throat was tightening. She'd stood stiff up and said they lived
where they could afford to live and made the best of it. Preaching to him!
Then she'd walked stiff off without a word more. That was her. Trying to
be holy with her shoulders curved around and her neck in the air. Like he
was a fool. He knew yankees let niggers in their front doors and let them

set on their sofas but he didn't know his own daughter that was raised proper would stay next door to them—and then think he didn't have no more sense than to want to mix with them. Him!

He got up and took a paper off another chair. He might as well appear to be reading when she came through again. No use having her standing there staring at him, believing she had to think up something for him to do. He looked over the paper at the window across the alley. The geranium wasn't there yet. It had never been this late before. The first day he'd seen it, he had been sitting there looking out the window at the other window and he had looked at his watch to see how long it had been since breakfast. When he looked up, it was there. It startled him. He didn't like flowers, but the geranium didn't look like a flower. It looked like the sick Grisby boy at home and it was the color of the drapes the old ladies had in the parlor and the paper bow on it looked like the one behind Lutish's uniform she wore on Sundays. Lutish had a fondness for sashes. Most niggers did, Old Dudley thought.

The daughter came through again. He had meant to be looking at the paper when she came through. "Do me a favor, will you?" she asked as if she had just thought up a favor he could do.

He hoped she didn't want him to go to the grocery again. He got lost the time before. All the blooming buildings looked alike. He nodded.

"Go down to the third floor and ask Mrs. Schmitt to lend me the shirt pattern she uses for Jake."

Why couldn't she just let him sit? She didn't need the shirt pattern. "All right," he said. "What number is it?"

"Number 10—just like this. Right below us three floors down."

Old Dudley was always afraid that when he went out in the dog runs, a door would suddenly open and one of the snipe-nosed men that hung off the window ledges in his undershirt would growl, "What are you doing here?" The door to the nigger's apartment was open and he could see a woman sitting in a chair by the window. "Yankee niggers," he muttered. She had on rimless glasses and there was a book in her lap. Niggers don't think they're dressed up till they got on glasses, Old Dudley thought. He remembered Lutish's glasses. She had saved up thirteen dollars to buy them. Then she went to the doctor and asked him to look at her eyes and tell her how thick to get the glasses. He made her look at animals' pictures through a mirror and he stuck a light through her eyes and looked in her head. Then he said she didn't need any glasses. She was so mad she burned the corn bread three days in a row, but she bought her some glasses anyway at the ten cent store. They didn't cost her but $1.98 and she wore them every Saddey. "That was niggers," Old Dudley chuckled. He realized he had made a noise, and covered his mouth with his hand. Somebody might hear him in one of the apartments.

He turned down the first flight of stairs. Down the second he heard footsteps coming up. He looked over the banisters and saw it was a woman—a fat woman with an apron on. From the top, she looked kind er like Mrs. Benson at home. He wondered if she would speak to him. When they were four steps from each other, he darted a glance at her but she wasn't looking at him. When there were no steps between them, his eyes fluttered up for an instant and she was looking at him cold in the face. Then she was past him. She hadn't said a word. He felt heavy in his stomach.

He went down four flights instead of three. Then he went back up one and found number 10. Mrs. Schmitt said O. K., wait a minute and she'd get the pattern. She sent one of the children back to the door with it. The child didn't say anything.

Old Dudley started back up the stairs. He had to take it more slowly. It tired him going up. Everything tired him, looked like. Not like having Rabie to do his running for him. Rabie was a light-footed nigger. He could sneak in a hen-house 'thout even the hens knowing it and get him the fattest fryer in there and not a squawk. Fast too. Dudley had always been slow on his feet. It went that way with fat people. He remembered one time him and Rabie was hunting quail over near Molton. They had 'em a hound dog that could find a covey quickern any fancy pointer going. He wasn't no good at bringing them back but he could find them every time and then set like a dead stump while you aimed at the birds. This one time the hound stopped cold-still. "Dat gonna be a big 'un," Rabie whispered, "I feels it." Old Dudley raised the gun slowly as they walked along. He had to be careful of the pine needles. They covered the ground and made it slick. Rabie shifted his weight from side to side, lifting and setting his feet on the waxen needles with unconscious care. He looked straight ahead and moved forward swiftly. Old Dudley kept one eye ahead and one on the ground. It would slope and he would be sliding forward dangerously or in pulling himself up an incline, he would slide back down.

"Ain't I better get dem birds dis time, boss?" Rabie suggested. "You ain't never easy on yo' feets on Monday. If you falls in one dem slopes, you gonna scatter dem birds fo' you gits dat gun up."

Old Dudley wanted to get the covey. He could er knocked four out it easy. "I'll get 'em," he muttered. He lifted the gun to his eye and leaned forward. Something slipped beneath him and he slid backward on his heels. The gun went off and the covey sprayed into the air.

"Dem was some mighty fine birds we let get away from us," Rabie sighed.

"We'll find another covey," Old Dudley said, "now get me out of this damn hole."

He could er got five er those birds if he hadn't fallen. He could er shot 'em off like cans on a fence. He drew one hand back to his ear and extended the other forward. He could er knocked 'em out like clay pigeons. Bang! A squeak on the staircase made him wheel around—his arms still holding the invisible gun. The nigger was clipping up the steps toward him, an amused smile stretching his trimmed mustache. Old Dudley's mouth dropped open. The nigger's lips were pulled down like he was trying to keep from laughing. Old Dudley couldn't move. He stared at the clear-cut line the nigger's collar made against his skin.

"What are you hunting, old timer?" the Negro asked in a voice that sounded like a nigger's laugh and a white man's sneer.

Old Dudley felt like a child with a pop-pistol. His mouth was open and his tongue was rigid in the middle of it. Right below his knees felt hollow. His feet slipped and he slid three steps and landed sitting down.

"You better be careful," the Negro said. "You could easily hurt yourself on these steps," and he held out his hand for Old Dudley to pull up on. It was a long narrow hand and the tips of the fingernails were clean and cut squarely. They looked like they might have been filed. Old Dudley's hands hung between his knees. The nigger took him by the arm and pulled up. "Whew!" he gasped, "you're heavy. Give a little help here." Old Dudley's knees unbended and he staggered up. The nigger had him by the arm. "I'm going up anyway," he said. "I'll help you." Old Dudley looked frantically around. The steps behind him seemed to close up. He was walking with the nigger up the stairs. The nigger was waiting for him on each step. "So you hunt?" the nigger was saying. "Well, let's see. I went deer hunting once. I believe we used a Dodson 38 to get those deer. What do you use?"

Old Dudley was staring through the shiny tan shoes. "I use a gun," he mumbled.

"I like to fool with guns better than hunting," the nigger was saying. "Never was much at killing anything. Seems kind of a shame to deplete the game reserve. I'd collect guns if I had the time and the money, though." He was waiting on every step till Old Dudley got on it. He was explaining guns and makes. He had on grey socks with a black fleck in them. They finished the stairs. The nigger walked down the hall with him, holding him by the arm. It probably looked like he had his arm locked in the nigger's.

They went right up to Old Dudley's door. Then the nigger asked, "You from around here?"

Old Dudley shook his head looking at the door. He hadn't looked at the nigger yet. All the way up the stairs, he hadn't looked at the nigger. "Well," the nigger said, "it's a swell place—once you get used to it." He patted Old Dudley on the back and went into his own apartment. Old Dudley went into his. The pain in his throat was all over his face now, leaking out his eyes.

He shuffled to the chair by the window and sank down in it. His throat was going to pop. His throat was going to pop on account of a nigger—a damn nigger that patted him on the back and called him "old timer." Him that knew such as that couldn't be. Him that had come from a good place. A good place. A place where such as that couldn't be. His eyes felt strange in their sockets. They were swelling in them and in a minute there wouldn't be any room left for them there. He was trapped in this place where niggers could call you "old timer." He wouldn't be trapped. He wouldn't be. He rolled his head on the back of the chair to stretch his neck that was too full.

A man was looking at him. A man was in the window across the alley looking straight at him. The man was watching him cry. That was where the geranium was supposed to be and it was a man in his undershirt, watching him cry, waiting to watch his throat pop. Old Dudley looked back at the man. It was supposed to be the geranium. The geranium belonged there, not the man. "Where is the geranium?" he called out of his tight throat.

"What you cryin' for?" the man asked. "I ain't never seen a man cry like that."

"Where is the geranium?" Old Dudley quavered. "It ought to be there. Not you."

"This is my window," the man said. "I got a right to set here if I want to."

"Where is it?" Old Dudley shrilled. There was just a little room left in his throat.

"It fell off if it's any of your business," the man said.

Old Dudley got up and peered over the window ledge. Down in the alley, way six floors down, he could see a cracked flower pot scattered over a spray of dirt and something pink sticking out of a green paper bow. It was down six floors. Smashed down six floors.

Old Dudley looked at the man who was chewing gum and waiting to see the throat pop. "You shouldn't have put it so near the ledge," he murmured. "Why don't you pick it up?"

"Why don't you, pop?"

Old Dudley stared at the man who was where the geranium should have been.

He would. He'd go down and pick it up. He'd put it in his own window and look at it all day if he wanted to. He turned from the window and left the room. He walked slowly down the dog run and got to the steps. The steps dropped down like a deep wound in the floor. They opened up through a gap like a cavern and went down and down. And he had gone up them a little behind the nigger. And the nigger had pulled him up on his feet and kept his arm in his and gone up the steps with him and said he hunted deer, "old timer," and seen him holding a gun that wasn't there and sitting on the steps like a child. He had shiny tan shoes and he was trying not to laugh and the whole business was laughing. There'd probably be niggers with black flecks in their socks on every step, pulling down their mouths so as not to laugh. The steps dropped down and down. He wouldn't go down and have niggers pattin' him on the back. He went back to the room and the window and looked down at the geranium.

The man was sitting over where it should have been. "I ain't seen you pickin' it up," he said.

Old Dudley stared at the man.

"I seen you before," the man said. "I seen you settin' in that old chair every day, starin' out the window, looking in my apartment. What I do in my apartment is my business, see? I don't like people looking at what I do."

It was at the bottom of the alley with its roots in the air.

"I only tell people once," the man said and left the window.

Judgement Day

FLANNERY O'CONNOR

Tanner was conserving all his strength for the trip home. He meant to walk as far as he could get and trust to the Almighty to get him the rest of the way. That morning and the morning before, he had allowed his daughter to dress him and had conserved that much more energy. Now he sat in the chair by the window—his blue shirt buttoned at the collar, his coat on the back of the chair, and his hat on his head—waiting for her to leave. He couldn't leave until she got out of the way. The window looked out on a brick wall and down into an alley full of New York air, the kind fit for cats and garbage. A few snow flakes drifted past the window but they were too thin and scattered for his failing vision.

The daughter was in the kitchen washing dishes. She dawdled over everything, talking to herself. When he had first come, he had answered her, but that had not been wanted. She glowered at him as if, old fool that he was, he should still have had sense enough not to answer a woman talking to herself. She questioned herself in one voice and answered herself in another. With the energy he had conserved yesterday letting her dress him, he had written a note and pinned it in his pocket. IF FOUND DEAD SHIP EXPRESS COLLECT TO COLEMAN PARRUM, CORINTH, GEORGIA. Under this he had continued: COLEMAN SELL MY BELONGINGS AND PAY THE FREIGHT ON ME & THE UNDERTAKER. ANYTHING LEFT OVER YOU CAN KEEP. YOURS TRULY T.C. TANNER. P.S. STAY WHERE YOU ARE. DON'T LET THEM TALK YOU INTO COMING UP HERE. ITS NO KIND OF PLACE. It had taken him the better part of thirty minutes to write the paper; the script was wavery but decipherable with patience. He controlled one hand by holding the other on top of it. By the time he had got it written, she was back in the apartment from getting her groceries.

Today he was ready. All he had to do was push one foot in front of the other until he got to the door and down the steps. Once down the steps, he would get out of the neighborhood. Once out of it, he would hail a taxi cab and go to the freight yards. Some bum would help him onto a car. Once he got in the freight car, he would lie down and rest. During the night the train would start South, and the next day or the morning after, dead or alive, he would be home.

If he had had good sense he would have gone the day after he arrived; better sense and he would not have arrived. He had not got desperate until two days ago when he had heard his daughter and son-in-law taking leave of each other after breakfast. They were standing in the front door, she seeing him off for a three-day trip. He drove a long distance moving van. She must have handed him his leather head-gear. "You ought to get you a hat," he heard her say, "a real one."

"And sit all day in it," the son-in-law said, "like him in there. All he does is sit all day with that hat on. Sits all day with that damn black hat on his head. Inside!"

"Well, you don't even have you a hat," she said. "Nothing but that leather cap with flaps. People that are somebody wear hats. Other kinds wear those leather caps like you got on."

"People that are somebody!" he cried. "People that are somebody! That kills me! That really kills me!" The son-in-law had a stupid muscular face and a yankee voice to go with it.

"My daddy is here to stay," his daughter said. "He ain't going to last long. He was somebody when he was somebody. He never worked for nobody in his life but himself, and he had people—other people—working for him."

"Niggers is what he had working for him," the son-in-law said. "That's all. I've worked a nigger or two myself."

"Those were just nawthun niggers you worked," she said, her voice suddenly going lower so that Tanner had to lean forward to catch the words. "It takes brains to work a real nigger. You got to know how to handle them."

"Yah so I don't have brains," the son-in-law said.

"You got them," she said. "You don't always use them."

One of the sudden, very occasional, feelings of warmth for the daughter came over Tanner. Every now and then she said something that might make you think she had a little sense stored away somewhere for safe keeping.

"He didn't have the brains to hang on to what he did have," the son-in-law said. "He has a stroke when he sees a nigger in the building, and she tells me he can handle a . . ."

"Shut up talking so loud," she said. "That's not why he had the stroke."

There was a silence. "Where you going to bury him?" the son-in-law asked, taking a different tack.

"Right here in New York," she said. "Where do you think? We got a lot. I'm not taking that trip down there again with anybody."

"You stick to your guns," he said. "I just wanted to make sure."

When she returned to the room, Tanner had had both hands gripped on the chair arms. His eyes were trained on her like the eyes of an angry corpse. "You promised you'd bury me there," he said. "Your promise ain't any good. Your promise ain't any good. Your promise ain't any good." His voice was so dry it was barely audible. He began to shake, his hands, his head, his feet. "Bury me here and burn in hell!" he cried and fell back into his chair.

The daughter shuddered to attention. "You ain't dead yet!" She threw out a ponderous sigh. "You got a long time to be worrying about that." She turned and began to pick up parts of the newspaper scattered on the floor. She had grey hair that hung to her shoulders and a round face, beginning to wear. "I do every last living thing for you," she muttered, "and this is the way you carry on." She stuck the papers under her arm and said, "And don't throw hell at me. I don't believe in it. That's a lot of hardshell Baptist hooey." Then she went into the kitchen.

He kept his mouth stretched taut, his top plate gripped between his tongue and the roof of his mouth. Still the tears ran down his cheeks; he wiped each one furtively on his shoulder.

Her voice rose from the kitchen. "As bad as having a child. He wanted to come and now he's here, he don't like it."

He had not wanted to come.

"Pretended he didn't but I could tell. I said if you don't want to come I can't make you. If you don't want to live like decent people there's nothing I can do about it."

"As for me," her higher voice said, "when I die that ain't the time I'm going to start getting choosey. They can lay me in the nearest spot. When I pass from this world I'll be considerate of them that stay in it. I won't be thinking of just myself."

"Certainly not," the other voice said, "you never been that selfish. You're the kind that looks out for other people."

"Well I try," she said, "I try."

He laid his head on the back of the chair for a moment and the hat tilted down over his eyes. He had raised three boys and her. The three boys were gone, two in the war and one to the devil and there was nobody left who felt a duty toward him but her, married and childless, and living in New York City like Mrs. Big. After he lost the place, she had come down in person to offer him a home with her. The son-in-law brought her and leaned against a tree with a cigaret hanging out of his mouth. He never said a word but hello. She had put her face in the door of the shack and had stared, expressionless, for a second. Then all at once she had screamed and jumped back.

"What's that on the floor?"

"Coleman," he said.

The old Negro was curled up on a pallet asleep at the foot of Tanner's bed, a stinking skin full of bones, arranged in what seemed vaguely human form. When Coleman was young, he had looked like a bear; now that he was old he looked like a monkey. With Tanner it was the opposite: when he was young he had looked like a monkey but when he got old, he looked like a bear.

The daughter stepped back onto the ground. The bottoms of two cane chairs were tilted against the side of the shack but she declined to take a seat. She stepped out about ten feet as if it took that much space to clear the odor. Then she spoke her piece.

"If you don't have any pride I have and I know my duty and I was raised to do it. My mother raised me to do it. She was from plain people but not the kind that liked to settle in with niggers."

At that point Coleman roused up and slid out the door, a doubled-up shadow which Tanner just caught sight of gliding away.

He shouted so both she and Coleman could hear. "Who you think cooks? Who you think cuts my firewood and empties my slops? He's paroled to me. That scoundrel has been on my hands for thirty years. He ain't a bad nigger."

She was unimpressed. "Whose shack is this anyway?" she had asked. "Yours or his? It looks like him and you built it. Whose land is it on?"

"Him and me built it," he said. "You go on back up there. I wouldn't come with you for no million dollars or no sack of salt."

"Whose land is it?" she persisted.

"Some people that live in Florida," he said evasively. He had known then that it was land up for sale but he thought it was too sorry for anyone to buy. He should have known different.

Later in the summer when he saw the brown porpoise-shaped figure striding across the field, he knew at once what had happened; no one had to tell him. If that nigger had owned the whole world except for one runty rutted pea-field and he acquired it, he would walk across it that way, beating the weeds aside, his thick neck swelled, his stomach a throne for his gold watch and chain. Doctor Foley. He was only part black. The rest was Indian and white.

He was everything to the niggers—druggist and undertaker and general counsel and real estate man and sometimes he got the evil eye off them and sometimes he put it on. Be prepared, he said to himself, watching him approach, to take something off him, nigger though he be. Be prepared, because you ain't got a thing to hold up to him but the skin you come in, and that's no more use to you now than what a snake would shed. You don't have a chance with the government against you.

He was sitting on the porch in the piece of straight chair tilted against the shack. "Good evening, Foley," he said and nodded as the doctor came up and stopped short at the edge of the clearing, as if he had only just that minute seen him though it was plain he had sighted him as he crossed the field.

"I be out here to look at my property," the doctor said. "Good evening." His voice was quick and high.

Ain't been your property long, Tanner said to himself. "I seen you coming," he said.

"I acquired this here recently," the doctor said and proceeded without looking at him again to walk around to one side of the shack. In a moment he came back and stopped in front of him. Then he stepped boldly to the door of the shack and put his head in. Coleman was in there that time too, asleep. He looked for a moment and then turned aside. "I know that nigger," he said. "Coleman Parrum—how long does it take him to sleep off that stump liquor you all make?"

Tanner took hold of the knobs on the chair bottom and held them hard. "This shack ain't in your property. Only on it, by mistake," he said.

The Doctor removed his cigar momentarily from his mouth. "It ain't my mistake," he said and smiled.

He had only sat there, looking ahead.

"It don't pay to make this kind of mis-take," the doctor said.

"I never found nothing that payed yet," Tanner muttered.

"Everything pays," the Negro said, "if you knows how to make it," and he remained there smiling, looking the squatter up and down. Then he turned and went around the other side of the shack. There was a silence. He was looking for the still.

Then would have been the time to kill him. There was a gun inside the shack and he could have done it as easy as not, but, from childhood, he had been weakened for that kind of violence by the fear of hell. He had never killed one, he had always handled them with his wits and with luck. He was known to have a way with niggers. There was an art to handling them. The secret of handling a nigger was to show him his brains didn't have a chance against yours; then he would jump on your back and know he had a good thing there for life. He had had Coleman on his back for thirty years.

Tanner had first seen Coleman when he was working six of them at a saw mill in the middle of a pine forest fifteen miles from nowhere. They were as sorry a crew as he had worked, the kind that on Monday they didn't show up. What was in the air had reached them. They thought there was a new Lincoln elected who was going to abolish work. He managed them with a very sharp penknife. He had had something wrong with his kidney then that made his hands shake and he had taken to whittling to force that waste motion out of sight. He did not intend them to see that his hands shook of their own accord and he did not intend to see it himself or to countenance it. The knife had moved constantly, violently, in his quaking hands and here and there small crude figures—that he never looked at again and could not have said what they were if he had—dropped to the ground. The Negroes picked them up and took them home; there was not much time between them and darkest Africa. The knife glittered constantly in his hands. More than once he had stopped short and said in an off-hand voice to some half-reclining, head-averted Negro, "Nigger, this knife is in my hand now but if you don't quit wasting my time and money, it'll be in your gut shortly." And the Negro would begin to rise—slowly, but he would be in the act—before the sentence was completed.

A large black loose-jointed Negro, twice his own size, had begun hanging around the edge of the saw mill, watching the others work and when he was not watching, sleeping, in full view of them, sprawled like a gigantic bear on his back. "Who is that?" he had asked. "If he wants to work, tell him to come here. If he don't, tell him to go. No idlers are going to hang around here."

None of them knew who he was. They knew he didn't want to work. They knew nothing else, not where he had come from, nor why, though he was probably brother to one, cousin to all of them. Tanner had ignored him for a day; against the six of them he was one yellow-faced scrawny white man with shaky hands. He was willing to wait for trouble, but not forever. The next day the stranger came again. After the six Tanner worked had seen the idler there for half the morning, they quit and began to eat, a full thirty minutes before noon. He had not risked ordering them up. He had gone to the source of the trouble.

The stranger was leaning against a tree on the edge of the clearing, watching with half-closed eyes. The insolence on his face barely covered the wariness behind it. His look said, this ain't much of a white man so why he come on so big, what he fixing to do?

He had meant to say, "Nigger, this knife is in my hand now but if you ain't out of my sight . . ." but as he drew closer he changed his mind. The Negro's eyes were small and bloodshot. Tanner supposed there was a knife on him somewhere that he would as soon use as not. His own penknife moved, directed solely by some intruding intelligence that worked in his hands. He had no idea what he was carving, but when he reached the negro, he had already made two holes the size of half dollars in the piece of bark.

The Negro's gaze fell on his hands and was held. His jaw slackened. His eyes did not move from the knife tearing recklessly around the bark. He watched as if he saw an invisible power working on the wood.

He looked himself then and, astonished, saw the connected rims of a pair of spectacles.

He held them away from him and looked through the holes past a pile of shavings and on into the woods to the edge of the pen where they kept their mules.

"You can't see so good, can you, boy?" he said, and began scraping the ground with his foot to turn up a piece of wire. He picked up a small piece of haywire; in a minute he found another shorter piece and picked that up. He began to attach these to the bark. He was in no hurry now that he knew what he was doing. When the spectacles were finished, he handed them to the Negro. "Put these on," he said. "I hate to see anybody can't see good."

There was an instant when the Negro might have done one thing or an-

other, might have taken the glasses and crushed them in his hand or
grabbed the knife and turned it on him. He saw the exact instant in the
muddy liquor-swollen eyes when the pleasure of having a knife in this
white man's gut was balanced against something else, he could not tell
what.

The Negro reached for the glasses. He attached the bows carefully behind his ears and looked forth. He peered this way and that with exaggerated solemnity. And then he looked directly at Tanner and grinned, or
grimaced, Tanner could not tell which, but he had an instant's sensation of
seeing before him a negative image of himself, as if clownishness and captivity had been their common lot. The vision failed him before he could decipher it.

"Preacher," he said, "what you hanging around here for?" He picked up
another piece of bark and began, without looking at it, to carve again. "This
ain't Sunday."

"This here ain't Sunday?" the Negro said.

"This is Friday," he said. "That's the way it is with you preachers—drunk
all week so you don't know when Sunday is. What you see through those
glasses?"

"See a man."

"What kind of a man?"

"See the man make theseyer glasses."

"Is he white or black?"

"He white!" the Negro said as if only at that moment was his vision sufficiently improved to detect it. "Yessuh, he white!" he said.

"Well, you treat him like he was white," Tanner said. "What's your
name?"

"Name Coleman," the Negro said.

And he had not got rid of Coleman since. You make a monkey out of one
of them and he jumps on your back and stays there for life, but let one
make a monkey out of you and all you can do is kill him or disappear. And
he was not going to hell for killing a nigger. Behind the shack he heard the
doctor kick over a bucket. He sat and waited.

In a moment the doctor appeared again, beating his way around the
other side of the house, whacking at scattered clumps of Johnson grass with
his cane. He stopped in the middle of the yard.

"You don't belong here," he began. "I could have you prosecuted."

Tanner remained there, dumb, staring across the field.

"Where's your still?" the doctor asked.

"If it's a still around here, it don't belong to me," he said and shut his
mouth tight.

The Negro laughed softly. "Down on your luck, ain't you?" he murmured. "Didn't you used to own a little piece of land over acrost the river
and lost it?"

He had continued to study the woods ahead.

"If you want to run the still for me, that's one thing," the doctor said. "If you don't, you might as well be packing up."

"The governmint ain't got around yet to forcing the white folks to work for the colored," Tanner said.

The doctor polished the stone in his ring with the ball of his thumb. "I don't like the governmint no bettern you," he said. "Where you going instead? You going to the city and get you a soot of rooms at the Biltmo' Hotel?"

Tanner said nothing.

"The day coming," the doctor said, "when the white folks IS going to be working for the colored and you might's well to git ahead of the crowd."

"That day ain't coming for me," Tanner said shortly.

"Done come for you," the doctor said. "Ain't come for the rest of them."

Tanner's gaze drove on past the farthest blue edge of the treeline into the pale afternoon sky. "I got a daughter in the north," he said. "I don't have to work for you."

The doctor took his watch from his watch pocket and looked at it and put it back. He gazed for a moment at the back of his hands. He appeared to have measured and to know secretly the time it would take the world to turn upsidedown. "She don't want no old daddy like you," he said. "Maybe she say she do, but that ain't likely. Even if you rich," he said, "they don't want you. They got they own ideas. The black ones they rears and they pitches. I made mine," he said, "and I ain't done none of that." He looked again at Tanner. "I be back here next week," he said, "and if you still here, I know you going to work that still for me." He remained there a moment, rocking on his heels, waiting for some answer. Finally he turned and started beating his way back through the overgrown path.

Tanner had continued to look across the field as if his spirit had been sucked out of him into the woods and nothing was left on the chair but a shell. If he had known it was a question of this—sitting here looking out of this window all day in this no-place, or just running a still for a nigger, he would have run the still for the nigger. He would have been a nigger's white nigger any day. Behind him he heard the daughter come in from the kitchen. His heart beat faster. He heard her plump herself down on the sofa. She was not yet ready to go. He did not turn and look at her.

She sat there silently a few moments. Then she began. "The trouble with you is," she said, "you sit in front of that window all the time where there's nothing to look out at. You need some inspiration and an out-let. If you would let me pull your chair around to look at the TV, you would quit thinking about morbid stuff, death and hell and judgment. My Lord."

"The Judgement is coming," he muttered. "The sheep'll be separated from the goats. Them that kept their promises from them that didn't. Them that did the best they could with what they had from them that didn't. Them that honored their father and their mother from them that cursed them. Them that . . ."

She heaved a mammoth sigh that all but drowned him out. "What's the use in me wasting my good breath?" she asked. She rose and went back in the kitchen and began knocking things about.

She was so high and mighty! At home he had been living in a shack but there was at least air around it. He could put his feet on the ground. Here she didn't even live in a house. She lived in a pigeon-hutch of a building, with all stripes of foreigner, all of them twisted in the tongue. It was no place for a sane man. The first morning here she had taken him sightseeing and he had seen in fifteen minutes exactly how it was. He had not been out of the apartment since. He never wanted to set foot again on the underground railroad or the steps that moved under you while you stood still or any elevator to the thirty-fourth floor. When he was safely back in the apartment again, he had imagined going over it with Coleman. He had to turn his head every few seconds to make sure Coleman was behind him. Keep to the inside or these people'll knock you down, keep right behind me or you'll get left, keep your hat on, you damn idiot, he had said, and Coleman had come on with his bent running shamble, panting and muttering, What we doing here? Where you get this fool idea coming here?

I come to show you it was no kind of place. Now you know you were well off where you were.

I knowed it before, Coleman said. Was you didn't know it.

When he had been here a week, he had got a post card from Coleman that had been written for him by Hooten at the railroad station. It was written in green ink and said, "This is Coleman—X—howyou boss." Under it Hooten had written from himself, "Quit frequenting all those nitespots and come on home, you scoundrel, yours truly, WT Hooten." He had sent Coleman a card in return, care of Hooten, that said, "This place is alrite if you like it. Yours truly, T.C. Tanner." Since the daughter had to mail the card, he had not put on it that he was returning as soon as his pension check came. He had not intended to tell her but to leave her a note. When the check came, he would hire himself a taxi to the bus station and be on his way. And it would have made her as happy as it made him. She had found his company dour and her duty irksome. If he had sneaked out, she would have had the pleasure of having tried to do it and to top that off, the pleasure of his ingratitude.

As for him, he would have returned to squat on the doctor's land and to take his orders from a nigger who chewed ten-cent cigars. And to think less about it than formerly. Instead he had been done in by a nigger actor, or one who called himself an actor. He didn't believe the nigger was any actor.

There were two apartments on each floor of the building. He had been with the daughter three weeks when the people in the next hutch moved out. He had stood in the hall and watched the moving-out and the next day he had watched a moving-in. The hall was narrow and dark and he stood in the corner out of the way, offering only a suggestion every now and then to the movers that would have made work easier for them if they had paid any attention. The furniture was new and cheap so he decided the people moving in might be a newly married couple and he would just wait around until they came and wish them well. After a while a large Negro in a light blue suit came lunging up the stairs, carrying four bulging canvas suitcases, his head lowered against the strain. Behind him stepped a young tan-skinned woman with bright copper-colored hair. The Negro dropped the suitcases with a thud in front of the door of the next apartment.

"Be careful, Sweetie," the woman said. "My make-up is there."

It broke upon him then just what was happening.

The Negro was grinning. He took a swipe at one of her hips.

"Quit it," she said, "there's an old guy watching."

They both turned and looked at him.

"Had-do," he said and nodded. Then he turned quickly into his own door.

His daughter was in the kitchen. "Who you think's rented that apartment over there?" he asked, his face alight.

She looked at him suspiciously. "Who?" she muttered.

"A nigger!" he said in a gleeful voice. "A South Alabama nigger if I ever saw one. And got him this high-yeller, high-stepping woman with a red wig and they two are going to live next door to you!" He slapped his knee. "Yes siree!" he said. "Damn if they ain't!" It was the first time since coming up here that he had had occasion to laugh.

Her face squared up instantly. "All right now you listen to me," she said. "You keep away from them. Don't you go over there trying to get friendly with him. They ain't the same around here and I don't want any trouble with niggers, you hear me? If you have to live next to them, just you mind your business and they'll mind theirs. That's the way people were meant to get along in this world. Everybody can get along if they just mind their business. Live and let live." She began to wrinkle her nose like a rabbit, a stupid way she had. "Up here everybody minds their own business and everybody gets along. That's all you have to do."

"I was getting along with niggers before you were born," he said. He went back out into the hall and waited. He was willing to bet the nigger would like to talk to someone who understood him. Twice while he waited, he forgot and in his excitement, spit his tobacco juice against the baseboard. In about twenty minutes, the door of the apartment opened again and the Negro came out. He had put on a tie and a pair of horn-rimmed spectacles and Tanner noticed for the first time that he had a small almost invisible goatee. A real swell. The Negro came on without appearing to see there was anyone else in the hall.

"Haddy, John," Tanner said and nodded, but the Negro brushed past without hearing and went rattling rapidly down the stairs.

Could be deaf and dumb, Tanner thought. He went back into the apartment and sat down but each time he heard a noise in the hall, he got up and went to the door and stuck his head out to see if it might be the Negro. Once in the middle of the afternoon, he caught the Negro's eye, or thought he did, just as he was rounding the bend of the stairs again but before he could get out a word, the man was in his own apartment and had slammed the door. He had never known one to move that fast unless the police were after him.

He was standing in the hall early the next morning when the woman came out of her door alone, walking on high gold-painted heels. He wished to bid her good morning or simply to nod but instinct told him to beware. She didn't look like any kind of woman, black or white, he had ever seen before and he remained pressed against the wall, frightened more than anything else, and feigning invisibility.

The woman gave him a flat stare, then turned her head away and stepped wide of him as if she were skirting an open garbage can. He held his breath until she was out of sight. Then he waited patiently for the man.

The Negro came out about ten o'clock.

This time Tanner advanced squarely in his path. "Good morning, Preacher," he said. It had been his experience that if a Negro tended to be sullen, this title usually cleared up his expression.

The Negro stopped abruptly.

"I seen you move in," Tanner said. "I ain't been up here long myself. It ain't much of a place if you ask me. I reckon you wish you were back in South Alabama."

The Negro did not take a step or answer. His eyes began to move. They moved from the top of the black hat, down to the collarless blue shirt, neatly buttoned at the neck, down the faded galluses to the grey trousers and the high-top shoes and up again, very slowly, while some unfathomable dead-cold rage seemed to stiffen and shrink him.

"I thought you might know somewhere around here we could find us a pond and fish, Preacher," Tanner said in a voice growing thinner but still with considerable hope in it.

A seething noise came out of the Negro before he spoke. "I'm not from South Alabama," he said in a breathless wheezing voice. "I'm from New York City. And I'm not a preacher! I'm an actor."

Tanner chortled. "It's a little actor in most preachers, ain't it?" he said and winked. "I reckon you just preach on the side."

"I don't preach!" the Negro cried and rushed past him as if a swarm of bees had suddenly come down on him out of nowhere. He dashed down the stairs and was gone.

Tanner stood there for some time before he went back in the apartment. The rest of the day he sat in his chair and debated whether he would have one more try at making friends with him. Every time he heard a noise on the stairs he went to the door and looked out, but the Negro did not return until late in the afternoon. Tanner was standing in the hall waiting for him when he reached the top of the stairs. "Good evening, Preacher," he said.

The Negro stopped and gripped the banister rail. A tremor racked him from his head to his crotch. Then he began to come forward slowly. When he was close enough he lunged and grasped Tanner by both shoulders. "I don't take no crap," he whispered, "off no wool-hat red-neck son-of-a-bitch peckerwood old bastard like you." He caught his breath. And then his voice came out in the sound of an exasperation so profound that it rocked on the verge of a laugh. It was high and piercing and weak. "And I'm not a preacher! I'm not a Christian. I don't believe in that crap. There ain't no Jesus and there ain't no God."

The old man felt his heart inside him hard and tough as an oak knot. "And you ain't black," he said. "And I ain't white!"

The Negro slammed him against the wall. He yanked the black hat down over his eyes. Then he grabbed his shirt front and shoved him backwards to his open door and knocked him through it. From the kitchen the daughter saw him blindly hit the edge of the inside hall door and fall reeling into the living room.

Hard as his head was, the fall cracked it and when he got over the concussion he had a little stroke.

For days his tongue appeared to be frozen in his mouth. When it unthawed it was twice its normal size and he could not make her understand him. What he wanted to know was if the government check had come. He meant to buy a bus ticket with it and go home. After a few weeks, he made her understand. "It came," she said, "and it'll just pay the first two weeks doctor-bill and please tell me how you're going home when you can't talk or walk or think straight and you got one eye crossed yet? Just please tell me that?"

It had come to him then slowly just what his present situation was. He would never see Corinth again. At least he would have to make her understand that he must be sent home to be buried. They could have him shipped back in a refrigerated car so that he would keep for the trip. He didn't want any undertaker up here messing with him. Let them get him off at once and he would come in on the early morning train and they could wire Hooten to get Coleman and Coleman would do the rest. I'm not letting no nigger bury you, she said, but quit talking morbid. You'll be up and around in a while. After a lot of argument, he wrung the promise from her. She would ship him back. It had only been, he saw now, to shut him up.

After that he slept peacefully and improved a little. In his waking dreams he could feel the cold early morning air of home coming in through the cracks of the pine box. He saw Coleman waiting, red-eyed, on the station platform and Hooten standing there with his green eyeshade and black alpaca sleeves, waiting for the train to stop. Hooten would be thinking: if the old fool had stayed at home where he belonged, he wouldn't be arriving on the 6:03 in no box. Coleman would turn the borrowed mule and cart so that they could slide the box off the platform onto the open end of the wagon. When the coffin was off the train the two of them, shut-mouthed, would inch the loaded coffin toward the wagon. From inside he would begin to scratch on the wood. They would drop the box as if it had caught fire.

They stood looking at each other, then at the box.

"That him," Coleman would say. "He in there his self."

"Naw," Hooten would say, "must be a rat got in there with him."

"That him. This here one of his tricks."

"If it's a rat he might as well stay."

"That him. Git a crowbar."

Hooten would go grumbling off and get the crowbar and come back and begin to pry open the lid. Even before he had the upper end pried open, Coleman would be jumping up and down, wheezing and panting from excitement. Tanner would give a thrust upward with both hands and spring up in the box. "Judgement Day! Judgement Day!" he would cry. "Don't you two fools know it's Judgement Day?"

Now that he knew exactly what her promises were worth, he would do as well to trust to the note pinned in his coat and to any stranger who found him dead in the street or in the boxcar or wherever. There was nothing to be looked for from her except that she would do things her way. She came out of the kitchen again, holding her hat and coat and rubber boots.

"Now listen," she said, "I have to go to the store. Don't you try to get up and walk around while I'm gone. You've been to the bathroom and you shouldn't have to go again. I don't want to find you on the floor when I get back."

You won't find me atall when you get back, he said to himself. This was the last time he would see her flat dumb face. Then he felt guilty. She had been good to him and he had been nothing but a nuisance to her.

"Do you want you a glass of milk before I go?" she asked.

"No," he said. Then he drew breath and said, "You got a nice place here. It's a nice part of the country. I'm sorry if I've give you a lot of trouble getting sick. It was my fault trying to be friendly with that city nigger." And I'm a dammed liar besides, he said to himself to kill the taste such a statement made in his mouth.

For a moment she stared as if he were losing his mind. Then she seemed to think better of it. "Now don't saying something pleasant like that once in a while make you feel better?" she asked and sat down on the sofa.

His knees itched to unbend. Git on, git on, he fumed silently. Make haste and go.

"It's great to have you here," she said in return. "I wouldn't have you any other place. My own daddy." She gave him a big smile and hoisted her right leg up and began to pull on her boot. "I wouldn't wish a dog out on a day like this," she said, "but I got to go. You can sit here and hope I don't slip and break my neck." She stamped the booted foot on the floor and then began to tackle the other one.

He turned his eyes to the window. The snow was beginning to stick and freeze to the outside pane. When he looked at her again, she was standing there like a big doll stuffed into its hat and coat. She drew on a pair of green knitted gloves. "Okay," she said, "I'm gone. You sure you don't want anything?"

"No," he said, "go ahead on."

"Well so long then," she said.

He raised the hat enough to reveal a bald palely speckled head. The hall door closed behind her. He began to tremble with excitement. He reached behind him and drew the coat into his lap. When he got it on, he waited until he had stopped panting, then he gripped the arms of the chair and pulled himself up. His body felt like a great heavy bell whose clapper swung from side to side but made no noise. Once up, he remained standing a moment, swaying until he got his balance. A sensation of terror and defeat swept over him. He would never make it. He would never get there dead or alive. He pushed one foot forward and did not fall and his confidence returned. "The Lord is my shepherd," he muttered, "I shall not want." He began moving toward the sofa where he would have support. He reached it! He was on his way.

By the time he got to the door, she would be down the four flights of steps and out of the building. He got past the sofa and crept along by the wall, keeping his hand on it for support. Nobody was going to bury him here. He was as confident as if the woods of home lay at the bottom of the stairs. He reached the front door of the apartment and opened it and peered into the hall. This was the first time he had looked into it since the actor had knocked him down. It was dank-smelling and empty. The thin piece of linoleum stretched its moldy length to the door of the other apartment, which was closed. "Nigger actor," he said.

The head of the stairs was ten or twelve feet from where he stood and he bent his attention to getting there without creeping around the long way with a hand on the wall. He held his arms a little way out from his sides and pushed forward directly. He was half way there when all at once his legs disappeared, or felt as if they had. He looked down, bewildered, for they were still there. He fell forward and grasped the banister post with both hands. Hanging there, he gazed for what seemed the longest time he had ever looked at anything down the steep unlighted steps; then he closed his eyes and pitched forward. He landed upsidedown in the middle of the flight.

He felt presently the tilt of the box as they took it off the train and got it on the baggage wagon. He made no noise yet. The train jarred and slid away. In a moment the baggage wagon was rumbling under him, carrying him back to the station side. He heard footsteps rattling closer and closer to him and he supposed that a crowd was gathering. Wait until they see this, he thought.

"He in there," Coleman said, "one of his tricks."

"It's a damm rat in there," Hooten said.

"It's him. Git the crowbar."

In a moment a shaft of greenish light fell on him. He pushed through it and cried in a weak voice, "Judgement Day! Judgement Day. You idiots didn't know it was Judgement Day, did you?"

"Coleman?" he murmured.

The Negro bending over him had a large surly mouth and sullen eyes.

This must be the wrong station, Tanner thought. Those fools put me off too soon. Who is this nigger? It ain't even daylight here.

At the Negro's side was another face, a woman's, pale, topped with a pile of copper-glinting hair and twisted as if she had just stepped in a pile of dung.

"Oh," Tanner murmured, "it's you."

The actor leaned closer and grasped him by the front of his shirt. "Judgement day," he said in a mocking voice. "There's not any judgement day, old man. Except this. Maybe this here is judgement day for you."

Tanner tried to catch hold of a banister spoke to raise himself but his hand grasped air. The two faces, the black one and the pale one, appeared to be wavering. By an effort of will he kept them focussed before him while he lifted his hand, as light as a breath, and said in his jauntiest voice, "Hep me up, Preacher. I'm on my way home!"

His daughter found him when she came in from the grocery store. His hat had been pulled down over his face and his head and arms thrust between the spokes of the banister; his feet dangled over the stairwell like those of a man in the stocks. She tugged at him frantically and then flew for the police. They cut him out with a saw and said he had been dead about an hour.

She buried him in New York City, but after she had done it she could not sleep at night. Night after night she turned and tossed and very definite lines began to appear in her face, so she had him dug up and shipped the body to Corinth. Now she rests well at night and her good looks have mostly returned.

Guests of the Nation

FRANK O'CONNOR

I

At dusk the big Englishman, Belcher, would shift his long legs out of the ashes and say "Well, chums, what about it?" and Noble or me would say "All right, chum" (for we had picked up some of their curious expressions), and the little Englishman, Hawkins, would light the lamp and bring out the cards. Sometimes Jeremiah Donovan would come up and supervise the game and get excited over Hawkins's cards, which he always played badly, and shout at him as if he was one of our own "Ah, you divil, you, why didn't you play the tray?"

But ordinarily Jeremiah was a sober and contented poor devil like the big Englishman, Belcher, and was looked up to only because he was a fair hand at documents, though he was slow enough even with them. He wore a small cloth hat and big gaiters over his long pants, and you seldom saw him with his hands out of his pockets. He reddened when you talked to him, tilting from toe to heel and back, and looking down all the time at his big farmer's feet. Noble and me used to make fun of his broad accent, because we were from the town.

I couldn't at the time see the point of me and Noble guarding Belcher and Hawkins at all, for it was my belief that you could have planted that pair down anywhere from this to Claregalway and they'd have taken root there like a native weed. I never in my short experience seen two men to take to the country as they did.

They were handed on to us by the Second Battalion when the search for them became too hot, and Noble and myself, being young, took over with a natural feeling of responsibility, but Hawkins made us look like fools when he showed that he knew the country better than we did.

"You're the bloke they calls Bonaparte," he says to me. "Mary Brigid

800

O'Connell told me to ask you what you done with the pair of her brother's socks you borrowed."

For it seemed, as they explained it, that the Second used to have little evenings, and some of the girls of the neighbourhood turned in, and, seeing they were such decent chaps, our fellows couldn't leave the two Englishmen out of them. Hawkins learned to dance "The Walls of Limerick," "The Siege of Ennis," and "The Waves of Tory" as well as any of them, though, naturally, he couldn't return the compliment, because our lads at that time did not dance foreign dances on principle.

So whatever privileges Belcher and Hawkins had with the Second they just naturally took with us, and after the first day or two we gave up all pretense of keeping a close eye on them. Not that they could have got far, for they had accents you could cut with a knife and wore khaki tunics and overcoats with civilian pants and boots. But it's my belief that they never had any idea of escaping and were quite content to be where they were.

It was a treat to see how Belcher got off with the old woman of the house where we were staying. She was a great warrant to scold, and cranky even with us, but before ever she had a chance of giving our guests, as I may call them, a lick of her tongue, Belcher had made her his friend for life. She was breaking sticks, and Belcher, who hadn't been more than ten minutes in the house, jumped up from his seat and went over to her.

"Allow me, madam," he says, smiling his queer little smile, "please allow me"; and he takes the bloody hatchet. She was struck too paralytic to speak, and after that, Belcher would be at her heels, carrying a bucket, a basket, or a load of turf, as the case might be. As Noble said, he got into looking before she leapt, and hot water, or any little thing she wanted, Belcher would have it ready for her. For such a huge man (and though I am five foot ten myself I had to look up at him) he had an uncommon shortness—or should I say lack?—of speech. It took us some time to get used to him, walking in and out, like a ghost, without a word. Especially because Hawkins talked enough for a platoon, it was strange to hear big Belcher with his toes in the ashes come out with a solitary "Excuse me, chum," or "That's right, chum." His one and only passion was cards, and I will say for him that he was a good card-player. He could have fleeced myself and Noble, but whatever we lost to him Hawkins lost to us, and Hawkins played with the money Belcher gave him.

Hawkins lost to us because he had too much old gab, and we probably lost to Belcher for the same reason. Hawkins and Noble would spit at one another about religion into the early hours of the morning, and Hawkins worried the soul out of Noble, whose brother was a priest, with a string of questions that would puzzle a cardinal. To make it worse even in treating of holy subjects, Hawkins had a deplorable tongue. I never in all my career met a man who could mix such a variety of cursing and bad language into an argument. He was a terrible man, and a fright to argue. He never did a stroke of work, and when he had no one else to talk to, he got stuck in the old woman.

He met his match in her, for one day when he tried to get her to complain profanely of the drought, she gave him a great come-down by blaming it entirely on Jupiter Pluvius (a deity neither Hawkins nor I have ever heard of, though Noble said that among the pagans it was believed that he had something to do with the rain). Another day he was swearing at the capitalists for starting the German war when the old lady laid down her iron, puckered up her little crab's mouth, and said: "Mr. Hawkins, you can say what you like about the war, and think you'll deceive me because I'm only a simple poor countrywoman, but I know what started the war. It was the Italian Count that stole the heathen divinity out of the temple in Japan. Believe me, Mr. Hawkins, nothing but sorrow and want can follow the people that disturb the hidden powers."

A queer old girl, all right.

II

We had our tea one evening, and Hawkins lit the lamp and we all sat into cards. Jeremiah Donovan came in too, and sat down and watched us for a while, and it suddenly struck me that he had no great love for the two Englishmen. It came as a great surprise to me, because I hadn't noticed anything about him before.

Late in the evening a really terrible argument blew up between Hawkins and Noble, about capitalists and priests and love of your country.

"The capitalists," says Hawkins with an angry gulp, "pays the priests to tell you about the next world so as you won't notice what the bastards are up to in this."

"Nonsense, man!" says Noble, losing his temper. "Before ever a capitalist was thought of, people believed in the next world."

Hawkins stood up as though he was preaching a sermon.

"Oh, they did, did they?" he says with a sneer. "They believed all the things you believe, isn't that what you mean? And you believe that God created Adam, and Adam created Shem, and Shem created Jehoshophat. You believe all that silly old fairytale about Eve and Eden and the apple. Well, listen to me, chum. If you're entitled to hold a silly belief like that, I'm entitled to hold my silly belief—which is that the first thing your God created was a bleeding capitalist, with morality and Rolls-Royce complete. Am I right, chum?" he says to Belcher.

"You're right, chum" says Belcher with his amused smile, and got up from the table to stretch his long legs into the fire and stroke his moustache. So, seeing that Jeremiah Donovan was going, and that there was no knowing when the argument about religion would be over, I went out with him. We strolled down to the village together, and then he stopped and started blushing and mumbling and saying I ought to be behind, keeping guard on the prisoners. I didn't like the tone he took with me, and anyway I was bored with life in the cottage, so I replied by asking him what the hell we wanted guarding them at all for. I told him I'd talked it over with Noble, and that we'd both rather be out with a fighting column.

"What use are those fellows to us?" says I.

He looked at me in surprise and said: "I thought you knew we were keeping them as hostages."

"Hostages?" I said.

"The enemy have prisoners belonging to us," he says, "and now they're talking of shooting them. If they shoot our prisoners, we'll shoot theirs."

"Shoot them?" I said.

"What else did you think we were keeping them for?" he says.

"Wasn't it very unforeseen of you not to warn Noble and myself of that in the beginning?" I said.

"How was it?" says he. "You might have known it."

"We couldn't know it, Jeremiah Donovan," says I. "How could we when they were on our hands so long?"

"The enemy have our prisoners as long and longer," says he.

"That's not the same thing at all," says I.

"What difference is there?" says he.

I couldn't tell him, because I knew he wouldn't understand. If it was only an old dog that was going to the vet's, you'd try and not get too fond of him, but Jeremiah Donovan wasn't a man that would ever be in danger of that.

"And when is this thing going to be decided?" says I.

"We might hear tonight," he says. "Or tomorrow or the next day at latest. So if it's only hanging round here that's a trouble to you, you'll be free soon enough."

It wasn't the hanging round that was a trouble to me at all by this time. I had worse things to worry about. When I got back to the cottage the argument was still on. Hawkins was holding forth in his best style, maintaining that there was no next world, and Noble was maintaining that there was; but I could see that Hawkins had had the best of it.

"Do you know what, chum?" he was saying with a saucy smile. "I think you're just as big a bleeding unbeliever as I am. You say you believe in the next world, and you know just as much about the next world as I do, which is sweet damn-all. What's heaven? You don't know. Where's heaven? You don't know. You know sweet damn-all! I ask you again, do they wear wings?"

"Very well, then," says Noble, "they do. Is that enough for you? They do wear wings."

"Where do they get them, then? Who makes them? Have they a factory for wings? Have they a sort of store where you hands in your chit and takes your bleeding wings?"

"You're an impossible man to argue with," says Noble. "Now, listen to me—" And they were off again.

It was long after midnight when we locked up and went to bed. As I blew out the candle I told Noble what Jeremiah Donovan was after telling me. Noble took it very quietly. When we'd been in bed about an hour he asked me did I think we ought to tell the Englishmen. I didn't think we should, because it was more than likely that the English wouldn't shoot our men, and even if they did, the brigade officers, who were always up and down with the Second Battalion and knew the Englishmen well, wouldn't be likely to want them plugged. "I think so too," says Noble. "It would be great cruelty to put the wind up them now."

"It was very unforeseen of Jeremiah Donovan anyhow," says I.

It was next morning that we found it so hard to face Belcher and Hawkins. We went about the house all day scarcely saying a word. Belcher didn't seem to notice; he was stretched into the ashes as usual, with his usual look of waiting in quietness for something unforeseen to happen, but Hawkins noticed and put it down to Noble's being beaten in the argument of the night before.

"Why can't you take a discussion in the proper spirit?" he says severely. "You and your Adam and Eve! I'm a Communist, that's what I am. Communist or anarchist, it all comes to much the same thing." And for hours he went round the house, muttering when the fit took him. "Adam and Eve! Adam and Eve! Nothing better to do with their time than picking bleeding apples!"

III

I don't know how we got through that day, but I was very glad when it was over, the tea things were cleared away, and Belcher said in his peaceable way: "Well, chums, what about it?" We sat round the table and Hawkins took out the cards, and just then I heard Jeremiah Donovan's footstep on the path and a dark presentiment crossed my mind. I rose from the table and caught him before he reached the door.

"What do you want?" I asked.

"I want those two soldier friends of yours," he says, getting red.

"Is that the way, Jeremiah Donovan?" I asked.

"That's the way. There were four of our lads shot this morning, one of them a boy of sixteen."

"That's bad," I said.

At that moment Noble followed me out, and the three of us walked down the path together, talking in whispers. Feeney, the local intelligence officer, was standing by the gate.

"What are you going to do about it?" I asked Jeremiah Donovan.

"I want you and Noble to get them out; tell them they're being shifted again; that'll be the quietest way."

"Leave me out of that," says Noble under his breath.

Jeremiah Donovan looks at him hard.

"All right," he says. "You and Feeney get a few tools from the shed and dig a hole by the far end of the bog. Bonaparte and myself will be after you. Don't let anyone see you with the tools. I wouldn't like it to go beyond ourselves."

We saw Feeney and Noble go round to the shed and went in ourselves. I left Jeremiah Donovan to do the explanations. He told them that he had orders to send them back to the Second Battalion. Hawkins let out a mouthful of curses, and you could see that though Belcher didn't say anything, he was a bit upset too. The old woman was for having them stay in spite of us, and she didn't stop advising them until Jeremiah Donovan lost his temper and turned on her. He had a nasty temper, I noticed. It was pitch-dark in the cottage by this time, but no one thought of lighting the lamp, and in the darkness the two Englishmen fetched their topcoats and said good-bye to the old woman.

"Just as a man makes a home of a bleeding place, some bastard at headquarters thinks you're too cushy and shunts you off," says Hawkins, shaking her hand.

"A thousand thanks, madam," says Belcher. "A thousand thanks for everything"—as though he'd made it up.

We went round to the back of the house and down towards the bog. It was only then that Jeremiah Donovan told them. He was shaking with excitement.

"There were four of our fellows shot in Cork this morning and now you're to be shot as a reprisal."

"What are you talking about?" snaps Hawkins. "It's bad enough being mucked about as we are without having to put up with your funny jokes."

"It isn't a joke," says Donovan. "I'm sorry, Hawkins, but it's true," and begins on the usual rigmarole about duty and how unpleasant it is.

I never noticed that people who talk a lot about duty find it much of a trouble to them.

"Oh, cut it out!" says Hawkins.

"Ask Bonaparte," says Donovan, seeing that Hawkins isn't taking him seriously. "Isn't it true, Bonaparte?"

"It is," I say, and Hawkins stops.

"Ah, for Christ's sake, chum!"

"I mean it, chum," I say.

"You don't sound as if you mean it."

"If he doesn't mean it, I do," says Donovan, working himself up.

"What have you against me, Jeremiah Donovan?"

"I never said I had anything against you. But why did your people take out four of our prisoners and shoot them in cold blood?"

He took Hawkins by the arm and dragged him on, but it was impossible to make him understand that we were in earnest. I had the Smith and Wesson in my pocket and I kept fingering it and wondering what I'd do if they put up a fight for it or ran, and wishing to God they'd do one or the other. I knew if they did run for it, that I'd never fire on them. Hawkins wanted to know was Noble in it, and when we said yes, he asked us why Noble wanted to plug him. Why did any of us want to plug him? What had he done to us? Weren't we all chums? Didn't we understand him and didn't he understand us? Did we imagine for an instant that he'd shoot us for all the so-and-so officers in the so-and-so British Army?

By this time we'd reached the bog, and I was so sick I couldn't even answer him. We walked along the edge of it in the darkness, and every now and then Hawkins would call a halt and begin all over again, as if he was wound up, about our being chums, and I knew that nothing but the sight of the grave would convince him that we had to do it. And all the time I was hoping that something would happen; that they'd run for it or that Noble would take over the responsibility from me. I had the feeling that it was worse on Noble than on me.

IV

At last we saw the lantern in the distance and made towards it. Noble was carrying it, and Feeney was standing somewhere in the darkness behind him, and the picture of them so still and silent in the bogland brought it home to me that we were in earnest, and banished the last bit of hope I had.

Belcher, on recognizing Noble, said: "Hallo, chum," in his quiet way, but Hawkins flew at him at once, and the argument began all over again, only this time Noble had nothing to say for himself and stood with his head down, holding the lantern between his legs.

It was Jeremiah Donovan who did the answering. For the twentieth time, as though it was haunting his mind, Hawkins asked if anybody thought he'd shoot Noble.

"Yes, you would," says Jeremiah Donovan.

"No, I wouldn't, damn you!"

"You would, because you'd know you'd be shot for not doing it."

"I wouldn't, not if I was to be shot twenty times over. I wouldn't shoot a pal. And Belcher wouldn't—isn't that right, Belcher?"

"That's right, chum," Belcher said, but more by way of answering the question than of joining in the argument. Belcher sounded as though whatever unforeseen thing he'd always been waiting for had come at last.

"Anyway, who says Noble would be shot if I wasn't? What do you think I'd do if I was in his place, out in the middle of a blasted bog?"

"What would you do?" asks Donovan.

"I'd go with him wherever he was going, of course. Share my last bob with him and stick by him through thick and thin. No one can ever say of me that I let down a pal."

"We had enough of this," says Jeremiah Donovan, cocking his revolver. "Is there any message you want to send?"

"No, there isn't."

"Do you want to say your prayers?"

Hawkins came out with a cold-blooded remark that even shocked me and turned on Noble again.

"Listen to me, Noble," he says. "You and me are chums. You can't come over to my side, so I'll come over to your side. That show you I mean what I say? Give me a rifle and I'll go along with you and the other lads."

Nobody answered him. We knew that was no way out.

"Hear what I'm saying?" he says. "I'm through with it. I'm a deserter or anything else you like. I don't believe in your stuff, but it's no worse than mine. That satisfy you?"

Noble raised his head, but Donovan began to speak and he lowered it again without replying.

"For the last time, have you any messages to send?" says Donovan in a cool, excited sort of voice.

"Shut up, Donovan! You don't understand me, but these lads do. They're not the sort to make a pal and kill a pal. They're not the tools of any capitalist."

I alone of the crowd saw Donovan raise his Webley to the back of Hawkin's neck, and as he did so I shut my eyes and tried to pray. Hawkins had begun to say something else when Donovan fired, and as I opened my eyes at the bang, I saw Hawkins stagger at the knees and lie out flat at Noble's feet, slowly and as quiet as a kid falling asleep, with the lantern-light on his lean legs and bright farmer's boots. We all stood very still, watching him settle out in the last agony.

Then Belcher took out a handkerchief and began to tie it about his own eyes (in our excitement we'd forgotten to do the same for Hawkins), and, seeing it wasn't big enough, turned and asked for the loan of mine. I gave it to him and he knotted the two together and pointed with his foot at Hawkins.

"He's not quite dead," he says. "Better give him another."

Sure enough, Hawkins's left knee is beginning to rise. I bend down and put my gun to his head; then, recollecting myself, I get up again. Belcher understands what's in my mind.

"Give him his first," he says. "I don't mind. Poor bastard, we don't know what's happening to him now."

I knelt and fired. By this time I didn't seem to know what I was doing.

Belcher, who was fumbling a bit awkwardly with the handkerchiefs, came out with a laugh as he heard the shot. It was the first time I heard him laugh and it sent a shudder down my back; it sounded so unnatural.

"Poor bugger!" he said quietly. "And last night he was so curious about it all. It's very queer, chums, I always think. Now he knows as much about it as they'll ever let him know, and last night he was all in the dark."

Donovan helped him to tie the handkerchiefs about his eyes. "Thanks, chum," he said. Donovan asked if there were any messages he wanted sent.

"No, chum," he says. "Not for me. If any of you would like to write to Hawkins's mother, you'll find a letter from her in his pocket. He and his mother were great chums. But my missus left me eight years ago. Went away with another fellow and took the kid with her. I like the feeling of a home, as you may have noticed, but I couldn't start again after that."

It was an extraordinary thing, but in those few minutes Belcher said more than in all the weeks before. It was just as if the sound of the shot had started a flood of talk in him and he could go on the whole night like that, quite happily, talking about himself. We stood round like fools now that he couldn't see us any longer. Donovan looked at Noble, and Noble shook his head. Then Donovan raised his Webley, and at that moment Belcher gives his queer laugh again. He may have thought we were talking about him, or perhaps he noticed the same thing I'd noticed and couldn't understand it.

"Excuse me, chums," he says. "I feel I'm talking the hell of a lot, and so silly, about my being so handy about a house and things like that. But this thing came on me suddenly. You'll forgive me, I'm sure."

"You don't want to say a prayer?" asks Donovan.

"No, chum," he says. "I don't think it would help. I'm ready, and you boys want to get it over."

"You understand that we're only doing our duty?" says Donovan.

Belcher's head was raised like a blind man's, so that you could only see his chin and the tip of his nose in the lantern-light.

"I never could make out what duty was myself," he said. "I think you're all good lads, if that's what you mean. I'm not complaining."

Noble, just as if he couldn't bear any more of it, raised his fist at Donovan, and in a flash Donovan raised his gun and fired. The big man went over like a sack of meal, and this time there was no need of a second shot.

I don't remember much about the burying, but that it was worse than all the rest because we had to carry them to the grave. It was all mad lonely with nothing but a patch of lantern-light between ourselves and the dark, and birds hooting and screeching all round, disturbed by the guns. Noble went through Hawkins's belongings to find the letter from his mother, and then joined his hands together. He did the same with Belcher. Then, when we'd filled the grave, we separated from Jeremiah Donovan and Feeney and took our tools back to the shed. All the way we didn't speak a word. The kitchen was dark and cold as we'd left it, and the old woman was sitting

over the hearth, saying her beads. We walked past her into the room, and
Noble struck a match to light the lamp. She rose quietly and came to the
doorway with all her cantankerousness gone.

"What did ye do with them?" she asked in a whisper, and Noble started
so that the match went out in his hand.

"What's that?" he asked without turning round.

"I heard ye," she said.

"What did you hear?" asked Noble.

"I heard ye. Do ye think I didn't hear ye, putting the spade back in the
houseen?"

Noble struck another match and this time the lamp lit for him.

"Was that what ye did to them?" she asked.

Then, by God, in the very doorway, she fell on her knees and began
praying, and after looking at her for a minute or two Noble did the same
by the fireplace. I pushed my way out past her and left them at it. I stood at
the door, watching the stars and listening to the shrieking of the birds
dying out over the bogs. It is so strange what you feel at times like that that
you can't describe it. Noble says he saw everything ten times the size, as
though there were nothing in the whole world but that little patch of bog
with the two Englishmen stiffening into it, but with me it was as if the patch
of bog where the Englishmen were was a million miles away, and even Noble and the old woman, mumbling behind me, and the birds and the bloody
stars were all far away, and I was somehow very small and very lost and
lonely like a child astray in the snow. And anything that happened to me
afterwards, I never felt the same about again.

I Stand Here Ironing

TILLIE OLSEN

I stand here ironing, and what you asked me moves tormented back and forth with the iron.

"I wish you would manage the time to come in and talk with me about your daughter. I'm sure you can help me understand her. She's a youngster who needs help and whom I'm deeply interested in helping."

"Who needs help." . . . Even if I came, what good would it do? You think because I am her mother I have a key, or that in some way you could use me as a key? She has lived for nineteen years. There is all that life that has happened outside of me, beyond me.

And when is there time to remember, to sift, to weigh, to estimate, to total? I will start and there will be an interruption and I will have to gather it all together again. Or I will become engulfed with all I did or did not do, with what should have been and what cannot be helped.

She was a beautiful baby. The first and only one of our five that was beautiful at birth. You do not guess how new and uneasy her tenancy in her now-loveliness. You did not know her all those years she was thought homely, or see her poring over her baby pictures, making me tell her over and over how beautiful she had been—and would be, I would tell her—and was now, to the seeing eye. But the seeing eyes were few or nonexistent. Including mine.

I nursed her. They feel that's important nowadays. I nursed all the children, but with her, with all the fierce rigidity of first motherhood, I did like the books then said. Though her cries battered me to trembling and my breasts ached with swollenness, I waited till the clock decreed.

Why do I put that first? I do not even know if it matters, or if it explains anything.

She was a beautiful baby. She blew shining bubbles of sound. She loved motion, loved light, loved color and music and textures. She would lie on the floor in her blue overalls patting the surface so hard in ecstasy her hands and feet would blur. She was a miracle to me, but when she was eight months old I had to leave her daytimes with the woman downstairs to whom she was no miracle at all, for I worked or looked for work and for Emily's father, who "could no longer endure" (he wrote in his good-bye note) "sharing want with us."

I was nineteen. It was the pre-relief, pre-WPA world of the depression. I would start running as soon as I got off the streetcar, running up the stairs, the place smelling sour, and awake or asleep to startle awake, when she saw me she would break into a clogged weeping that could not be comforted, a weeping I can hear yet.

After a while I found a job hashing at night so I could be with her days, and it was better. But it came to where I had to bring her to his family and leave her.

It took a long time to raise the money for her fare back. Then she got chicken pox and I had to wait longer. When she finally came, I hardly knew her, walking quick and nervous like her father, looking like her father, thin, and dressed in a shoddy red that yellowed her skin and glared at the pockmarks. All the baby loveliness gone.

She was two. Old enough for nursery school they said, and I did not know then what I know now—the fatigue of the long day, and the lacerations of group life in the kinds of nurseries that are only parking places for children.

Except that it would have made no difference if I had known. It was the only place there was. It was the only way we could be together, the only way I could hold a job.

And even without knowing, I knew. I knew the teacher that was evil because all these years it has curdled into my memory, the little boy hunched in the corner, her rasp, "why aren't you outside, because Alvin hits you? that's no reason, go out, scaredy." I knew Emily hated it even if she did not clutch and implore "don't go Mommy" like the other children, mornings.

She always had a reason why we should stay home. Momma, you look sick, Momma. I feel sick. Momma, the teachers aren't there today, they're sick. Momma, we can't go, there was a fire there last night. Momma, it's a holiday today, no school, they told me.

But never a direct protest, never rebellion. I think of our others in their three-, four-year-oldness—the explosions, the tempers, the denunciations, the demands—and I feel suddenly ill. I put the iron down. What in me demanded that goodness in her? And what was the cost, the cost to her of such goodness?

The old man living in the back once said in his gentle way: "You should smile at Emily more when you look at her." What *was* in my face when I looked at her? I loved her. There were all the acts of love.

It was only with the others I remembered what he said, and it was the face of joy, and not of care or tightness or worry I turned to them—too late for Emily. She does not smile easily, let alone almost always as her brothers and sisters do. Her face is closed and sombre, but when she wants, how fluid. You must have seen it in her pantomimes, you spoke of her rare gift for comedy on the stage that rouses a laughter out of the audience so dear they applaud and applaud and do not want to let her go.

Where does it come from, that comedy? There was none of it in her when she came back to me that second time, after I had had to send her away again. She had a new daddy now to learn to love, and I think perhaps it was a better time.

Except when we left her alone nights, telling ourselves she was old enough.

"Can't you go some other time, Mommy, like tomorrow?" she would ask. "Will it be just a little while you'll be gone? Do you promise?"

The time we came back, the front door open, the clock on the floor in the hall. She rigid awake. "It wasn't just a little while. I didn't cry. Three times I called you, just three times, and then I ran downstairs to open the door so you could come faster. The clock talked loud. I threw it away, it scared me what it talked."

She said the clock talked loud again that night I went to the hospital to have Susan. She was delirious with the fever that comes before red measles, but she was fully conscious all the week I was gone and the week after we were home when she could not come near the new baby or me.

She did not get well. She stayed skeleton thin, not wanting to eat, and night after night she had nightmares. She would call for me, and I would rouse from exhaustion to sleepily call back: "You're all right, darling, go to sleep, it's just a dream," and if she still called, in a sterner voice, "now go to sleep, Emily, there's nothing to hurt you." Twice, only twice, when I had to get up for Susan anyhow, I went in to sit with her.

Now when it is too late (as if she would let me hold and comfort her like I do the others) I get up and go to her at once at her moan or restless stirring. "Are you awake, Emily? Can I get you something?" And the answer is always the same: "No, I'm all right, go back to sleep, Mother."

They persuaded me at the clinic to send her away to a convalescent home in the country where "she can have the kind of food and care you can't manage for her, and you'll be free to concentrate on the new baby." They still send children to that place. I see pictures on the society page of sleek young women planning affairs to raise money for it, or dancing at the affairs, or decorating Easter eggs or filling Christmas stockings for the children.

They never have a picture of the children so I do not know if the girls still wear those gigantic red bows and the ravaged looks on the every other Sunday when parents can come to visit "unless otherwise notified"—as we were notified the first six weeks.

Oh it is a handsome place, green lawns and tall trees and fluted flower beds. High up on the balconies of each cottage the children stand, the girls in their red bows and white dresses, the boys in white suits and giant red ties. The parents stand below shrieking up to be heard and the children shriek down to be heard, and between them the invisible wall "Not To Be Contaminated by Parental Germs or Physical Affection."

There was a tiny girl who always stood hand in hand with Emily. Her parents never came. One visit she was gone. "They moved her to Rose Cottage" Emily shouted in explanation. "They don't like you to love anybody here."

She wrote once a week, the labored writing of a seven-year-old. "I am fine. How is the baby. If I write my letter nicly I will have a star. Love." There never was a star. We wrote every other day, letters she could never hold or keep but only hear read—once. "We simply do not have room for children to keep any personal possessions," they patiently explained when we pieced one Sunday's shrieking together to plead how much it would mean to Emily, who loved so to keep things, to be allowed to keep her letters and cards.

Each visit she looked frailer. "She isn't eating," they told us.

(They had runny eggs for breakfast or mush with lumps, Emily said later, I'd hold it in my mouth and not swallow. Nothing ever tasted good, just when they had chicken.)

It took us eight months to get her released home, and only the fact that she gained back so little of her seven lost pounds convinced the social worker.

I used to try to hold and love her after she came back, but her body would stay stiff, and after a while she'd push away. She ate little. Food sickened her, and I think much of life too. Oh she had physical lightness and brightness, twinkling by on skates, bouncing like a ball up and down up and down over the jump rope, skimming over the hill; but these were momentary.

She fretted about her appearance, thin and dark and foreign-looking at a time when every little girl was supposed to look or thought she should look a chubby blonde replica of Shirley Temple. The doorbell sometimes rang for her, but no one seemed to come and play in the house or be a best friend. Maybe because we moved so much.

There was a boy she loved painfully through two school semesters. Months later she told me how she had taken pennies from my purse to buy him candy. "Licorice was his favorite and I brought him some every day, but he still liked Jennifer better'n me. Why, Mommy?" The kind of question for which there is no answer.

School was a worry to her. She was not glib or quick in a world where glibness and quickness were easily confused with ability to learn. To her overworked and exasperated teachers she was an overconscientious "slow learner" who kept trying to catch up and was absent entirely too often.

I let her be absent, though sometimes the illness was imaginary. How different from my now-strictness about attendance with the others. I wasn't working. We had a new baby, I was home anyhow. Sometimes, after Susan grew old enough, I would keep her home from school, too, to have them all together.

Mostly Emily had asthma, and her breathing, harsh and labored, would fill the house with a curiously tranquil sound. I would bring the two old dresser mirrors and her boxes of collections to her bed. She would select beads and single earrings, bottle tops and shells, dried flowers and pebbles, old postcards and scraps, all sorts of oddments; then she and Susan would play Kingdom, setting up landscapes and furniture, peopling them with action.

Those were the only times of peaceful companionship between her and Susan. I have edged away from it, that poisonous feeling between them, that terrible balancing of hurts and needs I had to do between the two, and did so badly, those earlier years.

Oh there are conflicts between the others too, each one human, needing, demanding, hurting, taking—but only between Emily and Susan, no, Emily toward Susan that corroding resentment. It seems so obvious on the surface, yet it is not obvious. Susan, the second child, Susan, golden- and curly-haired and chubby, quick and articulate and assured, everything in appearance and manner Emily was not; Susan, not able to resist Emily's precious things, losing or sometimes clumsily breaking them; Susan telling jokes and riddles to company for applause while Emily sat silent (to say to me later: that was *my* riddle, Mother, I told it to Susan); Susan, who for all the five years' difference in age was just a year behind Emily in developing physically.

I am glad for that slow physical development that widened the difference between her and her contemporaries, though she suffered over it. She was too vulnerable for that terrible world of youthful competition, of preening and parading, of constant measuring of yourself against every other, of envy, "If I had that copper hair," "If I had that skin. . . ." She tormented herself enough about not looking like the others, there was enough of the unsureness, the having to be conscious of words before you speak, the constant caring—what are they thinking of me? without having it all magnified by the merciless physical drives.

Ronnie is calling. He is wet and I change him. It is rare there is such a cry now. That time of motherhood is almost behind me when the ear is not one's own but must always be racked and listening for the child cry, the child call. We sit for a while and I hold him, looking out over the city spread in charcoal with its soft aisles of light. "*Shoogily*," he breathes and curls closer. I carry him back to bed, asleep. *Shoogily*. A funny word, a family word, inherited from Emily, invented by her to say: *comfort*.

In this and other ways she leaves her seal, I say aloud. And startle at my saying it. What do I mean? What did I start to gather together, to try and make coherent? I was at the terrible, growing years. War years. I do not remember them well. I was working, there were four smaller ones now, there was not time for her. She had to help be a mother, and housekeeper, and shopper. She had to set her seal. Mornings of crisis and near hysteria trying to get lunches packed, hair combed, coats and shoes found, everyone to school or Child Care on time, the baby ready for transportation. And always the paper scribbled on by a smaller one, the book looked at by Susan then mislaid, the homework not done. Running out to that huge school where she was one, she was lost, she was a drop; suffering over the unpreparedness, stammering and unsure in her classes.

There was so little time left at night after the kids were bedded down. She would struggle over books, always eating (it was in those years she developed her enormous appetite that is legendary in our family) and I would be ironing, or preparing food for the next day, or writing V-mail to Bill, or tending the baby. Sometimes, to make me laugh, or out of her despair, she would imitate happenings or types at school.

I think I said once: "Why don't you do something like this in the school amateur show?" One morning she phoned me at work, hardly understandable through the weeping: "Mother, I did it. I won, I won; they gave me first prize; they clapped and clapped and wouldn't let me go."

Now suddenly she was Somebody, and as imprisoned in her difference as she had been in anonymity.

She began to be asked to perform at other high schools, even in colleges, then at city and statewide affairs. The first one we went to, I only recognized her that first moment when thin, shy, she almost drowned herself into the curtains. Then: Was this Emily? The control, the command, the convulsing and deadly clowning, the spell, then the roaring, stamping audience, unwilling to let this rare and precious laughter out of their lives.

Afterwards: You ought to do something about her with a gift like that— but without money or knowing how, what does one do? We have left it all to her, and the gift has as often eddied inside, clogged and clotted, as been used and growing.

She is coming. She runs up the stairs two at a time with her light graceful step, and I know she is happy tonight. Whatever it was that occasioned your call did not happen today.

"Aren't you ever going to finish the ironing, Mother? Whistler painted his mother in a rocker. I'd have to paint mine standing over an ironing board." This is one of her communicative nights and she tells me everything and nothing as she fixes herself a plate of food out of the icebox.

She is so lovely. Why did you want me to come in at all? Why were you concerned? She will find her way.

She starts up the stairs to bed. "Don't get me up with the rest in the morning." But I thought you were having midterms." "Oh, those," she comes back in, kisses me, and says lightly, "in a couple of years when we'll all be atom-dead they won't matter a bit."

She has said it before. She *believes* it. But because I have been dredging the past, and all that compounds a human being is so heavy and meaningful in me, I cannot endure it tonight.

I will never total it all. I will never come in to say: She was a child seldom smiled at. Her father left me before she was a year old. I had to work her first six years when there was work, or I sent her home and to his relatives. There were years she had care she hated. She was dark and thin and foreign-looking in a world where the prestige went to blondeness and curly hair and dimples, she was slow where glibness was prized. She was a child of anxious, not proud, love. We were poor and could not afford for her the soil of easy growth. I was a young mother, I was a distracted mother. There were the other children pushing up, demanding. Her younger sister seemed all that she was not. There were years she did not want me to touch her. She kept too much in herself, her life was such she had to keep too much in herself. My wisdom came too late. She has much to her and probably little will come of it. She is a child of her age, of depression, of war, of fear.

Let her be. So all that is in her will not bloom—but in how many does it? There is still enough left to live by. Only help her to know—help make it so there is cause for her to know—that she is more than this dress on the ironing board, helpless before the iron.

Nomad and Viper

AMOS OZ

I

The famine brought them.

They fled north from the horrors of famine, together with their dusty flocks. From September to April the desert had not known a moment's relief from drought. The loess was pounded to dust. Famine had spread through the nomads' encampments and wrought havoc among their flocks.

The military authorities gave the situation their urgent attention. Despite certain hesitations, they decided to open the roads leading north to the Bedouins. A whole population—men, women, and children—could not simply be abandoned to the horrors of starvation.

Dark, sinuous, and wiry, the desert tribesmen trickled along the dirt paths, and with them came their emaciated flocks. They meandered along gullies hidden from town dwellers' eyes. A persistent stream pressed northward, circling the scattered settlements, staring wide-eyed at the sights of the settled land. The dark flocks spread into the fields of golden stubble, tearing and chewing with strong, vengeful teeth. The nomads' bearing was stealthy and subdued; they shrank from watchful eyes. They took pains to avoid encounters. Tried to conceal their presence.

If you passed them on a noisy tractor and set billows of dust loose on them, they would courteously gather their scattered flocks and give you a wide passage, wider by far than was necessary. They stared at you from a distance, frozen like statues. The scorching atmosphere blurred their appearance and gave a uniform look to their features: a shepherd with his staff, a woman with her babes, an old man with his eyes sunk deep in their sockets. Some were half-blind, or perhaps feigned half-blindness from some vague alms-gathering motive. Inscrutable to the likes of you.

How unlike our well-tended sheep were their miserable specimens: knots of small, skinny beasts huddling into a dark, seething mass, silent and subdued, humble as their dumb keepers.

The camels alone spurn meekness. From atop tall necks they fix you with tired eyes brimming with scornful sorrow. The wisdom of age seems to lurk in their eyes, and a nameless tremor runs often through their skin.

Sometimes you manage to catch them unawares. Crossing a field on foot, you may suddenly happen on an indolent flock standing motionless, noonstruck, their feet apparently rooted in the parched soil. Among them lies the shepherd, fast asleep, dark as a block of basalt. You approach and cover him with a harsh shadow. You are startled to find his eyes wide open. He bares most of his teeth in a placatory smile. Some of them are gleaming, others decayed. His smell hits you. You grimace. Your grimace hits him like a punch in the face. Daintily he picks himself up, trunk erect, shoulders hunched. You fix him with a cold blue eye. He broadens his smile and utters a guttural syllable. His garb is a compromise: a short, patched European jacket over a white desert robe. He cocks his head to one side. An appeased gleam crosses his face. If you do not upbraid him, he suddenly extends his left hand and asks for a cigarette in rapid Hebrew. His voice has a silken quality, like that of a shy woman. If your mood is generous, you put a cigarette to your lips and toss another into his wrinkled palm. To your surprise, he snatches a gilt lighter from the recesses of his robe and offers a furtive flame. The smile never leaves his lips. His smile lasts too long, is unconvincing. A flash of sunlight darts off the thick gold ring adorning his finger and pierces your squinting eyes.

Eventually you turn your back on the nomad and continue on your way. After a hundred, two hundred paces, you may turn your head and see him standing just as he was, his gaze stabbing your back. You could swear that he is still smiling, that he will go on smiling for a long while to come.

And then, their singing in the night. A long-drawn-out, dolorous wail drifts on the night air from sunset until the early hours. The voices penetrate to the gardens and pathways of the kibbutz and charge our nights with an uneasy heaviness. No sooner have you settled down to sleep than a distant drumbeat sets the rhythm of your slumber like the pounding of an obdurate heart. Hot are the nights, and vapor-laden. Stray clouds caress the moon like a train of gentle camels, camels without any bells.

The nomads' tents are made up of dark drapes. Stray women drift around at night, barefoot and noiseless. Lean, vicious nomad hounds dart out of the camp to challenge the moon all night long. Their barking drives our kibbutz dogs insane. Our finest dog went mad one night, broke into the henhouse, and massacred the young chicks. It was not out of savagery that the watchmen shot him. There was no alternative. Any reasonable man would justify their action.

II

You might imagine that the nomad incursion enriched our heat-prostrated nights with a dimension of poetry. This may have been the case for some of our unattached girls. But we cannot refrain from mentioning a whole string of prosaic, indeed unaesthetic disturbances, such as foot-and-mouth disease, crop damage, and an epidemic of petty thefts.

The foot-and-mouth disease came out of the desert, carried by their live-stock, which had never been subjected to any proper medical inspection. Although we took various early precautions, the virus infected our sheep and cattle, severely reducing the milk yield and killing off a number of animals.

As for the damage to the crops, we had to admit that we had never man-aged to catch one of the nomads in the act. All we ever found were the tracks of men and animals among the rows of vegetables, in the hayfields, and deep inside the carefully fenced orchards. And wrecked irrigation pipes, plot markers, farming implements left out in the fields, and other objects.

We are not the kind to take such things lying down. We are no believers in forbearance or vegetarianism. This is especially true of our younger men. Among the veteran founders there are a few adherents of Tolstoyan ideas and such like. Decency constrains me not to dwell in detail on certain isolated and exceptional acts of reprisal conducted by some of the young-sters whose patience had expired, such as cattle rustling, stoning a nomad boy, or beating one of the shepherds senseless. In defense of the perpetra-tors of the last-mentioned act of retaliation I must state clearly that the shepherd in question had an infuriatingly sly face. He was blind in one eye, broken-nosed, drooling; and his mouth—on this the men responsible were unanimous—was set with long-curved fangs like a fox's. A man with such an appearance was capable of anything. And the Bedouins would certainly not forget this lesson.

The pilfering was the most worrisome aspect of all. They laid hands on the unripe fruit in our orchards, pocketed the faucets, whittled away piles of empty sacks in the fields, stole into the henhouses, and even made away with the modest valuables from our little houses.

The very darkness was their accomplice. Elusive as the wind, they passed through the settlement, evading both the guards we had posted and the ex-tra guards we had added. Sometimes you would set out on a tractor or a

battered jeep toward midnight to turn off the irrigation faucets in an outlying field and your headlights would trap fleeting shadows, a man or a night
beast. An irritable guard decided one night to open fire, and in the dark he
managed to kill a stray jackal.

Needless to say, the kibbutz secretariat did not remain silent. Several
times Etkin, the secretary, called in the police, but their tracking dogs betrayed or failed them. Having led their handlers a few paces outside the
kibbutz fence, they raised their black noses, uttered a savage howl, and
stared foolishly ahead.

Spot raids on the tattered tents revealed nothing. It was as if the very
earth had decided to cover up the plunder and brazenly outstare the victims. Eventually the elder of the tribe was brought to the kibbutz office,
flanked by a pair of inscrutable nomads. The short-tempered policemen
pushed them forward with repeated cries of "Yallah, yallah."

We, the members of the secretariat, received the elder and his men politely and respectfully. We invited them to sit down on the bench, smiled at
them, and offered them steaming coffee prepared by Geula at Etkin's special request. The old man responded with elaborate courtesies, favoring us
with a smile which he kept up from the beginning of the interview till its
conclusion. He phrased his remarks in careful, formal Hebrew.

It was true that some of the youngsters of his tribe had laid hands on our
property. Why should he deny it. Boys would be boys, and the world was
getting steadily worse. He had the honor of begging our pardon and re-
storing the stolen property. Stolen property fastens its teeth in the flesh of
the thief, as the proverb says. That was the way of it. What could one do
about the hotheadedness of youth? He deeply regretted the trouble and
distress we had been caused.

So saying, he put his hand into the folds of his robe and drew out a few
screws, some gleaming, some rusty, a pair of pruning hooks, a stray knife-
blade, a pocket flashlight, a broken hammer, and three grubby bank notes,
as a recompense for our loss and worry.

Etkin spread his hands in embarrassment. For reasons best known to
himself, he chose to ignore our guest's Hebrew and to reply in broken Arabic, the residue of his studies during the time of the riots and the siege. He
opened his remarks with a frank and clear statement about the brotherhood of nations—the cornerstone of our ideology—and about the quality
of neighborliness of which the peoples of the East had long been justly
proud, and never more so than in these days of bloodshed and groundless
hatred.

To Etkin's credit, let it be said that he did not shrink in the slightest from
reciting a full and detailed list of the acts of theft, damage, and sabotage
that our guest—as the result of oversight, no doubt—had refrained from
mentioning in his apology. If all the stolen property were returned and the
vandalism stopped once and for all, we would be wholeheartedly willing to

open a new page in the relations of our two neighboring communities. Our children would doubtless enjoy and profit from an educational courtesy visit to the Bedouin encampment, the kind of visit that broadens horizons. And it went without saying that the tribe's children would pay a return visit to our kibbutz home, in the interest of deepening mutual understanding.

The old man neither relaxed nor broadened his smile, but kept it sternly at its former level as he remarked with an abundance of polite phrases that the gentlemen of the kibbutz would be able to prove no further thefts beyond those he had already admitted and for which he had sought our forgiveness.

He concluded with elaborate benedictions, wished us health and long life, posterity and plenty, then took his leave and departed, accompanied by his two barefooted companions wrapped in their dark robes. They were soon swallowed up by the wadi that lay outside the kibbutz fence.

Since the police had proved ineffectual—and had indeed abandoned the investigation—some of our young men suggested making an excursion one night to teach the savages a lesson in a language they would really understand.

Etkin rejected their suggestion with disgust and with reasonable arguments. The young men, in turn, applied to Etkin a number of epithets that decency obliges me to pass over in silence. Strangely enough, Etkin ignored their insults and reluctantly agreed to put their suggestion before the kibbutz secretariat. Perhaps he was afraid that they might take matters into their own hands.

Toward evening, Etkin went around from room to room and invited the committee to an urgent meeting at eight-thirty. When he came to Geula, he told her about the young men's ideas and the undemocratic pressure to which he was being subjected, and asked her to bring along to the meeting a pot of black coffee and a lot of good will. Geula responded with an acid smile. Her eyes were bleary because Etkin had awakened her from a troubled sleep. As she changed her clothes, the night fell, damp and hot and close.

III

Damp and close and hot the night fell on the kibbutz, tangled in the dust-laden cypresses, oppressed the lawns and ornamental shrubs. Sprinklers scattered water onto the thirsty lawn, but it was swallowed up at once: perhaps it evaporated even before it touched the grass. An irritable phone rang vainly in the locked office. The walls of the houses gave out a damp vapor. From the kitchen chimney a stiff column of smoke rose like an arrow into the heart of the sky, because there was no breeze. From the greasy sinks came a shout. A dish had been broken and somebody was bleeding. A fat house-cat had killed a lizard or a snake and dragged its prey onto the baking concrete path to toy with it lazily in the dense evening sunlight. An ancient tractor started to rumble in one of the sheds, choked, belched a stench of oil, roared, spluttered, and finally managed to set out to deliver an evening meal to the second shift, who were toiling in an outlying field. Near the Persian lilac Geula saw a bottle dirty with the remains of a greasy liquid. She kicked at it repeatedly, but instead of shattering, the bottle rolled heavily among the rosebushes. She picked up a big stone. She tried to hit the bottle. She longed to smash it. The stone missed. The girl began to whistle a vague tune.

Geula was a short, energetic girl of twenty-nine or so. Although she had not yet found a husband, none of us would deny her good qualities, such as the dedication she lavished on local social and cultural activities. Her face was pale and thin. No one could rival her in brewing strong coffee—coffee to raise the dead, we called it. A pair of bitter lines were etched at the corners of her mouth.

On summer evenings, when the rest of us would lounge in a group on a rug spread on one of the lawns and launch jokes and bursts of cheerful song heavenward, accompanied by clouds of cigarette smoke, Geula would shut herself up in her room and not join us until she had prepared the pot of scalding, strong coffee. She it was, too, who always took pains to ensure that there was no shortage of biscuits.

What had passed between Geula and me is not relevant here, and I shall make do with a hint or two. Long ago we used to stroll together to the orchards in the evening and talk. It was all a long time ago, and it is a long time since it ended. We would exchange unconventional political ideas or argue about the latest books. Geula was a stern and sometimes merciless critic: I was covered in confusion. She did not like my stories, because of the extreme polarity of situations, scenery, and characters, with no intermediate shades between black and white. I would utter an apology or a denial, but Geula always had ready proofs and she was a very methodical thinker. Sometimes I would dare to rest a conciliatory hand on her neck, and wait for her to calm down. But she never relaxed completely. If once or twice she leaned against me, she always blamed her broken sandal or her aching head. And so we drifted apart. To this day she still cuts my stories out of the periodicals, and arranges them in a cardboard box kept in a special drawer devoted to them alone.

I always buy her a new book of poems for her birthday. I creep into her room when she is out and leave the book on her table, without any inscription or dedication. Sometimes we happen to sit together in the dining hall. I avoid her glance, so as not to have to face her mocking sadness. On hot days, when faces are covered in sweat, the acne on her cheeks reddens and she seems to have no hope. When the cool of autumn comes, I sometimes find her pretty and attractive from a distance. On such days Geula likes to walk to the orchards in the early evening. She goes alone and comes back alone. Some of the youngsters come and ask me what she is looking for there, and they have a malicious snicker on their faces. I tell them that I don't know. And I really don't.

IV

Viciously Geula picked up another stone to hurl at the bottle. This time she did not miss, but she still failed to hear the shattering sound she craved. The stone grazed the bottle, which tinkled faintly and disappeared under one of the bushes. A third stone, bigger and heavier than the other two, was launched from ridiculously close range: the girl trampled on the loose soil of the flower bed and stood right over the bottle. This time there was a harsh, dry explosion, which brought no relief. Must get out.

Damp and close and hot the night fell, its heat pricking the skin like broken glass. Geula retraced her steps, passed the balcony of her room, tossed her sandals inside, and walked down barefoot onto the dirt path.

The clods of earth tickled the soles of her feet. There was a rough friction, and her nerve endings quivered with flickers of vague excitement. Beyond the rocky hill the shadows were waiting for her: the orchard in the last of the light. With determined hands she widened the gap in the fence and slipped through. At that moment a slight evening breeze began to stir. It was a warmish summer breeze with no definite direction. An old sun rolled westward, trying to be sucked up by the dusty horizon. A last tractor climbed back to the depot, panting along the dirt road from the outlying plots. No doubt it was the tractor that had taken the second-shift workers their supper. It seemed shrouded in smoke or summer haze.

Geula bent down and picked some pebbles out of the dust. Absently she began to throw them back again, one by one. There were lines of poetry on her lips, some by the young poets she was fond of, others her own. By the irrigation pipe she paused, bent down, and drank as though kissing the faucet. But the faucet was rusty, the pipe was still hot, and the water was tepid and foul. Nevertheless she bent her head and let the water pour over her face and neck and into her shirt. A sharp taste of rust and wet dust filled her throat. She closed her eyes and stood in silence. No relief. Perhaps a cup of coffee. But only after the orchard. Must go now.

V

The orchards were heavily laden and fragrant. The branches intertwined, converging above the rows of trunks to form a shadowy dome. Underfoot the irrigated soil retained a hidden dampness. Shadows upon shadows at the foot of those gnarled trunks. Geula picked a plum, sniffed and crushed it. Sticky juice dripped from it. The sight made her feel dizzy. And the smell. She crushed a second plum. She picked another and rubbed it on her cheek till she was spattered with juice. Then, on her knees, she picked up a dry stick and scratched shapes in the dust. Aimless lines and curves. Sharp angles. Domes. A distant bleating invaded the orchard. Dimly she became aware of a sound of bells. She was far away. The nomad stopped behind Geula's back, as silent as a phantom. He dug at the dust with his big toe, and his shadow fell in front of him. But the girl was blinded by a flood of sounds. She saw and heard nothing. For a long time she continued to kneel on the ground and draw shapes in the dust with her twig. The nomad waited patiently in total silence. From time to time he closed his good eye and stared ahead of him with the other, the blind one. Finally he reached out and bestowed a long caress on the air. His obedient shadow moved in the dust. Geula stared, leapt to her feet, and leaned against the nearest tree, letting out a low sound. The nomad let his shoulders drop and put on a faint smile. Geula raised her arm and stabbed the air with her twig. The nomad continued to smile. His gaze dropped to her bare feet. His voice was hushed, and the Hebrew he spoke exuded a rare gentleness:

"What time is it?"

Geula inhaled to her lungs' full capacity. Her features grew sharp, her glance cold. Clearly and dryly she replied:

"It is half past six. Precisely."

The Arab broadened his smile and bowed slightly, as if to acknowledge a great kindness.

"Thank you very much, miss."

His bare toe had dug deep into the damp soil, and the clods of earth crawled at his feet as if there were a startled mole burrowing underneath them.

Geula fastened the top button of her blouse. There were large perspiration stains on her shirt, drawing attention to her armpits. She could smell the sweat on her body, and her nostrils widened. The nomad closed his blind eye and looked up. His good eye blinked. His skin was very dark; it was alive and warm. Creases were etched in his cheeks. He was unlike any man Geula had ever known, and his smell and color and breathing were also strange. His nose was long and narrow, and a shadow of a mustache showed beneath it. His cheeks seemed to be sunk into his mouth cavity. His lips were thin and fine, much finer than her own. But the chin was strong, almost expressing contempt or rebellion.

The man was repulsively handsome, Geula decided to herself. Unconsciously she responded with a mocking half-smile to the nomad's persistent grin. The Bedouin drew two crumpled cigarettes from a hidden pocket in his belt, laid them on his dark, outstretched palm, and held them out to her as though proffering crumbs to a sparrow. Geula dropped her smile, nodded twice, and accepted one. She ran the cigarette through her fingers, slowly, dreamily, ironing out the creases, straightening it, and only then did she put it to her lips. Quick as lightning, before she realized the purpose of the man's sudden movement, a tiny flame was dancing in front of her. Geula shielded the lighter with her hand even though there was no breeze in the orchard, sucked in the flame, closed her eyes. The nomad lit his own cigarette and bowed politely.

"Thank you very much," he said in his velvety voice.

"Thanks," Geula replied. "Thank you."

"You from the kibbutz?"

Geula nodded.

"Goo-d." An elongated syllable escaped from between his gleaming teeth. "That's goo-d."

The girl eyed his desert robe.

"Aren't you hot in that thing?"

The man gave an embarrassed, guilty smile, as if he had been caught red-handed. He took a slight step backward.

"Heaven forbid, it's not hot. Really not. Why? There's air, there's water. . . ." And he fell silent.

The treetops were already growing darker. A first jackal sniffed the oncoming night and let out a tired howl. The orchard filled with a scurry of small, busy feet. All of a sudden Geula became aware of the throngs of black goats intruding in search of their master. They swirled silently in and out of the fruit trees. Geula pursed her lips and let out a short whistle of surprise.

"What are you doing here, anyway? Stealing?"

The nomad cowered as though a stone had been thrown at him. His hand beat a hollow tattoo on his chest.

"No, not stealing, heaven forbid, really not." He added a lengthy oath in his own language and resumed his silent smile. His blind eye winked nervously. Meanwhile an emaciated goat darted forward and rubbed against his leg. He kicked it away and continued to swear with passion:

"Not steal, truly, by Allah not steal. Forbidden to steal."

"Forbidden in the Bible," Geula replied with a dry, cruel smile. "Forbidden to steal, forbidden to kill, forbidden to covet, and forbidden to commit adultery. The righteous are above suspicion."

The Arab cowered before the onslaught of words and looked down at the ground. Shamefaced. Guilty. His foot continued to kick restlessly at the loose earth. He was trying to ingratiate himself. His blind eye narrowed. Geula was momentarily alarmed: surely it was a wink. The smile left his lips. He spoke in a soft, drawn-out whisper, as though uttering a prayer.

"Beautiful girl, truly very beautiful girl. Me, I got no girl yet. Me still young. No girl yet. Yaaa," he concluded with a guttural yell directed at an impudent goat that had rested its forelegs against a tree trunk and was munching hungrily at the foliage. The animal cast a pensive, skeptical glance at its master, shook its beard, and solemnly resumed its munching.

Without warning, and with amazing agility, the shepherd leapt through the air and seized the beast by the hindquarters, lifted it above his head, let out a terrifying, savage screech, and flung it ruthlessly to the ground. Then he spat and turned to the girl.

"Beast," he apologized. "Beast. What to do. No brains. No manners."

The girl let go of the tree trunk against which she had been resting and leaned toward the nomad. A sweet shudder ran down her back. Her voice was still firm and cool.

"Another cigarette?" she asked. "Have you got another cigarette?"

The Bedouin replied with a look of anguish, almost of despair. He apologized. He explained at length that he had no more cigarettes, not even one, not even a little one. No more. All gone. What a pity. He would gladly, very gladly, have given her one. None left. All gone.

The beaten goat was getting shakily to its feet. Treading circumspectly, it returned to the tree trunk, disingenuously observing its master out of the corner of its eye. The shepherd watched it without moving. The goat reached up, rested its front hoofs on the tree, and calmly continued munching. The Arab picked up a heavy stone and swung his arm wildly. Geula seized his arm and restrained him.

"Leave it. Why. Let it be. It doesn't understand. It's only a beast. No brains, no manners."

The nomad obeyed. In total submission he let the stone drop. Then Geula let go of his arm. Once again the man drew the lighter out of his belt. With thin, pensive fingers he toyed with it. He accidentally lit a small flame, and hastily blew at it. The flame widened slightly, slanted, and died. Nearby a jackal broke into a loud, piercing wail. The rest of the goats, meanwhile, had followed the example of the first and were absorbed in rapid, almost angry munching.

A vague wail came from the nomad encampment away to the south, the dim drum beating time to its languorous call. The dusky men were sitting around their campfires, sending skyward their single-noted song. The night took up the strain and answered with dismal cricket-chirp. Last glimmers of light were dying away in the far west. The orchard stood in darkness. Sounds gathered all around, the wind's whispering, the goats' sniffing, the rustle of ravished leaves. Geula pursed her lips and whistled an old tune. The nomad listened to her with rapt attention, his head cocked to one side in surprise, his mouth hanging slightly open. She glanced at her watch. The hands winked back at her with a malign, phosphorescent glint, but said nothing. Night.

The Arab turned his back on Geula, dropped to his knees, touched his forehead on the ground, and began mumbling fervently.

"You've got no girl yet," Geula broke into his prayer. "You're still too young." Her voice was loud and strange. Her hands were on her hips, her breathing still even. The man stopped praying, turned his dark face toward her, and muttered a phrase in Arabic. He was still crouched on all fours, but his pose suggested a certain suppressed joy.

"You're still young," Geula repeated, "very young. Perhaps twenty. Perhaps thirty. Young. No girl for you. Too young."

The man replied with a very long and solemn remark in his own language. She laughed nervously, her hands embracing her hips.

"What's the matter with you?" she inquired, laughing still. "Why are you talking to me in Arabic all of a sudden? What do you think I am? What do you want here, anyway?"

Again the nomad replied in his own language. Now a note of terror filled his voice. With soft, silent steps he recoiled and withdrew as though from a dying creature. She was breathing heavily now, panting, trembling. A single wild syllable escaped from the shepherd's mouth: a sign between him and his goats. The goats responded and thronged around him, their feet pattering on the carpet of dead leaves like cloth ripping. The crickets fell silent. The goats huddled in the dark, a terrified, quivering mass, and disappeared into the darkness, the shepherd vanishing in their midst.

Afterward, alone and trembling, she watched an airplane passing in the dark sky above the treetops, rumbling dully, its lights blinking alternately with a rhythm as precise as that of the drums: red, green, red, green, red. The night covered over the traces. There was a smell of bonfires on the air and a smell of dust borne on the breeze. Only a slight breeze among the fruit trees. Then panic struck her and her blood froze. Her mouth opened to scream but she did not scream, she started to run and she ran barefoot with all her strength for home and stumbled and rose and ran as though pursued, but only the sawing of the crickets chased after her.

VI

She returned to her room and made coffee for all the members of the secretariat, because she remembered her promise to Etkin. Outside the cool of evening had set in, but inside her room the walls were hot and her body was also on fire. Her clothes stuck to her body because she had been running, and her armpits disgusted her. The spots on her face were glowing. She stood and counted the number of times the coffee boiled—seven successive boilings, as she had learned to do it from her brother Ehud before he was killed in a reprisal raid in the desert. With pursed lips she counted as the black liquid rose and subsided, rose and subsided, bubbling fiercely as it reached its climax.

That's enough, now. Take clean clothes for the evening. Go to the showers.

What can that Etkin understand about savages. A great socialist. What does he know about Bedouins. A nomad sniffs out weakness from a distance. Give him a kind word, or a smile, and he pounces on you like a wild beast and tries to rape you. It was just as well I ran away from him.

In the showers the drain was clogged and the bench was greasy. Geula put her clean clothes on the stone ledge. I'm not shivering because the water's cold. I'm shivering with disgust. Those black fingers, and how he went straight for my throat. And his teeth. And the goats. Small and skinny like a child, but so strong. It was only by biting and kicking that I managed to escape. Soap my belly and everything, soap it again and again. Yes, let the boys go right away tonight to their camp and smash their black bones because of what they did to me. Now I must get outside.

VII

She left the shower and started back toward her room, to pick up the coffee and take it to the secretariat. But on the way she heard crickets and laughter, and she remembered him bent down on all fours, and she was alarmed and stood still in the dark. Suddenly she vomited among the flowering shrubs. And she began to cry. Then her knees gave way. She sat down to rest on the dark earth. She stopped crying. But her teeth continued to chatter, from the cold or from pity. Suddenly she was not in a hurry any more, even the coffee no longer seemed important, and she thought to herself: There's still time. There's still time.

Those planes sweeping the sky tonight were probably on a night-bombing exercise. Repeatedly they roared among the stars, keeping up a constant flashing, red, green, red, green, red. In counterpoint came the singing of the nomads and their drums, a persistent heartbeat in the distance: One, one, two, One, one, two. And silence.

VIII

From eight-thirty until nearly nine o'clock we waited for Geula. At five to nine Etkin said that he could not imagine what had happened; he could not recall her ever having missed a meeting or been late before; at all events, we must now begin the meeting and turn to the business on the agenda.

He began with a summary of the facts. He gave details of the damage that had apparently been caused by the Bedouins, although there was no formal proof, and enumerated the steps that had been taken on the committee's initiative. The appeal to good will. Calling in the police. Strengthening the guard around the settlement. Tracking dogs. The meeting with the elder of the tribe. He had to admit, Etkin said, that we had now reached an impasse. Nevertheless, he believed that we had to maintain a sense of balance and not give way to extremism, because hatred always gave rise to further hatred. It was essential to break the vicious circle of hostility. He therefore opposed with all the moral force at his disposal the approach— and particularly the intentions—of certain of the younger members. He wished to remind us, by way of conclusion, that the conflict between herds-men and tillers of the soil was as old as human civilization, as seemed to be evidenced by the story of Cain, who rose up against Abel, his brother. It was fitting, in view of the social gospel we had adopted, that we should put an end to this ancient feud, too, just as we had put an end to other ugly phenomena. It was up to us, and everything depended on our moral strength.

The room was full of tension, even unpleasantness. Rami twice inter-rupted Etkin and on one occasion went so far as to use the ugly word "rub-bish." Etkin took offense, accused the younger members of planning terrorist activities, and said in conclusion, "We're not going to have that sort of thing here."

Geula had not arrived, and that was why there was no one to cool down the temper of the meeting. And no coffee. A heated exchange broke out between me and Rami. Although in age I belonged with the younger men, I did not agree with their proposals. Like Etkin, I was absolutely opposed to answering the nomads with violence—for two reasons, and when I was given permission to speak I mentioned them both. In the first place, noth-ing really serious had happened so far. A little stealing perhaps, but even that was not certain: every faucet or pair of pliers that a tractor driver left in a field or lost in the garage or took home with him was immediately blamed on the Bedouins. Secondly, there had been no rape or murder. Hereupon Rami broke in excitedly and asked what I was waiting for. Was I perhaps waiting for some small incident of rape that Geula could write poems about and I could make into a short story? I flushed and cast around in my mind for a telling retort.

But Etkin, upset by our rudeness, immediately deprived us both of the right to speak and began to explain his position all over again. He asked us how it would look if the papers reported that a kibbutz had sent out a lynch mob to settle scores with its Arab neighbors. As Etkin uttered the phrase "lynch mob," Rami made a gesture to his young friends that is commonly used by basketball players. At this signal they rose in a body and walked out in disgust, leaving Etkin to lecture to his heart's content to three elderly women and a long-retired member of Parliament.

After a moment's hesitation I rose and followed them. True, I did not share their views, but I, too, had been deprived of the right to speak in an arbitrary and insulting manner.

IX

If only Geula had come to the meeting and brought her famous coffee with her, it is possible that tempers might have been soothed. Perhaps, too, her understanding might have achieved some sort of compromise between the conflicting points of view. But the coffee was standing, cold by now, on the table in her room. And Geula herself was lying among the bushes behind the Memorial Hall, watching the lights of the planes and listening to the sounds of the night. How she longed to make her peace and to forgive. Not to hate him and wish him dead. Perhaps to get up and go to him, to find him among the wadis and forgive him and never come back. Even to sing to him. The sharp slivers piercing her skin and drawing blood were the fragments of the bottle she had smashed here with a big stone at the beginning of the evening. And the living thing slithering among the slivers of glass among the clods of earth was a snake, perhaps a venomous snake, perhaps a viper. It stuck out a forked tongue, and its triangular head was cold and erect. Its eyes were dark glass. It could never close them, because it had no eyelids. A thorn in her flesh, perhaps a sliver of glass. She was very tired. And the pain was vague, almost pleasant. A distant ringing in her ears. To sleep now. Wearily, through the thickening film, she watched the gang of youngsters crossing the lawn on their way to the fields and the wadi to even the score with the nomads. We were carrying short, thick sticks. Excitement was dilating our pupils. And the blood was drumming in our temples.

Far away in the darkened orchards stood somber, dust-laden cypresses, swaying to and fro with a gentle, religious fervor. She felt tired, and that was why she did not come to see us off. But her fingers caressed the dust, and her face was very calm and almost beautiful.

The Shawl

CYNTHIA OZICK

Stella, cold, cold, the coldness of hell. How they walked on the roads together, Rosa with Magda curled up between sore breasts, Magda wound up in the shawl. Sometimes Stella carried Magda. But she was jealous of Magda. A thin girl of fourteen, too small, with thin breasts of her own, Stella wanted to be wrapped in a shawl, hidden away, asleep, rocked by the march, a baby, a round infant in arms. Magda took Rosa's nipple, and Rosa never stopped walking, a walking cradle. There was not enough milk; sometimes Magda sucked air; then she screamed. Stella was ravenous. Her knees were tumors on sticks, her elbows chicken bones.

Rosa did not feel hunger; she felt light, not like someone walking but like someone in a faint, in trance, arrested in a fit, someone who is already a floating angel, alert and seeing everything, but in the air, not there, not touching the road. As if teetering on the tips of her fingernails. She looked into Magda's face through a gap in the shawl: a squirrel in a nest, safe, no one could reach her inside the little house of the shawl's windings. The face, very round, a pocket mirror of a face: but it was not Rosa's bleak complexion, dark like cholera, it was another kind of face altogether, eyes blue as air, smooth feathers of hair nearly as yellow as the Star sewn into Rosa's coat. You could think she was one of *their* babies.

Rosa, floating, dreamed of giving Magda away in one of the villages. She could leave the line for a minute and push Magda into the hands of any woman on the side of the road. But if she moved out of line they might shoot. And even if she fled the line for half a second and pushed the shawl-bundle at a stranger, would the woman take it? She might be surprised, or afraid; she might drop the shawl, and Magda would fall out and strike her head and die. The little round head. Such a good child, she gave up screaming, and sucked now only for the taste of the drying nipple itself. The neat grip of the tiny gums. One mite of a tooth tip sticking up in the bottom

831

gum, how shining, an elfin tombstone of white marble, gleaming there. Without complaining, Magda relinquished Rosa's teats, first the left, then the right; both were cracked, not a sniff of milk. The duct crevice extinct, a dead volcano, blind eye, chill hole, so Magda took the corner of the shawl and milked it instead. She sucked and sucked, flooding the threads with wetness. The shawl's good flavor, milk of linen.

It was a magic shawl, it could nourish an infant for three days and three nights. Magda did not die, she stayed alive, although very quiet. A peculiar smell, of cinnamon and almonds, lifted out of her mouth. She held her eyes open every moment, forgetting how to blink or nap, and Rosa and sometimes Stella studied their blueness. On the road they raised one burden of a leg after another and studied Magda's face. "Aryan," Stella said, in a voice grown as thin as a string; and Rosa thought how Stella gazed at Magda like a young cannibal. And the time that Stella said "Aryan," it sounded to Rosa as if Stella had really said "Let us devour her."

But Magda lived to walk. She lived that long, but she did not walk very well, partly because she was only fifteen months old, and partly because the spindle of her legs could not hold up her fat belly. It was fat with air, full and round. Rosa gave almost all her food to Magda, Stella gave nothing; Stella was ravenous, a growing child herself, but not growing much. Stella did not menstruate. Rosa did not menstruate. Rosa was ravenous, but also not; she learned from Magda how to drink the taste of a finger in one's mouth. They were in a place without pity, all pity was annihilated in Rosa, she looked at Stella's bones without pity. She was sure that Stella was waiting for Magda to die so she could put her teeth into the little thighs.

Rosa knew Magda was going to die very soon; she should have been dead already, but she had been buried away deep inside the magic shawl, mistaken there for the shivering mound of Rosa's breasts; Rosa clung to the shawl as if it covered only herself. No one took it away from her. Magda was mute. She never cried. Rosa hid her in the barracks, under the shawl, but she knew that one day someone would inform; or one day someone, not even Stella, would steal Magda to eat her. When Magda began to walk Rosa knew that Magda was going to die very soon, something would happen. She was afraid to fall asleep; she slept with the weight of her thigh on Magda's body; she was afraid she would smother Magda under her thigh. The weight of Rosa was becoming less and less; Rosa and Stella were slowly turning into air.

Magda was quiet, but her eyes were horribly alive, like blue tigers. She watched. Sometimes she laughed—it seemed a laugh, but how could it be? Magda had never seen anyone laugh. Still, Magda laughed at her shawl when the wind blew its corners, the bad wind with pieces of black in it, that made Stella's and Rosa's eyes tear. Magda's eyes were always clear and tearless. She watched like a tiger. She guarded her shawl. No one could touch it; only Rosa could touch it. Stella was not allowed. The shawl was Magda's own baby, her pet, her little sister. She tangled herself up in it and sucked on one of the corners when she wanted to be very still.

Then Stella took the shawl away and made Magda die.

Afterward Stella said: "I was cold."

And afterward she was always cold, always. The cold went into her heart: Rosa saw that Stella's heart was cold. Magda flopped onward with her little pencil legs scribbling this way and that, in search of the shawl; the pencils faltered at the barracks opening, where the light began. Rosa saw and pursued. But already Magda was in the square outside the barracks, in the jolly light. It was the roll-call arena. Every morning Rosa had to conceal Magda under the shawl against a wall of the barracks and go out and stand in the arena with Stella and hundreds of others, sometimes for hours, and Magda, deserted, was quiet under the shawl, sucking on her corner. Every day Magda was silent, and so she did not die. Rosa saw that today Magda was going to die, and at the same time a fearful joy ran in Rosa's two palms, her fingers were on fire, she was astonished, febrile: Magda, in the sunlight, swaying on her pencil legs, was howling. Ever since the drying up of Rosa's nipples, ever since Magda's last scream on the road, Magda had been devoid of any syllable; Magda was a mute. Rosa believed that something had gone wrong with her vocal cords, with her windpipe, with the cave of her larynx; Magda was defective, without a voice; perhaps she was deaf; there might be something amiss with her intelligence; Magda was dumb. Even the laugh that came when the ash-stippled wind made a clown out of Magda's shawl was only the air-blown showing of her teeth. Even when the lice, head lice and body lice, crazed her so that she became as wild as one of the big rats that plundered the barracks at daybreak looking for carrion, she rubbed and scratched and kicked and bit and rolled without a whimper. But now Magda's mouth was spilling a long viscous rope of clamor.

"Maaaa—"

It was the first noise Magda had ever sent out from her throat since the drying up of Rosa's nipples.

"Maaaa . . . aaa!"

Again! Magda was wavering in the perilous sunlight of the arena, scribbling on such pitiful little bent shins. Rosa saw. She saw that Magda was grieving for the loss of her shawl, she saw that Magda was going to die. A tide of commands hammered in Rosa's nipples: Fetch, get, bring! But she did not know which to go after first, Magda or the shawl. If she jumped out into the arena to snatch Magda up, the howling would not stop, because Magda would still not have the shawl; but if she ran back into the barracks to find the shawl, and if she found it, and if she came after Magda holding it and shaking it, then she would get Magda back, Magda would put the shawl in her mouth and turn dumb again.

Rosa entered the dark. It was easy to discover the shawl. Stella was heaped under it, asleep in her thin bones. Rosa tore the shawl free and flew—she could fly, she was only air—into the arena. The sunheat murmured of another life, of butterflies in summer. The light was placid, mellow. On the other side of the steel fence, far away, there were green meadows speckled with dandelions and deep-colored violets; beyond them, even farther, innocent tiger lilies, tall, lifting their orange bonnets. In the barracks they spoke of "flowers," of "rain": excrement, thick turd-braids, and the slow stinking maroon waterfall that slunk down from the upper bunks, the stink mixed with a bitter fatty floating smoke that greased Rosa's skin. She stood for an instant at the margin of the arena. Sometimes the electricity inside the fence would seem to hum; even Stella said it was only an imagining, but Rosa heard real sounds in the wire: grainy sad voices. The farther she was from the fence, the more clearly the voices crowded at her. The lamenting voices strummed so convincingly, so passionately, it was impossible to suspect them of being phantoms. The voices told her to hold up the shawl, high; the voices told her to shake it, to whip with it, to unfurl it like a flag. Rosa lifted, shook, whipped, unfurled. Far off, very far, Magda leaned across her air-fed belly, reaching out with the rods of her arms. She was high up, elevated, riding someone's shoulder. But the shoulder that carried Magda was not coming toward Rosa and the shawl, it was drifting away, the speck of Magda was moving more and more into the smoky distance. Above the shoulder a helmet glinted. The light tapped the helmet and sparkled it into a goblet. Below the helmet a black body like a domino and a pair of black boots hurled themselves in the direction of the electrified fence. The electric voices began to chatter wildly. "Maamaa, maaamaaa," they all hummed together. How far Magda was from Rosa now, across the whole square, past a dozen barracks, all the way on the other side! She was no bigger than a moth.

All at once Magda was swimming through the air. The whole of Magda traveled through loftiness. She looked like a butterfly touching a silver vine. And the moment Magda's feathered round head and her pencil legs and balloonish belly and zigzag arms splashed against the fence, the steel voices went mad in their growling, urging Rosa to run and run to the spot where Magda had fallen from her flight against the electrified fence; but of course Rosa did not obey them. She only stood, because if she ran they would shoot, and if she tried to pick up the sticks of Magda's body they would shoot, and if she let the wolf's screech ascending now through the ladder of her skeleton break out, they would shoot; so she took Magda's shawl and filled her own mouth with it, stuffed it in and stuffed it in, until she was swallowing up the wolf's screech and tasting the cinnamon and almond depth of Magda's saliva; and Rosa drank Magda's shawl until it dried.

A Conversation with My Father

GRACE PALEY

My father is eighty-six years old and in bed. His heart, that bloody motor, is equally old and will not do certain jobs any more. It still floods his head with brainy light. But it won't let his legs carry the weight of his body around the house. Despite my metaphors, this muscle failure is not due to his old heart, he says, but to a potassium shortage. Sitting on one pillow, leaning on three, he offers last-minute advice and makes a request.

"I would like you to write a simple story just once more," he says, "the kind de Maupassant wrote, or Chekhov, the kind you used to write. Just recognizable people and then write down what happened to them next."

I say, "Yes, why not? That's possible." I want to please him, though I don't remember writing that way. I *would* like to try to tell such a story, if he means the kind that begins: "There was a woman . . ." followed by plot, the absolute line between two points which I've always despised. Not for literary reasons, but because it takes all hope away. Everyone, real or invented, deserves the open destiny of life.

Finally I thought of a story that had been happening for a couple of years right across the street. I wrote it down, then read it aloud. "Pa," I said, "how about this? Do you mean something like this?"

> Once in my time there was a woman and she had a son. They lived nicely, in a small apartment in Manhattan. This boy at about fifteen became a junkie, which is not unusual in our neighborhood. In order to maintain her close friendship with him, she became a junkie too. She said it was part of the youth culture, with which she felt very much at home. After a while, for a number of reasons, the boy gave it all up and left the city and his mother in disgust. Hopeless and alone, she grieved. We all visit her.

"O.K., Pa, that's it," I said, "an unadorned and miserable tale."

"But that's not what I mean," my father said. "You misunderstood me on

835

purpose. You know there's a lot more to it. You know that. You left everything out. Turgenev wouldn't do that. Chekhov wouldn't do that. There
are in fact Russian writers you never heard of, you don't have an inkling of,
as good as anyone, who can write a plain ordinary story, who would not
leave out what you have left out. I object not to facts but to people sitting in
trees talking senselessly, voices from who knows where. . . ."

"Forget that one, Pa, what have I left out now? In this one?"

"Her looks, for instance."

"Oh. Quite handsome, I think. Yes."

"Her hair?"

"Dark, with heavy braids, as though she were a girl or a foreigner."

"What were her parents like, her stock? That she became such a person.
It's interesting, you know."

"From out of town. Professional people. The first to be divorced in their
county. How's that? Enough?" I asked.

"With you, it's all a joke," he said. "What about the boy's father? Why
didn't you mention him? Who was he? Or was the boy born out of
wedlock?"

"Yes," I said. "He was born out of wedlock."

"For Godsakes, doesn't anyone in your stories get married? Doesn't anyone have the time to run down to City Hall before they jump into bed?"

"No," I said. "In real life, yes. But in my stories, no."

"Why do you answer me like that?"

"Oh, Pa, this is a simple story about a smart woman who came to N.Y.C.
full of interest love trust excitement very up to date, and about her son,
what a hard time she had in this world. Married or not, it's of small consequence."

"It is of great consequence," he said.

"O.K.," I said.

"O.K. O.K. yourself," he said, "but listen. I believe you that she's good-
looking, but I don't think she was so smart."

"That's true," I said. "Actually that's the trouble with stories. People start
out fantastic. You think they're extraordinary, but it turns out as the work
goes along, they're just average with a good education. Sometimes the
other way around, the person's a kind of dumb innocent, but he outwits
you and you can't even think of an ending good enough."

"What do you do then?" he asked. He had been a doctor for a couple of
decades and then an artist for a couple of decades and he's still interested
in details, craft, technique.

"Well, you just have to let the story lie around till some agreement can be
reached between you and the stubborn hero."

"Aren't you talking silly now?" he asked. "Start again," he said. "It so
happens I'm not going out this evening. Tell the story again. See what you
can do this time."

"O.K.," I said. "But it's not a five-minute job." Second attempt:

Once, across the street from us, there was a fine handsome woman, our neighbor. She had a son whom she loved because she'd known him since birth (in helpless chubby infancy, and in the wrestling, hugging ages, seven to ten, as well as earlier and later). This boy, when he fell into the fist of adolescence, became a junkie. He was not a hopeless one. He was in fact hopeful, an ideologue and successful converter. With his busy brilliance, he wrote persuasive articles for his high-school newspaper. Seeking a wider audience, using important connections, he drummed into Lower Manhattan newsstand distribution a periodical called *Oh! Golden Horse!*

In order to keep him from feeling guilty (because guilt is the stony heart of nine tenths of all clinically diagnosed cancers in America today, she said), and because she had always believed in giving bad habits room at home where one could keep an eye on them, she too became a junkie. Her kitchen was famous for a while—a center for intellectual addicts who knew what they were doing. A few felt artistic like Coleridge and others were scientific and revolutionary like Leary. Although she was often high herself, certain good mothering reflexes remained, and she saw to it that there was lots of orange juice around and honey and milk and vitamin pills. However, she never cooked anything but chili, and that no more than once a week. She explained, when we talked to her, seriously, with neighborly concern, that it was her part in the youth culture and she would rather be with the young, it was an honor, than with her own generation.

One week, while nodding through an Antonioni film, this boy was severely jabbed by the elbow of a stern and proselytizing girl, sitting beside him. She offered immediate apricots and nuts for his sugar level, spoke to him sharply, and took him home.

She had heard of him and his work and she herself published, edited, and wrote a competitive journal called *Man Does Live by Bread Alone*. In the organic heat of her continuous presence he could not help but become interested once more in his muscles, his arteries, and nerve connections. In fact he began to love them, treasure them, praise them with funny little songs in *Man Does Live*. . . .

> the fingers of my flesh transcend
> my transcendental soul
> the tightness in my shoulders end
> my teeth have made me whole

To the mouth of his head (that glory of will and determination) he brought hard apples, nuts, wheat germ, and soybean oil. He said to his old friends, From now on, I guess I'll keep my wits about me. I'm going on the natch. He said he was about to begin a spiritual deep-breathing journey. How about you too, Mom? he asked kindly.

His conversion was so radiant, splendid, that neighborhood kids his age began to say that he had never been a real addict at all, only a journalist along for the smell of the story. The mother tried several times to give up what had become without her son and his friends a lonely habit. This effort only brought it to supportable levels. The boy and his girl took their electronic mimeograph and moved to the bushy edge of another borough. They were very strict. They said they would not see her again until she had been off drugs for sixty days.

At home alone in the evening, weeping, the mother read and reread the seven issues of *Oh! Golden Horse!* They seemed to her as truthful as ever. We often crossed the street to visit and console. But if we mentioned any of our children who were at college or in the hospital or dropouts at home, she would cry out, My baby! My baby! and burst into terrible, face-scarring, time-consuming tears. The End.

First my father was silent, then he said, "Number One: You have a nice sense of humor. Number Two: I see you can't tell a plain story. So don't waste time." Then he said sadly, "Number Three: I suppose that means she was alone, she was left like that, his mother. Alone. Probably sick?"

I said, "Yes."

"Poor woman. Poor girl, to be born in a time of fools, to live among fools. The end. The end. You were right to put that down. The end."

I didn't want to argue, but I had to say, "Well, it is not necessarily the end, Pa."

"Yes," he said, "what a tragedy. The end of a person."

"No, Pa," I begged him. "It doesn't have to be. She's only about forty. She could be a hundred different things in this world as time goes on. A teacher or a social worker. An ex-junkie! Sometimes it's better than having a master's in education."

"Jokes," he said. "As a writer that's your main trouble. You don't want to recognize it. Tragedy! Plain tragedy! Historical tragedy! No hope. The end."

"Oh, Pa," I said. "She could change."

"In your own life, too, you have to look it in the face." He took a couple of nitroglycerin. "Turn to five," he said, pointing to the dial on the oxygen tank. He inserted the tubes into his nostrils and breathed deep. He closed his eyes and said, "No."

I had promised the family to always let him have the last word when arguing, but in this case I had a different responsibility. That woman lives across the street. She's my knowledge and my invention. I'm sorry for her. I'm not going to leave her there in that house crying. (Actually neither would Life, which unlike me has no pity.)

Therefore: She did change. Of course her son never came home again. But right now, she's the receptionist in a storefront community clinic in the East Village. Most of the customers are young people, some old friends. The head doctor has said to her, "If we only had three people in this clinic with your experiences. . . ."

"The doctor said that?" My father took the oxygen tubes out of his nostrils and said, "Jokes. Jokes again."

"No, Pa, it could really happen that way, it's a funny world nowadays."

"No," he said. "Truth first. She will slide back. A person must have character. She does not."

"No, Pa," I said. "That's it. She's got a job. Forget it. She's in that storefront working."

"How long will it be?" he asked. "Tragedy! You too. When will you look it in the face?"

Big Blonde

DOROTHY PARKER

Hazel Morse was a large, fair woman of the type that incites some men when they use the word "blonde" to click their tongues and wag their heads roguishly. She prided herself upon her small feet and suffered for her vanity, boxing them in snub-toed, high-heeled slippers of the shortest bearable size. The curious things about her were her hands, strange terminations to the flabby white arms splattered with pale tan spots—long, quivering hands with deep and convex nails. She should not have disfigured them with little jewels.

She was not a woman given to recollections. At her middle thirties, her old days were a blurred and flickering sequence, an imperfect film, dealing with actions of strangers.

In her twenties, after the deferred death of a hazy widowed mother, she had been employed as a model in a wholesale dress establishment—it was still the day of the big woman, and she was then prettily colored and erect and high-breasted. Her job was not onerous, and she met numbers of men and spent numbers of evenings with them, laughing at their jokes and telling them she loved their neckties. Men liked her, and she took it for granted that the liking of many men was a desirable thing. Popularity seemed to her to be worth all the work that had to be put into its achievement. Men liked you because you were fun, and when they liked you they took you out, and there you were. So, and successfully, she was fun. She was a good sport. Men liked a good sport.

No other form of diversion, simpler or more complicated, drew her attention. She never pondered if she might not be better occupied doing something else. Her ideas, or, better, her acceptances, ran right along with those of the other substantially built blondes in whom she found her friends.

840

When she had been working in the dress establishment some years she met Herbie Morse. He was thin, quick, attractive, with shifting lines about his shiny, brown eyes and a habit of fiercely biting at the skin around his finger nails. He drank largely; she found that entertaining. Her habitual greeting to him was an allusion to his state of the previous night.

"Oh, what a peach you had," she used to say, through her easy laugh. "I thought I'd die, the way you kept asking the waiter to dance with you."

She liked him immediately upon their meeting. She was enormously amused at his fast, slurred sentences, his interpolations of apt phrases from vaudeville acts and comic strips; she thrilled at the feel of his lean arm tucked firm beneath the sleeve of her coat; she wanted to touch the wet, flat surface of his hair. He was as promptly drawn to her. They were married six weeks after they had met.

She was delighted at the idea of being a bride; coquetted with it, played upon it. Other offers of marriage she had had, and not a few of them, but it happened that they were all from stout, serious men who had visited the dress establishment as buyers; men from Des Moines and Houston and Chicago and, in her phrase even funnier places. There was always something immensely comic to her in the thought of living elsewhere than New York. She could not regard as serious proposals that she share a western residence.

She wanted to be married. She was nearing thirty now, and she did not take the years well. She spread and softened, and her darkening hair turned her to inexpert dabblings with peroxide. There were times when she had little flashes of fear about her job. And she had had a couple of thousand evenings of being a good sport among her male acquaintances. She had come to be more conscientious than spontaneous about it.

Herbie earned enough, and they took a little apartment far uptown. There was a Mission-furnished dining-room with a hanging central light globed in liver-colored glass; in the living-room were an "over-stuffed suite," a Boston fern, and a reproduction of the Henner "Magdalene" with the red hair and the blue draperies; the bedroom was in gray enamel and old rose, with Herbie's photograph on Hazel's dressing-table and Hazel's likeness on Herbie's chest of drawers.

She cooked—and she was a good cook—and marketed and chatted with the delivery boys and the colored laundress. She loved the flat, she loved her life, she loved Herbie. In the first months of their marriage, she gave him all the passion she was ever to know.

She had not realized how tired she was. It was a delight, a new game, a holiday, to give up being a good sport. If her head ached or her arches throbbed, she complained piteously, babyishly. If her mood was quiet, she did not talk. If tears came to her eyes, she let them fall.

She fell readily into the habit of tears during the first year of her marriage. Even in her good sport days, she had been known to weep lavishly and disinterestedly on occasion. Her behavior at the theater was a standing joke. She could weep at anything in a play—tiny garments, love both unrequited and mutual, seduction, purity, faithful servitors, wedlock, the triangle.

"There goes Haze," her friends would say, watching her. "She's off again."

Wedded and relaxed, she poured her tears freely. To her who had laughed so much, crying was delicious. All sorrows became her sorrows; she was Tenderness. She would cry long and softly over newspaper accounts of kidnaped babies, deserted wives, unemployed men, strayed cats, heroic dogs. Even when the paper was no longer before her, her mind revolved upon these things and the drops slipped rhythmically over her plump cheeks.

"Honestly," she would say to Herbie, "all the sadness there is in the world when you stop to think about it!"

"Yeah," Herbie would say.

She missed nobody. The old crowd, the people who had brought her and Herbie together, dropped from their lives, lingeringly at first. When she thought of this at all, it was only to consider it fitting. This was marriage. This was peace.

But the thing was that Herbie was not amused.

For a time, he had enjoyed being alone with her. He found the voluntary isolation novel and sweet. Then it palled with a ferocious suddenness. It was as if one night, sitting with her in the steam-heated living-room, he would ask no more; and the next night he was through and done with the whole thing.

He became annoyed by her misty melancholies. At first, when he came home to find her softly tired and moody, he kissed her neck and patted her shoulder and begged her to tell her Herbie what was wrong. She loved that. But time slid by, and he found that there was never anything really, personally, the matter.

"Ah, for God's sake," he would say. "Crabbing again. All right, sit here and crab your head off. I'm going out."

And he would slam out of the flat and come back late and drunk.

She was completely bewildered by what happened to their marriage. First they were lovers; and then, it seemed without transition, they were enemies. She never understood it.

There were longer and longer intervals between his leaving his office and his arrival at the apartment. She went through agonies of picturing him run over and bleeding, dead and covered with a sheet. Then she lost her fears for his safety and grew sullen and wounded. When a person wanted to be with a person, he came as soon as possible. She desperately wanted him to want to be with her; her own hours only marked the time till

he would come. It was often nearly nine o'clock before he came home to
dinner. Always he had had many drinks, and their effect would die in him,
leaving him loud and querulous and bristling for affronts.

He was too nervous, he said, to sit and do nothing for an evening. He
boasted, probably not in all truth, that he had never read a book in his life.
"What am I expected to do—sit around this dump on my tail all night?"
he would ask, rhetorically. And again he would slam out.

She did not know what to do. She could not manage him. She could not
meet him.

She fought him furiously. A terrific domesticity had come upon her, and
she would bite and scratch to guard it. She wanted what she called "a nice
home." She wanted a sober, tender husband, prompt at dinner, punctual at
work. She wanted sweet, comforting evenings. The idea of intimacy with
other men was terrible to her; the thought that Herbie might be seeking
entertainment in other women set her frantic.

It seemed to her that almost everything she read—novels from the drugstore lending library, magazine stories, women's pages in the papers—
dealt with wives who lost their husbands' love. She could bear those, at that,
better than accounts of neat, companionable marriage and living happily
ever after.

She was frightened. Several times when Herbie came home in the evening, he found her determinedly dressed—she had had to alter those of
her clothes that were not new, to make them fasten—and rouged.

"Let's go wild tonight, what do you say?" she would hail him. "A person's
got lots of time to hang around and do nothing when they're dead."

So they would go out, to chop houses and the less expensive cabarets. But
it turned out badly. She could no longer find amusement in watching Herbie drink. She could not laugh at his whimsicalities, she was so tensely
counting his indulgences. And she was unable to keep back her remonstrances—"Ah, come on, Herb, you've had enough, haven't you? You'll
feel something terrible in the morning."

He would be immediately enraged. All right, crab; crab, crab, crab, crab,
that was all she ever did. What a lousy sport *she* was! There would be scenes,
and one or the other of them would rise and stalk out in fury.

She could not recall the definite day that she started drinking, herself.
There was nothing separate about her days. Like drops upon a window-
pane, they ran together and trickled away. She had been married six
months; then a year; then three years.

She had never needed to drink, formerly. She could sit for most of a
night at a table where the others were imbibing earnestly and never droop
in looks or spirits, nor be bored by the doings of those about her. If she
took a cocktail, it was so unusual as to cause twenty minutes or so of jocular
comment. But now anguish was in her. Frequently, after a quarrel, Herbie

would stay out for the night, and she could not learn from him where the time had been spent. Her heart felt tight and sore in her breast, and her mind turned like an electric fan.

She hated the taste of liquor. Gin, plain or in mixtures, made her promptly sick. After experiment, she found that Scotch whisky was best for her. She took it without water, because that was the quickest way to its effect.

Herbie pressed it on her. He was glad to see her drink. They both felt it might restore her high spirits, and their good times together might again be possible.

" 'Atta girl," he would approve her. "Let's see you get boiled, baby."

But it brought them no nearer. When she drank with him, there would be a little while of gaiety and then, strangely without beginning, they would be in a wild quarrel. They would wake in the morning not sure what it had all been about, foggy as to what had been said and done, but each deeply injured and bitterly resentful. There would be days of vengeful silence.

There had been a time when they had made up their quarrels, usually in bed. There would be kisses and little names and assurances of fresh starts. . . . "Oh, it's going to be great now, Herb. We'll have swell times. I was a crab. I guess I must have been tired. But everything's going to be swell. You'll see."

Now there were no gentle reconciliations. They resumed friendly relations only in the brief magnanimity caused by liquor, before more liquor drew them into new battles. The scenes became more violent. There were shouted invectives and pushes, and sometimes sharp slaps. Once she had a black eye. Herbie was horrified next day at sight of it. He did not go to work; he followed her about, suggesting remedies and heaping dark blame on himself. But after they had had a few drinks—"to pull themselves together"—she made so many wistful references to her bruise that he shouted at her and rushed out and was gone for two days.

Each time he left the place in a rage, he threatened never to come back. She did not believe him, nor did she consider separation. Somewhere in her head or her heart was the lazy, nebulous hope that things would change and she and Herbie settle suddenly into soothing married life. Here were her home, her furniture, her husband, her station. She summoned no alternatives.

She could no longer bustle and potter. She had no more vicarious tears; the hot drops she shed were for herself. She walked ceaselessly about the rooms, her thoughts running mechanically round and round Herbie. In those days began the hatred of being alone that she was never to overcome. You could be by yourself when things were all right, but when you were blue you got the howling horrors.

She commenced drinking alone, little, short drinks all through the day. It was only with Herbie that alcohol made her nervous and quick in offense. Alone, it blurred sharp things for her. She lived in a haze of it. Her life took on a dreamlike quality. Nothing was astonishing.

A Mrs. Martin moved into the flat across the hall. She was a great blonde woman of forty, a promise in looks of what Mrs. Morse was to be. They made acquaintance, quickly became inseparable. Mrs. Morse spent her days in the opposite apartment. They drank together, to brace themselves after the drinks of the nights before.

She never confided her troubles about Herbie to Mrs. Martin. The subject was too bewildering to her to find comfort in talk. She let it be assumed that her husband's business kept him much away. It was not regarded as important; husbands, as such, played but shadowy parts in Mrs. Martin's circle.

Mrs. Martin had no visible spouse; you were left to decide for yourself whether he was or was not dead. She had an admirer, Joe, who came to see her almost nightly. Often he brought several friends with him—"The Boys," they were called. The Boys were big, red, good-humored men, perhaps forty-five, perhaps fifty. Mrs. Morse was glad of invitations to join the parties—Herbie was scarcely ever at home at night now. If he did come home, she did not visit Mrs. Martin. An evening alone with Herbie meant inevitably a quarrel, yet she would stay with him. There was always her thin and wordless idea that, maybe, this night, things would begin to be all right.

The Boys brought plenty of liquor along with them whenever they came to Mrs. Martin's. Drinking with them, Mrs. Morse became lively and good-natured and audacious. She was quickly popular. When she had drunk enough to cloud her most recent battle with Herbie, she was excited by their approbation. Crab, was she? Rotten sport, was she? Well, there were some that thought different.

Ed was one of The Boys. He lived in Utica—had "his own business" there, was the awed report—but he came to New York almost every week. He was married. He showed Mrs. Morse the then current photographs of Junior and Sister, and she praised them abundantly and sincerely. Soon it was accepted by the others that Ed was her particular friend.

He staked her when they all played poker; sat next her and occasionally rubbed his knee against hers during the game. She was rather lucky. Frequently she went home with a twenty-dollar bill or a ten-dollar bill or a handful of crumpled dollars. She was glad of them. Herbie was getting, in her words, something awful about money. To ask him for it brought an instant row.

"What the hell do you do with it?" he would say. "Shoot it all on Scotch?"

"I try to run this house half-way decent," she would retort. "Never thought of that, did you? Oh, no, his lordship couldn't be bothered with that."

Again, she could not find a definite day, to fix the beginning of Ed's proprietorship. It became his custom to kiss her on the mouth when he came in, as well as for farewell, and he gave her little quick kisses of approval all through the evening. She liked this rather more than she disliked it. She never thought of his kisses when she was not with him.

He would run his hand lingeringly over her back and shoulders.

"Some dizzy blonde, eh?" he would say. "Some doll."

One afternoon she came home from Mrs. Martin's to find Herbie in the bedroom. He had been away for several nights, evidently on a prolonged drinking bout. His face was gray, his hands jerked as if they were on wires. On the bed were two old suitcases, packed high. Only her photograph remained on his bureau, and the wide doors of his closet disclosed nothing but coat-hangers.

"I'm blowing," he said. "I'm through with the whole works. I got a job in Detroit."

She sat down on the edge of the bed. She had drunk much the night before, and the four Scotches she had had with Mrs. Martin had only increased her fogginess.

"Good job?" she said.

"Oh, yeah," he said. "Looks all right."

He closed a suitcase with difficulty, swearing at it in whispers.

"There's some dough in the bank," he said. "The bank book's in your top drawer. You can have the furniture and stuff."

He looked at her, and his forehead twitched.

"God damn it, I'm through, I'm telling you," he cried. "I'm through."

"All right, all right," she said. "I heard you, didn't I?"

She saw him as if he were at one end of a cannon and she at the other. Her head was beginning to ache bumpingly, and her voice had a dreary, tiresome tone. She could not have raised it.

"Like a drink before you go?" she asked.

Again he looked at her, and a corner of his mouth jerked up.

"Cockeyed again for a change, aren't you?" he said. "That's nice. Sure, get a couple of shots, will you?"

She went to the pantry, mixed him a stiff highball, poured herself a couple of inches of whisky and drank it. Then she gave herself another portion and brought the glasses into the bedroom. He had strapped both suitcases and had put on his hat and overcoat.

He took his highball.

"Well," he said, and he gave a sudden, uncertain laugh. "Here's mud in your eye."

"Mud in your eye," she said.

They drank. He put down his glass and took up the heavy suitcases.

"Got to get a train around six," he said.

She followed him down the hall. There was a song, a song that Mrs. Martin played doggedly on the phonograph, running loudly through her mind. She had never liked the thing.

"Night and daytime,
Always playtime.
Ain't we got fun?"

At the door he put down the bags and faced her.

"Well," he said. "Well, take care of yourself. You'll be all right, will you?"

"Oh, sure," she said.

He opened the door, then came back to her, holding out his hand.

" 'By, Haze," he said. "Good luck to you."

She took his hand and shook it.

"Pardon my wet glove," she said.

When the door had closed behind him, she went back to the pantry.

She was flushed and lively when she went in to Mrs. Martin's that evening. The Boys were there, Ed among them. He was glad to be in town, frisky and loud and full of jokes. But she spoke quietly to him for a minute.

"Herbie blew today," she said. "Going to live out west."

"That so?" he said. He looked at her and played with the fountain pen clipped to his waistcoat pocket.

"Think he's gone for good, do you?" he asked.

"Yeah," she said. "I know he is. I know. Yeah."

"You going to live on across the hall just the same?" he said. "Know what you're going to do?"

"Gee, I don't know," she said. "I don't give much of a damn."

"Oh, come on, that's no way to talk," he told her. "What you need—you need a little snifter. How about it?"

"Yeah," she said. "Just straight."

She won forty-three dollars at poker. When the game broke up, Ed took her back to her apartment.

"Got a little kiss for me?" he asked.

He wrapped her in his big arms and kissed her violently. She was entirely passive. He held her away and looked at her.

"Little tight, honey?" he asked, anxiously "Not going to be sick, are you?"

"Me?" she said. "I'm swell.

II

When Ed left in the morning, he took her photograph with him. He said he wanted her picture to look at, up in Utica. "You can have that one on the bureau," she said.

She put Herbie's picture in a drawer, out of her sight. When she could look at it, she meant to tear it up. She was fairly successful in keeping her mind from racing around him. Whisky slowed it for her. She was almost peaceful, in her mist.

She accepted her relationship with Ed without question or enthusiasm. When he was away, she seldom thought definitely of him. He was good to her; he gave her frequent presents and a regular allowance. She was even able to save. She did not plan ahead of any day, but her wants were few, and you might as well put money in the bank as have it lying around.

When the lease of her apartment neared its end, it was Ed who suggested moving. His friendship with Mrs. Martin and Joe had become strained over a dispute at poker; a feud was impending.

"Let's get the hell out of here," Ed said. "What I want you to have is a place near the Grand Central. Make it easier for me."

So she took a little flat in the Forties. A colored maid came in every day to clean and to make coffee for her—she was "through with that house-keeping stuff," she said, and Ed, twenty years married to a passionately do-mestic woman, admired this romantic uselessness and felt doubly a man of the world in abetting it.

The coffee was all she had until she went out to dinner, but alcohol kept her fat. Prohibition she regarded only as a basis for jokes. You could always get all you wanted. She was never noticeably drunk and seldom nearly so-ber. It required a larger daily allowance to keep her misty-minded. Too lit-tle, and she was achingly melancholy.

Ed brought her to Jimmy's. He was proud, with the pride of the transient who would be mistaken for a native, in his knowledge of small, recent res-taurants occupying the lower floors of shabby brownstone houses; places where, upon mentioning the name of an habitué friend, might be obtained strange whisky and fresh gin in many of their ramifications. Jimmy's place was the favorite of his acquaintances.

There, through Ed, Mrs. Morse met many men and women, formed quick friendships. The men often took her out when Ed was in Utica. He was proud of her popularity.

She fell into the habit of going to Jimmy's alone when she had no engage-ment. She was certain to meet some people she knew, and join them. It was a club for her friends, both men and women.

The women at Jimmy's looked remarkably alike, and this was curious, for, through feuds, removals, and opportunities of more profitable con-tacts, the personnel of the group changed constantly. Yet always the new-comers resembled those whom they replaced. They were all big women and stout, broad of shoulder and abundantly breasted, with faces thickly clothed in soft, high-colored flesh. They laughed loud and often, showing opaque and lusterless teeth like squares of crockery. There was about them the health of the big, yet a slight, unwholesome suggestion of stubborn preservation. They might have been thirty-six or forty-five or anywhere between.

They composed their titles of their own first names with their husbands' surnames—Mrs. Florence Miller, Mrs. Vera Riley, Mrs. Lilian Block. This gave at the same time the solidity of marriage and the glamour of freedom. Yet only one or two were actually divorced. Most of them never referred to their dimmed spouses; some, a shorter time separated, described them in terms of great biological interest. Several were mothers, each of an only child—a boy at school somewhere, or a girl being cared for by a grandmother. Often, well on toward morning, there would be displays of Kodak portraits and of tears.

They were comfortable women, cordial and friendly and irrepressibly matronly. Theirs was the quality of ease. Become fatalistic, especially about money matters, they were unworried. Whenever their funds dropped alarmingly, a new donor appeared; this had always happened. The aim of each was to have one man, permanently, to pay all her bills, in return for which she would have immediately given up other admirers and probably would have become exceedingly fond of him; for the affections of all of them were, by now, unexacting, tranquil, and easily arranged. This end, however, grew increasingly difficult yearly. Mrs. Morse was regarded as fortunate.

Ed had a good year, increased her allowance and gave her a sealskin coat. But she had to be careful of her moods with him. He insisted upon gaiety. He would not listen to admissions of aches or weariness.

"Hey, listen," he would say, "I got worries of my own, and plenty. Nobody wants to hear other people's troubles, sweetie. What you got to do, you got to be a sport and forget it. See? Well, slip us a little smile, then. That's my girl."

She never had enough interest to quarrel with him as she had with Herbie, but wanted the privilege of occasional admitted sadness. It was strange. The other women she saw did not have to fight their moods. There was Mrs. Florence Miller who got regular crying jags, and the men sought only to cheer and comfort her. The others spent whole evenings in grieved recitals of worries and ills; their escorts paid them deep sympathy. But she was instantly undesirable when she was low in spirits. Once, at Jimmy's, when she could not make herself lively, Ed had walked out and left her.

"Why the hell don't you stay home and not go spoiling everybody's evening?"he had roared.

Even her slightest acquaintances seemed irritated if she were not conspicuously light-hearted.

"What's the matter with you, anyway?" they would say. "Be your age, why don't you? Have a little drink and snap out of it."

When her relationship with Ed had continued nearly three years, he moved to Florida to live. He hated leaving her; he gave her a large check and some shares of a sound stock, and his pale eyes were wet when he said good-by. She did not miss him. He came to New York infrequently, perhaps two or three times a year, and hurried directly from the train to see her. She was always pleased to have him come and never sorry to see him go.

Charley, an acquaintance of Ed's that she had met at Jimmy's, had long admired her. He had always made opportunities of touching her and leaning close to talk to her. He asked repeatedly of all their friends if they had ever heard such a fine laugh as she had. After Ed left, Charley became the main figure in her life. She classified him and spoke of him as "not so bad." There was nearly a year of Charley; then she divided her time between him and Sydney, another frequenter of Jimmy's; then Charley slipped away altogether.

Sydney was a little, brightly dressed, clever Jew. She was perhaps nearest contentment with him. He amused her always; her laughter was not forced.

He admired her completely. Her softness and size delighted him. And he thought she was great, he often told her, because she kept gay and lively when she was drunk.

"Once I had a gal," he said, "used to try and throw herself out of the window every time she got a can on. Jee-*zuss*," he added, feelingly.

Then Sydney married a rich and watchful bride, and then there was Billy. No—after Sydney came Ferd, then Billy. In her haze, she never recalled how men entered her life and left it. There were no surprises. She had no thrill at their advent, nor woe at their departure. She seemed to be always able to attract men. There was never another as rich as Ed, but they were all generous to her, in their means.

Once she had news of Herbie. She met Mrs. Martin dining at Jimmy's, and the old friendship was vigorously renewed. The still admiring Joe, while on a business trip, had seen Herbie. He had settled in Chicago, he looked fine, he was living with some woman—seemed to be crazy about her. Mrs. Morse had been drinking vastly that day. She took the news with mild interest, as one hearing of the sex peccadilloes of somebody whose name is, after a moment's groping, familiar.

"Must be damn near seven years since I saw him," she commented. "Gee. Seven years."

More and more, her days lost their individuality. She never knew dates, nor was sure of the day of the week.

"My God, was that a year ago!" she would exclaim, when an event was recalled in conversation.

She was tired so much of the time. Tired and blue. Almost everything could give her the blues. Those old horses she saw on Sixth Avenue—struggling and slipping along the car-tracks, or standing at the curb, their heads dropped level with their worn knees. The tightly stored tears would squeeze from her eyes as she teetered past on her aching feet in the stubby, champagne-colored slippers.

The thought of death came and stayed with her and lent her a sort of drowsy cheer. It would be nice, nice and restful, to be dead.

There was no settled, shocked moment when she first thought of killing herself; it seemed to her as if the idea had always been with her. She pounced upon all the accounts of suicides in the newspapers. There was an epidemic of self-killings—or maybe it was just that she searched for the stories of them so eagerly that she found many. To read of them roused reassurance in her; she felt a cozy solidarity with the big company of the voluntary dead.

She slept, aided by whisky, till deep into the afternoons, then lay abed, a bottle and glass at her hand, until it was time to dress and go out for dinner. She was beginning to feel toward alcohol a little puzzled distrust, as toward an old friend who has refused a simple favor. Whisky could still soothe her for most of the time, but there were sudden, inexplicable moments when the cloud fell treacherously away from her, and she was sawed by the sorrow and bewilderment and nuisance of all living. She played voluptuously with the thought of cool, sleepy retreat. She had never been troubled by religious belief and no vision of an afterlife intimidated her. She dreamed by day of never again putting on tight shoes, of never having to laugh and listen and admire, of never more being a good sport. Never.

But how would you do it? It made her sick to think of jumping from heights. She could not stand a gun. At the theater, if one of the actors drew a revolver, she crammed her fingers into her ears and could not even look at the stage until after the shot had been fired. There was no gas in her flat. She looked long at the bright blue veins in her slim wrists—a cut with a razor blade, and there you'd be. But it would hurt, hurt like hell, and there would be blood to see. Poison—something tasteless and quick and painless—was the thing. But they wouldn't sell it to you in drugstores, because of the law.

She had few other thoughts.

There was a new man now—Art. He was short and fat and exacting and hard on her patience when he was drunk. But there had been only occasionals for some time before him, and she was glad of a little stability. Too, Art must be away for weeks at a stretch, selling silks, and that was restful. She was convincingly gay with him, though the effort shook her.

"The best sport in the world," he would murmur, deep in her neck. "The best sport in the world."

One night, when he had taken her to Jimmy's, she went into the dressing-room with Mrs. Florence Miller. There, while designing curly mouths on their faces with lip-rouge, they compared experiences of insomnia.

"Honestly," Mrs. Morse said, "I wouldn't close an eye if I didn't go to bed full of Scotch. I lie there and toss and turn and toss and turn. Blue! Does a person get blue lying awake that way!"

"Say, listen, Hazel," Mrs. Miller said, impressively, "I'm telling you I'd be awake for a year if I didn't take veronal. That stuff makes you sleep like a fool."

"Isn't it poison, or something?" Mrs. Morse asked.

"Oh, you take too much and you're out for the count," said Mrs. Miller. "I just take five grains—they come in tablets. I'd be scared to fool around with it, but five grains, and you cork off pretty."

"Can you get it anywhere?" Mrs. Morse felt superbly Machiavellian.

"Get all you want in Jersey," said Mrs. Miller. "They won't give it to you here without you have a doctor's prescription. Finished? We'd better go back and see what the boys are doing."

That night, Art left Mrs. Morse at the door of her apartment; his mother was in town. Mrs. Morse was still sober, and it happened that there was no whisky left in her cupboard. She lay in bed, looking up at the black ceiling.

She rose early, for her, and went to New Jersey. She had never taken the tube, and did not understand it. So she went to the Pennsylvania Station and bought a railroad ticket to Newark. She thought of nothing in particular on the trip out. She looked at the uninspired hats of the women about her and gazed through the smeared window at the flat, gritty scene.

In Newark, in the first drug-store she came to, she asked for a tin of talcum powder, a nailbrush, and a box of veronal tablets. The powder and the brush were to make the hypnotic seem also a casual need. The clerk was entirely unconcerned. "We only keep them in bottles," he said, and wrapped up for her a little glass vial containing ten white tablets, stacked one on another.

She went to another drug-store and bought a face-cloth, an orange-wood stick, and a bottle of veronal tablets. The clerk was also uninterested.

"Well, I guess I got enough to kill an ox," she thought, and went back to the station.

At home, she put the little vials in the drawer of her dressing-table and stood looking at them with a dreamy tenderness.

"There they are, God bless them" she said, and she kissed her finger-tip and touched each bottle.

The colored maid was busy in the living-room.

"Hey, Nettie," Mrs. Morse called. "Be an angel, will you? Run around to Jimmy's and get me a quart of Scotch."

She hummed while she awaited the girl's return.

During the next few days, whisky ministered to her as tenderly as it had done when she first turned to its aid. Alone, she was soothed and vague, at Jimmy's she was the gayest of the groups. Art was delighted with her.

Then, one night, she had an appointment to meet Art at Jimmy's for an early dinner. He was to leave afterward on a business excursion, to be away for a week. Mrs. Morse had been drinking all the afternoon; while she dressed to go out, she felt herself rising pleasurably from drowsiness to high spirits. But as she came out into the street the effects of the whisky deserted her completely, and she was filled with a slow, grinding wretchedness so horrible that she stood swaying on the pavement, unable for a moment to move forward. It was a gray night with spurts of mean, thin snow, and the streets shone with dark ice. As she slowly crossed Sixth Avenue, consciously dragging one foot past the other, a big, scarred horse pulling a rickety express-wagon crashed to his knees before her. The driver swore and screamed and lashed the beast insanely, bringing the whip back over his shoulder for every blow, while the horse struggled to get a footing on the slippery asphalt. A group gathered and watched with interest.

Art was waiting, when Mrs. Morse reached Jimmy's.

"What's the matter with you, for God's sake?" was his greeting to her.

"I saw a horse," she said. "Gee, I—a person feels sorry for horses. I—it isn't just horses. Everything's kind of terrible, isn't it? I can't help getting sunk."

"Ah, sunk, me eye," he said. "What's the idea of all the bellyaching? What have you got to be sunk about?"

"I can't help it," she said.

"Ah, help it, me eye," he said. "Pull yourself together, will you? Come on and sit down, and take that face off you."

She drank industriously and she tried hard, but she could not overcome her melancholy. Others joined them and commented on her gloom, and she could do no more for them than smile weakly. She made little dabs at her eyes with her handkerchief, trying to time her movements so they would be unnoticed, but several times Art caught her and scowled and shifted impatiently in his chair.

When it was time for him to go to his train, she said she would leave, too, and go home.

"And not a bad idea, either," he said. "See if you can't sleep yourself out of it. I'll see you Thursday. For God's sake, try and cheer up by then, will you?"

"Yeah," she said. "I will."

In her bedroom, she undressed with a tense speed wholly unlike her usual slow uncertainty. She put on her nightgown, took off her hair-net and passed the comb quickly through her dry, vari-colored hair. Then she took the two little vials from the drawer and carried them into the bathroom. The splintering misery had gone from her, and she felt the quick excitement of one who is about to receive an anticipated gift.

She uncorked the vials, filled a glass with water and stood before the mirror, a tablet between her fingers. Suddenly she bowed graciously to her reflection, and raised the glass to it.

"Well, here's mud in your eye," she said.

The tablets were unpleasant to take, dry and powdery and sticking obstinately half-way down her throat. It took her a long time to swallow all twenty of them. She stood watching her reflection with deep, impersonal interest, studying the movements of the gulping throat. Once more she spoke aloud.

"For God's sake, try and cheer up by Thursday, will you?" she said. "Well, you know what he can do. He and the whole lot of them."

She had no idea how quickly to expect effect from the veronal. When she had taken the last tablet, she stood uncertainly, wondering, still with a courteous, vicarious interest, if death would strike her down then and there. She felt in no way strange, save for a slight stirring of sickness from the effort of swallowing the tablets, nor did her reflected face look at all different. It would not be immediate, then; it might even take an hour or so.

She stretched her arms high and gave a vast yawn.

"Guess I'll go to bed," she said. "Gee, I'm nearly dead."

That struck her as comic, and she turned out the bathroom light and went in and laid herself down in her bed, chuckling softly all the time.

"Gee, I'm nearly dead," she quoted. "That's a hot one!"

III

Nettie, the colored maid, came in late the next afternoon to clean the apartment, and found Mrs. Morse in her bed. But then, that was not unusual. Usually, though, the sounds of cleaning waked her, and she did not like to wake up. Nettie, an agreeable girl, had learned to move softly about her work.

But when she had done the living-room and stolen in to tidy the little square bedroom, she could not avoid a tiny clatter as she arranged the objects on the dressing-table. Instinctively, she glanced over her shoulder at the sleeper, and without warning a sickly uneasiness crept over her. She came to the bed and stared down at the woman lying there.

Mrs. Morse lay on her back, one flabby, white arm flung up, the wrist against her forehead. Her stiff hair hung untenderly along her face. The bed covers were pushed down, exposing a deep square of soft neck and a pink nightgown, its fabric worn uneven by many launderings; her great breasts, freed from their tight confiner, sagged beneath her arm-pits. Now and then she made knotted, snoring sounds, and from the corner of her opened mouth to the blurred turn of her jaw ran a lane of crusted spittle.

"Mis' Morse," Nettie called. "Oh, Mis' Morse! It's terrible late."

Mrs. Morse made no move.

"Mis' Morse," said Nettie. "Look, Mis' Morse. How'm I goin' get this bed made?"

Panic sprang upon the girl. She shook the woman's hot shoulder.

"Ah, wake up, will yuh?" she whined. "Ah, please wake up."

Suddenly the girl turned and ran out in the hall to the elevator door, keeping her thumb firm on the black, shiny button until the elderly car and its Negro attendant stood before her. She poured a jumble of words over the boy, and led him back to the apartment. He tiptoed creakingly in to the bedside; first gingerly, then so lustily that he left marks in the soft flesh, he prodded the unconscious woman.

"Hey, there!" he cried, and listened intently, as for an echo.

"Jeez. Out like a light," he commented.

At his interest in the spectacle, Nettie's panic left her. Importance was big in both of them. They talked in quick, unfinished whispers, and it was the boy's suggestion that he fetch the young doctor who lived on the ground floor. Nettie hurried along with him. They looked forward to the limelit moment of breaking their news of something untoward, something pleasurably unpleasant. Mrs. Morse had become the medium of drama. With no ill wish to her, they hoped that her state was serious, that she would not let them down by being awake and normal on their return. A little fear of this determined them to make the most, to the doctor, of her present condition. "Matter of life and death," returned to Nettie from her thin store of reading. She considered startling the doctor with the phrase.

The doctor was in and none too pleased at interruption. He wore a yellow and blue striped dressing-gown, and he was lying on his sofa, laughing with a dark girl, her face scaly with inexpensive powder, who perched on the arm. Half-emptied highball glasses stood beside them, and her coat and hat were neatly hung up with the comfortable implication of a long stay.

Always something, the doctor grumbled. Couldn't let anybody alone after a hard day. But he put some bottles and instruments into a case, changed his dressing-gown for his coat and started out with the Negroes.

"Snap it up there, big boy," the girl called after him. "Don't be all night."

The doctor strode loudly into Mrs. Morse's flat and on to the bedroom, Nettie and the boy right behind him. Mrs. Morse had not moved; her sleep was as deep, but soundless, now. The doctor looked sharply at her, then plunged his thumbs into the lidded pits above her eyeballs and threw his weight upon them. A high, sickened cry broke from Nettie.

"Look like he tryin' to push her right on th'ough the bed," said the boy. He chuckled.

Mrs. Morse gave no sign under the pressure. Abruptly the doctor abandoned it, and with one quick movement swept the covers down to the foot of the bed. With another he flung her nightgown back and lifted the thick, white legs, cross-hatched with blocks of tiny, iris-colored veins. He pinched them repeatedly, with long, cruel nips, back of the knees. She did not awaken.

"What's she been drinking?" he asked Nettie, over his shoulder.

With the certain celerity of one who knows just where to lay hands on a thing, Nettie went into the bathroom, bound for the cupboard where Mrs. Morse kept her whisky. But she stopped at the sight of the two vials, with their red and white labels, lying before the mirror. She brought them to the doctor.

"Oh, for the Lord Almighty's sweet sake!" he said. He dropped Mrs.

Morse's legs, and pushed them impatiently across the bed. "What did she want to go taking that tripe for? Rotten yellow trick, that's what a thing like that is. Now we'll have to pump her out, and all that stuff. Nuisance, a thing like that is; that's what it amounts to. Here, George, take me down in the elevator. You wait here, maid. She won't do anything."

"She won't die on me, will she?" cried Nettie.

"No," said the doctor. "God, no. You couldn't kill her with an ax."

IV

After two days, Mrs. Morse came back to consciousness, dazed at first, then with a comprehension that brought with it the slow, saturating wretchedness.

"Oh, Lord, oh, Lord," she moaned and tears for herself and for life striped her cheeks.

Nettie came in at the sound. For two days she had done the ugly, incessant tasks in the nursing of the unconscious, for two nights she had caught broken bits of sleep on the living-room couch. She looked coldly at the big, blown woman in the bed.

"What you been tryin' to do, Mis' Morse?" she said, "What kine o' work is that, takin' all that stuff?"

"Oh, Lord," moaned Mrs. Morse, again, and she tried to cover her eyes with her arms. But the joints felt stiff and brittle, and she cried out at their ache.

"Tha's no way to ack, takin' them pills," said Nettie. "You can thank you' stars you heah at all. How you feel now?"

"Oh, I feel great," said Mrs. Morse. "Swell, I feel."

Her hot, painful tears fell as if they would never stop.

"Tha's no way to take on, cryin' like that," Nettie said. "After what you done. The doctor, he says he could have you arrested, doin' a thing like that. He was fit to be tied, here."

"Why couldn't he let me alone?" wailed Mrs. Morse. "Why the hell couldn't he have?"

"Tha's terr'ble, Mis' Morse, swearin' an' talkin' like that," said Nettie, "after what people done for you. Here I ain' had no sleep at all for two nights, an' had to give up goin' out to my other ladies!"

"Oh, I'm sorry, Nettie," she said. "You're a peach. I'm sorry I've given you so much trouble. I couldn't help it. I just got sunk. Didn't you ever feel like doing it? When everything looks just lousy to you?"

"I wouldn' think o' no such thing," declared Nettie. "You got to cheer up. Tha's what you got to do. Everybody's got their troubles."

"Yeah," said Mrs. Morse. "I know."

"Come a pretty picture card for you," Nettie said. "Maybe that will cheer you up."

She handed Mrs. Morse a post-card. Mrs. Morse had to cover one eye with her hand, in order to read the message; her eyes were not yet focusing correctly.

It was from Art. On the back of a view of the Detroit Athletic Club he had written: "Greeting and salutations. Hope you have lost that gloom. Cheer up and don't take any rubber nickels. See you on Thursday."

She dropped the card to the floor. Misery crushed her as if she were between great smooth stones. There passed before her a slow, slow pageant of days spent lying in her flat, of evenings at Jimmy's being a good sport, making herself laugh and coo at Art and other Arts; she saw a long parade of weary horses and shivering beggars and all beaten, driven, stumbling things. Her feet throbbed as if she had crammed them into the stubby champagne-colored slippers. Her heart seemed to swell and harden.

"Nettie," she cried, "for heaven's sake pour me a drink, will you?"

The maid looked doubtful.

"Now you know, Mis' Morse," she said, "you been near daid. I don' know if the doctor he let you drink nothin' yet."

"Oh, never mind him," she said. "You get me one, and bring in the bottle. Take one yourself."

"Well," said Nettie.

She poured them each a drink, deferentially leaving hers in the bathroom to be taken in solitude, and brought Mrs. Morse's glass in to her.

Mrs. Morse looked into the liquor and shuddered back from its odor. Maybe it would help. Maybe, when you had been knocked cold for a few days, your very first drink would give you a lift. Maybe whisky would be her friend again. She prayed without addressing a God, without knowing a God. Oh, please, please, let her be able to get drunk, please keep her always drunk.

She lifted the glass.

"Thanks, Nettie," she said. "Here's mud in your eye."

The maid giggled. "Tha's the way, Mis' Morse," she said. "You cheer up, now."

"Yeah," said Mrs. Morse. "Sure."

The Witness

ANN PETRY

It had been snowing for twenty-four hours, and as soon as it stopped, the town plows began clearing the roads and sprinkling them with a mixture of sand and salt. By nightfall the main roads were what the roadmaster called clean as a whistle. But the little winding side roads and the store parking lots and the private walkways lay under a thick blanket of snow.

Because of the deep snow, Charles Woodruff parked his station wagon, brand-new, expensive, in the road in front of the Congregational church rather than risk getting stuck in the lot behind the church. He was early for the minister's class so he sat still, deliberately savoring the new-car smell of the station wagon. He found himself sniffing audibly and thought the sound rather a greedy one and so got out of the car and stood on the snow-covered walk, studying the church. A full moon lay low on the horizon. It gave a wonderful luminous quality to the snow, to the church, and to the branches of the great elms dark against the winter sky.

He ducked his head down because the wind was coming in gusts straight from the north, blowing the snow so it swirled around him, stinging his face. It was so cold that his toes felt as though they were freezing and he began to stamp his feet. Fortunately his coat insulated his body against the cold. He hadn't really planned to buy a new coat but during the Christmas vacation he had been in New York City and he had gone into one of those thickly carpeted, faintly perfumed, crystal-chandeliered stores that sell men's clothing and he had seen the coat hanging on a rack—a dark gray cashmere coat, lined with nutria and adorned by a collar of black Persian lamb. A tall, thin salesman who smelled of heather saw him looking at the coat and said: "Try it on, sir—it's toast-warm, cloud-light, guaranteed to make you feel like a prince—do try it on, here let me hold your coat, sir." The man's voice sounded as though he were purring and he kept brushing against Woodruff like a cat, and managed to sell him the coat, a narrow-brimmed felt hat, and a pair of fur-lined gloves.

If Addie had been alive and learned he had paid five hundred dollars for an overcoat, she would have argued with him fiercely, nostrils flaring, thin arched eyebrows lifted. Standing there alone in the snow, in front of the church, he permitted himself a small indulgence. He pretended Addie was standing beside him. He spoke to her, aloud: "You always said I had to dress more elegantly than my students so they would respect my clothes even if they didn't respect my learning. You said—"

He stopped abruptly, thinking he must look like a lunatic, standing in the snow, stamping his feet and talking to himself. If he kept it up long enough, someone would call the state police and a bulletin about him would go clattering out over the teletype: "Attention all cruisers, attention all cruisers, a black man, repeat, a black man is standing in front of the Congregational church in Wheeling, New York; description follows, description follows, thinnish, tallish black man, clipped moustache, expensive (extravagantly expensive, outrageously expensive, unjustifiably expensive) overcoat, felt hat like a Homburg, eyeglasses glittering in the moonlight, feet stamping in the moonlight, mouth muttering in the moonlight. Light of the moon we danced. Glimpses of the moon revisited . . ."

There was no one in sight, no cars passing. It was so still it would be easy to believe that the entire population of the town had died and lay buried under the snow and that he was the sole survivor, and that would be ironic because he did not really belong in this all-white community.

The thought of his alien presence here evoked an image of Addie— dark-skinned, intense, beautiful. He was sixty-five when she died. He had just retired as professor of English at Virginia College for Negroes. He had spent all of his working life there. He had planned to write a grammar to be used in first-year English classes, to perfect his herb garden, catalogue his library, tidy up his files, and organize his clippings—a wealth of material in those clippings. But without Addie these projects seemed inconsequential—like the busy work that grade school teachers devise to keep children out of mischief. When he was offered a job teaching in a high school in a small town in New York, he accepted it quickly.

Everybody was integrating and so this little frozen Northern town was integrating, too. Someone probably asked why there were no black teachers in the school system and the school board and the Superintendent of Schools said they were searching for 'one'—and the search yielded that brand-new black widower, Charles Woodruff (nigger in the woodpile, he thought, and then, why that word, a word he despised and never used so why did it pop up like that, does a full moon really affect the human mind) and he was eager to escape from his old environment and so for the past year he had taught English to academic seniors in Wheeling High School.

No problems. No hoodlums. All of his students were being herded toward college like so many cattle. He referred to them (mentally) as the Willing Workers of America. He thought that what was being done to them was a crime against nature. They were hard-working, courteous, pathetic. He introduced a new textbook, discarded a huge anthology that was filled with mutilated poetry, mutilated essays, mutilated short stories. His students liked him and told him so. Other members of the faculty said he was lucky but just wait until another year—the freshmen and the sophomores were "a bunch of hoodlums"—"a whole new ball game—"

Because of his success with his English classes, Dr. Shipley, the Congregational minister, had asked him if he would assist (Shipley used words like "assist" instead of "help") him with a class of delinquent boys—the class met on Sunday nights. Woodruff felt he should make some kind of contribution to the life of this small town which had treated him with genuine friendliness so he had said yes.

But when he first saw those seven boys assembled in the minister's study, he knew that he could neither help nor assist the minister with them—they were beyond his reach, beyond the minister's reach. They sat silent, motionless, their shoulders hunched as though against some chill they found in the air of that small book-lined room. Their eyelids were like shutters drawn over their eyes. Their long hair covered their foreheads, obscuring their eyebrows, reaching to the collars of their jackets. Their legs, stretched out straight in front of them, were encased in pants that fit as tightly as the leotards of a ballet dancer.

He kept looking at them, studying them. Suddenly, as though at a signal, they all looked at him. This collective stare was so hostile that he felt himself stiffen and sweat broke out on his forehead. He assumed that the same thing had happened to Dr. Shipley because Shipley's eyeglasses kept fogging up, though the room was not overly warm.

Shipley had talked for an hour. He began to get hoarse. Though he paused now and then to ask a question and waited hopefully for a reply, there was none. The boys sat mute and motionless.

After they left, filing out, one behind the other, Woodruff had asked Shipley about them—who they were and why they attended this class in religion.

Shipley said, "They come here under duress. The Juvenile Court requires their attendance at this class."

"How old are they?"

"About sixteen. Very bright. Still in high school. They're all sophomores—that's why you don't know them. Rambler, the tall thin boy, the ringleader, has an IQ in the genius bracket. As a matter of fact, if they weren't so bright, they'd be in reform school. This class is part of an effort to—well—to turn them into God-fearing responsible young citizens."

"Are their families poor?"

"No, indeed. The parents of these boys are—well, they're the backbone of the great middle class in this town."

After the third meeting of the class where the same hostile silence prevailed, Woodruff said, "Dr. Shipley, do you think we are accomplishing anything?" He had said "we" though he was well aware that these new young outlaws spawned by the white middle class were, praise God, Shipley's problem—the white man's problem. This cripplingly tight shoe was usually on the black man's foot. He found it rather pleasant to have the position reversed.

Shipley ran his fingers through his hair. It was very short hair, stiff-looking, crew-cut.

"I don't know," he said frowning. "I really don't know. They don't even respond to a greeting or a direct question. It is a terribly frustrating business, an exhausting business. When the class is over, I feel as though I had spent the entire evening lying prone under the unrelieved weight of all their bodies."

Woodruff, standing outside the church, stamping his feet, jumped and then winced because he heard a sound like a gunshot. It was born on the wind so that it seemed close at hand. He stood still, listening. Then he started moving quickly toward the religious education building which housed the minister's study.

He recognized the sound—it was made by the car the boys drove. It had no muffler and the snorting, back-firing sounds made by the spent motor were like a series of gunshots. He wanted to be out of sight when the boys drove up in their rusted car. Their lithe young bodies were a shocking contrast to the abused and ancient vehicle in which they traveled. The age of the car, its dreadful condition, was like a snarled message aimed at the adult world: All we've got is the crumbs, the leftovers, whatever the fat cats don't want and can't use; the turnpikes and the throughways and the seventy-mile-an-hour speedways are filled with long, low, shiny cars built for speed, driven by bald-headed, big-bellied rat finks and we're left with the junk, the worn-out beat-up chassis, the thin tires, the brakes that don't hold, the transmission that's shot to hell. He had seen them push the car out of the parking lot behind the church. It wouldn't go in reverse.

Bent over, peering down, picking his way through the deep snow lest he stumble and fall, Woodruff tried to hurry and the explosive sound of that terrible engine kept getting closer and closer. He envisioned himself as a black beetle in a fur-collared coat silhouetted against the snow trying to scuttle out of danger. Danger: Why should he think he was in danger? Perhaps some sixth sense was trying to warn him and his beetle's antenna (did beetles have antennae, did they have five senses and some of them an additional sense, extrasensory—) picked it up—by the pricking of my thumbs, something wicked this way comes.

Once inside the building he drew a deep breath. He greeted Dr. Shipley, hung his hat and coat on the brass hat rack, and then sat down beside

Shipley behind the old fumed oak desk. He braced himself for the entrance of the boys.

There was the sound of the front door opening followed by the click-clack sound of their heavy boots, in the hall. Suddenly they were all there in the minister's study. They brought cold air in with them. They sat down with their jackets on—great quilted dark jackets that had been designed for European ski slopes. At the first meeting of the class, Dr. Shipley had suggested they remove their jackets and they simply sat and stared at him until he fidgeted and looked away obviously embarrassed. He never again made a suggestion that was direct and personal.

Woodruff glanced at the boys and then directed his gaze away from them, thinking, if a bit of gilt braid and a touch of velvet were added to their clothing, they could pass for the seven dark bastard sons of some old and evil twelfth-century king. Of course they weren't all dark. Three of them were blond, two had brown hair, one had red hair, only one had black hair. All of them were white. But there was about them an aura of something so evil, so dark, so suggestive of the far reaches of the night, of the black horror of nightmares, that he shivered deep inside himself whenever he saw them. Though he thought of them as being black, this was not the blackness of human flesh, warm, soft to the touch, it was the blackness and the coldness of the hole from which D. H. Lawrence's snake emerged.

The hour was almost up when to Woodward's surprise, Rambler, the tall boy, the one who drove the ramshackle car, the one Shipley said was the leader of the group, began asking questions about cannibalism. His voice was husky, low in pitch, and he almost whispered when he spoke. Woodruff found himself leaning forward in an effort to hear what the boy was saying. Dr. Shipley leaned forward, too.

Rambler said, "Is it a crime to eat human flesh?"

Dr. Shipley said, surprised, "Yes. It's cannibalism. It is a sin and it is also a crime." He spoke slowly, gently, as though he were wooing a timid, wild animal that had ventured out of the woods and would turn tail and scamper back if he spoke in his normal voice.

"Well, if the cats who go for this human flesh bit don't think it's a sin and if they eat it because they haven't any other food, it isn't a sin for them, is it?" The boy spoke quickly, not pausing for breath, running his words together.

"There are many practices and acts that are acceptable to non-Christians which are sinful. Christians condemn such acts no matter what the circumstances."

Woodruff thought uncomfortably, why does Shipley have to sound so pompous, so righteous, so from-off-the-top-of-Olympus? The boys were all staring at him, bright-eyed, mouths slightly open, long hair obscuring their foreheads. Then Rambler said, in his husky whispering voice, "What about you, Doc?"

Dr. Shipley said, "Me?" and repeated it, his voice losing its coaxing tone, rising in pitch, increasing in volume. "Me? What do you mean?"

"Well, man, you're eatin' human flesh, ain't you?"

Woodruff had no idea what the boy was talking about. But Dr. Shipley was looking down at his own hands with a curious self-conscious expression and Woodruff saw that Shipley's nails were bitten all the way down to the quick.

The boy said, "It's self-cannibalism, ain't it, Doc?"

Shipley put his hands on the desk, braced himself, preparatory to standing up. His thin, bony face had reddened. Before he could move, or speak, the boys stood up and began to file out of the room. Rambler leaned over and ran his hand through the minister's short-cut, bristly hair and said, "Don't sweat it, Doc."

Woodruff usually stayed a half-hour or more after the class ended. Dr. Shipley liked to talk and Woodruff listened to him patiently, though he thought Shipley had a second-rate mind and rambled when he talked. But Shipley sat with his head bowed, a pose not conducive to conversation and Woodruff left almost immediately after the boys, carrying in his mind's eye a picture of all those straight, narrow backs with the pants so tight they were like elastic bandages on their thighs, and the oversized bulky jackets and the long, frowsy hair. He thought they looked like paper dolls, cut all at once, exactly alike with a few swift slashes of scissors wielded by a skilled hand. Addie could do that —take paper and fold it and go snip, snip, snip with the scissors and she'd have a string of paper dolls, all fat, or all thin, or all bent over, or all wearing top hats, or all bearded Santas or all Cheshire cats. She had taught arts and crafts in the teacher-training courses for elementary-school teachers at Virginia College and so was skilled in the use of crayon and scissors.

He walked toward his car, head down, picking his way through the snow and then he stopped, surprised. The boys were standing in the road. They had surrounded a girl. He didn't think she was a high school girl though she was young. She had long blond hair that spilled over the quilted black jacket she was wearing. At first he couldn't tell what the boys were doing but as he got closer to them, he saw that they were moving toward their ancient car and forcing the girl to move with them though she was resisting. They were talking to each other and to her, their voices companionable, half-playful.

"So we all got one in the oven."

"So it's all right if it's all of us."

The girl said, "No."

"Aw, come on, Nellie, hurry up."

"It's colder'n hell, Nellie. Move!"

They kept pushing her toward the car and she turned on them and said, "Quit it."

"Aw, get in."

One of them gave her a hard shove, sent her closer to the car and she screamed and Rambler clapped his hand over her mouth and she must have bitten his hand because he snatched it away and then she screamed again because he slapped her and then two of them picked her up and threw her on the front seat and one of them stayed there, holding her.

Woodruff thought, There are seven of them, young, strong, satanic. He ought to go home where it was quiet and safe, mind his own business— black man's business; leave this white man's problem for a white man, leave it alone, not his, don't interfere, go home to the bungalow he rented—ridiculous type of architecture in this cold climate, developed for India, a hot climate, and that open porch business—

He said, "What are you doing?" He spoke with the voice of authority, the male schoolteacher's voice and thought, Wait, slow down, cool it, you're a black man speaking with a white man's voice.

They turned and stared at him; as they turned, they all assumed what he called the stance of the new young outlaw: the shoulders hunched, the hands in the pockets. In the moonlight he thought they looked as though they belonged in a frieze around a building—the hunched-shoulder posture repeated again and again, made permanent in stone. Classic.

"What are you doing?" he said again, voice louder, deeper.

"We're standin' here."

"You can see us, can't you?"

"Why did you force that girl into your car?"

"You're dreamin'."

"I saw what happened. And that boy is holding her in there."

"You been readin' too much."

They kept moving in, closing in on him. Even on this cold, windy night he could smell them and he loathed the smell—cigarettes, clothes washed in detergents and not rinsed enough and dried in automatic driers. They all smelled like that these days, even those pathetic college-bound drudges, the Willing Workers of America, stank so that he was always airing out his classroom. He rarely ever encountered the fresh clean smell of clothes that had been washed in soap and water, rinsed in boiling water, dried in the sun—a smell that he associated with new-mown hay and flower gardens and —Addie.

There was a subtle change in the tone of the voice of the next speaker. It was more contemptuous and louder.

"What girl, ho-daddy, what girl?"

One of them suddenly reached out and knocked his hat off his head, another one snatched his glasses off and threw them in the road and there was the tinkling sound of glass shattering. It made him shudder. He was half-blind without his glasses, peering about, uncertain of the shape of objects—like the woman in the Thurber cartoon, oh, yes, of course, three balloons and an H or three cats and a dog—only it was one of those scrambled alphabet charts.

They unbuttoned his overcoat, went through the pockets of his pants, of his jacket. One of them took his wallet, another took his car keys, picked up his hat, and then was actually behind the wheel of his station wagon and was moving off in it.

He shouted, "My car. Damn you, you're stealing my car—" his brand-new station wagon; he kept it immaculate, swept it out every morning, washed the windows. He tried to break out of that confining circle of boys and they simply pushed him back toward their car.

"Don't sweat it, man. You goin' ride with us and this little chick-chick."

"You goin' be our pro-tec-shun, ho-daddy. You goin' be our protec-shun."

They took his coat off and put it around him backward without putting his arms in the sleeves and then buttoned it up. The expensive coat was just like a strait jacket—it pinioned his arms to his sides. He tried to work his way out of it by flexing his muscles, hoping that the buttons would pop off or a seam would give, and thought, enraged, they must have stitched the goddamn coat to last for a thousand years and put the goddamn buttons on the same way. The fur collar pressed against his throat, choking him.

Woodruff was forced into the back seat, two boys on each side of him. They were sitting half on him and half on each other. The one holding his wallet examined its contents. He whistled. "Hey!" he said, "Ho-daddy's got one hundred and forty-four bucks. We got us a rich ho-daddy—"

Rambler held out his hand and the boy handed the money over without a protest, not even a sigh. Then Rambler got into the front seat behind the wheel. The girl was quiet only because the boy beside her had his hand around her throat and from the way he was holding his arm, Woodruff knew he was exerting a certain amount of pressure.

"Give the man a hat," Rambler said.

One of the boys felt around until he found a cap. They were so close to each other that each of his movements slightly disrupted their seating arrangement. When the boy shifted his weight, the rest of them were forced to shift theirs.

"Here you go," the boy said. He pulled a black wool cap down on Woodruff's head, over his eyes, over his nose.

He couldn't see anything. He couldn't breathe through his nose. He had to breathe through his mouth or suffocate. The freezing cold air actually hurt the inside of his mouth. The overcoat immobilized him and the steady pressure of the fur collar against his windpipe was beginning to interfere with his normal rate of breathing. He knew that his whole circulatory system would gradually begin to slow down. He frowned, thinking what a simple and easily executed method of rendering a person helpless—just an overcoat and a knit cap. Then he thought, alarmed, If they should leave me out in the woods like this, I would be dead by morning. What do they want of me anyway?

He cleared his throat preparatory to questioning them but Rambler started the car and he could not make himself heard above the sound of the engine. He thought the noise would shatter his eardrums and he wondered how these boys could bear it—the terrible cannon fire sound of the engine and the rattling of the doors and the windows. Then they were off and it was like riding in a jeep—only worse because the seat was broken and they were jounced up out of the seat and then back down into a hollowed-out place, all of them on top of each other. He tried to keep track of the turns the car made but he couldn't, there were too many of them. He assumed that whenever they stopped it was because of a traffic light or a stop sign.

It seemed to him they had ridden for miles and miles when the car began to jounce up and down more violently than ever and he decided they had turned onto a rough, rutted road. Suddenly they stopped. The car doors were opened and the boys pushed him out of the car. He couldn't keep his balance and he stumbled and fell flat on his face in the snow and they all laughed. They had to haul him to his feet for his movements were so constricted by the overcoat that he couldn't get up without help.

The cap had worked up a little so that he could breathe more freely and he could see anything that was in his immediate vicinity. Either they did not notice that the cap had been pushed out of place or they didn't care. As they guided him along he saw that they were in a cemetery that was filled with very old tombstones. They were approaching a small building and his station wagon was parked to one side. The boy who had driven it opened the door of the building and Woodruff saw that it was lighted inside by a big bulb that dangled from the ceiling. There were shovels and a grease-encrusted riding mower, bags of grass seed, and a bundle of material that looked like the artificial grass used around new graves.

Rambler said, "Put the witness here."

They stood him against the back wall, facing the wall.

"He's here and yet he ain't here."

"Ho-daddy's here—and yet—he ain't here."

"He's our witness."

And then Rambler's voice again, "If he moves, ice him with a shovel."

The girl screamed and then the sound was muffled, only a kind of far-off moaning sound coming through something. They must have gagged her. All the sounds were muffled—it was like trying to see something in a fog or hear something when other sounds overlay the one thing you're listening for. What had they brought him here for? They would go away and leave him with the girl but the girl would know that he hadn't—

How would she know? They had probably blindfolded her, too. What were they doing? He could see shadows on the wall. Sometimes they moved, sometimes they were still, and then the shadows moved again and then there would be laughter. Silence after that and then thuds, thumps, silence again. Terrible sounds behind him. He started to turn around and someone poked him in the back, sharply, with the handle of a shovel or a rake. He began to sweat despite the terrible cold.

He tried to relax by breathing deeply and he began to feel as though he were going to faint. His hands and feet were numb. His head ached. He had strained so to hear what was going on behind him that he was afraid he had impaired his own hearing.

When Rambler said, "Come on, ho-daddy, it's your turn," he was beginning to lose all feeling in his arms and legs.

Someone unbuttoned his coat, plucked the cap off his head. He let his breath out in a long drawn-out sigh. He doubted that he could have survived much longer with that pressure on his throat. The boys looked at him curiously. They threw his coat on the hard-packed dirt floor and tossed the cap on top of it. He thought that the black knit cap they'd used, like a sailor's watch cap, was as effective a blindfold as could be found—providing, of course, the person couldn't use his hands to remove it.

The girl was lying on the floor, half-naked. They had put some burlap bags under her. She looked as though she were dead.

They pushed him toward her saying, "It's your turn."

He balked, refusing to move.

"You don't want none?"

They laughed. "Ho-daddy don't want none."

They pushed him closer to the girl and someone grabbed one of his hands and placed it on the girl's thigh, on her breasts, and then they laughed again. They handed him his coat, pulled the cap down on his head.

"Let's go, ho-daddy. Let's go."

Before he could put his coat back on they hustled him outdoors. One of them threw his empty wallet at him and another aimed his car keys straight at his head. The metal stung as it hit his cheek. Before he could catch them the keys disappeared in the snow. The boys went back inside the building and emerged carrying the girl, half-naked, head hanging down limply the way the head of a corpse would dangle.

"The girl—" Woodruff said.

"You're our witness, ho-daddy. You're our big fat witness."

They propped the girl up in the back seat of their car. "You're the only witness we got," they repeated it, laughing. "Take good care of yourself."

"She'll freeze to death like that," he protested.

"Not Nellie."

"She likes it."

"Come on, man, let's go, let's go," Rambler said impatiently.

Woodruff's arms and hands were so numb that he had trouble getting his coat on. He had to take his gloves off and poke around in the snow with his bare hands before he could retrieve his wallet and the car keys. The pain in his hands was as sharp and intense as if they had been burned.

Getting into his car be began to shake with fury. Once he got out of this wretched cemetery he would call the state police. Young animals. He had called them outlaws; they weren't outlaws, they were animals. In his haste he dropped the keys and had to feel around on the floor of the car for them.

When he finally got the car started he was shivering and shaking and his stomach was quivering so that he didn't dare try to drive. He turned on the heater and watched the tiny taillight on Rambler's car disappear—an old car and the taillight was like the end of a pencil glowing red in the dark. The loud explosive sound of the engine gradually receded. When he could no longer hear it, he flicked on the light in his car and looked at his watch. It was quarter past three. Wouldn't the parents of those godforsaken boys wonder where they were at that hour? Perhaps they didn't care—perhaps they were afraid of them—just as he was.

Though he wanted to get home as quickly as possible, so he could get warm, so he could think, he had to drive slowly, peering out at the narrow rutted road because he was half blind without his glasses. When he reached the cemetery gates he stopped, not knowing whether to turn right or left for he had no idea where he was. He took a chance and turned right and followed the macadam road, still going slowly, saw a church on a hill and recognized it as the Congregational church in Brooksville, the next town, and knew he was about five miles from home.

By the time he reached his own driveway, sweat was pouring from his body just like water coming out of a showerhead—even his eyelashes were wet; it ran down his ears, dripped off his nose, his lips, even the palms of his hands.

In the house he turned on the lights, in the living room, in the hall, in his bedroom. He went to his desk, opened a drawer and fished out an old pair of glasses. He had had them for years. They looked rather like Peter Cooper's glasses—he'd seen them once in the Cooper Union Museum in New York—small-lensed, with narrow, silvery-looking frames. They evoked an image of a careful scholarly man. When he had started wearing glasses, he had selected frames like Peter Cooper's. Addie had made him stop wearing them. She said they gave him the look of another era, made it easy for his students to caricature him—the tall, slender figure, slightly stooped, the steel-rimmed glasses. She said that his dark, gentle eyes looked as though they were trapped behind those little glasses.

Having put on the glasses, he went to the telephone and stood with one hand resting on it, sweating again, trembling again. He turned away, took off his overcoat and hung it on a hanger and placed it in the hall closet.

He began to pace up and down the living room—a pleasant spacious room, simply furnished. It had a southern exposure and there were big windows on that side of the room. The windows faced a meadow. The thought crossed his mind, lightly, like the silken delicate strand of a cobweb, that he would have to leave here and he brushed it away—not quite away, a trace remained.

He wasn't going to call the police. Chicken. That was the word his students used. Fink was another one. He was going to chicken out. He was going to fink out.

Why wasn't he going to call the police? Well, what would he tell them? That he'd been robbed? Well, that was true. That he'd been kidnapped? Well, that was true, too, but it seemed like a harsh way of putting it. He'd have to think about that one. That he'd been witness to a rape? He wasn't even certain that they had raped the girl. No? Who was he trying to kid? Himself? Himself.

So why wasn't he going to the police? He hadn't touched the girl. But those horrible little hoods, toads rather, why toads, toe of frog ingredient of witches' brew, poisonous substance in the skin—bufotenine, a hallucinogen found in the skin of the frog, of the toad. Those horrible toadlike hoods would say he had touched her. Well, he had. Hadn't he? They had made sure of that. Would the police believe him? The school board? The PTA? "Where there's smoke there must be fire." "I'm not going to let my daughter stay in his class."

He started shivering again and made himself a cup of tea and sat down on the window seat in the living room to drink it and then got up and turned off the lights and looked out at the snow. The moonlight was so bright that he could see wisps of tall grass in the meadow—yellow against the snow. Immediately he thought of the long blond hair of that starvation-thin young girl. Bleached hair? Perhaps. It didn't lessen the outrage. She was dressed just like the boys—big quilted jacket, skin-tight pants, even her hair worn like theirs, obscuring the forehead, the sides of the face.

There was a sudden movement outside the window and he frowned and leaned forward, wondering what was moving about at this hour. He saw a pair of rabbits, leaping, running, literally playing games with each other. He had never before seen such free joyous movement, not even children at play exhibited it. There was always something unrelaxed about the eyes of children, about the way they held their mouths, wrinkled their foreheads—they looked as though they had been cornered and were impelled to defend themselves or that they were impelled to pursue some object that forever eluded them.

Watching this joyous heel-kicking play of the rabbits, he found himself thinking, I cannot continue to live in the same small town with that girl and those seven boys. The boys knew, before he did, that he wasn't going to report this—this incident—these crimes. They were bright enough to know that he would quickly realize how neatly they had boxed him in and thus would keep quiet. If he dared enter a complaint against them they would accuse him of raping the girl, would say they found him in the cemetery with her. Whose story would be believed? "Where there's smoke there's fire."

Right after that he started packing. He put his clothes into a foot locker. He stacked his books on the floor of the station wagon. He was surprised to find among the books a medical textbook that had belonged to John—Addie's brother.

He sat down and read all the material on angina pectoris. At eight o'clock he called the school and said he wasn't feeling well (which was true) and that he would not be in. Then he called the office of the local doctor and made an appointment for that afternoon.

When he talked to the doctor he described the violent pain in his chest that went from the shoulder down to his finger tips on the left side, causing a squeezing, crushing sensation that left him feeling faint, dizzy.

The doctor, a fat man in an old tweed jacket and a limp white shirt, said after he examined him, "Angina. You'll have to take three or four months off until we can get this thing under control."

"I will resign immediately."

"Oh, no. That isn't necessary. Besides I've been told you're the best English teacher we've ever had. It would be a great pity to lose you."

"No," Woodruff said, "it is better to resign." Come back here and look at that violated little girl? Come back here? Ever?

He scarcely listened to the detailed instructions he was to follow, did not even glance at the three prescriptions he was handed, for he was eager to be on his way. He composed a letter of resignation in his mind. When he went back to the bungalow he wrote it quickly and then put it on the front seat of the station wagon to be mailed en route.

Then he went back into the house and stayed there just long enough to call his landlord. He said he'd had a heart attack and was going back to Virginia to convalesce, that he had turned the thermostat down to sixty-five and he would return the house keys by mail. The landlord said, My goodness, you just paid a month in advance, I'll mail you a refund, what's your new address, so sorry, ideal tenant.

Woodruff hung up the receiver and said, "Peace be with you, brother—" There was already an echo in the room though it wasn't empty—all he'd removed were his books and his clothes.

He put on his elegant overcoat. When he got back to Virginia, he would give the coat away, his pleasure in it destroyed now for he would always remember the horrid feel of the collar tight across his throat, even the feel of the fabric under his finger tips would evoke an image of the cemetery, the tool shed, and the girl.

He drove down the road rather slowly. There were curves in the road and he couldn't go fast, besides he liked to look at this landscape. It was high rolling land. Snow lay over it—blue-white where there were shadows cast by the birch trees and the hemlocks, yellow-white and sparkling in the great meadow where he had watched the heel-kicking freedom of the rabbits at play.

At the entrance to the highway he brought the car to a halt. As he sat there waiting for an opportunity to get into the stream of traffic, he heard close at hand the loud explosive sound of an engine—a familiar sound. He was so alarmed that he momentarily experienced all the symptoms of a heart attack, the sudden terrible inability to breathe and the feeling that something was squeezing his chest, kneading it so that pain ran through him as though it were following the course of his circulatory system.

He knew from the sound that the car turning off the highway, entering the same road that he was now leaving, was Rambler's car. In the sunlight, silhouetted against the snow, it looked like a junkyard on wheels, fenders dented, sides dented, chassis rusted. All the boys were in the car. Rambler was driving. The thin blond girl was in the front seat—a terrible bruise under one eye. For a fraction of a second Woodruff looked straight into Rambler's eyes, just visible under the long, untidy hair. The expression was cold, impersonal, analytical.

After he got on the highway, he kept looking in the rearview mirror. There was no sign of pursuit. Evidently Rambler had not noticed that the car was loaded for flight—books and cartons on the seats, foot locker on the floor, all this was out of his range of vision. He wondered what they were doing. Wrecking the interior of the bungalow? No. They were probably waiting for him to return so they could blackmail him. Blackmail a black male.

On the turnpike he kept going faster and faster—eighty-five miles an hour, ninety, ninety-five, one hundred. He felt exhilarated by this tremendous speed. It was clearing his mind, heartening him, taking him out of himself.

He began to rationalize about what had happened. He decided that Rambler and his friends didn't give a damn that he Woodruff, was a black man. They couldn't care less. They were very bright boys, bright enough to recognize him for what he was: a black man in his sixties, conditioned all his life by the knowledge that "White woman taboo for you" (as one of his African students used to say). The moment he attempted to intervene there in front of the church, they decided to take him with them. They knew he wasn't going to the police about any matter which involved sex and a white girl, especially where there was the certainty that all seven of them would accuse him of having relations with the girl. They had used his presence in that tool shed to give an extra exquisite fillip to their dreadful game.

He turned on the radio and waited impatiently for music, any kind of music, thinking it would distract him. He got one of those stations that play what he called thump-and-blare music. A husky-voiced woman was shouting a song—not singing, shouting:

I'm gonna turn on the big beat
I'm gonna turn up the high heat
For my ho-daddy, ho-daddy,
For my ho-daddy, ho-daddy.

He flipped the switch, cutting off the sound and he gradually diminished the speed of the car, slowing, slowing, slowing. "We got us a rich ho-daddy." That's what one of the boys had said there in front of the church when he plucked the money out of Woodruff's wallet. A rich ho-daddy? A black ho-daddy. A witness. Another poor scared black bastard who was a witness.

The Fall of the House of Usher

EDGAR ALLAN POE

Son cœur est un luth suspendu;
Sitôt qu'on le touche il résonne.

—*De Béranger*

During the whole of a dull, dark, and soundless day in the autumn of the
year, when the clouds hung oppressively low in the heavens, I had been
passing alone, on horseback, through a singularly dreary tract of country,
and at length found myself, as the shades of the evening drew on, within
view of the melancholy House of Usher. I know not how it was—but, with
the first glimpse of the building, a sense of insufferable gloom pervaded
my spirit. I say insufferable; for the feeling was unrelieved by any of that
half-pleasurable, because poetic, sentiment with which the mind usually receives even the sternest natural images of the desolate or terrible. I looked
upon the scene before me—upon the mere house, and the simple landscape features of the domain—upon the bleak walls—upon the vacant eye-
like windows—upon a few rank sedges—and upon a few white trunks of
decayed trees—with an utter depression of soul which I can compare to no
earthly sensation more properly than to the after-dream of the reveller
upon opium—the bitter lapse into every-day life—the hideous dropping
off of the veil. There was an iciness, a sinking, a sickening of the heart—an
unredeemed dreariness of thought which no goading of the imagination
could torture into aught of the sublime. What was it—I paused to think—
what was it that so unnerved me in the contemplation of the House of
Usher? It was a mystery all insoluble; nor could I grapple with the shadowy
fancies that crowded upon me as I pondered. I was forced to fall back upon
the unsatisfactory conclusion, that while, beyond doubt, there *are* combina-
tions of very simple natural objects which have the power of thus affecting
us, still the analysis of this power lies among considerations beyond our
depth. It was possible, I reflected, that a mere different arrangement of the
particulars of the scene, of the details of the picture, would be sufficient to
modify, or perhaps to annihilate its capacity for sorrowful impression; and,
acting upon this idea, I reined my horse to the precipitous brink of a black

and lurid tarn that lay in unruffled lustre by the dwelling, and gazed down—but with a shudder even more thrilling than before—upon the re-modelled and inverted images of the gray sedge, and the ghastly tree-stems, and the vacant and eye-like windows.

Nevertheless, in this mansion of gloom I now proposed to myself a so-journ of some weeks. Its proprietor, Roderick Usher, had been one of my boon companions in boyhood; but many years had elapsed since our last meeting. A letter, however, had lately reached me in a distant part of the country—a letter from him—which, in its wildly importunate nature, had admitted of no other than a personal reply. The MS. gave evidence of ner-vous agitation. The writer spoke of acute bodily illness—of a mental disor-der which oppressed him—and of an earnest desire to see me, as his best and indeed his only personal friend, with a view of attempting, by the cheerfulness of my society, some alleviation of his malady. It was the man-ner in which all this, and much more, was said—it was the apparent *heart* that went with his request—which allowed me no room for hesitation; and I accordingly obeyed forthwith what I still considered a very singular summons.

Although, as boys, we had been even intimate associates, yet I really knew little of my friend. His reserve had been always excessive and habit-ual. I was aware, however, that his very ancient family had been noted, time out of mind, for a peculiar sensibility of temperament, displaying itself through long ages, in many works of exalted art, and manifested, of late, in repeated deeds of munificent yet unobtrusive charity, as well as in a pas-sionate devotion to the intricacies, perhaps even more than to the orthodox and easily recognizable beauties, of musical science. I had learned, too, the very remarkable fact, that the stem of the Usher race, all time-honored as it was, had put forth, at no period, any enduring branch; in other words, that the entire family lay in the direct line of descent, and had always, with very trifling and very temporary variation, so lain. It was this deficiency, I con-sidered, while running over in thought the perfect keeping of the character of the premises with the accredited character of the people, and while spec-ulating upon the possible influence which the one, in the long lapse of cen-turies, might have exercised upon the other—it was this deficiency, perhaps, of collateral issue, and the consequent undeviating transmission, from sire to son, of the patrimony with the name, which had, at length, so identified the two as to merge the original title of the estate in the quaint and equivocal appellation of the "House of Usher"—an appellation which seemed to include, in the minds of the peasantry who used it, both the fam-ily and the family mansion.

I have said that the sole effect of my somewhat childish experiment—that of looking down within the tarn—had been to deepen the first singu-lar impression. There can be no doubt that the consciousness of the rapid increase of my superstition—for why should I not so term it?—served mainly to accelerate the increase itself. Such, I have long known, is the paradoxical law of all sentiments having terror as a basis. And it might have been for this reason only, that, when I again uplifted my eyes to the house itself, from its image in the pool, there grew in my mind a strange fancy—a fancy so ridiculous, indeed, that I but mention it to show the vivid force of the sensations which oppressed me. I had so worked upon my imagination as really to believe that about the whole mansion and domain there hung an atmosphere peculiar to themselves and their immediate vicinity—an atmosphere which had no affinity with the air of heaven, but which had reeked up from the decayed trees, and the gray wall, and the silent tarn—a pestilent and mystic vapor, dull, sluggish, faintly discernible, and leaden-hued.

Shaking off from my spirit what *must* have been a dream, I scanned more narrowly the real aspect of the building. Its principal feature seemed to be that of an excessive antiquity. The discoloration of ages had been great. Minute fungi overspread the whole exterior, hanging in a fine tangled web-work from the eaves. Yet all this was apart from any extraordinary dilapidation. No portion of the masonry had fallen; and there appeared to be a wild inconsistency between its still perfect adaptation of parts, and the crumbling condition of the individual stones. In this there was much that reminded me of the specious totality of the old wood-work which has rotted for long years in some neglected vault, with no disturbance from the breath of the external air. Beyond this indication of extensive decay, however, the fabric gave little token of instability. Perhaps the eye of a scrutinizing observer might have discovered a barely perceptible fissure, which, extending from the roof of the building in front, made its way down the wall in a zigzag direction, until it became lost in the sullen waters of the tarn.

Noticing these things, I rode over a short causeway to the house. A servant in waiting took my horse, and I entered the Gothic archway of the hall. A valet, of stealthy step, thence conducted me, in silence, through many dark and intricate passages in my progress to the *studio* of his master. Much that I encountered on the way contributed, I know not how, to heighten the vague sentiments of which I have already spoken. While the objects around me—while the carvings of the ceilings, the sombre tapestries of the walls, the ebon blackness of the floors, and the phantasmagoric armorial trophies which rattled as I strode, were but matters to which, or to such as which, I had been accustomed from my infancy—while I hesitated not to acknowledge how familiar was all this—I still wondered to find how unfamiliar were the fancies which ordinary images were stirring up. On one of the staircases, I met the physician of the family. His countenance, I thought, wore a mingled expression of low cunning and perplexity. He accosted me with trepidation and passed on. The valet now threw open a door and ushered me into the presence of his master.

The room in which I found myself was very large and lofty. The windows were long, narrow, and pointed, and at so vast a distance from the black oaken floor as to be altogether inaccessible from within. Feeble gleams of encrimsoned light made their way through the trellissed panes, and served to render sufficiently distinct the more prominent objects around; the eye, however, struggled in vain to reach the remoter angles of the chamber, or the recesses of the vaulted and fretted ceiling. Dark draperies hung upon the walls. The general furniture was profuse, comfortless, antique, and tattered. Many books and musical instruments lay scattered about, but failed to give any vitality to the scene. I felt that I breathed an atmosphere of sorrow. An air of stern, deep, and irredeemable gloom hung over and pervaded all.

Upon my entrance, Usher arose from a sofa on which he had been lying at full length, and greeted me with a vivacious warmth which had much in it, I at first thought, of an overdone cordiality—of the constrained effort of the *ennuyé* man of the world. A glance, however, at his countenance convinced me of his perfect sincerity. We sat down; and for some moments, while he spoke, I gazed upon him with a feeling half of pity, half of awe. Surely, man had never before so terribly altered, in so brief a period, as had Roderick Usher! It was with difficulty that I could bring myself to admit the identity of the wan being before me with the companion of my early boyhood. Yet the character of his face had been at all times remarkable. A cadaverousness of complexion; an eye large, liquid, and luminous beyond comparison; lips somewhat thin and very pallid, but of a surpassingly beautiful curve; a nose of a delicate Hebrew model, but with a breadth of nostril unusual in similar formations; a finely moulded chin, speaking, in its want of prominence, of a want of moral energy; hair of a more than web-like softness and tenuity;—these features, with an inordinate expansion above the regions of the temple, made up altogether a countenance not easily to be forgotten. And now in the mere exaggeration of the prevailing character of these features, and of the expression they were wont to convey, lay so much of change that I doubted to whom I spoke. The now ghastly pallor of the skin, and the now miraculous lustre of the eye, above all things startled and even awed me. The silken hair, too, had been suffered to grow all unheeded, and as, in its wild gossamer texture, it floated rather than fell about the face, I could not, even with effort, connect its Arabesque expression with any idea of simple humanity.

In the manner of my friend I was at once struck with an incoherence—an inconsistency; and I soon found this to arise from a series of feeble and futile struggles to overcome an habitual trepidancy—an excessive nervous agitation. For something of this nature I had indeed been prepared, no less by his letter, than by reminiscences of certain boyish traits, and by conclusions deduced from his peculiar physical confirmation and temperament. His action was alternately vivacious and sullen. His voice varied rapidly from a tremulous indecision (when the animal spirits seemed utterly in abeyance) to that species of energetic concision—that abrupt, weighty, unhurried, and hollow-sounding enunciation—that leaden, self-balanced, and perfectly modulated guttural utterance, which may be observed in the lost drunkard, or the irreclaimable eater of opium, during the periods of his most intense excitement.

It was thus that he spoke of the object of my visit, of his earnest desire to see me, and of the solace he expected me to afford him. He entered, at some length, into what he conceived to be the nature of his malady. It was, he said, a constitutional and a family evil, and one for which he despaired to find a remedy—a mere nervous affection, he immediately added, which would undoubtedly soon pass off. It displayed itself in a host of unnatural sensations. Some of these, as he detailed them, interested and bewildered me; although, perhaps, the terms and the general manner of their narration had their weight. He suffered much from a morbid acuteness of the senses; the most insipid food was alone endurable; he could wear only garments of certain texture; the odors of all flowers were oppressive; his eyes were tortured by even a faint light; and there were but peculiar sounds, and these from stringed instruments, which did not inspire him with horror.

To an anomalous species of terror I found him a bounden slave. "I shall perish," said he, "I *must* perish in this deplorable folly. Thus, thus, and not otherwise, shall I be lost. I dread the events of the future, not in themselves, but in their results. I shudder at the thought of any, even the most trivial, incident, which may operate upon this intolerable agitation of soul. I have, indeed, no abhorrence of danger, except in its absolute effect—in terror. In this unnerved, in this pitiable, condition I feel that the period will sooner or later arrive when I must abandon life and reason together, in some struggle with the grim phantasm, FEAR."

I learned, moreover, at intervals, and through broken and equivocal hints, another singular feature of his mental condition. He was enchained by certain superstitious impressions in regard to the dwelling which he tenanted, and whence, for many years, he had never ventured forth—in regard to an influence whose supposititious force was conveyed in terms too shadowy here to be re-stated—an influence which some peculiarities in the mere form and substance of his family mansion had, by dint of long sufferance, he said, obtained over his spirit—an effect which the *physique* of the gray walls and turrets, and of the dim tarn into which they all looked down, had, at length, brought about upon the *morale* of his existence.

He admitted, however, although with hesitation, that much of the peculiar gloom which thus afflicted him could be traced to a more natural and far more palpable origin—to the severe and long-continued illness—indeed to the evidently approaching dissolution—of a tenderly beloved sister, his sole companion for long years, his last and only relative on earth.

"Her decease," he said, with a bitterness which I can never forget, "would leave him (him, the hopeless and the frail) the last of the ancient race of the Ushers." While he spoke, the lady Madeline (for so was she called) passed through a remote portion of the apartment, and, without having noticed my presence, disappeared. I regarded her with an utter astonishment not unmingled with dread; and yet I found it impossible to account for such feelings. A sensation of stupor oppressed me as my eyes followed her retreating steps. When a door, at length, closed upon her, my glance sought instinctively and eagerly the countenance of the brother; but he had buried his face in his hands, and I could only perceive that a far more than ordinary wanness had overspread the emaciated fingers through which trickled many passionate tears.

The disease of the lady Madeline had long baffled the skill of her physicians. A settled apathy, a gradual wasting away of the person, and frequent although transient affections of a partially cataleptical character were the unusual diagnosis. Hitherto she had steadily borne up against the pressure of her malady, and had not betaken herself finally to bed; but on the closing in of the evening of my arrival at the house, she succumbed (as her brother told me at night with inexpressible agitation) to the prostrating power of the destroyer; and I learned that the glimpse I had obtained of her person would thus probably be the last I should obtain—that the lady, at least while living, would be seen by me no more.

For several days ensuing, her name was unmentioned by either Usher or myself; and during this period I was busied in earnest endeavors to alleviate the melancholy of my friend. We painted and read together, or I listened, as if in a dream, to the wild improvisations of his speaking guitar. And thus, as a closer and still closer intimacy admitted me more unreservedly into the recesses of his spirit, the more bitterly did I perceive the futility of all attempts at cheering a mind from which darkness, as if an inherent positive quality, poured forth upon all objects of the moral and physical universe in one unceasing radiation of gloom.

I shall ever bear about me a memory of the many solemn hours I thus spent alone with the master of the House of Usher. Yet I should fail in any attempt to convey an idea of the exact character of the studies, or of the occupations, in which he involved me, or led me the way. An excited and highly distempered ideality threw a sulphureous lustre over all. His long improvised dirges will ring forever in my ears. Among other things, I hold painfully in mind a certain singular perversion and amplification of the wild air of the last waltz of Von Weber. From the paintings over which his elaborate fancy brooded, and which grew, touch by touch, into vaguenesses at which I shuddered the more thrillingly, because I shuddered knowing not why—from these paintings (vivid as their images now are before me) I would in vain endeavor to educe more than a small portion which should lie within the compass of merely written words. By the utter simplicity, by the nakedness of his designs, he arrested and overawed attention. If ever mortal painted an idea, that mortal was Roderick Usher. For me at least, in the circumstances then surrounding me, there arose out of the pure abstractions which the hypochondriac contrived to throw upon his canvas, an intensity of intolerable awe, no shadow of which felt I ever yet in the contemplation of the certainly glowing yet too concrete reveries of Fuseli.

One of the phantasmagoric conceptions of my friend, partaking not so rigidly of the spirit of abstraction, may be shadowed forth, although feebly, in words. A small picture presented the interior of an immensely long and rectangular vault or tunnel, with low walls, smooth, white, and without interruption or device. Certain accessory points of the design served well to convey the idea that this excavation lay at an exceeding depth below the surface of the earth. No outlet was observed in any portion of its vast extent, and no torch or other artificial source of light was discernible; yet a flood of intense rays rolled throughout, and bathed the whole in a ghastly and inappropriate splendor.

I have just spoken of that morbid condition of the auditory nerve which rendered all music intolerable to the sufferer, with the exception of certain effects of stringed instruments. It was, perhaps, the narrow limits to which he thus confined himself upon the guitar which gave birth, in great measure, to the fantastic character of his performances. But the fervid *facility* of his *impromptus* could not be so accounted for. They must have been, and were, in the notes, as well as in the words of his wild fantasies (for he not unfrequently accompanied himself with rhymed verbal improvisations), the result of that intense mental collectedness and concentration to which I have previously alluded as observable only in particular moments of the highest artificial excitement. The words of one of these rhapsodies I have easily remembered. I was, perhaps, the more forcibly impressed with it as he gave it, because, in the under or mystic current of its meaning, I fancied that I perceived, and for the first time, a full consciousness on the part of Usher of the tottering of his lofty reason upon her throne. The verses, which were entitled "The Haunted Palace," ran very nearly, if not accurately, thus:—

I.

In the greenest of our valleys,
*   By good angels tenanted,*
Once a fair and stately palace—
*   Radiant palace—reared its head.*
In the monarch Thought's dominion—
*   It stood there!*
Never seraph spread a pinion
*   Over fabric half so fair.*

II.

Banners yellow, glorious, golden,
   On its roof did float and flow
(This—all this—was in the olden
      Time long ago);
And every gentle air that dallied,
      In that sweet day,
Along the ramparts plumed and pallid,
      A winged odor went away.

III.

Wanderers in that happy valley
   Through two luminous windows saw
Spirits moving musically
   To a lute's well-tuned law;
Round about a throne, where sitting
      (Porphyrogene!)
In state his glory well befitting,
   The ruler of the realm was seen.

IV.

And all with pearl and ruby glowing
   Was the fair palace door,
Through which came flowing, flowing, flowing
   And sparkling evermore,
A troop of Echoes whose sweet duty
      Was but to sing,
In voices of surpassing beauty,
   The wit and wisdom of their king.

V.

But evil things, in robes of sorrow,
   Assailed the monarch's high estate;
(Ah, let us mourn, for never morrow
   Shall dawn upon him, desolate!)
And, round about his home, the glory
      That blushed and bloomed
Is but a dim-remembered story
   Of the old time entombed.

VI.

And travellers now within that valley,
   Through the red-litten windows see
Vast forms that move fantastically
   To a discordant melody;
While, like a rapid ghastly river,
   Through the pale door;

> *A hideous throng rush out forever,*
> *And laugh—but smile no more.*

I well remember that suggestions arising from this ballad led us into a train of thought wherein there became manifest an opinion of Usher's which I mention not so much on account of its novelty (for other men have thought thus), as on account of the pertinacity with which he maintained it. This opinion, in its general form, was that of the sentience of all vegetable things. But in his disordered fancy, the idea had assumed a more daring character, and trespassed, under certain conditions, upon the kindgom of inorganization. I lack words to express the full extent, or the earnest *abandon* of his persuasion. The belief, however, was connected (as I have previously hinted) with the gray stones of the home of his forefathers. The conditions of the sentence had been here, he imagined fulfilled in the method of collocation of these stones—in the order of their arrangement, as well as in that of the many *fungi* which overspread them, and of the decayed trees which stood around—above all, in the long undisturbed endurance of this arrangement, and in its reduplication in the still waters of the tarn. Its evidence—the evidence of the sentience—was to be seen, he said (and I here started as he spoke) in the gradual yet certain condensation of an atmosphere of their own about the waters and the walls. The result was discoverable, he added, in that silent yet importunate and terrible influence which for centuries had moulded the destinies of his family, and which made *him* what I now saw him—what he was. Such opinions need no comment, and I will make none.

Our books—the books, which, for years, had formed no small portion of the mental existence of the invalid—were, as might be supposed, in strict keeping with this character of phantasm. We pored together over such works as the "Ververt et Chartreuse" of Gresset; the "Belphegor" of Machiavelli; the "Heaven and Hell" of Swedenborg; the "Subterranean Voyage of Nicholas Klimm" of Holberg; the "Chiromancy" of Robert Flud, of Jean D'Indaginé, and of Dela Chambre; the "Journey into the Blue Distance" of Tieck; and the "City of the Sun" of Campanella. One favorite volume was a small octavo edition of the "Directorium Inquisitorium," by the Dominican Eymeric de Gironne; and there were passages in Pomponius Mela, about the old African Satyrs and Œgipans, over which Usher would sit dreaming for hours. His chief delight, however, was found in the perusal of an exceedingly rare and curious book in quarto Gothic—the manual of a forgotten church—the *Vigiliæ Mortuorum Secundum Chorum Ecclesiæ Maguntinæ.*

I could not help thinking of the wild ritual of this work, and of its probable influence upon the hypochondriac, when, one evening, having informed me abruptly that the lady Madeline was no more, he stated his intention of preserving her corpse for a fortnight (previously to its final interment), in one of the numerous vaults within the main walls of the building. The worldly reason, however, assigned for this singular proceeding, was one which I did not feel at liberty to dispute. The brother had been led to his resolution (so he told me) by consideration of the unusual character of the malady of the deceased, of certain obtrusive and eager inquiries on the part of her medical men, and of the remote and exposed situation of the burial-ground of the family. I will not deny that when I called to mind the sinister countenance of the person whom I met upon the staircase, on the day of my arrival at the house, I had no desire to oppose what I regarded as at best but a harmless, and by no means an unnatural, precaution.

At the request of Usher, I personally aided him in the arrangements for the temporary entombment. The body having been encoffined, we two alone bore it to its rest. The vault in which we placed it (and which had been so long unopened that our torches, half smothered in its oppressive atmosphere, gave us little opportunity for investigation) was small, damp, and entirely without means of admission for light; lying, at great depth, immediately beneath that portion of the building in which was my own sleeping apartment. It had been used, apparently, in remote feudal times, for the worst purposes of donjon-keep, and in later days, as a place of deposit for powder, or some other highly combustible substance, as a portion of its floor, and the whole interior of a long archway through which we reached it, were carefully sheathed with copper. The door, of massive iron, also, similarly protected. Its immense weight caused an unusually sharp, grating sound, as it moved upon its hinges.

Having deposited our mournful burden upon tressels within this region of horror, we partially turned aside the yet unscrewed lid of the coffin, and looked upon the face of the tenant. A striking similitude between the brother and sister now first arrested my attention; and Usher, divining, perhaps, my thoughts, murmured out some few words from which I learned that the deceased and himself had been twins, and that sympathies of a scarcely intelligible nature had always existed between them. Our glances, however, rested not long upon the dead—for we could not regard her unawed. The disease which had thus entombed the lady in the maturity of youth, had left, as usual in all maladies of a strictly cataleptical character, the mockery of a faint blush upon the bosom and the face, and that suspiciously lingering smile upon the lip which is so terrible in death. We replaced and screwed down the lid, and, having secured the door of iron, made our way, with toil, into the scarcely less gloomy apartments of the upper portion of the house.

And now, some days of bitter grief having elapsed, an observable change came over the features of the mental disorder of my friend. His ordinary manner had vanished. His occupations were neglected or forgotten. He roamed from chamber to chamber with hurried, unequal, and objectless step. The pallor of his countenance had assumed, if possible, a more ghastly hue—but the luminousness of his eye had utterly gone out. The once occasional huskiness of his tone was heard no more; and a tremendous quaver, as if of extreme terror, habitually characterized his utterance. There were times, indeed, when I thought his unceasingly agitated mind was laboring with some oppressive secret, to divulge which he struggled for the necessary courage. At times, again, I was obliged to resolve all into the mere inexplicable vagaries of madness, for I beheld him gazing upon vacancy for long hours, in an attitude of the profoundest attention, as if listening to some imaginary sound. It was no wonder that his condition terrified—that it infected me. I felt creeping upon me, by slow yet certain degrees, the wild influences of his own fantastic yet impressive superstitions.

It was, especially, upon retiring to bed late in the night of the seventh or eighth day after the placing of the lady Madeline within the donjon, that I experienced the full power of such feelings. Sleep came not near my couch—while the hours waned and waned away. I struggled to reason off the nervousness which had dominion over me. I endeavored to believe that much, if not all of what I felt, was due to the bewildering influence of the gloomy furniture of the room—of the dark and tattered draperies, which, tortured into motion by the breath of a rising tempest, swayed fitfully to and fro upon the walls, and rustled uneasily about the decorations of the bed. But my efforts were fruitless. An irrepressible tremor gradually pervaded my frame; and, at length, there sat upon my very heart an incubus of utterly causeless alarm. Shaking this off with a gasp and a struggle, I uplifted myself upon the pillows, and, peering earnestly within the intense darkness of the chamber, hearkened—I know not why, except that an instinctive spirit prompted me—to certain low and indefinite sounds which came, through the pauses of the storm, at long intervals, I knew not whence. Overpowered by an intense sentiment of horror, unaccountable yet unendurable, I threw on my clothes with haste (for I felt that I should sleep no more during the night), and endeavored to arouse myself from the pitiable condition into which I had fallen, by pacing rapidly to and fro through the apartment.

I had taken but few turns in this manner, when a light step on an adjoining staircase arrested my attention. I presently recognized it as that of Usher. In an instant afterward he rapped, with a gentle touch, at my door, and entered, bearing a lamp. His countenance was, as usual, cadaverously wan—but, moreover, there was a species of mad hilarity in his eyes—an evidently restrained *hysteria* in his whole demeanor. His air appalled me—but any thing was preferable to the solitude which I had so long endured, and I even welcomed his presence as a relief.

"And you have not seen it?" he said abruptly after having stared about him for some moments in silence—"you have not then seen it?—but, stay! you shall." Thus speaking, and having carefully shaded his lamp, he hurried to one of the casements, and threw it freely open to the storm.

The impetuous fury of the entering gust nearly lifted us from our feet.

It was, indeed, a tempestuous yet sternly beautiful night, and one wildly singular in its terror and its beauty. A whirlwind had apparently collected its force in our vicinity; for there were frequent and violent alterations in the direction of the wind; and the exceeding density of the clouds (which hung so low as to press upon the turrets of the house) did not prevent our perceiving the life-like velocity with which they flew careering from all points against each other, without passing away into the distance. I say that even their exceeding density did not prevent our perceiving this—yet we had no glimpse of the moon or stars, nor was there any flashing forth of the lightning. But the under surfaces of the huge masses of agitated vapor, as well as all terrestrial objects immediately around us, were glowing in the unnatural light of a faintly luminous and distinctly visible gaseous exhalation which hung about and enshrouded the mansion.

"You must not—you shall not behold this!" said I, shuddering, to Usher, as I led him, with a gentle violence, from the window to a seat. "These appearances, which bewilder you, are merely electrical phenomena not uncommon—or it may be that they have their ghastly origin in the rank miasma of the tarn. Let us close this casement;—the air is chilling and dangerous to your frame. Here is one of your favorite romances. I will read, and you shall listen: —and so we will pass away this terrible night together."

The antique volume which I had taken up was the "Mad Trist" of Sir Launcelot Canning; but I had called it a favorite of Usher's more in sad jest than in earnest; for, in truth, there is little in its uncouth and unimaginative prolixity which could have had interest for the lofty and spiritual ideality of my friend. It was, however, the only book immediately at hand; and I indulged a vague hope that the excitement which now agitated the hypochondriac, might find relief (for the history of mental disorder is full of similar anomalies) even in the extremeness of the folly which I should read. Could I have judged, indeed, by the wild overstrained air of vivacity with which he hearkened, or apparently hearkened, to the words of the tale, I might well have congratulated myself upon the success of my design.

I had arrived at that well-known portion of the story where Ethelred, the hero of the Trist, having sought in vain for peaceable admission into the dwelling of the hermit, proceeds to make good an entrance by force. Here, it will be remembered, the words of the narrative run thus:

"And Ethelred, who was by nature of a doughty heart, and who was now mighty withal, on account of the powerfulness of the wine which he had drunken, waited no longer to hold parley with the hermit, who, in sooth, was of an obstinate and maliceful turn, but, feeling the rain upon his shoulders, and fearing the rising of the tempest, uplifted his mace outright, and, with blows, made quickly room in the plankings of the door for his gauntleted hand; and now pulling therewith sturdily, he so cracked, and ripped, and tore all asunder, that the noise of the dry and hollow-sounding wood alarumed and reverberated throughout the forest."

At the termination of this sentence I started and, for a moment, paused; for it appeared to me (although I at once concluded that my excited fancy had deceived me)—it appeared to me that, from some very remote portion of the mansion, there came, indistinctly to my ears, what might have been, in its exact similarity of character, the echo (but a stifled and dull one certainly) of the very cracking and ripping sound which Sir Launcelot had so particularly described. It was, beyond doubt, the coincidence alone which had arrested my attention; for, amid the rattling of the sashes of the casements, and the ordinary commingled noises of the still increasing storm, the sound, in itself, had nothing, surely, which should have interested or disturbed me. I continued the story:

"But the good champion Ethelred, now entering within the door, was sore enraged and amazed to perceive no signal of the maliceful hermit; but, in the stead thereof, a dragon of a scaly and prodigious demeanor, and of a fiery tongue, which sate in guard before a palace of gold, with a floor of silver; and upon the wall there hung a shield of shining brass with this legend enwritten—

> *Who entereth herein, a conqueror hath bin;*
> *Who slayeth the dragon, the shield he shall win.*

And Ethelred uplifted his mace, and struck upon the head of the dragon, which fell before him, and gave up his pesty breath, with a shriek so horrid and harsh, and withal so piercing, that Ethelred had fain to close his ears with his hands against the dreadful noise of it, like the whereof was never before heard."

Here again I paused abruptly, and now with a feeling of wild amazement—for there could be no doubt whatever that, in this instance, I did actually hear (although from what direction it proceeded I found it impossible to say) a low and apparently distant, but harsh, protracted, and most unusual screaming or grating sound—the exact counterpart of what my fancy had already conjured up for the dragon's unnatural shriek as described by the romancer.

Oppressed, as I certainly was, upon the occurrence of this second and most extraordinary coincidence, by a thousand conflicting sensations, in which wonder and extreme terror were predominant, I still retained sufficient presence of mind to avoid exciting, by any observation, the sensitive nervousness of my companion. I was by no means certain that he had noticed the sounds in question; although, assuredly, a strange alteration had, during the last few minutes, taken place in his demeanor. From a position fronting my own, he had gradually brought round his chair, so as to sit with his face to the door of the chamber; and thus I could but partially perceive his features, although I saw that his lips trembled as if he were murmuring inaudibly. His head had dropped upon his breast—yet I knew that he was not asleep, from the wide and rigid opening of the eye as I caught a glance of it in profile. The motion of his body, too, was at variance with this idea—for he rocked from side to side with a gentle yet constant and uniform sway. Having rapidly taken notice of all this, I resumed the narrative of Sir Launcelot, which thus proceeded:

"And now, the champion, having escaped from the terrible fury of the dragon, bethinking himself of the brazen shield, and of the breaking up of the enchantment which was upon it, removed the carcass from out of the way before him, and approached valorously over the silver pavement of the castle to where the shield was upon the wall; which in sooth tarried not for his full coming, but fell down at his feet upon the silver floor, with a mighty great and terrible ringing sound."

No sooner had these syllables passed my lips, than—as if a shield of brass had indeed, at the moment, fallen heavily upon a floor of silver—I became aware of a distinct, hollow, metallic, and clangorous, yet apparently muffled, reverberation. Completely unnerved, I leaped to my feet; but the measured rocking movement of Usher was undisturbed. I rushed to the chair in which he sat. His eyes were bent fixedly before him, and throughout his whole countenance there reigned a stony rigidity. But, as I placed my hand upon his shoulder, there came a strong shudder over his whole person; a sickly smile quivered about his lips; and I saw that he spoke in a low, hurried, and gibbering murmur, as if unconscious of my presence. Bending closely over him, I at length drank in the hideous import of his words.

"Now hear it?—yes, I hear it, and *have* heard it. Long—long—long—many minutes, many hours, many days, have I heard it—yet I dared not—oh, pity me, miserable wretch that I am!—I dared not—I *dared* not speak! *We have put her living in the tomb!* Said I not that my senses were acute? I *now* tell you that I heard her first feeble movements in the hollow coffin. I heard them—many, many days ago—yet I dared not—*I dared not speak!* And now—to-night—Ethelred—ha! ha!—the breaking of the hermit's door, and the death-cry of the dragon, and the clangor of the shield—say, rather, the rending of her coffin, and the grating of the iron hinges of her prison, and her struggles within the coppered archway of the vault! Oh! whither shall I fly? Will she not be here anon? Is she not hurrying to upbraid me for my haste? Have I not heard her footstep on the stair? Do I not distinguish that heavy and horrible beating of her heart? Madman!"—here he sprang furiously to his feet, and shrieked out his syllables, as if in the effort he were giving up his soul—*"Madman! I tell you that she now stands without the door!"*

As if in the superhuman energy of his utterance there had been found the potency of a spell, the huge antique panels to which the speaker pointed threw slowly back, upon the instant, their ponderous and ebony jaws. It was the work of the rushing gust—but then without those doors there *did* stand the lofty and enshrouded figure of the lady Madeline of

Usher. There was blood upon her white robes, and the evidence of some bitter struggle upon every portion of her emaciated frame. For a moment she remained trembling and reeling to and fro upon the threshold—then, with a low moaning cry, fell heavily inward upon the person of her brother, and in her violent and now final death-agonies, bore him to the floor a corpse, and a victim to the terrors he had anticipated.

From that chamber, and from that mansion, I fled aghast. The storm was still abroad in all its wrath as I found myself crossing the old causeway. Suddenly there shot along the path a wild light, and I turned to see whence a gleam so unusual could have issued; for the vast house and its shadows were alone behind me. The radiance was that of the full, setting, and blood-red moon, which now shone vividly through that once barely discernible fissure, of which I have before spoken as extending from the roof of the building, in a zigzag direction, to the base. While I gazed, this fissure rapidly widened—there came a fierce breath of the whirlwind—the entire orb of the satellite burst at once upon my sight—my brain reeled as I saw the mighty walls rushing asunder—there was a long tumultuous shouting sound like the voice of a thousand waters—and the deep and dank tarn at my feet closed sullenly and silently over the fragments of the *"House of Usher."*

Flowering Judas

KATHERINE ANNE PORTER

Braggioni sits heaped upon the edge of a straight-backed chair much too small for him, and sings to Laura in a furry, mournful voice. Laura has begun to find reasons for avoiding her own house until the latest possible moment, for Braggioni is there almost every night. No matter how late she is, he will be sitting there with a surly, waiting expression, pulling at his kinky yellow hair, thumbing the strings of his guitar, snarling a tune under his breath. Lupe the Indian maid meets Laura at the door, and says with a flicker of a glance towards the upper room, "He waits."

Laura wishes to lie down, she is tired of her hairpins and the feel of her long tight sleeves, but she says to him, "Have you a new song for me this evening?" If he says yes, she asks him to sing it. If he says no, she remembers his favorite one, and asks him to sing it again. Lupe brings her a cup of chocolate and a plate of rice, and Laura eats at the small table under the lamp, first inviting Braggioni, whose answer is always the same: "I have eaten, and besides, chocolate thickens the voice."

Laura says, "Sing, then," and Braggioni heaves himself into song. He scratches the guitar familiarly as though it were a pet animal, and sings passionately off key, taking the high notes in a prolonged painful squeal. Laura, who haunts the markets listening to the ballad singers, and stops every day to hear the blind boy playing his reed-flute in Sixteenth of September Street, listens to Braggioni with pitiless courtesy, because she dares not smile at his miserable performance. Nobody dares to smile at him. Braggioni is cruel to everyone, with a kind of specialized insolence, but he is so vain of his talents, and so sensitive to slights, it would require a cruelty and vanity greater than his own to lay a finger on the vast cureless wound of his self-esteem. It would require courage, too, for it is dangerous to offend him, and nobody has this courage.

Braggioni loves himself with such tenderness and amplitude and eternal charity that his followers—for he is a leader of men, a skilled revolutionist, and his skin has been punctured in honorable warfare—warm themselves in the reflected glow, and say to each other: "He has a real nobility, a love of humanity raised above mere personal affections." The excess of this self-love has flowed out, inconveniently for her, over Laura, who, with so many others, owes her comfortable situation and her salary to him. When he is in a very good humor, he tells her, "I am tempted to forgive you for being a *gringa, gringita!*" and Laura, burning, imagines herself leaning forward suddenly, and with a sound back-handed slap wiping the suety smile from his face. If he notices her eyes at these moments he gives no sign.

She knows what Braggioni would offer her, and she must resist tena-ciously without appearing to resist, and if she could avoid it she would not admit even to herself the slow drift of his intention. During these long eve-nings which have spoiled a long month for her, she sits in her deep chair with an open book on her knees, resting her eyes on the consoling rigidity of the printed page when the sight and sound of Braggioni singing threaten to identify themselves with all her remembered afflictions and to add their weight to her uneasy premonitions of the future. The gluttonous bulk of Braggioni has become a symbol of her many disillusions, for a revo-lutionist should be lean, animated by heroic faith, a vessel of abstract vir-tues. This is nonsense, she knows it now and is ashamed of it. Revolution must have leaders, and leadership is a career for energetic men. She is, her comrades tell her, full of romantic error, for what she defines as cynicism in them is merely "a developed sense of reality." She is almost too willing to say, "I am wrong, I suppose I don't really understand the principles," and afterward she makes a secret truce with herself, determined not to surren-der her will to such expedient logic. But she cannot help feeling that she has been betrayed irreparably by the disunion between her way of living and her feeling of what life should be, and at times she is almost contented to rest in this sense of grievance as a private store of consolation. Some-times she wishes to run away, but she stays. Now she longs to fly out of this room, down the narrow stairs, and into the street where the houses lean to-gether like conspirators under a single mottled lamp, and leave Braggioni singing to himself.

Instead she looks at Braggioni, frankly and clearly, like a good child who understands the rules of behavior. Her knees cling together under sound blue serge, and her round white collar is not purposely nun-like. She wears the uniform of an idea, and has renounced vanities. She was born Roman Catholic, and in spite of her fear of being seen by someone who might make a scandal of it, she slips now and again into some crumbling little church, kneels on the chilly stone, and says a Hail Mary on the gold rosary she bought in Tehuantepec. It is no good and she ends by examining the altar with its tinsel flowers and ragged brocades, and feels tender about the battered doll-shape of some male saint whose white, lace-trimmed drawers hang limply around his ankles below the hieratic dignity of his velvet robe. She has encased herself in a set of principles derived from her early training, leaving no detail of gesture or of personal taste untouched, and for this reason she will not wear lace made on machines. This is her private heresy, for in her special group the machine is sacred, and will be the salvation of the workers. She loves fine lace, and there is a tiny edge of fluted cobweb on this collar, which is one of twenty precisely alike, folded in blue tissue paper in the upper drawer of her clothes chest.

Braggioni catches her glance solidly as if he had been waiting for it, leans forward, balancing his paunch between his spread knees, and sings with tremendous emphasis, weighing his words. He has, the song relates, no father and no mother, nor even a friend to console him; lonely as a wave of the sea he comes and goes, lonely as a wave. His mouth opens round and yearns sideways, his balloon cheeks grow oily with the labor of song. He bulges marvelously in his expensive garments. Over his lavender collar, crushed upon a purple necktie, held by a diamond hoop: over his ammunition belt of tooled leather worked in silver, buckled cruelly around his gasping middle: over the tops of his glossy yellow shoes Braggioni swells with ominous ripeness, his mauve silk hose stretched taut, his ankles bound with the stout leather thongs of his shoes.

When he stretches his eyelids at Laura she notes again that his eyes are the true tawny yellow cat's eyes. He is rich, not in money, he tells her, but in power, and this power brings with it the blameless ownership of things, and the right to indulge his love of small luxuries. "I have a taste for the elegant refinements," he said once, flourishing a yellow silk handkerchief before her nose. "Smell that? It is Jockey Club, imported from New York." Nonetheless he is wounded by life. He will say so presently. "It is true everything turns to dust in the hand, to gall on the tongue." He sighs and his leather belt creaks like a saddle girth. "I am disappointed in everything as it comes. Everything." He shakes his head. "You, poor thing, you will be disappointed too. You are born for it. We are more alike than you realize in some things. Wait and see. Some day you will remember what I have told you, you will know that Braggioni was your friend."

Laura feels a slow chill, a purely physical sense of danger, a warning in her blood that violence, mutilation, a shocking death, wait for her with lessening patience. She has translated this fear into something homely, immediate, and sometimes hesitates before crossing the street. "My personal fate is nothing, except as the testimony of a mental attitude," she reminds herself, quoting from some forgotten philosophic primer, and is sensible enough to add, "Anyhow, I shall not be killed by an automobile if I can help it."

"It may be true I am as corrupt, in another way, as Braggioni," she thinks in spite of herself, "as callous, as incomplete," and if this is so, any kind of death seems preferable. Still she sits quietly, she does not run. Where could she go? Uninvited she has promised herself to this place; she can no longer imagine herself as living in another country, and there is no pleasure in remembering her life before she came here.

Precisely what is the nature of this devotion, its true motives, and what are its obligations? Laura cannot say. She spends part of her days in Xochimilco, near by, teaching Indian children to say in English, "The cat is on the mat." When she appears in the classroom they crowd about her with smiles on their wise, innocent, clay-colored faces, crying "Good morning, my titcher!" in immaculate voices, and they make her desk a fresh garden of flowers every day.

During her leisure she goes to union meetings and listens to busy important voices quarreling over tactics, methods, internal politics. She visits the prisoners of her own political faith in their cells, where they entertain themselves with counting cockroaches, repenting of their indiscretions, composing their memoirs, writing out manifestoes and plans for their comrades who are still walking about free, hands in pockets, sniffing fresh air. Laura brings them food and cigarettes and a little money, and she brings messages disguised in equivocal phrases from the men outside who dare not set foot in the prison for fear of disappearing into the cells kept empty for them. If the prisoners confuse night and day, and complain, "Dear little Laura, time doesn't pass in this infernal hole, and I won't know when it is time to sleep unless I have a reminder," she brings them their favorite narcotics, and says in a tone that does not wound them with pity, "Tonight will really be night for you," and though her Spanish amuses them they find her comforting, useful. If they lose patience and all faith, and curse the slowness of their friends in coming to their rescue with money and influence, they trust her not to repeat everything, and if she inquires, "Where do you think we can find money, or influence?" they are certain to answer, "Well, there is Braggioni, why doesn't he do something?"

She smuggles letters from headquarters to men hiding from firing squads in back streets in mildewed houses, where they sit in tumbled beds and talk bitterly as if all Mexico were at their heels, when Laura knows positively they might appear at the band concert in the Alameda on Sunday morning, and no one would notice them. But Braggioni says, "Let them sweat a little. The next time they may be careful. It is very restful to have them out of the way for a while." She is not afraid to knock on any door in any street after midnight, and enter in the darkness, and say to one of these men who is really in danger: "They will be looking for you—seriously—tomorrow morning after six. Here is some money from Vicente. Go to Vera Cruz and wait."

She borrows money from the Rumanian agitator to give to his bitter enemy the Polish agitator. The favor of Braggioni is their disputed territory, and Braggioni holds the balance nicely, for he can use them both. The Polish agitator talks love to her over café tables, hoping to exploit what he believes is her secret sentimental preference for him, and he gives her misinformation which he begs her to repeat as the solemn truth to certain persons. The Rumanian is more adroit. He is generous with his money in all good causes, and lies to her with an air of ingenuous candor, as if he were her good friend and confidant. She never repeats anything they may say. Braggioni never asks questions. He has other ways to discover all that he wishes to know about them.

Nobody touches her, but all praise her gray eyes, and the soft, round under lip which promises gaiety, yet is always grave, nearly always firmly closed: and they cannot understand why she is in Mexico. She walks back and forth on her errands, with puzzled eyebrows, carrying her little folder of drawings and music and school papers. No dancer dances more beautifully than Laura walks, and she inspires some amusing, unexpected ardors, which cause little gossip, because nothing comes of them. A young captain who had been a soldier in Zapata's army attempted, during a horseback ride near Cuernavaca, to express his desire for her with the noble simplicity befitting a rude folk-hero; but gently, because he was gentle. This gentleness was his defeat, for when he alighted, and removed her foot from the stirrup, and essayed to draw her down into his arms, her horse, ordinarily a tame one, shied fiercely, reared and plunged away. The young hero's horse careened blindly after his stable-mate, and the hero did not return to the hotel until rather late that evening. At breakfast he came to her table in full charro dress, gray buckskin jacket and trousers with strings of silver buttons down the leg, and he was in a humorous, careless mood. "May I sit with you?" and "You are a wonderful rider. I was terrified that you might be thrown and dragged. I should never have forgiven myself. But I cannot admire you enough for your riding."

"I learned to ride in Arizona," said Laura.

"If you will ride with me again this morning, I promise you a horse that will not shy with you," he said. But Laura remembered that she must return to Mexico City at noon.

Next morning the children made a celebration and spent their playtime writing on the blackboard, "We lov ar titcher," and with tinted chalks they drew wreaths of flowers around the words. The young hero wrote her a letter: "I am a very foolish, wasteful, impulsive man. I should have first said I love you, and then you would not have run away. But you shall see me again." Laura thought, "I must send him a box of colored crayons," but she was trying to forgive herself for having spurred her horse at the wrong moment.

A brown shock-haired youth came and stood in her patio one night and sang like a lost soul for two hours, but Laura could think of nothing to do about it. The moonlight spread a wash of gauzy silver over the clear spaces of the garden, and the shadows were cobalt blue. The scarlet blossoms of the Judas tree were dull purple, and the names of the colors repeated themselves automatically in her mind, while she watched not the boy, but his shadow, fallen like a dark garment across the fountain rim, trailing in the water. Lupe came silently and whispered expert counsel in her ear: "If you will throw him one little flower, he will sing another song or two and go away." Laura threw the flower, and he sang a last song and went away with the flower tucked in the band of his hat. Lupe said, "He is one of the organizers of the Typographers Union, and before that he sold corridos in the Merced market, and before that, he came from Guanajuato, where I was born. I would not trust any man, but I trust least those from Guanajuato."

She did not tell Laura that he would be back again the next day, and the next, nor that he would follow her at a certain fixed distance around the Merced market, through the Zocolo, up Francesco I. Madero Avenue, and so along the Paseo de la Reforma to Chapultepec Park, and into the Philosopher's Footpath, still with that flower withering in his hat, and an indivisible attention in his eyes.

Now Laura is accustomed to him, it means nothing except that he is nineteen years old and is observing a convention with all propriety, as though it were founded on a law of nature, which in the end it might very well prove to be. He is beginning to write poems which he prints on a wooden press, and he leaves them stuck like handbills in her door. She is pleasantly disturbed by the abstract, unhurried watchfulness of his black eyes which will in time turn easily toward another object. She tells herself that throwing the flower was a mistake, for she is twenty-two years old and knows better; but she refuses to regret it, and persuades herself that her negation of all external events as they occur is a sign that she is gradually perfecting herself in the stoicism she strives to cultivate against that disaster she fears, though she cannot name it.

She is not at home in the world. Every day she teaches children who remain strangers to her, though she loves their tender round hands and their charming opportunistic savagery. She knocks at unfamiliar doors not knowing whether a friend or a stranger shall answer, and even if a known face emerges from the sour gloom of that unknown interior, still it is the face of a stranger. No matter what this stranger says to her, nor what her message to him, the very cells of her flesh reject knowledge and kinship in one monotonous word. No. No. No. She draws her strength from this one holy talismanic word which does not suffer her to be led into evil. Denying everything, she may walk anywhere in safety, she looks at everything without amazement.

No, repeats this firm unchanging voice of her blood; and she looks at Braggioni without amazement. He is a great man, he wishes to impress this simple girl who covers her great round breasts with thick dark cloth, and who hides long, invaluably beautiful legs under a heavy skirt. She is almost thin except for the incomprehensible fullness of her breasts, like a nursing mother's, and Braggioni, who considers himself a judge of women, specu lates again on the puzzle of her notorious virginity, and takes the liberty of speech which she permits without a sign of modesty, indeed, without any sort of sign, which is disconcerting.

"You think you are so cold, *gringita!* Wait and see. You will surprise yourself someday! May I be there to advise you!" He stretches his eyelids at her, and his ill-humored cat's eyes waver in a separate glance for the two points of light marking the opposite ends of a smoothly drawn path between the swollen curve of her breasts. He is not put off by that blue serge, nor by her resolutely fixed gaze. There is all the time in the world. His cheeks are bellying with the wind of song. "O girl with the dark eyes," he sings, and reconsiders. "But yours are not dark. I can change all that. O girl with the green eyes, you have stolen my heart away." Then his mind wanders to the song, and Laura feels the weight of his attention being shifted elsewhere. Singing thus, he seems harmless, he is quite harmless, there is nothing to do but sit patiently and say, "No," when the moment comes. She draws a full breath, and her mind wanders also, but not far. She dares not wander too far.

Not for nothing has Braggioni taken pains to be a good revolutionist and a professional lover of humanity. He will never die of it. He has the malice, the cleverness, the wickedness, the sharpness of wit, the hardness of heart, stipulated for loving the world profitably. He *will never die of it.* He will live to see himself kicked out from his feeding trough by other hungry world-saviors. Traditionally he must sing in spite of his life which drives him to bloodshed, he tells Laura, for his father was a Tuscany peasant who drifted to Yucatan and married a Maya woman: a woman of race, an aristocrat. They gave him the love and knowledge of music, thus: and under the rip of his thumbnail, the strings of the instrument complain like exposed nerves.

Once he was called Delgadito by all the girls and married women who ran after him; he was so scrawny all his bones showed under his thin cotton clothing, and he could squeeze his emptiness to the very backbone with his two hands. He was a poet and the revolution was only a dream then; too many women loved him and sapped away his youth, and he could never find enough to eat anywhere, anywhere! Now he is a leader of men, crafty men who whisper in his ear, hungry men who wait for hours outside his office for a word with him, emaciated men with wild faces who waylay him at the street gate with a timid, "Comrade, let me tell you . . ." and they blow the foul breath from their empty stomachs in his face.

He is always sympathetic. He gives them handfuls of small coins from his own pockets, he promises them work, there will be demonstrations, they must join the unions and attend the meetings, above all they must be on the watch for spies. They are closer to him than his own brothers, without them he can do nothing—until tomorrow, comrade!

Until tomorrow. "They are stupid, they are lazy, they are treacherous, they would cut my throat for nothing," he says to Laura. He has good food

and abundant drink, he hires an automobile and drives in the Paseo on
Sunday morning, and enjoys plenty of sleep in a soft bed beside a wife who
dares not disturb him; and he sits pampering his bones in easy billows of
fat, singing to Laura, who knows and thinks these things about him. When
he was fifteen, he tried to drown himself because he loved a girl, his first
love, and she laughed at him. "A thousand women have paid for that," and
his tight little mouth turns down at the corners. Now he perfumes his hair
with Jockey Club, and confides to Laura: "One woman is really as good as
another for me in the dark. I prefer them all."

His wife organizes unions among the girls in the cigarette factories, and
walks in picket lines, and even speaks at meetings in the evening. But she
cannot be brought to acknowledge the benefits of true liberty. "I tell her I
must have my freedom, net. She does not understand my point of view."
Laura has heard this many times. Braggioni scratches the guitar and medi-
tates. "She is an instinctively virtuous woman, pure gold, no doubt of that.
If she were not, I should lock her up, and she knows it."

His wife, who works so hard for the good of the factory girls, employs
part of her leisure lying on the floor weeping because there are so many
women in the world, and only one husband for her, and she never knows
where nor when to look for him. He told her: "Unless you can learn to cry
when I am not here, I must go away for good." That day he went away and
took a room at the Hotel Madrid.

It is this month of separation for the sake of higher principles that has
been spoiled not only for Mrs. Braggioni, whose sense of reality is beyond
criticism, but for Laura, who feels herself bogged in a nightmare. Tonight
Laura envies Mrs. Braggioni, who is alone, and free to weep as much as she
pleases about a concrete wrong. Laura has just come from a visit to the
prison, and she is waiting for tomorrow with a bitter anxiety as if tomorrow
may not come, but time may be caught immovably in this hour, with herself
transfixed, Braggioni singing on forever, and Eugenio's body not yet discovered by the guard.

Braggioni says: "Are you going to sleep?" Almost before she can shake
her head, he begins telling her about the May-day disturbances coming on
in Morelia, for the Catholics hold a festival in honor of the Blessed Virgin,
and the Socialists celebrate their martyrs on that day. "There will be two independent processions, starting from either end of town, and they will
march until they meet, and the rest depends. . . ." He asks her to oil and
load his pistols. Standing up, he unbuckles his ammunition belt, and
spreads it laden across her knees. Laura sits with the shells slipping
through the cleaning cloth dipped in oil, and he says again he cannot understand why she works so hard for the revolutionary idea unless she loves
some man who is in it. "Are you not in love with someone?" "No," says
Laura. "And no one is in love with you?" "No." "Then it is your own fault.
No woman need go begging. Why, what is the matter with you? The legless

beggar woman in the Alameda has a perfectly faithful lover. Did you know that?"

Laura peers down the pistol barrel and says nothing, but a long, slow faintness rises and subsides in her; Braggioni curves his swollen fingers around the throat of the guitar and softly smothers the music out of it, and when she hears him again he seems to have forgotten her, and is speaking in the hypnotic voice he uses when talking in small rooms to a listening, close-gathered crowd. Some day this world, now seemingly so composed and eternal, to the edges of every sea shall be merely a tangle of gaping trenches, of crashing walls and broken bodies. Everything must be torn from its accustomed place where it has rotted for centuries, hurled skyward and distributed, cast down again clean as rain, without separate identity. Nothing shall survive that the stiffened hands of poverty have created for the rich and no one shall be left alive except the elect spirits destined to procreate a new world cleansed of cruelty and injustice, ruled by benevolent anarchy: "Pistols are good, I love them, cannon are even better, but in the end I pin my faith to good dynamite," he concludes, and strokes the pistol lying in her hands. "Once I dreamed of destroying this city, in case it offered resistance to General Ortiz, but it fell into his hands like an overripe pear."

He is made restless by his own words, rises and stands waiting. Laura holds up the belt to him: "Put that on, and go kill somebody in Morelia, and you will be happier," she says softly. The presence of death in the room makes her bold. "Today, I found Eugenio going into a stupor. He refused to allow me to call the prison doctor. He had taken all the tablets I brought him yesterday. He said he took them because he was bored."

"He is a fool, and his death is his own business," says Braggioni, fastening his belt carefully.

"I told him if he had waited only a little while longer, you would have got him set free," says Laura. "He said he did not want to wait."

"He is a fool and we are well rid of him," says Braggioni, reaching for his hat.

He goes away. Laura knows his mood has changed, she will not see him any more for a while. He will send word when he needs her to go on errands into strange streets, to speak to the strange faces that will appear, like clay masks with the power of human speech, to mutter their thanks to Braggioni for his help. Now she is free, and she thinks, I must run while there is time. But she does not go.

Braggioni enters his own house where for a month his wife has spent many hours every night weeping and tangling her hair upon her pillow. She is weeping now, and she weeps more at the sight of him, the cause of all her sorrows. He looks about the room. Nothing is changed, the smells are good and familiar, he is well acquainted with the woman who comes toward him with no reproach except grief on her face. He says to her tenderly: "You are so good, please don't cry any more, you dear good creature." She says, "Are you tired, my angel? Sit here and I will wash your feet." She brings a bowl of water, and kneeling, unlaces his shoes, and when from her knees she raises her sad eyes under her blackened lids, he is sorry for everything, and bursts into tears. "Ah, yes, I am hungry, I am tired, let us eat something together," he says, between sobs. His wife leans her head on his arm and says, "Forgive me!" and this time he is refreshed by the solemn, endless rain of her tears.

Laura takes off her serge dress and puts on a white linen nightgown and goes to bed. She turns her head a little to one side, and lying still, reminds herself that it is time to sleep. Numbers tick in her brain like little clocks, soundless doors close of themselves around her. If you would sleep, you must not remember anything, the children will say tomorrow, good morning, my teacher, the poor prisoners who come every day bringing flowers to their jailer. 1-2-3-4-5—it is monstrous to confuse love with revolution, night with day, life with death—ah Eugenio!

The tolling of the midnight bell is a signal, but what does it mean? Get up, Laura, and follow me: come out of your sleep, out of your bed, out of this strange house. What are you doing in this house? Without a word, without fear she rose and reached for Eugenio's hand, but he eluded her with a sharp, sly smile and drifted away. This is not all, you shall see—Murderer, he said, follow me, I will show you a new country, but it is far away and we must hurry. No, said Laura, not unless you take my hand, no; and she clung first to the stair rail, and then to the topmost branch of the Judas tree that bent down slowly and set her upon the earth, and then to the rocky ledge of a cliff, and then to the jagged wave of a sea that was not water but a desert of crumbling stone. Where are you taking me? she asked in wonder but without fear. To death, and it is a long way off, and we must hurry, said Eugenio. No, said Laura, not unless you take my hand. Then eat these flowers, poor prisoner, said Eugenio in a voice of pity, take and eat: and from the Judas tree he stripped the warm bleeding flowers, and held them to her lips. She saw that his hand was fleshless, a cluster of small white petrified branches, and his eye sockets were without light, but she ate the flowers greedily for they satisfied both hunger and thirst. Murderer! said Eugenio, and Cannibal! This is my body and my blood. Laura cried No! and at the sound of her own voice, she awoke trembling, and was afraid to sleep again.

Mannequin

JEAN RHYS

Twelve o'clock. Déjeuner chez Jeanne Veron, Place Vendôme.

Anna, dressed in the black cotton, chemise-like garment of the manne-quin off duty was trying to find her way along dark passages and down complicated flights of stairs to the underground room where lunch was served.

She was shivering, for she had forgotten her coat, and the garment that she wore was very short, sleeveless, displaying her rose-coloured stockings to the knee. Her hair was flamingly and honestly red; her eyes, which were very gentle in expression, brown and heavily shadowed with kohl; her face small and pale under its professional rouge. She was fragile, like a delicate child, her arms pathetically thin. It was to her legs that she owed this daz-zling, this incredible opportunity.

Madame Veron, white-haired with black eyes incredibly distinguished, who had given them one sweeping glance, the glance of the connoisseur, smiled imperiously and engaged her at an exceedingly small salary. As a beginner, Madame explained, Anna could not expect more. She was to wear the jeune fille dresses. Another smile, another sharp glance.

Anna was conducted from the Presence by an underling who helped her to take off the frock she had worn temporarily for the interview. Aspirants for an engagement are always dressed in a model of the house.

She had spent yesterday afternoon in a delirium tempered by a feeling of exaggerated reality, and in buying the necessary make up. It had been such a forlorn hope, answering the advertisement.

The morning had been dreamlike. At the back of the wonderfully decor-ated salons she had found an unexpected sombreness; the place, empty, would have been dingy and melancholy, countless puzzling corridors and staircases, a rabbit warren and a labyrinth. She dispaired of ever finding her way.

898

In the mannequins' dressing-room she spent a shy hour making up her face—in an extraordinary and distinctive atmosphere of slimness and beauty; white arms and faces vivid with rouge; raucous voices and the smell of cosmetics; silken lingerie. Coldly critical glances were bestowed upon Anna's reflection in the glass. None of them looked at her directly. . . . A depressing room, taken by itself, bare and cold, a very inadequate conservatory for these human flowers. Saleswomen in black rushed in and out, talking in sharp voices; a very old woman hovered, helpful and shapeless, showing Anna where to hang her clothes, presenting to her the black garment that Anna was wearing, going to lunch. She smiled with professional motherliness, her little, sharp, black eyes travelling rapidly from la nouvelle's hair to her ankles and back again.

She was Madame Pecard, the dresser.

Before Anna had spoken a word she was called away by a small boy in buttons to her destination in one of the salons: there, under the eye of a vendeuse, she had to learn the way to wear the innocent and springlike air and garb of the jeune fille. Behind a yellow, silken screen she was hustled into a leather coat and paraded under the cold eyes of an American buyer. This was the week when the spring models are shown to important people from big shops all over Europe and America: the most critical week of the season. . . . The American buyer said that he would have that, but with an inch on to the collar and larger cuffs. In vain the saleswoman, in her best English with its odd Chicago accent, protested that that would completely ruin the chic of the model. The American buyer knew what he wanted and saw that he got it.

The vendeuse sighed, but there was a note of admiration in her voice. She respected Americans: they were not like the English, who, under a surface of annoying moroseness of manner, were notoriously timid and easy to turn round your finger.

"Was that all right?" Behind the screen one of the saleswomen smiled encouragingly and nodded. The other shrugged her shoulders. She had small, close-set eyes, a long thin nose and tight lips of the regulation puce colour. Behind her silken screen Anna sat on a high white stool. She felt that she appeared charming and troubled. The white and gold of the salon suited her red hair.

A short morning. For the mannequin's day begins at ten and the process of making up lasts an hour. The friendly saleswoman volunteered the information that her name was Jeannine, that she was in the lingerie, that she considered Anna rudement jolie, that noon was Anna's lunch hour. She must go down the corridor and up those stairs, through the big salon then. . . . Anyone would tell her. But Anna, lost in the labyrinth, was too shy to ask her way. Besides, she was not sorry to have time to brace herself for the ordeal. She had reached the regions of utility and oilcloth: the decorative salons were far overhead. Then the smell of food—almost visible, it was so cloudlike and heavy—came to her nostrils, and high-noted, and sibilant, a buzz of conversation made her draw a deep breath. She pushed a door open.

She was in a big, very low-ceilinged room, all the floor space occupied by long wooden tables with no cloths. . . . She was sitting at the mannequin's table, gazing at a thick and hideous white china plate, a twisted tin fork, a wooden-handled stained knife, a tumbler so thick it seemed unbreakable.

There were twelve mannequins at Jeanne Veron's: six of them were lunching, the others still paraded, goddesslike, till their turn came for rest and refreshment. Each of the twelve was of a distinct and separate type: each of the twelve knew her type and kept to it, practising rigidly in clothing, manner, voice and conversation.

Round the austere table were now seated: Babette, the gamine, the traditional blonde enfant: Mona, tall and darkly beautiful, the femme fatale, the wearer of sumptuous evening gowns. Georgette was the garçonne: Simone with green eyes Anna knew instantly for a cat whom men would and did adore, a sleek, white, purring, long-lashed creature. . . . Eliane was the star of the collection.

Eliane was frankly ugly and it did not matter: no doubt Lilith, from whom she was obviously descended, had been ugly too. Her hair was henna-tinted, her eyes small and black, her complexion bad under her thick make-up. Her hips were extraordinarily slim, her hands and feet exquisite, every movement she made was as graceful as a flower's in the wind. Her walk . . . But it was her walk which made her the star there and earned her a salary quite fabulous for Madame Veron's, where large salaries were not the rule. . . . Her walk and her "chic of the devil" which lit an expression of admiration in even the cold eyes of American buyers.

Eliane was a quiet girl, pleasant-mannered. She wore a ring with a beautiful emerald on one long, slim finger, and in her small eyes were both intelligence and mystery.

Madame Pecard, the dresser, was seated at the head of the mannequin's table, talking loudly, unlistened to, and gazing benevolently at her flock.

At other tables sat the sewing girls, pale-faced, black-frocked—the workers, heroically gay, but with the stamp of labour on them: and the saleswomen. The mannequins, with their sensual, blatant charms and their painted faces were watched covertly, envied and apart.

Babette the blonde enfant was next to Anna, and having started the conversation with a few good, round oaths at the quality of the sardines, announced proudly that she could speak English and knew London very well. She began to tell Anna the history of her adventures in the city of coldness, dark and fogs. . . . She had gone to a job as a mannequin in Bond Street and the villainous proprietor of the shop having tried to make love to her and she being rigidly virtuous, she had left. And another job, Anna must figure to herself, had been impossible to get, for she, Babette, was too small and slim for the Anglo-Saxon idea of a mannequin.

She stopped to shout in a loud voice to the woman who was serving: "Hé, my old one, don't forget your little Babette. . . ."

Opposite, Simone the cat and the sportive Georgette were having a low-voiced conversation about the tristesse of a monsieur of their acquaintance. "I said to him," Georgette finished decisively, "Nothing to be done, my rabbit. You have not looked at me well, little one. In my place would you not have done the same?"

She broke off when she realized that the others were listening, and smiled in a friendly way at Anna.

She too, it appeared, had ambitions to go to London because the salaries were so much better there. Was it difficult? Did they really like French girls? Parisiennes?

The conversation became general.

"The English boys are nice," said Babette, winking one divinely candid eye. "I had a chic type who used to take me to dinner at the Empire Palace. Oh, a pretty boy. . . ."

"It is the most chic restaurant in London," she added importantly.

The meal reached the stage of dessert. The other tables were gradually emptying; the mannequins all ordered very strong coffee, several a liqueur. Only Mona and Eliane remained silent; Eliane, because she was thinking of something else; Mona, because it was her type, her genre to be haughty.

Her hair swept away from her white, narrow forehead and her small ears: her long earrings nearly touching her shoulders, she sipped her coffee with a disdainful air. Only once, when the blonde enfant, having engaged in a passage of arms with the waitress and got the worst of it was momentarily discomfited and silent, Mona narrowed her eyes and smiled an astonishingly cruel smile.

As soon as her coffee was drunk she got up and went out.

Anna produced a cigarette, and Georgette, perceiving instantly that here was the sportive touch, her genre, asked for one and lit it with a devil-may-care air. Anna eagerly passed her cigarettes round, but the Mère Pecard interfered weightily. It was against the rules of the house for the mannequins to smoke, she wheezed. The girls all lit their cigarettes and smoked. The Mère Pecard rumbled on: "A caprice, my children. All the world knows that mannequins are capricious. It is not so?" She appealed to the rest of the room.

As they went out Babette put her arm around Anna's waist and whispered: "Don't answer Madame Pecard. We don't like her. We never talk to her. She spies on us. She is a camel."

*   *   *

That afternoon Anna stood for an hour to have a dress draped on her. She showed this dress to a stout Dutch lady buying for the Hague, to a beautiful South American with pearls, to a silver-haired American gentleman who wanted an evening cape for his daughter of seventeen, and to a hook-nosed odd English lady of title who had a loud voice and dressed, under her furs, in a grey jersey and stout boots.

The American gentleman approved of Anna, and said so, and Anna gave him a passionately grateful glance. For, if the vendeuse Jeannine had been uniformly kind and encouraging, the other, Madame Tienne, had been as uniformly disapproving and had once even pinched her arm hard.

About five o'clock Anna became exhausted. The four white and gold walls seemed to close in on her. She sat on her high white stool staring at a marvelous nightgown and fighting an intense desire to rush away. Anywhere! Just to dress and rush away anywhere, from the raking eyes of the customers and the pinching fingers of Irene.

"I will one day. I can't stick it," she said to herself. "I won't be able to stick it." She had an absurd wish to gasp for air.

Jeannine came and found her like that.

"It is hard at first, hein? . . . One asks oneself: Why? For what good? It is all idiot. We are all so. But we go on. Do not worry about Irene." She whispered: "Madame Veron likes you very much. I heard her say so."

At six o'clock Anna was out in the rue de la Paix; her fatigue forgotten, the feeling that now she really belonged to the great, maddening city possessed her and she was happy in her beautifully cut tailor-made and a beret.

Georgette passed her and smiled; Babette was in a fur coat.

All up the street the mannequins were coming out of the shops, pausing on the pavements a moment, making them as gay and as beautiful as beds of flowers before they walked swiftly away and the Paris night swallowed them up.

The Secret Room

ALAIN ROBBE-GRILLET

To Gustave Moreau

The first thing to be seen is a red stain, of a deep, dark, shiny red, with almost black shadows. It is in the form of an irregular rosette, sharply outlined, extending in several directions in wide outflows of unequal length, dividing and dwindling afterward into single sinuous streaks. The whole stands out against a smooth, pale surface, round in shape, at once dull and pearly, a hemisphere joined by gentle curves to an expanse of the same pale color—white darkened by the shadowy quality of the place: a dungeon, a sunken room, or a cathedral—glowing with a diffused brilliance in the semidarkness.

Farther back, the space is filled with the cylindrical trunks of columns, repeated with progressive vagueness in their retreat toward the beginning of a vast stone stairway, turning slightly as it rises, growing narrower and narrower as it approaches the high vaults where it disappears.

The whole setting is empty, stairway and colonnades. Alone, in the foreground, the stretched-out body gleams feebly, marked with the red stain—a white body whose full, supple flesh can be sensed, fragile, no doubt, and vulnerable. Alongside the bloody hemisphere another identical round form, this one intact, is seen at almost the same angle of view; but the haloed point at its summit, of darker tint, is in this case quite recognizable, whereas the other one is entirely destroyed, or at least covered by the wound.

In the background, near the top of the stairway, a black silhouette is seen fleeing, a man wrapped in a long, floating cape, ascending the last steps without turning around, his deed accomplished. A thin smoke rises in twisting scrolls from a sort of incense burner placed on a high stand of ironwork with a silvery glint. Nearby lies the milkwhite body, with wide streaks of blood running from the left breast, along the flank and on the hip.

It is a fully rounded woman's body, but not heavy, completely nude, lying on its back, the bust raised up somewhat by thick cushions thrown down

903

on the floor, which is covered with Oriental rugs. The waist is very narrow, the neck long and thin, curved to one side, the head thrown back into a darker area where, even so, the facial features may be discerned, the partly opened mouth, the wide-staring eyes, shining with a fixed brilliance, and the mass of long, black hair spread out in a complicated wavy disorder over a heavily folded cloth, of velvet perhaps, on which also rest the arm and shoulder.

It is a uniformly colored velvet of dark purple, or which seems so in this lighting. But purple, brown, blue also seem to dominate in the colors of the cushions—only a small portion of which is hidden beneath the velvet cloth, and which protrude noticeably, lower down, beneath the bust and waist—as well as in the Oriental patterns of the rugs on the floor. Farther on, these same colors are picked up again in the stone of the paving and the columns, the vaulted archways, the stairs, and the less discernible surfaces that disappear into the farthest reaches of the room.

The dimensions of this room are difficult to determine exactly; the body of the young sacrificial victim seems at first glance to occupy a substantial portion of it, but the vast size of the stairway leading down to it would imply rather that this is not the whole room, whose considerable space must in reality extend all around, right and left, as it does toward the faraway browns and blues among the columns standing in line, in every direction, perhaps toward other sofas, thick carpets, piles of cushions and fabrics, other tortured bodies, other incense burners.

It is also difficult to say where the light comes from. No clue, on the columns or on the floor, suggests the direction of the rays. Nor is any window or torch visible. The milkwhite body itself seems to light the scene, with its full breasts, the curve of its thighs, the rounded belly, the full buttocks, the stretched-out legs, widely spread, and the black tuft of the exposed sex, provocative, proffered, useless now.

The man has already moved several steps back. He is now on the first step of the stairs, ready to go up. The bottom steps are wide and deep, like the steps leading up to some great building, a temple or theater; they grow smaller as they ascend, and at the same time describe a wide, helical curve, so gradually that the stairway has not yet made a half-turn by the time it disappears near the top of the vaults, reduced then to a steep, narrow flight of steps without handrail, vaguely outlined, moreover, in the thickening darkness beyond.

But the man does not look in this direction, where his movement nonetheless carries him; his left foot on the second step and his right foot already touching the third, with his knee bent, he has turned around to look at the spectacle for one last time. The long, floating cape thrown hastily over his shoulders, clasped in one hand at his waist, has been whirled around by the rapid circular motion that has just caused his head and chest to turn in the opposite direction, and a corner of the cloth remains suspended in the air as if blown by a gust of wind; this corner, twisting around upon itself in the form of a loose S, reveals the red silk lining with its gold embroidery.

The man's features are impassive, but tense, as if in expectation—or perhaps fear—of some sudden event, or surveying with one last glance the total immobility of the scene. Though he is looking backward, his whole body is turned slightly forward, as if were continuing up the stairs. His right arm—not the one holding the edge of the cape—is bent sharply toward the left, toward a point in space where the balustrade should be, if this stairway had one, an interrupted gesture, almost incomprehensible, unless it arose from an instinctive movement to grasp the absent support.

As to the direction of his glance, it is certainly aimed at the body of the victim lying on the cushions, its extended members stretched out in the form of a cross, its bust raised up, its head thrown back. But the face is perhaps hidden from the man's eyes by one of the columns, standing at the foot of the stairs. The young woman's right hand touches the floor just at the foot of this column. The fragile wrist is encircled by an iron bracelet. The arm is almost in darkness, only the hand receiving enough light to make the thin, outspread fingers clearly visible against the circular protrusion at the base of the stone column. A black metal chain running around the column passes through a ring affixed to the bracelet, binding the wrist tightly to the column.

At the top of the arm a rounded shoulder, raised up by the cushions, also stands out well lighted, as well as the neck, the throat, and the other shoulder, the armpit with its soft hair, the left arm likewise pulled back with its wrist bound in the same manner to the base of another column, in the extreme foreground; here the iron bracelet and the chain are fully displayed, represented with perfect clarity down to the slightest details.

The same is true, still in the foreground but at the other side, for a similar chain, but not quite as thick, wound directly around the ankle, running twice around the column and terminating in a heavy iron ring embedded in the floor. About a yard farther back, or perhaps slightly farther, the right foot is identically chained. But it is the left foot, and its chain, that are the most minutely depicted.

The foot is small, delicate, finely modeled. In several places the chain has broken the skin, causing noticeable if not extensive depressions in the flesh. The chain links are oval, thick, the size of an eye. The ring in the floor resembles those used to attach horses; it lies almost touching the stone pavement to which it is riveted by a massive iron peg. A few inches away is the edge of a rug; it is grossly wrinkled at this point, doubtless as a result of the convulsive, but necessarily very restricted, movements of the victim attempting to struggle.

The man is still standing about a yard away, half leaning over her. He looks at her face, seen upside down, her dark eyes made larger by their surrounding eyeshadow, her mouth wide open as if screaming. The man's posture allows his face to be seen only in a vague profile, but one senses in it a violent exaltation, despite the rigid attitude, the silence, the immobility. His back is slightly arched. His left hand, the only one visible, holds up at some distance from the body a piece of cloth, some dark-colored piece of clothing, which drags on the carpet, and which must be the long cape with its gold-embroidered lining.

This immense silhouette hides most of the bare flesh over which the red stain, spreading from the globe of the breast, runs in long rivulets that branch out, growing narrower, upon the pale background of the bust and the flank. One thread has reached the armpit and runs in an almost straight, thin line along the arm; others have run down toward the waist and traced out, along one side of the belly, the hip, the top of the thigh, a more random network already starting to congeal. Three or four tiny veins have reached the hollow between the legs, meeting in a sinuous line, touching the point of the V formed by the outspread legs, and disappearing into the black tuft.

Look, now the flesh is still intact: the black tuft and the white belly, the soft curve of the hips, the narrow waist, and, higher up, the pearly breasts rising and falling in time with the rapid breathing, whose rhythm grows more accelerated. The man, close to her, one knee on the floor, leans farther over. The head, with its long, curly hair, which alone is free to move somewhat, turns from side to side, struggling; finally the woman's mouth twists open, while the flesh is torn open, the blood spurts out over the tender skin, stretched tight, the carefully shadowed eyes grow abnormally larger, the mouth opens wider, the head twists violently, one last time, from right to left, then more gently, to fall back finally and become still, amid the mass of black hair spread out on the velvet.

At the very top of the stone stairway, the little door has opened, allowing a yellowish but sustained shaft of light to enter, against which stands out the dark silhouette of the man wrapped in his long cloak. He has but to climb a few more steps to reach the threshold.

Afterward, the whole setting is empty, the enormous room with its purple shadows and its stone columns proliferating in all directions, the monumental staircase with no handrail that twists upward, growing narrower and vaguer as it rises into the darkness, toward the top of the vaults where it disappears.

Near the body, whose wound has stiffened, whose brilliance is already growing dim, the thin smoke from the incense burner traces complicated scrolls in the still air: first a coil turned horizontally to the left, which then straightens out and rises slightly, then returns to the axis of its point of origin, which it crosses as it moves to the right, then turns back in the first direction, only to wind back again, thus forming an irregular sinusoidal curve, more and more flattened out, and rising, vertically, toward the top of the canvas.

The Conversion of the Jews

PHILIP ROTH

"You're a real one for opening your mouth in the first place," Itzie said. "What do you open your mouth all the time for?"

"I didn't bring it up, Itz, I didn't," Ozzie said.

"What do you care about Jesus Christ for anyway?"

"I didn't bring up Jesus Christ. He did. I didn't even know what he was talking about. Jesus is historical, he kept saying. Jesus is historical." Ozzie mimicked the monumental voice of Rabbi Binder.

"Jesus was a person that lived like you and me," Ozzie continued. "That's what Binder said—"

"Yeah? . . . So what! What do I give two cents whether he lived or not. And what do you gotta open your mouth!" Itzie Lieberman favored closed-mouthedness, especially when it came to Ozzie Freedman's questions. Mrs. Freedman had to see Rabbi Binder twice before about Ozzie's questions and this Wednesday at four-thirty would be the third time. Itzie preferred to keep *his* mother in the kitchen; he settled for behind-the-back subtleties such as gestures, faces, snarls and other less delicate barnyard noises.

"He was a real person, Jesus, but he wasn't like God, and we don't believe he is God." Slowly, Ozzie was explaining Rabbi Binder's position to Itzie, who had been absent from Hebrew School the previous afternoon.

"The Catholics," Itzie said helpfully, "they believe in Jesus Christ, that he's God." Itzie Lieberman used "the Catholics" in its broadest sense—to include the Protestants.

Ozzie received Itzie's remark with a tiny head bob, as though it were a footnote, and went on. "His mother was Mary, and his father probably was Joseph," Ozzie said. "But the New Testament says his real father was God."

"His *real* father?"

"Yeah," Ozzie said, "that's the big thing, his father's supposed to be God."

"Bull."

907

"That's what Rabbi Binder says, that it's impossible—"

"Sure it's impossible. That stuff's all bull. To have a baby you gotta get laid," Itzie theologized. "Mary hadda get laid."

"That's what Binder says: 'The only way a woman can have a baby is to have intercourse with a man.' "

"He said *that,* Ozz?" For a moment it appeared that Itzie had put the theological question aside. "He said that, intercourse?" A little curled smile shaped itself in the lower half of Itzie's face like a pink mustache. "What you guys do, Ozz, you laugh or something?"

"I raised my hand."

"Yeah? Whatja say?"

"That's when I asked the question."

Itzie's face lit up. "Whatja ask about—intercourse?"

"No, I asked the question about God, how if He could create the heaven and earth in six days, and make all the animals and the fish and the light in six days—the light especially, that's what always gets me, that He could make the light. Making fish and animals, that's pretty good—"

"That's damn good." Itzie's appreciation was honest but unimaginative: it was as though God had just pitched a one-hitter.

"But making light . . . I mean when you think about it, it's really something," Ozzie said. "Anyway, I asked Binder if He could make all that in six days, and He could *pick* the six days He wanted right out of nowhere, why couldn't He let a woman have a baby without having intercourse."

"You said intercourse, Ozz, to Binder?"

"Yeah."

"Right in class?"

"Yeah."

Itzie smacked the side of his head.

"I mean, no kidding around," Ozzie said, "that'd really be nothing. After all that other stuff, that'd practically be nothing."

Itzie considered a moment. "What'd Binder say?"

"He started all over again explaining how Jesus was historical and how he lived like you and me but he wasn't God. So I said I under*stood* that. What I wanted to know was different."

What Ozzie wanted to know was always different. The first time he had wanted to know how Rabbi Binder could call the Jews "The Chosen People" if the Declaration of Independence claimed all men to be created equal. Rabbi Binder tried to distinguish for him between political equality and spiritual legitimacy, but what Ozzie wanted to know, he insisted vehemently, was different. That was the first time his mother had to come.

Then there was the plane crash. Fifty-eight people had been killed in a plane crash at La Guardia. In studying a casualty list in the newspaper his mother had discovered among the list of those dead eight Jewish names (his grandmother had nine but she counted Miller as a Jewish name);

because of the eight she said the plane crash was "a tragedy." During free-discussion time on Wednesday Ozzie had brought to Rabbi Binder's attention this matter of "some of his relations" always picking out the Jewish names. Rabbi Binder had begun to explain cultural unity and some other things when Ozzie stood up at his seat and said that what he wanted to know was different. Rabbi Binder insisted that he sit down and it was then that Ozzie shouted that he wished all fifty-eight were Jews. That was the second time his mother came.

"And he kept explaining about Jesus being historical, and so I kept asking him. No kidding, Itz, he was trying to make me look stupid."

"So what he finally do?"

"Finally he starts screaming that I was deliberately simple-minded and a wise guy, and that my mother had to come, and this was the last time. And that I'd never get bar-mitzvahed if he could help it. Then, Itz, then he starts talking in that voice like a statue, real slow and deep, and he says that I better think over what I said about the Lord. He told me to go to his office and think it over." Ozzie leaned his body towards Itzie. "Itz, I thought it over for a solid hour, and now I'm convinced God could do it."

Ozzie had planned to confess his latest transgression to his mother as soon as she came home from work. But it was a Friday night in November and already dark, and when Mrs. Freedman came through the door she tossed off her coat, kissed Ozzie quickly on the face, and went to the kitchen table to light the three yellow candles, two for the Sabbath and one for Ozzie's father.

When his mother lit the candles she would move her two arms slowly towards her, dragging them through the air, as though persuading people whose minds were half made up. And her eyes would get glassy with tears. Even when his father was alive Ozzie remembered that her eyes had gotten glassy, so it didn't have anything to do with his dying. It had something to do with lighting the candles.

As she touched the flaming match to the unlit wick of a Sabbath candle, the phone rang, and Ozzie, standing only a foot from it, plucked it off the receiver and held it muffled to his chest. When his mother lit candles Ozzie felt there should be no noise; even breathing, if you could manage it, should be softened. Ozzie pressed the phone to his breast and watched his mother dragging whatever she was dragging, and he felt his own eyes get glassy. His mother was a round, tired, gray-haired penguin of a woman whose gray skin had begun to feel the tug of gravity and the weight of her own history. Even when she was dressed up she didn't look like a chosen person. But when she lit candles she looked like something better; like a woman who knew momentarily that God could do anything.

After a few mysterious minutes she was finished. Ozzie hung up the phone and walked to the kitchen table where she was beginning to lay the two places for the four-course Sabbath meal. He told her that she would have to see Rabbi Binder next Wednesday at four-thirty, and then he told her why. For the first time in their life together she hit Ozzie across the face with her hand.

All through the chopped liver and chicken soup part of the dinner Ozzie cried; he didn't have any appetite for the rest.

On Wednesday, in the largest of the three basement classrooms of the synagogue, Rabbi Marvin Binder, a tall, handsome, broad-shouldered man of thirty with thick strong-fibered black hair, removed his watch from his pocket and saw that it was four o'clock. At the rear of the room Yakov Blotnik, the seventy-one-year-old custodian, slowly polished the large window mumbling to himself, unaware that it was four o'clock or six o'clock, Monday or Wednesday. To most of the students Yakov Blotnik's mumbling, along with his brown curly beard, scythe nose, and two heel-trailing black cats, made of him an object of wonder, a foreigner, a relic, towards whom they were alternately fearful and disrespectful. To Ozzie the mumbling had always seemed a monotonous, curious prayer; what made it curious was that old Blotnik had been mumbling so steadily for so many years, Ozzie suspected he had memorized the prayers and forgotten all about God.

"It is now free-discussion time," Rabbi Binder said. "Feel free to talk about any Jewish matter at all—religion, family, politics, sports—"

There was silence. It was a gusty, clouded November afternoon and it did not seem as though there ever was or could be a thing called baseball. So nobody this week said a word about that hero from the past, Hank Greenberg—which limited free discussion considerably.

And the soul-battering Ozzie Freedman had just received from Rabbi Binder had imposed its limitation. When it was Ozzie's turn to read aloud from the Hebrew book the rabbi had asked him petulantly why he didn't read more rapidly. He was showing no progress. Ozzie said he could read faster but that if he did he was sure not to understand what he was reading. Nevertheless, at the rabbi's repeated suggestion Ozzie tried, and showed a great talent, but in the midst of a long passage he stopped short and said he didn't understand a word he was reading, and started in again at a drag-footed pace. Then came the soul-battering.

Consequently when free-discussion time rolled around none of the students felt too free. The rabbi's invitation was answered only by the mumbling of feeble old Blotnik.

"Isn't there anything at all you would like to discuss?" Rabbi Binder asked again, looking at his watch. "No questions or comments?"

There was a small grumble from the third row. The rabbi requested that Ozzie rise and give the rest of the class the advantage of his thought.

Ozzie rose. "I forget it now," he said, and sat down in his place.

Rabbi Binder advanced a seat towards Ozzie and poised himself on the edge of the desk. It was Itzie's desk and the rabbi's frame only a dagger's-length away from his face snapped him to sitting attention.

"Stand up again, Oscar," Rabbi Binder said calmly, "and try to assemble your thoughts."

Ozzie stood up. All his classmates turned in their seats and watched as he gave an unconvincing scratch to his forehead.

"I can't assemble any," he announced, and plunked himself down.

"Stand up!" Rabbi Binder advanced from Itzie's desk to the one directly in front of Ozzie; when the rabbinical back was turned Itzie gave it five-fingers off the tip of his nose, causing a small titter in the room. Rabbi Binder was too absorbed in squelching Ozzie's nonsense once and for all to bother with titters. "Stand up, Oscar. What's your question about?"

Ozzie pulled a word out of the air. It was the handiest word. "Religion."

"Oh, now you remember?"

"Yes."

"What is it?"

Trapped, Ozzie blurted the first thing that came to him. "Why can't He make anything He wants to make!"

As Rabbi Binder prepared an answer, a final answer, Itzie, ten feet behind him, raised one finger on his left hand, gestured it meaningfully towards the rabbi's back, and brought the house down.

Binder twisted quickly to see what had happened and in the midst of the commotion Ozzie shouted into the rabbi's back what he couldn't have shouted to his face. It was a loud, toneless sound that had the timbre of something stored inside for about six days.

"You don't know! You don't know anything about God!"

The rabbi spun back towards Ozzie. "What?"

"You don't know—you don't—"

"Apologize, Oscar, apologize!" It was a threat.

"You don't—"

Rabbi Binder's hand flicked out at Ozzie's cheek. Perhaps it had only been meant to clamp the boy's mouth shut, but Ozzie ducked and the palm caught him squarely on the nose.

The blood came in a short, red spurt on to Ozzie's shirt front.

The next moment was all confusion. Ozzie screamed, "You bastard, you bastard!" and broke for the classroom door. Rabbi Binder lurched a step backwards, as though his own blood had started flowing violently in the opposite direction, then gave a clumsy lurch forward and bolted out the door after Ozzie. The class followed after the rabbi's huge blue-suited back, and before old Blotnik could turn from his window, the room was empty and everyone was headed full speed up the three flights leading to the roof.

*   *   *

If one should compare the light of day to the life of man: sunrise to birth; sunset—the dropping down over the edge—to death; then as Ozzie Freedman wiggled through the trapdoor of the synagogue roof, his feet kicking backwards bronco-style at Rabbi Binder's outstretched arms—at that moment the day was fifty years old. As a rule, fifty or fifty-five reflects accurately the age of late afternoons in November, for it is in that month, during those hours, that one's awareness of light seems no longer a matter of seeing, but of hearing: light begins clicking away. In fact, as Ozzie locked shut the trapdoor in the rabbi's face, the sharp click of the bolt into the lock might momentarily have been mistaken for the sound of the heavier gray that had just throbbed through the sky.

With all his weight Ozzie kneeled on the locked door; any instant he was certain that Rabbi Binder's shoulder would fling it open, splintering the wood into shrapnel and catapulting his body into the sky. But the door did not move and below him he heard only the rumble of feet, first loud then dim, like thunder rolling away.

A question shot through his brain. "Can this be *me*?" For a thirteen-year-old who had just labeled his religious leader a bastard, twice, it was not an improper question. Louder and louder the question came to him—"Is it me? Is it me?"—until he discovered himself no longer kneeling, but racing crazily towards the edge of the roof, his eyes crying, his throat screaming, and his arms flying every-whichway as though not his own.

"Is it me? Is it me ME ME ME ME! It has to be me—but is it!"

It is the question a thief must ask himself the night he jimmies open his first window, and it is said to be the question with which bridegrooms quiz themselves before the altar.

In the few wild seconds it took Ozzie's body to propel him to the edge of the roof, his self-examination began to grow fuzzy. Gazing down at the street, he became confused as to the problem beneath the question: was it, is-it-me-who-called-Binder-a-bastard? or, is-it-me-prancing-around-on-the-roof? However, the scene below settled all, for there is an instant in any action when whether it is you or somebody else is academic. The thief crams the money in his pockets and scoots out the window. The bridegroom signs the hotel register for two. And the boy on the roof finds a streetful of people gaping at him, necks stretched backwards, faces up, as though he were the ceiling of the Hayden Planetarium. Suddenly you know it's you.

"Oscar! Oscar Freedman!" A voice rose from the center of the crowd, a voice that, could it have been seen, would have looked like the writing on scroll. "Oscar Freedman, get down from there. Immediately!" Rabbi Binder was pointing one arm stiffly up at him; and at the end of that arm, one finger aimed menacingly. It was the attitude of a dictator, but one—the eyes confessed all—whose personal valet had spit neatly in his face.

Ozzie didn't answer. Only for a blink's length did he look towards Rabbi Binder. Instead his eyes began to fit together the world beneath him, to sort out people from places, friends from enemies, participants from spectators. In little jagged starlike clusters his friends stood around Rabbi Binder, who was still pointing. The topmost point on a star compounded not of angels but of five adolescent boys was Itzie. What a world it was, with those stars below, Rabbi Binder below . . . Ozzie, who a moment earlier hadn't been able to control his own body, started to feel the meaning of the word control: he felt Peace and he felt Power.

"Oscar Freedman, I'll give you three to come down."

Few dictators give their subjects three to do anything; but, as always, Rabbi Binder only looked dictatorial.

"Are you ready, Oscar?"

Ozzie nodded his head yes, although he had no intention in the world—the lower one or the celestial one he'd just entered—of coming down even if Rabbi Binder should give him a million.

"All right then," said Rabbi Binder. He ran a hand through his black Samson hair as though it were the gesture prescribed for uttering the first digit. Then, with his other hand cutting a circle out of the small piece of sky around him, he spoke. "One!"

There was no thunder. On the contrary, at that moment, as though "one" was the cue for which he had been waiting, the world's least thunderous person appeared on the synagogue steps. He did not so much come out the synagogue door as lean out, onto the darkening air. He clutched at the doorknob with one hand and looked up at the roof.

"*Oy!*"

Yakov Blotnik's old mind hobbled slowly, as if on crutches, and though he couldn't decide precisely what the boy was doing on the roof, he knew it wasn't good—that is, it wasn't-good-for-the-Jews. For Yakov Blotnik life had fractionated itself simply: things were either good-for-the-Jews or no-good-for-the-Jews.

He smacked his free hand to his in-sucked cheek, gently. "*Oy, Gut!*" And then quickly as he was able, he jacked down his head and surveyed the street. There was Rabbi Binder (like a man at an auction with only three dollars in his pocket, he had just delivered a shaky "Two!"); there were the students, and that was all. So far it-wasn't-so-bad-for-the-Jews. But the boy had to come down immediately, before anybody saw. The problem: how to get the boy off the roof?

Anybody who has ever had a cat on the roof knows how to get him down. You call the fire department. Or first you call the operator and you ask her for the fire department. And the next thing there is great jamming of brakes and clanging of bells and shouting of instructions. And then the cat is off the roof. You do the same thing to get a boy off the roof.

That is, you do the same thing if you are Yakov Blotnik and you once had a cat on the roof.

When the engines, all four of them, arrived, Rabbi Binder had four times given Ozzie the count of three. The big hook-and-ladder swung around the corner and one of the firemen leaped from it, plunging headlong towards the yellow fire hydrant in front of the synagogue. With a huge wrench he began to unscrew the top nozzle. Rabbi Binder raced over to him and pulled at his shoulder.

"There's no fire . . ."

The fireman mumbled back over his shoulder and, heatedly, continued working at the nozzle.

"But there's no fire, there's no fire . . ." Binder shouted. When the fireman mumbled again, the rabbi grasped his face with both his hands and pointed it up at the roof.

To Ozzie it looked as though Rabbi Binder was trying to tug the fireman's head out of his body, like a cork from a bottle. He had to giggle at the picture they made: it was a family portrait—rabbi in black skullcap, fireman in red fire hat, and the little yellow hydrant squatting beside like a kid brother, bareheaded. From the edge of the roof Ozzie waved at the portrait, a one-handed, flapping, mocking wave; in doing it his right foot slipped from under him. Rabbi Binder covered his eyes with his hands.

Firemen work fast. Before Ozzie had even regained his balance, a big, round, yellowed net was being held on the synagogue lawn. The firemen who held it looked up at Ozzie with stern, feelingless faces.

One of the firemen turned his head towards Rabbi Binder. "What, is the kid nuts or something?"

Rabbi Binder unpeeled his hands from his eyes, slowly, painfully, as if they were tape. Then he checked: nothing on the sidewalk, no dents in the net.

"Is he gonna jump, or what?" the fireman shouted.

In a voice not at all like a statue, Rabbi Binder finally answered. "Yes, yes, I think so . . . He's been threatening to . . ."

Threatening to? Why, the reason he was on the roof, Ozzie remembered, was to get away; he hadn't even thought about jumping. He had just run to get away, and the truth was that he hadn't really headed for the roof as much as he'd been chased there.

"What's his name, the kid?"

"Freedman," Rabbi Binder answered. "Oscar Freedman."

The fireman looked up at Ozzie. "What is it with you, Oscar? You gonna jump, or what?"

Ozzie did not answer. Frankly, the question had just arisen.

"Look, Oscar, if you're gonna jump, jump—and if you're not gonna jump, don't jump. But don't waste our time, willya?"

Ozzie looked at the fireman and then at Rabbi Binder. He wanted to see Rabbi Binder cover his eyes one more time.

"I'm going to jump."

And then he scampered around the edge of the roof to the corner, where there was no net below, and he flapped his arms at his sides, swishing the air and smacking his palms to his trousers on the downbeat. He began screaming like some kind of engine, "Wheeeee . . . wheeeeee," and leaning way out over the edge with the upper half of his body. The firemen whipped around to cover the ground with the net. Rabbi Binder mumbled a few words to Somebody, and covered his eyes. Everything happened quickly, jerkily, as in a silent movie. The crowd, which had arrived with the fire engines, gave out a long, Fourth-of-July fireworks oooh-aahhh. In the excitement no one had paid the crowd much heed, except, of course, Yakov Blotnik, who swung from the doorknob counting heads. *Fier und tsvansik . . . finf und tsvantsik . . . Oy, Gut!*" It wasn't like this with the cat.

Rabbi Binder peeked through his fingers, checked the sidewalk and net. Empty. But there was Ozzie racing to the other corner. The firemen raced with him but were unable to keep up. Whenever Ozzie wanted to he might jump and splatter himself upon the sidewalk, and by the time the firemen scooted to the spot all they could do with their net would be to cover the mess.

"Wheeeee . . . wheeeee . . . "

"Hey, Oscar," the winded fireman yelled, "What the hell is this, a game or something?"

"Wheeeee . . . wheeeee . . . "

"Hey, Oscar—"

But he was off now to the other corner, flapping his wings fiercely. Rabbi Binder couldn't take it any longer—the fire engines from nowhere, the screaming suicidal boy, the net. He fell to his knees, exhausted, and with his hands curled together in front of his chest like a little dome, he pleaded, "Oscar, stop it, Oscar. Don't jump, Oscar. Please come down . . . Please don't jump."

And further back in the crowd a single voice, a single young voice, shouted a lone word to the boy on the roof.

"Jump!"

It was Itzie. Ozzie momentarily stopped flapping.

"Go ahead, Ozz—jump!" Itzie broke off his point of the star and courageously, with the inspiration not of a wise-guy but of a disciple, stood alone. "Jump, Ozz, jump!"

Still on his knees, his hands still curled, Rabbi Binder twisted his body back. He looked at Itzie, then, agonizingly, back to Ozzie.

"OSCAR, DON'T JUMP! PLEASE, DON'T JUMP . . . please please . . . "

"Jump!" This time it wasn't Itzie but another point of the star. By the time Mrs. Freedman arrived to keep her four-thirty appointment with Rabbi Binder, the whole little upside down heaven was shouting and pleading for Ozzie to jump, and Rabbi Binder no longer was pleading with him not to jump, but was crying into the dome of his hands.

Understandably Mrs. Freedman couldn't figure out what her son was doing on the roof. So she asked.

"Ozzie, my Ozzie, what are you doing? My Ozzie, what is it?"

Ozzie stopped wheeeeeing and slowed his arms down to a cruising flap, the kind birds use in soft winds, but he did not answer. He stood against the low, clouded, darkening sky—light clicked down swiftly now, as on a small gear—flapping softly and gazing down at the small bundle of a woman who was his mother.

"What are you doing, Ozzie?" She turned towards the kneeling Rabbi Binder and rushed so close that only a paper-thickness of dusk lay between her stomach and his shoulders.

"What is my baby doing?"

Rabbi Binder gaped up at her but he too was mute. All that moved was the dome of his hands; it shook back and forth like a weak pulse.

"Rabbi, get him down! He'll kill himself. Get him down, my only baby . . . "

"I can't," Rabbi Binder said, "I can't . . . " and he turned his handsome head towards the crowd of boys behind him. "It's them. Listen to them."

And for the first time Mrs. Freedman saw the crowd of boys, and she heard what they were yelling.

"He's doing it for them. He won't listen to me. It's them." Rabbi Binder spoke like one in a trance.

"For them?"

"Yes."

"Why for them?"

"They want him to . . . "

Mrs. Freedman raised her two arms upward as though she were conducting the sky. "For them he's doing it!" And then in a gesture older than pyramids, older than prophets and floods, her arms came slapping down to her sides. "A martyr I have. Look!" She tilted her head to the roof. Ozzie was still flapping softly. "My martyr."

"Oscar, come down, *please*," Rabbi Binder groaned.

In a startlingly even voice Mrs. Freedman called to the boy on the roof. "Ozzie, come down, Ozzie. Don't be a martyr, my baby."

As though it were a litany, Rabbi Binder repeated her words. "Don't be a martyr, my baby. Don't be a martyr."

"Gawhead, Ozz—*be* a Martin!" It was Itzie. "Be a Martin, be a Martin," and all the voices joined in singing for Martindom, whatever *it* was. "Be a Martin, be a Martin . . . "

Somehow when you're on a roof the darker it gets the less you can hear. All Ozzie knew was that two groups wanted two new things: his friends were spirited and musical about what they wanted; his mother and the rabbi were even-toned, chanting, about what they didn't want. The rabbi's voice was without tears now and so was his mother's.

The big net stared up at Ozzie like a sightless eye. The big, clouded sky pushed down. From beneath it looked like a gray corrugated board. Suddenly, looking up into that unsympathetic sky, Ozzie realized all the strangeness of what these people, his friends, were asking: they wanted him to jump, to kill himself; they were singing about it now—it made them that happy. And there was an even greater strangeness: Rabbi Binder was on his knees, trembling. If there was a question to be asked now it was not "Is it me?" but rather "Is it us? . . . "

Being on the roof, it turned out, was a serious thing. If he jumped would the singing become dancing? Would it? What would jumping stop? Yearningly, Ozzie wished he could rip open the sky, plunge his hands through, and pull out the sun; and on the sun, like a coin, would be stamped JUMP or DON'T JUMP.

Ozzie's knees rocked and sagged a little under him as though they were setting him for a dive. His arms tightened, stiffened, froze, from shoulders to fingernails. He felt as if each part of his body were going to vote as to whether he should kill himself or not—and each part as though it were independent of *him*.

The light took an unexpected click down and the new darkness, like a gag, hushed the friends singing for this and the mother and rabbi chanting for that.

Ozzie stopped counting votes, and in a curiously high voice, like one who wasn't prepared for speech, he spoke.

"Mamma?"

"Yes, Oscar."

"Mamma, get down on your knees, like Rabbi Binder."

"Oscar—"

"Get down on your knees," he said, "or I'll jump."

Ozzie heard a whimper, then a quick rustling, and when he looked down where his mother had stood he saw the top of a head and beneath that a circle of dress. She was kneeling beside Rabbi Binder.

He spoke again. "Everybody kneel." There was the sound of everybody kneeling.

Ozzie looked around. With one hand he pointed towards the synagogue entrance. "Make *him* kneel."

There was a noise, not of kneeling, but of body-and-cloth stretching. Ozzie could hear Rabbi Binder saying in a gruff whisper, ". . . or he'll *kill* himself," and when next he looked there was Yakov Blotnik off the doorknob and for the first time in his life upon his knees in the Gentile posture of prayer.

As for the firemen—it is not as difficult as one might imagine to hold a net taut while you are kneeling.

Ozzie looked around again; and then he called to Rabbi Binder.

"Rabbi?"

"Yes, Oscar."

"Rabbi Binder, do you believe in God?"

"Yes."

"Do you believe God can do Anything?" Ozzie leaned his head out into the darkness. "Anything?"

"Oscar, I think—"

"Tell me you believe God can do Anything."

There was a second's hesitation. Then: "God can do Anything."

"Tell me you believe God can make a child without intercourse."

"He can."

"Tell me!"

"God," Rabbi Binder admitted, "can make a child without intercourse."

"Mamma, you tell me."

"God can make a child without intercourse," his mother said.

"Make *him* tell me." There was no doubt who *him* was.

In a few moments Ozzie heard an old comical voice say something to the increasing darkness about God.

Next, Ozzie made everybody say it. And then he made them all say they believed in Jesus Christ—first one at a time, then all together.

When the catechizing was through it was the beginning of evening. From the street it sounded as if the boy on the roof might have sighed.

"Ozzie?" A woman's voice dared to speak. "You'll come down now?"

There was no answer, but the woman waited, and when a voice finally did speak it was thin and crying, and exhausted as that of an old man who has just finished pulling the bells.

"Mamma, don't you see—you shouldn't hit me. He shouldn't hit me. You shouldn't hit me about God, Mamma. You should never hit anybody about God—"

"Ozzie, please come down now."

"Promise me, promise me you'll never hit anybody about God."

He had asked only his mother, but for some reason everyone kneeling in the street promised he would never hit anybody about God.

Once again there was silence.

"I can come down now, Mamma," the boy on the roof finally said. He turned his head both ways as though checking the traffic lights. "Now I can come down . . ."

And he did, right into the center of the yellow net that glowed in the evening's edge like an overgrown halo.

Kalicz

EVELYN SCOTT

Kalicz worked quickly in the dusk. It was dusk outside. Here it was always dusk. The molders were putting oil on the molds over the molding sand that was burnt black as a charcoaled face. Kalicz took the bellows from them and blew off the loose sand so that the casting would be perfect. But he was not one of those who made the parts, who cast the parts, who riveted the parts. He was a laborer only. His mother, when he and she had come here, on the long way, on the ship, on the waters that wash all countries, had scolded him to learn a trade; but he had never cared to learn a trade or to do any work but such as could please God and the little Christ Child Himself.

In Poland, on November 29, 1860, on the anniversary of the great revolution of thirty years back, there were political outbreaks in the churches and streets, in Warsaw and in all the principal cities of Poland, and the family of the count, the family for whom Marja, the mother of Kalicz (because he had no other name, because at about the time he was born Marja went to live at Kalicz), because the family of the count, suspected by those who made the government of the Czar and were the Czar's rulers in Poland, because the Pan and Pani were abroad to escape the trouble; and Marja went to Kalicz to live, and there had a child, born to her maybe as the son of the coachman, or maybe the child of a man in the weis who was known for his strange behavior, and known never to have done a day's work in his life, and to be wild in his ways with women, Marja had borne a child, and, because the child had no father, had christened him Kalicz. That was what Kalicz knew. And when the Pan and Pani had left Poland forever, he and his mother had left Poland forever, but in a different ship. And this was because people who were like the count and like his mother who served the count and his family and had served them for generations, and Marja, the mother of Kalicz, worked in the folwark and did the churning and made

920

the butter, because people who knew the count and knew Marja and Kalicz and had traveled over the greater part of the world, these people said that America was a place for people who had always been the friends of Poland, and where the count and his friends had themselves come to raise money for Poland to pay the soldiers to fight the Russians and to fight all heretics, for these reasons when the count left the mąjatek and the folwark and all he had, and believed he would never see Poland more, he gave Marja the money to live on there under the Russian landlords for her whole life. But she liked to wander. And when the new people had come and she did not like the new people, she told Kalicz to come with her, and she and Kalicz walked for maybe a whole year, and came to the shores of what maybe was called the Black Sea, and took a boat.

Now Kalicz walked up and down in the dark. The belts ran in the ceiling over his head, and they ran from the engine, and there were many belts turning wheels, and these wheels turned belts that turned other wheels, and this was the existence of Kalicz, the son of Marja, in the foundry, on the East River, in America where they made the war. For the war that destroyed Poland, and destroyed the folwark, and turned the property over into the hands of a Russian landlord, that war had also come to America, to Kalicz in the foundry where they were making the castings for the cannon and the castings for the ships. For Marja said that Kalicz would never be a good workman and never learn to speak English well, and the foreman of the foundry said that Kalicz would never to learn to speak English well.

He walked along slowly. The floor was of earth, and when he walked on it slowly nobody heard him, and nobody knew that he was coming. He did not walk that way for any reason, but because he had walked a great deal in churches—in the grand church at Warsaw where he had followed the count, and in the little wooden kosciol at the town of Kalicz from which he got his name. In that place he had been accustomed to sit in the church door and take alms, because the priest had given his permission, because Kalicz was a man who thought of God and did not work. Some said that he was crazy, or an idiot; others, that he was a wiseacre. But Kalicz corrected them in either case. He was humble, as he told them, and (as he did not tell them) very vain of his humility. When the other workmen gibed at him here, he did not take offense.

Kalicz had a white, meek face, not at all ugly. His mother, indeed, when she looked at him, called him her 'pretty boy.' He was thirty-six years old. He always kept his eyes downcast, when he was among strangers—and all those in this world are strangers. It was only, as in the old days, when he had roamed the country in search of an understanding of the ways of God, that he had looked at the sky. He was meek, and he was lowly, but his body was very strong; one needed it in these times of antichrist. Killing and burning, killing and burning. On the last day when the angels struggle with the hosts of Evil it will be like that! Already, coming back to his work at noon, Kalicz had observed the darkness on the sunshine, and his mother had said that the negro quarter of New York was burning, that a mob of the Evil had set fire to a negro orphanage which had two hundred little negro girls in it. Kalicz was like the Lord God Himself. He had no name. He had no father. And when he saw the works of destruction all around him, he had to bear it patiently.

Kalicz walked by the core-makers, and saw the hollow cores of baked sand mixed with oil. He walked by the bench-molders and saw all the dies that were used for the things that were not all created for the devastation of the world, but were some of them for ornament. He walked until he came to smoking molds. And then he had to take up, in his soft, shapeless hands, the spread, thin handles of the ladle, and support his burden. But when the ladle was empty, as it was this moment, it had little weight.

Kalicz walked behind the man ahead who was helping him to carry the ladle to the cupola. And when he reached the cupola, and set the ladle lined with clay upon the floor, the flames from the cupola were already bursting out. Under the spout of the cupola the big ladle was set upon wooden horses. The ladle was cold now, since the last pouring, and was lined with a silver, warty skin. But the cupola was charged. When the man who had stopped the spout with the bobstick, jumped back, pure, fiery water bubbled forth and fell whole, flickering, into the pail. The iron spattered, and the red embers, cooling—but not before they had shriveled the leather—fell on the men's shoes, and some of the men stepped back, frowning and blaspheming; but others did not appear to notice it. Kalicz stepped back a little, because the air that came out of the cupola was glowing hot; and he saw it shining rosy on the faces of all the men, as though it came, not out of the furnace, but out of the mouth of the Devil. For the Devil, in this time of evil, was all-powerful, more powerful, until his day should come, than the Almighty.

The embers that lay on the floor were like glass fruit fallen, ripe and hot. And the iron that brimmed the pail was whole and like glass. It shone with a great light, as if the Spirit of All Things swelled, alive, in the pail. Jets came up from it, clean spray came from it, and the jets were like bloody dew. The jets were as the dew of blood that spouted from the seven wounds of Jesus Christ Our Lord, on Crucifixion Day. And the iron, like a pot of lurid, sparkling jelly, held in its flesh the radiance of the Holy Ghost. There were a hundred and fifty pounds of iron in the ladle, and the iron looked like nothing at all, just as if it were nothing at all, and no more to be caught and kept in the pail, than was the sun without. Sometimes the iron was too heavy for a man to carry; then the ladle was not a hand ladle, but a crane ladle, and the crane, that was a great thing with iron claws, came down, with a grinding sound, all the chains and ropes that worked the crane making a grinding sound. And the iron that came out of the cupola and poured into the ladle was a thousand tons. And it, too, might have been as nothing.

But the light that sprang from it was as if the sun lay in a casket in the middle of the foundry, and basked itself, and the men basked together, in the light of the sun, and it was as in the beginning when the sun was near and there was neither day nor night.

Kalicz seized again his end of the forked handle of the ladle, and raised it up, and staggered, though it was not so much heavy, this ladleful, as awkward to carry. And the man ahead, who had spat upon his own hands and cursed a little for comfort, also had picked up his end of the ladle, and the two walked together through the dusty gloom, Kalicz and the man, carefully, because the iron in the ladle bulged, and flickered. And the light that was to light the world lay like the heart of all things, bulging over the pail and often dripping down the pail's sides, but not so much dripping as burning over, like burning water, that spouted, that sparkled, and then grew cold. And Kalicz had the idea that fire was not so much to blame, but that fire was a material thing and had no soul until it was heated and was hot in the cupola, like the pigs of iron that were piled in the shed outside the foundry, and that fire had its good uses and its evil uses, that fire was of God, originally, and that fire here, put to these uses, was of man and of the Devil, of the Evil One, who used fire for the torment of the wicked, but that might be because fire was of God and became, when the Evil were immersed in it, painful to them.

There was a heavy, dinning sound, like wind blowing, and it never stopped, in the place where Kalicz and the man walked with the iron that was red-hot like the heart of God, so that no man could approach it or look on it unless he blinked and his eyes watered. But the heart of God was a cold thing, even to sinners it was a cold thing. And the liquid bubbling, sparkling in the pot, was like boiling ice that had caught the sun. Never had Kalicz heard of ice that was hot, or seen ice boil, but the iron in the ladle, and the iron in the reservoir, and the iron that coursed down the conduit into the mold for the casting of the cylinder, when Kalicz and the man with him emptied the ladle into the reservoir and the iron ran down into the mold for the casting of a cylinder, *that* glowed like ice, but ice in which the sun is caught, and the sun melted, and fire and ice blended, as if the sun melted all the polar regions. And perhaps it was like that in the beginning of the world the priest had talked about.

Little burning streams, that were like the coiling of serpents, that were like the rotting and decaying of the spirit into the cold death of flesh into cold iron, like bodies rotting and decaying when the souls have left them, these ran bright and dying, over the floor. And when the iron gushed down into the cold mold and seeped through it, there was the loud pop of an explosion, and the men stepped back. But the iron always made a heavy sound when it ran into the mold. Once had Kalicz seen a man killed by an explosion, and the mold burst with the gases and the man did not step back in time, and was horribly burned, and was dead, because he, Kalicz guessed, was a soul God wished to save here and now, before it was too late, and the man would not descend from earth to purgatory, and would not go straight to hell, but would ascend to God, whose heart is tender for all sinners, and sit in heaven with Him. Why did God allow the fire and the iron to be used to make cannon? Kalicz was troubled, worried. There was a reason for this and there must be a reason for all things on earth, but what? He wondered sometimes if God had sent him here, in this place, to save the soul from sin and turn the iron to some good use. Because Poland and America were all one to God, and God's children did not fight, and it was said that in America brother fought with brother. Kalicz believed that all negroes were descended from Ham, not through Abel, but through Cain, and it was because Cain had killed his brother that God had punished them. But Kalicz believed that they had suffered enough. Maybe when the war was over the negroes would come again into white faces, and the faces of those who burned the negroes and tormented all the negroes would be black as coal. For I have sinned, Kalicz said to himself, yet God tells me if I carry my sin for a thousand years, I shall be forgiven in the end. He wanted to tell all the workmen that carried all the ladles that they would be forgiven. The priest at Cracow—yes, Kalicz had been to Cracow, too—he and Marja had been everywhere, to Cracow, too, because they had often been, after the count's trouble, like the Son of Man, who had nowhere to lay his head—the priest at Cracow declared that not even the nobles would go to heaven because they gave the church so little money. But Kalicz did not believe that. He did not believe that the priest had told the truth, or was a true man of God. The priest was, maybe, a false priest, and like these here in America who had no God; and here there were always the grimy men carrying the ladles, the floor where the earth was black with the dust of the iron, the molds smoking, the castings in the molds smoking and covered all over with the blue flames of the gases that sprang from the crevices in the molds, and the molds with the castings were covered all over with blue fire like the fire of the Devil, for the fire out of the Devil's mouth is always evil and is made with phosphorus. The iron, when it came from the cupola, would be pure and glow with a white light like the light of the sun, and the sparks that jetted from the cupola would be like the rain of the stars themselves on the last day, and the lightnings that sprang from the cupola would be bright as the candles on the altars of the churches. But when the fire was poured into the castings that made the guns and the boilers and the engines of the ships to carry guns, it was turned to evil and burned blue, and there were *pop-pop* sounds all through the shed and through the foundry like the sounds the guns make, and the men's faces as they stared downward on the small molds and upward on the big molds were like the faces of Satan's foul imps, and the molds and the castings burning with little flames of blue were like the devil's altars, not the altars in a church. Because all was given over to the devil. The Corliss engine that turned the wheel that turned the belts that turned the other wheels—it was fed with the fire, and the steam, and had a flaming breath, but it ran by itself. Day and night, day and night it ran and was hungry, and was always red-hot. And the air in the foundry with the castings was white with steam. The men were sometimes hidden from each other in the steam.

Kalicz's punishment was to work here where Evil reigned, for God had told Kalicz not to be a man, and never to look on woman as Adam in his original sin looked on Eve, and Kalicz was thought generally never to have come to manhood because he had no beard, and people who had known him said this, his mother, Marja, was the man, and Kalicz, her son, was not a man. And there had been a time when Kalicz had been troubled because no hair grew on his face or anywhere on his body, and he knew none of the pleasures of being a man. Marja had three hairs in three moles on her chin, and she was not a man. But the priest told Kalicz he must be content as God had made him and must do God's work. But the Jewish girl had come to Cracow from Warsaw, because in Warsaw, or some other place, there was a pogrom. The people of Christ had risen up to destroy the Jews and the homes of the Jews, and the family of the Jewish girl had fled to Cracow where there was no pogrom—at least in that year there was no pogrom. And Kalicz had pitied the Jewish girl because she and her family had suffered the wrath of God, but not the compassion and forgiveness of the Son of God who forgives all who confess the True Church. But there are no Jews in the True Church. Kalicz pitied the Jewish girl, and he used to follow her. And he followed her until, one day, she was frightened. And he saw that she had not understood what he wanted, which was to tell her that in all things we are brothers, and that even among the Jews there may be Brothers in Christ. But Kalicz had an infirmity in his speech, and when he tried to talk he became confused. And when he could not tell the Jewish girl what it was necessary to tell her to bring her comfort, he ran after her, and followed her into the Jewish quarter of the city, among the evil of her own race, and he caught at her shawl. But she believed that he had intended something different. And she cried out, and the people of her own race came and thought that Kalicz was attacking her. And he had to slink away. But he continued to want to save her. But when Kalicz told the priest, the priest thought the same as the girl, that Kalicz had seen a woman who was a Jewess and had followed her, not for the sake of her soul, but for the satisfaction of a base desire. And Kalicz was shamed, because what the priest said had seemed at the time to be true, and because Kalicz was not a man, and did not even know how to behave himself properly in the company of women. Yes, his desire for the Jewish girl, after the talk with the priest, had grown and grown, though the priest said that no Jews could be saved. For the Jews, like the Russians, who are worse than the Jews, belong to the damned who have no true religion. And Kalicz had scourged himself. But he had never forgotten the Jewish girl. And he had never quite given up the idea that even the Jewish women who, like the Russians, are often beautiful, may be saved for God and the Church. Marja could shed tears over her son, who would never grow to manhood, and Kalicz was patient with her. In America, Kalicz and Marja lived in a loft not far from the foundry, and Marja, who was small, so short that she was no taller than a child of twelve, worked in a factory for making pants. And Marja sang in America just as she had always sung in Poland. She was a little brisk woman, with a cheery face, who wore a black handkerchief, and moved about all the time and could never sit still and was always busy. Marja had the soul of a cricket that will chirp no matter where. In New York she had bought a hen and a cock, and the hen laid an egg now and then, and the cock lived in the loft, and the cock went to rest on the rafters, and the cock crowed every morning and waked up Marja and Kalicz and was better than a clock and was not a machine and cost less and was more company. Marja called the cock 'Kochanek' (dearest), and Kalicz she called 'Kochanek,' also, for she loved both. In America there were few Poles, but Marja was very gay, even when sad. In Cracow where Marja had lived a long time she had learned to dance the Krakowiak, and she could dance very spryly for an old woman. Marja knew all the dances of all the towns and the countries she had lived in, and she could dance obertases, and Cracoviennes, and the mazurka, and the hop-sa-sa, and even dance the polka like a lady. In Cracow, she had worn two earrings, one in each ear, but on the ship coming to America she had lost an earring, and now she wore only one. But she was saving to buy herself another earring. Kalicz often wondered how it was that Marja, who was never troubled by the decrees of God, and who had lived a sinful life and committed the sin of her sex long after the time of life when it is common, still seemed to be a good woman, and was never troubled by her conscience. Kalicz loved his mother and she loved him.

"Nech będzie pochwalony," Marja used to say in Poland when she met a man or a woman on the street. And the man or the woman would answer, "Na wieki wickow," which was the pious way to greet people and not as it is done in America. Marja was a woman who greeted everybody piously, but she was not pious, and did not love churches, though she was proud of her son. Kalicz could not understand, but he knew the Lord forgave her. Kalicz knew that his mother had one day been drawing water from the studnia and had met a stranger there and they had spoken to one another, and the next thing the gossips said was that Marja, besides entertaining the stranger in her own cottage on boiled potatoes, had been free with him in other ways, and the next day he had left the town. And Marja never answered anybody's questions. When they tried to question her or abuse her, she began to sing and to praise God. Kalicz could not understand how his old mother, who was gray-haired, and must be well on to fifty, had this attraction for men who were always younger, and boys like himself. Marja was not lazy. She could carry big sacks of flour, almost as heavy as the iron, and could work like a man. Maybe God then forgave her for other things, because in this world, whether it appears so or not, all is arranged justly.

Kalicz saw the last pail of swollen, glowing iron run out from the cupola, and the men were swearing and were much excited, because they said New York was burning. New York was burning up and there was rioting in the streets not six blocks away, and they told the boss they wanted to quit work. And the boss was scared. And Kalicz, who had only been two years in America and only understood a little English, knew that the boss was scared and would let the men quit work earlier than usual. And the men were saying that the rioting was about the draft, but they had nothing to do with the draft, because they were engaged in what was known as 'vital labor,' and they could not be called on the draft, because they were especially excused, because they made the guns. But Kalicz was an ordinary laborer and might be called upon the draft because he could be replaced.

Kalicz listened, but he did not say anything. He listened and trembled a little, because he was not a man to fight, and he feared death as much as the others did; even after the promises of God he feared death. The men did not wash their hands that were greasy and smelled of oil and dust, and he did not wash his hands. The belts were still running and some of the castings were still hot in the molds, but many men, excited like children, were leaving the foundry to go home, and some were alarmed and wondered if their homes were burning, but if their homes were burning they only cursed.

Kalicz saw the last spill of myriad coals scattered on the ground when the cupola was emptied and left to cool, and he picked up his hat that was battered and put it on and he picked up his coat and hung it on his arm and he walked on with his eyes bent down on the ground as if he were looking for something. Nobody noticed him. The workmen were running to get their hats and coats and shouting to each other, and the boss said he would have to close the foundry for a few days if the rioting kept up, and he was afraid, and the foundry had to be locked up carefully, and the boss was especially afraid of fire which was already only three blocks off, and the fire engines could be heard, but the foundry was on the river and by the water and if the fire came they could put it out, and the boss was going to leave a special watchman to watch the foundry. But he did not want Kalicz to help. Kalicz was in the way.

He went out of the dim, smoking air of the foundry and it was already dark, and the fire that was burning up some negro houses was much farther off than he had imagined, but there was a glow in the sky. It was quiet around the water. There were some people in the streets and they were going home. They all seemed afraid of each other. A man passed Kalicz and looked at him, and Kalicz, shuffling along slowly, glanced up sidewise and looked at the man. And Kalicz thought both he and the man must look as if they were afraid of each other. And Kalicz was troubled. Why had man turned against man, and why had people who were brothers in the eyes of Christ begun suddenly to rob and burn and to murder?

Some workmen from his own foundry passed him in the dim street. One of them was running. The others began to run, too. And one who had reached a corner and was waiting there called, "I got to go down there where the trouble is anyhow and see what it's all about." And the others seemed to want to see, too.

Kalicz was frightened. He had to follow them, because the way they were going was the way home. He hesitated. Just beside him, only a little ahead, nearer where the men were, was a big wall like a box going up into the sky. And the big wall, that was not half finished, was flanked by lumber and a little scaffolding. Kalicz knew that this was the big grain elevator that was being built and would be like the Tower of Babel, and would go right up into the sky. They were building more and more things that would go right up into the sky and would affront God. Son, the fine women were never meant for you, Kalicz could hear his mother saying. Rolling her sleeves up, when she was at work, she would go on talking in her little raucous voice, or she would sing shrilly. But Kalicz knew that even Marja was not so happy in America as she once had been. None of them were happy in America. He was oppressed by a great sorrow for the world. Marja always told him that she was never tired, that she could do the work of ten men at least. But he had caught her crying. And he had been a bad son to her, because he had never grown to proper manhood, nor here in America had he ever done God's work properly. The work done for money and for hunger is never done for the love of Christ. Kalicz believed as long as the Powers of Evil were reigning in America he must work in the foundry. In Poland he had received alms and praised God.

The flood of light on the dusky sky stirred him. He was certain that he owed some duty to this burning world. What could it be? When he had reached New York, he had meant to do as before, and had made inquiry if there were any churches. But the people had shown him no churches, and the churches they had were not the True Church, and here all that was preached and was called the Word of God was intermingled with a foreign tongue.

Kalicz, standing by the water, hearing the water lap under the wharves, and seeing the faint huge shape of the grain elevator high above him like some heathen effigy, was troubled because already God had begun to destroy this world of Evil, and to destroy it with fire. He longed to ask God to desist. But who was Kalicz to question God? Two hundred little negro girls had been burned. Two hundred little negro virgins had been claimed by God's Word and had gone to Him in Heaven. But the foundry would be destroyed. Would the belts running and the engines turning the great wheel be destroyed, and would the cupola itself be melted, and would the steam machines that bound the souls of men be melted? Kalicz could not hate anybody. The greatest hate he felt now for the factory and the foundry was more like a thorn pricking his heart than a hate that could consume or seek revenge. Yet he was not sorry. The men who were enslaved by the engines would be freed. The men who had cursed Kalicz and had abused Kalicz and had called Kalicz a dirty Polack would be freed and they would forget how to curse. The boss would be freed. But only if the foundries that made the ammunitions and the factories that enslaved and destroyed the souls of men were destroyed.

Kalicz took off his small, round hat and turned it and turned it in his formless little hands. There was a great responsibility upon him to do something at the end of the world before it was too late. There was no joy in America. He gazed up and down the dingy street of warehouses and by the new elevator that he could just make out in the dark, and thought there was no joy in America. Men were enslaved and did not know the joy there is in believing on Jesus Christ Our Lord, and not in machinery. But the fire that was destroying the world of evil had begun in the wrong place. It should have begun here first.

There were a few dim steps leading down to the yard of the new elevator. Sidling carefully, because it was too gloomy, and too near night for him to see very well. Kalicz went down to the yard. He laid his hat on the ground—no, he picked it up and replaced it on his soft, fine black hair. He went on, walking like a blind man, and he found an armful of excelsior, some scattered wood. He took the wood and the excelsior and laid them up against the wall of the new elevator. There were two elevators, this one and one a little beyond. They had cost three hundred thousand dollars. Kalicz went on piling up planks and kindling. When he had made three nice heaps against the new wall, he took some matches from his pocket and lighted the heaps. He was cold, he was shivering. Yet he thought that was what ought to be done. If God was destroying the world and was destroying the houses and the homes of people, it was not that which should be destroyed first, but the factories and the engines, and the foundries where the engines lived and were making armament. Kalicz hoped that he would not attract God's anger, yet if he had done so, so be it. God had once been angry with His only Son, and Him had He crucified.

Kalicz was not angry with anybody. It was very quiet. The water plashed on the posts of the wharf. There were night sounds, some cries very distant; but all the workmen had gone home from the factories and nobody passed. Kalicz watched the fire burn. It crackled in the kindling, spread more lushly up the planks and soon was towering farther, sending a reflection like a curtain of gold over the whole face of the night, so that Kalicz could not see anything at all but the fire burning. With the back of his hand he wiped his bland brow. Maybe the people to whom he tried to do good would punish him, would be angered with him for making way with that which cost so much money, which had taken so long to make, and would not understand that their real interest did not lie in pleasing those who employed them, but in pleasing Jesus Christ.

He blinked dazedly. The fire was growing bigger than he had expected. He was uneasy before it. He hoped that it would consume only that which had to be consumed, the demons and pestilential spirits—even the big wheel, that turned in the shed, half in the ceiling, and half under the earth. It never tired. Or, if it hesitated for an instant, the piston, which was as bright as a steel bone, and indicated that the wheel lived without eating, would thrust at it suddenly, and the wheel, that was as big as the sun seen when it sinks in the ocean, would begin to move again. Kalicz crossed himself. Unlike the fire that shines from heaven, and that shines fine in the cupola before the soul mixes with matter, is steam, which some say issues from mountains. All that belongs in the sky is of God, while all those forces active in the bowels of the earth are given over to the Devil. Before man learned to imprison steam he depended for everything on God's bounty and the work of his own hands. Kalicz had failed to please the Jewess, but he had never since been able to reconcile himself to God's will. He had asked for a wife. A wife, Marja said, was not to be had for the asking. Kalicz saw plainly that one thing he had sold his birthright to the factory for had been for an answer to his prayer for a wife. He had deceived God and sometimes he had deceived himself. But that was the truth. The love of Christ, so all-sufficing, had not appeared to him enough. O God, humble me, God forgive me, Kalicz thought, crossing himself. Eleven thousand black virgins have been sacrificed to the lust of the wheel and the engines. Save us from further sin and the penalties of sin.

Far out on the river a steamship moved. He saw its hollow lights and heard the shuffling whistle, while the hulk passed mysteriously. That also is of the monster. Naked like a bone of the unburied dead, a steel arm pushes, and the wheel, glad to obey, revolves its glittering eye in a halo sacrilegiously borrowed from the saints.

Hearing the steamboat, and realizing how numerous were the wheel's progeny, Kalicz panted, sweated, resumed a more diligent labor to pile the wood higher, until the monolith of Babel should be lit like marble.

There was a moon rising. With its rosy hair spread out, it showed like a sign above the roofs of the warehouses. There were angels in the dark clouds rushing from upper New York over the moon's face. They spread themselves over the moon of blood, over the moon of iron. They covered the lamps in the houses of Brooklyn. The moon hung like beaten iron in the sky. The wheel turned. The wheel turned and the spokes that were fashioned of the bones of the workers turned in the wheel and flashed over New York. The moon was cold and the earth was cold.

Kalicz threw more wood on the blaze. The whited sepulchre was igniting. Flames ran along up the new boards in the scorching walls. Exorcised demons flitted high in the cloud of smoke. With the stare of a blind man, Kalicz lifted his head and gazed at the high, infinitesimal windows of the elevators, and saw the demons quaking, the demons howling, the glass shattered. The silver glass burst asunder. The eye of fire looked out from the window. Fire was purified of all its dross, and there was only water and light, where the flames shone molten and the East River was enmeshed in blood, where the East River was like brass, where the East River flowed out to the Harbor that was blood. Kalicz was a very, very humble man of God. He was scarcely mindful of the hoodlums that were collecting and were prancing about him, or of the frightened people who were pointing at him, saying, "This is the man! This is he who called himself King of the Jews!"

Yellow Woman

LESLIE SILKO

I

My thigh clung to his with dampness, and I watched the sun rising up through the tamaracks and willows. The small brown water birds came to the river and hopped across the mud, leaving brown scratches in the alkali-white crust. They bathed in the river silently. I could hear the water, almost at our feet where the narrow fast channel bubbled and washed green ragged moss and fern leaves. I looked at him beside me, rolled in the red blanket on the white river sand. I cleaned the sand out of the cracks between my toes, squinting because the sun was above the willow trees. I looked at him for the last time, sleeping on the white river sand.

I felt hungry and followed the river south the way we had come the afternoon before, following our footprints that were already blurred by lizard tracks and bug trails. The horses were still lying down, and the black one whinnied when he saw me but he did not get up—maybe it was because the corral was made out of thick cedar branches and the horses had not yet felt the sun like I had. I tried to look beyond the pale red mesas to the pueblo. I knew it was there, even if I could not see it, on the sandrock hill above the river, the same river that moved past me now and had reflected the moon last night.

The horse felt warm underneath me. He shook his head and pawed the sand. The bay whinnied and leaned against the gate trying to follow, and I remembered him asleep in the red blanket beside the river. I slid off the horse and tied him close to the other horse. I walked north with the river again, and the white sand broke loose in footprints over footprints.

"Wake up."

He moved in the blanket and turned his face to me with his eyes still closed. I knelt down to touch him.

"I'm leaving."

He smiled now, eyes still closed. "You are coming with me, remember?" He sat up now with his bare dark chest and belly in the sun.

"Where?"

"To my place."

"And will I come back?"

He pulled his pants on. I walked away from him, feeling him behind me and smelling the willows.

"Yellow Woman," he said.

I turned to face him. "Who are you?" I asked.

He laughed and knelt on the low, sandy bank, washing his face in the river. "Last night you guessed my name, and you knew why I had come."

I stared past him at the shallow moving water and tried to remember the night, but I could only see the moon in the water and remember his warmth around me.

"But I only said that you were him and that I was Yellow Woman—I'm not really her—I have my own name and I come from the pueblo on the other side of the mesa. Your name is Silva and you are a stranger I met by the river yesterday afternoon."

He laughed softly. "What happened yesterday has nothing to do with what you will do today, Yellow Woman."

"I know—that's what I'm saying—the old stories about the ka'tsina spirit and Yellow Woman can't mean us."

My old grandpa liked to tell those stories best. There is one about Badger and Coyote who went hunting and were gone all day, and when the sun was going down they found a house. There was a girl living there alone, and she had light hair and eyes and she told them that they could sleep with her. Coyote wanted to be with her all night so he sent Badger into a prairie-dog hole, telling him he thought he saw something in it. As soon as Badger crawled in, Coyote blocked up the entrance with rocks and hurried back to Yellow Woman.

"Come here," he said gently.

He touched my neck and I moved close to him to feel his breathing and to hear his heart. I was wondering if Yellow Woman had known who she was—if she knew that she would become part of the stories. Maybe she'd had another name that her husband and relatives called her so that only the ka'tsina from the north and the storytellers would know her as Yellow Woman. But I didn't go on; I felt him all around me, pushing me down into the white river sand.

Yellow Woman went away with the spirit from the north and lived with him and his relatives. She was gone for a long time, but then one day she came back and she brought twin boys.

"Do you know the story?"

"What story?" He smiled and pulled me close to him as he said this. I was afraid lying there on the red blanket. All I could know was the way he felt, warm, damp, his body beside me. This is the way it happens in the stories. I was thinking, with no thought beyond the moment she meets the ka'tsina spirit and they go.

"I don't have to go. What they tell in stories was real only then, back in time immemorial, like they say."

He stood up and pointed at my clothes tangled in the blanket. "Let's go," he said.

I walked beside him, breathing hard because he walked fast, his hand around my wrist. I had stopped trying to pull away from him, because his hand felt cool and the sun was high, drying the river bed into alkali. I will see someone, eventually I will see someone, and then I will be certain that he is only a man—some man from nearby—and I will be sure that I am not Yellow Woman. Because she is from out of time past and I live now and I've been to school and there are highways and pickup trucks that Yellow Woman never saw.

It was an easy ride north on horseback. I watched the change from the cottonwood trees along the river to the junipers that brushed past us in the foothills, and finally there were only piñons, and when I looked up at the rim of the mountain plateau I could see pine trees growing on the edge. Once I stopped to look down, but the pale sandstone had disappeared and the river was gone and the dark lava hills were all around. He touched my hand, not speaking, but always singing softly a mountain song and looking into my eyes.

I felt hungry and wondered what they were doing at home now—my mother, my grandmother, my husband, and the baby. Cooking breakfast, saying, "Where did she go?—maybe kidnaped," and Al going to the tribal police with the details: "She went walking along the river."

The house was made with black lava rock and red mud. It was high above the spreading miles of arroyos and long mesas. I smelled a mountain smell of pitch and buck brush. I stood there beside the black horse, looking down on the small, dim country we had passed, and I shivered.

"Yellow Woman, come inside where it's warm."

II

He lit a fire in the stove. It was an old stove with a round belly and an enamel coffeepot on top. There was only the stove, some faded Navajo blankets, and a bedroll and cardboard box. The floor was made of smooth adobe plaster, and there was one small window facing east. He pointed at the box.

"There's some potatoes and the frying pan." He sat on the floor with his arms around his knees pulling them close to his chest and he watched me fry the potatoes. I didn't mind him watching me because he was always watching me—he had been watching me since I came upon him sitting on the river bank trimming leaves from a willow twig with his knife. We ate from the pan and he wiped the grease from his fingers on his Levis.

"Have you brought women here before?" He smiled and kept chewing, so I said, "Do you always use the same tricks?"

"What tricks?" He looked at me like he didn't understand.

"The story about being a ka'tsina from the mountains. The story about Yellow Woman."

Silva was silent, his face was calm.

"I don't believe it. Those stories couldn't happen now," I said.

He shook his head and said softly, "But someday they will talk about us, and they will say, 'Those two lived long ago when things like that happened.'"

He stood up and went out. I ate the rest of the potatoes and thought about things—about the noise the stove was making and the sound of the mountain wind outside. I remembered yesterday and the day before, and then I went outside.

I walked past the corral to the edge where the narrow trail cut through the black rim rock. I was standing in the sky with nothing around me but the wind that came down from the mountain peak behind me. I could see faint mountain images in the distance miles across the vast spread of mesa and valleys and plains. I wondered who was over there to feel the mountain wind on those sheer blue edges—who walks on the pine needles in those blue mountains.

"Can you see the pueblo?" Silva was standing behind me.

I shook my head. "We're too far away."

"From here I can see the world." He stepped out on the edge. "The Navajo reservation begins over there." He pointed to the east. "The Pueblo boundaries are over here." He looked below us to the south, where the narrow trail seemed to come from. "The Texans have their ranches over there, starting with that valley, the Concho Valley. The Mexicans run some cattle over there too."

"Do you ever work for them?"

"I steal from them," Silva answered. The sun was dropping behind us and shadows were filling the land below. I turned away from the edge that dropped forever into the valleys below.

"I'm cold," I said; "I'm going inside." I started wondering about this man who could speak the Pueblo language so well but who lived on a mountain and rustled cattle. I decided that this man Silva must be Navajo, because Pueblo men didn't do things like that.

"You must be a Navajo."

Silva shook his head gently. "Little Yellow Woman," he said, "you never give up, do you? I have told you who I am. The Navajo people know me, too." He knelt down and unrolled the bedroll and spread the extra blankets out on a piece of canvas. The sun was down, and the only light in the house came from outside—the dim orange light from sundown.

I stood there and waited for him to crawl under the blankets.

"What are you waiting for?" he said, and I lay down beside him. He undressed me slowly like the night before beside the river—kissing my face gently and running his hands up and down my belly and legs. He took off my pants and then he laughed.

"Why are you laughing?"

"You are breathing so hard."

I pulled away from him and turned my back to him.

He pulled me around and pinned me down with his arms and chest. "You don't understand, do you, little Yellow Woman? You will do what I want."

And again he was all around me with his skin slippery against mine, and I was afraid because I understood that his strength could hurt me. I lay beneath him and I knew that he could destroy me. But later, while he slept beside me, I touched his face and I had a feeling—the kind of feeling for him that overcame me that morning along the river. I kissed him on the forehead and he reached out for me.

When I woke up in the morning he was gone. It gave me a strange feeling because for a long time I sat there on the blankets and looked around the little house for some object of his—some proof that he had been there or maybe that he was coming back. Only the blanket and the cardboard box remained. The .30-30 that had been leaning in the corner was gone, and so was the knife I had used the night before. He was gone, and I had my chance to go now. But first I had to eat, because I knew it would be a long walk home.

I found some dried apricots in the cardboard box, and I sat down on a rock at the edge of the plateau rim. There was no wind and the sun warmed me. I was surrounded by silence. I drowsed with apricots in my mouth, and I didn't believe that there were highways or railroads or cattle to steal.

When I woke up, I stared down at my feet in the black mountain dirt. Little black ants were swarming over the pine needles around my foot. They must have smelled the apricots. I thought about my family far below me. They would be wondering about me, because this had never happened to me before. The tribal police would file a report. But if old Grandpa weren't dead he would tell them what happened—he would laugh and say, "Stolen by a ka'tsina, a mountain spirit. She'll come home—they usually do." There are enough of them to handle things. My mother and grandmother will raise the baby like they raised me. Al will find someone else, and they will go on like before, except that there will be a story about the day I disappeared while I was walking along the river. Silva had come for me; he said he had. I did not decide to go. I just went. Moonflowers blossom in the sand hills before dawn just as I followed him. That's what I was thinking as I wandered along the trail through the pine trees.

It was noon when I got back. When I saw the stone house I remembered that I had meant to go home. But that didn't seem important any more, maybe because there were little blue flowers growing in the meadow behind the stone house and the gray squirrels were playing in the pines next to the house. The horses were standing in the corral, and there was a beef carcass hanging on the shady side of a big pine in front of the house. Flies buzzed around the clotted blood that hung from the carcass. Silva was washing his hands in a bucket full of water. He must have heard me coming because he spoke to me without turning to face me.

"I've been waiting for you."

"I went walking in the big pine trees."

I looked into the bucket full of bloody water with brown-and-white animal hairs floating in it. Silva stood there letting his hand drip, examining me intently.

"Are you coming with me?"

"Where?" I asked him.

"To sell the meat in Marquez."

"If you're sure it's O.K."

"I wouldn't ask you if it wasn't," he answered.

He sloshed the water around in the bucket before he dumped it out and set the bucket upside down near the door. I followed him to the corral and watched him saddle the horses. Even beside the horses he looked tall, and I asked him again if he wasn't Navajo. He didn't say anything; he just shook his head and kept cinching up the saddle.

"But Navajos are tall."

"Get on the horse," he said, "and let's go."

The last thing he did before we started down the steep trail was to grab the .30-30 from the corner. He slid the rifle into the scabbard that hung from his saddle.

"Do they ever try to catch you?" I asked.

"They don't know who I am."

"Then why did you bring the rifle?"

"Because we are going to Marquez where the Mexicans live."

III

The trail leveled out on a narrow ridge that was steep on both sides like an animal spine. On one side I could see where the trail went around the rocky gray hills and disappeared into the southeast where the pale sandrock mesas stood in the distance near my home. On the other side was a trail that went west, and as I looked far into the distance I thought I saw the little town. But Silva said no, that I was looking in the wrong place, that I just thought I saw houses. After that I quit looking off into the distance; it was hot and the wildflowers were closing up their deep-yellow petals. Only the waxy cactus flowers bloomed in the bright sun, and I saw every color that a cactus blossom can be: the white ones and the red ones were still buds, but the purple and the yellow were blossoms, open full and the most beautiful of all.

Silva saw him before I did. The white man was riding a big gray horse, coming up the trail toward us. He was traveling fast and the gray horse's feet sent rocks rolling off the trail into the dry tumbleweeds. Silva motioned for me to stop and we watched the white man. He didn't see us right away, but finally his horse whinnied at our horses and he stopped. He looked at us briefly before he loped the gray horse across the three hundred yards that separated us. He stopped his horse in front of Silva, and his young fat face was shadowed by the brim of his hat. He didn't look mad, but his small, pale eyes moved from the blood-soaked gunny sacks hanging from my saddle to Silva's face and then back to my face.

"Where did you get the fresh meat?" the white man asked.

"I've been hunting," Silva said, and when he shifted his weight in the saddle the leather creaked.

"The hell you have, Indian. You've been rustling cattle. We've been looking for the thief for a long time."

The rancher was fat, and sweat began to soak through his white cowboy shirt and the wet cloth stuck to the thick rolls of belly fat. He almost seemed to be panting from the exertion of talking, and he smelled rancid, maybe because Silva scared him.

Silva turned to me and smiled. "Go back up the mountain, Yellow Woman."

The white man got angry when he heard Silva speak in a language he couldn't understand. "Don't try anything, Indian. Just keep riding to Marquez. We'll call the state police from there."

The rancher must have been unarmed because he was very frightened and if he had a gun he would have pulled it out then. I turned my horse around and the rancher yelled, "Stop!" I looked at Silva for an instant and there was something ancient and dark—something I could feel in my stomach—in his eyes, and when I glanced at his hand I saw his finger on the trigger of the .30-30 that was still in the saddle scabbard. I slapped my horse across the flank and the sacks of raw meat swung against my knees as the horse leaped up the trail. It was hard to keep my balance, and once I thought I felt the saddle slipping backward; it was because of this that I could not look back.

I didn't stop until I reached the ridge where the trail forked. The horse was breathing deep gasps and there was a dark film of sweat on its neck. I looked down in the direction I had come from, but I couldn't see the place. I waited. The wind came up and pushed warm air past me. I looked up at the sky, pale blue and full of thin clouds and fading vapor trails left by jets.

I think four shots were fired—I remember hearing four hollow explosions that reminded me of deer hunting. There could have been more shots after that, but I couldn't have heard them because my horse was running again and the loose rocks were making too much noise as they scattered around his feet.

Horses have a hard time running downhill, but I went that way instead of uphill to the mountain because I thought it was safer. I felt better with the horse running southeast past the round gray hills that were covered with cedar trees and black lava rock. When I got to the plain in the distance I could see the dark green patches of tamaracks that grew along the river; and beyond the river I could see the beginning of the pale sandrock mesas. I stopped the horse and looked back to see if anyone was coming; then I got off the horse and turned the horse around, wondering if it would go back to its corral under the pines on the mountain. It looked back at me for a moment and then plucked a mouthful of green tumbleweeds before it trotted back up the trail with its ears pointed forward, carrying its head daintily to one side to avoid stepping on the dragging reins. When the horse disappeared over the last hill, the gunny sacks full of meat were still swinging and bouncing.

IV

I walked toward the river on a wood-hauler's road that I knew would eventually lead to the paved road. I was thinking about waiting beside the road for someone to drive by, but by the time I got to the pavement I had decided it wasn't very far to walk if I followed the river back the way Silva and I had come.

The river water tasted good, and I sat in the shade under a cluster of silvery willows. I thought about Silva, and I felt sad at leaving him; still, there was something strange about him, and I tried to figure it out all the way back home.

I came back to the place on the river bank where he had been sitting the first time I saw him. The green willow leaves that he had trimmed from the branch were still lying there, wilted in the sand. I saw the leaves and I wanted to go back to him—to kiss him and to touch him—but the mountains were too far away now. And I told myself, because I believe it, he will come back sometime and be waiting again by the river.

*   *   *

I followed the path up from the river into the village. The sun was getting low, and I could smell supper cooking when I got to the screen door of my house. I could hear their voices inside—my mother was telling my grandmother how to fix the Jell-o and my husband, Al, was playing with the baby. I decided to tell them that some Navajo had kidnaped me, but I was sorry that old Grandpa wasn't alive to hear my story because it was the Yellow Woman stories he liked to tell best.

Gimpel the Fool

ISAAC BASHEVIS SINGER

I

I am Gimpel the fool. I don't think myself a fool. On the contrary. But that's what folks call me. They gave me the name while I was still in school. I had seven names in all: imbecile, donkey, flax-head, dope, glump, ninny, and fool. The last name stuck. What did my foolishness consist of? I was easy to take in. They said, "Gimpel, you know the rabbi's wife has been brought to childbed?" So I skipped school. Well, it turned out to be a lie. How was I supposed to know? She hadn't had a big belly. But I never looked at her belly. Was that really so foolish? The gang laughed and hee-hawed, stomped and danced and chanted a good-night prayer. And instead of raisins they give when a woman's lying in, they stuffed my hand full of goat turds. I was no weakling. If I slapped someone he'd see all the way to Cracow. But I'm really not a slugger by nature. I think to myself: Let it pass. So they take advantage of me.

I was coming home from school and heard a dog barking. I'm not afraid of dogs, but of course I never want to start up with them. One of them may be mad, and if he bites there's not a Tartar in the world who can help you. So I made tracks. Then I looked around and saw the whole market place wild with laughter. It was no dog at all but Wolf-Leib the Thief. How was I supposed to know it was he? It sounded like a howling bitch.

When the pranksters and leg-pullers found that I was easy to fool, every one of them tried his luck with me. "Gimpel, the Czar is coming to Frampol: Gimpel, the moon fell down in Turbeen; Gimpel, little Hodel Furpiece found a treasure behind the bathhouse." And I like a golem believed everyone. In the first place, everything is possible, as it is written in the Wisdom of the Fathers. I've forgotten just how: Second, I had to believe when the whole town came down on me! If I ever dared to say, "Ah, you're kidding!"

there was trouble. People got angry. "What do you mean! You want to call everyone a liar?" What was I to do? I believed them, and I hope at least that did them some good.

I was an orphan. My grandfather who brought me up was already bent toward the grave. So they turned me over to a baker, and what a time they gave me there! Every woman or girl who came to bake a batch of noodles had to fool me at least once. "Gimpel, there's a fair in heaven; Gimpel, the rabbi gave birth to a calf in the seventh month; Gimpel, a cow flew over the roof and laid brass eggs." A student from the yeshiva came once to buy a roll, and he said, "You, Gimpel, while you stand here scraping with your baker's shovel the Messiah has come. The dead are arisen." "What do you mean?" I said. "I heard no one blowing the ram's horn!" He said, "Are you deaf?" And all began to cry, "We heard it, we heard!" Then in came Rietze the Candle-dipper and called out in her hoarse voice, "Gimpel, your father and mother have stood up from the grave. They are looking for you."

To tell the truth, I knew very well that nothing of the sort had happened, but all the same, as folks were talking, I threw on my wool vest and went out. Maybe something had happened. What did I stand to lose by looking? Well, what a cat music went up! And then I took a vow to believe nothing more. But that was no go either. They confused me so that I didn't know the big end from the small.

I went to the rabbi to get some advice. He said, "It is written, better to be a fool all your days than for one hour to be evil. You are not a fool. They are the fools. For he who causes his neighbor to feel shame loses Paradise himself." Nevertheless the rabbi's daughter took me in. As I left the rabbinical court she said, "Have you kissed the wall yet?" I said, "No; what for?" She answered, "It's the law; you've got to do it after every visit." Well, there didn't seem to be any harm in it. And she burst out laughing. It was a fine trick. She put one over on me, all right.

I wanted to go off to another town, but then everyone got busy matchmaking, and they were after me so they nearly tore my coat tails off. They talked at me and talked until I got water on the ear. She was no chaste maiden, but they told me she was virgin pure. She had a limp, and they said it was deliberate, from coyness. She had a bastard, and they told me the child was her little brother. I cried, "You're wasting your time. I'll never marry that whore." But they said indignantly, "What a way to talk! Aren't you ashamed of yourself? We can take you to the rabbi and have you fined for giving her a bad name." I saw then that I wouldn't escape them so easily and I thought: They're set on making me their butt. But when you're married the husband's the master, and if that's all right with her it's agreeable to me too. Besides, you can't pass through life unscathed, nor expect to.

I went to her clay house, which was built on the sand, and the whole gang, hollering and chorusing, came after me. They acted like bear-baiters. When we came to the well they stopped all the same. They were afraid to start anything with Elka. Her mouth would open as if it were on a hinge, and she had a fierce tongue. I entered the house. Lines were strung from wall to wall and clothes were drying. Barefoot she stood by the tub, doing the wash. She was dressed in a worn hand-me-down gown of plush. She had her hair put up in braids and pinned across her head. It took my breath away, almost, the reek of it all.

Evidently she knew who I was. She took a look at me and said, "Look who's here! He's come, the drip. Grab a seat."

I told her all; I denied nothing. "Tell me the truth," I said, "are you really a virgin, and is that mischievous Yechiel actually your little brother? Don't be deceitful with me, for I'm an orphan."

"I'm an orphan myself," she answered, "and whoever tries to twist you up, may the end of his nose take a twist. But don't let them think they can take advantage of me. I want a dowry of fifty guilders, and let them take up a collection besides. Otherwise they can kiss my you-know-what." She was very plainspoken. I said, "It's the bride and not the groom who gives a dowry." Then she said, "Don't bargain with me. Either a flat 'yes' or a flat 'no'—Go back where you came from."

I thought: No bread will ever be baked from *this* dough. But ours is not a poor town. They consented to everything and proceeded with the wedding. It so happened that there was a dysentery epidemic at the time. The ceremony was held at the cemetery gates, near the little corpse-washing hut. The fellows got drunk. While the marriage contract was being drawn up I heard the most pious high rabbi ask, "Is the bride a widow or a divorced woman?" And the sexton's wife answered for her, "Both a widow and divorced." It was a black moment for me. But what was I to do, run away from under the marriage canopy?

There was singing and dancing. An old granny danced opposite me, hugging a braided white *chalah*. The master of revels made a "God 'a mercy" in memory of the bride's parents. The schoolboys threw burrs, as on Tishe b'Av fast day. There were a lot of gifts after the sermon: a noodle board, a kneading trough, a bucket, brooms, ladles, household articles galore. Then I took a look and saw two strapping young men carrying a crib. "What do we need this for?" I asked. So they said, "Don't rack your brains about it. It's all right, it'll come in handy." I realized I was going to be rooked. Take it another way though, what did I stand to lose? I reflected: I'll see what comes of it. A whole town can't go altogether crazy.

II

At night I came where my wife lay, but she wouldn't let me in. "Say, look here, is this what they married us for?" I said. And she said, "My monthly has come." "But yesterday they took you to the ritual bath, and that's afterward, isn't it supposed to be?" "Today isn't yesterday," said she, "and yesterday's not today. You can beat it if you don't like it." In short, I waited.

Not four months later she was in childbed. The townsfolk hid their laughter with their knuckles. But what could I do? She suffered intolerable pains and clawed at the walls. "Gimpel," she cried. "I'm going. Forgive me." The house filled with women. They were boiling pans of water. The screams rose to the welkin.

The thing to do was to go to the House of Prayer to repeat Psalms, and that was what I did.

The townsfolk liked that, all right. I stood in a corner saying Psalms and prayers, and they shook their heads at me. "Pray, pray!" they told me. "Prayer never made any woman pregnant." One of the congregation put a straw to my mouth and said, "Hay for the cows." There was something to that too, by God!

She gave birth to a boy. Friday at the synagogue the sexton stood up before the Ark, pounded on the reading table, and announced, "The wealthy Reb Gimpel invites the congregation to a feast in honor of the birth of a son." The whole House of Prayer rang with laughter. My face was flaming. But there was nothing I could do. After all, I *was* the one responsible for the circumcision honors and rituals.

Half the town came running. You couldn't wedge another soul in. Women brought peppered chick-peas, and there was a keg of beer from the tavern. I ate and drank as much as anyone, and they all congratulated me. Then there was a circumcision, and I named the boy after my father, may he rest in peace. When all were gone and I was left with my wife alone, she thrust her head through the bed-curtain and called me to her.

"Gimpel," said she, "why are you silent? Has your ship gone and sunk?"

"What shall I say?" I answered. "A fine thing you've done to me! If my mother had known of it she'd have died a second time."

She said, "Are you crazy, or what?"

"How can you make such a fool," I said, "of one who should be the lord and master?"

"What's the matter with you?" she said. "What have you taken in into your head to imagine?"

I saw that I must speak bluntly and openly. "Do you think this is the way to use an orphan?" I said. "You have borne a bastard."

She answered, "Drive this foolishness out of your head. The child is yours."

"How can he be mine?" I argued. "He was born seventeen weeks after the wedding."

She told me then that he was premature. I said, "Isn't he a little too premature?" She said, she had had a grandmother who carried just as short a time and she resembled this grandmother of hers as one drop of water does another. She swore to it with such oaths that you would have believed a peasant at the fair if he had used them. To tell the plain truth, I didn't believe her; but when I talked it over next day with the schoolmaster he told me that the very same thing had happened to Adam and Eve. Two they went up to bed and four they descended.

"There isn't a woman in the world who is not the granddaughter of Eve," he said.

That was how it was; they argued me dumb. But then, who really knows how such things are?

I began to forget my sorrow. I loved the child madly, and he loved me too. As soon as he saw me he'd wave his little hands and want me to pick him up, and when he was colicky I was the only one who could pacify him. I bought him a little bone teething ring and a little gilded cap. He was forever catching the evil eye from someone, and then I had to run to get one of those abracadabras for him that would get him out of it. I worked like an ox. You know how expenses go up when there's an infant in the house. I don't want to lie about it; I didn't dislike Elka either, for that matter. She swore at me and cursed, and I couldn't get enough of her. What strength she had! One of her looks could rob you of the power of speech. And her orations! Pitch and sulphur, that's what they were full of, and yet somehow also full of charm. I adored her every word. She gave me bloody wounds though.

In the evening I brought her a white loaf as well as a dark one, and also poppyseed rolls I baked myself. I thieved because of her and swiped everything I could lay hands on: macaroons, raisins, almonds, cakes. I hope I may be forgiven for stealing from the Saturday pots the women left to warm in the baker's oven. I would take out scraps of meat, a chunk of pudding, a chicken leg or head, a piece of tripe, whatever I could nip quickly. She ate and became fat and handsome.

I had to sleep away from home all during the week, at the bakery. On Friday nights when I got home she always made an excuse of some sort. Either she had heartburn, or a stitch in the side, or hiccups, or headaches. You know what women's excuses are. I had a bitter time of it. It was rough. To add to it, this little brother of hers, the bastard, was growing bigger. He'd put lumps on me, and when I wanted to hit back she'd open her mouth and curse so powerfully I saw a green haze floating before my eyes. Ten times a day she threatened to divorce me. Another man in my place would have taken French leave and disappeared. But I'm the type that bears it and says nothing. What's one to do? Shoulders are from God, and burdens too.

One night there was a calamity in the bakery; the oven burst, and we almost had a fire. There was nothing to do but go home, so I went home. Let me, I thought, also taste the joy of sleeping in bed in mid-week. I didn't want to wake the sleeping mite and tiptoed into the house. Coming in, it seemed to me that I heard not the snoring of one but, as it were, a double

snore, one a thin enough snore and the other like the snoring of a slaughtered ox. Oh, I didn't like that! I didn't like it at all. I went up to the bed,
and things suddenly turned black. Next to Elka lay a man's form. Another
in my place would have made an uproar, and enough noise to rouse the
whole town, but the thought occurred to me that I might wake the child. A
little thing like that—why frighten a little swallow, I thought. All right
then, I went back to the bakery and stretched out on a sack of flour and till
morning I never shut an eye. I shivered as if I had had malaria. "Enough
of being a donkey," I said to myself. "Gimpel isn't going to be a sucker all
his life. There's a limit even to the foolishness of a fool like Gimpel."

In the morning I went to the rabbi to get advice, and it made a great commotion in the town. They sent the beadle for Elka right away. She came,
carrying the child. And what do you think she did? She denied it, denied
everything, bone and stone! "He's out of his head," she said. "I know nothing of dreams or divinations." They yelled at her, warned her, hammered
on the table, but she stuck to her guns: it was a false accusation, she said.

The butchers and the horse-traders took her part. One of the lads from
the slaughterhouse came by and said to me, "We've got our eye on you,
you're a marked man." Meanwhile the child started to bear down and
soiled itself. In the rabbinical court there was an Ark of the Covenant, and
they couldn't allow that, so they sent Elka away.

I said to the rabbi, "What shall I do?"

"You must divorce her at once," said he.

"And what if she refuses?" I asked.

He said, "You must serve the divorce. That's all you'll have to do."

I said, "Well, all right, Rabbi. Let me think about it."

"There's nothing to think about," said he. "You mustn't remain under
the same roof with her."

"And what if she refuses?" I asked.

"Let her go, the harlot," said he, "and her brood of bastards with her."

The verdict he gave was that I mustn't even cross her threshold—never
again, as long as I should live.

During the day it didn't bother me so much. I thought: It was bound to
happen, the abscess had to burst. But at night when I stretched out upon
the sacks I felt it all very bitterly. A longing took me, for her and for the
child. I wanted to be angry, but that's my misfortune exactly, I don't have it
in me to be really angry. In the first place—this was how my thoughts
went—there's bound to be a slip sometimes. You can't live without errors.
Probably that lad who was with her led her on and gave her presents and
what not, and women are often long on hair and short on sense, and so he
got around her. And then since she denies it so, maybe I was only seeing
things? Hallucinations do happen. You see a figure or a mannikin or something, but when you come up closer it's nothing, there's not a thing there.

And if that's so, I'm doing her an injustice. And when I got so far in my thoughts I started to weep. I sobbed so that I wet the flour where I lay. In the morning I went to the rabbi and told him that I had made a mistake. The rabbi wrote on with his quill, and he said that if that were so he would have to reconsider the whole case. Until he had finished I wasn't to go near my wife, but I might send her bread and money by messenger.

III

Nine months passed before all the rabbis could come to an agreement. Letters went back and forth. I hadn't realized that there could be so much erudition about a matter like this.

Meanwhile Elka gave birth to still another child, a girl this time. On the Sabbath I went to the synagogue and invoked a blessing on her. They called me up to the Torah, and I named the child for my mother-in-law—may she rest in peace. The louts and loudmouths of the town who came into the bakery gave me a going over. All Frampol refreshed its spirits because of my trouble and grief. However, I resolved that I would always believe what I was told. What's the good of *not* believing? Today it's your wife you don't believe; tomorrow it's God Himself you won't take stock in.

By an apprentice who was her neighbor I sent her daily a corn or a wheat loaf, or a piece of pastry, rolls or bagels, or, when I got the chance, a slab of pudding, a slice of honeycake, or wedding strudel—whatever came my way. The apprentice was a goodhearted lad, and more than once he added something on his own. He had formerly annoyed me a lot, plucking my nose and digging me in the ribs, but when he started to be a visitor to my house he became kind and friendly. "Hey, you, Gimpel," he said to me, "you have a very decent little wife and two fine kids. You don't deserve them."

"But the things people say about her," I said.

"Well, they have long tongues," he said, "and nothing to do with them but babble. Ignore it as you ignore the cold of last winter."

One day the rabbi sent for me and said, "Are you certain, Gimpel, that you were wrong about your wife?"

I said, "I'm certain."

"Why, but look here! You yourself saw it."

"It must have been a shadow," I said.

"The shadow of what?"

"Just of one of the beams, I think."

"You can go home then. You owe thanks to the Yanover rabbi. He found an obscure reference in Maimonides that favored you."

I seized the rabbi's hand and kissed it.

I wanted to run home immediately. It's no small thing to be separated for so long a time from wife and child. Then I reflected: I'd better go back to work now, and go home in the evening. I said nothing to anyone, although as far as my heart was concerned it was like one of the Holy Days. The women teased and twitted me as they did every day, but my thought was: Go on, with your loose talk. The truth is out, like the oil upon the water. Maimonides says it's right, and therefore it is right!

At night, when I had covered the dough to let it rise, I took my share of bread and a little sack of flour and started homeward. The moon was full and the stars were glistening, something to terrify the soul. I hurried onward, and before me darted a long shadow. It was winter, and a fresh snow had fallen. I had a mind to sing, but it was growing late and I didn't want to wake the householders. Then I felt like whistling, but I remembered that you don't whistle at night because it brings the demons out. So I was silent and walked as fast as I could.

Dogs in the Christian yards barked at me when I passed, but I thought: Bark your teeth out! What are you but mere dogs? Whereas I am a man, the husband of a fine wife, the father of promising children.

As I approached the house my heart started to pound as though it were the heart of a criminal. I felt no fear, but my heart went thump! thump! Well, no drawing back. I quietly lifted the latch and went in. Elka was alseep. I looked at the infant's cradle. The shutter was closed, but the moon forced its way through the cracks. I saw the newborn child's face and loved it as soon as I saw it—immediately—each tiny bone.

Then I came nearer to the bed. And what did I see but the apprentice lying there beside Elka. The moon went out all at once. It was utterly black, and I trembled. My teeth chattered. The bread fell from my hands, and my wife waked and said, "Who is that, ah?"

I muttered, "It's me."

"Gimpel?" she asked. "How come you're here? I thought it was forbidden."

"The rabbi said," I answered and shook as with a fever.

"Listen to me, Gimpel," she said, "go out to the shed and see if the goat's all right. It seems she's been sick." I have forgotten to say that we had a goat. When I heard she was unwell I went into the yard. The nannygoat was a good little creature. I had a nearly human feeling for her.

With hesitant steps I went up to the shed and opened the door. The goat stood there on her four feet. I felt her everywhere, drew her by the horns, examined her udders, and found nothing wrong. She had probably eaten too much bark. "Good night, little goat," I said. "Keep well." And the little beast answered with a "Maa" as though to thank me for the good will.

I went back. The apprentice had vanished.

"Where," I asked, "is the lad?"

"What lad?" my wife answered.

"What do you mean?" I said. "The apprentice. You were sleeping with him."

"The things I have dreamed this night and the night before," she said, "may they come true and lay you low, body and soul! An evil spirit has taken root in you and dazzles your sight." She screamed out, "You hateful creature! You moon calf! You spook! You uncouth man! Get out, or I'll scream all Frampol out of bed!"

Before I could move, her brother sprang out from behind the oven and struck me a blow on the back of the head. I thought he had broken my neck. I felt that something about me was deeply wrong, and I said, "Don't make a scandal. All that's needed now is that people should accuse me of raising spooks and *dybbuks*." For that was what she had meant. "No one will touch bread of my baking."

In short, I somehow calmed her.

"Well," she said, "that's enough. Lie down, and be shattered by wheels."

Next morning I called the apprentice aside. "Listen here, brother!" I said. And so on and so forth. "What do you say?" He stared at me as though I had dropped from the roof or something.

"I swear," he said, "you'd better go to an herb doctor or some healer. I'm afraid you have a screw loose, but I'll hush it up for you." And that's how the thing stood.

To make a long story short, I lived twenty years with my wife. She bore me six children, four daughters and two sons. All kinds of things happened, but I neither saw nor heard. I believed, and that's all. The rabbi recently said to me, "Belief in itself is beneficial. It is written that a good man lives by his faith."

Suddenly my wife took sick. It began with a trifle, a little growth upon the breast. But she evidently was not destined to live long; she had no years. I spent a fortune on her. I have forgotten to say that by this time I had a bakery of my own and in Frampol was considered to be something of a rich man. Daily the healer came, and every witch doctor in the neighborhood was brought. They decided to use leeches, and after that to try cupping. They even called a doctor from Lublin, but it was too late. Before she died she called me to her bed and said, "Forgive me, Gimpel."

I said, "What is there to forgive? You have been a good and faithful wife."

"Woe, Gimpel!" she said. "It was ugly how I deceived you all these years. I want to go clean to my Maker, and so I have to tell you that the children are not yours."

If I had been clouted on the head with a piece of wood it couldn't have bewildered me more.

"Whose are they?" I asked.

"I don't know," she said. "There were a lot . . . but they're not yours." And as she spoke she tossed her head to the side, her eyes turned glassy, and it was all up with Elka. On her whitened lips there remained a smile.

I imagined that, dead as she was, she was saying, "I deceived Gimpel. That was the meaning of my brief life."

IV

One night, when the period of mourning was done, as I lay dreaming on the flour sacks, there came the Spirit of Evil himself and said to me, "Gimpel, why do you sleep?"

I said, "What should I be doing? Eating *kreplach*?"

"The whole world deceives you," he said, "and you ought to deceive the world in your turn."

"How can I deceive all the world?" I asked him.

He answered, "You might accumulate a bucket of urine every day and at night pour it into the dough. Let the sages of Frampol eat filth."

"What about the judgment in the world to come?" I said.

"There is no world to come," he said. "They've sold you a bill of goods and talked you into believing you carried a cat in your belly. What nonsense!"

"Well then," I said, "and is there a God?"

He answered, "There is no God, either."

"What," I said, "*is* there, then?"

"A thick mire."

He stood before my eyes with a goatish beard and horn, long-toothed and with a tail. Hearing such words, I wanted to snatch him by the tail, but I tumbled from the flour sacks and nearly broke a rib. Then it happened that I had to answer the call of nature, and, passing, I saw the risen dough, which seemed to say to me, "Do it!" In brief, I let myself be persuaded.

At dawn the apprentice came. We kneaded the bread, scattered caraway seeds on it, and set it to bake. Then the apprentice went away, and I was left sitting in the little trench of the oven, on a pile of rags. Well, Gimpel, I thought, you've revenged yourself on them for all the shame they've put on you. Outside the frost glittered, but it was warm beside the oven. The flames heated my face. I bent my head and fell into a doze.

I saw in a dream, at once, Elka in her shroud. She called to me, "What have you done, Gimpel?"

I said to her, "It's all your fault," and started to cry.

"You fool!" she said. "You fool! Because I was false is everything false too? I never deceived anyone but myself. I'm paying for it all, Gimpel. They spare you nothing here."

I looked at her face. It was black; I was startled and waked, and remained sitting dumb. I sensed that everything hung in the balance. A false step now and I'd lose Eternal Life. But God gave me His help. I seized the long shovel and took out the loaves, carried them into the yard, and started to dig a hole in the frozen earth.

My apprentice came back as I was doing it. "What are you doing, boss?" he said and grew pale as a corpse.

"I know what I'm doing," I said, and I buried it all before his very eyes.

Then I went back home, took my hoard from its hiding place, and divided it among the children. "I saw your mother tonight," I said. "She's turning black, poor thing."

They were so astonished they couldn't speak a word.

"Be well," I said, "and forget that such a one as Gimpel ever existed." I put on my short coat, a pair of boots, took the bag that held my prayer shawl in one hand, my stock in the other, and kissed the *mezzuzah*. When people saw me in the street they were greatly surprised.

"Where are you going?" they said.

I answered, "Into the world." And so I departed from Frampol.

I wandered over the land, and good people did not neglect me. After many years I became old and white; I heard a great deal, many lies and falsehoods, but the longer I lived the more I understood that there were really no lies. Whatever doesn't really happen is dreamed at night. It happens to one if it doesn't happen to another, tomorrow if not today, or a century hence if not next year. What difference can it make? Often I heard tales of which I said, "Now this is a thing that cannot happen." But before a year had elapsed I heard that it actually had come to pass somewhere.

Going from place to place, eating at strange tables, it often happens that I spin yarns—improbable things that could never have happened—about devils, magicians, windmills, and the like. The children run after me, calling, "Grandfather, tell us a story." Sometimes they ask for particular stories, and I try to please them. A fat young boy once said to me, "Grandfather, it's the same story you told us before." The little rogue, he was right.

So it is with dreams too. It is many years since I left Frampol, but as soon as I shut my eyes I am there again. And whom do you think I see? Elka. She is standing by the washtub, as at our first encounter, but her face is shining and her eyes are as radiant as the eyes of a saint, and she speaks outlandish words to me, strange things. When I wake I have forgotten it all. But while the dream lasts I am comforted. She answers all my queries, and what comes out is that all is right. I weep and implore, "Let me be with you." And she consoles me and tells me to be patient. The time is nearer than it is far. Sometimes she strokes and kisses me and weeps upon my face. When I awaken I feel her lips and taste the salt of her tears.

No doubt the world is entirely an imaginary world, but it is only once removed from the true world. At the door of the hotel where I lie, there stands the plank on which the dead are taken away. The gravedigger Jew has his spade ready. The grave waits and the worms are hungry; the shrouds are prepared—I carry them in my beggar's sack. Another *shnorrer* is waiting to inherit my bed of straw. When the time comes I will go joyfully. Whatever may be there, it will be real, without complication, without ridicule, without deception. God be praised: there even Gimpel cannot be deceived.

Translated by Saul Bellow

The Chrysanthemums

JOHN STEINBECK

The high grey-flannel fog of winter closed off the Salinas Valley from the sky and from all the rest of the world. On every side it sat like a lid on the mountains and made of the great valley a closed pot. On the broad, level land floor the gang ploughs bit deep and left the black earth shining like metal where the shares had cut. On the foot-hill ranches across the Salinas River, the yellow stubble fields seemed to be bathed in pale cold sunshine, but there was no sunshine in the valley now in December. The thick willow scrub along the river flamed with sharp and positive yellow leaves.

It was a time of quiet and of waiting. The air was cold and tender. A light wind blew up from the southwest so that the farmers were mildly hopeful of a good rain before long; but fog and rain do not go together.

Across the river, on Henry Allen's foot-hill ranch there was little work to be done, for the hay was cut and stored and the orchards were ploughed up to receive the rain deeply when it should come. The cattle on the higher slopes were becoming shaggy and rough-coated.

Elisa Allen, working in her flower garden, looked down across the yard and saw Henry, her husband, talking to two men in business suits. The three of them stood by the tractor-shed, each man with one foot on the side of the little Fordson. They smoked cigarettes and studied the machine as they talked.

Elisa watched them for a moment and then went back to her work. She was thirty-five. Her face was lean and strong and her eyes were as clear as water. Her figure looked blocked and heavy in her gardening costume, a man's black hat pulled low down over her eyes, clod-hopper shoes, a fig-ured print dress almost completely covered by a big corduroy apron with four big pockets to hold the snips, the trowel and scratcher, the seeds and the knife she worked with. She wore heavy leather gloves to protect her hands while she worked.

She was cutting down the old year's chrysanthemum stalks with a pair of short and powerful scissors. She looked down toward the men by the tractor-shed now and then. Her face was eager and mature and handsome; even her work with the scissors was over-eager, over-powerful. The chrysanthemum stems seemed too small and easy for her energy.

She brushed a cloud of hair out of her eyes with the back of her glove, and left a smudge of earth on her cheek in doing it. Behind her stood the neat white farmhouse with red geraniums close-banked around it as high as the windows. It was a hard-swept-looking little house, with hard-polished windows, and a clean mud-mat on the front steps.

Elisa cast another glance toward the tractor-shed. The strangers were getting into their Ford coupé. She took off a glove and put her strong fingers down into the forest of new green chrysanthemum sprouts that were growing around the old roots. She spread the leaves and looked down among the close-growing stems. No aphids were there, no sow bugs or snails or cutworms. Her terrier fingers destroyed such pests before they could get started.

Elisa started at the sound of her husband's voice. He had come near quietly, and he leaned over the wire fence that protected her flower garden from cattle and dogs and chickens.

"At it again," he said. "You've got a strong new crop coming."

Elisa straightened her back and pulled on the gardening glove again. "Yes. They'll be strong this coming year." In her tone and on her face there was a little smugness.

"You've got a gift with things," Henry observed. "Some of those yellow chrysanthemums you had this year were ten inches across. I wish you'd work out in the orchard and raise some apples that big."

Her eyes sharpened. "Maybe I could do it, too. I've a gift with things, all right. My mother had it. She could stick anything in the ground and make it grow. She said it was having planters' hands that knew how to do it."

"Well, it sure works with flowers," he said.

"Henry, who were those men you were talking to?"

"Why, sure, that's what I came to tell you. They were from the Western Meat Company. I sold those thirty head of three-year-old steers. Got nearly my own price, too."

"Good," she said. "Good for you."

"And I thought," he continued, "I thought how it's Saturday afternoon, and we might go into Salinas for dinner at a restaurant, and then to a picture show—to celebrate, you see."

"Good," she repeated. "Oh, yes. That will be good."

Henry put on his joking tone. "There's fights tonight. How'd you like to go to the fights?"

"Oh, no," she said breathlessly. "No, I wouldn't like fights."

"Just fooling, Elisa. We'll go to a movie. Let's see. It's two now. I'm going to take Scotty and bring down those steers from the hill. It'll take us maybe two hours. We'll go in town about five and have dinner at the Cominos Hotel. Like that?"

"Of course I'll like it. It's good to eat away from home."

"All right, then. I'll go get up a couple of horses."

She said: "I'll have plenty of time to transplant some of these sets, I guess."

She heard her husband calling Scotty down by the barn. And a little later she saw the two men ride up the pale yellow hillside in search of the steers.

There was a little square sandy bed kept for rooting the chrysanthemums. With her trowel she turned the soil over and over, and smoothed it and patted it firm. Then she dug ten parallel trenches to receive the sets. Back at the chrysanthemum bed she pulled out the little crisp shoots, trimmed off the leaves of each one with her scissors and laid it on a small orderly pile.

A squeak of wheels and plod of hoofs came from the road. Elisa looked up. The country road ran along the dense bank of willows and cottonwoods that bordered the river, and up this road came a curious vehicle, curiously drawn. It was an old spring-wagon, with a round canvas top on it like the cover of a prairie schooner. It was drawn by an old bay horse and a little grey-and-white burro. A big stubble-bearded man sat between the cover flaps and drove the crawling team. Underneath the wagon, between the hind wheels, a lean and rangy mongrel dog walked sedately. Words were painted on the canvas, in clumsy, crooked letters. "Pots, pans, knives, sisors, lawn mores, Fixed." Two rows of articles, and the triumphantly definitive "Fixed" below. The black paint had run down in little sharp points beneath each letter.

Elisa, squatting on the ground, watched to see the crazy, loose-jointed wagon pass by. But it didn't pass. It turned into the farm road in front of her house, crooked old wheels skirling and squeaking. The rangy dog darted from between the wheels and ran ahead. Instantly the two ranch shepherds flew out at him. Then all three stopped, and with stiff and quivering tails, with taut straight legs, with ambassadorial dignity, they slowly circled, sniffing daintily. The caravan pulled up to Elisa's wire fence and stopped. Now, the newcomer dog, feeling out-numbered, lowered his tail and retired under the wagon with raised hackles and bared teeth.

The man on the wagon seat called out: "That's a bad dog in a fight when he gets started."

Elisa laughed. "I see he is. How soon does he generally get started?"

The man caught up her laughter and echoed it heartily. "Sometimes not for weeks and weeks," he said. He climbed stiffly down, over the wheel. The horse and the donkey drooped like unwatered flowers.

Elisa saw that he was a very big man. Although his hair and beard were greying, he did not look old. His worn black suit was wrinkled and spotted with grease. The laughter had disappeared from his face and eyes the moment his laughing voice ceased. His eyes were dark, and they were full of the brooding that gets in the eyes of teamsters and of sailors. The calloused hands he rested on the wire fence were cracked, and every crack was a black line. He took off his battered hat.

"I'm off my general road, ma'am," he said. "Does this dirt road cut over across the river to the Los Angeles highway?"

Elisa stood up and shoved the thick scissors in her apron pocket. "Well, yes, it does, but it winds around and then fords the river. I don't think your team could pull through the sand."

He replied with some asperity: "It might surprise you what them beasts can pull through."

"When they get started?" she asked.

He smiled for a second. "Yes. When they get started."

"Well," said Elisa, "I think you'll save time if you go back to the Salinas road and pick up the highway there."

He drew a big finger down the chicken wire and made it sing. "I ain't in any hurry, ma'am. I go from Seattle to San Diego and back every year. Takes all my time. About six months each way. I aim to follow nice weather."

Elisa took off her gloves and stuffed them in the apron pocket with the scissors. She touched the under edge of her man's hat, searching for fugitive hairs. "That sounds like a nice kind of a way to live," she said.

He leaned confidentially over the fence. "Maybe you noticed the writing on my wagon. I mend pots and sharpen knives and scissors. You got any of them things to do?"

'Oh, no," she said quickly. "Nothing like that." Her eyes hardened with resistance.

"Scissors is the worst thing," he explained. "Most people just ruin scissors trying to sharpen 'em, but I know how. I got a special tool. It's a little bobbit kind of thing, and patented. But it sure does the trick."

"No. My scissors are all sharp."

"All right, then. Take a pot," he continued earnestly, "a bent pot, or a pot with a hole. I can make it like new so you don't have to buy no new ones. That's a saving for you."

"No," she said shortly. "I tell you I have nothing like that for you to do."

His face fell to an exaggerated sadness. His voice took on a whining undertone. "I ain't had a thing to do today. Maybe I won't have no supper tonight. You see I'm off my regular road. I know folks on the highway clear from Seattle to San Diego. They save their things for me to sharpen up because they know I do it so good and save them money."

"I'm sorry," Elisa said irritably. "I haven't anything for you to do."

His eyes left her face and fell to searching the ground. They roamed about until they came to the chrysanthemum bed where she had been working. "What's them plants, ma'am?"

The irritation and resistance melted from Elisa's face. "Oh, those are chrysanthemums, giant whites and yellows. I raise them every year, bigger than anybody around here."

"Kind of a long-stemmed flower? Looks like a quick puff of colored smoke?" he asked.

"That's it. What a nice way to describe them."

"They smell kind of nasty till you get used to them," he said.

"It's a good bitter smell," she retorted, "not nasty at all."

He changed his tone quickly. "I like the smell myself."

"I had ten-inch blooms this year," she said.

The man leaned farther over the fence. "Look. I know a lady down the road a piece, has got the nicest garden you ever seen. Got nearly every kind of flower but no chrysanthemums. Last time I was mending a copper-bottom washtub for her (that's a hard job but I do it good), she said to me: 'If you ever run acrost some nice chrysanthemums I wish you'd try to get me a few seeds.' That's what she told me."

Elisa's eyes grew alert and eager. "She couldn't have known much about chrysanthemums. You *can* raise them from seed, but it's much easier to root the little sprouts you see there."

"Oh," he said. "I s'pose I can't take none to her, then."

"Why yes you can," Elisa cried. "I can put some in damp sand, and you can carry them right along with you. They'll take root in the pot if you keep them damp. And then she can transplant them."

"She'd sure like to have some, ma'am. You say they're nice ones?"

"Beautiful," she said. "Oh, beautiful." Her eyes shone. She tore off the battered hat and shook out her dark pretty hair. "I'll put them in a flower-pot, and you can take them right with you. Come into the yard."

While the man came through the picket gate Elisa ran excitedly along the geranium-bordered paths to the back of the house. And she returned carrying a big red flower-pot. The gloves were forgotten now. She kneeled on the ground by the starting bed and dug up the sandy soil with her fingers and scooped it into the bright new flower-pot. Then she picked up the little pile of shoots she had prepared. With her strong fingers she pressed them into the sand and tamped around them with her knuckles. The man stood over her. "I'll tell you what to do," she said. "You remember so you can tell the lady."

"Yes, I'll try to remember."

"Well, look. These will take root in about a month. Then she must set them out, about a foot apart in good rich earth like this, see?" She lifted a handful of dark soil for him to look at. "They'll grow fast and tall. Now remember this: In July tell her to cut them down, about eight inches from the ground."

"Before they bloom?" he asked.

"Yes, before they bloom." Her face was tight with eagerness. "They'll grow right up again. About the last of September the buds will start."

She stopped and seemed perplexed. "It's the budding that takes the most care," she said hesitantly. "I don't know how to tell you." She looked deep into his eyes, searchingly. Her mouth opened a little, and she seemed to be listening. "I'll try to tell you," she said. "Did you ever hear of planting hands?"

"Can't say I have, ma'am."

"Well, I can only tell you what it feels like. It's when you're picking off the buds you don't want. Everything goes right down into your fingertips. You watch your fingers work. They do it themselves. You can feel how it is. They pick and pick the buds. They never make a mistake. They're with the plant. Do you see? Your fingers and the plant. You can feel that, right up your arm. They know. They never make a mistake. You can feel it. When you're like that you can't do anything wrong. Do you see that? Can you understand that?"

She was kneeling on the ground looking up at him. Her breast swelled passionately.

The man's eyes narrowed. He looked away self-consciously. "Maybe I know," he said. "Sometimes in the night in the wagon there——"

Elisa's voice grew husky. She broke in on him: "I've never lived as you do, but I know what you mean. When the night is dark—why, the stars are sharp-pointed, and there's quiet. Why, you rise up and up! Every pointed star gets driven into your body. It's like that. Hot and sharp and—lovely."

Kneeling there, her hand went out toward his legs in the greasy black trousers. Her hesitant fingers almost touched the cloth. Then her hand dropped to the ground. She crouched low like a fawning dog.

He said: "It's nice, just like you say. Only when you don't have no dinner, it ain't."

She stood up then, very straight, and her face was ashamed. She held the flower pot out to him and placed it gently in his arms. "Here. Put it in your wagon, on the seat, where you can watch it. Maybe I can find something for you to do."

At the back of the house she dug in the can pile and found two old and battered aluminum saucepans. She carried them back and gave them to him. "Here, maybe you can fix these."

His manner changed. He became professional. "Good as new I can fix them." At the back of his wagon he set a little anvil, and out of an oily toolbox dug a small machine hammer. Elisa came through the gate to watch him while he pounded out the dents in the kettles. His mouth grew sure and knowing. At a difficult part of the work he sucked his underlip.

"You sleep right in the wagon?" Elisa asked.

"Right in the wagon, ma'am. Rain or shine I'm dry as a cow in there."

"It must be nice," she said. "It must be very nice. I wish women could do such things."

"It ain't the right kind of a life for a woman."

Her upper lip raised a little, showing her teeth. "How do you know? How can you tell?" she said.

"I don't know, ma'am," he protested. "Of course I don't know. Now here's your kettles, done. You don't have to buy no new ones."

"How much?"

"Oh, fifty cents'll do. I keep my prices down and my work good. That's why I have all them satisfied customers up and down the highway."

Elisa brought him a fifty-cent piece from the house and dropped it in his hand. "You might be surprised to have a rival some time. I can sharpen scissors, too. And I can beat the dents out of little pots. I could show you what a woman might do."

He put his hammer back in the oily box and shoved the little anvil out of sight. "It would be a lonely life for a woman, ma'am, and a scarey life, too, with animals creeping under the wagon all night." He climbed over the single-tree, steadying himself with a hand on the burro's white rump. He settled himself in the seat, picked up the lines. "Thank you kindly, ma'am," he said. "I'll do like you told me; I'll go back and catch the Salinas road."

"Mind," she called, "if you're long in getting there, keep the sand damp."

"Sand, ma'am? . . . Sand? Oh, sure. You mean around the chrysanthe-mums. Sure I will." He clucked his tongue. The beasts leaned luxuriously into their collars. The mongrel dog took his place between the back wheels. The wagon turned and crawled out the entrance road and back the way it had come, along the river.

Elisa stood in front of her wire fence watching the slow progress of the caravan. Her shoulders were straight, her head thrown back, her eyes half-closed, so that the scene came vaguely into them. Her lips moved silently, forming the words "Good-bye—good-bye." Then she whispered: "That's a bright direction. There's a glowing there." The sound of her whisper star-tled her. She shook herself free and looked about to see whether anyone had been listening. Only the dogs had heard. They lifted their heads to-ward her from their sleeping in the dust, and then stretched out their chins and settled asleep again. Elisa turned and ran hurriedly into the house.

In the kitchen she reached behind the stove and felt the water tank. It was full of hot water from the noonday cooking. In the bathroom she tore off her soiled clothes and flung them into the corner. And then she scrubbed herself with a little block of pumice, legs and thighs, loins and chest and arms, until her skin was scratched and red. When she had dried herself she stood in front of a mirror in her bedroom and looked at her body. She tightened her stomach and threw out her chest. She turned and looked over her shoulder at her back.

After a while she began to dress, slowly. She put on her newest under-clothing and her nicest stockings and the dress which was the symbol of her prettiness. She worked carefully on her hair, pencilled her eyebrows and rouged her lips.

Before she was finished she heard the little thunder of hoofs and the shouts of Henry and his helper as they drove the red steers into the corral. She heard the gate bang shut and set herself for Henry's arrival.

His step sounded on the porch. He entered the house calling: "Elisa, where are you?"

"In my room, dressing. I'm not ready. There's hot water for your bath. Hurry up. It's getting late."

When she heard him splashing in the tub, Elisa laid his dark suit on the bed, and shirt and socks and tie beside it. She stood his polished shoes on the floor beside the bed. Then she went to the porch and sat primly and stiffly down. She looked toward the river road where the willow-line was still yellow with frosted leaves so that under the high grey fog they seemed a thin band of sunshine. This was the only colour in the grey afternoon. She sat unmoving for a long time. Her eyes blinked rarely.

Henry came banging out of the door, shoving his tie inside his vest as he came. Elisa stiffened and her face grew tight. Henry stopped short and looked at her. "Why—why, Elisa. You look so nice!"

"Nice? You think I look nice? What do you mean by 'nice'?"

Henry blundered on. "I don't know. I mean you look different, strong and happy."

"I am strong? Yes, strong. What do you mean 'strong'?"

He looked bewildered. "You're playing some kind of a game," he said helplessly. "It's a kind of a play. You look strong enough to break a calf over your knee, happy enough to eat it like a watermelon."

For a second she lost her rigidity. "Henry! Don't talk like that. You didn't know what you said." She grew complete again. "I'm strong," she boasted. "I never knew before how strong."

Henry looked down toward the tractor-shed, and when he brought his eyes back to her, they were his own again. "I'll get out the car. You can put on your coat while I'm starting."

Elisa went into the house. She heard him drive to the gate and idle down his motor, and then she took a long time to put on her hat. She pulled it here and pressed it there. When Henry turned the motor off she slipped into her coat and went out.

The little roadster bounced along on the dirt road by the river, raising the birds and driving the rabbits into the brush. Two cranes flapped heavily over the willow-line and dropped into the river-bed.

Far ahead on the road Elisa saw a dark speck. She knew.

She tried not to look as they passed it, but her eyes would not obey. She whispered to herself sadly: "He might have thrown them off the road. That wouldn't have been much trouble, not very much. But he kept the pot," she explained. "He had to keep the pot. That's why he couldn't get them off the road."

The roadster turned a bend and she saw the caravan ahead. She swung full around toward her husband so she could not see the little covered wagon and the mis-matched team as the car passed them.

In a moment it was over. The thing was done. She did not look back.

She said loudly, to be heard above the motor: "It will be good, tonight, a good dinner."

"Now you've changed again," Henry complained. He took one hand from the wheel and patted her knee. "I ought to take you in to dinner oftener. It would be good for both of us. We get so heavy out on the ranch."

"Henry," she asked, "could we have wine at dinner?"

"Sure we could. Say! That will be fine."

She was silent for a while; then she said: "Henry, at those prize-fights, do the men hurt each other very much?"

"Sometimes a little, not often. Why?"

"Well, I've read how they break noses, and blood runs down their chests. I've read how the fighting gloves get heavy and soggy with blood."

He looked around at her. "What's the matter, Elisa? I didn't know you read things like that." He brought the car to a stop, then turned to the right over the Salinas River bridge.

"Do any women ever go to the fights?" she asked.

"Oh, sure, some. What's the matter, Elisa? Do you want to go? I don't think you'd like it, but I'll take you if you really want to go."

She relaxed limply in the seat. "Oh, no. No. I don't want to go. I'm sure I don't." Her face was turned away from him. "It will be enough if we can have wine. It will be plenty." She turned up her coat collar so he could not see that she was crying weakly—like an old woman.

Rain in the Heart

PETER TAYLOR

When the drilling was over they stopped at the edge of the field and the drill sergeant looked across the flat valley toward the woods on Peavine Ridge. Among the shifting lights on the treetops there in the late afternoon the drill sergeant visualized pointed roofs of houses that were on another, more thickly populated ridge seven miles to the west.

Lazily the sergeant rested the butt end of his rifle in the mud and turned to tell the squad of rookies to return to their own barracks. But they had already gone on without him and he stood a moment watching them drift back toward the rows of squat buildings, some with their rifles thrown over their shoulders, others toting them by the leather slings in suitcase fashion.

On the field behind the sergeant were the tracks which he and the twelve men had made during an hour's drilling. He turned and studied the tracks for a moment, wondering whether or not he could have told how many men had been tramping there if that had been necessary for telling the strength of an enemy. Then with a shrug of his shoulders he turned his face toward Peavine Ridge again, thinking once more of that other ridge in the suburban area where his bride had found furnished rooms. And seeing how the ridge before him stretched out endlessly north and south he was reminded of a long bus and streetcar ride that was before him on his journey to their rooms this night. Suddenly throwing the rifle over his shoulder, he began to make his way back toward his own barrack.

The immediate approach to the barrack of the noncommissioned officers was over a wide asphalt area where all formations were held. As the sergeant crossed the asphalt, it required a special effort for him to raise his foot each time. Since his furlough and wedding trip to the mountains, this was the first night the sergeant had been granted leave to go in to see his wife. When he reached the stoop before the entrance to the barrack he lingered by the bulletin board. He stood aimlessly examining the notices

962

posted there. But finally drawing himself up straight he turned and walked erectly and swiftly inside. He knew that the barrack would be filled with men ready with stale, friendly, evil jokes.

As he hurried down the aisle of the barrack he removed his blue denim jacket, indicating his haste. It seemed at first that no one had noticed him. Yet he was still filled with a dread of the jokes which must inevitably be directed at him today. At last a copper-headed corporal who sat on the bunk next to his own, whittling his toenails with his knife, had begun to sing:

> *"Yes, she jumped in bed*
> *And she covered up her head—"*

Another voice across the aisle took up the song here:

> *"And she vowed he couldn't find her."*

Then other voices, some faking soprano, other simulating the deepest choir bass, from all points of the long room joined in:

> *"But she knew damn well*
> *That she lied like hell*
> *When he jumped right in beside her."*

The sergeant blushed a little, pretended to be very angry, and began to undress for his shower. Silently he reminded himself that when he started for town he must take with him the big volume of Civil War history, for it was past due at the city library. *She* could have it renewed for him tomorrow.

In the shower too the soldiers pretended at first to take no notice of him. They were talking of their own plans for the evening in town. One tall and bony sergeant with a head of wiry black hair was saying, "I've got a strong deal on tonight with a WAC from Vermont. But of course we'll have to be in by midnight."

Now the copper-headed corporal had come into the shower. He was smaller than most of the other soldiers, and beneath his straight copper-colored hair were a pair of bright gray-green eyes. He had a hairy potbelly that looked like a football. "My deal's pretty strong tonight, too," he said, addressing the tall soldier beside him. "She lives down the road a way with her family, so I'll have to be in early too. But then you and me won't be all fagged out tomorrow, eh, Slim!"

"No," the tall and angular soldier said, "we'll be able to hold our backs up straight and sort of carry ourselves like soldiers, as some won't feel like doing."

The lukewarm shower poured down over the chest and back of the drill sergeant. This was his second year in the Army and now he found himself continually surprised at the small effect that the stream of words of the soldiers had upon him.

Standing in the narrow aisle between his own bunk and that of the copper-headed corporal, he pulled on his clean khaki clothes before an audience of naked soldiers who lounged on the two bunks.

"When I marry," the wiry-headed sergeant was saying, "I'll marry me a WAC who I can take right to the front with me."

"You shouldn't do that," the corporal said, "she might be wounded in action." He and the angular, wiry-headed sergeant laughed so bawdily and merrily that the drill sergeant joined in, hardly knowing what were the jokes they'd been making. But the other naked soldiers, of more regular shapes, found the jokes not plain enough, and they began to ask literally:

"Can a WAC and a soldier overseas get married?"

"If a married WAC gets pregnant, what happens?"

"When I get married," said one soldier who was stretched out straight on his back with his eyes closed and a towel thrown across his loins, "it'll be to a nice girl like the sergeant here's married."

The sergeant looked at him silently.

"But wherever," asked Slim, "are *you* going to meet such a girl like that in such company as you keep?"

The soldier lying on his back opened one eye: "I wouldn't talk about my company if I was you. I've saw you and the corporal here with them biddy-dolls at Midway twiest."

The corporal's eyes shone. He laughed aloud and fairly shouted. "And *he* got *me* the date both times, Buck."

"Well," said Buck, with his eyes still closed and his hands folded over his bare chest, "when I marry it won't be to one of them sort. Nor not to one of your WACs neither, Slim."

Slim said, "Blow it out your barracks bag."

One of those more regularly shaped soldiers seemed to rouse himself as from sleep to say, "That's why y'like 'em, ain't it, Slim? Y'like 'em because they know how?" His joke was sufficiently plain to bring laughter from all. They all looked toward Slim. Even the soldier who was lying down opened one eye and looked at him. And Slim, who was rubbing his wiry mop of black hair with a white towel, muttered, "At least I don't pollute little kids from the roller rink like some present."

The naked soldier named Buck who was stretched out on the cot opened his eyes and rolled them in the direction of Slim. Then he closed his eyes meditatively and suddenly opened them again. He sat up and swung his feet around to the floor. "Well, I did meet an odd number the other night," he said. "She was drinking beer alone in Connor's Café when I comes in and sits on her right, like this." He patted his hand on the olive-drab blanket, and all the while he talked he was not looking at the other soldiers.

Rather his face was turned toward the window at the end of his cot, and with his lantern jaw raised and his small, round eyes squinting, he peered into the rays of sunlight. "She was an odd one and wouldn't give me any sort of talk as long as I sit there. Then I begun to push off and she says out of the clear, 'Soldier, what did the rat say to the cat?' I said that I don't know and she says, 'This pussy's killin' me.' " Now all the other soldiers began to laugh and hollo. But Buck didn't even smile. He continued to squint up into the light and to speak in the same monotone. "So I said, 'Come on,' and jerked her up by the arm. But, you know, she was odd. She never did say much but tell a nasty joke now and then. She didn't have a bunch of small talk, but she come along and did all right. But I do hate to hear a woman talk nasty."

The potbellied corporal winked at the drill sergeant and said, "Listen to him. He says he's going to marry a nice girl like yours, but I bet you didn't run up on yours in Connor's Café or the roller rink."

Buck whisked the towel from across his lap and drawing it back he quickly snapped it at the corporal's little, hairy potbelly. The drill sergeant laughed with the rest and watched for a moment the patch of white that the towel made on the belly which was otherwise still red from the hot shower.

Now the drill sergeant was dressed. He combed his sandy-colored hair before a square hand mirror which he had set on the windowsill. The sight of himself reminded him of her who would already be waiting for him on that other ridge. She with her soft, Southern voice, her small hands forever clasping a handkerchief. This was what his own face in the tiny mirror brought to mind. How unreal to him were these soldiers and their hairy bodies and all their talk and their rough ways. How temporary. How different from his own life, from his real life with her.

He opened his metal footlocker and took out the history book in which he had been reading of battles that once took place on this campsite and along the ridge where he would ride the bus tonight. He pulled his khaki overseas cap onto the right side of his head and slipped away, apparently unnoticed, from the soldiers gathered there. They were all listening now to Slim who was saying, "Me and Pat McKenzie picked up a pretty little broad one night who was deaf and dumb. But when me and her finally got around to shacking up she made the damnedest noises you ever heard."

With the book clasped under his arm the drill sergeant passed down the aisle between the rows of cots, observing here a half-dressed soldier picking up a pair of dirty socks, there another soldier shining a pair of prized garrison shoes or tying a khaki tie with meticulous care. The drill sergeant's thoughts were still on her whose brown curls fell over the white collar of her summer dress. And he could dismiss the soldiers as he passed them as good fellows each, saying, "So long, Smoky Joe," to one who seemed to be retiring even before sundown, and "So long, Happy Jack," to another who scowled at him. They were good rough-and-ready fellows all, Smoky Joe,

Happy Jack, Slim, Buck, and the copper-headed one. But one of them called to him as he went out the door, "I wouldn't take no book along. What you think you want with a book this night?" And the laughter came through the open windows after he was outside on the asphalt.

The bus jostled him and rubbed him against the civilian workers from the camp and the mill workers who climbed aboard with their dinner pails at the first stop. He could feel the fat thighs of the middle-aged women rubbing against the sensitive places of his body, and they—unaware of such personal feelings—leaned toward one another and swapped stories about their outrageous bosses. One of the women said that for a little she'd quit this very week. The men, also mostly middle-aged and dressed in over-alls and shirt-sleeves, seemed sensible of nothing but that this suburban bus somewhere crossed Lake Road, Pidgeon Street, Jackson Boulevard, and that at some such intersection they must be ready to jerk the stop cord and alight. "The days are getting a little shorter," one of them said.

The sergeant himself alighted at John Ross Road and transferred to the McFarland Gap bus. The passengers on this bus were not as crowded as on the first. The men were dressed in linen and seersucker business suits, and the women carried purses and wore little tailored dresses and straw hats. Those who were crowded together did not make any conversation among themselves. Even those who seemed to know one another talked in whispers. The sergeant was standing in the aisle but he bent over now and again and looked out the windows at the neat bungalows and larger dwelling houses along the roadside. He would one day have a house such as one of those for his own. His own father's house was the like of these, with a screened porch on the side and a fine tile roof. He could hear his father saying, "A house is only as good as the roof over it." But weren't these the things that had once seemed prosaic and too binding for his notions? Before he went into the Army had there not been moments when the thought of limiting himself to a genteel suburban life seemed intolerable by its restrictions and confinement? Even by the confinement to the company of such people as those here on the bus with him? And yet now when he sometimes lay wakeful and lonesome at night in the long dark barrack among the carefree and garrulous soldiers or when he was kneed and elbowed by the worried and weary mill hands on a bus, he dreamed longingly of the warm companionship he would find with her and their sober neighbors in a house with a fine roof.

The rattling, bumping bus pulled along for several miles over the road atop the steep ridge which it had barely managed to climb in first gear. At the end of the bus line he stepped out to the roadside and waited for his streetcar. The handful of passengers that were still on the bus climbed out too and scattered to all parts of the neighborhood, disappearing into doorways of brick bungalows or clapboard two-storieds that were perched among evergreens and oak trees and maple and wild sumac on the crest and on the slopes of the ridge. *This* would be a good neighborhood to settle down in. The view was surely a prize—any way you chose to look.

But the sergeant had hardly more than taken his stand in the grass to wait for the streetcar, actually leaning a little against a low wall that bordered a sloping lawn, when he observed the figure of a woman standing in the shadow of a small chinaberry tree which grew beside the wall.

The woman came from behind the tree and stood by the wall. She was within three or four steps of the sergeant. He looked at her candidly, and her plainness from the very first made him want to turn his face away toward the skyline of the city in the valley. Her flat-chested and generally ill-shaped figure was clothed with a baglike gingham dress that hung at an uneven knee length. On her feet was a pair of flat-heeled brown oxfords. She wore white, ankle-length socks that emphasized the hairiness of her muscular legs. On her head a dark felt hat was drawn down almost to her eyebrows. Her hair was straight and of a dark color less rich than brown and yet more brown than black, and it was cut so that a straight not wholly greaseless strand hung over each cheek and turned upward just the slightest bit at the ends.

And in her hands before her the woman held a large bouquet of white and lavender sweet peas. She held them, however, as though they were a bunch of mustard greens. Or perhaps she held them more as a small boy holds flowers, half ashamed to be seen holding anything so delicate. Her eyes did not rest on them. Rather her eyes roved nervously up and down the car tracks. At last she turned her colorless, long face to the sergeant and asked with an artificial smile that showed her broad gums and small teeth. "Is this where the car stops?"

"I think so," he said. Then he did look away toward the city.

"I saw the yellow mark up there on the post, but I wasn't real sure," she pursued. He had to look back at her, and as he did so she said, "Don't that uniform get awful hot?"

"Oh, yes," he said. He didn't want to say more. But finally a thought of his own good fortune and an innate kindness urged him to speak again. "I sometimes change it two or three times a day."

"I'd sure say it would get hot."

After a moment's silence the sergeant observed, "This is mighty hot weather."

"It's awful hot here in the summer," she said. "But it's always awful here in some way. Where are you from?"

He still wanted to say no more. "I'm from West Tennessee."

"What part?" she almost demanded.

"I'm from Memphis. It gets mighty hot there."

"I oncet know somebody from there."

"Memphis gets awfully hot in the summer too."

"Well," she said, drawing in a long breath, "you picked an awful hot place to come to. I don't mind heat so much. It's just an awful place to be. I've lived here all my life and I hate it here."

The sergeant walked away up the road and leaned forward looking for the streetcar. Then he walked back to the wall because he felt that she would think him a snob. Unable to invent other conversation, he looked at the flowers and said, "They're very pretty."

"Well, if you like 'em at all," she said, "you like 'em a great lot more than I do. I hate flowers. Only the other day I say to Mother that if I get sick and go the hospital don't bring any flowers around me. I don't want any. I don't like 'em."

"Why, those are pretty," he said. He felt for some reason that he must defend their worth. "I like all flowers. Those are especially hard to grow in West Tennessee."

"If you like 'em you like 'em more than I do. Only the other day I say to my Sunday School teacher that if I would die it'd save her a lot of money because I don't want anybody to send no flowers. I hate 'em. And it ain't just these. I hate all flowers."

"I think they're pretty." he insisted. "Did you pick 'em down there in the valley?"

"They was growing wild in a field and I picked them because I didn't have nothin' else to do. Here," she said, pushing the flowers into his hands, "you take 'em. I hate 'em."

"No, no, I wouldn't think of taking your flowers. Here, you must take them back."

"I don't want 'em. I'll just throw 'em away."

"Why, I can't take your flowers."

"You have 'em, and I ain't going to take 'em back. They'll just lay there and die if you put them on the wall."

"I feel bad accepting them. You must have gone to a lot of trouble to pick them."

"They was just growing wild at the edge of a field, and the lady said they was about to take her garden. I don't like flowers. I did her a favor, and you can do me one."

"There's nothing I like better," he said, feeling that he had been ungracious. "I guess I would like to raise flowers, and I used to work in the garden some." He leaned forward, listening for the sound of the streetcar.

For a minute or two neither of them spoke. She shifted from foot to foot and seemed to be talking to herself. From the corner of his eye he watched her lips moving. Finally she said aloud, "Some people act like they're doing you a favor to pay you a dollar a day."

"That's not much in these times," he observed.

"It's just like I was saying to a certain person the other day, 'If you are not willing to pay a dollar and a half a day you don't want nobody to work for you very bad.' But I work for a dollar just the same. This is half of it right here." She held up a half dollar between her thumb and forefinger. "But last week I pay for all my insurance for next year. I put my money away instead of buying things I really want. You can't say that for many girls."

"You certainly can't."

"Not many girls do that."

"I don't know many that do."

"No sirree," she said, snapping the fingers of her right hand, "the girls in this place are awful. I hate the way they act with soldiers downtown. They go to the honky-tonks and drink beer. I don't waste anybody's money drinking beer. I put my own money away instead of buying things I might really want."

The sergeant stepped out into the middle of the road and listened for the streetcar. As he returned to the wall, a Negro man and woman rode by in a large blue sedan. The woman standing by the wall watched the automobile go over the streetcar tracks and down the hill. "There's no Negro in this town that will do housework for less than two and a half a day, and they pay us whites only a dollar."

"Why will they pay Negroes more?" he asked.

"Because they can boss 'em," she said hastily. "Just because they can boss 'em around. I say to a certain person the other day, 'You can't boss me around like a nigger, no ma'am.' "

"I suppose that's it." He now began to walk up and down in front of her, listening and looking for the streetcar and occasionally raising the flowers to his nose to smell them. She continued to lean against the wall, motionless and with her humorless face turned upward toward the car wire where were hanging six or eight rolled newspapers tied in pairs by long dirty strings. "How y'reckon them papers come to be up there?" she asked.

"Some of the neighborhood kids or paperboys did it, I guess."

"Yea. That's it. Rich people's kids's just as bad as anybody's."

"Well, the paperboys probably did it whenever they had papers left over. I've done it myself when I was a kid."

"Yea," she said through her nose. "But kids just make me nervous. And I didn't much like bein' a kid neither."

The sergeant looked along one of the steel rails that still glimmered a little in the late sunlight and remembered good times he had had walking along the railroad tracks as a child. Suddenly he hoped his first child would be a boy.

"I'll tell you one thing, soldier," the woman beside him was saying, "I don't spend my money on lipstick and a lot of silly clothes. I don't paint myself with a lot of lipstick and push my hair up on top of my head and walk around downtown so soldiers will look at me. You don't find many girls that don't do that in this awful place, do ya?"

"You certainly don't find many." The sergeant felt himself blushing.

"You better be careful, for you're going to drop some of them awful flowers. I don't know what you want with 'em."

"Why, they're pretty," he said as though he had not said it before.

Now the blue sedan came up the hill again and rolled quietly over the car tracks. Only the Negro man was in the sedan, and he was driving quite fast.

"How can a nigger like that own a car like that?"

"He probably only drives for some of the people who live along here."

"Yea. That's it. That's it. Niggers can get away with anything. I guess you've heard about 'em attacking that white girl down yonder."

"Yes . . . Yes."

"They ought to kill 'em all or send 'em all back to Africa."

"It's a real problem, I think."

"I don't care if no man black or white never looks at me if I have to put on a lot of lipstick and push my hair up and walk around without a hat."

The sergeant leaned forward, craning his neck.

"I'm just going to tell you what happened to me downtown the other day," she persisted. "I was standing looking in a store window on Broad when a soldier comes up behind me, and I'm just going to tell you what he said. He said he had a hotel room, and he asked me if I didn't want to go up to the room with him and later go somewhere to eat and that he'd give me some money too."

"I know," the sergeant said. "There's a mighty rough crowd in town now."

"But I just told him, 'No thanks. If I can't make money honest I don't want it,' is what I told him. I says, 'There's a girl on that corner yonder at Main that wants ya. Just go down there.' "

The sergeant stood looking down the track, shaking his head.

"He comes right up behind me, you understand, and tells me that he has a room in a hotel and that we can go there and do what we want to do and then go get something to eat and he will give me money besides. And I just told him, 'No thanks. There's a girl on that corner yonder at Main that wants ya. Just go down there.' So I went off up the street a way and then I come back to where I was looking at a lot of silly clothes, and a man in a blue shirt who was standing there all the time says that the soldier had come back looking for me."

The sergeant stretched out his left arm so that his wristwatch appeared from under his sleeve. Then he crooked his elbow and looked at the watch.

"Oh, you have *some* wait yet," she said.

"How often do they run?"

"I don't know," she said without interest, "just every so often. I told him, y'see, if I can't make money honest I don't want it. You can't say that for many girls." Whenever his attention seemed to lag, her speech grew louder.

"No, you can't," he agreed.

"I save my money. Soldier, I've got two hundred and seven dollars in the bank, besides my insurance paid up for next year." She said nothing during what seemed to be several minutes. Then she asked. "Where do your mother and daddy live?"

"In West Tennessee."

"Where do you stay? Out at the camp?" She hardly gave him time to answer her questions now.

"Well, I stay out at camp some nights."

"*Some* nights? Where do you stay other nights?" She was grinning.

"I'm married and stay with my wife. I've just been married a little while but we have rooms up the way here."

"Oh, are you a married man? Where is she from? I hope she ain't from here."

"She's from Memphis. She's just finished school."

The woman frowned, blushed deeply, then she grinned again showing her wide gums. "I'd say you are goin' to take her the flowers. You won't have to buy her any."

"I do wish you'd take some of them back."

The woman didn't answer him for a long time. Finally, when he had almost forgotten what he had said last, she said without a sign of a grin, "I don't want 'em. The sight of 'em makes me sick."

And at last the streetcar came.

It was but a short ride now to the sergeant's stop. The car stopped just opposite the white two-story house. The sergeant alighted and had to stand on the other side of the track until the long yellow streetcar had rumbled away. It was as though an ugly, noisy curtain had at last been drawn back. He saw her face through an upstairs window of the white house with its precise cupola rising ever higher than the tall brick chimneys and with fantastic lacy woodwork ornamenting the tiny porches and the cornices. He saw her through the only second-story window that was clearly visible between the foliage of trees that grew in the yard.

The house was older than most of the houses in the suburban neighborhood along this ridgetop, and an old-fashioned iron fence enclosed its yard. He had to stop a moment to unlatch the iron gate, and there he looked directly up into the smiling countenance at the open window. She spoke to him in a voice even softer than he remembered.

Now he had to pass through his landlady's front hall and climb a crooked flight of stairs before reaching his rooms, and an old-fashioned bell had tinkled when he opened the front door. At this tinkling sound an old lady's voice called from somewhere in the back of the house, "Yes?" But he made no answer. He hurried up the steps and was at last in the room with his wife.

They sat on the couch with their knees touching and her hand in his.

Just as her voice was softer, her appearance was fairer even than he had remembered. He told her that he had been rehearsing this moment during every second of the past two hours, and simultaneously he realized that what he was saying was true, that during all other conversations and actions his imagination had been going over and over the present scene.

She glanced at the sweet peas lying beside his cap on the table and said that when she had seen him in the gateway with the flowers she had felt that perhaps during the time they were separated she had not remembered him even as gentle and fine as he was. Yet she had been afraid until that moment by the window that in her heart she had exaggerated these virtues of his.

The sergeant did not tell her then how he had come into possession of the flowers. He knew that the incident of the cleaning woman would depress her good spirits as it had his own. And while he was thinking of the complete understanding and sympathy between them he heard her saying, "I know you are tired. You're probably not so tired from soldiering as from dealing with people of various sorts all day. I went to the grocery myself this morning and coming home on the bus I thought of how tiresome and boring the long ride home would be for you this evening when the buses are so crowded." He leaned toward her and kissed her, holding her until he realized that she was smiling. He released her, and she drew away with a laugh and said that she had supper to tend to and that she must put the sweet peas in water.

While she was stirring about the clean, closet-like kitchen, he surveyed in the late twilight the living room that was still a strange room to him, and without lighting the table or floor lamps he wandered into the bedroom, which was the largest room and from which an old-fashioned bay window overlooked the valley. He paused at the window and raised the shade. And he was startled by a magnificent view of the mountains that rose up on the other side of the city. And there he witnessed the last few seconds of a sunset—brilliant orange and brick red—beyond the blue mountains.

They ate at a little table that she drew out from the wall in the living room. "How have I merited such a good cook for a wife?" he said and smiled when the meal was finished. They stacked the dishes unwashed in the sink, for she had put her arms about his neck and whispered, "Why should I waste one moment of the time I have you here when the days are so lonesome and endless."

They sat in the living room and read aloud the letters that had come during the past few days.

For a little while she worked on the hem of a tablecloth, and they talked.

They spoke of their friends at home. She showed him a few of their wedding presents that had arrived late. And they kept saying how fortunate they were to have found an apartment so comfortable as this. Here on the ridge it was cool almost every night.

Afterward he took out his pen and wrote a letter to his father. He read the letter aloud to her.

Still later it rained. The two of them hurried about putting down windows. Then they sat and heard it whipping and splashing against the window glass when the wind blew.

By the time they were both in their nightclothes the rain had stopped. He sat on a footstool by the bed reading in the heavy, dark history book. Once he read aloud a sentence which he thought impressive: "I have never seen the Federal dead lie so thickly on the ground save in front of the sunken wall at Fredericksburg." This was a Southern general writing of the battle fought along this ridgetop.

"What a very sad-sounding sentence," she said. She was brushing her hair in long, even strokes.

Finally he put down the book but remained sitting on the stool to polish his low-quartered military shoes. She at her dressing table looked at his reflection in the mirror before her, and said, "It's stopped raining."

"It stopped a good while ago," he said. And he looked up attentively, for there had seemed to be some regret in her voice.

"I'm sorry it stopped," she said, returning his gaze.

"You should be glad," he said. "I'd have to drill in all that mud tomorrow."

"Of course I'm glad," she said. "But hasn't the rain made us seem even more alone up here?"

The sergeant stood up. The room was very still and close. There was not even the sound of a clock. A light was burning on her dressing table, and through the open doorway he could see the table lamp that was still burning in the living room. The table there was a regular part of the furnishing of the apartment. But it was a piece of furniture they might have chosen themselves. He went to the door and stood a moment studying the effect she had achieved in her arrangement of objects on the table. On the dark octagonal top was the white lamp with the urn-shaped base. The light the lamp shed contrasted the shape of the urn with the global shape of a crystal vase from which sprigs of ivy mixed with periwinkle sprang in their individual wiriness. And a square, crystal ashtray reflecting its exotic lights was placed at an angle to a small round silver dish.

He went to the living room to put out the light. Yet with his hand on the switch he hesitated because it was such a pleasing isolated arrangement of objects.

Once the light was out he turned immediately to go back into the bedroom. And now he halted in the doorway again, for as he entered the bedroom his eye fell on the vase of sweet peas she had arranged. It was placed on top of a high bureau and he had not previously noticed it. Up there the flowers looked somehow curiously artificial and not like the real sweet peas he had seen in the rough hands of the woman this afternoon. While he was gazing thus he felt his wife's eyes upon him. Yet without turning to her he went to the window, for he was utterly preoccupied with the impression he had just received and he had a strange desire to sustain the impression long enough to examine it. He kept thinking of that woman's hands.

Now he raised the shade and threw open the big window in the bay, and standing there barefoot on a small hooked rug he looked out at the dark mountains and at the lines and splotches of lights in the city below. He heard her switching off the two small lamps at her dressing table. He knew that it had disturbed her to see him so suddenly preoccupied, and it was as though he tried to cram all of a whole day's reflections into a few seconds. Had it really been the pale flowers that had impressed him so? Or had it been the setting of his alarm clock a few minutes before and the realization that after a few more hours here with her he must take up again that other life that the yellow streetcar had carried away with it this afternoon? He could hear the voices of the boys in the barrack, and he saw the figure of the woman by the stone wall under the chinaberry tree.

Now he could hear his wife moving to switch off the overhead light. There was a click. The room being dark, things outside seemed much brighter. On the slope of the ridge that dropped off steeply behind the house the dark treetops became visible. And again there were the voices of the boys in the barrack. Their crudeness, their hardness, even their baseness—qualities that seemed to be taking root in the very hearts of those men—kept passing like objects through his mind. And the bitterness of the woman waiting by the streetcar tracks pressed upon him.

His wife had come up beside him in the dark and slipped her arm about his waist. He folded his arms tightly about her. She spoke his name. Then she said, "These hours we have together are so isolated and few that they must sometimes not seem quite real to you when you are away." She too, he realized, felt a terrible unrelated diversity in things. In the warmth of her companionship, he felt a sudden contrast with the cold fighting he might take part in on a battlefield that was now distant and almost abstract.

The sergeant's eyes had now grown so accustomed to the darkness inside and outside that he could look down between the trees on the slope of the ridge. He imagined there the line after line of Union soldiers that had once been thrown into the battle to take this ridge at all cost. The Confederate general's headquarters were not more than two blocks away. If he and she had been living in those days he would have seen ever so clearly the Cause for that fighting. And *this* battlefield would not be abstract. He would have stood here holding back the enemy from the very land which was his own, from the house in which she awaited him.

But here the sergeant stopped and smiled at himself. He examined the sergeant he had just imagined in the Confederate ranks and it was not himself at all. He compared the Confederate sergeant to the sergeant on the field this afternoon who had stood a moment puzzling over the tracks that twelve rookies had made. *The sergeant is I,* he said to himself desperately, *but it is not that morning in December of '62 when the Federal dead were lying so thick on the ground.* He leaned down and kissed his wife's forehead, and taking her up in his arms he carried her to their bed. *It is only a vase of flowers,* he remarked silently, rhetorically to himself as his wife drew her arms tighter about his neck. *Three bunches from a stand of sweet peas that had taken the lady's garden.* As he let her down gently on the bed she asked, "Why did you look so strangely at the vase of flowers? What did they make you think about so long by the window?"

For a moment the sergeant was again overwhelmed by his wife's perception and understanding. He would tell her everything he had in his mind. What great fortune it was to have a wife who could understand and to have her here beside him to hear and to comprehend everything that was in his heart and mind. But as he lay in the dark trying to make out the line of her profile against the dim light of the window, there came through the rain-washed air outside the rumbling of a streetcar. And before he could even speak the thoughts which he had been thinking, all those things no longer seemed to matter. The noise of the streetcar, the irregular rumble and uncertain clanging, brought back to him once more all the incidents of the day. He and his wife were here beside each other, but suddenly he was hopelessly distracted by this new sensation. The streetcar had moved away now beyond his hearing, and he could visualize it casting its diffused light among the dark foliage and over the white gravel between the tracks. He was left with the sense that no moment in his life had any relation to another. It was as though he were living a thousand lives. And the happiness and completeness of his marriage could not seem so large a thing.

Impulsively, almost without realizing what he was doing, he sat up on the other side of the bed. "I wasn't really thinking about the flowers," he said. "I guess I was thinking of how nicely you had arranged things on the living-room table."

"Oh," she said, for by his very words *I guess* it was apparent that she felt him minimizing the importance of his own impressions this evening and of their own closeness. In the dark he went to the small rocking chair on which his clothes were hanging and drew a cigarette from his shirt pocket. He lit it and sat on the edge of the little rocker, facing the open window, and he sat smoking his cigarette until quite suddenly the rain began to fall again. At the very first sound of the rain he stood up. He moved quickly to the window and put out his cigarette on the sill near the wire screen. The last bit of smoke sifted through the wire mesh. The rain was very noisy among the leaves. He stumbled hurriedly back through the dark and into the bed where he clasped his wife in his arms.

"It's begun to rain again," she said.

"Yes," the sergeant said. "It's much better now."

The Secret Life of Walter Mitty

JAMES THURBER

"We're going through!" The Commander's voice was like thin ice breaking. He wore his full-dress uniform, with the heavily braided white cap pulled down rakishly over one cold gray eye. "We can't make it, sir. It's spoiling for a hurricane, if you ask me." "I'm not asking you, Lieutenant Berg," said the Commander. "Throw on the power lights! Rev her up to 8,500! We're going through!" The pounding of the cylinders increased: ta-pocketa-pocketa-pocketa-*pocketa-pocketa*. The Commander stared at the ice forming on the pilot window. He walked over and twisted a row of complicated dials. "Switch on No. 8 auxiliary!" he shouted. "Switch on No. 8 auxiliary!" repeated Lieutenant Berg. "Full strength in No. 3 turret!" shouted the Commander. "Full strength in No. 3 turret!" The crew, bending to their various tasks in the huge, hurtling eight-engined Navy hydroplane, looked at each other and grinned. "The Old Man'll get us through," they said to one another. "The Old Man ain't afraid of Hell!" . . .

"Not so fast! You're driving too fast!" said Mrs. Mitty. "What are you driving so fast for?"

"Hmm?" said Walter Mitty. He looked at his wife, in the seat beside him, with shocked astonishment. She seemed grossly unfamiliar, like a strange woman who had yelled at him in a crowd. "You were up to fifty-five." Walter Mitty drove on toward Waterbury in silence, the roaring of the SN202 through the worst storm in twenty years of Navy flying fading in the remote, intimate airways of his mind. "You're tensed up again," said Mrs. Mitty. "It's one of your days. I wish you'd let Dr. Renshaw look you over."

Walter Mitty stopped the car in front of the building where his wife went to have her hair done. "Remember to get those overshoes while I'm having my hair done," she said. "I don't need overshoes," said Mitty. She put her mirror back into her bag. "We've been all through that," she said, getting out of the car. "You're not a young man any longer." He raced the engine a little. "Why don't you wear your gloves? Have you lost your gloves?" Walter Mitty reached in a pocket and brought out the gloves. He put them on, but after she had turned and gone into the building and he had driven on to a red light, he took them off again. "Pick it up, brother!" snapped a cop as the light changed, and Mitty hastily pulled on his gloves and lurched ahead. He drove around the streets aimlessly for a time, and then he drove past the hospital on his way to the parking lot.

. . . "It's the millionaire banker, Wellington McMillan," said the pretty nurse. "Yes?" said Walter Mitty, removing his gloves slowly. "Who has the case?" "Dr. Renshaw and Dr. Benbow, but there are two specialists here, Dr. Remington from New York and Dr. Pritchard-Mitford from London. He flew over." A door opened down a long, cool corridor and Dr. Renshaw came out. He looked distraught and haggard. "Hello, Mitty," he said. "We're having the devil's own time with McMillan, the millionaire banker and close personal friend of Roosevelt. Obstreosis of the ductal tract. Tertiary. Wish you'd take a look at him." "Glad to," said Mitty.

In the operating room there were whispered introductions: "Dr. Remington, Dr. Mitty, Dr. Pritchard-Mitford, Dr. Mitty." "I've read your book on streptothricosis," said Pritchard-Mitford, shaking hands. "A brilliant performance, sir." "Thank you," said Walter Mitty. "Didn't know you were in the States, Mitty," grumbled Remington. "Coals to Newcastle, bringing Mitford and me up here for a tertiary." "You are very kind," said Mitty. A huge, complicated machine, connected to the operating table, with many tubes and wires, began at this moment to go pocketa-pocketa-pocketa. "The new anesthetizer is giving way!" shouted an interne. "There is no one in the East who knows how to fix it!" "Quiet, man!" said Mitty, in a low, cool voice. He sprang to the machine, which was now going pocketa-pocketa-queep-pocketa-queep. He began fingering delicately a row of glistening dials. "Give me a fountain pen!" he snapped. Someone handed him a fountain pen. He pulled a faulty piston out of the machine and inserted the pen in its place. "That will hold for ten minutes," he said. "Get on with the operation." A nurse hurried over and whispered to Renshaw, and Mitty saw the man turn pale. "Coreopsis has set in," said Renshaw nervously. "If you would take over, Mitty?" Mitty looked at him and at the craven figure of Benbow, who drank, and at the grave, uncertain faces of the two great specialists. "If you wish," he said. They slipped a white gown on him; he adjusted a mask and drew on thin gloves; nurses handed him shining. . . .

"Back it up, Mac! Look out for that Buick!" Walter Mitty jammed on the brakes. "Wrong lane, Mac," said the parking-lot attendant, looking at Mitty closely. "Gee. Yeh," muttered Mitty. He began cautiously to back out of the lane marked "Exit Only." "Leave her sit there," said the attendant. "I'll put her away." Mitty got out of the car. "Hey, better leave the key." "Oh," said Mitty, handing the man the ignition key. The attendant vaulted into the car, backed it up with insolent skill, and put it where it belonged.

They're so damn cocky, thought Walter Mitty, walking along Main Street; they think they know everything. Once he had tried to take his chains off, outside New Milford, and he had got them wound around the axles. A man had had to come out in a wrecking car and unwind them, a young, grinning garageman. Since then Mrs. Mitty always made him drive to the garage to have the chains taken off. The next time, he thought, I'll wear my right arm in a sling; they won't grin at me then. I'll have my right arm in a sling and they'll see I couldn't possibly take the chains off myself. He kicked at the slush on the sidewalk. "Overshoes," he said to himself, and he began looking for a shoe store.

When he came out into the street again, with the overshoes in a box under his arm, Walter Mitty began to wonder what the other thing was his wife had told him to get. She had told him, twice, before they set out from their house for Waterbury. In a way he hated these weekly trips to town— he was always getting something wrong. Kleenex, he thought, Squibb's, razor blades? No. Toothpaste, toothbrush, bicarbonate, carborundum, initiative and referendum? He gave it up. But she would remember it. "Where's the what's-its-name?" she would ask. "Don't tell me you forgot the what's-its-name." A newsboy went by shouting something about the Waterbury trial.

. . . "Perhaps this will refresh your memory." The District Attorney suddenly thrust a heavy automatic at the quiet figure on the witness stand. "Have you ever seen this before?" Walter Mitty took the gun and examined it expertly. "This is my Webley-Vickers 50.80," he said calmly. An excited buzz ran around the courtroom. The Judge rapped for order. "You are a crack shot with any sort of firearms, I believe?" said the District Attorney, insinuatingly. "Objection!" shouted Mitty's attorney. "We have shown that the defendant could not have fired the shot. We have shown that he wore his right arm in a sling on the night of the fourteenth of July." Walter Mitty raised his hand briefly and the bickering attorneys were stilled. "With any known make of gun," he said evenly, "I could have killed Gregory Fitzhurst at three hundred feet *with my left hand*." Pandemonium broke loose in the courtroom. A woman's scream rose above the bedlam and suddenly a lovely, dark-haired girl was in Walter Mitty's arms. The District Attorney struck at her savagely. Without rising from his chair, Mitty let the man have it on the point of the chin. "You miserable cur!" . . .

"Puppy biscuit," said Walter Mitty. He stopped walking and the buildings of Waterbury rose up out of the misty courtroom and surrounded him again. A woman who was passing laughed. "He said 'Puppy biscuit,'" she said to her companion. "That man said 'Puppy biscuit' to himself." Walter Mitty hurried on. He went into an A. & P., not the first one he came to but a smaller one farther up the street. "I want some biscuit for small, young dogs," he said to the clerk. "Any special brand, sir?" The greatest pistol shot in the world thought a moment. "It says 'Puppies Bark for It' on the box," said Walter Mitty.

His wife would be through at the hairdresser's in fifteen minutes, Mitty saw in looking at his watch, unless they had trouble drying it; sometimes they had trouble drying it. She didn't like to get to the hotel first; she would want him to be there waiting for her as usual. He found a big leather chair in the lobby, facing a window, and he put the overshoes and the puppy biscuit on the floor beside it. He picked up an old copy of *Liberty* and sank down into the chair. "Can Germany Conquer the World through the Air?" Walter Mitty looked at the pictures of bombing planes and of ruined streets.

. . . "The cannonading has got the wind up in young Raleigh, sir," said the sergeant. Captain Mitty looked up at him through tousled hair. "Get him to bed," he said wearily. "With the others. I'll fly alone." "But you can't, sir," said the sergeant anxiously. "It takes two men to handle that bomber and the Archies are pounding hell out of the air. Von Richtman's circus is between here and Saulier." "Somebody's got to get that ammunition dump," said Mitty. "I'm going over. Spot of brandy?" He poured a drink for the sergeant and one for himself. War thundered and whined around the dugout and battered at the door. There was a rending of wood and splinters flew through the room. "A bit of a near thing," said Captain Mitty carelessly. "The box barrage is closing in," said the sergeant. "We only live once, Sergeant," said Mitty, with his faint, fleeting smile. "Or do we?" He poured another brandy and tossed it off. "I never see a man could hold his brandy like you, sir," said the sergeant. "Begging your pardon, sir." Captain Mitty stood up and strapped on his huge Webley-Vickers automatic. "It's forty kilometers through hell, sir," said the sergeant. Mitty finished one last brandy. "After all," he said softly, "what isn't?" The pounding of the cannon increased; there was the rat-tat-tatting of machine guns, and from somewhere came the menacing pocket-pocketa-pocketa of the new flame-throwers. Walter Mitty walked to the door of the dugout humming "Auprès de Ma Blonde." He turned and waved to the sergeant. "Cheerio!" he said. . . .

Something struck his shoulder. "I've been looking all over this hotel for you," said Mrs. Mitty. "Why do you have to hide in this old chair? How did you expect me to find you?" "Things close in," said Walter Mitty vaguely. "What?" Mrs. Mitty said. "Did you get the what's-its-name? The puppy biscuit? What's in that box?" "Overshoes," said Mitty. "Couldn't you have put them on in the store?" "I was thinking," said Walter Mitty. "Does it ever occur to you that I am sometimes thinking?" She looked at him. "I'm going to take your temperature when I get you home," she said.

They went out through the revolving doors that made a faintly derisive whistling sound when you pushed them. It was two blocks to the parking lot. At the drugstore on the corner she said, "Wait here for me. I forgot something. I won't be a minute." She was more than a minute. Walter Mitty lighted a cigarette. It began to rain, rain with sleet in it. He stood up against the wall of the drugstore, smoking. . . . He put his shoulders back and his heels together. "To hell with the handkerchief," said Walter Mitty scornfully. He took one last drag on his cigarette and snapped it away. Then, with that faint, fleeting smile playing about his lips, he faced the firing squad; erect and motionless, proud and disdainful, Walter Mitty the Undefeated, inscrutable to the last.

The Three Hermits

LEO TOLSTOY

AN OLD LEGEND CURRENT
IN THE VOLGA DISTRICT

And in praying use not vain repetitions as the Gentiles do: for they think that they shall be heard for their much speaking. Be not therefore like them, for your Father knoweth what things ye have need of, before ye ask Him.

Matthew vi: 7,8.

A Bishop was sailing from Archangel to the Solovétsk Monastery, and on the same vessel were a number of pilgrims on their way to visit the shrines at that place. The voyage was a smooth one. The wind favorable and the weather fair. The pilgrims lay on deck, eating, or sat in groups talking to one another. The Bishop, too, came on deck, and as he was pacing up and down he noticed a group of men standing near the prow and listening to a fisherman, who was pointing to the sea and telling them something. The Bishop stopped, and looked in the direction in which the man was pointing. He could see nothing, however, but the sea glistening in the sunshine. He drew nearer to listen, but when the man saw him, he took off his cap and was silent. The rest of the people also took off their caps and bowed.

"Do not let me disturb you, friends," said the Bishop. "I came to hear what this good man was saying."

"The fisherman was telling us about the hermits," replied one, a tradesman, rather bolder than the rest.

"What hermits?" asked the Bishop, going to the side of the vessel and seating himself on a box. "Tell me about them. I should like to hear. What were you pointing at?"

"Why, that little island you can just see over there," answered the man, pointing to a spot ahead and a little to the right. "That is the island where the hermits live for the salvation of their souls."

"Where is the island?" asked the Bishop. "I see nothing."

"There, in the distance, if you will please look along my hand. Do you see that little cloud? Below it, and a bit to the left, there is just a faint streak. That is the island."

The Bishop looked carefully, but his unaccustomed eyes could make out nothing but the water shimmering in the sun.

"I cannot see it," he said. "But who are the hermits that live there?"

"They are holy men," answered the fisherman. "I had long heard tell of them, but never chanced to see them myself till the year before last."

And the fisherman related how once, when he was out fishing, he had been stranded at night upon that island, not knowing where he was. In the morning, as he wandered about the island, he came across an earth hut, and met an old man standing near it. Presently two others came out, and after having fed him and dried his things, they helped him mend his boat.

"And what are they like?" asked the Bishop.

"One is a small man and his back is bent. He wears a priest's cassock and is very old; he must be more than a hundred, I should say. He is so old that the white of his beard is taking a greenish tinge, but he is always smiling, and his face is as bright as an angel's from heaven. The second is taller, but he also is very old. He wears a tattered peasant coat. His beard is broad, and of a yellowish grey color. He is a strong man. Before I had time to help him, he turned my boat over as if it were only a pail. He too is kindly and cheerful. The third is tall, and has a beard as white as snow and reaching to his knees. He is stern, with overhanging eyebrows; and he wears nothing but a piece of matting tied round his waist."

"And did they speak to you?" asked the Bishop.

"For the most part they did everything in silence, and spoke but little even to one another. One of them would just give a glance, and the others would understand him. I asked the tallest whether they had lived there long. He frowned, and muttered something as if he were angry; but the oldest one took his hand and smiled, and then the tall one was quiet. The oldest one only said: 'Have mercy upon us,' and smiled."

While the fisherman was talking, the ship had drawn nearer to the island.

"There, now you can see it plainly, if your Lordship will please to look," said the tradesman, pointing with his hand.

The Bishop looked, and now he really saw a dark streak—which was the island. Having looked at it a while, he left the prow of the vessel, and going to the stern, asked the helmsman:

"What island is that?"

"That one," replied the man, "has no name. There are many such in this sea."

"Is it true that there are hermits who live there for the salvation of their souls?"

"So it is said, your Lordship, but I don't know if it's true. Fisherman say they have seen them; but of course they may only be spinning yarns."

"I should like to land on the island and see these men," said the Bishop. "How could I manage it?"

"The ship cannot get close to the island," replied the helmsman, "but you might be rowed there in a boat. You had better speak to the captain."

The captain was sent for and came.

"I should like to see these hermits," said the Bishop. "Could I not be rowed ashore?"

The captain tried to dissuade him.

"Of course it could be done," said he, "but we should lose much time. And if I might venture to say so to your Lordship, the old men are not worth your pains. I have heard say that they are foolish old fellows, who understand nothing, and never speak a word, any more than the fish in the sea."

"I wish to see them," said the Bishop, "and I will pay you for your trouble and loss of time. Please let me have a boat."

There was no help for it; so the order was given. The sailors trimmed the sails, the steersman put up the helm, and the ship's course was set for the island. A chair was placed at the prow for the Bishop, and he sat there, looking ahead. The passengers all collected at the prow, and gazed at the island. Those who had the sharpest eyes could presently make out the rocks on it, and then a mud hut was seen. At last one man saw the hermits themselves. The captain brought a telescope and, after looking through it, handed it to the Bishop.

"It's right enough. There are three men standing on the shore. There, a little to the right of that big rock."

The Bishop took the telescope, got it into position, and he saw the three men: a tall one, a shorter one, and one very small and bent, standing on the shore and holding each other by the hand.

The captain turned to the Bishop.

"The vessel can get no nearer in than this, your Lordship. If you wish to go ashore, we must ask you to go in the boat while we anchor here."

The cable was quickly let out; the anchor cast, and the sails furled. There was a jerk, and the vessel shook. Then, a boat having been lowered, the oarsmen jumped in, and the Bishop descended the ladder and took his seat. The men pulled at their oars and the boat moved rapidly towards the island. When they came within a stone's throw, they saw three old men: a tall one with only a piece of matting tied round his waist, a shorter one in a tattered peasant coat, and a very old one bent with age and wearing an old cassock—all three standing hand in hand.

The oarsmen pulled in to the shore, and held on with the boathook while the Bishop got out.

The old men bowed to him, and he gave them his blessing, at which they bowed still lower. Then the Bishop began to speak to them.

"I have heard," he said, "that you, godly men, live here saving your own souls and praying to our Lord Christ for your fellow men. I, an unworthy servant of Christ, am called, by God's mercy, to keep and teach His flock. I wished to see you, servants of God, and to do what I can teach you, also."

The old men looked at each other smiling, but remained silent.

"Tell me," said the Bishop, "what you are doing to save your souls, and how you serve God on this island."

The second hermit sighed, and looked at the oldest, the very ancient one. The latter smiled, and said:

"We do not know how to serve God. We only serve and support ourselves, servant of God."

"But how do you pray to God?" asked the Bishop.

"We pray in this way," replied the hermit. "Three are ye, three are we, have mercy upon us."

And when the old man said this, all three raised their eyes to heaven, and repeated:

"Three are ye, three are we, have mercy upon us!"

The Bishop smiled.

"You have evidently heard something about the Holy Trinity," said he. "But you do not pray aright. You have won my affection, godly men. I see you wish to please the Lord, but you do not know how to serve Him. That is not the way to pray; but listen to me, and I will teach you. I will teach you, not a way of my own, but the way in which God in the Holy Scriptures has commanded all men to pray to Him."

And the Bishop began explaining to the hermits how God had revealed Himself to men; telling them of God the Father, and God the Son, and God the Holy Ghost.

"God the Son came down on earth," said he, "to save men, and this is how He taught us all to pray. Listen, and repeat after me: 'Our Father.'"

And the first old man repeated after him, "Our Father," and the second said, "Our Father," and the third said, "Our Father."

"Which art in heaven," continued the Bishop.

The first hermit repeated, "Which art in heaven," but the second blundered over the words, and the tall hermit could not say them properly. His hair had grown over his mouth so that he could not speak plainly. The very old hermit, having no teeth, also mumbled indistinctly.

The Bishop repeated the words again, and the old men repeated them after him. The Bishop sat down on a stone, and the old men stood before him, watching his mouth, and repeating the words as he uttered them. And all day long the Bishop labored, saying a word twenty, thirty, a hundred times over, and the old men repeated it after him. They blundered, and he corrected them, and made them begin again.

The Bishop did not leave off till he had taught them the whole of the Lord's Prayer so that they could not only repeat if after him, but could say it by themselves. The middle one was the first to know it, and to repeat the whole of it alone. The Bishop made him say it again and again, and at last the others could say it too.

It was getting dark and the moon was appearing over the water, before the Bishop rose to return to the vessel. When he took leave of the old men they all bowed down to the ground before him. He raised them, and kissed each of them, telling them to pray as he had taught them. Then he got into the boat and returned to the ship.

And as he sat in the boat and was rowed to the ship he could hear the three voices of the hermits loudly repeating the Lord's Prayer. As the boat drew near the vessel their voices could no longer be heard, but they could still be seen in the moonlight, standing as he had left them on the shore, the shortest in the middle, the tallest on the right, the middle one on the left. As soon as the Bishop had reached the vessel and got on board, the anchor was weighed and the sails unfurled. The wind filled them and the ship sailed away, and the Bishop took a seat in the stern and watched the island they had left. For a time he could still see the hermits, but presently they disappeared from sight, though the island was still visible. At last it too vanished, and only the sea was to be seen, rippling in the moonlight.

The pilgrims lay down to sleep, and all was quiet on deck. The Bishop did not wish to sleep, but sat alone at the stern, gazing at the sea where the island was no longer visible, and thinking of the good old men. He thought how pleased they had been to learn the Lord's Prayer; and he thanked God for having sent him to teach and help such godly men.

So the Bishop sat, thinking, and gazing at the sea where the island had disappeared. And the moonlight flickered before his eyes, sparkling, now here, now there, upon the waves. Suddenly he saw something white and shining, on the bright path which the moon cast across the sea. Was it a sea-gull, or the little gleaming sail of some small boat? The Bishop fixed his eyes on it, wondering.

"It must be a boat sailing after us," thought he, "but it is overtaking us very rapidly. It was far, far away a minute ago, but now it is much nearer. It cannot be a boat, for I can see no sail; but whatever it may be, it is following us and catching us up."

And he could not make out what it was. Not a boat, nor a bird, nor a fish! It was too large for a man, and besides a man could not be out there in the midst of the sea. The Bishop rose, and said to the helmsman:

"Look there, what is that, my friend? What is it?" the Bishop repeated, though he could now see plainly what it was—the three hermits running upon the water, all gleaming white, their grey beards shining, and approaching the ship as quickly as though it were not moving.

The steersman looked, and let go the helm in terror.

"Oh, Lord! The hermits are running after us on the water as though it were dry land!"

The passengers, hearing him, jumped up and crowded to the stern.

They saw the hermits coming along hand in hand, and the two outer ones beckoning the ship to stop. All three were gliding along upon the water without moving their feet. Before the ship could be stopped, the hermits had reached it, and raising their heads, all three as with one voice, began to say:

'We have forgotten your teaching, servant of God. As long as we kept repeating it we remembered, but when we stopped saying it for a time, a word dropped out, and now it has all gone to pieces. We can remember nothing of it. Teach us again.'

The Bishop crossed himself, and leaning over the ship's side, said:

"Your own prayer will reach the Lord, men of God. It is not for me to teach you. Pray for us sinners."

And the Bishop bowed low before the old men; and they turned and went back across the sea. And a light shone until daybreak on the spot where they were lost to sight.

Translated by Louise and Aylmer Maude

Fern

JEAN TOOMER

Face flowed into her eyes. Flowed in soft cream foam and plaintive ripples, in such a way that wherever your glance may momentarily have rested, it immediately thereafter wavered in the direction of her eyes. The soft suggestion of down slightly darkened, like the shadow of a bird's wing might, the creamy brown color of her upper lip. Why, after noticing it, you sought her eyes, I cannot tell you. Her nose was aquiline, Semitic. If you have heard a Jewish cantor sing, if he has touched you and made your own sorrow seem trivial when compared with his, you will know my feeling when I follow the curves of her profile, like mobile rivers, to their common delta. They were strange eyes. In this, that they sought nothing—that is, nothing that was obvious and tangible and that one could see, and they gave the impression that nothing was to be denied. When a woman seeks, you will have observed, her eyes deny. Fern's eyes desired nothing that you could give her; there was no reason why they should withhold. Men saw her eyes and fooled themselves. Fern's eyes said to them that she was easy. When she was young, a few men took her, but got no joy from it. And then, once done, they felt bound to her (quite unlike their hit and run with other girls), felt as though it would take them a lifetime to fulfill an obligation which they could find no name for. They became attached to her, and hungered after finding the barest trace of what she might desire. As she grew up, new men who came to town felt as almost everyone did who ever saw her: that they would not be denied. Men were everlastingly bringing her their bodies. Something inside of her got tired of them, I guess, for I am certain that for the life of her she could not tell why or how she began to turn them off. A man in fever is no trifling thing to send away. They began to leave her, baffled and ashamed, yet vowing to themselves that some day they would do some fine thing for her: send her candy every week and not let her know whom it came from, watch out for her wedding-day and give her a magnificent something with no name on it, buy a house and deed it to her, rescue her from some unworthy fellow who had tricked her into marrying him. As you know, men are apt to idolize or fear that which they cannot understand, especially if it be a woman. She did not deny them, yet the fact was that they were denied. A sort of superstition crept into their consciousness of her being somehow above them. Being above them meant that she was not to be approached by anyone. She became a virgin. Now a virgin in a small southern town is by no means the usual thing, if you will believe me. That the sexes were made to mate is the practice of the South. Particularly, black folks were made to mate. And it is black folks whom I have been talking about thus far. What white men thought of Fern I can arrive at only by analogy. They let her alone.

Anyone, of course, could see her, could see her eyes. If you walked up the Dixie Pike most any time of day, you'd be most like to see her resting listless-like on the railing of her porch, back propped against a post, head tilted a little forward because there was a nail in the porch post just where her head came which for some reason or other she never took the trouble to pull out. Her eyes, if it were sunset, rested idly where the sun, molten and glorious, was pouring down between the fringe of pines. Or maybe they gazed at the gray cabin on the knoll from which an evening folk-song was coming. Perhaps they followed a cow that had been turned loose to roam and feed on cotton-stalks and corn leaves. Like as not they'd settle on some vague spot above the horizon, though hardly a trace of wistfulness would come to them. If it were dusk, then they'd wait for the search-light of the evening train which you could see miles up the track before it flared across the Dixie Pike, close to her home. Wherever they looked, you'd follow them and then waver back. Like her face, the whole countryside seemed to flow into her eyes. Flowed into them with the soft listless cadence of Georgia's South. A young Negro, once, was looking at her, spellbound, from the road. A white man passing in a buggy had to flick him with his whip if he was to get by without running him over. I first saw her on her porch. I was passing with a fellow whose crusty numbness (I was from the North and suspected of being prejudiced and stuck-up) was melting as he found me warm. I asked him who she was. "That's Fern," was all I could get from him. Some folks already thought that I was given to nosing around; I let it go at that, so far as questions were concerned. But at first sight of her I felt as if I heard a Jewish cantor sing. As if his singing rose above the unheard chorus of a folk song. And I felt bound to her. I too had my dreams: something I would do for her. I have knocked about from town to town too much not to know the futility of mere change of place. Besides, picture if you can, this cream-colored solitary girl sitting at a tenement window looking down on the indifferent throngs of Harlem. Better that she listens to folk songs at dusk in Georgia, you would say, and so would I. Or, suppose she came up North and married. Even a doctor or a lawyer, say, one who would be sure to get along—that is, make money. You and I know, who have had experience in such things, that love is not a thing like prejudice which can be bettered by changes of town. Could men in Washington, Chicago, or New York, more than the men of Georgia, bring her something left vacant by the bestowal of their bodies? You and I who know men in these cities will have to say, they could not. See her out and out a prostitute along State Street in Chicago. See her move into a southern town where white men are more aggressive. See her become a white man's concubine . . . Something I must do for her. There was myself. What could I do for her? Talk, of course. Push back the fringe of pines upon new horizons. To what purpose? and what for? Her? Myself? Men in her case seem to lose their selfishness. I lost mine before I touched her. I ask you, friend (it makes no difference if you sit in the Pullman or the Jim Crow as the train crosses her road), what thoughts would come to you—that is, after you'd finished with the thoughts that leap into men's minds at the sight of a pretty woman who will not deny them; what thoughts would come to you, had you seen her in a quick flash, keen and intuitively, as she sat there on her porch when your train thundered by? Would you have got off at the next station and come back for her to take her where? Would you have completely forgotten her as soon as you reached Macon, Atlanta, Augusta, Pasadena, Madison, Chicago, Boston, or New Orleans? Would you tell your wife or sweetheart about a girl you saw? Your thoughts can help me, and I would like to know. Something I would do for her . . .

One evening I walked up the Pike on purpose, and stopped to say hello. Some of her family were about, but they moved away to make room for me. Damn if I knew how to begin. Would you? Mr. and Miss So-and-So, people, the weather, the crops, the new preacher, the frolic, the church benefit, rabbit and possum hunting, the new soft drink they had at old Pap's store, the schedule of the trains, what kind of town Macon was, Negro's migration north, boll-weevils, syrup, the Bible—to all these things she gave a yassur or nassur, without further comment. I began to wonder if perhaps my own emotional sensibility had played one of its tricks on me. "Let's take a walk," I at last ventured. The suggestion, coming after so long an isolation, was novel enough, I guess, to surprise. But it wasn't that. Something told me that men before me had said just that as a prelude to the offering of their bodies. I tried to tell her with my eyes. I think she understood. The thing from her that made my throat catch, vanished. Its passing left her visible in a way I'd thought, but never seen. We walked down the Pike with people on all the porches gaping at us. "Doesn't it make you mad?" She meant the row of petty gossiping people. She meant the world. Through a canebrake that was ripe for cutting, the branch was reached. Under a sweet-gum tree, and where reddish leaves had dammed the creek a little, we sat down. Dusk, suggesting the almost imperceptible procession of giant trees, settled with a purple haze about the cane. I felt strange, as I always do in Georgia, particularly at dusk. I felt that things unseen to men were tangibly immediate. It would not have surprised me had I had a vision. People have them in Georgia more often than you would suppose. A black woman once saw the mother of Christ and drew her in charcoal on the courthouse wall . . . When one is on the soil of one's ancestors, most anything can come to one . . . From force of habit, I suppose, I held Fern in my arms—that is, without at first noticing it. Then my mind came back to her. Her eyes, unusually weird and open, held me. Held God. He flowed in as I've seen the country-side flow in. Seen men. I must have done something—what, I don't know, in the confusion of my emotion. She sprang up. Rushed some distance from me. Fell to her knees, and began swaying, swaying. Her body was tortured with something it could not let out. Like boiling sap it flooded arms and fingers till she shook them as if they burned her. It found her throat, and spattered inarticulately in plaintive, convulsive sounds, mingled with calls to Christ Jesus. And then she sang, brokenly. A Jewish cantor singing with a broken voice. A child's voice, uncertain, or an old man's. Dusk hid her; I could hear only her song. It seemed to me as though she were pounding her head in anguish upon the ground. I rushed to her. She fainted in my arms.

There was talk about her fainting with me in the canefield. And I got one or two ugly looks from town men who'd set themselves up to protect her. In fact, there was talk of making me leave town. But they never did. They kept a watch-out for me, though. Shortly after, I came back North. From the train window I saw her as I crossed her road. Saw her on her porch, head tilted a little forward where the nail was, eyes vaguely focused on the sunset. Saw her face flow into them, the countryside and something that I call God, flowing into them . . . Nothing ever really happened. Nothing ever came to Fern, not even I. Something I would do for her. Some fine unnamed thing . . . And, friend, you? She is still living, I have reason to know. Her name, against the chance that you might happen down that way, is Fernie May Rosen.

A & P

JOHN UPDIKE

In walks these three girls in nothing but bathing suits. I'm in the third checkout slot, with my back to the door, so I don't see them until they're over by the bread. The one that caught my eye first was the one in the plaid green two-piece. She was a chunky kid, with a good tan and a sweet broad soft-looking can with those two crescents of white just under it, where the sun never seems to hit, at the top of the backs of her legs. I stood there with my hand on a box of HiHo crackers trying to remember if I rang it up or not. I ring it up again and the customer starts giving me hell. She's one of these cash-register-watchers, a witch about fifty with rouge on her cheekbones and no eyebrows, and I know it made her day to trip me up. She'd been watching cash registers for fifty years and probably never seen a mistake before.

By the time I got her feathers smoothed and her goodies into a bag—she gives me a little snort in passing, if she'd been born at the right time they would have burned her over in Salem—by the time I get her on her way the girls had circled around the bread and were coming back, without a pushcart, back my way along the counters, in the aisle between the checkouts and the Special bins. They didn't even have shoes on. There was this chunky one, with the two-piece—it was bright green and the seams on the bra were still sharp and her belly was still pretty pale so I guessed she just got it (the suit)—there was this one, with one of those chubby berry-faces, the lips all bunched together under her nose, this one, and a tall one, with black hair that hadn't quite frizzed right, and one of these sunburns right across under the eyes, and a chin that was too long—you know, the kind of girl other girls think is very "striking" and "attractive" but never quite makes it, as they very well know, which is why they like her so much—and then the third one, that wasn't quite so tall. She was the queen. She kind of led them, the other two peeking around and making their shoulders round. She didn't look around, not this queen, she just walked straight on slowly, on these long white prima-donna legs. She came down a little hard on her heels, as if she didn't walk in her bare feet that much, putting down her heels and then letting the weight move along to her toes as if she was testing the floor with every step, putting a little deliberate extra action into it. You never know for sure how girls' minds work (do you really think it's a mind in there or just a little buzz like a bee in a glass jar?) but you got the idea she had talked the other two into coming in here with her, and now she was showing them how to do it, walk slow and hold yourself straight.

She had on a kind of dirty-pink—beige maybe, I don't know—bathing suit with a little nubble all over it and, what got me, the straps were down. They were off her shoulders looped loose around the cool tops of her arms, and I guess as a result the suit had slipped a little on her, so all around the top of the cloth there was this shining rim. If it hadn't been there you wouldn't have known there could have been anything whiter than those shoulders. With the straps pushed off, there was nothing between the top of the suit and the top of her head except just *her*, this clean bare plane of the top of her chest down from the shoulder bones like a dented sheet of metal tilted in the light. I mean, it was more than pretty.

She had sort of oaky hair that the sun and salt had bleached, done up in a bun that was unravelling, and a kind of prim face. Walking into the A & P with your straps down, I suppose it's the only kind of face you *can* have. She held her head so high her neck, coming up out of those white shoulders, looked kind of stretched, but I didn't mind. The longer her neck was, the more of her there was.

She must have felt in the corner of her eye me and over my shoulder Stokesie in the second slot watching, but she didn't tip. Not this queen. She kept her eyes moving across the racks, and stopped, and turned so slow it made my stomach rub the inside of my apron, and buzzed to the other two, who kind of huddled against her for relief, and then they all three of them went up the cat-and-dog-food-breakfast-cereal-macaroni-rice-raisins-seasonings-spreads-spaghetti-soft-drinks-crackers-and cookies aisle. From the third slot I look straight up this aisle to the meat counter, and I watched them all the way. The fat one with the tan sort of fumbled with the cookies, but on second thought she put the package back. The sheep pushing their carts down the aisle—the girls were walking against the usual traffic (not that we have one-way signs or anything)—were pretty hilarious. You could see them, when Queenie's white shoulders dawned on them, kind of jerk, or hop, or hiccup, but their eyes snapped back to their own baskets and on they pushed. I bet you could set off dynamite in an A & P and the people would by and large keep reaching and checking oatmeal off their lists and muttering "Let me see, there was a third thing, began with A, asparagus, no, ah, yes, applesauce!" or whatever it is they do mutter. But there was no doubt, this jiggled them. A few houseslaves in pin curlers even looked around after pushing their carts past to make sure what they had seen was correct.

You know, it's one thing to have a girl in a bathing suit down on the beach, where what with the glare nobody can look at each other much anyway, and another thing in the cool of the A & P, under the fluorescent lights, against all those stacked packages, with her feet paddling along naked over our checkerboard green-and-cream rubber-tile floor.

"Oh Daddy," Stokesie said beside me. "I feel so faint."

"Darling," I said. "Hold me tight." Stokesie's married, with two babies chalked up on his fuselage already, but as far as I can tell that's the only difference. He's twenty-two, and I was nineteen this April.

"Is it done?" he asks, the responsible married man finding his voice. I forgot to say he thinks he's going to be manager some sunny day, maybe in 1990 when it's called the Great Alexandrov and Petrooshki Tea Company or something.

What he meant was, our town is five miles from a beach, with a big summer colony out on the Point, but we're right in the middle of town, and the women generally put on a shirt or shorts or something before they get out of the car into the street. And anyway these are usually women with six children and varicose veins mapping their legs and nobody, including them, could care less. As I say, we're right in the middle of town, and if you stand at our front doors you can see two banks and the Congregational church and the newspaper store and three real-estate offices and about twenty-seven old freeloaders tearing up Central Street because the sewer broke again. It's not as if we're on the Cape, we're north of Boston and there's people in this town haven't seen the ocean for twenty years.

The girls had reached the meat counter and were asking McMahon something. He pointed, they pointed, and they shuffled out of sight behind a pyramid of Diet Delight peaches. All that was left for us to see was old McMahon patting his mouth and looking after them sizing up their joints. Poor kids, I began to feel sorry for them, they couldn't help it.

Now here comes the sad part of the story, at least my family says it's sad, but I don't think it's so sad myself. The store's pretty empty, it being Thursday afternoon, so there was nothing much to do except lean on the register and wait for the girls to show up again. The whole store was like a pinball machine and I didn't know which tunnel they'd come out of. After a while they come around out of the far aisle, around the light bulbs, records at discount of the Caribbean Six or Tony Martin Sings or some such gunk you wonder they waste the wax on, sixpacks of candy bars, and plastic toys done up in cellophane that fall apart when a kid looks at them anyway. Around they come, Queenie still leading the way, and holding a little gray jar in her hand. Slots Three through Seven are unmanned and I could see her wondering between Stokes and me, but Stokesie with his usual luck draws an old party in baggy gray pants who stumbles up with four giant cans of pineapple juice (what do these bums *do* with all that pineapple juice? I've often asked myself) so the girls come to me. Queenie puts down the jar and I take it into my fingers icy cold. Kingfish Fancy Herring Snacks in Pure Sour Cream: 49¢. Now her hands are empty, not a ring or a bracelet, bare as God made them, and I wonder where the money's coming from. Still with that prim look she lifts a folded dollar bill out of the hollow at the center of her nubbled pink top. The jar went heavy in my hand. Really, I thought that was so cute.

Then everybody's luck begins to run out. Lengel comes in from haggling with a truck full of cabbages on the lot and is about to scuttle into that door marked MANAGER behind which he hides all day when the girls touch his eye. Lengel's pretty dreary, teaches Sunday school and the rest, but he doesn't miss that much. He comes over and says, "Girls, this isn't the beach."

Queenie blushes, though maybe it's just a brush of sunburn I was noticing for the first time, now that she was so close. "My mother asked me to pick up a jar of herring snacks." Her voice kind of startled me, the way voices do when you see the people first, coming out so flat and dumb yet kind of tony, too, the way it ticked over "pick up" and "snacks." All of a sudden I slid right down her voice into her living room. Her father and the other men were standing around in ice-cream coats and bow ties and the women were in sandals picking up herring snacks on toothpicks off a big glass plate and they were all holding drinks the color of water with olives and sprigs of mint in them. When my parents have somebody over they get lemonade and if it's a real racy affair Schlitz in tall glasses with "They'll Do It Every Time" cartoons stencilled on.

"That's all right," Lengel said. "But this isn't the beach." His repeating this struck me as funny, as if it had just occurred to him, and he had been thinking all these years the A & P was a great big dune and he was the head lifeguard. He didn't like my smiling—as I say he doesn't miss much—but he concentrates on giving the girls that sad Sunday-school-superintendent stare.

Queenie's blush is no sunburn now, and the plump one in plaid, that I liked better from the back—a really sweet can—pipes up, "We weren't doing any shopping. We just came in for the one thing."

"That makes no difference," Lengel tells her, and I could see from the way his eyes went that he hadn't noticed she was wearing a two-piece before. "We want you decently dressed when you come in here."

"We *are* decent," Queenie says suddenly, her lower lip pushing, getting sore now that she remembers her place, a place from which the crowd that runs the A & P must look pretty crummy. Fancy Herring Snacks flashed in her very blue eyes.

"Girls, I don't want to argue with you. After this come in here with your shoulders covered. It's our policy." He turns his back. That's policy for you.

Policy is what the kingpins want. What the others want is juvenile delinquency.

All this while, the customers had been showing up with their carts but, you know, sheep, seeing a scene, they had all bunched up on Stokesie, who shook open a paper bag as gently as peeling a peach, not wanting to miss a word. I could feel in the silence everybody getting nervous, most of all Lengel, who asks me, "Sammy, have you rung up their purchase?"

I thought and said "No" but it wasn't about that I was thinking. I go through the punches, 4, 9, GROC, TOT—it's more complicated than you think, and after you do it often enough, it begins to make a little song, that you hear words to, in my case "Hello *(bing)* there, you *(gung)* hap-py *pee*-pul *(splat)*!"—the *splat* being the drawer flying out. I uncrease the bill, tenderly as you may imagine, it just having come from between the two smoothest scoops of vanilla I had ever known were there, and pass a half and a penny into her narrow pink palm, and nestle the herrings in a bag and twist its neck and hand it over, all the time thinking.

The girls, and who'd blame them, are in a hurry to get out, so I say "I quit" to Lengel quick enough for them to hear, hoping they'll stop and watch me, their unsuspected hero. They keep right on going, into the electric eye; the door flies open and they flicker across the lot to their car, Queenie and Plaid and Big Tall Goony-Goony (not that as raw material she was so bad), leaving me with Lengel and a kink in his eyebrow.

"Did you say something, Sammy?"

"I said I quit."

"I thought you did."

"You didn't have to embarrass them."

"It was they who were embarrassing us."

I started to say something that came out "Fiddle-de-doo." It's a saying of my grandmother's, and I know she would have been pleased.

"I don't think you know what you're saying," Lengel said.

"I know you don't," I said. "But I do." I pull the bow at the back of my apron and start shrugging it off my shoulders. A couple customers that had been heading for my slot begin to knock against each other, like scared pigs in a chute.

Lengel sighs and begins to look very patient and old and gray. He's been a friend of my parents for years. "Sammy, you don't want to do this to your Mom and Dad," he tells me. It's true, I don't. But it seems to me that once you begin a gesture it's fatal not to go through with it. I fold the apron, "Sammy" stitched in red on the pocket, and put it on the counter, and drop the bow tie on top of it. The bow tie is theirs, if you've ever wondered. "You'll feel this for the rest of your life," Lengel says, and I know that's true, too, but remembering how he made the pretty girl blush makes me so scrunchy inside I punch the No Sale tab and the machine whirs "pee-pul" and the drawer splats out. One advantage to this scene taking place in summer, I can follow this up with a clean exit, there's no fumbling around getting your coat and galoshes, I just saunter into the electric eye in my white shirt that my mother ironed the night before, and the door heaves itself open, and outside the sunshine is skating around on the asphalt.

I look around for my girls, but they're gone, of course. There wasn't anybody but some young married screaming with her children about some candy they didn't get by the door of a powder-blue Falcon station wagon. Looking back in the big windows, over the bags of peat moss and aluminum lawn furniture stacked on the pavement, I could see Lengel in my place in the slot, checking the sheep through. His face was dark gray and his back stiff, as if he'd just had an injection of iron, and my stomach kind of fell as I felt how hard the world was going to be to me hereafter.

Everyday Use

ALICE WALKER

FOR YOUR GRANDMAMA

I will wait for her in the yard that Maggie and I made so clean and wavy yesterday afternoon. A yard like this is more comfortable than most people know. It is not just a yard. It is like an extended living room. When the hard clay is swept clean as a floor and the fine sand around the edges lined with tiny, irregular grooves anyone can come and sit and look up into the elm tree and wait for the breezes that never come inside the house.

Maggie will be nervous until after her sister goes: she will stand hope-lessly in corners homely and ashamed of the burn scars down her arms and legs, eyeing her sister with a mixture of envy and awe. She thinks her sister has held life always in the palm of one hand, that "no" is a word the world never learned to say to her.

You've no doubt seen those TV shows where the child who has "made it" is confronted, as a surprise, by her own mother and father, tottering in weakly from backstage. (A pleasant surprise, of course: What would they do if parent and child came on the show only to curse out and insult each other?) On TV mother and child embrace and smile into each other's faces. Sometimes the mother and father weep, the child wraps them in her arms and leans across the table to tell how she would not have made it without their help. I have seen these programs.

Sometimes I dream a dream in which Dee and I are suddenly brought to-gether on a TV program of this sort. Out of a dark and soft-seated limou-sine I am ushered into a bright room filled with many people. There I meet a smiling, gray, sporty man like Johnny Carson who shakes my hand and tells me what a fine girl I have. Then we are on the stage and Dee is em-bracing me with tears in her eyes. She pins on my dress a large orchid, even though she has told me once that she thinks orchids are tacky flowers.

In real life I am a large, big-boned woman with rough, man-working hands. In the winter I wear flannel nightgowns to bed and overalls during the day. I can kill and clean a hog as mercilessly as a man. My fat keeps me hot in zero weather. I can work outside all day, breaking ice to get water for washing; I can eat pork liver cooked over the open fire minutes after it comes steaming from the hog. One winter I knocked a bull calf straight in the brain between the eys with a sledge hammer and had the meat hung up to chill before nightfall. But of course all this does not show on television. I am the way my daughter would want me to be: a hundred pounds lighter, my skin like an uncooked barley pancake. My hair glistens in the hot bright lights. Johnny Carson has much to do to keep up with my quick and witty tongue.

But that is a mistake. I know even before I wake up. Who ever knew a Johnson with a quick tongue? Who can even imagine me looking a strange white man in the eye? It seems to me I have talked to them always with one foot raised in flight, with my head turned in whichever way is farthest from them. Dee, though. She would always look anyone in the eye. Hesitation was no part of her nature.

"How do I look, Mama?" Maggie says, showing just enough of her thin body enveloped in pink skirt and red blouse for me to know she's there, almost hidden by the door.

"Come out into the yard," I say.

Have you ever seen a lame animal, perhaps a dog run over by some careless person rich enough to own a car, sidle up to someone who is ignorant enough to be kind to him? That is the way my Maggie walks. She has been like this, chin on chest, eyes on ground, feet in shuffle, ever since the fire that burned the other house to the ground.

Dee is lighter than Maggie, with nicer hair and a fuller figure. She's a woman now, though sometimes I forget. How long ago was it that the other house burned? Ten, twelve years? Sometimes I can still hear the flames and feel Maggie's arms sticking to me, her hair smoking and her dress falling off her in little black papery flakes. Her eyes seemed stretched open, blazed open by the flames reflected in them. And Dee. I see her standing off under the sweet gum tree she used to dig gum out of; a look of concentration on her face as she watched the last dingy gray board of the house fall in toward the red-hot brick chimney. Why don't you do a dance around the ashes? I'd wanted to ask her. She had hated the house that much.

I used to think she hated Maggie, too. But that was before we raised the money, the church and me, to send her to Augusta to school. She used to read to us without pity; forcing words, lies, other folks' habits, whole lives upon us two, sitting trapped and ignorant underneath her voice. She washed us in a river of make-believe, burned us with a lot of knowledge we didn't necessarily need to know. Pressed us to her with the serious way she read, to shove us away at just the moment, like dimwits, we seemed about to understand.

Dee wanted nice things. A yellow organdy dress to wear to her graduation from high school; black pumps to match a green suit she'd made from an old suit somebody gave me. She was determined to stare down any disaster in her efforts. Her eyelids would not flicker for minutes at a time. Often I fought off the temptation to shake her. At sixteen she had a style of her own: and knew what style was.

I never had an education myself. After second grade the school was closed down. Don't ask me why: in 1927 colored asked fewer questions than they do now. Sometimes Maggie reads to me. She stumbles along good-naturedly but can't see well. She knows she is not bright. Like good looks and money, quickness passed her by. She will marry John Thomas (who has mossy teeth in an earnest face) and then I'll be free to sit here and I guess just sing church songs to myself. Although I never was a good singer. Never could carry a tune. I was always better at a man's job. I used to love to milk till I was hooked in the side in '49. Cows are soothing and slow and don't bother you, unless you try to milk them the wrong way.

I have deliberately turned my back on the house. It is three rooms, just like the one that burned, except the roof is tin; they don't make shingle roofs any more. There are no real windows, just some holes cut in the sides, like the portholes in a ship, but not round and not square, with rawhide holding the shutters up on the outside. The house is in a pasture, too, like the other one. No doubt when Dee sees it she will want to tear it down. She wrote me once that no matter where we "choose" to live, she will manage to come see us. But she will never bring her friends. Maggie and I thought about this and Maggie asked me, "Mama, when did Dee ever *have* any friends?"

She had a few. Furtive boys in pink shirts hanging about on washday after school. Nervous girls who never laughed. Impressed with her they worshiped the well-turned phrase, the cute shape, the scalding humor that erupted like bubbles in lye. She read to them.

When she was courting Jimmy T she didn't have much time to pay to us, but turned all her faultfinding power on him. He *flew* to marry a cheap gal from a family of ignorant flashy people. She hardly had time to recompose herself.

When she comes I will meet—but there they are!

Maggie attempts to make a dash for the house, in her shuffling way, but I stay her with my hand. "Come back here," I say. And she stops and tries to dig a well in the sand with her toe.

It is hard to see them clearly through the strong sun. But even the first glimpse of leg out of the car tells me it is Dee. Her feet were always neat-looking, as if God himself had shaped them with a certain style. From the other side of the car comes a short, stocky man. Hair is all over his head a foot long and hanging from his chin like a kinky mule tail. I hear Maggie suck in her breath. "Uhnnnh," is what is sounds like. Like when you see the wriggling end of a snake just in front of your foot on the road. "Uhnnnh."

Dee next. A dress down to the ground, in this hot weather. A dress so loud it hurts my eyes. There are yellows and oranges enough to throw back the light of the sun. I feel my whole face warming from the heat waves it throws out. Earrings gold, too, and hanging down to her shoulders. Brace-lets dangling and making noises when she moves her arm up to shake the folds of the dress out of her armpits. The dress is loose and flows, and as she walks closer, I like it. I hear Maggie go "Uhnnnh" again. It is her sister's hair. It stands straight up like the wool on a sheep. It is black as night and around the edges are two long pigtails that rope about like small lizards dis-appearing behind her ears.

"Wa-su-zo-Tean-o!" she says, coming on in that gliding way the dress makes her move. The short stocky fellow with the hair to his navel is all grinning and he follows up with "Asalamalakim, my mother and sister!" He moves to hug Maggie but she falls back, right up against the back of my chair. I feel her trembling there and when I look up I see the perspiration falling off her chin.

"Don't get up," says Dee. Since I am stout it takes something of a push. You can see me trying to move a second or two before I make it. She turns, showing white heels through her sandals, and goes back to the car. Out she peeks next with a Polaroid. She stoops down quickly and lines up picture after picture of me sitting there in front of the house with Maggie cowering behind me. She never takes a shot without making sure the house is in-cluded. When a cow comes nibbling around the edge of the yard she snaps it and me and Maggie *and* the house. Then she puts the Polaroid in the back seat of the car, and comes up and kisses me on the forehead.

Meanwhile Asalamalakim is going through the motions with Maggie's hand. Maggie's hand is as limp as a fish, and probably as cold, despite the sweat, and she keeps trying to pull it back. It looks like Asalamalakim wants to shake hands but wants to do it fancy. Or maybe he don't know how peo-ple shake hands. Anyhow, he soon gives up on Maggie.

"Well," I say. "Dee."

"No, Mama," she says. "Not 'Dee,' Wangero Leewanika Kemanjo!"

"What happened to 'Dee'?" I wanted to know.

"She's dead," Wangero said. "I couldn't bear it any longer being named after the people who oppress me."

"You know as well as me you was named after your aunt Dicie," I said. Dicie is my sister. She named Dee. We called her "Big Dee" after Dee was born.

"But who was *she* named after?" asked Wangero.

"I guess after Grandma Dee," I said.

"And who was she named after?" asked Wangero.

"Her mother," I said, and saw Wangero was getting tired. "That's about as far back as I can trace it," I said. Though, in fact, I probably could have carried it back beyond the Civil War through the branches.

"Well," said Asalamalakim, "there you are."

"Uhnnnh," I heard Maggie say.

"There I was not," I said, "before 'Dicie' cropped up in our family, so why should I try to trace it that far back?"

He just stood there grinning, looking down on me like somebody inspecting a Model A car. Every once in a while he and Wangero sent eye signals over my head.

"How do you pronounce this name?" I asked.

"You don't have to call me by it if you don't want to," said Wangero.

"Why shouldn't I?" I asked. "If that's what you want us to call you, we'll call you."

"I know it might sound awkward at first," said Wangero.

"I'll get used to it," I said. "Ream it out again."

Well, soon we got the name out of the way. Asalamalakim had a name twice as long and three times as hard. After I tripped over it two or three times he told me to just call him Hakim-a-barber. I wanted to ask him was he a barber, but I didn't really think he was, so I didn't ask.

"You must belong to those beef-cattle peoples down the road," I said. They said "Asalamalakim" when they met you, too, but they didn't shake hands. Always too busy: feeding the cattle, fixing the fences, putting up salt-lick shelters, throwing down hay. When the white folks poisoned some of the herd the men stayed up all night with rifles in their hands. I walked a mile and a half just to see the sight.

Hakim-a-barber said, "I accept some of their doctrines, but farming and raising cattle is not my style." (They didn't tell me, and I didn't ask, whether Wangero [Dee] had really gone and married him.)

We sat down to eat and right away he said he didn't eat collards and pork was unclean. Wangero, though, went on through the chitlins and corn bread, the greens and everything else. She talked a blue streak over the sweet potatoes. Everything delighted her. Even the fact that we still used the benches her daddy made for the table when we couldn't afford to buy chairs.

"Oh, Mama!" she cried. Then turned to Hakim-a-barber. "I never knew how lovely these benches are. You can feel the rump prints," she said, running her hands underneath her and along the bench. Then she gave a sigh and her hand closed over Grandma Dee's butter dish. "That's it!" she said. "I knew there was something I wanted to ask you if I could have." She jumped up from the table and went over in the corner where the churn stood, the milk in it clabber by now. She looked at the churn and looked at it.

"This churn top is what I need," she said. "Didn't Uncle Buddy whittle it out of a tree you all used to have?"

"Yes," I said.

"Uh huh," she said happily. "And I want the dasher, too."

"Uncle Buddy whittle that, too?" asked the barber.

Dee (Wangero) looked up at me.

"Aunt Dee's first husband whittled the dash," said Maggie so low you almost couldn't hear her. "His name was Henry, but they called him Stash."

"Maggie's brain is like an elephant's," Wangero said, laughing. "I can use the churn top as a centerpiece for the alcove table," she said, sliding a plate over the churn, "and I'll think of something artistic to do with the dasher."

When she finished wrapping the dasher the handle stuck out. I took it for a moment in my hands. You didn't even have to look close to see where hands pushing the dasher up and down to make butter had left a kind of sink in the wood. In fact, there were a lot of small sinks; you could see where thumbs and fingers had sunk into the wood. It was beautiful light yellow wood, from a tree that grew in the yard where Big Dee and Stash had lived.

After dinner Dee (Wangero) went to the trunk at the foot of my bed and started rifling through it. Maggie hung back in the kitchen over the dish-pan. Out came Wangero with two quilts. They had been pieced by Grandma Dee and then Big Dee and me had hung them on the quilt frames on the front porch and quilted them. One was in the Lone Star pattern. The other was Walk Around the Mountain. In both of them were scraps of dresses Grandma Dee had worn fifty and more years ago. Bits and pieces of Grandpa Jarrell's Paisley shirts. And one teeny faded blue piece, about the piece of a penny matchbox, that was from Great Grandpa Ezra's uniform that he wore in the Civil War.

"Mama," Wangero said sweet as a bird. "Can I have these old quilts?"

I heard something fall in the kitchen, and a minute later the kitchen door slammed.

"Why don't you take one or two of the others?" I asked. "These old things was just done by me and Big Dee from some tops your grandma pieced before she died."

"No," said Wangero. "I don't want those. They are stitched around the borders by machine."

"That'll make them last better," I said.

"That's not the point," said Wangero. "These are all pieces of dresses Grandma used to wear. She did all this stitching by hand. Imagine!" She held the quilts securely in her arms, stroking them.

"Some of the pieces, like those lavender ones, come from old clothes her mother handed down to her," I said, moving up to touch the quilts. Dee

(Wangero) moved back just enough so that I couldn't reach the quilts. They already belonged to her.

"Imagine!" she breathed again, clutching them closely to her bosom.

"The truth is," I said, "I promised to give them quilts to Maggie, for when she marries John Thomas."

She gasped like a bee had stung her.

"Maggie can't appreciate these quilts!" she said. "She'd probably be backward enough to put them to everyday use."

"I reckon she would," I said. "God knows I been saving 'em for long enough with nobody using 'em. I hope she will!" I didn't want to bring up how I had offered Dee (Wangero) a quilt when she went away to college. Then she had told me they were old-fashioned, out of style.

"But they're *priceless!*" she was saying now, furiously; for she has a temper. "Maggie would put them on the bed and in five years they'd be in rags. Less than that!"

"She can always make some more," I said. "Maggie knows how to quilt."

Dee (Wangero) looked at me with hatred. "You just will not understand. The point is these quilts, *these* quilts!"

"Well," I said, stumped. "What would *you* do with them?"

"Hang them," she said. As if that was the only thing you *could* do with quilts.

Maggie by now was standing in the door. I could almost hear the sound her feet made as they scraped over each other.

"She can have them, Mama," she said, like somebody used to never winning anything, or having anything reserved for her. "I can 'member Grandma Dee without the quilts."

I looked at her hard. She had filled her bottom lip with checkerberry snuff and it gave her face a kind of dopey, hangdog look. It was Grandma Dee and Big Dee who taught her how to quilt herself. She stood there with her scarred hands hidden in the folds of her skirt. She looked at her sister with something like fear but she wasn't mad at her. This was Maggie's portion. This was the way she knew God to work.

When I looked at her like that something hit me in the top of my head and ran down to the soles of my feet. Just like when I'm in church and the spirit of God touches me and I get happy and shout. I did something I never had done before: hugged Maggie to me, then dragged her on into the room, snatched the quilts out of Miss Wangero's hands and dumped them into Maggie's lap. Maggie just sat there on my bed with her mouth open.

"Take one or two of the others," I said to Dee.

But she turned without a word and went out to Hakim-a-barber.

"You just don't understand," she said, as Maggie and I came out to the car.

"What don't I understand?" I wanted to know.

"Your heritage," she said. And then she turned to Maggie, kissed her, and said, "You ought to try to make something of yourself, too, Maggie. It's really a new day for us. But from the way you and Mama still live you'd never know it."

She put on some sunglasses that hid everything above the tip of her nose and her chin.

Maggie smiled; maybe at the sunglasses. But a real smile, not scared. After we watched the car dust settle I asked Maggie to bring me a dip of snuff. And then the two of us sat there enjoying, until it was time to go in the house and go to bed.

Roselily

ALICE WALKER

Dearly Beloved,

She dreams; dragging herself across the world. A small girl in her mother's white robe and veil, knee raised waist high through a bowl of quicksand soup. The man who stands beside her is against this standing on the front porch of her house, being married to the sound of cars whizzing by on highway 61.

we are gathered here

Like cotton to be weighed. Her fingers at the last minute busily removing dry leaves and twigs. Aware it is a superficial sweep. She knows he blames Mississippi for the respectful way the men turn their heads up in the yard, the women stand waiting and knowledgeable, their children held from mischief by teachings from the wrong God. He glares beyond them to the occupants of the cars, white faces glued to promises beyond a country wedding, noses thrust forward like dogs on a track. For him they usurp the wedding.

in the sight of God

Yes, open house. That is what country black folks like. She dreams she does not already have three children. A squeeze around the flowers in her hands chokes off three and four and five years of breath. Instantly she is ashamed and frightened in her superstition. She looks for the first time at the preacher, forces humility into her eyes, as if she believes he is, in fact, a man of God. She can imagine God, a small black boy, timidly pulling the preacher's coattail.

to join this man and this woman

She thinks of ropes, chains, handcuffs, his religion. His place of worship. Where she will be required to sit apart with covered head. In Chicago, a word she hears when thinking of smoke, from his description of what a cinder was, which they never had in Panther Burn. She sees hovering over the heads of the clean neighbors in her front yard black specks falling, clinging, from the sky. But in Chicago. Respect, a chance to build. Her children at last from underneath the detrimental wheel. A chance to be on top. What a relief, she thinks. What a vision, a view, from up so high.

in holy matrimony.

Her fourth child she gave away to the child's father who had some money. Certainly a good job. Had gone to Harvard. Was a good man but weak because good language meant so much to him he could not live with Roselily. Could not abide TV in the living room, five beds in three rooms, no Bach except from four to six on Sunday afternoons. No chess at all. She does not forget to worry about her son among his father's people. She wonders if the New England climate will agree with him. If he will ever come down to Mississippi, as his father did, to try to right the country's wrongs. She wonders if he will be stronger than his father. His father cried off and on throughout her pregnancy. Went to skin and bones. Suffered nightmares, retching and falling out of bed. Tried to kill himself. Later told his wife he found the right baby through friends. Vouched for, the sterling qualities that would make up his character.

It is not her nature to blame. Still, she is not entirely thankful. She supposes New England, the North, to be quite different from what she knows. It seems right somehow to her that people who move there to live return home completely changed. She thinks of the air, the smoke, the cinders. Imagines cinders big as hailstones; heavy, weighing on the people. Wonders how this pressure finds its way into the veins, roping the springs of laughter.

If there's anybody here that knows a reason why

But of course they know no reason why beyond what they daily have come to know. She thinks of the man who will be her husband, feels shut away from him because of the stiff severity of his plain black suit. His religion. A lifetime of black and white. Of veils. Covered head. It is as if her children are already gone from her. Not dead, but exalted on a pedestal, a stalk that has no roots. She wonders how to make new roots. It is beyond her. She wonders what one does with memories in a brand-new life. This had seemed easy, until she thought of it. "The reasons why . . . the people who" . . . she thinks, and does not wonder where the thought is from.

these two should not be joined

She thinks of her mother, who is dead. Dead, but still her mother. Joined. This is confusing. Of her father. A gray old man who sold wild mink, rabbit, fox skins to Sears, Roebuck. He stands in the yard, like a man waiting for a train. Her young sisters stand behind her in smooth green dresses, with flowers in their hands and hair. They giggle, she feels, at the absurdity of the wedding. They are ready for something new. She thinks the man beside her should marry one of them. She feels old. Yoked. An arm seems to reach out from behind her and snatch her backward. She thinks of cemeteries and the long sleep of grandparents mingling in the dirt. She believes that she believes in ghosts. In the soil giving back what it takes.

together,

In the city. He sees her in a new way. This she knows, and is grateful. But is it new enough? She cannot always be a bride and virgin, wearing robes and veil. Even now her body itches to be free of satin and voile, organdy and lily of the valley. Memories crash against her. Memories of being bare to the sun. She wonders what it will be like. Not to have to go to a job. Not to work in a sewing plant. Not to worry about learning to sew straight seams in workingmen's overalls, jeans, and dress pants. Her place will be in the home, he has said, repeatedly, promising her rest she had prayed for. But now she wonders. When she is rested, what will she do? They will make babies—she thinks practically about her fine brown body, his strong black one. They will be inevitable. Her hands will be full. Full of what? Babies. She is not comforted.

let him speak

She wishes she had asked him to explain more of what he meant. But she was impatient. Impatient to be done with sewing. With doing everything for three children, alone. Impatient to leave the girls she had known since childhood, their children growing up, their husbands hanging around her, already old, seedy. Nothing about them that she wanted, or needed. The fathers of her children driving by, waving, not waving; reminders of times she would just as soon forget. Impatient to see the South Side, where they would live and build and be respectable and respected and free. Her husband would free her. A romantic hush. Proposal. Promises. A new life! Respectable, reclaimed, renewed. Free! In robe and veil.

or forever hold

She does not even know if she loves him. She loves his sobriety. His refusal to sing just because he knows the tune. She loves his pride. His blackness and his gray car. She loves his understanding of her *condition*. She thinks she loves the effort he will make to redo her into what he truly wants. His love of her makes her completely conscious of how unloved she was before. This is something; though it makes her unbearably sad Melancholy. She blinks her eyes. Remembers she is finally being married, like other girls. Like other girls, women? Something strains upward behind her eyes. She thinks of the something as a rat trapped, cornered, scurrying to and fro in her head, peering through the windows of her eyes. She wants to live for once. But doesn't know quite what that means. Wonders if she has ever done it. If she ever will. The preacher is odious to her. She wants to strike him out of the way, out of her light, with the back of her hand. It seems to her he has always been standing in front of her, barring her way.

his peace.

The rest she does not hear. She feels a kiss, passionate, rousing, within the general pandemonium. Cars drive up blowing their horns. Firecrackers go off. Dogs come from under the house and begin to yelp and bark. Her husband's hand is like the clasp of an iron gate. People congratulate. Her children press against her. They look with awe and distaste mixed with hope at their new father. He stands curiously apart, in spite of the people crowding about to grasp his free hand. He smiles at them all but his eyes are as if turned inward. He knows they cannot understand that he is not a Christian. He will not explain himself. He feels different, he looks it. The old women thought he was like one of their sons except that he had somehow got away from them. Still a son, not a son. Changed.

She thinks how it will be later in the night in the silvery gray car. How they will spin through the darkness of Mississippi and in the morning be in

Chicago, Illinois. She thinks of Lincoln, the president. That is all she knows about the place. She feels ignorant, *wrong,* backward. She presses her worried fingers into his palm. He is standing in front of her. In the crush of well-wishing people, he does not look back.

Blackberry Winter

ROBERT PENN WARREN

It was getting into June and past eight o'clock in the morning, but there was a fire—even if it wasn't a big fire, just a fire of chunks—on the hearth of the big stone fireplace in the living room. I was standing on the hearth, almost into the chimney, hunched over the fire, working my bare toes slowly on the warm stone. I relished the heat which made the skin of my bare legs warp and creep and tingle, even as I called to my mother, who was somewhere back in the dining room or kitchen, and said: "But it's June, I don't have to put them on!"

"You put them on if you are going out," her voice called.

I tried to assess the degree of authority and conviction in the tone, but at that distance it was hard to decide. I tried to analyze the tone, and then I thought what a fool I had been to start out the back door and let her see that I was barefoot. If I had gone out the front door or the side door she would never have known, not till dinner time anyway, and by then the day would have been half gone and I would have been all over the farm to see what the storm had done and down to the creek to see the flood. But it never had crossed my mind that they would try to stop you from going barefoot in June, no matter if there had been a gully-washer and a cold spell.

Nobody had ever tried to stop me in June as long as I could remember, and when you are nine years old what you remember seems forever, for you remember everything and everything is important and stands big and full and fills up Time and is so solid that you can walk around and around it like a tree and look at it. You are aware that time passes, that there is a movement in time, but that is not what Time is. Time is not a movement, a flowing, a wind then, but is, rather, a kind of climate in which things are, and when a thing happens it begins to live and keeps on living and stands solid in Time like the tree which you can walk around. And if there is a

1011

movement, the movement is not Time itself, any more than a breeze is climate, and all the breeze does is to shake a little the leaves on the tree which is live and solid. When you are nine, you know that there are things which you don't know, but you know that when you know something you know it. You know how a thing has been and you know that you can go barefoot in June. You do not understand that voice from back in the kitchen which says that you cannot go barefoot outdoors and run to see what has happened and rub your feet over the wet shivery grass and make the perfect mark of your foot in the smooth, creamy red mud and then muse on it as though you had suddenly come upon that single mark on the glistening auroral beach of the world. You have never seen a beach, but you have read the book and how the footprint was there.

The voice had said what it had said, and I looked savagely at the black stockings and the strong, scuffed brown shoes which I had brought from my closet as far as the hearth rug. I called once more, "But it's June," and waited.

"It's June," the voice replied from far away, "but it's blackberry winter."

I had lifted my head to reply to that, to make one more test of what was in that tone, when I happened to see the man.

The fireplace in the living room was at the end, for the stone chimney was built, as in so many of the farmhouses in Tennessee, at the end of a gable; and there was a window on each side of the chimney. Out of the window on the north side of the fireplace I could see the man. When I saw the man I did not call out what I had intended, but, engrossed by the strangeness of the sight, watched him, still far off, come along the path by the edge of the woods.

What was strange was that there should be a man there at all. That path went along the yard fence between the fence and the woods which came right down to the yard, and then on back past the chicken runs and on by the woods until it was lost to sight where the woods bulged out and cut off the back field. There the path disappeared into the woods. It led on back, I knew, through the woods and to the swamp, skirted the swamp, where the big trees gave way to sycamores and water oaks and willows and tangled cane, and then led on to the river. Nobody ever went back there except people who wanted to gig frogs in the swamp or to fish in the river or to hunt in the woods, and those people, if they didn't have a standing permission from my father, always stopped to ask permission to cross the farm. But the man whom I now saw wasn't, I could tell even at that distance, a sportsman. And what would a sportsman have been doing down there after a storm? Besides, he was coming from the river, and nobody had gone down there that morning. I knew that for a fact, because if anybody had passed the house, certainly if a stranger had passed, the dogs would have made a racket and would have been out on him. But this man was coming up from the river, and had come up through the woods. I suddenly had vision of him moving up the grassy path in the woods, in the green twilight under the big trees, not making any sound on the path, while now and then, like drops off the eaves, a big drop of water would fall from a leaf or bough and strike a stiff oak leaf lower down with a small, hollow sound like a drop of water hitting tin. That sound, in the silence of the woods, would be very significant.

When you are a boy and stand in the stillness of woods, which can be so still that your heart almost stops beating and makes you want to stand there in the green twilight until you feel your very feet sinking into and clutching the earth like roots and your body breathing slow through its pores like the leaves—when you stand there and wait for the next drop to drop with its small, flat sound to a lower leaf, that sound seems to measure out something, to put an end to something, to begin something, and you cannot wait for it to happen and are afraid it will not happen, and then, when it has happened, you are waiting again, almost afraid.

But the man whom I saw coming through the woods in my mind's eye did not pause and wait, growing into the ground and breathing with the enormous, soundless breathing of the leaves. Instead, I saw him moving in the green twilight inside my head as he was moving at that very moment along the path by the edge of the woods, coming toward the house. He was moving steadily but not fast, with his shoulder hunched a little and his head thrust forward, like a man who has come a long way and has a long way to go. I shut my eyes for a couple of seconds, thinking that when I opened them he would not be there at all. There was no place for him to have come from, and there was no reason for him to come where he was coming, toward our house. But I opened my eyes, and there he was, and he was coming steadily along the side of the woods. He was not yet even with the back chicken yard.

"Mama," I called.

"You put them on," the voice said.

"There's a man coming," I called, "out back."

She did not reply to that, and I guessed that she had gone to the kitchen window to look. She would be looking at the man and wondering who he was and what he wanted, the way you always do in the country, and if I went back there now she would not notice right off whether or not I was barefoot. So I went back to the kitchen.

She was standing by the window. "I don't recognize him," she said, not looking around at me.

"Where could he be coming from?" I asked.

"I don't know," she said.

"What would he be doing down at the river? At night? In the storm?"

She studied the figure out the window, then said: "Oh, I reckon maybe he cut across from the Dunbar place."

That was, I realized, a perfectly rational explanation. He had not been down at the river in the storm, at night. He had come over this morning. You could cut across from the Dunbar place if you didn't mind breaking through a lot of elder and sassafras and blackberry bushes which had about taken the old cross path, which nobody ever used any more. That satisfied me for a moment, but only for a moment. "Mama," I asked, "what would he be doing over at the Dunbar place last night?"

Then she looked at me, and I knew that I had made a mistake, for she was looking at my bare feet. "You haven't got your shoes on," she said.

But I was saved by the dogs. That instant there was a bark which I recognized as Sam, the collie, and then a heavier, churning kind of bark which was Bully, and I saw a streak of white as Bully tore round the corner of the back porch and headed out for the man. Bully was a big, bone-white bulldog, the kind of dog which they used to call a farm bulldog but which you don't see any more, heavy chested and heavy headed, but with pretty long legs. He could take a fence as light as a hound. He had just cleared the white paling fence toward the woods when my mother ran out to the back porch and began calling, "Here you, Bully! Here you!"

Bully stopped in the path, waiting for the man, but he gave a few more of those deep, gargling, savage barks, which reminded you of something down a stone-lined well. The red clay mud, I saw, was splashed up over his white chest and looked exciting like blood.

The man, however, had not stopped walking even when Bully took the fence and started at him. He had kept right on coming. All he had done was to switch a little paper parcel which he carried from the right hand to the left, and then reach into his pants pocket to get something. Then I saw the glitter and knew that he had a knife in his hand, probably the kind of mean knife just made for devilment and nothing else, with a blade as long as the blade of a frog-sticker which will snap out ready when you press a button in the handle. That knife must have had a button in the handle, or else how could he have had the blade out glittering so quick and with just one hand?

Pulling his knife against the dogs was a funny thing to do, for Bully was a big, powerful brute and fast, and Sam was all right. If those dogs had meant business, they might have knocked him down and ripped him before he got a stroke in. He ought to have picked up a heavy stick, something to take a swipe at them with and something which they could see and respect when they came at him. But he apparently did not know much about dogs. He just held the knife blade close against the right leg, low down, and kept on moving down the path.

Then my mother had called, and Bully had stopped. So the man let the blade of the knife snap back into the handle, and dropped it into his pocket, and kept on coming. Many women would have been afraid with the strange man who they knew had that knife in his pocket. That is, if they were alone in the house with nobody but a nine-year-old boy. And my

mother was alone, for my father had gone off and Dellie the cook was
down at her cabin because she wasn't feeling well. But my mother wasn't
afraid. She wasn't a big woman, but she was clear and brisk about everything she did, and looked everybody and everything right in the eye from
her own blue eyes in her tanned face. She had been the first woman in the
country to ride a horse astride (that was back when she was a girl and long
before I was born), and I have seen her snatch up a pump gun and go out
and knock a chicken hawk out of the air like a busted skeet when he came
over her chicken yard. She was a steady and self-reliant woman, and when
I think of her now after all the years she has been dead, I think of her
brown hands, not big but somewhat square for a woman's hands, with
square-cut nails. They looked as a matter of fact, more like a young boy's
hands than a grown woman's. But back then it never crossed my mind that
she would ever be dead.

She stood on the back porch and watched the man enter the back gate,
where the dogs (Bully had leapt back into the yard) were dancing and muttering and giving sidelong glances back to my mother to see if she meant
what she said. The man walked right by the dogs, almost brushing them,
and didn't pay them any attention. I could see now that he wore old khaki
pants and a dark wool coat with stripes in it, and a gray felt hat. He had on
a gray shirt with blue stripes in it, and no tie. But I could see a tie, blue and
reddish, sticking in his side coat pocket. Everything was wrong about what
he wore. He ought to have been wearing blue jeans or overalls and a straw
hat or an old black felt hat, and the coat, granting that he might have been
wearing a wool coat and not a jumper, ought not to have had those stripes.
Those clothes, despite the fact that they were old enough and dirty enough
for any tramp, didn't belong there in our back yard, coming down the path,
in Middle Tennessee, miles away from any big town, and near a mile off
the pike.

When he got almost to the steps, without having said anything, my
mother, very matter-of-factly, said, "Good morning."

"Good morning," he said, and stopped and looked her over. He did not
take off his hat, and under the brim you could see the perfectly unmemorable face, which wasn't old and wasn't young, or thick or thin. It was grayish and covered with about three days of stubble. The eyes were a kind of
nondescript, muddy hazel, or something like that, rather bloodshot. His
teeth, when he opened his mouth, showed yellow and uneven. A couple of
them had been knocked out. You knew that they had been knocked out,
because there was a scar, not very old, there on the lower lip just beneath
the gap.

"Are you hunting work?" my mother asked him.

"Yes," he said—not "yes mam"—and still did not take off his hat.

"I don't know about my husband, for he isn't here," she said, and didn't
mind a bit telling the tramp, or whoever he was, with the mean knife in his

pocket, that no man was around, "but I can give you a few things to do. The storm has drowned a lot of my chicks. Three coops of them. You can gather them up and bury them. Bury them deep so the dogs won't get at them. In the woods. And fix the coops the wind blew over.

"And down yonder beyond that pen by the edge of the woods are some drowned poults. They got out and I couldn't get them in. Even after it started to rain hard. Poults haven't got any sense."

"What are them things—poults?" he demanded, and spat on the brick walk. He rubbed his foot over the spot, and I saw that he wore a black, pointed-toe low shoe, all cracked and broken. It was a crazy kind of shoe to be wearing in the country.

"Oh, they're young turkeys," my mother was saying. "And they haven't got any sense. I oughtn't to try to raise them around here with so many chickens, anyway. They don't thrive near chickens, even in separate pens. And I won't give up my chickens." Then she stopped herself, and resumed briskly on the note of business. "When you finish that, you can fix my flower beds. A lot of trash and mud and gravel has washed down. Maybe you can save some of my flowers if you are careful."

"Flowers," the man said, in a low, impersonal voice which seemed to have a wealth of meaning, but a meaning which I could not fathom. As I think back on it, it probably was not pure contempt. Rather, it was a kind of impersonal and distant marvelling that he should be on the verge of grubbing in a flower bed. He said the word, and then looked off across the yard.

"Yes, flowers," my mother replied with some asperity, as though she would have nothing said or implied against flowers. "And they were very fine this year." Then she stopped, and looked at the man. "Are you hungry?" she demanded.

"Yeah," he said.

"I'll fix you something," she said, "before you get started." She turned to me. "Show him where he can wash up," she commanded, and went into the house.

I took the man to the end of the porch where a pump was and where a couple of wash pans sat on a low shelf for people to use before they went into the house. I stood there while he laid down his little parcel wrapped in newspaper and took off his hat and looked around for a nail to hang it on. He poured the water and plunged his hands into it. They were big hands, and strong looking, but they did not have the creases and the earth-color of the hands of men who work outdoors. But they were dirty, with black dirt ground into the skin and under the nails. After he had washed his hands, he poured another basin of water and washed his face. He dried his face, and with the towel still dangling in his grasp, stepped over to the mirror on the house-wall. He rubbed one hand over the stubble on his face. Then he carefully inspected his face, turning first one side and then the other, and stepped back and settled his striped coat down on his shoulders. He had the movements of a man who has just dressed up to go to church or a party—the way he settled his coat and smoothed it and scanned himself in the mirror.

Then he caught my glance on him. He glared at me for an instant out of the bloodshot eyes, then demanded in a low, harsh voice, "What are you looking at?"

"Nothing," I managed to say, and I stepped back a step from him.

He flung the towel down, crumpled, on the shelf, and went toward the kitchen door and entered without knocking.

My mother said something to him that I could not catch. I started to go in again, then thought about my bare feet, and decided to go back of the chicken yard, where the man would have to come to pick up the dead chicks. I hung around behind the chicken house until he came out.

He moved across the chicken yard with a fastidious, not quite finicking motion, looking down at the curdled mud flecked with bits of chicken-droppings. The mud curled up over the soles of his black shoes. I stood back from him some six feet and watched him pick up the first of the drowned chicks. He held it up by one foot and inspected it.

There is nothing deader looking than a drowned chick. The feet curl in that feeble, empty way which back when I was a boy, even if I was a country boy who did not mind hog-killing or frog-gigging, made me feel hollow in the stomach. Instead of looking plump and fluffy, the body is stringy and limp with the fluff plastered to it, and the neck is long and loose like a little string of rag. And the eyes have that bluish membrane over them which makes you think of a very old man who is sick about to die.

The man stood there and inspected the chick. Then he looked all around as though he didn't know what to do with it.

"There's a great big old basket in the shed," I said, and pointed to the shed attached to the chicken house.

He inspected me as though he had just discovered my presence, and moved toward the shed.

"There's a spade there, too," I added.

He got the basket and began to pick up the other chicks, picking each one up slowly by a foot and flinging it into the basket with a nasty, snapping motion. Now and then he would look at me out of the bloodshot eyes. Every time he seemed on the verge of saying something, but he did not. Perhaps he was building up to say something to me, but I did not wait that long. His way of looking at me made me so uncomfortable that I left the chicken yard.

Besides, I had just remembered that the creek was in flood, over the bridge, and that people were down there watching it. So I cut across the farm toward the creek. When I got to the big tobacco field I saw that it had not suffered much. The land lay right and not many tobacco plants had washed out of the ground. But I knew that a lot of tobacco round the country had washed right out. My father had said so at breakfast.

My father was down at the bridge. When I came out of the gap in the osage hedge into the road, I saw him sitting on his mare over the heads of the other men who were standing around admiring the flood. The creek was big here, even in low water, for only a couple of miles away it ran into the river, and when a real flood came the red water got over the pike where it dipped down to the bridge, which was an iron bridge, and ran high over the floor and even the side railings of the bridge. Only the upper iron work would show, with the water boiling and frothing red and white around it. That creek rose so fast and so heavy because a few miles back it came down out of the hills, where the gorges filled up with water in no time when a rain came. The creek ran in a deep bed with limestone bluffs along both sides until it got within three quarters of a mile of the bridge, and when it came out in flood from between those bluffs it was boiling and hissing and steaming like water from a fire hose.

Whenever there was a flood, people from half the county would come down to see the sight. After a gully-washer there would not be any work to do anyway. If it didn't ruin your crop, you couldn't plow and you felt like taking a holiday to celebrate. If it did ruin your crop, there wasn't anything to do except to try to take your mind off the mortgage, if you were rich enough to have a mortgage, and if you couldn't afford a mortgage you needed something to take your mind off how hungry you would be by Christmas. So people would come down to the bridge and look at the flood. It made something different from the run of days.

There would not be much talking after the first few minutes of trying to guess how high the water was this time. The men and kids just stood around, or sat their horses or mules, as the case might be, or stood up in the wagon beds. They looked at the strangeness of the flood for an hour or two, and then somebody would say that he had better be getting on home to dinner and would start walking down the gray, puddled limestone pike, or would touch heel to his mount and start off. Everybody always knew what it would be like when he got down to the bridge, but people always came. It was like church or a funeral. They always came, that is, if it was summer and the flood unexpected. Nobody ever came down in winter to see high water.

When I came out of the gap in the bowdock hedge, I saw the crowd, perhaps fifteen or twenty men and a lot of kids, and I saw my father sitting his mare Nellie Gray. He was a tall, limber man and carried himself well. I was always proud to see him sit a horse, he was so quiet and straight, and when I stepped through the gap of the hedge that morning, the first thing that happened was, I remember, the warm feeling I always had when I saw him up on a horse, just sitting. I did not go toward him, but skirted the crowd on the far side, to get a look at the creek. For one thing, I was not sure what he would say about the fact that I was barefoot. But the first thing I knew, I heard his voice calling, "Seth!"

I went toward him, moving apologetically past the men, who bent their large, red, or thin, sallow faces above me. I knew some of the men, and knew their names, but because those I knew were there in a crowd, mixed with the strange faces, they seemed foreign to me, and not friendly. I did not look up at my father until I was almost within touching distance of his heel. Then I looked up and tried to read his face, to see if he was angry about my being barefoot. Before I could decide anything from that impassive, high-boned face, he had leaned over and reached a hand to me. "Grab on," he commanded.

I grabbed on and gave a little jump, and he said, "Up-see-daisy!" and whisked me, light as a feather, up to the pommel of his McClellan saddle.

"You can see better up here," he said, slid back on the cantle a little to make me more comfortable, and then, looking over my head at the swollen, tumbling water, seemed to forget all about me. But his right hand was laid on my side, just above my thigh, to steady me.

I was sitting there as quiet as I could, feeling the faint stir of my father's chest against my shoulders as it rose and fell with his breath, when I saw the cow. At first, looking up the creek, I thought it was just another big piece of driftwood steaming down the creek in the ruck of water, but all at once a pretty good size boy who had climbed part way up a telephone pole by the pike so that he could see better yelled out, "Golly-damn, look at that-air cow!"

Everybody looked. It was a cow all right, but it might just as well have been driftwood, for it was dead as a chunk, rolling and roiling down the creek, appearing and disappearing, feet up or head up, it didn't matter which.

The cow started up the talk again. Somebody wondered whether it would hit one of the clear places under the top girder of the bridge and get through or whether it would get tangled in the drift and trash which had piled against the upright girders and braces. Somebody remembered how about ten years before so much driftwood had piled up on the bridge that it was knocked off its foundations. Then the cow hit. It hit the edge of the drift against one of the girders, and hung there. For a few seconds it seemed as though it might tear loose, but then we saw that it was really caught. It bobbed and heaved on its side there in a slow, grinding, uneasy fashion. It had a yoke around its neck, the kind made out of a forked limb to keep a jumper behind fence.

"She shore jumped one fence," one of the men said.

And another: "Well, she done jumped her last one, fer a fack."

Then they began to wonder about whose cow it might be. They decided
it must belong to Milt Alley. They said that he had a cow which was a
jumper, and kept her in a fenced-in piece of ground up the creek. I had
never seen Milt Alley, but I knew who he was. He was a squatter and lived
up the hills a way on a shirt-tail patch of set-on-edge land, in a cabin. He
was pore white trash. He had lots of children. I had seen the children at
school, when they came. They were thin-faced, with straight, sticky-look-
ing, dough-colored hair, and they smelled something like old sour buttermilk, not because they drank so much buttermilk but because that is the
sort of smell which children out of those cabins tend to have. The big Alley
boy drew dirty pictures which he showed to the little boys at school.

That was Milt Alley's cow. It looked like the kind of cow he would have,
a scrawny, old, sway-backed cow, with a yoke around her neck. I wondered
if Milt Alley had another cow.

"Poppa," I said, "do you think Milt Alley has got another cow?"

"You say 'Mr. Alley'," my father said, quietly.

"Do you think he has?"

"No telling," my father said.

Then a big gangly boy, about fifteen, who was sitting on a scraggly little
old mule with a piece of croker sack thrown across the saw-tooth spine, and
who had been staring at the cow, suddenly said to nobody in particular,
"Reckin anybody ever et drownt cow?"

He was the kind of boy who might just as well as not have been the son of
Milt Alley, with his faded and patched overalls ragged at the bottom of the
pants and the mud-stiff brogans hanging off his skinny, bare ankles below
the level of the mule's belly. He had said what he did, and then looked embarrassed and sullen when all the eyes swung at him. He hadn't meant to
say it, I am pretty sure now. He would have been too proud to say it, just as
Milt Alley would have been too proud. He had just been thinking out loud,
and the words had popped out.

There was an old man standing there on the pike, an old man with a
white beard. "Son," he said to the embarrassed and sullen boy on the mule,
"you live long enough and you'll find a man will eat anything when the time
comes."

"Time gonna come fer some folks this year," another man said.

"Son," the old man said, "in my time I et things a man don't like to think
on. I was a sojer and I rode with Gin'l Forrest, and them things we et when
the time come. I tell you. I et meat what got up and run when you taken out
yore knife to cut a slice to put on the fire. You had to knock it down with a
carbeen butt, it was so active. That-air meat would jump like a bullfrog, it
was so full of skippers."

But nobody was listening to the old man. The boy on the mule turned his
sullen face from him, dug a heel into the side of the mule and went off up

the pike with a motion which made you think that any second you would hear mule bones clashing inside that lank and scrofulous hide.

"Cy Dundee's boy," a man said, and nodded toward the figure going up the pike on the mule.

"Reckin Cy Dundee's young-uns seen times they'd settle fer drownt cow," another man said.

The old man with the beard peered at them both from his weak, slow eyes, first at one and then at the other. "Live long enough," he said, "and a man will settle for what he kin git."

Then there was silence again, with the people looking at the red, foam-flecked water.

My father lifted the bridle rein in his left hand, and the mare turned and walked around the group and up the pike. We rode on up to our big gate, where my father dismounted to open it and let me myself ride Nellie Gray through. When he got to the lane that led off from the drive about two hundred yards from our house, my father said, "Grab on." I grabbed on, and he let me down to the ground. "I'm going to ride down and look at my corn," he said. "You go on." He took the lane, and I stood there on the drive and watched him ride off. He was wearing cowhide boots and an old hunting coat, and I thought that that made him look very military, like a picture. That and the way he rode.

I did not go to the house. Instead, I went by the vegetable garden and crossed behind the stables, and headed down for Dellie's cabin. I wanted to play with Jebb, who was Dellie's little boy, about two years older than I was. Besides, I was cold. I shivered as I walked, and I had goose flesh. The mud which crawled up between my toes with every step I took was like ice. Dellie would have a fire, but she wouldn't make me put on shoes and stockings.

Dellie's cabin was of logs, with one side, because it was on a slope, set on limestone chunks, with a little porch attached to it, and had a little white-washed fence around it and a gate with plow-points on a wire to clink when somebody came, in, and had two big white oaks in the yard and some flow-ers and a nice privy in the back with some honeysuckle growing over it. Del-lie and Old Jebb, who was Jebb's father and who lived with Dellie and had lived with her for twenty-five years even if they never had got married, were careful to keep everything nice around their cabin. They had the name all over the community for being clean and clever negroes. Dellie and Jebb were what they used to call "white folks' niggers." There was a big dif-ference between their cabin and the two other cabins farther down where the other tenants lived. My father kept the other cabins weatherproof, but he couldn't undertake to go down and pick up after the litter they strewed. They didn't take the trouble to have a vegetable patch like Dellie and Jebb or to make preserves from wild plums, and jelly from crab apples the way Dellie did. They were shiftless, and my father was always threatening to get shed of them. But he never did. When they finally left, they just up and left on their own, for no reason, to go and be shiftless somewhere else. Then some more came. Meanwhile they lived down there, Matt Rawson and his family, and Sid Turner and his, and I played with their children all over the farm when they weren't working. But when I wasn't around they were mean sometimes to Little Jebb. That was because the other tenants down there were jealous of Dellie and Jebb.

I was so cold that I ran the last fifty yards to Dellie's gate. As soon as I had entered the yard, I saw that the storm had been hard on Dellie's flowers. The yard was, as I have said, on a slight slope, and the water running across had gutted the flower beds and washed out all the good black woods-earth which Dellie had brought in. What little grass there was in the yard was plastered sparsely down on the ground, the way the drainage water had left it. It reminded me of the way the fluff was plastered down on the skin of the drowned chicks which the strange man had been picking up, up in my mother's chicken yard.

I took a few steps up the path to the cabin, and then I saw that the drainage water had washed a lot of trash and filth out from under Dellie's house. Up toward the porch the ground was not clean any more. Old pieces of rag, two or three rusted cans, pieces of rotten rope, some hunks of old dog dung, broken glass, old paper, and all sorts of things like that had washed out from under Dellie's house to foul her clean yard. It looked just as bad as the yards of the other cabins, or worse. It was worse, as a matter of fact, because it was a surprise. I had never thought of all that filth being under Dellie's house. It was not anything against Dellie that the stuff had been under her cabin. Trash will get under any house. But I did not think of that when I saw the foulness washed out on the ground which Dellie sometimes used to sweep with a twig broom to make nice and clean.

I picked my way past the filth, being careful not to get my bare feet on it, and mounted to Dellie's door. When I knocked, I heard her voice telling me to come in.

It was dark inside the cabin, after the daylight, but I could make out Dellie piled up in bed under a quilt, and Little Jebb crouching by the hearth, where a low fire simmered. "Howdy," I said to Dellie, "how you feeling?"

Her big eyes, the whites surprising and glaring in the black face, fixed on me as I stood there, but she did not reply. It did not look like Dellie, or act like Dellie, who would grumble and bustle around our kitchen, talking to herself, scolding me or Little Jebb, clanking pans, making all sorts of unnecessary noises and mutterings like an old-fashioned black stream thrasher engine when it has got up an extra head of steam and keeps popping the governor and rumbling and shaking on its wheels. But now Dellie just lay there on the bed, under the patchwork quilt, and turned the black face, which I scarcely recognized, and the glaring white eyes to me.

"How you feeling?" I repeated.

"I'se sick," the voice said croakingly out of the strange black face which was not attached to Dellie's big, squat body but stuck out from under a pile of tangled bedclothes. Then the voice added: "Mighty sick."

"I'm sorry," I managed to say.

The eyes remained fixed on me for a moment, then they left me and the head rolled back on the pillow. "Sorry," the voice said, in a flat way which wasn't question or statement or anything. It was just the empty word put into the air with no meaning or expression, to float off like a feather or a puff of smoke, while the big eyes, with the white like the peeled white of hard-boiled eggs, stared at the ceiling.

"Dellie," I said after a minute, "there's a tramp up at the house. He's got a knife."

She was not listening. She closed her eyes.

I tiptoed over to the hearth where Jebb was, and crouched beside him. We began to talk in low voices. I was asking him to get out his train and play train. Old Jebb had put spool wheels on three cigar boxes and put wire links between the boxes to make a train for Jebb. The box that was the locomotive had the top closed and a length of broomstick for a smokestack. Jebb did not want to get the train out, but I told him I would go home if he didn't. So he got out the train, and the colored rocks, and fossils of crinoid stems, and other junk he used for the load, and we began to push it around, talking the way we thought trainmen would talk, making a chuck-chucking sound under the breath for the noise of the locomotive and now and then uttering low, cautious toots for the whistle. We got so interested in playing train that the toots got louder. Then, before he thought, Jebb gave a good, loud *toot-toot*, blowing for a crossing.

"Come here," the voice said from the bed.

Jebb got up slow from his hands and knees, giving me a sudden, naked, inimical look.

"Come here!" the voice said.

Jebb went to the bed. Dellie propped herself up weakly on one arm, muttering, "Come closter."

Jebb stood closer.

"Last thing I do, I'm gonna do it," Dellie said. "Done tole you to be quiet."

Then she slapped him. It was an awful slap, more awful for the kind of weakness which it came from and which it brought to focus. I had seen her slap Jebb before, but the slapping had been the kind of easy slap you would expect from a good-natured, grumbling negro woman like Dellie. But this was different. It was awful. It was so awful that Jebb did not make a sound. The tears just popped out and ran down his face, and his breath came sharp, like gasps.

Dellie fell back. "Caint even be sick," she said to the ceiling. "Git sick and they won't even let you lay. They tromp all over you. Caint even be sick." Then she closed her eyes.

I went out of the room. I almost ran to the door, and I did run across the porch and down the steps and across the yard, not caring whether or not I stepped on the filth which had washed out from under the cabin. I ran almost all the way home. Then I thought of my mother catching me with bare feet. So I went down to the stables.

I heard a noise in the crib, and opened the door. There was Big Jebb, sitting on an old nail keg, shelling corn into a bushel basket. I went in, pulling the door shut behind me, and crouched on the floor near him. I crouched there for a couple of minutes before either of us spoke, and watched him shelling the corn.

He had very big hands, knotted and grayish at the joints, with calloused palms which seemed to be streaked with rust with the rust coming up between the fingers to show from the back. His hands were so strong and tough that he could take a big ear of corn and rip the grains right off the cob with the palm of his hand, all in one motion, like a machine. "Work long as me," he would say, "and the good Lawd'll give you a hand lak cassion won't nuthen hurt." And his hands did look like cast iron, old cast iron streaked with rust.

He was an old man, up in his seventies, thirty years or more older than Dellie, but he was strong as a bull. He was a squat sort of man, heavy in the shoulders, with remarkably long arms, the kind of build they say the river natives have on the Congo from paddling so much in their boats. He had a round bullet-head, set on powerful shoulders. His skin was very black, and the thin hair on his head was now grizzled like tufts of old cotton batting. He had small eyes and a flat nose, not big, and the kindest and wisest old face in the world, the blunt, sad, wise face of an old animal peering tolerantly out on the goings-on of the merely human creatures before him. He was a good man, and I loved him next to my mother and father. I crouched there on the floor of the crib and watched him shell corn with the rusty cast-iron hands while he looked down at me out of the little eyes set in the blunt face.

"Dellie says she's mighty sick," I said.

"Yeah," he said.

"What's she sick from?"

"Woman-mizry," he said.

"What's woman-mizry?"

"Hit comes on 'em," he said. "Hit just comes on 'em when the time comes."

"What is it?"

"Hit is the change," he said. "Hit is the change of life and time."

"What changes?"

"You too young to know."

"Tell me."

"Time come and you find out ever-thing."

I knew that there was no use in asking him any more. When I asked him things and he said that, I always knew that he would not tell me. So I continued to crouch there and watch him. Now that I had sat there a little while I was cold again.

"What you shiver fer?" he asked me.

"I'm cold. I'm cold because it's blackberry winter," I said.

"Maybe 'tis and maybe 'taint," he said.

"My mother says it is."

"Ain't sayen Miss Sallie doan know and ain't sayen she do. But folks doan know ever-thing."

"Why isn't it blackberry winter?"

"Blackberry winter just a leetle cold spell. Blackberry winter come earlier ner this. Hit come and then hit go away, and hit is growed summer of a sudden lak a gunshot. Ain't no tellen hit will go way this time."

"It's June," I said. "It will go way."

"June," he replied with great contempt. "That what folks say. What June mean? Maybe hit is come cold to stay."

"Why?"

"Cuz this-here old yearth is tahrd. Hit is tahrd and ain't gonna perduce. Lawd let hit come rain one time forty days and forty nights, cuz He was tahrd of sinful folks. Maybe this-here old yearth say to the Lawd, Lawd I done plum tahrd, Lawd lemme rest. And Lawd say, yearth you done yore best, you give 'em cawn and you give 'em taters, and all they think on is they gut, and yearth, you kin take a rest."

"What will happen?"

"Folks will eat up ever-thing. The yearth won't perduce no more. Folks cut down all the trees and burn 'em cause they cold, and the yearth won't grow no more. I been tellen 'em. I been tellen folks. Sayen, maybe this year, hit is the time. But they doan listen to me, how the yearth is tahrd. Maybe this year they find out."

"Will everything die?"

"Ever-thing and ever-body, hit will be so."

"This year?"

"Ain't no tellen. Maybe this year."

"My mother said it is blackberry winter," I said confidently, and got up.

"Ain't sayen nuthen agin Miss Sallie," he said.

I went to the door of the crib. I was really cold. Running I had got up a sweat and now I was worse.

I hung on the door, looking at Jebb, who was shelling corn again.

"There's a tramp came to the house," I said. I had almost forgotten the tramp.

"Yeah."

"He came by the back way. What was he doing down there in the storm?"

"They comes and they goes," he said, "and ain't no tellen."

"He had a mean knife."

"The good ones and the bad ones, they comes and they goes. Storm or sun, light or dark. They is folks and they comes and they goes lak folks."

I hung on the door, shivering.

He studied me a moment, then said: "You git on to the house. You ketch yore death. Then what yore Mammy say?"

I hesitated.

"You git," he said.

When I came to the back yard, I saw my father standing by the back porch and the tramp walking toward him. They began talking before I reached them, but I got there just as my father was saying, "I'm sorry, but I haven't got any work. I got all the hands I need on the place now. I won't need any extra until wheat thrashing."

The stranger made no reply, just looking at my father.

My father took out his leather coin purse, and got out a half-dollar. He held it toward the man. "This is for half a day," he said.

The man looked at the coin, and then at my father, making no motion to take the money. But that was the right amount. A dollar a day was what you paid them back in 1910. And the man hadn't even worked half a day.

Then the man reached out and took the coin. He dropped it into the right side pocket of his coat. Then he said, very slowly and without feeling: "I didn't want to work on your f. . . . .g farm."

He used the word which they would have frailed me to death for using.

I looked at my father's face, and it was suddenly streaked white under the sunburn. Then he said: "Get off this place. Get off this place or I won't be responsible."

The man dropped his right hand into his pants pocket. It was the pocket where he kept the knife. I was just about to yell to my father about the knife when the hand came back out with nothing in it. The man gave a kind of twisted grin, showing where the teeth had been knocked out above the new scar. I thought that instant how maybe he had tried before to pull a knife on somebody else and had got his teeth knocked out.

So now he just gave that twisted, sickish grin out of the unmemorable, grayish face, and then spat on the brick path. The glob landed just about six inches from the toe of my father's right boot. My father looked down at it, and so did I. I thought that if the glob had hit my father's boot something would have happened. I looked down and saw the bright glob, and on one side of it my father's strong cowhide boots, with the brass eyelets and the leather thongs, heavy boots splashed with good red mud and set solid on the bricks, and on the other side the pointed-toe, broken black shoes on which the mud looked so sad and out of place. Then I saw one of the black shoes move a little, just a twitch first, then a real step backward.

The man moved in a quarter circle to the end of the porch, with my father's steady gaze upon him all the while. At the end of the porch, the man reached up to the shelf where the wash pans were to get his little newspaper-wrapped parcel. Then he disappeared around the corner of the house, and my father mounted the porch and went into the kitchen without a word.

I followed around the house to see what the man would do. I wasn't afraid of him now, no matter if he did have the knife. When I got around in front, I saw him going out the yard gate and starting up the drive toward the pike. So I ran to catch up with him. He was sixty yards or so up the drive before I caught up.

I did not walk right up even with him at first, but trailed him, the way a kid will, about seven or eight feet behind, now and then running two or three steps in order to hold my place against his longer stride. When I first came up behind him, he turned to give me a look, just a meaningless look, and then fixed his eyes up the drive and kept on walking.

When we had got around the bend in the drive which cut the house from sight, and were going along by the edge of the woods, I decided to come up even with him. I ran a few steps, and was by his side, or almost, but some feet off to the right. I walked along in this position for a while, and he never noticed me. I walked along until we got within sight of the big gate that let on the pike.

Then I said: "Where did you come from?"

He looked at me then with a look which seemed almost surprised that I was there. Then he said: "It ain't none of yore business."

We went on another fifty feet.

Then I said: "Where are you going?"

He stopped, studied me dispassionately for a moment, then suddenly took a step toward me and leaned his face down at me. The lips jerked back, but not in any grin, to show where the teeth were knocked out and to make the scar on the lower lip come white with the tension instead of red.

He said: "Stop following me. You don't stop following me and I cut yore throat, you little son-of-a-bitch."

Then he went on to the gate, and up the pike.

That was thirty-five years ago. Since that time my father and mother have died. I was still a boy, but a big boy, when my father got cut on the blade of a mowing machine, and died of lockjaw. My mother sold the place and went to town to live with her sister. But she never took hold after my father's death, and she died within three years, right in strong middle life. My aunt always said: "Sallie just died of a broken heart, she was so devoted." Dellie is dead too, but she died, I heard, quite a long time after we sold the farm.

As for Little Jebb, he grew up to be a mean and ficey negro. He killed another negro in a fight and got sent to the penitentiary, where he is yet, the last I heard tell. He probably grew up to be mean and ficey from just being picked on so much by the children of the other tenants, who were jealous of Jebb and Dellie for being thrifty and clever and being white folks' niggers.

Old Jebb lived forever. I saw him ten years ago, and he was about a hundred then, and not looking much different. He was living in town, on relief—that was back in the Depression—when I went to see him. He said to me: "Too strong to die. When I was a young feller just comen on and seen how things wuz, I prayed the Lawd. I said, oh Lawd, gimme strength and make me strong fer to do and to in-dure. The Lawd harkened to my prayer. He give me strength. I was in-duren proud fer being strong and me much man. The Lawd give me my prayer and my strength. But now He done gone off and fergot me and left me alone with my strength. A man doan know what to pray fer, and him mortal."

Jebb is probably living yet, as far as I know.

That is what has happened since the morning when the tramp leaned his face down at me and showed his teeth and said: "Stop following me. You don't stop following me and I cut yore throat, you little son-of-a-bitch." That was what he said, for me not to follow him. But I did follow him, all the years.

Why I Live at the P.O.

EUDORA WELTY

I was getting along fine with Mama, Papa-Daddy and Uncle Rondo until my sister Stella-Rondo just separated from her husband and came back home again. Mr. Whitaker! Of course I went with Mr. Whitaker first, when he first appeared here in China Grove, taking "Pose Yourself" photos, and Stella-Rondo broke us up. Told him I was one-sided. Bigger on one side than the other, which is a deliberate, calculated falsehood: I'm the same. Stella-Rondo is exactly twelve months to the day younger than I am and for that reason she's spoiled.

She's always had anything in the world she wanted and then she'd throw it away. Papa-Daddy gave her this gorgeous Add-a-Pearl necklace when she was eight years old and she threw it away playing baseball when she was nine, with only two pearls.

So as soon as she got married and moved away from home the first thing she did was separate! From Mr. Whitaker! This photographer with the popeyes she said she trusted. Came home from one of those towns up in Illinois and to our complete surprise brought this child of two.

Mama said she like to made her drop dead for a second. "Here you had this marvelous blonde child and never so much as wrote your mother a word about it," says Mama. "I'm thoroughly ashamed of you." But of course she wasn't.

Stella-Rondo just calmly takes off this *hat,* I wish you could see it. She says, "Why, Mama, Shirley-T.'s adopted, I can prove it."

"How?" says Mama, but all I says was, "H'm!" There I was over the hot stove, trying to stretch two chickens over five people and a completely unexpected child into the bargain, without one moment's notice.

"What do you mean—'H'm!'?" says Stella-Rondo, and Mama says, "I heard that, Sister."

I said that oh, I didn't mean a thing, only that whoever Shirley-T. was, she was the spit-image of Papa-Daddy if he'd cut off his beard, which of course he'd never do in the world. Papa-Daddy's Mama's papa and sulks.

Stella-Rondo got furious! She said, "Sister, I don't need to tell you you got a lot of nerve and always did have and I'll thank you to make no future reference to my adopted child whatsoever."

"Very well," I said. "Very well, very well. Of course I noticed at once she looks like Mr. Whitaker's side too. That frown. She looks like a cross between Mr. Whitaker and Papa-Daddy."

"Well, all I can say is she isn't."

"She looks exactly like Shirley Temple to me," says Mama, but Shirley-T. just ran away from her.

So the first thing Stella-Rondo did at the table was turn Papa-Daddy against me.

"Papa-Daddy," she says. He was trying to cut up his meat. "Papa-Daddy!" I was taken completely by surprise. Papa-Daddy is about a million years old and's got this long-long beard. "Papa-Daddy, Sister says she fails to understand why you don't cut off your beard."

So Papa-Daddy l-a-y-s down his knife and fork! He's real rich. Mama says he is, he says he isn't. So he says, "Have I heard correctly? You don't understand why I don't cut off my beard?"

"Why," I says, "Papa-Daddy, of course I understand, I did not say any such of a thing, the idea!"

He says, "Hussy!"

I says, "Papa-Daddy, you know I wouldn't any more want you to cut off your beard than the man in the moon. It was the farthest thing from my mind! Stella-Rondo sat there and made that up while she was eating breast of chicken."

But he says, "So the postmistress fails to understand why I don't cut off my beard. Which job I got you through my influence with the government. 'Bird's nest'—is that what you call it?"

Not that it isn't the next to smallest P.O. in the entire state of Mississippi.

I says, "Oh, Papa-Daddy," I says, "I didn't say any such of a thing, I never dreamed it was a bird's nest, I have always been grateful though this is the next to smallest P.O. in the state of Mississippi, and I do not enjoy being referred to as a hussy by my own grandfather."

But Stella-Rondo says, "Yes, you did say it too. Anybody in the world could of heard you, that had ears."

"Stop right there," says Mama, looking at *me*.

So I pulled my napkin straight back through the napkin ring and left the table.

As soon as I was out of the room Mama says, "Call her back, or she'll starve to death," but Papa-Daddy says, "This is the beard I started growing on the Coast when I was fifteen years old." He would of gone on till night-fall if Shirley-T. hadn't lost the Milky Way she ate in Cairo.

So Papa-Daddy says, "I am going out and lie in the hammock, and you can all sit here and remember my words: I'll never cut off my beard as long as I live, even one inch, and I don't appreciate it in you at all." Passed right by me in the hall and went straight out and got in the hammock.

It would be a holiday. It wasn't five minutes before Uncle Rondo suddenly appeared in the hall in one of Stella-Rondo's flesh-colored kimonos, all cut on the bias, like something Mr. Whitaker probably thought was gorgeous.

"Uncle Rondo!" I says. "I didn't know who that was! Where are you going?"

"Sister," he says, "get out of my way, I'm poisoned."

"If you're poisoned stay away from Papa-Daddy," I says. "Keep out of the hammock. Papa-Daddy will certainly beat you on the head if you come within forty miles of him. He thinks I deliberately said he ought to cut off his beard after he got me the P.O., and I've told him and told him and told him, and he acts like he just don't hear me. Papa-Daddy must of gone stone deaf."

"He picked a fine day to do it then," says Uncle Rondo, and before you could say "Jack Robinson" flew out in the yard.

What he'd really done, he'd drunk another bottle of that prescription. He does it every single Fourth of July as sure as shooting, and it's horribly expensive. Then he falls over in the hammock and snores. So he insisted on zigzagging right on out to the hammock, looking like a half-wit.

Papa-Daddy woke up with this horrible yell and right there without moving an inch he tried to turn Uncle Rondo against me. I heard every word he said. Oh, he told Uncle Rondo I didn't learn to read till I was eight years old and he didn't see how in the world I ever got the mail put up at the P.O., much less read it all, and he said if Uncle Rondo could only fathom the lengths he had gone to to get me that job! And he said on the other hand he thought Stella-Rondo had a brilliant mind and deserved credit for getting out of town. All the time he was just lying there swinging as pretty as you please and looping out his beard, and poor Uncle Rondo was *pleading* with him to slow down the hammock, it was making him as dizzy as a witch to watch it. But that's what Papa-Daddy likes about a hammock. So Uncle Rondo was too dizzy to get turned against me for the time being. He's Mama's only brother and is a good case of a one-track mind. Ask anybody. A certified pharmacist.

Just then I heard Stella-Rondo raising the upstairs window. While she was married she got this peculiar idea that it's cooler with the windows shut and locked. So she has to raise the window before she can make a soul hear her outdoors.

So she raises the window and says, *"Oh!"* You would have thought she was mortally wounded.

Uncle Rondo and Papa-Daddy didn't even look up, but kept right on with what they were doing. I had to laugh.

I flew up the stairs and threw the door open! I says, "What in the wide world's the matter, Stella-Rondo? You mortally wounded?"

"No," she says, "I am not mortally wounded but I wish you would do me the favor of looking out that window there and telling me what you see."

So I shade my eyes and look out the window.

"I see the front yard," I says.

"Don't you see any human beings?" she says.

"I see Uncle Rondo trying to run Papa-Daddy out of the hammock," I says. "Nothing more. Naturally, it's so suffocating-hot in the house, with all the windows shut and locked, everybody who cares to stay in their right mind will have to go out and get in the hammock before the Fourth of July is over."

"Don't you notice anything different about Uncle Rondo?" asks Stella-Rondo.

"Why, no, except he's got on some terrible-looking flesh-colored contraption I wouldn't be found dead in, is all I can see," I says.

"Never mind, you won't be found dead in it, because it happens to be part of my trousseau, and Mr. Whitaker took several dozen photographs of me in it," says Stella-Rondo. "What on earth could Uncle Rondo *mean* by wearing part of my trousseau out in the broad open daylight without saying so much as 'Kiss my foot,' *knowing* I only got home this morning after my separation and hung my negligee up on the bathroom door, just as nervous as I could be?"

"I'm sure I don't know, and what do you expect me to do about it?" I says. "Jump out the window?"

"No, I expect nothing of the kind. I simply declare that Uncle Rondo looks like a fool in it, that's all," she says. "It makes me sick to my stomach."

"Well, he looks as good as he can," I says. "As good as anybody in reason could." I stood up for Uncle Rondo, please remember. And I said to Stella-Rondo, "I think I would do well not to criticize so freely if I were you and came home with a two-year-old child I had never said a word about, and no explanation whatever about my separation."

"I asked you the instant I entered this house not to refer one more time to my adopted child, and you gave me your word of honor you would not," was all Stella-Rondo would say, and started pulling out every one of her eyebrows with some cheap Kress tweezers.

So I merely slammed the door behind me and went down and made some green-tomato pickle. Somebody had to do it. Of course Mama had turned both the niggers loose; she always said no earthly power could hold one anyway on the Fourth of July, so she wouldn't even try. It turned out that Jaypan fell in the lake and came within a very narrow limit of drowning.

So Mama trots in. Lifts up the lid and says, "H'm! Not very good for your Uncle Rondo in his precarious condition, I must say. Or poor little adopted Shirley-T. Shame on you!"

That made me tired. I says, "Well, Stella-Rondo had better thank her lucky stars it was her instead of me came trotting in with that very peculiar-looking child. Now if it had been me that trotted in from Illinois and brought a peculiar-looking child of two, I shudder to think of the reception I'd of got, much less controlled the diet of an entire family."

"But you must remember, Sister, that you were never married to Mr. Whitaker in the first place and didn't go up to Illinois to live," says Mama, shaking a spoon in my face. "If you had I would of been just as overjoyed to see you and your little adopted girl as I was to see Stella-Rondo, when you wound up with your separation and came on back home."

"You would not," I says.

"Don't contradict me, I would," says Mama.

But I said she couldn't convince me though she talked till she was blue in the face. Then I said, "Besides, you know as well as I do that that child is not adopted."

"She most certainly is adopted," says Mama, stiff as a poker.

I says, "Why, Mama, Stella-Rondo had her just as sure as anything in this world, and just too stuck up to admit it."

"Why, Sister," said Mama. "Here I thought we were going to have a pleasant Fourth of July, and you start right out not believing a word your own baby sister tells you!"

"Just like Cousin Annie Flo. Went to her grave denying the facts of life," I remind Mama.

"I told you if you ever mentioned Annie Flo's name I'd slap your face," says Mama, and slaps my face.

"All right, you wait and see," I says.

"I," says Mama, "I prefer to take my children's word for anything when it's humanly possible." You ought to see Mama, she weighs two hundred pounds and has real tiny feet.

Just then something perfectly horrible occurred to me.

"Mama," I says, "can that child talk?" I simply had to whisper! "Mama, I wonder if that child can be—you know—in any way? Do you realize," I says, "that she hasn't spoken one single, solitary word to a human being up to this minute? This is the way she looks," I says, and I looked like this.

Well, Mama and I just stood there and stared at each other. It was horrible!

"I remember well that Joe Whitaker frequently drank like a fish," says

Mama. "I believed to my soul he drank *chemicals*." And without another word she marches to the foot of the stairs and calls Stella-Rondo.

"Stella-Rondo? O-o-o-o-o! Stella-Rondo!"

"What?" says Stella-Rondo from upstairs. Not even the grace to get up off the bed.

"Can that child of yours talk?" asks Mama.

Stella-Rondo says, "Can she what?"

"Talk! Talk!" says Mama. "Burdyburdyburdyburdy!"

So Stella-Rondo yells back, "Who says she can't talk?"

"Sister says so," says Mama.

"You didn't have to tell me, I know whose word of honor don't mean a thing in this house," says Stella-Rondo.

And in a minute the loudest Yankee voice I ever heard in my life yells out, "OE'm Pop-OE the Sailor-r-r-r Ma-a-an!" and then somebody jumps up and down in the upstairs hall. In another second the house would of fallen down.

"Not only talks, she can tap-dance!" calls Stella-Rondo. "Which is more than some people I won't name can do."

"Why, the little precious darling thing!" Mama says, so surprised. "Just as smart as she can be!" Starts talking baby talk right there. Then she turns on me. "Sister, you ought to be thoroughly ashamed! Run upstairs this instant and apologize to Stella-Rondo and Shirley-T."

"Apologize for what?" I says. "I merely wondered if the child was normal, that's all. Now that she's proved she is, why, I have nothing further to say."

But Mama just turned on her heel and flew out, furious. She ran right upstairs and hugged the baby. She believed it was adopted. Stella-Rondo hadn't done a thing but turn her against me from upstairs while I stood there helpless over the hot stove. So that made Mama, Papa-Daddy and the baby all on Stella-Rondo's side.

Next, Uncle Rondo.

I must say that Uncle Rondo has been marvelous to me at various times in the past and I was completely unprepared to be made to jump out of my skin, the way it turned out. Once Stella-Rondo did something perfectly horrible to him—broke a chain letter from Flanders Field—and he took the radio back he had given her and gave it to me. Stella-Rondo was furious! For six months we all had to call her Stella instead of Stella-Rondo, or she wouldn't answer. I always thought Uncle Rondo had all the brains of the entire family. Another time he sent me to Mammoth Cave, with all expenses paid.

But this would be the day he was drinking that prescription, the Fourth of July.

So at supper Stella-Rondo speaks up and says she thinks Uncle Rondo ought to try to eat a little something. So finally Uncle Rondo said he would

try a little cold biscuits and ketchup, but that was all. So *she* brought it to
him:

"Do you think it wise to disport with ketchup in Stella-Rondo's flesh-
colored kimono?" I says. Trying to be considerate! If Stella-Rondo couldn't
watch out for her trousseau, somebody had to.

"Any objections?" asks Uncle Rondo, just about to pour out all the
ketchup.

"Don't mind what she says, Uncle Rondo," says Stella-Rondo. "Sister has
been devoting this solid afternoon to sneering out my bedroom window at
the way you look."

"What's that?" says Uncle Rondo. Uncle Rondo has got the most terrible
temper in the world. Anything is liable to make him tear the house down if
it comes at the wrong time.

So Stella-Rondo says, "Sister says, 'Uncle Rondo certainly does look like a
fool in that pink kimono!'"

Do you remember who it was really said that?

Uncle Rondo spills out all the ketchup and jumps out of his chair and
tears off the kimono and throws it down on the dirty floor and puts his foot
on it. It had to be sent all the way to Jackson to the cleaners and re-pleated.

"So that's your opinion of your Uncle Rondo, is it?" he says. "I look like
a fool, do I? Well, that's the last straw. A whole day in this house with nothing to do, and then to hear you come out with a remark like that behind my
back!"

"I didn't say any such of a thing, Uncle Rondo," I says, "and I'm not saying who did, either. Why, I think you look all right. Just try to take care of
yourself and not talk and eat at the same time," I says. "I think you better
go lie down."

"Lie down my foot," says Uncle Rondo. I ought to of known by that he
was fixing to do something perfectly horrible.

So he didn't do anything that night in the precarious state he was in—
just played Casino with Mama and Stella-Rondo and Shirley-T. and gave
Shirley-T. a nickel with a head on both sides. It tickled her nearly to death,
and she called him "Papa." But at 6:30 A.M. the next morning, he threw a
whole five-cent package of some unsold one-inch firecrackers from the
store as hard as he could into my bedroom and they every one went off.
Not one bad one in the string. Anybody else, there'd be one that wouldn't
go off.

Well, I'm just terribly susceptible to noise of any kind, the doctor has always told me I was the most sensitive person he had ever seen in his whole
life, and I was simply prostrated. I couldn't eat! People tell me they heard
it as far as the cemetery, and old Aunt Jep Patterson, that had been holding
her own so good, thought it was Judgment Day and she was going to meet
her whole family. It's usually so quiet here.

And I'll tell you it didn't take me any longer than a minute to make up my mind what to do. There I was with the whole entire house on Stella-Rondo's side and turned against me. If I have anything at all I have pride.

So I just decided I'd go straight down to the P.O. There's plenty of room there in the back, I says to myself.

Well! I made no bones about letting the family catch on to what I was up to. I didn't try to conceal it.

The first thing they knew, I marched in where they were all playing Old Maid and pulled the electric oscillating fan out by the plug, and everything got real hot. Next I snatched the pillow I'd done the needlepoint on right off the davenport from behind Papa-Daddy. He went "Ugh!" I beat Stella-Rondo up the stairs and finally found my charm bracelet in her bureau drawer under a picture of Nelson Eddy.

"So that's the way the land lies," says Uncle Rondo. There he was, piecing on the ham. "Well, Sister, I'll be glad to donate my army cot if you got any place to set it up, providing you'll leave right this minute and let me get some peace." Uncle Rondo was in France.

"Thank you kindly for the cot and 'peace' is hardly the word I would select if I had to resort to firecrackers at 6:30 A.M. in a young girl's bedroom," I says back to him. "And as to where I intend to go, you seem to forget my position as postmistress of China Grove, Mississippi," I says. "I've always got the P.O."

Well, that made them all sit up and take notice.

I went out front and started digging up some four-o'clocks to plant around the P.O.

"Ah-ah-ah!" says Mama, raising the window. "Those happen to be my four-o'clocks. Everything planted in that star is mine. I've never known you to make anything grow in your life."

"Very well," I says. "But I take the fern. Even you, Mama, can't stand there and deny that I'm the one watered that fern. And I happen to know where I can send in a box top and get a packet of one thousand mixed seeds, no two the same kind, free."

"Oh, where?" Mama wants to know.

But I says, "Too late. You 'tend to your house, and I'll 'tend to mine. You hear things like that all the time if you know how to listen to the radio. Perfectly marvelous offers. Get anything you want free."

So I hope to tell you I marched in and got that radio, and they could of all bit a nail in two, especially Stella-Rondo, that it used to belong to, and she well knew she couldn't get it back, I'd sue for it like a shot. And I very politely took the sewing-machine motor I helped pay the most on to give Mama for Christmas back in 1929, and a good big calendar, with the first-aid remedies on it. The thermometer and the Hawaiian ukulele certainly were rightfully mine, and I stood on the step-ladder and got all my water-melon-rind preserves and every fruit and vegetable I'd put up, every jar.

Then I began to pull the tacks out of the bluebird wall vases on the archway to the dining room.

"Who told you you could have those, Miss Priss?" says Mama, fanning as hard as she could.

"I bought 'em and I'll keep track of 'em," I says. "I'll tack 'em up one on each side the postoffice window, and you can see 'em when you come to ask me for your mail, if you're so dead to see 'em."

"Not I! I'll never darken the door to that post office again if I live to be a hundred," Mama says. "Ungrateful child! After all the money we spent on you at the Normal."

"Me either," says Stella-Rondo. "You can just let my mail lie there and *rot*, for all I care. I'll never come and relieve you of a single, solitary piece."

"I should worry," I says. "And who you think's going to sit down and write you all those big fat letters and postcards, by the way? Mr. Whitaker? Just because he was the only man ever dropped down in China Grove and you got him—unfairly—is he going to sit down and write you a lengthy correspondence after you come home giving no rhyme nor reason whatsoever for your separation and no explanation for the presence of that child? I may not have your brilliant mind, but I fail to see it."

So Mama says, "Sister, I've told you a thousand times that Stella-Rondo simply got homesick, and this child is far too big to be hers," and she says, "Now, why don't you all just sit down and play Casino?"

Then Shirley-T. sticks out her tongue at me in this perfectly horrible way. She has no more manners than the man in the moon. I told her she was going to cross her eyes like that some day and they'd stick.

"It's too late to stop me now," I says. "You should have tried that yesterday. I'm going to the P.O. and the only way you can possibly see me is to visit me there."

So Papa-Daddy says, "You'll never catch me setting foot in that post office, even if I should take a notion into my head to write a letter some place." He says, "I won't have you reachin' out of that little old window with a pair of shears and cuttin' off any beard of mine. I'm too smart for you!"

"We all are," says Stella-Rondo.

But I said, "If you're so smart, where's Mr. Whitaker?"

So then Uncle Rondo says, "I'll thank you from now on to stop reading all the orders I get on postcards and telling everybody in China Grove what you think is the matter with them," but I says, "I draw my own conclusions and will continue in the future to draw them." I says, "If people want to write their inmost secrets on penny postcards, there's nothing in the wide world you can do about it, Uncle Rondo."

"And if you think we'll ever *write* another postcard you're sadly mistaken," says Mama.

"Cutting off your nose to spite your face then," I says. "But if you're all determined to have no more to do with the U. S. mail, think of this: What will Stella-Rondo do now, if she wants to tell Mr. Whitaker to come after her?"

"Wah!" says Stella-Rondo. I knew she'd cry. She had a conniption fit right there in the kitchen.

"It will be interesting to see how long she holds out," I says. "And now— I am leaving."

"Good-bye," says Uncle Rondo.

"Oh, I declare," says Mama, "to think that a family of mine should quarrel on the Fourth of July, or the day after, over Stella-Rondo leaving old Mr. Whitaker and having the sweetest little adopted child! It looks like we'd all be glad!"

"Wah!" says Stella-Rondo, and has a fresh conniption fit.

"*He* left *her*—you mark my words," I says. "That's Mr. Whitaker. I know Mr. Whitaker. After all, I knew him first. I said from the beginning he'd up and leave her. I foretold every single thing that's happened."

"Where did he go?" asks Mama.

"Probably to the North Pole, if he knows what's good for him," I says.

But Stella-Rondo just bawled and wouldn't say another word. She flew to her room and slammed the door.

"Now look what you've gone and done, Sister," says Mama. "You go apologize."

"I haven't got time, I'm leaving," I says.

"Well, what are you waiting around for?" asks Uncle Rondo.

So I just picked up the kitchen clock and marched off, without saying "Kiss my foot" or anything, and never did tell Stella-Rondo goodbye.

There was a nigger girl going along on a little wagon right in front.

"Nigger girl," I says, "come help me haul these things down the hill, I'm going to live in the post office."

Took her nine trips in her express wagon. Uncle Rondo came out on the porch and threw her a nickel.

And that's the last I've laid eyes on any of my family or my family laid eyes on me for five solid days and nights. Stella-Rondo may be telling the most horrible tales in the world about Mr. Whitaker, but I haven't heard them. As I tell everybody, I draw my own conclusions.

But oh, I like it here. It's ideal, as I've been saying. You see, I've got everything cater-cornered, the way I like it. Hear the radio? All the war news. Radio, sewing machine, book ends, ironing board and that great big piano lamp—peace, that's what I like. Butter-bean vines planted all along the front where the strings are.

Of course, there's not much mail. My family are naturally the main people in China Grove, and if they prefer to vanish from the face of the earth, for all the mail they get or the mail they write, why, I'm not going to open my mouth. Some of the folks here in town are taking up with me and some turned against me. I know which is which. There are always people who will quit buying stamps just to get on the right side of Papa-Daddy.

But here I am, and here I'll stay. I want the world to know I'm happy.

And if Stella-Rondo should come to me this minute, on bended knees, and *attempt* to explain the incidents of her life with Mr. Whitaker, I'd simply put my fingers in both my ears and refuse to listen.

Roman Fever

EDITH WHARTON

I

From the table at which they had been lunching two American ladies of ripe but well-cared-for middle age moved across the lofty terrace of the Roman restaurant and, leaning on its parapet, looked first at each other, and then down on the outspread glories of the Palatine and the Forum, with the same expression of vague but benevolent approval.

As they leaned there a girlish voice echoed up gaily from the stairs leading to the court below. "Well, come along, then," it cried, not to them but to an invisible companion, "and let's leave the young things to their knitting" and a voice as fresh laughed back: "Oh, look here, Babs, not actually *knitting*—" "Well, I mean figuratively," rejoined the first. "After all, we haven't left our poor parents much else to do . . ." and at that point the turn of the stairs engulfed the dialogue.

The two ladies looked at each other again, this time with a tinge of smiling embarrassment, and the smaller and paler one shook her head and colored slightly.

"Barbara!" she murmured, sending an unheard rebuke after the mocking voice in the stairway.

The other lady, who was fuller, and higher in color, with a small determined nose supported by vigorous black eyebrows, gave a good-humored laugh. "That's what our daughters think of us!"

Her companion replied by a deprecating gesture. "Not of us individually. We must remember that. It's just the collective modern idea of Mothers. And you see—" Half guiltily she drew from her handsomely mounted black handbag a twist of crimson silk run through by two fine knitting needles. "One never knows," she murmured. "The new system has certainly given us a good deal of time to kill; and sometimes I get tired just looking—even at this." Her gesture was now addressed to the stupendous scene at their feet.

The dark lady laughed again, and they both relapsed upon the view, contemplating it in silence, with a sort of diffused serenity which might have been borrowed from the spring effulgence of the Roman skies. The luncheon-hour was long past, and the two had their end of the vast terrace to themselves. At its opposite extremity a few groups, detained by a lingering look at the outspread city, were gathering up guidebooks and fumbling for tips. The last of them scattered, and the two ladies were alone on the air-washed height.

"Well, I don't see why we shouldn't just stay here," said Mrs. Slade, the lady of the high color and energetic brows. Two derelict basket-chairs stood near, and she pushed them into the angle of the parapet, and settled herself in one, her gaze upon the Palatine. "After all, it's still the most beautiful view in the world."

"It always will be, to me," assented her friend Mrs. Ansley, with so slight a stress on the "me" that Mrs. Slade, though she noticed it, wondered if it were not merely accidental, like the random underlinings of old-fashioned letterwriters.

"Grace Ansley was always old-fashioned," she thought; and added aloud, with a retrospective smile: "It's a view we've both been familiar with for a good many years. When we first met here we were younger than our girls are now. You remember?"

"Oh, yes, I remember," murmured Mrs. Ansley, with the same undefinable stress—"There's the headwaiter wondering," she interpolated. She was evidently far less sure than her companion of herself and of her rights in the world.

"I'll cure him of wondering," said Mrs. Slade, stretching her hand toward a bag as discreetly opulent-looking as Mrs. Ansley's. Signing to the headwaiter, she explained that she and her friend were old lovers of Rome, and would like to spend the end of the afternoon looking down on the view— that is, if it did not disturb the service? The headwaiter, bowing over her gratuity, assured her that the ladies were most welcome, and would be still more so if they would condescend to remain for dinner. A full moon night, they would remember. . . .

Mrs. Slade's black brows drew together, as though references to the moon were out-of-place and even unwelcome. But she smiled away her frown as the headwaiter retreated. "Well, why not? We might do worse. There's no knowing, I suppose, when the girls will be back. Do you even know back from *where*? I don't!"

Mrs. Ansley again colored slightly. "I think those young Italian aviators we met at the Embassy invited them to fly to Tarquinia for tea. I suppose they'll want to wait and fly back by moonlight."

"Moonlight—moonlight! What a part it still plays. Do you suppose they're as sentimental as we were?"

"I've come to the conclusion that I don't in the least know what they are," said Mrs. Ansley. "And perhaps we didn't know much more about each other."

"No; perhaps we didn't."

Her friend gave her a shy glance. "I never should have supposed you were sentimental, Alida."

"Well, perhaps I wasn't." Mrs. Slade drew her lids together in retrospect; and for a few moments the two ladies, who had been intimate since childhood, reflected how little they knew each other. Each one, of course, had a label ready to attach to the other's name; Mrs. Delphin Slade, for instance, would have told herself, or any one who asked her, that Mrs. Horace Ansley, twenty-five years ago, had been exquisitely lovely—no, you wouldn't believe it, would you? . . . though, of course, still charming, distinguished. . . . Well, as a girl she had been exquisite; far more beautiful than her daughter Barbara, though certainly Babs, according to the new standards at any rate, was more effective—had more *edge* as they say. Funny where she got it, with those two nullities as parents. Yes; Horace Ansley was— well, just the duplicate of his wife. Museum specimens of old New York. Good-looking, irreproachable, exemplary. Mrs. Slade and Mrs. Ansley had lived opposite each other—actually as well as figuratively—for years. When the drawingroom curtains in No. 20 East 73rd Street were renewed, No. 23, across the way, was always aware of it. And of all the movings, buyings, travels, anniversaries, illnesses—the tame chronicle of an estimable pair. Little of it escaped Mrs. Slade. But she had grown bored with it by the time her husband made his big *coup* in Wall Street, and when they bought in upper Park Avenue had already begun to think: "I'd rather live opposite a speak-easy for a change; at least one might see it raided." The idea of seeing Grace raided was so amusing that (before the move) she launched it at a woman's lunch. It made a hit, and went the rounds—she sometimes wondered if it had crossed the street, and reached Mrs. Ansley. She hoped not, but didn't much mind. Those were the days when respectability was at a discount, and it did the irreproachable no harm to laugh at them a little.

A few years later, and not many months apart, both ladies lost their husbands. There was an appropriate exchange of wreaths and condolences, and a brief renewal of intimacy in the half-shadows of their mourning; and now, after another interval, they had run across each other in Rome, at the same hotel, each of them the modest appendage of a salient daughter. The similarity of their lot had again drawn them together, lending itself to mild jokes, and the mutual confession that, if in old days it must have been tiring to "keep up" with daughters, it was now, at times, a little dull not to.

No doubt, Mrs. Slade reflected, she felt her unemployment more than poor Grace ever would. It was a big drop from being the wife of Delphin Slade to being his widow. She had always regarded herself (with a certain conjugal pride) as his equal in social gifts, as contributing her full share to the making of the exceptional couple they were: but the difference after his death was irremediable. As the wife of the famous corporation lawyer, always with an international case or two on hand, every day brought its exciting and unexpected obligation: the impromptu entertaining of eminent colleagues from abroad, the hurried dashes on legal business to London, Paris or Rome, where the entertaining was so handsomely reciprocated; the amusement of hearing in her wake: "What, that handsome woman with the good clothes and the eyes is Mrs. Slade—*the* Slade's wife? Really? Generally the wives of celebrities are such frumps."

Yes; being *the* Slade's widow was a dullish business after that. In living up to such a husband all her faculties had been engaged; now she had only her daughter to live up to, for the son who seemed to have inherited his father's gifts had died suddenly in boyhood. She had fought through that agony because her husband was there, to be helped and to help; now, after the father's death, the thought of the boy had become unbearable. There was nothing left but to mother her daughter; and dear Jenny was such a perfect daughter that she needed no excessive mothering. "Now with Babs Ansley I don't know that I *should* be so quiet," Mrs. Slade sometimes half-enviously reflected; but Jenny, who was younger than her brilliant friend, was that rare accident, an extremely pretty girl who somehow made youth and prettiness seem as safe as their absence. It was all perplexing—and to Mrs. Slade a little boring. She wished that Jenny would fall in love—with the wrong man, even; that she might have to be watched, out-manoeuvred, rescued. And instead, it was Jenny who watched her mother, kept her out of draughts, made sure that she had taken her tonic. . . .

Mrs. Ansley was much less articulate than her friend, and her mental portrait of Mrs. Slade was slighter, and drawn with fainter touches. "Alida Slade's awfully brilliant; but not as brilliant as she thinks," would have summed it up; though she would have added, for the enlightenment of strangers, that Mrs. Slade had been an extremely dashing girl; much more so than her daughter, who was pretty, of course, and clever in a way, but had none of her mother's—well, "vividness," some one had once called it. Mrs. Ansley would take up current words like this, and cite them in quotation marks, as unheard-of-audacities. No; Jenny was not like her mother. Sometimes Mrs. Ansley thought Alida Slade was disappointed; on the whole she had had a sad life. Full of failures and mistakes; Mrs. Ansley had always been rather sorry for her. . . .

So these two ladies visualized each other, each through the wrong end of her little telescope.

II

For a long time they continued to sit side by side without speaking. It seemed as though, to both, there was a relief in laying down their somewhat futile activities in the presence of the vast Memento Mori which faced them. Mrs. Slade sat quite still, her eyes fixed on the golden slope of the Palace of the Caesars, and after a while Mrs. Ansley ceased to fidget with her bag, and she too sank into meditation. Like many intimate friends, the two ladies had never before had occasion to be silent together, and Mrs. Ansley was slightly embarrassed by what seemed, after so many years, a new stage in their intimacy, and one with which she did not yet know how to deal.

Suddenly the air was full of that deep clangor of bells which periodically covers Rome with a roof of silver. Mrs. Slade glanced at her wristwatch. "Five o'clock already," she said, as though surprised.

Mrs. Ansley suggested interrogatively: "There's bridge at the Embassy at five." For a long time Mrs. Slade did not answer. She appeared to be lost in contemplation, and Mrs. Ansley thought the remark had escaped her. But after a while she said, as if speaking out of a dream: "Bridge, did you say? Not unless you want to. . . . But I don't think I will, you know."

"Oh, no," Mrs. Ansley hastened to assure her. "I don't care at all. It's so lovely here; and so full of old memories, as you say." She settled herself in her chair, and almost furtively drew forth her knitting. Mrs. Slade took sideway note of this activity, but her own beautifully cared-for hands remained motionless on her knee.

"I was just thinking," she said slowly, "what different things Rome stands for to each generation of travelers. To our grandmothers, Roman fever; to our mothers, sentimental danger—how we used to be guarded!—to our daughters, no more dangers than the middle of Main Street. They don't know it—but how much they're missing!"

The long golden light was beginning to pale, and Mrs. Ansley lifted her knitting a little closer to her eyes. "Yes; how we were guarded!"

"I always used to think," Mrs. Slade continued, "that our mothers had a much more difficult job than our grandmothers. When Roman fever stalked the streets it must have been comparatively easy to gather in the girls at the danger hour; but when you and I were young, with such beauty calling us, and the spice of disobedience thrown in, and no worse risk than catching cold during the cool hour after sunset, the mothers used to be put to it to keep us in—didn't they?"

She turned again toward Mrs. Ansley, but the latter had reached a delicate point in her knitting. "One, two, three—slip two; yes, they must have been," she assented, without looking up.

Mrs. Slade's eyes rested on her with a deepened attention. "She can knit—in the face of *this*! How like her. . . ."

Mrs. Slade leaned back, brooding, her eyes ranging from the ruins which faced her to the long green hollow of the Forum, the fading glow of the church fronts beyond it, and the outlying immensity of the Colosseum. Suddenly she thought: "It's all very well to say that our girls have done away with sentiment and moonlight. But if Babs Ansley isn't out to catch that young aviator—the one who's a Marchese—then I don't know anything. And Jenny has no chance beside her. I know that too. I wonder if that's why Grace Ansley likes the two girls to go everywhere together? My poor Jenny as a foil—!" Mrs. Slade gave a hardly audible laugh, and at the sound Mrs. Ansley dropped her knitting.

"Yes—?"

"I—oh, nothing. I was only thinking how your Babs carries everything before her. That Campolieri boy is one of the best matches in Rome. Don't look so innocent, my dear—you know he is. And I was wondering, ever so respectfully, you understand . . . wondering how two such exemplary characters as you and Horace had managed to produce anything quite so dynamic." Mrs. Slade laughed again, with a touch of asperity.

Mrs. Ansley's hands lay inert across her needles. She looked straight out at the great accumulated wreckage of passion and splendor at her feet. But her small profile was almost expressionless. At length she said: "I think you overrate Babs, my dear."

Mrs. Slade's tone grew easier. "No; I don't. I appreciate her. And perhaps envy you. Oh, my girl's perfect; if I were a chronic invalid I'd—well, I think I'd rather be in Jenny's hands. There must be times . . . but there! I always wanted a brilliant daughter . . . and never quite understood why I got an angel instead."

Mrs. Ansley echoed her laugh in a faint murmur. "Babs is an angel too."

"Of course—of course! But she's got rainbow wings. Well, they're wandering by the sea with their young men; and here we sit . . . and it all brings back the past a little too acutely."

Mrs. Ansley had resumed her knitting. One might almost have imagined (if one had known her less well, Mrs. Slade reflected) that, for her also, too many memories rose from the lengthening shadows of those august ruins. But no; she was simply absorbed in her work. What was there for her to worry about? She knew that Babs would almost certainly come back engaged to the extremely eligible Campolieri. "And she'll sell the New York house, and settle down near them in Rome, and never be in their way . . . she's much too tactful. But she'll have an excellent cook, and just the right people in for bridge and cocktails . . . and a perfectly peaceful old age among her grandchildren."

Mrs. Slade broke off this prophetic flight with a recoil of self-disgust. There was no one of whom she had less right to think unkindly than of Grace Ansley. Would she never cure herself of envying her? Perhaps she had begun too long ago.

She stood up and leaned against the parapet, filling her troubled eyes with the tranquilizing magic of the hour. But instead of tranquilizing her the sight seemed to increase her exasperation. Her gaze turned toward the Colosseum. Already its golden flank was drowned in purple shadow, and above it the sky curved crystal clear, without light or color. It was the moment when afternoon and evening hang balanced in mid-heaven.

Mrs. Slade turned back and laid her hand on her friend's arm. The gesture was so abrupt that Mrs. Ansley looked up, startled.

"The sun's set. You're not afraid, my dear?"

"Afraid—?"

"Of Roman fever or pneumonia? I remember how ill you were that winter. As a girl you had a very delicate throat, hadn't you?"

"Oh, we're all right up here. Down below, in the Forum, it does get deathly cold, all of a sudden . . . but not here."

"Ah, of course you know because you had to be so careful." Mrs. Slade turned back to the parapet. She thought: "I must make one more effort not to hate her." Aloud she said: "Whenever I look at the Forum from up here I remember that story about a great-aunt of yours, wasn't she? A dreadfully wicked great-aunt?"

"Oh yes; Great-aunt Harriet. The one who was supposed to have sent her young sister out to the Forum after sunset to gather a night-blooming flower for her album. All our great-aunts and grandmothers used to have albums of dried flowers."

Mrs. Slade nodded. "But she really sent her because they were in love with the same man—"

"Well, that was the family tradition. They said Aunt Harriet confessed it years afterward. At any rate, the poor little sister caught the fever and died. Mother used to frighten us with the story when we were children."

"And you frightened *me* with it, that winter when you and I were here as girls. The winter I was engaged to Delphin."

Mrs. Ansley gave a faint laugh. "Oh, did I? Really frightened you? I don't believe you're easily frightened."

"Not often; but I was then. I was easily frightened because I was too happy. I wonder if you know what that means?"

"I—yes. . . ." Mrs. Ansley faltered.

"Well, I suppose that was why the story of your wicked aunt made such an impression on me. And I thought: 'There's no more Roman fever, but the Forum is deathly cold after sunset—especially after a hot day. And the Colosseum's even colder and damper'."

"The Colosseum—?"

"Yes. It wasn't easy to get in, after the gates were locked for the night. Far from easy. Still, in those days it could be managed; it was managed, often. Lovers met there who couldn't meet elsewhere. You knew that?"

"I—I daresay. I don't remember."

"You don't remember? You don't remember going to visit some ruins or other one evening, just after dark, and catching a bad chill? You were supposed to have gone to see the moon rise. People always said that expedition was what caused your illness."

There was a moment's silence; then Mrs. Ansley rejoined: "Did they? It was all so long ago."

"Yes. And you got well again—so it didn't matter. But I suppose it struck your friend—the reason given for your illness, I mean—because everybody knew you were so prudent on account of your throat, and your mother took such care of you. . . . You *had* been out late sight-seeing, hadn't you, that night?"

"Perhaps I had. The most prudent girls aren't always prudent. What made you think of it now?"

Mrs. Slade seemed to have no answer ready. But after a moment she broke out: "Because I simply can't bear it any longer—!"

Mrs. Ansley lifted her head quickly. Her eyes were wide and very pale. "Can't bear what?"

"Why—you not knowing that I've always known why you went."

"Why I went—?"

"Yes. You think I'm bluffing, don't you? Well, you went to meet the man I was engaged to—and I can repeat every word of the letter that took you there."

While Mrs. Slade spoke Mrs. Ansley had risen unsteadily to her feet. Her bag, her knitting and gloves, slid in a panic-stricken heap to the ground. She looked at Mrs. Slade as though she were looking at a ghost.

"No, no—don't," she faltered out.

"Why not? Listen, if you don't believe me. 'My one darling, things can't go on like this. I must see you alone. Come to the Colosseum immediately after dark tomorrow. There will be somebody to let you in. No one whom you need fear will suspect'—but perhaps you've forgotten what the letter said?"

Mrs. Ansley met the challenge with an unexpected composure. Steadying herself against the chair she looked at her friend, and replied: "No; I know it by heart too."

"And the signature? 'Only *your* D.S.' Was that it? I'm right, am I? That was the letter that took you out that evening after dark?"

Mrs. Ansley was still looking at her. It seemed to Mrs. Slade that a slow struggle was going on behind the voluntarily controlled mask of her small quiet face. "I shouldn't have thought she had herself so well in hand," Mrs. Slade reflected, almost resentfully. But at this moment Mrs. Ansley spoke, "I don't know how you knew. I burnt that letter at once."

"Yes; you would, naturally—you're so prudent!" The sneer was open now. "And if you burnt the letter you're wondering how on earth I know what was in it. That's it, isn't it?"

Mrs. Slade waited, but Mrs. Ansley did not speak.

"Well, my dear, I know what was in that letter because I wrote it!"

"You wrote it?"

"Yes."

The two women stood for a minute staring at each other in the last golden light. Then Mrs. Ansley dropped back into her chair. "Oh," she murmured, and covered her face with her hands.

Mrs. Slade waited nervously for another word or movement. None came, and at length, she broke out: "I horrify you."

Mrs. Ansley's hands dropped to her knee. The face they uncovered was streaked with tears. "I wasn't thinking of you. I was thinking—it was the only letter I ever had from him!"

"And I wrote it. Yes, I wrote it! But I was the girl he was engaged to. Did you happen to remember that?"

Mrs. Ansley's head drooped again. "I'm not trying to excuse myself. . . . I remembered. . . ."

"And still you went?"

"Still I went."

Mrs. Slade stood looking down on the small bowed figure at her side. The flame of her wrath had already sunk, and she wondered why she had ever thought there would be any satisfaction in inflicting so purposeless a wound on her friend. But she had to justify herself.

"You do understand? I'd found out—and I hated you, hated you. I knew you were in love with Delphin—and I was afraid; afraid of you, of your quiet ways, your sweetness . . . your . . . well, I wanted you out of the way, that's all. Just for a few weeks; just till I was sure of him. So in a blind fury I wrote that letter. . . . I don't know why I'm telling you now."

"I suppose," said Mrs. Ansley slowly, "it's because you've always gone on hating me."

"Perhaps. Or because I wanted to get the whole thing off my mind." She paused. "I'm glad you destroyed the letter. Of course I never thought you'd die."

Mrs. Ansley relapsed into silence, and Mrs. Slade, leaning above her, was conscious of a strange sense of isolation, of being cut off from the warm current of human communion. "You think me a monster!"

"I don't know. . . . It was the only letter I had, and you say he didn't write it?"

"Ah, how you care for him still!"

"I cared for that memory," said Mrs. Ansley.

Mrs. Slade continued to look down on her. She seemed physically reduced by the blow—as if, when she got up, the wind might scatter her like a puff of dust. Mrs. Slade's jealousy suddenly leapt up again at the sight. All these years the woman had been living on that letter. How she must have loved him, to treasure the mere memory of its ashes! The letter of the man her friend was engaged to. Wasn't it she who was the monster?

"You tried your best to get him away from me, didn't you? But you failed; and I kept him. That's all."

"Yes. That's all."

"I wish now I hadn't told you. I'd no idea you'd feel about it as you do; I thought you'd be amused. It all happened so long ago, as you say; and you must do me the justice to remember that I had no reason to think you'd ever taken it seriously. How could I, when you were married to Horace Ansley two months afterward? As soon as you could get out of bed your mother rushed you off to Florence and married you. People were rather surprised—they wondered at its being done so quickly; but I thought I knew. I had an idea you did it out of *pique*—to be able to say you'd got ahead of Delphin and me. Girls have such silly reasons for doing the most serious things. And your marrying so soon convinced me that you'd never really cared."

"Yes. I suppose it would," Mrs. Ansley assented.

The clear heaven overhead was emptied of all its gold. Dusk spread over it, abruptly darkening the Seven Hills. Here and there lights began to twinkle through the foliage at their feet. Steps were coming and going on the deserted terrace—waiters looking out of the doorway at the head of the stairs, then reappearing with trays and napkins and flasks of wine. Tables were moved, chairs straightened. A feeble string of electric lights flickered out. Some vases of faded flowers were carried away, and brought back replenished. A stout lady in a dust coat suddenly appeared, asking in broken Italian if any one had seen the elastic band which held together her tattered Baedeker. She poked with her stick under the table at which she had lunched, the waiters assisting.

The corner where Mrs. Slade and Mrs. Ansley sat was still shadowy and deserted. For a long time neither of them spoke. At length Mrs. Slade began again: "I suppose I did it as a sort of joke—"

"A joke?"

"Well, girls are ferocious sometimes, you know. Girls in love especially. And I remember laughing to myself all that evening at the idea that you were waiting around there in the dark, dodging out of sight, listening for every sound, trying to get in—Of course I was upset when I heard you were so ill afterward."

Mrs. Ansley had not moved for a long time. But now she turned slowly toward her companion. "But I didn't wait. He'd arranged everything. He was there. We were let in at once," she said.

Mrs. Slade sprang up from her leaning position. "Delphin there? They let you in?—Ah, now you're lying!" she burst out with violence.

Mrs. Ansley's voice grew clearer, and full of surprise. "But of course he was there. Naturally he came—"

"Came? How did he know he'd find you there? You must be raving!"

Mrs. Ansley hesitated, as though reflecting. "But I answered the letter. I told him I'd be there. So he came."

Mrs. Slade flung her hands up to her face. "Oh, God—you answered! I never thought of your answering. . . ."

"It's odd you never thought of it, if you wrote the letter."

"Yes. I was blind with rage."

Mrs. Ansley rose, and drew her fur scarf about her. "It is cold here. We'd better go. . . . I'm sorry for you," she said as she clasped the fur about her throat.

The unexpected words sent a pang through Mrs. Slade. "Yes; we'd better go." She gathered up her bag and cloak. "I don't know why you should be sorry for me," she muttered.

Mrs. Ansley stood looking away from her toward the dusky secret mass of the Colosseum. "Well—because I didn't have to wait that night."

Mrs. Slade gave an unquiet laugh. "Yes; I was beaten there. But I oughtn't to begrudge it to you, I suppose. At the end of all these years. After all, I had everything; I had him for twenty-five years. And you had nothing but that one letter that he didn't write."

Mrs. Ansley was again silent. At length she turned toward the door of the terrace. She took a step, and turned back, facing her companion.

"I had Barbara," she said, and began to move ahead of Mrs. Slade toward the stairway.

The Use of Force

WILLIAM CARLOS WILLIAMS

They were new patients to me, all I had was the name, Olson. Please come down as soon as you can, my daughter is very sick.

When I arrived I was met by the mother, a big startled looking woman, very clean and apologetic who merely said, Is this the doctor? and let me in. In the back, she added. You must excuse us, doctor, we have her in the kitchen where it is warm. It is very damp here sometimes.

The child was fully dressed and sitting on her father's lap near the kitchen table. He tried to get up, but I motioned for him not to bother, took off my overcoat and started to look things over. I could see that they were all very nervous, eyeing me up and down distrustfully. As often, in such cases, they weren't telling me more than they had to, it was up to me to tell them; that's why they were spending three dollars on me.

The child was fairly eating me up with her cold, steady eyes, and no expression to her face whatever. She did not move and seemed, inwardly, quiet; an unusually attractive little thing, and as strong as a heifer in appearance. But her face was flushed, she was breathing rapidly, and I realized that she had a high fever. She had magnificent blonde hair, in profusion. One of those picture children often reproduced in advertising leaflets and the photogravure sections of the Sunday papers.

She's had a fever for three days, began the father and we don't know what it comes from. My wife has given her things, you know, like people do, but it don't do no good. And there's been a lot of sickness around. So we tho't you'd better look her over and tell us what is the matter.

As doctors often do I took a trial shot at it as a point of departure. Has she had a sore throat?

Both parents answered no together, No . . . No, she says her throat don't hurt her.

"Does your throat hurt you?" added the mother to the child. But the lit-

1051

tle's girl's expression didn't change nor did she move her eyes from my face.

Have you looked?

I tried to, said the mother, but I couldn't see.

As it happens we had been having a number of cases of diphtheria in the school to which this child went during that month and we were all, quite apparently, thinking of that, though no one had as yet spoken of the thing.

Well, I said, suppose we take a look at the throat first. I smiled in my best professional manner and asking for the child's first name I said, come on, Mathilda, open your mouth and let's take a look at your throat.

Nothing doing.

Aw, come on, I coaxed, just open your mouth wide and let me take a look. Look, I said opening both hands wide, I haven't anything in my hands. Just open up and let me see.

Such a nice man, put in the mother. Look how kind he is to you. Come on, do what he tells you to. He won't hurt you.

At that I ground my teeth in disgust. If only they wouldn't use the word "hurt" I might be able to get somewhere. But I did not allow myself to be hurried or disturbed but speaking quietly and slowly I approached the child again.

As I moved my chair a little nearer suddenly with one catlike movement both her hands clawed instinctively for my eyes and she almost reached them too. In fact she knocked my glasses flying and they fell, though unbroken, several feet away from me on the kitchen floor.

Both the mother and father almost turned themselves inside out in embarrassment and apology. You bad girl, said the mother, taking her and shaking her by one arm. Look what you've done. The nice man . . .

For heaven's sake, I broke in. Don't call me a nice man to her. I'm here to look at her throat on the chance that she might have diphtheria and possibly die of it. But that's nothing to her. Look here, I said to the child, we're going to look at your throat. You're old enough to understand what I'm saying. Will you open it now by yourself or shall we have to open it for you?

Not a move. Even her expression hadn't changed. Her breaths however were coming faster and faster. Then the battle began. I had to do it. I had to have a throat culture for her own protection. But first I told the parents that it was entirely up to them. I explained the danger but said that I would not insist on a throat examination so long as they would take the responsibility.

If you don't do what the doctor says you'll have to go to the hospital, the mother admonished her severely.

Oh yeah? I had to smile to myself. After all, I had already fallen in love with the savage brat, the parents were contemptible to me. In the ensuing struggle they grew more and more abject, crushed, exhausted while she surely rose to magnificent heights of insane fury of effort bred of her terror of me.

The father tried his best, and he was a big man but the fact that she was his daughter, his shame at her behavior and his dread of hurting her made him release her just at the critical moment several times when I had almost achieved success, till I wanted to kill him. But his dread also that she might have diphtheria made him tell me to go on, go on though he himself was almost fainting, while the mother moved back and forth behind us raising and lowering her hands in an agony of apprehension.

Put her in front of you on your lap, I ordered, and hold both her wrists.

But as soon as he did the child let out a scream. Don't, you're hurting me. Let go of my hands. Let them go I tell you. Then she shrieked terrifyingly, hysterically. Stop it! Stop it! You're killing me!

Do you think she can stand it, doctor! said the mother.

You get out, said the husband to his wife. Do you want her to die of diphtheria?

Come on now, hold her, I said.

Then I grasped the child's head with my left hand and tried to get the wooden tongue depressor between her teeth. She fought, with clenched teeth, desperately! But now I also had grown furious—at a child. I tried to hold myself down but I couldn't. I know how to expose a throat for inspection. And I did my best. When finally I got the wooden spatula behind the last teeth and just the point of it into the mouth cavity, she opened up for an instant but before I could see anything she came down again and gripping the wooden blade between her molars she reduced it to splinters before I could get it out again.

Aren't you ashamed, the mother yelled at her. Aren't you ashamed to act like that in front of the doctor?

Get me a smooth-handled spoon of some sort, I told the mother. We're going through with this. The child's mouth was already bleeding. Her tongue was cut and she was screaming in wild hysterical shrieks. Perhaps I should have desisted and come back in an hour or more. No doubt it would have been better. But I have seen at least two children lying dead in bed of neglect in such cases, and feeling that I must get a diagnosis now or never I went at it again. But the worst of it was that I too had got beyond reason. I could have torn the child apart in my own fury and enjoyed it. It was a pleasure to attack her. My face was burning with it.

The damned little brat must be protected against her own idiocy, one says to one's self at such times. Others must be protected against her. It is social necessity. And all these things are true. But a blind fury, a feeling of adult shame, bred of a longing for muscular release are the operatives. One goes on to the end.

In a final unreasoning assault I overpowered the child's neck and jaws. I forced the heavy silver spoon back of her teeth and down her throat till she gagged. And there it was—both tonsils covered with membrane. She had fought valiantly to keep me from knowing her secret. She had been hiding that sore throat for three days at least and lying to her parents in order to escape just such an outcome as this.

Now truly she *was* furious. She had been on the defensive before but now she attacked. Tried to get off her father's lap and fly at me while tears of defeat blinded her eyes.

Kew Gardens

VIRGINIA WOOLF

From the oval-shaped flower-bed there rose perhaps a hundred stalks spreading into heart-shaped or tongue-shaped leaves half-way up and un-furling at the tip red or blue or yellow petals marked with spots of colour raised upon the surface; and from the red, blue or yellow gloom of the throat emerged a straight bar, rough with gold dust and slightly clubbed at the end. The petals were voluminous enough to be stirred by the summer breeze, and when they moved, the red, blue and yellow lights passed one over the other, staining an inch of the brown earth beneath with a spot of the most intricate colour. The light fell either upon the smooth, grey back of a pebble, or, the shell of a snail with its brown, circular veins, or falling into a raindrop, it extended with such intensity of red, blue and yellow the thin walls of water that one expected them to burst and disappear. Instead, the drop was left in a second silver grey once more, and the light now set-tled upon the flesh of a leaf, revealing the branching thread of fibre be-neath the surface, and again it moved on and spread its illumination in the vast green spaces beneath the dome of the heart-shaped and tongue-shaped leaves. Then the breeze stirred rather more briskly overhead and the colour was flashed into the air above, into the eyes of the men and women who walk in Kew Gardens in July.

The figures of these men and women straggled past the flower-bed with a curiously irregular movement not unlike that of the white and blue but-terflies who crossed the turf in zig-zag flights from bed to bed. The man was about six inches in front of the woman, strolling carelessly, while she bore on with greater purpose, only turning her head now and then to see that the children were not too far behind. The man kept this distance in front of the woman purposely, though perhaps unconsciously, for he wished to go on with his thoughts.

"Fifteen years ago I came here with Lily," he thought. "We sat somewhere over there by a lake and I begged her to marry me all through the hot afternoon. How the dragonfly kept circling round us: how clearly I see the dragonfly and her shoe with the square buckle at the toe. All the time I spoke I saw her shoe and when it moved impatiently I knew without looking up what she was going to say: the whole of her seemed to be in her shoe. And my love, my desire, were in the dragonfly; for some reason I thought that if it settled there, on that leaf, the broad one with the red flower in the middle of it, if the dragonfly settled on the leaf she would say 'Yes' at once. But the dragonfly went round and round: it never settled anywhere—of course not, happily not, or I shouldn't be walking here with Eleanor and the children. Tell me, Eleanor. D'you ever think of the past?"

"Why do you ask, Simon?"

"Because I've been thinking of the past. I've been thinking of Lily, the woman I might have married. . . . Well, why are you silent? Do you mind my thinking of the past?"

"Why should I mind, Simon? Doesn't one always think of the past, in a garden with men and women lying under the trees? Aren't they one's past, all that remains of it, those men and women, those ghosts lying under the trees, . . . one's happiness, one's reality?"

"For me, a square silver shoe buckle and a dragonfly—"

"For me, a kiss. Imagine six little girls sitting before their easels twenty years ago, down by the side of a lake, painting the water-lilies, the first red water-lilies I'd ever seen. And suddenly a kiss, there on the back of my neck. And my hand shook all the afternoon so that I couldn't paint. I took out my watch and marked the hour when I would allow myself to think of the kiss for five minutes only—it was so precious—the kiss of an old grey-haired woman with a wart on her nose, the mother of all my kisses all my life. Come, Caroline, come, Hubert."

They walked on past the flower-bed, now walking four abreast, and soon diminished in size among the trees and looked half transparent as the sunlight and shade swam over their backs in large trembling irregular patches.

In the oval flower-bed the snail, whose shell had been stained red, blue and yellow for a space of two minutes or so, now appeared to be moving very slightly in its shell, and next began to labour over the crumbs of loose earth which broke away and rolled down as it passed over them. It appeared to have a definite goal in front of it, differing in this respect from the singular high stepping angular green insect who attempted to cross in front of it, and waited for a second with its antennae trembling as if in deliberation, and then stepped off as rapidly and strangely in the opposite direction. Brown cliffs with deep green lakes in the hollows, flat, blade-like trees that waved from root to tip, round boulders of grey stone, vast crumpled surfaces of a thin crackling texture—all these objects lay across the snail's progress between one stalk and another to his goal. Before he had decided whether to circumvent the arched tent of a dead leaf or to breast it there came past the bed the feet of other human beings.

This time they were both men. The younger of the two wore an expression of perhaps unnatural calm; he raised his eyes and fixed them very steadily in front of him while his companion spoke, and directly his companion had done speaking he looked on the ground again and sometimes opened his lips only after a long pause and sometimes did not open them at all. The elder man had a curiously uneven and shaky method of walking, jerking his hand forward and throwing up his head abruptly, rather in the manner of an impatient carriage horse tired of waiting outside a house; but in the man these gestures were irresolute and pointless. He talked almost incessantly; he smiled to himself and again began to talk, as if the smile had been an answer. He was talking about spirits—the spirits of the dead, who, according to him, were even now telling him all sorts of odd things about their experiences in Heaven.

"Heaven was known to the ancients as Thessaly, William, and now, with this war, the spirit matter is rolling between the hills like thunder." He paused, seemed to listen, smiled, jerked his head and continued:

"You have a small electric battery and a piece of rubber to insulate the wire—isolate?—insulate?—well, we'll skip the details, no good going into details that wouldn't be understood—and in short the little machine stands in any convenient position by the head of the bed, we will say, on a neat mahogany stand. All arrangements being properly fixed by workmen under my direction, the widow applies her ear and summons the spirit by sign as agreed. Women! Widows! Women in black—"

Here he seemed to have caught sight of a woman's dress in the distance, which in the shade looked a purple black. He took off his hat, placed his hand upon his heart, and hurried towards her muttering and gesticulating feverishly. But William caught him by the sleeve and touched a flower with the tip of his walking-stick in order to divert the old man's attention. After looking at it for a moment in some confusion the old man bent his ear to it and seemed to answer a voice speaking from it, for he began talking about the forests of Uruguay which he had visited hundreds of years ago in company with the most beautiful young woman in Europe. He could be heard murmuring about forests in Uruguay blanketed with the wax petals of tropical roses, nightingales, sea beaches, mermaids, and women drowned at sea, as he suffered himself to be moved on by William, upon whose face the look of stoical patience grew slowly deeper and deeper.

Following his steps so closely as to be slightly puzzled by his gestures came two elderly women of the lower middle class, one stout and ponderous, the other rosy cheeked and nimble. Like most people of their station they were frankly fascinated by any signs of eccentricity betokening a disordered brain, especially in the well-to-do; but they were too far off to be certain whether the gestures were merely eccentric or genuinely mad. After they had scrutinized the old man's back in silence for a moment and given each other a queer, sly look, they went on energetically piecing together their very complicated dialogue:

"Nell, Bert, Lot, Cess, Phil, Pa, he says, I says, she says, I says, I says—"
"My Bert, Sis, Bill, Grandad, the old man, sugar,

> *Sugar, flour, kippers, greens,*
> *Sugar, sugar, sugar."*

The ponderous woman looked through the pattern of falling words at
the flowers standing cool, firm, and upright in the earth, with a curious expression. She saw them as a sleeper waking from a heavy sleep sees a brass
candlestick reflecting the light in an unfamiliar way, and closes his eyes and
opens them, and seeing the brass candlestick again, finally starts broad
awake and stares at the candlestick with all his powers. So the heavy woman
came to a standstill opposite the oval-shaped flower-bed, and ceased even
to pretend to listen to what the other woman was saying. She stood there
letting the words fall over her, swaying the top part of her body slowly
backwards and forwards, looking at the flowers. Then she suggested that
they should find a seat and have their tea.

The snail had now considered every possible method of reaching his goal
without going round the dead leaf or climbing over it. Let alone the effort
needed for climbing a leaf, he was doubtful whether the thin texture which
vibrated with such an alarming crackle when touched even by the tips of his
horns would bear his weight; and this determined him finally to creep beneath it, for there was a point where the leaf curved high enough from the
ground to admit him. He had just inserted his head in the opening and was
taking stock of the high brown roof and was getting used to the cool brown
light when two other people came past outside on the turf. This time they
were both young, a young man and a young woman. They were both in the
prime of youth, or even in that season which precedes the prime of youth,
the season before the smooth pink folds of the flower have burst their
gummy case, when the wings of the butterfly, though fully grown, are motionless in the sun.

"Lucky it isn't Friday," he observed.
"Why? D'you believe in luck?"
"They make you pay sixpence on Friday."
"What's sixpence anyway? Isn't it worth sixpence?"
"What's 'it'—what do you mean by 'it'?"
"O, anything—I mean—you know what I mean."

Long pauses came between each of these remarks; they were uttered in
toneless and monotonous voices. The couple stood still on the edge of the
flower-bed, and together pressed the end of her parasol deep down into
the soft earth. The action and the fact that his hand rested on the top of
hers expressed their feelings in a strange way, as the short insignificant
words also expressed something, words with short wings for their heavy
body of meaning, inadequate to carry them far and thus alighting awk-

wardly upon the very common objects that surrouded them, and were to their inexperienced touch so massive; but who knows (so they thought as they pressed the parasol into the earth) what precipices aren't concealed in them, or what slopes of ice don't shine in the sun on the other side? Who knows? Who has ever seen this before? Even when she wondered what sort of tea they gave you at Kew, he felt that something loomed up behind her words, and stood vast and solid behind them; and the mist very slowly rose and uncovered—O, Heavens, what were those shapes?—little white tables, and waitresses who looked first at her and then at him; and there was a bill that he would pay with a real two shilling piece, and it was real, all real, he assured himself, fingering the coin in his pocket, real to everyone except to him and to her; even to him it began to seem real; and then—but it was too exciting to stand and think any longer, and he pulled the parasol out of the earth with a jerk and was impatient to find the place where one had tea with other people, like other people.

"Come along, Trissie; it's time we had our tea."

"Wherever *does* one have one's tea?" she asked with the oddest thrill of excitement in her voice, looking vaguely round and letting herself be drawn on down the grass path, trailing her parasol; turning her head this way and that way forgetting her tea, wishing to go down there and then down there, remembering orchids and cranes among wild flowers, a Chinese pagoda and a crimson crested bird; but he bore her on.

Thus one couple after another with much the same irregular and aimless movement passed the flower-bed and were enveloped in layer after layer of green blue vapour, in which at first their bodies had substance and a dash of colour, but later both substance and colour dissolved in the green-blue atmosphere. How hot it was! So hot that even the thrush chose to hop, like a mechanical bird, in the shadow of the flowers, with long pauses between one movement and the next; instead of rambling vaguely the white butter-flies danced one above another, making with their white shifting flakes the outline of a shattered marble column above the tallest flowers; the glass roofs of the palm house shone as if a whole market full of shiny green umbrellas had opened in the sun; and in the drone of the aeroplane the voice of the summer sky murmured its fierce soul. Yellow and black, pink and snow white, shapes of all these colours, men, women, and children were spotted for a second upon the horizon, and then, seeing the breadth of yellow that lay upon the grass, they wavered and sought shade beneath the trees, dissolving like drops of water in the yellow and green atmosphere, staining it faintly with red and blue. It seemed as if all gross and heavy bodies had sunk down in the heat motionless and lay huddled upon the ground, but their voices went wavering from them as if they were flames lolling from the thick waxen bodies of candles. Voices. Yes, voices. Wordless voices, breaking the silence suddenly with such depth of contentment, such passion of desire, or, in the voices of children, such freshness of surprise; breaking the silence? But there was no silence; all the time the motor omnibuses were turning their wheels and changing their gear; like a vast nest of Chinese boxes all of wrought steel turning ceaselessly one within another the city murmured; on the top of which the voices cried aloud and the petals of myriads of flowers flashed their colours into the air.

The Man Who Was Almost a Man

RICHARD WRIGHT

Dave struck out across the fields, looking homeward through paling light. Whut's the use talkin wid em niggers in the field? Anyhow, his mother was putting supper on the table. Them niggers can't understan nothing. One of these days he was going to get a gun and practice shooting, then they couldn't talk to him as though he were a little boy. He slowed, looking at the ground. Shucks, Ah ain scareda them even ef they are biggern me! Aw, Ah know whut Ahma do. Ahm going by ol Joe's sto n git that Sears Roebuck catlog n look at them guns. Mebbe Ma will lemme buy one when she gits mah pay from ol man Hawkins. Ahma beg her t gimme some money. Ahm ol ernough to hava gun. Ahm seventeen. Almos a man. He strode, feeling his long loose-jointed limbs. Shucks, a man oughta hava little gun aftah he done worked hard all day.

He came in sight of Joe's store. A yellow lantern glowed on the front porch. He mounted steps and went through the screen door, hearing it bang behind him. There was a strong smell of coal oil and mackerel fish. He felt very confident until he saw fat Joe walk in through the rear door, then his courage began to ooze.

"Howdy, Dave! Whutcha want?"

"How yuh, Mistah Joe? Aw, Ah don wanna buy nothing. Ah jus wanted t see ef yuhd lemme look at tha catlog erwhile."

"Sure! You wanna see it here?"

"Nawsuh. Ah wants t take it home wid me. Ah'll bring it back termorrow when Ah come in from the fiels."

"You plannin on buying something?"

"Yessuh."

"Your ma lettin you have your own money now?"

"Shucks. Mistah Joe, Ahm gittin t be a man like anybody else!"

Joe laughed and wiped his greasy white face with a red bandanna.

"Whut you plannin on buyin?"

Dave looked at the floor, scratched his head, scratched his thigh, and smiled. Then he looked up shyly.

"Ah'll tell yuh, Mistah Joe, ef yuh promise yuh won't tell."

"I promise."

"Waal, Ahma buy a gun."

"A gun? What you want with a gun?"

"Ah wanna keep it."

"You ain't nothing but a boy. You don't need a gun."

"Aw, lemme have the catlog, Mistah Joe. Ah'll bring it back."

Joe walked through the rear door. Dave was elated. He looked around at barrels of sugar and flour. He heard Joe coming back. He craned his neck to see if he were bringing the book. Yeah, he's got it. Gawddog, he's got it!

"Here, but be sure you bring it back. It's the only one I got."

"Sho, Mistah Joe."

"Say, if you wanna buy a gun, why don't you buy one from me? I gotta gun to sell."

"Will it shoot?"

"Sure it'll shoot."

"Whut kind is it?"

"Oh, it's kinda old . . . a left-hand Wheeler. A pistol. A big one."

"Is it got bullets in it?"

"It's loaded."

"Kin Ah see it?"

"Where's your money?"

"What yuh wan fer it?"

"I'll let you have it for two dollars."

"Just two dollahs? Shucks, Ah could buy tha when Ah git mah pay."

"I'll have it here when you want it."

"Awright, suh. Ah be in fer it."

He went through the door, hearing it slam again behind him. Ahma git some money from Ma n buy me a gun! Only two dollahs! He tucked the thick catalogue under his arm and hurried.

"Where yuh been, boy?" His mother held a steaming dish of black-eyed peas.

"Aw, Ma, Ah jus stopped down the road t talk wid the boys."

"Yuh know bettah t keep suppah waitin."

He sat down, resting the catalogue on the edge of the table.

"Yuh git up from there and git to the well n wash yosef! Ah ain feedin no hogs in mah house!"

She grabbed his shoulder and pushed him. He stumbled out of the room, then came back to get the catalogue.

"Whut this?"

"Aw, Ma, it's jusa catlog."

"Who yuh git it from?"

"From Joe, down at the sto."

"Waal, thas good. We kin use it in the outhouse."

"Naw, Ma." He grabbed for it. "Gimme ma catlog, Ma."

She held onto it and glared at him.

"Quit hollerin at me! Whut's wrong wid yuh? Yuh crazy?"

"But Ma, please. It ain mine! It's Joe's! He tol me t bring it back t im termorrow."

She gave up the book. He stumbled down the back steps, hugging the thick book under his arm. When he had splashed water on his face and hands, he groped back to the kitchen and fumbled in a corner for the towel. He bumped into a chair; it clattered to the floor. The catalogue sprawled at his feet. When he had dried his eyes he snatched up the book and held it again under his arm. His mother stood watching him.

"Now, ef yuh gonna act a fool over that ol book, Ah'll take it n burn it up."

"Naw, Ma, please."

"Waal, set down n be still!"

He sat down and drew the oil lamp close. He thumbed page after page, unaware of the food his mother set on the table. His father came in. Then his small brother.

"Whutcha got there, Dave?" his father asked.

"Jusa catlog," he answered, not looking up.

"Yeah, here they is!" His eyes glowed at blue-and-black revolvers. He glanced up, feeling sudden guilt. His father was watching him. He eased the book under the table and rested it on his knees. After the blessing was asked, he ate. He scooped up peas and swallowed fat meat without chewing. Buttermilk helped to wash it down. He did not want to mention money before his father. He would do much better by cornering his mother when she was alone. He looked at his father uneasily out of the edge of his eye.

"Boy, how come yuh don quit foolin wid tha book n eat yo suppah?"

"Yessuh."

"How you n ol man Hawkins gitten erlong?"

"Suh?"

"Can't yuh hear? Why don yuh lissen? Ah ast yu how wuz yuh n ol man Hawkins gittin erlong?"

"Oh, swell, Pa. Ah plows mo lan than anybody over there."

"Waal, yuh oughta keep you mind on whut yuh doin."

"Yessuh."

He poured his plate full of molasses and sopped it up slowly with a chunk of cornbread. When his father and brother had left the kitchen, he still sat and looked again at the guns in the catalogue, longing to muster courage enough to present his case to his mother. Lawd, ef Ah only had tha pretty one! He could almost feel the slickness of the weapon with his fingers. If he had a gun like that he would polish it and keep it shining so it would never rust. N Ah'd keep it loaded, by Gawd!

"Ma?" His voice was hesitant.

"Hunh?"

"Ol man Hawkins give yuh mah money yit?"

"Yeah, but ain no usa yuh thinking bout throwin nona it erway. Ahm keeping tha money sos yuh kin have cloes to go to school this winter."

He rose and went to her side with the open catalogue in his palms. She was washing dishes, her head bent low over a pan. Shyly he raised the book. When he spoke, his voice was husky, faint.

"Ma, Gawd knows Ah wans one of these."

"One of whut?" she asked, not raising her eyes.

"One of these," he said again, not daring even to point. She glanced up at the page, then at him with wide eyes.

"Nigger, is yuh gone plumb crazy?"

"Aw, Ma—"

"Git outta here! Don yuh talk t me bout no gun! Yuh a fool!"

"Ma, Ah kin buy one fer two dollahs."

"Not ef Ah knows it, yuh ain!"

"But yuh promised me one—"

"Ah don care what Ah promised! Yuh ain nothing but a boy yit!"

"Ma, ef yuh lemme buy one Ah'll *never* ast yuh fer nothing no mo."

"Ah tol yuh t git outta here! Yuh ain gonna toucha penny of tha money fer no gun! Thas how come Ah has Mistah Hawkins t pay yo wages to me, cause Ah knows yuh ain got no sense."

"But, Ma, we needa gun. Pa ain got no gun. We needa gun in the house. Yuh kin never tell whut might happen."

"Now don yuh try to maka fool outta me, boy! Ef we did hava gun, yuh wouldn't have it!"

He laid the catalogue down and slipped his arm around her waist.

"Aw, Ma, Ah done worked hard alla summer n ain ast yuh fer nothing, is Ah, now?"

"Thas whut yuh spose t do!"

"But Ma, Ah wans a gun. Yuh kin lemme have two dollahs outta mah money. Please, Ma. I kin give it to Pa. . . . Please, Ma! Ah loves yuh, Ma."

When she spoke her voice came soft and low.

"What yu wan wida gun, Dave? Yuh don need no gun. Yuh'll git in trouble. N ef yo pa jus thought Ah let yuh have money t buy a gun he'd hava fit."

"Ah'll hide it, Ma. It ain but two dollahs."

"Lawd, chil, whut's wrong wid yuh?"

"Ain nothin wrong, Ma. Ahm almos a man now. Ah wans a gun."

"Who gonna sell yuh a gun?"

"Ol Joe at the sto."

"N it don cos but two dollahs?"

"Thas all, Ma. Jus two dollahs. Please, Ma."

She was stacking the plates away; her hands moved slowly, reflectively. Dave kept an anxious silence. Finally, she turned to him.

"Ah'll let yuh git tha gun ef yuh promise me one thing."

"What's tha, Ma?"

"Yuh bring it straight back t me, yuh hear? It be fer Pa."

"Yessum! Lemme go now, Ma."

She stooped, turned slightly to one side, raised the hem of her dress, rolled down the top of her stocking, and came up with a slender wad of bills.

"Here," she said. "Lawd knows yuh don need no gun. But yer pa does. Yuh bring it right back t me, yuh hear? Ahma put it up. Now ef yuh don, Ahma have yuh pa lick yuh so hard yuh won fergit it."

"Yessum."

He took the money, ran down the steps, and across the yard.

"Dave! Yuuuuuh Daaaaave!"

He heard, but he was not going to stop now. "Naw, Lawd!"

The first movement he made the following morning was to reach under his pillow for the gun. In the gray light of dawn he held it loosely, feeling a sense of power. Could kill a man with a gun like this. Kill anybody, black or white. And if he were holding his gun in his hand, nobody could run over him; they would have to respect him. It was a big gun, with a long barrel and a heavy handle. He raised and lowered it in his hand, marveling at its weight.

He had not come straight home with it as his mother had asked; instead he had stayed out in the fields, holding the weapon in his hand, aiming it now and then at some imaginary foe. But he had not fired it; he had been afraid that his father might hear. Also he was not sure he knew how to fire it.

To avoid surrendering the pistol he had not come into the house until he knew that they were all asleep. When his mother had tiptoed to his bedside late that night and demanded the gun, he had first played possum; then he had told her that the gun was hidden outdoors, that he would bring it to her in the morning. Now he lay turning it slowly in his hands. He broke it, took out the cartridges, felt them, and then put them back.

He slid out of bed, got a long strip of old flannel from a trunk, wrapped the gun in it, and tied it to his naked thigh while it was still loaded. He did not go in to breakfast. Even though it was not yet daylight, he started for Jim Hawkins' plantation. Just as the sun was rising he reached the barns where the mules and plows were kept.

"Hey! That you, Dave?"

He turned. Jim Hawkins stood eying him suspiciously.

"What're yuh doing here so early?"

"Ah didn't know Ah wuz gittin up so early, Mistah Hawkins. Ah was fixin t hitch up ol Jenny n take her t the fiels."

"Good. Since you're so early, how about plowing that stretch down by the woods?"

"Suits me, Mistah Hawkins."

"O.K. Go to it!"

He hitched Jenny to a plow and started across the fields. Hot dog! This was just what he wanted. If he could get down by the woods, he could shoot his gun and nobody would hear. He walked behind the plow, hearing the traces creaking, feeling the gun tied tight to his thigh.

When he reached the woods, he plowed two whole rows before he decided to take out the gun. Finally, he stopped, looked in all directions, then untied the gun and held it in his hand. He turned to the mule and smiled.

"Know whut this is, Jenny? Naw, yuh wouldn know! Yuhs jusa ol mule! Anyhow, this is a gun, n it kin shoot, by Gawd!"

He held the gun at arm's length. Whut t hell, Ahma shoot this thing! He looked at Jenny again.

"Lissen here, Jenny! When Ah pull this ol trigger, Ah don wan yuh t run n acka fool now!"

Jenny stood with head down, her short ears pricked straight. Dave walked off about twenty feet, held the gun far out from him at arm's length, and turned his head. Hell, he told himself, Ah ain afraid. The gun felt loose in his fingers; he waved it wildly for a moment. Then he shut his eyes and tightened his forefinger. Bloom! A report half deafened him and he thought his right hand was torn from his arm. He heard Jenny whinnying and galloping over the field, and he found himself on his knees, squeezing his fingers hard between his legs. His hand was numb; he jammed it into his mouth, trying to warm it, trying to stop the pain. The gun lay at his feet. He did not quite know what had happened. He stood up and stared at the gun as though it were a living thing. He gritted his teeth and kicked the gun. Yuh almos broke mah arm! He turned to look for Jenny; she was far over the fields, tossing her head and kicking wildly.

"Hol on there, ol mule!"

When he caught up with her she stood trembling, walling her big white eyes at him. The plow was far away; the traces had broken. Then Dave stopped short, looking, not believing. Jenny was bleeding. Her left side was red and wet with blood. He went closer. Lawd, have mercy! Wondah did Ah shoot this mule? He grabbed for Jenny's mane. She flinched, snorted, whirled, tossing her head.

"Hol on now! Hol on."

Then he saw the hole in Jenny's side, right between the ribs. It was round, wet, red. A crimson stream streaked down the front leg, flowing fast. Good Gawd! Ah wuzn't shootin at tha mule. He felt panic. He knew he had to stop that blood, or Jenny would bleed to death. He had never seen so much blood in all his life.He chased the mule for half a mile, trying to catch her. Finally she stopped, breathing hard, stumpy tail half arched. He caught her mane and led her back to where the plow and gun lay. Then he stopped and grabbed handfuls of damp black earth and tried to plug the bullet hole. Jenny shuddered, whinnied, and broke from him.

"Hol on! Hol on now!"

He tried to plug it again, but blood came anyhow. His fingers were hot and sticky. He rubbed dirt into his palms, trying to dry them. Then again he attempted to plug the bullet hole, but Jenny shied away, kicking her heels high. He stood helpless. He had to do something. He ran at Jenny; she dodged him. He watched a red stream of blood flow down Jenny's leg and form a bright pool at her feet.

"Jenny . . . Jenny," he called weakly.

His lips trembled. She's bleeding t death! He looked in the direction of home, wanting to go back, wanting to get help. But he saw the pistol lying in the damp black clay. He had a queer feeling that if he only did something, this would not be; Jenny would not be there bleeding to death.

When he went to her this time, she did not move. She stood with sleepy, dreamy eyes; and when he touched her she gave a low-pitched whinny and knelt to the ground, her front knees slopping in blood.

"Jenny . . . Jenny . . ." he whispered.

For a long time she held her neck erect. He picked up the gun and held it gingerly between his thumb and forefinger. He buried it at the foot of a tree. He took a stick and tried to cover the pool of blood with dirt—but what was the use? There was Jenny lying with her mouth open and her eyes walled and glassy. He could not tell Jim Hawkins he had shot his mule. But he had to tell something. Yeah, Ah'll tell em Jenny started gittin wil n fell on the joint of the plow. . . . But that would hardly happen to a mule. He walked across the field slowly, head down.

It was sunset. Two of Jim Hawkins' men were over near the edge of the woods digging a hole in which to bury Jenny. Dave was surrounded by a knot of people, all of whom were looking down at the dead mule.

"I don't see how in the world it happened," said Jim Hawkins for the tenth time.

The crowd parted and Dave's mother, father, and small brother pushed into the center.

"Where Dave?" his mother called.

"There he is," said Jim Hawkins.

His mother grabbed him.

"Whut happened, Dave? Whut yuh done?"

"Nothin."

"C'mon, boy, talk," his father said.

Dave took a deep breath and told the story he knew nobody believed.

"Waal," he drawled. "Ah brung ol Jenny down here sos Ah could do mah plowin. Ah plowed bout two rows, just like yuh see." He stopped and pointed at the long rows of upturned earth. "Then somethin musta been wrong wid ol Jenny. She wouldn ack right a-tall. She started snortin n kickin her heels. Ah tried t hol her, but she pulled erway, rearin n goin on. Then when the point of the plow was stickin up in the air, she swung erroun n twisted herself back on it. . . . She stuck herself n started t bleed. N fo Ah could do anything, she wuz dead."

"Did you ever hear of anything like that in all your life?" asked Jim Hawkins.

There were white and black standing in the crowd. They murmured. Dave's mother came close to him and looked hard into his face. "Tell the truth, Dave," she said.

"Looks like a bullet hole to me," said one man.

"Dave, whut yuh do wid the gun?" his mother asked.

The crowd surged in, looking at him. He jammed his hands into his pockets, shook his head slowly from left to right, and backed away. His eyes were wide and painful.

"Did he hava gun?" asked Jim Hawkins.

"By Gawd, Ah tol yuh tha wuz a gun wound," said a man, slapping his thigh.

His father caught his shoulders and shook him till his teeth rattled.

"Tell whut happened, yuh rascal! Tell whut. . . ."

Dave looked at Jenny's stiff legs and began to cry.

"Whut yuh do wid tha gun?" his mother asked.

"What wuz he doin wida gun?" his father asked.

"Come on and tell the truth," said Hawkins. "Ain't nobody going to hurt you. . . ."

His mother crowded close to him.

"Did yuh shoot tha mule, Dave?"

Dave cried, seeing blurred white and black faces.

"Ahh ddinn gggo tt sshooot hher. . . . Ah ssswear ffo Gawd Ahh ddin. . . . Ah wuz a-tryin t sssee ef the old gggun would sshoot—"

"Where yuh git the gun from?" his father asked.

"Ah got it from Joe, at the sto."

"Where yuh git the money?"

"Ma give it t me."

"He kept worryin me, Bob. Ah had t. Ah tol im t bring the gun right back t me. . . . It was fer yuh, the gun."

"But how yuh happen to shoot that mule?" asked Jim Hawkins.

"Ah wuzn shootin at the mule, Mistah Hawkins. The gun jumped when

Ah pulled the trigger. . . . N fo Ah knowed anythin Jenny was there a-bleedin."

Somebody in the crowd laughed. Jim Hawkins walked close to Dave and looked into his face.

"Well, looks like you have bought you a mule, Dave."

"Ah swear fo Gawd, Ah didn go t kill the mule, Mistah Hawkins!"

"But you killed her!"

All the crowd was laughing now. They stood on tiptoe and poked heads over one another's shoulders.

"Well, boy, looks like yuh done bought a dead mule! Hahaha!"

"Ain tha ershame."

"Hohohohoho."

Dave stood, head down, twisting his feet in the dirt.

"Well, you needn't worry about it, Bob," said Jim Hawkins to Dave's father. "Just let the boy keep on working and pay me two dollars a month."

"Whut yuh wan fer yo mule, Mistah Hawkins?"

Jim Hawkins screwed up his eyes.

"Fifty dollars."

"Whut yuh do wid tha gun?" Dave's father demanded.

Dave said nothing.

"Yuh wan me t take a tree n beat yuh till yuh talk!"

"Nawsuh!"

"Whut yuh do wid it?"

"Ah throwed it erway."

"Where?"

"Ah . . . Ah throwed it in the creek."

"Waal, c mon home. N firs thing in the mawnin git to tha creek n fin tha gun."

"Yessuh."

"Whut yuh pay fer it?"

"Two dollahs."

"Take tha gun n git yo money back n carry it to Mistah Hawkins, yuh hear? N don fergit Ahma lam you black bottom good fer this! Now march yosef on hom, suh!"

Dave turned and walked slowly. He heard people laughing. Dave glared, his eyes welling with tears. Hot anger bubbled in him. Then he swallowed and stumbled on.

That night Dave did not sleep. He was glad that he had gotten out of killing the mule so easily, but he was hurt. Something hot seemed to turn over inside him each time he remembered how they had laughed. He tossed on his bed, feeling his hard pillow. N Pa says he's gonna beat me. . . . He remembered other beatings, and his back quivered. Naw, naw, Ah sho don wan im t beat me tha way no mo. Dam em all! Nobody ever gave him anything. All he did was work. They treat me like a mule, n then they beat me.

He gritted his teeth. N Ma had t tell on me.

Well, if he had to, he would take old man Hawkins that two dollars. But that meant selling the gun. And he wanted to keep that gun. Fifty dollars for a dead mule.

He turned over, thinking how he had fired the gun. He had an itch to fire it again. Ef other men kin shoota gun, by Gawd, Ah kin! He was still, listening. Mebbe they all sleeping now. The house was still. He heard the soft breathing of his brother. Yes, now! He would go down and get that gun and see if he could fire it! He eased out of bed and slipped into overalls.

The moon was bright. He ran almost all the way to the edge of the woods. He stumbled over the ground, looking for the spot where he had buried the gun. Yeah, here it is. Like a hungry dog scratching for a bone, he pawed it up. He puffed his black cheeks and blew dirt from the trigger and barrel. He broke it and found four cartridges unshot. He looked around; the fields were filled with silence and moonlight. He clutched the gun stiff and hard in his fingers. But, as soon as he wanted to pull the trigger, he shut his eyes and turned his head. Naw, Ah can't shoot wid mah eyes closed n mah head turned. With effort he held his eyes open; then he squeezed. *Blooooom!* He was stiff, not breathing. The gun was still in his hands. Dammit, he'd done it! He fired again. *Blooooom!* He smiled. *Blooooom! Blooooom! Click, click.* There! It was empty. If anybody could shoot a gun, he could. He put the gun into his hip pocket and started across the fields.

When he reached the top of a ridge he stood straight and proud in the moonlight, looking at Jim Hawkins' big white house, feeling the gun sagging in his pocket. Lawd, ef Ah had just one mo bullet Ah'd taka shot at tha house. Ah'd like t scare ol man Hawkins jusa little. . . . Jusa enough t let im know Dave Saunders is a man.

To his left the road curved, running to the tracks of the Illinois Central. He jerked his head, listening. From far off came a faint *hoooof-hoooof; hoooof-hoooof.* . . . He stood rigid. Two dollahs a mont. Les see now. . . . Tha means it'll take bout two years. Shucks! Ah'll be dam!

He started down the road, toward the tracks. Yeah, here she comes! He stood beside the track and held himself stiffly. Here she comes, erroun the ben. . . . C mon, yuh slow poke! C mon! He had his hand on his gun; something quivered in his stomach. Then the train thundered past, the gray and brown box cars rumbling and clinking. He gripped the gun tightly; then he jerked his hand out of his pocket. Ah betcha Bill wouldn't do it! Ah betcha. . . . The cars slid past, steel grinding upon steel. Ahm ridin yuh ter night, so hep me Gawd! He was hot all over. He hesitated just a moment; then he grabbed, pulled atop of a car, and lay flat. He felt his pocket; the gun was still there. Ahead the long rails were glinting in the moonlight, stretching away, away to somewhere, somewhere where he could be a man. . . .

QUESTIONS AND COMMENTARIES FOR DISCUSSION AND WRITING

Discussion questions have been provided for each selection, but no attempt has been made to provide the same type or amount of information for all the stories. For some stories very different approaches have been taken. Selected works by the author and critical and biographical works are cited. Movie versions and recordings of the stories are noted where possible. (Consult *Video Log, Phono Log,* or your audio-visual librarian for more information on movies and records.) Commentaries are provided for selected stories by both relatively new writers and classic writers—writers whose work poses problems or illustrates special techniques. Most of the commentaries have been deliberately written to illustrate basic types of literary papers: description, analysis, comparison and contrast, interpretation, personal evaluation or appreciation, papers on theme, on certain techniques, and a research paper.

Note: The date of publication given in the Chronological History usually refers to publication of the story in an author's collection. Some dates in the following material refer to first publication in a magazine.

CIVIL PEACE (1972) p. 1

CHINUA ACHEBE (Ogidi, Nigeria, 1930)
 1. What are some of the implications of the title?
 2. How universal is the ironic Civil War-Civil Peace parallel? Compare Jonathan's situation as a survivor of the war with his situation having survived the perils of peace.
 3. Where is Enugu?
 4. The point of view is omniscient, with a tight focus on Jonathan. What is the tone of Achebe's narration?
 5. Contrast the way Jonathan talks with the way the thieves talk. What is the tone in this scene?
 6. What influences Jonathan's attitude about "egg-rasher"?
 7. Given the context Achebe creates, what are some possible meanings of

the ambiguous line given four times throughout the story, "Nothing puzzles God"?

Commentary

When you encounter dialect, or an unusual word, recall and consider the general context the author has created and then examine closely the immediate context created by the lines preceding and following the sentence in which the word or phrase appears. For instance, the bureaucratic word "exgratia" seems so strange to Jonathan himself that he calls it "egg-rasher." It is a "windfall," "like Christmas," and it comes from the state treasury. The context tells you that it is money "given out of" *(ex)* "thanks" *(gratia)* for turning in rebel money.

Reading dialect is difficult for modern readers, who seldom encounter it and have little interest in reading it. Many writers who use it enjoy the sound of words and the expressiveness of dialect phrases and want to share that enjoyment with readers. Notice that Jonathan does not speak in dialect (see the last paragraph, for instance) as heavily as the thieves do. What does the contrast imply? (See page 4 for an example of both Jonathan's and the thieves' speech.) It is comic, satirical, and ironic that Jonathan calls for help in dialect. Perhaps the implication is that to Jonathan, as well as to the reader, these thieves seem strange and terrifying, as if they came out of the "forest holes." Consider also the possibility that Achebe is suggesting the problem of communication among people of different factions and tribes.

British novelist-critic Anthony Burgess, whose *Clockwork Orange* relies heavily upon a made-up dialect, describes Achebe's "predominant theme" as "the threat to native civilizations which the great world may call primitive but which are in fact vital, rich, and happy." Achebe "also shows remarkable power in the rendering of Umuaro speech and thought" *(The Novel Now).* "I was born in the colonial era," Achebe writes, "grew up in the heady years of nationalist protest and witnessed Africa's resumption of independence. . . . It was not . . . the same Africa but a different Africa created in the image of Europe. . . ." He declares that he is a political writer: "My politics is concerned with universal human communication across racial and cultural boundaries as a means of fostering respect for all people."

The dialect stories in this anthology offer an opportunity to study language and expressions produced by people who are forced to use the language of captors or foreign rulers. Turn your frustration into surrender to a sense of foreign voices, as if a tourist who only half comprehends (even as a Maine Yankee feels in Alabama). Compare Achebe's handling of Nigerian dialect (based on the English of British Colonists) with Charles Chesnutt's handling of dialect in "The Wife of His Youth," (based on the English of the American Southern slave society). Compare it with the Chinese dialect in "Food For All His Dead" by Frank Chin (p. 236).

"Civil Peace" is a deliberately simple tale, an omniscient narrative focusing on Jonathan. Achebe doesn't present events from Jonathan's point of view; he summarizes Jonathan's story, offers only one satirically illustrative scene. The comical dialogue in dialect expresses a serious point. The tone is not Jonathan's but Achebe's. Jonathan's plight is an ironic, sometimes satirical tale of survival in war and peace. The ironic tone is set by the title "Civil Peace," which suggests that the peace after a Civil War is much like the war itself. Note that a soldier confiscated Jonathan's bicycle and a "tief man" extorts, threatening shooting, money given to Jonathan by the victorious government, but not to the thieves ("We sef no get even aninni."). They may, or may not, be defeated rebels. The leader jeeringly calls for "soja" to help Jonathan, as if knowing soldiers must have treated him in a similar fashion during the war.

"Civil Peace," like most of Achebe's fiction, is set in Eastern Nigeria. After Colonists withdrew, the pattern of the Civil War in Nigeria in the late 1960s was repeated, sometimes several times over, in many African countries. But the situation Achebe describes has also been true in European, British, and American Civil Wars.

This is an example of an essay that treats several elements of a story.

WRITING SUGGESTION: Derive a topic for a paper from question #2.

This story appears in *Girls at War*, 1972. Novel: *Things Fall Apart*, 1958. Achebe has also written two books of verse, two juvenile novels, a book of essays, *Morning Yet on Creation Day*, 1975, and edited *The Insider: Stories of War and Peace from Nigeria*, 1971. About: Arthur Ravenscroft, *Chinua Achebe*. Wilfred Cartey, *Whispers from a Continent: The Literature of Contemporary Black Africa*.

NEW BEST FRIENDS (1982) p. 6

ALICE ADAMS (Fredericksburg, Virginia, 1926)
1. What meanings of "friends" emerge from the various contexts Adams creates? Why does Jonathan's heart sink at the end?
2. What point of view technique does Adams use? On which character's perceptions does she focus? What are the advantages (and possible disadvantages) of this point of view for this story?
3. How does Adams' use of present tense contribute to the story's effects?
4. What contrasts does New York City provide to the Southern town of Hilton?
5. Compare and contrast the characters.
6. Analyze the effect of the "relocation" on Jonathan, on Sarah. What is Sarah's problem?
7. Is the title ironic?
8. Is the structure effective?

WRITING SUGGESTION: Analyze the effectiveness of the structure of "New Best Friends."

This story appeared in *The New Yorker* and is included in *Return Trips*, 1983. Stories: *Beautiful Girl*, 1979; *To See You Again*, 1982. Novels: *Listening to Billie*, 1978; *Second Chances*, 1988. About: *Contemporary Novelists*, 4th ed. *Dictionary of Literary Biography Yearbook*, 1986.

THE SILENCE OF THE LLANO (1982) p. 17

RUDOLFO ANAYA (Hispanic-American. Pastura, New Mexico, 1937)
1. What point of view technique does Anaya employ and what relation is there between that and his style?
2. What motifs lend unity of effect to the story?
3. What parallels exist between the characters?
4. After the rape, the story becomes ambiguous. Is the ambiguity accidental or deliberate?
5. Discuss pro and con: The girl is better off at the end.

WRITING SUGGESTION: Analyze the effect of isolation and solitude upon the characters.

This story appears in *The Silence of the Llano*, 1982. Novel: *Bless Me, Ultima*, 1971. Nonfiction: *A Chicano in China*, 1986; co-editor (with Simon J. Ortiz) of *A Ceremony of Brotherhood, 1680–1980*, 1981. About: Paul Vassallo, ed., *The Magic of Words: Rudolfo Anaya and His Writings*, 1982.

SEEDS (1921) p. 31

SHERWOOD ANDERSON (Camden, Ohio, 1876–1941)
1. How does Anderson structure the story to suggest that the woman from Iowa is not the main character?
2. Why do you suppose the narrator tells (or writes) this story?
3. Why does Anderson have the doctor and the young artist make the same statements?
4. Discuss pro and con: Sex is a male preconception of what a woman, such as the one in this story, needs.

Commentary

The image of the repressed woman and the theme of the grotesque are at the vital center of Anderson's fiction. It is strange, then, that "Seeds" is rarely anthologized and seldom discussed. Perhaps it is too enigmatic. Given enough consideration, it may prove to be one of his finest achievements.

"Seeds" appears in *The Triumph of the Egg* (1921), which contains Anderson's most famous story, "The Egg" (adapted by him for the stage as "The

Triumph of the Egg"). "The Dumb Man," the first story in this collection, is very brief and lined as blank verse, and sets the tone for the entire book. Anderson gives a sense of himself as he sets the image of the woman hovering over all the stories.

There is a story—I cannot tell it—I have no words. . . .

The story concerns three men in a house in a street.

If I could say the words I would sing the story.

I would whisper it into the ears of women, of mothers.

I would run through the streets saying it over and over. . . .

Upstairs in the house there is a woman standing with her back to a wall, in half darkness by a window.

That is the foundation of my story and everything I will ever know is distilled in it. . . .

I have no words to tell what happened in my story.

I cannot tell the story.

The white silent one may have been Death . . .

I keep thinking about the dandified man who laughed all through my story. . . .

If I could understand him I could understand everything.

I could run through the world telling a wonderful story.

I would no longer be dumb.

Why was I not given words?

Why am I dumb?

I have a wonderful story to tell but know no way to tell it.

Three years later, in *A Storyteller's Story*, Anderson spoke of himself in similar phrases. "I tell you what—words have color, smell; one may sometimes feel them with the fingers as one touches the cheek of a child." Words are "the materials of a story writer's craft . . . the little words that must be made to run into sentences and paragraphs, now slow and haltingly, now quickly, swiftly, now singing like a woman's voice in a dark house in a dark street at midnight, now viciously, threateningly, like wolves running in a winter forest of the North."

Anderson had planted seeds for "Seeds" two years earlier in his most important and influential book, *Winesburg, Ohio* (1919), a cycle of stories (Hemingway, Faulkner, Steinbeck, and Welty also published story cycles). Anderson opens with "The Book of the Grotesque," a story about an aging writer. He writes: "All of the men and women the writer had ever known had become grotesques. . . . It was the truths that made the people grotesques. The old man had quite an elaborate theory concerning the matter.

It was his notion that the moment one of the people took one of the truths to himself, called it his truth, and tried to live his life by it, he became a grotesque and the truth he embraced became a falsehood." This passage clearly describes the father in "The Egg." The narrator of "Seeds" also speaks of grotesques. "The woman—you see—was like a young tree choked by a climbing vine. . . . She was a grotesque . . ." (p. 36). The grotesque became a pervasive theme in American fiction, especially Southern literature, as illustrated by Faulkner's "A Rose for Emily" (300) and the two stories by Flannery O'Connor (pp. 775 and 785). In *Winesburg, Ohio,* the stories "Surrender" (under the heading "Godliness, Part III") and "Adventure," about two repressed women in a small, Midwestern town, illuminate "Seeds," in which a young woman from a small Iowa town takes her repressions into the big city, Chicago.

The above quotations may help us understand the narrator of "Seeds." The first person narrator is usually the main character of the story he or she tells because the effect on him or her of the story, and of the storytelling process, is more meaningful than the story he or she tells. "Seeds" is a good example of this principle. The lame woman's psychic dilemma is certainly important and moving (is it sexual or a need for love?). But if the young woman's internal and external conflicts were Anderson's primary concern, why would he involve LeRoy and the narrator, especially in the way that he does? Her effect on them is more powerful than her effect on the reader, and their comments reveal far more about themselves than about her. In that light, LeRoy stands out more as the protagonist than the woman.

The relationship between LeRoy and the narrator is, considering all the implications, as complex as that between LeRoy and the woman. When we consider that the narrator begins, not with LeRoy, but with his own obsessive memory of a psychoanalyst tormented by the grotesque lives of his patients, we may begin to see that Anderson's main interest is in the narrator. And at the end, when the unnamed narrator (who may or may not be Anderson himself) quotes what LeRoy told him only "yesterday" and we realize that LeRoy uses phrases the same as or similar to those of the doctor, we may have cause to wonder whether the painter-writer LeRoy and the narrator are the same person. When we note further that the narrator himself uses the same words to describe both his own behavior with the doctor and LeRoy's ("I became passionately in earnest" (p. 32) and "A passionate earnestness took possession of him" (p. 36)) we may feel even more convinced of the possibility that LeRoy and the narrator—and perhaps even the doctor—are the same person. (Or perhaps the narrator is a patient of the doctor.) We must also pause to wonder whether we are forcing an ingenious interpretation, because Anderson's stories are usually more straightforward on the surface, while generating complex implications. We are left, in any case, with the prospect of a rewarding answer to this question: What motivates the narrator to tell this story?

This is an example of an essay showing the use of a writer's other work to illuminate theme and technique in a particular work.

For examples of the objective correlative, consider the woman's lameness and the narrator's compulsion to tell her story and LeRoy's (which is perhaps his own).

Compare with "Paul's Case," (p. 174).

WRITING SUGGESTION: A psychological interpretation.

Stories: *Horses and Men*, 1923; *Death in the Woods*, 1933. Novel: *Poor White*, 1920; *Dark Laughter*, 1925. About: Brom Weber, *Sherwood Anderson;* Irving Howe, *Sherwood Anderson;* Welford Dunaway, *Sherwood Anderson*.

THE REUNION (1983)   p. 37

MAYA ANGELOU (Black American. St. Louis, Missouri, 1932)
1. What is Birdland a reference to? What does the name Philomena mean? Is there any significance in her nickname "Meanie"?
2. Is Philomena telling or writing her story? To whom and why?
3. Is it true that Beth Ann has everything? What does Philomena have?
4. Why does Beth Ann assert that Willard is "mine. He belongs to me"?
5. Mistakingly thinking that Beth Ann has left, Philomena imagines what she would have said to Beth Ann. By contrast, what *does* she say to her?
6. Beth's father has sex with black women. Might he have been Philomena's father?
7. What are some of the possible meanings of the last, ambiguous line?
8. Discuss pro and con: Ironically, Philomena is now free and she has her music, but she is still in bondage to her past.

WRITING SUGGESTION: Consider the problem of identity.

This story appears in *Confirmation: An Anthology of African-American Women*, 1983, compiled by Imamu Amiri Baraka and Imina Baraka. Autobiography: *I Know Why the Caged Bird Sings*, 1970. Angelou has also written several plays and books of poetry. Her latest work is *All God's Children Need Traveling Shoes*, 1986. About: "The Black Scholar Interviews Maya Angelou," *Black Scholar*, 8 (Jan.–Feb. 1977), 44–53. *Dictionary of Literary Biography*, Vol. 38: *Afro-American Writers After 1955*.

SIGNIFICANT MOMENTS IN THE LIFE OF MY MOTHER (1986)   p. 42

MARGARET ATWOOD (Ottawa, Canada, 1939)
1. Atwood presents twelve "moments," an unusual technique producing a structure that is rather loose, and episodic. What holds these moments together in a kind of unity of effect?

First person narratives are almost always primarily about the narrator. This story is a good example. "Significant Moments in My Life" might be the title for the implicit story. The line ". . . the air was heavy with things that were known but not spoken" (top of p. 44) applies in various ways to the narrator's own life and story. Consider the phrase "suddenly I was always cold" (bottom of p. 53) as well as that whole paragraph.

2. In what ways are the twelve moments significant?

Consider the mother's apparent view of why each story she tells is significant; sometimes the daughter (the narrator) is significant to her. Next, determine what unspoken significance each moment might have for the narrator as a character whom Atwood is gradually creating out of the developing context.

3. Where does the mother tell of significant moments in the daughter's life?

See the "hair" moment (p. 44) and the related moment (p. 53). See the "sense of smell" moment (p. 50).

4. What parallels between the daughter and the mother do you see?

The enigmatic opening moment may imply a parallel (p. 42). See the "hair" moments (pp. 44 and 53). See the beginning of the second paragraph; mother and daughter tell stories, but for what different reasons? See page 50, second paragraph of the new section: the narrator compares her childhood with her mother's. See page 52: the opening and closing sentences implicitly apply in various ways to mother and daughter. The daughter is often significant in the life of her mother and vice versa.

5. What are some implications of the dark ending?

Notice the many negative notes sounded in the final section beginning on page 53. Why does the mother have "few stories to tell about these times"? Why might the mother be afraid of the narrator? What might the narrator mean by "language"? Notice that the first complete sentence on page 48 prepares the reader for the last line of the story. What might "great disaster" suggest?

6. Describe the attitudes about the sexes, and about parents and children conveyed in this story.

Consider especially the moments that begin on pages 46, 48 and 49. Why do repressed people seem preoccupied with crude stories about panties embarrassingly falling down and urine?

7. Discuss pro and con: The narrator's tone is generally sarcastic and condescending, or superior.

See, for instance, pages 44, 47, 48, 50 and 54. Does the tone ever shift or vary?

WRITING SUGGESTION: Derive the topic for a paper from questions 4, 6, or 7.

This story appeared in *Queen's Quarterly* and is included in *Bluebeard's Egg*, 1983. Novels: *The Handmaid's Tale*, 1986; *Cat's Eye*, 1988. Nonfiction: *Survival: A Thematic Guide to Canadian Literature*. About: Katherine Van Spanckeren and Jan Garden Castro, *Margaret Atwood: Visions and Forms*. Jerome H. Rosenberg, *Margaret Atwood*. Barbara Hill Rigney, *Madness and Sexual Politics in the Feminist Novel: Studies in Bronte, Woolf, Lessing and Atwood*.

GOING TO MEET THE MAN (1965)   p. 55

JAMES BALDWIN (Black American. Harlem, New York, 1924–1987)
1. How does his use of point of view enable Baldwin, regarded as a radical black writer, simultaneously to empathize with Jesse and to severely criticize his attitudes and actions as representative of certain white racists?
2. How is sex related to racism and violence in Jesse's life, past and present?
3. Is Grace's sexual response to Jesse at the end ambiguous? We know Jesse fantasizes that Grace is black, but does Grace fantasize that Jesse is black, or is she the unwilling object of his racist male fantasies?
4. How do Jesse's memories affect his state of mind, his attitudes in the present?

Commentary

Baldwin probably wrote this story during the time of the Civil Rights Voter Registration campaign in the summer of 1964. As a Northern black man, he condemned white racists in Mississippi and elsewhere. He could have condemned Jesse and others like him directly by using the omniscient point of view, or he could have let the young black leader express his outrage and hatred directly in the first person. But Baldwin chose to tell his story through the third person, central intelligence point of view technique: the reader is to assume that everything passes through the consciousness of Jesse. Using several other techniques—context, implication, irony, flashback, parallels, motifs—Baldwin communicates his condemnation of racism while simultaneously making it possible for all readers, black or white, to empathize with Jesse, especially as an innocent child being taught to hate "niggers." The effect of this simultaneity is to express the hideous power of racism while explaining how it is born and nurtured in individuals. Baldwin also dramatizes the process by which religion and family in some social contexts promote racism, and how sex and violence help perpetuate it.

In the first several pages, Baldwin introduces themes that he will develop, with variations, throughout—the association of sex, violence, and pain with racial attitudes and behavior, for instance. He also introduces motifs that enhance those themes in changing contexts: singing, smell, fire, animals, light and dark, childhood, family feeling, religion, sex, violence, cars.

To stimulate the reader's participation, Baldwin sets up various parallels. He first presents the black child's meeting with Jesse the adult, then parallels it with Jesse's own childhood witnessing of the burning of the black man; also, the black child, Otis, in Jesse's childhood parallels the black child in Jesse's adult life. Sex between Jesse and his wife, stimulated by racial violence, is paralleled by Jesse's parents' sex after the burning of the castrated black man.

The flashback device helps to stress these parallels, but the very use of that device expresses one of the themes: that racists are nurtured in the family circle. Notice that Jesse flashes back first to the effect of the burning on his parents and himself before he remembers the cause. The effect has dominated his life.

The point of view and various other technical devices help stimulate the reader's awareness of ironies that stress the irrationality of racism. Consider the title, the names Jesse and Grace, such phrases as "will they never learn?", "I am a good man," good "niggers," "they like me, they hate me," duty, role models, the castration of the black man, being free and not free, love and hatred (the boy loves his father who hates "niggers"), the dying black man's eyes looking into the boy's, as well as the fact that Jesse thinks the older blacks sing for his soul, too, and that the mother takes good care of dogs and Jesse before she takes her child to watch the "nigger" burn. Baldwin suffuses the story with controlled ironies of every type.

Baldwin's vision of himself as an artist seems to have predisposed him to write from within the consciousness of a racist. "The artist," he wrote, "cannot allow any consideration to supersede his responsibility to reveal all that he can possibly discover concerning the mystery of the human being." "One discovers that life is tragic, and therefore unutterably beautiful." Writing out of that and other paradoxes confuses some readers, perhaps because America "is devoted to the death of paradox." Devoted as he was to creating works of art, Baldwin believed that the artist is "responsible to—and for—the social order." He developed an ethical vision of life in his fiction, within an historical perspective.

Baldwin's early works may illuminate "Going to Meet the Man." In his first novel, *Go Tell It On the Mountain* (1953), he developed some of the same themes. He tells of a boy's religious conversion, one that is socially and ethnically conditioned (Baldwin was a preacher himself for three years in his early youth). Baldwin's reputation as a master of the personal, often polemical essay is based on three collections: *Notes of a Native Son* (1955), *Nobody Knows My Name: Further Notes of a Native Son* (1961) ("Native Son" pays homage to Richard Wright's novel of that name), and *The Fire Next Time* (1963). In 1964, the year before the collection of stories *Going to Meet the Man* appeared, Baldwin's controversial play *Blues for Mister Charlie* was produced.

This is an example of a paper on a technique—point of view—working in relation to other techniques to express a socially relevant theme.

WRITING SUGGESTIONS: 1) Argue pro or con (or both): Black and white writers can write from the point of view of members of each other's race; 2) Compare the way Baldwin, a black male, writes out of the consciousness of a male racist with the way Flannery O'Connor, a white female, writes out of the consciousness of a male racist in two versions of the same short story (pp. 775, 785). Eudora Welty let a male racist speak in the first person in two versions of "Where Is the Voice Coming From," both reprinted in John Kuehl's *Creative Writing and Rewriting*.

This story first appeared in *Going to Meet the Man*, 1965, Baldwin's only collection. Novels: *Giovanni's Room*, 1956; *If Beale Street Could Talk*, 1974. About: Fern Marja Eckman, *The Furious Passage of James Baldwin*; Addison Gayle, Jr., "Of Race and Rage," in *The Way of the World: The Black Novels in America*; Stanley Macebuh, *James Baldwin: A Critical Study*; John Reese Moore, "An Embarrassment of Riches: Baldwin's 'Going to Meet the Man,' " in *The Sounder Few*, 121–136, R. H. W. Dillard, et al, eds.; Therman B. O'Daniel, ed., *James Baldwin: A Critical Evaluation*; Carolyn Wedin Sylvander, *James Baldwin*; J. Weatherby, *James Baldwin: Artist on Fire*.

MY MAN BOVANNE (1972)   p. 69

TONI CADE BAMBARA (Black American. New York City, 1939)
   1. To whom or for whom, if anybody, is Miss Hazel Peoples telling or writing this story?
   2. Comment on Bambara's ability to portray Hazel's way of talking, as in the phrase, "I was just talkin on the drums"?
   3. What makes the dance image effective in this story?
   4. How does the thematic motif of blindness apply to young and old?
   5. In the context set up in this story, what is ironic about speeches concerning the mistreatment of all blacks? What is meant by "grassroots"?

Compare with Gaines' "Just Like a Tree" (p. 352).

WRITING SUGGESTION: Examine identity and family crisis in this story.

This story appears in *Gorilla, My Love*, 1972. Stories: *The Sea Birds Are Still Alive: Collected Short Stories*, 1977. Novel: *The Salt Eaters*, 1980. About: Claudia Tate, "Toni Cade Bambara," in *Black Women Writers At Work*; Nancy D. Hargrove, "Youth in Toni Cade Bambara's *Gorilla, My Love*," in *Women Writers of the Contemporary South. Dictionary of Literary Biography*, vol. 38: *Afro-American Writers after 1955*.

LOST IN THE FUNHOUSE (1967)   p. 74

JOHN BARTH (Cambridge, Maryland, 1930)
  1. Discuss pro and con: "It is impossible to discuss this story," a student
     once said. "It is one of life's horrors."
  2. What point of view technique does Barth employ? What is the relation
     between point of view and style in this story?
  3. Find 20 puns.
  4. Consider the implications of the title. What is the funhouse? Who is
     lost in it? Is it fun? For whom?
  5. Barth is famous for his effective oral renditions of his work, and espe-
     cially for his public readings of this story, in which his recorded voice
     is heard reading some parts as he delivers others live. How do you
     imagine he would plot such a reading?
  6. As a review of the basics of the techniques of fiction, look up in the
     glossary or dictionary the key literary terms Barth uses.
  7. Discuss pro and con: Barth's satire of conventional literary theory
     only makes the art of fiction clearer for the reader.
  8. Speculate: Does Ambrose grow up to be the author of a story like this
     one?
  9. What do the allusions refer to?

Commentary

When a literature class sets itself the task of dealing with a difficult story,
students sometimes wish that the author were there to comment. As a way
of bringing Barth into the classroom, here are some of his comments:

"As a writer . . . my objective has been to attempt to assimilate as well as
I can the twentieth century aspects of my medium, to invent some myself,
and, at the same time . . . to preserve the appeal that narrative has always
had to the imagination: the simple appeals of suspense, of *story*, with which
I've been in love since the beginning" (*Dictionary of Literary Biography: American Novelists Since World War II*, volume 2, 23.) In 1967, the year "Lost in the
Funhouse" appeared in *The Atlantic Monthly*, the same magazine published
Barth's essay on "The Literature of Exhaustion," a reference to the "used-
upness of certain possibilities."

The book *Lost in the Funhouse* is subtitled "Fiction for Print, Tape, Live
Voice," and, as Barth said in the Author's Note, is "neither a collection nor
a selection, but a series" of pieces; some "were composed expressly for
print, others were not." Although "Lost in the Funhouse" was intended for
print, it too has been performed as reader's theater. According to Barth,
" 'Glossolalia' will make no sense unless heard in live or recorded voices,
male and female, or read as if so heard; 'Echo' is intended for monophonic
authorial recording, either disc or tape; 'Autobiography,' for monophonic
tape and visible but silent author. . . ." "Title" was "done" in six different

media. "On with the story. On with the story" ends the Author's Note.

But the paperback edition included "Seven Additional Author's Notes." Some of Barth's observations: "The title 'Autobiography' means 'self-composition': the antecedent of the first-person pronoun is not I, but the story, speaking of itself. I am its father; its mother is the recording machine." "The triply schizoid monologue entitled 'title' addresses itself simultaneously to three matters: the 'Author's' difficulties with his companion, his analogous difficulties with the story he's in process of composing, and the not dissimilar straits in which, I think mistakenly, he imagines his culture and its literature to be." "The deuteragonist of 'Life-Story,' antecedent of the second-person pronoun, is you."

Such writing provoked *Life's* reviewer Webster Schott to attack the book as "a grinding bore" and advise Barth to drop literature and embrace life.

When Rust Hills, fiction editor at *Esquire* for several decades and at *The Saturday Evening Post* earlier, asked Barth to choose his favorite story for a collection Hills was editing, Barth chose "Lost in the Funhouse." It was "written for print," he said in a comment preceding the story, "and occurs midway through the series of which it is the title story. I meant to look back—at the narrator Ambrose's earlier youth, at the earlier 'Ambrose' stories in the series, and at some classic manners and concerns of the conventional realist-illusionist short story—and also 'forward,' to some less conventional narrative matters and concerns as well as to some future, more mythic avatars of the narrator. Finally, I meant it to be accessible, entertaining, perhaps moving; for I have no use for merely cerebral inventions, merely formalistic tours de force, and the place and time—tidewater Maryland, World War Twotime—are pungent in my memory. In short, my choice for this anthology, like the story itself, is partly sentimental" (*Writer's Choice*).

Barth spoke about his writing more generally with writer-critic Joe David Bellamy in 1972.

"As you compose, particularly if you have a theoretical turn of mind, you're likely to be interested in working out any theoretical notions that you might be afflicted with about the medium you're working in."

"I tend to regard it [realism] as a kind of aberration in the history of literature."

"The process is the content, more or less," Barth said of his fiction.

Bellamy responded: "I'm thinking of other examples in 'Lost in the Funhouse' which do that in different ways. Do you think there's a basic conflict between that kind of anti-illusionistic writing and the storytelling impulse? That is, when you start talking about the equipment of the story and deliberately break the illusion of the story, do you possibly disrupt the impulse you have toward storytelling and forego those qualities?"

"No," Barth said, "I don't think there's a conflict, only a kind of tension, which can be used. When we talk about it this way it all sounds dreadfully self-conscious, involuted, vertiginous, dull. In the actual execution it doesn't have to be at all; it can be charming, entertaining; it can even be illusionist. . . .

"The trick, always, is to be at the same time entertaining. I still regard literature as a form of pleasure; and while there are lots of pleasures . . . I myself like a kind of fiction that, if it's going to be self-conscious, is at least comic about its own self-consciousness. Otherwise, self-consciousness can be a bloody bore. What is more loathsome than the self-loathing of a self one loathes?" *(The New Fiction: Interviews with Innovative American Writers)*

Twelve years later, Barth told George Plimpton that he liked what Vladimir Nabokov said "he wanted from his novels: 'aesthetic bliss.' Let me change masters for a moment and say that I prefer Henry James's remark that the first obligation of the writer—which I would also regard as his last obligation—is to be interesting. *To be interesting.* To be interesting one beautiful sentence after another. To be interesting; not to change the world."

"Would you ever make a compromise in your books to gain more readers?" Plimpton asked.

"I would," Barth replied, "but I can't. I start every new project saying, 'This one's going to be simple, this one's going to be simple.' It never turns out to be. My imagination evidently delights in complexity for its own sake. Much of life, after all, and much of what we admire is essentially complex. . . . There are writers whose gift is to make terribly complicated things simple. But I know my gift is the reverse: to take relatively simple things and complicate them to the point of madness" *(Writers at Work,* Seventh Series).

WRITING SUGGESTION: Explain to a friend Barth's method in this story, using some of the statements quoted above.

This story first appeared in *The Atlantic Monthly,* 1967, and was included in *Lost in the Funhouse,* 1968. Novellas: *Chimera,* 1972. Novels: *The Sot Weed Factor,* 1960; *The Tidewater Tales. A Novel,* 1987. About: Beverly Gray Bienstock, "Lingering on the Autognostic Verge: John Barth's *Lost in the Funhouse,*" *Modern Fiction Studies,* 19 (Spring 1973), 69–78; Charles B. Harris, *Passionate Virtuosity: The Fiction of John Barth;* Ihab Hassan, in *Contemporary Novelists;* Gerhard Joseph, *John Barth;* Carol A. Kyle, "The Unity of Anatomy: The Structure of Barth's *Lost in the Funhouse,*" *Critique,* XIII No. 3 (1972), 31–43; David Morrell, *John Barth: An Introduction.* Jac Tharpe, *John Barth: The Comic Sublimity of Paradox.*

THE KING OF JAZZ (1977)   p. 93

DONALD BARTHELME (Philadelphia, Pennsylvania, 1931–1989)
   1. Specifically, in which sentences in the narrative and dialogue does Barthelme most effectively reveal the effect of jazz upon his style (his

choice of words, syntax, repetition of phrases and the rhythm of sentences)?

2. At which points do the various kinds of "changes" occur?

3. What explains the effect of the one long paragraph in the story?

Commentary

Philip Stevick, editor of an influential anthology of experimental fiction, *Anti-story,* has said of Barthelme that he is "the most imitated fictionist in the United States today" (the "term "fictionist" seems more appropriate for such writers than "short story writer"). Jerome Klinkowitz, another critic who writes about innovative writers, asked Barthelme, "When you improvise, do you think of the chord changes or the melody?" Barthelme replied: "All I want is just a trace of skeleton—three bones from which the rest may be reasoned out." A character in Barthelme's "See the Moon" says, "Fragments are the only forms I trust." Barthelme refuses to accept that as his general aesthetics, but when Klinkowitz posed "collage" as a key term for modern art in all media, Barthelme responded: "The point of collage is that unlike things are stuck together to make, in the best case, a new reality. This new reality, in the best case, may be or imply a comment on the other reality from which it came, and may be also much else. It's an *itself,* if it's successful" (*The New Fiction: Interviews with Innovative American Writers,* Joe David Bellamy, ed.).

In a speech in 1985, Barthelme said that for him: "Writing is a process of dealing with not-knowing, a forcing of what and how. . . . art is always a meditation upon external reality rather than a representation of external reality." Referring to writers, he said, "It's our good fortune to be able to imagine realities, other possibilities." To illustrate his point, he told a story: "Once when I was in Elaine de Kooning's studio on Broadway, at a time when the metal sculptor Herbert Ferber occupied the studio immediately above, there came through the floor a most horrible crashing and banging. 'What in the world is that?' I asked, and Elaine said, 'Oh, that's Herbert thinking.' " He also listed some criticisms of innovative or post-modernists "fictionists" and "ardently" contested them: "that this kind of writing has turned its back on the world, is in some sense not about the world but about its own processes, that it is . . . chilly, that it excludes readers by design, speaks only to the already tenured, or that it does not speak at all, but instead, like Frost's Secret, sits in the center of a ring and Knows" ("Not-Knowing," *Voicelust: Eight Contemporary Fiction Writers on Style,* edited by Allen Wier and Don Hendrie, Jr.).

Note: Barthelme draws much of his raw material, clichés, and jargon from popular culture. His first book of short fiction, *Come Back, Dr. Caligari,* 1964 (perhaps a satirical allusion to "Come back, Shane") included a fiction about Batman and Robin, "The Joker's Greatest Triumph," and one of his few novels is the satire *Snow White,* 1967.

WRITING SUGGESTION: Derive a topic from the above commentary. Perhaps include Barth's "Lost in the Funhouse," (p. 74) and draw on the commentary on that story.

This story appears in *Great Days,* 1979. Stories: *Come Back, Dr. Caligari,* 1964; *Sixty Stories,* 1981. Novels: *Snow White,* 1967; *The Dead Father,* 1975. About: John Ditsky, " 'With Ingenuity and Hard Work, Distracted': The Narrative Style of Donald Barthelme," *Style* IV (Summer 1975), 388–400; Lois Gordon, *Donald Barthelme.*

SHIFTING (1977) p. 97

ANNE BEATTIE (Washington, D.C., 1947)
1. Looking at the first few passages and the last line, get a fix on the point of view technique and its relation to style. Are they well-chosen for the effect Beattie seems to want to have on the reader?
2. Compare the three men in relation to Natalie.
3. Contrast the two cars.
4. How does "shifting" function as a metaphor throughout the story?
5. How do the sculpture and the photographs illuminate aspects of Natalie's situation?

WRITING SUGGESTION: Derive a topic from questions 2, 4, or 5.

This story appeared in *The New Yorker* and is included in *Secrets and Surprises,* 1979. Stories: *Distortions,* 1976. Novels: *Chilly Scenes of Winter,* 1976 (made into a movie); *Alex Katz,* 1987. About: Pico Iyer, "The World According to Beattie," *Partisan Review,* L (1983), 548–553; John Gerlach, "Through 'The Octascope': A View of Ann Beattie," *Studies in Short Fiction* 17 (Fall, 1980), 489–494; Christina Murphy, *Ann Beattie.*

LOOKING FOR MR. GREEN (1951) p. 108

SAUL BELLOW (Jewish American, born in La Chine, Quebec, Canada, 1915)
1. What would Bellow have lost had he written the story in the first person from George's point of view?
2. The locale is Chicago during the depression of the 1930s. Discuss pro and con: This story is not dated.
3. What is the function of Raynor in the story?
4. How does the widow immigrant, Mrs. Staika, contrast with the woman Grebe encounters at the end?
5. What is the effect of the flashback structure?
6. What role does "luck" play in the lives of the characters?
7. Notice that Grebe thinks he has found, but never meets, Mr. Green. Is the last line an example of ironic ambiguity?

WRITING SUGGESTION: An interviewer asked Bellow: "How much are you conscious of the reader when you write? Is there an ideal audience that you write for?" Apply Bellow's answer to the story in some way: "I have in mind another human being who will understand me. I count on this. Not on perfect understanding, which is Cartesian, but on approximate understanding, which is Jewish. And on a meeting of sympathies, which is human."

This story appeared in *Commentary*, 1951, and is included in *Mosby's Memoirs and Other Stories*, 1968. Three of Bellow's novels won the National Book Award: *The Adventures of Augie March*, 1953, *Herzog*, 1964, and *Mr. Sammler's Planet*, 1970. *Humboldt's Gift*, 1975, won the Pulitzer Prize. Bellow was awarded the Nobel Prize in 1976. Novella: *A Theft*, 1988. Nonfiction: *To Jerusalem and Back: A Personal Account*, 1976. About: John J. Clayton, *Saul Bellow: In Defense of Man;* Keith Michael Opdahl, *The Novels of Saul Bellow: An Introduction;* Daniel Fuchs, *Saul Bellow: Vision and Revision;* Earl Rovit, *Saul Bellow. Writers at Work*, Third Series.

AN OCCURRENCE AT OWL CREEK BRIDGE (1891)
p. 125

AMBROSE BIERCE (Horse Cave Creek, Ohio, 1842–?)
1. What are some implications of the key words "an" and "occurrence" in the title?
2. Discuss pro and con: Bierce uses the omniscient point of view to enable him to bring off the surprise ending.
3. Is the flashback effective?
4. What vision of life emerges from this story? Ironic? Cynical? Pessimistic?
5. How crucial to the effect of this story is a knowledge of the history of the Civil War?

Commentary

"We are all," Bierce declared, "dominated by our imaginations and our views are creatures of our view-points. . . . In literature, as in all art, manner is everything and matter nothing. . . ." Style is more important than content. Stuart C. Woodruff summed up his study of the fiction: "Bierce's own views were always precariously balanced between the polarities of his response to art and to life. One viewpoint saw imagination as man's greatest endowment; another saw it as the curse of illusions painfully exposed" (*The Short Stories of Ambrose Bierce: A Study in Polarity*, 1964).

Note: The date of Bierce's death is uncertain; he is believed to have disappeared mysteriously in Mexico while fighting with Pancho Villa in 1914.

From Fiction to Film: Ambrose Bierce's An Occurrence at Owl Creek Bridge," edited by Gerald R. Barrett and Thomas L. Erskine, offers the story, the script, and critical articles on both. *Story into Film,* edited by Ulrich Ruchti and Sybil Taylor, offers a comparison of the story and the French movie script (printed side by side), with commentary by the director and the editors. A recording is also available.

WRITING SUGGESTION: This is probably the only short story ever adapted three times into a movie. What is inherently cinematic about this story? How might it be adapted to the movies three different ways?

This story appears in *Tales of Soldiers and Civilians,* 1891 (reissued, with some revisions, as *In the Midst of Life,* 1898). Nonfiction: *The Devil's Dictionary,* 1911. Stories: *Can Such Things Be?,* 1893. About: M. E. Grenander, *Ambrose Bierce;* Robert A. Wiggins, *Ambrose Bierce;* Napier Wilt, "Ambrose Bierce and the Civil War," *American Literature,* I (1929), 260–285; Stuart C. Woodruff, *The Short Stories of Ambrose Bierce: A Study in Polarity,* 1964.

THE GARDEN OF FORKING PATHS (1956)   p. 133

JORGE LUIS BORGES (Buenos Aires, Argentina, 1899–1986)

1. Find and discuss passages that suggest the way the fictionist may want you to approach his fiction. Consider, for instance, the passage on p. 131 that begins: "The Garden of Forking Paths is an enormous riddle, or parable . . ." and ends ". . . prohibits its mention."
2. What questions and implications are raised by the first two missing pages of Yu Tsun's deposition, and by the footnote?
3. Why does Borges make his narrator tell the reader very early that he has "outwitted" Madden, thus apparently undercutting the element of suspense?
   How does that strategy, used more than once, affect the reader's response to the story from segment to segment?
4. Borges, speaking metaphorically, has called this a detective story. Who is the detective and what is his mode of operation?
5. Specifically, how do the narrator's ways of perceiving, his imaginings, his meditations on space and time and other matters, anticipate and parallel particular aspects of his visit with Stephen Albert?
6. What are some of the thematic implications of Yu Tsun's killing of the man to whom he was grateful?
7. What questions remain unanswered, and why?

Commentary

To some degree every work of fiction functions on this principle: seldom say exactly what you mean. Some passages in fiction, especially early passages, suggest ways in which the writer wants the reader to approach the reading of the story. The following passage illustrates both the preceding statements: Arthur says Ts'ui Pen's novel "is an enormous riddle, or parable, whose theme is time; this recondite cause prohibits its mention" (p. 139). On page 138 there is another such passage. And here is another: "To omit a word always, to resort to inept phrases and obvious periphrases, is perhaps the most emphatic way of stressing it" (p. 139).

Because two pages are supposedly missing from Yu Tsun's deposition, we wonder whether those pages may not contain important elements. How can we trust any of the story? Notice the technical consequence of the missing pages; the fiction begins with a narrative hook: ". . . and I hung up the receiver." Who is the "manuscript editor"? Look at the first line of the footnote. The editor's obvious prejudice suggests that he might be Captain Madden himself. Did he suppress the first two pages? Did the editor edit only the first paragraph, only Yu Tsun's deposition, or both? While answers to these questions are irrelevant to truth, they stimulate and enhance the workings of the reader's imagination. What matters to us here is not facts but the shape of Borges' imagination.

By making his narrator tell the reader very early that he has "mocked" Madden, Borges only "apparently" undercuts the element of suspense in his story, for we only wonder all the more how he mocked him. From segment to segment of the story, the enigmatic utterances and behavior of the narrator (explained later, but never fully) keep the element of suspense alive.

Borges plays the more important elements off the detective elements. In another work in *Ficciones*, Borge speaks of a "detective story mechanism" with a "mystic undercurrent." In "Garden," detective story suspense and "mystic" elements enhance each other. Even Stephen Albert uses detective story elements as metaphors (see p. 138). The mystic dimension or undercurrent is suggested in the same paragraph, in which Yu Tsun feels one way but will act in another. Borges' mode of operation is to turn up clues and leave them with the reader. That's why there are no definite answers to the seven questions posed above.

Most of the thematic implications of this fiction apply to all men generally, but Yu Tsun's killing of the man to whom he was grateful has particular implications. Because he thinks the culmination of his "innumerable ancestors" lies in him, he wants to prove to the Chief "that a yellow man could save" the German armies. Review the passages in his conversation with Albert concerning the garden and time. In this place, at this time, as this person, out of a mortal pride in his race that overwhelms his intuition of belonging to the labyrinth of time-space consciousness his grandfather described, Tsun kills Albert, and feels "innumerable contrition and weariness."

Although as a detective story this fiction ends with the obvious questions answered, its "mystic undercurrent" throws up all sorts of unresolved and perhaps unresolvable ambiguities. For instance, is there any relation between the two letters? What other questions remain unanswered?

Why is Tsun, a Chinese, in the service of Germany? Why is Madden, an Irishman, in the service of England? What other questions do these questions raise? For instance, did Madden, too, want word to reach Berlin?

WRITING SUGGESTION: Take issue with one of the comments in the essay above.

This story is from *Ficciones*, 1962. Stories: *A Personal Anthology*, 1961; *Labyrinths*, 1962; *Doctor Brodie's Report*, 1970; *The Book of Land*, 1975. No novels. Nonfiction: *Borges on Writing*, Norman Thomas di Giovanni, ed. About: Jaime Alazark, "Kabbalistic Traits in Borges's Narration," *Studies in Short Fiction* VII (Winter 1971), 78–82; George R. McMurray, *Jorges Luis Borges;* Carlos Navarro, "The Endlessness in Borges' Fiction," *Modern Fiction Studies,* XIX (Autumn 1973), 395–405; Carter Wheelock, *The Mythmaker: A Study of Motif and Symbol in the Short Stories of Jorges Luis Borges; Writers at Work*, Fourth Series.

THE DEMON LOVER (1946)   p. 141

ELIZABETH BOWEN (Dublin, Ireland, 1899–1973)

1. What typical and atypical elements of ghost stories are at work in this story?
2. What words denoting death and decay does Bowen use?
3. What details and images, sometimes repeated, make this story vivid from moment to moment?
4. What line on page 145 renders the ending ambiguous?
5. What does this story convey about the lingering effects of war?

WRITING SUGGESTIONS: 1) Derive a topic from question 1; 2) Compare with "Yellow Woman" by Leslie Silko (p. 932).

This story appears in *The Demon Lover*, 1946. Stories: *Encounters*, 1923; *A Day in the Dark*, 1965. Most famous novels: *The House in Paris*, 1936, and *The Death of the Heart*, 1938. About: Walter Allan, ed., "Notes on Writing a Novel," in *Writers on Writing;* Allan E. Austin, *Elizabeth Bowen;* Joycelyn Brooke, *Elizabeth Bowen;* William Webster Heath, *Elizabeth Bowen: An Introduction to Her Novels.*

REST CURE (1931)   p. 147

KAY BOYLE (St. Paul, Minnesota, 1903)

1. Kay Boyle says the death of the English novelist D. H. Lawrence inspired her to write this story. For the story to have its effect, must the reader know this?
2. Boyle says she wanted to show two things in this story: the individual

"being persecuted, as usual, by the conformist," and "the loneliness of man." In what ways did she achieve her purpose?

3. Describe the roles of the wife and the male visitor in contributing to Boyle's stated purpose.

4. Beyond her stated purpose, what does Boyle achieve? For instance, what is the effect of the role of the father in the story?

5. What is the function of the sun and the flowers in the story?

6. Does Boyle express any aspect of D. H. Lawrence as man and artist that is also expressed in Lawrence's own short story "The Rocking Horse Winner" on page 582?

7. Boyle claims Lawrence as an influence on her writing. In a comparison of "Rest Cure" with "The Rocking Horse Winner" do you discern indications of that influence?

WRITING SUGGESTION: Whit and Hallie Burnett, editors of *Story*, in which "Rest Cure" first appeared, asked writers to choose a story for a book they were editing, *The Modern Short Story in the Making*, and to comment on their choice. Boyle said that in "Rest Cure" she wanted to show the individual "being persecuted, as usual, by the conformist." Show how her comment does or does not apply to the story.

This story appears in *First Lover and Other Stories*, 1933. Stories: *The White Horses of Vienna and Other Stories*, 1936; *Fifty Stories*, 1980. Novels: *Generation Without Farewell*, 1960. About: Richard C. Carpenter, "Kay Boyle," *College English*, XV (November 1953), 81–87; Sandra Whipple Spanier, *Kay Boyle, Artist and Activist*. Interview in *Fiction! Interviews with Northern California Novelists*, Dan Tooker and Roger Hofheins, eds.

THE GUEST (1957)   p. 153

ALBERT CAMUS (Frenchman, born in Mondovi, Algeria, 1913–1960)

1. This story offers a good example of the third person, central intelligence point of view. Are there any lapses? Where?

2. What are some possible meanings of the title?

3. Where is Tinguit? What is the setting in time?

4. Why did Camus create a family killing, not a political one?

5. Compare Daru and Balducci with regard to colonization, revolution, and the prisoner.

6. What in Daru's character explains why he refuses to hand over the prisoner?

7. Discuss the theme of isolation (solitude, silence, landscape, weather) versus brotherhood.

8. In what sense does Daru become a stranger in the land of his birth?

9. What is implied about Daru's future in the final paragraph?

Compare with Achebe's "Civil Peace" (1).

WRITING SUGGESTION: Derive a topic from question 7.

This story appears in *The Exile and the Kingdom,* 1957, Camus' only book of stories. Novels: *The Stranger,* 1942; *The Plague,* 1947; *The Fall,* 1957. Play: *Caligula,* 1944. Nonfiction: *The Myth of Sisyphus,* 1942; *The Rebel,* 1951. Nobel Prize, 1957. Essays: *Resistance, Rebellion, and Death,* 1961. About: Lev Braun, *Witness of Decline: Albert Camus, Moralist of the Absurd;* Germaine Bree, *Camus;* Donald Lavere, *The Unique Creation of Albert Camus.*

WHAT WE TALK ABOUT WHEN WE TALK ABOUT LOVE (1981)   p. 164

RAYMOND CARVER (Clatskanie, Oregon, 1938–1988)
   1. What are some possible implications of key words in the title, "we" and "love"?
   2. How does the word "talk" apply to each of the characters?
   3. Does Laura's attitude change?
   4. What are the functions of Ed (and his suicide) and the old couple in the story?
   5. What does the last line suggest?
   6. What is ironic about Mel's use of the four letter word?
   7. Discuss pro and con: This story is a good example of the need for censorship in this country.

Commentary

Carver has said that he doesn't think fiction has to affect social change to justify itself. "It just has to be there for the fierce pleasure we take in doing it, and the different kind of pleasure that's taken in reading something that's durable and made to last, as well as beautiful in and of itself. Something that throws off these sparks—a persistent and steady glow, however dim" (*Writers at Work,* Seventh Series, p. 327). He says that in writing the stories in *What We Talk About When We Talk About Love* every move was "intentional" and "calculated." Many of his readers find a "fierce" pleasure in Carver's economical prose, which has been called "minimalist," a term he abhorred. He is also known for writing often in the present tense. The influence of Carver is readily seen in creative writing workshops and in the published stories of many new young writers, male and female.

Compare with the stories by Adams (p. 6) and Beattie (p. 97).

WRITING SUGGESTION: Write a paper in response to this question: In what sense is this story more about the narrator than about Mel?

This story is from the collection of the same name, 1981. Stories: *Will You Please Be Quiet, Please* (1976); *Where I'm Calling From, New and Selected Stories* (1988). Carver also published books of poems. About: Marc Chenetir, "Living on/off the 'Reserve': Performance, Interrogation, and Negativity in the works of Raymond Carver," in *Critical Angles;* Arthur M. Saltzman, *Understanding Raymond Carver;* Interview in *Reasons to Believe,* 1–27, Michael Schumacher, ed.; *Dictionary of Literary Biography, Yearly,* 1984 and 1988; *Contemporary Novelists,* 4th ed.

PAUL'S CASE (1905)   p. 174

WILLA CATHER (Gore, Virginia, 1873–1947)

1. In what ways do Paul's artistic ideals conflict with the middle class's materialistic ideas?
2. In her choice of details, how does Cather employ the device of ironic contrast to describe Paul and his ideal world and to describe the real environment and its inhabitants?
3. How does Cather's style evolve out of the point of view she employs?
4. Why is the story called "Paul's Case"? What implications, if any, contribute to make up a psychological diagnosis of Paul's behavior?

Commentary

"A Study in Temperament" was Cather's subtitle for "Paul's Case" in the 1905 version published in *The Troll Garden.* Although Paul is not a practicing artist, the story is a study in the artistic temperament. The reader follows Paul's responses to literature, music, opera, painting. Each form of art can provide him with "the spark, the indescribable thrill that made his imagination master of his sense." Paul truly lives only in the theatre, and at Carnegie Hall "the rest was but a sleep and a forgetting."

In his pursuit of the ideals of art, Paul comes into conflict with people who pursue the materialistic ideals of middle-class America at the turn of the century. Criticism of American values is implied in Cather's description of the environment in which Paul was born and grew up. Those values are clearly set forth in the passages dealing with the "clerk to one of the magnates of a great steel company." Paul does not simply refuse to conform; he actively rejects and rebels in pursuit of what he, and perhaps Cather, considers to be superior values. Living in his rich imagination in the kingdom of art, he finds lying to those who live in the so-called real world, the kingdom of iron, easy.

Paul's single link with the kingdom of iron is his admitted envy of the legendary iron kings who are wealthy enough to live sophisticated, refined, romantic lives in exotic cities. When he steals their money, he is able to make his ideal into reality. In the sense of power money provides, he finds peace, but only briefly. Then, "All the world becomes Cordelia Street." In Cather's vision, a Darwinian determinism works against an obsolete species; Paul apes the old-world aristocratic aestheticism that is ill-adapted to the new world of iron. Cather contrasts Pittsburgh with New York, the holy city of art; Cordelia Street with the streets of New York; Paul's house with the Schenley Hotel in Pittsburgh and the Waldorf in New York. Cather enhances these details with symbolic images: the reality of Cordelia Street is symbolized in tepid, dark water in contrast to the "blue-and-white Mediterranean shore bathed in perpetual sunshine" that symbolizes Paul's romantic dream world.

The point of view technique that would enable Cather to show the contrast and conflict between the two apparently irreconcilable kingdoms of iron and art is inevitably omniscient. In the opening two pages, she poses the conflict very clearly, giving the reader Paul's and his teacher's view of his predicament. After several passages, she focuses on Paul; the reader experiences Paul's responses to aspects of the two opposed kingdoms. The contrast between the two is emphasized by the omniscient narrator's abrupt shift from Pittsburgh to the train en route to New York. It may be effectively argued that if Cather's primary purpose is more to persuade her reader to empathize with Paul than to articulate a vision of life, the third-person, central intelligence point of view would have been the inevitable choice.

Cather's rather formal style, appropriate to the omniscient point of view, enables her to put some distance between the reader and Paul. Comparison of the 1905 *Troll Garden* version of this story with the 1920 *Youth and the Bright Medusa* version reveals Cather's effort to tone down the omniscient voice in those passages intended to focus on Paul's own interior responses. She cut the following lines, among others: "It was not the first time that Paul had steered through treacherous waters"; "Even under the glow of his wine he was never boisterous, though he found the stuff like a magician's wand for wonder-building."

There is very little in Cather's use of point of view or in her style to justify a literal response to the title. Perhaps it is to be taken ironically. Who thinks of Paul as a "case"? Ironically, even the stock theatre people "agreed with the faculty and his father, that Paul's was a bad case." One may find in this story intimations of a psychological "study" of the artistic temperament with Paul as a case in point.

In 1975, Larry Rubin argued that it was Cather's covert intention to offer Paul as a homosexual case. If so, one must conclude that Cather's perception of homosexuals, especially of the artistic homosexual temperament, is rather stereotypical. Perhaps the characteristics of Paul's temperament presented by Cather are simply those of the artistic sensibility as she observed it at the turn of the century. To conclude that Paul is homosexual is to alter drastically our response to questions 1 and 2 and to narrow the focus of the vision of life Cather presents in this story.

PBS offers a movie version of this story, written by playwright Ron Cowan. Part of the script and an essay on the story by novelist Rosellen Brown appear in *The American Short Story,* Vol. 2 (Dell, 1980), edited by Calvin Skaggs.

WRITING SUGGESTION: Dispute one or several of the interpretations given above, or agree and/or disagree with the following statement by one of the masters of the short story, Katherine Anne Porter: "Willa Cather was the first writer to express a horror of middle- and lower-class poverty and to give an appalling picture of life in the provinces of this country for the gifted or even just romantic, self-indulgent dreamer like Paul in 'Paul's Case.' The story of a strange boy who simply wanted luxury, a pathological liar, a real 'case' in the clinical sense of the word, this is in one way the most contemporary of Miss Cather's stories: the number of boys like Paul has increased" (a note added in 1961 for the Signet Classic edition to her preface to the 1952 edition of *The Troll Garden*).

This story appeared in *McClure's* and is included in *The Troll Garden*, 1905; it was revised and reprinted in *Youth and the Bright Medusa*, 1920. Stories: *Obscure Destinies*, 1932; *The Old Beauty and Others*, 1948. Novels: *My Antonia*, 1918; *Death Comes for the Archbishop*, 1927. Nonfiction: *Willa Cather on Writing*, 1949. About: E. K. Brown, *Willa Cather, A Critical Biography;* Larry Rubin, "The Homosexual Motif in Willa Cather's 'Paul's Case,' " *Studies in Short Fiction* XII (1975), 127–31; Dorothy Van Ghent, *Willa Cather.*

WILLOW GAME (1986) p. 190

DENISE CHAVEZ (Hispanic-American. Las Cruces, New Mexico, 1948)
  1. Discuss the function of the trees as three metaphors for the different worlds of the narrator's childhood.
  2. How is Ricky a human parallel to the trees metaphor?
  3. Analyze the lyrical, nostalgic style of the narrator.
  4. Is the use of photographs effective? How?

Commentary

Henry James said that the function of the critic is to point out. Point out what? Things that will move the reader to respond more intensely to aspects of the story. If we apply James's principle, in the hope that it might be one of many helpful ways of looking at the way fiction makes its effects, to "Willow Game," the title itself should be noticed, predisposing us to pay attention when trees, especially a willow, and games are mentioned. Look next at the first paragraph, where an author usually introduces key elements. In the first sentence, notice that the narrator was a child before she became aware that there was such a concept as the South. The next sentence implies she has had experiences of different kinds in all other parts of the nation. Notice that she returns to the very different time-frame of her childhood, when all directions were within a single neighborhood but leading to different little worlds. Notice, in a more general way, that up to the last paragraph on page 193, the narrator marks those worlds off by describing three trees and three houses and their inhabitants.

Notice, in the second paragraph, that flowers are described in a religious context and then, in the third paragraph, in a neighborhood context. Notice also an early indication that the style will be lyrical: "yet the asking lay calmly with us." Notice, in the third paragraph of page 191, that along with the flowers such things as the burning sanitary napkin made up the narrator's childhood environment, and notice, at the bottom of page 191, that humor also contributes to the tone of the story: "the cousin who always got soap in her nose." Notice the narrator's lingering focus on the three trees—Apricot (p. 191), Marking-Off Tree (p. 192), Willow (bottom of p. 192). Notice that she uses religious terms in describing the trees, starting with the inclusive term "trinity of trees," along with a kind of pagan emphasis in capitalizing their names. Notice that she begins with the beautiful, fruitful tree, describes next the tree that is like the old wino, and saves the Willow for last. Notice at the top of page 195 that the ailing of the Willow is associated with Ricky's "emerging manhood" and his irrational behavior.

Notice that Ricky hates his brother, while the narrator loves her sister (bottom of p. 194). Notice that Ricky and his brother play separately with a tetherball, a sharp contrast to the mystery and beauty and solace of the sister's Willow. Ricky kills the willow because the sisters have what he is incapable of having. Notice that Ricky is taken away; then the Willow is taken away. But notice that a part of the stump always remains, even after the new willow that the narrator's mother plants is "thriving." Just as her memory of the Willow and all other beautiful and fruitful things live on in the narrator's memory, so does Ricky, a kind of person the narrator has probably encountered in her travels ("backdrop of the traveling me" is "the wall of trees" along the highway). Notice that the new willow (no capital W) "stands in the center of the block . . . between." Between what? Between past and present, childhood and adulthood, innocence and knowledge, illusion and reality, fantasy and fact, sacred and secular—a kind of marking-off tree.

The process of noticing and pointing out in the examination of this story is by no means complete. Many other elements remain unnoticed. Look, for instance, at the narrator's use of the photograph metaphor as a way of getting a fix on key images in her sometimes lyrical, sometimes painful nostalgic recall of her childhood. Her allusions to the shifting time contexts for individual memories are always worth noticing because the time and place setting of Chavez's story is the narrator's memory. After the question, "Notice what?" comes the logical question, Why? The reader becomes more intensely aware of what is noticed and responds more intensely. The next step is to notice repetitions, variations, and further developments of what has been noticed. This process helps make all the elements interact and cohere so that the reader may experience the full emotional, imaginative, and intellectual effect of the story.

WRITING SUGGESTION: 1) Compare this story with "Just Like a Tree" in its use of trees as metaphors. 2) Compare the use of photographs in various stories in this anthology.

This story appears in *The Last of the Menu Girls,* 1986, Chavez's first book and winner of the Puerto del Sol award. Play: *Plaza,* 1984 (14 other plays produced). Novel: *Face of An Angel,* in progress.

THE SWIMMER (1964) p. 197

JOHN CHEEVER (Quincy, Massachusetts, 1912–1982)
 1. The point of view is omniscient. Describe the author's style. Notice his choice of detail, and his direct address to "you."
 2. The swimmer's wife's name is Lucinda. Why do you suppose Cheever names the river Lucinda also?
 3. What is revealed at each of the swimming pools?
 4. Where are the signs that something is wrong?
 5. Why is Cheever's allusion to Aphrodite appropriate? What other allusions do you find?

WRITING SUGGESTION: Consider the swimmer as metaphor.

This story is from *The Brigadier and the Golf Widow* (1964). A movie version of "The Swimmer" appeared on PBS in 1964 and as a feature film in 1968. Stories: *The Enormous Radio,* 1953; *Collected Stories,* 1978. Novel: *Falconer,* 1977. Most of Cheever's stories, including this one, appeared first in *The New Yorker.* About: *Dictionary of Literary Biography: American Novelists Since World War II,* vol. 2; Samuel Coale, *John Cheever;* Scott Donaldson, ed. *Conversations with John Cheever;* Lynne Waldeland, *John Cheever.* Cheever's daughter, Susan, has published a biography, *Home Before Dark.*

GOOSEBERRIES (1918) p. 207

ANTON CHEKHOV (Taganrog, Russia, 1860–1904)
 Readers of Chekhov stories—or of Chekhovian stories, for his influence on many other writers has been profound—sometimes complain of not "getting the point." In such stories, far more questions are indirectly raised through implication than are literally raised or answered. But to some extent all stories, from start to finish, raise questions. And the reader carries on a silent, sometimes half-conscious interrogation of a story. The answers to many questions are latent in the very wording of the questions. "Gooseberries" offers a good opportunity for seeing that process at work, from start to finish.
 1. Why does Chekhov, as omniscient narrator, attribute, beginning in

the first paragraph, the same perceptions and feelings to Ivan and Burkin?

2. Why does Chekhov interrupt Ivan's story again (p. 207)?

3. What effect does the interruption have on Burkin, as expectant listener to a story?

4. Why does Chekhov continuously describe the weather and the landscape, particularly the rain and the millpond water?

5. Why does Chekhov make Pelageya "so beautiful"?

6. Why does Chekhov make Ivan enjoy his swim so vigorously?

7. How does the swim affect the mood of the three men as a group?

8. Why does Chekhov create such a large and varied audience for the story Ivan had started to tell only Burkin (p. 209, third full paragraph)?

9. What does Ivan reveal about himself as he gives background for the story of his brother Nikolay (p. 209, fourth full paragraph and fifth paragraph, ending on p. 214, especially the last sentence)?

10. Do you suppose what Ivan says about farms applies to Alehin? Is Ivan insensitive to Alehin's possible response?

11. What is Ivan's tone as he describes his brother's dream (p. 210)? His marriage (pp. 210–211)?

12. Why does Burkin interrupt Ivan's story (p. 211)?

13. Why does Ivan caricature his brother (fourth paragraph, "Last year...." (p. 211)?

14. How does our memory of Alehin's farm affect our response as we read of Ivan's brother and his farm (p. 211)?

15. What does Ivan reveal, directly and by implication, about himself and his beliefs in his ironic, sarcastic, and satirical descriptions of his brother's mode of life (pp. 211–212)?

16. Within the context Chekhov has created up to this point (p. 212), what is the effect of Ivan's sudden declaration, "But the point just now is not he, but myself"?

17. What vision of life does Ivan describe to his listeners (p. 213)?

18. What possible reactions might Burkin and Alehin be having to Ivan's vision?

19. What is "the change that took place" in Ivan as a result of visiting his happy brother (pp. 213–214)?

20. Why does Ivan "look angrily at Burkin" (p. 213)?

21. Does Chekhov imply here that Ivan and Burkin have discussed these matters before?

22. Given the immediate context Chekhov has created, what is implied by Ivan's speech on page 214, first full paragraph?

23. What is implied by "If I were young!" (p. 214)?

24. Why are Alehin and Burkin "not satisfied" with Ivan's story?

25. How does Chekhov conjure up an external (historical) context for his story (214)?

26. What function does Pelageya serve in Chekhov's story at various points?
27. What kind of a story does a person like Alehin hope to hear?
28. What function does Alehin serve in Chekhov's story?
29. Chekhov opened with a focus on Ivan and Burkin; he returns to them for a moment at the end. With what differences?
30. What do the crucifix and Ivan's final exclamation contribute to the story's effect?
31. Why does Chekhov leave the reader focused upon Burkin?
32. How does Ivan's pipe function as an objective correlative (an external object that expresses some aspect of a subjective state)?
33. While "Gooseberries" is a simple, literal title for Ivan's story about his brother, what does it suggest about Ivan's and Alehin's and Burkin's own stories?
34. How might one argue that Burkin, considering the story's context and the implications it generates, is the main character, thus partially explaining how a Chekhovian story works?

WRITING SUGGESTION: Show the influence of Chekhov upon James Joyce's "The Dead" (p. 504) and Katherine Mansfield's "Bliss" (p. 604).

The Collected Works, 1899–1902, includes several novellas (Chekhov wrote no novels) and plays, the best-known of which are *The Three Sisters,* 1910, and *The Cherry Orchard,* 1904. About: Peter M. Bitsilli, *Chekhov's Art: A Stylistic Analysis;* Irina Kirk, *Anton Chekhov;* Thomas Winner, *Chekhov and His Prose;* Logan Spiers, *Tolstoy and Chekhov.*

THE DARLING (1899) p. 216

ANTON CHEKHOV

1. What are some implications of the title? Is Olenka a darling? What are some of the consequences of being thought a darling? Notice Olenka calls Sasha a darling.
2. Characterize Olenka. Is she naïve?
3. What is the effect upon Olenka of loving four very different males?
4. Define love in the context of this story.
5. Is the ending ambiguous?

WRITING SUGGESTION: Compare Chekhov's storytelling techniques in the two very different stories, "Gooseberries" and "The Darling."

Information about Chekhov's works appears above under "Gooseberries."

THE WIFE OF HIS YOUTH (1889) p. 226

CHARLES CHESNUTT (Black American. Cleveland, Ohio, 1858–1932)

1. As a consequence of using the omniscient point of view, Chesnutt is

able to withhold from the reader the surprise ending that the character Ryder already knows. Is there any other function of the omniscient point of view?

2. Why doesn't Ryder's wife recognize him?
3. What is effective stylistically or rhetorically about Ryder's speech at
   the end?
4. Discuss pro and con: The Blue Veins are racists.

Compare with other surprise-ending stories—"A Rose for Emily" (p.
300), "The Story of An Hour" (p. 246), "Haircut" (p. 573).

WRITING SUGGESTIONS: 1) Prejudice and class structure; 2) Dialect
and "good" English in light of the contemporary debate over the use of
Black English.

This story appears in *The Wife of His Youth and Other Stories of the Color
Line,* 1889, Chesnutt's only book of stories, published the same year as first
novel, *The Conjure Woman.* Other novels: *The House Behind the Cedars,* 1900;
The Marrow of Tradition, 1901; *The Colonel's Dream,* 1905. About: William J.
Andrews, *The Literary Career of Charles W. Chesnutt;* Helen M. Chesnutt,
Charles W. Chesnutt: Pioneer of the Color Line; Francis Richardson Keller, *An
American Crusade: The Life of Charles W. Chesnutt;* Sylvia Lyons Render,
Charles W. Chesnutt; Dictionary of Literary Biography, volumes 12, 50, and 78;
David Ray, "On Charles Chesnutt's *The Wife of His Youth,*" *Rediscoveries,* II,
David Madden and Peggy Bach, eds.

FOOD FOR ALL HIS DEAD (1962)   p. 236

FRANK CHIN (Chinese-American. Berkeley, California, 1940)
1. What are some implications of key words in the title? What is meant
   by "food"? Who does "his" refer to? Who are the "dead"?
2. What are the various conflicts in this story?
3. How effective is Chin's technique of juxtaposing the public speeches
   with narrative?
4. In what sense is the story partly about language?
5. How does Chin employ generational motifs to enhance Johnny's
   problem?
6. What is Sharon's function?
7. How does Chin expand the context of cultural rebellion by alluding to
   other minorities?

Commentary

Even though the protagonist is keenly conscious of his predicament and is
articulate when he speaks about it to his father and to Sharon, Chin uses

the techniques of contrast and juxtaposition to give the reader an even more complex perspective than Johnny's own. Johnny's normal cultural conflict with his father is stalled, both because his father is dying—a secret they share and lie about (unaware that the mother knows)—and because he must take care of him. This predicament is made more painful on this particular day, when his father's Old World culture is celebrating with speeches and parades, and his father is one of the speakers. Another facet of Johnny's dilemma is that he is ashamed of aspects of his Chinese heritage while being attracted to aspects of the general American culture (see examples on pp. 239, 240). A further complication is Chinese-American pride in being part of America (see the italicized passages throughout).

Johnny's conflict with his dying father and the dying Old World Chinese heritage also throws him into conflict with his mother (pp. 244–245), with Sharon (pp. 241, 244), and with the American culture in which he aspires to participate.

Johnny's external conflicts are all the more anguished because he is simultaneously experiencing internal conflicts. He is not sure how he feels about his father, his family in general, Sharon, Chinatown and his cultural heritage, San Francisco and the engulfing American culture. These external and internal conflicts aggravate each other, rendering Johnny's attitudes ambiguous, his behavior indecisive. He is in a transitional stage between childhood and manhood, freedom and captivity, Chinatown and broader San Francisco, the Old World and the New. His father forces him to say whether he will stay or leave; even though his reply upsets his father, it is rather irresolute.

To dramatize facets of this web of conflicts, Chin develops a pattern of contrasts: Sharon and Johnny's sister with the other characters in their reactions to Johnny; old and young, with Johnny nostalgic for his childhood (pp. 241, 243) and eager for liberty as a young man; Johnny's speech and the dialect of his father and of Sharon (pp. 238, 239, 241); ceremonies, of the parade and later of the funeral; and Chinese and Indian cultures, expressed in Johnny's satirical speech (p. 242).

Another technique Chin uses is juxtaposition, the most obvious being that between the italicized speeches and the thoughts and actions which precede or follow. For instance, on page 239, Johnny is thinking that his father is dying (the implication in this context is that the old ways he believes in are dying too); Johnny is proud that his father is brave. This thought is juxtaposed to the statement in italics about bowing in respect; that speech is then juxtaposed to the lion dancers, who exemplify the old ways, and the boys beating a drum in the back seat of a red convertible, exemplifying the new ways. Johnny respects his father to some extent, but he is neither a lion dancer nor a boy in the car, participating in the parade. The effect of the juxtaposition is to stress for the reader images and insights of which Johnny himself is only superficially aware.

Frank Chin has said that he wants his fiction to convey "the kind of sensibility that is neither Chinese of China nor white-American. The sensibility derived from the peculiar experience of a Chinese born in this country some thirty years ago with all the stigmas attached to his race, but felt by himself alone as an individual human being."

This story provides a good example of how attention to general and immediate context may enable the reader to figure out the meaning of a foreign word. See page 241: Sharon's red *cheongsam;* see page 244, Johnny's mother's *cheongsam,* the second, more important instance. Note: "food" in the title refers to the Chinese tradition of offering food to dead on festive anniversaries.

Compare this story with Bambara's "My Man Bovanne" (p. 69) and other stories of generational conflict. Compare also Chin's use of dialect to Achebe's in "Civil Peace" (p. 1) as well as other stories.

WRITING SUGGESTION: "All my writing," says Frank Chin, ". . . . is Chinaman backtalk." Show how that statement applies to this story.

This story appeared in *Contact* and is included in *Chinaman Pacific & Frisco R. R. Co.,* 1988. Plays: *The Chickencoop Chinaman; The Year of the Dragon: Two Plays.* Editor: *The Big AIIIEEEEE,* 1989. Nonfiction: *Memoirs of a Chinese-American,* 1988. Chin has work in *The Young American Writers,* Richard Kostelanetz, ed.; *19 Necromancers from Now,* Ishamel Reed, ed.; *Asian American Authors,* Kai-yu Hsu, ed. About: *Contemporary Authors,* Vol. 33.

THE STORY OF AN HOUR (1884) p. 246

KATE CHOPIN (St. Louis, Missouri, 1851–1904)

1. Would Chopin have been able to create the ironic twist of fate in the surprise ending with the use of any other point of view technique?
2. Describe the several ironies in the story.
3. What are the implications of Mrs. Mallard's use of the word "free"?
4. How does Chopin prepare for the surprise ending?

Compare with "The Wife of His Youth" (p. 226), "A Rose for Emily" (p. 300), and "Haircut" (p. 572).

WRITING SUGGESTIONS: 1) Discuss how different writers use the surprise ending; 2) Examine the relevance of this story today.

This story appears in *Bayou Folk,* 1894. Stories: *A Night in Arcadia,* 1897. Novel: *The Awakening,* 1899. About: Susan Lohafer, *Coming to Terms with the Short Story,* 115–132; Per Seyersted, *Kate Chopin: A Critical Biography.*

THE BRIDE COMES TO YELLOW SKY (1898) p. 249

STEPHEN CRANE (Newark, New Jersey, 1871–1900)
1. What are the effects in style and in structure of Crane's use of the omniscient point of view technique?
2. Since Crane uses an omniscient narrator, who usually tells everything himself, does the reader need the question-asking drummer as a device for getting background or exposition?
3. What elements of the western genre are at work in this story?
4. Describe Crane's tone.

WRITING SUGGESTION: Consider the implications of the bride's attitudes and reactions.
This story appears in *The Open Boat and Other Tales of Adventure*, 1898. Novelist James Agee wrote the screenplay for the movie version of this story and also for Crane's "The Blue Hotel" (see *Agee on Film*, volume two, 1960). Novel: *The Red Badge of Courage*, 1895. Crane also wrote poetry and journalism. About: Frank Bergon, *Stephen Crane's Artistry;* John Berryman, *Stephen Crane;* Edwin Cady, *Stephen Crane*, 1962; Chester L.Wolford, *The Anger of Stephen Crane: Fiction and the Epic Tradition*.

THE SAILOR-BOY'S TALE (1942) p. 259

ISAK DINESEN (Baroness Karen Blixen-Finecke) (Rungsted, Denmark, 1885–1962)
1. What makes this a tale? Consider the title, point of view, style, and the characters and events.
2. Why would Simon want to identify himself with the falcon?
3. Caught in a conflict between his friend and the girl, why does Simon give in to the impulse to kill?
4. What is the theme or moral point of this tale? Is it a story of initiation into young manhood, or of man's relationship to nature?
5. How does Dinesen make the reader accept the supernatural element?

WRITING SUGGESTION: Derive a topic from question 4.
This story appears in *Winter's Tales*, 1942. Stories: *Seven Gothic Tales*, 1934; *Last Tales*, 1957; *Anecdotes of Destiny*, 1958; *Ehrengard*, 1963; *Carnival Entertainments and Posthumous Tales*, 1977. Memoir: *Out of Africa*, 1937, (made into a movie, 1987). About: Eric O. Johannesson, *The World of Isak Dinesen;* Robert Langbaum, *The Gayety of Vision: A Study of Isak Dinesen's Art;* Carson McCullers, *The Mortgaged Heart;* Sara Stambaugh, "The Witch and the Goddess," in *The Stories of Isak Dinesen: A Feminist Reading;* Judith Thurman, *Isak Dinesen: The Life of a Storyteller*.

KING OF THE BINGO GAME (1944) p. 268

RALPH ELLISON (Black American. Oklahoma City, Oklahoma, 1914)
1. Ellison's use of the third person, central intelligence point of view is very effective. Does he ever lapse from it?
2. Is the style appropriate to the mentality of the unnamed protagonist?
3. How is the title ironic?

Commentary

"I wasn't, and am not," said Ellison, in 1954, "*primarily* concerned with injustice, but with art" (*Writers at Work*, Second Series, 322).

A few years later, he expanded on his vision of the purpose of fiction: "When successful in communicating its vision of experience, that magic thing occurs between the world of the novel and the reader—and indeed, between reader and reader in their mutual solitude—which we know as communion." Fiction, says Ellison, is concerned "with action depicted in words; and it operates by amplifying and giving resonance to a special complex of experience until, through the eloquence of its statement, that specific part of life speaks metaphorically for the whole." What Ellison says about the novel applies full force to the short story as well: "And I believe that the primary social function of the novel (the function from which it takes its form and which brought it into being) is that of seizing from the flux and flow of our daily lives those abiding patterns of experience which, through their repetition and consequence in our affairs, help to form our sense of reality and from which emerge our sense of humanity and our conception of human value." Ellison is concerned about affecting all readers: ". . . how does one persuade readers with least knowledge of literature to recognize the broader values implicit in their lives? How, in a word, do we affirm that which *is* stable in human life beyond and despite all processes of social change? How give the reader that which we [fiction writers] do have in abundance, all the countless untold and wonderful variations on the themes of identity and freedom and necessity, life and death, and with all the mystery of personality undergoing its endless metamorphosis?" ("Society, Morality, and the Novel," in *The Living Novel*, Granville Hicks, ed.).

WRITING SUGGESTION: Examine the patterns of irony.

This story appeared in the magazine *Tomorrow*. Enough excellent stories for a book remain uncollected. Novel: *Invisible Man*, 1952, winner of the National Book Award; since about 1953, Ellison has been at work on a second, eagerly awaited novel. Essays: *Shadow and Act*, 1964. About: Edward Guereshi, "Anticipations of Invisible Man: Ralph Ellison's 'King of the Bingo Game,'" *Negro American Literature Forum*, VI (Winter 1972), 122–124; Robert G. O'Meally, *The Craft of Ralph Ellison*.

FLYING HOME (1944)   p. 276

RALPH ELLISON

1. What effects does Ellison's use of point of view have on the various elements in this story?
2. How does Ellison indicate or imply Todd's alienation from his fellow blacks?
3. What are the implications of the various metaphors of flight?

Commentary

Todd's problem in "Flying Home" is not that he, as a black man, wants to fly as high as the white man, but that his pride spurs him to fly beyond the reach of his fellow black men. His forced landing in the field makes him fearful of the displeasure of white officers and exposes him to persecution by the white landowner, appropriately named Graves. But more critical than that external conflict is the internal conflict between his aspiration to fly above his roots (p. 279, last line) and the need every human being has to feel part of a community (p. 291, last paragraph). Todd's attitude develops from one of alienation to one of communion: "A new current of communication flowed between the man and boy and himself" (p. 291). Images and metaphors of flight enhance the reader's sense of Todd's internal progress from "pride to passion to purpose" (Ellison's phrase regarding his novel *Invisible Man*).

Until the end, the flight imagery is consistently ironic; contrasting images of non-flight enhance the force of the irony. The irony derives from Todd's inability to perceive what the reader perceives. The most effective point of view technique, then, for Ellison's delineation of Todd's internal conflict is third-person, central intelligence, with a sudden, bold shift in the middle to first person for Todd's first experiences with airplanes. The reader is locked inside Todd's consciousness, his keen intelligence, but simultaneously has enough distance to see irony in the images of flight, from start to finish.

Ellison repeatedly provides allusions to Icarus, the young son of Dedalus, architect of the labyrinth built to contain the deadly Minotaur. To escape their own captivity in the labyrinth, Dedalus constructs wings of wax for himself and his son. He warns his son not to fly too close to the sun, but in his youthful pride, Icarus flies too near, the sun melts his wings, and he falls into the sea. Ellison's references to the sun and the old man's calling Todd "son" in the opening paragraphs introduce this external context.

One effect of flying too near the sun out of pride is the feverish inability to distinguish reality from illusion. When Todd wakes, he is unable to "tell if they [the two faces] were black or white," or whether the voices are inside or outside his head. Because he is a pilot, one of the blacks "coulda sworn he was white."

The offer of an ox to carry him back to the airfield humiliates Todd (p. 277). Ellison reinforces the ironies of flight consistently with such contrasts. "That buzzard knocked me back a hundred years" is the first ironic flight metaphor (p. 278). The bird of death foils the black hero's attempt to fly above his history. With his keen intelligence, Todd is conscious of many ironies. "Ironies danced within him like the gnats circling the old man's head." But the reader is more alert to the irony of flight in Todd's own choice of simile—"like the gnats"—and his elaboration of it around the head of his opposite, the old man, who is representative of his past. Todd is most aware on page 279, from "Between ignorant black men and condescending whites. . . ." to the end of that long paragraph. Note especially "his course of flight" and "flying blind." The reader should not forget that, whether Todd himself is fully conscious of them or not, the ironic images of flight derive from Todd's consciousness and are not the author's contrivance.

Just after Todd's long, painful meditation on ironic metaphors of flight, Ellison juxtaposes this contrast: "He sighed, seeing the oxen making queer, prehistoric shadows against the dry brown earth." Todd seems unaware of the irony in the fact that the boy, who has just seen a black pilot crash land, is "crazy" about airplanes. Nor does he think of the ironic connotations of the name of the plane he flies: "An Advanced Trainer."

The story title suggests a general irony. Today, he is "flying home" to his roots. "It came to him suddenly that there was something sinister about the conversation, that he was flying unwillingly into unsafe and uncharted regions. If he could only be insulting and tell this old man who was trying to help him to shut up!" (p. 280) When the old man speaks of flight, he often uses anti-flight images. He tells Todd that his plane looked like "a pitchin' hoss." The old man's voice streams "around Todd's thoughts like air flowing over the fuselage of a flying plane" (p. 280).

Before the spin, Todd sees a boy's kite, remembers his own as a child; but the boy, like Todd's childhood self, is "invisible." Todd knows he is flying too high, too steep, and too fast (like Icarus). The buzzard is a comic agent of his undoing.

After the old man tells about seeing some jimcrows flying out of a dead horse and after Todd mistakes a bird for a plane coming to his rescue, the old man tells a tall tale about the time he went to heaven. His tale is a kind of parable meant to make Todd see his own situation in a new light. Just as Todd flies an Advanced Trainer, the old man was supposed to use a harness to fly, but he rebels. "I had to let eve'ybody know that old Jefferson could fly good as anybody else" (p. 282). He speeds, stunts, flies to the stars and around the moon, "raisin' hell," scaring the white angels, "free at last." When he starts flying with only one wing, Saint Peter gives him a parachute and a map of Alabama and escorts him to the pearly gates, an ending as comic as the end of Todd's flight when he hits the buzzard (p. 283). Humiliated by the old man's mockery, Todd consciously uses a flight metaphor:

"Maybe we are a bunch of buzzards feeding on a dead horse, but we can hope to be eagles, can't we?" But in his pride, Todd prefers to be an eagle soaring above buzzards like the old man. When the old man asks Todd whether he wasn't scared "they might shoot you for a cow," he seems to be invoking the nursery rhyme about the cow jumping over the moon.

As his memory of the first time he ever saw a plane comes to him, Todd likens it to another flying insect, a wasp. He got stung twice: once when he mistook a model for a real plane and again when he mistook a real plane for a toy such as the one he had begged his mother to buy for him (pp. 285 and 286). The shift from third person, central intelligence point of view to Todd's first person narration of his memory is rather artificial, but thematically it is appropriate if the reader imagines that Todd has lapsed into an intense state of semi-conscious fever as when he was a child—a kind of feverish interior monologue. This tale of childhood parallels and contrasts with the old man's imaginary tall tale about his own experience with flight. Also, in this section, the attitude that a black man who wants to fly must be crazy is reiterated when Todd's mother says, "AIRPLANE! Boy, is you crazy?" (p. 286). We see that in childhood Todd developed a predisposition to think of airplane flight in bird terms: "each fighting bird became a soaring plane (p. 285).

It is the old man who calls Todd out of his fevered return to childhood: "Hey, son!" As another plane flies over, Todd "feared that somehow a horrible recurring fantasy of being split in twain by the whirling blades of a propeller had come true." Todd is like the invisible boy at the end of the kite string. Old man Graves makes the rules "down here," a contast to the freedom up there in the sky. Ellison suggests the Icarus metaphor again when he writes, "The closer I spin toward the earth the blacker I become, flashed through his mind" (p. 289). Todd relapses into his fevered memory of childhood in which a plane drops white cards reading "Niggers Stay From the Polls," like a telegram from God. Now the sun, "like a fiery sword," becomes the whirling propeller. "And seeing it soar he was caught, transfixed between a terrible horror and a horrible fascination." Ellison develops the racism context further, just before Graves appears with the straightjacket, the ultimate contrast to flight, to "harness" Todd, to turn this "crazy" "black eagle" into a "fly" (p. 290).

Throughout the story the metaphors of flight have, by contrast, given force to the abstract theme of prideful isolation. Lying on his back, straightjacketed, the opposite of solo flight, Todd is carried "gently" away by the boy and the old man. "And it was as though he had been lifted out of his isolation, back into the world of men." Now the ironic flight metaphors recede from his consciousness. "Far away he heard a mockingbird liquidly calling." But Ellison himself leaves Todd suspended in ambiguous images. Todd does not consciously realize what the reader perceives: that he has placed his hope in a boy who is "crazy" about airplanes and an old man who obeys the violent white landowner.

This is an example of an analysis essay that deals with a single image in a story, as derived from the point of view.

WRITING SUGGESTION: Write an essay on the dangers of isolation as one rises in the world.

This story appears in *Cross Section, 1944,* Edwin Seaver, ed. See notes after "King of the Bingo Game" above.

THE RED CONVERTIBLE (1974)   p. 292

LOUISE ERDRICH (Native American-German. Little Falls, Minnesota, 1954)

1. Is the title effective? Why does Erdrich add the subtitle?
2. How does the narrator relate Henry and the car to each other?
3. Where does the narrator begin to transfer some of his feelings about Henry to the car?
4. Why are the boots important?
5. Is the sudden ending convincing? What does it imply?
6. What do the historical allusions refer to?

Commentary

What I find most impressive about "The Red Convertible" is Louise Erdrich's ability to convey a sense of the psyches of two brothers. Lyman Larmatine is moved to tell, or write, about his relationship with his brother. It would be impossible for him to describe directly the psychic trauma of his brother or his own deeper reactions to his brother's mental problems. When he makes an attempt, he says such vague things as "the change was no good." I doubt that even the author, in a work of fiction, at least, could describe such a state well enough to evoke a sufficient response from a reader. Lyman associates certain objects and events with his brother's trauma and his own reactions. As a writer of fiction, Erdrich chooses, arranges, and describes those objects and events in such a way as to evoke a sense of the inexpressible.

As he begins to tell, or to write, Lyman is so full of a sense of his relationship with his brother that he tells the whole story in the first paragraph in figures of speech he will develop throughout his story. His distinction as "the first one to drive a convertible on our reservation" will prove irrelevant compared to the event in which his brother's "boots filled with water on a windy night." Not until the end does the reader discover that phrases like "he bought out my share," "Henry owns the whole car," and "his youngest brother . . . walks everywhere he goes" are not facts but loaded figures of speech.

From the first reference, "And of course it was an Olds. A red Olds," Lyman uses a tone that endows the car with special, almost mythic, qualities.

When the brothers first see it, it looks "as if it was alive. I thought of the word *repose*." They take an impulsive, epic drive in it to Alaska. The last drive is momentous, too. The brothers are together in the car once again, going to see "the high water." "You feel like your whole life is starting," says Lyman. I feel the car's importance for the brothers is an analogue to changes in their lives.

While the red convertible and the trips the brothers take in it are the focal images of Lyman's story, other objects and events seem to me to have a similar effect. Susy's hair "twirling" around him is another suggestion of Henry's joyous response to life's possibilities. But when he returns from Vietnam, Henry's laugh resembles "a man choking, a sound that stopped up the throats of other people around him." Henry's trauma is so suppressed, though visible in his moods and his relation to such objects as the television, that other people, Lyman particularly, respond empathetically but apprehensively. One of the most powerful images is of Henry "sitting still in his chair gripping the armrests with all his might, as if the chair itself was moving at a high speed and if he let go at all he would rocket forward and maybe crash right through the set" (p. 295). Erdrich's skill in embodying objects with a sense of the mental states of her characters is illustrated in her further development of the TV image in the next paragraph, enhanced by the image soon after of Henry "eating his own blood mixed in with the food." I doubt that an abstract, clinical description could make me feel as strong a sense of Henry's mental state.

Erdrich's use of the car and TV set not only make sense artistically, they strike me as being grounded in psychic reality. I know by Lyman's own testimony and by Henry's reaction to the car's pitiful state of disrepair (p. 296) that from the start they made it the center of major events in their lives and consciously endowed it with aspects of their identities, as individuals and as Indians. Lyman is an instinctual psycho-therapist. To lure Henry back to what was once a life-enhancing object in his life and away from an object that intensifies Henry's deathlike stillness, Lyman renders both the car and the TV in need of repair.

Their little sister Bonita senses that the repair of the car is an occasion that should be preserved in a photograph. The power of the photograph after Henry drowns is expressed in Lyman's reaction when, looking up from watching TV himself now, he sees the photograph—sees Henry's face—expressive even then of the fact that despite the therapeutic repairing of the car, "The whole war . . . would keep on going." He tried to hide the picture in a bag in the closet. But even as he is telling the story, he admits, "I still see that picture now, as if it tugs at me, whenever I pass that closet door." Just as Henry and the car under water continue to "run," the photograph in the closet is "very clear in my mind." The photograph is another object in Lyman's life that is in "repose," but alive.

For me, these objects are all like catalysts that bring Henry's and Lyman's emotions together. They drive to the water, which is also a mirror of

Henry's psyche. "It was just at its limit, hard swollen glossy like an old gray scar." Lyman says, "I knew I was feeling what Henry was going through at that moment." The car ride fails to express how both really feel now. In the fist fight they vent repressed emotions and express frustration over the failure of the car therapy. Henry's "mood is turning again." When he jumps into the dangerous current after a wild, laughing dance somewhat reminiscent of his attempt to "know what it was like to have long pretty hair," I am moved to wonder whether he is fleeing a future transfixed before the TV.

In the last paragraph, Lyman makes the car roll into the river, and the phrase "running and running" metaphorically expresses the idea that although Henry has drowned and the car is under water, the experience is still "running" in Lyman's psyche as in his story.

Whether her use of the car and other objects and events were a solution to the writer's problem of describing the psychological disintegration of a relationship between brothers or whether she responded initially, as her narrator does, to the power of association of the objects themselves, Erdrich's skill is impressive, making "The Red Convertible" a story with lasting effect.

This is an example of a personal evaluation or appreciation essay.

WRITING SUGGESTION: Examine the metaphor of identity used in this story.

This story appeared in *Mississippi Review* and is included in *Love Medicine,* 1984 (a novel made up of related stories). Novels: *The Beet Queen,* 1986; *Tracks,* 1988. Poems: *Jacklight,* 1984. About: Contemporary Literary Criticism, Vol. 39.

A ROSE FOR EMILY (1930)　p. 300

WILLIAM FAULKNER (New Albany, Mississippi, 1887–1962)
 1. Why does Faulkner choose an anonymous narrator (sex unknown) who never says "I" but often says "we"?
 2. Is the narrator writing or speaking?
 3. How does Faulkner handle chronological time as opposed to time in memory?
 4. What does Miss Emily symbolize for the townspeople?
 5. How does Faulkner use the rose as ironic symbol?
 6. What are some of the symbolic and ironic motifs developed in the story?
 7. Why does Faulkner use deliberate ambiguity?
 8. Discuss pro and con: The surprise ending is a cheap trick.

Commentary

Young Faulkner managed to compress into this, his first published story, enough material for a novel and many of the elements that came to be characteristic of his fiction; that is one effect of his unusual use of the first person point of view technique and his control of the motifs that flow from it. As representative of the citizens of the small town of Jefferson, Mississippi, the "we" narrator feels a compulsion to tell—in a complicated manner, shifting back and forth in time without trying to make clear transitions—the story of an aristocratic woman who represents something important to the community.

To ask the basic questions—who, what, where, when, and why—about this unusual "we" mode of narration is to stir up many possibilities. The Southern oral tradition of storytelling seems most appropriate, but the style, consisting of such phrases as "diffident deprecation" suggests the written mode.

The community's sense of time is predominately chronological, but it is also, like Emily's, the confused, psychological time sense of memory. Like many women of the defeated upperclass in the Deep South, Miss Emily withdrew from the chronological time of reality into the timelessness of illusion. Emily's refusal to accept the fact of her father's death suggests the refusal of some aristocrats to accept the death of the Old South even when faced with the evidence of its corpse. Perversely, "She would have to cling to that which had robbed her, as people will." But the modern generations insist on burying the decaying corpse of the past. Miss Emily preserves all the dead, in memory if not literally. "See Colonel Sartoris," she tells the new town fathers, as if Sartoris were alive. The townspeople are like Miss Emily in that they persist in preserving her "dignity" as the last representative of the Old South (her death ends the Grierson line); after she is dead, the narrator preserves her in this story. Early, the narrator invokes such concepts as "tradition," "duty," "hereditary obligation," and "custom," suggesting a perpetuation in the community consciousness of those old values.

Even though Miss Emily was a child during the Civil War, she represents to several generations the Old Deep South of the Delta cotton plantation aristocracy. She is a visible hold-over of a by-gone era of romance, chivalry, and the Lost Cause. The insanity of clinging to exposed illusions is suggested by the fact that Miss Emily's great-aunt went "crazy" and that Miss Emily later appears "crazy" to the townspeople. Just after the narrator refers to Miss Emily as like an "idol" and to her great aunt as "crazy," Faulkner presents this image, symbolic of the aristocracy: "We had long thought of them as a tableau, Miss Emily a slender figure in white in the background, her father a straddled silhouette in the foreground, his back to her and clutching a horsewhip, the two of them framed by the back-flung front door." Miss Emily is, then, symbolic of the Religion of Southernness that survived military defeat and material destruction. The children of Colonel Sartoris' generation are sent to learn china-painting from Miss Emily in "the same spirit that they were sent to church." It is because "we" see her as resembling "those angels in colored church windows" that her affair with a Yankee makes her "a bad example to the young people."

The rose is a symbol of the age of romance in which the aristocracy were obsessed with delusions of grandeur, pure women being a symbol of the ideal in every phase of life. Perhaps the narrator offers this story as a "rose" for Emily. As a lady might press a rose between the pages of a history of the South, Emily keeps her own personal rose, her lover, preserved in the bridal chamber where a rose color pervades everything. Miss Emily's rose is ironically symbolic because her lover was a modern Yankee, whose corpse has grinned "profoundly" for forty years, as if he, or Miss Emily, had played a joke on all of the townspeople.

A pattern of motifs that interact, contrasting with or paralleling each other, sometimes symbolically, sometimes ironically, flows naturally from the reservoir of communal elements in the narrator's saturated consciousness as he tells the story: death images, modern technology, legal images, race relations, the house (especially, the window), the Civil War, decay, smell, doors, hair. Most of the motifs, spaced effectively throughout, are repeated at least three times, enabling the reader to respond at any given point to all the elements simultaneously.

By confining himself to the "We" pronoun, the narrator gives the reader the impression that the whole town is bearing witness to the behavior of a heroine, about whom they have ambivalent attitudes, ambiguously expressed. The ambiguity derives in part from the community's lack of access to facts, stimulating the narrator to draw on his own and the communal imagination to fill out the picture, creating a collage of images. The narration gives the impression of coming out of a communal consciousness, creating the effect of a peculiar omniscience.

Imitators of the surprise ending device, made famous in modern times by O. Henry, have given that device a bad name by using it mechanically to provoke a superficial thrill. But the "long gray strand of iron-gray hair," the charged image that ends the story, shocks the reader into a sudden, intuitive re-experiencing and reappraisal of the stream of images, bringing order and meaning to the pattern of motifs.

WRITING SUGGESTION: Examine the various types of symbolism in this story.

This story appeared in *The Forum*, 1930; a revised version is included in *These Thirteen*, 1931, and in *Collected Stories*, 1950. It was made into a short movie. Novels: *The Sound and the Fury*, 1929; *As I Lay Dying*, 1930; *Sanctuary*, 1931; *Light in August*, 1934; *Absalom, Absalom!*, 1936. About: Cleanth Brooks, *William Faulkner: Toward Yoknapatawpha and Beyond;* Judith Fetterley, *The Resisting Reader: A Feminist Approach to American Fiction*, 12–22; Sally R. Page. *Faulkner's Women: Characterization and Meaning;* Frederick Karl, *William Faulkner, American Writer*, 1988; *Writers at Work*, First Series.

THAT EVENING SUN (1931) p. 308

WILLIAM FAULKNER

1. Why does Quentin's style change after the first few paragraphs?
   Note that in the first published version Faulkner separated the second, third, and fourth sentences in the last paragraph on page 316 with semicolons: "There was some fire there; Nancy built it up; it was already hot." Why do you suppose he changed the punctuation and a few words in that sentence?

2. Why does Quentin make abrupt transitions from one time and place to another? What is the effect of Quentin's almost compulsive use of "he said/she said"?

3. The obvious narrative concerns Nancy's waiting to be killed by Jesus. How might one argue that an implied narrative, complex enough for a novel, concerns Quentin's feelings about his sister Caddy?
   Interpreting a story in light of a writer's other work is somewhat risky; a work of art should stand alone. But this story is a problematic work of art because Quentin as a character and Quentin as narrator do not quite make sense without some knowledge of his role in two novels by Faulkner—*The Sound and the Fury* (1929), in which he commits suicide, ostensibly because he desires his sister, Caddy, and *Absalom, Absalom!* (1935)—as well several other short stories. In one possible interpretation of "That Evening Sun," Quentin starts out to write about a childhood experience focussed on Nancy, but the shift in his style suggests that he regresses in the act of writing to a childhood mental state in which he sensed, unconsciously, his sister's dangerous fascination with the sex and violence surrounding Nancy. This interpretation requires some very complex investigation; here, commentary is limited to Faulkner's revision process, after first publication of the story, which only suggests support for this interpretation. For instance, look at the end of the first full paragraph on page 310. The first version continued with:

> "And it was Winter, too.
>
> " 'Where did you get a watermelon in the Winter?' Caddy said.
>
> " 'I didn't,' Jubah [Jesus' name in the first version] said. 'It wasn't me that give it to her. But I can cut it down, same as if was.' "

In the revision, the sexual reference to "vine" and Caddy's direct question are much more explicit.

On page 314, after the line "Caddy asked Mother," Faulkner originally had Mother say, "I can't have Negroes sleeping in the house." He changed "house" to "bedrooms"; his revision emphasizes the atmosphere of sexuality surrounding Nancy and white men.

4. To show how writers revise for the purpose of implying rather than literally stating, Faulkner's earlier version of the final passages of "That Evening Sun" is given below. Compare with the revised version published in his collection *These Thirteen* (1931), (reprinted on pp. 308–321).

Considering the context he has carefully prepared, identify Faulkner's cuts and additions. What is the effect of each cut and addition?

Father carried Jason on his back. We went out Nancy's door; she was sitting before the fire. "Come and put the bar up," father said. Nancy didn't move. She didn't look at us again. We left her there, sitting before the fire with the door opened, so that it wouldn't happen in the dark.

"What, father?" Caddy said. "Why is Nancy scared of Jubah? What is Jubah going to do to her?"

"Jubah wasn't there," Jason said.

"No," father said. "He's not there. He's gone away."

"Who is it that's waiting in the ditch?" Caddy said. We looked at the ditch. We came to it, where the path went down into the thick vines and went up again.

"Nobody," father said.

There was just enough moon to see by. The ditch was vague, thick, quiet. "If he's there, he can see us, can't he?" Caddy said.

"You made me come," Jason said on father's back. "I didn't want to."

The ditch was quite still, quite empty, massed with honeysuckle. We couldn't see Jubah, any more than we could see Nancy sitting there in her house, with the door open and the lamp burning, because she didn't want it to happen in the dark. "I don't got tired," Nancy said. "I just a nigger. It ain't no fault of mine."

But we could still hear her. She began as soon as we were out of the house, sitting there above the fire, her long brown hands between her knees. We could still hear her when we had crossed the ditch, Jason high and close and little about father's head.

Then we had crossed the ditch, walking out of Nancy's life. Then her life was sitting there with the door open and the lamp lit, waiting, and the ditch between us and us going on, the white people going on, dividing the impinged lives of us and Nancy.

"Who will do our washing now, father?" I said.

"I'm not a nigger," Jason said.

"You're worse," Caddy said, "you are a tattletale. If something was to jump out, you'd be scairder than a nigger."

"I wouldn't," Jason said.

"You'd cry," Caddy said.

Caddy!" father said.

"I wouldn't," Jason said.

"Scairy cat," Caddy said.

"Candace!" father said.

5. When it was published in *The American Mercury* in March 1931, this story was called "That Evening Sun Go Down." Why do you suppose Faulkner revised the title?

6. Earlier in the story, Faulkner made other revisions that affect reader response.

   In the first published version, Jesus' name was Jubah. How does that affect the irony of his name on page 313?

   In the middle of page 315, Caddy tells Jason, "You were asleep in Mother's room." In the first version, "in Mother's room" does not appear. Why do you suppose Faulkner added that phrase?

   On page 319, just before section V, the line "I'm going to tell" did not appear in the first version. Why do you suppose Faulkner added that line?

   On page 317, after Section IV begins, the last phrase of the fourth line read "because he was little" in the first version. Why do you suppose Faulkner changed it to read "where he sat on Nancy's lap"?

7. After the story appeared in *The American Mercury* and Faulkner revised it for *These Thirteen*, short story writer Whit Burnett included the original magazine version, not the revised version, eleven years later in an anthology he edited, *This Is My Best* (1942). However, the end of the story is missing. In that version, the story ends at the conclusion of the paragraph that begins: "Who is it that's waiting in the ditch?" Suppose Faulkner authorized that ending. Why do you suppose he would do so? What different effect does that ending create?

WRITING SUGGESTION: For a research paper, compare all the versions cited above, including one more in *The American Mercury Reader*, 1944, Lawrence E. Spivak and Charles Angoff, eds.

See note after "A Rose For Emily," above.

About: Joseph M. Garrison, "The Past and the Present in 'That Evening Sun,' " *Studies in Short Fiction* XIII (1976), 371–73; Jim Lee, "The Problem of Nancy in Faulkner's 'That Evening Sun,' "; *South Central Bulletin* Vol. XXI (Winter 1961); Philip Momberger, "Faulkner's 'The Village' and 'That Evening Sun': The Tale in Context," *The Southern Literary Journal* XI (Fall 1978), 20–31; Charles Nilon, *Faulkner and the Negro*, 44–7; Barry Sanders, "Faulkner's Fire Imagery in 'That Evening Sun,' " *Studies in Short Fiction* V (Fall 1967), 69–71; Robert Slabey, "Quentin Compson's 'Lost Childhood,' " *Studies in Short Fiction* I (Spring 1964), 173–83.

BABYLON REVISITED (1935)   p. 322

F. SCOTT FITZGERALD (St. Paul, Minnesota, 1896–1940)
1. What is the point of view?
2. Fitzgerald's style is considered especially distinctive. What are some of the features of his style?
3. Some critics say the story's five parts are analogous to the five acts of a tragedy. How might that claim be supported?
4. Explain the two words of the title as applied to facets of the story.
5. The locale is Paris in the 1930s. How does Fitzgerald evoke America of the Depression era?
6. How does Charlie's presence recreate the past for Marion?
7. How is Charlie haunted by his past character through Lorraine?
8. What do the various allusions refer to?

WRITING SUGGESTION: The implications of Charlie's past and his future.

This story first appeared in *The Saturday Evening Post*, 1931, and is included in *Taps at Reveille*, 1935. Stories: *Flappers and Philosophers*, 1920; *Tales of the Jazz Age*, 1922; *All the Sad Young Men*, 1926. Novel: *The Great Gatsby*, 1925. About: Matthew J. Bruccoli, *Some Sort of Epic Grandeur;* Richard D. Lehan, *F. Scott Fitzgerald and the Craft of Fiction;* James E. Miller, Jr., *The Fictional Techniques of F. Scott Fitzgerald.*

COMMUNIST (1987)   p. 339

RICHARD FORD (Jackson, Mississippi, 1944)
1. When is the narrator telling or writing this story? What does his telling it express about him now?
2. Explain the implications of the title.
3. How are the geese and the guns objective correlatives to subjective states of the characters?
4. What aspects of the masculine mystique are exemplified in the story?

Compare with "The Last Day in the Field" (p. 408).

WRITING SUGGESTION: Consider the implications of the roles of mother and lover in this story.

This story appeared in *Antaeus*, 1985, and is reprinted in *Rock Springs*, 1987. Novels: *A Piece of My Heart*, 1976; *The Ultimate Good Luck*, 1981; *The Sports-writer*, 1986. About: *Contemporary Literary Criticism*, Vol. 46.

JUST LIKE A TREE (1967)   p. 352

ERNEST GAINES (Black-American. Oscar, Louisiana, 1933)
1. What is the effect of Gaines' point of view strategy?
2. Why does Gaines not let Aunt Fe talk in a section of her own?
3. What kind of emphasis distinguishes one section from another?
4. Discuss the characteristics of Gaine's style. How does he adjust that style to each character's way of speaking? For instance, compare Leola's way of talking with Anne-Marie Duvall's.
5. How do folk elements interact with contemporary elements?

Commentary

One of the major effects of Gaines' story is that the reader experiences a sense of community and its triumph over various forces that threaten it. Talk is one means people use to maintain community cohesiveness. It is appropriate then that Gaines uses a series of first-person narrators to give the reader ten views of this community of southern rural blacks. Each narrator has his or her own personal concern and bias of perception. Separateness is one force that always threatens community; but it is also a reason for needing a sense of community. With one exception, each narrator reaches out and contributes in some way to the feeling they all have that they belong to each other. Thus Gaines conveys a sense of separateness and community simultaneously. He also shows how each narrator is viewed by at least one of the others. Leola says of James, for instance, "Right from the start I can see I ain't go'n like that nigger," partly because he does not contribute to a sense of community.

To show the power of community feeling, Gaines gives the different reactions of the narrators to the passing Aunt Fe, a major figure in the life of the community. Each narrator expresses attitudes about her and we see what she represents to each person in the story. The ten narrators are representative of the many relatives and neighbors. By not devoting a section to Aunt Fe herself, Gaines dramatizes her importance. We imagine her thoughts and feelings.

It is very unusual for a writer to employ ten narrators in a novel, much less a story (see Gaines' novel A Gathering of Old Men). Gaines uses each narrator to lend a different emphasis to his vision of community, focused on Aunt Fe. The sequence is carefully patterned; the end of each section impinges expressively upon the beginning of the next. The story opens with a child's view and closes with an old woman's. Gaines orchestrates his ten almost choric voices with uncommon control and unity of effect.

Although we cannot quite imagine situations in which these ten narrators would speak as they do here, the reader is expected to accept as a convention for this story Gaines' use of first person. These ten narrators speak in the Southern oral tradition, a major means of creating, sustaining, and preserving a sense of community. Most of them use dialect, to varying degrees, from the heavy vernacular of Aunt Clo to the hip lingo of James to the Standard English of Anne-Marie. This variety helps make each narrative distinctive. All use the vivid, imaginative figures of speech and rhythmic patterns found in the oral tradition. Aunt Clo's expanded metaphor of the tree is a classic example—like gospel blues and jazz in the use of repetition and variation.

The sense of community Gaines expresses here is based on rural folk traditions of farming, of visiting neighbors and relatives on special occasions, of caring for the young, the old, the sick, and the destitute, of the black-white social order, of coping with changes. Gaines shows assaults on these folk traditions of the past that continue, in some jeopardy, today.

The dominant metaphor, the charged image of the story, is the tree; Leola early alludes to the one in the yard and later Anne-Marie, the white aristocrat, notices it; Aunt Clo turns it into a metaphor of Aunt Fe's situation. Other motifs and images reinforce the effect of such elements as those discussed here.

Compare with "My Man Bovanne" (p. 69).

WRITING SUGGESTION: Argue that Gaines' point-of-view strategy is the only one possible for *this* story.

This story appeared in *The Sewanee Review* and is included in *Bloodline*, 1968. Novels: *The Autobiography of Miss Jane Pittman*, 1971 (made into a movie in 1974); *In My Father's House*, 1978; *A Gathering of Old Men*, 1983 (made into a movie in 1983). Gaines' short story "The Sky Is Gray" was made into a movie for The American Short Story series on PBS. About: Jack Hicks, "To Make These Bones Live: History and Community in Ernest Gaines' Fiction," *Black American Literature Forum* XI (1977), 9–19; Ruth Laney, "A Conversation with Ernest Gaines," *The Southern Review* X (1974), 1–14.

ACCEPTANCE OF THEIR WAYS (1957)   p. 371

MAVIS GALLANT (Montreal, Quebec, Canada, 1922)
1. The reader's perception of Mrs. Freeport and Mrs. Garnett is controlled by Lily's point of view, but what implications enable the reader to see the irony in Lily's attitudes and judgments about the other two women?
2. What effect have the men in their pasts had upon these three women?
3. On a narrative level, not much happens in this story, but what does Gallant develop on the level of character interaction and psychological processes? Why, for instance, is Mrs. Garnett important in Mrs. Freeport's life and how is Lily affected by her own role in the household?

Compare with "Gooseberries" (p. 207), "Bliss" (p. 664), and "The Dead" (p. 504).

WRITING SUGGESTION: Discuss food as a metaphor.

This story appears in *My Heart Is Broken,* 1964. Stories: *The End of the World,* 1974; *Overhead is Balloon: Stories of Paris,* 1985. Novels: *Green Water, Green Sky,* 1959. About: "Mavis Gallant Issue" of *Canadian Fiction,* 28; Grazia Mendes, *Mavis Gallant: Narrative Patterns and Devices.*

A VERY OLD MAN WITH ENORMOUS WINGS (1972)   p. 378

GABRIEL GARCÍA MÁRQUEZ (Aracataca, Columbia, 1928)

1. How did the title affect your attitude toward the story?
2. Which elements in this story are likely to appeal to children? Which elements are likely not to appeal to them?
3. In what ways does the style of the first paragraph prepare a context for the events that follow?
4. What do the time and locale contribute to the tale-like quality?
5. Cite instances in which the author seems to reverse the reader's expectations.
6. What is the effect of Márquez's mingling of fantastic and realistic elements?
7. How do some of the images evoke the atmosphere of the tale?
8. Which element dominates the tale—imagination or meaning?
9. Does this fantasy tale comment meaningfully, by implication, on real life? Explain.
10. Discuss the humorous and satirical elements.
11. Compare Dinesen's tale-telling strategies, devices, and techniques (p. 259) with Márquez's.

Commentary

The title informs the reader instantly, as the titles of most stories do, that one is entering the realm of fantasy: an old man with wings. That the man is "very" old and that his wings are "enormous" suggest a humorous, perhaps satirical approach. One suspects that this is a tale depicting in a satirical vein the childlike behavior of adults.

The style of the first paragraph prepares a context for the events that follow. The third-person omniscient point of view partly dictates a style that creates a sense of distance from the characters, especially the somewhat Biblical tone. The complex structure of Márquez's sentences enables him to spring unexpected statements upon the reader in the paragraph's first and last sentences. These stylistic elements tend to prepare the reader for the bizarre episodes and developments to come.

The time and the locale contribute to the tale-like quality. Although a small isolated South American village is suggested, time and place are unspecified, as is consistent with the expectations of readers of tales. The locale described is exotic, and the types of people make it seem more exotic. By contrast, the Angel's foreign language suggests Norway and the sea, and other places, including heaven and hell.

Márquez raises, as most tale-tellers do, our expectations about certain elements in his tale, then deliberately reverses those expectations. The reader, and the villagers, expect stereotypical appearance and behavior from an angel. Márquez reverses such expectations and offers opportunities to reevaluate them in a spirit of comedy and satire. The reader expects that the angel will become a carnival-like attraction and that Pelayo and Elisenda will make money charging admission. The reversal comes when the spider woman, a real person who becomes an insect, draws all attention away from the angel, who becomes a man. The reader expects such people as the villagers to kill the angel, but Márquez reverses our expectations when the angel regains enough strength to fly away, a pseudo-happy ending to a nightmare experience.

The effect of Márquez's mingling of realistic and fantastic elements makes the reader tend to believe one moment and disbelieve the next, but there generally is a "willing suspension of disbelief." The characters' lives are so routine and ritualized and their responses so predetermined that they domesticate the fantastic even as they make a side show of it.

Images of crabs, odors, sickness, ether, and hens evoke the atmosphere of the tale. These often-repeated images interact harmoniously to create the atmosphere of sickness and decay that pervades the story. For instance, they are effectively related to the angel.

Saul Bellow has said that "by refusing to write about anything with which he is not thoroughly familiar, the American writer confesses the powerlessness of the imagination and accepts its relegation to an inferior place." Although this tale has meaning, as most tales do, Márquez seems to be simply enjoying his imagination at play, spinning off bizarre possibilities from the main situation. Márquez's general conception and the specific facets of his story are so well created that what we feel at work, even more than thematic development, is the playful energy of the author's imagination, especially in passages that consist of a series of summary statements. There is an indulgence (though not over-indulgence) in the bizarre that suggests the author is almost compulsively playing. In a sense, no matter how serious any author's intentions, playfulness is at the heart of the creative process.

Although fantasy stories are often considered "escape entertainment," fantasy may be employed as a means of criticizing, directly or by implication, the actual world. Almost every paragraph of this story contains an entertaining element, but each makes a meaningful commentary on the actual world, expressing a generally critical attitude.

In many humorous stories, the humor is ordinary (one line jokes) and benign, and the satirical targets are rather predictable; there is often a reconciliation of contending forces that leaves the reader satisfied, complacent. But in Márquez's tale the humor is dark, uneasy, leaving the reader brooding on the story's implications. The major satirical target is the inability of people—the peasants, the church, the medical profession—to respond with generosity and imagination to the extraordinary, even to a creature out of their own religious tradition. They exhibit their worst traits in reaction to the angel.

Márquez's strategy is to plunge directly into his fantasy tale of man-meets-angel, employing the omniscient voice of the traditional tale-teller, offering a general narrative summary.

WRITING SUGGESTION: Analyze the appeal of fantasy.

This story appears in *Leaf Storm,* 1972. Stories: *No One Writes to the Colonel,* 1962; *Innocent Erendira,* 1978. Novels: *One Hundred Years of Solitude,* 1967; *Love in the Time of Cholera,* 1988. About: Claudia Dreifus, "Playboy Interview: Gabriel García Márquez," *Playboy,* XXX (February 1983), 65–77, 172–178; Regina Janes, *Gabriel García Márquez: Revolutions in Wonderland;* George R. McMurray, *Gabriel García Márquez;* Roger M. Peel, "The Short Stories of Gabriel García Márquez," *Studies in Short Fiction* VIII (Winter 1978), 150–68; *Writers at Work,* Sixth Series.

BALTHAZAR'S MARVELOUS AFTERNOON (1968)
p. 384

GABRIEL GARCÍA MÁRQUEZ
1. What is Balthazar's attitude toward his cage-making craft?
2. How do the various characters differ in their responses to the cage?
3. Why does Balthazar offer as a gift the cage he had made for money? How does that affect the attitudes of himself and his friends?

This story appears in *No One Writes to the Colonel,* 1968. See note above at "A Very Old Man With Enormous Wings."

THE TERMITARY (1980) p. 390

NADINE GORDIMER (Springs, South Africa, British, 1923)
1. Why does Gordimer choose a first-person narrator? Is the narrator male or female, or is the author intentionally ambiguous about the narrator's sex? What effect does your answer have on the symbolic elements in the story?
2. What is the function of the males in the story?
3. What parallels does the narrator see between the house above and the

termitary below? Between the inhabitants of the house and those of
the termitary?

4. What does the termitary symbolize? What does the queen termite
symbolize? Are the symbols established (as the cross is) or private (peculiar to this story)?

5. Where does Gordimer use the technique of juxtaposition to suggest
symbolic relations between characters and between other elements?

6. What motifs enhance the effect of these symbols?

Commentary

Most symbols are interwoven among other major elements in a story, but
"The Termitary" is somewhat unique in offering an excellent example of
overt symbolism that derives from a compulsion of character. The narration evolves directly out of the anonymous narrator's gradual awareness of
the symbolic relation between the mother and the termite queen. The first
person point of view keeps the focus tightly on the symbolic pattern. The
narrator ends with a self-conscious symbolic statement.

It is rather unusual for a first person narrator to be so conscious of symbolism. Gordimer's narrator develops a private symbol; even the title she
gives her story is a made-up name for the termite's nest. The first person
narrative lends dramatic immediacy to a rather meditative story that the
omniscient or third-person, central intelligence point of view would have
rendered too sluggish.

The ambiguity of the sex of the narrator may at first seem curious, but
on closer examination may prove to reinforce Gordimer's rare use of symbolism. While the narrator, haunted by the negative image of the mother as
termite queen, may wish to avoid awareness of his or her own sex as a possible parallel or contrast to the mother's situation, the ambiguity enables
male and female readers to identify with the voice of the narrator. The attitudes and assumptions of male and female readers are able to come into
play more freely in response to aspects of the literal family situation and
the symbolic pattern. The sex of all the children is ambiguous. "If a child is
sick, she doesn't have to go to school" is the only suggestion that the narrator, like the author, may be a woman, but the ambiguity seems deliberate.
The namelessness and sexlessness of the children helps to keep the focus
on the symbolic relationship between the mother and the termite queen.
The children are only observers in the symbolic rite that Gordimer delineates. One of the children, the narrator, grows up to become a self-
conscious witness; the details of his or her own life are buried in the reminiscent meditation.

The function of the males in the narrator's symbolic memoir is clear. All
the visitors to the isolated house, in an isolated town, in an isolated part of
South Africa, are males. They attend to the needs of the mother as the
males in the termitary attend to the termite queen. The narrator's father is

simply the male who fertilized her mother (the number of their children is deliberately not stated).

The narrator describes the termitary as having passages and rooms much like the house above it. The narrator also describes the nuptial ceremony of the termites. Having given up her transparent, dragon-fly wings of freedom for the humdrum existence of isolation and "parturition," the termite queen—and the mother—are captives in their separate termitaries. The frustration the mother feels—because it is always she who must assume responsibility for all decisions and actions to carry out the running of her domain—is expressed in her complaint, "I'm not like any other woman."

The narrator consciously parallels the children with the termite children. The exterminators bring the captured queen into the kitchen where the mother is mixing a cake, the children all around her. Later, the narrator finds a book in the library, *The Soul of the White Ant*, in which the children of termites are described in terms that recall the mother and her children in the kitchen.

If the termitary has become a conscious, compelling private symbol for the narrator, some readers may be tempted to enhance it with other elements that seem to refer to established symbols. Gordimer may have intended an inversion of religious symbolism; on the other hand, such speculation may be a good example of symbol-hunting.

To stress the symbolic relationships the narrator does see, Gordimer uses the device of juxtaposition. "I haven't got a home like other women" is juxtaposed to "Workmen were treated as . . . house guests . . ." "Ordinary black ants" are juxtaposed to "My father. . . ."

The pattern of motifs leads the narrator to see the symbolic relationships between the mother and the house and the queen and the termitary and enhances their effect upon the reader: the doctor attends the sick female child as the males attend the captive queen. Motifs of isolation are numerous. All motifs suggest the termitary: the numerous smells allude to the queen and her termitary.

This story appears in *A Soldier's Embrace*, 1980. Stories: *Selected Stories*, 1980; *Something Out There*, 1984. Novels: *The Soft Voice of the Serpent*, 1952; *July's People*, 1981; *A Sport of Nature*, 1987. Essays: *The Essential Gesture*, 1988. About: Ursula Laredo, "Nadine Gordimer," *Contemporary Novelists;* Stephen Clingman, *The Novels of Nadine Gordimer: History from the Inside;* John Cooke, *The Novels of Nadine Gordimer: Private Lives, Public Landscapes;* Christopher Heywood, *Nadine Gordimer. Writers at Work*, Sixth Series.

A SOLDIER'S EMBRACE (1980)   p. 396
NADINE GORDIMER

1. After the lawyer tells her of his experience, why doesn't the wife tell her husband about kissing the white soldier and the black soldier?

2. What is the nature of the relationship of the lawyer's wife and the lawyer to Chipande?
3. How does Gordimer prepare for the white couple's decision to leave? Why do they leave?

Compare with "Civil Peace" (p. 1) and "The Guest" (p. 153).

WRITING SUGGESTION: Discuss pro and/or con: "Never does Gordimer use character or situation to make a political point" (Peggy Bach, generalizing about the stories in *A Soldier's Embrace*).

This story appeared in *Harper's,* and is included in *A Soldier's Embrace.* See note above at "The Termitary."

THE LAST DAY IN THE FIELD (1945)   p. 408

CAROLINE GORDON (Todd County, Kentucky, 1895–1981)
1. What are some implications of the key words in the title?
2. Describe the tone of the first person narration.
3. How is the old hunter a teacher to the young one?
4. What parallels are there between the dogs and the two hunters?
5. What are some of the motifs in the story?
6. Discuss aspects of the themes of mortality, mutability, and man in harmony with nature.
7. What implications are there in the story that the old hunter might have considered suicide?

Commentary

Caroline Gordon has said that great writers offer the reader enjoyment, a deep and lasting experience, while good, but lesser, writers offer amusement, which passes quickly. The reader, too, she says, "has his role to play. There is indeed a moment in the creation of any work of art when reader and author are assigned the same role." Summing up her comments on *How to Read a Novel* (1957), she says: "The reader who prefers enjoyment to amusement and the author who realizes that it is his duty to provide it have the same lifelong preoccupation. Each bends over the great, flowing stream of human consciousness, intent on deciphering the characters of his 'only book'. There is a peculiar pleasure in store for each: the moment when they realize that they are, after all, engaged in the same task—when they salute each other in the shock of recognition."

Gordon's comments describe her own fiction and her own readers. Thomas McGuane, who has written novels and nonfiction on sports and who has a ranch and hunts in Montana, testifies to the enjoyment Gordon's novel *Aleck Maury, Sportsman* (1934, reissued 1980 with an Afterword by Gordon) has given him: ". . . there are sections of this book which seem to me to have been written by God. . . . When I read . . . *Aleck Maury, Sportsman* for the first time, I put it down, unable to describe a single one of its passages; the trance was so deep. I had no irony or reservations about this book. It reminded me that a work of art can have the standing of things which are impervious to irony.

"Still, I wish I could see into the process a bit. Peter Taylor told me that he thought that this was the book that Caroline Gordon was 'born to write.' But that only deepened its status as an outcropping of landscape, a weather pattern, a shoal of fish at the mouth of the river" (in *Rediscoveries, II,* David Madden and Peggy Bach eds.).

Aleck Maury is the narrator of "The Last Day in the Field" and the protagonist of "Old Red," another important short story by Gordon.

WRITING SUGGESTION: Derive a topic from question 6.

This story appears in *The Forest of the South,* 1945. Stories: *Old Red,* 1963. Novels: *None Shall Look Back,* 1937; *Green Centuries,* 1941; *The Women on the Porch,* 1944; *The Malefactors,* 1956. Criticism: *The House of Fiction* (with Allan Tate), 1950. About: Frederick P. W. McDowell, *Caroline Gordon;* W. J. Stuky, *Caroline Gordon;* Ann Waldron, *Caroline Gordon and the Southern Review.*

THE DESTRUCTORS (1955)   p. 415

GRAHAM GREENE (Berkhamsted, Hertfordshire, England, 1904)
  1. Why does Greene's omniscient narration focus on Blackie rather than T.? Is the shift on page 430 to a focus on Old Misery effective?
  2. Would "The Destroyers" have been as good a title?
  3. How does T. differ from Blackie? From the other boys?
  4. Is this story a study in destructive mentality? What might have shaped it in T.? How is he able to bring it out in the other boys?

WRITING SUGGESTION: Base a paper on the following statement by Greene: "The creative writer perceives his world once and for all in childhood and adolescence, and his whole career is an effort to illustrate his private world in terms of the great public world we all share" ("The Young Dickens," *Collected Essays*).

This story appears in *Twenty-one Stories,* 1955. Stories: *A Sense of Reality,* 1963; *May We Borrow Your Husband?* 1967. Novels: *The Heart of the Matter,* 1949; *Dr. Fischer of Geneva, or The Bomb Party,* 1980. Autobiography: *A Sort of Life.* About: Gwenn R. Boardman, *Graham Greene: The Aesthetics of Exploration;* David Lodge, *Graham Greene;* Martin Turnell, *Graham Greene: A Critical Essay.*

THE MINISTER'S BLACK VEIL (1837)   p. 427

NATHANIEL HAWTHORNE (Salem, Massachusetts, 1804–1864)
1. What makes this story a parable? As a parable, what does it teach?
2. What elements in the story suggest a psychological portrayal of the minister as an individual?
3. What aspects of human nature do the members of the congregation exhibit in their responses to the minister from his first appearance to his death, and afterwards?

WRITING SUGGESTION: Examine the use of parable to express psychological insights.

This story appears in *Twice-Told Tales,* 1837. Stories: *Mosses from an Old Manse,* 1846; *The Snow-Image and Other Twice-Told Tales,* 1851. Novels: *The Scarlet Letter,* 1850; *The House of the Seven Gables,* 1851. About: Terence Martin, *Nathaniel Hawthorne;* F. O. Matthiessen, *The American Renaissance;* Mary Rohrberger, *Hawthorne and the Modern Short Story.*

THE KILLERS (1927)   p. 438

ERNEST HEMINGWAY (Oak Park, Illinois, 1899–1961)
1. How does the killers' mission affect Nick, George, Sam, Ole, and the killers themselves?
2. Discuss pro and con: Ole Andreson is the protagonist of "The Killers."
3. " 'The Killers,' " said Ernest Hemingway, "probably had more left out of it than anything I ever wrote." Does Hemingway imply that Ole will be killed eventually? If so, why does Hemingway not depict the killing?
4. How does Hemingway use the following techniques to express the effect on the characters and on the reader of the killers' mission: point of view, style, context and implication, contrast, repetition.

Commentary

"The Killers" is a classic example of a rare type of narration: objective omniscient point of view. Hemingway records events with a camera-eye objectivity. It is as though we are watching scenes in a play or a movie. Note the photographer simile and the reference to movies on page 411. Using a style that is relatively free of adjectives and figurative language, Hemingway presents realistic details selectively. Except for one possible slip, he never tells us what the characters think or feel. But with each line, he further develops a context—preparations for a ritual gangland slaying in a small town near Chicago in the mid-1920s—that enables him to imply a great deal.

The technique of contrast helps to develop the context and to stimulate implications. The way the killers look, talk, and behave contrasts with their deadly preparations. The flat tone of the narrative passages contrasts with the killers' purpose; in the Nick-Ole dialogue, Nick's urgent warning contrasts with Ole's flat tone. Hemingway's narrative tone suggests impersonal forces of death; Ole's tone suggests resignation to the inevitable.

Al's accusation, "You talk too goddamn much," and his evaluation, "It's sloppy," reflect Hemingway's attitude about a style that is overwritten. He consciously forged a style that is distinctive, simultaneously describing surface reality while implying a character's subjective reality. "If a writer of prose knows enough about what he is writing about," he said, "he may omit things that he knows and the reader . . . will have a feeling of those things as strongly as though the writer had stated them. The dignity of movement of an ice-berg is due to only one eighth being above water." But once a story is finished, "the alteration of a word can throw an entire story out of key." Notice the effect if you omit the word "amuse" from the lunch-room scene and the word "wall" from the Nick-Ole scene. A major feature of Hemingway's economic, compressed, concrete style is repetition, in both narration ("counter," "clock," etc.) and dialogue ("bright boy," etc.) to achieve unity of effect. Notice that Hemingway repeated almost all key words twice close together and then later one or more times.

Is "The Killers" simply a realistic account of how two men set up a gangland slaying that didn't come off? If so, why does Hemingway focus so much on Nick? Is Ole the protagonist? If so, why is he in only one short scene and why do we return to the lunch room with Nick? Is this really a story about Nick's initiation into the world's violence? If so, why doesn't Hemingway consistently focus on Nick? In discussing this ambiguity, it may be interesting to keep in mind the fact that Hemingway ended the first draft of this story (one of three that he wrote on the same day in Madrid in 1926) with the exit of the killers. The last line was, "Somebody else has got to do it." The Nick-Ole, then the Nick-George scenes, were added later.

Other Considerations:

Until guns are mentioned several pages into the story, how does the title generate implications?

How does Hemingway generate suspense? Notice the increasingly urgent references to the clock.

Notice the various levels of tension that exist among the characters. A different kind of tension is sustained between the surface melodrama and its implied effect on Nick.

Notice that to heighten tension and terror, Hemingway uses comic incongruity: the descriptions of the killers, the banal talk of food, etc.

Notice the proportion and pattern of narration and dialogue. How does Hemingway use dialogue to suggest or imply thoughts and feelings?

Notice the repetition of the word "think," ending with "you better not think about it."

This story influenced hardboiled gangster and private detective fiction and movies. "The Killers" was adapted to the movies twice: in 1946, with Burt Lancaster and Ava Gardner, and in 1964, with Ronald Reagan (his last role) and Angie Dickinson; both versions ignore the implied emphasis on Nick as a witness; instead, they literally develop what Nick and the reader only imagine about Ole's earlier relationship with the mob and the inevitable killing.

Nick is a more obvious protagonist (usually the first person narrator) of twenty-three other stories, collected in *The Nick Adams Stories* (1972) and in *The Complete Short Stories of Ernest Hemingway* (1987).

Compare Nick with Quentin Compson in "That Evening Sun" (312). Quentin appears in three other stories and in two of William Faulkner's novels.

WRITING SUGGESTION: Analyze Hemingway's style.

Like Nick, Hemingway experienced a series of initiations and rituals and lived by or admired several kinds of codes of conduct that are depicted in his stories, novels, and nonfiction: expatriate, "lost generation" behavior in Paris and Spain, *The Sun Also Rises* (1926); war, *A Farewell to Arms* (1929) and *For Whom the Bell Tolls* (1940); bullfighting, *Death in the Afternoon* (1932); hunting, *The Green Hills of Africa* (1935); fishing, *The Old Man and the Sea* (1952); writing, *A Moveable Feast* (1964).

This story appears in *Men Without Women*, 1927. Stories: *In Our Time*, 1924; *The Short Stories of Ernest Hemingway*, 1952. About: Carlos Baker *Hemingway: The Writer as Artist* (1963, third edition); *Ernest Hemingway; a Life Story*, 1969; *Writers at Work*, Second Series.

THANK YOU, MA'M (1958)   p. 446

LANGSTON HUGHES (Black American. Joplin, Missouri, 1902–1967)
1. Describe the character traits of the woman and the boy.
2. Why does the woman respond to the boy as she does?
3. What effect does the woman have on the boy? How profound is that effect?
4. What are the possible implications of the last paragraph?
5. This is a brief story. Are the characters fully developed?

WRITING SUGGESTION: Derive a topic from question 3 or question 4.

This story appears in *Sudden Fiction: American Short Short Stories*, 1986. Stories: *The Ways of White Folks*, 1934; *Something In Common*, 1963. Novel, *Not Without Laughter*, 1930. About: Faith Berry, *Langston Hughes: Before and Beyond Harlem;* James Emanuel, *Langston Hughes;* Arnold Rampersad, *The Life of Langston Hughes.*

THE GILDED SIX-BITS (1933)   p. 450

ZORA NEAL HURSTON (Black American. Eatonville, Florida, 1901–1960)
   1. Hurston collected folklore. Are there any elements characteristic of folktales in this story?
   2. In the first sentence, Hurston stresses the ethnic. Does her emphasis on race relations or on male-female relations within a certain group of blacks focus on a certain time and place?
   3. Comment on the structure of the story. How important is it?
   4. What contributes to Joe's eventual forgiving of Missie May?
   5. Describe Hurston's style as omniscient narrator. (See, for instance, p. 455.)

WRITING SUGGESTION: Compare and contrast Hurston's use of dialect to Achebe's (or another writer's).

   This story appeared in *Story*. Novels: *Their Eyes Were Watching God*, 1937; *Seraph on the Suwanee*, 1948. Other works: *Mules and Men*, 1935, a collection of Black folklore; *Tell My Horse*, 1938, a collection of Jamaican and Haitian folklore. About: Robert Hemenway, *Zora Neal Hurston;* Lillie P. Howard, *Zora Neal Hurston*.

THE BEAST IN THE JUNGLE (1903)   p. 460

HENRY JAMES (New York City, 1843–1916)
   1. How necessary to the overall effect of this novella is it that James does not give us direct access to May's thoughts?
   2. What is John Marcher's secret?
   3. Why do neither John nor May refrain from naming "it" or the "thing"? (See, for instance, pp. 465 and 464) Why is "it" refered to in the abstract—as "something" (p. 469), the question (p. 479), the obsession (p. 467), and the vision (pp. 471, 477)?
   4. What does May get out of "watching" with John?
   5. What is ironic about May's speeches on pages 465 and 475? What is ironic about John's thoughts and perceptions on pages 462, 463, 469, 477, 478?
   6. How do the following function in this story: knowledge, experience, imagination, consciousness, ignorance? An early instance is given, followed by a later one; find the most important: For knowledge, see pages 464 and 483; for experience, see page 493; for imagination, see pages 461 and 476; for ignorance, see pages 463 and 481; for consciousness, see pages 466 and 469.
   7. Why do you suppose one critic called this novella "a lyric meditation"?

8. What are the salient characteristics of James' style?
9. How does James make deliberate use of clichés?
10. Is the novella length necessary for this story?
11. Tell the story of May Bartram as implied by the story of John Marcher.
12. What do the names Marcher and May suggest in the context of this story?

Notes on *some* of the questions above (the numbers correspond):

1. Even though he uses "we" (p. 472) and "I" (p. 485) as an old-fashioned omniscient narrator would, James pioneered the third person, central intelligence (his own phrase) point of view technique.

3. Because he has confined the reader to the consciousness of a narrator who knows quite clearly what they refer to, James often uses pronouns that may seem vague. The effect is that the reader, forced to pay attention, becomes involved. Pronouns such as "it" and "thing" often, in James' fiction, frequently allude to something unspoken between two major characters.

4. Consider the possibility that before she sees clearly that John will never love her, May's life is rich with emotional, imaginative, and intellectual intensities as she watches and waits. Can that be said of John as well?

5. Part IV is rich with both direct and indirect ironies, especially on pages 482 and 483. May, for example, seems almost always to speak ironically.

8. James' use of long, complex, parenthetical sentences proves too difficult for many readers. They feel as Marcher himself does when he tries to understand what May is saying: "If he could but know what she meant." But readers who get the feel and flow of James' style enjoy it, find it witty, even exhilarating. Try reading a dialogue scene aloud (for example, pp. 472–475) with a friend; then read a narrative passage alone, aloud (for example, the middle of p. 487 to p. 489). The parenthetical delay between subject and verb sometimes creates a momentary suspense within a sentence that emphasizes a thought or an image and provides a certain delight.

9. James deliberately uses clichés, but transforms them in a rich and complex context. See, for example, "whistle in the dark," page 474.

10. Even readers who consider this one of James' masterpieces wonder whether it isn't too long. Sean O'Faolain, a short story writer and critic, ridicules its length in *The Short Story*.

11. Most fiction makes the greatest impact when the writer uses the technique of implication and James uses it more deliberately than most. Line by line, one may infer May Bartram's story from the thoughts and perceptions conveyed through Marcher's point of view.

Commentary

As was noted in the commentary on Denise Chavez's "Willow Game," James believed that the function of the critic is "to point out." To continue that function for James' own novella, below is a list of key words, with page numbers for their early appearances and, in some instances, for a major later appearance. Find the most important appearance.

beast, ... p. 470 and p. 488;   watch, ... p. 467 and p. 472;
lost or loss, . p. 460 and p. 463;   wait, ... p. 484;
miss, ... p. 463 and p. 488;   fate, ... p. 481, p. 492;
suffer, ... p. 461 and p. 477;   light, ... p. 481 and p. 482;
afraid, ... p. 467 and p. 473;   unspoken, . . p. 481 and p. 483;
fear, ... p. 481;   alone, ... p. 465;
friendship, . p. 463 and p. 470;   violence, ... p. 466;
love, ... p. 466;   curiosity, ... p. 473;
nothing, ... p. 460 and p. 483;   interest, ... p. 472;
never, ... p. 482;   egotism, ... p. 475;
time, ... p. 462 and p. 478;   ordinary, ... p. 476;
accident, . . . p. 461 and p. 478;   failure, ... p. 478;
catastrophe, . . . p. 462 and 476;   real truth, ... p. 470.

James also said of the critic that "To criticise is to appreciate, to appropriate, to take intellectual possession, to establish in fine a relation with the criticised thing and make it one's own."

James' notes for this story and his preface to a revised version in his collected works may be illuminating.

NOTES: "(Lamb House, August 27th, 1901). . . . a very tiny *fantaisie* probably—in small notion that comes to me of a man haunted by the fear, more and more throughout his life, that *something will happen to him:* he doesn't quite know what. . . . the years go by and the stroke doesn't fall. Yet 'It *will* come, it will still come,' he finds himself believing—and indeed saying to some one, some second-consciousness in the anecdote. . . . Finally I think it must be *he* who sees—not the 2nd consciousness. Mustn't indeed the 2nd consciousness be some woman, and it be she who *helps* him to see? She has always loved him—yes, *that*, for the story, 'pretty,' and he, saving, protecting, exempting his life (always, really, with and *for* the fear), has ever known it. . . . her hidden passion, but never guesses. It is to her that he tells his fear—yes, she is the '2nd consciousness.' At first she *feels,* herself, for him, his feeling of his fear, and is tender, reassuring, protective. Then she reads, as I say, his real case, and is, though unexpressedly, *lucid.* The years go by and *she sees the thing not happen.* At last one day they are somehow, some day, face to face over it, and then she speaks. 'It *has,* the great thing you've always lived in dread of, had the foreboding of—it *has* happened to you.' . . . She is dying, or ill when she says it. He *then* DOESN'T understand, doesn't see—or so far, only as to agree with her, ruefully, that that very well *may* be it: that nothing has happened. . . . *What* she has said to him has in a way, by its truth, created the need for her, made him want her, *positively* want her, more. But she is gone, he has lost her, and *then* he sees all she has meant. She has loved him. *(It must come for the READER thus, at this moment).* . . . *That* was what might have happened, and what *has* happened is that it didn't."

PREFACE to *The Altar of the Dead and Other Tales* (1907–1909)
   [John Marcher] was to have been . . . condemned to keep counting with the unreasoned prevision of some extraordinary fate; the conviction, lodged in his brain, part and parcel of his imagination from far back, that experience would be marked for him, and whether for good or for ill, by some rare distinction, some incalculable violence or unprecedented stroke. . . . Therefore as each item of experience comes, with its possibilities, into view, he can but dismiss it under this sterilizing habit of the failure to find it good enough and thence to appropriate it. . . .
   . . . He is afraid to recognise what he incidentally misses, since what his high belief amounts to is . . . that he shall have felt and vibrated more [than anyone else]. . . . Such a course of existence naturally involves a climax— the final flash of the light under which he reads his lifelong riddle and sees his conviction proved. He has indeed been marked and indeed suffered his fortune—which is precisely to have been the man in the world to whom nothing whatever was to happen. My picture leaves him overwhelmed. . . .

WRITING SUGGESTIONS: (1) Discuss pro and con: John Marcher is a man to whom nothing was to happen. (2) Discuss pro and con: May Bartram is a woman to whom nothing was to happen.
   This novella appears in *The Better Sort*, 1903. Novels: *Daisy Miller*, 1879; *The Bostonians*, 1886; *Turn of the Screw*, 1898; *Portrait of a Lady*, 1881; *The Wings of the Dove*, 1902; *The Ambassadors*, 1903. About: Martha Banta, *Henry James and the Occult: The Great Extension;* Leon Edel, *Henry James;* Caroline Gordon and Allen Tate, *The House of Fiction*, 228–231; David Smit, "The Leap of the Beast: The Dramatic Style of Henry James' 'The Beast in the Jungle,' " *Henry James Review*, IV (Spring 1983), 219–230.

A WHITE HERON (1886)   p. 495

SARAH ORNE JEWETT (South Berwick, Maine, 1849–1909)
   1. What are some of the features of Jewett's use of the omniscient point of view?
   2. Where does the author use the rhetorical device of personification?
   3. John Crowe Ransom, poet and critic, defined sentimentality as a negative element in poetry and fiction as "emotion in excess of the occasion." Discuss pro and con: the last line is too sentimental.
   4. What does the hero symbolize?

5. Is the author's shift in tense effective?
6. What is the conflict the girl is involved in? To what extent does she resolve it?

Compare with "The Silence of Llano" (p. 17), "Willow Game" (p. 180), "The Sailor-Boy's Story" (p. 259).

WRITING SUGGESTION: Jewett wrote in a literary era of regionalism and local color. Of which is this story an example?

From *A White Heron*, 1886. Stories: *Deephaven*, 1877; *Country By Ways*, 1881; *A Native of Winby*, 1893. Novels: *The Country of Pointed Firs*, 1896; *A Country Doctor*, 1884. About: Richard Cary, *Sarah Orne Jewett;* Josephine Donovan, *Sarah Orne Jewett;* Eugene Hillhouse Poole, "The Child Is Sarah Orne Jewett," *Appreciation of Sarah Orne Jewett*, Richard Cary, ed.; Margaret Farrand Thorp, *Sarah Orne Jewett*.

THE DEAD (1916)   p. 504

JAMES JOYCE (Dublin, Ireland, 1882–1941)
1. Joyce's omniscient narrator focuses mainly on Gabriel. What is the effect of opening and closing with an omniscient view of the setting and of shifting periodically from a focus on Gabriel to more general views? How does that strategy contribute to the theme of the novella?
2. In what ways are the setting and the time more important here than in most stories?
3. Describe the characters and their relationships. How does each exemplify some facet of Irish temperament or politics?
4. How does each character provide a contrast or a parallel to some aspects of Gabriel's personality?
5. Discuss the symbolism of the snow and the rain.
6. How does Gabriel's response to Gretta's mood prove to be ironic?
7. Trace the motifs: light and dark, the goose and other food, the goloshes and other garments, mirrors, music.
8. Who are the dead?
9. Is the length of this novella justified?

WRITING SUGGESTION: Discuss manifestations of the theme of being "thought-tormented."

This story appears in *Dubliners*, 1916. Novels: *A Portrait of the Artist as a Young Man*, 1917; *Ulysses*, 1922; *Finnegans Wake*, 1939. About: Robert Sholes and A. Walton Litz, eds., *Dubliners: Text, Criticism, and Notes;* Richard Ellmann, *James Joyce;* Marilyn French, "Missing Pieces in Joyce's Dubliners," *Twentieth Century Literature*, XXIV (Winter 1978), 465–471; Caroline Gordon and Allen Tate, *The House of Fiction*, 279–282; A. Walton Litz,

James Joyce; Andrew Lytle, "A Reading of Joyce's 'The Dead,' " *Sewanee Review,* LXXVII (Spring 1969), 193–216.

IN THE PENAL COLONY (1919)   p. 537

FRANZ KAFKA (Prague, Czechoslovakia, 1883–1914)

1. What are the allegorical meanings of this story on political and quasi-religious levels?
2. As the story develops, the situations of the officer, the Explorer, and the prisoner are reversed. What revelations or recognitions do these reversals cause in each of the characters?
3. As a metaphor or symbol, what does the machine itself represent? How does its function and meaning change?

Commentary

While this novella has meaning and impact on the realistic level, the allegorical extensions, which create most of the difficulties for interpretation, are more profound. A peculiar logic and vivid detail constitute Kafka's own type of realism: nothing is illogical but everything, as in a dream, seems wrong. No critical scheme can fully account for the very peculiar kinds of tension, uniquely Kafka's that emerge in that undefined region between realistic rendering and allegorical meaning.

An Explorer witnesses an execution in an oriental penal colony (his Western ideas of justice and humanity influencing his reactions). The operation of the ingenious, complex machine is explained to him by the sole advocate of its inventor, the former Commandant, who planned the entire colony as well. The Explorer and the reader are horrified by the inhumane and grossly unjust judicial procedure and by the monstrous instrument of execution. The condemned man is an unsympathetic, uncouth person, "a submissive dog," whose crime is that he threatened to eat an officer who had beaten him for malingering. He, too, is fascinated by the machine, although ignorant of its purpose and even of the fact that he has been condemned. The soldier, probably of the same class as the prisoner, is indifferent, bored by the familiar.

The officer, speaking the language of the civilized (French), which only he and the Explorer comprehend, tries to win the Explorer's support for this manner of administering justice. The new Commandant is an enemy of such savage methods. But though the officer's plea wins the Explorer's sympathy, it fails to alleviate his revulsion. In order to impress the observer with the humanity and efficiency of his outmoded methods, the officer frees the prisoner and replaces him on the bed, to the gratification of the condemned man, the awe of the soldier, and the discomfort of the Explorer, who feels himself to be the cause of this turn of events. The officer's demonstration of faith in the machine, in this form of punishment which must now revert to him in his failure, is a horrible fiasco—the machine butchers him. The Explorer leaves the colony with the conviction that since man has it in him to devise such apparatuses and to submit to them, this kind of inhumanity will become reestablished.

The plot is based on two movements resulting in reversals that involve recognitions. The major reversal occurs through the officer, who moves from the status of judge and executioner to the status of victim, in order to elicit the Explorer's support by a sacrificial act. The minor recognition is the officer's, who recognizes that the critical moment for proving his point demands that he offer himself as victim. The major recognition comes to the Explorer (and the reader) when he realizes that his moral position does not really negate the indestructible reality of that which he opposes; he realizes that the underlying absurdity of man's predicament in the world renders his moral objections powerless except as formal protests. The minor reversal of situation occurs for the Explorer: from indifferent non-involvement as observer to morally ineffectual involvement as executioner ("executioner" because his reluctance to support him drives the officer to self-crucifixion). Consequently, a reversal occurs for the condemned man but is not followed by recognition.

The machine itself also undergoes a change: from its function as an exquisite apparatus of capital punishment—which the officer, under his deluded vision, believes to elicit redemption from the victim—to a machine for perpetrating "plain murder." The story describes the general change of the old order from a state of incipient ruin to one of collapse. The Explorer recognizes that this collapse is a slow rebirth.

The allegory is about man's dilemma as a social creature living in an age of complexity—overwhelmed with guilt, the causes of which remain largely enigmatic, cut off from religious redemption by the confusing, conflicting and insidiously demoralizing forces in society, alienated from the controlling bureaucratic systems (civil, military, religious) that have dominion over him. Estranged from his religion by a technological civilization in which machines usurp all the provinces by which man was formerly defined, man himself becomes an anonymous shape moving through a labyrinth of undiscernable, non-purposeful causes and effects. Even the superiors, the governing officials, are unsafe in their total commitment to the man-conceived processes of justice; as the officer learns, the machine, when put to its final test, revolts and eats him alive just as the condemned man had threatened to do.

In the machine, in the forms of justice and way of life the old Commandant sets up, the temporal encroaches upon the jurisdiction of the spiritual. The condemned man is supposed to experience, as the end result of this "exquisite" form of torture and capital punishment, a kind of religious recognition of his guilt at the moment prior to death when he first learns his crime "in his wounds"; but the knowledge is tortured into him from without (a temporal process) not awakened within his soul (a spiritual process). Perhaps God does accept as one of redemption that moment when the condemned man recognizes his crime, but for those who administer the System there is no such redemption. By "System" is meant the entire, complex undecipherable hieroglyph in which the social structure as conceived by the higher officials is described.

Although the Explorer may retain his belief that the System is unjust (it is not clear whether he changes his mind), he goes away feeling that, horrible and absurd though it may be, the system will reappear because it is in man's nature to sustain it out of the guilt that both distorts and perhaps redeems him. One might relate the entire allegory to, or place the major emphasis upon, the story's obvious religious elements, relegating the idea of the System to the nature of the Universe created and controlled by a cruel, stern but somehow benevolent God. Although this does not seem as interesting or supportable as the temporal emphasis, if a terrible civil apparatus invests itself with religious attributes, the two-headed monster that results is a complex and meaningful personification of all man's problems.

This is an example of an essay that describes plot and meaning simultaneously, as in the long second paragraph, and goes on to express the allegorical meaning and the moments of recognition experienced by the characters.

WRITING SUGGESTION: Compare with Hawthorne's "The Minister's Black Veil" (p. 427).

This story appears in *The Penal Colony*, 1948, and in *The Complete Stories*, 1971, which also includes the famous novella, "Metamorphosis." Novels: *The Trial*, 1925; *The Castle*, 1926; *Amerika*, 1927. About: Max Brod, *Franz Kafka;* Wilhelm Emrich, *Franz Kafka: A Critical Study;* Ronald D. Gray, *Franz Kafka.*

NO NAME WOMAN (1976)   p. 558

MAXINE HONG KINGSTON (Chinese-American. Stockton, California, 1940)

1. This excerpt is from Kingston's *The Woman Warrior,* a work of nonfiction. It was chosen for this fiction anthology as an example of the way fiction techniques may be used in nonfiction. Describe some of those techniques at work in this excerpt.
2. Compare this piece with Frank Chin's "Food for All His Dead" (p. 236). Are the people described in Kingston's nonfiction any less real or meaningful than those in Chin's fiction? Or are they real and meaningful in different ways?
3. How do the events Kingston recounts to us seem to have affected her?
4. Does Kingston's style reflect the effect that the events she writes about had on her?

5. Describe the cultural and time context Kingston seems to bring to the events she recounts.
6. Does this place have relevance for those outside the Chinese culture described in it?

WRITING SUGGESTION: Why does Kingston tell this story?

This is an excerpt from *The Woman Warrior*, 1976. Novels: *China Men*, 1980; *Tripmaster Monkey: His Fake Book*, 1989. About: Sidonie Smith, *A Poetics of Women's Autobiography: Marginality and the Fictions of Self-Representation*.

BLOOMINGDALE'S (1986) p. 568

PERRI KLASS (Tunapuna, Trinidad, 1959)
1. What do the statements in brackets reveal about the narrator? Who is she and what is her relation to Maggie?
2. What do the details (the blue plastic propeller, for instance) suggest about the kind of life offered these young women by their educators?
3. Why does Maggie react so violently when the woman lifts her ankles?

WRITING SUGGESTION: Compare Maggie with the narrator of Oates' "How I Contemplated the World . . ." (p. 722).

This story appears in *I Am Having An Adventure*, 1986. Novel: *Recombination*, 1986. Nonfiction: *A Not Entirely Benign Procedure*, 1987. About: *Contemporary Authors*, Vol. 126 (includes interview).

HAIRCUT (1925) p. 573

RING LARDNER (Niles, Michigan, 1885–1933)
1. Because the author intends for what they say to be taken as either ironic or untrustworthy by the reader, the literary term for characters like Whitey is "unreliable narrator." Considering the implied listener, what is ironic about the things Whitey tells his customer?
2. Most first person narratives are about the narrators. What does Whitey reveal about himself?
3. The customer is sitting in for the reader, so to speak. How do you suppose he responds to what he is being told?
4. Why does Whitey admire Jim?
5. How effective is Whitey at telling jokes or making cracks?
6. When the writer deliberately uses an unreliable narrator, he must reach the reader through implication. Since we can assume that Jim knows as well as Whitey what Jim says in the final paragraph, what might Larner be implying about Jim's action with Paul?

Compare this surprise ending with "A Rose for Emily" (p. 300), "The Story of an Hour" (p. 246), "The Wife of His Youth" (p. 226), or the "The Necklace" (p. 691). Compare for irony with "Why I Live at the P.O." (p. 1029).

WRITING SUGGESTION: Derive a topic from the above questions.

This story appeared in *Liberty* and is included in *The Love Nest*, 1926. Stories: *How to Write Short Stories*, 1924; *Round Up*, 1929. About: Otto Friedrich, *Ring Lardner;* Elizabeth Evans, *Ring Lardner;* Jonathan Yardley, *Ring: A Biography of Ring Lardner.*

THE ROCKING HORSE WINNER (1926)　p. 582

D. H. LAWRENCE (Nottinghamshire, England, 1885–1933)
1. What characteristics of a tale does Lawrence use in this story?
2. What characteristics of the fantasy genre does this story have?
3. Why do the voices in the house suddenly go mad?
4. What does the rocking horse symbolize?
5. Is this an allegory of the worship of religion, of money?
6. Why does the boy die at the end?

WRITING SUGGESTIONS: 1) Examine the elements that make this story adaptable to the movies. 2) Consider the differences in form: purely literary elements and cinematic elements.

This story appears in *The Lovely Lady*, 1933. This short story, the feature-length movie script, and criticism of both are found in Gerald R. Barrett and Thomas L. Erskine, *From Fiction to Film: D. H. Lawrence's "The Rocking-Horse Winner"*. Stories: *The Prussian Officer*, 1914; *England, My England*, 1922; *The Woman Who Rode Away*, 1928; *The Lovely Lady*, 1933; *A Modern Lover*, 1934. Novels: *Sons and Lovers*, 1913; *The Rainbow*, 1915; *Women in Love*, 1920; *Lady Chatterley's Lover*, 1928. Essays: *Studies in Classic American Literature*, 1923. About: Caroline Gordon and Allen Tate, *The House of Fiction*, 348–351; Harry T. Moore, *The Life and Works of D. H. Lawrence.*

THE ONES WHO WALK AWAY FROM OMELAS (1975)　p. 595

URSULA LE GUIN (Berkeley, California, 1929)
1. What characteristics of the science fiction genre does this story have? What characteristics of fantasy?
2. Describe the narrator's attitude and tone? Note use of "our," "I," "we," "you" (see p. 596).
3. Who are the "ones" and why do they "walk away from Omelas"? Where do they go?

4. Compare this story with "Lost in the Funhouse." LeGuin builds into the story the narrator's problems writing it. Is this, like Barth's story, an example of metafiction?

WRITING SUGGESTION: What keeps this from being more a speculative essay than a work of fiction?

This story appeared in *New Dimensions* and is included in *The Wind's Twelve Quarters*, 1975. Novels: *The Planet of Exile*, 1966; *City of Illusions*, 1967; *The Left Hand of Darkness*, 1969; *Always Coming Home*, 1985. About: Bernard Selinger, *LeGuin and Identity in Contemporary Fiction;* Charlotte Spivak, *Ursula K. LeGuin; Ursula K. LeGuin*, Harold Bloom, ed.

TO ROOM 19 (1967)   p. 601

DORIS LESSING (Kermanshah, Persia, 1919)
1. What point of view does Lessing employ? Describe its special characteristics in this story.
2. How much does the style rely upon nuance or implication?
3. Discuss Lessing's conscious use of literary clichés. Compare with Barth's "Lost in the Funhouse" (p. 74).
4. In spite of, or perhaps because of, the author's bullying tone of condescension or contempt in almost every line, does Susan come alive as a character?
5. What does the room offer Susan?
6. Is Susan's suicide plausible?
7. Is this story itself somehow an intellectual exercise *about* an intelligent woman?
8. Is this a novella?

WRITING SUGGESTION: Consider the importances of having a room of one's own. (Virginia Woolf, author of "Kew Gardens," p. 1055, wrote a book on this subject called *A Room of One's Own*, 1929).

This story appears in *A Man and Two Women*, 1958. Stories: *The Habit of Loving*, 1957; *The Temptation of Jack Orkney*, 1972. Novels: *The Grass Is Singing*, 1950; *Children of Violence*, 1952–59 (5 vols.); *The Golden Notebook*, 1962. About: Dorothy Brewster, *Doris Lessing;* Inta Ezergailis, *Women Writers: Divided Self;* Claire Sprague, *Re-Reading Doris Lessing; Narrative Patterns of Doubling and Repetitions;* Mona Knapp, *Doris Lessing*.

GOLD COAST (1969)   p. 627

JAMES ALAN McPHERSON (Black-American. Savannah, Georgia, 1943)

1. Discuss the relationship between the narrator Robert and Sullivan. What are some of the ironies of this relationship?
2. Characterize Robert by examining his attitude toward Sullivan and all the other characters.
3. To what extent is Robert's role as janitor expressive of class and race relations?

WRITING SUGGESTION: Consider how McPherson's depiction of whites differs from other black writers in this anthology.

This story appears in *Hue and Cry*, 1969. Stories: *Elbow Room*, 1978. About: Edith Blicksilver, "The Image of Women in Selected Short Stories by James Alan McPherson," *CLA Journal*, 22 (June 1979): 390–401. *Dictionary of Literary Biography*, vol. 38.

THE WHISPER OF MADNESS (1938)   p. 645

NAGUIB MAHFOUZ (Cairo, Egypt, 1911)
1. How does Mahfouz's use of the ominiscient point of view enable him to tell about a "whisper of madness" in the life of a "sane" person without having to present a convincing psychological analysis?
2. What provokes a "complete change" in the silent man?
3. Having decided that he is free, why does the man begin to question everything and indulge in eccentric behavior?

WRITING SUGGESTION: Compare with "The Swimmer" (p. 197).

This story appears in *The Whisper of Madness*, 1938. Among his forty novels are *Midaq Alley, The Thief and the Dogs,* and *Miramar,* published in one volume in 1989. Filmwriter and playwright. Nobel Prize winner. (The Nobel Lecture, in *Poets and Writers,* vol. 17, no. 4, July–Aug. 1989, 13–16). About: Matityahu Peled, Religion, My Own: The Literary Works of Naguib Mahfouz (see bibliography).

THE MAGIC BARREL (1954)   p. 650

BERNARD MALAMUD (Jewish-American. Brooklyn, New York, 1914)
1. What characteristics of a folk tale does this story have?
2. What do we learn about the Jewish way of life from this story?
3. What is universal about the story—that is, beyond narrow ethnic limits?
4. Compare the Jewish dialect here with other ethnic dialects in other stories?
5. What is magic about the barrel?
6. How are Leo and Salzman alike, by implication if not literally?

7. What revelations about himself does Leo experience?
8. Why does Leo desire the woman who suggests evil?
9. What is implied by the last line?

WRITING SUGGESTION: Discuss pro and con: Saltzman planned the outcome from the beginning.

This story appears in *The Magic Barrel*, 1958. Stories: *Idiots First*, 1963; *A Malamud Reader*, 1967; *Pictures of Fidelman: An Exhibition*, 1969; *Rembrandt's Hat*, 1973. Novels: *The Assistant*, 1958; *The Natural*, 1952 (made into a movie, 1984); *The Fixer*, 1967 (winner of both the National Book Award and the Pulitzer Prize, made into a movie). About: Sheldon J. Hershinow, *Bernard Malamud;* Sidney Richman, *Bernard Malamud. Writers at Work*, Sixth Series.

BLISS (1924)   p. 664

KATHERINE MANSFIELD (Wellington, New Zealand, 1888–1923)
1. What psychological mechanisms or devices does Bertha use?
2. Discuss pro and con: Mansfield employs deliberate ambiguity.
3. What point of view technique does Mansfield employ?
4. How does the surprise ending affect all other elements in the story?
5. What other technical devices does Mansfield use?

Commentary

Mansfield is a psychological realist who analyzes impressionistically a single moment in her characters' lives. Bertha's moments of bliss make her want, for a moment, to touch her husband. Later, she has a "miraculous" moment when she is certain Pearl feels what she feels. The time setting for the story is only a few hours—a moment in Bertha's life—but one prefigured in her past, and one that presages her future. Bertha's moment of bliss precedes another, inseparable, key moment: her "strange . . . terrifying" realization that she desires her husband.

The reader follows Bertha's unconscious use of several psychological devices: instead of expressing her feelings, she, as is her habit, represses them; instead of acting on her feelings, she projects them onto other people, especially Pearl. Bertha's perceptions and emotions throughout the evening predispose her to project impulsively onto the scene what she believes, or imagines, she sees. Mansfield shows the reader how—in a moment, or a series of moments—faulty human perceptions generate rare, romantic emotions that, given the nature of their stimulus, may be doomed to shatter against reality.

The complex nature of this story makes a single interpretation virtually indefensible. One possibility is to read "Bliss" soley as an expression of Bertha's moment of bliss from start to finish; from neither Bertha nor the author does the reader receive clear, literal expressions of negative feelings Bertha might have about the scene between Harry and Pearl at the end. Mansfield's intentional ambiguity raises many questions. Why is Bertha "overcome, suddenly, by a feeling of bliss" on this particular day? What other questions arise?

Though readers may not be certain of the validity of a single interpretation of the story, they may be certain that the techniques which enable us to experience Bertha's moments are functioning. As an artist, Mansfield is an impressionist; just as impressionist painters offer a single image charged with emotion, she focuses on a single image—Bertha standing with Pearl communing with the pear tree, and a single emotion, bliss.

The image is sharpened and the emotion intensified by the controlled use of two major techniques: point of view and the style that evolves most naturally out of it. The point of view is third-person central intelligence; that is, all elements of the story are to be taken by the reader as having been filtered through Bertha's perceptions. As Bertha responds emotionally, imaginatively, and, to a lesser extent, intellectually, the reader receives her psychological impressions via a style carefully controlled, paragraph by paragraph, to suit Bertha, on this particular day, at each instant. Appropriately, in a story focusing on bliss, Mansfield's style activates all the reader's senses.

The surprise ending is one of those literary devices most often open to abuse or misinterpretation. Commercial writers use this device to stimulate a transitory thrill. The serious writer knows that a surprise ending may lead the reader to disregard everything that precedes it. If misunderstood, the surprise ending may generate numerous misleading, distorting ambiguities. When the reader comes, with Bertha, to the surprise ending, Mansfield provides a dramatic demonstration of how Bertha's perceptions have been flawed.

Having chosen the point of view technique most effective for her purposes, Mansfield cannot tell the reader what actually happened between Harry and Pearl. But how does she use the following devices to prepare the reader's emotions, imagination, and intellect to re-evaluate retroactively (in a second reading perhaps) all Bertha's assumptions, preconceptions, and perceptions: the surprise ending, the pattern of implied ironies, implication, the theatre, fire, color motifs, comic contrast, parallels, symbolic images?

WRITING SUGGESTION: Compare with other surprise ending stories—"Haircut" (p. 573), "A Rose for Emily" (p. 300), "The Story of an Hour" (p. 246), "The Necklace" (p. 691).

This story appeared in *The English Review,* and is included in *Bliss,* 1920. Stories: *In a German Pension,* 1911; *The Garden Party,* 1922; *The Dove's Nest,* 1923. About: Sylvia Berkman, *Katherine Mansfield: A Critical Study;* Saralyn

R. Daly, *Katherine Mansfield;* C. A. Hankin, *Katherine Mansfield and Her Confessional Stories.*

BROOKLYN (1961)   p. 675

PAULE MARSHALL (Black American. Brooklyn, New York, 1927)
1. What are the thematic subjects raised in this story? What is the dominant theme?
2. What is Berman's problem? What is Miss Williams' problem? What problem do they share?
3. Miss Williams stimulates in Berman a recognition of all his failures. What are they?
4. What is the effect on Miss Williams of Berman's sexual attraction to her?
5. At the end, what does Miss Williams have, ironically, that Berman wants more than sex?
6. Why is the story called "Brooklyn"?
7. To what do the literature, art, and politics allusions refer?

WRITING SUGGESTION: Compare this story by a black woman about a Jewish man's lust for a black woman with "Going to Meet the Man" by a black man about a white man.
   This story appears in *Soul Clap Hands and Sing,* 1961. Novels: *Brown Girl, Brownstones,* 1959 (made into CBS movie, 1960); *The Chosen Place, the Timeless People,* 1969.

THE NECKLACE (1884)   p. 691

GUY DE MAUPASSANT (Chateau de Miromesnil, France, 1850–1893)
1. What makes this an example of traditional omniscient point of view technique?
2. Analyze the author's narrative technique by locating the turning points in the story.
3. Discuss pro and con: The use of coincidence makes the story implausible.
4. Describe Madame Loisel's character and values before she loses the necklace. After the loss of the necklace, do her values change?
5. Is the ending a happy or an unhappy one? (Review the opening.)
6. The omniscient narrator knows all and may tell all. Is De Maupassant justified in withholding the surprise ending?

WRITING SUGGESTION: Does the surprise ending enhance the theme or distract from it?

This story appears in *Day and Night Stories*, 1885. Stories: *La Maison Tellier*, 1881; *Mademoiselle Fifi*, 1882; *The Sister Rondoli*, 1884; *The Useless Beauty*, 1890. Novels: *A Woman's Life*, 1883; *Bel Ami*, 1885. About: Francis Steegmuller, *Maupassant: A Lion in the Path*; Edward D. Sullivan, *Maupassant: The Short Stories.*

PATRIOTISM (1966)   p. 698

YUKIO MISHIMA (Tokyo, Japan, 1925–1970)
1. What seems to be Mishima's attitude about the events he describes? He often comments directly on what he is depicting. Look, for instance, at the next to last sentence of Part I.
2. What is the effect of opening with the very short section?
3. How does Mishima's use of photographs relate to other elements in the story?
4. What are some characteristics of Japanese husband-wife relationships in the military in the 1930s as evidenced by this story? (See pp. 698, 703)
5. Why does Mishima focus on the sexual relationship between the husband and the wife? (p. 699)
6. What is the effect of Mishima's return to the photograph (and introduction of other photographs) at the end of Part II?
7. For the story to have its effect, does the reader need to know more about what happened in Japan on February 26, 1936?
8. Why does Mishima return to the sexual relationship on pp. 701, 704, 705, 706?
9. Why does the soldier commit suicide? (p. 702)
10. What makes Mishima's description of sensory details particularly important and effective in this story? (pp. 704, 712, 714, 716, etc.)
11. "Each moment had its own vital strength" (p. 704). How does Mishima support that observation throughout the story?
12. What does the title mean? (The word appears also on p. 705, and the idea again on p. 706).
13. How does their impending suicide give the husband and wife new perspective on various aspects of themselves and their lives? (See the focus on "face" pp. 705, 707; see also pp. 710, 713, 716).
14. What paradoxes, ironies, and wonders does Mishima pose in the light of suicide? (pp. 705, 709, 711)
15. How does sex become part of the suicide ritual, along with the drinking of sake, bathing, the wearing of appropriate clothing, etc? (See p. 707)
16. How are death and sex related? (pp. 708, 709)
17. How does Mishima's use of the omniscient point of view technique, with the focus shifting back and forth from husband to wife, en-

hance the effect of all the other elements in the story? (See throughout, but note pp. 708, 709, 714)

18. What are the various rituals the husband and the wife perform? (For example, the farewell notes, p. 710; prayers, p. 711; see also, p. 715)
19. Has Mishima's style up to page 711, where it is particularly prominent, been appropriate for this story of ritual suicide? Note the style from page 711 to the end.
20. What turning point is suggested on page 712 in the paragraph that begins "Resting the sword"?
21. Has Mishima created a context rich enough to give you a sense of what the word *seppuku* might mean? (p. 713)
22. On page 716, the wife releases the bolt to the front door. Where does Mishima prepare earlier for that action?
23. Is this story too exotic for Western readers?
24. Mishima, a doctrinaire homosexual, himself committed suicide years after he wrote this story. Does knowledge of such biographical information enhance our responses to his story?

WRITING SUGGESTION: Examine the role of women in 1930s Japan as suggested in this story.

This story appears in *Death in Midsummer*, 1966. Novels: *Confessions of a Mask*, 1949; *The Sailor Who Fell from Grace with the Sea*, 1965. About: Jean Nathan, *Mishima: A Biography;* Gwenn B. Petersen, *The Moon in the Water: Understanding Tanizaki, Kawabata, and Mishima.*

HOUSE MADE OF DAWN: THREE SKETCHES (1966)   p. 717

N. SCOTT MOMADAY (Native American, Kiowa. Lawton, Oklahoma, 1934)

1. How does Momaday's use of style in his description of the natural and cultural setting express aspects of the characters Francisco, Abel, and Angela?
2. How does Momaday use the device of contrast and comparison to give an impression of what it means both to belong to and to be alienated from Indian culture?
3. Discuss the implications of the contest between the Albino Indian and Abel.

Compare with the novel version of these three sketches. Compare with "The Red Convertible," p. 292 and "Yellow Woman," p. 932.

WRITING SUGGESTION: Discuss the role of nature in the story.

This early version appeared in *The Southern Review* in 1966 and, much revised, is included in *House Made of Dawn,* 1968, Pulitzer Prize winner. *Angle of Geese and Other Poems,* 1974. *The Names: A Memoir,* 1976. About: *Ancestral Voice: Conversations with N. Scott Momaday,* 1989.

SLANT-EYED AMERICANS (1940)   p. 727

TOSHIO MORI (Japanese-American, Oakland, California, 1910)
1. How does Mori use the technique of contrast? Look, for instance, at the narrator's people as flower gardeners and Kazuo as a soldier.
2. Who were the Nisei soldiers of World War II?
3. What famous radio drama is alluded to on page 739?
4. How does Mori prepare for the implied irony of the ending?
5. The implied irony of the ending depends upon the reader's knowledge of treatment of the Japanese Americans after Pearl Harbor. What happened?
6. What does the narrator's story imply about himself?

WRITING SUGGESTION: Compare this story with "Patriotism" (p. 698): This story appears in *Yokohama California,* 1949. Stories: *The Chauvinist and Other Stories,* 1979. Novel: *Woman from Hiroshima,* 1979.

1919 (1973)   p. 732

TONI MORRISON (Chloe Anthony Wofford) (Black-American. Lorain, Ohio, 1931)
1. What aspects of the story of Shadrach in Daniel (Chapter 3) in the Old Testament ironically parallel or contrast with elements in "1919"?
2. How do the story's point of view, style, and structure express its meaning?
3. What is the story's dominant image and how do other images relate to it?

Commentary

While a reader should not make too much of the parallels and contrasts between Morrison's Shadrack and the Shadrach of the Old Testament, and while the story's power does not rely heavily on a knowledge of the Book of Daniel, some comparisons can provide ironic perspectives. Because they suicidally refused to obey King Nebuchadnezzar's decree that all men worship "an image of gold," Shadrach, Meshach, and Abednego were "cast into the midst of a burning fiery furnace"; because they had faith, they were delivered out of the furnace by an angel of God. The King then decreed a severe punishment for anyone interfering with the religion of the three men. Morrison's Shadrack, a black man from Ohio, is, on a very cold day, flung into the "fiery furnace" of World War I. The hospital, the street, and the jail prove to be like the furnace where Shadrack struggles to deliver himself from the fiery crucible of his own skin, bones, and mind. It is Shadrack himself who makes a decree for the welfare of all men: "he instituted National Suicide Day."

"1919" is part of Morrison's novel *Sula*, which is composed of several stories, somewhat in the manner of Hemingway's *In Our Time* and Sherwood Anderson's *Winesburg, Ohio*. "1919" does not depend upon the context of the novel; it has its own unity of effect. The effect of a story is usually most powerful when the point of view, the style, and the structure in themselves, as technical choices, express the essence of a story's emotion, imagination, and meaning. In "1919," an ordinary black man leaves his small Midwestern hometown, goes through the hell of war, then the hell of his own fears, and emerges to offer a way of partial salvation for all men. The omniscient point of view is appropriate for such a fable. Morrison's style creates a tale-like aura, especially when she speaks as the omniscient narrator, as she does near the end: "Easily, quietly, Suicide Day became a part of the fabric of the life up in the Bottom of Medallion, Ohio." Within this general reference to the community, Morrison gives a very detailed description of Shadrack's private travail.

Shadrack's personal odyssey into the hell of war and the hell of shock ends in the town, where it is focused in the dominant or charged image of his hands. When he awakes from a year-long coma, he is afraid that only his hands exist. Shadrack's fears focus upon his hands until, in the jail cell, he finally sees his face. His hands become "courteously still," because he is convinced that he is now psychologically and physically whole. But he still must "order and focus experience" to make "a place for fear as a way of controlling it." He puts fear in its place each January 3, on National Suicide Day.

In addition to the face motif, other images are related to the hands image: for example, images of order and of disorder. The negative images in the passage on page 735 effectively suggest Shadrack's trauma.

WRITING SUGGESTION: Examine symbolism in the story.

This story was incorporated into the novel *Sula*, 1973. Novels: *The Bluest Eye*, 1970; *Song of Solomon*, 1977; *Tar Baby*, 1981; *The Beloved*, 1987. About: Jane B. Bakerman, "Failures of Love: Female Initiation in the Novels of Toni Morrison," *American Literature* LII (January 1981), 541–63; *Contemporary Authors*, Vols. 29–30; *Contemporary Literary Criticism*, vols. 4, 10, and 20; *Contemporary Novelists*, third edition.

HOW I MET MY HUSBAND (1968)   p. 738

ALICE MUNRO (Wingham, Ontario, Canada, 1931)
1. How does the narrator's references to the future affect our responses to the events and attitudes expressed in the story?

2. Describe the narrator. Notice her insights, perceptions, revelations.
3. How does the title affect our responses throughout the story? Compare with the effect of another "How I" title, the Oates story on page 752.
4. Does the surprise ending work? How does Munro prepare for its effect?
5. With regard to the story up to the "surprise," what is a possible implication of the last line?
6. Is the narrator writing or telling her story or does the author rely on convention in her use of first person?

WRITING SUGGESTION: What kind of life do you imagine for the narrator?

This story appeared in *McCall's* and is included in *Something I've Been Meaning to Tell You,* 1974. Stories:*Who Do You Think You Are,* 1978; *Dance of the Happy Shades,* 1968; *Moons of Jupiter,* 1983. Novel: *Lives of Girls and Women,* 1971. About: *Contemporary Authors,* vol. 116; E. D. Blodgett, *Alice Munro;* Dahlie Hallvard, *Alice Munro and Her Works;* W. R. Martin, *Alice Munro: Paradox and Parallel;* Louis K. Mackendrick, ed. *Probably Fictions: Alice Munro's Narrative Acts.*

HOW I CONTEMPLATED THE WORLD FROM THE DETROIT HOUSE OF CORRECTION AND BEGAN MY LIFE OVER AGAIN (1969)   p. 752

JOYCE CAROL OATES (Lockport, New York, 1938)

1. Is the form of this story experimental? If so, in what ways? Is its use inevitable? Explain.
2. What is the effect of the "notes" device? Of the category labelling? Of the nameless narrator's shift from "the girl" to "I"? Of the omissions of names and passages? Of the shifts in tense?
3. Which passages contribute to the development of a conception about the seemingly chaotic raw material the narrator compiles? How do all the references to hands cohere into a general conception about the narrator's experiences?
4. What do the sections concerning Detroit's weather and Sioux Drive contribute to our sense of the narrator's predicament?
5. Discuss ways Oates creates a brooding specter of violence over Detroit and around the narrator. Why do the girls beat her up?
6. Does the story end happily? Explain.

Commentary

The diary, notebook, or journal format as a technique for story-telling is almost as old as the short story itself. What makes Oates's technique in this story somewhat unique and experimental is the making of "notes for an essay for English class" in slapdash outline form under three general headings. This method of telling a story through labeled, impressionistic (and sometimes expressionistic) fragments is now, 20 years after publication of Oates's story, not unusual. But numbered subsections (here imitating the outline format) are rarely employed in this particular technique. The kind of girl the narrator is, the occasion for her making the notes, and her ironic, sardonic, defiant and mock-submissive attitude gives the technique an even more bizarre aura of experimentalism. Long titles and subtitles frequently indicate a comic or satirical tale; Oates's title, however, immediately suggests an experimental approach.

As in several of Oates's stories, the basic raw material here is that of *True Confessions*. The girl is very conscious that she is writing, and the intrusions of that consciousness are startling. She writes first in fear, contempt, and mockery of the assignment, then in serious compulsion, and finally in terrified self-awareness.

It is important to stress the inevitability of Oates's innovative technique. This expression of the girl's consciousness, her mental weather and environment, could not have been presented in any other way. Had the girl told or written the narrative in a conventional way, it is unlikely that we would get such a startling impression of her mental state. What is most crucial is the way she examines her own personality and contemplates in strained tranquility the other characters. The technique is the story ("the medium is the message"); the story is what happens psychologically in this technique.

One effect of this "notes" technique is that it gives us a more natural sense of the way a precocious sixteen-year-old, upper-class juvenile delinquent feels about herself. Another effect is that the implied fact that she didn't end up writing the essay itself is dramatized; the notes themselves express her inability to describe her experience in a smooth, coherent fashion. This expository method activates our emotions and intelligence; we get impressions of the girl's life that our own imagination is forced to enhance.

The girl is consciously ironic, sardonic, and parodic in tone and intent. By calling herself "the girl," the narrator at first is consciously mocking the adult expectation that she be objective, but gradually she reaches seriously for an objective perspective on herself and her own experiences. When she lapses into "me" or "I" she expresses to some degree an inability to get out of herself. The shifts express the disassociation of her personality, suggesting a slightly schizoid quality in her make-up. She can't leave in the "deleted" passage in VII, 4. The effect of this character-motivated act is that the reader's imagination is activated to fill in the cut-out space.

The "Sioux Drive" and "Detroit" sections enhance our sense of the narrator's predicament. They are objective correlatives, external manifestations of the narrator's inner weather. Her notes reflect the interplay of internal and external environments. The girl flees the weathers of home.

The weathers of places merge; the weathers of the characters merge. The mental climates of Simon and the girl become inextricably entwined. The weather, physical and psychological, conjures up a brooding specter of violence over Detroit and Bloomfield, the jagged, spastic utterances of the notes themselves clashing in juxtapositions.

In the subtitle, the girl promises a "a happy ending." But she does precisely what the main title says; the life she begins over again is exactly the same. Only fear prevents her from repeating the runaway phase of her life, but is she cured of kleptomania, and the suppressed sexuality of which it is an expression? Is she cured of stealing for thrills, attention, and revenge? Nothing has changed. She has been beaten into submission. A kind of living death is evoked at the end, and some readers may imagine suicide. Her choices are aggressive, critical acts of rejection. In "VII Events," she asks, "Would I lie down with him in all that filth and craziness? Over and over again."

"I am interested in formal experimentation, yes, but generally this grows out of a certain plot. The form and the style seem naturally suited to the story that has to be told," Oates told Joe David Bellamy in an interview. When he asked her about her writing habits, she said, "I spend a lot of time looking at the river. Everything is flowing away, flowing by. . . . At times my head seems crowded; there is a kind of pressure inside it, almost a frightening physical sense of confusion, fullness, dizziness. Strange people appear in my thoughts and define themselves slowly to me: first their faces, then their personalities and quirks and personal histories, then their relationships with other people, who very slowly appear, and a kind of 'plot' then becomes clear to me as I figure out how all these people come together and what they are doing. I can see them at times very closely, and indeed I 'am' them—my personality merges with theirs. . . . so I try to put this all together, working very slowly never hurrying the process. I can't hurry it any more than I can prevent it. When the story is more or less coherent and has emerged from the underground, then I can begin to write quite quickly. . . . It is sometimes such a *duty* to remain sane and accountable" (*"The New Fiction: Interviews with Innovative American Writers*).

This story appeared in *TriQuarterly* and is included in *The Wheel of Love*, 1970. Stories: *Assignation Stories*, 1988. Novels: *A Garden of Earthly Delights*, 1967; *Do With Me What You Will*, 1973, *Bellefleur*, 1980; *You Must Remember This*, 1988. Nonfiction: *On Boxing*, 1987; *Woman Writer, Occasions and Opportunities*, 1988. About: David Madden, "The Violent World of Joyce Carol Oates," in *The Poetic Image in Six Genres*, 25–46; Sue S. Park, "A Study in Counterpoint: Joyce Carol Oates's 'How I Contemplated the World from the Detroit House of Correction and Began My Life Over Again,' " *Modern Fiction Studies* XXII (1976), 213–24; Joanne V. Creighton, *Joyce Carol Oates;* Ellen G. Friedman, *Joyce Carol Oates;* Linda Wagner, ed., *Critical Essays on Joyce Carol Oates;* Eileen Teper Bender, *Joyce Carol Oates, Artist in Residence; Writers at Work*, Fifth Series.

WRITING SUGGESTION: Compare the narrator in this story with the protagonist in "Bloomingdale's" (p. 508), "Significant Moments in the Life of My Mother" (p. 42), and "Paul's Case" (p. 174).

THE JOURNEY (1974) p. 766

EDNA O'BRIEN (Tuamgraney, County Clare, Ireland, 1930)
1. Why is the third person central intelligence point of view effective for this story?
2. "Why do I love him . . . this Boyce?" the woman asks herself. Why do you suppose she does?
3. What "divides" them?
4. Why are they afraid of each other?
5. What's her general situation in life?
6. What is the relation between sex and politics in this story? Consider that three countries—Ireland, England, and Scotland—and trade unionism are involved.
7. How does Boyce's wife and his friends affect the lovers' relationship?

WRITING SUGGESTION: Considering the way the story was tending, does the conclusion seem appropriate? Consider the title, among other things.

This story appeared in the *New Yorker* and was included in *A Scandalous Woman*, 1974. Stories: *The Love Object*, 1968; *A Rose in the Heart*, 1979. Novels: *The Country Girls*, 1960; *Pagan Place*, 1970; *High Road*, 1988. Nonfiction: *Mother Ireland*, 1976. About: *Contemporary Authors*, New Revision Series, vol. 6; *Contemporary Novelists*, 4th ed.; Grace Eckley, *Edna O'Brien*; *Writers at Work*, Seventh Series.

THE GERANIUM (1946) p. 775

FLANNERY O'CONNOR (Savannah, Georgia, 1925–1964)
1. What point of view technique does O'Connor use in this story?
2. What various effects does O'Connor achieve by juxtaposing characters, events, and attitudes in the present with those in the past?
3. What are the dominant images or motifs in the present as compared with the past?
4. How do the old man's attitudes about blacks in the present compare and contrast with those in the past?

Compare with "Judgement Day," (p. 785) which follows *The Geranium*.

WRITING SUGGESTION: Discuss the relation between irony and point of view in this story.

For publication information about this story, as well as commentary, see below under "Judgement Day." Stories: *A Good Man Is Hard to Find*, 1955. *Everything That Rises Must Converge*, 1965. Novels: *Wise Blood*, 1952; *The Violent Bear It Away*, 1960. Essays: *Mystery and Manners*, 1969. About: Robert Coles, *Flannery O'Connor's South;* Sister Kathleen Feeley, *Flannery O'Connor: Voice of the Peacock;* John R. May, *The Pruning Word: The Parables of Flannery O'Connor;* Martha Stephens, *The Question of Flannery O'Connor;* Dorothy Walters, *Flannery O'Connor.*

JUDGEMENT DAY (1965)   p. 785

FLANNERY O'CONNOR

1. Consider for this story the same questions asked above about "The Geranium."
2. Compare this story with "The Geranium." Compare and contrast, for instance, the old man's attitudes about blacks in the present and the past in the two stories.
3. Obviously, O'Connor has told a very similar story in two totally different ways. In "Judgement Day" she has reconceived "The Geranium." What is her new conception?
4. What new elements appear in the second version of the story? What do they contribute to O'Connor's new conception?
6. What elements are the same, or very much the same, in both versions?
7. Do the elements carried over from the first version work effectively in the second?
8. What changes has O'Connor made in the character of the old man? In the character of his black friend? In the character of the black man in New York?
9. Does O'Connor carry any lines over from the first version into the last?
10. Most of the techniques O'Connor used in "The Geranium" she also used in the revised version, "Judgement Day." How does she use the following differently in the revised version?
    a) point of view
    b) flashbacks
    c) imagery, motifs
    d) juxtaposition of present and past
    e) irony
    f) other techniques and devices

Commentary

A comparison of "The Geranium" with "Judgement Day" reveals a dramatic example of the importance of the revision process to the creation of major elements in a short story. Flannery O'Connor was twenty-one when "The Geranium," her first published story, appeared in *Accent* (1946). When "Judgement Day," her last published story, appeared posthumously in *Everything that Rises Must Converge* (1965), she was acknowledged the world over as a master of the modern short story. In the years between, she had greatly matured as an artist and her vision of black-white relationships in the South and the North had become more complex.

O'Connor was an ideal student of creative writing. "The Geranium" is a perfect example of a story obviously written to certain technical specifications. She knew *how* intellectually to write a short story and she could practice what she knew, but not at a very high level. One may imagine what a pleasure it must have been for her to employ her mature talent to revise and improve this story twenty years—and great fame—later. Her effort is a dramatic demonstration of a writer's compulsion to "get it right." But this is also an exceptional case. No other writer known to this editor has rewritten a first published story after so many years, and certainly not one who, in failing health, knew that the new version would also be her final published story. Exceptional also is the radical reconceiving of the first version. "Judgement Day" is also seven pages longer.

"The Geranium" appears in *The Collected Stories* (1971). The version that appears in the Library of America edition of her collected works (1988) is the version that appears in O'Connor's Master's of Fine Arts thesis collection for the writing workshop at the University of Iowa and is somewhat different from the version that appeared in *Accent* magazine. O'Connor wrote an intermediate version of the story in 1955 called "An Exile in the East," which she almost included in her first collection, *A Good Man Is Hard to Find* (1955); it later appeared in *South Carolina Review* (November 1978). As she lay dying of Lupus, she finished "Judgement Day" and one other story for inclusion in her last book of stories *Everything That Rises Must Converge*. Within a few days of her death, she made a good number of revisions but they arrived too late for incorporation in the book. However, the version reprinted in her collected stories does not include those changes either. The version reprinted in the Library of America collected works does.

Note: In the process of working with the two published versions of "Judgement Day" an error, recognized too late for correction in the body of this text, was made. The text used in this anthology is the one printed in the Library of America edition of the collected works, but the authority consulted for the spelling of "judgement" and for the capitalization of "Negro" was the collected stories published by Farrar, Straus and Giroux in 1971. The American spelling of "judgment" and the lower case "Negro" were among the changes that did not reach O'Connor's agent in time. One might conjecture that she lower-cased "Negro" because the story is presented solely through the consciousness of Tanner, a racist.

WRITING SUGGESTIONS: 1) Examine the paradoxes and ironies in Southern black-white relationships presented in "The Geranium" and "Judgement Day"; 2) Compare "The Geranium" and "Judgement Day"; 3) Argue Pro or Con: "Judgement Day" is a greater achievement than "The Geranium."

See note above at "The Geranium."

GUESTS OF THE NATION (1931)   p. 800

FRANK O'CONNOR (Cork, Ireland, 1903–1966)

1. What makes the opening effective (see the first 5 paragraphs)?
2. Examine the fourth paragraph, page 815. ". . . and he took the bloody hatchet." Within the context of the entire story, what makes the adjective "bloody" effective?
3. In what general and specific ways is Bonaparte's use of colloquial expressions a contribution to the impact of this story? Notice the dialogue as well.
4. How well has O'Connor developed the character of Bonaparte, the narrator?
5. What effect does the incident he tells about have on Bonaparte?
6. Describe the conflict in this story.
7. Where does O'Connor most effectively use the technique of implication?
8. Bonaparte as narrator is haunted by Hawkins and Belcher. How well does O'Connor develop them as minor characters?
9. Is the style O'Connor uses always appropriate for Bonaparte as narrator?
10. What makes the ending effective?

Commentary

" 'Guests of the Nation' is the only story I have admitted from my first book," said Frank O'Connor in his foreword to *The Stories of Frank O'Connor*, 1956, "and it has been greatly revised. It was written originally under the influence of the great Jewish storyteller, Isaac Babel [*The Red Cavalry*]." The revised version is the one reprinted in this anthology. In his introduction to the *Collected Stories*, 1981, Richard Ellmann claims that the latest version of all the stories is reprinted; that is not true of "Guests of the Nation;" Ellmann reprints the first version as it appeared in O'Connor's first collection, *Guests of the Nation* (1931). Indeed, anthologists seldom use the revised version; perhaps its existence is little known. Ironically, when the editors of the Special Anthology Edition of O'Connor's study of the short story, *The Lonely Voice* (1963) added "Guests of the Nation" two years after his death in 1966, they reprinted the *first* version just after his closing comment on revision: ". . . the rest is rereading and rewriting. The writer should never forget that he is also a reader, though a prejudiced one, and if he cannot read his own work a dozen times he can scarcely expect a reader to look at it twice. . . . Most of my stories have been rewritten a dozen times, a few of them fifty times."

In an interview published in *Writers at Work* (1959), O'Connor answered the question, "Do you rewrite?": "Endlessly, endlessly, endlessly. And keep on rewriting, and after it's published, and then after it's published in book form, I usually rewrite it again. I've rewritten versions of most of my early stories and one of these days, God help, I'll publish these as well." Readers who compare the first published version of 1931 with the revised version published in 1956 will appreciate more fully O'Connor's statements in this interview on the technique of the short story. Raymond Carver, whose own story appears on page 164, said, "It's instructive and heartening both to look at the early drafts of great writers." (*Writers at Work*, Seventh Series.)

"Oh, naturally I admire Chekhov extravagantly," O'Connor said; "I think every short-story writer does. He's inimitable, a person to read and admire and worship—but never, never, never to imitate. He's got all the most extraordinary technical devices, and the moment you start imitating him without those technical devices, you fall into a sort of rambling narrative, as I think even a good story writer like Katherine Mansfield did." (Did she? In "Bliss"?) "I was cursed at birth with a passion for techniques. . . ." O'Connor often made clear the purpose of his use of techniques: to affect the reader: "The moment you grab somebody by the lapels and you've got something to tell, that's a real story. It means you want to tell him and think the story is interesting in itself."

The questions listed above are of the sort commonly asked when studying short stories. Below, comments on the passages O'Connor revised for the 1956 version are numbered to correspond to the 10 questions asked above. They are provided to suggest the way writers revise to achieve the effects we study, effects O'Connor himself studied and taught.

1. In the first three paragraphs of the 1931 version, O'Connor exhibited his passion for revision by making 15 of the almost 70 changes, major and minor. There and throughout the story, he reduced wordiness; he reduced the use of distracting and inappropriate parentheses; he toned down the heavy dialect; he turned long paragraphs into several (he made six of the first three). More importantly, he began, in those opening paragraphs, to get rid of "literary" words and phrases because they were incongruous with Bonaparte's background. For instance, he changed "seldom did I perceive his hands outside the pockets of that pants" to "you seldom saw him with his hands out of his pockets" (second paragraph, p. 820). Certain phrases gave the impression he was telling his story, contradicted in the last para-

graph by this line: "It is so strange what you feel at such moments, and not to be written afterwards" (p. 809). O'Connor cut "written afterwards"; while the oral tone and wording is one of the story's achievements in the 1956 version, it is ambiguous whether Bonaparte writes or tells his story.

2. O'Connor inserted "bloody" in the 1956 version.

3. Even as he cut the phonetic spelling of dialect in most instances, O'Connor changed many flat or literary phrases to colloquialism. For instance, "talked too much" became "too much old gab" (p. 801). Critic-novelist Caroline Gordon has pointed out that, "The narrator's easy flow of colloquial speech contributes to the tonal unity." *(The House of Fiction)*.

4. O'Connor cut, added, and reworded often to enhance the development of Bonaparte as a character. Many changes cluster on pages 803 and 804. O'Connor inserted: "I didn't like the tone he took with me, and anyway I was bored with life in the cottage" (top of p. 803). On page 803, the paragraph that begins "I couldn't tell him" is the result of substitutions, cuts, and additions, resulting in a fuller expression of Bonaparte's attitude. To imply rather than overtly state Bonaparte's feelings, O'Connor revised the first sentence of the third paragraph from the bottom of page 803; the 1931 version read: "I cannot explain it even now, how sad I felt, but I went back to the cottage a miserable man." O'Connor cut out of the 1931 version a paragraph that even more obviously expressed Bonaparte's attitude (after paragraph four, p. 804). In the 1931 version, the long passage of dialogue was crammed confusingly into a long paragraph. In breaking it up, O'Connor not only provided ease of reading, he placed a sharper focus on Bonaparte as a character.

5. Comments under 4 apply as well here. It is well to point out here that O'Connor changed nothing in the last line.

6. A major conflict, worked out externally and internally, is between the impulse to universal brotherhood and duty to one's country. In the passage near the bottom of page 805, O'Connor felt the need to insert, "I never noticed that people who talk a lot about duty find it much trouble to them." Hawkins' statement, "They're not the sort to make a pal and kill a pal. They're not the tools of any capitalist" (just below the middle of p. 807) is much more succinct and clear than in the 1931 version.

7. To imply how Bonaparte feels, O'Connor made four cuts (p. 806). For instance, the first line of the fifth paragraph originally read: "By this time I began to perceive in the dusk the desolate edges of the bog that was to be their last earthly bed, and, so great a sadness overtook my mind, I could not answer him." O'Connor inserted into the 1956 version the last two sentences of that paragraph.

8. Readers may imagine that Bonaparte is moved to tell this story not only because he is haunted by the fact of Hawkins' and Belcher's deaths but by the different manner in which each faced death. To bring Belcher more alive before he must die, O'Connor inserted several passages into the 1956 version (see the last paragraph on p. 806 and the first two sentences of the

fourth full paragraph, p. 808). To this more real Belcher, Noble reacts by raising "his fist at Donovan" (p. 808); in the 1931 version, he "signals to Donovan" to shoot to get it over with. Noble's reactions serve to emphasize or imply Bonaparte's.

9. Many of the passages O'Connor cut (some of which are quoted above) were wrong for Bonaparte. For instance, out of the last paragraph on page 808 he cut the italicized phrases "we had to carry *the warm corpses a few yards before we sunk them in the windy bog*." He also cut from that paragraph "and went back along the desolate edge of the treacherous bog without a word."

10. In the last paragraph, O'Connor made about as many changes as he did in the first, mostly cuts. A close comparison of the two versions of the final paragraph would reinforce many of the points made above; as stated earlier, the 1931 version is available in numerous anthologies and in the *Collected Stories*. Caroline Gordon praised the author's use of the word "damned" in "the damned shrieking of the birds," but O'Connor the passionate reviser cut it out.

WRITING SUGGESTIONS: 1) Compare this story with Chekhov's "Gooseberries" (p. 207) and Mansfield's "Bliss" (p. 664) to show Chekhov's influence on Mansfield and O'Connor (p. 800) and to agree or disagree, perhaps, with O'Connor's charge that Mansfield lacks Chekhov's technique. 2) Compare the two versions of "Guests of the Nation" to show the effects, positive and/or negative, of a single type of revision throughout.

O'Connor published 14 volumes of short stories: the best of these are to be found in *Collected Stories*, 1981. Many of his stories appeared in *The New Yorker*. Novels: *The Saint and Mary Kate*, 1932; *Dutch Interior*, 1940. Criticism: *The Mirror in the Roadway*, 1957; *The Backward Look: A Survey of Irish Literature*, 1967. About: James H. Matthews, *Frank O'Connor*; Richard F. Peterson, "Frank O'Connor and the Modern Irish Short Story," *Modern Fiction Studies*, XXVIII (Spring 1982), 53–67; Maurice Wohlgelernter, *Frank O'Connor: An Introduction*.

I STAND HERE IRONING (1956)   p. 810

TILLIE OLSEN (Omaha, Nebraska, 1913)
   1. Why do you suppose the teacher's call "to come and talk" about Emily stimulates this interior monologue addressed to the teacher?
   2. How does Olsen's use of the pronoun "you" and the act of ironing enhance the effect upon the reader of the mother's monologue?
   3. To what extent does the mother share the teacher's optimistic vision of Emily's future?

WRITING SUGGESTION: Emily's implied view of her mother.
   This story appeared in *Pacific Spectator*, 1956, and was included in *Tell Me*

a Riddle, 1961 (and won the O. Henry Award in 1961). Novel: *Yonnondio,* 1974 (lost in 1932, but recovered). Essays: *Silences,* 1978. About: Abigal Martin, *Tillie Olsen;* Elaine Neil Orr, *Tillie Olsen and a Feminist Spiritualist*

NOMAD AND VIPER (1963)   p. 817

AMOS OZ (Jerusalem, Israel, 1939)
1. Who is the main character, the narrator or Geula? Why does the narrator not focus on Geula earlier than Part III?
2. What is the effect of remembering at the end that the narrator has been describing events that have already occurred?
3. How is the narrator able to tell about Geula's experience with the Arab, and her feelings and thoughts? *Why* does he tell about them?

Commentary

This story is so rich with material some readers may lose sight of the fact that the unnamed narrator tells us almost nothing about himself; he figures in only one scene, the meeting of the secretariat at the end. In the first four pages, he describes the conflict between nomads and the residents of his kibbutz (Jewish commune) in the Israeli desert. Geula is not even mentioned until page 820, and her own story does not begin until two pages later, in the third of nine parts. To the reader who is anxious to achieve orientation, the question naturally arises: what is the subject and theme and who is the main character of this story?

If this is mainly a story of nomad-kibbutz conflict, the story of a young woman's near sexual encounter seems distracting. If this is mainly a story of a young woman's near sexual encounter, the background material on the nomad-kibbutz conflict presented at the beginning seems much too long. Do the conflict and the encounter complement each other? If so, what story, together, do they make? Above all, how does the narrator fit into any of these three possible perspectives? A hard focus on the narrator answers those questions, while posing further complexities.

As a young member of the secretariat who is fully aligned neither with the idealistic elders nor with the vengeful youths, the narrator has a strong interest in describing the social and historical material he offers at the beginning. And as a somewhat distant friend of Geula, he has a plausible reason for telling *her* story. But what *is* her story? We can know only what he tells us, and most of what he tells us only Geula would know and would be unlikely to tell him even if, having dealt with the snake incident at the end, we conclude that she did not die of a viper bite (the narrator's title *does* designate that the snake was a viper and thus venomous).

This is a story whose unity of effect depends upon a clear focus on the narrator's function. One viable explanation is that the narrator is the main character. The reader responds to *his* response to the elements in the historical, religious-cultural-political conflict and to the circumstances of Geula's life—and death. The reader responds even more intensely to what the narrator imagines. If one concludes that Geula is dead and, given the context, that the one-eyed shepherd may have been "lynched" in the raid in which the narrator participated, one may then posit double guilt and hope of redemption as the narrator's impetus to tell this story.

Notice that when the narrator, who has referred to the nomads as "they" and to his own people as "we" first uses "I" he explains the beating of the one-eyed shepherd with the blatant rationalization of the racist. The narrator is of a people who suffered from similarly facile stereotyping; a historically persecuted minority rules here in the desert. One may wonder whether *he* beat the shepherd before and whether he beat him again in the raid at the end—or killed him. The narrator, as if by psychological necessity, leaves many implied questions unanswered. Context supports, at the very least, feelings of guilt as an accomplice to persecution of the nomad and as violator of social ideals that grew out of the persecution of Jews themselves.

Because this guilt would be easier for him to deal with, the narrator begins his story with a kind of omniscient overview of the conflict. Guilt about Geula is more intensely personal. Even after he has set Part III for the beginning of her story, he delays it by indulging in a long, lyrical scene-setting passage into which Geula almost seems to intrude (p. 822). He describes her in the most general terms as a troubled woman of twenty-nine who has "not yet found a husband." Earlier he had suggested that such "unattached" women may have found "poetry" in the invasion of the nomads (Part II, first sentence, p. 819).

After a space break, he plunges into an obviously self-justifying declaration that, "What had passed between Geula and me is not relevant here." That he places a book of poems in her room on each of her birthdays suggests not only his indecisiveness and his romantic temperament but also that he has continued to encourage her to expect more from him.

Our response to everything the narrator tells us is further complicated by our awareness that, as a romantic young writer, he has found in the persecution of the nomads and the death of Geula rich material for an interesting story. In a style that is often very literary and sometimes self-indulgent, he imaginatively presents the kibbutz-nomad conflict, and he totally imagines Geula's experiences in the orchard—a young male's fantasy about a near sexual union of enemies. He even fantasizes that she hallucinates being raped (VI, p. 828).

As Oz presents them, through this narrator, the two major elements of this story make sense only as willful manifestations of the temperament and imagination of an indecisive, romantic young writer. As we read about Geula's encounter in the orchard with the young Arab, we must never lose sight of the fact that the narrator is imagining everything and writing it all down for us to read. His consciousness, then, is the subject of the story. He is simultaneously manipulating his own emotions and ours for psychological and literary reasons and effects.

WRITING SUGGESTION: Compare with "The Guest" (p. 153), "A Soldier's Embrace" (p. 396), and "The Shawl" (p. 831).

This story appears in *Where the Jackals Howl*, 1981, revised edition. Other fiction: *Elsewhere Perhaps*, 1966; *Unto Death, Two Novellas*, 1971; *A Perfect Peace* (1982); *In The Land of Israel*, 1983. Editor: *Stories from the Kibbutz*, 1968. About: *Contemporary Authors*, 53–56; *Contemporary Literary Criticism*, Vol. 5; A. S. Grossman, Interview in *The Partisan Review*, vol. 53, no. 3, 1986, 427–38; Leon I. Yudkin, "The Jackal and the Other Place: The Stories of Amos Oz," *1948 and After: Aspects of Israeli Fiction*, 135–48.

THE SHAWL (1980)   p. 831

CYNTHIA OZICK (Jewish American, New York City, 1928)
1. What does the shawl represent to Magda? Stella? Rosa?
2. What other images does Ozick repeat to represent aspects of the holocaust?
3. Beyond the holocaust, what universal implications does this story generate?

WRITING SUGGESTION: Compare with "Nomad and Viper" (p. 817).

This story first appeared in *The New Yorker*, 1980, and is included in *The Shawl*, 1989. Stories: *The Pagan Rabbi*, 1971; *Bloodshed and Three Novellas*, 1976; *Levitation: Five Fictions*, 1981. Novels: *Trust*, 1966; *The Cannibal Galaxy*, 1983; *Messiah of Stockholm*, 1987. Essays: *Art and Ardor*, 1983. About: Harold Bloom, ed., *Cynthia Ozick;* Joseph Lowin, *Cynthia Ozick*; Sanford Pinsker, *The Uncompromising Fictions of Cynthia Ozick*.

A CONVERSATION WITH MY FATHER (1974)   p. 835

GRACE PALEY (Jewish American, New York City, 1922)
1. Look at the second paragraph. What does the father mean?
2. Look at the de Maupassant and Chekhov stories in the anthology. Is Paley's story like either in any way?
3. Who is Turgenev?
4. Discuss pro and con: Follow the argument between father and daughter and argue for either side throughout.
5. Who does Paley seem to suggest wins the argument?
6. Compare this story with others in this anthology that deal with the writing process. See Barth's "Lost in the Funhouse" (p. 74) and Le Guin's "The Ones Who Walk Away from Omelas" (p. 595).
7. Most of Paley's stories are as short as this one (she has written no nov-

els). Is this story a good example of minimalism? or miniaturism? (Define this term.)
8. How do you interpret the last line?

WRITING SUGGESTION: This story comes from a volume called *Enormous Changes at the Last Minute*. Paley's epigraph is: "Everyone in this book is imagined into life except the father. No matter what story he has to live in, he's my father. I. Goodside, M. D., artist, and storyteller." Argue that the first person narrator in a work of fiction is never to be taken literally as the author, that the narrator is always a product of the author's imagination.

This story appeared in *New American Review, 13*, 1972, and is included in *Enormous Changes at the Last Minute*, 1974. Stories: *The Little Disturbances of Man: Stories of Men and Women in Love*, 1959; *Later the Same Day*, 1985. About: Joan Lidoff, "Clearing Her Throat: An Interview with Grace Paley," *Shenandoah*, 32 (1981): 3–26; Blanche Gelfant, "Grace Paley: Fragments for a Portrait in College," *New England Review*, 3 (Winter 1980): 276–293. Harriet Shapiro, "Grace Paley: 'Art Is on the Side of the Underdog,'" *Ms.*, 2 (May 1974): 43–45.

BIG BLONDE (1929)   p. 840

DOROTHY PARKER (West End, New Jersey, 1893–1967)
1. Compare the demands made upon Hazel by her husband to those made by other men. Are there any differences?
2. Is Hazel different in any way from the other women in the story?
3. What kind of person is Hazel, as determined by circumstances?
4. What kind of person might Hazel be if her circumstances were more compatible with her better qualities?
5. Describe the blonde mystique.
6. How does this story contribute to our understanding of alcoholism and suicide?
7. How does the beaten horse (pp. 868, 872) function as a metaphor in this story?
8. What is implied about Hazel by the ending?
9. Compare this story with Chekhov's "The Darling."

WRITING SUGGESTION: This story appeared in 1929. To what extent do male-female relationships like those described here still exist?

This story appeared in *The Bookman*, 1929, and is included in *Laments for the Living*, 1930; Stories: *Here Lies*, 1939; *After Such Pleasures*, 1933. About: *Writers at Work*, First Series; Leslie Ronald Frewin, *The Late Mrs. Dorothy Parker;* John Keats, *You Might As Well Live: The Life and Times of Dorothy Parker;* Arthur F. Kinney, *Dorothy Parker;* Marion Meade, *What Fresh Hell Is This?*.

THE WITNESS (1971)   p. 858

ANN PETRY (Black American. Old Saybrook, Connecticut, 1908)

1. How does the point of view technique enhance Petry's portrayal of the character of Charles Woodruff? What are the external and internal sources of conflict Woodruff is engaged in?
2. What are the thematic implications of Woodruff's encounter with the boys? Beyond the rape itself, to what is he a witness?
3. Besides implication, what other devices does Petry use to develop character and theme effectively?
4. Up to the entrance of the boys, Woodruff simply stands outside the church; most of the story is devoted to exposition that contributes more to character development than to plot. Obvious exposition is usually dull. What does Petry do to that opening section to make it interesting, to hold the reader?

Commentary

Told through the third-person central intelligence of Charles Woodruff, "The Witness" appears to be yet another story of racial cruelty; that's the way Woodruff views his ordeal until he realizes "that Rambler and his friends didn't give a damn that Woodruff was a Black man." The entire episode is a momentary distraction from the emptiness of their pampered, protected lives. Petry uses a stock racial situation as a way of setting off in sharp relief another problem: the violent potential of the bright upper-middle-class young. This is a classic example of a writer's strategy: to depict one problem while seeming to depict another. Apparently writing about racial conflict, Petry depicts a problem that transcends race.

With Woodruff, the reader must be distracted from this central theme if it is to have the impact of a sudden realization; and with this point of view, we can experience Woodruff's own self-deception up to his partial realization. The reader may see even more clearly than Woodruff that the conflict of generations overwhelms the racial conflict. To stress her point that race is not the cental issue, Petry contrasts Woodruff with Shipley. In his observations, thoughts, insights and behavior, Woodruff proves himself to be a sensitive, intelligent, warm man, able to cope with most kids. Despite the fact that an elderly black is sitting in judgment on them, they are much more hostile and disrespectful at first to Reverend Shipley—a disrespect Woodruff himself feels.

Should he stand and fight or flee? Petry ends the story with the implied question: should Woodruff have fled?

Woodruff is a witness, then, to more than the rape of a white girl by a gang of white boys, to more than the humiliation once again of a black man. He is witness to a purely gratuitous impulse to violate and degrade, physically and psychologically. To escape the boredom and blandness of a middle-class comfort and the predictability of a routine, more-planned life, these kids cultivate the streak of pure meanness that is perhaps dormant in most people. That the victim is one of their own contemporaries and an old man dramatizes the undirected nature of their viciousness. The psychological rape is the most severe and its victims are not just Woodruff, but Shipley and the girl as well—and by implication the boys themselves ("self-cannibals"). The story is no more about physical rape itself than it is about the plight of the assimilated professional, middle-class black male. Nor is it mainly about the irony of racial discrimination in the North. Woodruff himself is prejudiced, not in racial so much as in generational terms.

In addition to implication, a few of the devices Petry uses to develop character and theme are contrast, parallelism, irony, and allusion.

Woodruff himself seems aware of the irony of his official relationship with the boys: a black man asked to help white boys behave decently. An ironic reversal he must experience in humiliation is the way the boys reverse the salesman's pitch about the coat.

A discussion as to whether the story is weakened by the long passages of exposition may be instructive. Woodruff simply stands outside the church for what seems an implausibly long time, and that act in itself is not sufficiently interesting. But Petry uses a number of devices and techniques to make that opening section far from dull.

The exposition is structured clearly in chronological stages: the remote past, with Woodruff's wife; the recent past, with his move to New York as a widower; the immediate past, with the boys, the immediate present, with the boys. Not until near the end of the exposition section does narrative interest pick up, with the entrance of the boys. But meanwhile, Petry provides us with some vivid description, past and present, keenly expressed.

Compare with "Geranium" (p. 775) and "Judgement Day" (p. 785).

WRITING SUGGESTION: Derive a topic from issues posed in the commentary above.

This story, in a quite different version, appeared in *Redbook*, February, 1971; this revised version is from *Miss Muriel*, 1971. Novels: *The Street*, 1946, *Country Place*, 1947, *The Narrows*, 1953. About: David Madden, "Ann Petry's "The Witness,'" *Studies in Black Literature* (Winter 1975), 24–26; John O'Brien, ed., *Interviews with Black Writers; Contemporary Authors*, New Revised Series, Vol. 4; *Contemporary Novelists; Dictionary of Literary Biography*, vol. 76; *Critique*, Vol. 16, no. 1, 1974.

THE FALL OF THE HOUSE OF USHER (1839) p. 873

EDGAR ALLAN POE (Boston, Massachusetts, 1809–1849)
 1. What characteristics of the gothic horror story does this story exhibit?

2. How does Poe create atmosphere? (p. 875)
3. How are people part of the setting?
4. What is the role of imagination (p. 875), superstitition, and the supernatural in this story?
5. What is the role of the arts, music and painting, and of exotic books and arcane knowledge?
6. What relation does the narrator develop between Usher and the house, between the facade of the house, for instance, and his description of Usher's face? (p. 876)
7. What is Madeline's malady?
8. How important are the various kinds of allusions?
9. Describe Poe's style; compare it with other first person narratives in this anthology.
10. Where does Poe seem to suggest the subconscious as we know it in modern psychology?
11. Why is the narrator necessary to the effect of this story?
12. How might this story be read primarily as a depiction of a psychological process within the narrator?

Commentary

Almost all Poe's short stories are told in the first person; his narrators obsessively, compulsively describe and analyze, almost in essay fashion, the experience of a bizarre psychological phenomenon. It was a convention in early fiction that dealt with an unusual event to lend credibility to the tale by having another character tell the reader what he witnessed. But Poe goes beyond that convention. Ostensibly, the narrator in this story describes and analyzes his own reactions to witnessing the psychological and physical plight of his boyhood friend, Roderick Usher and Usher's twin sister, Madeline; the effect, he tells us, will last forever. Many descriptions of this story leave out the narrator as an active character, placing the focus on Usher and his sister.

With such a focus, the reader has experienced what has become a stereotypical Gothic horror story: in a decaying castle, situated in a desolate landscape, madness destroys the last members of an aristocratic family. For that reason, many readers of serious fiction only reluctantly consent to study Poe's fiction seriously. Such readers might concede that Usher is a forerunner of the modern alienated hero.

But other serious readers regard that approach to Poe as a misreading of his purpose, in this and many of his other stories. If one accepts the premise that first person narration in serious fiction expresses more about the narrator than about an ostensible hero or main character, and if one agrees that this Poe story, at least, deserves serious attention, then "The Fall of the House of Usher" becomes far more interesting than many readers have supposed.

It is not unusual for there to be no extended dialogue in a Poe story, but why is there not a single exchange between the unnamed narrator and Usher? And why is the narrator unnamed? Where does he come from? What does he do in life? Where does he go when he flees? It is not unusual for such basic implied questions to go unanswered in a Poe story. But continued interrogation of the story on this single point may prove provocative.

Why does the narrator emphasize his own reactions to what he witnesses rather than describing characters and events somewhat objectively? Notice that in the first three and a half pages, even before he enters the room where Usher rises from a sofa, the narrator describes his own quite extreme physical and mental state. With the rest of the story well in mind, examine every word of the first paragraph. Notice that when he describes Usher's supposed mental state, the narrator uses terms that are similar to the ones he had used earlier in describing his own: "a sense of insufferable gloom pervaded my spirit," "an utter depression of soul," which he compares to "the after-dream of the reveller upon opium," "a sickening of the heart," "shadowy fancies."At the end of the incomplete paragraph on p. 877, he compares, for instance, Usher to the opium eater. And on page p. 878, end of second complete paragraph, he describes Usher as pouring forth "unceasing radiation of gloom" from his dark mind.

Why does the narrator describe Usher's face in phrases similar to those he earlier used to describe the facade of his house? Notice that his second description of Usher's house as a kind of living organism (first paragraph, p. 896) closely parallels his description of Usher's mind. Why does Poe have the narrator describe his intimate sharing of the arts and of ideas and sensations with Usher before he allows him to tell us Usher and his dead twin sister Madeline had always shared "sympathies"? Notice that the narrator becomes increasingly aware of the terrifying effect upon him of Usher's condition: ". . . it infected me. I felt creeping upon me . . . the wild influences of his own fantastic yet impressive superstitions. . . . An irrepressible tremor gradually pervaded my frame. . . . there sat upon my very heart an incubus of utterly causeless alarm" (p. 883). And the "whirlwind" becomes an outward expression of their inner turmoil.

Still, the narrator attempts to calm Usher. Notice that he uses "we," "our," "us" more frequently to describe perceptions and emotions as they face the storm together (last paragraph, p. 883). Then, as the climax nears, he returns to a dominant attention to his own thoughts and feelings (see next to last paragraph, p. 885), and except for Usher's one long speech (p. 886), the narrator expresses his own reactions in the same extreme (one might say hysterical) style in which he began the story. The fact that the narrator, who so often remarks on Usher's tendency to hallucinate, actually saw everything—including Madeline falling on Usher, bearing him to the floor "a corpse, and a victim to the terrors he had anticipated"—becomes much more pertinent when the reader makes him the main character.

One supportable interpretation is that there is only one character in this story and that he is Roderick Usher himself, a split personality (symbolized by the zigzag fissure in the facade of the house), and that the narrator and Usher are the same person. This interpretation would posit a sister, but not necessarily in the situation described in the story. The tarn and its vapor and the tunnels deep under the house would then suggest the subconscious, and so on.

Whether the reader takes the narrator to be simply that, a character who simply facilitates Poe's telling of the story of Roderick Usher, or responds to the narrator as an expression of psychological processes at work in the narrator's mind, or sees the narrator and Usher as two sides of a split personality, it is more than likely that Poe himself knew exactly the effect he wanted this story to have. In his famous essay "The Philosophy of Composition," describing how he calculated every moment of his long poem, "The Raven," he demonstrated his ability to execute an intention. His conception of the art of the short story is described in his review of Hawthorne's *Twice-Told Tales*. The skillful artist, ". . . having deliberately conceived a certain *single effect* to be wrought . . . then invents such incidents . . . combines such events, and discusses them in such tone as may best serve him in establishing this preconceived effect. If his very first sentence tend not to the out-bringing of this effect, then in his very first step has he committed a blunder. In the whole composition there should be no word written of which the tendency, direct or indirect, is not to the one pre-established design. And by such means, with such care and skill, a picture is at length painted which leaves in the mind of him who contemplates it with a kindred art, a sense of the fullest satisfaction."

While it is certainly true that the most carefully planned and consciously executed work of art always has effects on the reader that the author never imagines, one may assume that when Poe created the narrator of "The Fall of the House of Usher" he had far more clearly in mind than simply telling the Usher tale. That tale is there for everyone to enjoy, but to neglect the narrator is to miss an equally fine, quite different, experience.

WRITING SUGGESTION: Examine how this story might be read primarily as a depiction of a psychological process within the narrator.

This story appears in *Tales*, 1845. Stories: *Tales of the Grotesque and Arabesque*, (2 vols.), 1840. Novel: *The Narrative of Arthur Gordon Pym*, 1838. About: Caroline Gordon and Allen Tate, *The House of Fiction;* Daniel Hoffman, *Poe Poe Poe Poe Poe Poe Poe;* D. H. Lawrence, *Studies in Classic American Literature*, 110–116; Renata R. Mautner, "The Self, the Mirror, The Other: " 'The Fall of the House of Usher,' " *Poe Studies*, X (December 1977), 33–35; Robert N. Mollinger, *Psychoanalysis and Literature: An Introduction;* Ulian Symons, *The Tell-Tale Heart: The Life and Works of Edgar Allan Poe;* Allen Tate, "Our Cousin, Mr. Poe," *Partisan Review*, XVI (December 1949); J. Gerald Kennedy, *Poe, Death, and the Life of Writing.*

FLOWERING JUDAS (1930)   p. 888

KATHERINE ANNE PORTER (Indian Creek, Texas, 1890–1980)

1. How does the structure of the story contribute to its effects?
2. How does Porter use the device of juxtaposing brief scenes?
3. How does Porter employ symbolic patterns?
4. What thematic elements are enhanced by juxtaposition, structure, and symbolism?

Commentary

The omniscient author's psychological analysis of and philosophical reflections on Laura's predicament and the self-delusory processes that follow from her predicament are everywhere in the story, suffusing the very style that creates a tissue of images. Overwhelming her own overt interpretations when they threaten to intimidate the life of the story, the images embody Porter's meaning with expressive vitality. Ultimately, of course, this vitality cannot be separated from the vitality of her meditations about Laura. The story exfoliates from a tight intermingling of showing and telling. And that story, were it not for the author's technique of dramatically juxtaposing tableaux, is so rich and multifaceted as to require the scope of a novel.

As the elements of Laura's exterior and interior worlds intermingle, they cohere in a developing pattern of images which expands from the charged image that Porter sets forth in the first paragraph. Paralyzed, Laura is locked into this image, as though in a small box stage set, and we see her at a distance, as though through a window. With each image Porter shows us, we feel that Laura is withdrawing more and more deeply into herself, that her will is becoming more and more paralyzed. The controlling image (Laura and Braggioni sitting opposite each other by the table) is a simplified visual and thematic expression of the entire story; this image recurs at strategic points in the pattern, creating that sense of simultaneity that makes a work of art cohere and seem inevitable. The tableau is motionless—yet it vibrates from within, sending its electrical charge in a radial fashion out into the other images connected to it.

The energy of the story is transmitted in the kinetic juxtaposition of one charged image to another. Porter's technique of creating a dynamic interplay among images strategically spaced in an unfolding pattern is appropriate for the rendering of Laura's state of mind—self-delusion producing paralysis of will. The contrast between the static quality of the images and the immediacy of the historical present tense generates a tension that enhances the effect of Porter's basic image technique. Figuratively, Laura and Braggioni reveal two perspectives on a single person; each exhibits aspects of the other. They also contrast with each other. But finally, Laura's personality embodies many aspects of Braggioni's, carrying them to a negative extreme.

This story delineates a maze of ambiguity of roles, from Laura and Braggioni, to the minor characters. Everyone seems to be both a savior and a Judas to everyone else. The author conceives these complex savior-Judas relationships paradoxically and ironically, and enhances them with a controlled atmosphere of ambiguity; this nexus of savior-Judas analogies extends from the inner psychological realm of Laura and Braggioni out into the public realm and up to a symbolic level.

Porter handles the intermingling of interior and exterior worlds so adroitly that the dream passage comes with a controlled abruptness, and the change in tone does not jar, but seems inevitable. Here Porter, though she is describing a dream that is happening in the present, shifts into the past tense to enhance our feeling that Laura's life, its capacity for responding to possibilities, is over, whether she literally dies soon after the story ends or not.

The ambiguous title enables the reader to interpret all the story's images. The Judas tree is so named because of the belief that Judas hanged himself from such a tree. So the tree itself and Porter's title ultimately have both positive and negative connotations, and the story depicts in its charged images the textures of both betrayers and betrayed.

Laura wakes, but not to enlightenment, for the dominating idea in her life, as in the nightmare, is denial, and with this "No," Porter appropriately ends the story. When we discover Laura sitting at the table in the initial, persistent charged image, she has already lost in her conflict between ideal aspiration and actuality. What self-knowledge she has she fails to employ in an act of self-discovery.

While this story is not concerned with religion in itself, suggestive religious terms and motifs recur throughout the story. The images are almost like black parodies of religious elements as analogies to patterns of human behavior and relationships on secular levels.

Politics is closer than religion to Porter's concern for her characters as people alive or dying in the secular world. Politics functions almost expressionistically. Institutionalized religion and political ideals, perverted in revolution, become escapes from ordinary love. Failure to distinguish illusion from reality in the conflict between ideal aspirations and brutal actuality produces Laura's self-delusion and the "No" with which she arms herself against the world. Thus, she waits in fear; a sense of overwhelming futility paralyzes her.

In preparation for the public violence that is imminent, Laura, who so intensely fears violence to herself, oils and loads Braggioni's pistols; no more grotesque half-parody of Freudian symbols can be imagined. A psychological examination of Laura will reveal the organic unity of the story more closely. In light of what psychological forces may one look at Laura? The reader sees what Laura fails to see. If one examines the story from beginning to end, keeping in mind the pattern of images delineated earlier, one may see how each of these aspects of Laura's psychological and physical predicament is embodied in charged images that recur and cluster. For Porter's comments on the writing of this story, see David Madden, "The Charged Image in Katherine Anne Porter's 'Flowering Judas,'" *Studies in Short Fiction* VII, 2 (Spring 1970), 277–89.

Compare with "How I Contemplated the World . . . ." (p. 752).

WRITING SUGGESTION: Derive a topic from the above commentary and questions.

This story appears in *Flowering Judas,* 1930. Novellas: *Pale Horse, Pale Rider: Three Short Novels,* 1939. Stories: *The Leaning Tower,* 1944. Novel: *Ship of Fools,* 1962. Essays: *The Collected Essays,* 1970; *The Never-Ending Wrong,* 1977. About: Charles Allen, "Katherine Anne Porter: Psychology as Art," *Southwest Review* XLI (Summer, 1956); Joan Givner, *Katherine Anne Porter: A Life;* George Hendrick, *Katherine Anne Porter;* Robert Penn Warren "Irony with a Center: Katherine Anne Porter," *Kenyon Review* IV (Winter 1942); Ray B. West, Jr., *Katherine Anne Porter;* Jane Karuse DeMouy, *Katherine Anne Porter's Women: The Eye of Her Fiction.*

MANNEQUIN (1927)   p. 898

JEAN RHYS (Roseau, Dominica, 1894–1979)
1. Is the title effective?
2. "Mannequin" was published in 1927 in a collection called *The Left Bank.* How does the sub-title "Sketches and studies of a present-day Bohemian in Paris"—suggest how one might read this piece? Which of the two terms seems to fit this piece most helpfully? What is this a *study* or *sketch* of?
3. Are there patterns of images that give unity of effect to this piece?
4. The point of view is omniscient. Is that effective for this kind of fiction?
5. Describe the author's tone.

WRITING SUGGESTION: In a preface to the collection, critic-novelist Ford Madox Ford said that Rhys had an instinct for form: "these sketches begin exactly where they should and end exactly when their job is done." What do you think he might have meant by that statement?

This story appears in *The Left Bank,* 1927. Stories: *Tigers Are Better-Looking,* 1963. Novels: *Quartet,* 1928; *After Leaving Mr. MacKenzie,* 1930; *Voyage in the Dark,* 1934; *Good Morning Midnight,* 1939. *Wide Sargasso Sea,* 1966 (an attempt to finish the story of Charlotte Bronte's *Jane Eyre*). Autobiography: *Smile Please,* 1979. About: Arnold E. Davidson, *Jean Rhys;* Nancy R. Harrison, *Jean Rhys and the Novel as Women's Text;* Peter Wolfe, *Jean Rhys.*

THE SECRET ROOM (1962)   p. 903

ALAIN ROBBE-GRILLET (Brest, France, 1922)

1. Robbe-Grillet deliberately uses geometrical terminology, formal phrases, and passive verbs to describe the fragments of the total image seen by a universal viewer. What is the effect of this technique on the reader? To start, examine the first paragraph.
2. At the end, Robbe-Grillet introduces a new element—"the canvas." In what sense is the idea of a canvas, a painting, not new to the reader at that point? Consider the way the author has directed our eyes throughout.
3. The event and the painting of it exist simultaneously. Discuss that statement.
4. There is nothing unrealistic in the scene Robbe-Grillet describes, but his technique pushes reality to such an extreme it becomes like fantasy. Discuss that statement.
5. The action described is a melodramatic cliché. How does Robbe-Grillet's handling of imagination transform that cliché?
6. All the elements of a traditional story—character, conflict, plot, action, suspense—are here, but how does Robbe-Grillet handle them differently?
7. What movement do you discern in the snapshot? Why does Robbe-Grillet introduce movement into an otherwise deliberately static tableau?
8. This fiction conveys a strong sensuality, even sexuality. How do you account for that effect? By what is described or what is implied?
9. How may the controlled contemplation of a scene be considered an appropriate focus for a work of fiction?

Commentary

Geometric terminology, formal phrases, and passive verbs characterize Alain Robbe-Grillet's style in most of his fiction; even the images in his movies emphasize the geometrical, the formal, the passive or static. In "The Secret Room," the use of such an unusual style is most justified. The reader is asked to look with the narrator at a tableau depicting a female sacrificial victim from several actual (literally on canvas) and imagined perspectives. "The first thing to be seen" sets the cold, objective, formal tone, enhancing the similar qualities of the geometrical terminology; the passive verbs help to lend a static, arrested quality to the details, fragments we are asked to examine. The effect is to anesthetize the reader's emotions as each fragment contributes to a more and more melodramatic image, so that when we reach the fourth from last paragraph in which the man stabs the woman we respond with greater intensity than if the entire scene had been depicted in a conventional way, chronologically. The active verbs leave us with an image that is static, but vibrant.

The reader who knows that Gustav Moreau was an early French symbolist surrealist painter will suspect that the style and images are static because the narrator is looking at a painting. That the last word of the piece is "canvas" suggests that Robbe-Grillet would prefer that one only suspect a painting is being examined. What we see with the narrator stimulates his imagination, which introduces into the "empty" room a male figure in the act of fleeing from the bloody deed. Because we are looking at a painting, the images superimposed upon the static painted image are themselves static, as if painted. Moving back in time and space, we contemplate the murderer in various attitudes, looking again and again at the victim, who becomes more and more human. The imagined violent action disrupts the dynamic still point of art.

The event of the sacrificial murder and the painting of it are made to exist simultaneously in this double act of viewing a painting and imagining the event that produced the painted image. This kind of action exhibits the technique and the content of much modern experimental art. To view a non-objective painting is to experience the subject and the creative process simultaneously; they exist inseparably in time and space. In this story, the events of imagining and of depicting what is imagined exist simultaneously in the perceptions of the reader, who is collaborating with Robbe-Grillet imaginatively, emotionally, and intellectually.

If the scene and the action seem surrealistic it is not because there is anything unrealistic about it, but because of Robbe-Grillet's unusual, somewhat bizarre technique and his conception about what we see. His technique and style push realism to such an extreme that it seems like fantasy; we aren't used to perceiving things in the way he enables us to see them in this piece. The action described is a melodramatic cliché—a man in a cape manacles the hands and feet of a beautiful young nude woman and stabs her, among columns and shadows and burning incense in a secret room, then flees up a stone stairway.

By rendering these traditional elements in fragments, using a formal, passive style, and a technique that controls the juxtaposition of those fragments, and by mingling art and reality, Robbe-Grillet enables us to reexamine our attitudes towards these elements, to experience them differently. The impact of these static images, what makes their interplay dynamic, is paradoxically our sense of the movement of our eyes from one static image to another. That's what makes a painting exciting—the movement of our eyes, controlled by the sense of movement conveyed by the composition and the color dynamics. We experience that living moment of the victim's convulsed reaction to the knife thrust all the more intensely for its erupting in a setting of stony repose. Robbe-Grillet suggests that our most powerful perceptions as well as our sensory, emotional, imaginative, and even intellectual responses work by contraries and paradoxes: inertia suggests movement, furious movement suggests stillness.

This formal fiction conveys a strong sensuality, even sexuality, although with a decidedly decadent aura. Even when the style is geometrical and formal, the author dwells lovingly upon the young woman; but there is a certain sensuality even in his description of the man's postures and in the interplay of all the forms in the picture.

Making innovative use of the raw materials of conventional fiction, Robbe-Grillet enables the reader to have a fictive experience that is basically contemplative rather than narrative. We experience fragments of a narrative in a controlled contemplative mode. But it is still a fictive experience; the elements are certainly far removed from the practical elements of a nonfictive piece and our responses in no way resemble the contemplative uses to which we put basically informational nonfictive material. Just as the materials, the subject matter, and the basic fictive elements are those of conventional fiction, experienced from different perspectives, so our responses are similar; they come in different sequences, out of different contexts.

WRITING SUGGESTION: Discuss pro and/or con: This story is too obscure.

This story appears in *Snapshots*, 1962. Novels: *The Erasers*, 1953; *The Voyeur*, 1955; *Jealousy*, 1957; *Topology of a Phantom City*, 1976; *Ghosts in the Mirror*, 1988. Criticism: *For a New Novel*, 1963. About: Bruce Archer Morrisette, "The Evolution of Narrative Viewpoint in Robbe-Grillet," *Novel*, I (Fall 1967), 24–33; Patricia Deduck, *Realism, Reality, and the Fictional Theory of Alain Robbe-Grillet;* Bruce Archer Morrisette, *The Novels of Robbe-Grillet;* Ben Stoltzfus, *Alain Robbe-Grillet: The Body of the Text.*

THE CONVERSION OF THE JEWS (1959)   p. 907

PHILIP ROTH (Jewish American, Newark, New Jersey, 1933)
 1. In which passages does Roth speak most directly as omniscient author?
 2. What is Roth's tone?
 3. How does humor function in the story?
 4. How does Ozzie differ from each of the other characters regarding religion?
 5. Discuss pro and con: This story is not primarily about religion; Ozzie is not particularly religious.
 6. How does Roth use irony?
 7. What are the implications of key words in the title?
 8. Discuss the relation of violence and power in regard to organized religions.

WRITING SUGGESTIONS: 1) Compare the way Jewish writers portray Jews with the way Southern minority writers in this anthology portray their minority ethnic groups. 2) On the subject of children and religion, compare this story with "Going to Meet the Man" (p. 55).

This story appeared in *The Paris Review* and is included in *Goodbye, Columbus,* 1959. Novels: *When She Was Good,* 1967; *Portnoy's Complaint,* 1969; *My Life as a Man,* 1974; *Anatomy Lesson,* 1983. Nonfiction: *Reading Myself and Others,* 1975; *Facts, A Novelist's Autobiography,* 1988. About: *Writers at Work,* Seventh Series.

KALICZ (1929)   p. 920

EVELYN SCOTT (Clarksville, Tennessee, 1893–1963)

1. How is Scott's complex omniscient style appropriate for this story?
2. How does Scott's style change as Kalicz identifies himself with Christ?
3. What do the historical, religious, and other allusions refer to?
4. Discuss the religious elements in the story.
5. What is the relation between sex and violence and the religious elements affecting Kalicz? (See, for instance, pp. 941 and 943.)
6. What is ironic about this statement: "Kalicz is not angry with anybody."
7. Trace images of fire and water, heaven and hell, throughout the story.
8. What is Scott suggesting about the violent effect of zealous beliefs in war?
9. This story appears in Scott's enormous, experimental Civil War novel of 1929, *The Wave*. "Kalicz," like all the components of this novel, is a self-contained unit, and was often anthologized in the thirties. According to Peggy Bach, Scott's biographer, the concept of *The Wave* is that in war each person is caught up like a drop of water, separate but a part of the whole, on a wave of communal energy or violence, but simultaneously on the wave of one's own psychic energy as stimulated by war. What images of water and of wave-like energy do you find in this story?

"Kalicz" is reprinted here as a contribution to the rediscovery effort of Peggy Bach, who persuaded publishers to reprint *The Wave* and several other works by Scott, a major writer of the 1920s whose many writings have suffered neglect since the 1940s. Bach's comment on "Kalicz" may aid discussion and writing about the story. "Any religious implication . . . is overt, not in the least hidden. Kalicz works in a foundry on the East River in New York making cannons from molten iron. The illegitimate son of Marja, he thinks that because he has no real father and thus no real name, he is like Jesus. He reflects on the struggle of the angels with evil and compares all things in the foundry to Biblical times and the coming of the Lord. Kalicz fears the draft; he is caught up in the draft rioting and feels he owes some duty to this burning world. He burns a huge grain elevator, and as the mob comes for him, he imagines them yelling: 'This is the man! This is he who called himself King of the Jews!' Robert Welker contends that Scott employed religious symbolism in several episodes [of *The Wave*]. Actually each episode of *The Wave* could be disassembled and one could find whatever symbolism one is looking for, but if this symbolism is read, it perhaps may be the predilection of readers of the 1950s and 1960s to hunt for religious and mystic symbolism, rather than a deliberate intention of Scott's. One must return to the place of the individual in the force and disorder of the war, and in that context, symbolism, religious or otherwise, does not function importantly in the novel."

In an interview, Bach clarified: all religious references are in Kalicz's mind, not symbolically imposed upon him by Scott. One must consider what all the other characters think of Kalicz. See Peggy Bach, "*The Wave:* Evelyn Scott's Civil War," *The Southern Literary Journal*, XVII, no. 2, Spring 1985, 18–32 (her other articles on Scott are cited there). See also Robert Welker, "*Liebestod* With a Southern Accent," *Reality and Myth: Essays in American Literature*, ed. William E. Walker and Robert Welker, 1964.

WRITING SUGGESTION: Discuss pro and/or con: Religion in this story is not important. What matters is how it affects the mind and behavior of Kalicz.

Novels: The trilogy, *The Narrow House*, 1921, *Narcissus*, 1922, *The Golden Door*, 1925. Ideals: *A Book of Farce and Comedy*, 1927; *Migrations: An Arabesque in Histories*, 1927; *A Calender of Sin, American Melodramas*, 1931; *Eva Gay: A Romantic Novel*, 1933; *The Shadow of a Hawk*, 1941. Memoir: *Escapade*, 1923. Memoir-History: *Background in Tennessee*, 1937. Criticism: *On William Faulkner's "The Sound and The Fury,"* 1929.

YELLOW WOMAN (1974) p. 932

LESLIE SILKO (Native American. Laguna Pueblo, New Mexico, 1948)

1. What characteristics of a folk-tale does the story have?
2. What does "yellow" in the title refer to?
3. How can Silva be explained by reality? Can we be certain he is not a supernatural being?
4. What is the appeal of Silva for the narrator?
5. Why is the narrator glad to leave Silva?
6. Discuss pro and con: Indians may hold onto superstition as one way to hold onto something the white man cannot control.
7. Is the narrator writing or telling or does Silko rely on convention? To whom or for whom or for what reason might the narrator be telling or writing this story?

WRITING SUGGESTION: Compare with "The Red Convertible" (p. 692).

This story appears in *The Man to Send the Rain Clouds*, Kenneth Rosen, ed., 1974. Stories: *Laguna Woman*, 1974; *Storyteller*, 1981. Novel: *Ceremony*, 1977. About: *The Delicacy and Strength of Lace: Letters Between Leslie Marmon Silko and James Wright*, Anne Wright, ed.; *Contemporary Literary Criticism*, Vol. 23; Dexter Fisher, "Stories and Their Tellers—A Conversation with Leslie Silko," *The Third Woman: Minority Women Writers of the United States*, Dexter Fisher, ed.; Ambrose Lucero, "For the People: Leslie Silko's Storyteller," *Minority Voices*, V (Spring–Fall 1981), 1–10; Jarold Ramsey, "The Teacher of Modern American Indian Writing as Ethnographer and Critic," *College English*, XLI (October 1979), 163–169; Per Seyersted, *Leslie Marmon Silko*.

GIMPEL THE FOOL (1957) p. 941

ISAAC BASHEVIS SINGER (Radzymin, Poland, 1904)

1. Most of Singer's short stories may be described as tales. This one is unusual in that the subject of the tale is also the teller. Even so, what characteristics of a tale enhance this story?
2. What do the key words of the title suggest?
3. Considering the attitude about life expressed in the first paragraph and in the last few paragraphs, what statements and events between them support Gimpel's vision of himself and life?
4. Is Gimpel's attitude and behavior believable?
5. Discuss pro and con: "If the fool would persist in his folly he would become wise."
6. Why does Gimpel resist the temptation for revenge, to deceive the world?
7. What do the allusions mean? To Dybbuk, for instance?
8. Locate Frampol, Poland, on the map.
9. What picture of life for the Jews in small Polish villages emerges from this story?

WRITING SUGGESTION: Discuss the following observation: With the last few pages, Singer suggests for your imagination a whole story, perhaps a novel.

This story appears in *Gimpel the Fool*, 1957. Stories: *The Spinoza of Market Street*, 1961; *A Friend of Kafka*, 1970; *The Death of Methuselah*, 1988. Novels: *The Family Moskat*, 1950; *The Magician of Lublin*, 1960 (movie version titled *The Magician*); *Shosha*, 1978 (Nobel Prize winner, 1978). About: Irving Malin, *Isaac Bashevis Singer;* Sanford Pinsker, *The Schlemiel as Metaphor: Studies in the Yiddish and American Jewish Novel;* Marcia Allentuck, ed., *The Achievement of Isaac Bashevis Singer;* Barbara Frey Waxman, "Isaac Bashevis Singer's Spirit of Play: Games and Tricks in Some of Singer's Short Stories," *Studies in American Jewish Literature*, N. S. I. (1981), 3–13.

THE CHRYSANTHEMUMS (1937)   p. 953

JOHN STEINBECK (Salinas, California, 1902–1968)

1. Discuss pro and con: The story would have been more effective had Steinbeck used third person, central intelligence point of view instead of omniscient.
2. What does the chrysanthemum symbolize?
3. Does Eliza want to be as free as men are?
4. What effect on Eliza do clothes have?
5. Trace the change in Eliza—for us, for her husband, for herself.
6. What insights into the nature of male-female relationships does this story stimulate?

Commentary

In this story Steinbeck shows a woman experiencing a change in attitude toward herself, her husband and other men, and toward life in general. Two different published versions of this famous story exist—one that appears in various anthologies and one in *The Long Valley* (1938), a collection of related stories. Both versions are ambiguous about the nature of Eliza's change. But the fact that Steinbeck revised key passages of the *Harper's* magazine (October 1937) version for reprint in *The Long Valley* suggests that he wanted to emphasize certain aspects of her character. (*The Long Valley* version is used in this anthology.) For example, look at the end of the sixth paragraph on page 958. In the *Harper's* version this passage did not appear: "Every pointed star gets driven into your body. It's like that. Hot and sharp and—lovely." Now look at the end of the seventh paragraph on that page. Steinbeck also added this line in revision: "She crouched low like a fawning dog." What effect, in the immediate context, do those additions have? Do these passages affect the way you respond to the six questions asked above?

Here are two other revisions that may affect the way you respond to the questions above and to any other questions you may have. Look at the passage on page 960 beginning "Far ahead. . . ." Compare that revised version with this *Harper's* version:

> Far ahead on the road Elisa saw a speck in the dust. She suddenly felt empty. She did not hear Henry's talk. She tried not to look; she did not want to see the little heap of sand and green shoots, but she could not help herself. The chrysanthemums lay in the road close to the wagon tracks. But not the pot; he had kept that. As the car passed them, she remembered the good bitter smell and a little shudder went through her. She felt ashamed of her strong planter's hands, that were no use, lying palms up in her lap.

> [The next paragraph is the same in both versions. But Steinbeck makes cuts and changes in the next paragraph.]

> In a moment they had left behind them the man who had not known or needed to know what she said, the bargainer. She did not look back.

In the first version, Steinbeck had literally stated what perhaps he thought later it would be more effective to imply.

WRITING SUGGESTION: Compare Eliza with Bertha in Mansfield's "Bliss" (p. 664).

This story appears in *The Long Valley*, 1938. Stories: *The Pastures of Heaven*, 1932; *The Red Pony*, 1937. Novels: *The Grapes of Wrath*, 1939; *Tortilla Flat*, 1935; *Of Mice and Men*, 1937; *Cannery Row*, 1945; *East of Eden*, 1952 (all of these were made into movies). Nonfiction: *Journal of a Novel (East of Eden)*, 1969. About: Elizabeth E. McMahan, " 'The Chrysanthemums,': Study of a Woman's Sexuality," *Modern Fiction Studies*, XI (Winter 1968–1969), 453–458; Marillyn Mitchel, "Steinbeck's Strong Women: Feminine Identity in the Short Stories," *Southwest Review*, LXI (Summer 1976), 304–325; William Osborne, "The Texts of Steinbeck's 'The Chrysanthemums,' " *Modern Fiction Studies*, XII (Winter 1966–1967), 479–484; Warren French, *John Steinbeck*.

RAIN IN THE HEART (1945)   p. 962

PETER TAYLOR (Trenton, Tennessee, 1917)
1. Is Taylor's use of the omniscient point of view effective for this story?
2. Why does he not name the sergeant and his wife, even though he names Buck, etc.?
3. What sense of race relations during the forties do you get from this story?
4. Where is this story set?
5. What does the scene with the soldiers contribute to the scene with the sergeant and his wife?
6. What does the scene with the woman at the streetcar stop contribute to the scene with the sergeant and his wife?
7. What does the sergeant's reading about the Civil War contribute to the scene with his wife?
8. What is ironic about the insights the sergeant has in the last two pages?

WRITING SUGGESTIONS: 1) Compare with the other two Civil War stories by Bierce (p. 125) and Scott (p. 920); 2) Compare with other Southern writers—Faulkner (p. 300), Welty (p. 1029), Warren (p. 1011)—who are from the region around Memphis. Do they have anything in common?

This story appeared in *The Sewanee Review* and was included in *The Old Order*, 1985. Stories: *A Long Fourth*, 1948; *Happy Families Are All Alike*, 1959; *The Collected Stories of Peter Taylor*, 1970; *In the Miro District*, 1977. Novels: *A Woman of Means*, 1950; *Summons to Memphis*, 1986. About: Albert Joseph Griffith, *Peter Taylor*; Hubert H. Alexander, ed., *Conversations with Peter Taylor*.

THE SECRET LIFE OF WALTER MITTY (1942)   p. 977

JAMES THURBER (Columbus, Ohio, 1894–1961)
  1. In which genre would you place this story, satirical humor or light satire?
  2. How does Thurber use the device of juxtaposition to contrast reality and daydream for comic and satirical effect?
  3. What about male-female relationships does Thurber satirize?
  4. What about the masculine mystique does Thurber satirize?
  5. Where does Thurber use the device of repetition for comic effect?
  6. Which details mock Mitty's fantasies?
  7. What about this story lends itself to movie adaptation?

WRITING SUGGESTION: Why satire appeals to some readers.

   This story appears in *My World—and Welcome to It!*, 1942. Stories: *Is Sex Necessary?* 1929, (with E. B. White); *The Middle-Aged Man on the Flying Trapeze*, 1935; *The Thurber Carnival*, 1945; *Credos and Curios*, 1962. Memoir: *My Life and Hard Times*, 1933. About: Charles Shivley Holmes, *The Clocks of Columbus: The Literary Career of James Thurber;* Richard Cook, *The Art of James Thurber.*

THE THREE HERMITS (1906)   p. 982

LEO TOLSTOY (Yasnaya Polyana, Russia, 1828–1910)
  1. What motivates the Bishop to tell the three hermits that they do not know how to serve God?
  2. Why does the Bishop reverse his judgment about the hermits' prayer?
  3. What makes the technique of religious allegory with a surprise ending effective for this tale?

WRITING SUGGESTION: Compare with other surprise-ending stories: "The Necklace" (p. 691), "Haircut" (p. 573), and "A Rose for Emily" (p. 300).

   This story appears in *Twenty-three Tales*, 1906. Novels: *War and Peace*, 1869; *Anna Karenina*, 1877. Autobiography: *Childhood*, 1852; *Boyhood*, 1854; *Youth*, 1857. About: R. F. Christian, *Tolstoy: A Critical Introduction;* Edward Wasiolek, *Tolstoy: The Major Fiction;* Logan Speirs, *Tolstoy and Chekhov;* Ernest J. Simmons, *Introduction to Tolstoy's Writings.*

FERN (1923)   p. 988

JEAN TOOMER (Black American. Washington, D.C., 1894–1967)
  1. How does his being an alien from the North affect the narrator's storytelling?

2. What is the effect of the narrator's direct address to his listener or reader? Is he telling or writing?
3. How might it be apt to call this piece a meditation on Fern's eyes?
4. What is the narrator's "emotional sensibility"?
5. Discuss pro and con: The narrator's romanticization of Fern inadvertently robs her, to some degree, of her humanity.
6. Is this story a sketch or a study? See Rhy's "Mannequin," page 898.

Commentary

"From my point of view I am naturally and inevitably an American," wrote Toomer, in response to a request from *Liberator* magazine for some biographical notes. "I have strived for a spiritual fusion analogous to the fact of racial intermingling. Without denying a single element in me, with no desire to subdue one to the other, I have sought to let them function as complements. I have tried to let them live in harmony. Within the last two or three years, however, my growing need for artistic expression has pulled me deeper and deeper into the Negro group. . . .

"A visit to Georgia last fall was the starting point of almost everything of worth that I have done. I heard folk-songs come from the lips of Negro peasants. I saw the rich dusk beauty that I had heard many false accents about, and of which till then, I was somewhat skeptical. And a deep part of my nature, a part that I had repressed, sprang suddenly to life and responded to them. Now I cannot conceive of myself as aloof and separated. My point of view has not changed; it has deepened, it has widened."

Along with Zora Neal Hurston, Langston Hughes, and Charles Chesnutt, Jean Toomer was a collector of black folklore.

WRITING SUGGESTION: How are the feelings Toomer expresses in the above quotation revealed in this story?

This story appears in *Cane*, 1923. Autobiography: *Essentials: Definitions and Aphorisms*, 1931. About: Brian Joseph Benson, *Jean Toomer;* Fritz Gysin, *The Grotesque in American Negro Fiction: Jean Toomer, Richard Wright, Ralph Ellison;* Cynthia Earl Kerman, *The Lives of Jean Toomer: A Hunger for Wholeness;* Darwin T. Turner, *Three Afro-American Writers and Their Search for Identity* (Jean Toomer, Countee Cullen, Zora Neal Hurston).

A & P (1962)   p. 992

JOHN UPDIKE (Shillington, Pennsylvania, 1932)
1. How does his narration express facets of the narrator's character?
2. How would knowing whether the narrator is telling or writing his story affect its elements?
3. How do the details—brand names, etc.—evoke and affect the setting and what happens in it?

4. How do the girls change the atmosphere of the A & P?
5. How does Updike show the attitudes of people in a setting toward that setting?
6. Lengle tells the narrator, "You'll feel this the rest of your life." To what extent might that be true? Does that line affect what the narrator says later on?
7. What does the ending suggest?
8. How does Updike show how two external things—the A & P and the girls—become internalized?

WRITING SUGGESTION: Why do you suppose that out of the hundred or so stories Updike has published this is the one most often anthologized?

This story appears in *Pigeon Feathers,* 1962. Stories: *The Same Door,* 1959; *The Music School,* 1966; *Bech: A Book,* 1970; *Museums and Women,* 1972; *Too Far to Go: The Maples Stories,* 1979; *Trust Me,* 1987. Novels: *Rabbit, Run,* 1960 (made into a movie), *Rabbit Redux,* 1971, *Rabbit Is Rich,* 1981; *Couples,* 1968; *Marry Me,* 1976. About: Robert Detweiler, *John Updike;* Joyce Carol Oates, "Updike's American Comedies," *Modern Fiction Studies,* XXI (1975), 459–472; Suzanne Uphaus, *John Updike.*

EVERYDAY USE (1973)   p. 998

ALICE WALKER (Black American. Eatonton, Georgia, 1944)
1. The shift in tenses early in the story raises a question as to whether the mother is telling (or writing or thinking) the story as it happens, up to the point where it all becomes past tense. What is the point of view strategy?
2. Considering the fact that the mother says she has no education, does the style of her first person narration seem to fit her? If not, is Walker asking the reader to accept a certain artificiality here?
3. Why does Walker include the dedication and what purpose does it serve?
4. What does the title mean?
5. Discuss pro and con: This story is an attack on mindless rejection of one's culture, followed by mindless acceptance?
6. Compare with "My Man Bovanne" (p. 69).

WRITING SUGGESTION: How does the ending comment on the rest of the story?

This story appears in *In Love and Trouble: Stories of Black Women,* 1973. Stories: *You Can't Keep a Good Woman Down,* 1982. Novels: *The Third Life of Grange Copeland,* 1970; *Meridien,* 1976; *The Color Purple,* 1982 (made into a movie, 1985); *The Temple of My Familiar,* 1989. Essays: *Living by the Word,*

1988. About: *Contemporary Novelists,* Fourth Edition. *Dictionary of Literary Biography,* Vols. 6, 33.

ROSELILY (1972)   p. 1006

ALICE WALKER
1. Compare the style of this third person, central intelligence point of view story with Walker's first person story "Everyday Use."
2. How effective is the device of interpersing the wedding ceremony ritual with Roselily's feelings?
3. What is the effect of Walker's use of present tense? Is it appropriate for this story?
4. Many elements are introduced into this brief story—characters, settings, problems. How well does Walker orchestrate these elements so that they interact?

WRITING SUGGESTION: Derive a topic from Walker's comments below.

Alice Walker: ". . . in our . . . society, it is the narrowed and narrowing view of life that often wins.

"Recently, I . . . was asked . . . what I considered the major difference between the literature written by black and by white Americans. I had not spent a lot of time considering this question, since it is not the difference between them that interests me, but, rather, the way black writers and white writers seem to me to be writing one immense story—the same story, for the most part—with different parts of this immense story coming from a multitude of different perspectives. Until this is generally recognized, literature will always be broken into bits, black and white, and there will always be questions, wanting neat answers, such as this."

"I have often been asked why, in my own life and work, I have felt such a desperate need to know and assimilate the experiences of earlier black women writers, most of them unheard of by you and by me, until quite recently; why I felt a need to study them and to teach them.

". . . My discovery of them—most of them out of print, abandoned, discredited, maligned, nearly lost—came about, as many things of value do, almost by accident. . . .

"Mindful that throughout my four years at a prestigious black and then a prestigious white college I had heard not one word about early black women writers, one of my first tasks was simply to determine whether they had existed . . ." ("Saving the Life that is Your Own: The Importance of Models in the Artist's Life," *In Search of Our Mother's Gardens: Womanist Prose,* 1983).

This story appears in *In Love and Trouble,* 1973. See note above under "Everyday Use."

BLACKBERRY WINTER (1947) p. 1011

ROBERT PENN WARREN (Guthrie, Kentucky, 1905–1989)
1. How do the title and going barefoot contribute to the theme of the story?
2. What is the effect of references to the future on our sense of the narrator's story?
3. What effect does the scene at the bridge have on the scenes with the tramp, before and after?
4. Why does the narrator tell or write this story?
5. What kind of relationship does the boy have with his parents?
6. What attracts the boy to the tramp?
7. Is the element of repetition in the style effective?
8. What do the allusions contribute to the story's effect?

WRITING SUGGESTION: Compare the boy with Eliza in Steinbeck's "Chrysanthemums" (p. 953) as to their responses to strangers.

This story appears in *The Circus in the Attic,* 1947. Novels: *Night Rider,* 1939; *All the King's Men,* 1946 (made into a play, a movie, and an opera); *World Enough and Time,* 1950; *A Place to Come To,* 1977. Biography: *John Brown: The Making of a Martyr,* 1929. Essays: *Selected Essays,* 1958. Editor: *Understanding Poetry* and *Understanding Fiction* (see Warren's essay on "Blackberry Winter") with Cleanth Brooks, 1938. About: Charles Bohner, *Robert Penn Warren;* James H. Justus, *The Achievement of Robert Penn Warren; Robert Penn Warren Talking,* Floyd C. Atkins and John T. Hiers, eds.; Katherine Snipes, *Robert Penn Warren.*

WHY I LIVE AT THE P.O. (1941) p. 1029

EUDORA WELTY (Jackson, Mississippi, 1919)
1. Which lines indicate that Sister is *telling* her story? To whom do you suppose she is telling it?
2. Where does Welty use colloquialisms and clichés for comic effect?
3. How well does Welty handle transitional devices?
4. Explain the comic effect of repetition, as on p. 1032.
5. What makes the humorous moments effective? (See p. 1033).
6. Discuss pro and con: The blinding effect of egocentricity and pride is the theme of this story.

Commentary

Katherine Anne Porter, who promoted Eudora Welty's fiction early in her career, once said that Sister, the narrator of "Why I Live at the P.O.," was suffering from schizophrenia. Welty commented, "It never occurred to me while I was writing the story (and it still doesn't) that I was writing about someone in serious mental trouble. I was trying to write about the way people who live away off from nowhere have to amuse themselves by dramatizing every situation that comes along by exaggerating it—'telling it.' . . . It's just the way they keep life interesting—they make an experience out of the ordinary. I wasn't trying to do anything but show that. I thought it was cheerful, on the whole" (*Conversations with Eudora Welty,* Peggy Prenshaw, ed.)

Sister's mental condition may not be as serious as Porter claimed, but neither is to be taken as lightly as the author suggests. In the way she explains why she has been living at the P.O. for the past five days, Sister exhibits a powerfully integrated egocentric personality sullenly suffering from wounded pride. Over a year ago, her younger sister ran away with Mr. Whitaker, a traveling photographer who first went out with Sister herself. Sister's references, in dialogue and in telling her story to her listener, to Mr. Whitaker are all negative. Was he perhaps no more important to Sister than the other people, events, and objects over which she has had conflicts all her life? Has her egocentricity and excessive pride alienated and isolated her from members of her family and others all her life? "If I have anything at all I have pride," she says (p. 1036). Sister is young, but the reader may well imagine that she will behave all the rest of her life as she does on this fourth of July and on the occasion of her sister's return home with a two-year-old child (was Stella-Rondo pregnant by Mr. Whitaker before they left town?).

Sister's personality has clearly been shaped by the people around her. They all behave and talk the same way. Sister simply behaves more spectacularly and speaks with more blisteringly sarcastic innuendo. The source of humor in this story is the egocentricity and petty vanity and pride of the entire family and the medium is the oral storytelling tradition of the Deep South. Comic irony derives from the blindness of all the characters to the fact that almost every ugly thing they say about someone else clearly applies to themselves. Just as Sister is the most dramatic actor in this domestic comedy, she is also the target of Welty's sharpest ironies. Each time she claims that one person turned another against her, the reader recalls that Sister's own behavior and sarcasm has already caused that effect, either just previously or, as implied by the context, in the recent past (See pp. 1030, 1031, 1034.)

The reader may further assume, then, that Sister caused Mr. Whitaker to turn against her. As entertaining as it is to listen to her, she probably alienated most of the townspeople when she told them her story (they already know she reads their mail); with each sarcasm, she is now, as she tells it again, turning both her fictional listener and the reader against her. Who is her present listener? Note that on page 1033, she says to her listener, "You ought to see Mama. . . ." China Grove is a small hamlet and the P.O. is the second smallest in Mississippi. Is Sister's immediate listener then a stranger, someone just passing through, or someone like Mr. Whitaker? And is she in the process of turning yet another person against her, a person she ego-centrically assumes will be on her side and find her "sensitive," a trait in which she takes excessive pride?

The comic irony of the story derives then from character; Welty en-hances the humor with her adroit use of various elements and devices. The title itself sounds a humorous note, and all the names of the characters, including Sister, alert the reader to expect humor: Stella-Rondo, Shirley-T., and the redundant Papa-Daddy. In context, all the colloquial expres-sions and clichés they speak are humorous, sometimes hilarious: "made her drop dead for a second," "trying to stretch two chickens over five people," "conniption fit." The lives of these people are cluttered with comic objects: Add-a-Pearl necklace, "cheap Kress tweezers", chain letters, box tops, movie star photos, charm bracelets, and the vast inventory of objects Sister lays claim to in her whirlwind exit of the house. As she tells her story, we may imagine the background clutter of weird objects in the tiny post office, including the sewing-machine *motor*.

Sudden comic actions provoke laughter. "He would have gone on until midnight if Shirley-T. hadn't lost the Milky Way she ate in Cairo" (p. 1031). Uncle Rondo runs out into the yard dressed in Stella-Rondo's flesh-colored kimono (p. 1031). " 'I told you if you ever mentioned Annie Flo's name I'd slap your face,' says Mama, and slaps my face" (p. 1033). Welty even em-ploys a little slapstick with Uncle Rondo's firecracker revenge (p. 1035). In a series of comic actions, Sister collects all her possessions and has them hauled off in a little wagon in nine trips to the P. O.

Another source of humor is Sister's use of swift transitions from one comic incident to another. An early and typical example:

" 'She looks exactly like Shirley Temple to me,' says Mama, but Shirley-T. just ran away from her.

"So the first thing Stella Rondo did at the table was turn Pappa-Daddy against me." (p. 1030)

Sister's affected but fluid phrasing lends a comic, satirical tone to the story. And the repetition of phrases that are comic in context stimulates the comic pace. In the excellent example on page 1032, Sister introduces the phrase "mortally wounded" in her narration and it is repeated in dialogue.

Welty has said that a partial inspiration for this story was seeing an iron-ing board in a little post office, "but what the story grew out of was some-thing much more than that. I mean, it was a lifelong listening to talk on my own block where I grew up as a child. . . ." (*Conversations*, p. 285). In an in-terview, Bill Ferris, director of the Center for Southern Folklore, praised Welty for often choosing "the spoken word for your primary vehicle rather than a more abstract literary frame." "In much of your work I have a feel-ing that I really am hearing the voice of the people, hearing words as they are spoken. 'Why I Live at the P. O.,' I guess, is the most famous. . . ."

Welty responded: "I think the ability to use dialogue, or the first person . . . is just as essential as the knowledge of place and other components of a story. But I think it has a special importance, because you can use it in fiction to do very subtle things and very many things at once—like giving a notion of the speaker's background, furthering the plot, giving the sense of the give-and-take between characters. Dialogue gives a character's age, background, upbringing, everything, without the author's having to explain it on the side. He's doing it out of his own mouth. And also, other things—like a character may be telling a lie which he will show to the reader, but perhaps not to the person to whom he's talking, and perhaps not even realize it himself. Sometimes he's deluded. All these things can come out in dialogue. And you get that, of course, by your ear, by listening to the rhythms and habits and so on of everyday speech everywhere" (*Conversations*, pp. 178, 179). "Why I Live at the P.O." exhibits an unusually effective interaction between first person narration and dialogue, with the narrator dominating even the dialogue.

WRITING SUGGESTIONS: 1) Trace the patterns of irony in this story; 2) Compare Welty's use of the unreliable narrator with Lardner's in "Haircut" (p. 573).

This story appeared in *The Atlantic Monthly* and is included in *A Curtain of Green*, 1941. Stories: *The Wide Net*, 1943; *The Golden Apples,* 1949, a cycle of stories; *The Bride of Innisfallen*, 1955. *Stories*, 1980. Novels: *The Robber Bridegroom,* 1942; *Delta Wedding*, 1946; *The Ponder Heart*, 1954; *Losing Battles,* 1970; *The Optimist's Daughter*, 1973 (winner of the Pulitzer Prize). Essays: *The Eye of the Story*, 1977. Autobiography: *One Writer's Beginnings*, 1984. About: Alfred Appel, *A Season of Dreams: The Fiction of Eudora Welty;* J. A. Bryant, *Eudora Welty;* Peggy Whitman Prenshaw, ed., *Conversations with Eudora Welty;* Ruth M. Vande Kieft, *Eudora Welty.*

ROMAN FEVER (1936) p. 1040

EDITH WHARTON (New York City, 1862–1937)
1. What point of view technique does Wharton use and how does she use it?
2. Why does Mrs. Slade tell Mrs. Ansley the truth now?
3. Discuss Wharton's use of the Roman ruins as a metaphor for memories of the past.
4. What are the implications of the last line?
5. What does the title mean?

WRITING SUGGESTIONS: 1) Discuss the following comment as it applies to this story: "My last page," wrote Edith Wharton, "is always latent in my first"; 2) Compare with Henry James' novella *Daisy Miller*.

This story appeared in *Liberty* and is included in *The World Over*, 1934. Stories: *The Great Inclination*, 1899; *Ghosts*, 1937. Novels: *House of Mirth,*

1905; *The Age of Innocence,* 1920. Autobiography: *A Backward Glance,* 1934. Essays: *The Writing of Fiction,* 1925. About: Louis Auchincloss, *Edith Wharton: A Woman in Her Time;* R. W. B. Lewis, *Edith Wharton: A Biography;* Millicent Bell, *Edith Wharton and Henry James;* Richard H. Lawson, *Edith Wharton;* Cynthia Griffin, *A Feast of Words;* Percy Lubbock, *Portrait of Edith Wharton.*

THE USE OF FORCE (1938)   p. 1051

WILLIAM CARLOS WILLIAMS (Rutherford, New Jersey, 1883–1963)
  1. Discuss the difference between plot and conflict in this story.
  2. "The Use of Force" is primarily an external conflict story, but how is it also an internal conflict story?
  3. In what different ways does the "crisis situation" affect the doctor and the child? Who is the protagonist?
  4. Discuss the conflict in this story, using these concepts: suspense, unity, plausibility, foreshadowing.
  5. Brief though it is, "The Use of Force" poses and develops several kinds of conflict. What are they? For instance, what conflict preceded the doctor's visit? What social issues create a context of conflict for the major conflict?
  6. In what minor conflicts is the doctor embroiled?

Commentary

This story has all the classic elements of plot: the posing of the problem, rising action, climax, denouement. The conflict is clearly between the doctor and the girl. The title itself describes an external type of conflict: the doctor attacks the child with force and she defends herself with force. The stages in the development of this external conflict are clear. But this external conflict also produces an internal conflict for the doctor. As an adult, a professional on whom society, the parents and even the child must depend, the doctor must think and act rationally, especially when contending with a force that is almost as natural and devoid of social, ethical, and rational restraint as a cyclone—the terror and physical fury of a child. But the purity of the child's negative rage is what undermines the doctor's control. He becomes simultaneously a child, like the girl, and an adult who worries about his unprofessional conduct. To distract himself from becoming conscious of his anger at the child, he recognizes his irritation with the behavior of the parents. Simultaneously, he tries to persuade himself that basically he adores the child. Finally he admits, "I tried to hold myself down but I couldn't." Having tried on cold professional grounds to rationalize his own violence, he must face the fact that what he feels is "blind fury . . . adult shame."

For the reader to feel this internal conflict intimately in so brief a story, it is necessary that Williams tell it in the first person. The narrator describes his conflict and then tells how he feels about his role in it. The inner conflict remains unresolved because it is an unresolvable conflict inherent in human nature itself. The obvious crisis situation is significant to both characters, and neither will be quite the same again. But it is the doctor, perhaps, on whom the conflict has the maximum effect: he must deal both immediately and ever after with the implications of the unresolved internal conflict that extends beyond his supposed victory in the external conflict. The first-person point of view gives force to his observations on his own behavior by withholding from the reader the outcome of his conflict with the child; the reader is free to develop personal attitudes unaffected by the doctor's and to enjoy the suspense. Recognition of the shocking plausibility of the conflict's effect—that a child's irrational rage can infect a doctor and incite his violent response—is a major consequence of the narrator's internal conflict. The doctor's dilemma is foreshadowed in the description of the child and in the implication that the parents have failed in a task for which they assume the doctor's success.

Other external conflicts create a context for the doctor's internal and external conflicts: preceding the doctor's visit, a conflict between the parents and the child; a still developing conflict between the father and the mother; and the doctor's minor conflicts with the parents. The setting creates a context in which the doctor's conflict develops. The doctor poses a larger social context when he refers to the cases of diphtheria in the school the girl attends. The doctor is then a protagonist in conflict with parents and child on behalf of society. The minor external conflicts are resolved, but the doctor's external conflict with the child has shockingly posed an internal conflict that will remain unresolved.

WRITING SUGGESTIONS: 1) Derive a topic from the commentary and questions above; 2) the implications of child abuse.

This story appears in *Life Along the Passaic River*, 1938. Stories: *The Knife of the Times*, 1932; *The Farmer's Daughters: The Collected Stories*, 1961. Novels: *A Voyage to Pagany*, 1928; *The Build-up*, 1952. Essays: *In the American Grain*, 1925. Nonfiction: *The Autobiography of William Carlos Williams*, 1951. About: R. F. Dietrich, "Connotations of Rape in 'The Use of Force,'" *Studies in Short Fiction* III (1966), 446–450; Linda W. Wagner, "Williams' 'The Use of Force": An Expansion,' *Studies in Short Fiction* IV (1967), 351–53.

KEW GARDENS (1921)   p. 1055

VIRGINIA WOOLF (London, England, 1882–1941)
  1. Why does Woolf describe plants and lower animals first?
  2. Why are the people not fully drawn as characters?

3. Why does Woolf return again and again to the snail and the flowers?
4. Identify the point of view technique Woolf employs and describe her style. What effect do these elements have on everything the reader sees and hears?
5. Kew Gardens may be described as an ecological system. What elements impinge upon each other in this system?
6. How does Woolf's method of impingement contrast with the juxta-position-of-fragments method used by Oates in "How I Contemplated the World . . .." (p. 752).

Commentary

Even though the garden is cultivated rather than wild, Woolf focuses first upon plants, snails, insects, and then upon water and earth to suggest that all elements in this fiction are of somewhat equal importance. The human beings are introduced merely as "men and women who walk in Kew Gardens" and are encapsulated in a generalization near the end: "Thus one couple after another with much the same irregular and aimless movement pass the flowerbed" as the snail and insects move and breezes, light, and colours move over them all. In a very short space, Woolf intimates a great deal about the lives of four couples, but she does not fully develop them as characters because she wants to give an impression of a process, rather than delineate the action of a conventional plot. And to express the relatively equal function of each element in the garden, Woolf devotes as much attention to one element as to another, returning as often to the snail and to the flowers as to the human "figures." Notice the things that all these elements share.

Woolf's experimental use of the omniscient point of view may seem confusing. One commentator has simplified the problem by deciding that Woolf records the impressions of a person sitting on a bench. But who might that person be? And how is he or she affected by the sights and sounds in Kew Gardens? Given such an explanation, one might easily dismiss this piece as a prose poem or a precious sketch. But Woolf has deliberately avoided implying that a character is observing events in the garden. Rather she has imagined a pure, god-like omniscient perspective, and the style evolves out of that point-of-view stategy.

In the opening paragraph, Woolf chooses words and phrases that describe the flower-bed in semi-scientific or geometrical terms, anticipating to some degree the style and intention of Robbe-Grillet in many of his works, and in "The Secret Room" (p. 903) specifically. She meshes these objective terms with figurative language. To convey a sense of elements impinging upon each other, the omniscient narrator must achieve and sustain a complex style.

Woolf dramatizes the kinetic or fluid impingement of one element upon another in the garden so that the reader may experience it as an ecological system. The process is set in motion in the first paragraph. The breeze stirs the light which activates a spectrum of colors which impinge upon the motionless pebble, then upon the moving snail, and so on. Many forms of life and many types of inanimate objects impinge upon each other. The human figures are of various ages, both sexes, and various classes.

Man-made mechanical objects are integrated with inanimate natural objects. Shoes, buckles, and the parasol function no less than the pebble in this ecosystem. Things organic appear mechanical, things mechanical appear lifelike. For example, "The thrush chose to hop like a mechanical bird, in the shadow of the flowers." Words, as real as flowers, become objects. Voices become like the breeze. Woolf stimulates all the senses. She emphasizes what the living creatures see. Smells are implied. The young couple experience the sense of touch most intensely. And the piece ends with a swelling sense of sound—mechanical city sounds and the clamor of animals.

Mental processes are simultaneously separate from and an integral part of this all-inclusive ecological system. Here Woolf also extends the garden image to a wider context. Memory is part of that mental process and contributes to the talk. Time is the ambience in which events in this small space occur.

WRITING SUGGESTION: Derive a topic from the commentary and questions above.

This story appears in *A Haunted House,* 1944. Stories: *Monday or Tuesday,* 1921. Novels: *To the Lighthouse,* 1927; *Orlando,* 1928; *Between the Acts,* 1941. Biography: *Roger Fry,* 1940. Criticism: *The Common Reader,* 1925. Essays: *A Room of One's Own,* 1929; *A Writer's Diary,* 1953. About: E. M. Forster, *Virginia Woolf;* Katherine Mansfield, *Novels and Novelists.* S. P. Mittal, *The Aesthetic Venture: Virginia Woolf's Poetics of the Novel;* Lyndall Gordon, *Virginia Woolf, A Writer's Life;* Quentin Bell, *Virginia Woolf, a Biography;* Jane Marcus, *Art and Anger: Reading Like A Woman.*

THE MAN WHO WAS ALMOST A MAN (1940)   p. 1061

RICHARD WRIGHT (Black-American. Natchez, Mississippi, 1908–1960)

1. For its effect Wright's story depends on irony—the contrast between Dave's "self-image" and the image he presents to the world. Find the ways in which Dave unknowingly behaves like a child and the ways he is treated by others as a child.
2. Is the ending one more example of Dave's acting like a child or does it suggest that he is about to become an adult?
3. Compare this story and "King of the Bingo Game" (p. 268) by Ellison in terms of technique, style, and handling of story elements. Discuss in particular the differences in their handling of point of view.

Commentary

Wright depicts a child who thinks he thinks like a man but doesn't. The effect is pathetic irony. Wright makes the initiation or the rite of passage from adolescence to manhood an ironic metaphor for the relationship that existed between many blacks and whites, and among blacks themselves, in the agrarian South up until the 1950s. Dave's motivation is quickly established: whites and blacks treat him as if he were a boy. In the scene with Joe, the white storekeeper—as in the first scene with his mother, the scene at supper, and the scene in which he begs his mother for two dollars of his own money—Dave's behavior is consistently childish.

The concept of manhood and the possession of a gun are inseparable in the culture Dave has inherited from the white man. Ironically, he is not as powerless as he thinks; he has the power of a child. Although his mother talks to him as if he were a child, his childlike show of affection and his reasoning succeed with her. In possession of the gun, he feels "a sense of power." The power is solely destructive, aimed at both the powerless race from which he springs and at the powerful race that subjugates him: he can "kill anybody, black or white." Wright implies that the "foe" will not always be "imaginary." Ironically, the destructiveness lies partly in the fact that Dave really is not yet a man. The innocent bystander, the mule, is his victim, and Wright implies at the end that she is not the last victim of Dave's almost innocent lust for the power to destroy. That power is also self-destructive. Having accidentally shot the mule, he, like a child, chases it and only helps to make the wound fatal. The child must face the adult fact that foolish acts can not be undone, that guns often backfire. The simplicity of the story's actions, and the cold logic of their progression, makes the reader feel that they are inevitable.

At the scene of the accident, the child who was unable to handle the power of an adult (a bogus power that is also the undoing of many adults) becomes a child again, surrounded by whites, interrogated aggressively by his parents. Just as Joe, who sold him the gun, laughed at him, and his mother ridiculed him, and his father sternly watched him, the whole crowd watches, ridicules, and laughs at him. "If anybody could shoot a gun, he could." That is the point Dave misses—because "anybody" can shoot a gun, the ability to shoot is a fallacious basis on which to build a concept of manhood. Wright's last line suggests that true maturity is unlikely for a person enslaved to such a concept of manhood: "away to somewhere, somewhere where he could be a man. . . ." Leaving home, with a gun in his pocket, Dave will always, Wright suggests, be the man who was "almost a man."

In terms of characterization, conflict, and theme, this story is deceptively simple, blunt, almost deterministic in its execution and effect. The third person central intelligence point of view produces a style that meshes Wright's diction, at times, with Dave's. Examine carefully the first two paragraphs. Dave's thoughts—phonetically spelled, highly colloquial, and grammatically in the language of an uneducated field hand—are reproduced with naturalistic fidelity. Wright's formal poetic phrases offer contrast and perspective. One of Wright's techniques is the use of dialogue, with its effect of dramatic immediacy. From the time Dave goes into Joe's store to the time he acquires the gun, the story is told almost entirely in dialogue; a few descriptions of action are handled in short sentences in a simple, objective vocabulary.

WRITING SUGGESTION: Derive a topic from the commentary and questions above.

This story appears in *Eight Men,* 1961. Stories: *Uncle Tom's Children: Five Long Stories,* 1940. Novel: *Native Son,* 1940. Autobiography: *Black Boy: A Record of Childhood and Youth,* 1954. Nonfiction: *12 Million Black Voices: A Folk History of the Negro in the United States,* 1941; autobiographical essay in *The God That Failed,* 1950; *Richard Wright Reader,* 1978, Ellen Wright and Michel Fabre, editors. About: David Bakish, *Richard Wright;* Russell Carl Brignano, *Richard Wright: An Introduction to the Man and His Works;* Edward Margolies, *The Art of Richard Wright;* James Baldwin, *Notes on a Native Son,* 24–25.

USEFUL BOOKS NOT CITED EARLIER

Walter Allen, *The Short Story in English*
Wayne C. Booth, *The Rhetoric of Fiction*
R. V. Cassill, *Writing Fiction*
John Gardner, *On Moral Fiction*
Wallace Hildick, *Word for Word; Writing With Care*
John Keuhl, *Creative Writing and Rewriting*
Percy Lubbock, *The Craft of Fiction*
David Madden, *Revising Fiction; Studies in the Short Story,* sixth edition; *The Fiction Tutor*
Charles E. May, *Short Story Theories*
James Moffett, *Points of View*
Frank O'Connor, *The Lonely Voice*
Sean O'Faolain, *Short Stories: A Study in Pleasure*
William Peden, *The American Short Story: Continuity and Change, 1940–1975*
Danforth Ross, *The American Short Story*
Mark Schorer, "Technique as Discovery," *The World We Imagine*
Ray B. West, *The Short Story in America: 1900–1950*

COPYRIGHT
ACKNOWLEDGMENTS

1192